HELEN VAN SLYKE

THREE COMPLETE NOVELS

A Necessary Woman

Sisters and Strangers

Always Is Not Forever

AVENEL BOOKS · NEW YORK

Previously published in separate volumes under the titles:
A Necessary Woman copyright © 1979 by Helen Van Slyke
Sisters and Strangers copyright © 1978 by Helen Van Slyke
Always is Not Forever copyright © 1977 by Helen Van Slyke

This 1982 edition is published by Avenel Books,
distributed by Crown Publishers, Inc.,
by arrangement with Doubleday & Company, Inc.

Manufactured in the United States of America

Library of Congress Cataloging in Publication Data

Van Slyke, Helen, 1919–1979
  Helen Van Slyke, three complete novels.

  Contents: A necessary woman—Sisters and strangers
—Always is not forever.
  I. Title.
PS3572.A54A6   1982   813'.54   82-11349

ISBN: 0-517-391392

h g f e d c b a

CONTENTS

HELEN VAN SLYKE had a distinguished business career before leaving it in 1972 to devote her full time to a writing career. She was Fashion Editor of the Washington *Evening Star*; Advertising Director of Henri Bendel; Vice-President of Norman, Craig, and Kummel, an advertising agency; President of the House of Fragrance; Vice-President of Creative Activities for Helena Rubenstein; and President of the Fashion Group, Inc.

She contributed articles to *Vogue, Harper's Bazaar,* and the *Saturday Evening Post*. Her other books include *The Best Place to Be, The Mixed Blessing, The Heart Listens, All Visitors Must Be Announced,* and *The Rich and the Righteous*. Helen Van Slyke's books have a wide appeal, especially for the modern career woman. Van Slyke was particularly sensitive to tensions and desires of the career woman, one of the reasons her books were bestsellers. Helen Van Slyke died in 1979.

A Necessary Woman

Introduction

WITHOUT REALIZING WHAT she was doing, Mary put her hand to her lips, as though to retrace the kiss. She'd kissed Michael thousands of times these past fifteen years, in dozens of different ways. Shyly, at first. Passionately later. And, later still, comfortingly, compassionately, reassuringly, almost maternally. As though he were her child rather than her husband.

The kiss she'd given him less than an hour ago at the gangway was all of those and none of them. It was a lying "I'll miss you too" motion. A Judas kiss. Perhaps the kiss of death for the marriage that suited him well and was, for her, a kind of love-hate union filled with disappointment and a sense of failure. Not only his failure but her own.

She leaned against the polished mahogany railing of the big white ship, watching San Francisco recede into the fog. Sixty-nine days from now when she sailed back into this harbor, she would have made THE DECISION. That was how she thought of it. Two words. Capitalized. At the end of this South Pacific cruise she would have decided whether or not to stay married to Michael Morgan.

"She would have decided." The realization of her own thought processes brought a mirthless smile to her lips. As though it were all up to her. But that's how it was and always had been in her marriage. Not only in her marriage; in almost the whole thirty-eight years of her life. From girlhood, she'd made her own decisions, not selfishly but as though she felt from her earliest days she was expected to be self-sufficient. She learned to seem calm and self-assured, and people admired her control, her capacity for dealing with the difficult business of living. "Disciplined," they called her. "Efficient and organized," they said.

How little they knew her, any of them. Beneath the unflappable surface, the serene exterior, was another Mary Farr Morgan. That one was the eternal, unquenchable female longing to be protected and to admire the protector. That hidden Mary did what she hated to do, like millions of other women who accepted a leading role that had somehow been thrust upon them. There were so many like her. Women forced into a dominant position. The eternal earth-mothers. Her sisters-under-the-skin. Some, like Mary, climbed their way to modest success in business, literally supporting their husbands with their earnings. Others stayed at home, but their influence was equally great. They took charge of the husband's paycheck, set rules for the couple's social life, planned the vacations and spoke as the voice of authority to the children. They did what was required, whatever their station in life, some willingly, others with resigned awareness of the strength that held the family together: their strength.

Did they chafe under their ties to men who couldn't measure up to their dreams? Wish, as she did, to respect a husband as well as love him? She didn't know about all those others. She knew only that she'd pledged her life to an engaging, adoring, undemanding man-child who accepted her as lover and provider, and who had come to expect her to chart the course of their life together. She wasn't sure she could go on with it. She wanted something more than a charming little boy who'd never grow up.

Respect. In the end, it always came back to that. Though they lived in apparent harmony, her love had slowly diminished in proportion to her respect for Michael. Why was it so important to her that he be the stronger one in their relationship? Why did she care so much for the surface things, allowing them to overshadow what should matter more: his ungrudging pride in her success, his unconcern about the lack of his own, his unfailing gentleness and eternal optimism? He was a good man in so many ways and yet she saw him as a failure.

Standing alone on the deck, she played devil's advocate. By whose standards was Michael a failure? The world's, because he'd never had a good job, never kept even a mediocre one? Society's, because her generation expected the man to be the wage earner and decision-maker? Her own inbred belief that her husband should be the leader in their marriage?

I'm the result of early conditioning, Mary thought sadly. If I'd been born twenty years later, perhaps none of those things would matter to me. I could handle my lovable loser because I wouldn't see him as one. I'd consider him a partner, contributing the things of which he's capable. Doing his own thing, as the kids say. I wouldn't want him to be my master. I wouldn't wish him to be smarter and stronger than I. I wouldn't look down on him because he's vulnerable and spoiled and weak.

But I can't handle that kind of rational, 1977 approach. I'm a product of another time. Like so many other wives, I want to be the secondary partner. It's the way I think things were meant to be. I pretend to be modern and "liberated," but I'm hopelessly old-fashioned. The eternal, starry-eyed, woman's-magazine-type romantic, eager to give herself fully to a man's demands, secretly fascinated by the male ego.

I must be crazy. Other women would kill for a husband so handsome, so gentle, so amenable to my every wish. Michael is an expert lover, though it's been years since I've been able to respond as I want. Even in bed, my mind won't rest. I accept him. I even want him. But this creeping resentment takes the joy out of lovemaking. He must notice, but he doesn't comment. He simply accepts, as he accepts everything I do, unquestioningly, loyally, almost deferentially.

On the surface, we're the prototype of the perfect couple, she thought wearily: well-suited and happy, living proof that fidelity and compatibility are alive and well within the confines of matrimony. And one of us is tortured with doubts.

She stared into the cold, gray February waters of the Pacific. Why do I blame Michael for what he is? How much of this is my fault? Much of it. Most of it, probably. What compels me to take charge? Why do I have this unwilling thirst for power, this drive that translates itself into domination? Ego. God knows I don't feel egotistical, but I must be. Inside, I must believe that I, and only I, can keep myself safe. Maybe, unwittingly, I never gave Michael a chance to be what I want him to be. I was always too quick with answers, too impatient to let him solve his own problems, too frightened to put my trust in him. Maybe I really like it this way. Perhaps I couldn't put myself in a minor role in any marriage, no matter how strong or dependable my partner.

Some women are born like that. They want to be helpless and it's impossible for them. They know what's right and do what's wrong. And they end up hurting others and themselves through the misguided belief that they know best.

Am I one of those? What do I want? A different kind of marriage with the same man? That's impossible. Neither of us is going to change. It's too late for that.

But, God, how I wish we could.

PART I

Chapter 1

THIRTY-EIGHT YEARS and a thousand decisions preceded that bleak winter morning when Mary Farr Morgan sailed toward the South Pacific. And through them all she had always felt alone. Her earliest memories were those of existing apart, even from her parents and her sister and brother. In later years, she would feel some closeness to Patricia, who was nearly seven when Mary was born. And she would make an uneasy truce with the aging parents who still lived in the old Riverside Drive apartment in New York. A continent between them made for a less tense relationship than she'd had in her girlhood. And maturity helped her to realize that in their own way they loved her and her sister, even though they mourned the only son, who died so young and whom they loved most of all, in death as they had in life.

But through the early years, the youngest of the Farr children wore a protective cloak of independence, a defense against the instinctive knowledge that Camille and John Farr thought Patricia more beautiful and John Jr. more promising than their last-born. She yearned for her parents' admiration and determined to earn it. In school her marks were higher, her awards more plentiful, her recognition greater than her pretty sister's. But her mother and father accepted her accomplishments as something to be expected of her. "The child *should* have brains," she once overheard Camille say. "Poor thing, she'll never get through life on her looks, the way Patricia will."

The words hurt, but they also strengthened Mary's determination to be the star of the family. There was no longer a drive to outshine John Jr. as there'd been in the first eight years of her life, for the boy was no longer there. It was so senseless. One minute he was a lively ten-year-old and the next he was dead under the wheels of a car that couldn't stop when John ran in front of it. In that moment and forever after, her parents made no secret of their feelings. Overwhelmed by grief, they spoke what was in their hearts, not caring what their words did to their surviving children. To the people who came to pay sympathy calls, Camille said the same thing over and over. "We've lost the best one," she told them, her voice full of anguish and self-pity. "We've lost the best one."

John Farr Sr. said little, but the tragedy turned him into a remote and bitter man. After Mary's birth, Camille had had a hysterectomy. There'd be no son to replace the one he lost, and he seemed consumed by sorrow. Young as she was, Mary sensed that if—unspeakable thought—he'd had to give up one of his

7

children he'd have sacrificed one of the girls. He never said that, of course, but the child knew it at the time and became more convinced of it as she grew older. She came to feel sorry for him, remembering how much he loved John, but she was angry, too. Angry at both her parents for loving her brother more. Angry at them for not appreciating how hard she tried to make them happy. She realized what "partial" meant, and resented it. People weren't supposed to favor one child, she thought. When she grew up and had children she'd love them equally.

And yet, despite the anger, she wanted to please them, to bask in their praise, at least to have them say she never gave them a moment's worry.

Not so Patricia. Patricia didn't seem to know that the favorite was dead. She was sorry her brother had been killed but not sensitive enough to realize that his death had left an unfillable void in her parents' lives. Thick-skinned, self-centered, boy-crazy at fifteen, Patricia gave no thought to the terrible impact the tragedy had on all their lives. Once, years later, when they were grown, Mary tried to explain that John had been more important to their parents than either of them. Patricia had just stared at her. "You're crazy. They loved us all the same. I don't know what gets into you, Mary. They were good to us, weren't they?"

"Good, yes. But they never loved us blindly, the way they did him."

Patricia, already married and with a baby of her own, had shrugged. "Love. At eighteen I don't know what you think it is. Some kind of magic potion, I expect. They aren't very affectionate, I suppose. At least not by your standards. But you always want people falling down in worship at your feet. Don't expect it. It's not all that important anyway."

Mary didn't argue the point, but she knew Patricia was wrong. Love was important and John Jr. had had it. He wasn't considerate of his parents. He disobeyed them and they adored him all the more. He worried them with his boyish escapades and they never punished him. He got more hugs and kisses than she and Patricia, more praise for every halfway important thing he did. Yes, they loved him more. He could do no wrong. He was idolized. And someday she'd find someone who'd give her that same kind of blind devotion. Meanwhile, she'd make her mother and father proud of her. Not as proud as they'd have been of John if he'd lived, but impressed enough to feel she was worthy of their love.

As far as her parents were concerned, it never quite worked out that way. They thought it was a good idea when she got a secretarial job at a local radio station after she graduated high school. They seemed to be quite pleased that she'd focused her intelligence on the business world, but they were hardly impressed.

"You should meet some nice young men there," Camille said.

"Is that all you want for me, Mother? A nice young man?" Mary had been disappointed that they weren't more excited about her job. "What about a career? Don't you think I might be on the way to becoming a success?"

John Farr had looked up from his newspaper. "Success is marriage and a family, Mary. If you accomplish that, we'll be satisfied."

She'd wanted to scream. "You still think I'm the ugly duckling, don't you? You probably think nobody will ever love me, but I might be lucky enough to trap somebody, the way Patricia did!"

"Mary Louise Farr!" When her mother used her full name, Mary knew she was angry. "How dare you speak that way about your sister!"

"Well, it's true, isn't it? If Stan Richton hadn't had to marry her, your precious beauty might still be single and on your hands!"

"Go to your room!" John Farr's eyes blazed. "And never say such things again while you're living under this roof!"

Mary's defiance totally collapsed. It was terrible of her to remind them that Patricia had been pregnant when she married. They'd been so ashamed, so fearful "people would know." John Jr. would never have found himself in the predicament Stanley Richton did. He'd have had more respect for women. He'd never have taken advantage of a young girl as Patricia's boy friend did. They'd said that to her when she told them she "had to get married." Patricia hadn't seemed bothered by the oblique comparison, but Mary found herself thinking, even now. Even after all these years everything is measured against my brother. Stan Richton is a nice fellow. He's no more to blame than Patricia is. He loves her. She's lucky to be marrying someone who loves her. I wonder what John would have been like if he'd lived. Would he ever have disappointed them the way Patricia has, or the way I do?

She'd apologized that evening and a month later found herself a one-room apartment on West End Avenue. Camille and John made only a feeble protest when she moved out. Mary felt they were actually relieved that they no longer had to pretend. With Patricia married and Mary on her own, they could rid themselves of the last responsibilities of parenthood and concentrate on the memory of the boy who never became a man. But when she said this to her sister, Patricia frowned. "You're really obsessive. I don't think they spend as much time dwelling on that memory as you do. You know, you're not easy to understand, Mary. You're a good-looking girl, you've gotten yourself a good job and now a place of your own. Will you ever start to relax and believe you don't have to prove something every minute?"

Mary bounced her one-year-old niece on her knee and seriously considered her sister's remarks. It was true, she supposed. She had turned into a reasonably pretty young woman. At least people said so, though privately she thought her looks were no more than passable. On her driver's license they read like a remarkably average description: hair, brown; eyes, brown; height, 5' 5"; weight, 110; birth date, April 10, 1938. The motor-vehicle statistics did not detail her flawless skin, the slim, perfect figure or the alert, interested expression that was so appealing. But Mary could never think of herself as attractive. In her mind, she'd always compare her looks with Patricia's almost theatrical blondness, with her sister's melting blue eyes and striking, five-foot-eight figure.

It was also true, though, that she had a better mind than Patricia, who'd drifted from one stupid little job to the next until she married. Mary's job was exciting, unimportant as it was. She loved the super-charged atmosphere of the radio station's newsroom, the vitality of the men who worked there, the daily challenge of making herself more and more indispensable so that one day she might really get into communications herself. That was her dream. A strange dream for an introverted loner, but one she cherished. Someday she'd like to have her own radio show. She'd be famous and admired and loved. She supposed, deep down,

she did believe in herself, but Patricia didn't understand that she had to prove
it.

"I'm relaxed," she said. "I really am, Pat. I like having my own place. I've
even begun to do a little entertaining."

"Really? Intimate candlelit dinners for two?"

"Not exactly. More like sit-on-the-floor suppers for five or six. Chili and red
wine and candles stuck in Chianti bottles."

"How Bohemian!"

Mary smiled. "At least it proves I'm relaxed."

"How's your love life?"

The question made her uncomfortable. At her sister's age, Patricia had had
more "invitations" than she could accept and Mary was secretly ashamed that
she knew why Pat had been so sought after. She had, to put it mildly, a freewheeling reputation. Damn it, call it what it was: Patricia was always a pushover,
an easy lay. I can't be like that. In 1957 my morals are left over from *Little
Women*. And my date book reflects it.

As though she read Mary's mind, Patricia laughed. "Relaxed, are you? Come
on. You're about as Bohemian as Elsie Dinsmore! I'll bet you're still a virgin!"

"None of your damned business!" But a blush confirmed it. "Anyway, what
if I am? Does that make me some kind of a freak?"

"Not a freak. But possibly an oddity." Patricia picked up little Jayne and
held the baby close. "Look at your Aunt Mary, sweetheart. She may be the
only chaste woman of nineteen you'll ever see."

Walking home from the Richton apartment, Mary was furious. What was so
terrible about not falling into bed with every man who asked you? Why did she
feel embarrassed about having no "love life" as Patricia called it? Pat should
be glad her sister had a sense of discrimination, an unwillingness to experiment
until she felt love. She had no right to criticize Mary for decent behavior.
Particularly when that behavior was the result of watching her sister's flagrant
sexuality. And where had Pat's behavior gotten her? Into marriage to a man she
didn't care any more for than a dozen others. Into unplanned motherhood. Into
a dull little apartment and a stagnant life. She's dumb, Mary thought. No matter
how beautiful she is, she's stupid and out of control of her destiny.

It was then she decided she'd never be out of control of hers.

A light touch on her shoulder brought her back to the present. Jayne, a twenty-
one-year-old reproduction of her mother, was standing beside her on the deck,
smiling quizzically.

"What are you doing up here, Aunt Mary? It's freezing!"

"I was just about to come to the cabin. Thought I'd let you get settled before
I unpacked. There's hardly room enough for both of us to be flinging things
around at the same time."

"It is a little small for two, but when you consider that it's free . . ."

". . . it's practically palatial," Mary finished for her. "You're right, darling.
I shouldn't complain. I still can't believe people really win things like this as
door prizes at charity balls. Especially me. I've never won anything before in
my life!"

"Well, you sure got off to a good start. Sixty-nine days in the South Pacific. Tahiti, Tonga, Australia, New Zealand, Hong Kong, Japan, even Red China! I can't believe it myself! And I do feel a little guilty. You should have taken Uncle Mike instead of me. A second honeymoon. I'm surprised he isn't furious."

"He couldn't make it, Jaynie. I told you. He's on the verge of a big deal." One more little lie. What did it matter? Anyway, it was only a half lie. Michael really believed he was going to get the great job he always said was just around the corner. There'd been so many of those corners in the past fifteen years. Mary no longer believed in them, but he still did. At least he said he did. The truth was, she hadn't asked him to come along. She had to get away from him, to put the perspective of time and distance between them and their marriage. It had been Fate, that insane business of winning a trip for two. It was her chance to think things through, as calmly and dispassionately as possible, without the silent reproach of his presence.

He had no idea what was in her mind. He'd been happy about her good fortune, delighted that she'd sent for her only niece from New York to share the trip with her. If he was hurt, or surprised that she didn't invite him, he covered those emotions with the quick response that he "couldn't leave just now because something big is on the fire."

"Have a good time, baby," he'd said as he left the ship. "I'll be counting the days until you come home."

"Are you sure you'll be all right?" The question was involuntary, an automatic reaction, as though he couldn't get along without her. Long-standing habits are hard to break.

"Don't worry. I'll be fine. Lonesome but fine. And I'll cable you the minute the new job's sewed up."

"Yes. Do that."

Damn him, Mary thought now. Why was he always so generous, so infuriatingly unselfish? Another man would have insisted on coming along, or demanded she stay home if he couldn't go. But not Michael. Never Michael. If just once he'd put his foot down, "put her in her place" as her father would have said. If only he would assert himself.

"Coming, Aunt Mary? They've sounded the first call for lunch."

She nodded. "I'm on my way."

The phrase struck her as bitterly ironic. She really was on her way, in quite a different sense.

Chapter 2

CABIN 320 ON the port side of Adriatic Deck was far from the plushest of accommodations on H.M.S. *Prince of Wales* but, small though it was, it was compactly designed and scrupulously clean. Still, one bed under the portholes and another near the bath, a small dressing table, plus two chairs and a coffee table left very little "walking-around space," and Mary looked with dismay at the three small closets and six less than capacious drawers in the dresser.

"Good Lord! How are the two of us going to manage in here for two months? There's hardly enough room for one person's clothes!"

Jayne had the flexibility of the young. "Not to worry. I'll take one of the bigger closets and you can have the other, plus that teeny one in the corner. And I only need a couple of dresser drawers. I've already met our stewardess and found out the suitcases go under the beds and our life jackets are in that counter thing over there and there's an ice bucket and glasses hidden in . . ."

"Whoa!" Mary clapped her hands over her ears. "I can't stand such efficiency! You've probably already learned your way around the whole ship."

"Far from it. It's enormous. But I have been studying the floor plan—or is it deck plan?—in this brochure. Look." Jayne thrust a small pamphlet under her aunt's nose. "We're here, on Adriatic. The hospital and theater are on this same deck."

"Nice." Mary's tone was ironic. "We can be entertained and seasick without having to take the elevator."

Her niece grinned. " 'Lift,' please. Not 'elevator.' And is that any kind of attitude for a woman on a pleasure cruise?"

"Sorry. I guess I'm just a little apprehensive. I've never been on a ship before, and my maiden voyage is ambitious, to say the least."

"It's okay." Jayne sounded like the older of the two. "I know how you must feel, particularly leaving Uncle Mike for so long. You miss him already, don't you?"

Mary was evasive. "It's our longest separation in fifteen years."

"You're not sorry?"

"No. Honestly. Married people should get away from each other now and then." She stopped before she revealed too much. "Show me more about the ship."

"Okay. The deck above us is Caribbean. Then comes Indian Deck where the reception desk is, plus the shops and beauty salon. Moving right along, we ascend to Dominion Deck where we find the Westminster Dining Room and the London Lounge with bingo in the afternoon and entertainment in the evening. Behind that is the swimming pool and sun deck."

Mary was suddenly absorbed in the ship's layout. "I see. And one flight up is the Promenade Deck with the British Bar and the Soho Club—whatever they are—plus the library and writing room. Above that is the Bridge Deck where the captain hangs out."

"Right. And on the very top is the sports deck and the Trafalgar Room, a kind of observation bar where they serve midnight supper."

"It'll take us sixty-nine days to find our way around." Mary studied the plan again. "Also looks like a very liquid cruise. Let's see. I count three bars plus whatever drinking one does in the dining room and the London Lounge."

"Well, there are nearly five hundred passengers on this little twenty-two-thousand-ton dinghy."

Mary frowned. "And I'm afraid ninety per cent of them will be over sixty-five. Anyone with enough time and money for a cruise like this has to be rich and retired. I hope you won't be bored, Jaynie. It'll be terrible if there aren't any young people. It doesn't matter to me. I'm just here for the sight-seeing and the chance to unwind, but you might get terribly restless with no one your own age around.''

"Come on. You're my age. I mean, what's seventeen years difference, especially with somebody like you?''

"Almost eighteen,'' Mary said. But she felt ridiculously pleased. She adored this child. No, not child; young woman. Jayne was an adult, even though she could be her daughter. At such moments, Mary regretted not having children of her own. Perhaps if I'd had babies, she thought, things might be different with Michael and me. But I didn't dare. I was afraid to put such responsibilities in his hands. I never really had enough faith in him to think he could provide for a family if I stopped working. Even in the beginning I knew I'd have to take on the job of seeing that we had a good life. Wait. Did I *have* to? Or did I *want* to?

She was aware that Jayne was rattling on. "Anyway, I'm sure the ship's officers are bound to be attractive. And there's a whole group of entertainers—singers, dancers, impressionists. I won't be bored, Aunt Mary. It's the most exciting experience of my life and I have you to thank for it.''

"Me and that lovely old dowager who drew my number out of the lottery box.''

Jayne bowed her head in mock solemnity. "Bless her ample bosom, wherever she is.''

They began to giggle like schoolgirls.

"And bless your mother for letting you come with me.''

"And Daddy for ponying up for a bunch of new clothes!''

"And Charlie Burke for giving me a leave of absence from the station as long as I promise to tape one interview a week while I'm gone.''

Mary stopped laughing. Charlie Burke was not only her boss, he was also in love with her. There'd been nothing between them, nothing physical, not even a declaration on his part, but they both knew how he felt about her. Charlie was the only one who knew she wasn't happy with Michael. They had a drink sometimes after work and Charlie had a way of getting her to say things she could say to no one else. Perhaps she felt a closeness to him because he, too, was trapped in a marriage from which his conscience would not let him escape. Tracey Burke was an alcoholic. Had been for years. His friends urged him to divorce her, but Charlie couldn't. "What would happen to her, Mary? I'm all she has. If I left her, it would be like abandoning a child. Tracey needs me. God knows I'd like to be free, but I can't be that inhumane.''

"You have your life to consider, too, Charlie. Years of it.''

He'd looked at her knowingly. "So have you. How much does an individual owe himself, at the expense of someone else?''

She hadn't answered. It was a question she asked herself over and over again, never finding an answer she could live with. Sometimes she thought that if she ever left Michael there could be a future with Charlie. He was her kind of man: strong, successful, secure enough to handle a wife with a career of her own and still be "head of the house.'' He was all the things she thought she wanted in a husband, and perhaps if she made the first move . . . No. Charlie wouldn't leave his wife. She wasn't sure she could live with his guilt if he did. Nor with her own. He'd have an affair with her, gladly. Maybe one that would be as firm and long lasting as a marriage. But that wasn't what she wanted. What she wanted was impossible. What she wanted was a strong Michael. And those two words were contradictory. She pulled away from her thoughts. Plenty of time for them in the days and nights ahead.

"Hey, I'm sorry," she said. "I got lost there for a minute, trying to figure out a dozen interviews! Come on, Jaynie love, let's go to lunch and see whom we drew for tablemates."

Mary felt a momentary letdown when she and Jayne entered the Westminster Dining Room. It was big but surprisingly severe despite its beautifully set tables with fresh flowers, its wide windows with a view of the sea and its seemingly endless array of captains and waiters hovering solicitously around the diners. She'd expected something like the pictures she'd seen of the dining salon of the old *Queen Mary* or the *France* with its curving staircase down which elaborately gowned women made their entrances. She'd imagined great opulence and, again, as in their cabin, she'd found tasteful simplicity but no lush elegance.

She introduced herself to the maître d', who responded enthusiastically.

"Mrs. Morgan! Delighted to have you and your niece aboard. We have you at the purser's table. Mr. Telling's. I'm sure you'll be quite happy there."

Jayne whispered to her aunt as they followed the man. "Purser's table. That's a good sign. All the snappiest people are put at officers' tables and the purser's is super. He gives a lot of parties."

"How do you know?" Mary hissed back.

"I read it in the New York *Times*."

They were the last to arrive. Five other people already were halfway through their lunch. The maître d' made the introductions. "Mrs. Morgan, Miss Richton, this is Mrs. DeVries and Mrs. Lawrence, Colonel Stanford, Mr. Spalding and Mr. Andrews. I'm sorry Mr. Telling will not join you for luncheon. He's very busy at sailing time but he'll be down for dinner. Enjoy your meal."

They took their places, murmuring acknowledgments of the introductions and apologies for their tardiness. Mary found a vacant chair on her right. Obviously she was on the left of the absent Mr. Telling. On his right was Mrs. Lawrence, an attractive woman in her fifties who leaned over and struck up a conversation.

"You'll like George Telling," she said. "Charming young man. This is the third voyage I've made with him."

"Oh?" Mary did not conceal her surprise. "You've made this trip three times, Mrs. Lawrence?"

"Please call me Peggy. My dear, I've made this trip *five* times. In all, I've done twenty-five cruises on this ship. I'm aboard eight months of the year, and have been for the past three years. So if there's anything you want to know, don't hesitate to ask me."

"Thank you, I shall. It's my first cruise and I feel literally at sea." Mary tried to hide her curiosity. Eight months of the year on this ship? Incredible! She wondered who Mrs. Lawrence was. Rich, obviously. Idle, undoubtedly. Probably bored with some empty life at home. "Where are you from, Mrs. . . . uh, Peggy?"

"Chicago. Lovely city but lonely for a widow. My husband died three and a half years ago. And you?"

"I live in San Francisco now. I was raised in New York."

Gail DeVries, a plump, white-haired, smiling woman in her seventies, spoke up. "I know who you are, Mrs. Morgan. You're Mary Farr Morgan. The lady who has that marvelous radio show. I never miss it. I'm really delighted to meet you." She turned to the man between her and Mary. "Maybe you don't know that Mrs. Morgan is a celebrity, Mr. Andrews, but in our town she is. Why, she's as famous in San Francisco as Barbara Walters is across the country!"

Mary smiled. "Hardly, I'm afraid. I just do a local half-hour interview program."

Christopher Andrews had a clipped, public school English accent. "I'm sure you do it very well, Mrs. Morgan. I admire successful women. They have to work so much harder for recognition, even in your country."

Across the table, Colonel Stanford snorted. "No offense, ma'am, but I can't agree. This woman's thing is getting out of hand. Not because I'm a Southerner, but I like a woman to be soft and dependent. Appears to me they're mighty aggressive these days."

Jayne, sitting next to him, turned on her most brilliant smile. "Why, Colonel, I can't believe you're a male chauvinist! You're much too attractive."

The elderly man smiled. "You a Southern girl?"

"No. I live in New York."

"Well, you got the winning ways of a Southern girl. Bet you'll have that young man next to you wound around your finger before we get to Tahiti."

All eyes went to Terry Spalding on Jayne's right and a little ripple of indulgent laughter for the colonel's tactlessness spread around the table. Only Terry looked uncomfortable, fiddling with the heavy gold bracelet on his wrist.

"Don't worry, Mr. Spalding," Jayne said lightly, "I promise not to pursue you."

"I'm not worried, Miss Richton. It would be a pleasure."

Like hell it would, Mary thought. Just our luck. A young, handsome man at the table and even a blind woman could tell he's gay. Really, the colonel was too much! He probably had no contact with men like Terry Spalding, but everyone else must realize. She caught Jayne's eye and the girl gave her a half smile as though to say, I know. Ain't it a shame?

"Don't let it trouble you," the voice beside her said quietly. "Your niece will find plenty of company on the trip."

Her smile thanked him. "I do want her to have a good time. Young people should find every day exciting."

"Only young people?"

She turned and looked squarely at him for the first time. Andrews was an attractive man. About fifty, she guessed. Not handsome, as Michael was, nor intense in the way of Charlie Burke. His features were irregular, the nose a little too short and the jaw a bit too square. It was hard to tell while he was seated, but Mary thought he was probably no more than medium height, almost stocky, though one could see he was more muscular than fat. Funny, his rugged looks were somehow at odds with his cultured voice. It was an intriguing combination.

"You're English, I gather, Mr. Andrews."

"Australian, actually. And the name is Christopher."

"Australian? I thought they spoke with a different accent. I mean . . ." She stopped, feeling gauche.

"You thought Australians spoke a crude language all their own. Well, many of them do, in a way. The workingman's lingo is practically undecipherable to Americans. I was born in Sydney, but I went to school in England and I spend half the year traveling on business."

"What do you do?"

"I'm in antiques." The expression on her face amused him. He lowered his voice. "Don't worry. Terry Spalding and I are cut from different cloth. I've never worn a gold bracelet in my life."

They exchanged understanding smiles.

"You're aboard for the whole trip?" Christopher asked.

"Yes. You?"

"No. I leave the ship in Sydney. I was in the States on a project and decided to go home the easy way. A little vacation from February tenth to March sixth. Quite a few of us do that. You'll find that about half the ship changes in Australia, people boarding and debarking there. But that's almost a month away. We'll see a great deal of each other before then, I hope."

"That would be very nice," Mary said almost primly. Christopher smiled again and turned to chat with Gail DeVries. Instantly, Peggy Lawrence began to talk with Mary across the purser's vacant chair.

"I hope you and your niece will join us after dinner tonight. The captain and I and a few people always sit at a table in the rear of the London Lounge. Tomorrow he'll have a 'welcome aboard' cocktail party for all the passengers before dinner, but I'd like you to meet him in advance."

"That would be lovely. I suppose you know him very well by now."

Mrs. Lawrence gave a smug little smile. "Yes. Very well. In fact, I always have the suite next to his on Promenade Deck. You must come to some of our cocktail parties. Just a few of the officers and some select people." She lowered her voice even more. "Not all of them at this table, I might add. But Tony . . . I mean Captain Robin . . . will like you, as I do. In fact, Mary, I do hope we'll spend a lot of time together."

It took a minute for Mary to realize what was going on. Peggy Lawrence obviously was more than a friend of the captain's. Of course. That explained her constant presence on the ship, her proprietary air about the vessel and its master. Good Lord, what a life, following a sea captain around the world! Mary wondered whether Captain Robin was married. Could be. Poor Peggy. What a wasted existence. She seemed nice enough, but Mary had a sudden, uneasy feeling that Mrs. Lawrence would swallow her up if she wasn't careful. It could turn out to be difficult if she were trapped with this woman day and night for more than two months. She's the kind who'll confide all her troubles, Mary thought. I don't need that. I have enough of my own.

Unexpectedly, she realized she'd much prefer to spend the next few weeks in the company of Christopher Andrews. There was something about him that she found enormously attractive. In the next breath she was appalled by her thoughts. She hadn't come on this cruise looking for romance. Anything but.

What on earth was she thinking of? Besides, for all she knew, Christopher Andrews had a wife and six children in Australia. And, she reminded herself, I have a husband at home. It might be a good, safe thing if she allowed Peggy Lawrence to take over her life. At least it would keep her from some foolish, reckless act. Come on, Mary, she said silently, get yourself together. You've been aboard two hours and you're imagining all kinds of crazy things including a shipboard flirtation with an Australian! What on earth was the matter with her? She'd done one rash, unthinking thing in her life: falling in love with Michael. And it had led her to this state of desperate confusion. She wasn't about to clutter up her life again with an infatuation. Even though they'd exchanged only a few brief sentences, she had a sinking feeling that in her present state of mind she could fall all too easily into the arms of Christopher Andrews.

Deliberately, she turned her attention to the portly old gentleman across the table.

"Tell me, Colonel Stanford, what part of the South are you from?"

"Atlanta, Miz Morgan. Gateway to the South. Beautiful city. You ever been there?"

"No. I've always wanted to go. I hear it's charming. Have you lived there all your life?"

"Yes, ma'am. All seventy-nine years of it." He launched into an account of the city and the life there. A good life. A gracious life. Mary listened with genuine interest to his amusing anecdotes, told with old-fashioned charm. He'll be my first taped interview, she decided: a man who's lived long and well and is still actively enjoying life. My listeners will enjoy and identify with that. And it's the kind of thing Charlie likes.

"You travel a great deal, I take it," Mary said when she could get a word in.

"One cruise a year for the last eight years. My children and grandchildren think I'm crazy. Think I'm going to die aboard someday. I told 'em, fine if I do. I'm enjoying my money now, so they needn't count on inheriting from me. And it would save a lot of fuss and nonsense if I was buried at sea. Gail would take care of it."

"Gail?"

"Miz DeVries there, talking to young Andrews. She and I are friends. Met on a North Cape cruise eight years ago. Decided we'd get together once a year and go on a trip somewhere." The colonel's eyes twinkled. "No hanky-panky, you understand. We just enjoy each other's company."

Mary laughed with delight as did Jayne, who'd been listening intently. Peggy Lawrence raised her eyebrows to indicate she thought the colonel was a silly old fool. Mary found him warm and funny, a character made to order.

"Colonel, would you tape a radio interview with me? It was a condition of my leave of absence that I bring back tapes of fascinating people I meet on the trip, and I think you're completely captivating." She smiled and added, "Even if you don't have much use for working women."

"Me on the radio? Well, now, Miz Morgan, I'd consider that an honor. I surely would. Your place or mine?"

The whole table, which had suddenly stopped talking, burst into affectionate laughter. All except Peggy Lawrence, who smiled stiffly and excused herself.

"Seems like Miz Lawrence isn't too happy with me," the old man said.

"Pay her no mind, Beau," Gail DeVries said. "We've sailed with her often enough to know how she is."

"Beau?" Jayne repeated. "Is that your first name, Colonel?"

"Sure is. Beauregarde Calhoun Stanford. Retired Colonel, U.S.A. Ain't that a mouthful?"

"I love it," Jayne said. "In fact, I think I'm in love with you."

The colonel patted her hand. "You know what, little lady? You wouldn't be the first."

"Nor, I daresay, the last," Mary said. She felt relaxed and happy. Contemplating an interview always did that for her. When everything else seemed complex and confusing, the professional in her took over. She couldn't wait to do her first tape of the trip. And she'd find eleven more personalities just as delightful. It was a relief to know she could justify her long absence from the station by bringing back some top-notch material. For a moment she forgot about the real purpose of the cruise. For the first time in days, her thoughts were not with Michael.

Chapter 3

MICHAEL SEATED HIMSELF at the typewriter in Mary's "office" and rolled a thin sheet of airmail paper into the machine. It was strange to be sitting at her desk in the small room of the high-rise apartment on Taylor Street. He was used to seeing his wife in this chair, absorbed in preparing the weekly interviews for her radio show. Gently, almost reverently, he touched the things she dealt with: the silver stamp box, the letter opener with her initials, the old china cup he'd found in a junk shop, a cup that said "Love the Giver." It was crammed full of pens and pencils and Michael absently fingered them, thinking how often he'd watched her automatically reach into that container. She probably no longer saw the words inscribed on it. He forced himself to consider that perhaps they were no longer true for her. Not that anything had been said. Not that either of them was willing to admit the strain between them. But Michael knew. He sensed her discontent in the overly considerate way she treated him, as though her restlessness made her guilty. And he knew she was only a dutiful wife in bed, not an eager one. It was the kind of thing men knew, even when women tried to fool them. He'd failed her. He'd lied to her from the start and he lied every day, pretending it was just a matter of time before he became the success she wanted him to be.

He swiveled around in the desk chair and looked out of the window. From this vantage point he could see much of San Francisco. It was an exciting view, but it reproached him. He had no right to be enjoying such comfortable living when he contributed virtually nothing to it. So what else is new? he asked himself. You never have contributed to any of the women who've taken care of you. Not to your mother, the widow who struggled to put you through school. Not to your first wife, who gave up on you when you were twenty-eight and still "trying to find yourself." And not to Mary, who married you two years later, believing you were what you were not.

Fifteen years of marriage to Mary. Fifteen years of unimportant jobs easily obtained and quickly lost or more quickly left because they didn't offer enough of a future. Who the hell was he kidding? He'd always had enough looks and charm to get himself into an organization, but not enough guts to stay with anything for the long, slow climb upward. Damn you and your stupid vanity, Michael Morgan. Nothing's ever good enough for you. Nothing is "worthy of your talents." What talents, for God's sake? Why don't you admit that at forty-five you're never going to be anything but a loser?

Because I don't believe it, he answered himself. Even at my age, there must be someone smart enough to recognize my capabilities. I've been an insurance salesman, a junior account man in an advertising agency, an assistant buyer in a department store, a dozen other things, not necessarily in that order. But it all adds up to experience. All I need is the right chance in the right place. Maybe Harry Carson will be the answer. If he really will back me in that men's boutique, I know I can make a success of it. I love good clothes and I know about buying and promoting. All I need is the money.

As always, optimism returned. This time, things would be different. He'd be in his own business, not subject to the petty demands of a stupid employer who had no vision. This time he'd succeed and Mary would be happy, as she'd been in the early years of their marriage.

Smiling to himself, confident once more, he lit a cigarette and consulted her travel schedule. She'd been gone three days. Probably too late for mail to catch her in Tahiti, and the ship's brochure suggested that no mail be sent to the exotic port of Nuku Alofa in Tonga. (Small wonder. They probably had no post office.) He'd write to her in Auckland, New Zealand. By the time she heard, she'd have been gone eighteen days. He hoped she'd miss him on every one of them. Using two fingers, the old hunt-and-peck system, he began:

Sunday, Feb.13, 1977

Darling,

Sitting in your chair, at your typewriter, makes me feel closer to you, even though you're so many miles away. I try to imagine you on your way to Tahiti, to Papeete and Moorea and Tonga . . . those exotically named islands of sunshine and smiling natives. Tell me every detail about them. Do you feel like Mary Martin in *South Pacific?* Don't meet a handsome French planter and never return to me!

A lot of exciting things are going on in our home town this week, but I'm planning nothing much. If you were here, maybe we'd go to see Eva Le Gallienne in *The Royal Family* at the Curran. Or trot down to the U.S.F. gym to watch Charlton Heston and Lloyd Bridges and Rob Reiner and James Franciscus play celebrity tennis for the Muscular Dystrophy Benefit today. If you'd been here, I'd even have let you drag me to the symphony last night to hear Sarah Caldwell conduct during Women in Music Week! (That shows how much I miss you!)

I've been pretty much in the house since you left. Not that people haven't been kind about inviting this lonely soul to dinner. I just haven't felt like going. I did break down and say I'd go to Rae's for supper tonight. She's having a few people for a "pre-valentine buffet" and I agreed to come, even though my heart is on the high seas.

Mostly, I'm getting facts and figures together for my meeting with Harry Carson on the 25th. He seems very high on the idea of backing me in the boutique and I've even been scouting possible locations. Seems to me that Sutter Street would be the best if we can find the space there. Of course, there are three or four other men's clothing stores there, but mine would be completely different, much more inventive, if Harry goes along with my ideas, as, of course, he must if we're to succeed.

Charlie Burke called yesterday and said to give you his love when I wrote, and to tell you that things are okay at the station and they'll be filling in with the interviews you taped before you left. I called Patricia and told her you and Jayne got off safely on Thursday and that the ship looked wonderful.

But not as wonderful as you, my darling. And not as wonderful as you'll look when you come sailing back to me.

All my love,
Michael

He reread the letter. It was no literary masterpiece, but he was no writer. As in all things, he'd done the best he could.

On the day before they were to arrive in Tahiti, Mary realized how quickly she'd become accustomed to this strange new life at sea. The past eight days had given her a chance to learn her way around the ship and to settle into the easy routine. It wasn't difficult to see why people became infatuated with cruising. It was the most pampered, trouble-free (face it), mindless way to spend the long days and nights.

On the pillow at bedtime was the program for the next day, every hour charted if one chose to follow the schedule. There were deck games and exercise groups and dance classes in the morning. Bridge lessons and movies and bingo in the afternoon. Cocktails and elaborate entertainment after dinner, and late-night entertainment and dancing until all hours in the Soho Club, which turned out to be the ship's cabaret. One could swim or sun or read in a deck chair; play Ping-Pong or shuffleboard; have a massage and sauna, a shampoo and set. One could eat five times a day and order food in the cabin at any hour. And one certainly could drink. The British Bar began serving cocktails at ten o'clock in the morning and not a few people were there waiting when the bar opened. Nothing was left to chance. The daily bulletin even told you how to dress in the evening—casual, informal or formal, depending upon the activities offered.

Almost every evening she found an invitation under her door. At first, they were the formally engraved kind: "Captain Anthony Robin cordially invites you to the Captain's Reception at 6:45 P.M. in the London Lounge." But as she came to know more people, the engraved invitations meant for all passengers gave way to those specially typed on the ship's available invitation cards. People were constantly giving luncheon parties in the card room, tea dances in the Soho, cocktail gatherings in their cabins. The officers invited selected passengers to predinner drinks in their quarters, and she and Christopher quickly became part of the small "in" group asked to lunch or cocktails with the captain, with whom she was now on a "Tony-Mary" basis. At these select occasions in his quarters, Peggy Lawrence was very much the hostess, openly proprietary about the tall gray-haired captain, who was undeniably handsome in his immaculate white uniform with all the gold braid.

It was quickly taken for granted that she and Christopher were a twosome, and with good reason. They spent their days together, swimming and sunning, met for cocktails in the Trafalgar Room before dinner on the rare evening when they were not at a party, danced far into the night at the Soho. Mary knew she shouldn't be spending all her time with him. People probably thought they were sleeping together. They were not, though Christopher made it plain that he hoped they would. So far, she'd been able to lightly turn off his hints, but there was a long way to go before they parted. She also worried that she spent so little time with Jayne and said so one morning after the stewardess brought breakfast to their cabin.

"I feel as though I'm neglecting you, baby. I almost never see you except at breakfast and dinner."

"Neglecting me? Don't be silly. You're living it up, and so am I. That's what a cruise is for, isn't it? To throw your inhibitions into the drink?"

Over her coffee, Mary stared sharply at her niece. Did Jayne also think her aunt was having a shipboard affair? It was true she came back to the cabin very late every night, sometimes after Jayne was in bed. Maybe the girl assumed she was in Christopher's cabin for an hour or two after the last bar closed. She wasn't. Often they left the Soho when the band departed and wandered up to the deserted sun deck. That's where they did their talking. That's where Mary learned her new friend was a widower and quite rich. He told her about his house in Sydney, his two married sons, about his life at home and his travels around the world. And it was here that she told him something of her life in San Francisco with Michael. She did not tell him of her doubts about her marriage, nor confide the ambivalent feelings about her husband. But Christopher was bright. He read between the lines, knew she was in the most vulnerable state of her adult life.

"I didn't think I had too many inhibitions," Mary said now. "But if I have, they're still with me."

Jayne looked amused. "Aunt Mary, I know you're not sleeping with Christopher. Maybe you should. It might be just what you need. *I*'ve been to bed with George Telling."

Mary was genuinely shocked. Not only by the fact that Jayne was having an affair with the young purser but that she could announce it so calmly. She also wondered why she was surprised. Jayne was almost the only young girl aboard. Mary had seen the way the officers looked at her, had been aware of the glances Jayne and Telling exchanged across the dinner table, had seen them wandering off by themselves after dinner. Still, she hadn't really thought . . .

She tried to sound unalarmed, matter-of-fact. "Darling, is that wise? I mean, you've only known him a week. And I don't want to see you getting a reputation as a . . . a . . ."

"The expression is 'crew chaser,' " Jayne said. "I know. We have a couple of them aboard. That pathetic middle-aged woman who carries the crossword-puzzle book around with her and is always asking the officers to help her with the difficult words. And your good friend Peggy. In a way she's a crew chaser, too. Even if it's the captain.''

"Peggy's a mature woman. And Tony's a grown-up man. They have a long-standing relationship, Jayne. In fact, they hope to marry.''

"*She* hopes to marry is more like it. George says Tony has been a bachelor too long. He's not going to give up this little dictatorship for a house in the Chicago suburbs where he'd live off Peggy's money and die of boredom at the country club.''

Mary wanted to tell her that it wouldn't be that way, according to Peggy, but the trend of this conversation was getting off the subject. "I'm not concerned with Peggy and Tony,'' she said. "I'm concerned with you. After all, your mother left you in my charge. I'd feel responsible if you got into trouble.''

Jayne finished off her scrambled eggs. "Dear heart, I'm not going to get in trouble. You didn't really think at twenty-one with four years of college behind me I was an innocent child, did you? I know what I'm doing. And I recognize a shipboard romance when I see one. Tomorrow or sixty days from now George Telling and I will kiss each other good-bye and go our own ways. And we'll have had a helluva good time. Believe me, Aunt Mary, I know what I'm doing.'' She paused. "Do you?''

Mary didn't answer.

"You don't have to pretend with me,'' Jayne said gently. "Do you think for one minute I believed Uncle Mike's 'big deal' kept him from coming on this trip? I'll bet a million bucks you never asked him. You wanted to get away from him, didn't you? Good Lord, I can understand that! Fifteen years with the same man and never a night apart! Who wouldn't need a break?'' She hesitated. "It's none of my business, but I wish you'd make it a *real* change. Have an honest-to-God affair. It would do you good. You'd probably be a lot more content with Uncle Mike when you got home.''

"It wouldn't work that way for me,'' Mary said. "I don't think I could ever look him in the eye if I'd been unfaithful.''

"Unfaithful is as much a state of mind as of body. Listen, just wanting to go to bed with Christopher makes you as much of an adultress as actually doing it. And you do want to sleep with him. You have a lousy poker face, Aunt M.''

Mary pushed the tray away angrily. "You're quite mistaken, I have no intention of it. Christopher knows I'm married. Our generation doesn't take sex as lightly as yours. Maybe our emotions don't run any deeper, but our principles might. I don't like what you're doing, Jayne. I can't stop you. I can't become a watchdog. I won't spoil your trip and mine by following you around every minute, but I can't approve of the careless way you give yourself to strangers.''

"*Give myself to strangers!* I don't believe you really said that! It sounds like something out of a nineteenth-century novel. Aunt Mary, you amaze me. I thought you were so with it, so today, and suddenly you've gone all over Victorian on me. I always thought you were the most broad-minded woman I know. I meant it when I said I felt you were my age. I always have.''

Mary's eyes filled with tears. "Until now. That's what you really mean. Oh,

Jaynie, I'm sorry. You have a right to your life. I just don't want to see you turn into a promiscuous, careless young woman.''

''Like my mother.''

The words caught Mary like a stab in her middle.

''I've known for a long time, Aunt Mary. About Mother and Daddy having to get married.''

''You've known? How could you know?''

''Mother told me once when she was furious with me about something. I was about fourteen, I think. I remember her saying, 'If it hadn't been for you, I'd never have landed in this stupid marriage with your idiotic father. If I hadn't gotten pregnant I'd have had a glamorous life.' Words to that effect. Enough to let me know I wasn't exactly a planned-for child.''

''My God! That's monstrous! How could Patricia do such a thing to you?''

Jayne shrugged her shoulders. ''No matter. I brooded for a while but I got over it. The puint is, I'm not stupid the way Mother was. Or still is. I'm not likely to get pregnant and if, God forbid, I did, I'd know what to do about it. She probably 'slept around' to be popular. I don't 'sleep around' in that sense, but I'm sensible enough to gratify my urges when I want to. Just as men do. A double standard doesn't make sense to my generation.''

''Does fidelity make sense?'' Mary's question came slowly.

''If it makes you happy, yes. If it doesn't, it's hypocritical.''

''As simple as that.''

''Yes, darling aunt, as simple as that.''

Mary thought of that revealing conversation as she lay in a deck chair sunning herself after a morning swim. Tomorrow they'd be in Tahiti. Christopher knew the island well and promised to take her sight-seeing. Jayne already had plans for the day and Mary refused to think what they were. From the chair next to her, Christopher reached over and took her hand.

''If you weren't wearing those sunglasses, I probably could tell what you're thinking. Big thoughts?''

Mary smiled. ''Fairly sizable but not awfully important.''

''Such as?''

''Such as how content I am. How wonderfully removed from everything. How much I'm looking forward to seeing the place Gauguin loved.''

''I'm afraid you'll find it changed. Gauguin would.''

''Everything changes.''

''Yes,'' Christopher said. ''Everything and nothing.''

Mary didn't answer. Instead, she sat up, pushed her glasses on top of her head and looked at the island of Moorea, which was clearly visible from the ship. They lay at anchor for the day in Cook's Bay, but Christopher had decided that they'd not go ashore.

''It's a waste of time,'' he'd said over late-night drinks. ''Absolutely nothing there except the Bali Hai Hotel, which was started by three of your enterprising young business executives who went looking for a better life.''

''Americans?''

He nodded. ''Your twentieth-century explorers. Made a good thing of it, too.

It's a lovely spot, but it's off-limits to cruise passengers unless you're on one of the ship tours, and God knows you want to avoid *those* organized expeditions!''

Mary had looked wistful. ''I may have to join them, just the same, after you leave the ship in Sydney. I can't go sight-seeing on my own. Not even with Jayne. You're going to spoil me with personalized tours of Tahiti and Tonga. Not to mention New Zealand and Australia. What will I do when you go?''

''Maybe I won't go.''

Sitting at the little table in the Soho, she'd stared at him in the half darkness. ''Not go?'' she repeated. ''But of course you will. That's home.''

''Well, I had this idea that I'd check out things at the office and if there's nothing crucial I might stay on the ship a while longer. I've already inquired, and I can keep my cabin until we get to Yokohama.''

Mary felt a surge of excitement. ''Really? You mean we could see all the other places together? Oh, Christopher, how marvelous!'' She stopped. ''But I don't want you to change your plans for me. You've seen this part of the world many times. Even Red China. You've already managed to get in there.''

''But not with you. I've never seen any of it with someone I care about.''

They were coming dangerously close to a subject she was afraid to face. The thoughts she'd had the first time they met came flooding back: I mustn't let myself get involved with anyone. Being attracted to another man will distort my thinking about Michael. Yet the chemistry between her and Christopher was irresistible. Unwillingly, she kept comparing his confident, masterful ways with Michael's docile temperament, finding that she loved having her life ordered for her, feeling more feminine than she ever had.

''I don't want to be selfish,'' she'd said last night.

''Why not? I am.''

This morning, looking at the craggy peaks of the French Polynesian island, she wondered whether Christopher would stay on the ship and knew she wanted him to. Wanted it very much.

February 26, 1977

Dearest Michael,

So far, it's been an interesting trip. The ship is full of characters and though most of them are on the geriatric side (one of my tablemates calls this the Three C's Cruise—canes, crutches and cardiac cases) there are some pleasant people aboard and Jayne is managing to have fun. So am I. You know how much I've always wanted to see this part of the world and it's almost living up to my expectations. I didn't leave the ship at Moorea, but had a pleasant day in Papeete, though Gauguin would never know it now! I drove miles around this lush, killingly hot island, stopping occasionally for a cold beer and lunch at the Hotel Tahara in Arue. Frankly, it was touristy, with Astroturf at the swimming pool and a quartet of elderly native musicians, old men and women with phony, toothless grins and greedy eyes. I must admit my high-flown dreams of Tahiti are now deflated. It's a plastic island, overpriced, overpopulated, and, for my money, overrated. Nonetheless, I can say I've seen it.

More to my liking, peculiarly enough, was Tonga, even though the heat was even more oppressive and the poverty sickening. Still the people seemed more friendly, standing by the roadside, shaded by their parasols, waving as I drove by. I was fascinated by the birds they call "flying foxes" which hang from the trees like yards of black crepe. (On the rare occasions when a white one appears it's supposed to mean a royal death. One came two weeks before the last queen, Salote Tupou III, died. Spooky, I call it.)

There is nothing to buy on these islands. They sell shell necklaces, wicker baskets, bad carvings and tacky cotton dresses. The same ones in every market, so they must have a production line somewhere! Probably suffering sunstroke, I bought two dreadful "at home" costumes off the fence near the pier. Eight dollars apiece and at whose home I'd ever wear them, I cannot possibly imagine!

In two days I shall be able to post this in New Zealand where we will arrive on what will be, to me, the 28th. I'm not sure what that is in San Francisco as we lost a day when we crossed the dateline. (They promise to give it back on the return trip.) The ship's newspaper coyly headlined the event with the words "February 24 canceled due to lack of interest."

I taped my first interview with a delicious old colonel who sits at my table in the dining room, another with a priest on Tonga. I'll mail them to Charlie when we reach Sydney.

Hope your meeting went well and that everyone is taking care of you for me. Jayne sends love, and so, of course, do I.

Mary

She frowned as she addressed and sealed the letter. It would not be what Michael hoped for, but she couldn't bring herself to say she missed him or wished he were there. It was as impersonal as a letter to a friend, a travelogue which said little more than that she was alive and well. Worse, it was a lie. For by implication she'd said she was alone on her sight-seeing expeditions. I've never lied to him before, Mary thought, but this time I have no choice. What was that old Irish saying? Something about "Words spoken you are a slave to; those not said you are the master of." At least hers was a lie of omission. Not like those unforgettable ones Michael had told her over the years. She remembered them all. They began the day they met.

Chapter 4

MARY MET MICHAEL MORGAN two weeks after she arrived in San Francisco in June 1961. She was two months past her twenty-third birthday, uneasy about being a continent away from everyone she knew, terrified of the long chance she was taking by accepting the job at the San Francisco radio station and thrilled by the prospect of turning it into something nearer her ultimate goal.

The station was a network affiliate of the one in New York where she'd worked for five years, climbing from her first job as a girl Friday in the newsroom to executive secretary to the station manager. It was in this latter spot, a highly responsible one, that she met Charlie Burke, an old friend of her boss. Charlie came to New York every couple of months on business and he and Mary had fallen into the habit of having dinner together on the evenings he was free. They liked and respected each other. Theirs was a no-nonsense relationship. He told her frankly about his wife's drinking problem but he did not suggest that Mary might help him forget his troubles. Perhaps, she thought later, Charlie knew even then what a little Puritan I was.

For her part, Mary talked more freely than she ever had to anyone. She told him about the still-idolized brother, dead these fourteen years, about her parents, her married sister and the niece she adored.

"You'll marry and have your own kids," Charlie had said.

"I guess so. But first I'd like to see what I can accomplish on my own."

"A career woman instead of a wife? That's your choice?"

"I don't see why it has to be a choice. Lots of women manage both."

"I'm not so sure about that." Charlie was very serious. "It's tough handling two jobs. I know some working wives with real ambition, not women just supplementing the family income. They have a hard time deciding where the priorities are. The only way a career woman can succeed in that kind of double life is either to have a husband who's very secure in his own right or one who doesn't mind being dominated."

Mary had laughed. "That's old-fashioned propaganda. My Lord, Charlie, do you have such a low opinion of women?"

"Not at all. If anything, the low opinion is of men. Most of them think with their egos." He grinned. "Notice I said 'most,' not all. There are a few rare birds who wouldn't feel threatened by a bright wife." The grin faded. "I like to think I'm one of them. You know, Mary, if I were unattached, I'd be the perfect husband for you."

"Well, then, I'll just have to find a second Charlie Burke, won't I? Where might he hang out? In California?"

"More so than in New York, I suspect. This is a competitive city. We're much less nervous in the West."

"Okay. I'll move to San Francisco. Find me a job and I'll find the unthreatenable husband."

"Do you mean that?"

She was taken aback. She'd been rattling on blithely but Charlie apparently was prepared to take her seriously.

"I don't know. I've never really thought about leaving New York."

"Well, think about it. And don't take too much time. The assistant station manager at our place is leaving next month. I think you'd be damned good for the job."

Six weeks later she was in San Francisco and two weeks after that she met Michael. He was twenty-nine, separated from his wife, and a charmer. They were introduced at a cocktail party given by one of the girls at the station and the attraction was mutual and instantaneous. He immediately asked her to dinner and she didn't hesitate to accept.

Over coffee they exchanged facts about themselves. He told her he'd been born in Los Angeles, that his widowed mother still lived there and he had no brothers or sisters. He'd gone to U.C.L.A. until the Army grabbed him and shipped him to Korea. When he came home, he married his childhood sweetheart.

"It just didn't work out. We had nothing in common anymore. She's a nice girl. Successful, too. She's a fashion model in L.A. We parted amiably six months ago. I expect she'll get a Mexican divorce when she has time."

"I'm sorry," Mary said.

"Don't be. It wasn't a bad experience for either of us."

Much later she'd learn that was the first lie. A year after she and Michael were married, his mother told her about that first marriage.

"Linda's a nice girl," Mrs. Morgan said. "She really loved Michael, but she couldn't stand his irresponsibility. It made her terribly unhappy that he left everything up to her. She isn't a competent person the way you are, Mary. She didn't know how to handle him. It was a bitter thing, that separation. Linda felt she'd failed miserably. She hadn't, of course. She just wasn't mature enough to understand that some men aren't interested in taking charge. And some women need things demanded of them."

The conversation took place at a strange time in Mary's life, a time when she was beginning to realize that Michael had no compunction about twisting the truth if he thought it made someone happy to do so. She had just learned that he'd lied to her about what he did for a living. She could hardly believe it. During the year of their courtship and the year since their marriage, she thought Michael was a sales executive with United Airlines. That's what he told her when they met and that was the farce he continued until she inadvertently discovered the truth. She'd accepted his explanation of his constant traveling. It made sense that someone in sales would be away three or four days some weeks, talking with travel agents, scouting business in various cities across the country. She hated his being away so much and was surprised that they paid him so little for such an important job. She asked him often why he didn't look for something better, something that would let him be at home every night.

"I'm a good salesman," he'd answered. "It's only a matter of time before I get into top management, honey. I know the pay isn't terrific, but it will be. I'm sorry most of the expenses are on your shoulders, but that won't be forever."

"I don't mind that. It's not important. I just want you to be even more successful, and I hate all the traveling you have to do."

"That's a young executive's life, babe."

She was proud of him and lonely without him and she believed implicitly in him and his future until the devastating day when one of the men at the radio station said casually, "Flew in from Denver last night with your husband, Mary. Helluva nice guy."

"Oh? You and Michael were on the same flight?"

"Sure. That's one of his regular runs, isn't it?"

She didn't understand what he meant, but she pretended to. "Yes, of course. He travels a great deal."

"Most of those guys do." The man laughed. "You've got a wild sense of humor. 'Travels a great deal.' That's a good one. What else does an airline steward do?"

Airline steward! She was stunned, but simply smiled, hoping her surprise didn't show.

On the way to their apartment—it was a smaller one then, a little walk-up just off Powell Street that Mary had found when she first arrived and into which Michael moved six months before they were married—she wondered what he'd say when she told him she'd learned what his real job was. Or maybe he planned to tell her now, on the theory that her co-worker might do so. How had he managed so long not to run into anyone they knew? And why had he lied about his work?

He was waiting for her, arms outstretched, martinis ready and dinner on the stove. She ignored his greeting, dropped her handbag in the bedroom and came back to face him. She went straight to the point.

"Michael, I was talking to Winkie Kaufman at the station today. He says he came in on your flight last night."

"Yes, he did."

She waited but Michael did not go on. His back was to her as he stirred the martinis and poured them into chilled glasses.

"Why, Michael?"

"Why what?"

"Why have you lied about your job? Why did you pretend you were a sales executive? Are you ashamed of what you do?"

He put the glasses down carefully. "No. I thought you might be."

She was aghast. "You thought I'd be ashamed? For God's sake, Michael, what kind of person do you think I am? I wouldn't care if you were a street cleaner! I love you. It doesn't matter to me whether you're a big executive or simply doing an honest job of work. There's nothing wrong with what you do. It's a very responsible job. But it was wrong to lie about it. Wrong and snobbish." She nearly added, "And stupid, too." He must have known that sooner or later he'd be found out. How blind with love she'd been not to have sensed, long ago, that his hours didn't make sense.

He handed her a glass and she accepted it automatically. "I just wanted you to think I was important," he said. "I want you to be proud of me, Mary. I was afraid you'd be embarrassed if you had to say your husband was a flight attendant. I'm not going to be one forever, you know. This was just a way to get my foot in the door. In fact, I'm planning to give it up if I'm not promoted soon. I've stayed with this longer than I have with anything. I'm thirty-one and I know there's something better for me in the field of aviation. I thought it would make you happier if you believed I'd already gotten where I expect to be. I did it for you. That's the God's truth. Your happiness is all I care about."

She didn't know what to say. He should know happiness couldn't be built on deceit. Of all sins, lying was the one she found hardest to forgive. And yet, looking at him, loving him so, her anger disappeared. He was so eager to please her, so anxious to appear larger than life in her eyes. He was like an unhappy little boy who'd lied to his mother rather than risk her disapproval or lose her love.

"Michael, darling, I don't care what you do. Always remember that. Just tell the truth about it. Please."

He knelt and put his head against her breast. "You're so wonderful, Mary. So understanding. I will make good. You'll see. And I won't lie to you again. Not ever. You have my word of honor."

She'd cradled him, saying that was all she wanted, that she loved him more than anything in the world.

That night he made love to her more passionately than ever. And that night, for the first time, even while she responded ecstatically, a small corner of her mind opened itself to a disturbing ray of doubt. She tried to tell it to go away, that he'd seen how silly and superficial it was to lie in order to make himself a big man, that he'd never do it again.

And to her knowledge, he hadn't. In fact, he seemed relieved not to have to pretend, secure in the knowledge that what he did couldn't change her love for him. She refused to think, cynically, that knowing she'd provide for them both made Michael less ambitious, more relaxed about waiting for his "big break."

Slowly, unwillingly, his casual attitude began to annoy her. Wishing she didn't feel that way, she began to resent it when he refused jobs he considered "beneath him" or ones that involved traveling.

"I know you're unhappy when I'm away," he said. "So I wouldn't consider it again."

She said nothing because that's what she had said in the beginning. Like any young bride, she wanted her husband beside her at night. Michael was only giving her what he thought she wanted: his presence. He couldn't see that his idleness had become more distressing to her than his absence. It's my own fault, Mary thought. I nagged him to stay home and now I hate it when I go off to work in the morning and he's still asleep. I hate it when I come home in the evening and find he's done nothing about getting a job.

He had, of course, had many jobs over the years, all of them low-paying and short-term. He'd long since given up even the gesture of offering any contribution to their joint expenses. He really didn't seem to mind being—in that old-fashioned phrase—a "kept man."

Fortunately, or perhaps unfortunately, as his prospects waned, Mary's grew. Five years after she joined the station, Charlie Burke suggested she might try a local show of her own if she was still interested. He knew, from the early days, where her ambitions lay.

"You still want to be on the air?" The question had come casually.

"You know I'd love to, but I might be the biggest flop in the history of broadcasting."

"You might. That's why I think we should test it. Think you could do it in addition to your regular duties for a few weeks? That way we could get an idea whether you'd attract enough sponsors to make it worthwhile for us and you. And if it didn't work, you'd still have your job. I know you need it."

She'd glanced at him sharply. They didn't have their quiet dinners anymore. But even when they talked privately she couldn't tell him about Michael's attitude, wouldn't have humiliated Michael or herself that way. Still, Charlie knew. They had many mutual friends, sometimes went to the same parties, and no matter how important Michael made his current job sound, Charlie was smart enough to know what it really was.

"Thanks, Charlie. Were you thinking of a daily or a weekly?"

"Weekly, probably. We'll hype it and see if it attracts listeners and sponsors."

She'd gone home bubbling with excitement when she told Michael. He'd been as pleased for her as she was for herself.

"That's wonderful, sweetheart! With your personality you can't help but be a smash! Imagine, my wife a big radio star!"

"Well, hardly," she'd laughed. "It's just a trial run. It might not take off at all."

But she'd known it would. She worked hard on her scripts, developed a format that wasn't exactly original, but she gave it a new twist. Instead of the stale "famous people interviews," she went looking for "real people" with lives and problems to which the listeners could relate. The research was time consuming but worth it. She found interesting middle-class housewives who did things outside the home; registered nurses who treated the terminally ill; volunteers who worked with retarded children; teenagers who couldn't get along with their parents. Her genuine interest in people drew out the best in a line of "unfamous" interviewees from divorced fathers who wanted custody of their children to adopted children who sought their mothers. She was ahead of her time in picking topics many people cared about and few radio talk shows selected. There were enough other programs to accommodate visiting actors and actresses, writers pushing their books and politicians wanting their say. She didn't care about those easy choices. She sought out, sometimes with difficulty, people whose lives were intriguing or inspirational and always "just plain human." She worked hard to find them and to make them articulate and involving. And the formula, so basically simple that it escaped other broadcasters, worked. Word-of-mouth about "The Mary Farr Morgan Show" quickly spread and sponsors became interested. Within three months, she was locally famous. It was back-breaking, handling the preparation and not neglecting her duties at the station. She worked late at night at home, preparing her shows, badgered everyone she knew for suggested guests, read every newspaper for human-interest stories she could follow up. She lost ten pounds and gained a confidence she'd never had. In six months she was firmly established and the show became her sole career.

Without being immodest about it, her success did not surprise her. She'd waited years for this chance and she had no intention of failing. She now was a San Francisco celebrity and even something of a national name through newspaper and magazine interviews. She brought a great deal of revenue to the station and her compensation rose accordingly until she was able to rent the big apartment on Taylor Street and have the luxury of a daily cleaning woman. It was not that she became rich or world famous, but she was satisfyingly successful, known and, most important of all to her, loved by thousands of people in and around her adopted city.

But the approval she wanted more than any other still eluded her. She called her parents in New York when Charlie offered her the first chance. Camille answered and listened courteously as Mary almost shyly told her what had happened.

"That's very nice, dear," her mother said.

"Well, of course, it's only a test. I might not be able to make it work."

"But you'll still have your regular job in case it doesn't."

Damn you, Mary thought. Couldn't you at least pretend to have some faith in me? Just once. Just once couldn't you show you care? I know you do. You must. I'm your child. She suppressed a sigh. "How's Daddy?"

"He's fine. Right now he's watching Walter Cronkite. It's seven o'clock here, you know."

"Yes, Mother, I know there's a three-hour time difference."

She waited for Camille to ask about Michael. The Farrs hadn't come to California for Mary's wedding, but she and Michael had made three trips back East. Each time they'd stayed at a hotel and visited with the Farrs in the big old apartment. There would have been plenty of room for them to stay, but the invitation did not come and Mary was too proud to ask. Her mother and father had treated their son-in-law politely, but he was a stranger to them. They did not take easily to strangers.

"Michael's started a new job, by the way. He's working with a brokerage house here."

"I see."

Camille's two-word response spoke volumes. In the past three years Michael had had six jobs, and each time Mary had been foolish enough to call home and tell her parents about them. Each time he took a new position she pretended it was a step upward, but the Farrs were not fooled. They knew a man who changed jobs so often was not to be relied on.

"I'll tell your father your news," Camille said. "I know he'll be happy for you. We really should hang up now, Mary. These calls are very expensive and I hate to see you wasting your money."

Mary smiled bitterly at the other end of the phone. Why couldn't she be soft and loving? Other mothers would be thrilled to have their children call from California.

"It's not that expensive. We can afford it. Tell me, how's Patricia? And Stanley? And how's Jayne? She must be growing like a weed."

"They seem to be all right. Stanley's doing well in the hardware business and little Jayne likes the private school they insist on sending her to. I don't know why the public schools aren't good enough. They were for you and your brother and sister."

"Things have changed, Mother." Impulsively, she added, "New York has changed. Even your neighborhood. Have you and Daddy ever thought of moving here? The weather's so nice in California and living is easier."

"We're too old to be uprooted, Mary."

"That's silly. You're only in your sixties."

"We still like New York. Besides, I wouldn't want to be so far from my only grandchild."

Did she imagine the emphasis on the word "only"? Camille never mentioned it, but her daughter was sure she wondered why Mary and Michael had no children. My God, Mary thought, she makes me feel guilty about everything, including my unwillingness to give birth. I wonder if Patricia feels guilty that she stopped after one? Not likely. Patricia never feels guilty about anything.

"Well, give my love to Daddy."

"I will. Thank you for calling."

The stilted phrase made her angry. She had a thing about it, no matter who said it. It sounded so cold. Like signing a letter "Very truly yours." Formal and disinterested.

"I'll be in touch, Mother. Let you know what's happening."

"Be sure to do that. Good-bye, Mary."

"Good night."

"Good night" indeed, Mary thought as she hung up. Better it *should* be good-bye. They didn't care, these remote parents of hers. Why should *she?* Why was she the one who yearned for family ties? Most children complained of too many of them. She was lucky to have such independent, self-sufficient parents. To have a sister who lived her own life with barely more than an exchange of Christmas and birthday cards. I don't miss any of them, she told herself resolutely. I have my own life, my career, my apartment, a place I've made for myself in this community.

She realized she was thinking "my." Not "our." As though she wasn't half of a couple. A tear slid down her face. This wasn't the way she meant it to be.

But this was the way it was.

Chapter 5

PEGGY LAWRENCE AWAKENED early. For a minute she didn't remember why she felt so unusually happy and then it all came back to her in delicious detail. Last night, Tony had agreed that they'd marry when the ship had a three-day layover in Hong Kong. Almost a third of the passengers would be taking the special tour into China and the ship would be quiet. They'd slip off, have a quiet civil ceremony and honeymoon in one of the most glamorous cities in the world.

She was so excited she had to tell someone. She rolled over and looked at the bedside clock. Seven A.M. In another hour they'd be docking in New Zealand. Maybe Mary would be awake. She and Christopher planned to get an early start so Mary could get in as much sight-seeing as possible before they sailed at midnight. God knows what they wanted to see in Auckland. The Ellerslie Race-course? The War Memorial Museum with all those beat-up Maori relics? Or a look at the city from the top of Mount Eden? She'd never seen any of them. In most ports, she left the ship only long enough to pick up a few trinkets for people back home. Sometimes she didn't disembark at all. It really depended on what Tony wanted to do.

Everything depended on that. For three years she'd chased him shamelessly around the world. She knew what people said about her. The "repeaters," those who'd sailed before on the *Prince of Wales,* knew that the rich and elegant Mrs. Lawrence was hellbent on marrying the captain. They probably laughed at her behind her back, certain she'd never get him, thinking she made a complete ass of herself. She didn't give a damn. Any more than she cared that the crew and the officers were so deferential to her, so scrupulously correct in her presence because they knew that any lapse of conduct would be reported within minutes to "the Old Man." Now they'd see that she was smarter than any of them gave her credit for. Soon she'd be rid of all of them. Tony would take early retirement and live with her in the big house in Highland Park in the summer. They'd winter in her place in Naples, Florida. They'd go to England frequently to see his eighty-five-year-old mother and his brothers and sisters and nieces and nephews. The thought of her wonderful new life was too much to contain. She picked up the phone and dialed 302. A sleepy voice answered.

"Mary?"

"No. Jayne. Who's this?"

"Peggy Lawrence. Is your aunt there?"

Jayne opened one eye and saw Mary at the bathroom mirror putting on her makeup. "Yeah. Hold on a minute." She put her hand over the receiver and called out, "Aunt Mary, it's Mrs. Lawrence calling in the middle of the night."

Mary hurried to the phone, holding her finger in front of her lips. "Hush. She'll hear you."

"No, she won't. Anyway, who cares? Who calls at this hour? Honest to God, she acts like you're her dearest friend."

Mary took the receiver. "Good morning, Peggy. How are you?"

"Absolutely wonderful! I have such news! Can you come up for coffee?"

Mary hesitated. "Well, I don't know. Christopher and I are going ashore early . . ."

"Please, Mary. Just for a few minutes."

"Well, all right. I'll be up in about ten minutes."

Jayne was thoroughly awake now. She propped herself up in bed and pushed the bell for the stewardess. "You want breakfast, Aunt Mary?"

"No thanks, dear, I'll have a bite with Peggy."

"I don't know why you're so nice to that boring woman."

"She isn't boring. Well, maybe a *little*, but I feel sorry for her."

"Sorry! She thinks she's Queen Elizabeth!"

Mary shook her head. "That's a big, brave act. She's a frightened, lonely lady."

"Oh, come on!"

"No, she really is, Jayne. She's one of those women who can't live without a husband. I doubt she's had a happy day since Mr. Lawrence died." Mary finished dressing as she talked. "She's desperate to get married again. She doesn't know how to live alone. And I don't think she has that many friends here at or at home."

"So she picks on you. How can you put up with it?"

"Sweetie, it's temporary. I'll never see her again after this trip. It doesn't kill me to spend a little time with her every day." Not when I have Christopher the rest of the time, she added silently. It's frightening how quickly I've made him part of my life. I mustn't. Even if he doesn't leave the ship at Sydney, I must get used to the idea of never seeing him again after Japan. He's not part of The Decision. I can't let him be. I don't even know that he wants to be. She picked up a sweater and prepared to depart. "You and George have plans for the day?"

"Nope. He has to stay aboard."

"Oh."

"Don't look so conscience-stricken. I'll be okay. In fact, you'll never guess what I'm going to do."

"What?"

"Go sight-seeing with Terry Spalding. He's even more lonely than the lovely Peggy. You know, I think it's a damn shame the way everybody ignores him because he's a little limp in the wrist. He's a sweet boy."

Mary smiled. For all Jayne's assumed sophistication, she was a softie, too. Spending a day with that lonely young man was a nice thing to do. Particularly when Jayne could have gone ashore with one of the other officers or even joined the three or four other young people aboard.

"You're a good kid, Miss Richton."

Jayne waved her off. "Might as well have two patsys in the family. Have a good time with Chris."

"Christopher," Mary corrected. "Never Chris. He hates it."

"Veddy soddy, old girl. Have a good time with Christopher."

I always do, Mary thought as she took the lift to Promenade. I love the way he takes over. I feel womanly when I'm with him. Even that thing with the interview. He respects my work, but to him it's something totally apart from us. She'd wanted to do him as one of her interviews.

"Come on, Christopher. Please do it," she'd begged a few days ago. "You're a wonderful subject and my listeners would be so interested. They're mad for antiques and decorating."

He'd only laughed. "Not a chance, luv. No Colonel Stanford, I."

She'd been defensive. "The colonel is a darling man. He gave me a wonderful interview."

"I couldn't agree more on both counts." Christopher had turned serious. "But that part of your life is your own, Mary. It doesn't involve me in any way whatsoever. I'm interested in the woman, not the radio personality." He'd looked at her steadily. "They are two separate people, aren't they? I mean, one could, if necessary, live without the other?"

If anyone else had asked me that I'd have unhesitatingly said no, she thought. To Michael, or even Charlie, she would have replied that she couldn't be complete without her work; that nothing could take its place. But to Christopher she said nothing. Simply smiled and said lightly, "Well, you're my first turndown. I suppose it had to come sooner or later."

They'd left it at that, Mary remembered, as she tapped lightly at the door of Peggy's suite, but her silence had been disturbingly significant.

Peggy flung open the door and embraced her visitor. "Oh, Mary, thank you for coming up! Come in. Sit down. What can I get you?"

"Just coffee. Maybe a piece of toast. What on earth has happened, Peggy? You look positively radiant."

"I am radiant!" she gave the breakfast order to her stewardess, who hovered in the corridor. Then she closed the door and perched on the sofa next to Mary. "You won't believe it. Tony and I are going to be married in Hong Kong! Isn't that sensational?"

Mary leaned over and kissed her cheek. "I'm delighted for both of you! You'll make him a good wife, Peggy."

"Of course I will. That's all I know how to do—make a man happy. I'm a born wife, Mary. I'm miserable without someone to fuss over. I need to be married. I need to belong to someone. Without a husband, I'm only half alive."

"Yes, I'm sure you are. I couldn't be more pleased for you."

"I knew you'd understand. The others on this ship, well, I know they think I'm pretentious and possessive, but they don't know how lost I feel as a single woman. You realize what an important thing marriage is. You're so much more self-sufficient than I, but even so, you know how secure a wedding ring makes a woman feel."

Mary hesitated. "I'm glad you're going to be married, Peggy, but I think you're secure with Tony as it is. A piece of paper doesn't make that much difference when a relationship is as firm as yours."

"Oh, but it does! It makes all the difference! It's a public declaration that I'm loved and in love."

"And that means so much to you." It was a statement rather than a question.

"Of course. Every real woman feels that way. Even the young ones will learn that sooner or later. From the beginning, men and women were meant to marry, not just couple, like animals. I know that sounds hopelessly outdated. We're all supposed to be individuals these days, with identities of our own. But I never felt that way. Even though I've been sleeping with Tony for years, I never feel right about it. I always feel as though he might leave me."

"And marriage will remove that fear?"

Peggy looked almost apologetic. "Yes. Oh, I know that's silly. Plenty of husbands leave their wives, but that won't happen to us. I loved my first husband and he loved me. When he died, I thought my life was over. I really did. But it isn't. I want to live as I did before, married and happy."

As though one thing guaranteed the other, Mary thought. How amazed this remarkably naïve woman would be if she knew the thoughts that are constantly in my head, the questions and doubts. Right now, I feel that marriage is nothing but a legal burden or, at best, an act of duty. I could belong more to Christopher having an affair with him than I can to Michael being his wife. I want to be loved. But maybe I don't want to be married.

She glanced at her watch. "Do you think that coffee is coming soon? I have to meet Christopher at the gangway at a quarter past eight."

Peggy leaped to her feet and pressed the buzzer imperiously. "I'm so sorry! I can't imagine what happened to that silly girl. She's his stewardess, too." Peggy smiled dreamily. "Soon, I'll be bringing him his breakfast. He's going to leave the ship and we'll live ashore."

They were silent while the stewardess set up the breakfast table. After the girl left, Mary said, "Tony's going to give up the sea? It's been his life, Peggy. Are you sure he'll be happy?"

"Of course he'll be happy. He's only five years from retirement anyway." She poured the coffee. "I'll make him happy, Mary. I'll love him so much he'll *have* to be happy."

You'll love him the way Michael loves me, Mary thought. Too abjectly, too undemandingly. Will Tony react as I do, eventually smothering under the self-lessness? Perhaps not. Perhaps he'll be delighted. He's quite used to being obeyed. She realized Peggy had asked her something and she hadn't heard. "I'm sorry, Peggy, what did you say?"

"I said would you be my matron of honor."

"Me? I . . . I'm flattered, but we really don't know each other that well."

"There's no one else, Mary. Nobody's going to fly out from Chicago to stand up for me, and there's no one aboard."

"But, Peggy, I can't. I'm going into China while the ship's in Hong Kong. I'm sorry, really I am."

The woman looked as though she were going to cry. "You'll hate China. It's primitive and full of Communists. Hong Kong is such fun. Oh, please, Mary. It would mean so much to me. To both of us."

"I . . . I can't, Peggy. I'd love to, but I do want to see the People's Republic. And I promised Jayne and Christopher." Peggy had begun to weep. It was foolish. What difference did it make to this middle-aged woman whether she had an "attendant" at her wedding? But her distress made Mary waver. "Let me see," she hedged. "It's almost a month away. Let's see what happens." She hated herself for being so silly. Sillier than Peggy. But she couldn't bring herself to stick with a flat refusal. Peggy cheered up instantly.

"I knew you would! Thank you, Mary. You don't know how happy you've made me!"

"Absolutely and positively not," Christopher said. "You're not going to miss the trip into China for the sake of some dotty, mid-life matron who's behaving like a bloody idiot. I won't allow it. If you can't see how ridiculous that is, my dear Mary, then I'm forced to make the decision for you. It's quite absurd, the whole thing."

She'd waited until the end of the lovely day in Auckland to tell him what Peggy had asked of her. It had been a glorious twelve hours. They'd driven to the top of Mount Eden and looked at the beautiful city below, laughing at the incongruous touch of five cows placidly grazing among the tourists. They'd visited the War Museum and lunched at a "typical tea shoppe," browsed through a quaint, reconstructed section called "Parnell," where Christopher bought her a little painting as a souvenir of the day. Now they were dining elegantly at Ponsonby's, an expensive restaurant that had once been a firehouse and was as "gourmet" as any in San Francisco or New York.

Mary sighed. He was right, of course. China was the place she looked forward to most. Few people had been there and she knew she'd get several good interviews, perhaps not with the Chinese (though she hoped for that) but at least with some of her fellow passengers who would give their impressions of Canton. Or, as the Chinese called it, Kwangchow.

"I hate to disappoint her. She's counting on me."

Christopher gave an exasperated snort. "Good Lord, Mary, must you always behave as though the world will end if you don't live up to everyone's expectations? From what I've come to know of you in the past eighteen days, I'd say you have an obsessive desire to please. First it was to please your parents, who obviously didn't appreciate your efforts. Then you had to succeed in your job to prove Charlie Burke's faith in you. Don't deny it. I'm certain that was part of the motivation. I can tell, from the obligated way you speak of it. You fret that you might not be giving Jayne as much attention as you should. And heaven knows what debt you feel you owe your husband! Now it's Peggy, a woman you scarcely know." He paused. "I'm sorry, darling, I don't mean to be hard on you. You're a lovely, giving woman. But there's enough of the amateur psychiatrist in me to recognize that you have either a strong streak of masochism or an inflated ego that makes you feel you're indispensable. People who let the weak or greedy drink their blood sometimes have a need to play God. Very often they're enjoying a secret sense of power, believing they're sacrificing themselves."

The words stung. But they made her feel more confused than angry. What if Christopher was right? What if all the efforts to please really were prompted by righteousness rather than compassion? He knew virtually nothing about Michael, yet he'd hinted at what might be true. Perhaps she stayed with him because it made her feel powerful to believe he couldn't live without her. She was quiet for so long that Christopher finally reached across the table and took her hand, stroking it in a now familiar gesture of tenderness.

"I didn't mean to hurt you. I just got so damned mad when you told me you'd even consider missing the trip of a lifetime for such an unimportant reason. Forgive me?"

"Of course. You're right. I know that. I just didn't have the heart to refuse her on the spot. I'll tell her I can't do it. She'll be just as married without my being there."

"Good girl."

"You do think you'll be able to stay aboard and go with us, don't you?"

"Ninety-nine per cent certain. Unless there's some dire emergency in Sydney. And I'm sure there isn't or they'd have called by now or sent a wireless. But even if the highly unlikely happened and I couldn't go, you still must do it. It's an experience you'll never forget. It's another world. A far cry from what you've seen in your Chinatown."

"I'm only sorry I'll have so little time in Hong Kong."

"Big deal. We can go back there anytime."

She felt her heart begin to race. It was the first time Christopher had spoken of the future as though he intended they spend it together. I must be terribly transparent, Mary thought. He must know that the thought of never seeing him again gives me nightmares. She half wanted to pick up the lead he'd obviously given, but she was afraid. Afraid he might ask her to leave Michael and marry him. Afraid because she wouldn't know how to answer if he did. She needed time. Perhaps I'm hoping for some miraculous revelation, she thought. Something that will tell me the right thing to do. His mention of a wireless reminded her that she'd had no word from Michael about the outcome of his February 25 meeting with Harry Carson. It must have been inconclusive or he'd have let her know. Surely there'd be a letter waiting when she got back to the ship, but it would have been written long before. No news was good news, she told herself. Or was it?

They returned to the ship an hour before sailing.

"Meet you on the Promenade at midnight to watch us cast off?"

Mary shook her head reluctantly. "I think I'll turn in. It's been a long, wonderful day, but I'm sure you've had enough of my company."

Christopher didn't answer, but his small smile told her how silly that remark had been.

Jayne was already in the cabin when she returned. A small pile of mail lay on Mary's bed, and Jayne was busy reading her own. She looked up when her aunt came in.

"Have a good day?"

Mary nodded. "Lovely. What about you?"

"Not bad. Poor Terry. He was so damned grateful for company. Even mine."

Mary glanced at her letters, anxious to get at them. Mail from home was so important when you were traveling. It kept you in touch with the familiar, even the part you were running from. She forced herself to continue the conversation with Jayne. After all, she'd run out on her all day. Damn. There I go again, she thought. Thinking I didn't do my duty. Maybe Christopher's right. Maybe I do think I'm indispensable. This young woman is quite capable of leading her life without me. I've seen her no more than three times in the past fifteen years. Still, from force of habit, she made herself sound interested in Jayne's day.

"You like Terry Spalding, don't you?"

"I'm sorry as hell for him, Aunt Mary. I think he hates being the way he is, but he can't help it. You know, he took this trip to recover from a love affair. His boy friend decided to go straight. Or pretend to. He's marrying some older woman, would you believe! Terry's heartbroken. Practically suicidal. He told me the story of his life. Classic. Possessive mother. Frail childhood. All that junk. He's only twenty-six and his life's been a living hell since Day One."

Mary shook her head. "That way of life is hard for me to understand."

"A lot of life-styles are hard to understand." Jayne gave her a knowing look. "Mother's, for instance. If she's always been so unhappy with Daddy, why in hell has she stuck around? Why didn't she split early, while she was still young enough to find somebody else?"

"Maybe she didn't know what to do, Jaynie. She's never been equipped to make a decent living. Besides, your father is a dear man. Maybe she loves him more than you realize."

"No way. She despises him. Poor Daddy. He's spent the last twenty-two years making up for a lack of contraception."

The coarse statement shocked Mary. At a loss for an answer, she said, "Mind if I look over my mail?"

"Be my guest. I'm done in. It's not easy playing Freud and Ann Landers all in one day. Good night, Aunt Mary."

"Night, dear."

Mary undressed and climbed into her bed. By the light of the night lamp she opened the letter from Michael written three days after she sailed. It sounded like him: boyish and open. No subtlety there. She wondered if he'd had a good time at Rae Spanner's Valentine party. For a brief moment, she felt a twinge of jealousy. Rae was one of her closest friends, a rich widow who entertained lavishly and usually had a cluster of younger men around her. But she'd always had a special fondness for Michael. Mary sensed this would be a golden opportunity for Rae to move in and try to get something started with her friend's husband. She wasn't above it, that was for sure. But Michael wouldn't. Or would he? Sixty-nine days without sex was a long time for a man. She smiled ruefully. For a woman, too, she thought. But if Michael decided to go to bed with someone, he wouldn't pick one of their friends. He'd pick some total stranger. Someone she'd never know about.

What kind of thoughts were these? Was she already predicting Michael's unfaithfulness to justify the possibility of her own? Or was she searching for an excuse to break up her marriage with a clear conscience?

Impatiently, she discarded this train of thought, concentrating instead on the vaguely disquieting part of the letter about his meeting with Carson. "Harry must go along with my ideas." The phrase stuck in her mind like a warning bell. She knew what would happen. Michael would make all kinds of demands for autonomy in the business capitalized by Carson. He'd probably blow the whole deal with his inflated ideas of his own knowledge. She sent him a silent entreaty. "Be sensible, be realistic." She wanted him to succeed. His employable years were going by too fast. Whether she was around or not, he had to be self-sustaining.

Quickly she skimmed three other notes from friends, chatty little letters telling her what was happening in their circle. She looked for a letter from her parents or Patricia, but there was none. Not surprising. Pat had probably written to Jayne, and her parents never wrote at all, Well, I haven't done any writing either, Mary thought. Just a few postcards from Tahiti and Tonga.

She saved the fat envelope from Charlie Burke until last, knowing she'd enjoy it. There was a long letter on the yellow paper he typed on in the office. A little clipping fell out and she read it first. It was from the radio column in the *Examiner,* saying merely that Mary Farr Morgan was on an extended assignment in the Far East and her shows would be pretaped for the next two months. "Mary on tape somehow gives us a feeling of loss," the columnist wrote. "The shows are good, but we'll be glad to have San Francisco's 'voice of human interest' back, with all her warmth and spontaneity, in mid-April." Across the top of the column Charlie had scrawled, "See? *Everybody* loves you!"

Smiling, she began to read the long letter from her boss.

Dearest Nellie Bly,

You should receive this in New Zealand, the home of the Kiwi bird. You know about that poor thing. It can't fly. It did once, but when it stopped soaring, its wings became ineffectual—proving, as an elderly, impotent roué once said, that what you don't use, you lose. This, of course, accounts for the notorious reputation of sailors in port. (And lone passengers at sea? Ah, no. Not my Mary!)

Did I ever tell you that once, way back when, Tracey and I took a South American cruise? I was young and boringly introspective in those days and fancied someday I'd be a serious writer. I kept a full and alarmingly pretentious diary during that trip, recording "impressions." A few days after you left, I looked up that collection of musty reminiscences and found that the words I'd so painstakingly inscribed now sound as though they were written with a quill.

But for the sheer hell of it, I've copied my lofty thoughts about cruise ships, wondering if your feeling about them may in any way match my young condescension. If so, you would express them far better, with

more simplicity than a twenty-two-year-old Charlie Burke managed. Promise
not to laugh? Okay, here's what I wrote:

"It's especially fitting that they call a cruise ship 'she,' for she is
pregnant with a thousand adult embryos who long to stay forever warm
and sheltered in this great white womb. How lovely to be hidden from
a harsh and noisy world which demands decisions and discipline. How
easy to have each day neatly planned, each hour secure and unchallenging.
Effortless is the life of the floating fetus, snug in the belly of the mother
ship. Passengers? No. Prisoners of pleasure, swaddled in blissful boredom,
floating undisturbed, figuratively curled in the prenatal position, silently
begging never to be born.

"And when, indeed, they emerge into the daylight, they are as infants,
force-fed five times a day. The bartenders are their wet nurses, the
stewardesses their nannies, the captain their father figure, the other passengers their playmates.

"And play they do. They play 'dress up' at their costume parties, form
secret societies with dirty passwords, give tea parties worthy of the Mad
Hatter. The bars are their playpens, the swimming pool their wading
pond, the outdoor games their recess activities. In ports, they dutifully
take their airings in big perambulator buses. Restless and fretful, they
suffer these lessons in geography, buy their toy souvenirs, squirm and
complain and rush home to their sea-going nurseries.

"Rich babies with too much time and money. Old babies running from
the specter of death. Hungry, hopeful babies in search of love or comfort
or forgetfulness. Poor babes-at-sea. Poor, rootless, fading flower-children
in a bed weeded of all things ugly, a bed watered with self-indulgence
and fertilized with the manure of mindlessness.

"Have pity on them, these captives willingly suspended above the
bright blue water. Ask them not to grow, for they do not wish to grow.
Rather, let them sail on endlessly, forever amused and entertained in the
ways little people demand—pampered and petted and, above all, never
left alone. For, wrenched from this world of make-believe, they are buds
that cannot bloom elsewhere, frail blossoms that, transplanted to the cruel
earth, wither and die.''

Now, my dearest Mary, can you believe your hard-bitten boss ever
wrote such high-flown drivel? You can see I had the cynicism of the
very young, the pseudo-superiority of the cruel, remote and misinformed
observer. How clever I thought I was. How much above it all. How
condescending.

I'm sure that your "great white womb" holds a very different kind
of embryo. Or if not, you will not see it through such prematurely world-
weary eyes. Tell me about it as it appears to you, my lovely friend. Tell
me it is a delicious, light-hearted time and that you are surrounded by
kind and gentle and loving people.

Your first tapes will tell me whether you've found them. I doubt not
that you have. For they would come flocking to you.

Charlie

She dropped the letter on the floor by her bed, snapped off the light and lay
back, listening to the shouts and noises of the ship's departure and thinking of
what she'd just read. An odd kind of letter from home. One expected local and

personal news, an account of the writer's doings such as she'd received from her other friends. Nothing so trite from Charlie. He was trying to tell her something, warn her, perhaps, that she dwelt temporarily in a make-believe land. She doubted he'd ever taken a cruise, or that the "diary" had been written more than twenty minutes before mailing. There'd always been a kind of ESP between them. Even thousands of miles away he must sense that she felt like another person. The "old Mary Morgan" would not have become infatuated with another man, would not have ignored the speculation of others or virtually abandoned the young woman in her charge.

Yes, Charlie somehow knew that on shipboard everyone became an irresponsible child. The pretended "youthful impressions" were his way of telling her to remember that she had to return to a real world, that she could not be one of those who floated undisturbed forever above the bright blue water.

It's as though I've told him about Christopher, Mary thought. As though he knows the temptations and is begging me not to be blinded by the unreality of this time and place.

Chapter 6

SUNDAY DINNER WITH her parents was such a bore. Patricia looked around the living room of the Farr apartment and thought how accurate a picture it was of its occupants. Nothing had changed in years, except for the addition of a big, monstrously ugly television set that stared at her from a place of honor in front of the never-used fireplace. The wall over the couch was crowned by three hand-tinted photographs in oval gilt frames, pictures of herself and Mary and John as children, taken thirty-five years ago. She studied them with distaste. She'd been a smirking twelve-year-old, full of airs and graces. John, at seven, looked resentful. And five-year-old Mary had an air of false bravado, her chin lifted but her eyes shy. There were no later pictures of any of them, though there were several of Jayne in frames on the round table in front of the window, Jayne as a fat baby. Jayne at her first communion, her high school and college graduations. At least she has an ongoing life for them, Patricia thought. The rest of us have been halted in time, as though we all ceased to exist when John died.

My God, I'm beginning to sound like Mary! She always believed that nobody mattered but the boy; that they cared for nothing after they lost him. Perhaps she was right. After thirty years, they still spoke of him, endlessly retelling stories about his childish exploits now transformed into deeds of an angel who stayed on earth such a brief, sweet time. It was like living with a ghost more real to them than the children who survived. Patricia shuddered.

She looked at Stanley Richton, fifty, paunchy and balding and wondered how she could ever have let herself be seduced by him. Hell, she'd let herself be seduced by everybody, never dreaming she'd spend the rest of her life paying for it. But to end up with Stanley! Dull, devoted Stanley, who aspired to nothing more than running his crummy little hardware business and eventually retiring to some place like Sarasota where he could watch the baseball teams in spring training.

She felt like screaming. She was forty-six years old and nothing was ever going to happen to her, ever. All she had to look forward to was another thirty years of mediocrity. She'd end up as a grandmother and a baby-sitter. She who should have used her beauty as a wedge to wealth and happiness. She might have been an actress, or at least the chic wife of some rich and exciting man.

Even Mary, plain, boring Mary, had made something of her life. She had a glamorous career and was a celebrity, even if it was only in San Francisco. Mary had a handsome husband who looked ten years younger than he was. Mary was lucky. Imagine winning a twenty-five-thousand-dollar trip in a drawing! That was more money than Stanley earned in a year.

Patricia resented the fact that Jayne had been invited to share this windfall. She should have asked me, Pat thought. If she wasn't going to take Michael, it would have been much more appropriate to take someone near her own age who'd speak her language. But no. Mary had to invite a twenty-one-year-old, as though she felt more at ease with her niece than with her sister. Damn it, my kid has plenty of time ahead of her to travel. I've never been anywhere and I'm not likely to go. It wasn't fair. Mary had never even invited her to visit. Not once in more than fifteen years.

A wild idea came into her head. If Mary wouldn't invite her to San Francisco, she'd invite herself. Why not? Mary'd always avoided asking the family because she said she had no guest room. She'd turned the second bedroom into her "office" and the convertible couch was "too uncomfortable." Baloney. Mary didn't want her. Well, Mary wasn't there, and Pat was sure that Michael would gladly sleep on the sofa if she wrote and told him she'd like to come for a visit. The more she thought of it, the better an idea it seemed.

She interrupted the boring conversation Stan and her father were having about the rate of unemployment in New York.

"We had a postcard from Jayne yesterday. Mailed from Tahiti on February the twentieth."

"Yes," Camille said. "We had one from Mary."

Stanley nodded. "Jayne sounds as though she's having a good time. Wonderful opportunity for her. Nice of Mary to take her. Travel is so broadening."

Patricia winced. She might not be intellectual, but Stanley's clichés drove her wild. "Speaking of traveling," she said, "I thought I might go to San Francisco and meet them when they return. It would be fun to see a ship dock."

Her husband didn't seem perturbed. "Well, we'll see. They don't get back until the twentieth of April. It's only the fifth of March, honey."

"I thought I might go early and stay at Mary's apartment. I've never been to San Francisco and it wouldn't cost anything except the plane fare. I'm sure we can swing *that*." Pat's voice was heavy with sarcasm.

"Patricia, I'm not sure that would look right." Camille was disapproving. "What would people say if you stayed in the apartment with Michael, unchaperoned?"

"Unchaperoned! For God's sake, Mother, I'm forty-six years old and Michael's forty-five! Besides, he's my brother-in-law! What the hell kind of foolishness are you talking?"

"Patricia! Don't speak to your mother that way!" John Farr was once again the stern parent. "Besides, she happens to be quite right. It would look very peculiar if you spent a long time in Mary's apartment when she isn't there. A day or two, perhaps, if Stanley agrees you may go. But no prolonged stay."

Rage boiled up within her. "You obviously have a wonderful opinion of me, all of you. What do you think I'm going to do? Climb into bed with my sister's husband? If I were going to do that, I could manage it just as well in two days as two weeks! You don't trust me, Daddy, do you? You never have."

"Have you ever given us reason to?"

"Oh, fine! Dandy! I'm never allowed to forget that I was pregnant before I was married. You're chewing on your old disgrace like cows with their cuds. Always living in the past. I'm the slut, Mary's the grind and your dead son is still alive and well and holier than any of us! Well, it's 1977! John's rotted in his grave and I've been a bored wife for a hundred years. Get that through your heads, will you?"

She ran from the room, leaving the others in uncomfortable silence. Finally, Stanley got to his feet.

"I'm sorry," he said. "Patricia's not herself these days. I think she must be going through 'the change.' I'd better take her home. Thanks for the nice dinner."

John and Camille didn't answer, and Patricia didn't return to say good-bye.

In the bus on the way home, Stanley said quietly, "Honey, you shouldn't have gotten so upset with your folks. They're old. Sometimes I think they don't realize we've all grown up."

"Have we?" Patricia asked bitterly. "It doesn't seem to me we're any different than we were twenty-two years ago. Same dumpy apartment. Same stupid friends. Same boring life."

"I'm sorry. You know I'd like to give you all the things you want."

She turned on him. "How could you? You have no idea what I want."

"Tell me."

Patricia stared out the window, thinking, What do I want? Excitement. The company of interesting people. A sable coat. A diamond the size of Elizabeth Taylor's. Freedom. My beauty back. And my youth. God, I want another chance at life! Finally she said, "I just want a little holiday, Stanley. That's all. I know you can't get away, but there's no reason why I shouldn't go out and welcome Jayne home, is there? And if I'm going to make such a long trip, would it be so terrible to spend a little extra time beforehand? Mary doesn't have room for Jayne and me to stay on, but I'm sure Michael wouldn't mind if I slept on the couch in her office. I wouldn't be in his way."

"But what would you do all alone in a strange city?"

"Just walk around. Take the cable car. Go to Ghiradelli Square and the Cannery and Fisherman's Wharf. Have a drink at the Top of the Mark. See Chinatown and I. Magnin and Telegraph Hill. I've heard so much about San Francisco. I'd like to see it. Is that asking too much?"

She could be so appealing when she wanted to. Stanley never could resist her.

"No. I suppose it isn't," he said. "All right, honey. Write to Mike, if you want to. If he can spare his wife for two months I guess I can spare mine for two weeks."

She squeezed his hand. "Thank you, darling. I really love you, you know."
Suggestively, she moved closer to him on the seat. "Wait until we get home.
I'll show you how much."

On the afternoon of March 6, H.M.S. *Prince of Wales* moved slowly into the
harbor of Sydney, Australia. Mary and Christopher stood at the prow on Promenade
Deck, crammed in among dozens of other passengers who'd chosen this same
spot for the magnificent view. Below them they could see the crew also clustered
at the railing for a sight not to be missed. Everyone, it seemed, had a camera
to capture this moment. It was a perfect day, with a brilliant blue sky and bright
sunshine dancing on the waters and bouncing off the white sails of what appeared
to be a thousand little pleasure boats coming dangerously near the big liner. One
or two reckless motorboat drivers kept cutting back and forth in their path,
scaring Mary to death. It seemed to her that all of Sydney must be on the water
that day. There could be no one left in the great buildings that made up the
skyline of the city.

"That's the opera house on the left," Christopher said. "You probably recognize
it from pictures. It took nineteen years to build and ended up costing $125 million
American dollars." He laughed. "The original estimate was ten million."

Mary stared, speechless at the sight of the great building with its roof of huge
"shells," actually glass and concrete vaults, the highest of which, she'd been
told, measured two hundred and twenty-one feet, about the height of a twenty-
two-story building.

"And on the other side," Christopher said, pointing to his right, "is our
famous Harbor Bridge, the largest arch bridge in the world. We call it 'the coat
hanger' and, incidentally, at night it's lighted only on the chic-er East Side. We,
too, can be snobs, my darling Mary, even though a mere two hundred years ago
this was a penal colony. See that little island, there? That's where the convicts
were kept in 1788. As you say in your advertisements, we've come a long way,
baby!"

She looked up at him, laughing. "It's beautiful beyond belief. I can see why
you want to live here."

"Can you? That's good."

Mary looked away, pretending interest in the view. They'd been lovers for
three days and three nights, and Christopher wanted her to leave Michael and
marry him. Lying in his arms, happy despite her conscience, she hadn't been
able to give him an answer. She'd told him at last about Michael, how devoted
he was, how hard he tried to make her happy.

"I came on this trip to think about my life, my marriage," she said. "I thought
that getting away for a few weeks would clarify it all." She laughed ruefully.
"And now I'm more confused than ever."

"Because of me," Christopher said.

"Yes. Because of you."

"You do love me, Mary. And I love you. I can make you happy, darling.
I'm the kind of man you should have. One who'll protect you and care for you
and share a full life with you. You can't stay with Michael out of pity or concern
for his future. He's a grown man. Perhaps the kindest thing you could do for

him would be to make him stand on his own feet. He'll never do that, you know, as long as you're there to take care of everything.''

"I know. I know that's true. But I don't know what he'd do if I left him. He . . . he loves me very much, Christopher.''

He'd stroked her hair gently. "How could he help it? Sweetheart, I won't pressure you. You have to make up your own mind. About a lot of things. But I need you, too. As much, perhaps more, than Michael, but in a different way. I want a woman with intelligence and grace. I've wanted that forever, it seems. Someone who'll make her life mine. It would be a very different life for you, Mary. I realize that. You'd live in Australia and travel with me. There'd be no radio show, no job at all because I'd want you always at my side. But I believe the gains would be worth the sacrifices, my love. I want you to have your identity, but a different kind.''

With her first glimpse of his country, those words came back to her now, just as the memory of that first night of love returned in vivid detail. They'd had a wonderful time in New Zealand, visiting friends of his in Wellington, a charming couple who lived in a typically upper-middle-class "British" house, full of chintz and flowers and fireplaces and sherry before dinner. They'd explored the tiny town of Picton set against great green hills and deep water, a funny little town of two spotless streets and a dear little park where children played around statues of Mickey Mouse and Donald Duck and everyone seemed cheerful and happy. She'd never known such a hospitable country, such warm and welcoming people. She even managed to do an interview with one of the ladies on the town's Hospitality Committee. How amazed her listeners would be to hear this lovely, cultivated woman describe life in this remote place, proudly explaining how the volunteers in their cars met every cruise ship and took the passengers sight-seeing, refusing to let them pay for the "petrol," even though the hosts were of modest means.

"We're quite proud of Picton," her interviewee said. "We do hope more of you lovely Americans will come and visit us.''

Mary had been thoroughly enchanted, almost euphoric as they sailed that evening through Queen Charlotte Sound and the narrow straits, the ship daintily picking its way so close to land that one felt able to stretch out a hand and touch the shore.

That night, she and Christopher sat over late-night drinks in the Trafalgar Room. They were the only people in the bar at the very top of the ship.

"Like having your own yacht, isn't it?''

Mary nodded contentedly. "Um. Fabulous. What are those lights over there?''

"Japanese fishing fleet. They're brightly lighted to attract the fish. And the brightest light of all is the 'mother ship.' ''

The phrase made her think of Charlie's letter. "It's unreal. Like a picture postcard. There's even a full moon. Do you believe a full moon makes people go crazy?''

"I don't know. Is it supposed to?''

"That's what they say.''

Christopher's hand tightened on her own. "Mary. Darling. Haven't we waited long enough?''

She hesitated for a second. In three days they'd be in Sydney. She might lose him forever. She would never know what it was like to be loved by him. In the soft light, she turned to face him. She felt certain and happy.

"Yes," she said, "more than long enough."

"Will you be all right this afternoon? I have to look after my business and break the news to my children and the office that I'm leaving again for another month."

She realized Christopher was speaking to her. She'd been so caught up in her thoughts she'd almost forgotten that they were about to dock in Sydney.

"Of course I'll be all right. You don't suppose anything will change your plans?"

He shook his head. "It was virtually impossible before. Now it's absolutely impossible. I have one month to make myself indispensable for a lifetime. I love you, darling."

"And I love you." How easily and surely the words came, though uncertainty about the future remained.

"I'll be back to pick you up about seven. We'll go to dinner at Eliza's. It's one of our smarter restaurants. I want you to see how civilized Australia is, and we only have two days here. We have a lot of ground to cover."

When Christopher left the ship, she returned to her cabin to answer her mail. To friends, she dashed off brief postcards, smiling as she remembered reading somewhere that it didn't do to write long or frequent letters home when one was away, lest people think you had nothing better to do than spend time at a desk. She did write to her parents, telling them things they could have read in any travel brochure. She frowned as she set down the inane, almost impersonal words to John and Camille, thinking how sad it was that she couldn't confide in them or ask the advice she so desperately needed.

There was no one to give her such advice. Not even Charlie, although he, of all people, would understand. Instead, she told him how she'd loved his "diary" and how accurate he was, in general, about the attitude of people on long cruises. "Fortunately," she wrote, "there are a handful of attractive, mature, un-lost souls among all the 'babes-at-sea.' They, and the interesting ports, keep Jayne and me from jumping overboard to escape the mere monotony of the days aboard. I'll tell you about them when I see you, dear friend."

Will I? Mary wondered. Will I ever be able to tell anyone about Christopher? Only if I link my life with his. If I decide not to, I'll never be able to speak his name again. It would hurt much too much. It would never stop hurting.

The noises of a ship in port swirled around her, the sounds of disembarking passengers and arriving visitors, the babble of strange voices and odd accents. How interested Michael would be in all this, she suddenly thought. It's like a big party. And Michael adores big parties.

Resolutely, she began a letter to her husband. She'd put it off until last, wishing she didn't have to communicate at all with the man to whom she'd been unfaithful. It seemed to her that whatever she wrote would be revealing, as though Michael could read between the lines. That was nonsense, of course. He'd be delighted to hear from her. She'd probably have another letter from him when the Sydney mail was distributed. She began by thanking him for his letter and saying she hoped by this time he'd had a good meeting with Harry Carson about the proposed men's shop. She rattled on about Wellington and Picton and the tapes she'd made and sent to Charlie. Not a word about her fellow passengers, none of them. She didn't dare, lest some inadvertent comment about Christopher pique Michael's curiosity. Instead (was it a subconscious defense mechanism?), she devoted a whole paragraph to inquiries about Rae Spanner's Valentine party. Had it been fun? Who was there? Did Rae have a new young man in her life? Or was Michael her beau for the evening?

I don't even care, Mary thought. How terrible. I'm almost hoping he's having a fling with Rae. Anything to make my own indiscretion justifiable.

It was a bleak thought. My God, an inner voice said, how deceitful you've become, Mary Morgan! What a crazed, torn creature you are. Worse than when you left San Francisco.

But there was no turning back now. She'd begun her joyous affair. There was no way to retreat between here and Yokohama. Surprised by her lack of guilt, she realized she didn't want to. For the first time in her life she felt physically and spiritually complete.

Michael was depressed, an unusual state for him. Even in the worst of times he was an optimist. When one thing didn't work out, he was soon ready to think about the next. But on this March morning, a few days after his meeting with Harry Carson, his mood was pessimistic.

Not that Carson had canceled the deal. He'd spent two hours going over Michael's projection for the men's boutique, first reading it all the way through, his face expressionless, the fat, ugly cigar he chewed on staying unlit in his mouth. Each time Michael tried to interrupt with an explanation, Harry raised a big hairy hand to silence him.

"Lemme get the whole picture, Mike. Then we'll discuss it."

Michael had been forced to sit for half an hour in uncomfortable silence as the "money man" slowly read his proposal. At last, Carson put down the papers and grunted.

"Not a bad outline, Mike. Lot of things wrong with it, of course, but could be the nut of something good if we make some changes."

"I'm glad you like it, Harry."

"I don't like it. That is, I don't hate it, but I don't like it."

"What the hell does that mean?"

"It means you're not much further along than you were the day you made the first proposal, pally."

Michael stared at him. "What are you talking about? I've spent weeks getting all the data together—the operating overhead, the promotional costs, the inventory investment, the resources . . ."

Carson interrupted him. "And it's crap. You're smoking opium with this plan! French designer labels, custom-made clothes, advertising in *Vogue*, free drinks at five o'clock, delivery by limousine! What the hell do you think I'm going to invest in, a society tea party? Men don't want that junk. Give 'em decent threads, well priced. Keep the overhead down. Buy from the big resources at the right cost. Have plenty special sale days. Give me those things in a proposal and we might be able to talk business.''

Michael felt his anger rising. ''We might be able to *talk* it, but we certainly wouldn't *have* it! For Christ's sake, Harry, you're talking about a store no different than twenty-five others in this town!''

''That's right. The ones that make money.''

''But there's too much competition!'' He tried to calm down. ''Listen, I'm not on an ego trip. I know this is the way to go. You've got to offer the public something special if you want to build a new business. You have to invest, innovate, experiment.''

''Not with my money. I'm all for doing what's tried and tested. I got no interest in some snotty little shop that might appeal to a few fairies.'' Harry flicked the papers back at him contemptuously. ''If you want to go home and draft a plan for an honest-to-God store that won't lose a bundle for five years before it gets in the black, if ever, I'll be glad to meet with you again. But don't give me this jet-set garbage. I'm not sinking my dough into a damned boutique that only friends of yours and your wife's would come into. I want volume, Morgan. And profit.''

''You'd have them,'' Michael protested. ''And don't underrate Mary's friends. She's a very influential woman in this town. Why, she'd plug the shop on the air, interview people about it. Customers would flock in!''

Carson looked at him with disgust. ''Counting on your wife to save your hide, huh? I hear that's your specialty. Well, forget it. I don't believe she can do it this time. And even if she could, I don't buy that as enough reason for starting a risky business. I'll tell you again, Morgan. You want to start a solid, no-frills men's store I'm interested in investing. But *my* way and *only* my way. You want to redo the plan my way or not?''

Michael had wanted to tell him what he could do with ''his way,'' but instead he said, ''I don't know, Harry. I'll have to think about it. It would be hard for me to head up something I don't believe in. I don't know that I could succeed with a premise I thought was wrong.''

The other man threw back his head and barked a grating laugh. ''Man, that's a good one! When did all those high-flown ideals ever pay off for you? When did you ever make more than twelve thousand dollars a year in your whole life? 'Believe in something'? I'll tell you what to believe in—the almighty buck. I didn't get to be a millionaire by chasing rainbows, and neither will you. Copy what works. Search the world and steal the best. That's the only way to make money. And you *do* want to make money, don't you, Morgan? Or would you rather live on ideals and your wife's income?''

His face red above his tight white collar, Michael rose. ''I'll think about it, Harry, and get back to you.''

''Sure. The offer stands. On my terms.''

Damn it, Michael thought now as he paced the apartment, I can't do it his way. I can't start another dumb clothing store and let Harry Carson destroy every valid idea I have for a shop that's in touch with the times. But it's his way or nothing. His way. Old-fashioned. Boring. Cheap. All the things I despise.

But what are the alternatives? Look for another backer? They're probably all the same, these rich old fools who don't know the world has changed. Try to find another idea? I don't have one. I've run out of ideas and I'm running out of time. I almost promised Mary this would work.

Hating it, he sat down and began to draw up a plan pedestrian enough for Harry Carson's approval. He'd swallow his pride, bitter medicine as it was.

Chapter 7

THE MORNING AFTER they left Sydney, Gail DeVries cornered Mary in the British Bar where eleven o'clock bouillon was being served for those who did not care to start the day with bloody marys or brandy milk punches.

"Come talk with me," the little white-haired woman said. "We never get a chance to visit except at dinner, and lord knows it's hard to get a word in between Beau and Peggy Lawrence!"

Mary smiled. She didn't know her well, but Gail seemed to be the kind of woman Mary would like to be thirty years from now: active, cheerful, a motherly sort who didn't indulge in self-pity or complaints and who took her advancing years in stride. She and Colonel Stanford were obviously fond of each other and enjoyed their annual trip. The arrangement apparently suited them well. Maybe, Mary reflected, it was a better arrangement than marriage. They led their own lives ten months of the year and looked forward to a fresh renewal of friendship each winter.

They seated themselves in a far corner of the bar.

"Would you like a drink?" Gail asked.

"No, thanks. I can't start this early. What about you?"

"Never touch it until cocktail time. Easy to fall into the trap of too much drinking on a cruise. You know, it fascinates me. People who wouldn't dream of having a drink before six o'clock at home are up here at ten in the morning, waiting for the bar to open. There's a different mentality at sea, don't you think? There's a kind of to-hell-with-it attitude that's pervasive. Maybe that's why so many people like it."

"My boss thinks it's a little like going back to the womb. That most of the passengers want to behave like infants—fed, amused, pampered, with nothing demanded of them."

"Your boss sounds like a smart man."

"He is. And a lovely one. When we get back, you must meet him."

"I'd love to. And your husband, too."

Mary took a sip of her clear soup, avoiding an answer. Gail looked at her affectionately.

"Look, Mary, it's none of my business and you can tell me to shut up and stop being a meddlesome old lady, but I think you have problems, and if talking about them will help, I'll be glad to listen. I don't know you very well, but I'm old enough to be your mother. I have daughters your age. Lovely girls. And the one thing I'm grateful for is that they feel able to confide in me. You may not want to, but if you do, I give you my word that whatever you say will never leave this table."

Feeling ridiculous, Mary's eyes filled with tears. She needed to talk to someone. Someone with experience and compassion who would listen and react objectively. Many times in the past month she'd thought of confiding in Jayne, but she couldn't. They were too close in their relationship and too far apart in their views about things.

"Thank you, Gail. Yes, I would like to talk. And I know you won't repeat what I tell you."

As though someone had carefully lifted a cork from a bottle, Mary began to pour out her heart. She told the older woman about Michael and her marriage, trying to explain the conflict within her.

"I feel so shallow, caring that he's not strong and successful. I don't even think it's all his fault. I've helped to make him that way, demanding nothing of him, hiding the fact that I blame him for becoming the person I helped create. I'm not happy with him, Gail, but I can't stand the thought of what might happen to him if I desert him. It's all so mixed up. I don't know where my loyalties lie. Sometimes I think I might do him a great favor to push him out on his own. Maybe he'd find the right kind of wife for him, one who'd be dependent, who'd insist he support her. Maybe one who'd give him children before it's too late. Or maybe that's just a cop-out I've made up to let me live with my conscience. I don't know. Christopher says . . . " She stopped. "Christopher and I are in love. I'm sure you've guessed that. It's not just a shipboard romance. He wants me to marry him. I met his sons in Sydney. They were wonderful. I could see how happy they were that their father had found someone to care for again. I could have a good life with Christopher. I could even give up my work, much as I love it. But there'd be Michael. The memory of what I'd done to him. The realization of what I *have* done to him all these years. I don't know if I could live with that." She stopped, surreptitiously wiping away her tears. "I'm sorry. I shouldn't be slobbering all over you. You can't make the decision for me. Nobody can. It's just so good to say things aloud to another woman. I've told Christopher a little of what I feel, but it's not the same. Mostly I just go over it in my head, again and again, until I think I'm going mad."

Gail sat quietly for a moment before she said, "What would happen, Mary, if Michael suddenly did become successful at something? Would you be content with him then? Does your ability to love him hinge on this one thing? If he changed, could you care for him as you once did?" She paused. "Do you really want him to succeed? Or do you just want out of this marriage, no matter what?"

"I don't know. As God is my judge, I don't know. I can't tell the difference between love and responsibility anymore. I think I don't want him to be dependent on me, but maybe I do, in a crazy way. I must have wanted him to be in the past or I wouldn't have made things so easy for him. What is it with strong women and weak men, Gail? Do we seek them or do they gravitate toward us? I know quite a few women who have passive husbands like Michael. They seem content with the arrangement. But I'm not. The balance is wrong. No matter what people say about equality between the sexes, marriage is like business— somebody has to be in charge. And I don't want to be in charge."

"And with Christopher you wouldn't be."

"No. He's strong and secure. But this didn't start because of him. I've been fretting about Michael and me for years. I took this trip to make a decision about us. I didn't know I'd meet someone else. Had no idea of it. Women who take cruises thinking they're going to meet a man are just plain stupid. The odds were a million to one I'd meet Christopher.'' She smiled sadly. ''In a way, I'm almost sorry I did. This didn't start because of him,'' Mary repeated, ''but it's become much more complex because he's shown me what I'm missing. When I left home, I thought it would be Michael or nothing. I thought if I couldn't have a good marriage with such a kind and loving man I'd never be capable of succeeding at any marriage. I never really said it even to myself, but I know I'd decided that if I divorced Michael I'd never marry again. That I wasn't cut out for marriage. That I couldn't give enough of myself, even though I wanted to. Now, I don't know. I wish this ship would sail on forever so I'd never have to come to grips with the decisions, either of them.''

''You and Michael or you and Christopher?''

''Yes. They're separate but entwined.''

Gail's eyes were full of sympathy. ''I've been listening to you very carefully, Mary, as though you were my own daughter. You know I can't advise you. You're too sensible to expect I'll have the magic answer. But I wonder if you're hearing yourself. You say you can't give enough of yourself, but the fact is you do nothing but give. Maybe for selfish reasons, but I doubt it. I think you've spent your life trying to please other people. Maybe it's time to think about yourself. You seem so full of guilt in every direction, dear Mary. Why is that? Was it instilled in you early on, this feeling of obligation? You seem to feel it for Michael and even for Christopher. What makes you so lacking in healthy selfishness?''

Mary thought of the early years, the almost fanatical desire to make her parents love her, the insane notion that she could replace their dead son. Even her career, though it was something she wanted, was in part dedicated to pleasing Charlie, to making him feel he'd been right in giving her a chance. Maybe I even took Jayne on this trip to please my sister, she thought. Or maybe I wanted to show off to Patricia by giving her daughter something she could never offer. God, I'm so addled! Much more of this introspection and I'll go out of my head! For a moment the anger at herself was directed at Gail DeVries. How dare she meddle in my life? What gave this old woman the right to stir up long-suppressed thoughts?

Instantly, she was sorry for her silent reaction. Gail was being kind. Sensible. She was only trying to make Mary see herself and work through to her own solutions. She wasn't prying. It was honest concern, not idle curiosity, that made her encourage the younger woman to talk. And Mary was grateful. Nothing was solved, but just hearing all her fears put into words made them less terrifying.

''I can't tell you how much I appreciate your letting me pour out this living soap opera,'' Mary said. ''It must be a riveting bore for you. I'm sorry I went on so.''

''Mary, don't. Don't say such a thing. I like you. I only wish I could help.''

''You have. Just by listening.''

''And I will, any time you want to talk. Think of me as your surrogate mother.''

I wish you were my mother, Mary thought. If you had been, maybe I'd be a different person. No, that wasn't fair. She wasn't going to blame her messed-up life on her parents or her childhood. She didn't hold with all the psychiatric crutches. Intelligent humans should be able to cope with their own problems without whining that their formative years were to blame for their later troubles. Oh, some people truly needed help. She knew that. But most people grew up and lived through the heartbreaks that life handed out and didn't expect things to be fair. I have to be one of those, Mary thought. I'm strong enough to sort this out if I'm disciplined and in control. Gail probably is right. I should coldly, clinically think of myself and stop worrying about other people, as though I'm a necessary woman, indispensable to their happiness and well-being. Self-preservation is the first law. I must start trying to obey the law.

As Mary was keeping secrets from her, so Jayne was not telling her aunt what had transpired in her life. Behind the flippancy was a young woman easily hurt and more insecure than the world ever would have imagined. The knowledge of the accident of her birth wounded her deeply, though she'd have died before she admitted it to anyone. Like Mary, she yearned to be loved. But unlike her, Jayne went seeking it, cynically telling herself that she came by her promiscuity naturally, a self-destructive inheritance from the mother she hated.

She'd slept with boys from her sophomore days in high school, but she didn't fall in love until her senior year in college. Russell King was a classmate, captain of the football team, class president, big man on campus. And, to her surprise and joy, this paragon returned her love. She wanted to marry him, but he insisted they wait. He was going on to law school, would have to work his way through, as he'd worked part time to supplement the football scholarship that had gotten him to college.

"I'll help," Jayne had said. "I'll get a job. We can live. It will be wonderful."

"No, darling. It would be terrible. Years of struggling to make ends meet. Me feeling guilty that you were paying the bills. You ending up hating me because you were supporting me. I couldn't live that way, Jay. It's not for me. Look. We're young. We have time. We'll see each other and be secretly engaged. The time will go fast and we'll have years ahead of us."

"I don't want to wait years! If you won't marry me, then we'll live together. What's the point of all this sneaking around with dates and secret engagements?" She stopped suddenly. "It's your family, isn't it? Your bloody, uptight family. They'd disapprove if you were openly cohabiting."

Russell had been angry. "All right, part of it *is* my family! They're poor people but they've given me everything they could. They're old-fashioned and they won't change. And I'm damned if I'll repay them by rubbing their noses in a situation they can't understand and would be devastated by. Damn it, Jayne, they'd consider themselves disgraced!" He'd calmed down. "We can go on just as we are. They'll get to know you better. We'll ease into some arrangement sooner or later. Take it easy, babe. Things will work out."

"No, they won't. We'll drift apart. We're not kids. At least I'm not a kid. But I think you are." The words came slowly, disparagingly. "I think you're nothing but a damned mama's boy, still scared to death you'll get a spanking if you misbehave."

"Don't be ridiculous! I'm just trying to show some decency and consideration!"

"For whom?"

"For everybody! Including you! Please, Jayne, don't be childish. If we love each other, we can wait awhile. Think it over and you'll see I'm right."

"No, thanks. *You* think it over. And when you grow up, get in touch with me."

She'd expected him to call the next day, but he hadn't. She waited three weeks and called him, swallowing her pride and saying she loved him and she'd see him on his terms. But it had been different, somehow. They still talked of the future and she pretended she could wait, no matter how long it took, but inside she knew she had to do something to force him into action. He was the only man she wanted. The only one she'd ever want, and she couldn't budge him. Why should he budge? she asked herself one day. He had what he wanted. He slept with her whenever he felt like it. He lived comfortably at home with his parents, had a part-time job in a law office and went to school. Nothing disturbed him and nothing would. Unless she made it happen. She considered getting pregnant and rejected the idea. She wasn't her mother and Russell wasn't her father. He'd never fall into that trap. She wouldn't want him that way, even if he did.

No, the only way was not to see him. Let him miss her so much he'd change his mind. But she didn't think she'd have the willpower not to see him. That was when Aunt Mary's invitation came like a miracle and she leapt at it. She'd be gone almost three months. By the time she returned, he'd be so crazy for her he'd do anything she wanted.

Lying on her bed in the cabin the day after they left Sydney, Jayne reread the letter for the twentieth time.

I wanted to tell you before you left, but I wasn't sure, myself, that what I felt for Pamela wasn't simply infatuation. I realize I haven't been honest with you for the past few months, but I didn't want to hurt you by telling you I'd met someone else until I was quite sure of my feelings for her, and hers for me.

We decided last week to become engaged and be married in June. She's lovely, Jayne, and my family is delighted. Her father is the senior partner in one of the most successful law firms in New York and I will, in time, be joining it. Until then, we'll live in her parents' house in Greenwich, and she'll continue her course in psychology while I work toward my degree.

Darling Jayne, I know you will be surprised by this, but not too disappointed in me, I hope. I would rather have told you in person, as I've told Pam about you, but as I said, I had to make sure of my feelings. I know how strong and sensible you are and although I'm conceited enough to think you may be sorry, I'm also aware that you, of all people, are realistic enough to want the truth from me, instead of having someone send you a clipping of our engagement announcement from the New York *Times*.

I shall never forget the wonderful times we had, nor what a terrific girl you are. I would like to have you as a friend, always, and if you think that's possible, please call me when you return. I wish for you everything good in this world, and I know you will have it.

Love,
Russ

Bastard. She let the letter flutter from her fingers. Selfish, scheming bastard. Liar. Opportunist. Shallow fool. How could she have loved such a spineless wonder? It was all quite clear. His precious Pamela was a rich lawyer's daughter. There'd be no years of struggle, no working wife whose support would wound his precious damned male chauvinist pride. He'd been seeing this girl all the time he was sleeping with her, pretending love while he was coldly calculating his future. She couldn't even cry. She felt leaden with loss, even though the logical part of her tried to be glad she was rid of this egotist before it was too late.

Funny. It was almost as though she knew this "Dear Jayne" letter was coming. Until she shared the purser's bed, she'd been with no one but Russell since the day they met. If she hadn't sensed it was over, why had she started the tawdry little affair with George Telling, someone she didn't give a damn about? Instinctively, she must have been beginning to rebuild her confidence, proving to herself that she could enjoy and be enjoyed by another man. No. Not so. She'd felt guilty about it, unfaithful to Russell. Before New Zealand, she'd already broken it off with George. That nonsense about his not being able to go ashore in Auckland was just a lie invented for Mary's benefit. Choosing to spend her time with Terry Spalding was her way of staying out of trouble until she got home.

She hadn't really thought her romance with Russell was over. She'd honestly thought absence would do the trick. The little fling with Telling hadn't been a presentment; it had been an impulse brought on by the glamour and unreality of shipboard life. She'd truly believed, until this letter arrived yesterday, that her plan would work. What blinders women wear when they don't wish to see the truth about men! If a girl friend had told her she was in love with a young man who wouldn't marry her, wouldn't even live with her because it would distress his family, she'd have thought her friend the world's biggest damned fool. "If he's in love with you, he won't ask you to wait years," she'd have said to someone else. "He won't take a chance on losing you. It wouldn't matter to him who paid the bills as long as you were together."

That's what she would have said, lofty in her wisdom, to someone else. But we can't analyze our own situations with such reasonable objectivity. The men we love are always perfect. Of course they are, otherwise we wouldn't love them, would we? They're an extension of our good taste, a mirror image of our own perfection. They can't fail, because we've chosen them.

Like hell. They're lousy bastards, all of them. Insensitive, like Russell. She thought of the condescending words. "Strong, sensible, realistic" was she? He "wished her everything good" did he? He hoped to "have her as a friend." It was outrageous! How dare he sit there smugly writing his little kiss-off letter and probably thinking she should be grateful for having known him at all. Well, she wasn't grateful. She hoped he was miserable in his well-chosen, secure little future. She hated his guts.

Tears came at last. She didn't hate him. She wanted him. She would die, thinking of him married to someone else. If only she were there, instead of thousands of miles away, maybe she could change his mind. Suddenly she hated the ship. Sobbing, alone, she unreasonably hated even Mary, who'd brought her to this God-forsaken part of the world. If she hadn't left New York, this wouldn't have happened. She'd have fought for Russell. Used every trick she knew to keep him. She wished she were dead. There was no hope, no consolation, no future.

Slowly, she sat up. At least she had her pride. No one knew how deep her feeling for him went. There'd been no one to confide in, thank God; so there was no one to pity her. I couldn't stand that, Jayne thought.

Taking deep breaths, she tried to compose herself before Mary returned to the cabin. She'd be the same flippant, nonchalant person the world thought she was. Maybe she'd take up with George again, or find some other attractive man aboard. But there were no attractive men. Mary had the only eligible, available one and he was a hundred years old. Fifty, at least. Forget it. A man was the last thing she wanted now. Maybe ever.

Terry Spalding was beginning to feel better. The pain of his lover's betrayal was slowly diminishing, as was the desperation that had caused him to take every penny he had in the world and spend it on this escape cruise. He'd never forget Paul. He'd never stop loving him. People didn't understand how deep the feelings between people of the same sex could go. He didn't expect them to. It was rare when you found someone like Jayne who sympathized without condemnation.

He was grateful for Jayne's friendship and he enjoyed her company although he didn't understand why she'd chosen to spend all her time with him this past week. She was a lusty, blatantly heterosexual girl who could have had any man on the ship. The officers were always inviting her to parties, asking her to dance, suggesting she go ashore with them. But since Auckland she'd seemed distinterested, preferring to spend her time with him. He was happy and thankful for that. He began to feel a strong attachment to her, not in any romantic way of course, but he'd developed a genuine fondness for her.

It won't last, he told himself realistically. Her devotion to me won't last. She feels sorry for me, that's all. But he hoped Jayne wouldn't find anyone else on this trip. She was the only thing that made it bearable for him. She was so amusing, so relaxing to be with. He could tell her anything and know she'd be interested and compassionate.

If I could spend my life with any woman, it would be Jayne, he thought. But that's out of the question for me. I'm not like Paul. I couldn't marry to provide myself with a cover of "respectability." That's what Paul did. In addition to wanting money and security, he wanted to appear "normal" for the sake of his business career in the brokerage house where he worked.

I couldn't do that, Terry thought. Thank God I don't have to. In the theater, it didn't matter what sexual persuasion you followed. People liked you for yourself, respected you for your talent, kept their noses out of your private life. Jayne would fit in with them. They'd like her. When the big chance comes and I get to New York, I hope I'll see her. He stopped. What was he talking about? By that time Jayne would be married to some Brooks Brothers type and she'd have forgotten all about the "waif" she'd been so kind to.

But I'll never forget her, Terry thought. She doesn't know it, but she saved my life.

Chapter 8

"WELL, NOW THAT you've had a quick look at my country, what do you think of it?"

Mary smiled lovingly at the long-legged figure sprawled in one of the deep leather chairs that flanked the picture windows of the Trafalgar Room. "You *know* what I think. Sydney is fabulous and everyone was so kind. It's lovely to meet people who actually like Americans. I've heard that in other foreign countries we're not so popular."

Christopher smiled back at the beautiful woman in the long, pale-green chiffon gown. They'd made a pact to dress for dinner every night, whether or not the daily program indicated "formal attire." He didn't give a damn what others wore. "I like to see you in evening clothes," he'd said. "I like watching you enter a room looking better than any other woman in the place." He thought now she'd never looked more desirable. "Australians are crazy about Yanks," he said in answer to her comment. "It's been that way since World War II. The British wrote us off. They had to, you know. There was no way they could protect us. But, as we say, you Americans came like the morning mail. We'll never forget it."

"I'm glad we did."

"To you, it's schoolbook history," Christopher teased. "You were just a kid. What, three, four years old when that war broke out? God, it seems impossible! I'm an old man compared to you. I'll be fifty-two in August. You're just a baby."

"Some baby! I'll be thirty-nine next month, for heaven's sake!"

Christopher widened his eyes in pretended astonishment. "As old as that! Fancy! And you're still a real Sheila."

"Sheila?"

"Sorry. I keep forgetting you don't speak Australian. 'Sheila' is our slang word for a good-looking woman."

"Why 'Sheila'? What's the derivation?"

"I haven't the faintest idea. English is our official language, but we've done weird things to it. There really are three kinds of English in our language. The original Australian is just about extinct. It's the tongue of the Aborigines and you never hear it except maybe in the outback. New Australian is the English you recognize, and Old Australian, spoken by most of the native-born, is called Aussie-English. It's full of slang words and expressions like 'Sheila' and some people think it's close to Cockney. I suppose it is, at that. We do say things like 'a bag of fruit' to mean 'a nice suit.' And most of the Australian you hear in the street is spoken through closed lips, with a definite slur.''

"You don't talk that way."

"No, darling. I was educated in England, remember? But I can speak Aussie-English as well as the next bloke."

"Tell me some more."

Christopher considered. "All right. You're the kind of woman who makes any man take a 'dekko.' 'Dekko' means a look, not a twenties or thirties art form. And our waiter is a 'bloody little bottler,' which translates into someone who gives you particularly good service. I promise you I'll never 'bung on a blue,' meaning I won't get into a fistfight, particularly with a 'Pommy,' which is the word for an Englishman. I do know the derivation of 'Pommy.' Supposedly it comes from the letters P.O.H.M. which stood for 'Prisoners of Her Majesty' and which the original convict settlers wore on their backs. Had enough?''

Mary was laughing. "No. Tell me more."

"I will not. You're turning me into the biggest fool this side of the black stump.''

"The *what?*"

"'The black stump' is an imaginary marker that designates the limits of unmeasurable distances. Therefore, the biggest fool this side of the black stump is the biggest fool in or out of this world. Simple, isn't it?''

"Absurd. I think I'd rather learn French."

Christopher sighed. "Such a difficult woman. Why couldn't I have taken up with a nice agreeable hero worshiper like Peggy Lawrence?''

"You don't have enough gold braid. Besides, I'd scratch her eyes out."

"Nicest thing you ever said to me." He leaned over and kissed her lightly.

Involuntarily, Mary drew back. "Christopher, don't. Someone might see."

"Let them. You don't think we're fooling anyone, do you? Darling, this ship is a floating small town. What the passengers don't see, the crew does. You don't honestly believe people don't know we make love in my cabin after lunch or that you sneak down the corridor late at night?''

Put so bluntly, the facts made her cringe. It was true. She wanted to believe that no one knew she was behaving in a way she'd never have believed possible: letting herself quietly into Christopher's cabin, sliding into bed beside him, forgetting for long, wonderful moments that there were any other hands than his.

"Don't look so ashamed. It's important and wonderful."

Mary nodded. "And frightening."

"It mustn't be," Christopher said. "You must never be frightened again. Promise me you won't."

She tried to look happy. "All right, I won't." Another lie. A little white one, the kind that made someone happy.

As though he read her mind, Christopher said, "At the race track, we call that a 'percentage lie.' You just want to please me, don't you? I know you're frightened, darling. Scared to death of the future. But it's going to be all right, Mary. No matter what, we're not going to lose each other.''

Jayne awakened abruptly, wondering what had jolted her from her sleep. The radium dial of her bedside clock said ten minutes before two. The ship was pitching and tossing ferociously, almost throwing her from her bed. Something slid off the dresser and fell to the floor. She snapped on her reading light, worried about what was happening. I've heard that the waters of the Great Barrier Reef are rough, she thought, but this is ridiculous! Damn! A full ashtray had gone skittering off the dresser and landed upside down on the clean white robe she'd dropped beside her bed. What a mess! She glanced over to see whether her aunt was awake. The other bed was empty. Of course. It was always empty until nearly dawn when Mary came sneaking back into the cabin. Jayne always pretended to be asleep. Poor thing, she thought every night, I'm sure she's guilty enough without having to face me.

Jayne picked up the ashtray, secured the other dresser-top items firmly and knelt on her bed to look out the porthole. The waves were so high they crashed against the glass, but in the intervals between each onslaught, she could see a little boat bobbing precariously on the churning sea. She thought she was dreaming as she watched a small figure leave the boat and scramble onto the ship through the crew-deck entrance. What was going on in the middle of the night?

She turned as the cabin door opened. Mary came in, looking worried. "Are you all right?"

"Sure. It's kicking up a helluva fuss out there."

"I know. Half the ship is awake. Christopher and I were just about to leave the Trafalgar Room when it started. Peggy came in, full of dire warnings about cyclones at sea."

"She would. Madam Captain. There isn't going to be one, is there?"

"Of course not. It's just a bad storm. Probably be clear and beautiful tomorrow when we cruise Whitsunday Passage. Did you see the pilot boarding just now?"

"Is that who that was? What pilot?"

"The special one who's supposed to board in Sydney. He was home watching 'the telly.' He thought we sailed today instead of yesterday, so he missed us. Had to fly to Brisbane and board a few minutes ago in all this storm. He guides us through the Passage. Poor man. I don't know how he ever got aboard."

"It wasn't easy," Jayne said. "I thought I was seeing things." She looked out into the black, stormy night again. "There won't be much sleep for anybody tonight."

"No. Peggy says the waves are coming all the way up to Promenade." Mary sat down on her bed with a lurch. "Wow! This *is* rough! I was hanging onto the walls all the way back to the cabin."

"Maybe you'd feel safer with Christopher. Don't stay here on my account. I'm perfectly okay."

Mary didn't answer.

"I'm sorry, Aunt Mary. That wasn't meant to be a nasty crack. I just meant I think it's silly that we're playing games. I know you spend most of every night with Christopher. I'm all for it. I told you long ago I thought it was a good idea. You don't have to pretend with me. I'm glad you're happy." Her voice broke. "I'm glad one of us is happy."

"Jayne, what is it?" Mary forgot her own problems. "What's wrong?"

"Nothing."

"That's not true. You're miserable about something."

The sympathy in her aunt's voice got to her. Damn it, she hadn't meant anybody to know about Russell, but now it came pouring out, all of it, the whole story, told between choking sobs. Mary ached with pity for her, remembering how it felt to be that age, recalling how desperately in love with Michael she'd been, how she'd have been suicidal if he hadn't married her. She didn't think the young took things so hard these days. Jayne seemed so independent, so self-assured. But human nature doesn't change, no matter what people say. Hearts ache in the seventies as they did in the fifties, as they have since the beginning of time. She staggered over to Jayne's bed and put her arms around the weeping girl.

"I'm so sorry, Jaynie. So terribly sorry."

Jayne wiped her eyes and tried to smile. "You can't win 'em all, to coin a phrase."

"Don't, honey. Don't try to be brave. You have a right to cry. I wish there were some words of comfort that weren't the old clichés. You know the answer—time. And some really nice young man who'll come along."

"Sure."

"I know you don't believe that now, but it's true." Mary hugged her. "Think you could get some sleep? Even with this rocking and rolling going on? Tomorrow will be a better day."

The girl nodded. "Thanks. Sorry I dumped all over you."

"I'm glad you did. Talking helps. I know that." She undressed and slid into her bed. Christopher was waiting for her. It was the first night since New Zealand that she hadn't been with him. He was probably disappointed, but she was too troubled to forget everything, even in his arms. Some nights it was better to lie quietly alone and try to make sense of things. In a little while she heard the sound of Jayne's even breathing. How wonderful it was to be young and resilient. Heartbroken as she was, Jayne's youth let her sleep, healing herself as she dreamed.

Not so with Mary. She lay awake all night, listening to the groaning and creaking of the ship as it fought the angry waters. Jayne would forget that selfish young man. In days to come she'd scarcely remember his name. If only I could do the same, Mary thought. There are two men in my life I'll never be able to forget. Because in a terrible, pulled-apart way I'm in love with both.

Michael picked up the mail and quickly skimmed it, happy to see a letter from Mary postmarked Sydney. Things took an unconscionable length of time to reach San Francisco from the other side of the world. He'd memorized the schedule. By the time he read her words from Australia, she was on her way to Bali. How he envied her that trip. He hadn't let her know how disappointed he was that she'd taken Jayne. Angry, really, though he didn't show it. Still, he didn't know how lonely he was going to be without her. In a way, he'd almost looked forward to the separation. It would be like being a bachelor again, he'd thought. And if some pretty young thing took his eye, well, what Mary didn't know would never hurt her.

But it hadn't worked out that way. He just hadn't been in the mood. Reading his wife's presumably lighthearted questions about Rae Spanner, he wondered what kept him from accepting her unmistakable invitation to stay on after the party. Rae was a damned good-looking woman and, he suspected, a sexy one. It wasn't his high moral character that kept him from cheating on Mary. He'd done that several times, unbeknownst to her, since their marriage. But they were always inconsequential adventures, most of them in Los Angeles when he went down to visit his mother, and they meant nothing to him. He supposed he was afraid that getting involved with Rae Spanner might lead to more serious trouble. She was not one to be brushed off, and rather than risk Mary's finding out, he'd pretended not to take her overtures seriously. He'd left the Valentine party early and had not seen her in the month since then.

In addition to his wariness about Rae, he'd been so damned caught up in trying to prepare a new proposal for Harry Carson that he'd hardly thought of anything else. He still hadn't finished it. It was boring and stupid to plan the kind of men's store Harry wanted. Michael hated the idea. He'd made a dozen false starts, knowing that anything so difficult to do must be wrong. But he had no choice.

He flipped through the bills, putting them aside, and threw the advertisements and charity pleas into the wastebasket. At the bottom of the pile was a letter addressed to him in a handwriting he did not recognize. Surprised, he read Patricia's brief note. He barely knew Mary's sister, had seen her only on those rare visits to New York, spoken to her once on the phone. Now she was asking if it would be possible for her to come and stay at the apartment until Mary and Jayne returned!

"I'd so like to meet the ship when it docks," Patricia wrote. "I miss my child terribly and can't wait to see her and Mary again. And since I don't know San Francisco at all, I thought it would be fun to spend some time in advance of April 20. I wouldn't get in your way, Michael, and I'll be perfectly happy on your extra couch. But if it isn't convenient, don't hesitate to say so. I'll understand if the idea of a houseguest fills you with horror—even if it's a member of the family!"

She's right, Michael thought. The idea of a houseguest does fill me with horror. It will be a pain in the behind. But how can I refuse Mary's only sister? God, I'll have to take her sight-seeing and out to dinner, or prepare meals for her here! She'll get in my way just when I need to be alone to get this silly business started. Still, I can't say no.

He dashed off a letter saying he'd be delighted to have her and to let him know when she planned to arrive.

With alarming speed she responded that she'd come on March 25 if that was agreeable. He shouldn't bother to meet her at the airport. She'd take a bus to the terminal and a taxi from there, so unless he heard further, he could plan to see her that Monday afternoon and she was so appreciative and looked forward so much to her first vacation in years.

Michael couldn't believe it. He'd thought she'd come a few days before the ship returned and here she was planning to stay nearly a month! What's more, her arrival was less than a week away! He muttered a four-letter word. He'd have to give her the bedroom, of course, and he didn't look forward to sleeping on the convertible. For that matter, he didn't look forward to the whole damned thing. He supposed he could have made some excuse, but Patricia knew the room was here. And Mary would be upset if he'd refused. She'd have a right to be angry since she paid the bills. It was really her apartment, Michael thought. He'd have to make her sister welcome.

Charlie Burke read his letter from Mary with pleasure and a sense of appreciation. She knew his diary was phony, written not only to satisfy the frustrated essayist within him but also to prepare her for the fact that most cruises were filled with boring people and she shouldn't be surprised if she found her fellow travelers less than stimulating. Apparently she had not. He wondered who the "handful of attractive, mature, un-lost souls" were. At least one of them must be a man.

He felt an unreasonable twinge of jealousy. He was fifty years old and married to a woman who'd live a long time, at least until she drank herself to death. Not that he wanted Tracey to die. He couldn't bring himself to wish that. But life with her was day after day, year after year of purgatory. A hundred times she'd told him she wanted to stop drinking, but of course she didn't. She made half-hearted attempts at psychiatry and gave it up after a few sessions; went to Alcoholics Anonymous meetings and quit after two weeks, saying they were a bunch of crazy extroverts who stood up and told the most disgusting things about their lives. She wasn't one of them, she told Charlie. She'd never been picked up drunk on the street or landed in the alcoholic ward of the City Hospital.

No, he'd thought, you haven't. Maybe it would be better if you had. Maybe it would shock you into realization of how sick you are. Instead, you drink quietly and steadily at home, knowing I'll come in and find you either passed out or incoherent. Or, on more than one occasion, raving mad and violent.

She'd been younger than Mary when she became a heavy drinker. A pretty woman in her early thirties. They'd been married almost ten years when she went into her depression and began to seek forgetfulness in the bottle. The doctors said she brooded over her inability to have children. She had three miscarriages in the first five years of their marriage, and they told her she could never go full term.

"Some women can't handle their barrenness," the doctors said. "They feel utter failures, to themselves and their husbands."

"But I don't care whether we have children," Charlie had protested. "I've told her that over and over. I've even said we could adopt if she wants babies so badly, but she refuses to listen to the idea."

"I know. These cases are beyond reason. Maybe analysis . . ."

Charlie had finally persuaded her to try it, but it didn't take. He knew it wouldn't. It couldn't, unless the patient really wanted it, and Tracey only went to please him. Just as she went to AA to please him, knowing full well she didn't believe in it. He gave up long ago, accepting the fact that this was their cross and they'd have to bear it. Unreasonably, he also felt some guilt for her condition. It wasn't only her childlessness that tore them apart, it was Tracey's feeling of inadequacy in other ways. She saw him become more and more successful in his business and felt herself being left behind. She didn't mix well with the wives of his associates and whenever they went to a business party she got drunk immediately, having fortified herself for the ordeal with several hefty shots of scotch before she left the house. She embarrassed him terribly at such times and there were terrible scenes when they got home. Eventually, he stopped taking her to these gatherings, an action which both relieved and angered her.

"I know I'm not smart enough for your friends," she said bitterly. "I'm just a dull, dreary housewife."

He'd lashed out sometimes. "You wouldn't be, damn it, if you'd stay sober! You think I've left you behind. Well, if I have, it's your own fault. You're as bright as any of those wives, except *they're* not falling-down drunk!''

She'd cry, then, and beg him not to leave her, she loved him so, she couldn't live without him. Charlie was always remorseful and apologetic. She couldn't help the way she was. It was despicable of him to say such cruel things to her.

It had been going on for five years when he met Mary and fell silently, hopelessly in love with her. He loved her in that fashion still. It was hard to be her friend, her mentor, when he wanted to be her lover. Yet there was comfort in seeing her every day, in watching her bloom into the personality he knew she could become. Half a loaf, but he settled for it. He even tried to like Michael, though he was convinced the man wasn't good enough for her. If he makes her happy, he's a good choice, Charlie tried to believe.

But Michael *wasn't* right for her. Charlie recognized that even before Mary told him a little of it. They seldom spoke of it these days. It was a taboo subject, just as his feelings for her were off limits in any conversation. He'd always felt that someday she'd meet someone who'd be all she deserved, and he wondered what would happen when that time came. Would she stay with Michael, out of pity and conscience, the way he stayed with Tracey? Or would she have the great good sense to grab at happiness while there still was time?

Funny. She mentioned no man in her letter, but Charlie felt this strange certainty that there was one. Good luck if there is, sweetheart, he said silently. Don't let him get away.

He opened the package of tapes that had arrived along with the letter and put the first one on the portable machine that was a duplicate of the one Mary carried. He listened with satisfaction to Colonel Beauregarde Calhoun Stanford. It was a wonderful interview. You could fall in love with this courtly gentleman of the old school, even forgive him his "chauvinist views," which he didn't recognize as such because he obviously adored women and wanted them on a pedestal to be worshiped.

Nice job, Charlie thought. He put on the second tape. Mary had interviewed her cabin stewardess, an unmistakably lower-class English girl with youthful charm and enthusiasm. She described life at sea, what it was like "below decks" in the crew dining room where a half-dozen languages were spoken, and in the bar where the staff obviously had a rollicking good time when they were off duty. She told, under Mary's skillful prodding, how wonderful it was to see the world and be paid for the privilege and how most of the youngsters aboard signed on for that very reason and would leave the ship after their contracts were up.

Good. A real "Upstairs, Downstairs" approach. Charlie was equally pleased with the interview with a Catholic priest on Tonga who spent his life helping the poor on the island, running a school for the children, assisting the adults in setting up meager farms to support their pathetically modest needs. And the lady in Picton was just fine.

The fifth tape was an interview with the English captain. The man spoke fluently of his long naval background, beginning with his experiences on a British cargo ship in World War II as a young sailor and moving easily into the more glamorous life he now lived. Charlie listened carefully. Mary seemed intensely interested in everything Anthony Robin had to say, expressing surprise that he'd never married, laughing indulgently when he replied that the ship was all the woman he could handle and the sea a demanding mistress.

Was this the one? Charlie wondered. Maybe. Maybe not. Mary's seeming fascination with his story might indicate that she had more than a professional interest in the man. On the other hand, she gave the same rapt attention to everyone she talked to. It was the secret of her success. People knew she cared. The interviewee was flattered by it and the sincerity of her interest came across to the listener. Probably he was only imagining there was something different in the way she spoke to the captain. Of course he was. Mary wasn't the kind to go chasing after the officers on a ship.

He snapped off the machine. Nearly two hours had passed as he sat listening to her voice. It was the best two hours he'd had since she left.

Chapter 9

BALI WAS A dream. Everything was as Mary had pictured it—the beautiful, graceful people in their exotic and brilliantly colored clothes; the ornate, golden temples of Balinese Hinduism; the breathtaking sight of Gunung Agung, the ten-thousand-foot peak towering above the rice paddies. It was unbearably hot, but they didn't mind. She and Christopher went ashore in a ship's launch, laughingly fended off the noisy souvenir sellers and tourist guides at the pier and found their own pixyish cab driver who took them to Ubud, a microscopic village forty kilometers from the main town of Benoa.

In a tiny art gallery, they drank coffee and bought a painting and, almost shyly, Mary asked the owner if she'd consent to talk into the machine for the American radio. Politely, the woman agreed. In halting, charmingly broken English, she told them something of life on the small Indonesian island. Under Mary's questioning, she described the food and its preparation, with emphasis on the steamed rice called *nasi*, word also used to mean food itself. She spoke reverently of her religion built around Sanghyang Widi, the Supreme Being of the Balinese, portrayed as a symbolic male figure with flames shooting out from his body. She described feast days and offerings to pacify evil spirits and, her eyes shining, the beauty of Balinese dances and drama, all rich with symbolism. Enchanted, Mary listened, interrupting only when the woman seemed to falter, and at the end she impulsively kissed the smooth cheek of her obliging "guest."

"The people in America will be so interested. We can't imagine this kind of peaceful, gentle life."

"Not always peaceful in Bali. Sometimes Agug spit fire."

Mary looked questioningly at Christopher.

"She means a volcanic eruption," he said. "Mount Agug and Mount Batur erupted in the early sixties. Wiped out whole villages and killed thousands in eastern Bali.''

''Gentleman is correct. But our mountains the home of gods. We look *up* for help. Not out to sea like some peoples.'' She smiled. ''We look up for love and protection. Always *up*. Bali once a flat land but gods raised mountains to live in. Agug most holy of all.''

''Thank you,'' Mary said. ''You've been wonderful.''

The woman bowed. ''You come back. Always welcome.''

Christopher answered for them. ''We'll be back, madame. You can count on it.''

Jayne was already in the shower when Mary returned carrying her painting, a lovely piece of batik and her precious tape. In a moment, the girl emerged, wrapped in a towel.

''That island was like a sneak preview of Hades! I've been standing under ice-cold water for ten minutes! Nice day?''

''Perfect. I even got a great interview. Did you have fun?''

Jayne nodded. ''I went ashore with Terry. Took a drive and ended up having a late lunch at the Hong Kong restaurant. It was so funny. Nobody spoke a word of English, but Terry had five pretty little Balinese waitresses hanging around the table watching him eat. They looked like they'd like to kidnap him.'' ·

Mary was noncommittal. ''He is a handsome young man.''

Jayne stepped into her bra and panties. ''You know,'' she said thoughtfully, ''I'm not sure Terry's gay. That is, I know he's gay, but I think he could be bisexual. He was flirting like crazy with those girls. I think he's even turned on by me.''

Mary tried not to show her dismay. Since the night of the storm, Jayne hadn't referred to her broken romance with Russell and Mary considerately hadn't reminded her of it. But now she said, ''Jayne, you're not getting any silly ideas about Terry, are you?''

''You mean like maybe trying to get him into bed? I've been thinking about it. Why not?''

''That's not the answer to your unhappiness. And you might create more for him.''

The girl raised her chin in a defiant gesture that reminded Mary of her own youthful rebellion. ''It might be the best thing I can do for both of us. Terry's never slept with a woman. It could change his whole life.''

''Darling, be sensible. You're not the first woman who's ever thought she was the one to change a man's sexual preference. Unfortunately, it rarely works.'' Mary tried to sound light-hearted. ''There's a little bit of conceit in that kind of thinking, my dear. As though only you in all the world could be so fascinating that Terry would 'see the light.' ''

''I'm not sure that isn't true.''

''Jayne, it isn't the answer for you,'' Mary said again. ''You're hurt. You're confused and rebounding. You won't get even with Russell this way. Don't do it.''

"What have I got to lose? My God, I'm not talking about marrying Terry! It's just an experiment. I've never tried it before." She sounded angry.

"You don't experiment with people's psyches! It's too much like playing God!"

Jayne didn't answer. Mary looked at the half-clad young body. How beautiful she was. Beautiful enough, perhaps, to stir even Terry. But it was no good. Mary knew other women who married gay men in the honest belief they could "reform" them. Strangely enough, some of the marriages lasted, though she wondered how they did. How could a woman share her husband with another man? Bad enough to fight a female rival, but a male would be impossible competition. She was being silly. Jayne had no intention of marrying the boy. She wasn't that foolish. But there was little doubt she was going to try to seduce him. It could be a disaster for both of them and yet there was no way to stop her. *The more I argue against it,* Mary thought, *the more she'll be determined to do it. I just have to hope that Terry isn't as curious as she is.*

Peggy Lawrence was furious. Damn Christopher Andrews! He was the one who'd talked Mary into going ahead with her plans for China instead of staying in Hong Kong to act as Peggy's matron of honor. The man had Mary twisted around his little finger and she couldn't see what a fool she was making of herself. Peggy had seen enough of these shipboard romances in the past three years to know they ended as abruptly as they began. Andrews was smooth. No doubt about that. And Mary was totally taken in. The whole ship was gossiping about her infatuation. Angry when Mary told her she couldn't do her the favor she asked, Peggy had told her just that.

"You're really making a spectacle of yourself," she'd said coldly. "Everyone knows you're a married woman. Besides, what kind of example do you think you're setting for your niece? Really, Mary, I'm shocked by your behavior!"

Not knowing whether to be upset or to laugh at the incongruity of Peggy's criticism, Mary chose to be calm. "I really doubt that Christopher and I are of that much interest to anyone. We're not children, after all. As for Jayne, she's a young adult, quite capable of making her assessments. I'm sorry to disappoint you about the wedding, Peggy. I know that's why you're upset. But it's not really Christopher's fault that I'm going to stay with my original plan. One of the main attractions of this cruise was the chance to go into China."

Despite her reasonable tone of voice, Mary was disturbed. It wasn't just the fact that she was being talked about, though she hated that. And heaven knows it wasn't as though she was doing anything Jayne thought even mildly shocking. Peggy's words had stirred up feelings she was continually trying to suppress. She tried not to think of Michael, alone at home, believing in her, trusting her implicitly.

And less important but not to be ignored was the fact that after this blow-up she'd have to face Peggy every day for another month. Discounting shore trips, that meant another twenty or so strained dinners at the same table with a woman who disapproved of her. Maybe after they were married Peggy and Tony would dine in his cabin. No, that wouldn't work. Part of the captain's duties was to preside at his own table of VIPs. *It's a stupid arrangement, their getting married* in the middle of a trip, Mary thought with annoyance. If Peggy weren't so hungry for a husband, she'd have the good sense to wait until Tony had shore leave. And how dare she criticize me anyway? If there's a spectacle aboard, she's it! Wrong. The truth was that Tony and Peggy were both free agents. Questionable taste as it might be for the captain to have his lady love aboard, there was no adultery involved, as there was with her.

Christopher was furious when she reported the conversation to him on the way to Singapore.

"That bloody bitch! How dare she talk to you that way?"

"Don't get so upset or you'll make me sorry I told you. We still have to look at her at dinner between here and Yokohama."

"Maybe I should try to get us a table for two."

"Christopher! Don't you dare! Good lord, if there's talk now, think what that would do! Besides, I'm traveling with Jayne, remember? I can't just waltz off and leave her."

"I could get a table for three."

"No. It's out of the question."

He looked at her, half amused. "You can be a very determined lady when you choose to, can't you? I'm quite sure you're used to making decisions and having them obeyed. All right. In this I concede, but don't think you're setting a precedent with me, my love! I'm stronger and tougher and meaner than you, even if I'm not as pretty."

"Gin."

Colonel Stanford turned a baleful eye on the woman across the card table. Gail DeVries smiled innocently.

"I've been having a great run of luck on this trip, haven't I, Beau? Let's see, we've played gin rummy every morning since San Francisco and you now owe me forty-seven dollars and fifty cents. I think I'll let you spend it on me in China."

"I don't think there'll be anything worth forty-seven dollars in China. Besides, little lady, I'm not sure they're going to let us in. You saw the brochure. They're recommending it only to people in good health, without handicaps."

"So? We're in good health and neither of us has a handicap."

"You don't think old age is a handicap?"

Gail bristled. "I certainly do not! We're not infirm, either of us. And as for all that warning nonsense about lots of walking and very few public toilets, who cares? I mean to go into China, Beau, and I certainly don't intend to let longevity stop me! My lord, the Chinese are supposed to revere old people!"

"The Chinese, maybe, but what about the Occidentals? They're the ones who'll decide whether we're up to making the trip."

"Well, I'm not going to let some whippersnapper of a young tour director decide whether I can go or not!" Gail was vehement. "I don't know if I'll ever get this way again, and I don't intend to miss it. I won't let you miss it, either. For heaven's sake, Beauregarde, you're not going to die in Canton!" She smiled. "It would be much too inconvenient."

She delighted him. How lucky he was to have a friend like this enthusiastic, cheerful woman. Other men his age were sitting in rockers on their children's front porches or, worse still, withering away in some old folks' home. But he had his trip with Gail to look forward to every year, and his weekly correspondence between times to keep him feeling alive and interested. His children and grandchildren didn't understand. To them, old people were stereotypes, useless, ancient things to be tucked quietly into a corner and given a decent amount of respect and attention. They were also sure he was squandering their inheritance on these expensive trips. Crazy kids. They didn't know there'd be plenty left for them if he died tomorrow.

Of course, all that silly talk about being buried at sea was just part of his conversational patter. He knew cruise ships had their own morgues aboard. They had to, on long voyages such as this. He'd never seen it, but he'd heard they had a place for three or four bodies. Statistically, it was to be expected that with a passenger list of primarily elderly people, they had to be prepared for the possibility of death aboard, and for handling the deceased until they reached the next port from which the unfortunate one could be shipped home. Gail knew how to handle that for him if it happened. They'd exchanged that information on their second cruise. She knew what to do if he died. And he knew what to do for her. Of course, the odds were it wouldn't occur. They were lucky, both of them, to be so robust. They'd probably take quite a few more trips together. He hoped so. It was a lifesaver for both of them, in more ways than one.

"All right," he said, packing up the cards and score pad. "China it is. Mary is going, isn't she?" Gail had told him what Mary had confided in her: that Peggy wanted her to stay in Hong Kong for the wedding.

"Yes, thank goodness, she's going. Christopher put his foot down. But her niece has decided against it. She and Terry are going to take in the sights in Hong Kong."

"I see. Well, I suppose it will be gay for the young folks."

She raised her eyebrows. Was her old friend deliberately making a play on words? They'd never discussed Terry. She wasn't sure whether Beau knew about him. Homosexuals were something he probably gave no thought to, and they'd never discussed Terry's "condition" as she thought of it. For that matter, she realized, Terry was a good deal less obvious than he'd been at the start of the trip. The jewelry had disappeared and he seemed, somehow, more confident, even more, well, manly. Maybe Jayne was having a good influence on him. Gail frowned. She certainly hoped that nice child wasn't deluding herself. In San Francisco, Gail had met many young men like Terry, friends of her granddaughters'. She knew about the "gay community," but she wasn't sure Beau had that much knowledge of it. He was not an unsophisticated man, but his life in Atlanta was different. She doubted, even now, he realized what Terry was. She wouldn't tell him. It might not sit well and she wouldn't want to upset him or have him upset Terry. She liked that boy. He was sweet and sensitive. She wished he were different. He and Jayne made such a handsome pair.

They'd arrive in Singapore on the twenty-first, just two days from now, and Jayne and Terry were making their plans for the shore excursion. There's such a change in him, the girl thought, as she listened to him reading from the information booklet the ship provided in advance of every port.

"We have to have a drink at Raffles," Terry said. "A Singapore Sling, naturally. In honor of Somerset Maugham. And we'll go to Chinatown. Do you know you can still see old women with bound feet from their youth? And we should have dinner at the open market on Orchard Street. How are you with chopsticks?"

"Terrific. No self-respecting New York girl grows up not knowing how to eat with chopsticks. Next to kosher delis we specialize in Chinese restaurants."

Terry laughed. "You make everything such fun, Jayne." He sobered. "When I came aboard, I never thought I'd have fun again."

"You feel better about Paul."

He swallowed hard at the mention of the name, but he was glad Jayne was always so direct. It was one of the things he liked best about her. "Yes, I feel better. I'm still hurt, but I've come around to feeling angry, too. That's healthy, I guess."

"You bet your damn boots it's healthy!" Jayne looked at him affectionately. They were still friends, nothing more, but she hadn't forgotten what she'd said to Mary in the cabin. At the time, it had been almost an effort to shock. She wasn't sure she'd meant it seriously. But now she was genuinely devoted to Terry. If she got him into bed, it would be more than an experiment. It might well be a loving experience. Terry was sensual, as she was. She looked at the lean, hard young body under the thin cotton shirt and felt genuine desire. But what about him? As though to test him, she said, casually, "How about Bugis Street? I hear that's where the action is after midnight."

He wasn't deceived. He knew what was in her mind. Bugis Street was famous. Or notorious. That's where the "girls" paraded their wares, moving up and down the wide alley, past street cafes, looking for clients. Some of them were female prostitutes, often accompanied by their pimps, openly inviting the willing sailors who flocked to Bugis Street. But there were even more who weren't girls at all, but who were also looking for business. Men "in drag" were a large part of the passing parade. Terry had heard all about them from friends who'd been to Singapore. There was even a changing room in the shape of a corner cafe. Young men disappeared into this shuttered structure and reappeared minutes later wearing extravagant female attire, clinging dresses slit to the hip, luxurious wigs and makeup. Bugis Street was decadence personified. Anything you wanted was there, yours for the taking at a gesture. Jayne knew about Bugis Street too. She was probing.

For a minute he resented it. If he wanted to pick up a young man, it wasn't her business. But he didn't. Not that he might not be happy to find a replacement for Paul someday, but when he did, it would be a civilized long-term arrangement. He wasn't one for this tawdry kind of chance encounter. He looked directly into Jayne's eyes.

"I think we should see Bugis Street," he said. "Together. I hear it's a unique spectacle."

Her eyes gave him a warm, approving response.

After Patricia announced her impending arrival in San Francisco, Michael dashed off a letter to Mary. With luck, she'd receive it before the ship left Hong Kong on March 29. In his note, he made light of the visit he dreaded.

> I can't say I really relish putting up with a female guest for such a long stay, but she seemed so anxious I couldn't very well say no. Anyway, I made a reservation for her and Jayne at the St. Francis for the night of April 20, in the devout hope they'll go home next day. I'm sure, fond as you are of Jayne, you'll have had plenty of her by that time. I'm damned sure I'll be glad to see the last of your sister, no matter how little trouble she is. And I certainly don't want anybody around to spoil our first night together after so long!
>
> Harry Carson and I are still talking about the boutique and I'm making a few minor changes in the plan. I'm sure it's in the bag and things will be rosy from there on.

In his mind, it was all true. He did feel unable to refuse Patricia's request. And he was eager to have Mary home. It seemed forever since he'd been to bed with her, and though their love life wasn't that great after fifteen years, it satisfied him. Most of the time.

As for Harry, well, he'd decided not to knuckle under to Harry's stupid demands. He'd make minor changes in the plan, but not many. If that fool didn't like them, he could go to hell. But Harry would go along in the end. Michael was sure of it.

When Patricia arrived less than a week later, he was stunned. Either he hadn't paid her much attention before or she'd undergone a transformation. In any case, she was a beauty.

"Michael!" She kissed him on the cheek. "It's so good to see you!" She stepped back and looked him over appraisingly. "I'd forgotten how handsome you are. My sister's a lucky woman."

He felt himself blushing like a schoolboy. "Good to see *you*, Patricia. How was the trip?"

"Fabulous. I felt as though I were running away from home." She gave a throaty laugh. "As a matter of fact, I am. Not literally, of course. Don't get nervous that you'll be stuck with me forever. But it's marvelous to have a change of scene! And you're a darling to take me in."

"Happy to have you here." To his own surprise, he found it was true. She was as ebullient as she was good-looking. She'll be nice to have around, Michael thought. I didn't realize how empty this place has been. He felt suddenly comforted. It was like having a part of Mary here, a gayer, more enthusiastic Mary. He couldn't believe Patricia was seven years older than her sister. She didn't look a day over thirty-five. The shining blond hair fell to her shoulders and the makeup, though too heavy, was skillfully applied to a perfect, unlined skin. Obviously, she worked hard at looking young. The effect was just a little cheap, he realized.

A little out of keeping for a woman her age. But it was dramatic, and combined with the good figure and the pantsuit, which emphasized the extraordinary length of her legs, it made for a woman any man would turn to stare at as she passed.

"Let me show you to the bedroom. I'm sure you'd like to unpack."

She held up a long, well-manicured hand in protest. "Now don't give me an argument. I'm not taking your room. I know Mary has a couch in her office and that will suit me just fine. All I need is a place to hang up a few things."

"Nonsense. Mary would kill me if I let you sleep there. Not that it's all that uncomfortable. I mean, I don't mind it, and you're our guest."

"Well, if you're sure. . . . But I do feel I'm inconveniencing you terribly, Michael."

"Not for a minute."

"You're very sweet. I can understand why Mary's so crazy about you."

Again, he felt vaguely uncomfortable and didn't know why. Hell, she was only being pleasant. Grateful that he allowed her to impose for such a lengthy stay. But he felt a surge of physical excitement. She was the most provocative woman he'd met in years. Patricia could make a banal conversation sound like an invitation to seduction. Ridiculous! Was he crazy, having such thoughts about his sister-in-law? It was disgusting. She'd slap his face if she could read his mind. He'd been too long without a woman, that was all. More than a month. He'd better sneak out one of these nights soon and find himself something. After all, a man had his needs. Maybe Rae. No. Better a stranger. There was that cute little secretary in Harry Carson's office. She gave him the eye every time he went in. Sure. Why not? If Mary left him alone so long she couldn't expect him to live like a monk. Next week when he went to see Harry, he'd see what else he could accomplish.

Chapter 10

"I WISH YOU were going into China with us."

Jayne, busily inspecting the mound of things she'd bought the first day in Hong Kong, shook her head. "Terry doesn't care about it. He wants to do the restaurants and night clubs and, of course, shop. Did you ever, in your life, see such a city for encouraging bankruptcy? We've been here eight hours and I've already bought enough stuff to open my own boutique on Madison Avenue!"

Mary looked with interest at the array that covered Jayne's bed: a palm-sized transistor radio, a camera, yards of silk fabric, an exquisite mandarin coat, assorted pieces of ivory. One lovely piece, in particular, caught her eye. It was a delicately carved ivory figure of a Chinese woman, a superb nude with carved flowers in her hair and a bouquet of them held against her breast. The gleaming figure rested on a teak base about twelve inches long, as though it were reclining on a bed.

"What's that fascinating thing?"

"Isn't it wonderful? They call it a 'doctor doll.' Unfortunately, it's a reproduction of the antique ones, but I love it just the same. Do you know about them, Aunt Mary? In the old days, Chinese ladies wouldn't undress in front of their doctors, so they had these dolls and could point to the spot where their complaint was. Terry bought it for me."

"It's beautiful." She hesitated. "I didn't know Terry was interested in female nudes."

"He is now," Jayne said. "In fact, he has been ever since we left Singapore."

There was no mistaking her meaning. So she did it, Mary thought. She actually seduced him. She admitted to herself that she was curious, but she'd bite off her tongue before she'd ask her niece to tell her more.

"Come on," the girl said, laughing. "You know you're dying to hear about it. Don't be so bloody tactful. I don't mind telling you. It's been great, Aunt Mary. For both of us. It's like introducing a child to the mysteries of the birds and bees. He's struck dumb by the magic. Oh, the first time was a little awkward, I admit. But since then, it's as though he can't live without me. And believe me, I don't mind. He's a beautiful person, spiritually as well as physically. God, when I compare him with that insensitive Russell. . ."

Mary didn't know what to say. Apparently she'd been wrong in her fears that Jayne would only further confuse herself and Terry by trying to have an affair with him. Obviously, it had worked well. So much for my curbstone psychology, she thought. Jayne's instincts are better than my limited knowledge. The girl was looking at her, waiting for a reaction.

"You still disapprove."

"No, darling, I just don't want to see either of you hurt by this."

Jayne's face softened and her voice became almost a whisper. "We won't be. I think it's the best thing that ever happened to me in my whole life. I didn't know a man could be so gentle, so worshipful and still so virile. He's tried before, Aunt Mary, but never with someone who cared for him. You know, he cried that first night. Actually wept. I held him in my arms for hours, soothing him as though he were a child. He's happy, and so am I."

Mary kept still. This was wrong. She still felt it. Jayne was the mother Terry was looking for. He was acting out a fantasy. No, I mustn't think such things! I have to believe she's the one-in-a-million woman who can change a young man like Terry. And I can only pray that they'll say good-bye in San Francisco without having done some terrible emotional damage to each other. She looked at Jayne, radiant in her new-found happiness. At least for the moment she's forgotten how miserable she was. That's something to be grateful for.

"Be careful, darling," Mary said. "That's all I ask."

"You mean don't get pregnant?"

"No, I mean take this for what it is—a very special moment in time that both of you will remember with gratitude and affection. You're both getting over bad love affairs, finding consolation with each other. Don't read more into it than that, Jayne dear. Don't try to continue it when the trip ends."

Her aunt's lack of belief in miracles stung the young woman. Mary didn't know what she was talking about. She hadn't been there during those hours of lovemaking, hadn't seen the joy in Terry's eyes. She was spouting textbook psychology and it infuriated Jayne.

"I hope you're going to take your own advice," she said. "Speaking of 'special moments in time,' I trust that's how you look on your own affair with Christopher. You do have a loving husband at home, as I recall. Or had you forgotten?"

The bitter outburst did not anger Mary. "I haven't forgotten," she said quietly. "Perhaps it's because I haven't forgotten that I'm so concerned about you. I don't want to see you make the same mistake I did."

"Don't tell me Michael was ever gay!"

"No. Of course not. But he also wanted someone to cling to. Someone always there to soothe and comfort and protect. You're very like me, Jayne. Perhaps that's why I love you so much and fear for you at the same time. You could fall into the same trap I did, choosing someone who needed your strength, a man who made you feel superhuman. You're strong, as I am. And our strength is our weakness where men are concerned. We mother them, excuse them, feel some misguided obligation to take care of them. It's wrong, Jaynie. We end up unhappy and unfulfilled, and guilty because of our feelings."

Her niece stared at her. "I didn't know," she said. "I didn't know how you felt. I always was kind of sorry for Uncle Mike. I thought you dominated him because you liked having a pet on a leash. I didn't know you felt empty and miserable. I'm sorry, Aunt Mary. You always seemed so much in charge of your life. I thought you had everything you wanted. Funny. I never thought you had problems of your own. All I saw was a career and a fancy apartment and a good-looking man who adores you. It never occurred to me that wasn't enough. I can see now why you're so attracted to Christopher. He's everything Mike isn't, I suppose—successful, demanding, unmanageable. What are you going to do about him?"

"I don't know. He wants me to marry him."

"And you want to."

"Yes, I do." It was strange to say it aloud for the first time. "But I don't know whether I can. I didn't tell you, but I came on this trip to think about whether or not I wanted to go on with my marriage. I was uncertain even before I met Christopher. He hasn't changed my thinking that much. I mean, I'm not one of those women who predicates her future on the next man. Even if there'd been no Christopher, I'd still have to decide by the time I got back whether I wanted to stay with Michael or set him free."

"Set *him* free?"

"Yes. I'm not sure that marriage to me isn't worse for him than marriage to him is for me. I've helped make him more dependent and helpless than he already was. I didn't want to. Not consciously. But I did. I'm torn between thinking it would be the greatest kindness I ever did both of us, or the greatest disaster."

Jayne looked at her with pity. "You still love him, don't you?"

"In a way. But I can't respect him, maybe because I can't respect myself. All my life I've wanted to be *somebody*, Jayne. I watched my mother, your grandmother, sublimate herself to her husband. She's no more than a mirror image of my father. I saw your own mother throw her life away because she couldn't resist flaunting her beauty. I never had beauty, Jayne, but I made up my mind somewhere early on that I'd be more in control of my life than either of those two handsome women. I'd find a man who adored me because I was competent and smart. One who'd love me because he needed me." Mary gave a little laugh. "Well, I did. And I have no right to blame him because he succeeded at that. He shouldn't pay for my conceit." She paused. "And Terry is too nice a boy to pay for yours. He needs you. He worships you. He's even discovered that with you 'normal sex' can be good. But that won't be enough for you in the long run, I'm afraid. And probably not for him, either.''

"I'm not going to marry him, Aunt Mary. I'm not going to marry anybody.''

"I'd hate to think you meant that. About not marrying anybody, I mean. When it's right, marriage is the best state of all.''

"Do you know any that are right? Would you call your parents' marriage ideal? Or mine? How about your own? And what do you think Peggy and Captain Robin's chances are when they do that dumb thing here? No, I'm not going to marry Terry or anybody else. I'll love someone and live with him. Terry, maybe. But no marriage. Marriage is strictly for procreation and I want no part of that.''

Mary sighed. Jayne had a right to be disillusioned about marriage. The knowledge of her own conception was enough to make her cynical about matrimony and its aftermath. Yet Mary was romantic enough to believe it could be good. It would be with Christopher, she thought. I know it would.

"Well, let's hope we both come out of our situations intact,'' she said finally. "You're a sensible girl, Jayne. Use the brains God gave you. That's all I ask.'' She managed to smile. "And I'll try to use the ones He gave me.''

"Right.'' Jayne obviously was glad to end the discussion. "You and Christopher going on the town tonight?''

"No. We're having an early dinner aboard. We have to get up at five o'clock. Breakfast is at six and we leave by train at seven. Which reminds me, I must put my jewelry in the safe-deposit box at the purser's desk. We mustn't wear any into China. Nothing but a wedding ring and a watch.''

"Why? Will it be stolen?''

"Not by the Chinese. I'm told you could leave all your money lying out on the dresser and if any of it was missing it would be because somebody in the tour group pinched it. The Chinese are very honest. And very moral. The Party doesn't allow them to be anything else. It's just that it isn't good taste to be overdressed in The People's Republic.'' Mary self-consciously fingered her new ring. "Look what Christopher bought me today.''

Jayne stared at the jade and diamond ring and whistled. "That's some gorgeous! It must have cost a fortune even in Hong Kong.''

"It did. I didn't want to take it, but he insisted.''

"An engagement ring?''

Mary looked troubled. "He'd like it to be, but I wouldn't accept it on that basis. I can't. Not now. Maybe not ever.''

The sadness in her voice tore at Jayne's heart. "Think about your own happiness, Aunt Mary. Please. And Christopher's too. He's a very, very nice man. As nice as you are a woman.''

Mary tried not to cry. Damn it, all she did these days was puddle up! She blinked back the tears and nodded. "I'll try,'' she said. "I'll really, truly try.''

Dressing for dinner, Christopher thought about the day. A lovely day. Lovelier even than Mary knew. He'd been afraid she might get suspicious when he left her for a couple of hours that afternoon, but she unquestioningly accepted his lie that he had to meet some business associates.

"Don't worry about it," she said. "I won't get lost. In fact, I think I'll head right back to the Ocean Terminal where we're docked. I'm dying to explore all those shops. Floors of them! A whole arcade full of gorgeous things right at the bottom of the gangway. What bliss! I'll meet you aboard later. Good luck with your meeting."

He'd put her in a cab, made sure the driver understood his instructions and watched her disappear. Then he took another and headed for Queen Mary Hospital. He'd not felt up to par since Singapore. Nothing serious, he was sure, but since that damned heart attack five years ago he took no chances. Queen Mary's was the center of Western medicine in this part of the world. He'd simply have a precautionary check.

On the way back to the ship he felt wonderful. The doctors diagnosed it as nothing. Maybe a touch of indigestion. Or too much wine every night at dinner. He was fit as the proverbial fiddle and delighted he'd gone to make sure. In the cab, he smiled to himself. Maybe it's a good omen, he thought. The Queen Mary Hospital was the setting for Han Suyin's book *Love Is a Many Splendored Thing*.

Terry stepped out of the shower, dried himself and walked, naked, to the closet. He opened the door and stood looking at his reflection in the full-length mirror on the inside. He'd never been vain about his firm young body though he'd often been complimented on it. His earliest memories were of his mother parading him, nude, in front of her women friends.

"Isn't he adorable, my little man? What a handsome fellow Mummy's precious is going to be!"

He'd only been four or five at the time but he remembered his embarrassment even then. In an instinctive gesture he'd tried to cover himself and he could still hear the ladies laughing as Theresa Spalding had picked him up and carried him out of the room, cuddling him to her. Damn her! Terry thought. She even named me for herself. Or as close as she could come.

It was years, many years, before he saw her as the destructive influence she was. In his childhood and adolescence, he'd hated the father who abandoned them when Terry was seven. It was a hatred fostered by Theresa, who reminded him over and over that Maurice Spalding was a cruel and unfaithful man who left his wife and only child to marry another woman.

"You're all I have, baby," she said. "Promise you'll never leave me. No one could ever love you as I do. You're my life."

He'd thought she was wonderful and stayed with her most of the time. At ten, he was playing bridge with her and her cronies. He went with her when she bought her clothes, hovered around when she cooked dinner, sat with her in the evenings watching the ugly, cathedral-shaped television set. They were one of the first in his mother's group to have the new TV, bought with the alimony check Maurice sent every month, year after year.

He'd read and studied enough to know now that his formative years almost predictably led him to compare all women to his mother and find them wanting. In high school, he had a few dates, but he found the giggling, overperfumed girls nauseating and he soon stopped seeing friends his own age. The girls were repulsive and the boys thought only of them or of football and basketball, neither of which Theresa would let him play lest he get hurt.

He didn't go to college. Maurice's money didn't stretch that far. After high school he got a job ushering in a movie theater and there he met other young men like himself, all of whom wanted to be actors. He decided he wanted that, too. Since Theresa wouldn't accept a penny from him, he used his small salary to pay for lessons at a drama school. He got a few small parts in local productions. He also took his first step into the gay community where, after a few chance encounters, he met Paul and fell desperately in love with him. Terry was twenty-two, still living at home. Paul was thirty, making a name for himself in the brokerage business and able to afford a nice apartment where he and Terry met several evenings a week. Terry never stayed overnight. Theresa would have disapproved. Theresa, in fact, disapproved of Paul, not because she knew what he was, but because she saw him as a rival for Terry's time, a serious threat to her own monopoly.

"I do wish you'd take out some nice girls, Terry darling, instead of spending all your time with that dreary young man."

"I don't know any nice girls, Mother."

"Of course you do! What about that pretty little Jo-Anne Peterson? Her mother's a dear friend of mine. I'm sure Jo-Anne would love to go out with such a handsome boy!"

He couldn't tell her that Jo-Anne was a tramp. Everybody knew what a nymphomaniac she was.

"She's not my type. Honest."

"Nonsense! You've never had a date with her. How would you know?"

She nagged and prodded until Terry finally agreed to call Jo-Anne. Not that Theresa wanted him to be interested in any girl. It was her way of trying to pry him away from Paul. He called and Jo-Anne agreed to see him. They went to a movie and he took her home.

"Why don't you come in? The family's away for the weekend. We could have some fun."

The idea made him sick. "No thanks, Jo-Anne. I'd better get home."

"Why? Mama waiting up for you?"

"No. She's visiting my aunt."

Jo-Anne leaned against him in the car, letting her hand run languidly across his leg. "It's true what they say, isn't it, Terry? You really are queer."

For some inexplicable reason, the condescending tone enraged and excited him. He'd never been with a woman, but now he got out of the car, opened the door on her side and almost dragged her out and into the house.

"I'll show you how queer I am!"

It had been terrible. He'd been awkward and fumbling, and though the aroused girl tried to help him, he could do nothing. He felt dirty and degraded, unable to look at her as he got into his clothes. Jo-Anne lay on her bed, laughing at him.

"Don't worry," she said. "The first time's the hardest." She giggled at the vulgar double entendre. "I mean, it'll be better next time."

He hadn't answered, but he knew there'd be no next time. Not with her. Not with any woman, the clutching, panting things.

A year later, Theresa Spalding died of cancer. Terry didn't attempt to notify his father. He left that to the lawyers. She left him the house, which he sold, and he moved in with Paul. For three years he was very happy. The career progressed slowly, but he didn't particularly care. He had a few thousand dollars in the bank and all his expenses paid by Paul.

And then in January, Paul told him he was getting married.

"I have to, Terry," he said. "You don't understand. I'm in a very macho business where the social side means a lot. I have to entertain and mix with my associates and their wives. I'm thirty-four and they're beginning to wonder why I'm single."

Terry was hurt and angry. "You mean they're beginning to suspect you're a closet queen," he said spitefully.

"If you want to put it that way."

"Damn you! How can you do this to me? It's been four years, Paul! Nobody but you."

"I'm sorry, Terry. Will you be all right?"

"What the hell do you care? You'll never want to see me again. I might embarrass you in front of your precious straight associates!"

"No, I won't see you. You're right about that. But I still care what happens to you. Do you need money?"

"No. I don't need anything. God help you, Paul. I hope you know what you're doing. And God help that poor stupid woman who's marrying you."

"She knows. She's older and very worldly, but she's made it a condition that I don't see you."

Devastated, Terry had booked himself on the cruise that left a week later. He was at loose ends. All he wanted was to get as far away from San Francisco as possible, from everything that reminded him of his lost love. For days on end he'd done nothing but think. He saw his mother as she really was—a sick, possessive, destroying woman. He saw Paul, who cared more for himself and his career than he did for Terry. And he saw himself, empty, caring for nothing.

Somehow Jayne had changed all that. She was at first a friend, the first woman friend he'd ever had. She was casual, undemanding, sympathetic. His affection for her became deeper and when he sensed she wanted to go to bed with him he was both grateful and afraid. What if it turned out to be another hideous experience like the one with Jo-Anne? Why should he even risk it? He didn't like women that way.

But when it happened, that crazy, half-drunken early morning when they came reeling back from Bugis Street, he'd found that a woman could be ardent but tender, slow in bringing him to a pitch of excitement and able to share his astonished pleasure without threatening to devour him.

Afterward, he'd wept with relief and she'd held him steadily until, to his further surprise, he made love to her again. And every night since then. Only four nights, but they were a revelation.

Standing in his cabin, he wondered whether he was in love with her. He loved her, but that was different. He didn't know how he'd continue to feel. If he met some man tomorrow . . . he couldn't predict what would happen.

But for now, he was happy.

Chapter 11

AT SHUM CHUN, the border, the tour group from the ship stepped off the train that had brought them from Hong Kong into this secret, mysterious world. The hundred and twenty tourists were divided into small groups, each assigned two guides, a young Chinese man and woman wearing blue Mao jackets and baggy pants. Mary and Christopher, Gail and Colonel Stanford were assigned to Group 7, instructed to wear their identification badges at all times and to follow their male guide, Mr. Li, who carried a placard bearing the number 7 on a long stick high above his head. His teammate, Miss Lu, shepherded them solicitously past the unsmiling border guards in green shirts with red lapels, blue trousers and the perennial Mao caps. But only the soldiers were grim-faced. Everywhere else, the visitors saw welcoming faces and a graciousness none of them expected.

Excited and curious, they crossed a long, covered bridge, passed immigration and entered the railroad station for the long walk through customs and money-changing areas before boarding the train that would take them to Kwangchow. It was a time-consuming, leisurely procedure that took them past endless reception rooms filled with white slip-covered chairs and couches and beautiful old teak furniture. At one point, they had a ''tea stop'' where sheets of propaganda material were distributed.

On the surprisingly comfortable train, they settled into chairs with footrests, drank tea from lovely covered mugs and accepted box lunches of small, delicious sandwiches, hard-boiled eggs and fruit. Mary looked with dismay at her ornamented cardboard container.

''Aside from the box, which is beautiful, I'm disappointed. It's like an American picnic!''

Christopher, busily snapping pictures of rice paddies, water buffaloes and straw-hatted farmers in the fields, smiled as he leaned across her to the window.

''Don't worry. You'll eat enough unidentifiable food in the next three days to satisfy you for life.''

She looked up at him. ''In the briefing on the ship they told us we weren't allowed to take pictures from the train, or photograph the police or military.''

''They also told us we'd have to carry our own bags, and I'm sure you noticed ours were put on trucks to cross the border. The Chinese are anxious to please their 'foreign friends.' You'll see.'' He sat back down beside her. ''There's a strange psychology here. For example, if there's something you want to do and you're refused permission, you just write a letter home saying you weren't allowed to do it. Next day, like magic, you'll suddenly receive the permission.''

''You mean they read the mail?''

''That would be a fair deduction. And monitor the phone calls as well.''

''Who'd make a phone call from China, for heaven's sake?''

''Anybody who wanted to have good service. The phone and cable service from here is better than in most parts of the Orient.''

Mary shook her head. ''Weird. So far, nothing seems as primitive as I expected. Unless maybe it's the fact that I've counted only three pieces of farm machinery in the last hour and a half. I thought their agricultural production had speeded up, but so far the rural area looks like a twelfth-century painting come to life.''

"Give 'em time. They've only been 'liberated' since 1949. And the rural farm communes weren't set up until '58. We'll see one of those tomorrow. 'Lokang,' it's called."

The two-hour train ride ended at another beautiful railroad station, spotless, modern, flanked by trees and dominated by an enormous portrait of Chairman Mao. They were efficiently settled into creaking buses which jolted their way to the Tung Fang Hotel. En route, Mary realized she saw no cars or taxis on the broad streets of Kwangchow; just thousands of bicycles ridden by men and women of all ages.

The hotel was another surprise. From the outside, it looked as modern as any in America, but once inside the doors, it became a fascinating combination of yesterday and today. There were, of course, no bellmen. She was prepared for that. She knew that in this new China there were no servants, that no one would carry a bag and that room service was unknown. Here, all were equal. Tipping was forbidden, as were gifts. They'd been told they might offer their guides a small gift, but nothing more important than a picture postcard from their home towns, or perhaps a souvenir lapel pin picked up for twenty-five cents in Australia or New Zealand. She was not, however, prepared for the room to which she was directed. The "old wing" in which she was housed was built in 1961 but it looked as though it had seen a hundred years of wear. The floors of her room were bare, and the paint job sloppy. The screens to the balcony were ill-fitting and the plumbing workable but antiquated. She hadn't expected luxury, but she was surprised by the griminess of the tub and the thin, worn towels. No matter. She could shower and dry herself and live for three days without a face cloth, which no one had told her to bring. On the ship, she'd been told to take cleansing tissue, medication, instant coffee, an alarm clock and liquor if she wanted a drink. None was sold in China. She wished they'd also mentioned light bulbs. There were two small lamps in her room, each of them with a bulb that couldn't have been over twenty-five watts.

In spite of this, she was intrigued by her quarters. The Chinese gave great thought to the amenities, if not the modern necessities, of life. Her room was large and faced onto a garden and a busy badminton court. On the dresser was a thermos of hot, boiled water, a delicate tea set; a bottle of Pearl River Orange Drink and one of Yuchuan beer, both warm. Close by were White Cloud cigarettes and a small box of matches. The desk was equipped with hotel stationery and a notice that her room was priced at twenty-two yuan a day, about twelve dollars. Under the twin beds were rather worn-looking slippers and over each bed heavy mosquito netting. She'd forgotten this was semitropical country and later she'd find the netting claustrophobic. A couple of mosquito bites were better than smothering. She only wished her briefing had also included the advice to bring bug spray. The room smelled of something unidentifiable. Bug killer? Disinfectant? Incense?

Mary sank into one of the big armchairs and thought that even if she couldn't do an interview with the Chinese, she could do a half hour of impressions on the train trip and the hotel alone. And probably three or four more programs on the rest of her adventure. It was wonderful to have a purpose in life. Her work was her passion. The thought brought a little frown to her face. Much as she loved Christopher, could she really be happy giving up this job she adored? It was a disturbing thought. Tiny as her career was, it held her to San Francisco, perhaps as much as did her obligation to Michael. Don't be a fool, she told herself. You can't have it all. Something has to give. Something has to . . . There was a light tap on her door.

"Ready?" Christopher called. "The troops are gathering at the bus. We're off to the Children's Palace."

She opened the door. "Welcome to the Ritz. How's your room?"

"About the same, but we weren't expecting Paris accommodations, were we? God, the terrible tourists are at it already, complaining that the bus is uncomfortable and the rooms are bad! You should hear them in the lobby."

"I don't want to. I have a feeling they'll get worse."

He looked around. "It's not bad, really. Bed looks comfortable enough."

"Except for that damned netting. I've never slept under such a contraption and I don't think I'll be able to."

Christopher gave her an exaggerated leer. "Ever made love under one?"

"No."

"Neither have I, but I'm willing to try."

She pushed him out the door. "None of that. The bus awaits. Anyway we're in a moral country. I'm sure the Chinese wouldn't talk that way."

In the empty hallway he kissed her. "The hell with that," he said. "I'm not Chinese."

The Children's Palace was enchanting, fascinating and somehow frightening.

"It's identical to those pictures of Pat Nixon's visit to China," Mary whispered as they were greeted by a gathering of small boys and girls waving bright red pompoms. "They must be programed in exactly how to greet visitors."

"In many things," Christopher said quietly. "Wait. You'll see. There's something scary about it."

She realized what he meant. The Kwangchow Children's Palace was an "educational center" for youngsters from seven to fifteen, set up, according to the eternal propaganda release, for "varied extracurricular activities to help the children develop themselves morally, intellectually and physically." It held ten thousand children at a time and received an average of six hundred thousand a year, every afternoon and on Sunday morning and each day during summer and winter vacations. On the surface, it was beautiful. The tiny gymnasts performed beautifully, the dancing class was delightful and the singing group was sweet. But in addition to the cultural parts, there was heavy emphasis on electric games and shooting, boys simulating war maneuvers and a playground called "Route of Long March for Little Red Army."

"They're like tiny robots," Gail DeVries said under her breath. "All following Chairman Mao's revolutionary line. Think of it. Thousands of them, millions of them, being brainwashed to obey orders. It makes one quite nervous, thinking of the future."

At dinner that night, Mary sat next to their female guide and was delighted by her. She was a young woman of twenty, attractive despite the fact that like all the Chinese girls she wore the regulation uniform and no makeup. Mary kept mentally comparing her to Jayne, who was almost the same age. It was like comparing creatures from two planets. Miss Lu was idealistic and dedicated to her political philosophy. Though she was outgoing, free with information and full of questions, she seemed surprisingly innocent and untouched.

Hoping she wouldn't be thought rude, Mary questioned her about her life. She was unmarried, of course. By government decree, young people couldn't marry until they were twenty-two.

"Most girls wait until they're twenty-five or twenty-six," Miss Lu said. "And most men until twenty-eight or thirty."

Was that to discourage large families?

"No, to give us more time for study."

She explained that separations were rare in marriages and could be obtained only with government approval. Chinese women could get the birth-control pill. "But only the married ones, of course," she told Mary almost primly. Life was good in China today, Miss Lu said proudly. "Wait until you see the commune tomorrow. Even the peasants are determined to carry out Chairman Mao's directives, with class struggle as the key link. We adhere to the Party's basic line and make greater contribution to the socialist revolution and construction. The Lokang People's Commune is led by the Party Central Committee and headed by Chairman Mhua Kuofeng," Miss Lu recited. "We follow the policy of self-reliance and hard struggle."

Life was good, Mary repeated in her head. Perhaps, in comparison to what it had been. But how would little Miss Lu know the wretched past? She wasn't born until years after the liberation. She wished she could show this young woman a world Miss Lu couldn't imagine. Maybe not a better one, in many ways, but one that would fascinate her as this one fascinated Mary. Miss Lu was looking at her, smiling happily, her glass of rice wine raised.

"Bottoms up!" she said.

Mary grinned. "Bottoms up!"

There were twenty-seven thousand people in the commune, which was eighteen miles and an hour and a quarter of torturous ride from the hotel over rough roads in a bus that had long since lost its springs. They were received ceremonially by the leader, fed tea, dried leechee nuts and wrapped prunes in a hall dominated by huge pictures of Mao, Lenin and Marx, conducted on a wearying tour of orchards, fruit-preserving factories and the community hospital.

The high point, for Mary, was a visit to a private family in their tiny brick house with a bare stone floor and wooden benches for the guests. Mary felt a little uncomfortable, as though she were prying, but the husband and wife and one remaining daughter who lived there seemed proud and pleased to have been chosen to entertain the foreigners. She looked around the main room with its bare light bulb hanging in the center, its photographs of the family of ten, its eternal picture of the Chairman, and she wondered how she dared complain about anything. Through the interpreter, the head of the house spoke cheerfully of their well-being. He had a wristwatch and a radio now, and his wife had a sewing machine. He earned 450 yuan a year, about $300, working from seven-thirty in the morning to five in the afternoon with a lunch break and a morning recess. He had six days off every month, two days in every ten, and his food and housing were free. His children, after working two years, could apply for the university, and he paid twenty cents per person per month for the family's medical care. Some of his sons wanted to go into the army, he said, but there were too many applicants. Not all volunteers could be accepted.

Going back on the bus, Mary was thoughtful.

"Incredible, isn't it?" Christopher said.

"Totally. Their philosophy isn't for me. Couldn't be. But I can see how it's right for them. In a way it's enviable, thinking first of the good of others. Imagine putting yourself after the state and the commune, Imagine believing so much in *anything*. What must it be like to be so grateful for so little?"

He took her hand. "Depends on what you think is 'little.' Enough to eat is sometimes a lot. So is a roof over your head. And protection for your health, and hope for your children. Success is measured by different yardsticks, my love. In the minds of these people, they're achieving success."

Everything seemed to conspire to keep him from becoming the success he should be, Michael decided as he left Harry Carson's office. The man was a damned fool who couldn't see beyond his nose. What did he want for his money, anyhow? A dumb manager who'd say "yessir," that's what he wanted. Some stupid slave who'd never venture an idea. Some idiot who'd do things the way Harry wanted them done.

He'd gone to Carson's office feeling optimistic. He'd revised the plan for the men's boutique, taking out some of the things that bothered Harry but leaving the general idea of a super-chic establishment intact. He couldn't bring himself to give his potential backer the kind of unimaginative, boring men's clothing store the man wanted. But he had compromised, hadn't he? He'd toned down some of the fancier things and he was sure Harry would meet him halfway.

The night before, he'd read the plan to Patricia and she'd thought it was wonderful.

"It's brilliant, Michael! It will be the talk of San Francisco!"

"Cross your fingers. I'm dealing with a square character who doesn't understand what's happening today. I hope to God he buys it."

"He will. How could he not? You have a real flair for this kind of thing. Not that I'm an expert, of course, but I am the modern consumer. I know a shop like that would attract me. I'd insist that Stanley buy all his clothes there. And there must be thousands of women like me, not to mention thousands of men who have the same kind of elegant taste you have. Why, it's more imaginative than anything in New York! I've never seen anything as original on Madison Avenue or Fifty-seventh Street or even in the men's department in Henri Bendel. Don't worry. Your Mr. Carson can't help but see how good it is."

He'd been enormously pleased and suddenly confident. It was true that Patricia wasn't a businesswoman. He suspected she really wasn't even too bright. But what she said made sense. She was the modern shopper. Women like her influenced what men bought. Even if the boutique was too chichi for some men, their fashion-conscious wives would push them there. That was an important point. He'd have to make sure he stressed that to Harry.

But he never had a chance. The tough businessman read through the revised proposal as he had the first one, refusing any comment during the process. When he finished, he leaned back and lit a cigar. Michael waited hopefully.

"You, Morgan, are the biggest damned jackass this side of the Rockies. What are you wasting my time for? I told you what I wanted. So why do you come back with the same jerky plan?"

"It isn't the same plan! I've made a lot of changes. Look, Harry, I know it's right. I was talking to my sister-in-law last night and she said . . ."

Carson snorted. "She said you were a genius, I suppose. Frankly, I don't give a damn what your relatives think. Or what *you* think. I'm a businessman and I know what *I* think. And what *I* think is that this is a piece of arrogant crap and I wouldn't put a plugged nickel into it!"

"Harry, you've got to realize . . ."

"I know what I've got to realize, pal. You can't take orders, for one thing. You're stubborn as a mule with a brain to match. When are you going to wise up, Morgan? If you're so smart, why ain't you rich?" He shoved the papers across the desk. "It's been nice meeting you. Hope you find a sucker dumb enough to go along with this."

Michael hesitated. He could still salvage it. If he backed down and agreed to plan it Harry's way, he probably could talk himself into one more chance. No, damn it, he wouldn't! He wasn't going to knuckle under to this bully. He wasn't going to fawn and meekly agree to something he didn't believe in. There'd be other men with vision. Or maybe he could swing it by himself. No. That was out of the question. He didn't have a dime of his own.

"You're the one who's dumb, Harry," he said as he gathered up his papers. "You'll see that when I get the boutique going."

Carson didn't look up. He'd already dismissed him.

Patricia was waiting when he let himself into the apartment. She'd been there four days and already felt at home. Michael had been lovely to her, taking her out every night to some elegant restaurant for dinner. They'd been to Ernie's and Lehr's Greenhouse and Emelio's. It was expensive and lovely and she wished it would go on forever. It was fun dining in beautiful places with an attractive man, a far cry from fixing dinner every night for a boring husband who wanted to eat at six o'clock and watch television for the rest of the evening.

And she was flattered that Michael had discussed his big proposal with her and complimented her on her insight about the appeal of the shop to women. Stanley never discussed his business with her. Not, God knows, that she gave a damn about nuts and bolts.

She was sure Michael was coming home with good news. She'd surprise him by cooking dinner in the apartment. They'd celebrate his success over an excellent meal and a good bottle of wine and she'd listen to him carefully as he told her every detail of his triumph. She looked at the carefully set table with the candles ready for lighting and checked the coq au vin on the stove. Everything was perfect.

Everything except Michael's face when she greeted him in the foyer. One look and she knew before he said it.

"Carson didn't buy it."

Patricia looked stricken. "I can't believe it. The man must be crazy! What happened?"

"He called it a piece of arrogant crap." Michael sounded defeated. "Maybe it is, Patricia. Maybe he's right and I'm just a stupid, impractical dreamer."

She was indignant. "Nothing of the sort! It's a wonderful idea. He's the one who's wrong. Not you." Without thinking, she put her arms around him and held him close. "You're ahead of your time, that's all it is, Michael. The world's not smart enough to see what you do. Don't worry. You'll find someone who appreciates you. You were just dealing with the wrong person. The right one will see how terrific your ideas are."

The words were like balm to his battered ego. And the warmth of her, pressed against him, was like being enveloped in a voluptuous cocoon. He held her close, felt the ripe figure under the thin cotton shirt, and realized she was trembling. As though he couldn't help it, he found her mouth and kissed it deeply.

"I . . . I cooked dinner for us," Patricia whispered.

Michael put his lips against her ear. "I don't want dinner, do you?"

Wordlessly, she shook her head.

Chapter 12

STANDING ALONE IN her cabin at midnight, Peggy watched the ship sail out of Hong Kong toward the Japan Inland Sea and Kobe. Life was wonderful. She turned the gold band on the third finger of her left hand and said, aloud, "Mrs. Anthony Robin. Peggy Lawrence Robin." Beautiful.

Almost until the last minute, she hadn't been sure Tony would go through with the marriage. She could admit to herself now how frightened she'd been the evening before they docked. Tony had come next door to her suite, looking worried.

"Peggy, we have to talk."

She made him a drink. "Yes, darling?"

"You know I love you." He'd fiddled with his glass. "But I'm still not sure we should get married right now."

She'd felt as though she'd turned to ice. She could feel herself shivering inside but she managed to sound calm.

"Why not?"

"It's not practical. I don't want to take early retirement, and if we get married I'll be away months at a time. Most of the year. It wouldn't be fair to you, you sitting at home while your husband is at sea."

She stared at him wordlessly.

"I know," Tony said. "I agreed to leave the ship, but I can't, Peggy. Try to understand. It's my life. In another five years I'll have to step down. But right now I'd miss it so much I'm afraid I'd make you miserable with my unhappiness."

"I'd make you happy, Tony. You don't know what it's like to have a wonderful, settled life. We'd travel whenever you wanted to, but it would be play, not work. We'd live in lovely houses and enjoy interesting friends.''

"*Your* houses. *Your* friends.''

"Darling, they'd be *ours!* You wouldn't be bored, I promise you.''

"Yes I would. I'd be useless. An aging ex-sea captain living off his rich wife. I couldn't stand it.''

She'd been frantic. The thought of not being married to Tony was unbearable. She had to belong, any way she could.

"All right, dearest. If you feel so strongly, we'll have to work this out so we'll both be content. We'll go ahead with our plans, get married day after tomorrow as we've arranged, and you'll continue to work as you want. I won't insist you leave the ship if it makes you so unhappy.''

"Peggy, be reasonable! Five years of almost constant separation? It wouldn't work.''

"We don't have to be separated. We can go on for the next five years as we have for the past three. I'll make the trips with you. I don't care where I am, as long as we're together.''

Tony sighed. "You don't understand. I couldn't have my wife aboard. It's against all regulations.''

"I wouldn't expect to share your cabin. I'd keep this one.''

"For God's sake be rational! You'd still be my wife! We don't even allow crew members to sail with their spouses! Even a dining-room waiter and a stewardess who marry can't be on the same ship together. It's a company rule. As for the captain having his wife in the next cabin, it's unthinkable.''

"Then we'd keep it a secret. Nobody would have to know we're married. I could keep on being Mrs. Lawrence, the constant passenger.''

Tony shook his head. "I don't understand you. In the first place, the news would get out through the grapevine. If it didn't, you'd be sure to tell someone. You couldn't keep that to yourself. And if you could, what would be the point of marriage? We might just as well go on as we are. Our affair is no secret.'' He began to get angry. "I've often wondered why I haven't been called on the carpet before this. The line doesn't like this kind of thing. God knows if you weren't such a good customer, guaranteeing them a hundred thousand dollars a year, they probably would find a way not to have a reservation for you!''

She began to weep. "I want to be your wife. I don't care if nobody else knows. *I'*ll know. I'll feel safe and protected. I can't stand being alone, Tony. I don't feel like a whole woman. It's me. How I feel inside. Can't you understand?''

He spoke more gently. "No, Peggy, I really can't. To be a secret wife seems like nothing to me.''

"Then believe it means *everything* to me! I swear to you, on my mother's grave, no one will know we're married. Please, Tony. Please, please do this for me.''

"I can't. It's not the kind of life you should have. I really think, dear, after this trip you shouldn't book any more cruises. I'll see you whenever I have leave. We'll be together ashore. And if you still want to marry me in five years, I'll be a happy man. I won't stop loving you, I promise. But you'll have to make a separate life while I'm away.''

She became hysterical. "Why don't you say what you really mean? It's not my life you're worried about is it? It's yours! You don't want to be tied down. You want to be the glamorous captain, flirting with all the hungry widows, strutting around giving your damned little orders! You don't love me. If you did, you'd want me to be your wife even if nobody knew but you and me. You'd want to own me, as I want to be owned. Tony, if you don't marry me, my life is over. I don't want it anymore. I couldn't live away from you."

"Sweetheart, don't talk nonsense. I love you dearly. I'm not looking for anyone else. I'm just trying to be sensible. It's only a matter of postponing our plans."

"For five years? At our age?"

"They'll go quickly, darling. We'll see each other often. You can't stay on the ship, Peggy. It's a futile life for you. You drink too much, have too many hours to kill. It's too confining. I promise you, it will be better my way."

"Get out," she said. "Leave me alone."

"We'll have a good time in Hong Kong."

"No. I don't want to see you again."

He tried to make a joke of it. "That's going to be pretty hard to avoid, love. We're almost a month away from San Francisco. Or are you planning to fly home?"

"Never mind what I'm planning. Just go."

He rose to leave. "See you in the morning."

Peggy didn't answer.

At 3:00 A.M. the phone by his bed rang. He could hardly make out the words but he recognized the voice.

"Peggy? What's the matter? Are you sick?"

She sounded very far away. "Just . . . wanted to say good-bye. Love you."

"What's going on? Peggy! Answer me!"

"Too tired . . . very sleepy . . ."

He slammed down the receiver and called the ship's doctor. "Get to Mrs. Lawrence's cabin on the double!" Tony pulled on a robe and raced next door. Thank God she hadn't locked herself in. He knew what had happened. Peggy had tried to commit suicide. Jesus! He'd never forgive himself!

Later, when the doctor brought her around, a weary Tony went back to his quarters from the ship's hospital, silently thanking God she was alive, and resigned to the fact that now he'd have to marry her as she'd planned. He'd leave the ship after this trip. Better that than living in fear that next time she'd succeed in taking her life. He couldn't handle that. Not for the sake of another few years in his job.

He'd ordered the doctor and nurse not to mention this unfortunate incident to anyone. Lucky for all of them, he thought, that it happened in the middle of the night when their hurried rush down to Adriatic Deck could be managed with no one around. Even the night stewards were dozing in their service rooms. He supposed he should have known Peggy would get her way somehow. Perhaps it was just as well. Better, in the long run, he consoled himself, than facing a lonely old age in some little house in Southampton watching ships commanded by younger men sail in and out of the harbor.

The doctor yawned and stretched. It was 6 A.M. and Peggy Lawrence was sleeping normally.

"Cup of coffee, Doctor?"

He took the cup the nurse offered. "Thanks."

"Will she be all right?"

"For God's sake, Martha, you know it was a fake! She didn't take enough pills to kill a two-year-old."

"Just enough to scare hell out of the captain."

"Exactly."

"I don't understand it," Martha said. "The scuttlebutt is they're getting married in Hong Kong. Why would she pull such a stunt?"

"Maybe the Old Man tried to back out."

The nurse looked thoughtful. "Well, he's hooked now. Did you hear him while we were working on her? 'Peggy, darling, you must live! We're going to be married in Hong Kong. Everything will be fine.'"

"Yeah, I heard him. I'll bet you fifty dollars Mrs. Lawrence did, too."

Tony had been frantic, Peggy thought now, as she remembered the scene. Some people would call it underhanded, pretending she'd taken a lethal dose of pills, but it was the only way to show him how much he loved her. It was for his own good as much as for hers, this justifiable means to an end. He'd been so close to throwing away their future. She couldn't let him do that. Men were such babies sometimes. They had to be figuratively hit over the head to do the sensible thing. He'd see that she knew best. And he'd never know what a good actress she was. He'd always think she preferred death to life without him.

As the ship headed slowly toward Japan, Peggy put a hundred-dollar bill into one envelope and a fifty into another. She addressed them to the doctor and nurse. "A most inadequate expression of my appreciation" she wrote on the cards she enclosed.

There was nothing like a little cash to make sure the captain's orders were carried out. Or to make sure the captain never knew the truth.

Jayne lay snugly in the curve of Terry's arm, listening to the departure noises outside. "I hate leaving Hong Kong," she said.

"Not sorry we didn't go to China?"

"Not a bit, though Aunt Mary said it was marvelous. She came back looking like a basket case this afternoon. Must have been some strenuous trip! Every minute programed, from official dinners to a look at the pandas in the zoo. She skipped the acupuncture operations but she said those who went were stunned. Apparently, they did a heart by-pass and a brain operation with the patients conscious and waving at the audience! Can you imagine?"

"I'd rather not."

"That's how she felt. So she and Christopher went to the ivory-carving factory instead."

"How did Gail and Colonel Stanford hold up?"

Jayne giggled. "Apparently, better than most. They told the Chinese they were a hundred years old and got super VIP treatment. Aunt Mary said the

Chinese practically carried those two around while the rest of them had to manage as best they could. They're marvelous, aren't they? I hope if I live that long I'll have as much pep as they do. It's kind of a shame they don't get married.''

"Why?"

"Why what?"

"Why is it a shame they don't get married? I think they have a great arrangement. They'd probably turn into two old, bored people if they saw each other every day. She'd hate his snoring and his dentures in a glass by the bed. And he'd be fed up with her daily reports of success or failure on the john in the morning.''

"Terry! You're terrible!"

"I know." He reached for her. "But you're wonderful. I'm going to miss you when this trip is over."

She lay close to him, feeling the beat of their hearts. "I'll miss you, too." There was a little silence before she said, "Terry, what are you going to do when you get back?"

"Do? I don't know. Look for a job, I guess."

"Will you see Paul?"

He disentangled himself and lay on his back, staring at the ceiling. "No. That's over. I told you. He doesn't want to see me ever again. I don't fit into his life."

"Will you find . . . I mean, will you look for . . ."

"Another man? I don't know, Jayne. I'm not sure now. You've made me take a step on a different road. At least I know I'm bisexual, if not thoroughly hetero. I'm not over Paul. Maybe I never will be. Most people never quite forget their first love. But it doesn't hurt so much anymore." He propped himself up on one elbow and looked at her. "Because of you, I can function. I don't mean just sexually. As a person. You've made me grow up. I think I can make it on my own now."

"Can you? Or would you like to find out what the therapy would be like on dry land?"

"What does that mean?"

"How would it grab you if I stayed in San Francisco for a while? The little I saw of it before sailing appealed to me. Maybe I could get a job there and stay a few months. There's nothing to take me back to New York anymore."

"No more Russell King, you mean."

Jayne sat up and lit a cigarette. "That's right. No more Russell King. You've helped me get my head on straight too, Terry. You've shown me what a thoughtful, considerate man really is. Let's face it. I don't want to lose you. Oh, I don't want to marry you. I'm not going to marry anybody. But maybe we could find a little apartment, share expenses, live together, at least until we're sure our broken wings are mended and we can fly back into the cold, cruel world alone.'' She laughed. "How's that for a poetic proposition?"

He sat up beside her. "Are you serious?"

"Totally."

"I'm not sure I'm in love with you, Jayne."

"Did anybody mention love?"

"I might hurt you. I don't know how I'll feel when I get back to reality. This isn't reality, you know, this shipboard life. I wouldn't want to get you into something . . .''

"Would you rather send me back to nothing?''

"Come on. You're being dramatic.''

"Not really. I hate living with my parents. My dad is a poor, dull, dominated man. And my mother is a selfish bitch.''

"Jayne!''

"Don't look so shocked. She is. Motherhood—especially unwilling motherhood—doesn't change a devil into a saint. She's made life hell for my father. And not so terrific for me. It's a terrible household I live in. I was planning to find a roommate and get an apartment in New York anyway. Why not in San Francisco?'' She smiled. "I promise I will not discuss my toilet problems with you. And I know you have your own teeth. You snore a little, but I can put up with that.''

He laughed. It was a crazy idea. Totally unexpected and probably impractical. But why not? They knew all there was to know about each other. They were congenial and physically compatible and there were no illusions on either side. Maybe it made sense. He still had a few dollars and he'd find work. Jayne would get a job. Her aunt would help her, if necessary. It was worth a try. They had nothing to lose. At least they weren't pretending. He wasn't insanely in love and neither was she, but at this stage of their lives they needed each other. If they were lucky, it might grow into something.

"You're sure?'' Terry asked again.

"I can't see anything against it, can you?''

"No. Not as long as we know it's a friendly experiment.''

She held out her hand. "Deal?''

Terry shook it firmly. "Deal,'' he said.

Charlie Burke shifted uncomfortably on his seat in the Fairmont Tower cocktail lounge. It was embarrassing to hear Mike Morgan go on about what a jerk Harry Carson was and how the fool had let a million-dollar opportunity slip through his fingers. Charlie didn't know Harry Carson, but he thought the man was probably right. Michael's idea sounded, even to his unknowledgeable ears, like a sophomoric dream. It isn't a plan, Charlie thought; it's an ego trip. Mary's husband sees himself as the suave proprietor of a fancy store, dispensing charm and fashion authority to a waiting world. His superior attitude grated. The guy was a four-flusher, nothing more. How in God's name had Mary put up with him all these years? And now Michael was going to ask him for money. He knew it, even before the man got around to the subject. He also knew he wouldn't get involved with this stupid scheme. Not even for Mary's sake.

"So, I thought, what the hell,'' Michael was saying, "if Carson's too dumb to know a good thing when it falls in his lap, there are plenty of smarter people around. I figure on forming my own corporation and offering shares to my friends. I'd hold fifty-one per cent of the stock, of course, but three or four other chums could get in on the ground floor for a few thousand dollars apiece. I wanted to give you a shot at it, Charlie. You've been damned good to Mary, and we'd like to show our appreciation.''

"I see. Does Mary know?"

"Not yet. I just got this brain wave a couple of days ago. She was in China, so I couldn't call her, but I'll probably get her on the phone, ship-to-shore, on her way to Kobe." He grinned. "I know she'll think it's a great idea. She'd never forgive me if I didn't offer you a piece of the action. Mary's devoted to you, you know."

"Mary's a very loyal woman."

"You better believe it." Michael took a sip of his scotch. "A lot of other women wouldn't have the faith she has. She's always had confidence in me, and this time I'm going to prove how right she is. Hell, Charlie, this one shop is only the beginning. We could have a chain of them. Los Angeles. Dallas. Chicago. New York. All the major markets. It's a gold mine."

More like a pipe dream, Charlie thought. Even if he got the idea going, Michael didn't have enough discipline to give it the kind of backbreaking time and effort needed to start a new business. He'd lose interest in a few months and be off on some other wild tangent. And that would be the end of it. Assuming it ever got started, which it probably never would.

"I appreciate your coming to me, Mike, but I'm afraid I can't take advantage of the offer. You see, I have pretty heavy expenses these days. Tracey's spending a few months in a sanatorium, for a rest, and it costs the earth. I'm really strapped for cash."

"Tracey's in a sanatorium? Hey, I'm sorry." Some "rest," Michael thought. She's drying out again. Poor old Charlie. To have to put up with that! "I know hospitals are killers," Mike went on, "but maybe that's all the more reason you should look for additional income. The boutique will pay off in six months, at the outside, and you'll be able to pick up some extra money."

"Sorry. I just can't swing the initial outlay."

"The bank will lend it to you. No problem."

Damn him, why doesn't he stop? Charlie fumed. There was no end to his nerve. Mary will die when she finds out he's going around to their friends trying to put the bite on them for this idiotic scheme.

"Wish I could get in on it, Mike. Good of you to think of me, but I'm old-fashioned. Hate owing money. I know that's out of step. Everybody borrows these days. I understand it even makes you a better credit risk to have a bank loan." He gave a little laugh. "But I'm square. I don't like to live beyond my means."

Michael shrugged. "No problem. I won't have trouble raising the money. Rae Spanner's already in for twenty-five thousand. A couple of other investors, plus my own share, and I'll be off and running. Refill, Charlie?"

"No thanks. I have to go back to the station this afternoon. We really miss Mary. She sent some terrific tapes, by the way. I suppose you know that."

"Yes. She said she was sending you some."

"Sounds like she's enjoying the trip. How are you making out, Mike?"

"Me? Fine. Oh, I miss Mary, of course, but her sister's staying at the apartment. Jayne's mother. She's a nice woman and a helluva good cook."

Charlie was surprised. "Oh? I didn't know Mary's sister was here. That should make it pleasant for you."

"It sure does. Patricia's good company."

"Listen, Mike, I have to leave, but maybe we can get together soon. I'll want to hear how you're doing on your project, and I'd like to meet Patricia."

"Right, Charlie. You run along. I think I'll have another one before I go home."

"Well, let me at least get the check."

Michael waved him off. "Wouldn't hear of it. This is on me. You buy next time."

Going down in the elevator, Charlie shook his head. Mike Morgan. Always the big shot. Offering deals. Picking up checks. Keeping up the façade of the charm boy. I wonder what he had to do to get twenty-five thousand dollars out of that man-eater Rae Spanner. Plenty, I'll bet. Poor Mary.

Michael ordered another scotch, flirting mildly with the waitress as he did. Not that he intended to do anything about her. He had enough on his hands these days. Yesterday, Rae Spanner had made it very clear what the conditions of her investment were: a little drop-in "visit" every afternoon from five to seven.

"You needn't worry," she'd said. "Mary will never know. Frankly, Michael, I don't think your scheme is worth a damn, but I've always had a yen for you. It's worth a few thousand."

He'd been genuinely shocked. "Listen, Rae, I've never yet sold the body. I'm offering a straight business deal."

She'd been amused. "*Are* you now? Well, so am I. My money for your affection, to put it delicately. A fair exchange on a temporary basis. Take it or leave it, Michael."

My God, he'd thought, has she no pride? She knows I don't give a damn for her. Oh, she's attractive, but I couldn't fall in love with her. And what if Mary found out? He'd almost laughed aloud. Why was he worrying about Mary finding out about Rae? If he wanted something to really squirm about, it should be his ongoing affair with Patricia.

Rae was waiting for his answer. "Well? What about it?"

He'd tried to find some face-saving way to agree. "Rae, you don't have to invest in my business to have me go to bed with you. I've been dying to, for years. Let's forget the money. I'm flattered as hell that you'd like me to drop in from time to time. Now that I know how you feel, I will."

He knew she wouldn't buy it. She needed strings attached. As he expected, she shook her head.

"Dear boy, that's much too indefinite for me. I'd rather have you in my debt. That way I know I can count on you. The money means nothing to me. I won't even miss it. Let's just say you're taking out a loan, with yourself as collateral."

He managed to smile. "A very discreet loan."

"Naturally."

"And the length of the loan?"

"That," Rae said, "will be up to me. Let's just call it 'payable on demand,' the way the banks do."

Chapter 13

"I HAVE A surprise for you," Christopher said.

"I'm not sure I can stand another one." Mary spoke softly, not to be overheard by the people at the next table in the cocktail lounge. "I'm still stunned by Jayne's plans to stay in San Francisco with Terry. She's making a terrible mistake and I don't know how to stop her."

"You can't, luv. She's legally of age. It's her parents' problem, not yours. Besides, those kids have another three weeks to go. They might change their minds before then."

Mary shook her head. "You don't know Jayne. She's like me. Stubborn."

He smiled. "I've noticed that."

Mary didn't answer. It wasn't stubbornness that kept her from saying yes to Christopher. It was fear. Fear of uprooting her whole life, changing everything about it. Was she never going to get over this feeling that no one was better equipped to make decisions? Christopher was no Michael. He could take charge. Insisted on taking charge. Wasn't this what she'd always wanted? Why was she so fearful? Was her concern for Michael or more for herself? It was no good living with a failure. It was agony, watching him try to prove himself to her and knowing he'd never make it. Maybe I'm masochistic, she thought. Maybe I can't be happy unless I'm suffering, agonizing over someone weaker than I. Disgusting! I see this same quality in Jayne and hate it for her just as, deep down, I hate it for myself.

"Hello, there." Christopher recalled her to the present.

"What? Oh, darling, I'm sorry. I was a million miles away."

"Several thousand, at least. Don't you want to hear about my surprise?"

She'd almost forgotten. "Of course. What is it?"

"I've arranged for a car to pick us up in Kobe and take us to Kyoto. We have twenty-four hours, and you can't miss seeing the spiritual home of the Japanese. I forbid it."

She smiled. *"Do* you now?"

"Yes, I do. There are a couple of hundred Shinto shrines and fifteen hundred Buddhist temples. And wait until you see the shogun's palace. The art work is fantastic! We're going to stay at Tawaraya. An authentic Japanese inn. None of your tourist stuff. God, it's all so beautiful, Mary! And we're shot with luck, getting there at cherry-blossom time." He looked at her balefully. "You don't want to go."

"I do! Of course I do! Bear with me, Christopher. I have a lot on my mind."

"I know. And not just Jayne. What do you hear from Mr. Morgan?"

"Nothing. I don't understand it. I thought surely there'd be a letter in Hong Kong."

"The mails are not entirely dependable, my dear. Perhaps he sent it too late."

"Yes. Knowing Michael, that's possible."

"Or," Christopher said slowly, "maybe he's doing very well without you."

She looked at him sharply. "I hope so."

"Do you, Mary? Do you really? Or is it important to you that Michael draw on your strength? Is that why you won't commit yourself to me? Are you afraid I don't need you enough? I do, you know. Not in the way your husband does, but equally as much. Maybe more.''

"I don't want to think about it, Christopher."

"I'm afraid you must darling. In less than a week we'll be in Yokohama. That's the point of no return. When I leave the ship, I have to know whether you're coming back to me. It's your decision, my love. I'd like to make it for you, but I can't. You know what I have to offer. You know what you have at home. I've said all I can say.''

Mary took his hand. "I love you. I want to come back. I just don't know whether I can.''

"Not good enough. You can. It's whether you want to. *Really* want to, I mean. Not just say you do.'' His fingers tightened on hers. "You have to trust someone sometime, my darling.''

She tried to sound cheerful. "Let's talk about something else. Isn't it incredible that Peggy and Tony actually got married? I didn't believe he'd go through with it, even though I said I did. I thought he'd back out. Everybody did. Peggy said it was just a nice quiet ceremony and they . . .''

"Shut up, sweetheart,'' Christopher said gently. "Stop trying to run away from the inevitable. You can't postpone it much longer. You must make up your mind.''

"I will,'' Mary said soberly. "I promise you, by Yokohama I will.''

Michael sat by the phone, debating whether to call. Mary would be so disappointed that the deal with Carson had fallen through. He didn't know how to tell her. He'd been so sure of it when she left. So certain that at last he'd be everything she wanted. In a panic, he thought this might be the last straw. These past few weeks she'd been surrounded by affluent men able to take their wives on long, expensive trips, dress them in Diors and diamonds, assure them security as wives and widows. Had Mary been comparing them with him? She didn't need him. She earned a good living. He'd kept their marriage alive on dreams and promises and on the deliberate appeal to her compassion. But he'd always thought that one day he could deliver. Damn Harry Carson. There was no way to start a business without him. Everybody he'd approached in the past forty-eight hours had turned him down. Even Charlie, who might have done it for Mary's sake, Only Rae had come through, and her lousy twenty-five thousand wasn't enough to get the enterprise going.

What a mess he'd gotten into! Like some damned male whore, dutifully turning up these past three afternoons at Rae's. It made him sick to his stomach, but a bargain was a bargain. He hoped she'd soon tire of her little game. She'd have to when Mary got home. He thought of returning the money and telling Rae to go to hell. But he hung on, hoping he could add to the stake. So far it hadn't happened, and it looked as though it never would.

And why in God's name had he gotten himself involved with Patricia? The first time it happened was just a reflex. He'd been so depressed. He'd needed comfort and forgetfulness. He hadn't meant it to go on, but how was a man to resist? Patricia was there, openly inviting him to make love to her in his own bed. Mary's bed. The woman was as hungry as he. More hungry, judging by the disparaging things she said about her husband. He felt rotten about the affair, even as he enjoyed the hours with her. But Patricia should be more ashamed than he. Her own sister's husband! And she seemed to have no conscience.

"We're not hurting Mary," she'd said at one point. "What's the big deal? She won't be deprived. You're terrific." She laughed. "Mike Morgan, the envy of the locker room!"

The crudeness made him cringe. It was one thing to have some young, willing bedmate. It was not even so terrible to cheat with one of Mary's "friends." But Patricia was different. Mary would die if she found out. Not that she would, of course. It would never enter her mind that her husband and her sister were sleeping together. Damn these women! He was extraordinarily virile, thank God, but how long could he handle two of them?

He needed to talk to his wife. Mary would be consoling, understanding about Carson. Of course she would. He could get rid of Rae, and Patricia would soon leave, in any case. Resolutely, he placed the call and sat back waiting for it to be completed.

Mary was at dinner when the maître d' told her she had a ship-to-shore call. She went to the phone at the bar in the dining room.

"Mrs. Morgan? Radio room here. We have a call coming through from San Francisco. Would you like to take it in your cabin, madame?"

She'd hurried down to 320 and in a few minutes the phone rang. She heard the radio operator telling San Francisco to go ahead, Mrs. Morgan was on the line. Michael's voice came through with surprising clarity.

"Darling, how are you? How's the trip?"

"Michael? Is anything wrong?"

There was a second's hesitation. "Did you get my letter in Hong Kong?"

"No. What is it?"

"Nothing. I just told you that Patricia's here for a visit."

"Patricia? There? Why?"

"She wanted a little vacation, and to be here when you and Jayne returned. Don't worry. We're getting along famously. How are you?"

"I'm fine. So is Jayne." How easy it was to lie. "What happened with Harry Carson?"

There was silence on the line.

"Michael? Are you there?"

"Yes. Everything's signed, sealed and delivered. Carson's wildly enthusiastic."

"Oh, Michael, I'm so happy for you!"

"Yeah, me, too. I told you I'd pull it off."

"It's wonderful! I'm so proud of you! You must be working very hard, but it's a good feeling, isn't it?"

"Sure is. Thought you'd be pleased."

"I'm delighted. I was so afraid he'd back out."

"You been having a good time?"

"It's been fascinating. How's Charlie?"

"He's okay, but Tracey's in some sanatorium, drying out, I guess. We had a drink a couple of nights ago."

"Poor Charlie. Give him my love. And try to see him as often as you can, Michael. He must be down in the dumps."

"Right. Well, I'd better hang up. The phone bill will look like the national debt. Just wanted to hear your voice, darling. I miss you. You must never go away again, unless I'm along."

"Yes. Take care of yourself. Give my love to Patricia. I'm sure Jayne sends hers, too."

She was trembling as she put down the receiver.

Her tablemates stared at her inquiringly when she returned to the dining room.

"Everything all right at home?" Gail DeVries asked.

"Fine." She didn't look at Christopher. "My husband just called to tell me he has a wonderful new business deal."

"Well!" Colonel Stanford said. "That's cause for celebration!" He beckoned to the wine steward. "I think we-all better have us a couple bottles of champagne and drink to his success."

Michael sat looking at the telephone. Why had he lied? He'd meant to tell her the truth, counting, as always, on her sympathy. But when he heard her voice, he couldn't do it. What was the point of spoiling her trip, anyway? Time enough to give her the bad news when she got home. But somehow he felt worse about deceiving her this way than he did about the infidelity. He should have come right out with it. Hell, what was he worrying about? Mary wasn't concerned about him. She was quick enough to go off and leave him. She always did what she wanted. Deliberately, he courted his anger. She was so bloody efficient, so damned lucky. Like falling into that job. He'd always thought Charlie Burke had more than a professional interest in her. For all he knew, they might have been sleeping together all these years. It wasn't fair. It was his rotten luck to be around women who always came up smelling like roses. His mother had been self-sufficient. So had his first wife. And so, of course, was Mary. They enjoyed taking care of him. So let them.

He got up and began to pace the room, full of self-justification. They used him, these women. They took advantage of his amiability to satisfy their need to dominate. He gave them more than they gave him, He saw himself as the victim of sharks, the prey of devouring females.

"Something wrong?" Patricia stood in the doorway.

"I just talked to Mary."

"Oh. I suppose she was upset when you told her about Harry Carson."

"I didn't tell her. That is, I told her everything was okay. That the deal was on."

Patricia's face was expressionless.

"Damn it," Michael said, "what was the use of telling her the truth now? What could she do about it out there in the middle of the Pacific?"

"Nothing. You were right. Dear Michael. You're so sweet, so considerate not to worry her. How many men would have that strength? Most of them are babies, thinking only of themselves. Take Stanley," she said bitterly. "If such a thing happened to him, he'd make my life miserable with his whining. He'd be impossible to live with. But you're different. You think of your wife first."

He looked uncomfortable. "I haven't thought too much of her since you've been here. That hasn't been so considerate."

"Nonsense. Call it fate. Call it whatever you want. Something made me come out here to you just when you needed a woman to comfort you." She held out her arms. "I needed comfort, too, you know. The kind you give me."

He held back. "Come on, Patricia, don't tell me you're frustrated. Not a woman like you."

She laughed. "I don't know whether that's an insult or a compliment. *A woman like me?* What kind of woman do you think I am?"

Michael didn't answer.

"You're afraid of hurting my feelings, aren't you, darling? Don't be. I know what I am. Sexy. Selfish. Unconventional, to say the least. But in a healthy way, Michael. Just as you are. We're two of a kind, my dear. Danger stimulates us. Tell the truth—isn't illicit lovemaking more exciting than the legal kind?"

For a moment he wondered whether Mary had confided in her. Did she know how dutiful and routine her sister had become in bed? No. Mary wouldn't talk about her feelings to anyone. Not even to him. She was a good wife. Patient, faithful, loving in her own way. But she didn't have Patricia's lustiness, her blatant sensuality. Mary wouldn't know about illicit love. Patricia, he suspected, knew plenty about it. He was sure he was not the only one who'd given her "comfort" in the years of her dull marriage.

She moved close to him now, rubbing the back of his neck, letting her hands move invitingly down his spine. I'm going to die from all this, he thought half humorously. Rae in the afternoon and Patricia whenever she can turn me on. For God's sake, I'm forty-five years old and I'm trying to live the sex life of a boy of twenty! And yet, almost with pride, he found himself responding.

The talk with Mary had been painful. She'd been wide-eyed when Jayne told her what she and Terry planned when they returned to San Francisco.

"I know you don't approve, Aunt Mary, but you must believe we know what we're doing. I told you before, I don't intend to marry him. There are no strings. We can break it off any time either of us feels like it."

Mary sighed. "Jayne, it's not that simple. You'll be emotionally involved, both of you. You're asking for trouble. You know so little about Terry."

Jayne was defensive. "I know everything about him. I certainly know as much about him as you do about Christopher."

"I haven't decided to link my life with Christopher's. Besides, my dear, I'm almost twice your age. I like to think I know a little more about the realities than you do. Jaynie, try to see this objectively. You know Terry's past. For now, he's fascinated with you. You're a new experience. Maybe he really does believe you've changed him, but what about tomorrow or a year from tomorrow? He could go back to being what he was. You'd be terribly hurt."

"No. We've discussed that. He's not sure what will happen. Neither am I. But who is? We're happy together, Aunt Mary. He adores me. He really does. And I love him. Not the way I loved Russell. More tenderly, because I know he needs me."

Mary was in despair. "Don't do it, Jayne. I beg you. Don't repeat my mistakes.

It's wrong to tie yourself to a dependent man. You're strong and patient and good, but you can't handle this. It's not enough to be a tower of strength. Believe me. I know. You end up feeling cheated and glued to your bargain out of pity and false pride. There are millions of women like us, settling for a half-life because the men they chose can't get along without them. Don't be one of us. You don't know what a vacant existence that is.''

It was like talking to a wall.

"I know you're only saying what you believe, Aunt Mary. I know you're trying to protect me. But you're assuming it's going to work out that way. How do you know Terry won't become a famous actor? I could end up living with a star.'' Jayne sounded reasonable. "But let's assume the worst. Let's assume Terry never makes anything of his life and I support him. That's not so tragic these days. Millions of women of my generation do that without being miserable about it. Times have changed. We don't expect a man to go out and kill a boar for supper, any more than we want him to drag us by the hair of our heads to his cave! We're willing to share responsibilities. We want to. You grew up seeing things differently. I know what you mean about the way some women feel. Even the ones who only manage the family budget, not those who've gone after real careers. They're women of your time, Aunt Mary. Not mine. They have a stereotyped idea of what a man should be, and if he doesn't live up to that conditioned image, they feel they've missed something. I don't buy that.''

"What do you buy, Jayne? Being a mother to your lover? Or are you going to turn into one of those hard-bitten dames who think it's amusing to have a man they can boss around?''

"Neither. I want a career of some kind, but that won't necessarily make me a barracuda, will it? It hasn't made you one.''

Mary made one last try. "Darling, you're going into something with impossible odds. Forget all we've said. Even if you believe the basic man-woman relationship has changed, which I don't, what about Terry's homosexuality? Won't you be plagued with doubts about him? Every time he's out, won't you wonder whether he's found some man?''

"Do you worry that Uncle Mike has found some woman?''

There was nothing more to say, Mary realized. No way to keep Jayne from getting into this perilous situation. They have to learn the hard way. They don't believe terrible things can happen to them, these naïve, opinionated young people. That's how it's always been. It's human nature. If Michael's mother or his ex-wife had tried to warn me about marrying him, I'd still have been positive it would be different with us. Just as Jayne is positive she and Terry can make a go of their arrangement. I wouldn't have listened either.

"All right. There's no point in discussing it further. I can see that. I don't know what your mother and father are going to say, but that's up to them and you to settle. If you decide to stay in San Francisco, I'll help any way I can— job-wise, apartment-wise, whatever. At least you'll know I'm there.''

Jayne looked at her evenly. "Thanks, Aunt Mary, but will you be there? What about Christopher?''

The words came almost as a shock. She'd been so embroiled in Jayne's plans, she hadn't thought of her own. It was possible she wouldn't be there. For a moment, she'd forgotten that.

"I don't know about Christopher," she said slowly. "I wish to God I did."

Watching Mary as she returned to the dinner table after her call from Michael, Jayne wondered whether the good news from home would make Mary's decision easier. She seemed numb, somehow, and she didn't look at Christopher as she joined in a toast to her husband's future. Michael's okay now, Jayne thought. She can leave him with a clear conscience. Why doesn't she look happier?

Peggy fussed around the captain's cabin, rearranging the fresh flowers, checking the liquor supply he kept for cocktail parties, straightening the pictures of his mother and the rest of his unknown family in England.

It was the next best thing to taking care of him in their own home, she thought. She could hardly wait for that, though it might not come as quickly as she'd hoped. Frowning, she interrupted Tony, who was going over some papers at his desk.

"Are you sure you won't be able to leave the ship in San Francisco?"

He didn't look up. "I told you, Peggy. I can't just quit on the spur of the moment. They'll have to find someone to take over my command. That means I'll have to stay on at least until we get back to England."

"But that's so far away! Back down the coast, through the Panama Canal, all the way across the Atlantic. It will be weeks before you're free."

"Don't complain. It should have been five years."

"Should have been?"

He didn't answer.

"Tony! Answer me! What do you mean, 'should have been'?"

He looked up angrily. "Don't give orders to me! I give the orders! And you know damned well what I mean. If you hadn't blackmailed me into marrying you in Hong Kong, I'd have had the time I wanted. I'd have married you gladly then, but no, you couldn't wait! You had to rig that damned fake suicide, didn't you? Make me feel you'd die if you didn't get me. Well, you've got me, in a manner of speaking."

She was outraged. That damned, sniveling doctor had told him. Taken her money, thanked her in his supercilious manner and run straight to the captain. No wonder Tony had acted so strangely the past couple of days. He'd been so loving and gentle on their brief honeymoon, but he'd turned horrid in the last forty-eight hours. Now she knew why. He was furious, knowing he'd been outsmarted. She felt a rush of fear. What if he decided to dissolve the marriage? Maybe he could divorce her, claiming fraud. She didn't like the sound of that phrase "in a manner of speaking." Peggy looked meek and repentant. It was the only way to handle him.

"Darling, I'm sorry. But it wasn't a fake. I just didn't know how many pills to take. I meant it, Tony. When I thought I was losing you, I didn't want to live."

He acted as though he didn't hear her.

"Please, believe me," she said. "You can't hate someone for loving you so much. I'll do anything you want. Anything to make you happy."

"Anything?"

"Yes. I swear it, darling. Anything you say."

"All right, Peggy. In that case, I'll tell you what you'll do. You'll get off this ship in San Francisco and go back to Chicago. You won't take any more cruises. Whenever I have leave, we'll spend it together, wherever you like. And that's the way we'll live for the next five years. The way I wanted it in the beginning."

"Tony! No! You can't! You promised!"

"No man is expected to stand by a promise made under the conditions you set up. I love you, Peggy. Strangely enough, I do. But I can't let you run my life. I'm going to stay with the ship until my retirement. You'll be my wife, and like the wives of other sea captains you'll be with me when I'm ashore. Later, we'll live the way you want to."

She stared at him. "You expect me to be alone for five years?"

"You won't be alone. I'll be with you some of the time. Many another woman has made that adjustment for much longer. Besides," Tony said sardonically, "you have what matters to you. You're a wife with a living husband. You belong to somebody. That's what really counts, isn't it?"

She began to cry, but she knew tears wouldn't help. This was an ultimatum. Take it or leave it. What choice did she have? He'd divorce her if she didn't go along with his decisions. Five years. It was a long time. But meanwhile, she would be Mrs. Anthony Robin. She'd have the security that meant so much to her. She'd be a married woman. The world would know she was wanted by a handsome, glamorous man. She'd not be one of those pathetic divorcées or widows, aimlessly adrift. It was better than nothing. Much better. And certainly she could change his mind before the five years were up. Peggy finally managed to smile.

"All right, darling," she said. "Your happiness is all I care about."

Chapter 14

AS SOON AS Jayne left the cabin that evening, Mary pushed the "on" button of the tape recorder and began to speak into the microphone.

"Good morning, friends. This is Mary Farr Morgan. There'll be no interview as such today. Instead, I'd like to share with you an unforgettable interlude. Try to capture a moment in time. Imprison a picture in your heart as one is imprisoned in mine.

"I'm sure most of you have a mental picture of Japan. I know I did. I visualized a small, bustling country rapidly becoming Westernized. In the years since World War II, we've bought Japanese cars and TV sets, seen pictures of Tokyo, a traffic-jammed city bigger and more crowded than New York, with American-style night clubs populated by young men and women in modern dress.

"Well, I haven't seen Tokyo yet. Probably it's as we imagine. But there's another, quieter Japan that still exists, and I've just returned from it. For the past twenty-four hours, I've been in the gracious city of Kyoto.

"Forgive my sentimentality, but I think that wherever I go I shall never forget the feeling of having been plucked from the hurried, noisy world of the twentieth century and transported back to a culture whose roots go deep into Japanese soil.

More than a thousand years deep. I won't bore you with statistics. Suffice to say that from 794 to 1869, Kyoto was the capital city of Japan and today is its fifth largest city with a population of nearly one and a half million.

"More interesting to me—and, I hope, to you—is the fact that Kyoto is still the cradle of Japanese civilization, the repository of its legends and the dramatic reminder of its sophisticated past. Not sophisticated in the world-weary sense, but in the elegant, unpretentious way that genuinely sophisticated people are, assured and elegant, conscious of their quality with no need to flaunt their riches.

"I arrived at night, under a full moon. I was driven through streets incredibly adhering to a modern, checkered design laid out in the original plan more than eleven hundred years ago. And I came at last to an oasis of sanity called Tawaraya, the inn made famous in the writings of Elizabeth Gray Vining, the American tutor of Crown Prince Akihito.

"Believe me, I could spend our whole half hour describing this inn managed by Mrs. Toshi Sato, whose family has run Tawaraya for eleven generations, or three hundred years. There are nineteen rooms, each with bath. And what rooms! Done in the traditional manner with sliding doors overlooking private gardens which are softly lighted at night. The main room is sparsely furnished with a low teak table and quote chairs unquote which really are pillows with rush backs and separate, kidney-shaped armrests of antique brocade. The no-color walls are bare except for one beautiful hanging. And precisely to its right, on the floor, is a perfect flower arrangement of two graceful blossoms in a wicker basket.

"I dined, solicitously served by a dignified elderly Japanese woman in traditional dress. I'm sure she was amused by my ineptitude with chopsticks and my thoroughly baffled expression when confronted by pressed seaweed and other exotic and still unidentified dishes, but she was much too polite to show it.

"Later, I explored details I'd been too entranced at first to discover. The bath was a miracle unto itself. The sleek, oversized wooden tub has a cover to keep the water hot. One soaps and rinses and then steps, rather gingerly, into the near-scalding water to relax. But the tub is not the only wonder of the perfectly appointed bathroom. There are stocks of kimonos and slippers, tissues, a comb and brush, razor, shampoo and body lotion and several toothbrushes. And there are modern concessions which I almost wished weren't there. A portable hair dryer and in the main room, a small television set. I found myself resenting their intrusion into this old-fashioned world, and I wanted to say, 'Don't. Please let me pretend I'm a pampered woman of a hundred years ago with smiling retainers to bring me tea and arrange my room for the night.'

"Dear friends, promise you'll never ask for an Occidental bedroom in Japan! Don't miss the ceremonial joy of watching the maid take your two flowered mattresses out of a secret closet in the wall and stack them on the floor, carefully covering them with thick padding. She adds clean white sheets, top and bottom, a striped blanket and over that a bright-pink quilt. Two small pillows are propped against one of the rush-back chairs which suddenly serves as a backboard. A standing paper lamp is set next to the bed and a calm descends that drives tension and pressures far into the still, moonlit night. You will rest as you never have before."

Mary snapped off the machine and sat thinking of the night as it really was.

Whatever would happen to her and Christopher in the days ahead, they had this euphoric memory to share. This was a world made for lovers. A private world, civilized and tranquil, where even the movements of love had a slow, graceful, dreamlike quality.

Almost reluctantly she went on to describe the next day in Kyoto. The breathtaking beauty of the gardens, all water and stone and cherry-blossom trees in full bloom.

("The Japanese don't plant flowers in their gardens," Christopher said. "Flowers die, but trees live forever and grow more beautiful with age.")

She described the shrines she visited. The glorious Shinto temple where she saw a baptism, called a "purification," in progress. Another where, for a few pennies, one bought a slip of paper with one's fortune. If the fortune was bad, you simply attached it to a tree outside the temple where it fluttered with hundreds of others, blowing its ill omen away, into the soft spring breeze.

With her listeners, she wandered through the seventeenth-century shogun's summer palace, stunned by the beauty of the intricately painted screen-walls, the decorative gold leaf that had endured for centuries, the "nightingale floors" that squeaked as one walked, as they'd once squeaked to warn the guards of intruders. In the area where the shogun's concubines lived, the "harem" scene was re-created with mannequins in authentic dress.

"Every night," Mary said, "each of the shogun's concubines offered him a cup of tea. The one he accepted was the lady chosen to be with him. The others had to wait their turn!"

("From this came the expression, 'You're not my cup of tea,' " Christopher solemnly explained. "Idiot!" Mary said. "You made that up!" He'd laughed. "Sure. But what a considerate rejection.")

The tape was coming to a close as Mary told of her experience with the famous "Bullet Train," known in Japan for its electrified smoothness and speed.

"I decided to take it back to Kobe to meet the ship, which sailed at six o'clock. My ticket was on the four-fifteen train and, knowing it was only a thirty-minute ride, I knew I had plenty of time. Unfortunately, at the station my guide informed me the train had been indefinitely delayed by, of all things, an encounter with a kite string! It didn't come into the Kyoto station until five o'clock and I nearly had heart failure racing up the dock to catch my floating home before it left for Yokohama! I made it. But barely!"

How they'd laughed, she and Christopher, at the idea of the super-streamlined train, the pride of Japan, stopped by a kite string. They were still laughing as they raced down the long dock toward the gangway. But the laughter turned to fear as Christopher suddenly stopped halfway and leaned against a post, his face gray. Mary ran on a few feet before she realized he wasn't following. She turned and rushed back.

"Christopher! What is it? What's wrong?"

He'd shaken his head and smiled. "Nothing. Just a little winded. I'll be okay in a second. Don't worry. They won't leave without us."

"I'm not worried about that! I'm worried about you!"

"It's okay." In a minute he straightened up. "See? Just had to catch my breath. The old boy ain't what he used to be."

"You're sure? Shouldn't I get a doctor?"

"Nope. I'm fine. Come along. We only have ten minutes."

No account of that terrifying episode went onto the tape. No mention of the fact that her "guide" was the charming, knowledgeable man she loved. She wished she could tell the world what it meant to spend this time with him. Poor Christopher, she thought, smiling. I can't even give him credit for some of the trivia I picked up. Like the reason the Japanese bow when they meet someone is because it's considered rude to look another person in the eye, and bowing is a graceful way to avoid such discourtesy. She ended her report with that little piece of information.

"Perhaps, more than anything, that simple gesture, so misunderstood by Westerners, symbolizes the courteous formality and the adherence to tradition one feels in this land. It also points up the vast difference between us. For, as Americans, we condemn a person who 'can't look you in the eye.' In Japan, it is just the opposite.

"So, until you and I figuratively 'look each other in the eye' in San Francisco, this is Mary Farr Morgan saying 'Sayonara' from the other side of the world."

She put the tape in its container and addressed it to Charlie. Tomorrow evening she'd mail it from Yokohama. A part of her life was going to the States. And another part was going back to Australia, hoping she'd join him there. She thought of Michael's call. She knew what she was going to do. Tonight she'd tell Christopher.

He lay on his bed, resting. The pain was gone now, but it had scared hell out of him back there on the dock. It was like the time before. A searing poker in his chest. Stupid damned doctors in Singapore! They'd told him he was fine.

Christopher propped himself up on the pillows. Well, he probably was. It might not have had anything to do with his heart. After all, he wasn't a kid. He couldn't make those wild sprints along two city blocks without running out of steam.

He sat up gingerly. Sure. He was fine. No point in seeing that silly little med student who passed for a doctor on this ship. In another day or so he'd be home. He'd have his own specialist check, just to be sure. Ridiculous to get so frightened every time he had a twinge. His doctor told him that if he lived sensibly he'd be good for another twenty years. Racing like a track star was hardly sensible. He wasn't infirm, but he had to be cautious.

Perhaps he should tell Mary his history. No. If she wasn't going to marry him, there was no point. And if she was, it was selfish to worry her needlessly. He had no intention of dying soon. If he thought that, he'd never have proposed, would never let her give up everything to be with him. He was all right. Everything was all right. He was certain she'd marry him. Why wouldn't she? That damned husband of hers was finally on his feet. She need have no guilts about "abandoning" him. She must realize that after the phone call, though they hadn't discussed it. Her "helpless child" needed her no more. Christopher sighed with pleasure. The conscience-haunting hurdle that stood between them was gone. And Mary loved him. If he needed reassurance, it had come in Kyoto. They'd go back one day and recapture that particular ecstasy. Meantime, so many ecstatic days lay ahead.

"Christopher will never understand. And I can't say I blame him." Jayne stared at her aunt, who was slowly dressing for dinner. "My God, Aunt Mary, I've never heard such an inverted rationale! First you can't leave Uncle Mike because he's a failure and now you have to stay with him because he's a success! I don't get it. I really don't. I'm beginning to think you're some kind of masochist!"

Mary turned slowly from the dressing table to face her niece. She looked drawn and unhappy even while she tried to sound light-hearted. "The same thought crossed my mind," she said. "All I need in my spring wardrobe is a hair shirt."

Jayne persisted. "Why are you doing this? Why are you going back to him? Don't you remember anything you told me weeks ago? I thought the whole purpose was to decide whether Michael could live without you. You led me to believe that you stayed with him only because he depended on you. Well, he's all set now. He doesn't have to lean on you, financially or emotionally. You're scot-free, Aunt Mary, and a super guy wants you. You could be happy, be the kind of woman you say you always wanted to be. And you're going to turn it down? I think you're crazy!"

"I don't blame you. I think maybe I am." Mary nervously twisted the jade ring on her finger. "How can I explain it to you?"

"Try."

Mary took a deep breath. Later she'd have to try to make Christopher understand. As Jayne said, he never would. How could he? She didn't really understand herself. She wasn't even sure that what she was doing was right. Maybe if she talked it out with Jayne, it would be clearer in her own mind. A kind of dress rehearsal for disaster, she thought mirthlessly. A practice session before I try to make Christopher see what I must do.

"I haven't forgotten what I told you," she said. "It was all true, Jaynie. It still is, I suppose. The respect I lost for Michael hasn't magically come back just because he's finally pulled off one of his impossible dreams. I haven't fallen in love with him again. But the thing of it is, everything he's ever done has been in an effort to make me proud of him. All the lies about his jobs, all the bravado about the big deals in the offing, all this was done to please me. To make me glad I married him. He loves me very much. More than I love him. He's never cared about being a success, except that he knows it's important to me. Now that he's broken his back to be what I wanted, could I possibly leave him? Wouldn't that negate everything he's tried to do? Wouldn't it make all the years of trying and failing meaningless? How can I walk out on him when he's done the very thing I felt I needed? Not the thing *he* needed. The thing *I* needed— his success. I can't let him feel it's all been in vain. I can't pat him on the head and say, 'Good boy, Michael. Now you don't need me anymore. Good-bye.' My God, Jayne, that would really destroy him! To have worked all these years toward an end that someone else wants and then be rewarded by desertion! I could have justified it more, in my own mind, when he was a failure. I could have convinced myself that he didn't care enough for me to try to make something of himself. I could have told myself he's a hopeless goof-off. But he's delivered what he believed I wanted. I believed it myself. Am I to repay all this pathetic striving by selfishly turning away from him? I can't. I want to, but I can't!''

Jayne stared at her, speechless. She really believes that, the girl thought. She honestly feels she has an obligation. That Michael doesn't care about himself. That his motivation has been her approval and nothing more.

"You're wrong, you know,'' Jayne finally said. "You're still doing the same number with a different twist. You still think he needs you. That this new career means nothing without you. Maybe you're afraid he won't make a success of it unless you're there. You still must be indispensable, mustn't you? I'm sorry, Aunt Mary, but I think you rather enjoy being a martyr. You must get your kicks out of self-sacrifice. I don't doubt you believe what you're saying, but it's dumb. Really dumb. Hell, it's more than that! It's sick! Why does everything have to depend on you? What is this wild ego of yours that makes you think Michael can't make it without you? He's a grown man, for God's sake! And what about Christopher? Doesn't it haunt you to know how unhappy he's going to be?''

Mary didn't fight back. "Everything you're saying is probably true, but I have to live with myself. I can't help how I feel. I know Michael isn't strong enough to be alone. Christopher is. In a few months Christopher will have forgotten me, but not standing by Michael would destroy him. I made my bed. I'm going to have to try to be content in it.''

Jayne snorted. "I never heard such hogwash! I could throw up! You're not doing anything admirable, Aunt Mary. You're still pampering an ego that won't stop. You may believe all those flimsy excuses about making Michael's efforts worthwhile, but I have my doubts. I think if you really told the truth, you'd admit that you don't *want* a strong man. That the thought of being second fiddle to Christopher scares hell out of you. That you can't stand the idea of giving up your career and your feeling of importance. I don't think it's Michael who's taking you back to your old life. I think you *like* your old life! I don't think you could live without it!''

Mary took the verbal beating without anger. For all she knew, Jayne might be right. She did love her work. She did love the attention it brought her. She couldn't deny that. As for the ego, the indispensability where Michael was concerned, maybe that was true, too. She didn't know. She only knew she couldn't deliver this final blow to a faithful, loving man who was trying to please her. Couldn't do it even if it meant giving up one she desperately loved.

"I know how I must sound,'' she said quietly. "In your place, I'd feel just as disgusted. Maybe I'm guilty of everything you say. Probably I am. But I won't be the first woman who stuck out of loyalty. Misguided, maybe. But still loyalty. There are principles involved here, Jayne. I'm not patting myself on the back, but I can't be as selfish as I probably should. Your mother and I were brought up to believe in the sanctity of marriage. I'm sure, in a different way, she's not been any happier than I. But she's stayed with your father, hasn't she? She hasn't walked out because she's bored.''

"Now you're really being ridiculous! Mother hasn't walked out because she has no place to walk to. You said so yourself. God! Don't point her out as the model of a perfect wife! She's cheated on Dad since Day One!''

Mary's voice was almost a whisper. "And I've cheated on Michael.''

Jayne sighed. "That's part of it, too, isn't it? You're feeling guilty as hell about this affair. Probably beating yourself up because you've been having a wonderful time while Michael's been home trying to get his damned project off the ground. Aunt Mary, get with it! This isn't the Victorian age! Everybody strays from the reservation. You don't honestly think Uncle Mike's been a paragon of virtue all these weeks, do you? If you tell me that, I'll faint. I swear I'll absolutely faint!"

In spite of her distress, Mary laughed. "I can't imagine you fainting no matter what." She sobered. "I envy you, Jayne. I really do. I think I'm a strong woman, but next to you, I'm Jell-O. You're so certain of things. Everything is so neatly black and white. You're not afraid of anything in the world are you?"

"Only of being maudlin."

Involuntarily, Mary recoiled.

"I'm sorry, Aunt Mary. I didn't mean to say that. But I can't stand what you're doing! Think about yourself. You talk of being 'unfulfilled,' of having made terrible mistakes, of not wanting to see me get into a situation like yours. Yet when you have a chance to escape, you won't. All this bull about loyalty and principles. What is that? Don't you see what you're going to do to Christopher? What you're going to do to yourself? No, of course you don't. You only see this fancied obligation to Michael. Don't do it. I beg you. You'll be sorry the rest of your life."

"You mean damned if I do, and damned if I don't."

"No. I only mean damned if you don't tell Christopher you're divorcing Michael and flying back to him as soon as you can."

"I can't, Jayne. I want to, but I can't."

"Then you don't really want to. You prefer to suffer rather than take a chance on someone else."

It was very much what Christopher had said to her. You have to really want it. You have to trust someone, sometime. I do trust, Mary thought. I know Christopher would take care of me. I trust Michael to be faithful and loving. It's my own emotions I don't trust. I don't even know when I'm lying to myself. I don't know what's true anymore.

I just know I have to go back and find out.

She'd never seen anyone look so bewildered and hurt. Then the look changed to incredulity.

"Mary, what are you saying? You're going to throw away everything we could have together because of this distorted thinking? It's not possible! It's upside down! My God, I could almost have made myself accept the fact that a woman like you wouldn't desert a helpless, dependent man. But to believe that you owe him some kind of thanks for finally succeeding! It's incredible. I won't allow it."

"I know. It seems sick. But I do owe him, Christopher. He's spent the past fifteen years trying to please me."

"And what happens in the next fifteen? Or the next thirty?"

Tears came to Mary's eyes. "Don't you think I've thought of that? Don't you know how hard it is for me to do this?"

"No." His voice was harsh. "I don't know that at all. All I see is some kind of warped feeling of obligation that isn't credible. You're doing a terrible thing, Mary. You're destroying two lives, yours and mine, for the sake of one that doesn't sound worth worrying about. What kind of man has to be constantly propped up to keep going? What kind of man would have let you take care of him all these years? Damn it, don't you see what he is? What he'll always be?"

"You don't understand." The words came from her choked throat. "I love you, Christopher. But I can't love at someone else's expense. Women feel differently than men about things like this. Michael is my husband, for better or for worse."

"Like hell! Michael is your child. And that's what you want, isn't it? A child to mother. Too bad you never had any. Or maybe it's just as well. You'd have smothered them, too!" He stopped, instantly remorseful. "Oh, God, darling, forgive me. I'm beside myself. I don't know what I'm saying. I can't believe this. I don't know how to stop you from making this terrible mistake. I want you so much, Mary. I love you more than I've ever loved any woman. I can't lose you. It's wrong. Hideously wrong."

"I have to do it, Christopher. I have to go home and give him a chance. It has nothing to do with my feeling for you. I'll love you the rest of my life, but I must do this."

He rose from the chair on the upper deck where they sat under the stars and walked to the railing. With his back to her he said, "Yokohama tomorrow. I had such hopes."

Mary closed her eyes. I wish I were dead, she thought. I can't bear it. She felt Christopher return to her side.

"It's our last night, darling."

"Yes. Oh, Christopher, I . . ."

"Hush. No more to be said. You go home and decide about your life, sweetheart. Our life. You'll hear from me. I'm not going to take this decision as final. I realize you think you must stay, but I'm betting that when you get there you'll see you're free to leave. That you've paid your dues. Fifteen years of them. That you've done everything a loving woman can do. And more. When you see that, my dearest Mary, I'll be waiting. You know where to find me."

"Don't wait," she pleaded. "Make a life for yourself with someone else. I want you to. I want you to be happy."

"You'll come to me," Christopher said. "It may take a while, but you'll come." He pulled her to her feet. "Meantime, my love, we have one more chance to be together before our temporary separation. And that's what it is, dear heart, a time for the unfinished business you must complete. I know you must. You'd never know peace until you did." He smiled sadly. "My wonderful, darling Mary. What rotten luck she's such a loyal, compassionate woman."

"An old-fashioned idiot, you mean."

Christopher gently stroked her hair. "Yes," he said, "that, too. But I wouldn't have you any other way, dearest. Even if it means letting you find out for yourself what I already know."

"That I'm wrong for Michael?"

"More importantly, that you're right for me."

Chapter 15

PATRICIA POURED A cup of coffee for Michael and handed it to him across the breakfast table. She'd been a guest in her sister's apartment for ten days, her brother-in-law's lover for nearly that long, and she hated to think of it coming to an end in another couple of weeks. I wish I could stay in San Francisco, she thought. I love this city. I could get a little apartment and see Michael now and then when Mary was at work. Forget it, she told herself. Who'd support her? Not Stanley. Not Michael, who didn't have a penny of his own. And she certainly wasn't going to start trying to earn a living at this late date. Maybe Jayne, she thought suddenly. Maybe the kid would like to work here and share an apartment with her mother. She decided to try the idea out on Michael.

"What would you think if I could talk Jayne into staying in San Francisco and the two of us took an apartment?"

The horrified look in Michael's eyes was her answer, though he quickly tried to cover his dismay.

"I don't know," he said casually. "Do you think you'd want to live here permanently? What about Stanley?"

"To hell with Stanley."

"He's your husband, Patricia. Even if we've chosen to ignore that fact." Michael looked uneasy. "Besides, I think you'd be bored here. All your friends are in New York."

"I make friends easily. Anyway, *you're* here."

Michael began to feel nervous. "Look, Pat, this whole business ends the minute Mary comes back. You do know that, don't you? I mean, my God, there's no way in the world I could see you after she returns!"

"Really? You couldn't see your sister-in-law?"

"You know what I mean."

"You bet I know. The cat's on her way home and playtime is over for the mouse. It's easy enough to dump me, Michael, but what are you going to do about your friend Rae?"

He was visibly startled. "What about Rae?"

"Oh, come on! Do you really think a woman like Rae Spanner could keep a triumph like that to herself? She called here yesterday, pretending she'd like to give a party for Mary and Jayne when they return, and saying how anxious she was to meet me. She was about as subtle as a see-through blouse."

"How did she know you were in town?"

"She said somebody named Charlie Burke mentioned it. And then she said she was amazed that you hadn't told her." Patricia imitated Rae's boarding-school voice. " 'I can't imagine why dear Michael didn't tell me himself. He drops by every afternoon. We're in a business venture together and we've become *very* close.' " Patricia laughed. "I got the picture. She's lent you money and she's extracting her pound of flesh."

Michael flushed. "All right, it's true, but I can't imagine why she'd want you to know any of that."

"Oh, Michael, you *are* naïve! Don't you see? She wants me to tell Mary."

"Tell Mary!"

"Of course. You don't really think she's going to settle for some temporary arrangement, do you? She's after you, dear boy. After you for keeps. Don't tell me you didn't suspect that."

He was growing angry. "What makes you so damned sure? You've never even met her. It seems to me you're jumping to a lot of conclusions based on one telephone call!"

Methodically, Patricia ticked off her reasons on the fingers of one hand. "Okay. Number one, Mary's mentioned her over the years. I know she's rich and single and used to buying what she wants. Number two, I know you'd do anything to get money to start your own business. Number three, I'm a street-smart girl from New York. I've heard that proprietary tone of voice before. Women understand other women, Michael. I know her type. I saw through that phony phone call even before she said more."

"Said more? What more?"

"Just a few little things. Like wasn't it too bad that someone as brilliant and attractive as you didn't have a rich wife to set him up in business. And how marvelous it was that Mary at least could do well enough to let the two of you live comfortably. And how she wondered what Mary's reaction would be when she came home and found you hadn't raised enough capital. She's a barracuda. If I were you, I'd pay her off and deny everything if she starts trouble. If you're lucky, Mary won't find out what's been going on there."

"You're not going to tell Mary, are you?"

Patricia grinned. "What's it worth to you?"

"Exactly what does that mean?"

"Is it worth your helping me talk Jayne into staying in San Francisco and getting a job to support her devoted mother? And is it worth an occasional visit to me while Mary's at work?"

He stared at her and then, unexpectedly, began to laugh. "That's funny! Oh, God, that's funny! Talk about your boomerangs! You'd really do that, wouldn't you? You'd threaten to tell Mary about my involvement with Rae, which isn't nearly as ugly as my involvement with you. And I'd be in the middle, wouldn't I? Because you know I'd never tell her about us." Michael stopped laughing. "It's hard to believe you and Mary are sisters. She's so damned honest and you're as devious as they come. Jesus, how could the two of you have come from the same parents?"

Patricia was unperturbed. "It happens that way, lots of times. Saints and sinners out of the same womb. Not that I think Mary's a saint. Not by any means. She's been self-centered since the day she was born. I don't think she could make a real commitment to anyone."

"She certainly made one to me!"

"Nope. With you she made an arrangement. She found herself a nice, big, handsome guy who wouldn't get in the way of her ambitions. That's not a commitment, Michael. A commitment means putting yourself in someone else's hands. Has Mary ever done that? Has she ever depended on you for a roof over her head and food in her mouth? Has she ever made you feel like a man? Hell, I've cheated all over the place but I've made more of a commitment to Stanley than Mary has to you."

"Shut up!" Without thinking, he reached across the table and slapped her hard across the mouth. Patricia hardly blinked. She simply put her hand to her face as though to cover the red finger-marks that appeared.

"Nice going," she said slowly.

Michael was horrified. He'd never hit a woman before. The act sickened and yet, strangely, excited him. Violence had never been his thing but he suddenly understood how it aroused all kinds of passions. Looking at Patricia, he realized she understood it, too.

Wordlessly, she rose from the table and walked slowly toward the bedroom. In silence, Michael followed.

Mary lay on her bed as though life had left her body. It was five o'clock in the afternoon and the ship was in port at Yokohama. Since five o'clock that morning, when she'd crept back to her cabin from Christopher's, she'd not left the room, had eaten nothing and spoken to no one except Jayne. The girl had gone now, to explore the city with Terry. She'd been reluctant to abandon Mary.

"Are you sure I shouldn't stay with you? I don't mind. There's nothing much to see here."

Mary shook her head. "No. You run along. I'm okay."

"You're not okay. You didn't see Christopher at all today. You didn't even say good-bye to him."

"I said good-bye to him last night, Jayne. We agreed not to see each other again. Too anticlimactic."

Too painful, you mean, Jayne thought. Too terrible. It was awful. She didn't tell Mary she'd run into Christopher on deck at lunchtime. He looked gray and devastated as he beckoned Jayne to a corner of the lounge.

"How is she?" he asked.

No need to ask whom he meant. "Lousy," Jayne said. "She hasn't gotten out of bed all day. Won't eat a thing. Hardly speaks. Why are you letting her do this? It's dead wrong for both of you. You know that. Can't you make her see what a stupid sacrifice this is?"

Christopher shook his head. "I can't force her to go against her conscience. I can only hope that she'll get home and see how wrong she is. I'm waiting for her. She knows that."

She wanted to shake both of them: Mary for being so stupid and Christopher for being so damned noble. I don't understand that generation, she thought. Who brainwashed them into all these ideas of duty? They're intelligent people and yet they're living by some outmoded code of conduct they find impossible to ignore. It was too bloody civilized. Where was the anger, the bitterness Mary should have felt? Where was the command Christopher should have exerted? Why did he take this lying down? Was there no fight in him that he accepted this with almost pious resignation?

He seemed to read her mind. "You're wondering why I don't raise hell, aren't you?"

"Frankly, yes. You're a strong man."

"And your aunt is a strong woman. It takes superhuman strength to do what she's doing, Jayne. She doesn't run away from her obligations, even if you and I think they're false ones. Don't mistake what she's doing for weakness or stupidity. And don't mistake my acceptance for lassitude. I'd fight for her if that would help. But it won't. I'd only add to the unhappiness she already feels. She's left me no choice but to wait and hope that she can come to me without lingering doubts and guilt. That's the only way it can every work for a woman like Mary. For me too. I fell in love with her for what she is. It would be childish of me to expect her to change."

"Do you think she'll ever see how undeserving of all this Michael really is?"

"Yes," Christopher said, "I think she'll see. I only hope it's in time."

Jayne looked at him curiously. "You mean you'll wait only so long."

"I'll wait as long as I can, but one never knows about tomorrow. Accidents happen. Sickness happens. Who can tell?" He pulled a note pad out of his pocket and scribbled on it. "I'd like you to give her my son James' address and telephone number. Mary knows where to reach me, but in case she should want to contact me while I'm on a business trip or something, give her this, will you? I travel a lot, but James always knows where I am."

"Will you be in San Francisco soon?"

Christopher shook his head. "No. I think I'll avoid it for a while. I'll write to Mary at the radio station. She knows that, but tell her again, will you? And tell her I love her more than anything in the world, though she knows that, too."

Looking down at Mary, who lay deathly still in her bed, Jayne took the scrap of paper out of her pocket.

"I saw Christopher this morning," she said. "He asked me to give you this. It's his son's address and phone in Sydney. In case Christopher's away when you're ready to reach him."

Mary opened her eyes and took the paper wordlessly.

"He said to tell you again that he loves you more than anything in the world."

A look of pain crossed Mary's face, but she said nothing.

Jayne made one more try. "Please, Aunt Mary, won't you . . ."

"Go away, darling. Please, just go away."

With Jayne gone and Christopher on his way to Tokyo to catch a flight back to Sydney, Mary finally gave way to her tears. She seldom cried, but now she sobbed uncontrollably, not even trying to stop. Let it all wash away, she thought. Let all the heartache and longing run out through my eyes. If only it would. If only she'd stop wishing she were free and on the plane with Christopher to start a whole new life. If only she'd never taken this trip at all. No. That she wouldn't wish. Not to have known Christopher was far worse than losing him. Not to have experienced mutual love and desire would have been to be cheated out of the greatest emotion of her life. I have that to cherish, she thought. Those memories to savor. The knowledge of his love to give me strength. I need strength. People think I'm so strong. Even Jayne, who knows more about me than most, thinks I'm made of steel, a woman who may bend but never break.

But I'm not. Just the opposite. Perhaps because I cannot bend, I will break into a million tiny pieces that can never be put together again.

It seemed so long ago that she'd stood on the deck and watched San Francisco disappear and thought about The Decision. Who'd have thought Michael would make it for her, pulling her back to share the success she wanted for him? And who'd have thought she'd go so unwillingly, so reluctantly, hating every step of the way?

She turned her head to the wall. She pictured Michael, exuberant with delight at her return, anxious to tell her every detail of his accomplishment, eager to take her to bed.

God, how will I go through with it? How will I pretend to make love to my husband when it's someone else I want? Won't he know? Won't he sense the change in me? Will I be able to play out this charade, thinking always of Christopher?

I suppose I should feel ashamed of my unfaithfulness, but I don't. I love Christopher. I love him still. When Michael's arms are around me, I'll be remembering another man's. When my husband tells me how wonderful life is going to be, I'll be thinking only of the one I could have had. It's not fair to Michael. But I've never been fair to him. Not really. Just as he's never been fair to me.

Angrily, she pounded the pillow. Nothing was fair. Everything was too late. Michael had come to manhood too late. And she'd come too late to love.

It was not until they were well at sea, on their way to Hawaii, that Mary finally found strength to dress and come out of the cabin. Late in the morning she wandered up to the British Bar and found Gail DeVries having a cup of consommé. The older woman cheerfully beckoned her over to a corner table.

"Where have you been hiding for three days? I rang your cabin the morning we arrived in Yokohama, but there was no answer. Beau and I were going up to Tokyo overnight and we thought you might like to join us."

Mary had heard the phone ring a couple of times after Jayne left, but she hadn't answered. She didn't want to talk to anyone except Christopher, yet she was terrified that if she did speak to him again she might not be able to go through with her agonizing decision.

"That was kind of you, Gail. I'm sorry to have missed it. I haven't been feeling too well."

"Nothing serious, I hope."

"I think you can imagine what it was."

Gail sighed and nodded. "You've let him go."

"Yes. Jayne thinks I'm the world's biggest fool. I'm not sure I don't agree with her. I've probably made the worst mistake of my life. I must be crazy. Nobody in his right mind would throw away such a chance."

"You're not crazy." Gail said. "Do you think you're the only woman in the world who felt compelled to stand by someone who needs her?"

"That's just the point. Michael doesn't need me now. For the first time in forty-five years he's independent. He's done something on his own, with no help from me. He's going to have an identity of his own."

"Fair enough. But it wouldn't be a complete identity unless he shared it with you, would it?"

"I suppose not," Mary said. "Deep down, I guess I think I owe him that satisfaction."

Gail patted her hand. "Why don't you admit it, Mary? You know it's more than that. You're not sure that Michael will make it even now. A new business venture is a risky thing. Aren't you afraid he'll fail again and there'll be nobody to pick up the pieces? Nobody but strong, dependable Mary? Isn't that part of it?"

Mary gazed out the window for a long moment. "Yes. That's part of it. I haven't even wanted to admit it to myself. I lied when I said Michael doesn't need me anymore. I know, in my heart, he'll need me more than ever now. It will be hard for him, more frightening than he'd ever admit. There'll be bad moments in the months ahead until the shop is on its feet. I can't desert him when he'll need all the support and reassurance he can get."

Gail shook her head. "Mary, Mary," she said despairingly. "Dear child, for a modest woman you have an inordinate sense of indispensability. Must you take perpetual care of every wounded bird? I don't mean to be hard on you. I know you're miserable enough without a lecture from me. I know what you're going through. I've been there, my dear."

Mary looked at her inquiringly.

"Isn't it boring," Gail said in quiet amusement, "how people always want to tell you their own stories instead of listening to yours? I suppose that's why psychiatrists are better than friends; the paid listener doesn't interrupt with his own experiences. Well, I've committed the unpardonable sin of bringing this conversation back to myself, so I might as well go on. Before I married Mr. DeVries, I was terribly in love with another young man." Her expression grew gentle. "Even now, I remember how wonderful he was. But I felt I had a duty to marry my husband because he was well off, whereas the one I loved had no money at all. You see, Mary, I supported my parents when I was young. My father was an invalid, barely scraping by on a pension, and my dear mother had three other children to care for. At sixteen, I was the breadwinner. Imagine, almost fifty years ago I was a typist, earning twelve dollars a week and taking care of six people. I had to make a decision. Marry the penniless one I loved and leave my family to shift for itself or marry Mr. DeVries, whom I liked and who would take care of the people who needed me. Obviously, you know which road I chose."

"How sad for you," Mary said. "How brave."

Gail smiled. "It wasn't brave. It was selfish. It was simply as though I had to do it or never know a moment's peace. And it worked out. I was very happy with my husband. I even grew to love him. We had a good life and nice children. I was glad I'd done my duty, when I saw my parents living comfortably and my brothers and sister educated and successful. I suppose I felt very saintly. But in retrospect, I can see that it was an unhealthy decision. I missed the great love of my life, Mary. I'm older now and hopefully wiser. If I had it to do all over again, I'd realize that nobody appointed me God. My family would have managed. But I didn't believe they could. I felt that with my defection they'd go under. I never thought that if I died they'd go on somehow. I didn't see that my vanity was more important to me than a solid sense of self-preservation."

Gail looked compassionately at her younger friend. "My story has some of the elements of your own. Or so it seems to me. The situation is different but the motivations are recognizable."

"Yes. You're saying I'm not necessary to Michael's survival any more than you were to your family's. But it's different, Gail. When this trip started, I was coming to the conclusion that he'd be better off if I kicked him out of the nest. Now I feel I have to support him emotionally if not financially. It's a matter of decent, civilized behavior."

"You're quibbling, my friend. It all comes down to the same thing, There's a streak of martyrdom in us, I suppose, though I find that most distasteful to contemplate. But the main flaw in our character is an overwhelming and exaggerated view of our role in life. In business, it's called autonomy or, more kindly, leadership. The company will collapse, the president thinks, if he doesn't make every decision. In private life, it's a compliment to ourselves and an insult to others."

"I can't see it that way. I wish I could."

"I know." Gail was sympathetic. "Perhaps you'll always be glad you did what you thought you had to do. I only hope that you don't wake up one day and wonder how your values could have gotten so mixed up when your intentions were so good. I don't want to think that, when you're older and time is racing by, you may feel some bitterness for the sacrifice you made. It will be too late then. There'll always be a hole in your life that not even self-righteousness can fill." She paused. "I know you'll never disappoint your husband. I hope he never truly disappoints you."

Mary smiled. *"Truly* disappoints me? Gail, it's happened a hundred times. The big deal that's always going to come through. The big job that never pans out. It's played like a broken record. Until now. Now it sounds as though he's really gotten his teeth into something. I don't think it will be the same kind of disappointment."

"I didn't mean that kind of letdown. I hope your Michael is always the devoted, adoring man you picture him to be. Constant failure has a funny effect on people sometimes. A man who can't succeed in business very often has to prove his manliness in other ways."

"Like running after other women, you mean? No. Not Michael. I don't think that would happen." A note of bitterness crept into Mary's voice. "Michael's too dependent to risk losing me through unfaithfulness. At least, he has been until now. Who knows what he'll be like when he has something to be proud about? But I don't think he'll disappoint me, Gail. Not that way." She hesitated. "And I couldn't really be outraged if he did, could I? I've no right to point a finger. Not anymore."

A voice behind them said, "Now what are you two pretty little ladies up to? You look mighty serious!"

They smiled up at Beauregarde.

"Girl talk," Gail said. "None of your business. I just told Mary we wanted her to go to Tokyo with us."

"Yes. I'm sorry I missed it, Colonel Stanford."

The old man snorted. "You didn't miss much. Biggest damned crowded place I ever saw. And the prices! Lord, I never saw prices like that in New York City! Little people in the streets. Big numbers on the menus."

"What kind of nonsense is that?" Gail said tartly. "You never worry about spending money. It's your children who're worried." She stood up. "Speaking of money, you're late for our gin game, Beau. I mean to liberate some more of your cash."

"She does, too," Beau said indulgently. "I think her daddy must have been a Mississippi riverboat gambler."

Mary watched them affectionately as they moved to their card table. Lovely people. They were what growing old should be. Not self-centered retreat or querulous hostility, but continued *joie de vivre* and a lively curiosity about new places and people. They were enjoying every day left to them, giving off love, and sharing, if it was wanted, the kind of wisdom that comes only with a lifetime of experience.

She thought of Gail's unexpected confession of her own lost love and the way she'd come to terms with it, not without regret but with realistic acknowledgment of why she'd done what she had. Not many women would admit they'd married for money. And not many would have analyzed their motives as dispassionately as Gail, seeing the flaws in their logic but rejecting self-pity. It was a lesson in discipline and self-control, a gentle reminder that most lives are not storybook perfect. She felt a rush of affection for Gail DeVries, once again comparing her to Camille Farr and wishing she could talk to her own mother as she could to this comparative stranger. She envied Gail's daughters a mother so worldly wise and independent, understanding of human frailties and so full of the saving grace of humor.

I hope I'll see Gail when we get home, Mary thought. I won't burden her with my problems, but it would be good to have another woman to turn to when the weight of my world gets too heavy to handle.

For the first time in days, she felt better. The burden of loss was still with her. Even the thought of Christopher brought unwilling tears to her eyes. But she'd survive. She'd take it day by day, step by step, remembering that the life line between her and Australia stretched strong and firm to take her back, when and if she felt free to go.

Meanwhile, she'd do the best she could. She'd let Michael know she was proud of him. She'd show him she trusted him and depended on him. Perhaps now she'd be able to put all of herself into her marriage as Gail had done, since that was the course she'd decided to take. Put up or shut up, she told herself. You've made up your mind to go home, so give it everything you've got. Don't even think about that life line, because if you do you'll be only half-hearted in your effort to be content as Michael's wife. You must make yourself believe it's the only possible choice and it's going to work. Otherwise, it never will.

She was not a religious person but she believed in some kind of Presence and she spoke to it now. Help me, she said silently. Help me do what's right. Give me peace and dignity. Show me how to accept these past few weeks of my life with gratitude and serenity, remembering them as a wonderful, impossible dream.

Chapter 16

PATRICIA DASHED INTO the apartment full of high spirits, her eyes shining with excitement. She was hardly inside the door when she burst out with her news.

"Guess what? I found an apartment!"

Michael, sprawled on the living-room couch, reading the evening paper, sat bolt upright.

"You *what?*"

"I said I found an apartment. For Jayne and me. Three rooms on Fillmore Street. A furnished sublet. We can have it for only six months while the owner is away, but that's great. By that time we'll be settled and can find a permanent place."

"You're out of your mind!"

"Not at all. I know exactly what I'm doing. I told you before," Patricia said patiently. "I have it all figured out. Jayne will get a job. Eventually, I may find a little something to do, too. The apartment isn't expensive and we can manage."

Michael stared at her. "I don't believe this! You're taking a hell of a lot for granted. What if Jayne doesn't want to stay in San Francisco? What if she can't get a job or, more likely, isn't willing to support you? Has it ever occurred to you, Patricia, that Jayne may have other plans? And what about Stanley? I can't believe he'll not lift a finger to stop you. You're his wife!"

Patricia didn't stop smiling but there was an edginess in her voice. "This is where I came in, I think. We've been all over this before. I told you, to hell with Stanley. It's a matter of supreme indifference to me whether he likes it or not."

"Well, for God's sake give him a chance to express an opinion! Maybe he'll take to the idea of living in California. Maybe he'd be happy to move out here, too. If you're so bound and determined to stay, it's a hell of a lot more practical to set up housekeeping with your husband than to expect a young girl to take care of you."

"I'm bored with Stanley," Patricia said calmly. "I've been bored with him for twenty-two years. I don't want him here and I don't intend to go back where he is. I'm going to enjoy the rest of my life, Michael. As for Jayne, I can talk her into the idea. Remember, you promised to help."

"You have no conscience about saddling that girl with a mother to support?"

"None. I've taken care of her for twenty-one years. She owes me. Besides, if I'm lucky I'll find a man. One who can marry me. A rich man, of course. That's what I always wanted. Then I'll be off her hands. It may take a year or two, but she can afford to give me that much. She hasn't given me much up to now."

"My God! You'd really do that. You'd sponge off Jayne."

"What's so terrible about that? She's my daughter. My flesh and blood." Patricia began to get angry. "I don't think you're in much of a position to talk about sponging off people!"

"*Touché.*" Michael smiled wearily. "Okay. Let's call a truce. It's none of my business. But I still think you're moving too fast, Pat. Why don't you wait until Jayne gets here? It's only a couple of weeks now."

Mollified, Patricia calmed down. "All right. Truce. But I've put a deposit on the place and I am going to take it."

"I'm sure you will. Just do me one favor, will you? Don't tell Stanley until we've all had a chance to talk, you and Jayne and Mary and I."

"That won't change my mind."

"I'm sure it won't, but it will be a more acceptable thing if Jayne believes she had some hand in the decision."

Patricia shrugged. "Makes no difference to me. The outcome will be the same."

When she left the room, Michael sat back and took a deep breath. He was playing for time. He couldn't afford to antagonize Patricia. But it was unthinkable that she'd move to San Francisco. He knew she'd never leave him alone. All that big talk about finding a rich man to marry her! What craziness was that? Didn't the woman know there weren't that many eligible men, rich or otherwise? And that those who were available would marry a woman who was very rich or very young? Patricia was neither. She looked good for her age. No question about that. But she was no competition for a twenty-two-year-old, which was what any rich, free man wanted. Youth was everything. Even money didn't speak as loudly as it once did. Look at Rae Spanner. She was attractive and loaded, but the only way she could get a man was to rent one.

The thought of Rae left a bad taste in his mouth. He hated those afternoons with her. She was getting more and more possessive and even less discreet. He'd faced her, angrily, when Patricia told him about her phone call. At first she pretended innocence.

"I didn't tell her anything, Michael darling. I can't help it if your sister-in-law draws inferences from simple statements."

"Simple statements! You practically spelled out our arrangement! You want her to tell Mary about us, don't you? That's the whole plot. You want Mary to leave me, so you can have a chance."

Rae laughed. "I must say that's about as conceited a conclusion as anyone could reach. Really, Michael! Do you think I'm madly in love with you? I'm not. You're a good lover. Period. Why on earth would I want Mary to divorce you? I like things just the way they are. I wouldn't have you as a husband on a bet. Support you? No way. You're worth twenty-five thousand dollars as a loan for value received. And not a penny more." Her eyes narrowed. "Sometimes I'm not sure you're worth even that. You haven't been exactly an enthusiastic participant in this deal. Let's say you're competent but scarcely imaginative in bed. Quite the opposite from what you are in business. There you have imagination but no skill."

Michael was furious. "What the hell does that mean?"

"Oh, darling, I know Harry Carson! He told me how insane your business ideas are. Like a child playing at storekeeping. You're never going to raise any more money, Michael. You're not smart enough. You won't be realistic. Everybody knows that—Harry and Charlie Burke and half of San Francisco. You're a dreamer. An amiable, nice-looking, dinner-party decoration. Good in bed when you want to be. But a go-getter? Never. You should be glad you have a wife to pay the bills. And friends like me to pretend they're making a profitable investment."

For a moment he was speechless. How dare she? How dare this rich tramp talk to him like that? He wanted to kill her. But when he answered, he sounded cool and assured.

"If you think the deal's so hopeless, Rae, let's call it off right now. I still have your money intact. It's only a fraction of the stake anyway. I don't need it. You see, you and Harry Carson are wrong. I'm already well financed for the shop."

He was lying and Rae knew it, but she simply raised her eyebrows and said, "Really? That's marvelous! I'm delighted to be misinformed!" She feigned distress. "I do apologize to you, dear. I was simply angry when you accused me of saying irresponsible things to your sister-in-law. I didn't. Obviously, she made up a whole story out of fragments of a conversation. Let's forget it. We've cleared the air. I believe in you. I know my money's safely invested, not that I give a damn." She came close, touching him. "Come to bed, Michael. It's a lovely, rainy afternoon."

He calmed down. The only financing he had was still safe and he would get more somehow. He had to. Hopefully before Mary came home and found out he'd lied. But he didn't want to make love to Rae that day. He knew he probably couldn't, even if he tried.

"I don't have time," he said. "I'd like to, but I have to meet a guy in half an hour. He's a money man from Chicago. Very interested in the boutique."

She pretended remorse. "You're still angry with me. I told you I'm sorry."

"I'm not angry. I honestly have to meet this fellow. I'll see you tomorrow."

"Promise?"

"Of course. I'm a man of my word."

Remembering it now, Michael shuddered. It was so ugly, the whole business. But you did anything when you were desperate. He could understand, a little, why women sold themselves. Money was the most important thing in the world. With it, you had confidence and power. Without it, you were nothing.

"Aunt Mary's birthday is day after tomorrow," Jayne said. "I think we should organize something."

"Like what?" Terry looked baleful. "She'll murder us if we trot out a cake and have the musicians come to the dinner table and sing 'Happy Birthday to You.' You know how she cringes every time they do that to somebody else. And she's been through every kind of gala known to man since we came aboard— the mandatory ones dreamed up by the cruise director and the impromptu kind put together by our fellow travelers."

Jayne made a face. "They're terrible, all of them. I can't stand all the organized fun the ship seems to think we enjoy, like those awful costume parties with people making fools of themselves. Remember that vulgar Mrs. Juniper, who stuffed a pillow over her stomach and carried a sign saying 'I should have danced all night'?"

"She wasn't as ridiculous as Mr. Fletcher, who wrapped himself in toilet paper and came as a 'high roller.' "

"How about the Smiths, who hopped in as a pair of Australian kangaroos?"

"Or the Kitridge family, who covered themselves with pots and pans and came as 'A conducted tour of the kitchen'?"

They began to laugh hysterically. "Why do people make such asses of themselves?" Jayne said. "Certainly not to win those silly cuff links and bookmarks for prizes!"

Terry shook his head. "Beats me. At least Gambling Night was kind of fun and the prizes were good. Christopher won that nice crystal vase for accumulating the most chips at the end of the evening, remember?"

Jayne nodded. "He gave it to Aunt Mary."

Silence fell between them. "I don't think she's going to feel much like celebrating her birthday," Terry said.

"I know. She's turned down all the invitations we've gotten so far for the rest of the trip—the Jeffersons' Balinese lunch party in the card room; the Endicotts' 1920s tea dance. She doesn't want to do anything since Christopher's gone." Jayne slammed her fist on the arm of the deck chair. "Damn them! Why are they being so silly? I don't understand Aunt Mary. She's such a fool!"

Terry, who knew the whole story, shook his head. "I don't understand it, but I can't criticize people for the way they choose to live. I've had too much criticism in my own life. People do what they think is right for them, Jayne. Even if the world doesn't agree. Your aunt knows herself better than you know her. You have to respect her feelings, even if you don't share them."

"You're right. It's just that I love her a lot. I don't want her to be unhappy. God knows what she's going to find when she gets home."

Terry looked puzzled. "What she's going to find?" he repeated. "I thought everything was under control. Your uncle has his business deal wrapped up. And your mother is there, waiting for you and Mary. You sound as though she's in for some kind of shock."

"Maybe she is. I hope I'm wrong, but I have a bad feeling about things, Terry. If Uncle Mike has lied to her, she'll go out of her mind. I don't know that he has, but if so it won't be the first time. And as for Mother, I've been nervous about that ever since I heard about it."

"Nervous? Why?"

"She's not your basic good influence. My mother has the morals of the proverbial alley cat. She's been alone in that apartment for weeks with Uncle Mike. If she hasn't seduced him by now, he's a bloody saint."

"Jayne! What a God-awful thing to say about your mother!"

"You don't know her. Unfortunately, I do. She can't keep her hands off anything in pants, even when she's home. I can imagine what she's like three thousand miles from my father, alone night after night with a good-looking man."

"Come on," Terry said, "you don't mean that. He's her brother-in-law. She wouldn't do that to her own sister."

"I'd like to think that," Jayne said. "I'd sure like to think it for Aunt Mary's sake." She gave a little shake, as though to brush off bad thoughts. "Anyway, we still have the birthday to celebrate on the tenth and we haven't solved it."

"I can't think of any party that hasn't been given on this floating palace. We've whooped it up on every deck from Promenade to Adriatic, from the Soho

Club to Colonel Stanford's cabin. If there's a nook or cranny on this ship that hasn't been used for a celebration, I sure don't know it.''

Jayne stared at him in delight. ''That's it! You've just come up with the answer!''

Terry looked blank. ''I have?''

''Sure. We've partied all over the passenger area, but we've never had a bash below decks, In the crew quarters! That's what we'll do for Mary. Have an after-hours party with the staff!''

Terry hesitated. ''I'm not sure that's such a terrific idea. The passengers aren't even supposed to go there. It's against regulations. Anyway, I don't know if Mary would enjoy it. And supposing she did, how would we arrange such a thing?''

Jayne was excited by the idea. ''No problem. I'll get Lars, the bartender in the Trafalgar room, to set it up for us. He loves Aunt Mary. She and Christopher were his regulars. I know he'll do it. We'll buy the booze and get mounds of caviar, and after the bars close we'll get a little group to go down and celebrate the birthday with the 'real people.' Aunt Mary will love it! We'll get Gail and the colonel and you and me. I'll tell Lars to invite Ron, and Geoffrey from the Soho bar, and George and Walter, our table waiters, and our cabin stewardess and the manicurist and hair stylist from the beauty salon. It'll be a ball!'' Jayne was bubbling. ''The only thing we have to be careful of is not to let Peggy know anything about it. 'The Eyes and Ears of the World' would tell the captain, and all those adorable people would be in trouble.''

Terry continued to look doubtful. ''I don't know, Jayne. It's risky. It might be terrible down there.''

''It isn't. It's super.''

''How do you know?''

She looked faintly embarrassed. ''Well, I went down one night. The night before we got to Singapore. Before you and I . . . Anyway, I was up in the Trafalgar late and Lars asked me if I'd like to go to a crew party. It was tremendous. Lars has a great cabin. He's decorated it with sheepskin rugs from New Zealand and he has the best stereo I've ever heard. And a million tapes. He even showed me how the crew hides things they're smuggling home to England. The customs people give them a hell of a going over in every port, but they have all sorts of secret spots for cameras and tape recorders and antiques they pick up.''

Terry didn't say anything.

''What's the matter, luv? Do you still think it's a terrible idea to have Aunt Mary's party there?''

He looked unhappy. ''It isn't that. I mean, I guess it would be fun. It's . . . well, did you sleep with Lars?''

For a moment she looked at him in surprise. He was jealous! Terry, the young man who'd never loved any woman, was actually jealous! She felt elated. He loved her. He really was ''cured'' and she'd done it. Gently, she reached for his hand. ''No, I didn't sleep with him,'' she said.

Terry was almost petulant. ''You had a thing with George Telling when we first came aboard.''

Jayne wanted to laugh, but she managed to stay very serious. "Yes, I did. A very brief thing. I guess it's par for the course for impressionable young females. All that starched white and gold braid and the romantic atmosphere of a ship at sea. But it didn't last, as you well know. George is nice, but he's dull. He's also quite conceited. I suppose he's so used to every unattached woman making a pass at him that he responds automatically. I felt like I was just one of a long list to be checked off as impersonally as he reviews the boarding cards. I don't like being an anonymous body. I've slept around a little. You and I haven't made a secret of our past. But I've always cared for the person I was with, Terry. Just as you did. George Telling could never fall in that category and I knew it. That's why I cut it off so fast. It was cheap. And dumb. And I don't like being either."

Terry brightened. "How do you like that? I was actually jealous. I might as well confess it. I was."

"You're kidding! You? Jealous?"

"Yes. And you know something else? I liked it."

"What a smashing idea!" Gail DeVries said when Jayne told her the idea for Mary's birthday party. "I love it. So will Beau. What do we do?"

"We meet in the Trafalgar at midnight and sneak down the service elevator back of the bar. I thought it would be more fun if it was a surprise, so I'm not going to tell Aunt Mary. I'll get her up there on some pretext or other. And, of course, don't mention it to you-know-who or she'll tell 'our leader.' "

Gail understood. "Not a word to Mary or Peggy. And I'll warn Beau. I think we ought to go through the formalities at the dinner table, though. Just so Mary won't suspect there's anything else, and Mrs. Captain won't decide to dream up something on her own."

"Good idea. Aunt Mary will hate the cake and the serenade, but she'll live through it."

"Yes," Gail said. "She's been living through much worse. My heart aches for her."

"Mine, too. Do you think she's doing the right thing?"

"There's no right or wrong in this, Jayne dear. There's only what her conscience dictates. Nothing any of us can do about that."

Gail turned brisk. "Well, now, I have only two problems. One is what kind of gift to give that darling Mary."

"And the other?"

The other woman laughed. "The other is how to keep Beauregarde Stanford awake until twelve o'clock at night!"

Every evening when Mary walked in to dinner she felt a pang, remembering the first time she'd met Christopher. They'd removed his chair and place setting after Yokohama and the table was now an uneven seven with Gail, rather than Christopher, on her left. She was glad they hadn't put some stranger at the table. After so many weeks, they'd almost become "family." She'd grown very fond of Terry, despite her reservations about Jayne's plans to live with him. She loved

Gail and Beau, tolerated George Telling and felt sorry for Peggy Lawrence Robin.

Peggy had confided, with a great show of bravado, the change in her plans. "Tony and I have agreed he'll finish his time with the line," she told Mary. "It's quite the most sensible thing to do. And, of course, he'll have a great deal of leave to spend with me."

"But I thought . . . That is, it will be years . . . " Mary floundered.

"Time goes quickly," Peggy said, "And it would be wrong of me to ask him to cut short a brilliant career."

She's lying, Mary thought, but I give her credit for putting a good face on things. At least she has what she wants. A ring on her finger. "Captain and Mrs." on her calling cards. To her, that's security, as necessary for her peace of mind as food for her body. Mary had heard about the "suicide attempt." The whole ship had, though she was sure Peggy didn't know that. She felt pity for the woman. How humiliating to be laughed at behind one's back. Thank heaven Peggy had no idea she was a joke among the passengers and the crew. Perhaps I am, too, Mary thought. Maybe everyone is laughing at the middle-aged married lady who had such an overt affair with a man they think abandoned her in Japan.

It didn't matter. Nothing mattered now except getting home and getting on with the business of her old life. She was anxious to see San Francisco again, to plunge herself into work. It would be hard, pretending to Michael that nothing had changed, but she'd made her choice and now the best thing was to rediscover the old Mary Farr Morgan. If, indeed, she still existed.

On the night of her birthday, she was horrified to see her table in the dining room decorated with an elaborate centerpiece from which rose brightly colored balloons. Oh, no! They weren't going to make a fuss! She didn't think anyone knew. Jayne. Of course. Jayne had told them. I'll kill that child, she thought.

She found half a dozen gifts heaped in front of her place. Laughing, protesting, she opened them, while George Telling ordered champagne. Jayne had given her a delicate gold chain, and Terry's gift was an exquisite Japanese fan. From Gail she received a large piece of beautiful silk with instructions to have it made into something as lovely as the wearer. Also enclosed was the card of Gail's own dressmaker in San Francisco, with a note saying it was good for "one gown for Mrs. Michael Morgan." From Colonel Stanford came a carved rose-quartz figure of a Chinese goddess to remind her of their trip to Kwangchow. And Peggy had given her an ornate jewel box from the gift shop aboard. It was hideous, emblazoned with the ship's insignia, but Mary exclaimed over it and smiled fondly at Peggy as she read the message: "Happy birthday from Tony and Peggy Robin. May we share many other happy cruises."

"I'm quite overwhelmed," Mary said. "I don't know how to thank you. You must have depleted Singapore and Hong Kong! And," she added quickly, "our own marvelous shop!"

There was caviar and wine and a trio from the band played that awful song and half the dining room joined in singing it. Mary yearned for dinner to be over so she could escape to her cabin. She wondered whether there'd be a message from Christopher. He'd always teased her about being an Aries. "I love Aries women,'' he said. "They're so totally unpredictable." But there was no word from Christopher. None from Michael, either, which surprised her. He always made a great fuss over birthdays and anniversaries, buying her costly gifts which were put on their joint charge account and ultimately paid for by her. He probably had some expensive, useless present awaiting her return.

At last, mercifully, dinner ended. Peggy asked her to join Tony's table in the lounge, but Mary declined apologetically. "Another time," she said, lightly. "I've had all the birthday I can stand! But I love all of you for being so kind."

Jayne followed her down to the cabin after dinner, helping her carry her packages.

"That was nice," Mary said. "Very sweet of them, though I know you tipped them off, you rat!"

"Sure. I love birthdays."

"Wait until you're thirty-nine and tell me how you feel about them then!"

"Pooh! Thirty-nine's not old." Jayne handed her a small package. "I didn't think you'd want to open this in public," she said quietly. "Christopher gave it to me the morning he left."

Mary's hand trembled as she took the box. "Thank you."

"Listen, I'm going up to meet Terry. Will you join us in the Trafalgar a little later for a drink? Gail and the colonel are coming up. It's a private celebration. Just the good buddies."

"Oh, Jayne, I'd rather not. Make my apologies, please."

"Aunt Mary, you can't stay in your shell. Besides, I promised Gail and the colonel you'd come. It would be mean of you to disappoint them after they've been so nice!"

Mary sighed. "All right. I'll be up in a little while."

"Great! See you later. No more fancy fuss, I promise."

She waited until Jayne closed the door to open her package. Inside was a jade heart pendant surrounded by diamonds, a work of art very like the ring she wore. There was also a note in Christopher's hand.

"My darling, this little gift says everything. It is my heart, yours to keep forever. I know I shall see you wear it one day. Until then, I close my eyes and think of it lying close to you, as I wish now and always to be. I adore you. Christopher."

She held the heart against her own and believed she felt it throb with the love of the man she'd sent away.

Chapter 17

JAYNE NUDGED HER aunt. "They just called 'B-twenty-two' and you didn't cover it on your card."

Mary looked up, startled. "What?"

"If you're going to play bingo, the object is to cover the board and win the money." Jayne's voice was half-impatient, half-amused. "The pot's fifty dollars for this game."

"Right. Sorry." Obediently, Mary did as she was told. "It doesn't matter, actually. I've never won anything in my life." She smiled. "Except this trip, of course." She put down the card and looked at her niece. "What on earth are we doing here, anyhow? Tomorrow we're in Hawaii. Practically the end of the trip and this is the first afternoon we've spent in the lounge playing this silly game."

"Beats me. It was your idea." Tactfully, Jayne didn't remind her that most of her afternoons in the past weeks had been spent with Christopher, doing more interesting things than playing bingo. She did say, "At least it's better than your staying in the cabin day and night."

Something of the old, spirited Mary returned. "That's an exaggeration! Didn't you see your ancient aunt kicking up her heels at her birthday party night before last? That was fun, Jayne. There really is another world on the crew deck, isn't there? It's like 'Upstairs Downstairs' with a 1977 setting."

Jayne grinned. "Except it's the *Prince of Wales* and not Eaton Place. And the staff's a lot more hip than Mr. Hudson and Mrs. Bridges. You did have fun, didn't you? I'm glad."

"I had a wonderful time. Much to my surprise, frankly. I loved the whole thing—sitting on the edge of Lars' bunk, listening to that wild stereo music, guzzling champagne and eating caviar. And looking at those great kids. It was the best birthday I ever had, Jaynie, and it was all thanks to you."

"It was good to hear you laugh again."

"I know. I've really been a drag this past week. I'm sorry."

"Hey, I understand! You have a right!"

"No, I really haven't. I've been a bloody bore, crying over what's done. I'm going to get my act together. Scout's honor. Other women have. I will, too." She thought of Gail DeVries, who'd also given up the man she passionately loved. Of course, years had healed that hurt, but Gail had made the best of things, had found a life in which she was content, one that justified her choice. I'll never be that strong, Mary thought, but I'll get over this. I'll make it work. It's too important not to work. "Gail and the colonel had a marvelous time at the party, Jayne. I'm so glad you asked them. They got right into the swing of things. You'd never guess they were old."

"They're not. They think young. I hope I can be like that at their age."

"Yes," Mary said. "Me, too." She looked at the little old ladies around them, intent on their hour of bingo, the most exciting part of their day. "I hope I can be productive till the day I die. Even when I'm too old to work, I want to be active and interested, enjoying everything, the way Gail does." She put down her card. "Come on, let's get out of here. Let's take a few laps around the deck and get the old blood pumping. Okay?"

Jayne sighed with relief. "I thought you'd never ask."

They were on their second lap when the deck steward stopped them. "Mrs. Morgan, they've been looking everywhere for you. Could you go down to the hospital, please, as quickly as possible?"

"The hospital? What for?"

"It's Mrs. DeVries, madame. She's been taken ill and she's asking for you."

"Ill? How ill?"

"I don't know, but Colonel Stanford is there. He sent the message to find you."

Jayne looked concerned. "Want me to go with you, Aunt Mary?"

"No. I'll let you know what's happening. See you in the cabin later."

Without waiting for the elevator she ran down the four flights from Promenade to Adriatic and rushed through the corridors to the ship's infirmary. Beau was in the waiting room, pacing back and forth, his face gray with anxiety.

"Mary! Thank God you're here! She's been asking for you."

"What is it? What's happened?"

"I'm not sure. An hour ago, we were in the middle of our afternoon gin game and she suddenly got this terrible pain in her chest. She didn't want to see the doctor. You know her. But I insisted. She's inside, and they sent word a few minutes ago that she wanted to see you."

Mary managed to sound calm, though she had a hideous premonition. She patted Beau on the arm reassuringly. "I'm sure it's nothing. Probably indigestion. What did she have for lunch?"

The old man passed a shaky hand across his eyes. "I don't recall. Soup, I think. And, oh yes, they had franks and beans. I remember telling her that junk food would kill her."

Mary acted unconcerned. "See? What did I tell you? Probably gas pains. Don't worry. I'll check it out and be right back."

She went down the hall, looking for the doctor, and met the nurse coming out of one of the rooms.

"I'm looking for Mrs. DeVries. She called for me. How is she?"

"Oh, I'm glad you're here, Mrs. Morgan. She's been anxious to see you."

Something in the girl's voice alarmed Mary.

"What's wrong with her? It isn't serious, is it?"

The professional mask appeared. "I think you'd better speak with the doctor. He's inside. I'll get him."

One look at the man's face confirmed Mary's worst fears even before he spoke to her.

"Mrs. DeVries is very ill, Mrs. Morgan. She's had a heart attack."

"Will . . . will she be all right?"

"I don't know. We're doing everything we can, but of course our facilities are limited here. Thank God we'll be in Hawaii tomorrow morning. If she can just hang on until then . . ."

"Hang on! You mean she may die?"

"There's a strong possibility she won't make it through tonight. I can't say for certain, one way or another, but if we can get her to the hospital in Honolulu she'll have a fighting chance. It depends on what happens between now and eight o'clock tomorrow morning."

Mary leaned against the corridor wall for support. "A helicopter," she said. "Can't we get a helicopter to lift her off this afternoon and fly her to Honolulu?"

"Too risky. I wouldn't dare move her. She'd never survive the trip."

Tears began to run down Mary's face. "Oh, my God! She can't . . . she mustn't . . ."

The doctor took her by the shoulders. "Mrs. Morgan, you must get yourself together! She's conscious and very brave and she wants to talk to you. Don't stay long. I shouldn't let her see anyone, but she's adamant. And under these conditions . . ." He shook his head. "Anyway, don't stay more than three minutes. And try not to let her get excited. I'll be right outside the door if you want me."

Gail looked very small and frail in the hospital bed, an oxygen mask over her face. She feebly indicated to Mary that she wanted it lifted off, and when Mary hesitated she gestured almost imperiously. Gently, Mary raised the mask.

"Gail, you shouldn't talk."

The cheerful voice was almost a whisper and the words came haltingly but precisely, as though she'd organized them.

"Mary, dear. Not going to make it. Saw my husband. Same thing." She fought for breath. "Tell Beau call my children. Can't face him. Tell him not be sad. You neither. Be happy, Mary. Wanted to tell you . . . you did right thing. Don't you regret it." Gail's breath became more labored. "Better put that . . . damned thing . . . back. . . ."

Hurriedly, Mary replaced the mask and Gail drew a deep breath. A little smile touched her face and she looked almost happy.

"I love you," Mary said. "We all love you. You'll be all right, darling. We'll get you into the hospital in Honolulu and you'll be fine. You and Beau will take another cruise next year."

The eyes thanked her as they denied it, then they closed gently. Mary rushed for the door, calling the doctor. In a moment he looked up from Gail's still form and shook his head.

"I'm sorry, Mrs. Morgan." He took her arm. "Really sorry. You'd better go now."

"Is she . . ."

"It's over. I was afraid she'd go fast. That's why I let her talk to you. She couldn't make it. I think she knew it, too."

Mary began to tremble. "Yes, she knew it." Mechanically, she moved toward the door. "I'd better tell Colonel Stanford."

"Wouldn't you rather I did that? He's an old man. The shock . . ."

"No. He's strong but he'll need me."

She didn't have to say the terrible words. When she walked back into the waiting room, Beau let out one terrible cry of pain and took her in his arms. Together they wept, the man who'd lost his dearest companion, and the woman who'd benefited by her wisdom and gained strength through her example. They stood, locked in sorrow, almost unable to believe the swift stroke of fate that overwhelmed them. At last, Beau stepped back and wiped his eyes with a great white handkerchief.

"Did she say anything, Mary?"

"She said you shouldn't be sad, Beau. Her last thoughts were of you. I think she didn't want to put you through those final moments. That's why she didn't call for you. She loved you too much."

"I loved her. Very much. She was my best friend."

"I know. In many ways, mine too. She's the mother I wish I'd had."

Beau nodded. "She cared about you a great deal, Mary. We talked about you a lot. She hated to see you so sad, but she felt you'd done the right thing. I remember her saying that if you were her daughter she'd be proud of you for your courage and your loyalty.'' He began to weep again. ''God knows she knew about those qualities. She had them in abundance. I can't believe she's gone. I just can't believe it.''

Mary put her arm around his shoulders. ''She'll never be gone, dear. She'll be with you on all the cruises in the future.''

He shook his head. ''No more. No more cruises for me. I'm an old man, Mary. I'll stay home where I belong.''

''She'd be furious if she heard you say that. She wants you to be happy. It was the last thing she said. She wants us both to be happy. We have to try, Beau, for her sake. She never let anything stop her. I know she expects the same of us.'' She led the old man out of the waiting room. ''Let me walk you back to your cabin. Try to get some rest.''

''No rest. I have to call one of her daughters. I have the numbers. Will you stay with me while I call?''

''Of course. Do you want me to do it for you?''

''No. I've met them. They're lovely girls. I have to break the news myself. See what they want done.'' He sighed. ''They're strong women, Gail's children. Like their mother. Like you, Mary. You're all stronger than we are. Your sex is more compassionate than mine, but more realistic, too. You know about birth and death. Women handle those things better than men. I like to pretend that women need protecting, but I know in the end they're the protectors. We lean on them, just as I'm leaning on you.''

Mary brushed the tears from her eyes as she and Beau walked slowly toward his cabin.

''We lean on each other,'' she said gently. ''We support and are supported. That's what friends are all about.''

And lovers, too, she thought suddenly. Michael needs me too much. And perhaps Christopher needs me too little. And I? Maybe I've never met the man who understands the happy medium. Maybe I never will.

Jayne burst into tears. ''It isn't true! I can't believe it! I saw her only this morning and she was fine!''

Mary hugged her. Death was incomprehensible to the young. Unacceptable. They acknowledged its existence, but not for themselves or anyone they cared for. Jayne has never had contact with it before, Mary thought. For that matter, neither have I. No, that isn't true. I remember my brother's death. I was never allowed to forget it. But I didn't grieve. I was old enough to understand but I didn't mourn. With the callousness of childhood, I suppose I was almost glad he was gone—the perfect one, the center of attention, the rival for my parents' love. One mourns selfishly, for oneself. For what is lost. For the things one took from the departed. John Jr. gave me nothing in eight years. Gail gave me hope and understanding in the brief time I knew her. For the first time, I know the overwhelming pain that comes with another human's death, the deprivation one feels knowing you'll never talk again to someone you need. I made her a surrogate mother and she believed in me more than my own ever has.

''Jayne, darling, listen carefully,'' she said at last. ''Colonel Stanford and I have spoken to Gail's daughters in San Francisco. There's no point in their flying to Hawaii to meet the ship tomorrow. Beau and I are going to fly back with . . . with Gail. We leave tomorrow afternoon at two twenty-five. I couldn't let him make the trip alone.''

"I'll get ready.''

"No, there's no point in your going. It would be easier if you stayed aboard for the last week and brought my things off the ship with yours. I'll meet you a week from tomorrow. I can't fly with all the luggage I brought for the cruise. You won't mind packing for me, will you? Someone on the ship is going to pack for the colonel so neither of us will have to worry about luggage on the plane. Gail's daughters will meet us at the airport. They're making the arrangements there. They sound like wonderful women.''

"They must be devastated.''

"Of course. Any child would be.''

Jayne looked out the porthole without answering. I wouldn't be, she thought. Oh, I'd feel sorry, I suppose. I'm sorry when anyone dies. But my mother wouldn't be missed the way Gail will be missed by her daughters. I'm certain of that. It must have been wonderful growing up with a woman so warm and caring. I never had that. Neither did Aunt Mary. Neither, for that matter, did Mother. And Terry had too much mother. Maybe that's why we've all turned out as we have. Early influences count. They do mold us, one way or another. For good or evil. In emulation or rebellion.

"Have you told Uncle Mike you're flying home?''

"Yes. I just sent a radiogram saying I was arriving on the evening of the thirteenth. There was no need to go into explanations.''

Jayne smiled without humor. "Mother will be furious, being kicked out of the apartment a week early.''

"Nonsense. For that matter, she can stay right where she's been these past weeks. It won't make any difference. That part of it might even work out well. It will give us a chance to visit before she goes back to New York. We haven't really spent much time together in the past fifteen years.''

"Lucky you.''

"Oh, come on, Jaynie. She's not so terrible. We all have our faults. Maybe we'll find we've both mellowed. Maybe we have more in common than we know.''

"Yes,'' Jayne said. "Maybe you have.''

Michael read the radiogram with surprise. "Mary's flying home tomorrow night,'' he said. "She'll be in at nine-fifteen.''

Patricia was startled. "Why on earth is she doing that? Will Jayne be with her?''

"She doesn't say why she's coming early.'' He read the message aloud. "Feeling fine. Arriving San Francisco April thirteen, United flight number ninety-six nine-fifteen P.M. Jayne staying aboard. Explain when I see you. Love. Mary.''

"I don't get it. She doesn't sound as though she's upset.''

Michael raised his eyebrows. "Why would she be upset?''

"How do I know? Maybe she's heard you don't have the deal after all. Or maybe she's heard about you and Rae. Or possibly somebody tipped her off about us.''

''I doubt any of those things. Nobody but you knows anything about the deal. And Rae certainly wouldn't tell her about that mess. As for us . . .'' He stopped. ''Patricia, you wouldn't be a big enough damned fool to . . .''

''Tell Mary I've been sleeping with you? Hardly. What would be the point of that?''

''None. But I don't get the point of a lot of things you do. Like planning to stay in San Francisco without discussing it with Stanley or Jayne.''

''That's a little different from telling your sister you've had an affair with her husband. For God's sake, Michael, what do you think I am? Give me credit for a little sensitivity. I might make love to my brother-in-law but I'm not crass enough to talk about it.''

''Bully for you.''

''And there's no need to be sarcastic! I didn't rape you. You've seemed to enjoy playing house these past weeks. *Any* house.''

''All right. I've been a bastard. I admit it. But strangely enough, I love my wife.''

''Sure. Like I love the Bank of Northern California.''

''Damn you!'' Michael's face flushed with anger. ''You're a bitch! All I want is to see you out of this house!''

Patricia shrugged. ''I'm going. As soon as Jayne gets back.''

''No. Tonight. I'll call the St. Francis and tell them to move up your reservation. You can stay there until Jayne gets back and you straighten things out with her.''

''Michael, don't be ridiculous. I'll move my clothes and bunk in the office when Mary gets here. My God, what do you want to do, make her really suspicious? She'd think it was odd that I suddenly checked into a hotel alone after staying here for weeks.'' Patricia laughed. ''Or do you think my presence in the next room will inhibit your performance with your wife?''

''I just want you out! I wish to God you'd never come! Boy, do I wish you'd never come! And believe me I'm not going to encourage you and Jayne to stay in this town!''

Patricia wagged a finger at him playfully. ''Naughty, naughty! Remember our little conversation.''

''You're bluffing. You'd never tell Mary about Rae and me.''

''Want to bet?''

He stormed out of the room. Why was Mary coming home early? Even if she was bored, why was she spending the money on air fare when there was only a week of the cruise left? She must know something. Maybe Charlie Burke had told her how Michael had tried to hit him up for money and she put two and two together and figured Carson was out of the picture. Or maybe Rae wrote her about the loan. Even Patricia might be lying. Who knows what that warped character might have done? But it was true that Mary's wire had not sounded upset. She'd said she was fine, so he wouldn't worry about her health. And she'd signed it ''love.'' He was sure she didn't know about his extramarital affairs. And if it were merely the business deal, she could wait one more week. What the hell could bring her flying home? Well, he'd soon know. Worse, he'd soon have to tell her the truth about another aborted dream.

PART II

Chapter 18

THE AIRPLANE FLEW swiftly and steadily toward San Francisco. Outside was black nothingness, but within half an hour they'd be on the ground, she and Beau, bringing Gail home to her children. Mary turned to look at the old man who sat stiffly, dry-eyed, in the seat beside her.

"You all right?"

He nodded. "I was just thinking how unpredictable everything is. I've been so sure, the last few years, that it would be Gail coping with my death on one of these trips. It worried me, I must admit. Her having to bring me back. All that talk about being buried at sea was just so much nonsense, of course. They don't do that. They take you off at the first port and send you home. And if it happens in some heathen country, it's a mess. So many complications and clearances. I was afraid Gail would have to go through that. She'd have managed. She could handle anything. But I didn't want her to." The colonel sighed. "I'll miss her, Mary. Doesn't seem like much to go on living for now."

She took the gnarled hand in her own. "I told you before—Gail wouldn't want you to feel that way. You have your children and grandchildren, Beau. You still have your health and your independence. Life doesn't stop, dear. It just stutters now and then."

He summoned up a little smile. "I know, but as you get older it takes longer and longer to get over things, which is bad because you have less and less time to spare. I'll be all right, little girl. I've had a good, long life. Nothing to complain about. A few rough spots here and there, but who doesn't have those?" He looked at her affectionately. "Don't fret about me. You have problems of your own. Gail told me. I hope you'll let me know what's happening to you, Mary. Maybe you'd even come to see me in Atlanta one day. We'd make you mighty welcome."

She squeezed his hand. "It's a promise. I'll stay in touch if you'll do the same."

"Never was much of a letter writer, but you'll hear from me. And I'm no substitute for Gail, but if you ever need me . . .''

Mary felt a lump in her throat. No more tears, she commanded herself. She'd shed so many in the past weeks. Tears for Christopher, tears for Gail and Beau, tears for herself. It was a new and unwelcome experience. She was not a woman who cried easily, and rarely over sad things. She was much more touched by happy events: sweet solemn weddings; the accomplishment of a handicapped child in the Kennedy Special Olympics; the reunion of returning soldiers with their loved ones after Viet Nam. A hundred joyous things moved her. She suffered but seldom wept over tragic ones. She felt deeply inside, but outwardly she was slow to weep. Perhaps the tight rein she kept on deep emotions during low moments was why she let herself go in the richly sentimental ones. Perhaps the unshed tears were always there, just below the surface, but she was too proud or disciplined or stubborn to let them flow. Until lately. Lately, it seemed, her pillow was always wet. Mary swallowed hard. She wouldn't break down when she saw Gail's daughters. Later, maybe, when she was home in her own bed.

A chill came over her. Michael would be in that bed, too. Michael would be at the airport, his happy, unsuspecting face turned eagerly toward her. Michael would be waiting for her to share his joy. Their joy.

She stared out the window. I'm right to go home, she told herself again, trying to believe it. I had no choice. Gail knew that. Even Christopher did. Where is Christopher now? Is he sitting alone, thinking of me? Is he trying to explain my convoluted reasoning to his sons? Is he back in his own social sphere, surrounded by attractive women who are delighted to have him home?

The musing brought physical pain. I mustn't be a dog in the manger. I can't expect him to go through life alone, moping over me, rejecting another love, hoping for what may not, probably will not, happen.

And yet she was ridiculously, childishly jealous. She wanted him to yearn only for her as much as she yearned for him. She wanted him never to forget, because she'd always remember.

In the waiting room, two groups who did not know their connection with each other watched nervously as the clock on the wall ticked off the last minutes before the arrival of Flight 96 from Honolulu. In one corner, Gail's daughters and their husbands sat quietly, handling their shock and sorrow with well-bred restraint. In another, Michael, Patricia and Charlie Burke talked among themselves, curious about Mary's premature return, pretending to be delighted.

Only Charlie truly was. He didn't understand the arrival by air, but since Mary's message said she was fine he wasn't worried. On the contrary, it was a bonus to have her home a week early. He'd missed her more than he'd imagined. For more than fifteen years he'd grown used to seeing her nearly every day, and the two months since her departure had seemed an eternity. They had so much to talk about. Her trip. What had happened at the radio station since she'd been away. Even his troubles with Tracey. His wife wasn't getting better in the sanatorium. Usually she came out of these "visits" looking and feeling like a new woman. For weeks she'd be sober and reasonable before she slipped gradually into her old ways. But this time was different. The years of drinking were taking a terrible physical toll. She was sober but ill. The doctors would not even give an anticipated date for her release.

Ashamed of the knowledge, Charlie admitted to himself that he did not miss her. It was peaceful to go home to a quiet house knowing there'd be no scenes, no hysterics. It was a relief to attend social functions without having to explain Tracey's absence or, worse still, her behavior when she accompanied him. He was tired of it. Terribly tired after twenty-five years of this difficult marriage. Hating himself for it, he dreaded her return. Dreaded it as much as he welcomed Mary's. Like an ardent young man, he wished he were alone to greet her, without Michael and that extraordinary sister. Two such different women, he thought. Patricia was loud, brassy, arrogant. She clung possessively to Michael as though he were *her* husband. Charlie glanced at her speculatively. She exuded an air of intimacy in her glances, her touch. Michael looked decidedly uncomfortable. Was something going on there? Good God, that was unthinkable! And yet it was strange that Michael called and asked Charlie to come to the airport with them. Almost as though he needed protection, an "outsider" to make the reunion go smoothly. Rot! Charlie told himself. He was imagining things. Michael was simply being considerate. He knew Mary would be happy to see her "boss," who was like one of the family.

"Another couple of minutes," Michael said. "The flight is on the ground. She should be coming through the gate soon. I hope she's all right."

"Of course, she is!" Patricia sounded petulant. "Her wire said she was fine. Really, Michael, you'd think Mary was made of spun sugar! I don't know what you're so fidgety about. If she was sick, she'd have said so."

"That's right," Charlie said. "I'll bet she just got cabin fever after two months on that ship and decided to cut out the last week at sea. After all, she saw everything she wanted to. The trip from Hawaii would only be a bore."

"Apparently Jayne isn't bored," Michael said.

Charlie smiled. "It's not a disease of the young. Jayne's probably found herself a beau she can't bear to leave. When I was her age, I was constantly interested in everything and everybody." The smile broadened. "I was also constantly in love."

Patricia looked at him coyly. "And now?"

"Now I'm an old married man. Creeping up on old age, though I can't say I feel it." He laughed. "I don't feel old, but I sure as hell feel married. Just like you two."

He added the last words deliberately, watching for a reaction. Michael looked away, pretending nonchalance, but Patricia stared at him boldly. You've made a pretty good guess, haven't you? her eyes said. So what? What are you going to do about it?

Nothing, his look said in return. I wouldn't hurt Mary, even if you would.

"She's coming!" Michael started forward and then stopped. "She's holding on to some old guy's arm. Who the hell is he, do you suppose?"

Patricia laughed. "Some old fogy she picked up on the plane, no doubt. You know Mary. Very big on waifs and strays."

A well-dressed woman standing nearby heard the remark. She turned and stared with distaste at Patricia before she and her sister moved forward to greet Colonel Stanford.

"How the hell was I to know they were the woman's daughters?" Patricia kicked off her shoes and sank down on the couch in Mary's living room. "Make us a drink, Michael. That airport scene was too much! My God, Mary, who but you would fly home with a perfect stranger in a pine box? I think you're crazy to cut a week off your trip for that. You hardly knew the woman or the old boy she traveled with.''

Mary leaned back in her chair and closed her eyes wearily. She felt drained. Gail's daughters had been wonderful. They and Beau couldn't stop expressing their appreciation, courteous even in their grief, but it had been an ordeal. There'd hardly been time to explain in the midst of introductions and words of thanks. She'd simply turned Beau over to these loving hands, kissed him and said she'd see him later. There was nothing more she could do. Gail's children would look after him until he was ready to return to Georgia. Just as they'd look after their mother through the last hours they had her.

"Beau Stanford is a lovely man," Mary said. "Anyone would have done as much. I didn't do it for Gail. I did it for the colonel." She corrected herself. "No, that's not entirely true. I wanted to do it for her, too. She was a very special lady. Like a mother to me on that trip."

"A mother?" Patricia echoed. "What did you need a mother for? Isn't the one you have enough to drive you crazy?"

Mary didn't answer.

"I think it was a wonderful thing to do," Charlie said. "Sad for the old boy. It must have been a terrible shock."

Patricia sighed impatiently. "For God's sake, Michael, what are you doing? Distilling that booze? I've never seen anybody make such a production out of mixing four drinks!"

She sounds so proprietary, Mary thought. As though this is her house. As though Michael is Stanley, whom she can order around. She wished suddenly that Patricia weren't here. Not that she wanted to be alone with Michael. Quite the contrary. She dreaded the moment when they retired. Michael wouldn't expect anything of her tonight. He could see she was exhausted. She simply didn't want to talk privately with him, didn't know how she could summon up the enthusiasm he'd expect as he told her about the boutique. I wish I were back on the ship, she thought. Back in Charlie's "watery womb." How will I ever be able to talk easily and naturally about the trip when Michael and I are by ourselves? I'm such a bad liar. He'll guess something happened to change my life.

"I think I'll run along. You look done in," Charlie said. "I hope you don't plan to come in to the station for the rest of the week. No need to. We didn't expect you back so soon anyway."

"I'll be in. I've missed it, Charlie. I'm anxious to see everyone. And I have some more tapes." She stopped. "No, I haven't. That is, I left them aboard for Jayne to bring with my luggage. Well, I'll come in anyway to see the gang."

"Want to have lunch tomorrow?"

"Love to. You can fill me in on the gossip." She rose and kissed him on the cheek. "Thanks for coming to the airport, Charlie. It was good to see all my family there."

When the door closed behind him, Patricia held out her glass to Michael for a refill. When he went into the kitchen for more ice, she looked at Mary.

"Poor Charlie. Nothing as sad as unrequited love, is there?"

"What are you talking about?"

"Oh, come on, Mary. That man's crazy about you."

"And I'm crazy about him."

"Does Michael know?"

Mary looked at her with annoyance. "There's nothing to know. Charlie is my oldest and dearest friend. He loves me. I love him. It is possible to love without being in love, Patricia. What we feel for each other is not, never has been and never will be physical. Michael knows that as well as Charlie and I do."

Patricia spat out a four-letter word. "Your intentions may be pure," she said, "but you give Charlie Burke the slightest come-on and he'll leap at it. Take it from me. I know the look. He may be a 'gentleman' but he'd sure as hell like not to be."

"Don't be absurd." Mary hoped she sounded convincing. Of course she knew Charlie was in love with her. Had been for years. But she denied it to her sister just as she denied it to herself. At one time, she'd imagined herself half in love with him too, but she'd never come between a husband and wife even if she could. She'd long since dismissed all thoughts of such a thing and now it was utterly out of the question. Since Christopher. Christopher made the difference. In this and everything.

Michael came back with Patricia's drink. He turned to Mary. "You want another, darling?"

She shook her head. "No, thanks. I had a couple on the plane. More than my quota for one evening."

"I know," Michael teased. "You're such a lush."

"Probably why Charlie Burke is so fond of her," Patricia said lazily. "She's such a contrast to his wife."

Mary went lightly past the barb. "How is Tracey, Michael?"

"Not good, I hear. She's been in the hospital for weeks and there's no telling when she'll be out. They say her liver is affected. Not surprising. It's a wonder she hasn't caved in before this. Damned shame. I hope nothing happens to her. Charlie would take it hard."

Patricia's voice dripped sarcasm. "I *bet* he would."

Michael turned on her. "My God, Patricia, you have a rotten mind! There never was a more devoted, faithful man than Charlie Burke! Jesus! You think nobody's happily married, just because you hate your own life! Well, let me tell you, there are some men who love their wives and suffer when they suffer, and Charlie Burke is one of them!"

Mary stared at him. She'd seldom heard Michael so violent. He sounded as though he hated Patricia, as though he'd like to harm her physically as well as attack her verbally. I suppose she has been a trial all these weeks, Mary thought. It really was colossal nerve of her to park herself on Michael for such a long time. He's probably fed up. Small wonder. She thought of Jayne's dislike of her mother. Probably she has reason, Mary decided. I've seen so little of Patricia these past fifteen years that I'd almost forgotten how abrasive she is. Un-insultable, as well, as she quickly proved. Michael's angry words didn't seem to bother her at all. She smiled as one would smile at a child having a temper tantrum.

"My, my! Aren't we the loyal friend! You men always stick together. I didn't know you were so fond of Charlie."

"Well, I am! So is Mary. We're very close to him."

"That's nice." Patricia sounded indifferent. "By the way, Mary, you haven't said much about Jayne. Has she had a good time?"

"Yes, I think so. I mean, I'm sure she has." Mary was relieved to be off the subject of Charlie Burke but hesitant about discussing Jayne. She was certain Patricia knew nothing of Russell King's defection and probably had never heard of Terry Spalding. It was up to Jayne to tell her mother about those things. Her aunt had no intention of discussing the girl's plans.

"Were there any interesting young men aboard?"

"One or two."

"I hope they weren't sailors!" Patricia laughed. "Every movie about cruises always has some dashing young officer in pursuit of the resident beauty. Jayne's so impressionable. She didn't get mixed up with the crew, did she?"

"What do you mean, 'mixed up'?"

"Now just what do you think I mean? Was she sleeping with the staff?"

"Patricia!"

"Don't sound so shocked. You don't have children. These days, girls much younger than Jayne know what it's all about. I know *she* does. She's been carrying on with Russell King for years."

Mary didn't answer that. She merely said, "I'm sure Jayne will tell you all about the trip when she gets home."

"I have something to tell, too, haven't I, Michael?"

"Don't involve me in this, Patricia."

She looked injured. "I'm not involving anybody except myself."

"And your daughter."

"What are you two talking about?"

Patricia gave her an innocent smile. "I've decided it would be marvelous if Jayne and I stayed in San Francisco. New York has changed so much I really can't stand it anymore."

Mary was stunned. "Move here? Permanently? You and Jayne? I don't understand. What about Stanley?"

"He'd hardly miss me."

"But how would you live?"

"Well, Jayne could certainly get some kind of job. I'm sure you'd help her. And rents here are less than New York. I found this darling place I know we can afford. I've even put a deposit on it."

Knowing Jayne's plans with Terry, Mary was aghast. For a moment she thought of telling Patricia that her daughter already planned to stay in San Francisco, with Terry, but in the next breath she decided against that. For all she knew, by the time the ship docked they might have changed their minds. But one thing was certain: Jayne would never consent to live with her mother, much less support her. It was foolish of Patricia to make such arrangements without discussing them with the other people involved. Foolish and selfish as always. She didn't give a damn what suited anyone else.

"Patricia," she said patiently, "I don't think you should move so fast on this. You have no idea whether Jayne would go along with that idea. And you're hardly being fair to Stanley, making such a big decision without even telling him what's in your mind. He *is* your husband. You can't just walk out on him with no warning.''

I know whereof I speak, Mary thought bitterly.

Patricia was unconvinced. "I told you. Stanley won't give a hoot. Or, if it comes to that, he's perfectly free to move to San Francisco. I don't care one way or another." That was a lie. She never wanted to see that boring man again, but leaving a loophole sounded more convincing. "As for Jayne, why wouldn't she be pleased? I had a letter from a friend in New York. She told me Russell King has dumped Jayne for some rich lawyer's kid, so I'm sure she'd be glad not to go back. Anyway, I've been looking around. There seem to be a lot more eligible young men here than there are back East." Patricia was pleased with herself. "I've thought it through very carefully. Change is good. It keeps you young. I was getting in a terrible rut. I didn't realize how deep a one until I came here."

There was no use arguing with her. She'd made up her mind. Anyway, the discussion was academic. When Jayne arrived and told her mother about Terry, that would put an end to Patricia's plans. Without Jayne to support her, Patricia couldn't leave Stanley. And unless Jayne had a change of heart, she intended to share a place with Terry. Mary looked at her watch, stood up and yawned.

"I'm exhausted. It's after midnight. I simply have to get to bed. You two stay up and talk if you like, but I'm turning in."

Patricia gave Michael an amused look. So much for your amorous ideas, she seemed to be saying. Michael rose when Mary did.

"It's time we all packed it in," he said. "You've had a long day, darling. An emotional one, too. You need a good night's rest."

Mary smiled gratefully. She kissed her sister on the cheek as she started toward the door. "Are you all right on the office couch? Anything you need?" Then she smiled. "Silly of me. You must be quite used to that awful convertible by now. I hope you haven't been too uncomfortable, Patricia."

"I've been very comfortable. Couldn't have asked for better accommodations."

Alone in their bedroom, Michael began to take off his clothes. Mary found a robe and gown and headed for the bath. Her husband looked up, surprised.

"Since when have you started undressing in the bathroom?"

She stopped short. She didn't want to undress in front of him, fearful it might precipitate the overture she dreaded.

"Force of habit," she laughed. "I've been rooming with Jayne too long. I got used to changing in the bathroom on the ship."

Michael looked amused. "Seems a little prudish somehow."

"I know. Silly. But I just don't take to the picture of two females prancing around naked in one room."

"How about a male and a female?"

"Husbands and wives are different." She quickly stepped out of her dress and underthings and put on the gown and robe, aware that Michael was watching her with a puzzled expression.

"You act as though you're almost afraid of me."

"Don't be ridiculous! I'm just so damned tired, Michael. I hardly know what I'm doing."

"I'm not going to try to make love to you tonight." He sounded almost hurt. "I'd like to, but I know you're not in the mood."

She didn't answer.

"Is something wrong, Mary? You seem different. Keyed up."

"Nothing's wrong, dear. I'm just done in. I'll be fine tomorrow. I want to hear about everything, especially the plans for the boutique, but I don't want to fall asleep in the middle of it. You don't mind, do you?"

"No, of course not. I can wait."

She brushed her teeth and fell into bed without even bothering to take off her makeup. Minutes later, Michael slipped in beside her. He kissed her lightly and said, "Good night, love. Sleep as long as you can. I'm so glad to have you home."

"Mmmm. Good night, Michael dear."

She turned her back to him and lay still. She was bone-weary but wide awake, almost too tired and far too troubled to fall asleep. So much to think about. So strange, somehow, to be here in this big, familiar bed with her husband beside her. He made her feel guilty with his devotion and understanding, his blissful ignorance of what was going on inside her head. And yet he sensed something. She wasn't surprised. She knew she was a terrible actress. How long could she sustain this role of the pulled-together, organized, happily married Mary? And what of Patricia? Of Jayne and Terry? Even Charlie was in her thoughts. So were Beau, and Gail's children. God! It was like a kaleidoscope of ever-moving, frightening images, with the central figure of Christopher weaving in and out among the pictures in her mind.

Much, much later, when Michael's regular breathing told her he was asleep, she crept quietly out of bed and went to the window. There it was. San Francisco. The place where she'd once been happy and where the restiveness had slowly begun to take shape. She'd tried to run, tried to think, and it had solved nothing. She was unhappier than ever.

For God's sake get yourself together, she thought angrily. You're here. You made The Decision. Get your own life in order, Mary Farr Morgan, and stop trying to play God. Other people's problems aren't yours. Not Jayne's or Patricia's or Charlie's. They'll have to work them out for themselves. You have enough to do to muddle through your own.

Chapter 19

CHRISTOPHER SAT ALONE at the desk in his study, a mass of color photographs taken aboard the ship spread out before him. He'd ordered a copy of every one in which he and Mary appeared, even the group shots at their table in the dining room and the ones in the lounge where they were sitting with boring strangers whose names he didn't remember. As long as he and Mary were in the picture together he'd bought two, one for her and one for himself, as though he knew they'd end up keeping separate albums. What will Mary do with hers? he wondered. How will she answer when her husband asks about the man who is constantly at her side? Probably she won't show them, but maybe she'll look at them secretly and remember.

Idly, he shuffled through the glossy prints. Pictures of them at the captain's reception for all the passengers and others taken at small parties in his quarters. Glimpses of them laughing at the participants in the masquerade parade and the ceremonial shenanigans that went on when they crossed the equator and "King Neptune" ordered some unlucky first-timers daubed with paint and thrown into the swimming pool. Mary had been afraid they'd grab her, but Christopher had reassured her. The victims were pre-chosen, usually members of the crew who had to suffer such embarrassment while the paying guests looked on.

He smiled at the sight of Mary at the railing, wide-eyed as they sailed into the harbor at Sydney. How she'd loved it! She'd been so at home with his children and they'd adored her. It had been wonderful seeing her in his place and more wonderful still when he'd told her he'd arranged his affairs to stay aboard with her until Yokohama. It was one of their most joyous nights, rich with lovemaking and the knowledge that they still had time together. Time. Christopher shook his head. It hung heavily on one's hands when the days and nights were lonely. Only a little more than a week since he'd seen her. And it seemed a year.

He went back to the pictures. He and Mary bargaining with the Balinese who came out in their funny-shaped boats to bob alongside the ship, offering to sell canes and carvings to the incoming visitors who shouted back at them from the decks high above the water. Mary in a swimsuit grinning at him from an adjoining deck chair; smiling up at him as they walked down the gangplank in Singapore; eager and solemn as they left the ship in Hong Kong en route to China. Mary everywhere, looking beautiful and young and in love. Studying the dozens of prints, it seemed to him that the ship's photographer had been omnipresent. He knew a good thing when he saw one, Christopher thought. He knew every picture he took of Mary and me was a guaranteed sale.

He set the pictures aside and idly toyed with other souvenirs of those blissful days: the silly little stuffed kiwi bird she'd bought for him in New Zealand; the tiny figure of a Balinese goddess carved of boar tusk and picked up for a dollar on the dock; a set of enameled Chinese pendants brought back from Kwangchow where there was little else to buy; a handful of wooden toothpicks from the inn in Kyoto, each a small masterpiece in itself, carved at the top with the exquisite detail the Japanese put into even the most mundane objects. Sentimental trinkets, monetarily valueless but precious in the recollections they evoked.

One memory was uncomfortable. Christopher frowned as he recalled the frightening attack he'd had on the dock in Kobe. It had been slight but ominous and as soon as he returned to Sydney he'd phoned his doctor, who was also one of his oldest friends. He'd been told to get right over to the office for a look-see. As Christopher buttoned his shirt after the examination, Charles Grahame had looked at him appraisingly.

"I can't find any further deterioration, Christopher, but you look like hell. For a man just back from a restful sea voyage, there's a bloody lot of strain in your face even under that tan. What have you been up to?"

Christopher, relieved that his heart was no worse, smiled. "I've been falling in love, Charles old boy."

"Oh? And trying to perform like an eighteen-year-old, I suppose."

"Right. I felt like an eighteen-year-old."

"Who's the lady?"

"An American. She lives in San Francisco. Has a little radio show there." He paused. "I asked her to marry me, Charles."

The doctor leaned back in his chair and pushed his glasses up on top of his head. "And?"

"And she won't. She can't. She's already married."

"I must have missed the article that said they outlawed divorces in the States. Or is this a one-sided passion?"

"No. She loves me too. She just can't bring herself to walk out on a weak husband. Presumably he's charming and devoted and utterly dependent." Christopher threw himself into the chair opposite the doctor's desk. "In point of fact, it's even more complicated than that. It's a nightmare."

"Want to talk about it?"

Christopher hesitated for a moment and then he said, "Yes, if you don't mind. I need to tell someone. I've been trying to understand it myself. One minute I do, and the next I don't."

He told Charles everything. The meeting, the instant attraction, the weeks of falling deeper and more passionately in love. He tried to explain Mary's feeling of pity and loyalty toward Michael as a failure and, later, her belief that she needed to be there when he finally was about to achieve the success she felt he wanted only for her sake. It sounded almost irrational as he set forth the facts. There was no adequate way to describe Mary's compassion or the torment she felt over her wrenching decision. No way to explain to another man how he tried to understand the workings of a woman's mind, pretending to comprehend and sympathize even when he couldn't. Christopher finally stopped, his voice trailing off in confusion and despair.

The doctor shook his head in amazement. "Good God, no wonder you look as though you've been through the wringer! Your Mary is either a saint or the biggest damned fool on two continents. As for you, where in hell is your backbone, man? Are you telling me you just walked away? That you accepted this like a broken dinner date? I've known you for thirty years, Christopher. You're strong, successful, intelligent. Why are you behaving like a lily-livered fool? For Christ's sake, go get her! Can't you see she's just begging you to be masterful?"

Christopher shook his head. "You don't understand. It wouldn't work unless she came to me voluntarily, without guilt. She has to work her way out of this herself."

"Balls! You're so in love with this woman you can't see the reality of it. Listen to me carefully, Christopher. I'm no psychiatrist, but every doctor has to treat the mind as well as the body. I hear a lot of stories all day long, meet a lot of men and women. I think I've picked up enough understanding of human nature to dare to give you some advice, not only as your doctor but as your friend. You've never met a woman like this one. She's probably much more aware than you are that this strength of hers is something she really doesn't want. Strong women, for the most part, want to be dominated. Not ordered around as though they have no intelligence, or physically battered by some insensitive oaf, but they're always looking for a leader. Sometimes it's subconscious. Sometimes they know it but don't know what to do about it. But in all cases, they know they need a man stronger and smarter and more solid than they. A man they can respect. A person to depend on. They can't make the step toward that man, but they're always hoping he'll take matters out of their hands and demand they put themselves under his protection." Charles leaned forward and looked Christopher in the eye. "I'll stake my reputation on the fact that Mary is one of those women. She doesn't *want* you to listen to reason, Christopher! She wants you to ignore her misguided maternal instincts toward her husband and refuse to take her emotional decision as the right one. You love her. She loves you. Life is short. For God's sake, friend, will you realize that you know what's best for her and hop the next plane to San Francisco?"

Christopher stared at him through the long, unusually impassioned speech. He'd never heard Charles so vehement and intense. What if he's right? What if Mary is silently begging me not to respect her wishes? What if they're not her wishes at all? He shook his head. Could he have been so wrong in the way he handled this? Was Mary disappointed that he hadn't behaved in the forceful way Charles suggested? No, she was much too intelligent for that. She believed in what she was doing. He had to respect that belief.

"Maybe you're right," he said slowly. "Maybe a lot of women do think that way, consciously or not, but I don't think Mary does. You don't know her, Charles. She has so much character, such a strong sense of obligation. She'll have to come around through her own process of reasoning. I can't just turn up on her doorstep and demand she leave her husband, even though I believe she wants to. She's her own person. She can't be made to obey, or even enticed into hurting someone."

Dr. Grahame sighed in despair. "She's hurting *you,* isn't she? Worse than that, she's hurting herself. If you love her so much, isn't it your damned duty to see that she's happy? Or are you afraid of the responsibility?"

Christopher thought of Jayne. Jayne also thought he'd behaved like a spineless ninny. He remembered their conversation the day he left the ship. The girl hadn't said much, but he hadn't wanted to hear even the few things she did say. He'd been too busy spouting about Mary's strength and obligations and excusing his acceptance under the guise of respect for Mary's feelings. Were Charles and Jayne right? Was he, in his own way, as weak as Michael? Maybe Mary felt he was. Maybe she had doubts about his ability to give her the protection the doctor was so sure she wanted.

"I don't know," Christopher said. "I wish I knew whether you were right. If I was sure you were, I'd go to San Francisco and force a confrontation with Mary and her husband. Clear the air once and for all. I don't know how long I can live in this limbo, wondering what will happen now that she's home."

Charles played idly with a paper clip on his desk. "I can't force you to do anything," he said almost indifferently. "I can only tell you what I believe, as your friend."

"And as my doctor? Can I expect to offer Mary a long life with me? That figures into this, too. I've never told her about my heart attack."

"As your doctor I can't give guarantees. Not even the unqualified assurance you'd like. But I can say, Christopher, that if you continue to live with moderate good sense you should have an average life expectancy. As far as I can see, the doctors in Singapore were right. And I don't think you had another incident in Kobe. You probably were responding to too much food and wine, too much excitement and, most significant of all, too much anxiety. Your heart attack is behind you. Sometimes it's a good thing—a warning to take better care of yourself. I wouldn't dwell on the health aspect, if I were you. Certainly not in terms of Mary."

"At least that's reassuring." Christopher grinned. "Let's hope I don't drop dead on the way out of your office."

"Try not to. It's beastly for my reputation."

They shook hands at the door. "Let me know what you decide," Charles said. "And don't wait too long. You should have another twenty years or so at least, but they go by mighty fast. I hope you're going to enjoy them with your American."

Sitting at his desk a week later, Christopher thought of his doctor's advice. He still didn't know what was fair to Mary. He was eager to have his first letter from her. He hoped she'd mailed one from Hawaii. If so, he'd have it in a day or two. Its tone, after a week's absence, should tell him what he wanted to know. He deliberately hadn't written to her. He'd put all he felt into the little note that was enclosed with the jade heart and now he waited impatiently for the response. Knowing nothing of Gail's death, he assumed it would be still another week before Mary reached San Francisco. He'd have a letter waiting for her at the office when she returned. Hopefully a letter of love that would acknowledge her own.

The apartment was very quiet when Mary awakened the next morning. She still felt desperately tired. It was eleven o'clock, but it must have been after four before she fell into an exhausted sleep. For a minute after she opened her eyes the room seemed strange, big and empty after the close confines of the cabin. Then everything came rushing back. Beau's sad face as they parted at the airport. Charlie's gentle welcome and Michael's flash of intuition in the bedroom. Patricia's crazy scheme. It was all jumbled in her head as she forced herself into consciousness.

She slipped on her robe and wandered out into the other rooms. Neither Michael nor Patricia was around and she was glad. The longer she could postpone any serious conversation with them the better. In the kitchen she found a breakfast tray set up and a note from Michael propped up on it.

"Darling," it said, "I didn't want to wake you. Had to leave for a business meeting. Patricia's gone on some errand of her own. Charlie called at ten to remind you of lunch. See you this afternoon. I love you. Michael."

She heated the coffee on the stove, drank a glass of orange juice and called the radio station. The switchboard operator was delighted to hear her voice.

"Welcome home, Mrs. Morgan! Was it wonderful?"

"Thanks, Susan. Glad to be home. Yes, it was terrific."

"Your tapes were fabulous! Mr. Burke let us hear them. Gosh, I'd give anything to make that trip! You're really lucky."

"I know." Would this gabby young woman never shut up? "Is Mr. Burke there?"

"Oh, sure. I'll connect you. You coming in, Mrs. Morgan? We're all dying to hear about everything."

"I'll be in, Susan. Will you please put Mr. Burke on?"

The girl caught the impatience in her voice and resented it. What was wrong with Mrs. Morgan? She was always so nice, so friendly with everybody. It would be a crying shame if she'd suddenly gone all high-hat just because she had a ritzy cruise. Susan assumed her professional manner, hoping Mary would notice that she, too, could be cool.

"I'll put you through to Mr. Burke's office. One moment, please."

The change in tone did not escape Mary. Damn. Susan was a darling child, and she'd hurt her feelings with her obvious reluctance to chat. She started to say something more friendly but the switchboard operator had already connected her with Charlie.

"Mary? Good morning. How do you feel?"

"Not too bad. A little jet lag, I guess. We're still on for lunch?"

"Absolutely, if you feel up to it. I'm looking forward. Michael doesn't mind if I steal you the first day, does he?"

"I'm sure he doesn't. In fact, he's already gone out. A meeting with Harry Carson, I should think."

There was a small silence on the other end of the wire.

"Charlie? Are you there?"

"What? Oh, sure. Where would you like to meet? You want to come to the office or go straight to the restaurant?"

"I'm such a late starter this morning, I'd better meet you there. Julius Castle as usual?"

"Perfect. One o'clock?"

She agreed and hung up, feeling a little better. It would be good to have a real visit with Charlie. Last night didn't count. They weren't alone, and anyway she'd been so tired she hardly knew what she was saying. In the intimate atmosphere of Julius Castle they could really talk. It was their favorite place, an attractive restaurant with good food and a wonderful view. And sufficiently out of the way so that few tourists found their way down the bottom of the hill on Greenwich Street to a restaurant favored by the "in" people of San Francisco.

As she dressed, she realized how strange she must have seemed last night. She'd told her husband and her sister and her best friend almost nothing about the trip and they hadn't pressed her for a "travelogue." They knew how tired I was, Mary thought. And how distraught over Gail. They were being considerate, waiting until I was ready to talk about the people and places I've seen these past sixty days. She stared at her reflection in the mirror as she put on her lipstick. Or can they see the change in me? Do they sense what's going on inside and feel as though a stranger has returned? I do feel remote from them, from everything that was once so familiar. I'm preoccupied with myself, with my future. Perhaps they are, too, she suddenly thought. Michael was unusually agreeable when I begged off from hearing about the boutique. It's not like him to be so patient about discussing one of his schemes. And there was that pregnant pause this morning on the telephone when she told Charlie that Mike probably was seeing Harry Carson. An uneasiness came over her. Something was wrong. There was something Michael didn't want her to know. Whatever it was, Charlie must know it, too. Maybe Patricia as well.

Now that she looked back on it, it was as though everyone was carefully waltzing around things they didn't want to reveal. Patricia's attitude toward Michael was odd. She'd noticed it last night, and this morning in retrospect it seemed even more peculiar. It was more than proprietary. Almost as though she had the upper hand and could make Michael jump when she snapped her fingers. His reaction confirmed it. Michael was always angry and defensive when someone tried to boss him. He hated authority. Of course he did. That's why he never stayed long in any job. And, Mary thought ruefully, why he's so attached to me, because I've never made demands on him or made him feel threatened.

But how could he feel threatened by Patricia? She was a domineering woman, but she had no weapons to use against Michael. Mary paused, the lipstick halfway to her mouth. Or did she? Did she know some secret Michael was trying to keep? Patricia was a devious woman. Always had been. Look at the way she was planning to dump poor Stanley and stay in San Francisco, demanding her daughter support her. She probably had this in mind even before she arrived. The excuse to meet the ship was very likely only a subterfuge to put a continent between herself and the husband she detested. And Jayne was merely a convenient means to an end.

Lord! I'm going crazy! My imagination is running away with me. I'm reading all sorts of implications into the simplest things. Michael was simply being sweet to me, as he always is. And I'm fantasizing that business with Patricia. Her attitude toward Michael is only what her attitude is toward everyone: arrogant and demanding. Why *shouldn't* Michael resent her? She's been too much underfoot for weeks. Well, she'll soon be on her way back to New York. Another six days and she'll find out Jayne has no intention of living with her. She'll come up against the only one who won't knuckle under: her own daughter.

And Charlie? There was no change in Charlie. If he seemed more subdued and introspective than usual, he was entitled. He must be out of his mind with anxiety about Tracey. Pathetic woman. If anyone ever had her finger on the self-destruct button it was Tracey Burke.

I see ghosts in every corner because I'm so haunted by my own fears, Mary told herself. Nobody here has changed. It's I who am different. And will never be the same.

"I hope Aunt Mary and the colonel are all right. God, what a terrible mission!"

Terry patted her hand. "They're all right, Jayne." He settled himself comfortably on the blanket they'd spread out on the white sandy beach. "I'm sorry Mary had to miss seeing Hawaii. It's so beautiful. I'm glad we flew over here to Kauai for the day. No wonder they call it the 'Garden Isle.' Do you suppose Eden was something like this?"

Jayne looked at him tenderly. He was like a beautiful boy, graceful and sensitive. Though she was younger by five years, she felt protective of him. He'd had a terrible life, really. She was glad she'd been the one to bring him some feeling of belonging, some sense of his place in the scheme of things. They'd be all right. Things would work out. She'd be lover, confidante and friend to him, as he was to her. We are an unlikely pair, Jayne thought, without regret. A couple of misfits who can't make it alone but might struggle through together.

"Eden?" she said in answer to his question. "Maybe. What we're wearing is damned close to fig leaves. I know that!"

Terry laughed. "You're beautiful."

She made a face at him. "You're ugly, but I suppose I have to put up with you."

He looked troubled. "Maybe you shouldn't, Jayne. Maybe we're crazy, thinking of taking an apartment at home. It might not work out. I wouldn't want to hurt you."

"Why do you keep saying that?" She ran her hand lightly across his chest. "Aren't you afraid I might hurt you?"

"No. You never would. You're like your aunt. You care about other people."

"Don't you, Terry?"

"I haven't cared about many in my life. Only two, really."

She lay back and stared up into the cloudless blue sky. I'm one of the two, she thought. And the other is Paul. But Paul was faithless. I never will be. She thought of Mary's warnings. Was she drawn to Terry because she wanted to mother him, to feel omnipotent because he needed her strength? Would she end up, as her aunt feared, feeling lonely and unfulfilled, the victim of her own attraction to the weak and helpless? No. She loved Terry in a way she'd loved no other man. She felt peaceful with him, confident they were products of a strange and merciful destiny. Still, she felt a twinge of fear. Terry wasn't as convinced as she. But that was natural. He'd lived a different kind of life. He was making a far bigger step than she. Bigger, perhaps, than even he realized.

"Terry?"

"Hmmm?"

"Do you want to call it off? Our plans, I mean. If you do, if you have second thoughts, I'll understand. I don't want to push you into something you're not ready for. Maybe we should take this step by step. I could live alone in San Francisco for a while at least, and so could you. We'd see each other and decide whether we wanted to live together. Would that make you happier?"

He rolled over and took her in his arms. "No, I don't want to call it off. Not as long as you're patient with me. I've never spent all my time with a woman, Jayne. Except my mother, and that was a sick thing. I love you. I can't live alone. I want to be with you."

They made love there on the deserted beach. It was romantic and unreal, as idealized as one of the South Pacific movies that had been filmed nearby. But we're not acting, Jayne thought dreamily. We were meant to find this life together.

Only when they dressed and prepared to leave did she remember one small, disturbing sentence. I can't live alone, Terry had said. Was that because he eagerly anticipated their life together or because he was afraid of his old temptations? She pushed the thought from her mind. It was unworthy of consideration. Terry was too fine to use her as a shield. He was through with his old life. She'd opened his eyes to a new one. She put her hand in his as they walked toward their rented jeep. "We'll have some surprises for the folks back on the Mainland, won't we?"

Terry's fingers tightened on hers. "Yes," he said softly, "tongues will wag. It won't be easy. I'm thinking of your family, for one thing. What will they say about all this?"

"I don't care what they say. I don't care what anyone says. People aren't important. Nothing's important but us. We know what we are, Terry. We know what we feel."

He stopped and kissed her. "Darling Jayne. You make everything right."

"And I always will, as best I can. As long as you want me, I'll want you. Nothing and nobody can change that."

Chapter 20

RAE SPANNER'S HOUSEKEEPER opened the door when Michael rang the buzzer at ten-thirty that morning. She'd already alerted her half-awake employer that Mr. Morgan was on his way up. The doorman had called on the house phone. In the evening he wouldn't be announced, Tessie thought with distaste; the evening shift knew him well from his daily five o'clock calls, visits whose purpose probably were no secret to the whole staff of the apartment. It was shocking. Everybody knew Mrs. Spanner's reputation. Too many young men had left the apartment in the early hours of the morning, having obviously spent the night. That was bad enough, but the regular afternoon visits from Mr. Morgan were disgusting. How could she? Mrs. Morgan was supposed to be one of her best friends. The housekeeper shook her head. Sometimes Tessie felt as though she lived in a brothel. A high-class one, to be sure, but a brothel all the same. Someday this wickedness would catch up with Mrs. Spanner, and Tessie only hoped she wouldn't be around when that day came.

"Good morning, sir," she said politely. "I've told Mrs. Spanner you're here. She'll be right out. Would you like some coffee?"

"No thanks, Tessie. I won't be staying long." He gave her that charming smile of his, the one that made her feel like a conspirator. "Not as long as usual."

Despite her impersonal manner, Tessie blushed. He meant he and Mrs. Spanner wouldn't retire to the bedroom a few minutes after he arrived. How could he be so brazen!

Rae appeared in one of her lacy negligees, looking elegant even at this hour, and obviously surprised to see Michael.

"Well! What on earth brings you here this morning?"

He glanced at Tessie, and Rae followed his look. She'd almost forgotten the woman was still in the room.

"That will be all, Tessie," she said. "I'll ring if I need you." She settled herself on the couch and patted the pillow beside her. "Sit down, Michael. What's going on?"

"Mary's home. She came in by plane last night."

"Oh?"

"A friend of hers, a woman she met on the cruise, died of a heart attack. Mary accompanied the body back from Hawaii."

"You can't be serious! A woman she barely knew?"

"That's Mary."

"Yes." Rae's voice was amused. "That's Mary. Big-hearted Mary. She would cut her trip short for such a pointless reason. So she's home. How is she?"

"She seems all right. She was terribly tired last night, of course, and still asleep when I left this morning. We really haven't had a chance to talk."

"I see." Rae calmly lit a cigarette, waiting.

Michael was nervous. "You know what this means, Rae. I can't come here anymore. Not the way I have been, I mean. You know that. You knew this arrangement had to end when Mary came back."

"Did I? I don't remember saying that. All I recall is our making a business deal. A loan with payment on demand. There wasn't a time limit on it as far as I know."

"For God's sake, don't be crazy! You know I can't keep coming here when my wife is in town!"

"Why? Is she going to quit her job? When does Mary ever get home before seven? If you like, we can move the hours up a little. If it would help, we could make it four-thirty to . . ."

"Stop it! How can you want somebody who doesn't want you?"

"It's easy, dear heart. It happens all the time. In fact"—Rae smiled cynically—"it's been my experience that people have a way of wanting what they can't get much more than they want what's offered. I suppose that makes me quite human. You now present more of a challenge than ever, Michael, and somehow that makes the game more interesting."

He stared at her. "I don't believe you! You're incredible! You'd actually *prefer* to have this affair going on right under Mary's nose, wouldn't you? It isn't enough we've made a fool of her when she wasn't around. You'd enjoy it more if you could see her, pretend to be her friend and laugh at her behind her back. God, have you no conscience?"

Rae was unperturbed. "Probably not. I find this kind of thing rather stimulating." She sat up straight and her tone was steely. "Don't be a child, Michael. You've gotten yourself into something complicated and this time you're not going to get off the hook."

"I'll get off the hook!" He pulled his checkbook out of his pocket and began to write furiously. "Here's your money, Rae. I've had it in a separate account. Here's a check for twenty-five thousand. Take it, and good riddance!"

Slowly, deliberately, she took the check and tore it into tiny pieces. "You can't cancel this kind of debt so easily. The money is incidental. It's the interest payments that count. You've been paying off the interest in a very unusual way, Michael. I think Mary would be more fascinated by that than she would be by the loan."

He looked at her through narrowed eyes. "That's blackmail!"

"Not unless I choose to use it." Rae smiled. "And if you continue to be a good boy, I won't."

She had him and he knew it. If she wanted to make trouble, she had more than her canceled check made out to him. She had Tessie and the whole damned staff to testify to his visits. She even had Patricia, if it came to that. She'd been clever all right, letting Patricia know by indirection what was going on. In a panic he tried reasoning with her.

"Listen, Rae, I know you could blow the whistle on me anytime you feel like it, but what's the point of going on with this? You're too attractive a woman to hold a man by threats. You don't need to. You're a realist, too. Good lord, do you really think I could make love to you under these conditions? You know what will happen if I continue to come here because you demand it. I'll be no good to you at all."

"It's a possibility," she conceded, "but I'll take my chances. I like going to bed with you, Michael, and you like going to bed period. So let's see how satisfied you are at home before we decide whether or not you can still be a lover to me. Maybe it won't be such an unwelcome diversion in the future. Especially when you tell Mary that you flunked finance. I wonder how she'll react to that?"

He was stunned. "What the hell do you mean?"

"Well, you have lied to her once again, haven't you? A woman like Mary might take her disappointment in you very much to heart. She's not tough, Michael. Not the way I am. Her emotions very much influence her actions. How do we know? Maybe she'll be so hurt she won't sleep with you. Then you'll be very glad to have this soft bed to run to."

"You really are crazy! You don't know Mary if you think she'd punish me for something I can't help."

Rae shrugged. "Maybe I'm wrong. It's just a wild guess. But it isn't the first time you've failed her. There's bound to be a breaking point, even for her. She might be fed up, my dear. Even angels must find their wings too heavy sometimes. She's hovered over you for a lot of years. Even our saintly Mary must know she doesn't need you. How long do you suppose she'll go on thinking it's her duty to be your protectress-in-residence?"

He was furious. "What kind of game are you playing? Do you really think you can brainwash me with that crap? I know Mary. She loves me. She understands me. But you . . . you're like all the others. God almighty! You and Patricia! Two of a kind! Both of you thinking there's nothing in life but sex!" He stopped abruptly, horrified at what he'd admitted.

Rae smiled. "Patricia, too? My, my, you *have* been busy! That's amusing, Michael. It really is. I love it! You going all over virtuous and all the time you've been sleeping with Mary's sister!" The smile turned to laughter. "Go away," she said. "You're too idiotic for words! You're worried about *me* when you have a real bombshell sitting under your own roof? That's funny! I mean you are the jackass of the world!" She stopped laughing and stood up. "Run along, Michael. You have a few things to sort out, I'd say. Oh, and why don't you take a couple of days off? I won't expect you until day after tomorrow. I imagine you'll need the time."

He let himself out of the apartment. How had he gotten so involved? He hadn't meant to, not with either of them. Things just happened to him that way.

He was too easygoing, too susceptible. Damn Rae Spanner! She was wrong, of course. Mary wouldn't turn away from him just because a business deal fell through. She never had. Still, she'd acted strangely even before she left on that trip. And last night, that business of starting to undress in the bathroom as though she wanted to be invisible. It wasn't natural. A woman who'd been without her husband for two months wouldn't . . . Hell, what was he thinking? That fast-talking Rae had gotten him all muddled. Mary didn't know the Carson thing was down the drain. And even when he told her, she'd sympathize. In every way.

Patricia rang the landlady's bell at the house on Fillmore Street. There was no real reason for her to visit the apartment on which she'd put a deposit, but it wouldn't hurt to let Mrs. Delaney know how enthusiastic she was. It would still be nearly a week before she could sign the lease and she didn't want the woman to give the place to someone else. She'd been reluctant enough to hold it as it was. Patricia smiled brightly when Mrs. Delaney opened the door.

"I hope I'm not disturbing you, but I just had to have another look at that adorable apartment!"

The woman was suspicious. "Why? You having second thoughts, Mrs. Richton? You did put a deposit on it, and I'm holding it in good faith. I could have rented it a dozen times since you were here. And for more money, at that."

"No, no! I haven't changed my mind! I just want to take a few measurements. You said it would be all right if I had some things of my own sent on from New York." Patricia laughed. "Heavens! Change my mind? On the contrary, I can't wait to move in! My daughter will be here in less than a week. She's been on a sixty-nine-day cruise to the Orient, you know. The minute she arrives, we'll come over and sign the lease."

Mrs. Delaney seemed mollified, but then she said, "A sixty-nine-day cruise? Your daughter work on the ship? She's not an entertainer, is she? I don't rent to theatrical people."

Patricia looked shocked. "An entertainer? Certainly not! She's my sister's guest on the voyage. A graduation present after college." Patricia put on her haughtiest air. "Perhaps you've heard of my sister—Mary Farr Morgan. She has a very popular radio program here in San Francisco."

Mrs. Delaney was impressed. "Mary Farr Morgan is your sister! Well, think of that! I never miss her! She's wonderful! I'm sorry, Mrs. Richton. Naturally, I didn't know you were related to Mrs. Morgan. Do you think she'll come here to visit? I'd love to meet her."

"I'm sure she will. We're very close. In fact, that's why I'm moving to California, to be near my only sister."

"I understand. It must be lonely for you, being a widow."

"Yes. Family becomes very important at a time like that."

"Well, you go right along and have another look around." Mrs. Delaney gave her the key. "It'll be a pleasure having you here."

As she walked up the two flights of stairs, Patricia idly wondered why she'd said Stanley was dead. Maybe because I feel as though he is, she thought. She'd only talked with him once since she'd been in San Francisco and even then she'd made the call. Stanley was too miserly to use long distance. He'd sounded rushed, worried about the money she was spending, emphasizing that she should get the charges from the operator and pay Mary for the call before she left.

Patricia had sighed at the pettiness of the man. "Don't worry. I will. It's very cheap to call in the evening."

"I don't want you imposing, that's all. It's enough you're making such a long visit. Your mother and father don't understand it. Tell you the truth, dear, neither do I."

"Is it so terrible for me to have a vacation once in my life? God knows you never take me anywhere!" She wanted to tell him it was a permanent vacation, but she controlled herself. "Anyway, I'm enjoying it. How are the folks?"

"Fine. Everything's fine. But we miss you and Jayne. I can't wait for April twenty-first!"

"I know. Well, I'd better hang up now."

"Yes. Have a good time."

"I will."

Yes, Patricia mused as she wandered through the sunlit living room of the apartment, Stanley really is dead. The walking dead. And if I stay with him I'll die of boredom. But I'm not going to stay with him. I'm going to live here in this clean, cheerful place. I'll start fresh, make a wonderful new life.

She could hardly wait for Jayne to return. She'll love it as much as I do, her mother thought. This is an exciting city for a young girl. Then a sickening thought struck her. What if Jayne decided to stay in San Francisco alone? She easily could. I've found her an apartment and there's no reason why she needs me. I'm an unnecessary expense. No. I'll make her see how much more comfortable it will be if I live with her. I'll do the cleaning and cooking and take care of things like dry cleaning and shoe repair. I'll make it sound like she has a live-in housekeeper who gets no salary. Well, maybe a few dollars here and there, but not as much as she'd have to pay an outsider.

It was a weak argument, but Patricia was not one to be deterred by logic. I'll talk her into it, she decided confidently. And Michael will help me convince her. He knows he has to. She'll buy it. I'll be pathetic, if necessary. She knows how miserable I am with her father. Yes, Jayne will break down. Underneath that independent attitude she has guilts. All daughters have. Patricia smiled. All except me.

Charlie was waiting at the restaurant when Mary arrived.

"Am I late?"

He glanced at his watch. "Nope. Right on time. I was early. Full of anticipation, you might say."

"That's nice. *You're* nice, Charlie. I'm so glad to see you! Last night hardly counted, I was so punchy."

"Terrible thing. You going to the funeral?"

Mary shook her head. "No, it's private. And honestly I hate funerals."

"Who loves 'em?"

"Lots of people. My mother, for one. She has everything planned for hers and Dad's. Right down to what they'll wear. They've even ordered their tombstones engraved, with just the last date blank.''

"Good lord!"

"It's funny. I mean strange. I've noticed whenever I interview old people they're eager to talk about death. Preoccupied with it, as though they enjoy the details. Isn't that odd, Charlie? You'd think the older you get the less you'd want to discuss it. Most times it's just the opposite. Kids have a greater horror of it than old people. Could it be that God gives you a kind of protective acceptance when the prospect gets terribly close?"

He shoved her drink gently toward her. "I think we could talk about more pleasant things on such a beautiful April day."

"Do you believe in God, Charlie?"

"I suppose so. Some kind of force, whatever you choose to call it—fate, destiny, something. Do you?"

Mary took a sip of her vermouth. "Yes. I mean, I don't think there's nothing except what we see here. I don't know about heaven and all that, but I'm sure we're put here for some reason. It would all be too ridiculous otherwise." She smiled. "Well, enough of that! Tell me what's been happening."

"I'm sure you have much more interesting things to tell. How was the trip? It sounded great."

"It was a dream. An absolute dream."

He looked at her searchingly. "Your tone doesn't go with the words. Something wrong?"

With her finger, Mary stirred the ice in her glass. "A few little things. Nothing that time won't take care of."

"Want to talk about them?"

"Not really. Not yet, anyway. Maybe later. I really do want to hear about the shop."

"Well, everybody loved your tapes. You have a sack of mail from your fans."

Her eyes lighted up. "Honest? Any from overseas?"

Charlie frowned. "Overseas? Not that I recall. Why would there be? It's a local show, remember?"

She seemed flustered. "I . . . I just meant I thought maybe I'd heard from some of the people I met while I was away. You know. The lady in Picton. Somebody like that."

"Maybe. I don't know, honey. I didn't go through the mail that closely." He paused. "What is it, Mary? You're jumpy as a cat. You must have a lot on your mind. Why don't you spill whatever it is? I've always been a pretty good listener, haven't I?"

Mary touched his hand lovingly. "The best. The best listener and the best friend. It's just that I'm not the most coherent explainer right now. I'm pretty mixed up."

"It's Michael, I suppose. We both know you went away to think about him and you. Did you think?"

"Of course. A lot."

"And?"

"As I said, I'm still mixed up. I can't talk about it until I'm clearer, Charlie. Not even to you. You understand, don't you?"

"Sure."

"I haven't even had a chance to talk to Michael."

"I assumed not."

Mary's eyes widened. "What does that mean?"

"Nothing. I just meant I know you were exhausted last night and he left early this morning. When would you have talked?"

She nodded. "Right. God, I *am* jumpy! Everything seems ominous to me. Every damned word and gesture seems scary."

"You're probably still tired. Have you considered that?"

"Yes. That must be part of it. But not all." She looked troubled. "One of the things that has me terribly worried is Jayne."

"You didn't get along together?"

"It isn't that. We got along beautifully. She's wonderful. Remarkable. It's just that she's about to make a terrible mistake and I don't know any way to stop her."

She told Charlie about Jayne's plans with Terry. "He's a delightful young man," she said, "but it's wrong. She's too young to handle such a complex situation. Women twice her age can't cope with it. It frightens me to death, knowing she believes she's the revelation Terry's been waiting for. What if he goes back to his friend Paul? Or some other man? What will that do to her? And what's Patricia going to say about all this? Not only does she expect Jayne to take an apartment here with her, but can you imagine what will happen when she hears about Terry's past? Jayne will tell her, you know. That child is too honest and too filled with evangelical zeal not to! And Patricia will hit the roof! She'll be furious, not only for Jayne but for herself. And God knows what she'll say to Terry!"

Charlie did not interrupt throughout the long recital except to order them both a second drink. When Mary wound down, he looked half annoyed, though his voice was gentle.

"Mary, why are you torturing yourself about this? Jayne isn't your child. I know you love her like your own, but she's Patricia's responsibility."

"But I feel responsible. If I hadn't taken her on that trip, she'd never have met Terry Spalding."

"Now that's plain silly! She's a grown girl. You didn't push her into the guy's arms. You really aren't making any sense. Blaming yourself for taking her on the trip! I never heard anything so lame-brained!"

"It's true, all the same."

"So it's true! My God, Mary, if we all went around blaming ourselves for every innocent move, we'd spend our lives saying *mea culpa*. Do you want me to feel guilty because I talked you into a job in San Francisco where you met Michael Morgan? Blaming yourself for Jayne's possible mistake is like blaming me for your unhappy marriage! What's going on in your head? You don't seem like the same woman who left here two months ago. You're behaving like a character in a soap opera! Where's the calm, pulled-together Mary the world admires? Where's that sensible woman I've always loved?"

The words came out of Mary like a stifled scream. "That calm, confident person doesn't exist! She never existed! I'm damned tired of being dependable and contained! I'm fed up with never being allowed to fret over the things other women worry about! Never permitted to be irrational or emotional! I'm not those things, Charlie. I've spent years pretending to be, but I'm not. I have my fears and my wants and needs like everybody else. Only nobody listens. Nobody wants to think I could have a problem . . . or worse yet, *be* one!''

The tears streamed down her face as she searched in her bag for a handkerchief. Charlie handed her his.

"You make me ashamed," he said quietly. "Ashamed of myself. Ashamed of us all. You're right. We take you for granted, don't we? We expect your knees never to buckle. We load our problems onto you and get annoyed when you react to your own in a very human, very understandable way."

Mary wiped her eyes. "No, I'm the one who's ashamed. Flying off the handle that way. You're right. I'm being stupid about Jayne. She's not my responsibility and this thing is not my fault. I don't know why I'm carrying on so about it."

"Maybe because it's only symptomatic," Charlie said. "My hunch is that real as Jayne's difficulties are, they're only part of what's bothering you. I know you still have your future with Michael to sort out. And I suspect there's something more, Mary. Something you've only hinted at." He held up his hand. "No, don't tell me what it is. You're not ready to talk about it yet. When you are, I'll be here, and I promise I'll listen with more understanding than I did a minute ago."

"Charlie, what the hell's the matter with me?"

He didn't pretend not to understand what she meant. "You want me to play curbstone analyst? Okay. I'll tell you what I think. You practically said it yourself a moment ago. You've spent your whole life trying to be what you think everybody expects. You've tried to be the successful son your parents lost; the mother your husband requires; the enviable image the women of this town look up to. I think you're always acting a part, Mary dear. Not that you're not good and kind and dependable. You are. But you're not perfect. You're fallible and mortal, a fact it's taken you thirty-nine years to discover. Something, or some *things,* have happened to crack that perfect shell, and the realization is throwing you. It's too much, too suddenly. Too much you think is demanded of you. Too much you demand of yourself. Why don't you consider yourself for a change? A good, gutsy dose of selfishness might be the best thing in the world for you. Hell, Mary, even the best actress in the world can't play a role seven days a week, three hundred and sixty-five days a year without taking time off!"

She silently considered his words. "I'm not sure I know what my real self is. I think I lost it somewhere along the way. Jayne thinks I have a martyr complex. Maybe she's right. Maybe I'm one of those terrible people who enjoys suffering in silence. God knows I do enough of it." She smiled sadly. "Until today, that is. I haven't been very silent today. I'm sorry to load all this onto you, Charlie. It must be a bore."

"There you go again, apologizing because you're behaving like an ordinary person. Mary, don't you know people are pleased to be asked for advice? It's like compliments—it's as important to know how to receive them as it is to give them. You never ask for help, never go to your friends and say 'Look, I'm in trouble. What should I do?' Do you have such a low opinion of yourself that you think you're not worth helping? Or such a high one that you think your friends aren't qualified to help?''

"Neither," Mary said. "There hasn't been anyone to go to, Charlie. Only you. Isn't it strange? I don't have a single close woman friend. Not one I can let down my hair with. Jayne is the closest I've come in my whole life to a woman with whom I can talk freely. Jayne. A child. Young enough to be my daughter.''

"What about your sister? Were you never able to talk with her? Not even when you were young?''

Mary shook her head. "Not really. Patricia's never been interested in anyone but herself. I remember once, years ago, trying to talk with her about our parents. About the way they cared for nothing after John Jr. died. She thought I was crazy. No, there's never been a woman I could confide in." She paused. "Except Gail DeVries. I did talk openly to her. I'd almost forgotten. I was looking forward to seeing her when we got home, thinking she was someone I could always go to for advice, like a mother who was sensible and caring. Is it possible that for a moment I blocked her out because I'm so sad that she died?''

"Are you sad or are you angry with her for leaving you just when you needed her most?''

Mary looked shocked. "What a terrible thing to say! Angry because someone died? Charlie, how could you think that of me?''

"Because very often people do almost hate their loved ones for dying. It's a kind of desertion. A rejection. They have a spontaneous, unreasonable anger, as though they've been betrayed. I hope you do feel that way about Gail. It would indicate that you're coming around to the degree of self-interest that's healthier than the patient understanding you've cultivated all through your life. Your willingness to forgive and forget is going to destroy you, Mary. I want to see you angry and rebellious, striking out against the unfairness of things, not accepting them as though you had no right to feelings of your own. *You* matter! *You*, Mary Farr Morgan, are important! Let the others survive—Jayne, Michael, Patricia, me. We drain you, Mary. We bleed you dry, hand you our troubles and make you the brunt of our selfishness, and you accept it, as though it's some God-imposed duty. I want you to stop it. I want you to think of nothing but what makes you happy, no matter who else you may think you hurt.''

Charlie stopped abruptly. He'd been on the verge of telling her not to overlook, once again, Michael's failure. To warn her that the man was going to let her down again, and to beg her not to put up with it still another time. But he couldn't do that. It was not his right. She'd find out soon enough. He looked at her, a world of longing in his eyes. There was something very important she was not telling him, something he sensed he didn't want to hear. Once again, as he had when he listened to the interview with Captain Robin, Charlie wondered whether she'd fallen in love with the man. Or if not with that man, some other. I want her to be in love with me, he thought. Subconsciously, all this advice about being happy may be my way of asking her to be with me when Tracey goes. And Tracey is going. She can't last more than another few months, if that.

God! What a monster I am! How can I even think such things when my wife is lying desperately ill? But she's not my wife anymore. She's a creature in another world, bound to me by the laws of this one. I've done all I can. Now I'm trying to hand Mary a dose of the medicine I've prescribed for myself, advising her to take whatever happiness she can while there's still time. Hoping she'll decide to take it with me.

"Mary?"

She looked at him with the glazed eyes of a sleepwalker.

"I didn't mean to be tough on you," Charlie said. "Whatever I said was said because I love you. You know that."

"Yes, I know that. I love you, too."

He nodded. Sure, she loved him. Hadn't she said he was her only friend? That will have to be enough, Charlie thought. It's better than nothing at all. No. Like hell it was. Men and women weren't meant to be friends. They were meant to be lovers or acquaintances, and nothing in between.

"Promise me you'll get all this out in the open," he said. "Whatever it is, stop bottling it up inside. Tell me, tell the people involved, tell *anybody,* but for God's sake stop trying to solve your problems alone! Nobody can, Mary. Everybody needs to talk out what's driving them up the wall. Even if you don't listen, even if you don't respect the advice, lay it on somebody!"

"Seems to me I've been laying it on you for the past hour."

"Not all of it. We both know that."

"No. Not all of it. Some of it. Some you already know." She sat up straighter. "Enough of this. Really. I appreciate your advice and I'll try to take it. It just isn't easy to start being somebody else after nearly forty years of living with yourself as you think you are." She was the old, sympathetic Mary again. "Tell me about Tracey. Is there anything I can do?"

Chapter 21

EIGHTEEN STEPS FORWARD and eighteen back. Michael counted them as he paced the living room, awaiting Mary's return from lunch. Three o'clock. Damn it, where was she? Probably telling Charlie Burke the story of her trip, giving him the play-by-play account she'd been too "tired" to tell last night. It wasn't natural. Nobody came home from such a long, exciting trip and barely talked about it. It was as though she was avoiding any personal conversation. The thought crossed his mind, as it had before, that she might somehow have heard the bad news about the boutique and didn't want to face the meaning of it.

Michael frowned. Well, what *was* the meaning of it? Deals fell through every day. That was business. She'd understand that; she was a businesswoman herself. Rae was wrong. Sure, Mary would be disappointed for him but she wouldn't let it come between them. That wasn't her style. Rae didn't know her the way he did.

Rae. The memory of the morning meeting returned like another dark cloud. The woman was insane, tearing up his check, refusing to let him go. He supposed, in a way, it was a compliment, some sort of testimony to his sexuality, but it was flattery he could live without. Damned nymphomaniac! Sooner or later,

Mary would find out about his borrowing Rae's money. And what he had to pay for that loan. Maybe he should tell her first. She'd be hurt, but she'd realize that he'd been driven to it out of desperation, and now was trapped by this insatiable woman. Mary was realistic enough to see how such things happened and how little they meant. Maybe she'd even get him out of it. If Rae knew that Mary knew, the hold would be broken.

He cheered up. Things would settle down now that his wife was home. There'd be some sticky minutes when he told her, but she'd appreciate his honesty. It would be more acceptable to her than being lied to. She could forgive anything except lies. They insulted her intelligence, she often said. She hated being made a fool of by people who thought she believed the transparent fabrications they invented. Yes, the truth was best. It wouldn't be pretty, but he'd be relieved.

He heard her key in the door and called out.

"Hi, honey. I'm in the living room."

She came in, put her handbag on a table and sank wearily into her favorite chair. Michael gave her a light kiss on the forehead before he took the chair opposite hers.

"Still tired from the trip?"

Mary nodded. "Jet lag, I guess. It'll probably take a day or two."

"Sure. How was your lunch? How was Charlie?"

"He's fine. Well, not really fine. He's worried about Tracey, of course. I'm afraid she's terribly sick. Poor woman. Poor Charlie. It hasn't been easy for either of them." Mary sat up straighter. "Well, enough of that. Tell me about your meeting. I assume it was with Harry Carson. I'm sorry I was so bushed last night, Michael. I'm really anxious to hear everything."

"I didn't have a meeting with Carson today."

"Oh? He canceled?"

"No. That is, not today. He canceled about three weeks ago, actually. Pulled out of the deal."

It took her a moment to understand. "Three weeks ago? But you called me on the ship a couple of weeks ago. You said everything was fine. What happened?"

"Carson's an idiot. The man's impossible! He doesn't want a man's boutique; he wants a mama-papa clothing store, for Christ's sake! I broke my back working up a plan that made sense in today's market and he wanted to water it down to nothing. I'd be nothing more than a damned small-time haberdasher! If he doesn't understand what's happening in men's fashions, that's *his* hard luck. I told him to take his money and stuff it! If he wants to set up a shop that could have come straight out of the thirties, he can get himself another boy. I'm not about to get myself involved with an operation that has no future."

Mary was speechless.

"You don't have to look so horrified," Michael said, defensively. "Hell, *I'm* sorry it didn't work out, too, but it was just one of those things. We agreed to disagree. That's show biz, honey. Nothing's certain until it's signed, sealed and delivered. I couldn't live with Carson's ideas. I'd have been miserable every day of my life."

She didn't seem to hear him. "You lied to me. You knew it had fallen through when you made that call." Mary spoke in a monotone, as though she couldn't believe it. "You deliberately let me think everything was fine. Why did you do that, Michael?"

"I did it for you, babe."

"For me?"

"Sure. Actually, I planned to tell you the truth. That's why I made the call. But when I heard your voice, I thought, Why should I spoil the rest of her trip? There's nothing Mary can do about it from thousands of miles away, so why not let her enjoy the cruise?" He looked wounded. "It seemed the only decent thing to do. I thought you'd appreciate it. God knows, it wasn't easy to pretend things were fine when I was so low. But I didn't see why both of us should suffer. I was being considerate, that's all."

"Considerate!" She began to laugh hysterically. "You thought you were being considerate?" Her body shook with laughter. "My God, you don't know how funny that is! It serves me right. It really serves me right!" Without warning, the laughter turned to tears. Mary buried her face in her hands and began to cry. What a fool I am! she thought as the tears flowed. What a blind, blundering self-righteous moron! I despise the part I was playing: the wonderful little wife, returning against her wishes to stand by the man who'd done it all for her. And it was a joke. A sick joke that changed the course of my life. She began to quiet down. But it's not my fault, she realized suddenly. If what I thought to be true really had been, I'd have been doing the right thing. Instead, I've been used again. Considerate? Michael wasn't being considerate. He'd been afraid to tell her, postponing it as long as he could. As always, he hated unpleasantness. He was buying time, hoping for a miracle, sure he could smooth it over when we were face to face. Or maybe counting on some magical solution turning up before I got here.

I hate him, Mary thought. I hate his unreality and his inflated ego and his injured air. I hate him for making a fool of me over and over again. I hate myself for letting him. She raised her head and looked into Michael's distressed, puzzled face.

"Hey," he said gently, "don't take it so hard. Look, I admit it's a bad break, but something else will come along." He came over and crouched by her chair, his eyes on a level with hers. "Take it easy, honey. Don't go to pieces this way." He reached out for her. "Don't cry, please. I can't stand to see you so upset."

She pushed him away roughly. "Don't try to smooth it over. It's too late for that."

He went back to his chair. Damn. This was worse than he expected. He knew she'd be disappointed, but he hadn't anticipated this loss of control or the physical rejection. It made him uneasy to see her this way. Mary was always so cool about things. It wasn't like her to get hysterical over a bad break. Desperately, he tried to salvage something.

"Hear me out," he said. "I know I have a good idea about that shop and I've decided to finance it independently. I've already raised twenty-five thousand dollars from one investor. It's just a matter of finding a couple of more angels. I can start on a shoestring. Borrow on my life insurance. I don't know whether you'd be willing, darling, but we do have a few thousand in our joint savings. Maybe . . ."

She was in control now, coldly in control, almost objective about this latest horror. "No, I'm not willing. I've worked hard for that nest egg, Michael. I won't risk it on one of your crazy schemes. I can't think of anybody in his right mind who'd invest in your adolescent dreams. You're insufferable. Your childish delusions about your own worth have made you a liar and a parasite and a cheat. Anyone who knows you at all would know they were throwing their money down the sewer if they gave it to you. You have an investor? He must be as infantile as you."

Rage boiled up in him. How dare she? Hadn't he tried to be what she wanted? Was it his fault people were too stupid to recognize talent when it was offered? Parasite? Damn her! She was the one who wanted a fancy apartment and nice clothes. She was the one who wanted him to be successful, just so *she* could be proud of him. He'd spent fifteen years trying to please her, and this was the thanks he got. Condescension and insults. He wouldn't stand for it. Crazy schemes, were they? An infantile investor? He'd show her who was the childish one. Uncaring, he struck back.

"Your friend Rae Spanner doesn't think I have childish delusions! She's given me twenty-five thousand to put into a shop and she's no stupid woman when it comes to money!"

Mary stared at him. "Rae Spanner? You asked Rae for money? How could you, Michael? How could you go to our friends?"

"What the hell's wrong with going to our friends? This is a solid business proposition. I just offered to let them in on the ground floor. Rae was smart enough to recognize a good thing. Not like your wonderful Charlie, who turned me down!"

Mary closed her eyes for a moment. Charlie, too. Both of them knowing this was another of Michael's pipe dreams. She was ashamed for him. If a smart moneyman like Harry Carson thought Michael's ideas were impractical, the others would know they were. Charlie wouldn't go along, even for her. But Rae? Rae was smart, too. Too smart to throw away that much money, even though she easily could spare it. Rae wasn't given to charity. She wanted something in return. And if it wasn't money to be made on her investment, it was something else. Something more than friendship. And Rae Spanner wasn't that good a friend. She had bought herself a new "diversion." I don't care, Mary thought dully. God help me, I don't even care. When she spoke, her voice was dispassionate, almost curious.

"Rae Spanner lent you twenty-five thousand dollars? What did you use for collateral, Michael?"

The flush that started from his collar and rose to his forehead was all the answer she needed.

"Don't tell me," Mary said. "I think I can guess."

Michael began to stammer. "Listen, Mary, I . . . I know it was stupid. It's meaningless. You know that. I was desperate. I couldn't stand the idea of telling you I'd failed. So when Rae . . . when Rae offered . . . well, I just thought . . ."

"You just thought what?"

"I don't know. I don't know what I thought. All right, it was dumb. I've admitted that. I'm sorry. Sorrier than I can tell you. But it was for you, Mary. All of it was for you."

She was incredulous. "My God!"

"I know that sounds crazy, but it's true. I've always wanted you to have the kind of life you deserve. Have I ever asked you to live on what I could earn? Have I ever asked you to give up your job and be a real wife, one who'd be willing to struggle with me, no matter how little we had?"

"No. I wish you had."

"Wish I had!" It was Michael's turn to laugh. "Now who's being funny? You've pushed me ever since we met. You've made me feel inadequate, inferior, always wanting in your eyes. You wish I had? Like hell, you do!"

"Yes, I do. I never wanted to be the stronger one. I didn't want to support us. I thought, under the circumstances, it was what any wife would do. God knows I never meant to make you feel less than a man. As for my working, you never offered me an option, Michael. You just assumed I'd take care of things while you wandered through life, chasing your ridiculous dreams. Yes, I wish you'd told me to lean on you. Yes, I wish you'd demanded your dignity. You're a man, not a child. Why haven't you acted like a man?"

"Because you didn't want one!" He was furious. "You're a castrating female, but I loved you. All I cared about was your well-being, your happiness. I thought you'd be miserable if I didn't go along with your life-style, admire your damned efficiency! I thought love and devotion were the best things I could give you. I was afraid to offer you less than you'd become used to. And what's my reward? Being called a parasite and a cheat because I have too much pride to kiss the rear end of a stupid bastard like Harry Carson? To be spat upon because I debased myself to get money out of Rae Spanner? It was for you, Mary. Can't you understand that? I was trying to live up to what you wanted!"

She put her hands over her ears. "Stop it! I don't want to hear any more. No more excuses. No more pretending. No more trying to make me feel guilty because you're too vain and shallow to think of anyone but yourself. I can't stand this life. It's destroying me. It's destroying both of us." She looked at him, wild-eyed. "You twist everything, Michael. You always have. You don't care what I want. You don't even *know* what I want."

He stared back at her. "All right. Tell me. What do you want?"

Slowly, she let her hands fall into her lap. He believes what he's saying, she thought. All those things about me. All those things about himself. She kept her eyes on her wedding ring, turning it slowly around and around on her finger.

"I want a divorce, Michael."

It was as though she'd struck him. "A divorce! What are you saying? I love you. And you love me. God almighty, every married couple has arguments, but they don't run to the divorce court! I was wrong about Rae. I'm sorry. And I was wrong not to tell you about Carson. But I meant well. I meant to succeed for your sake. You can't penalize me for one little lie and one mistaken infidelity. Not after all these years, Mary. Things will come right. This venture isn't the only game in town. I'll take any kind of job. I'll manage to pay the bills somehow. I'll provide for you, if that's what you want. Anything. I can do it, if I try. Mary, you can't do this to me!"

She felt light-headed, as though everything was drifting away. The anger had left, but the determination remained.

"I know you meant well," she said. "I'm civilized enough to forgive the thing with Rae. One mistake like that doesn't spell the end of a marriage these days." Hypocrite, she thought. Of course you can overlook the unfaithfulness. You were unfaithful yourself. With a twinge of conscience, she put Christopher out of her mind. "I don't want a divorce because you slept with someone. Or even because you lied about Carson. I want it because you can't help the way you are, any more than I can help the way I am. We just don't belong together, Michael. We've never been right for each other. We never will be. Funny. It's taken years for both of us to say what we feel about the other. All these years and no real communication until the end."

"You're wrong," he said desperately. "Mary, you're wrong. It's all out in the open now. We can start over in a healthy way. It hasn't been such a terrible marriage, has it? We never fought. We can make it work again. We can even make it better."

She shook her head. "I don't think we can. I don't know whose fault it's been. Mine. Yours. More likely both. We went wrong somewhere, a long time ago. I didn't ask enough, or too much. You offered too little or too much. I'm not sure. All I know is that we didn't understand each other's needs. We were too busy trying to please, and we were going at it the wrong way."

"But that can change! *I* can change!"

"No, you can't. Neither can I. It's not possible. I can never be the wife you need, the clinging vine who'll leave you no choice but to get out and support her. Maybe I could have done that once if you'd asked me. But not now, Michael. I'm not that love-struck girl anymore. I'd be too frightened, too unsure to do today what I might have been able to do fifteen years ago when I was young and anything seemed possible. I'm sorry. Truly sorry."

The color had left his face and he was trembling. "I love you," he said again. "Doesn't that mean anything?"

She wanted to run from the room. How could she do this to him? How could she abandon a man who depended so much on her? What would happen to him? I can't think about that, Mary told herself. He'll survive. There'll always be someone to take care of Michael.

"It means a great deal," she said. "I know you love me, in your way. I love you, too, in mine. I think we'll always love each other. But that isn't enough. We need mutual respect. And a feeling of security. We don't have that anymore. And after this, we could never get it back."

He seemed to sag. "You're determined about this. You really want me to leave."

She clutched the arms of her chair. "Yes. Yes, I do. Today."

"Today? You want me to leave today? I . . . I don't know where to go."

Go to Rae, she wanted to say bitterly. Or use her money to live on for a while. No. That was despicable of her. She no longer hated him. But she had to cut it off, now, while she still had the force of reason.

"Perhaps you could go to your mother for a while," she said gently. "It might be wise, for many reasons, to go down to Los Angeles." Damn it, I'm still planning his life for him, she thought. Will I never stop?

"Can't you give me a few days?" Michael asked. "Just time enough to make some plans?'' He saw her expression and shook his head. ''I know what you're thinking—that I'll hang around and try to make you change your mind. I won't. I promise you. I'll just stay until I find some kind of a job and get a room. It shouldn't take too long. I'll sleep on the office couch. Patricia can go to a hotel or, better still, go home.'' He smiled bitterly. ''Ironic. I wanted her to move out when I heard you were arriving. I thought she'd disrupt our second honeymoon. I didn't know she'd mess up our separation.''

Mary said nothing. It was terrible to see him beg. Beg for love. For forgiveness and another chance. Even for a place to sleep. She felt like the most heartless creature who ever lived, but she couldn't let him stay. Better the quick amputation than a painfully slow severing of the last shreds of their marriage.

''It's best you leave today, Michael. Do you . . . do you need some money?''

He gave her a long look. ''Right to the end, huh? Always Lady Bountiful. No thanks. I'll manage.'' He moved toward the door. ''I'll just take a few things now,'' he said politely. ''You won't mind if I come back later for the rest?''

''Michael, I'm sorry. Believe that.''

''Sure. Not to worry.''

She listened to him moving around the bedroom. She'd never done anything so cruel, never felt so selfish and remorseful. But she couldn't back down, no matter how much she pitied him. He'll be better off without me, she thought. I truly believe that. And I can't take it anymore. It wasn't the failure or the lies. It wasn't Rae. It wasn't even freedom to go to Christopher. She didn't know where she was headed. All she knew was that despite the sadness, she felt an enormous sense of relief. It was as though she realized for the first time how smothered she'd been by Michael's need of her. She'd been like a drowning person fighting for air, and even now, even in this terrible moment, she was ashamed to recognize that she felt as though she was coming up into a clean, healthy atmosphere. Michael sucked out the very breath of her life with his attachment to her. It had to come. It had taken a specific shock to finally move her toward this act of self-preservation. It was selfish, perhaps heartless. But it was necessary. She had to cut the cord that held them together, sever the life line that sustained something not worth keeping alive. It was, Mary thought, an emotional mercy killing, agonizing but inevitable.

Half an hour later she hadn't stirred from her chair. She heard Michael moving around in their bedroom, slamming closet doors, opening and closing the medicine chest. Then he came back, one-suiter in hand, and stood looking at her.

''I'll be in touch.''

Mary nodded. ''Where will you be staying?''

''I got a room at Stanford Court.''

Unthinkingly, she reverted to practicality. ''Stanford Court? Michael, isn't that fearfully expen . . .'' Mary's voice trailed off. It was so dumb of her to say things like that now! No wonder Michael smiled almost condescendingly.

''Don't worry. I won't charge it to you.''

''I know. That was stupid of me. I'm sorry, Michael,'' she said again. ''I really am. Sorry about everything.'' She felt miserable. She'd hurt him enough without reminding him once again that he took luxury for granted.

Her apology wiped the smile from his face. ''I'm trying to understand you,

Mary. I keep having the feeling something has happened to change you so drastically. Something *I* didn't do, I mean.'' He waited for an explanation, but she didn't respond. Michael sighed. ''Look, I want to ask you just one favor. Don't rush into a divorce, will you? Things have happened too fast. You've been home less than twenty-four hours. You want a separation. Okay. But don't take any final steps for a while. Let's give this a little time. Maybe we don't have to destroy something we both cared about a lot. I'll buckle down and try to be more realistic. I see, now, the mistakes I made. I can change, Mary, whether you believe it or not. Give me a chance to prove that to you. Please promise me you'll think this through before you do anything legal about it. It's the only thing I ask of you.''

She couldn't refuse. Even though she knew things would never change, she had to pretend to give him that chance. In a strange way, she wanted to. She hadn't ended her marriage in order to go to Christopher. Perhaps that's what she would do in time. But not now. At this moment she was too confused, too unhappy to think of the future. All she wanted was peace. Some kind of orderly, undramatic life. Later she'd know what to do about Christopher, but love of him wasn't the primary motivation in the step she'd taken.

''I won't do anything in a rush,'' she said. ''You have my word.''

''Thank you,'' Michael said quietly. And then he was gone.

She sat quietly in the gathering darkness, wondering what it was all about. It was cumulative, she supposed, the way most things are. Like suicide. People didn't kill themselves because of one unhappy moment, but rather because slowly, perhaps over a period of years, misery built in their minds until a final word or act or thought tipped them over the edge. That's how it was with her marriage. It wasn't this latest lie or Michael's admitted unfaithfulness. It wasn't even the knowledge that on the other side of the world a wonderful man waited for her to be free. It was the gathering of a hundred lies, a thousand trivial deceptions, a lifetime of vague uneasiness and uncertainty about so many things. She felt, again, the sad-happy sense of release, the pleasure of being alone, with no one to make demands on her. She'd write to Christopher and tell him what had happened. But she'd also have to tell him she needed more time. Time to be sure of what she was and what she really wanted. At this period she craved solitude. She felt as though she'd escaped from all the pressures, loving and otherwise, that addled her brain and tore at her emotions. Perhaps I'm incapable of giving, in the true, unselfish sense, Mary thought. Not material things. Not even love. She'd given Michael the former and Christopher the latter, but she was suddenly full of doubts as to whether she could wholly and gladly give herself.

I'm so tired, she thought, I want to sleep, to blot out everything and everyone.

A voice in the foyer put an end to those thoughts.

''Anybody home?'' Patricia sounded revoltingly cheerful.

Oh God, Mary thought. I'd forgotten all about her! ''I'm in the living room, Patricia.''

Her sister breezed in, snapping on a lamp as she entered. She was, Mary realized, a little drunk.

''What are you doing sitting here in the dark? Let's put on some lights. Start some music. Have a little drink." Patricia looked around. "Where's the head of the house?"

"Michael's not here."

"Oh? He must be having a big day. He was ready to leave when I went out this morning."

"He's been home since," Mary said. She couldn't bring herself to tell what had happened. Not quite yet. "Where have you been?"

Patricia unsteadily poured herself a drink at the bar. "Well, first I went over to the apartment. Jayne's and mine. Made a lot of character with the concierge when I told her who my famous sister was. And then I did some window shopping and had lunch. And then"—she flopped on the couch and grinned at Mary— "then guess what I did."

"I haven't the faintest idea."

"I called your boss, good old Charlie. And I invited him out for a drink."

"You called Charlie? What on earth for?"

"To ask him to give Jayne a job! And you know what? He said he would! Isn't that great? She'll be a receptionist. A hundred and forty a week to start. We can get by on that. And who knows? Maybe the kid will turn out to be a star, like her aunt. History could be repeating itself!" Patricia was triumphant. "How about that piece of news? Jayne will be thrilled! I know she will. Maybe she'll even realize her mother isn't as dim-witted as she thinks!"

Mary was dismayed. "Patricia, I really don't think you should take Jayne's life in your hands like this. There was no need to go to Charlie. I thought you'd wait until Jayne got back and you could discuss it with her. I could always have gone to Charlie then, if she decided she wanted to . . . to stay here and live with you."

"What's wrong with having it all set up? I know she's going to love the idea." A mean little smile crossed Patricia's face. "What's the matter? Are you jealous that I contacted your admirer and had a few drinks with him? Or maybe you're mad that you can't take credit for getting Jayne the job."

"Don't be ridiculous! What do I care if you see Charlie Burke? Or, for that matter, who speaks to him about Jayne? I simply think you take too much for granted. You can't tell people where and how to live, Patricia. Not even your daughter. She's grown up. She'll make her own decisions."

"Well, thank you very much!" Patricia's voice dripped sarcasm. "I'm delighted to hear you're such an expert on children, having had so many of your own!"

Mary was too exhausted to argue. "Skip it," she said. "Jayne will be home in five days. You two can thrash it out then."

"Right." Patricia sounded thoroughly satisfied, her victory assured. "When's Michael coming back?"

It was no longer possible to stall. "He isn't. He's left for good. We've agreed to separate. Michael's gone to Stanford Court."

"What?"

"You heard me. He's moved out."

Patricia seemed to sober up instantly. "What happened, for God's sake? This morning he was happy as a lark!"

"I don't want to go into it, Patricia. Not now."

"He told you about the Carson fiasco, didn't he?"

"Yes. That and several other things."

Patricia nervously lit a cigarette. "What other things?"

"It doesn't matter." Why didn't Patricia stop questioning her? She'd told her she didn't want to discuss it. Why didn't the woman have some consideration? Patricia was acting very strangely. Her stare seemed to penetrate Mary, as though she was trying to discover what was in her sister's mind. Oh, hell, there'd be no peace until she gave Patricia some kind of answer. "He's also borrowed money from Rae Spanner and had an affair with her." Mary's tone was leaden.

"Anything else?"

Mary gave a rueful little laugh. "Isn't that enough?" Then she looked grim. "It isn't just the deal, or even Rae. We haven't been happy for a long while, Patricia. A separation may be a good thing. We need to be alone, each of us, to think things through."

Patricia breathed more easily. Thank God Michael hadn't told Mary anything about them. She pretended sympathy. "I'm sorry. This must be very hard on you, dear. I'm glad I'm here right now when you need me. A good woman friend is important at a time like this, and we've always been friends, as well as sisters. Don't worry. I'll stay with you until Jayne comes. And even after that, I'll be nearby. It must have been fate, my deciding to move to San Francisco."

Mary was appalled. She didn't want Patricia around. She wanted to be alone. Totally, restfully, peacefully alone. And she'd never confide in Patricia. Never in a million years. It was absurd for her sister to act as though they were close.

"I thought . . . . well, that is, it would seem better somehow if you stayed in a hotel until Jayne arrives, Pat. I'm not very good company." Mary hesitated. "Not that I don't want you, but I know I'm going to be dull company for a while. It's difficult for you, too, I'm sure. I mean, there's only one bath and you must be awfully uncomfortable on that couch. I feel terribly inhospitable. I wish I had a guest room. Anyway, I insist you be my guest at a hotel until the ship arrives."

"Nonsense! Do you think I'd leave you alone, in your state of mind? I'm perfectly fine here. Don't worry about the cramped quarters. Michael and I managed just fine. It would be silly of you to spend your money putting me up for five days in a hotel. It costs the earth! Now you just relax. I won't get in your way. I'll keep the house tidy and cook you good dinners and we'll have lots of time to talk."

"But . . ."

"No buts about it! What's a family for if not to stand by when one of them needs help? It will be my pleasure, Mary, dear. A small enough gesture to repay your hospitality these past weeks. Now, you go have a nice, hot bath and climb into bed. I'll bring you a tray. You need rest after what you've been through. Men! Such ingrates! You've done so much for Michael. Now *you* deserve some consideration! You just do whatever you want and don't worry about me. I don't need to be treated like a guest. I'm quite at home here."

It was no use. Patricia wouldn't be moved with the kind of lame excuses Mary had given. And Mary couldn't bring herself to say, Go away. All I want is to be left alone.

"All right, Patricia. Thank you. I think I will go straight to bed. But don't bother about dinner, please. I'm not hungry. I don't think I could force a mouthful of food."

"I'll just do something light. Maybe a nice cheese soufflé. You run along and get comfortable. You look done in. I'll take care of everything. You'll see. It will work out fine. It will be just like it was when we were kids at home."

Mary smiled at her helplessly. God forbid, she thought.

Chapter 22

As THE SHIP edged its way gently toward its berth, Peggy Lawrence Robin watched from the window of her suite on Promenade Deck. Tony was busy, of course, supervising their arrival in San Francisco. Nervously, she smoothed back her long blond hair, done in the classic chignon she preferred, tucking in the stray tendrils and wondering, as she did so, why it was so important to look her best. Nobody would be there to meet her. She and Tony would have one evening together ashore before he left on the next cruise down the coast of California and through the canal to England. He was going home and happy about it. Happy to be free again, relieved to be rid, even temporarily, of a wife he didn't really want. The awareness filled Peggy with bitterness. She'd frightened him into marriage, but only because she believed he loved her as much as she loved him. The past weeks had shown her otherwise. The devoted, passionate captain of the past three years had turned into an almost indifferent companion. They'd spent less time together since their wedding than they had before. Tony seemed to invent excuses not to be with her. She kept her suite next to his, of course, but she was more often alone in it. Gone were the intimate dinners in his cabin. Since Hong Kong, he'd been at his table in the dining room every night, explaining that he had VIPs to entertain, leaving her, since Hawaii, with only Jayne and Terry and the purser for company at the big table for eight. She was bored and angry, and yet she was still pleased to be Mrs. Anthony Robin. She knew it was an obsession with her, this business of being a married woman, but it mattered, terribly. Even though she returned alone to Chicago, she'd come back as a woman some man wanted. Better, by far, to have an invisible husband than to be one of those rootless widows or divorcées she despised. In a few years she'd live with Tony. She could wait. Once he settled down and knew his seafaring days were over, he'd be content with her.

At least I know where I stand, she thought. I'm better off than Mary, who clearly was unhappy about returning to her husband, though she pretended not to be. She had nothing but scorn for Mary. "Miss Goody-Twoshoes." The woman was an idiot to let that rich Australian get away from her when it was obvious she was in love with him. Happily married women did not fall in love. Mary would be the type to go back to her marriage out of some idiotic sense of duty. I'll probably see her on the dock, Peggy mused. She'll come down to meet Jayne. It will be interesting to get a look at the unknown Michael Morgan, who'll undoubtedly be with her.

From her window, Peggy could see Jayne and Terry leaning over the railing, holding hands and talking animatedly as they looked toward the waiting crowd on the pier. What an odd couple they were! That combination had been the source of endless speculation ever since Singapore. It was hard to believe that Terry Spalding was attracted to a woman. And harder still to understand what a good-looking girl like Jayne saw in this delicate young man. And yet, crew gossip said they were sleeping together.

Peggy shrugged. Who cared? It was just another shipboard romance. She'd seen a hundred of them, though she had to admit that this one was more off-beat than most.

She put the last of her jewelry into the case she'd carry off the ship. Adieu to cruising, she thought with a tinge of regret. But *bon jour* to the status that more than took its place.

"I see her! I see Aunt Mary." Jayne jumped up and down like a child. "Over there, Terry!" She pointed to a slim woman in a neat navy suit. "And there's Mother, next to her! Good God, I never thought I'd be glad to see my mother, but I really am! I can't wait to introduce you!" Jayne's eyes sparkled. "I wonder where Uncle Mike is."

Terry tried to make out the features of Patricia Richton, still a blur from this distance and this height. As he came closer to meeting Jayne's mother, he grew increasingly nervous. What would the woman say when she heard her daughter's decision? She must know about me, he thought. Mary must have told her. But he doubted that Mary had gone into any detail about the future he and Jayne planned. She'd leave that up to them. Ridiculously, he scanned the crowd, half expecting Paul to be there. Insane. Paul didn't even know his former lover was on a cruise. It had taken all Terry's willpower not to tell him before he sailed, or to send him a postcard en route. He wondered whether the man he'd cared so much for had missed him, or was even curious as to his whereabouts. Probably not. Paul would be much too involved with the woman he must have married by now. The thought of Paul's wife left a bad taste. He pushed the mental picture aside. I mustn't think of him ever again. He's part of the past I want to forget. That's over and done with. I have Jayne. Darling, wonderful Jayne. She's given me something to care about, something to live for. He felt suddenly happy as he joined his excited companion in waving enthusiastically toward her family below.

For the first time in five days, Mary felt a little surge of pleasure as the ship nosed gently against its moorings. She'd be so glad to see Jayne again, to hear that incredibly understanding voice and see the affectionate smile. What a contrast she was to Patricia! It was as though Jayne was the elder and more dependable of the two. Patricia had driven Mary mad these past days. She was so damned solicitous, so overbearingly proprietary, so patently phony in her new role of "big sister," Mary could hardly wait for her to leave.

Yet, even while she was filled with joy at the prospect of seeing Jayne, the sight of the *Prince of Wales* engulfed her in a longing for Christopher and all the days and nights they'd spent together. In her purse was a letter from him which had arrived at the office yesterday. It was a tender, loving, undemanding message meant to be waiting for her when, as he thought, she stepped off the ship this afternoon. She hadn't written to him since her return. She'd made four or five starts but abandoned every one. She desperately wanted to communicate with him but was afraid to say too much or too little. I'll write tomorrow, Mary thought. Tomorrow night when Patricia's gone and I'm finally alone and can calmly and quietly tell him all that's happened. He'll be sad about Gail's death and the terrible blow it's been to Beau. He'll be happy Michael and I have separated. But how will he feel when I ask him to wait a little while longer for my decision? How much understanding can I expect from him or any man? Can I put into words the crazy, ambivalent feelings I have, not about him but about my whole life? I want him. And I'm scared to death of another marriage. It's as simple and complex as that.

There'd been no word from Michael since the day he left. He'd arranged to come by for more of his clothes at an hour he knew she'd be at the station. Patricia had been home when he came, and reported that Michael seemed well and was still at Stanford Court. He had no job yet, but he was "looking." What is he living on? Mary wondered as she listened in silence to Patricia's account of the visit. That's not my problem, she thought in the next breath. I can't worry about Michael anymore. He has to learn to worry about himself.

Patricia's eyes widened as the big, white ship, all flags flying, came closer to its destination. What a gorgeous floating hotel! Again, she felt jealous of Mary and Jayne. Someday I'll sail off on a boat like that, she thought. I don't know how or when, but I will. My life's going to change from now on. I feel it. At last, it will have some glamour. Now that I'm free, I can make it happen. There'll be some man, somewhere, who'll give me all the wonderful things I've dreamed of—the clothes and jewels and trips I was meant to have.

God knows who it would be. She hadn't met him yet. It certainly wasn't Michael, who'd never have a penny to his name. Or Charlie Burke, who was polite but obviously uninterested in her. I'll find him, Patricia thought. Through Jayne I'll probably meet a lot of attractive men in San Francisco. A young, pretty girl was a perfect lure. Her new beaus would have uncles or fathers interested in her still-beautiful and available mother. Stanley would be out of the picture soon. She'd be unattached and enchanting. She smiled at the thought, forgetting for a moment where she was or why she was here, She was almost surprised to feel Mary nudge her.

"There she is! There's Jayne up on Promenade! See her, Patricia? She sees us! She's waving!"

She followed Mary's finger. Yes, there was Jayne waving madly with her right arm. The left one, Patricia could see, was linked through that of a young man beside her.

"Who's that she's with?"

"That's Terry. Terry Spalding. He and Jayne became good friends on the trip."

"Oh? *How* good?"

Mary was evasive. She still had told Patricia nothing of Jayne's plans. She supposed she kept hoping they'd changed since Hawaii. Not that she didn't like Terry. She liked him very much. She simply couldn't shake the conviction that Jayne was going to do something she'd regret.

"They're very fond of one another," Mary said. "He's a nice young man."

"Live here?"

"Yes, I believe San Francisco is his home."

Patricia seemed pleased. "Perfect! He'll know a lot of people. It will make it easier for both of us to get into a social life." She took out a compact and carefully powdered her nose. "Is he rich? He must be if he can afford a cruise like this."

Mary looked at her with distaste. "I don't really know, but I don't think he has money. He's an actor."

"Probably has a rich family."

Jayne and Terry had disappeared from the railing with a final wave. Soon they'd be coming down the gangway, claiming their luggage. And mine, too, Mary thought. Poor Jayne, stuck with all my stuff. I hope customs doesn't give her too hard a time.

"Let's go over and wait for them by the gate, Patricia. It probably will take some time to get the baggage off and go through customs. We won't see them again until they've cleared."

"Okay. We have a lot of news for Jayne, haven't we? She'll be surprised about you and Michael. And wait until she hears about our apartment!"

Mary tried to change the subject. "Lord, what a crush! We're lucky Charlie insisted on sending us in a limousine. We'd never even *get* a taxi, much less load Jayne's luggage and mine and Terry's into one. See? The bags are put under the letter of your last name. I wonder what Jayne did about that. Probably put Richton tags on everything. Poor lamb, she'll have an awful lot to declare to the customs inspector. I'm afraid I bought much more than the duty-free hundred-dollar limit. I'll repay her, of course." Mary realized she was chattering like a magpie. What would Patricia think when she got a good look at Terry? Not that he was flagrantly gay. He'd toned down tremendously since that first day she and Jayne saw him in the dining room. Still, Patricia was a city girl. You didn't grow up in New York without developing the antennae that made you instantly recognize one of "the boys." Don't let her be rude to Terry, Mary prayed. No telling what the infatuated Jayne would do if her mother made some snide remark in front of him.

It seemed forever before the two young people, their mountain of luggage loaded onto a cart, pushed through the exit. Jayne threw her arms around Patricia while Terry hugged Mary. There was much laughter and introductions and excitement before Jayne said, "Where's Michael? Couldn't he come with you?"

"No," Mary said. "I'll explain later. Let's get out of here, shall we?"

Jayne seemed to understand without another word. "Sure. Let's go. Can we drop Terry? He's going to the St. Francis Hotel until . . . until he finds an apartment."

Patricia looked surprised. "Oh? You don't have an apartment here, Terry? I thought you lived in San Francisco."

"I do, Mrs. Richton. Live here, I mean. But I gave up my apartment just before the trip."

"I see. Well, I'm sure you'll find a wonderful one. The town is full of them. In fact . . ."

Mary hurriedly interrupted. "You and your mother will stay overnight with me, Jayne. Terry, will you come for dinner?"

"I'd love to, if I'm not intruding on a family reunion."

"Not a bit of it! I want to hear what's been going on this past week."

"Speaking of that," Jayne said, "did everything go all right on the flight home? How's the colonel?"

"He's doing all right, thank heavens. He's been staying with one of Gail's daughters but he leaves for Atlanta today. I spoke with him this morning. He said to be sure to give you and Terry his love. Such a rare human being, our Beau. He wants us to visit him one of these days, but I suppose we never will." Mary sounded regretful. "People lose touch when a voyage is over."

A familiar voice behind her spoke up. "I hope that won't hold true with us, Mary. You must come to Chicago!"

"Peggy!" Mary embraced the tall, fair-haired woman. "I'm so glad we got to see you. Patricia, this is Mrs. Lawrence. I'm sorry! I mean Mrs. *Robin*. She's our newlywed. She and the captain were married in Hong Kong. My sister, Patricia Richton, Peggy. Jayne's mother."

"How do you do." Peggy acknowledged the introduction. "I was hoping to meet your husband, Mary dear."

"He couldn't make it. How's Tony?"

"Fine. Busy right now, of course. We're spending the night at the Clift. Maybe you and Michael could come by this evening for a drink?"

"Oh, I'm so sorry we can't. How long are you staying?"

"Just overnight. Tony sails tomorrow and I'm flying back to Chicago." Peggy gave a tinkling little laugh. "Such is the life of a captain's wife! Well, another time, hopefully. I won't keep you. By the way, have you heard from Christopher?"

"As a matter of fact, I had a nice note from him yesterday." Mary hoped she sounded as casual as she tried to. "He seems fine."

"Perhaps he'll come and visit you and your husband one day. Such a charming man, my dear. So devoted to you. It would be a pity if you lost touch with him, too."

Bitch! Mary thought. You've never forgiven me for not coming to your ridiculous wedding, have you? You're probably sorry Michael isn't here so you could start him asking questions. Too bad you don't know it doesn't matter anymore. She smiled sweetly. "Yes, Christopher is a darling. I'm sure I'll stay in touch with him and a couple of other *good* friends." She didn't embrace Peggy again. "We must run, I'm afraid. Give my love to Tony. I do hope we'll all sail again, one day." Suddenly Mary regretted her rudeness. Impulsively, she kissed the other woman. "I hope you'll be happy, Peggy. Let me hear from you. If you get to San Francisco again . . ."

"I'll call you. That's a promise. Good-bye, Mary. Mrs. Richton. Terry, take good care of Jayne. You're lucky to have her." She waved her hand and disappeared.

"What was *that* all about?" Patricia asked.

"Nothing," Mary said. "I'll tell you about it later."

The atmosphere was strained when the three women finally reached Mary's apartment and deposited her luggage and Jayne's in the foyer. They'd had very little to say in the car after they let Terry out at his hotel, and the uneasy silence continued as they sat down in the living room to catch their breath. Jayne kicked off her shoes and she sighed deeply.

"Well," she said, "*that's* over! The worst part about a trip is the departure and return. Especially the return. Those customs boys are thorough, Aunt Mary. Fortunately, we didn't have anything madly expensive to declare. Did you have a problem with your jewelry when you went through customs in Hawaii?"

"No. Just paid a little duty on the jade."

Patricia perked up. "You didn't tell me you bought jade, Mary. How come you haven't shown it to me?"

"I don't know. I guess I forgot about it with all that's been going on." Another lie. The ring and heart Christopher had given her were hidden away. Patricia was all too wise about the value of things. She'd know Mary could never have afforded to buy such expensive jewelry. "There are just a couple of pieces," she said now. "I'll show them to you another time. There are a few little gifts in the luggage Jayne brought. Souvenirs, really, for all of you."

She hasn't told Mother about Christopher, Jayne realized. Well, that was no surprise. But maybe she'd told Michael. They hadn't mentioned him again, but Jayne sensed he wasn't going to be around. Everybody's hiding something, the girl thought. Aunt Mary's reluctant to talk about Michael. I'm nervous about telling Mother about Terry. And even Mother herself seems to be holding back some important piece of news.

"Maybe we'd all better talk," Jayne said in her forthright way. "You can cut the tension with a knife in here."

Mary nodded. "Michael's left," she said simply. "We've separated. The call he made to me on the ship was a packet of lies. There's no deal with Harry Carson. It was the last straw, Jaynie. I couldn't take it anymore." She looked knowingly at her niece. I didn't tell him about Christopher, the look said.

Jayne bit her lip. "I'm sorry, Aunt Mary. Will you get a divorce?"

"Not yet. He's asked me to wait and think it over. I told him I would." No need to mention Rae Spanner. Or to say she hadn't decided what to do about Christopher. Jayne would hear about Rae eventually, no doubt, and she'd understand now that Mary was in a turmoil about her lover.

"I have some happier news," Patricia said.

"What's that, Mother?"

"Charlie Burke's going to give you a receptionist's job at the radio station."

Jayne was amazed. "You're kidding! Aunt Mary told you I wanted to stay in San Francisco? Oh, Aunt Mary, thank you! It was wonderful of you to line up a job for me!"

"Your Aunt Mary didn't do it," Patricia said proudly. "*I* did. *I* talked to Charlie."

"*You* did? Then you don't mind that I won't be going back to New York?"

Patricia smiled broadly. "Mind? I'm delighted!" She turned to her sister. "See, Mary? You were wrong. You were afraid I was taking too much on myself, assuming Jayne would like to live here. I know my own child. I knew she'd want to stay!"

Before Mary could answer, Patricia rushed on. "And there's more, Jayne. I'm going to stay, too! I've found us the most adorable apartment. I'll be able to take care of it and you. We'll have a wonderful time meeting new people and doing different things! I'm so excited, honey! So glad you agree!''

It took Jayne a moment to digest what her mother was saying, and then she looked stunned. "You plan to stay, too? I don't understand. What about Daddy?''

"He'll manage. I doubt he'll miss us.''

"But . . . but you obviously don't know about Terry.''

Patricia looked at her sharply. "What about Terry?''

"I'm going to live with him. I plan to stay in San Francisco, but *Terry* and I are going to share an apartment.'' Jayne looked helplessly at Mary. "I thought you knew, Mother. I thought that's why you lined up the job for me. I assumed Aunt Mary must have told you.''

"I thought it was your place to tell your mother,'' Mary said softly. "I'm sorry, Jayne. I guess I was wrong to let her go on with this idea, but I didn't know whether you and Terry might not have changed your minds this past week.''

"Live with that boy?'' Patricia's voice began to rise. "What are you talking about, Jayne? You barely know him! No! I won't permit it! And what about me? I've made plans. I've even put a deposit on our apartment. I can't stay here unless I live with you! You tell him tonight. Tell him your mother is staying here and you're going to be with her!''

"I'm sorry, Mother. I can't. Terry and I intend to look for a place tomorrow. We've been talking about it for weeks. It's time for me to leave home anyway. I'd have done that in New York. Even if Terry hadn't come into the picture, I'd have gone out on my own. I'm sorry you're disappointed,'' Jayne said again, "but it is something you should have discussed with me before you went this far. Aunt Mary was right. You did take too much for granted.''

Patricia turned her rage on Mary. "What kind of sister are you? You knew about this all the time! You let me take that apartment and make my plans and all the time you knew what my ungrateful daughter was up to! It must have given you quite a kick! I'm sure you had a good laugh behind my back, seeing me make such a fool of myself!''

"Patricia, I didn't! It wasn't that way at all. I tried to tell you not to make plans, but you wouldn't listen. I didn't feel I had the right to tell you what Jayne was thinking, but I did everything I could to make you wait until she returned. But you were so sure of yourself you paid no attention.''

"I might have paid attention if you'd said she was sleeping with this actor from San Francisco! I might have guessed she'd figure some way to get her hooks into him!''

"Mother, stop it! Aunt Mary did all she could to stop you, I'm sure of that. But nobody can stop you when you make up your mind to do something. You never think about anybody but yourself. You don't give a damn what I do unless it inconveniences you! Well, that's just too bad!'' Jayne was in a rage. "You'll just have to go home where you belong. You have no right to walk out on Daddy. He's never given you any reason to leave him. For God's sake, how could you have done this to him even if I'd agreed to your idea? How could you desert a man who's so devoted to you?''

"How could your precious Aunt Mary throw out Michael?'' Patricia's answer was a snarl. "She wants to be free. So do I. You don't understand. You and your damned youth! You don't understand what it's like to be trapped in a dull, pointless existence with a man you've never given a damn about. My God! I have more reason than Mary! At least Michael is one hell of a lover! I can tell you that! Your father is a bore in bed as well as out of it! I haven't even had *that* going for me!'' She halted abruptly, silenced by the expression on the faces of the women opposite: shock on the part of Jayne, horror in Mary's eyes as they heard this unexpected confession. Patricia lifted her chin and tried to bluff it through. ''All right. I admit it. I slept with Michael. His wife went off and left him for two months. He was lonely. So was I. Don't sit there in moral judgment, you two! Don't you see how desperate I was about my life? Don't you see why I have to stay here, Jayne? Why I have to leave your father? I don't say it was right of me to go to bed with my sister's husband, but she asked for it, leaving him alone so long. Anyway, I wasn't the only one. That Rae Spanner . . .''

''Shut up!'' Mary screamed. ''Shut up, Patricia! Don't use my absence as an excuse for what you did! And don't pretend you were so desperate for affection you went to bed with my husband! You're using that to justify leaving Stanley. Well, if you're so unhappy, leave him! But don't blame it on me and don't expect Jayne to feel obligated to get you out of a marriage you got into because you were as wanton and uncaring then as you are now!'' Mary's eyes blazed. ''Leave this child alone! Leave us both alone, Patricia, now and forever! Go home. Go tonight. I'll get you a ticket on the next flight to New York, and I never want to see or hear from you again!''

Patricia seemed to collapse. ''Mary, I don't blame you for hating me. What I did was terrible. It was just an involuntary thing. Michael and I . . .''

Mary interrupted her. ''I don't want to hear about Michael and you,'' she said coldly. ''I'm tired of your ugly games. Fed up with your selfishness. You have no heart, Patricia.'' She seemed suddenly exhausted. ''My God, I might even have forgiven you if you'd fallen in love with my husband. But you don't love him or anyone. You played on Michael's weakness, just as you're trying to play on Jayne's. You disgust me. I can't bear to look at you.''

Jayne sat mutely through the terrible exchange, unwilling to hear her mother's dreadful words. Now she looked pityingly at both women, the betrayed and the betrayer. What Patricia had done was unspeakable, but she hadn't done it alone. Michael had been just as guilty and the hurt Mary felt must be doubly crushing. Not enough the thing with Rae Spanner, whoever *she* was, but to know that your own sister . . . Jayne shuddered. ''Aunt Mary's right, Mother,'' she said. ''I think you should go back tonight. I'll call Daddy and tell him where to meet you.''

Patricia looked at her imploringly. ''Jayne, please don't do this to me. Let me stay with you. We'll work it out just fine. I won't be in your way. You can still see Terry as much as you like. I tried so hard, Jaynie. I even got you that job. I thought things would be wonderful for us. We'd be pals, roommates . . .''

''No, I can't do that. Mothers and daughters aren't pals. Not even under the best of circumstances. I can't live with you. Even before tonight I knew that.''

Defeated, Patricia began to weep. ''All right. Get the ticket. Call your father. Tell him you're sending me home to die.''

"You won't die," Jayne said. There was no emotion in her voice. "You'll make the best of things, the way everybody else does." She got to her feet. "Where's your round-trip ticket?"

"I don't have one. I only bought one-way."

She never had the slightest intention of going back, Mary realized. She planned this all along. Planned to stay here with Jayne. Or maybe with Michael if she could get him. She probably knew before she arrived that she'd have an affair with my husband. I wonder if she was foolish enough to think he'd leave me for her? A cynical smile crossed Mary's lips. It would have served her right. If she'd gotten Michael, who would have supported her then? It was ludicrous. Insane. She wished they'd all go away. All of them. She desperately wanted to be alone.

"Mother, I don't have enough money for your air fare. Do you have a credit card?"

"Never mind, Jayne," Mary said wearily. "Charge it to me. Just get her the hell out of here."

Chapter 23

WHEN THE LONG-AWAITED letter finally arrived, Christopher was almost afraid to open it. Let it say what I want it to, he silently prayed. Let it be a message from Mary telling me she can't live without me. Slowly, almost fearfully, he slit open the envelope and began to read. It was a long letter, and as he carefully absorbed every line, Christopher felt his heart beat faster, his spirits alternately rise and fall with each paragraph.

He frowned and shook his head sadly as Mary told him of the sudden death of Gail DeVries and her return from Hawaii with the colonel. Damn it, if only he'd been aboard to help. She shouldn't have had to go through that alone, with a brokenhearted old man to care for and comfort. It took him a minute to realize she'd been home for more than two weeks before she sat down to write to him. The idea hurt, even while he recognized his own foolishness. I'm like a lovesick schoolboy, Christopher thought, expecting Mary to think of nothing but me when she's had so much else on her mind.

He read on. So Jayne and Terry had moved in together after all.

> They've taken a room in a house on Powell Street. I won't deny that it worries me. Jayne is working at "my" radio station. Charlie Burke was kind enough to give her a job that will support them both while Terry looks for something to do. God knows what that will be. I can't imagine there'd be much demand for actors in San Francisco, but I must say Jayne seems quite happy and carefree. Oh, for the optimism of youth, my darling Christopher! She is so sure things will work out for them. I wish I were as serene about it. Terry is a sweet young man and Jayne truly loves him. I believe he loves her, too. But I confess that I still have more than nagging doubts about this "conversion." To me, Terry seems restless and somehow tentative in this new situation. Jayne doesn't see this side of him. I hope I'm wrong, but I can't shake that awful feeling

in my bones about the whole arrangement. Jayne's mother was furious
about it, of course, but not for any of the reasons you might imagine.
She met Terry only once, briefly, when the ship arrived, and she has no
idea of his past. My sister is, to put it mildly, a selfish woman. The idea
of her daughter "living in sin" did not bother her, but the failure of her
own plans did. She was prepared to live with Jaynie in San Francisco
and let that child support her! There was a terrible scene when she found
that was not to be.

Get on with it! Christopher found himself thinking. I don't have that much
interest in Jayne and Terry. It's *us* I want to know about. It was as though Mary
was working up to the part of the letter that mattered to him, as though she was
afraid to put down the words that were personal and precious to them both. They
came at last.

Dearest, I know you must think I'm stalling, going on about everything
except what is the most important thing in the world to me—my love
and desire for you. Perhaps I am. Not that my longing to be with you
has diminished one iota. If anything, it grows stronger each day and each
night. How I long to be in your arms, my beloved Christopher. How
lost I am without your tenderness and your laughter. And how fearful I
am that you will not understand what keeps me from flying straight to
you when I tell you that I'm free to do so.

Michael moved out more than a week ago. The break came not because
of you and me. He doesn't know about us. It was simply the culmination
of all the things I thought of before I took the cruise, and a few more
that happened after I returned. I don't lie, even to myself, when I admit
that knowing you made it even more difficult to go on with my marriage.
But I'm not the kind of woman who leaves one man for another, no
matter how much she adores the new-found love. I'd have stayed with
Michael, sweetheart, even though I'd yearn, every waking and dreaming
moment, for you. I'm of that idiotic, irrational breed of females who
can't shake a sense of obligation to an innocent person. But Michael is
a man I can no longer forgive, as I might a naïve and naughty child.
Forget the infidelities which occurred while I was away. Who am I to
cast stones? No, the breaking point came not through his unfaithfulness,
unspeakable as it was, but, as I suppose I always knew it would, through
his lies and his sense of unreality. There was no "big deal" as he told
me. There never will be. And I know, at last, that I cannot pretend, as
I have for so long. I am ashamed of his shallowness—and my own. The
important thing is the ability to live with myself, and to look up to the
person with whom I share my life.

That comes effortlessly with you, my darling. You are my dream, my
ideal, my longed-for lover. More than anything, I want to set the wheels
in motion, get a divorce and be Mrs. Christopher Andrews. If only it
were that simple. But I gave Michael my word I'd wait awhile before
making the final break. Why was I so silly? I can't answer that. A
hangover, I suppose, from fifteen years of reluctance to knock the props
out from under him. Pity for his distress. Or, perhaps, a leftover feeling
of guilt which I know, logically, is absurd and which, emotionally, I am

prey to. But I did it. I gave my word that he'd have a chance to "prove himself." He won't. I know that. I'm sure he'd admit it too, if he could bear to be honest with himself. There will come a time when I can freely and gladly write finis to the episode. A time when I can belong to you, my love, in the way you need a woman to belong. Stay close to me with your letters and your support, dearest. Give me, I beg you, time to tie up the loose ends and rid myself of the real and imagined encumbrances.

I want to come to you, Christopher. I know that in my heart. And in time I will also know it in my head. I love you, darling, and I pray that when the miraculous moment comes you'll be waiting for your adoring Mary.

He read the last part of the letter again. The part about them. For a long moment, he sat staring into space. She was the most honest, the most compassionate woman he'd ever known. The least he could do would be to give her the time she pleaded for. And then his desolation changed to something near anger. No. He wouldn't wait indefinitely while she allowed that spineless husband of hers to pretend he could set things right. She owes Michael nothing. She knows that. She's afraid. There was fear between every line. But afraid of what? Afraid of entrusting her life to someone else? Of giving up her work, her independence? Fearful of moving to the other side of the world with someone she'd known such a short time? The end of her marriage had come. She was free, yet she delayed, with flimsy excuses about giving her word and feeling pity. She believed what she said. He didn't doubt that. She simply didn't understand that the break had to be swift and clean. She didn't know she was afraid, she who seemed so strong and fearless in every other way.

There's only one answer, Christopher decided. I must force her to choose between me and the invalid excuses she's making to herself. I mustn't go on being understanding and patient. Not for her sake or mine. She needs a strong hand for her own good. It was a chance, a risky move, but he saw, as the doctor had said, that subconsciously Mary was asking him to make the decision for her. And the only way he could do that would be to threaten not to wait. He might lose her by pushing her. But he'd certainly lose her if he permitted an endless period of separation. Geography and time. Too much of one, too little of the other.

Before he weakened, he took out pen and paper and answered the cry for help from the woman he loved.

Charlie Burke sat by the bedside, holding the hand of his dying wife. This gaunt woman who looks older than her years bears no resemblance to the Tracey I married, he thought. She was so beautiful then, so lively and full of fun. What happened to us? Where did our paths separate? She was unhappy for so long, unwilling or unable to follow where I was determined to lead. Perhaps I failed her, had too little patience, expected too much. All the stories he'd ever read, all the sad tales he'd ever heard of men "outgrowing their wives" came back to him. Always they blamed the woman. She didn't keep up, socially or intellectually, with an increasingly successful husband. She wanted the marriage to stay as it was in the beginning when they were young and on the same level of interest and ambition. The man changed and his wife stood still. That's the way all the sad stories went. Including his.

Charlie felt a lump in his throat, a sense of remorse for the things he should have done. If only he'd tried harder to understand, to be more tolerant of her limitations, perhaps she'd not have turned to drink for courage or forgetfulness. He'd been reasonably faithful. The phrase struck him as ridiculous. There was no such thing as "reasonably faithful." It was as impossible as being "a little bit pregnant." You either were or you weren't. And of course he hadn't been. He'd had his brief affairs over the years, but he'd never gotten himself seriously involved. Still, he sought comfort elsewhere and that, meaningful or not, was infidelity and self-indulgence. All those excuses he made to himself about the lack of love at home, the disgust he felt at living with a drunk, the anger at her unwillingness to be a partner he was proud of, all those were a cop-out. He should have been strong enough, considerate enough to work on the problems with her. Maybe if she'd felt more important to him, none of this would have happened.

He leaned over and kissed her forehead. In a drugged sleep, Tracey felt and heard nothing. The doctor said it was just a matter of days. Perhaps hours.

"I did care, Tracey," he said softly. "Please forgive me."

Wearing only a pair of brief swim trunks, Michael lay on a plastic chaise in the backyard of his mother's small house in North Hollywood. He'd arrived a week before and since then he'd spent every day baking in the hot Southern California sun.

Carrie Morgan had not been particularly surprised to get the phone call saying he'd like to come down alone for a while. She knew what that meant. She was only amazed that Mary hadn't gotten fed up years ago. Michael wasn't a bad human being, Carrie thought as she looked out the kitchen window and saw him lying motionless in her "patio." He was simply too handsome, too spoiled. Somewhere he'd developed the belief that the world owed him a living, that he never really had to work for it as other people did.

His mother sighed. Much of what he was was her fault, she supposed. She'd adored him, pampered him, supported him as best she could on the little she had. She'd been too easy on him, too quick to forgive. It was a blessing that all her attention hadn't turned him into one of those queer fellows you saw everywhere, the ones they said got that way because their mothers held on too tightly to them, were too protective and possessive.

Well, Carrie thought, there'd been no danger of his being a mama's boy. Michael had been anything but. A hell-raiser, in fact, despite his sweet nature. A lusty woman-chaser from his high school days. What he hadn't been was a man prepared to be a husband. His first wife, Linda, couldn't take it. And now Mary, though she stuck much longer, had reached the same inevitable conclusion: Michael was a spoiled child. No real woman could live with that forever. The day had to come when Mary reached the end of the rope. Carrie Morgan always knew that. That's why she wasn't surprised when he came home. He had nowhere else to go when his wife threw him out. Not, of course, that he'd ever admit that was what happened.

He'd arrived, bag and baggage, with some transparent story about there being more opportunities for him in Los Angeles than there were in San Francisco.

"Mary and I agreed I should come down here and look the situation over," he said. "In fact, it was her suggestion. We're both fed up with the North."

"I see. I must say I'm surprised, though, Michael. I thought Mary loved her job. She's done so well at it."

He'd been very casual. "Oh, she likes the job well enough, but it doesn't matter that much to her. That is, she'd prefer to live here when I get this project of mine going. Of course, she can't chuck the radio show until I do. You see, I have a great idea for a men's boutique, Mother. This is the place for it. San Francisco's much too uptight for the kind of swinging thing I have in mind. I figured down here it would be much easier to get backing and open up a shop. I'll get one of those good locations on Rodeo, probably. All I need is financing, and there's plenty of loose movie and TV money around here. It shouldn't be too tough to get started."

"And then Mary will come down?"

"Of course. What else?"

Carrie didn't answer. It was all lies, as usual. Maybe not the part about wanting to open a shop. That was typical of Michael's daydreams. Probably he'd tried it and failed in San Francisco. He'd tried so many things. He was lying when he pretended that he and Mary weren't separated; that it was just a matter of time before she joined him. Michael's marriage was over. His mother was certain of that, even if he chose to lie about it. Maybe he can't admit it even to himself, she thought, the old protectiveness returning. How often can a man try and fail?

"Well that's fine," she'd said cheerfully. "It will be nice to have you around for a while, son."

He grinned. "Glad to be here, Carrie-baby. You're still the best cook in the world!"

But he'd done nothing about looking for his financing since he'd arrived. He'd spent every day working on his tan. He'd made no phone calls or set up any business appointments. Probably he had no idea where to start. And there'd been no word from Mary. If Michael called his wife, Carrie wasn't aware of it. Certainly Mary hadn't tried to reach him.

Mrs. Morgan wished he'd come out with the truth, admit his marriage was over, make some sensible plans for the future. He could live with her for a while. She had room and it didn't cost that much extra to feed him, but a forty-five-year-old man couldn't just go on forever living off his mother, doing nothing but lying in the sun.

He'll talk when he's ready, Carrie told herself. There's no use pushing him. I already know the story. I've lived through it before.

Rae Spanner opened her morning mail and a check for twenty-three thousand dollars fell out. There was a brief note inside.

Dear Rae,
I'm returning your loan and hope you won't mind my keeping out two thousand dollars for the time being. I'm going down to L.A. to get a boutique started and I'm temporarily a little short of cash. I'll mail you

the balance in a couple of weeks when the interested parties there get all the papers filled out. Thanks very much for everything.

Michael

So that's where he was. Los Angeles. Of course. Where else would he go except home to Mother? Rae already knew the Morgans had split up. Everybody knew. The grapevine in their circle worked well. Mary's cleaning woman told a friend who told her employer who told . . . well, it went on and on. Within twenty-four hours, the news was all over town.

The only thing people didn't know was where Michael had gone. Rae made a shrewd guess that Mary herself might not be sure. She probably knows about Michael and me, Rae thought. I figured that when she didn't call. Not that she's called any of her old friends, as far as I know. The woman who works for her says she's living alone. The sister's gone back to New York. The only person she ever sees is her niece. And Charlie Burke. Maybe there's something going on there. There've always been rumors about those two, and now that Tracey Burke is dying. . . . Could be Charlie Burke was the reason for the breakup. No. As low an opinion as Rae had of her own sex, she couldn't make herself believe that Mary was already planning to step into Tracey's shoes. Some other woman, maybe, but not Mary. She was much too square for that kind of macabre planning.

What difference did it make why they'd separated. The fact was, they had, and that, Rae thought, is very good for me. In her cold, calculating way, Rae Spanner was in love with Michael. Until now, she hadn't thought of him as a husband. She'd settled for what she could get, never dreaming he'd leave Mary. Probably he hadn't wanted to. The shoe certainly was on the other foot. But that didn't matter either. The end result was the same.

All I have to do is give him time, she decided. He'll get fed up with Los Angeles. He won't do any better there than he did here. Michael is a sweet toy to be owned and cared for. An expensive possession that gives pleasure. I'm better equipped to own him than either of his two previous wives. They probably expected him to be a provider, the head of the house. It's not a role Michael's cut out for. He wants the good things of life handed to him as a reward for his charm. I'm willing to accept that. And I'm the first one who can afford it.

She glanced at the return address on the back of the envelope. She'd wait a couple of weeks and then make a quick trip to Los Angeles. She'd take a bungalow at the Beverly Hills, arrange quiet little dinners at the Hermitage or Le Restaurant, rent a shiny Mercedes for Michael to drive.

She wouldn't rush it, but she wouldn't wait too long. Just long enough for him to get bored in his mother's house. Long enough for him to realize that nobody in Los Angeles was going to back one of his crazy schemes, but not so long that he'd have a chance to meet one of those young, blond, tanned girls who seemed to be turned out on a production line in Southern California.

I really want him, Rae said to herself. I'm not blind to his shortcomings. Or mine. I need an attractive husband who can be manipulated. I'm getting too old to cruise around. Michael suits me fine. And I'll be the best thing that could happen to him.

When the phone rang at five o'clock in the morning, Mary was startled into frightened wakefulness. A call at this hour could only be bad news. As she reached for the receiver she wondered whether something had happened to one of her parents. Or Jayne. Or Michael. But it was a controlled, sad-sounding Charlie on the line.

"I'm sorry to call you at this hour, Mary, but I had to talk to someone."

She was instantly alert. "Tracey?"

"Yes. She died three hours ago."

"Oh, Charlie, I'm so sorry! Where are you? Are you all right?"

"Yes, I'm all right. As all right as I can be. I'm in our apartment. They called me at two o'clock this morning and told me. I've been walking around ever since, thinking, remembering how she used to be. She was wonderful, Mary, long ago. You never really knew her when she was happy. She was funny, then. A pixie of a girl. You'd have liked her."

Mary swallowed hard. "I always liked her, Charlie. I always wished I could help her somehow."

"I know. You were her only friend. She liked you too." There was a little silence and then Charlie said, "I hate to ask you, but could you help me with the . . . the arrangements? I have to pick out something for her to wear, and go to the funeral home and make a lot of decisions. There's no one . . ."

"Of course, dear. I'll be right over. I can get there within the hour."

"Thanks. I really appreciate it. It's a hell of an imposition, I know."

"Are you crazy? You're my best friend! Make some coffee and I'll be there before it's through perking."

As she hurriedly dressed, Mary felt grief for the man. God knows it hadn't been the best marriage in the world. Tracey had been a burden to Charlie and herself for so many years, a difficult, frightened, often hostile woman. But she had her appealing side, too. It wasn't hard to imagine what she'd been like as a young woman. Nor to guess the remorse Charlie now felt because, like any human being, he'd been driven nearly out of his mind by her behavior. It was sad to think Tracey had no friends closer than her husband's business associate. Mary stopped, suddenly comparing her own situation with Tracey's. I have no close women friends either, she realized again. I've lived for my work and for Michael. We had our circle of acquaintances, mostly couples, but there's no one I can go to with my troubles. There's Charlie, of course, but he's a man, with a man's point of view. And Jayne, young enough to be the daughter I never had, can't really understand the way I feel. If I died tomorrow, someone as remote as I am to Tracey would pick out my burial clothes. No. Jayne would do that. And that doesn't matter to me anyway. What I desperately need is a woman to talk to now, someone who can understand and identify. I'd hoped it would be Gail DeVries. At one time I even thought I could be close to Rae Spanner, a woman of my generation. That's a sick joke if I ever heard one. Friend? Rae is as loyal to me as Patricia is.

Since her traumatic departure, Mary had tried not to think of her sister. After her initial outburst, she'd forced herself not to let her mind dwell on Michael and Patricia's behavior. It was too ugly to visualize. Mary's work at the radio station brought her into daily contact with all kinds of sordid things. The public loved "juicy stories"—wife beaters, rapists, child molesters, incest, all the sickness of the human race covered in the news reports. She accepted these things in an objective way, but when horror struck close to home it was too loathsome to think about. It was as though a protective curtain had dropped. She could think of Michael's affair with Rae with distress, but with some understanding. She could not accept the idea of her sister in Mary's own bed with her husband. The idea made her physically ill. It was more than hate she felt for Patricia, it was revulsion.

No time to think of that now, Mary told herself firmly. My friend needs me. He's all alone over there, waiting.

When he opened the door, she saw he'd been crying. She held out her arms and embraced him soothingly. Charlie quickly wiped away his tears.

"You must think I'm a hypocrite," he said. "God knows Tracey and I weren't a devoted couple anymore. I didn't even think I'd cry when she went."

"Of course you'll cry. Death is part of life, Charlie, and we all mourn. Maybe we're crying for ourselves. That's all right, too. You can't lose someone who's been a part of your life for so long without feeling emptiness and regret."

"Yes. I regret so much. I let her down, Mary. I stopped loving her when she needed to be loved."

"She couldn't accept love," Mary said softly. "She was too full of her own insecurities to give or take it. I don't mean to speak unkindly of the dead, my dear, but you did all you could. No one could have done more. Most people wouldn't have done as much. You stuck by her. She always had someone to lean on. She knew that."

"Thanks," he said. "Thanks for coming over at this ungodly hour. Thanks for everything, Mary."

"I'm your friend," she said again. "I always will be."

The next few hours were a nightmare. Mary had never done this before. Death has never touched me in this intimate way, she thought, as she went through Tracey's closet, picking out a dress and underwear, taking them to the funeral home, telling the attendant how Tracey wore her hair and what kind of makeup she preferred. This was more real and more terrible than a few weeks ago when Gail died. These awful duties were thrust on Gail's daughters. Her heart ached for them as she thought of their going through what she and Charlie were enduring now. He'd pulled himself together. Even at the gruesome moment when an unctuous undertaker ("funeral directors" they called themselves these days) led them into a big room full of caskets, Charlie did not break down again, though she saw his eyes widen in horror. She knew her reaction was the same and she felt her knees begin to tremble.

"I'll leave you alone to make your choice," the man said. "You'll find the price on the back of every card." He discreetly withdrew, leaving Mary and Charlie surrounded by the wood and metal reminders of death.

"Let's get this over fast," Charlie said, looking around at the vast, morbid display. "God! You don't go bargain hunting for this kind of thing!"

They made a quick selection and fled from the room, back to the hushed office of the man in charge. Mary's head swam at the dozens of questions that had to be answered, the hundreds of details Charlie managed to give. Tracey's vital statistics, the information for the death notice in the papers, the arrangements for pallbearers and limousines and cemetery plots and flowers. She recoiled, as Charlie did, from queries about "slumber rooms" and "viewing hours."

"None of that," he said. "I want to remember my wife alive. I want her friends to remember her that way, too. I want the services simple and as soon as possible. Tomorrow morning, in fact."

The director looked shocked. "But Mr. Burke, there'll only be time for a notice in the afternoon paper. And your friends . . ."

"My friends will understand."

"Of course." The man's voice dripped practiced sympathy. "At times like these, the bereaved . . ."

"Thank you very much," Charlie said. "Good-bye."

Outside, they stood for a moment on the steps of the funeral home, gratefully breathing the clean, fresh morning air, watching the city go about its business of the day.

"Life goes on," Charlie said. "Not an original thought but something to hold on to. I'm sure that man in there thinks I'm heartless."

Mary took his arm. "No one who knows you could ever think that," she said. "The others don't count."

He looked at her. "What counts in this world, Mary? Love, loyalty, friendship, work? Everything comes and goes so fast. We don't cherish what we have. We don't appreciate what we're given. We're always looking for something more. Some new person to stimulate us, some new challenge to be met, some compliment to bolster our egos. Hell, what's it all about anyway? What do *you* want in this world, my friend? What would make you happy?"

Mary was silent for a moment. "I'm not sure. Peace, I suppose. Serenity. A sense of what I'm meant to be. A contentment with what I am."

"You're too young for those kinds of wishes. They're the desires of the old."

She smiled. "These days I'm feeling old, Charlie. Very old and torn apart."

"Want to talk about it? Really talk, I mean."

How kind he was. Even now, at this terrible hour of his life, he cared about her happiness. She shook her head.

"Not now, dear. Not until this is over. Maybe not for a while after that. But one thing is for sure—when the moment comes to pour out my heart, you'll be the one I'll come to."

Chapter 24

HE NEVER UNDERSTOOD his wife, Stanley Richton had long since realized, but the woman who returned from San Francisco was even more baffling than the one who left. Since her abrupt arrival two weeks before, Patricia had been colder and more uncommunicative than ever. In answer to his questions about Jayne,

Patricia simply said, "You might as well forget your precious daughter. She's moved in with some no-good actor she met on the ship. She won't be back."

Stanley stared at her. "Is that all you have to say?"

"What more is there?"

"For God's sake, Patricia, you're talking about our only child! Who is this man? Where are they living? Are they going to get married?"

"I don't know any of those answers. She didn't choose to enlighten me. She couldn't wait to get me out of town, that's all."

"You don't even have her address?" Stanley was incredulous. "You just left, like that? Not knowing anything of this man? Not having any idea whether she's going to be all right? I can't believe it! What does Mary have to say about it?"

Patricia's anger flared. "Mary? Why should Mary give a damn? She's much too wrapped up in herself to worry about her family!"

He tried to be reasonable. "That doesn't sound like Mary. She's devoted to Jayne."

"And I suppose I'm not?"

"I didn't mean that. I simply meant it doesn't fit Mary's character to let anyone she loves get involved in something so important without knowing more details than you seem to have. Mary must know this man pretty well if they were all on the ship together. Does she think he's a solid citizen? Is she in favor of this move? You must have discussed it with her. What did Mary say when Jayne decided to stay in San Francisco?"

Patricia was furious. "Mary, Mary, Mary! I'm sick to death of Mary! You think she's so marvelous. Well, let me tell you, Mary is the most selfish, egotistical, overbearing woman you'll ever have the misfortune to meet! All she cares about is *her* life, *her* job, *her* freedom! She's thrown Michael out. What do you think of that, Stanley? Chucked out her husband of fifteen years! He's not good enough for her. Not successful or famous enough. Not perfect enough for St. Mary! Don't talk to me about Mary! I think she put Jayne up to this. I think she encouraged it to keep our daughter near her. She's nothing but a damned, frustrated, barren woman who'd like to own a child without the bother of having one!"

"I think you're crazy," Stanley said slowly. "I think there's a lot you're not telling me. What happened between you and your sister? What did you do to her, Patricia?"

"What did *I* do to *her*? Why don't you ask me what *she* did to *me*?"

"All right. What did she do? What really happened out there?"

Patricia's eyes blazed. "I've already told you. She fostered this indecent relationship between Jayne and Terry What's-his-name. Then she made it clear that I wasn't welcome to stay in her apartment even for another day. What a bitch! No appreciation that I'd been there cooking and cleaning for her husband! No thanks that I even got Jayne a job so she could stay in San Francisco! She's a phony. A grade-A, first-class Judas. If you want to blame someone for your daughter's behavior, I can tell you where to point the finger!"

He hardly heard the last words. "*You* got Jayne a job so she could stay in San Francisco? You mean, even before she returned you'd made plans for her to stay? I don't understand. Did she write and tell you she wanted to stay? Did you already know about this Terry person?"

"No. Of course I didn't know. Do you think Jayne ever confides in me?"

"Then, why . . .?"

"Why did I get her the job? Because I thought we'd all move out there. You and I and Jayne. I thought we could start a new life. Mary has good connections. I thought she could help you get started in a business. I love California. You would, too. I couldn't presume to get a job for *you*, but I thought at least if Jayne was working it would tide the three of us over until you got settled. I even put a deposit on a nice apartment for us. But no. Our self-centered daughter had other ideas. To hell with us, she said. And Mary went along with her. I've never been so disappointed, Stanley." Patricia forced herself to sound unutterably sad. "I'm heartbroken that Jayne is so cruel and Mary so conniving. They're alike, those two. All for themselves and the devil take the rest of us."

He was thoroughly bewildered by the elaborate story and by Patricia's sudden switch from an angry woman to a disenchanted one. He could believe his wife had made plans to change their lives without so much as consulting him. It was like her. And why not? He'd always gone along with anything she wanted to do, even consenting to the California trip when he knew it was far too long a visit with Michael. Michael, he thought suddenly. Somehow, some way, this has something to do with Michael. Patricia's bitterness toward Mary was deeper than his sister-in-law's support of Jayne, if, indeed, she had approved the girl's decision. Something more had happened between the sisters. Something irrevocable. He thought what it might be and immediately dismissed the idea. No, not that. Not even Patricia would be capable of that. He felt a terrible sadness knowing he'd lost his daughter, probably forever. He worried about her. She was still just a baby in his eyes. She'd always be his baby. She wasn't the way Patricia painted her. Jayne was a warm and loving girl. As Mary was a gentle and generous woman. What's the real story? Stanley wondered. God help me, I may never know.

The senior Farrs, when Stanley and Patricia went to have dinner with them a week later, were equally appalled by the events in San Francisco. John Farr flew into a patriarchal rage when he heard how Jayne was living, and his anger was directed at Patricia.

"You permitted that? What kind of mother are you? You allowed that young girl to announce she is going to live in sin and you just washed your hands of it and came home? I've never heard anything so monstrous! Why didn't you stop her?"

His fury had no effect on Patricia. "What should I have done, Father dear? Locked her in a room? Dragged her by the hair, screaming, onto the next airplane?"

"Yes, by God, if you had to! It was your duty to stop her!"

"My duty! What about your duty? Are you going to order Mary to reconcile with her husband? Are you going to permit her to turn out a man who's never done anything but cater to her wishes and devote his life to her? If you're feeling so moral, why don't you do something about your own child?"

Stanley intervened. "Patricia, don't be foolish. Your father is talking about a twenty-one-year-old girl, not a thirty-nine-year-old woman. I'm sure your parents are upset, but Mary and Michael are adults. It's quite a different thing."

"Oh, is it? I don't think so. They're fatuous about Jayne and they don't give that much of a damn about Mary, that's all. Whatever love was left over from my dear, dead brother was reserved for their grandchild. I don't have much use for Mary, but she was right about one thing—our parents hardly knew we were alive, they were so busy mourning their dead son. I haven't heard any screaming about the actions of their daughter! Not that I care, but you'd think they'd be just as meddlesome about that as they are about Jayne! Why am *I* a bad mother, subject to all kinds of criticism because my child doesn't obey me? Why don't they try giving orders to their own?''

Camille Farr spoke for the first time. "We're heartsick about Mary's problems,'' she said. "There's never been a divorce in our family. Don't you think the failure of any of our children makes us wonder how much responsibility we had for it? But you know Stanley's right, Patricia. Trying to control a grown woman like Mary is unrealistic. Being firm with Jayne is something else again. I think you and Stanley should go out there and bring her back. You can't allow her to ruin her life.''

Patricia snorted. "Don't be naïve, Mother. She's already done that. You don't think your wonderful granddaughter is a virgin princess, do you? I'm not going near her. Let her learn her lesson the hard way.''

"Patricia!'' John Farr was horrified. "You can't mean that! I'm seventy-seven years old. As old as the century. I know things have changed. I'm aware of what goes on these days, young people living together out of wedlock, having illegitimate children, all the terrible things we read about every day. But that doesn't mean I condone it for my granddaughter. Nor do I condone the attitude of a mother who won't even attempt to protect her own child!''

"So don't condone it.'' Patricia shrugged. "If you think you can do something about it, go out there and try. Or let Stanley go. I don't do well in the heavy-parent role. I won't degrade myself that way, begging or threatening. She's made her bed and I'm sure she's enjoying it!''

"You're an unnatural mother,'' John Farr said heavily.

Patricia didn't blink. "Probably,'' she said. "If you recall, I never wanted to be one in the first place.''

Jayne saw Mary every day at work, sometimes had a quick lunch with her and, in the next couple of weeks, dined with her aunt a few times. But even when the two women were alone, they did not discuss Patricia. It was as though they wanted to put out of their minds the sickening scene that had taken place in Mary's apartment. Only once did Mary obliquely refer to her sister. It was over lunch at Lehr's Greenhouse Restaurant.

"Have you been in touch with your parents?''

"I dropped them a note, giving them my address and home phone number. Daddy wrote. He's terribly upset, of course. So are the grandparents. I guess I'm really a 'fallen woman' in their eyes.''

Mary understood the implication. Jayne had heard nothing from her mother, of course. She wondered what version of the whole story Patricia had given Stanley and the Farrs. Whatever it was, Patricia painted herself as the helpless victim. Camille's letter had confirmed that.

"I had a note from Mother," Mary said. "She and Dad are distressed, you're right about that. I don't know which one of us is the bigger sinner in their eyes— you for living with Terry or me for living without Michael. Mother went on and on about the sanctity of marriage and the disgrace of divorce." Mary gave a little smile. "I never mentioned divorce in my letter to them, but somebody did. Three guesses who."

"Aunt Mary, I've never really been able to tell you how terrible I feel about . . ."

"Hush. I know. You needn't say it. Let's face it, Jaynie, I wasn't faithful either."

"But you'd never have had an affair with your own . . ."

Mary interrupted again. "Let's drop it, okay?"

"Sure. But you don't mind my asking if you've heard from Christopher, do you?"

"I had a wonderful letter from him. He still feels the same."

"And you?"

"I feel the same, too."

"What are you going to do about it? You've taken the first step, leaving Michael. *Will* you divorce him and go to Australia? That's what you want, isn't it? My God, Aunt Mary, you're entitled! If you had qualms before, you certainly can't have them now."

Mary took a deep breath. "It's not that simple. I want Christopher, but that's another big step. Living on the other side of the world. Making all new friends. Giving up the work I love. You don't do these things lightly when you're my age, Jayne. You want to be sure. Very sure. I told Christopher that when I answered his letter. I asked him to be patient with me, that I'd promised Michael I wouldn't rush into a divorce. I need time, honey."

"Time for what?" Jayne had the impatience of the very young. "You know what you and Christopher felt for each other wasn't just a shipboard romance. You really love each other. You're perfect together. You're liable to blow it, Aunt Mary, if you let too much time go by. No man's going to wait forever. Especially an attractive one like that. He's been pretty damned patient, if you ask me. How long can you keep him dangling?"

Disturbed as she was, Mary was amused. It was as though the roles were reversed and she was the younger, getting advice from a more experienced woman. "Haven't you ever heard about 'absence making the heart grow fonder'?"

Jayne made a face. "Haven't you ever heard about 'out of sight out of mind'? And while we're spouting clichés, what about 'A bird in the hand is worth two in the Australian bush'?"

Mary put up her hands in mock surrender. "All right, all right! Don't lecture me anymore! Let's talk about you, for a change. How are things?"

"Great. I love the job."

"I know that. I also know you're doing well. Everybody at the station is crazy about you. I mean how are things with you and Terry?"

"We're settling in. He's having a hard time finding something to do. There isn't all that much work for an aspiring actor in San Francisco, but he'll get there. It's just a matter of the right break."

The words made Mary uneasy. If she stayed with Terry, Jayne was heading for a replay of her aunt's life. The girl was smart. She could go places, Mary thought. And God help her, she could end up as I did: taking care of a man who was always waiting for the big break. Mary chose her words carefully. "Has Terry thought of some other kind of work? There's an awful lot of competition in the theater. Has he ever considered another field?"

Jayne seemed astonished. "Another field? No, I don't think so. Why should he? This is the one he wants."

"Wanting isn't always the same as getting, Jaynie. People have to be realistic, too. Especially when they're sharing their lives with someone else."

"We're doing all right." Jayne set her jaw stubbornly. "It's only been a couple of weeks and he's out every day, looking."

"I see. Well, fine. I'm sure the right thing will come along." Mary picked up the menu. "Shall we order? What looks good to you?"

"Cottage cheese and fruit salad, I think."

Mary frowned. "Why don't you have something more substantial? They have a nice little steak here."

"Too much in the middle of a day."

"A hamburger, then."

Jayne sounded slightly annoyed. "Aunt Mary, please don't act as though I'm living on peanut butter and spaghetti at home. Terry and I eat very well. You don't have to make sure I have a solid meal at noon."

"I'm sorry. I didn't mean to insult you."

Jayne looked apologetic. "No, I'm the one who's sorry. I shouldn't have snapped like that at nothing at all."

"I understand. I do it myself quite a lot these days. It seems to be an unsettled time for a lot of people. Charlie, for one."

"How's he doing? He seems like himself at work, but of course he would."

Mary thought for a long moment. "He's all right. He feels sad and regretful, the way people do after someone dies and you wish you'd been kinder and more tolerant. But Charlie's an honest man. He wouldn't pretend to be destroyed by Tracey's death. That would be hypocritical. His life with her was hell for a lot of years. This is a release for him, as well as Tracey, terrible as it may sound. But that's the truth. She wasn't an easy woman to live with. It wasn't all her fault, but she really didn't try to help herself. She just gave in to her weaknesses and didn't put up a fight. I don't think she wanted to, in the end."

"You're spending a lot of time with him, aren't you?"

The unsubtle question made Mary smile. "We have dinner almost every night. But he's not a part of my indecision about Christopher, if that's what you're thinking. Once upon a time, I might have fallen in love with Charlie. We're well suited. Compatible. Yes, I could have visualized a life with Charlie once, but that was 1976 B.C."

"B.C.?"

"Before Christopher. What else? Come on, let's order."

"Right. One more question before we do, though. Where is Michael?"

"Los Angeles. He sent me a card. He's staying with his mother." Mary's eyes grew sad. "And, as usual, he's very enthusiastic about a new deal."

The positive attitude Jayne assumed when she spoke about her life with Terry was, in fact, an outward show of bravado designed to fool not only Mary but herself. Inside, little claws of doubt had begun to scratch at her confidence, making her unwillingly wonder whether she'd done the right thing in choosing to live with this sensitive but unpredictable young man. Characteristically, Jayne tried to ignore them. The subtle changes in their relationship were, she told herself, only those of any two people living under the same roof and coping with the mundane details of everyday life. A room and a hot plate in San Francisco did not provide the romantic ambiance of a cruise ship. The vacation atmosphere was over, and the reality of daily living, from shopping for groceries to watching TV in the evening, was an understandable letdown from the glamour of life at sea or the excitement of exotic ports.

If Terry seems different to me, she thought, I must seem different to him, too. The young woman who went sleepily to work every morning and returned tired and disheveled from fighting her way through the supermarket every evening was a different Jayne than that carefree creature who'd seduced him aboard the *Prince of Wales*. Terry was still sweet and gentle with her, but in only a few weeks of their new arrangement, passion had dwindled. They still made love, but the wonder and exaltation he'd felt on the ship no longer were there. It was, she sometimes felt, as though he had a duty toward her, a duty he seemed almost reluctant to assume.

He was moody these days, too. Often he sat for hours, simply staring into space, not speaking. She tried to find out what was wrong, but Terry always gave the same answer, one she could not fully accept.

"I'm depressed about finding work," he said. "This isn't an actor's town. Los Angeles or New York, maybe, but not here."

She tried to kid him out of it. "Come on! What do you mean, 'not here'? Of course there's work here! There's theater all over the place!"

"Sure. Most of it road-company stuff from New York. You don't think Debbie Reynolds hired local talent to do the revival of *Annie Get Your Gun* at the Orpheum, do you? Or maybe you think I could break into Vincent Gardenia's role in *Plaza Suite* down at the Curran?"

"No, honey, but there must be other things. Local companies. Or how about television?"

"Television?"

"Listen, the best years of my life were spent watching shows with a San Francisco setting! How about *Ironsides*? Or *The Streets of San Francisco*?"

He smiled patiently. "Jayne, dear, those shows are off the air now. Besides, they might have filmed them here but they didn't cast them here, except for extras, I suppose. No, I ought to do what I originally planned—go to New York, where at least there's opportunity."

I, she thought. Not *we*.

"Terry, are you sorry we got into this? We can get out of it in twenty minutes. We're not married. If you're unhappy living with me, please say so."

He looked genuinely alarmed. "No! You know I'm not sorry! My God, Jayne, don't even mention such a thing! You changed my life! I need you!" He calmed down. "I know I'm not easy to live with. Try to remember that it's a whole new world for me. The kind I've always wanted. I just get in the dumps, thinking I'll never make it in the theater. I adore you. You know that. I'm low, but not because of you. Believe that. Please believe that."

"Of course I believe it," she said soothingly. "So stop worrying, will you? It's only been a few weeks. Nobody falls into a job that fast. Not," she laughed, "unless they have pushy relatives like mine."

"I've done terrible things to you," Terry said soberly. "I've alienated you from your family. I've put the financial burden on you. Maybe you're the one who's unhappy, Jayne. If you are, tell me. I can take it. God knows I don't want to make you miserable."

"Do I look miserable? Sweetie, things are going to be fine. It's just an adjustment period we're going through. After all, neither one of us ever lived with . . ." She stopped, embarrassed. "I mean, not like this."

He knew she was thinking of his time with Paul. Does she sense that's what's really wrong? Terry wondered. Does she guess that I can't get him out of my mind—that I miss Paul and can't stop wanting to see him again? Not that I'm going to. That's over and done with. Ancient history. I have this wonderful girl and I'm going to be a man for her sake.

"Hey," Terry said, "what are we being so gloomy about? Tell you what. Let's go out for dinner tonight. What would you like? Chinese? Japanese? Italian? Russian? How about Indonesian? We could pretend we're back in Bali! San Francisco may not be heaven for actors but it's paradise for eaters. Come on, luv, what do you say?"

She got into the spirit of adventure. It was so good to hear Terry sounding enthusiastic and excited again.

"I choose Mexican," she said. "I'd kill for a good paella!"

"You've got it. How about Casa de Cristal on Post Street? They're famous for paella. The atmosphere is madly south of the border. And the price is right."

They had a wonderful evening and when they came home they made love almost as they had on the ship. Jayne was happy. I'm really in love with him, she thought. I'm as committed as though I were his wife. These moods of his will pass as soon as he's working and feeling like an equal partner. We did the right thing. It was meant to be. I'm making a vow to stop feeling so uncertain. I'm going to give my doubts a swift kick in the pants. We're young. We have our whole lives ahead of us. Yes, it's going to be fine once we get over the rough spots. Maybe we'll even decide to get married and have babies. She snuggled closer to a half-asleep Terry.

"I'm crazy for you," she said.

He reached for her hand. "You're an angel to put up with me."

Jayne smiled. "Naturally. Who else would bother with such a charming son of satan?"

But the vague sense of impending disaster sometimes came back to haunt her even while she pretended everything was perfect, as she did over lunch with Mary. Her love for Terry made her determined to succeed with him. Her pride would not allow her to fail. We'll show them, Jayne thought. We'll show Aunt Mary we knew what we were doing. We'll show my folks we're mature, modern people. Someday we'll even prove to Paul, whoever he is, that Terry never needed him at all. She didn't want to think of Russell King and his young bride. Her ex-lover had nothing to do with this. She hoped he was happy with his damned rich Pamela. As happy as she was with her decent, wonderful young man.

Chapter 25

ON THE ELEVENTH of May, Mary's phone rang as she was preparing for bed.

"Happy three-month anniversary," the voice said.

She couldn't believe it. "Christopher? Is it really you?"

The familiar laugh sounded as though it came from around the corner. "Who else are you having a three-month anniversary with? On February tenth, 1977, we had our first dinner. I think that rates a celebration phone call, don't you?"

She was so flabbergasted she said, inanely, "But it's May *eleventh*."

"Not in Australia."

"You're in *Australia*?"

"Sweetheart, if I were in San Francisco, I'd be pounding on your door. How are you, my love?"

"I . . . I'm fine. Stunned but fine. Oh, Christopher, it's wonderful to hear you! I miss you so much!"

"Me, too." He became very serious. "I had your letter a week ago, Mary. I've written five answers and torn them up. Words on paper won't do. At least, not for me. That's really why I'm calling." He paused. "I can't accept the future on your terms, darling."

"Can't accept . . ." Her heart sank. "You mean you've changed your mind about us?"

"No. Only about the indefinite time limit. I've practically memorized that letter. You say you love me, you want to be with me. Yet you beg me to wait, God knows how long, until you fulfill that pitiful promise to your husband. You say you hope I'll understand. I do understand, dearest. I understand you're frightened of making another mistake, that you still can't bear to hurt Michael, that you're trying to come to terms with the kind of selfishness you have trouble accepting. I understand all that, Mary, but I won't take it for an answer. I'm not going to wait. To hell with those doubts and promises you're clinging to. I've tried to be patient, but I've been wrong. If we love each other, we belong together. And soon. We're not children, sweetheart. I don't have years to hang around, waiting for the moment that suits everybody else. Not even the one that suits you."

She took a deep breath. "I know. I know you're right, but . . ."

"No 'buts.' I've gone along with you as far as I can. You're strong, dearest, but I'm stronger. You need that, Mary, if you're ever going to be the happy woman you should be."

She began to cry softly, half with joy, half with doubt. She tried to answer, but no words came. Christopher's voice became more gentle.

"Let's set the date," he said. "Mary? Are you listening?"

She swallowed hard. "Of course I am. Oh, Christopher, don't you think I want to know the very hour, the very minute I'll be with you? If only I could!"

"Why can't you? Is there anything in your life that can't be settled three months from now? I don't know where you Americans go for those quick divorces, but I'm sure you can find out. You can give your old friend Charlie plenty of notice, get rid of your apartment, do whatever you have to do. I don't give a bloody damn what plans you have to change or what promises you have to break. You belong to me and I'm coming to get you. We'll be married in San Francisco on August tenth. Six months from the day we met." He chuckled lovingly. "See what a romantic I am?" Then his tone became firm again. "I'm serious about this, Mary. Completely serious. I love you and I don't want to live without you, but somebody's got to make this decision and make it stick. It's no good going on this way. We'll lose each other if we do. If that has to happen, better now than a year or two years from now. I know I'm taking a desperate chance. Frankly, it scares hell out of me, but I have to do it. Shall I come for you on August tenth, my love, or shall we pretend it was all a wonderful dream and end it now?"

She was silent for a moment, gripping the receiver so tightly she felt her palm grow wet. He was right. It was unfair to ask him to wait for some unknown, far-off date. And unthinkable that she might lose him.

"Come for me," she said, gently. "I'll be waiting."

She heard his sigh of relief. "Thank God. You'll never regret it, dearest. I swear to you, we're going to be the most indecently happy people on this earth."

"Yes. We will. I feel happy already. Relieved. Free. Like a weight's been lifted. Oh, darling, if only you were here, holding me. You don't know how I've wanted you! Every single night since . . ."

"Stop it or I won't be able to wait until August!" He sounded boyishly eager. "Good God, woman, you drive me crazy even over the telephone!"

Mary laughed. "Wait until I get my hands on you! Make the days go fast, Christopher. Make them race by!"

"I'll give orders to the clock. Sweetheart, if I could only tell you . . ."

It was her turn to interrupt. "You don't have to. I know. And we have the rest of our lives to say it over and over—I love you, I love you, I love you."

After she hung up, Mary went to her jewelry case and took out the ring Christopher had bought for her in Hong Kong. She hadn't worn it since she left the ship. Now, for the first time in fifteen years, she took off her gold wedding band. Making a little vow to herself, she slipped the jade and diamond ring on the third finger of her left hand. She couldn't wear it in public yet. But three months from now . . . Smiling, she went to bed and fell asleep holding Christopher's ring next to her heart.

When she woke the next morning she thought for an instant that it had been a dream: Christopher's call and her promise to marry him in August. But his ring on her finger told her it was true. She had agreed to get her life in order and be ready to start a new one in three months. The thought overwhelmed her. The romantic in her felt nothing but soaring joy at the prospect; the practical side of her nature chilled her with the realization of the people she'd have to abandon, the utter upheaval she'd create. Was any love strong enough to weather such drastic change? Yes, Mary told herself as she slipped Michael's wedding band back on her finger. Ours is. The next few weeks would be agony, but they'd pass. She was frightened by the thought of burning all her bridges. Christopher knew that. But she'd do it. It was her life and she wasn't going to waste it through timidity. She felt strong and sure of herself. Thank you, God, she said silently. If Christopher had written, she might not have been convinced.

But the sound of his voice, the reminder of all the strong and wonderful things he was, brought her to full awareness of what she would not, could not let go.

Methodically, she mentally listed what she must do: tell Michael she wanted an immediate divorce and that she planned to remarry; tell Charlie she was leaving to move to Australia with a man she'd never mentioned to him; tell her parents all those things. Involuntarily, she shuddered. They'd be so shocked. None of them knew of Christopher's existence. Only Jayne knew. Jayne. In a strange way, she worried more about leaving her niece than any of the others. That was silly. The girl was young and self-sufficient. She'd chosen her life and she'd handle it. For that matter, they'd all handle things. She wasn't indispensable to any of them. They wouldn't die without her. The knowledge, so long denied, came as a relief. It was true, as she'd told Christopher, that she felt she'd shed a terrible weight. There'd be adventure and excitement ahead. And most of all, the kind of emotional security she'd never known in thirty-nine uneasy years.

Terry knew it was only a matter of time until it happened. Every day for a week, he'd had lunch in the little coffee shop where he used to regularly meet Paul for a hamburger. Every day he waited, hoping Paul would come in from his nearby office and there'd be an ''accidental'' meeting with his former lover. Terry loathed himself for it, but his desire to see the man was an obsession. He told himself that he only wanted to know, once and for all, that he was over his attraction. If he saw Paul again, heard about his marriage, made himself accept the fact that both their lives had changed, he'd be all right. Then he could give Jayne his wholehearted devotion. He could settle down and be content. Jayne deserved that. She didn't deserve this half-man he was, pretending to be happy with her and always thinking of the one person for whom he felt such longing.

He couldn't bring himself to call Paul. The sense of rejection was still there, as was the hurt and disappointment that had caused him to leave on the cruise without telling anyone where he was going. I ran, Terry thought. I was too cowardly to stay around and hear about his marriage. But I can take it now. I can face him and congratulate him and put him out of my mind forever. Until I do that, no matter how much I care for Jayne, I can't belong to her or anyone. Maybe, he thought hopefully, when I see him again it won't even bother me. Maybe I'll feel nothing, or even wonder why I was so bound to this selfish, conniving, ambitious man. I want it to be that way. I want to see him once more so I'll know what a fool I was, and how lucky I am to have something so much stronger and better.

But on the day Paul finally appeared, Terry knew instantly that his feelings had not changed. The sight of the tall, handsome figure coming in the door plunged him into despair, even as his pulse quickened. I wish we were still together, Terry thought. I wish he was coming to meet me.

For an instant, Terry thought of hiding behind the menu, sneaking out, if possible, unrecognized. Instead, he half rose from his seat in the booth where he was toying with a cup of coffee and gestured toward the man who was looking for a place to sit. The amazed, delighted look on Paul's face as he hurried toward him set Terry's heart racing.

''Terry! For God's sake, where have you been? I've been trying to find you for months!'' Paul slid into the seat opposite him. ''You look great! Jesus, I can't tell you how glad I am to see you!''

Terry tried to sound calm. ''I've been away. Took a long cruise to the South Pacific. How are you, Paul? How's the marriage going?''

''It isn't going. In fact, it never went. I didn't do it, Terry. I couldn't.''

''You didn't do it? Why not? I thought it was so important to you, to your career. What made you change your mind?''

''You.'' And then as though he'd said the most matter-of-fact thing in the world, he said, ''Have you ordered? Shall we get that out of the way before we talk? You want the usual?''

Terry nodded and sat silently as Paul gave their order to the waitress. He was in a state of shock, incapable of speech. Paul lit a cigarette and leaned back, looking at him intently.

''You,'' he repeated as though there'd been no interruption. ''Selfishly, I wanted to go through with the marriage. It made sense. She's a nice woman. She understood why I was marrying her. She even offered, finally, to have you share the apartment with us, if that would make me happy. A *ménage à trois*, I think it's called. But I knew you wouldn't do that. Hell, I wouldn't do it either. Two weeks after you and I split up, I told her I couldn't marry her. I said you were the only person I wanted to be with. I looked for you to tell you, Terry, but you'd vanished from the face of the earth.''

Terry still said nothing. Paul changed his plans because of me, he thought. He really couldn't let me go. He felt an overpowering wave of happiness. Paul cares more for me than for his ambitions. And I care more for him than anything in the world.

''Hello, there.'' Paul was smiling. ''You look like you've seen a ghost.''

Terry managed to return the smile. ''I think I have. You were dead to me, Paul. It's as though you've returned from the grave.''

''I'm very much alive, thank you. More so now than I've been for months. Can you forgive me for what I almost did, Terry? Can you understand how a person can almost rationalize himself into anything?''

''Yes.'' The thought of Jayne came into his head. ''I can understand.''

Paul sounded humble. ''Then we can forget all this ever happened? We can take up where we left off? I'm still in my apartment. *Our* apartment. It's all there waiting for you.'' He stopped, troubled by something in Terry's face. ''Unless you don't want to come back. Maybe you've changed your mind about us. Maybe there's someone else.''

Terry looked tortured. ''There is and there isn't. I have something to tell you, Paul.''

At the end of the recital, Paul said gravely, ''She sounds like a nice girl.''

''She is. A wonderful girl.''

''Does she want you to marry her?''

''No. That is, we haven't discussed that. It's been on a live-together basis. But she loves me, Paul.''

''And you?''

''I love her too.'' Terry pushed his untouched lunch aside. ''Who am I kidding? I'm fond of her. Devoted to her. Grateful to her. But that isn't love. I've used her, Paul. I thought she could make me forget you. I wanted desperately to forget you, but I couldn't. My God, why do you think I've been haunting this place for a week, hoping you'd come in? I couldn't bring myself to call you. I prayed I'd know, when I saw you, that I was through with you and that whole part of my life.'' He gave a mirthless laugh. ''But I knew what I'd always feel where you're concerned. I just had to confirm it, that's all.''

''And now?''

Terry looked miserable. ''I've got to tell her, of course. She'll pretend it's all right. She'll be casual about it. She puts on a very civilized façade, very liberal and liberated, but inside she's going to hurt. She'll feel rejected, Paul, and that's a lousy feeling. Take it from one who knows.''

''I deserved that.''

''I didn't say it to punish you. You did what you thought was best, just as I did. It's a damned shame we hurt two decent women in the process.''

''You've grown up a lot in a few months, Terry.''

''Yes. And I have Jayne to thank for it.''

Paul frowned. ''Maybe if I met her . . .''

''No. I don't want you to fight my battles for me. I'll tell her in my own way, in my own time.''

The earlier roles were reversed. Now it was Terry who was the stronger and more decisive.

''How much time?'' Paul asked.

''I don't know. A few days, a few weeks. I can't hit her between the eyes with this. I have to lead up to it, prepare her. Not that she isn't half prepared as it is. She's bright. She knows I'm restless and different than I was on the ship. I've pretended it was because of the no-job situation, but I don't think I'm fooling her. Life in a one-room, hot-plate pad is quite a change from a cruise ship. A big change for both of us. Jayne accepts it a lot more easily than I do, and I'm sure she thinks my surroundings are part of my depression.''

''Where are you living?''

Terry told him.

''My God, Terry, that's a dump!''

''I'm damned lucky to have any place, especially when I'm living on her salary.'' His face took on that stricken look again. ''God, I hate to hurt her this way! She's been mother, mistress, friend, and now . . .''

''You won't do her a favor by prolonging it, Terry.''

''I know. But I won't rush home today and pack. I want to be sure she's going to be okay before I walk out.''

''But we can see each other in the meantime?''

Terry hesitated. ''I'd like to say no, but I can't. Yes, we'll see each other.''

''And you'll come back to stay as soon as you can?''

Terry nodded. ''Yes. It's where I belong.''

Michael came onto the patio where his mother was sitting and threw himself onto his favorite chaise. He looked troubled.

''Who was on the phone?'' Carrie asked.

''It was Mary.''

"Oh? How is she?"

"I don't know. She just said she had to talk to me and that she'd fly down day after tomorrow for the day. I offered to go up there but she said no, it made more sense for her to come here."

"I see. She didn't say what she wanted to talk about?"

He shook his head. "No, but I can guess. I'm sure she wants a divorce."

Carrie looked surprised. "So soon? It's only been a month since you left. You told me last week it was a trial separation."

"I thought it was, but something in her voice tells me Mary doesn't want to go on this way. Oh, she was sweet. Almost too sweet. She sounded the way people do when they're talking to somebody who's terminally ill."

"Michael! What a dreadful thing to say!"

"All the same it's true, Mother. She wouldn't come flying down here unless it was terribly important. Something she had to tell me to my face. And what could it be except that she wants to end our marriage?"

"Perhaps not, dear. It could have something to do with her job. Maybe they want to transfer her somewhere. Or perhaps it's about the apartment. When is your lease up?"

Michael smiled. "Nice try, Mom, but you know damned well if it was something like that we could discuss it on the phone. This is the first word I've had from her in a month. And probably the last."

Carrie's heart went out to her son. She shared his instinct about this sudden visit from Mary. But why? Couldn't she wait, as she said she would? What was the rush? It was true that Michael had made no progress at all since he'd been in Los Angeles. Carrie had been meaning to speak to him about that. She'd planned to tell him he should go back to San Francisco and get a job, any job, to prove to his wife that he was really trying to be self-reliant. If only he'd be honest with her and with himself, Mary might well take him back. It was this dissembling, this bluffing that drove a woman crazy. She could accept a man as he was if he was manly enough to face facts, admit his shortcomings and say, I'm never going to be a world-beater, but I love you and I hope you can love me as I am.

But Michael had not been able to do that. He thought it mattered so much to Mary whether he was successful. He was incapable of understanding that it was not achievement that counted but mature recognition of one's abilities and limitations, and, above all, a willingness to face facts. Women are so much better at that, Carrie thought. They can overlook so many things if a man has enough genuine bigness to admit that he's merely average. But Michael couldn't bear to think of himself as average. He lived on dreams, saw a tycoon in the mirror when he shaved, lied to himself and everyone. He'd done it all his life. He was doing it still, pretending he was setting up meetings in Los Angeles with important bankers, talking flamboyantly about his plans and his future.

He's so dear, Carrie thought. So genuinely affectionate and kind. But there is this flaw. I've always known it. So have his wives. And none of us has been able to make Michael realize that we could love him for what he is if only he'd stop trying to make fools of us.

"If it's true," Carrie said gently, "if it's true that Mary's coming to discuss a divorce, what will you say to her, Michael?"

For the first time, he put up no defense. "What can I say, Mother? Oh, I'll try to talk her out of it. God knows I don't want it, but if she really wants to be free I won't stand in her way. She's been patient longer than most women would be. She's believed all my dreams, or at least pretended to. She's been loyal and uncomplaining. But she knows nothing will ever change. She's going on forty and if she ever has a chance to start over, this is it. I don't blame her. I blame myself for being a spoiled, selfish, blind bastard who never carried his share. Mary's too good for that. She deserves someone who'll look after her, make her feel like a wife instead of a caretaker." He paused. "Maybe she's already found him. Charlie Burke's wife died, you know. He's always been in love with Mary. Maybe now . . . I don't know."

Carrie wanted to cry. She'd never heard him sound so defeated. His unhappiness was her own. He was her child and it was painful to hear him admit failure. How miserable he was under that confident exterior. She longed to put her arms around him and soothe him as she had when he was a little boy, tell him things would be all right, that this was only temporary trouble which would pass. But it wasn't. She knew that. Mary was too self-sufficient for him. Her protectiveness had been the worst thing for Michael. She'd asked nothing of him. Consequently it became easier and easier for him to think nothing was required. Not that Mary didn't mean well. She'd loved her husband once, believed in him, was willing to give him time to find himself. But time had run out. Forty is the age of evaluation, Carrie thought. One suddenly realizes that half, or more than half, of one's life is gone. It's a frightening time when one takes stock and grows frantic about the future.

"Maybe you're jumping to conclusions, Michael." She tried to sound optimistic. "You don't really know why Mary's coming to see you."

"I know. You do, too, dear. Don't hate her for it, Mother. She has a right to a better life. She's paid her dues."

"Don't say that! You've been a wonderful husband in so many ways. You've adored her, been proud of her. You haven't envied her success as so many men would have. You haven't given her material things, perhaps, but you've been more than generous in other ways. You've been as loyal and uncomplaining as Mary has. It can't have been easy for you, either."

He smiled. "Bless your heart. The mother tiger to the end, aren't you? Your baby is never to blame. But I *am* to blame. I took the easy way. Loved her? Yes, I still do. Proud? Not really. Subconsciously, I've always been jealous of her, I suppose. I liked the comforts her success brought but I hated the fact that I didn't supply them. I didn't know how. I still don't."

"But you could, Michael! If you'd set your sights a little lower, ask Mary to let you take over the responsibility for both your lives, show her you can be depended on. You can start over, both of you. Maybe more modestly than the scale on which you live now, but you could make it. You could move here, the two of you. You'd get a job and . . ."

"Don't," he said. "Don't grasp at straws. You know it wouldn't work. People can't go backwards. The thirty-year-old man Mary married is no different than the forty-five-year-old one she now wants to leave. I was notoriously unsuccessful then and I haven't done one damned thing to change it since. I never will,

Mother. I'm not fooling myself. I'd hate a grubby life and Mary would hate it more. We're spoiled, both of us, and we're too old to start over like a couple of ambitious kids. Mary has her career and all the pleasant things that go with it. Even if she hasn't found someone else, you don't think she could give that up, do you? I couldn't ask her to, even if I could hold out some kind of promise of total rehabilitation, which I can't. No, it's over. I'm as sure of that as I am of my own name. I've seen this marriage disintegrating and I haven't done one damn thing to save it. I didn't want to look at it squarely because I kept hoping there were enough good times to hold it together. But I knew this would come. I knew it when Mary went away without me. I knew it in the way she kissed me good-bye. Hell, I denied it to myself. Like I deny everything I don't want to think about. But I *knew,* Mother. If I hadn't, I wouldn't have done some of the things I did while she was gone.''

She didn't ask what those things were. Women, she supposed. But the problem was deeper than unfaithfulness. It was, she now saw, an ongoing cancer whose roots lay somewhere in the years behind them. Carrie sighed.

"You always have a home here, Michael.''

"Thanks, dear. I know that. But I can't start living off you again. You're at the age where I should think about taking care of you, not the other way around.''

"I'm all right. You don't have to worry about me.''

"Of course I don't. But I also don't have to burden you with a forty-five-year-old dependent.''

"What will you do?''

"I'm not sure. But I won't kill myself, I promise you that.''

"Such a thought never entered my mind!''

Michael smiled again. "Hasn't it? Funny. It has mine, more than once. But I'm too much of a coward.''

"Stop talking like that! You're still young. Even if you lose Mary it's not the end of life. Maybe it will be the beginning. Maybe it's for the best.'' Carrie was terribly agitated. "Why are we speculating like this? We don't even know what's in Mary's mind.''

"Right. We're crossing bridges. We'll just have to wait and see. Cheer up, old girl. The thunderbolt has not yet struck. Maybe it won't.'' He patted her hand. "And if it does, I'll survive. Everybody survives.''

Carrie nodded. She wants to believe, Michael thought. Christ, so do I. But I don't. I don't believe in anything. He thought of the letter in his pocket. Rae Spanner was coming down to Los Angeles next week. He knew what that meant. She'd heard of the separation and she was moving in on him. Well, let her. He'd had enough of love. Love was for kids. Love was starry-eyed and romantic, looking toward the future, building and growing. Love was giving and sharing. I've been through that. Twice. With a remarkable lack of success. I'm as jaded and cynical as Rae, who's probably ready for a convenient arrangement in her declining years. Fair enough. So am I.

Mary knocked on Charlie Burke's office door and opened it. "May I come in?''

He looked up, surprised. "Sure. Got a problem?''

"I'm afraid so. Several." She took the chair opposite his desk. "Charlie I have to talk to you about something personal and professional."

"Okay. Want to go out to lunch?"

She shook her head. "No, I'd rather say this here. Maybe I can be less emotional."

Bad news. The thought flashed across his mind as though it were a news bulletin. "Shoot," he said.

"I . . . I'm giving notice, Charlie. I'd like to leave in three months. Sooner, if you can find a replacement." Mary's hands were clenched tightly in her lap. "I've been happy doing this job. I love it. I love you. I haven't been a great star, but it's been a wonderful experience and I'll miss it."

He managed to hide his surprise under the professional attitude he knew she wanted. "What's wrong? You have a better offer?"

"In a way. I'm going to be married in August. To a man I met on the ship. His name is Christopher Andrews. He lives in Australia. I'll be moving there."

This time, Charlie made no effort to conceal his amazement. "Married? Australia? Mary, what the hell are you talking about?"

"I'm flying to Los Angeles day after tomorrow to tell Michael. I wasn't sure until last night. I kept putting off the decision. It seemed so selfish. But then Christopher called. He won't wait for me forever, and he's right. He won't sit around while I try to come to terms with my conscience. It's August or never, and I can't lose him, Charlie. He's everything I've ever dreamed of. For one thing, I finally know what love is. It came late, but it came swiftly and surely and with such joy, such utter confidence. You'll like him. He's kind and gentle but he has the strength I need. I'm going to be happy with him, happy in a way I'd given up hoping I could be."

Charlie was nearly speechless. He stared at her for a moment and then he said, "Are you really sure, Mary? You hardly know the man. It's such a big step, giving up the work you like, moving so far away. I know it's over with you and Michael. I understand that. But aren't you rushing into something without enough thought? How much do you know about this Christopher? What if he isn't what you think? People get pretty dazzled by a shipboard romance, you know. Especially when they're not happy at home."

Her voice was quiet and contained. "I know. I've thought of all those things. I've thought of nothing else since he left the ship in Japan. Even when I came back, I was still hoping things could be different with Michael and me. I thought his dreams had come true, that he'd be established and I'd rediscover the feelings I'd lost. But it wasn't true, Charlie. It was more disappointment, more lies, more of everything that's made me so unhappy for years. I can't spend the rest of my life that way, not even for Michael, well-intentioned as he is. I want more than patience that was turning to condescension. I want a whole man."

"I understand that," Charlie said again. "But I don't want to see you make another mistake. Can't you spend some time with this man before you marry him? Can't you get to know him a little?"

"How? We're thousands of miles apart. Besides, I do know him. I know him better than I've ever known anyone. We're into each other's heads, Charlie, as well as into each other's hearts. We're not children. It's not just physical, it's a feeling that's hard to describe. He makes me laugh, he makes me comfortable. It's as though I've been close to him forever.'' She rose and began to pace the floor. ''You know me, dear friend. It took something powerful to give me courage for this. I've been frightened. Scared of the future. Terrified of hurting other people. Feeling like a damned heel about Michael. But I know I can't waste more weeks and years feeling half alive. And that's all I've been, Charlie. Half alive. Until I met Christopher. And then it was as though something inside me that had been dormant suddenly sprang into full bloom. I felt . . . I *feel* like a woman. Not dependable, understanding, disciplined good old Mary. A woman. With a man to share her life and make her proud and thankful. Can you understand that? Can you believe I know how right this is? Would I tear up my life and other people's lives if I weren't utterly, irrevocably certain?''

''No,'' Charlie said softly, ''no, you wouldn't. Funny. I sensed you'd met someone on the ship. In one of your tapes, the interview with the captain, I thought you were having some kind of romance with him. I had the wrong guy but the right instinct. Love was in your voice, Mary. But it was love for somebody else.'' He got up and took her hand. ''I'm happy for you, dear. I know what it must have taken to get to this decision. I'm going to miss you. Not only in the job but in my life.'' He stopped. No need to tell her what his own hopes had been. She didn't need that remorse on top of everything else. He supposed she knew he was in love with her. It didn't matter now. She'd found the one she wanted. ''We'll have dinner tonight, okay?''

Mary nodded, struggling to hold back tears of relief.

''You'll tell me all about Christopher. He must be one hell of a guy.''

''He is.'' The note of pride crept back into her voice, and with it Charlie felt his pain return. To hide it, he said, ''We should start thinking about your replacement, I suppose. I know the station would like to keep the show going. Any ideas?''

''A crazy one. I thought about it this morning.''

''Crazy like what?''

''Jayne. I know it sounds ridiculous, Charlie, but I could train her in three months. She's bright and ambitious and articulate. If you'd let her work with me around the clock I know I could teach her the techniques. She already has the interest in people that's so vital to this job. Would you give her a chance? You gave me one and it worked. Please. Will you?''

''I don't know, Mary. My God, she's thoroughly green! At least you'd worked around radio for a while. She's a baby. I'm not sure . . .''

''She's only a couple of years younger than I was, and a hundred years older in terms of experience and worldliness than I was at her age. I have a good feeling about it. Not just because she's my niece. She has vitality and enthusiasm and so much strength it almost scares me. I see myself in her. I also see a kind of compassion that's important. She cares about others. Maybe too much. But that vulnerability and caring will help her identify with the kind of people we like to have on the show. Real people. Unknown people.'' Mary's eyes were shining. ''Take a gamble, Charlie. You've never been afraid of a risk. And we have three months to see whether it will work.''

He laughed. ''You always could sell me anything. Okay, we'll give it six weeks. By that time we'll know whether Jayne can handle it. If she can't, we'll have to start looking for someone else. Unless," he said wistfully, "you change your mind in the meantime."

Mary shook her head. "I won't. It feels too right to me. And Jayne in my job feels right too. She'll be terrific."

"Let's hope, for your sake as well as hers. You and your damned tidy mind, Mary! You want to know she's earning a good living, don't you?"

"That's part of it. I admit I'd rest easier if I knew she was better off financially. But I wouldn't suggest it if I didn't think she'd be great. I swear it, Charlie. You know I have a sense of obligation to you, too."

"Fair enough. You want to tell her or should I?"

"You tell her about the job, but not until I've told her my plans. You're the first one after Christopher to know about those. I haven't spoken to Michael yet, as you know." Mary looked unhappy. "That's going to be the hardest part. I dread it. What will happen to him?"

"He'll manage, Mary. Everybody has to live with disappointment. Michael's no different than the rest of us."

Her eyes told him she knew what he meant, but all she said was, "You're the best man who ever lived, Charlie Burke."

"No," he said. "Only second best."

Chapter 26

ON THE SHORT flight back from Los Angeles to San Francisco, Mary sat dry-eyed and thoughtful, remembering the scene with Michael. Amazing how calm they'd both been, almost businesslike about this momentous event in their lives. The final parting was strangely anticlimactic, as though they both knew the actual decision had been made the night Michael left the apartment and neither believed they'd ever be together again, despite the words and promises exchanged.

Michael expected this, she thought. He hardly reacted when I told him about Christopher. All he'd said was, "Oh? Somehow I thought it would be Charlie. I hope he's a good man, Mary. You deserve one."

His passive acceptance troubled Mary more than a wild outburst of rage would have. This was a different Michael. He'd never been like this. This defeated, quiet, numb person was someone she didn't know. It was as though he didn't care, as though he already felt alone and the divorce was a mere formality. I'm worried about him, she realized. I don't know what I expected. Some kind of fight, I suppose. At least a strong protest or justifiable accusations about my own unfaithfulness, which, in a sense, matched his own. I expected emotion of some kind and there was none. Only this air of having given up on everything. That was worse than the anger she'd anticipated. If he'd been furious, she'd have felt less guilty. His resignation was the worst kind of mute accusation, the way one felt when one spanked a helpless puppy or sent a naughty child to bed without his supper.

In her mind, she relived the brief hour, a drama played out against the mundane background of the little house in which Michael grew up. Carrie had greeted her with reserve and Michael had given her only a quick kiss on the cheek before they retired to the patio, where his mother left them alone. Mary felt nervous and awkward as she said, almost formally, "You're looking well, Michael."

"Thanks. I've been soaking up a lot of sun."

A small silence fell between them before Mary said, "I don't quite know how to say this. I've done a lot of thinking in the past month. I know I promised to give it time, but . . ."

He interrupted as though he wanted to spare her. "I know. It's not a temporary separation. You want a divorce, don't you?"

She couldn't look at him. "Yes. Yes, I'm afraid I do." She managed to raise her eyes. "I met someone while I was away, Michael. He wants me to marry him."

"I see." There was no change in his expression as he made the remark about Charlie, no visible emotion when she said she was leaving the country. He simply listened, nodding as he might have nodded if she'd been talking about two other people. Mary found herself protesting that Christopher really wasn't the cause of the final break. As though she sought reassurance, she said, "We haven't been happy for a long while, Michael. This would have come in any case. I'm not right for you. You need someone who'll lean on you, make you feel nine feet tall. I've never been able to do that for you. I suppose it's not in me to have faith in anyone except myself."

The minute she said those last words she realized how ridiculous they sounded. Obviously she had faith in Christopher. She stopped, confused, aware she'd been babbling like an apologetic idiot. It was, almost for the first time in fifteen years, Michael who was in charge of the situation.

"It's all right," he said. "I understand. Funny, before you came I was prepared to try to talk you out of it. Now I know I can't. I know I shouldn't. You're generous to say you're not right for me, Mary. In a way that's true. But don't spare me. I'm more wrong for you than you are for me. I'm not going to stand in your way. I love you. I wish it were all different. But it isn't different. It won't ever be. You have a lot of years ahead. I can't ask you to spend them with a cripple."

"You're not a cripple! Michael, you're wonderful! You only need the right woman to bring out the strength in you."

He shook his head. "No. But never mind. That's not your problem. Your problems are over and I'm glad, for your sake, they have a happy ending. I mean that, Mary. I really do. God knows I'm miserable at the thought of losing you. But I'm not surprised. I lost you a long time ago. I wouldn't want you back because you felt sorry for me. I couldn't live with that. I've already had a glimpse of it. Pity instead of love in your eyes. Patience instead of passion when we made love. I hated it. I pretended it would pass when one of my wild schemes came through, but it wouldn't have, not even if I'd gotten lucky. You might have stuck it out if I'd gotten on my feet, but it wouldn't have been any good. We were too far apart, Mary dear. The gap already was too wide."

She blinked hard, trying to hold back the tears. "I didn't know you realized. God, how you must hate me!"

"Never. I could never hate you."

They sat in silence for another long moment. The sun was warm on Mary's face but inside she felt ice cold. How can I do this? she wondered. How can I walk away from more than a third of my life? If only he'd be bitter, outraged, accusatory. I could take that more easily than I can handle this selfless understanding, which is the worst punishment of all.

Michael watched her as though he was drinking in every detail to remember forever. Keep up the good work, old boy, he told himself. You've burdened her too long. This is your moment of atonement. At least you can set her free with some semblance of dignity, some gesture of independence.

"If you hadn't come to me," he lied, "I'd have come to you. I want out, too. We don't like loose ends, Mary. It's better this way. Better for both of us. I gather you'd like to move on this right away. So would I. I suppose Mexico is the most convenient place."

"Yes." She was surprised how small her voice sounded. "I suppose it is. I can fly down and . . ."

"Let me do that. I have nothing but time. I'll get working on it from here. Should be easy to arrange. There are no children involved, no property. I imagine the whole thing could be done in a couple of weeks."

"You needn't. I mean, I'm the one . . ."

"I'll take care of it. Call it my last gift to you. God knows I've given you few enough." He smiled gently. "And don't offer to pay for it, please. I can afford it. I owe you much more than that."

"No, you don't! You don't owe me anything, Michael. We had some wonderful years. I only wish . . ."

"Of course you do. So do I. But we're grownups, not romantic kids." He got to his feet. "You'd better go now, dear. I'll be in touch."

She hardly remembered leaving. She wanted to kiss him good-bye but she dared not. I've already done that, she thought sadly. I kissed him good-bye the day I sailed. Instead, she took his hand in both of hers and looked up at him, seeing again how handsome he was and how basically good.

"Good-bye, Michael. Thank you for everything."

He didn't answer, but with his free hand he reached out and gently stroked her hair.

Jayne called Terry from the office late the following morning. "Mind if I desert you this evening? Aunt Mary's asked me to have dinner. Says she has some girl talk."

"No, of course not. Go right ahead."

"There's leftover meat loaf in the fridge."

"Fine, but maybe I'll go out and grab a hamburger. You going to be late?"

"I don't think so, I'm going home with her straight from work. We'll probably have an early meal. I should be home by ten at the latest."

"Have a good time. Give Mary my love."

"Thanks, darling. I love you."

Terry winced. "Me, too." He hung up the phone feeling like dirt. She loved him and trusted him and he didn't deserve either. He'd told her nothing about seeing Paul again. He couldn't bring himself to do it, couldn't stand the pain she'd try to hide. But he'd have to tell her soon. It was only a few days, but already Paul was getting impatient. Well, at least they could have a few hours together this evening. Paul left work at five and Jayne wouldn't be back before ten. If only I didn't feel as I do, Terry thought. If only I had strength to call Paul now and say I never want to see him again. Instead, he slowly dialed his friend's private office number and said, "You free for dinner tonight?"

"I'm glad we're having an evening," Jayne said. She snuggled up on Mary's couch. "We haven't had much of a chance to talk lately."

"I know. How's Terry?"

"Okay. A little down in the dumps about nothing happening. He's starting to make the rounds of the advertising agencies now, hoping he can pick up some modeling jobs. Magazine ads or television commercials. He hates not earning any money. I keep telling him not to worry, I'll give him a chance to make up for it, but it bothers him."

Mary frowned. "And it doesn't bother you?"

"No. Only that it makes him unhappy. Otherwise, what difference does it make who earns the bread?"

"Yours is a different generation," Mary said. "I wish I could have felt that way." She took a sip of her drink. "Jaynie, I went to see Michael yesterday. He's going to get a Mexican divorce. And I'm going to marry Christopher in August."

There. It was out. The simple, bald facts that spanned years and could be told in an instant. Jayne raised her glass in salute.

"Well hooray! God bless! That is good news!" She quieted as she thought of the ramifications. "How did Michael take it?"

"Almost too well. He's being wonderful. I felt like a dog."

"Don't," Jayne said. "You did your best. You both did. When things don't work, there's no point in prolonging the agony. Tell me, what finally made you do it?"

Mary told her about the call from Christopher. "I knew in that instant I couldn't lose him. He forced my hand. And I'm glad he did. But I'm sad about Michael. He seems so . . . I don't know, mechanical. As though the life has gone out of him."

"He'll be okay, Aunt Mary. It's no good being with someone who wants to be somewhere else. Michael knows that."

"I'm sure. But right now it's pretty hard on both of us."

"It's going to be hard on everybody having you way off in Australia. I'm going to miss you. And Charlie must be desolate! Have you told him?"

"Yes." Mary bit her lip. She'd love to tell Jayne what was in store for her, but it would be better if the girl heard it from Charlie. It would seem more like a recognition from her employer than a favor from her aunt. "Charlie was great. As always."

"Super guy."

"He is that. God, I'm going to miss all of you! It terrifies me, this move. It's so far away."

"Not really. You can jet back in a few hours if you get homesick, which I doubt. And you'll be with Christopher.'' Jayne laughed. '' 'Mary Andrews.' Well, we'll just have to try to rise above that, won't we?''

Mary joined in her laughter. ''Thank God Mother didn't spell it 'Merry'! Oh, Jayne you are so good for me! You're always so *up*. It's a joy to be with you. I couldn't love you more if you were my own daughter.''

''Thank you. I feel the same.'' She paused. ''Speaking of which, have you told the New York contingent what's happening?''

''No, not yet. I don't know whether to call or write or fly back for a weekend. I should see Mother and Dad before I go. They're getting on, and I'd hate to leave the country without seeing them again.''

As though by mutual consent they did not mention Patricia. Jayne fiddled with her drink, absently stirring the ice cubes. Finally she said, ''I have some news for you, too. How do you fancy 'Wales' as a boy's name, as in 'Prince of Wales'? Or if it's a girl, do you think 'Singapore' is too outrageous?''

Mary stared at her. ''Are you saying what I think you are?''

''Yep. Pregnant. Found out yesterday. About two months along. Which pinpoints it to the first time Terry and I slept together in Singapore. Wouldn't you know I'd pick that fertile moment to be caught off guard? I quit the pills after the fling with our purser friend. Figured nothing was going to happen with Terry. Well, obviously it did.''

Mary felt sick. Pregnant by this young man? By this erratic free spirit with no job and no prospects? God! She tried to pull herself together.

''Does Terry know?''

''Not yet. I'm waiting for the appropriate moment. I have a feeling it's going to come as quite a shock. Heterosexual sex was enough of a surprise for the poor darling. I don't know how he'll react to fatherhood.'' Jayne seemed almost blithe about it. ''I expect he'll adjust. He once said he liked children. Not,'' she added somewhat balefully, ''that we were discussing them in this context. But actually, I think he'll be pleased.''

''So you'll be getting married.''

''I don't know. I suppose so.''

''You *suppose* so.''

''Well, yes, I'm sure we will. For the sake of the baby. I don't think it's fair to the kid otherwise.''

''How about fair to yourself? We may live in an enlightened society, Jayne, but unwed mothers are still viewed with some degree of disapproval by most people!'' Mary forgot her good intentions. ''Besides, it wouldn't sit well with the listeners. If you're going to take over my job, you'll be in the public eye. Pregnant's okay if you're married, but with that kind of show it would be impossible for an unmarried mother to gain acceptance from the audience. Maybe even from the station.''

Jayne sat bolt upright. ''If I'm going to do *what*?''

Mary sighed. ''Damn! I wasn't supposed to tell you. Charlie's decided to try you out in my spot. We both think that with three months' training you could take over the show.''

''You're kidding! I couldn't possibly, Aunt Mary! I'd love to, of course! Lord, what a break! But I have no experience. I don't know how to interview. I've never spoken a word on the air. It's crazy!''

"No, it isn't. You can do it. I know you can. We'd work hard together and you'd be great. You *will* be great. But, darling, you now understand why you must marry Terry. Unless . . . That is, are you sure you want to have this child? Things are unsettled with Terry. His career, I mean. And now with this new job coming up for you . . . it might be more sensible . . ."

"I want the baby, Aunt Mary. I'll have it with or without Terry, though I'm sure it will be with. God, it's all marvelous! If I make good, I'll get more money in the new job. Not as much as you, of course, but enough to live in a better place and afford a nurse for little what's-its-name. Isn't it *wild* how things work out?" She gave a whoop of delight. "I can even be grateful that it's radio and not TV! Nobody will see me bulge on the air!" She jumped up and threw her arms around Mary. "Oh, thank you, darling! Thanks for the chance. I'll try like hell to make you proud of me!"

Mary hugged her. "I'll always be proud of you, Jayne. I may think you're foolish sometimes. Headstrong, even. But I know whatever you do is honest."

Jayne backed off and looked at her affectionately. "I know you have doubts about Terry. You're right to. But we're going to be okay. Especially now." She gave Mary a little smile. "One thing's for sure—this is the appropriate time to tell him the big news. Crazy, but I have a hunch that child's going to be happy to hear he's going to have a child of his own."

Child, Mary thought uneasily. Yes, Terry is a child. Another Michael with even greater handicaps. Dear Lord, I hope Jayne can handle it. Please let her be right about Terry's reaction. Let her be right about him all the way. God forgive me, I wish she wouldn't marry him. Even more, I wish she wouldn't have this baby.

"Jaynie, what if . . . That is, suppose Terry doesn't want to be married? I mean, I hope you're right about his reaction, but what if you're wrong?"

"I told you, Aunt Mary. I'll have the baby anyway."

"Darling you can't do that. Raise a child alone? It's too much to tackle."

Jayne shook her head. "Thousands of women are doing it these days and it seems to work out fine. If Terry doesn't want to marry me, I won't force him. Remember me? I'm the product of the 'had to get married' syndrome. Do you think I'd want a child to grow up knowing what I've always known—that I was the reason two unwilling people had to live together? I said I'd marry because it was better for the baby. Well, it is, of course. Better to be legitimate and have two parents, but only if the parents want you and the marriage. Otherwise, the kid is better off with one who really loves it."

"But even so, Jayne, there's your career to consider."

"If my 'career' is shot down because I'm a mother without a husband, then we're still living in the Dark Ages, Aunt Mary. I don't really believe it would be. I don't think that audience of yours is as square as you believe it is. Or that the station is, either. But if they are, then I wouldn't know how to communicate with them anyway. I wouldn't be the right person for the job."

"You really feel strongly about this," Mary said slowly. "You really want this baby that much."

"Yes, I do. I'm not anti-abortion when it's a necessary thing, emotionally or physically. I'd have one if I hated the idea of a baby. But I'm hung up on the idea that this pregnancy was meant to be. For Terry, maybe, because I think it's important to him. But mostly for myself. I guess I'd like to give a child the kind of maternal love I never felt. I'd like it to feel safe and warm and protected. Maybe that's kinky. I know it sounds out of character for me, but it's what I feel. Just knowing I'm carrying a life is suddenly the most important thing in the world.'' Jayne laughed. ''Good Lord, listen to me! Talk about sounding holier-than-thou! But I mean it. I really do. Look, I'm still positive Terry's going to be happy about this. The whole conversation is academic. Why are we borrowing trouble?''

She's right, Mary thought. This is a different world. To be a single parent is not the oddity or the disgrace it once was. There are even organizations made up of unmarried mothers and fathers. I've interviewed some of them and respected them. Why am I so strait-laced when the subject hits home? Still, I can't help what 1 feel. Even knowing how wrong it was for Patricia and Stanley to marry, I'd like Jayne's baby to have its father's name, as she did. Even if they divorced after it was born, the child deserves that much of a break.

''Okay, kiddo,'' she said. ''You know what's right for you. And you know Terry much better than I do. Sorry to be a nag. For whatever it's worth, I'm with you.''

''It's going to be fine,'' Jayne said again. ''Not to worry. And I am thrilled about the job, even if it smacks of nepotism.''

''You mustn't think that! Charlie wouldn't give you this chance if he didn't think you were up to it!''

Jayne smiled. ''Come on. You and I know who suggested it. But I don't care. Hell, for years guys have been marrying the boss's daughter or inheriting the family business! Why shouldn't a woman try to step into her aunt's shoes if she's lucky enough to get the chance?''

It was after midnight when Terry fumblingly let himself into their room. He was very drunk and he hoped Jayne was asleep. He didn't want to talk to her tonight. Tomorrow, he thought. Tomorrow is Saturday. I'll tell her I can't stay any longer. Got to be free. Got to give her a break, too. Tomorrow. Time to talk. Saturday. S-Day. Separation Day. Surprise Day. Sad Day. Tears came to his eyes. Poor Jayne. Poor Terry, you lousy son of a bitch. He lurched and fell heavily against the dresser. The noise awakened Jayne, who'd fallen asleep waiting for him. By the dim light of the night-table lamp he saw her sit up and look at him.

''Hi,'' he said. ''Sorry I weakened you.'' He grinned foolishly. ''I mean sorry I wakened you.''

''That's okay. What time is it?''

''I dunno. Ten-thirty, maybe?''

Jayne glanced at the clock. ''Would you like to try for two hours later?'' There was no anger in her voice. ''You must have had a hell of a hamburger.''

''Yeah. Ran into somebody . . . some people I used to know. Had a couple drinks. Sorry. Meant to be here. Mished . . . missed the deadline.''

He's bombed out of his skull, Jayne realized. Odd. Terry almost never had more than a couple of drinks. Well, what the hell. He had a right. "No problem," she said. "You have fun?"

"Not very much. You?"

She hesitated. This was not the moment. Not when he was unable to think clearly. Tomorrow. Tomorrow they'd have all day to talk and plan.

"It was interesting," Jayne said. "Aunt Mary sends you her love."

Terry didn't answer.

Jayne turned on her side. "Take a couple of aspirins and get some sleep, you disreputable character. I'll fix you a bloody mary in the morning."

From eleven-thirty until noon, Mary sat staring at the telephone, trying to get up enough courage to make the call. What am I? she asked herself. A baby? I'm going into my fortieth year. I've been independent for more than half my life. I've been a wife and a working woman and I've asked nothing of my parents since the day I left home. And now I'm afraid to call and tell them what's happened. Afraid of their disapproval, dreading their lack of understanding. Why do I need those things from them at this stage of my life? Why have I always needed them and felt so angry and wounded when they weren't forthcoming? My God, I can be so superior about everybody else's problems, so damned judgmental about women like Patricia and Rae Spanner. So much the curbstone analyst in seeing how poor, pathetic Tracey Burke went wrong. I can even be righteous about Jayne's brave, foolish stand. But when it comes to my own feelings I behave like a child. I sit here wishing my mother and father would reassure me, tell me they love me, that they want only my happiness.

It was crazy. She'd been nervous and unhappy when she had to face Michael, but there'd been this overwhelming sense of relief when it was over. She wouldn't be relieved when she talked to Camille and John Farr. She'd feel as she'd always felt, inadequate, a failure, someone who never measured up to their expectations. What do they want from me? Mary wondered. Nothing. Nothing from either of their girls. They want nothing and they give nothing. It's been that way forever. It will never change.

She heard a church clock strike twelve. She took a deep breath and dialed the New York number, hearing the phone ring three times before her mother said hello.

"Hi, Mother, it's Mary."

"Well! For heaven's sake! Is something wrong?"

"No. That is, I hope you won't think it's wrong." Damn. There it was. The first words out of her mouth were half apologetic, half pleading. "What I mean is," Mary said quickly, "I have some happy news and I wanted to share it right away with you and Dad."

There was a pause. "I hope you're going to tell us you've come to your senses and gone back to your husband."

"No. In fact, just the opposite. Michael and I are getting a divorce."

"I see. And that's supposed to be good news? That your marriage is over? You know how we feel about vows, Mary. Michael may not be the great, glamorous man you seem to dream about, but he's always been devoted to you. You've never appreciated the fact you have a loyal husband."

If only you knew, Mary thought bitterly. If only you knew that my "loyal husband" and your other daughter . . . To hell with it. "I always appreciated him, Mother, but the marriage didn't work. We're not right for each other. We don't communicate. We're not in touch."

Camille snorted. "What kind of new-fangled nonsense is that? 'Communicate.' 'In touch.' You're *married,* Mary. It's hard to think of any situation in which two people are more 'in touch,' as you put it. What's the matter with you? Do you think, at your age, you're going to find some millionaire? You've always been above yourself. Patricia told us how you interfered in Jayne's life. Your father and I are worried sick about that child. Have you seen her? Is she still with that young man? Can't you do something about it?"

God help me, I could strangle her, Mary thought. She's delivered her lecture on my ingratitude and reminded me of my age. Now she wants to talk about the only subject that interests her: her granddaughter.

"Jayne seems to be doing very well," Mary said. Wait until you hear her latest development, she thought. Then you'll really have something to worry about. "I had dinner with her last night. She's going to take over my job at the radio station."

It took a few seconds for Camille to understand. "Your job? What are you talking about now? You're leaving your *job,* too?"

"Yes. In August. I'm going to be married to a man who lives in Australia. I met him on the cruise. I'm very much in love with him, Mother, and he loves me. I've told Michael. He was sweet about it. He's going to Mexico for the divorce."

"Sweet about it!" Camille's voice was almost a scream. "He just gave in to you, like that?"

"Yes. He loves me enough to understand."

"I suppose that means I don't."

"I didn't say that, Mother, but I hope you do. Both of you."

"Well, I don't, and neither will your father. You meet a man on a boat and as a result you divorce your husband and decide to marry some stranger. How could anyone understand that? You must be crazy, Mary! Australia? Do you intend to live there?"

"Of course. That's Christopher's home. That's his name, by the way, Christopher Andrews. He's an antique dealer. A widower with grown sons. You'd like him, Mother. He's substantial and mature and highly respected."

Camille seemed to hear nothing of that. "Moving to Australia? You can't do that! What about Jayne? You'd go thousands of miles away and leave that child in a strange city? What are you thinking of?"

All the instinct for survival rose in Mary. "I'm thinking that Jayne is a grown woman," she said. "And I'm remembering that I'm not her mother. Why hasn't her mother or her father come out here to 'rescue' her if that's the most important thing to you? Why is it up to me?"

"Because you encouraged this dreadful situation with that boy! Patricia told us. And you wouldn't even let your sister stay long enough to do something about it. You threw her out. She had no money to stay there and try to talk some sense into Jayne. But you're there. You started this, Mary, and now you're going to walk away from it. Selfish! Utterly selfish! You always have been, all your life! No wonder you couldn't hold a husband. No wonder your own sister is bitter about you. You took her child away from her and now when it's no longer convenient you're prepared to abdicate the responsibility!''

Mary was speechless. Finally she said, "Is that what you think of me, Mother? Is that the way you think it is?''

"Well, isn't it? What else can I think?''

"You might think of me. Just once. Just for a moment. You might want me to be happy. You might accept, even if you can't understand. I've begged all my life for your love, yours and Daddy's, but you've never given it. Even now, you don't care about me. You're only concerned with your grandchild. And you only believe the story you wish to believe . . . the lies Patricia told you. All right, if that's the way it is, I accept it. I'm sorry you're angry with me. Sorry you're disappointed. But I can't help that. If you don't choose to give me your support, there's nothing I can do about that, either. Except to say I wish it were different between us. I wish we . . . " Mary stopped. In a moment she would be in tears. How terrible it all was. How sad that there was such an impossible chasm between them. Her anger gave way to pity. She can't help it, Mary thought. She is what she is. Her standards are as rigid as her mind is narrow. She's my mother and it's impossible for me to reach her.

"I'm sure you'll be hearing from Jayne soon," Mary went on, quietly. "Try not to worry about her. She's enormously self-sufficient. She'll be all right. I know that's hard for you to believe, but it's true.''

"I can't think what your father will say when he hears all this.''

"You'll explain it, I'm sure. I'll be in touch before I leave. Good-bye, Mother. Kiss Dad for me.''

"Tell Jayne to call us collect, will you, please?''

"Yes, Mother. I'll tell her.''

She hung up and sat still for a long while. Then she put her head down on her arms and began to weep, for all that had never been, all that she'd longed for, all that would never happen. I wanted them to be proud of me and they never were, she thought. I wanted them to be standing by when I needed them. I wanted them to know I needed them, but I was afraid to say so. Afraid of being turned aside. Always hoping things would change and never daring to try to change them. I even hoped today. Foolish, childish hopes that they'd feel joy for me. And they don't care. Insensitive, small-minded people. I shouldn't give a damn what they think. But I do. I give such a damn I'd crawl on my hands and knees if only they'd pat my head and say they love me.

She reached for a handkerchief and dried her eyes. So be it. The last tie was severed. She had no one now. No one but Christopher. A stranger, her mother had called him. Dearest stranger. He knew her better than the people who'd given her birth.

Chapter 27

THE SOUND OF the running shower forced Terry to open his eyes and then quickly close them against the bright light of morning. He hadn't had many hangovers, but this one made up for a dozen missed. He lay quietly, waiting for his head to stop pounding and his stomach to settle down to only moderate nausea. It had been a terrible night. Paul had been impossible, raging at him to make up his goddamn mind, calling him a weakling and a coward and worse things, accusing him of playing games and demanding, finally, that Terry tell Jayne it was over and that he was leaving her to return to Paul.

Terry shuddered. People were always pushing him. His mother had pushed him, molded him into the little slave she wanted. Jayne had pushed him, gently, into an experience that dazzled and confused him and led, eventually, to this unfamiliar life he was trying to lead. And now Paul, pushing him into making the move he wanted but was reluctant to confess to the young woman who believed he was happy with her.

Well, he'd promised Paul he'd do it today and he would. If only he didn't feel so lousy this morning. It was going to be bad enough without adding physical discomfort to the emotional agony. He opened his eyes and saw Jayne standing beside the bed looking down on him with affectionate, amused sympathy.

"Poor old thing," she said. "You do feel like death, don't you? I'll bet even your hair hurts."

Terry groaned. "Everything hurts." He sat up gingerly. "You're right. My hair does hurt. So do my teeth and my toenails."

Jayne laughed and handed him a glass. "Here's the bloody mary I promised you. Go on. Drink it. It will help."

He took a sip and made a face. "Yuk. It tastes like medicine."

"It *is* medicine, you dope. Drink it down, have a shower and I'll do us some breakfast."

"I couldn't eat."

"Sure you can. You'd better. You'll need your strength for some big news."

Terry looked up at her, surprised. "Big news? What kind?"

"Good kind. Come on. Up and at 'em. Into the shower while I repair to what is laughingly known as our kitchenette." She was in a marvelous mood. "By the time you've washed away last night's sins, I'll be ready to feed you."

He stood under the shower for a long while, letting the soothing hot water run down his body, finally easing the downpour to cool and then cold. He felt a little better. The drink and the shower revived him. His body felt as though it was coming back to life, but his mind was in a turmoil. Jayne had news. Good news. What could it be? Probably something about the job. He hoped so. If she'd gotten a promotion and could live better, it would ease his mind when he told her he was leaving. Not that he contributed anything to this meager life-style, but at least he'd know she wasn't stuck in this miserable room while he was living in style in Paul's posh apartment. He'd let her tell her news first. Then he'd break his to her gently.

By the time he'd dried himself and put on a robe he felt reasonably human, almost optimistic. He even managed to smile as he took his place at the tiny table where they shared their meals, but the sight of eggs and bacon brought a wave of nausea. He fought back the queasy feeling and forced himself to eat. Jayne watched him like a concerned mother.

"Okay?" she asked.

"Great. I think I'll live." Terry refilled his coffee cup and hers. "All right, let's have your news."

"It comes in two parts," Jayne said. "First of all, Aunt Mary's going to marry Christopher and move to Australia. And they're going to let me try out for her job! If I make good, in three months the show will be mine. I'll be earning a lot more money and they can rent this wretched hole to some hippie who's been camping out in Union Square!"

Thank God, Terry thought. It was even better than he hoped. Not only will Jayne be able to live well but she'll have an exciting career to occupy her. She'll get over me quickly. She'll be so busy with her work, so involved with people that my defection will hardly leave a scar. In his relief, he forgot his hangover, jumped out of his chair and went over to hug her.

"Honey, that's terrific! I'm so happy for you! And there's no question about your making good. You'll be sensational! I'm glad for Mary, too. I never thought she'd do it." He went back to his seat. "So that's your two-part piece of news! I must say, they're two biggies!"

Jayne shook her head. "Uh-uh. That's only one part in two sections."

"Oh? What's the other?"

She hesitated and then said, "I was wondering whether you'd be happy in a *ménage à trois.*"

Terry stared at her. For a terrible moment he thought she'd found out about Paul and was suggesting they all live together, the way Paul's ex-fiancée had proposed to solve the problem. No. It couldn't be that. Jayne would have no part of such an arrangement.

"What are you talking about?"

Jayne looked half frightened. "We're going to be three in December. I'm pregnant, Terry. It seems our first close encounter in Singapore hit the jackpot."

His mouth fell open. "Pregnant? You're going to have a baby?"

"That's what the word usually means."

"But you can't! I mean . . . what about the new job? You won't be able to work. My mother told me what a terrible time that is for a woman."

Jayne smiled. "Darling, I'm sure your mother also told you what a death-defying experience she went through giving birth to you. That's hogwash. The kind of crap women tell impressionable kids to make them feel guilty all their lives. It's no big deal having a baby. I can work right up to the first labor pain. I'm healthy as an ox. And I'll be back on the job in no time." She stopped smiling. "I have a bigger worry than that, Terry. I don't know how you feel about the news. You, yourself. Do you hate the idea?"

He didn't know what to say. It was as though everything had fallen to pieces around him. Hate the idea? He more than hated it. He was horrified by it. It changed everything. He couldn't leave her now. He couldn't even tell her he'd considered it. Oh, God, why this? What had he gotten himself into? He felt trapped, torn between his own desires and the sense of decency that had to be bigger than his selfishness. You're an actor, Terry Spalding, he told himself. You'd better make this the best performance of your life. He'd only have to tell Jayne the truth. Tell her what he'd planned to say this morning and she'd let him go. He knew she would. But he couldn't do it. The baby was part of her "good news." She wanted it, obviously. He'd not suggest she get rid of it. Women died from abortions. His mother told him that, too. Besides, he instinctively knew that with or without him, Jayne would have her child.

As the silence lengthened, Jayne grew more uneasy. Aunt Mary is right, she thought. He isn't happy about it. Why did I expect him to be? How could I have deluded myself that he could become a different person in two months? He looked so stunned she felt sorry for him.

"You don't have to marry me, you know," she said softly. "In fact, I wouldn't want you to, unless that's what you wanted. Marriage was never part of our discussion. This needn't change it."

He disciplined his mind as though he were learning a new role in a play. It was important to speak the right words, assume the correct expression, make the right gestures.

"The baby doesn't change it, Jayne," he said. "I want to marry you. I've felt all along we should marry. The only reason I haven't mentioned it is because I can't support you yet. It didn't seem fair to tie you down to an unemployed actor. But if you're willing to take a chance on me, I'm all for it. You've opened a new world to me, a sane one. Something with reality and security. I love you very much. And I'll love the child as well."

Unexpectedly, she began to cry with relief. "Oh, Terry, I'm so damned glad! I kept telling myself I could take it if you walked out, but I knew part of me would die if you did. God, we all pretend to be so modern! I was prepared to have the baby alone if necessary. I was all set to put on a big act and say I understood that it wasn't a responsibility you contracted for. I even thought sometimes that you . . . that you might want your old life back. I didn't want to admit it even to myself, but I was scared as hell. Darling, you're everything I knew you were. The best. The greatest. The most wonderful guy who ever was."

If you only knew, he thought. If you had the least idea of the nightmare I've been living with, and how close I came to sharing it with you. She must never know about Paul, he told himself. Never know how close I came to leaving her for him. Paul. What will Paul say when he hears? He'll tell me I'm a bloody fool. Thank God he isn't a violent man or I think he'd kill me. Mustn't think about Paul. Mustn't think of anything but the part I have to play today and in the hundreds of thousands of days to come.

With an effort, he managed to smile. "Well, Mrs. Spalding-to-be, what's the first step?"

"The first step?"

"When do you want to get married and where?"

"I don't know. I hadn't thought that far."

"Okay. Let's fly to Vegas this afternoon and do it."

"This afternoon? You're kidding! We don't have to be in that big a rush.

Why not here, in a week or so? We could get the license on Monday and get married next Saturday. I'm sure Aunt Mary would have the ceremony at her apartment.''

"And who would we invite to this glittering event?"

"Well, Aunt Mary, of course. And Charlie Burke. And . . . maybe you have some friends you'd like to ask.''

"Nobody. And I'd rather not have any fuss, if you don't mind. Look, let's hop the plane before anybody talks us out of it.''

She looked at him curiously. "Who would?"

Terry groped for words. He hadn't meant to say that. He was thinking of Paul, of course. He had to do it before Paul heard his plan and skillfully maneuvered him into seeing it as a ridiculous sacrifice. "I don't know," Terry said. "Is Mary in favor of this? I mean, you told her about the baby, I imagine. What was her reaction?''

"Honest?"

"Honest.''

"I think she'd like me to have an abortion. But she knows I won't. It's not that she doesn't like you, Terry. She just wasn't certain how you'd feel. And she has some old-fashioned idea about the public not accepting an unmarried mother as a home-spun radio personality. Anyway, the problems have vanished and she'll be happy things turned out right for us. *She* wouldn't talk us out of it, or even try.''

"What about your family?"

"Mother will be furious, but I don't care. Dad will be warm and loving. The grandparents will sleep easier knowing I'm an honest woman." Jayne grinned mischievously. "And they'll all be thrilled when they have an eight-pound, seven-month 'premature' baby for Christmas.''

For a moment he felt a great surge of love for her that nearly drove the thought of Paul from his mind. She was wonderful. We'll be good together, Terry thought. In a way he was glad this had happened. It answered, once and for all, the indecision that plagued him. He had no choice now. There was nothing to do but forget the past and go forward. The old longings would vanish. He'd have to tell Paul. But by that time he'd be safely married. In time he'd even forget. Or only vaguely remember.

"Come on, lady. Get dressed for your wedding.''

The telegram came on Sunday morning, relayed over the phone by a bored-sounding Western Union operator. Stanley Richton listened attentively to the message addressed to Patricia and him.

"Terry and I married yesterday in Las Vegas. Very happy. Hope you feel the same. Much love. Jayne.''

"Would you like us to mail a copy of that to you, sir?"

"Yes, please. Thank you.''

He hung up slowly and went to find his wife. Patricia was engrossed in the voluminous Sunday New York *Times*, her attention focused on ads for clothes that were either too young or too expensive for her.

"Dear, that phone call was a telegram from Jayne. She and Terry were married yesterday in Las Vegas."

Patricia didn't look up.

"Pat, did you hear me? I said Jayne's married!"

"So? What do you want me to do about it? She didn't ask for our opinion, much less our approval. I'm surprised she bothered to inform us."

Stanley stared at her. "Is that all you have to say?"

"What else is there?"

"My God, our only child gets married and you act as though I've given you the weekend weather report!"

"The weather report has much more effect on me. Stanley, don't be such a stereotype of a father! Can't you see she's put us out of her life? I've accepted that. Why can't you?"

"Maybe because I *am* that stereotype, as you call it. Maybe because no matter what she does, she's my child. Yours, too, Patricia. No matter how tough you try to seem, 1 know you care about her. She's hurt you and you're trying to pretend she doesn't matter anymore, but that's impossible for me to accept. I know you love her, and I know she loves you."

Patricia shrugged and went back to her newspaper without answering. Stanley watched her for a moment and then left the room. He stood in the hall for a few seconds and then abruptly returned to continue the conversation. But he never did. What could you say to a woman who was sitting and staring at the wall, tears streaming down her cheeks?

Mary's housephone rang at eight o'clock Monday morning and the doorman said, "Your niece is downstairs, Mrs. Morgan. Can I send her up?"

"Certainly, Jerry. Thanks."

She stood at the open door, waiting for the elevator to bring Jayne up. When the young woman stepped out, she looked pretty and exceptionally happy.

"Well! What brings you here so early?"

"I thought I'd ride to work with you, Aunt Mary. We tried to phone you Saturday night and last night, but you weren't in, and I couldn't wait another minute to tell you."

Mary led the way into the living room. "Charlie and I were out both nights. Fact is, he was consoling me with expensive food and wine."

"Consoling you?"

"I had rather a nasty talk with your grandmother Saturday afternoon. It really put me into a blue funk. I'm over it now." She gave a little wave of her hand. "Anyway, I don't want to talk about it. I'm much more interested in what you can't wait to tell me."

"Okay. Terry and I got married Saturday in Las Vegas."

"You're kidding!"

"No way. Saturday morning I told him he was going to be a father. I must say he was staggered for a moment, but then he went into action like you wouldn't believe! I was all for a small wedding here next week, inconspicuous, of course, for obvious reasons, but he wouldn't hear of it. Next thing I knew I was on a flight to Nevada and a few hours later I was being legalized by the tackiest little justice of the peace you ever saw. We spent the night there and flew back yesterday afternoon.''

Mary groped for words. She was glad Terry had come through as Jayne believed he would, but it was typical of him to act on impulse. They could have waited a week. She'd loved to have given Jayne some kind of wedding, even the smallest, simplest one. Stop being so damned selfish! she told herself. You had the same kind of unattended ceremony. Maybe that's why you wanted something a little nicer, a little warmer, for Jayne. You're still playing mother, she thought. Quit it. Hadn't she just told her own that she wasn't responsible for Jayne?

"Well?" Jayne was waiting for her response. "Are you going to offer congratulations or condolences?"

"Darling, you just took my breath away! Congratulations, of course! That is, I know you congratulate the groom and wish the bride happiness, but whatever, you know I'm delighted for you both! Terry's really happy?"

"Delirious. In fact, he's starting out this morning to get any kind of job he can. He's going to sign up with one of the talent agencies here and hope they can find him work doing commercials. If not, he says he'll take whatever comes along, even if it's selling ties in Macy's. Oh, Aunt Mary, you'd be so pleased if you saw him now! It's as though I'd done something wonderful for him. He's stopped being the brooding, troubled guy I've seen these past weeks. He's acting as though he's shed troubles instead of taking on new ones! I thought he'd be okay, but I honestly never expected him to be so light-hearted about it.''

"That's wonderful!" Mary hugged her. "I couldn't be more delighted. Did you tell him about our job plans?"

"Sure. He was tickled to death. But I think it's all the more reason why he wants to be able to support us. It's a matter of pride, I suppose. Men are all alike, aren't they? The provider instinct is always there." Jayne stopped. "I'm sorry. That was tactless, wasn't it?"

"Not really. Michael had the instinct. He simply wasn't able to be realistic about it. I hope Terry will be. Force him to be, Jaynie. Don't make a child of him. No matter how successful you are, always make him think you depend on him, that you couldn't make it without him.''

"Yes. I will.''

"You're right, you know," Mary said as though she were thinking aloud. "It doesn't really matter who makes the money. What matters is the feeling of confidence a woman gives a man. How she handles herself. Whether she realizes where the values are. There are priorities that have nothing to do with dollars and cents. You have to know the difference between ants and elephants. Everything isn't of equal importance.''

"I know. I'll remember that, Aunt Mary.''

"Of course you will. You're a bright girl. Much brighter than I ever was.'' She became her brisk, cheerful self. "Come on, kiddo, let's get to the office. Charlie will want to discuss your future with you.''

"Should I mention . . .?''

"No. Not now. The marriage will come as enough of a surprise.''

Camille Farr's voice rose an octave. "Married? Jayne is married? To that young man she met on the ship?"

"Who else, Mother?" Patricia tried not to sound impatient over the telephone. "We got a wire yesterday. They were married in Las Vegas Saturday."

"How could she? You said he's an actor. Is he working?"

"I have no idea. I doubt it."

"Where are they going to live, Patricia? What are their plans? Will they be coming to New York? Your father and I want to meet him. I don't even know his last name!"

Patricia almost laughed as she realized she had to stop and think before she said, "Spalding. Terry Spalding. Wonderful," she said bitterly. "For a minute I couldn't remember it myself."

Camille sighed heavily. "It's terrible. Terrible. A young girl like that wasting her life. I don't understand this generation. No consideration for their families. Rushing into marriage this way."

"You weren't so happy when she was living with that boy. I thought you'd be relieved."

"No need to be nasty, Patricia. I've had almost more than I can bear. And heaven knows what this will do to your father. First Mary calling to say she was divorcing and remarrying and now . . ."

"What? What did you say about Mary?"

Camille repeated what she knew.

"Why on earth didn't you call and tell me, Mother? For God's sake, you didn't even let us know she'd phoned!"

Camille turned huffy. "After our recent conversations, I wasn't sure you'd be interested."

"Well, hell, she is my sister!"

"Don't swear, Patricia. It's becoming a terrible habit with you. In any case, I gave Mary a piece of my mind. I told her you'd told us what she did, encouraging this dreadful affair of Jayne's, throwing you out of her apartment before you could stop it. Believe me, I let her know exactly how selfishly she's behaved! For all I know, she may have been behind this marriage. She seems to have a great influence on your daughter's thinking. It's quite a coincidence that they're both marrying strangers they met on that boat. I wouldn't be surprised if Jayne was imitating Mary, now that Mary's taken this decision."

"Don't be crazy, Mother. That doesn't make sense."

"Then perhaps you'll tell me what does make sense about my grandchild rushing into marriage with a man she scarcely knows."

"She knows him." Patricia turned nasty. "She knows him intimately. For all I know, that may be why they got married. Jayne could be pregnant and stupid enough to go through with it."

"Patricia! You're talking about your own daughter!"

"Yes. It should sound familiar to you. History repeating itself."

There was a long silence on the other end of the line. "I think you should go out there," Camille said. "You and Stanley both. That child may need you." She sounded suddenly old and sad.

Patricia quieted down, too. "No, Mother, we won't go. I'm sure Mary's taking care of everything."

"But Mary's moving away. To Australia. Jayne will have no one! What if this man can't support her? What if he leaves her? Patricia, I'll never have a moment's peace until you have a heart-to-heart talk with Jayne!"

"I'm sorry. I can't do that. I don't ever want to see Mary again. As for Jayne, she knows where we are. Let her come to us."

At his little desk in his cluttered office, Stanley Richton chewed the end of his pen and tried to think of the right words to say to his daughter. Patricia flatly refused to call or write and was insistent that he not communicate either. If Jayne didn't have the decency to tell them her intentions, if she was so inconsiderate of them she simply sent a wire announcing her marriage, then she deserved nothing from them, Patricia said. Stanley did not agree. He didn't even believe Patricia meant what she said. He'd seen her crying. He knew she felt wounded by all that had happened, miserable inside. This estrangement had never been clear in his mind. Whatever happened in San Francisco when Jayne and Mary returned remained a mystery. All he knew was that Patricia had drawn her pride around her and that it would not allow her to reach out to her sister or her daughter.

It troubled him terribly, all of it. His child's sudden marriage, the new way of life she'd created without a word to her parents. And now that Mary was going away, he was even more disturbed. The thought of Jayne with no one but a stranger to turn to made him sick with anxiety. Be sensible, he told himself. Stop thinking of Terry Spalding as a stranger. He's your daughter's husband. Your son-in-law. She's his now. His to protect and care for. He must be a great guy. Jayne wouldn't pick out any other kind. He found his hand shaking slightly as he began to write.

My dearest Jayne,

Your mother and I were surprised, of course, to receive your telegram, but I hasten to tell you that we are as delighted as you hoped we'd be. Anything that makes you happy guarantees our feelings, because you are the center of our lives and the object of all our love and faith and pride.

Sometimes, my dear, people have trouble expressing their devotion. In these past few years, as you've become a young woman, I've wished I could treat you as I used to when you were a little girl. Remember the walks we used to take? Remember how I'd buy you hot dogs and ice cream in the park and you'd get sick to your stomach and your mother would give us both hell when we got home? She raised the roof because she loved us, because she didn't want you to ever feel physically sick or me to feel emotionally upset because I'd foolishly indulged you. So she read us both out. That was her way, Jaynie. She pretends to be hard sometimes, but it's only to cover how she really feels. She's afraid of weakness, in herself even more than in others. I admire her strength and I see it in you, in a very good way. I also see in you the sentimentality that is your father's heritage. It's not a bad combination, dear. Steel can be soft and candy can be hard, if you know what I mean. Your old man has never been very good with words, and that's as close as I can come to saying that in all good human beings there is both vulnerability and false pride, and sometimes we forget that every man and woman has a second person inside.

I didn't really mean this letter to go this way, dear heart. But I know you'll wonder why your mother hasn't been in touch, and I want you to know that she'd like to be. I said in the beginning that we are happy for anything that makes you happy. Your mother doesn't admit to that happiness right now, but it's there. I know her. She's angry and she feels rejected and it's hard for her to accept what's happened because she was not a part of it. But she loves you, Jayne. She's less sloppy about it than I, but she loves you as much. More than anyone or anything in the world. I know your Terry must be all the things I wish for you. All we both wish for you. You are incapable of loving someone who is not sensitive and honest and deeply caring. For those are your qualities, sweetheart, and your father believes that you would instinctively seek them in the man you marry.

Give him love from his new mother and father. Tell him we are proud to have a son. And remember always that you are my little girl, and that I am rejoicing with you and adoring you always.

                                                                Dad

P.S. We don't know what you'd like for a wedding gift, but this little check will, we hope, be useful. Buy something as beautiful as you are.

He wrote a check for a thousand dollars and then reread the letter. It was a terrible letter, he thought unhappily. He hadn't said any of the things he wanted to. He'd like to have told her his secret dream of one day walking down a big church aisle with her, all in white, on his arm. He wanted to say that she was the greatest accomplishment of his life, the thing that made all the dreariness and drudgery and day-by-day frustrations worthwhile. He wanted to beg her to come back with her husband, to live near him and her mother, to produce beautiful grandchildren who would be the joy of their later years.

But he couldn't say those things. He didn't know how to say some of them. Others he dared not say lest she feel some unnecessary guilt for being so far away. He'd liked to have said, Live and love, darling Jayne. Consume every hour of life with enjoyment. Be free and unafraid. And know that I am here if ever you need me.

He was tempted to tear the letter up and simply send the check and a short, warm note. It was unfair to apologize for Patricia. She'd be furious if she knew he was trying to explain her to her daughter. But Jayne would understand. They'd always understood each other, he and his child. They'd been conspirators, allies and friends. They'd shared more than forbidden treats in the park. They'd shared confidence and love. More closeness than she'd felt with Patricia. More closeness, in a way, than he'd felt with the woman who was his wife.

Poor Patricia. She's missed so much while she's nursed her anger, fed on her frustration, hidden all her gentle instincts under a layer of vanity and discontent. Stanley sighed as he sealed the envelope. No need to tell Jayne these things. She already knew them, too.

Chapter 28

CHRISTOPHER FROWNED AS he read Mary's latest letter. Its tone was adoring. She spoke, as she did every week, of her love for him and her confidence in their future. But between the lines he sensed waves of anxiety, not so much for them as for others, Jayne in particular. He'd been totally amazed when she wrote of Jayne's marriage to Terry Spalding. Despite his worldliness, Christopher found it hard to accept homosexuals and unable to believe they could change as completely as Terry seemed to have. I'm old-fashioned, he thought. I'd want to kill one of my boys if he'd gone that way. And if I had a daughter who'd chosen to marry a "convert," I'd do everything in my power to stop it. His heart ached for Mary. Though she totally denied it, he knew she was deeply troubled by the step Jayne had taken and the reason that precipitated it. Pregnant, for God's sake! No wonder Mary's agitation came through. It was a terrible time to leave this young woman who was like a daughter to her. Arranging the job thing was lucky, but that took care of only part of Jayne's problems. When Mary left, she'd be alone in San Francisco, emotionally dependent on a young man who'd never known such responsibility, one who might, at any moment, revert to his old ways and leave her alone with a baby to care for.

Damn young fools, both of them. Jayne shouldn't be having this child. Shouldn't be married to its father. Mary would be worried about her from August, when she left, until December when the baby was born. And even after that, he supposed. Bloody selfish kids. They never gave a thought to how they might mess up other people's lives.

An alarming thought struck him. What if Mary decided not to marry him until after Jayne had her baby? She hadn't mentioned such a possibility, but he realized that was what was really troubling him in all this. He reread that part of the letter. Since her marriage, Jayne had heard nothing from her parents, They'd probably disowned her, he thought. Not knowing that Patricia and Stanley were unaware of Terry's background or Jayne's condition, he could imagine their revulsion and grief, which would make Mary's feeling of responsibility all the greater. Yes, it was quite possible Mary was toying with the idea of postponing her own plans, to stay and give support and comfort to this heedless child. Well, he wouldn't permit it. Jayne was an adult and accountable for her actions. Mary would not be allowed to change the date they'd agreed on.

Not that she'd indicated any such thing. He'd been delighted to learn of her arrangements with her husband, relieved that Michael had not been difficult. She wrote positively of August and of his arrival and tried to pretend she felt nothing but happiness. He knew better. Blast the miles between us, he thought. If only I were there to reassure her.

Well, why not? Why did he have to wait until August to go to the States? He could go now, in June. See for himself what was happening. At times like this, a woman needed a man to take charge, to reinforce the rightness of her actions. He consulted his calendar. The next two weeks were impossible. But after that, there was no reason why he couldn't make a quick trip to San Francisco. He smiled, thinking how thrilled she would be. Hell, how thrilled *he* would be! The anticipation of being with her physically excited him, and even that fact amused him. She makes me feel young, he thought. Even thinking about her makes my heart race. Thank God the doctors tell me I'm in the pink. I can make Mary happy for years to come.

"How's everything going?" Charlie looked at his companion across the luncheon table.

Mary smiled at him. "In what direction?"

"Well, let's start with Jayne. Professionally."

"Swimmingly. She takes to this business like a natural. In the past three weeks I've had her with me at every taping. She absorbs like a sponge. Even makes constructive suggestions, Remember that interview with the Good Samaritan's widow? It was Jayne's idea to set up a fund for her and those four little children, and we've already gotten twenty-seven thousand dollars in donations from private citizens and business firms. It's terrific for that poor woman and not bad public relations for the station, either. Jayne's going to be fine, Charlie. She's blossoming in this field."

"And in others, I suspect."

For an instant, Mary's face darkened. "You've noticed. Yes, she's beginning to show a little. But only your eagle eye would spot it. It doesn't matter, does it? I mean, it won't spoil her chances for the job."

"I don't see why. Nobody knows about her private life, how long she's been married, any of that. She does have a husband. I can't see why anybody would object to her having a baby. When's she due?"

"Just before Christmas."

"She can tape in advance, the way you did when you went on the cruise. No problem."

"Right," Mary said. "No problem."

"You don't sound very convincing."

"Oh, Charlie, I'm crazy, that's all. It worries me to death that I'll be gone in August and she'll have to go through those last four months alone. And have the baby alone."

"Alone? What do you mean, 'alone'? She has Terry. And I'd be amazed if Patricia didn't come out for the event."

"She hasn't had a word from Patricia. A lovely letter from Stanley, but nothing from her mother. Not surprising, I suppose, knowing my sister. Still, you'd think if your child got married, you'd manage to forget your own disappointment long enough to be supportive of her."

"Don't they know she's pregnant?"

Mary shook her head. "Jayne won't tell them. Not yet. She says they'd only act like outraged Victorian parents. Personally, I think she's afraid they'll think less of her. Stanley, anyway. She adores her father."

"Not very realistic, is it? They can add."

"Of course. Jayne knows that, too. She's just postponing an unpleasant scene. I can't hate her for that, Charlie. None of us likes an ugly confrontation."

"No, I suppose not. Speaking of confrontations, what do you hear from Michael?"

"Nothing. That bothers me, too. I thought by now he'd let me know his plans."

"I assume you've gotten yourself a lawyer."

She looked surprised. "A lawyer? No. Do I need one? I thought since Michael was getting the divorce, he'd arrange things with someone in Mexico. Isn't that how it's usually done?"

"I can't be sure, not having gone through it, but things can get sticky, even in the most amiable of partings. You'd better find out about things like community property as well as the decree itself."

"Community property? We don't own anything, Charlie. The apartment's a rental and the furniture isn't valuable enough to ship to Australia, especially to the home of an antique dealer. I thought I'd give it to Jayne, as a matter of fact."

"No bank accounts? Savings? That kind of thing?"

"I'm ashamed to say we haven't been able to save much. We have a joint checking account with too much in it. I've been meaning to switch some over to a savings, but all this happened and I kind of forgot that I'd built it up so Michael could use it while I was away. But he hasn't asked for anything, and I assume he won't."

"What's the bank balance, if you don't mind my asking?"

Mary looked embarrassed. "I hate to admit that I don't know. About fifteen thousand, I think. The May statement came from the bank but I didn't even open it. There's been so much else on my mind. I'll check it tonight."

"Good idea." He shook his head. "I'm surprised Michael's so co-operative. It just doesn't ring true."

"He's a nice man, Charlie."

"Sure he is. But he's also a man who doesn't want to be divorced. A man who asked you to wait. A man who, to my surprise, didn't turn a hair when you told him there was someone else. Nice is one thing. Saintly is something else. Unless . . ."

"Unless what?"

Charlie hesitated. "He had a thing with Rae Spanner while you were away. Did you know?"

"Yes. I knew. I also know what you're thinking. You're thinking maybe Michael's being agreeable about the divorce because she's in the background."

"Could be. She's rich. And persistent. I hear she flew to Los Angeles last week." He reached for her hand. "I don't want to hurt you, but Michael's the sort who'll look for the next person to take care of him. He's not a bad guy, Mary, just a dependent one. If Rae has offered to set him up in style, it would be understandable that he might consider it. I have a hunch you'll be hearing from him soon. Since Rae's visit he might not feel the need to hang on to you after all."

She felt sick. "You make him sound horrible. Like an adventurer. There's more to Michael than that. There's a sweet, generous side as well."

"Of course there is, my dear. But he likes comfort and he knows he can't get it through what he can earn. It's a flaw, Mary. A weakness like alcoholism or drug addiction. He can't help it. He'll always need a strong woman. He always has, hasn't he?"

"Yes," she said reluctantly, "but I hoped he'd find someone who needed *him*. Someone who'd force him to take responsibility. A woman who'd restore his pride. Not Rae Spanner, for God's sake! She'd be the worst thing that could happen to Michael!"

"From your point of view, yes," Charlie said gently. "But from Michael's? I'm not sure. I think he's given up on himself a lot faster than you've given up on him. I think he knows Michael Morgan better than you do after fifteen years of living with him."

She thought back to the conversation in Carrie Morgan's backyard. Charlie was right. She never stopped trying to put her standards into Michael's head. Even now, when she'd left him, she was still trying to make him what she wanted him to be, not, probably, what he wanted to be himself. Was she doing that for him or for herself? Why do I have this compulsive thing about everybody else's future? she wondered. Does it lessen my own guilt? Reinforce my own ego? Why can't I let them all work out their lives for themselves? Michael. Jayne and Terry, too. I impose my ideals, my yardsticks of success and happiness on others. Wrong. I should leave them the hell alone.

She squeezed the hand that lay on hers. "You're right. I should butt out of everybody else's business and take care of my own. Thanks for the good advice. About everything. You're the big brother I always wanted."

He smiled his thanks. Terrific, he thought. Just what every man needs to hear from the woman he loves.

When she got home later that afternoon, Mary went through the pile of mail left untouched on her desk and found the bank statement showing her checking account balance as of the end of May. Incredulously, she looked at the figure. Three thousand dollars! That was impossible! The damned computers had made a mistake. Swiftly, she sorted through the canceled checks, noting the rent payments and utilities. She'd done her taxes before she left on the cruise and paid them in February. Even subtracting the money Michael used while she was away, there should have been thirteen thousand or so left. It took only a minute to see that the bank was not wrong. There was a check made out to "cash," signed and endorsed by her husband on their joint account, in the amount of ten thousand dollars. She stared at it, disbelieving. It was dated April 15, the day after Michael moved out.

Her first reaction was terrible disappointment that he'd done such an underhanded thing. And then sorrow turned to rage. How dare he? How dare he steal her money, the money she'd worked so hard for, the money that didn't belong to him in anything but the legal sense? The more she thought of it, the more furious she became. No wonder he hadn't mentioned community property. He knew he already had more than his share. He'd made a fool of her again. Deliberately, this time. Actually flaunting his dishonesty. He had to know that sooner or later she'd discover what he'd done. What did he think she'd do then—forgive him, as she always did? Consider it a small price for her freedom? Had it been his revenge for her "desertion" of him? Was this the way he repaid fifteen years of easy living at her expense?

She reached for the phone to call him in Los Angeles and confront him with her knowledge. But halfway through dialing his mother's number, she replaced the receiver. Charlie was right. Even in an "amiable parting," things could get sticky, he'd said. Well, this was sticky all right. It wasn't simply the money. It was an insult to her intelligence, a denial of her ability to judge people. In her wildest dreams, she'd never have believed Michael capable of cheating her. Lying to her, yes. Even being unfaithful. But this deliberately arrogant gesture showed her a side of him she didn't know existed. That was far more painful than the ten thousand dollars he'd appropriated out of who-knew-what emotion.

Money had never been that important to her. It always amazed her to see what greed could do to people, how families fought over estates and husbands and wives over property settlements. She'd have given Michael the money if he'd asked. Even that night when she was weary of everything about him and their marriage, she'd have made him a gift of it. But he hadn't asked. He'd simply taken, thumbing his nose at her in one last I'll-show-you gesture. The root of all evil, she thought. Love of money, the ultimate weapon of modern man.

She felt drained, the anger subsiding, an awful sense of futility taking its place. Let him have the money. She didn't care. But let him get out of her life once and for all, this stranger with a false face.

Hard as he tried, Paul couldn't keep his mind on his work. It had been more than two weeks since he'd seen or heard from Terry. Not since that last evening when he'd laid down the law and demanded Terry stop his nonsense and tell that woman exactly where things stood. Terry had agreed, promised he'd speak to her the next day. The kid had been drunk, but not so drunk he'd forget that promise. Paul had expected to hear from him that Saturday, but days passed without a word. He kept expecting the phone to ring, left word with his secretary that if Mr. Spalding called he was to be interrupted even if he was in a meeting. He stayed home at night, waiting to hear. He even went daily to the coffee shop where Terry had waited to find him. Nothing. Several times he thought of calling that dreary little studio apartment, but he held back. For the first time in their relationship, Terry had the upper hand. It was not an arrangement Paul liked and he certainly wasn't going to compound it by making an anxious overture. Damn him, he thought. Why doesn't he let me know what's happening? Maybe he's sick. Paul was suddenly alarmed. Worse, maybe he never made it home that night after he left my apartment. What if he'd been mugged or even killed? Terry was so drunk when he left, anything could have happened. He was a fool not to find out. What difference did it make if he humbled himself once more and called? He'd already confessed he couldn't live without him. What was one more admission of need? Anything was better than this uncertainty.

He dialed information, wondering as he did whether the phone Terry told him they'd had installed was under the name of Spalding or under her name. He couldn't remember it. Jayne something. Roberts? Rickman? No, Richton. That was it. Stupid of him not to have gotten Terry's number from him, but he hadn't thought he'd ever want to call there.

"We have a new listing for a Terrence Spalding," the operator said. "On Powell Street. Would that be the one, sir?"

"Yes." He jotted down the number. "Thank you."

Paul glanced at the expensive watch on his wrist. Nine-thirty. She'd have gone to work. He heard the phone ring three times and then Terry answered.

"Where the hell have you been?" Paul asked without preamble. "Christ, I thought something had happened to you! Why haven't you called? I've been crazy with worry!"

"I'm sorry."

"Sorry! Is that all you can say? What's going on? Not a word out of you in two weeks. And you're still living with her. What game are you playing now, Terry?''

"No game, Paul. Everything's very serious.''

He felt his stomach lurch. "She made trouble when you told her?''

There was a pause. "I didn't tell her. I didn't have a chance. Look, I know I should have been in touch with you, but I knew how angry you'd be.''

"Damn right I'm angry! I'm angry that you haven't had enough guts to tell her how things are. Just when do you plan to do that?''

"I . . . I don't think it's something we can discuss on the phone. Could I meet you someplace later today?''

"All right. Lunch? The usual place at twelve-thirty?''

"Yes. I'll be there.'' Terry's voice sounded strange.

"You sure you're all right? You sound funny.''

"I'm all right, Paul. See you in a little while.''

Paul sat for a moment after he hung up, digesting the conversation. Something was terribly wrong. He could hear it in Terry's almost frightened tone. That bitch! Somehow she's hanging on to him. Probably sniveling and saying she needs him. Playing on his soft-heartedness. The kid didn't know how to be tough. Well, I do. If he can't cut himself loose, I'll do it for him.

As he approached the coffee shop, Terry wondered how he'd get through it. So much had changed since the last time he was here. Then he was praying for a glimpse of Paul. Now he dreaded this last encounter, feeling as nauseous as he had when he was sure Paul was married. In spite of his nervousness, the irony of it struck him. A couple of weeks ago he'd cringed at the thought of meeting Paul the married man. Now the tables were turned. Thank God we're meeting in a public place, he thought. I'd be afraid to be alone with him when he hears what's happened.

Paul was waiting when he entered. Terry was struck again by the elegance of him. His clothes were so beautifully tailored, his jewelry expensive and discreet, even his thick hair carefully cut in a not-too-short, not-too-long style that suited the successful broker image he projected. By comparison, Terry thought, I look like what I am: an out-of-work actor. For a moment he wondered what attracted Paul to him. What is it, he thought, that makes a handsome man like this want to share his life with me? For that matter, what makes a beautiful, intelligent girl like Jayne love me and want to have my child? I have so little to offer either of them. Only adoration. I adore them, and they know it.

He slid into the seat opposite Paul and tried to compose his expression into a pleasant, noncommittal one. His companion obviously was making an effort to do the same.

"You're looking well, Terry. I had a vision of you lying battered and bruised in some hospital. You were pretty smashed last time I saw you.''

Terry managed to smile. "I had the worst hangover of my life the next day.''

"Oh? So bad you couldn't tell your friend what you promised? I can understand that. But I'm a little puzzled about a headache that's lasted two weeks.''

The waitress appeared.

"Just coffee, please,'' Terry said.

"That's all you want?" Paul asked. "No lunch?"

Terry shook his head. "I'm not hungry."

"In that case, neither am I. We'll just have two coffees."

The waitress sniffed. "I'll have to charge you the minimum. It's our busy time, you know. You might as well . . ."

Paul cut her off. "I don't give a damn if you charge fifty dollars! Just bring the coffee!" He settled back and looked at Terry. "Okay. Let's have it. What's wrong?"

No way to avoid it. Better to get it over fast. Terry took a deep breath. "I'm married, Paul. The day after I saw you, Jayne and I flew to Vegas and got married."

The other man said nothing. He simply sat there, waiting for an explanation.

"She . . . Jayne's pregnant. Going on three months. She wants the baby." Terry was sweating. "What else could I do? I couldn't abandon her, not when she's carrying my child. She didn't make demands, Paul. She said I didn't have to marry her, that we hadn't discussed marriage when we made the arrangement to live together. I could have walked out, but it would have been wrong. I couldn't leave her to have my baby alone."

Paul put a cigarette into a Dunhill holder and calmly lit it. "You seem very sure this is your baby," he said.

"Of course it's mine! Whose else would it be?"

"I don't know. Maybe she was pregnant when you met her."

"No! She wasn't. Jayne wouldn't do such a thing. She's the most honest woman I've ever known."

"She wouldn't have to go much, would she? How many women have you known?"

"Don't do this, Paul." Terry's voice was pleading. "Don't be clever and try to put doubts in my head about Jayne. Be angry. Be furious. I wouldn't blame you. You gave up a marriage because of me. I promised to come back to you. I wanted to. I would have. But now I can't." He suddenly spoke more strongly. "I'm not even sure I want to anymore. I can't hope you'll understand, but I'm happy, except for what I've done to you. Jayne and this child have given me a reason for being something more than I'd ever be if I had you to look after me. Maybe I needed that. Maybe I needed to grow up. If you're my friend, if you care about me, you'll try to understand that." He waited, expecting an outpouring of abuse, but Paul answered in a quiet, almost sympathetic way.

"Terry, I can't say I'm not thrown by this. Damned near desperate, I'm so disappointed. But in a funny way, I'm almost proud of you. The reason I care so much about you, I guess, is just because you are what you are, and you can't do anything but what you think is right. I could kill that woman for coming into your life, but she's here and she needs you. I suppose you need her, too, though I don't like to admit that." He stubbed out his cigarette. "We can't always have what we want in this life. I'm old enough to know that. Sometimes we have to settle for what we can get. What I'm saying is, I'd like to be friends with you and Jayne, if the two of you will let me. If you say no, I'll understand. Hell, I didn't even offer you that much a few months ago when I was going to walk out. But I hope you'll let me be on the fringes of your life. I promise you I won't cause trouble."

Terry could hardly believe what he was hearing. Paul being understanding, almost humble? It was the direct opposite of what he'd expected and relief flowed over him like a soothing breeze.

"I . . . I don't know what to say. Jesus, Paul, you're terrific! I wish I could have behaved as well when it was the other way around."

"Give me credit for a little maturity, Terry. I may be selfish but I'm realistic. I'd rather see you under any circumstances than not see you at all."

"But you do know . . ."

"I know it's over between us. The way it was, I mean. But we can be friends, can't we? You must trust me enough to know I wouldn't lie about anything so important. I want your friendship, Terry, if that's all I can have."

"Of course you can have it! Jayne's, too. You'll like each other. I'm so grateful, Paul. It's like having the best of both worlds."

The older man smiled. "I don't find it quite the best, frankly. The best would have been your coming back to me. But I know you won't. Don't worry, Terry. I'll find other companionship. But I don't have to lose touch with you, even if it's on a different basis."

Terry's face glowed. It was going to be all right. He'd explain it to Jayne frankly. The most understanding of women, she'd accept the reality of this sophisticated, civilized solution. Why couldn't they be friends? Ex-lovers often were. Even divorced people. Jayne and Paul were intelligent creatures. They'd be congenial. They might even grow fond of each other. "Say, you know what? Suddenly I'm hungry. What about you?"

"Let's order lunch," Paul said. "My appetite's come back too."

As he studied the menu, Paul secretly watched Terry's relaxed face. Incredible! He'd really swallowed all that bull about understanding and friendship. He was such a child, so completely without guile himself that he couldn't see how preposterously out of character Paul's proposal was. How could Terry possibly think he'd sit back and accept this gracefully, pretending to respect the young man for his decision? Terry might be able to convince Jayne that such an unlikely platonic friendship was possible, but if she believed that she was as big a fool as her husband. Be cool, Paul told himself. The only way to break up this marriage is to pretend to condone it. Ingratiate yourself. Subtly make Terry see what a mistake he's made. The kid couldn't be bullied into doing something against his damned conscience, but he could be seduced into the kind of discontent that would end this ridiculous alliance he'd made. Time. Time would take care of it. It was only a matter of handling things right.

Chapter 29

SINCE SHE'D BEEN living alone, Mary had developed the habit of waking at an ungodly hour each morning. Sometimes it was as early as five o'clock, the world still dark outside her window, quiet and peaceful as only a big city can be before it springs into action. She didn't mind this early return to reality. Sometimes she had terrible nightmares from which she was glad to escape. It was an actual relief to recognize the familiar surroundings, the feel of her own big bed, the sight of her dressing table on which a picture of herself and Michael remained, an enlarged snapshot taken of them on a happier day, years ago, at Fisherman's Wharf. She wondered why she kept the picture there, now that she was an unmarried woman. More habit than sentiment, she guessed. It was part of this room, as Michael's "valet," the wooden stand that used to hold his jacket and trousers, still was. She'd changed nothing, feeling it was all temporary. In less than two months she'd be on her way to a new house and a new bedroom to be shared with a new husband.

She liked this period of quiet contemplation, an hour or more of lying undisturbed by voices. The world was much too noisy the rest of the day. People talked too much, as though silence were dangerous. It was one of the good things about Christopher. He could sit silently beside her, holding her hand, communicating his thoughts without the need for words. Not so with Michael, who'd been a compulsive conversationalist. She wondered, idly, why that had been so. Perhaps it was to cover his insecurity, to reassure her and himself that his mind was always active, always planning a future, articulating schemes he tried to believe were real. She wondered if he'd continue to be that way. If he married Rae Spanner—and that triumphant woman was letting half of San Francisco know this was the plan now that Michael was free—would he try to convince her, too, that his success was just a step away? Probably not. Rae had no illusions as a young Mary had. She'd be bored with Michael's dreams, indifferent to his goals. Rae was buying companionship, social and sexual convenience. She was no starry-eyed girl believing in a future with a man who'd make her proud.

Funny, Mary thought. I feel no bitterness toward her or Michael. They're unhappy people, both of them, and well suited. Since the day she discovered Michael had virtually cleaned out their joint account, she'd had no contact with him. Charlie was outraged when she told him, but once the shock passed, she was almost indifferent.

"Let him keep the money," she said. "If he was that desperate, he must need it badly. I don't care."

Charlie thought she was mad to let herself be cheated, but she'd just shaken her head and told him to forget it. She wasn't quite sure, herself, why she felt that way. She'd felt so angry at first. So betrayed. But later it didn't seem to matter. It was ridiculous to think that perhaps, subconsciously, she felt the need to pay for her freedom. But it was possible. Charlie, Jayne, everyone told her the guilt was not hers, but somewhere inside she irrationally felt she'd failed. Perhaps it eased that sense of failure to know he'd behaved so badly about the money. His thirty pieces of silver, she thought whimsically. Strange it hurt more than the knowledge of his unfaithfulness with Rae and Patricia. Or maybe not strange. She'd cheated, too, but not in material things.

She lay back and watched the sky lighten. Fifteen years and nothing to show for it except memories, some good, some frightful. Memories and a sheaf of papers from a Mexican court severing the marriage of Mary and Michael Morgan. There were regrets. Things she wished she'd done differently. But there was this serenity, as well. Sometimes her peacefulness disturbed her. She didn't mind living alone. It was blissfully selfish. So much so that at times it worried her. Perhaps I shouldn't marry again, she thought anxiously. Maybe marriage is an unnatural state that deprives people of that most precious commodity: privacy. Instantly, she denied the idea. She loved Christopher. She wanted to live with him. It was the damned time and distance again. She hadn't seen him since the fourth of April. It was now almost the middle of June. There were moments of panic when she could hardly remember his face, when she wondered how she dare link her life with someone she'd known such a short time, when she felt frightened of a foreign country and of people and customs strange to her. At those times she reread his letters, gathering strength from them, knowing she'd be safe in his care. Her happiness would return then, and her certainty, and she wished again that August would come quickly.

There were days when she even wondered why she had to wait almost another two months. Jayne was catching on so quickly to the job she could step into it tomorrow. Mary had come to realize what an ambitious girl her niece really was, much more ambitious than Mary had ever been. I worked to make a living, her aunt thought, but Jayne really wants a big career. She's much more dedicated to power and success than I ever was. Much less frightened of failure. Jayne could handle failure if it came, God forbid. She'd pick herself up and start over, knowing she had brains and beauty and the kind of drive that young, liberated women had these days. But she wouldn't fail, not at this job or any in the future. She'd go onward and upward. Probably to local television. Maybe to national. Who knew where Jayne would be in fifteen years? A celebrity, most likely. One of those admirable women who managed a big job, a household, children and husband, neglecting none of them, being admired and appreciated by all.

And where would Terry be when that day came? The thought of him brought a frown of anxiety. It was such a strange marriage. Terry seemed to have grown up in the past few weeks. He'd even gotten a job, not much of one for a man of twenty-six, to be sure, but a real job nonetheless. He was working in a brokerage house, learning the business, starting at the bottom, and Mary gave him full marks for abandoning his hopeless love of the theater and settling down to something substantial. What troubled her was the way he'd gotten that job. When Jayne told her what he was doing, Mary had been more than a little surprised.

"Terry in stocks and bonds? I didn't know he had a head for finance."

Jayne laughed. "Neither did I. Neither did he. It was his friend Paul's suggestion. Paul got him the job in the firm where he's something of a big shot. And, I must say, it looks as though it might work."

"Paul? Who's Paul?"

"Paul Le Compte. Terry's former lover. The one he ran away from when he took the cruise." Jayne said it as casually as if she'd disclosed that Paul was a second cousin. "He's quite an interesting man, Aunt Mary. Very smooth. Terry and I have been seeing a lot of him lately. He has a really posh apartment near the Marina, with a view from his terrace that's to die from! Even a Japanese manservant who dishes up yummy dinners. We're together at least a couple of times a week. It's become quite a threesome."

Mary was shocked. "Jayne! You can't be serious! You're seeing the man Terry used to . . . to be attached to? The three of you are spending time together? It's the sickest thing I ever heard of! It's unnatural! How can you possibly be around a man you knew was your husband's . . ."

Jayne was unruffled. "Darling, it isn't a revival of Noel Coward. Everything's up-front these days. We don't play cute little sophisticated games. I know Paul still has a yen for Terry. Gullible, trusting Terry. He's such a child he really believes Paul is willing to settle for friendship. He's absolutely delighted that his old friend and I get on so well together. We both pretend to Terry that we're best buddies, but of course we know damned well all we're doing is keeping an eye on each other. Paul knows I know what he's up to. He also knows I have no intention of letting him win."

It was unreal. Mary stared at her helplessly. "Jayne, you don't know what you're doing. Letting Terry work with that man. The two of you spending evenings with him. It's insane! Don't you know how devious a man like that can be? Do you want to lose Terry?"

"Not at all. On the contrary, this is the way to keep him. If he felt he couldn't see Paul, he'd only be more anxious to. Forbidden fruit, that kind of thing. No, this way Terry's happy. I come off like the relaxed wife he wants me to be, a marvelous contrast to that all-consuming mother who turned him off women in the first place. And sooner or later, Paul will lose his cool. He'll make a mistake and Terry will sweep him out of his life. Our lives. But *Terry* has to do it. As long as there's the least idea that I'd keep him and Paul apart, he'll hang on to his old memories. When he sees that this new 'friendship' is just a trick, he'll be done with it once and forever."

Mary shook her head. "I don't understand. I think you're playing with fire."

"Come and see for yourself. Paul's been wanting to meet you. Why don't you have dinner with us Saturday night? I'm sure it will be fine with Paul, and you haven't seen Terry for weeks."

"I don't know. I'm not sure I have the stomach for that kind of thing. I'd probably feel ill at ease."

"Don't be silly. Why should you? I mean, we're not playing musical beds. It's rather fascinating, as a matter of fact. I must admit to you, Aunt Mary, that I'm amused seeing Paul grow more and more frustrated. He knows he's fighting a losing battle. I'm nasty enough to take some satisfaction from that. It's like a tug of war and my side is getting stronger with every pull."

Mary was still distressed. " 'A tug of war,' " she repeated. "With Terry in the middle. You're not being fair to him, Jayne."

The girl's eyes flashed. "I'm being more than fair. I'm protecting him from himself. I love Terry, but he's an innocent. I won't let him go back into that life with Paul. He's going to have a wife and a baby and a chance to grow into a self-respecting man instead of a dominated toy. Paul's kept him a child. He took up where Terry's mother left off. Terry's a late starter, but he'll make it. I'll see to that. There's good material in him. He just needs self-confidence and he's getting that with the first real job he ever had, and a pregnant wife who needs him." Jayne smiled reassuringly. "I know what you're thinking. That I'm directing his life. That I'll only make him weaker in the long run because I'm so much stronger. I know how to handle my strength, Aunt Mary. Terry will never feel threatened by me."

She believes that, Mary thought. I wish I could believe it, too. "I have to trust your judgment, Jayne. I remember my mistakes."

"I'm not you, Aunt Mary. And Terry isn't Michael. I don't mean that unkindly, but it's true. This is another time and another situation."

Yes, it is, Mary thought now as she slowly rose from her bed and went toward the kitchen. Jayne will never be torn as I was by some outmoded ideas of a woman's role in marriage. Or a man's. She's taken on a big job in her personal life, but she knows it's a challenge. I never did. I wasn't prepared, as she is, to cope.

I'm not looking forward to this dinner tonight. I don't really want to meet the man who was so important to Terry. Who still is, for that matter. I can't be as pulled together as Jayne is about this whole thing. I hate it. It repels me. More than that, it frightens me half to death.

Christopher snapped the lock on his suitcase and double-checked his ticket. On Sunday morning, San Francisco time, he'd be knocking on Mary's door. He supposed he was acting like an adolescent, not telling her he was arriving, but he wanted to surprise her. He could imagine the look on her face when he called. She'd think he was phoning from Sydney, and he could almost hear her gasp when she realized he was as close as the Fairmont Hotel. Darling, darling Mary. God, he'd missed her so much! Maybe he could talk her into an earlier date than August. She was free now and she said Jayne was going to be great in her job. If he could convince her that Jayne was also going to be perfectly okay, physically and emotionally, Mary could leave with an easy mind, every doubt overcome. Jayne will help me, he thought. She's always been on my side.

His son James drove him to the airport. "Be sure to give Mary our love," he said.

Christopher nodded. "I'm glad all of you like her. It's important to me, and it will make things easier for her."

"We think she's a knockout, Dad. Especially because she makes you so happy. I wish she'd come back with you now."

"I wish so, too. If I can talk her into it, she will. But we'll have to see. She's so conscientious about that job of hers, for one thing. Won't leave until she's sure things are under control."

"Do you think she'll miss working? It's going to be a big change for her."

"I don't know," Christopher said. "If she finds herself with too much time on her hands, I'm sure she'll dig up something to do. Very enterprising, these American ladies." He grinned at his son. "But I'm hoping she'll be busy looking after me. I'm a demanding old codger, you know."

James affectionately agreed. "Sure. You're a bloody martinet, you are, guv'ner. Give us all a pack of trouble, you do." He patted his father's shoulder as they pulled up to the airport. "Good luck," he said.

Christopher waved as he drove away. Nice boy, he thought. I have two nice boys. He thought briefly of Terry. Poor bugger. If he'd had the family love my kids did maybe he'd be a different young man. He hoped Jayne was really straightening him out. Hoped it for his own sake and Mary's, as well as for that unlikely young couple.

He wondered what Mary was doing at this moment. He tried to picture her in San Francisco and couldn't. But I know what she'll be doing this time tomorrow, by God! His own eagerness amused him, and anticipation made him look boyishly handsome. An attractive woman in the waiting area stared at him with unconcealed interest. Christopher smiled politely and buried himself in his newspaper. Since the day he met Mary, he didn't know any other woman existed. He'd waited most of his life for her, and thankfully the waiting soon would end.

Jayne and Terry picked her up in a taxi a little before seven on that Saturday evening.

"You look marvelous, Mary," Terry said. "Paul will be bowled over. He's a big admirer of yours anyway."

"Really? I'm surprised he ever has a chance to hear the program."

"It's only recently that he has," Jayne said meaningfully. "Now that I'm getting involved in it, he's gotten a little radio in his office and listens to every show. He's extremely bright and his comments are very helpful. I think you'll be interested in hearing some of them."

"I'm sure I will." It's starting already, Mary thought. We've begun the little cat-and-mouse game. Is Terry totally ignorant of what's going on? The young man in the seat between them seemed tense, almost desperate, holding Jayne's hand. He knows what's happening, Mary realized with alarm. He's not stupid. I thought he didn't see what he had no wish to, that he chose to be blind about the struggle that's taking place over him. But that's not so. He's in quiet agony over the way things are going between his wife and his friend. Why can't Jayne recognize an impossible situation and put an end to this farce?

Suddenly, Mary felt terribly anxious. Everything seemed unnatural, evil. She told herself she was being overly dramatic, imagining things, but she dreaded the evening with an agitated Terry, a falsely gay Jayne and the still unknown third member of the triangle. She hoped she could escape early without seeming rude.

Jayne chattered all the way to their destination while Terry said nothing. He had a troubled, faraway look. How changed he is, Mary thought. He's become a young man without hope. For a moment, she was ashamed of Jayne. She was as bad as Paul, maneuvering this boy's life. I hope she knows what she's doing, Mary prayed. I hope the end she believes in justifies the means.

Paul's high-floor, terraced apartment overlooking the Bay was as posh as Jayne promised. And Paul himself was as advertised: smooth and interesting. It wasn't difficult to see why anyone, male or female, could be attracted to him. He had an elegance about him that was more European than American. He even kissed Mary's hand when they were introduced, managing it gracefully and naturally, as most men did not.

"This is a long overdue pleasure," he said. "I've been looking forward to meeting you, Mrs. Morgan." He smiled. "Especially since I'm one of your great admirers."

Mary was determined to hide her feelings. She, too, smiled and said, "Please call me Mary. I'm delighted to be here. Jayne's told me how kind you've been to her and Terry."

He dismissed that with a deprecating gesture. "Terry and I are old friends. I was only too happy to find him interested in the boring world of brokers. As for Jayne, she's a delight. You're fortunate to have such a bright and beautiful niece.''

"I quite agree. I'm terribly proud of her." Mary looked around as they entered the living room. "What a lovely place! Jayne said it was beautiful but she didn't do it justice. Your taste runs toward the oriental, I see. So does mine. I find Chinese and Japanese furnishings the most beautiful of all, and you have so many magnificent examples.''

"I've been a collector for many years," Paul said. "Afraid I have an over-acquisitive nature. I can't resist anything I fall in love with, even if it's sometimes wildly overpriced.''

What a stilted, mannered exchange we're having, Mary thought. Like two fighters, sparring before the main event. What main event? This is not my battle. It's Jayne's and Paul's. I don't have to know what makes this man tick. It's not my problem, so why am I reading double meanings into everything he says? Why do I feel when he's talking about overpriced things he loves and must acquire that he really means Terry, not these inanimate objects? She accepted a glass of champage and lifted it in the direction of the two young people, who'd been silent since their arrival.

"To Jayne and Terry," she said. "A long and happy life.''

Paul raised his glass. "And to friendship.''

"I'll drink to that," Terry said. "All my best friends together at last." He swallowed his wine in a gulp and refilled his glass from the bottle in the cooler beside the cocktail table.

Jayne said nothing, but Mary saw her exchange a cynical smile with Paul. How can they do it? Mary wondered again. How can they play this waiting game, subtly edging each other toward some fatal error in calculation? Perhaps she was over-reacting, but there *was* something sinister about this outwardly perfect evening. All through dinner, though the conversation seemed easy and harmless, she had the feeling that every word from Jayne and Paul was fraught with terrible significance. I'm not alone, she realized. All four of us are on edge, Terry most of all. He was drinking too much. He'd had almost a whole bottle of champagne before and during dinner and was now starting on stingers when they returned to the living room for coffee. He was too keyed up, too obviously nervous. Can't Jayne see it? Mary thought. Can't she make him slow down? He's getting blind drunk. She's probably afraid to say anything to him. She'd sound like a nagging wife, and nothing would please Paul more. God! Is Terry worth all this? Can Jayne really care that much or does she just want to prove a point?

Mary was surprised to see the butler come in with a plate of brownies and put them on the low table in front of the sofa. Brownies? How totally out of character after a dinner of caviar mousse and sole amandine! Terry reached for one and only then did Jayne put out a restraining hand.

"Hey," she said lightly, "I don't think you need those after all the booze. You know Paul's brownies. That recipe's straight from Alice B. Toklas.''

"One won't hurt," Terry said. "I've had them often.''

"Not after a gallon of champagne and two stingers, silly. We'll have to call the rescue squad!''

"He can handle it, Jayne," Paul said calmly. "He's a big boy."

Jayne flushed. "You're supposed to be his friend, Paul. You should know better."

Mary was totally confused. What was all this about brownies? She watched Terry eat one of the little chocolate cakes, saw the distress in Jayne's eyes and the satisfaction in Paul's.

"Would you like one, Mary?" Paul held the plate toward her.

"No!" Jayne's voice was sharp. "She wouldn't like one. Paul, that's a terrible thing to do! I don't think Aunt Mary knows what they are."

"Oh, come, Jayne." His voice was condescending. "Your aunt is a worldly woman. Of course she knows."

Mary gave a little laugh. "I'm afraid I'm totally lost in all this. I honestly don't know what you're all talking about."

"Alice B. Toklas brownies aren't as innocent as they look," Jayne said. "They're full of marijuana. Maybe a little hashish, for all I know. Depends on how creative Paul's feeling when he makes them."

Mary's eyebrows lifted, but she tried not to seem shocked. "I see. Now that you mention it, I have heard of them, but I've not come in contact with them before. No thanks, Paul. I think I'll pass."

"Of course. As you like. Jayne doesn't care for them either."

"She doesn't know what she's missing." Terry took a second one before he could be stopped. "Dee-licious!"

Jayne looked half angry, half afraid. "Terry, stop! You know you can't handle that stuff." She bit her lip, knowing she was playing right into Paul's hands, acting like a prude. "No one can," she said. "It's dynamite, especially after you've been drinking. Paul will agree with me, honey. We don't want you to get sick."

"Never felt better." Terry got to his feet. "Who wants to dance?"

"Nobody," Jayne said. "Come on, darling. Sit down and relax."

Terry paid no attention. "Want to dance. Dance with me, Mary?"

She shook her head. "I don't think I could keep up with you." She glanced at her watch. "Besides, I really should be getting along. It's past eleven. Can I drop you and Jayne on my way?"

It was as though Terry didn't hear her. He was totally out of control, weaving his way around the room, humming to himself. The other three watched, the women anxiously, Paul with a permissive half-smile on his face.

"Don't worry about him, Jayne," Paul said. "He's high as a kite, but he's having fun. You don't want to be a downer, do you? Don't go yet, Mary. Please. It's early. And tomorrow's Sunday."

"It's been a lovely evening, Paul, but I really must . . ." She stopped. Terry had suddenly disappeared. "Where did Terry go?"

They'd taken their eyes off him for only a minute, but he'd vanished. Jayne stood up. "He's probably in the bathroom being sick. I'd better go get him and take him home."

"I'll go," Paul said. They were all standing now. "I'm sorry, Jayne. He used to be able to handle that stuff. I guess he doesn't have the tolerance for it anymore."

"There are a lot of things he can't tolerate anymore," Jayne said. "Including . . ."

Mary let out a small cry, interrupting her. "He's out there! Out on the terrace! My God, what is he doing?"

They rushed to the open door and stood frozen. Terry was balancing himself like a tightrope walker on top of the ledge that surrounded the terrace. Arms outstretched, dipping and weaving like an aerialist, he was picking his way along the high, precariously narrow concrete barrier. Sensing their presence, he glanced toward them and laughed.

"Look at me! Should have been in the circus!"

Jayne started toward him but her aunt held her back.

"Don't frighten him," she said quietly. "One misstep . . ." Her voice was barely louder than normal as she called out to Terry. "That's terrific, Terry. You're marvelous! But come on in, will you? It's too damned cold out there."

"It's nice." Terry's voice was happy. "Makes you feel like a bird. I can see a hundred miles, I bet. It's so pretty. I can see the Golden Gate Bridge, Jayne. Remember when we sailed under it?"

"Of course I do, darling. But we really have to go home now."

"Out there is Alcatraz." Terry was swaying on the edge. He giggled. "No more prisoners. Just tourists. That's nice. I used to be a prisoner, didn't I, Paul? I was your prisoner. No more. Got a wife now. Gonna have a baby." He began to sing. "Oh, if I had the wings of an angel . . ."

Paul's face was pale with fright. "Terry, for Christ's sake, get down from there! It's twelve stories, you fool!"

Terry kept smiling idiotically. "What's everybody so upset about? Come on, join me! Such a great view. Free. You feel free out here." He lurched dangerously and Paul raced toward him, heedless of Mary's warnings.

"Terry! No! Wait!"

The sudden, loud voice made the man on the ledge turn quickly. For a moment he looked puzzled as he realized he'd lost his balance. Terry seemed to fight for a split second and then, almost as though he was pleased, he raised his arms above his head and was gone.

Jayne's horrified screams split the silence of the night. Instinctively, Mary grabbed her, fearful the girl might try to follow. Paul stood as though rooted, not more than two feet from the wall, paralyzed with horror. None of them dared look over. They knew too well what they'd see lying on the street far below. For a few interminable seconds they were like a tableau, punctuated by Jayne's shrieks of anguish, which went on and on until they became part of the sirens that announced the arrival of the police.

Only two, maybe three minutes passed before the patrol car came. Mary remembered thinking, inanely, that it must have been close by. She stood holding Jayne in her arms, not knowing how to still her cries, not believing, quite yet, what had happened. She was aware that Paul did not move, and in one of those crazy flashes of clarity she wondered whether she was holding on to the wrong person. Paul looked as though he might be the one who'd insanely go after Terry. But when he heard the police sirens he turned and faced the two women. Over Jayne's hysterical screams, Mary heard him say, "I killed him. I killed

Terry." He brushed past them and disappeared into his bedroom. An awful premonition overtook Mary. Quickly she guided Jayne inside and turned to the Japanese butler, who stood, equally stunned, in the living room.

"Go see if Mr. Le Compte is all right."

The man nodded and approached the bedroom door as Mary forced Jayne to lie down on the couch. She sat beside her, holding her hand, patting her, relieved to hear the yelling begin to turn to sobs and moans.

"Door locked," the butler said over his shoulder.

"Can you force it? Try. It's important."

The man threw his shoulder hard against the door, but it didn't budge. "Door no open," he said.

"Go get help," Mary ordered. "Quickly!"

But before he could do so, the doorbell rang urgently. Paul's manservant opened it. A policeman and another man, apparently the building superintendent, stood in the entrance.

"Where's Mr. Le Compte?" the officer asked. "The super says the man on the street must have fallen from this apartment. He recognized him."

Mary pointed toward the bedroom. "In there, but it's locked. I think you'd better get in quickly, Officer. I'm afraid . . ."

"I have a master key," the superintendent offered.

The two men went in and came out quickly. The policeman's face was gray as he looked at Mary.

"I don't think you'd better go in there, ma'am. It's not a pretty sight."

Mary glanced at Jayne. The girl seemed only semiconscious, understanding nothing.

"Did he . . . ?"

"Yes, ma'am. A straight razor."

"Oh, my God!"

"Ambulance is on the way. Too late for either of them, I'm afraid, but maybe the doctor should look at the young lady."

"Yes," Mary said. "Yes, of course. She's my niece. That's her husband who . . . who fell. She's pregnant. This shock. I don't know."

"The doc'll be here in a few minutes." The policeman was kind, gentle. "Don't worry. She'll be all right." He seemed almost embarrassed. "Could you answer a few questions, please? Tell me what happened here?"

No, Mary thought, I can never tell you what happened. I don't know what happened. Terry was an actor. Was he really as out of control as he wanted us to believe or was he playing his final role? Was it an accident, or was this his way out of a situation he couldn't tolerate? She shuddered. What would happen now? Jayne might lose her baby. She was ashamed to realize she almost hoped that would be the case. Terry gone in this terrible way. Paul taking his own life. How responsible would Jayne feel for what happened? How much would she want a child to remind her every day of so many unanswered questions?

"Ma'am? Do you feel up to giving me a few facts?"

"Yes. The man . . . the man who fell is Terry Spalding. It was an accident. A silly game where he was pretending to be a tightrope walker." Her voice broke. "A silly, senseless game."

"I see. Sorry to ask, but had he been drinking? Or were there drugs?"

Mary wanted to deny both things. She already envisioned the publicity that would be so hard on Jayne. God knows what the papers would dig up about Terry and Paul. The butler knew. So did the super. He'd led them right to the apartment Terry once occupied. But there was no use lying about the liquor or the drugs. There would be an autopsy. They'd find out anyway.

"We had some champagne," she said. "And I believe there was some marijuana in a brownie Mr. Spalding ate."

The officer shook his head. Dumb bastard. Stoned out of his mind. Drugs. Car crashes. Homicides with Saturday Night Specials. Young guys like the one down there in the blanket. Girls, too, sometimes. And all the grief-stricken people they left behind.

"About Mr."—the policeman consulted his notebook—"Le Compte. Paul Le Compte. That right?"

Mary nodded.

"Clear case of suicide, of course. But could you give me any idea of why he did it? Had there been an argument of some kind?"

"No. No argument. We were all friends. It was just to be a quiet little dinner." Mary looked at the young officer helplessly. "I have no idea why Mr. Le Compte did what he did. I suppose he felt responsible for . . . for the other things, the champagne and the brownies." Suddenly she was exhausted. She wished the doctor would come and look after Jayne. The girl lay still now, eyes closed. She seemed to be barely breathing. "Where is that ambulance?" Mary said angrily. "Can't you see my niece needs care?"

"Just a minute, Mrs. . . . . sorry, I'm afraid I don't know your name."

"Morgan. Mary Farr Morgan."

He wrote it down carefully before he recognized it. "The lady on radio?"

"Yes."

"My wife listens to you every week!" He looked impressed for a few seconds before he became the professional again. "I guess I'll have to ask you to identify your nephew, Mrs. Morgan. Sorry, but I'm sure his wife isn't up to it."

"Can't that wait? I want to be sure she's all right."

"Sure. No rush. The morning will be okay." He seemed ill at ease. What the hell was a woman like Mary Farr Morgan doing mixed up in this kind of thing? A suicide. An accident, if it was. For all he knew, the guy in the bedroom might have pushed the other one over the side. Booze and drugs. Jesus! You never knew. When his wife talked about Mary Farr Morgan he always imagined some nice little old grandmotherly type. Not this good-looking dame who couldn't be more than forty. He was relieved when the ambulance guys arrived. The intern quickly examined the young woman and suggested she stay in the hospital overnight.

"It's nothing to worry about," the doctor said. "Everything seems okay, but she's in shock. In her condition, it pays to be careful. If you give me the name of her doctor, we'll notify him she's being admitted."

From somewhere in the back of her mind, Mary dredged up the name of the obstetrician Jayne had once mentioned.

"May I go with her in the ambulance?"

"Sure."

"What about . . . the others?"

"We'll take care of it," the doctor said. He looked at the policeman. "Identification?"

"Got it all. Mrs. Morgan will make it official tomorrow."

It's not happening, Mary told herself as she followed Jayne's now quiet form on the stretcher. None of it. Not the ambulances and the police cars. Not the morbidly curious crowds and the newspaper reporters and television crews who kept trying to ask her questions as she came out of the building. How did they get here so fast? she wondered. Time seemed to have stood still, but glancing at her watch she saw it was more than half an hour since Terry had stood on the ledge. She brushed the press aside.

"Not now," she said. "Please. I have to go to the hospital with my niece."

"Did he fall or did someone push him?"

"Maybe he jumped?"

"Why did Le Compte slash his throat?"

"Is it true that Spalding and Le Compte . . . ?"

Mary turned on them angrily. "Have you no decency? Can't you see there are more important things right now than your questions?"

A man she recognized from one of the TV stations caught her arm. "Hell, Mary, you, of all people, know this is just our job! You understand!"

She stared straight at him. "I don't care about your job. And I'm tired of understanding. You can quote me on that!"

"Some attitude from one of us," another reporter said nastily.

Mary didn't answer. I'm not one of you, she thought as she climbed silently into the ambulance. I'm not a radio commentator now. I'm a woman who's just seen two lives destroyed and another one jolted beyond endurance. What do you want of me, for God's sake? Headlines? Good quotes? You don't need me for that. You'll find plenty to write about, plenty of grist for the gossip mills. Say anything you want. I don't give a damn.

Chapter 30

MICHAEL QUIETLY OPENED the front door of Rae Spanner's apartment and picked up the Sunday paper. He tucked it under his arm and sneaked back to his own bed. Thank God, Rae didn't insist on sleeping in the same room with him. He could make love to her, but he didn't want to wake up next to this woman who'd so quickly come to take him for granted. She kept mentioning marriage, but Michael had side-stepped the issue since he moved in with her ten days ago. Who needs marriage? he thought. Marriage is for kids hellbent on overpopulating the world. I've tried it twice. So has Rae. Why should either of us risk being three-time losers at our age? And it wasn't as though either of them was hung up on "appearances." They were both free, and who cared if they lived together? Correction, he thought. Who cares if I live with Rae?

He'd drifted into the arrangement easily, almost fatalistically, after the divorce. He had little choice. No job. No prospects. And he couldn't stay forever at his mother's little house, it was driving him wild. Rae had come down and made another businesslike offer, this one involving his total time. He accepted indifferently. What did it matter? Besides, he was almost broke. The ten thousand he'd drawn out of his and Mary's checking account had dwindled alarmingly. It went fast when you bought clothes, rented a car, flew first-class to Mexico and back and paid the expenses of the divorce. He'd spent quite a lot on Rae when she was in Los Angeles, too. Good restaurants were expensive. A dinner for two could run more than a hundred dollars with wine, and he'd bought a number for her before his divorce. Not to mention all the entertaining he'd done before that, when he was trying to make contact with some of the Southern California big shots.

He felt bad about the money. Mary must know by now. Probably she hated him for it. Okay. Better she should hate him than feel sorry for him. He knew it was wrong to take it, but it was only a little more than he could have asked for under the community property laws anyhow. Half of fifteen thousand was what he was entitled to, if he'd cared to make a fuss. Not to mention the furnishings and other things. So it wasn't so terrible, after all.

He sighed, thinking of Mary. He wondered if she'd heard he'd moved in with Rae. Of course she had by now. The grapevine was fast and reliable. He dreaded the day he'd bump into her. Not that it wasn't finished. She had her Australian. But Michael still loved her. So much that he didn't want to see her again. Thank God she'd be moving away. The memory of her would slowly fade. She'd be somebody else's wife. He allowed himself a cynical smile. And I'll be Mr. Rae Spanner, he thought. No amount of logic was going to keep that dominating woman from having her way. Rae wanted to be married. It was only a question of time before he'd either agree or get out. He knew he'd agree. He wasn't likely to get a better offer.

He picked up the front section of the paper and sat bolt upright. A two-column headline at the bottom of the first page stunned him.

MARY FARR MORGAN'S NEPHEW
DIES IN PLUNGE FROM BALCONY
Second Man Suicide In Same Apartment

Shortly before midnight Saturday, Terrence Spalding, a nephew by marriage of radio commentator Mary Farr Morgan, fell or jumped to his death from the twelfth-story balcony of 1628 Marina Avenue, home of a mutual friend, Paul Le Compte. Minutes after the tragedy, Mr. Le Compte was found in the bedroom of the apartment, an apparent suicide from razor wounds.

According to police, Spalding, aged 26, was walking on the ledge of the wall-enclosed terrace when he lost his balance. Tashi Yoko, Le Compte's houseman, told reporters that there'd been a dinner party given by his employer and attended by Mr. Spalding and his wife, Jayne Richton Spalding, and her aunt, Ms. Morgan. Shortly after eleven, Mr. Yoko heard excited voices from the living room and came out to see Mr. Spalding balancing himself on the terrace railing while the others tried to coax him down.

"Mr. Terry was laughing," Mr. Yoko said. "He thought it was a joke. Then he fell. And Mr. Le Compte locked himself in his room and took a razor to his throat.''

Police tentatively confirmed the account. Rumors of drugs and alcohol could not be confirmed, they said, pending autopsies of the two bodies. It was reliably learned, however, that for several years before Mr. Spalding's marriage, he and Mr. Le Compte, a broker aged 33, shared the luxury apartment.

Ms. Spalding was hospitalized for extreme shock and Ms. Morgan could not be reached for comment. At the hospital early this morning, Charles Burke, a family friend and Ms. Morgan's employer, would say only that it had been a tragic accident and details would be released later.

Michael dropped the paper. Good Christ! Mary hadn't even mentioned Jayne being married when they talked in Los Angeles. For all he knew, she was living in San Francisco with her mother, the way Patricia planned it before the girl returned. He read the article again. The implications were horrendous. I should call Mary, he thought. She must be out of her mind. No. She'd be all right. She rose to occasions like this. Besides, Charlie Burke was very much in evidence. And there was no surprise to that.

Pan American Flight 816, nonstop from Sydney, arrived in San Francisco at 11:20 A.M. Christopher deplaned, feeling weary despite his anticipation. The damned time change was a nuisance. They'd picked up a whole day on the trip, so he'd left Australia at three o'clock Sunday afternoon, *his* time, and reached the States on Sunday morning *their* time. No matter what the clock or the calendar said, it was a long and tiring trip, and he'd be glad to get to the hotel and have a bath and a change of clothes before he saw Mary. Once again, he felt buoyed by the surprise in store for her. He'd call the minute he got to his room. They'd have lunch together. Or brunch, as the Americans called it. Maybe she'll pull something together for us at home, he thought hopefully. I want to be alone with her, to hold her in my arms. It seemed an eternity.

Mary lay across her bed, fully dressed as she'd been at the fateful dinner party. She couldn't sleep, though she'd been there for hours. All through the night, she'd been at Jayne's side at the hospital. She'd called Charlie soon after they arrived, and he'd come over and kept the vigil with her, though Jayne didn't know they were there. They'd heavily sedated the young woman, a blessing, no matter a temporary one.

The doctors and nurses had urged Mary to go home and get some rest. ''Your niece won't be awake for hours,'' they said. ''It's pointless for you to stay here. You've had a terrible shock, too, Mrs. Morgan.''

She'd refused to leave until Jayne woke and Mary could see for herself that the girl was all right. That had been at seven o'clock this morning. She'd opened her eyes, looked confused for a few seconds before memory returned. Mary took her hand and held on tightly, not knowing what to say.

''Terry's dead.'' Jayne's voice was leaden.

''Yes, darling. It was a tragic accident. A ghastly one.''

"*Was* it an accident?"

"Of course! You remember the condition he was in. He was just playing a prank, trying to frighten us. I'm so sorry, Jaynie. So terribly, terribly sorry."

The slender figure in the bed shuddered. "The baby. Is the baby all right?"

"It's fine," Mary said gently. "No problem."

"Thank God for that. At least I'll have his child. Paul can't take that away from me."

Mary drew on all her strength. Jayne didn't know Paul was dead, too. No reason to tell her at this moment. One horror at a time.

"Paul could never take anything away from you, sweetheart," she said. "He couldn't take Terry and he'll never be able to take Terry's child."

Jayne's eyelids were drooping. "I'm so tired. It's hard to remember. . . . Everything is a blur." Tears slid slowly down her cheeks. "I just know he's gone. I loved him, Aunt Mary. We were happy."

"I know, darling. You made him very happy. That's what you must remember."

"Don't want to sleep. Can't help it . . ." Jayne's voice drifted off.

"Sleep," Mary said. "It's your best medicine. I'll be right here."

Only then did she go to the morgue to identify, with horror, what remained of Terry. After, Charlie took her home. Hours ago. There were so many things to be done and she didn't have the energy to do them. Thank God for Charlie. He was seeing to the funeral arrangements, as he'd done all too recently for Tracey. But this time Mary was incapable of helping him. Neither of them knew what to do about Paul. If he had family, they were unaware of it. We'll have to find out, Mary thought. His office will know. Nothing can be done today, in any case. Nothing until after the autopsies. The thought made her cringe. She hated the idea of violating a body even after death, but that was the law in cases such as this.

She couldn't grieve for Paul, of course. She couldn't even sincerely mourn Terry's passing, except for the effect it would have on Jayne. She'd have given anything to undo the events of the past few months for Jayne's sake. If only I hadn't taken her on the cruise, Mary thought once more, none of this would have happened. That was stupid thinking, she realized, but she couldn't help it. But if she was irrationally blaming herself for Jayne's problems, God knows Patricia would blame her even more now.

Patricia! Mary suddenly sat up. She hadn't called Patricia and Stanley! They'd have to be told right away. Undoubtedly they'd want to come out, to be near Jayne, even though Stanley had never met Terry and Patricia had seen him only once, briefly, the day the ship returned. Still, he was their son-in-law. Their daughter's husband. Jayne would want them informed. Reluctantly, she reached for the phone. Half-past eleven. She hoped they'd be home at half-past two on a Sunday afternoon in New York.

"I think we're the only people left in New York on a weekend in June," Patricia said petulantly. "Other people have country houses, or at least get invited away for the weekend." She fanned herself. "It's so damned hot in here! Are you sure the air conditioner is working?"

"It's working," Stanley answered. "Feels perfectly comfortable to me."

"Well, I'm dying of the heat!"

"Maybe you're having a hot flash."

She knew he meant it as a joke, but it wasn't funny. "I'm having no such thing! What kind of a crack is that? I'm years away from those symptoms!"

"Okay, okay," Stanley said placatingly. "I didn't mean it, hon. I'm sorry you're uncomfortable. Maybe I can turn the air conditioner up higher."

"Turn it to 'frantic.' Then it and I will be even."

The phone rang and Patricia impatiently went to the bedroom to answer it. Probably her mother complaining about something. Her "hello" was tinged with irritation.

"Patricia? It's Mary."

"Mary?" Her voice dripped sarcasm. "Mary *who?*"

She ignored the sarcasm. "Patricia, I have some terrible news." As quickly and briefly as possible, Mary described what had happened the night before. "Jayne's all right," she said. "She'll probably be released from the hospital today. I'm going to bring her here to stay with me for a while."

Patricia listened incredulously. It was a dreadful story. Even so, she sensed that Mary was leaving out some details.

"This Le Compte man. Who was he?"

"A friend of Jayne and Terry's. He and Terry shared the apartment before, and he'd gotten Terry a job in the firm where he worked."

"Was he gay? Was Terry gay?"

Mary tried to suppress her annoyance and failed. "I don't know," she lied. "What difference does it make? They're dead, both of them."

"It all sounds very fishy to me."

"Patricia!" Mary was at the end of her rope. "This isn't the time for gossip! For God's sake, your daughter has just lost her husband! She's in shock! It's damned lucky this didn't bring on a miscarriage. I'd think you would . . ."

"Miscarriage? You mean Jayne's pregnant?"

Mary could have kicked herself. She should have known Jayne hadn't told her parents anything yet and probably didn't plan to until she was further along. Well, it didn't matter now. They'd have to know eventually, but it would have been better if they'd heard it from their daughter.

"Yes. She's going to have a baby in December." She could almost see Patricia ticking off seven months on her fingers. "That's right," Mary said boldly, "she was pregnant when they got married. You and Stanley would be the last people in the world to condemn her for that." Instantly she regretted her nasty crack. "I'm sorry. . . . That was uncalled for. I just meant . . ."

"I know what you meant. You never miss a chance to rub it in, do you? Well, at least my daughter and I know how to give of ourselves, which is more than anybody can say for you!"

Mary was too done in to fight. Patricia was hopeless. She was the guilty one, the amoral creature who'd slept with her own sister's husband, and she was behaving as though it was Mary, not she, who should be on the defensive. It was all too ugly, too absurd. *Give of herself.* Patricia didn't have an unselfish bone in her body. She thought of nothing but her own desires. Even now she probably was figuring out how she could make this tragedy work to her own advantage. Her next words confirmed that suspicion.

"I'll get a flight out there this afternoon. I presume you'll be willing to put me up, too, under these circumstances?"

Mary hesitated. She never wanted to lay eyes on Patricia again, but she was Jayne's mother. She had a right to be at the funeral of her daughter's husband. But that wasn't why she was coming. With Terry out of the way, Patricia probably hoped to expedite her original plan of sharing an apartment with Jayne. And now that the girl was pregnant, there would be an even stronger reason for Patricia to move in on her daughter and pretend to take care of her and the grandchild when it arrived. Jayne won't want that, Mary thought. She'll never live with her mother. She doesn't even like her.

"I could put you up for a few days," Mary said reluctantly, "but if you're planning a longer stay . . ."

"I'll make my plans when I get there, thank you."

"I'm sure you will." Mary tried to sound unconcerned. "What about Stanley? Won't he want to come, too?"

"I don't know. I really don't see how he can. We can't afford the trip for both of us. It would mean hotel expenses, too."

"If he wants to come, we'll manage." As she said it, Mary wondered how they would. Maybe Stanley could stay with Charlie. Or she could get a folding cot and put it in the living room. Or maybe both Patricia and Stanley could stay in the little place Jayne and Terry had shared. If it came to the worst, she'd pay for a hotel room for them. That would be best in any case. She couldn't face having Patricia under her roof. Why on earth had she said she would? "Now that I think of it," Mary said, "why don't I just arrange for you to stay in a hotel? It would be more comfortable for everybody and then Stanley can come too."

"I told you, Mary, we can't afford that expense."

"You can be my guest."

"We don't want your charity. No. Stanley had better stay home."

"For God's sake, Patricia, what difference whether you're here or in a hotel? You're a guest either way."

"I won't be beholden to you. Not after the things you've done."

In spite of herself, Mary began to laugh. Her sister was perfectly willing to move into the apartment, drink the liquor and eat the food, but letting Mary pay for a hotel was "charity." And always this reproachful thing, as though Patricia was the injured party in their broken relationship. To hell with it. I don't care where she stays, Mary thought. This is no time for family feuds. We seem to be forgetting that we have a grief-stricken young woman on our hands, and an ill-fated young man to lay to rest. Why are we squabbling over these petty details?

"Do whatever you like," Mary said. "I really don't care."

"I'll be there tonight. Please tell Jayne I'm coming."

Mary had hardly hung up when the phone rang. For a moment, when she heard Christopher's voice, she thought he must somehow have heard about the tragedy in Australia. But he sounded much too ebullient for that.

"Hello, sweetheart, what are you doing for lunch?"

"Christopher? Where are you?"

"Only a few blocks away, at the Fairmont."

"The Fairmont! Here? How? When?"

"Got in this morning. How are you, darling? When can I come over?"

She began to laugh hysterically, uncontrollably. Christopher was alarmed.

"Mary! What is it? What's wrong?"

Gasping, she finally managed to calm down. "Nothing. I mean, dear God, what next?"

He felt terribly let down. This was not the reaction he'd expected.

"You sound as though you're sorry I'm here," he said stiffly. "I suppose I should have let you know I was coming. I rather thought it would be a happy surprise."

She realized how her laughter and her first words must have sounded to him. He knew nothing of the past eighteen hours of her life.

"Oh, sweetheart, it is a happy surprise! The most wonderful thing that could have happened at this very moment. You're like a gift from heaven. It was just too much, suddenly, on top of everything else. I . . . I've dreamed for months of the moment when you'd arrive. I planned the things we'd do before we left together, the time we'd spend here as Mr. and Mrs. Andrews. I wanted our reunion to be full of laughter. Real, happy laughter, not hysteria. Christopher, the world's gone mad and you arrive in the middle of it . . . I mean, I'm happy, but it wasn't the way I planned it . . . that is . . ." She stopped, aware she was rambling.

"Calm down." His voice was firm, reassuring. "Tell me what's been going on here. Take it one step at a time."

"Yes." Again, she repeated the hideous story of Saturday night. "And now I'm bringing Jayne to stay in the apartment," she concluded, "and Patricia's flying in tonight, and we'll be surrounded by people and grief, and there'll be no privacy for us and no joy the way I imagined it. It's not fair!" She sounded like a disappointed child. "You're here and I want to spend every minute alone with you. Oh, God, that sounds so terribly selfish! I know I shouldn't be thinking of myself at a time like this. It's just that I didn't expect you until August, and to have you come when things are so dreadful and I'll be pulled apart by so many obligations and I haven't slept and I'm such a wreck and this isn't the way . . ."

"Be quiet!" There was love in the command. "Mary, darling, we're not children. What difference if this isn't the reunion we both imagined? I'm here at the time you need me most. It's a miracle. As though something told me to come. Dear heart, I don't care who's around. We don't need storybook settings, for God's sake! We have years to be alone together in any romantic spot you care to name. I'm not concerned about that now; I'm concerned about you. You're all that matters to me." He paused and said gently, "I'm coming right over. We'll get through this together."

"Yes," she said. "Please. Come right away, Christopher. I need you to hold me and never let me go."

"I never will. Never again."

Jayne woke for the second time and lay staring at the ceiling of the hospital room. She remembered it all vividly, now, in every unbearable detail. It's my fault, she thought in despair. My fault for trying to play God. I tampered with another person's life, so certain I knew what was best for him. I refused to believe Terry couldn't be happy in the kind of life I wanted. I was so arrogant about my ability to outwit Paul. I was wrong. Paul won in the end. And Terry? Terry knew what he was doing last night. He couldn't pretend any longer. A dry sob escaped her throat. I killed them both and I'll be punished for it. I deserve to be punished.

Why can't I cry? If only I could weep for Terry and the baby who'll never know him. Even for Paul, who cared in a way I'd never be capable of. For myself and my blind determination to have things my way.

And what now? Where am I headed with this baby inside me? Perhaps I should abort. It's not too late. Yes it is, she answered herself. Too late to release Terry. He's already done that for himself. Wrong to snuff out another life on top of those I've already taken. Not to have this child would make it all meaningless and futile. It's Terry's only chance at immortality. I'll love his son or daughter in the unselfish way I didn't love him.

"Jayne?"

She turned her head and saw Charlie in the doorway.

"How are you feeling, honey?"

She tried to smile. "Okay. What are you doing here? Why aren't you home getting some rest? I know you and Aunt Mary were here all night."

"Don't worry about us. I took Mary home a few hours ago. I don't think she slept, but she did lie down. Your mother's on the way."

"Oh, no!" It was an involuntary reaction she quickly tried to cover. "I mean, there's no need for her to make the trip."

"She wants to, I'm sure. In any case, Mary had to call her. I think in her own way your mother loves you very much, Jayne."

Jayne thought of her father's letter. I suppose she does love me. And in *my* crazy way I guess I love her, too. She's done some terrible things to people, but who am I to condemn her now?

"Is my father coming, too?"

"I don't know. There seemed to be some confusion about that." Charlie seemed nervous. "There's something else Mary just told me. Christopher Andrews has arrived in town."

"Christopher? How did he know?"

"He didn't. It was a weird coincidence." Charlie sat down next to the bed. "I know this isn't the moment to discuss it, but I have a hunch he'll want to take Mary back with him, and I wondered how you'd feel about taking over the show within the next few weeks, instead of waiting until August. You see, I don't think Mary will go unless you reassure her that you can handle things alone. Not just the job, but your whole life. I'm afraid she feels totally responsible for you, now that Terry's gone. She may give up the whole idea of Christopher because of some silly notion that none of this would have happened if she hadn't taken you on the cruise. We talked about that again last night, before we knew Christopher was arriving. I told her what nonsense it was to feel that way, but I'm not sure she believes me. You'll have to make her believe it, Jayne. You're the only one who can make her stop feeling guilty about any part of this."

"She wouldn't! She wouldn't give up the best thing in her life to stay here and look after me."

"Wouldn't she? She adores you. You're the child she never had. I even tried to be practical about it. Told her to remember that if she didn't leave, you couldn't step into her job. She said she'd thought of that. She said she was sure she could get a job at another station. She would, too. The way she's feeling right now, she'd resign and go to work someplace else, rather than deprive you."

Jayne was stunned. "That's insane, Charlie! What are we going to do?"

He shook his head. "I don't think there's anything I can do. Whether it's now, August or never, I'm afraid Mary's departure depends on how convincing you can be. I'm sorry to burden you with this, my dear, but Christopher's appearance puts a new light on things. We can't let Mary throw away the thing she wants most, out of some exaggerated sense of guilt or duty."

For a moment, Jayne forgot herself and Mary. This dear man. He loved Mary so much he was willing to drive her away. Not many other people would be so selfless. Wasn't it a temptation for him to agree with Mary, to say that she should, indeed, stay here and look after her niece and the unborn child? It would have been so easy for him to play on those very guilts he mentioned. Mary trusted his judgment, and rightly. He had only to encourage her and she'd break it off with Christopher, stay in San Francisco, get another job and, probably, one day marry Charlie. But he cared too much to do that. Jayne looked tenderly at his troubled face.

"You really love her a lot, don't you?"

Charlie smiled. "She's the most idiotic, pig-headed, insecure, vulnerable, strong and necessary woman in the whole damned world. And yes, I love her a lot."

"I know how to fix it," Jayne said.

Charlie nodded soberly. He guessed what was in her mind. He rose heavily and put his hand on Jayne's.

"You love her, too."

"Very much. Enough to hurt her if it will help."

It was impossible, Mary thought, that with all the grief and worry on her mind she could still respond like a schoolgirl when Christopher arrived and put his arms around her. She clung to him, trembling. He kissed her deeply and then held her at arm's length.

"You're more beautiful than ever."

Despite herself, she laughed. "Beautiful? With no sleep and all that's happened since last night? Christopher, my darling, love really is blind."

"I never saw you more clearly than I do at this moment. Never wanted you more."

"Nor I, you."

He forgot his weariness as Mary forgot her troubles. He pulled her close to him, feeling the soft, familiar shape of her body.

"Talking can come later," he said. "God, how I've missed you!"

Mary closed her eyes, feeling the wonderful weakening in her legs, the sense of floating on some all-enveloping cloud of desire that blotted out everything except this moment and this man. It was wrong, she thought briefly, to be so happy when others were so sad. No, not wrong. This feeling of delight was something apart. Rejecting it would not diminish Jayne's sorrow or bring Terry back to life.

Gladly, gratefully, she drew Christopher even closer toward her. For a little while, at least, the reunion would be all they imagined.

Chapter 31

OUTWARDLY, SHE APPEARED calm, a well-dressed, still-beautiful middle-aged woman in the window seat of economy class on the late-afternoon flight to San Francisco. But inside, Patricia was a mass of rage and frustration. She glanced to her left at Stanley's impassive face. He stared ahead, saying nothing to her, aware of her anger and unmoved by it. For once, he'd been more determined than she. This afternoon, when she reported Mary's bad news, Stanley had taken matters into his own hands.

"Start packing," he said. "We're going out there right away. That poor child must be going through hell!"

"I've already told Mary I'll be there tonight, dear. I knew you'd want me to go."

"Not *you*," Stanley said. "*Us*. You don't think I'm going to sit home at a time like this, do you? That's not just your child out there, Patricia. She's mine too."

She'd tried to placate him. "Of course she's ours. I know how you feel, but this is a mother's job, Stanley. Jayne will understand. Men just aren't good around grief. You know how you hate funerals."

"I love my daughter more than I hate funerals. I don't wish to discuss it. We're going together."

She began to be exasperated. "That's foolish! If you go, it will cost a fortune. Two plane fares. And we'll have to stay in a hotel. Jayne's going to be at Mary's and there'll be room for me, but not for you *and* me. For heaven's sake, be practical for once in your life! You can't do anything for Jayne!"

He stared at her coldly. "I beg to differ. Maybe I can do more for her than you can."

"Such as?"

Stanley took a deep breath. Hurting people was foreign to him and he hated it, but she left him no alternative. "Such as giving her the feeling of being loved and understood."

It was Patricia's turn to stare. "Are you saying *I* don't love and understand her?"

"No. I think you love her. Understand her? I'm not sure. We've always had a special closeness, Jayne and I. Maybe fathers and daughters manage that better than mothers and daughters. I don't know. I do know we've shared a bond of trust. Her hand has always been in mine. She's never felt threatened by me or competitive with me, and she knows I'm always on her side. Do you think she feels that way about you?"

"What you're saying is that you've always spoiled her rotten!" Patricia was furious. " 'Bond of trust,' indeed! She was always able to twist you around her little finger. I was the one who tried to keep her feet on the ground while you filled her head full of ideas about how wonderful she was! I was the heavy. Understand her? You bet I understand her. She's been selfish since the day she was born, thanks to you. Look what she's done, staying in California, marrying that simpering little actor, getting pregnant by him. And now I suppose she'll expect us to take care of her and her baby until she can find another man. My God, do you think I've liked being the disciplinarian? Don't you think I'd rather take your easy route, giving her everything, never criticizing her, always buying her love? But I couldn't do that. She had to learn that the world is cruel and people are rotten and everything doesn't come up smelling like roses, the way Daddy would like her to believe!"

Stanley shook his head. "And this is what you think a mother's job is? This is the comfort and solace you're going to offer her? No, Patricia. I'm not going to let you go out there alone and tell Jayne what a fool she's been. I'm not going to give you a chance to rub her nose in her mistakes. You'd like that. Just as you'd like to make Mary's life miserable. You're jealous of both of them. No," he said again, "you're not going to stir everybody up the way you did before. God knows what you did then. But this time I'll be watching you. You and I will go as loving parents to be with our widowed daughter. We'll be there to lend our support, not to make accusations or cause her more grief than she already has. I don't know what we're going to find when we get there. All I know is that the past is history and we have to see where Jayne wants to go from here."

She'd never heard him sound so confident and unmovable. Once again, Patricia tried to appeal to reason. "Stanley, you don't believe I'll be anything but sympathetic. Surely you can trust me to be understanding *now*, even if you don't think I've been in the past. And there *is* the money. Probably Jayne will want to come back to New York. There'll be the cost of that as well as Lord knows what other bills she may have. We can't afford double travel expense for no reason."

"There's every reason," he said quietly. "She needs both of us. As for the expense, how better could we spend our money? But if you're really worried about that, Patricia, why can't we stay in Jayne's apartment instead of a hotel? She'll be at Mary's. I'd think you'd prefer not to stay with your sister anyway, after the things you've said about her."

He had her. There was no way she could keep him from going. Damn him, Patricia thought now, as the plane flew swiftly westward, he's going to mess up everything. I was sure, in her vulnerable state, Jayne would leap at the idea I had before: that we could share an apartment. And Michael's free now. I could get back together with him. But no, Stanley has to tag along to ruin my life as he always has.

Mary lay in the crook of Christopher's arm, savoring the feel of him beside her.

"How long can you stay?"

"In San Francisco? As long as you need me, darling."

She gave a sad little smile. "That would be forever. I mean *really* how long?"

He gently disengaged his arm and sat up. "I'd planned ten days or so. A couple of weeks maybe. I thought perhaps I could talk you into winding up your affairs by then and going back with me, instead of waiting until August."

She raised herself to his eye level. "I can't, Christopher. Not now. Maybe if this thing hadn't happened to Jayne . . . But I can't leave her now. I was worried even before. I didn't have that much faith in Terry, but I'd convinced myself that at least she had a husband. Now she has no one. I'm sure she won't want to go back to New York. She couldn't live with her parents again, Patricia especially. And she's coming into a good job here that will mean she can support herself and her child. No, she'll want to stay, and she'll need me, darling."

"So do I."

"I know. But in a different way. You're not helpless and frightened, my love. You're not bereaved and alone and terribly young. We forget how young she is, Christopher."

He didn't answer for a minute. Then he said, "Answer me something honestly. If this hadn't happened, this thing with Jayne, and if I'd arrived this morning, would you have gone back with me? Would you even have come in August, knowing Jayne was pregnant and Terry was undependable? Or would you have asked me to wait longer? Until the baby was born, perhaps? Or until Jayne was safely remarried to someone you approved of? Would you have gone on and on, Mary, setting our life aside because you felt indispensable?"

"I . . . I can't answer those questions, darling. Nobody knows what he'll do in a terrible situation until he's faced with it. You know I love you. I love you more than anything in the world, but . . ."

"No," Christopher said, "you don't love me more than anything in the world. You love your conscience more. Forgive me for saying it, dearest, but you also love more the feeling of being needed. And you can't comprehend that my needs and your own are as important as Jayne's."

"That's not true! I'm not indispensable to her. I know that."

"Do you, Mary? Do you really?"

"Yes, of course."

"Then have some faith in her. She'll look after herself. She's strong. And unselfish. The *last* thing she'd want is to feel obligated to you, knowing you're giving up your life for hers."

"But I'm not giving it up. It's just a matter of . . ."

"Time?" he finished for her. "How much time? We lost a lot of our lives before we found each other. There aren't that many years to squander. I can't wait forever," he said quietly. "I can't live on dreams and promises and sacrifice. Perhaps I'm not as generous as you. I want to live with the woman I love and enjoy whatever time is left. I won't sit around for months and years, darling, while you fret over a lovely child who isn't even your own. She has parents for that, if there's worrying to be done. It's not your job, Mary. *I'm* your job. At least you led me to believe I was."

She sat with eyes closed. "I don't know. What you're saying is right. The logical part of me accepts it, but the emotional side . . . Please don't push me right now, Christopher. It's been such a hard time. Everything is so sad and frightening. Let me think. Just a few days, that's all I ask.''

He kissed her gently. "Of course, my love. Don't think this is easy for me, either. But it has to be done, and *now*. So that if, God forbid, you feel held here, we can try to accept that and go our own ways."

"Yes. You're right. It's not fair to prolong the agony. Or, the ecstasy.'' She managed to smile. "I'm blessed to have you. You're my comfort and my joy.''

He glanced at the bedside clock. "And your friendly reminder, as well,'' he said lightly. "Didn't you tell me you were going to pick up Jayne at four? It's three now. Hadn't we better move?''

"Will you go with me?''

"Naturally. I love that young woman. She fancies herself as invincible as her aunt.''

Mary got up reluctantly. "I'm ashamed of myself, being so happy these past couple of hours while Jayne is so miserable. I'd like to wish it all away, Christopher. More for my sake than anyone else's. I'd like to wish away last night and the next few days. I dread tonight when Patricia arrives. I hate the thought of seeing her. My own sister. I can't stand the thought of the act she'll put on at Terry's funeral, as though she gave a damn about a boy she scarcely knew. I don't want to see Jayne's suffering now and in time to come. I'm a terrible person. A heartless beast.''

He stood beside her, gathering her again in his arms. "No, you're not a terrible person. You're human, my love. You're admitting what most people would feel in your situation and not be honest enough to admit. There's nothing wrong with that, darling.'' He hugged her hard. "In fact,'' Christopher said, "it's the first hopeful sign of imperfection I've seen in you. And I like it. I like it very much indeed.''

Charlie was in the room when they arrived to collect Jayne. The girl, fully dressed, seemed composed, but her face was white and drawn and there were deep, dark circles under her eyes. The full impact of the tragedy struck Christopher when he saw her. Mary was right. She was so young to be widowed and friendless and with six months of pregnancy facing her. It was cruel of him to try to separate her and her aunt, but there was no choice. Mary would leave soon or she'd not leave at all.

Jayne managed a little smile of greeting when she saw him. "You must have a sixth sense, Christopher. How did you know to turn up at the right time?''

"I'm a witch. Or, rather, a warlock. Didn't you know? How are you, Jayne?''

"So-so.''

"Of course.'' He felt ill at ease. What was he expected to say? He could manage nothing more than a trite, "I'm sorry, dear. I liked Terry.'' He expected her to burst into tears, but she merely looked at him with her big eyes and nodded.

"I know. He liked you, too. So much has happened in the four months since we met, hasn't it? All our lives have changed. Yours and Aunt Mary's and mine. Even Charlie's.''

The mention of his name made Mary realize she hadn't introduced him to Christopher. For that matter, she hadn't uttered a word since she arrived. The sight of Jayne looking so small and helpless had brought back all the horror she'd almost forgotten in the past few precious hours, and she was speechless with sympathy. She rallied now and said, "I'm sorry. I forgot you two hadn't met. Charlie Burke, Christopher Andrews."

The men shook hands, quickly appraising each other. So this is the man Mary loves, Charlie thought. No wonder. There's power in him, not only in his grip but in the directness of his gaze. I like him, damn it.

"Glad to know you," Charlie said. "I guess congratulations are in order."

"Thank you. I know you hate to lose Mary, but I hear you have an excellent replacement." Christopher in turn was sizing up Mary's boss and best friend. Nice chap, he decided. A damned attractive man, this recent widower. No wonder Mary was so fond of him. For a split second, he entertained the crazy idea that Charlie might have something to do with Mary's reluctance to leave. No. Mary wasn't in love with Burke. She loved him. That was different.

"I'm shot with luck," Charlie said in answer to Christopher's compliment. "Jayne's going to be terrific in the job. She's had a good teacher."

There was an awkward silence before Mary said, "Well, young lady, are you ready to leave? You're all checked out. We stopped at the desk on the way up. I thought it best if you came home with me for a while, okay?"

"Fine." Jayne sounded as though it didn't matter where she went. "I hear Mother's on the way."

"Yes. She should be in some time this evening. I . . . I told her she could stay in the apartment, too."

"Really? *That* surprises me."

Mary felt the blood rush to her face. There was a slight edge to Jayne's voice. Or was she only imagining it?

"Our differences don't matter, Jayne. You're the only one we're thinking about."

Jayne seemed to accept that. "What time is she arriving?"

"I don't know, exactly."

"You mean nobody's going to meet her?"

Again, Mary was taken aback. What was this sudden concern for Patricia? Jayne knew the awful thing her mother had done. She'd been part of it. And she hadn't even been in touch with her since the night she put Patricia on the plane back to New York, the night of the ugly disclosures.

"I think somebody should go to the airport," Jayne continued. "I'll do it, if nobody else wants to. We can't let her get on a bus late at night, all alone."

"Darling, you can't! You're in no condition. Besides, we don't even know what flight she's on."

"Can't we call Daddy and find out?"

"I don't know," Mary said helplessly. "He might have decided to come with her."

"Then Grandma and Grandpa would know."

"We'll check it out," Christopher said. "I'll be glad to go and pick her up."

"You don't even know her!" The words burst, involuntarily, from Mary's lips and they sounded outraged. Hearing them, she stopped abruptly. What was the matter with her? Was she afraid Patricia would seduce Christopher as she had Michael? She must be going mad. It wasn't the ridiculous fear that her sister would be attractive to Christopher that frightened her. It was Jayne's concern that surprised and, yes, annoyed Mary. Jayne was acting as though she was actually eager to see her mother, as though all that had gone before was forgotten and she couldn't wait to rush into Patricia's arms. Mary felt a bleak, indefinable sense of loss, made stronger by Jayne's next words.

"I'm glad she's coming. I knew she would. I need her. She doesn't even know she's going to be a grandmother."

"Yes, she does," Mary said in a small voice. "I told her on the phone."

"You told her?" Jayne sounded reproachful. "I wish you hadn't, Aunt Mary. I was looking forward to doing that myself."

"I'm sorry. It just slipped out while we were talking."

"Talking? Or fighting?"

Christopher began to feel uneasy. Something was terribly wrong here. It was as though Jayne was deliberately trying to hurt her aunt.

"Look, my friends," he said, "why don't you continue this discussion at Mary's? We're anxious to get you out of here, Jayne, and I'm sure you're more than ready to leave."

"Right," Charlie agreed. "My car's nearby. I'll bring it around to the front door."

"Why don't you go with him, Christopher?" Mary said.

He started to protest and then sensed she wanted to be alone with her niece for a few minutes.

"Good enough. We'll be downstairs."

When the men left, Mary looked sharply at Jayne. "What's this all about, honey?"

"What's *what* all about?"

"Jayne, don't put on an act. You seem so cold toward me. And you sound as though you can't wait to see your mother."

"Is that so unnatural?"

"Under ordinary circumstances, no. But in view of your last meeting . . . and the fact that she's never so much as acknowledged your marriage . . ."

"You don't understand Mother, Aunt Mary. She just can't express the love she feels for both of us."

Mary was stunned. "Love for us? What are you saying? She tried to rearrange your life to suit herself. She didn't care whether she was destroying my marriage! She's acted as though neither of us exists ever since she left here! That's love? I don't want you to be alienated from your mother, but I don't understand this hundred-and-eighty-degree turn you're doing, being so anxious to see her, saying how much you need her, trying to convince me she cares but can't find the words to say so!"

Jayne hesitated for a split second before she said, "Are you jealous, Aunt Mary? I don't love you any the less. I'm grateful for all you've done for me. You're a terrific lady. But *she's* my mother."

"I see." God, it was funny. You never really knew people. She'd have bet her life that if it came to a choice, Jayne's loyalties would have been much more with her than with Patricia. Not so. In her hours of sorrow, the girl acted on instinct, reaching out for the one who gave her life. How clearly is she thinking? Mary wondered. Is she still in shock? Is grief overwhelming her usually rational view of things? And why do I feel so wounded by this rejection? Perhaps I am jealous. I'd begun to think of her as my own, more of a mother to her than the one who really is. Wishful thinking seems to be my specialty.

But sensible as she tried to be, Mary felt bitter. Where had Patricia been when Jayne was trying to handle her strange marriage? She hadn't cared what was happening to her daughter. Only Stanley and I cared. Or so it seemed. I'm not big enough to think that Patricia simply can't express love. I don't believe she knows that emotion. She's destructive and opportunistic. Jayne saw that once. She may remember it when she sees her mother again. Right now she's like a little girl, afraid and unhappy and clinging to "Mommy." Damn you, Patricia. You'd better be all she wants to believe you are. If you're not, I'll kill you.

"Aunt Mary?"

"Yes, dear?"

"Don't you think we'd better leave? They'll be waiting downstairs. And there's . . . there's a lot to do. Charlie's been wonderful, arranging things for Terry, but I still have to make some decisions. Like the service. I want Terry cremated, but there should be a service of some kind, and someone to say a few words about him." For the first time, Jayne's eyes filled with tears. "There's nobody, is there? His only friend is dead, too."

Mary forgot her feeling of having been betrayed. She went to Jayne and put her arms around her.

"Don't worry. We'll find a minister."

"No. I'd like it to be more personal. Terry wasn't religious. Do you think Christopher would do it? There won't be many people there. Just the family, I'm sure. And maybe some of the people from his office, or the radio station. But I'd like some kind of simple acknowledgment that he lived and did the best he could."

"Darling, I don't know. Christopher really didn't know him that well."

Jayne looked heartbreakingly sad. "None of us did," she said. "That was the trouble. None of us really knew him at all."

As long as she lived, Mary would not forget the sinking feeling she had when Patricia and Stanley walked into the apartment and Jayne rushed headlong into her mother's arms. She would not forget the petty sense of envy she felt as Patricia held her daughter, nor the look of triumph in her sister's eyes as she gazed over Jayne's head as though to say, See? Blood's thicker than water. I'm the one she needs.

Jayne turned from her mother, finally, to be embraced by Stanley.

"Oh, Daddy, I'm so glad you're both here! We called and Grandmother told us you were coming."

He soothed her as he had when she was a little girl who'd fallen and skinned her knee. "It's all right, baby. We're with you. We'll take care of you. There's nothing to worry about."

Mary stood silently, a little apart. Christopher and Charlie had left a little while before, reluctant to intrude on this intimate moment. Mary, herself, felt like an intruder. She wasn't part of this family. Not really. It was mother, father, child, joined in a closeness not even their nearest relatives could touch.

Gently, Stanley released his daughter. Jayne gave Mary a fleeting glance and then went over to sit close to Patricia, holding her hand, almost as though she was flaunting her dependence on her mother.

"Mary, how are you?" Stanley kissed her cheek. "This is all so terrible. Thank God you were around. I don't know what Jayne would have done without you."

"She's very brave, Stanley. I don't know where she gets her strength." Mary stopped, embarrassed, realizing how that must sound to him.

He smiled, understanding. "She comes from a long line of strong women," he said. "It's the Farr in her, I suppose."

"I didn't mean . . ."

"Don't be silly. It's not important where we get our strength. Only that we have it to draw on." They were speaking in low tones. "Have all the arrangements been made?" Stanley asked. "Is there anything I should do?"

"No. Charlie Burke has done everything. I . . . I identified the body this morning. It was ghastly." She shuddered and went on. "We've set the services for Tuesday morning. The casket will be closed, of course, but Jayne's asked Christopher to say a few words and he's agreed."

"Christopher? Who's Christopher?"

"Didn't Mother tell you? Jayne and I met him on the cruise. He's here at the moment." She didn't want to discuss the muddled state of her own affairs. "He knew Terry and liked him and, frankly, there's no one else. No friends. No family. Jayne told me that Terry once mentioned his father, but he hadn't seen him in years. We don't know how to get hold of him, or whether he's even alive."

"I see. And the other young man?"

Mary sighed. "Still at the morgue. We won't know until tomorrow when his office opens whether he has family or not."

Stanley glanced over at Jayne, who seemed deep in conversation with her mother. "Patricia seems to think there was something, well, abnormal about him and Terry. It doesn't matter now, if there was, unless it affects Jayne in any way."

"It doesn't affect her. It was part of Terry's past, but all that changed when he met Jayne." It was a lie, but a good lie, a "percentage lie," Christopher would have called it. "He was utterly faithful to Jayne and divinely happy with her, as she was with him. Whatever you may hear or read in the papers, don't believe there was anything unnatural about the relationship, or about that last evening. I was there. I know. They were all friends. Terry's death was an accident, brought on, I'm sorry to say, by drugs and alcohol. Paul's remorse was so great he couldn't live with it. Simple. Tragically simple."

Stanley sighed heavily. "She's going to have a baby."

"Yes. She's happy about that. It's like keeping part of her husband."

"Do you think, after all this is over, we can persuade her to go back with us?"

Mary looked toward the young woman who meant so much to her. Jayne seemed to be absorbed in whatever Patricia was saying, her head nodding in solemn agreement with her mother's words. She seemed oblivious to her aunt.

"I don't know," Mary said heavily. "I can't predict her reactions anymore."

Chapter 32

IT HAD SEEMED an eminently sensible idea last night, but this morning Mary told herself she was an idiot to have given the Richtons and Jayne her apartment while she took the miserable little room Terry and Jayne had shared for a few, brief, troubled weeks.

It was a terrible place. Depressing at any time and more so on this Monday morning with its reminders of Terry: his clothes crammed beside Jayne's in the small closet; his shaving things in the windowless bathroom; his copies of *Variety* and *The Hollywood Reporter* flung untidily on the floor beside the one comfortable chair. Poor, lost Terry. Even now, though she vividly remembered his last moments and, even more horribly, the broken shape of him she identified later, she could hardly believe he was dead. Jayne couldn't believe it, either. She was a different girl, a sleepwalker, going through the motions she thought were expected of her. And she seemed to have turned away from Mary. Her cruelty hurt.

Like last night.

When Mary suggested perhaps it would be more comfortable for them to use her place and she'd sleep in this one, she'd honestly expected Jayne to veto the idea. It had been only a polite offer, something one did automatically, but Patricia, predictably, had leapt at it.

"That makes sense," her sister said. "Stanley can take the couch in the office and Jayne and I will share your room. There are three of us and one of you, so it really would work out better, as long as you don't mind."

Mary looked at Jayne, but the girl was silent. She knows I'd planned on her staying here with me, Mary thought. Why doesn't she offer her apartment to her parents? That would work just as well. Instead, it was Stanley who protested.

"We can't do that, Patricia," he said. "No need to inconvenience Mary. We already talked about staying at Jayne's."

His wife gave him an angry look. "I'd like to be near my daughter tonight. It would seem to me you would, too."

"Well, of course, but . . ."

"It's all right," Mary said. "I don't mind if Jayne doesn't."

"Jayne would prefer it, wouldn't you, darling?" Patricia purred.

"Yes, I would."

So a surprised and wounded Mary had taken Jayne's key and come to this dreary "studio apartment." She called Christopher the moment she arrived and told him where she was. "It's frightful," she said. "God knows how those children stood it!"

"I don't want *you* to stand it. It's ridiculous for you to be there. I'll come and get you and bring you to the hotel. I have plenty of room. Besides, love, I want to be with you."

She'd been tempted. A clean, spacious suite at the Fairmont was appealing. So was the idea of being held and comforted by Christopher. But she was too upset, too confused to inflict herself on him.

"Not tonight," she said. "Tomorrow maybe I'll be able to change the arrangements. It was stupid of me to mention it. To be honest, I thought Jayne wouldn't want it. She knew I was just making a gesture. But something's happened to her, Christopher. Something beyond her grief, I mean. It's as though she's pulling away from me. As though she's almost trying to make me dislike her. I don't understand."

I do, he thought. She's setting you free, but you haven't come to that realization. Perhaps I wouldn't have either, if I hadn't had a drink with Charlie and heard about his discussion with Jayne in the hospital. This is her way of bringing us together. She has more heart and more sense than any of us. And more willingness to sacrifice. She'll give up your love if she has to, to make sure you have the happiness she wants for you.

But he couldn't say this to Mary. In time, it would dawn on her what Jayne had done, but before then she'd feel hurt and rejected, as bewildered as a woman whose devoted child had suddenly, inexplicably turned on her.

"I don't think Jayne's thinking straight right now," he said soothingly. "There's nothing in her but emptiness, Mary. It's understandable, an all-consuming absorption with her own loss. Don't judge Jayne these next few days. She won't be herself."

"Perhaps not. You make such sense, Christopher. I shouldn't be offended by the things she says and does. I forget the shock she's been through." Mary felt a little better. "You do understand if I don't come there tonight, don't you? It's not that I don't want you. There are just times when it's better to be alone."

"However you want it, dearest."

"Besides, they might need to reach me for something, and I can't very well tell them I'm staying at the hotel with you."

He couldn't resist laughing. "Mary, Mary, you are so bloody proper! What difference would it make if they did know you were here? We're free and a good bit over twenty-one."

She sounded slightly shocked. "But how would it look? Not twenty-four hours after this tragedy and me enjoying myself with you."

He didn't remind her that she'd "enjoyed herself" a little more than twelve hours after the tragedy. Her mind wasn't on him at this moment. She was physically and emotionally exhausted. He wouldn't add to the jumbled feelings Jayne deliberately had provoked.

"All right, darling. Try to get some sleep. Call me when you wake."

This morning she wished she'd accepted his offer. She'd slept hardly at all, though she couldn't remember ever being so tired. All night she'd lain awake in the lumpy bed, puzzled over the new, distant Jayne. She'd lied when she told Christopher he made sense about Jayne's attitude. It didn't make sense. She and her niece were closer than Patricia was to her daughter. Jayne knew the kind of woman her mother was. How could she turn to her this way, shutting me out? Mary wondered. Has she always secretly been on Patricia's side, perhaps even forgiving her the affair with Michael, possibly rationalizing that Mary had been no angel, either? No, that couldn't be. She simply responded unthinkingly to the ties that exist between mother and child, ties that remained intact, strained as they might be by all kinds of outward disappointments.

Me and my damned, frustrated maternal instincts! Mary thumped the thin pillow and tried to go to sleep. The love I felt I should have had from my own mother was what I tried to give first to Michael and then to Jayne. I smothered them with it, thinking I was doing the right thing. And ultimately they were both relieved to be free.

Never again, her mind said. Never again love more than you are loved in return.

In the bed beside her mother, Jayne also lay sleepless that Sunday night. She would not let herself think of Terry. He'd wanted to die. She knew that. He couldn't face the conflict within him, the tearing apart that never would be resolved no matter how hard he tried to make himself believe it could. He's gone. It's better for him. He never was of this world, somehow. Even with all he lived through, he didn't understand the games grownups play.

She mourned for him but accepted the inevitable as she now saw it. Almost as hard to bear was what she was doing to Mary. It wasn't easy, saying cold things to her aunt, pretending she preferred to be with Patricia. I hate my mother, she thought. I suppose I should be appalled by that idea, but it's true. Hate her pettiness, her insensitivity. Hate the triumph she feels because she believes I've come running back to her.

Just let me get through the next few days, Jayne silently prayed. Let me see Mary off to her new life with Christopher, convinced I don't need her. Even let her despise me, if that will take away the responsibility she feels. Then I'll tell Mother and Dad to go home where they belong. I'll lose myself in my new job, have my baby, take care of it myself. I'm not a girl, I'm a woman alone. And I can function as one, even if no one seems to believe that.

She felt sick, remembering the things Patricia said after Mary left. Once she was gone, Jayne let down her guard in front of her parents.

"We shouldn't have let her do that. It's an awful place. Aunt Mary's so generous, but there was no need to drive her out of her own house."

"I quite agree," Stanley said. "Your mother and I should be sleeping there."

Patricia looked disgusted. "You two are so naïve! You don't think that's where she's gone, do you? Really! If you're so concerned about her, why don't you call her boy friend's hotel room and ask to speak to her?"

"No, Mother. She wouldn't do that. Not tonight. To her, it would seem disrespectful."

"Disrespectful!" Patricia laughed. "You must be kidding! You don't seriously believe she's going to miss a chance to be with her lover! Grow up, Jayne. You, of all people, talking about respect! Where was her respect when she was sleeping with that man all over the South Pacific and poor Michael was here all alone, trying to prove himself to her? You think she's so high and mighty. So damned decent. Well, she certainly encouraged you to get yourself into a dirty mess! Marrying that fag! Approving of your affair with him before! Disrespectful!" Patricia said again. "She has the morals of a bitch in heat! I feel sorry for

Michael, discarded now that she has something better. You can bet she'd have hung on to him forever if she hadn't found a rich one!''

"Patricia, stop it!'' Stanley's words were a command. "I don't want to hear that kind of terrible talk about your sister. Mary's a fine woman. She gave Michael everything she could, probably more than he deserved. As for Jayne, Mary didn't push her into anything. She did what her heart told her. And I hardly think this is the time to speak ill of Terry, even if you have so little concern for your daughter's feelings!''

"Oh, shut up, Stanley. You don't know what you're talking about, so don't give us your opinions. I knew Michael. You didn't.''

Jayne bit her lips. You knew him all right, she thought. You're two of a kind, parasites both of you. How dare Patricia stand there and moralize after all she'd done? How dare she criticize Mary and me? She felt revulsion for this envious woman. You've fed off Daddy most of your life, but you won't feed off me. He's stuck with you, but I'm not. Jayne gave her mother a long, level look.

"We all see things through the eyes of our own experience, Mother," she said meaningfully. "That doesn't mean we see them as they are.''

Patricia stared back at her. My daughter loathes me, she realized. She really despises me. Would she be spiteful enough to tell Stanley about Michael and me? Never. Silly, sentimental Jayne wouldn't hurt her father that way. But why has she been playing this game since we arrived, pretending to be so glad to see me, almost ignoring her beloved Aunt Mary? What was she up to, this strong, defiant young woman who suddenly pretended to be so helpless? No matter. She and Mary thwarted my plans once before, but they won't do it again. I'm here. And here I mean to stay.

By the time Tuesday came, Mary thought she would drop with fatigue. She and Christopher had spent most of their time with Jayne and her parents and it was the most trying experience of a lifetime. Patricia was so "in charge," Stanley so clearly troubled and Jayne seemingly indifferent to her aunt.

Stubbornly, not understanding, herself, why she did it, Mary continued to sleep in the little apartment. Christopher said nothing more about the hotel. Nor, even in the few minutes they managed alone, did he discuss their future. He was waiting. He'd said all he could. It was up to Mary to decide the course of her life. She knew what his restraint meant. He was not a man to change his mind. Either she left with him or he left alone for all time.

Jayne's coolness toward her had culminated in a dreadful confrontation. Mary found her alone Monday afternoon and reported that Paul's office had contacted his sister in Des Moines. She was flying to San Francisco to take the body back for burial there.

"Des Moines? What an odd place for Paul to come from," Jayne said. "I'm sure he'll hate to go back. Not nearly chic enough for him.''

Mary was disturbed. "Darling, I know how you must feel about Paul. You have every right, but it doesn't become you to be so cynical.''

"Oh? What *does* become me, Aunt Mary?''

"The way you've always been. Those are the things that become you—the warmth, the generosity, the understanding. I know you're in a terrible state of mind right now, Jaynie, but you frighten me. I don't feel I know you, and that's crazy! I thought I knew you better than anyone did. And since Sunday night you've been, well, a stranger.''

"My husband just killed himself. What do you want me to be, the life of the party?''

Mary recoiled. "No, of course not. I understand your grief. But Terry didn't do that, Jayne. You saw it. He was clowning around. It was an accident.''

"Have it your way.''

Mary tried once more. "Why can't I reach you? Why are you closing doors between us?''

The girl turned on her angrily. "Because I want you and everyone else to stop peeking through keyholes! Stop masterminding everything, for God's sake! I've had it up to *here* with your sacrifice and your eternally knowing what's best for everybody! Leave me alone, Aunt Mary. You have no idea what I've been through, long before Saturday night. You think everything can be solved as long as you're standing by, ready to pick up the pieces. Well, everything can't! Sometimes the pieces are too complex to fit into this patchwork quilt you seem to think life is. We don't fall into neat little squares and circles and triangles you can stitch together. Some of us have funny, warped shapes. I don't fit into any pattern, so can't you please leave me the hell alone?''

Mary felt as though she'd been physically attacked. Jayne was making no sense. That's not the way I am, Mary thought. I don't consider myself omnipotent, not by any stretch of the imagination. She stopped. Or do I? Everything seems to point that way. At least it does to Jayne.

When she spoke, her voice was a quiet contrast to the near hysteria of the younger woman. "I didn't know you felt that way, Jayne. I'm sorry. I didn't realize you felt so . . . so supervised.''

"I do. By you. By my parents. Even by Charlie and Christopher. I feel everyone watching me, waiting to see what mistake I'll make next, just itching to get in and tell me how to run my life. Well, I want all of you out of it! You're driving me mad with this wait-and-see attitude. I'll manage. I don't need advice and help and jobs made for me and mothers ready to move in on me and people acting as though I can't . . . can't . . .'' She stopped, trembling, and then abruptly burst into tears and fled the room.

In a few minutes she heard the front door close and knew Mary had left the apartment. She took a deep breath and then dried her eyes. That finally did it, she thought. She'll go with Christopher now.

Such a pathetically sparse gathering. They occupied less than three pews in the funeral chapel. "The family" sat in the first one, and a smattering of unfamiliar men and women were dotted haphazardly on the benches in the rear. Mary recognized none of them as she entered. Probably people from Terry's office she supposed, though he'd hardly been there long enough to make friends. Here and there she saw young men unmistakably from the community of Terry and Paul's past, come for what reason? To pay their respects or to satisfy a morbid curiosity about the kind of woman Terry married? It made no difference. There were no blood relatives to wonder about Terry's odd friends, though she regretted Terry's father was not present. No amount of searching through the dead man's papers had produced a clue about the long-gone Maurice Spalding. Perhaps he was dead, too. As far as his son was concerned, he'd been dead for years.

Patricia and Stanley flanked Jayne, and Mary sat beside her brother-in-law, Charlie next to her and Christopher at the end of the row where he would soon rise and speak of the one they'd come to bid good-bye. It was an imposition to have asked Christopher to do this, but there'd been no choice. Of the people Jayne knew, Christopher was the only one who'd spent any time with her husband. Except me, Mary thought. And God knows I couldn't do it. It was sad to think this marriage had been so devoid of mutual friendships. Paul had been their only shared acquaintance, an ironic commentary on the state of this ill-fated union.

Since Jayne's tirade the day before, Mary had barely exchanged a dozen words with her, though she and Christopher continued to have meals with the Richtons, to stand by, as it were, until this final gesture had been made. Then no more, Mary thought sadly. Let them make their own plans from here on in. I'm making mine. As quickly as I can, I'll leave with Christopher. If Jayne wants to be on her own, let her. The thought came without bitterness, with only a kind of aching disappointment that Jayne did not care about her as Mary once believed she did.

As the soft organ music played and they waited for the signal for Christopher to speak, Patricia glanced over her shoulder toward the back of the chapel and was surprised to see Michael come in and sit alone in one of the back rows. She felt a little jolt of pleasure and surprise. He looked well, tanned and prosperous. She wondered what he was doing now that he was divorced. Every unattached woman in San Francisco must be after him, but she'd be in the race, too, once she'd sent Stanley back to New York and moved into an apartment with Jayne. Patricia gave him a little smile and a nod of recognition, but he seemed not to see her. He was staring straight at the back of Mary's head, as though he willed her, not her sister, to turn around and acknowledge him.

Don't get your hopes up, Michael, Patricia sent him a silent message. She's not coming back to you. In a minute you'll be listening to your replacement.

Charlie Burke's mind went back to another time, not long ago, when he'd been part of the ceremony of death. Tracey had been gone such a short time, but it seemed forever. He'd had none of the ''trappings,'' not even as much as these small gestures. He hadn't wanted a fuss. His wife wouldn't have wanted it either. Oh, hundreds of people would have turned out, but because of *him*, not for her. Tracey had no friends either, he thought. Like Terry, she never ''fit in.'' And like him, she probably welcomed the finality of release from a world she'd spent years trying to escape. Rest in peace, both of you, Charlie thought. You are the true victims of our age, not strong enough to survive and not weak enough to admit it.

Stanley felt a great knot of anxiety as he sat holding Jayne's hand. It was frightening to see her so calm, so utterly still and dry-eyed. Only twenty-one and pregnant with a child who'd never know its father. Widowed when she should have been still carefree and sought after, or safely married to a dependable young man who'd care for her. He wondered what had drawn her to Terry Spalding. From what he gleaned, Jayne's husband had been, at best, bisexual, weak and futureless. Yet there must have been something in him that Jayne saw and wanted. He wished he could have known Terry. Somewhere in his character was the key to Jayne's outlook on life. Somehow he filled a need, and Stanley didn't know what that need was. She's not like either of us, he thought. She's not hard like Patricia or passive as I am. What goes on inside my little girl's head? And will she ever permit any of us to know?

At the signal, Christopher rose slowly and took his place behind the podium. He looked over the small audience and allowed his gaze to come to rest on Jayne's unnaturally calm face. I know you, he thought, better than I knew Terry. I think when you asked me to do this you wanted me to talk to you, perhaps to help you understand yourself, even more than to eulogize your husband. He began to speak slowly, his eyes never leaving Jayne's.

"Never doubt love," Christopher said. "Never question it when it comes onstage, but be happy for its entrance. And do not weep when it makes its exit, for it leaves behind it the sweet aroma of caring, a fragrance to linger the rest of your life.

"Terry was an actor whose role was the very essence of love. He did not give off the powerful emanation of arrogance or the acrid smell of greed. His was not a nature that returned cruelty with hatred or selfishness with villainy. Nor was he a competitive man, consumed with ambition and enslaved by the material things of life. He worshiped beauty and was the consummate artist in the theater of life. In his mind and heart, all creatures were heroes and heroines. And every drama had a happy ending. Even his own.

"He was very young, but he had the wisdom of age even while he never lost the trusting qualities of childhood. His was an endless searching for truth in its finest form—a truth he found in the woman he married. In her he discovered the tenderness and compassion he worshiped. In her he found a friend who understood and appreciated the Terry all too few of us were privileged enough to know, or wise enough to recognize. He loved her in a way he never loved before. In a way that made up in depth what it was not fated to have in duration.

"I knew Terry only a few short weeks, and in an atmosphere in which few things are real. But he discovered reality and found it good. I saw him change and bloom and develop in that time, saw him give of himself and receive, in abundance, the devotion he deserved. He left too soon, too tragically, but he lived a lifetime in twenty-six swift-flowing years. He left us with grace, and with memories that will sweeten forever the air we breathe.

"He played his part well, right up to the final curtain. And we applaud him."

There was not a sound when Christopher took his seat. I did a rotten job, he thought. I had ugly thoughts about Terry once, thanking God my own sons did not have his "affliction." My hypocrisy came through in those vacant, inadequate words. I was terrible.

The little group stood silently as the casket was taken out. Only then did Jayne make her way to Christopher, reaching for his hand.

"Thank you," she said. "I know those words were meant for me, but Terry would have been glad."

"I wish I could have done better for you, Jayne."

The girl shook her head. "No one could have. I'll remember every word the rest of my life. You captured him the way he was, Christopher. I don't know anyone else who could have done that. I don't know anyone else big enough to understand."

Patricia touched her arm. "Time to leave, Jayne. We're going out the back way. I hear there's a crowd of photographers out front."

Jayne looked at Charlie Burke. "If they think we're news, we shouldn't disappoint them, isn't that right, Charlie?"

He nodded. "They'll see a lot of you from now on. You're one of them."

Overhearing the brief exchange, Mary felt a sense of shame, remembering Saturday night and the way she'd treated the press, brushing them off, angry with them when they were only trying to do the job for which they were paid. Jayne, so new to the world of reporting, was already much more the professional. Even in this moment of grief, she knows what it means to be a public figure, even a local one. She'll be much better at it than I ever was, Mary reflected. To me, the job was a way of earning a living. It will be that to Jayne, too, but much more. She senses the responsibility it bears, the obligation to her peers that takes precedence over her own need for privacy.

With a sense of dismay, Mary realized she felt envy. It had seemed the perfect solution to all their problems, this idea of Jayne stepping into her shoes. But until this moment, it had not struck her how much she was going to miss the recognition, the challenges, the exquisite feeling of satisfaction in a job well done. These would be Jayne's now, these interesting, stimulating sensations. She did not begrudge them, but she felt a terrible sense of impending loss for the life she was leaving. It was not true that her job had been only a paycheck. It had kept her vital and interested, made her feel important in her own right. Was it shallow to admit she'd miss the sense of being somebody? Not shallow, perhaps, but immature. What Christopher offered was much more important, deeper and more lasting. What had he said? "Never doubt love."

She didn't doubt it. But there were all kinds of love. Love of work. Love of a city and its people. Love even of power, a potent aphrodisiac, modest though the power might be. I love Christopher, she thought. But I love other things, too. Other people. My co-workers. The endlessly fascinating men and women I interview. I love Charlie. And Jayne. The real Jayne, not this strange person who'd appeared disguised in her skin, with none of her endearing qualities.

Again, she felt the bewilderment of the past few days. She could not fathom Jayne's sudden cruelty. What have I done to her? Mary wondered. What has brought on this bitterness, so abrupt and incisive, as though it were coldly calculated to alienate me?

And in a moment of blinding clarity she knew. My God! How could she have been so stupid not to have seen through Jayne's inexplicable "change of heart"? It was an act, all of it. An act for my benefit, Mary realized. Jayne knew my reluctance to leave her alone. She knew I'd lose Christopher if I kept delaying, pushing his patience to the brink. This is her way of releasing me from my feeling of responsibility. She really has tried to make me hate her. She's put on a merciless, merciful performance to let me leave without guilt. She knew rejection was the only thing I'd accept. There was no other way, even if I was devastated by her "treachery."

Mary's throat tightened at the thought of such generosity. Could I have done the same? No. Being loved has always been too important to me. I've craved it, bought it at any cost, needed it to sustain and nourish me. Jayne is bigger than that, and braver. This estrangement must have been even more of a hell for her than for me.

"Sweetheart?" She felt Christopher take her arm. "Hadn't we better leave now? The others have all gone."

Mary came to with surprise. It was as though she'd been standing there for hours, fascinated by revelations about herself and her niece. She looked around half-dazed, almost unaware of where she was. She saw the concern on Christopher's face.

"Are you all right?" His voice was anxious. "Do you want to go out the back door to avoid the photographers?"

She shook her head. "No, if Jayne can face them, I can. It's part of our job." She smiled. "For whatever it's worth, I'm still Mary Farr Morgan."

Chapter 33

THE SIX OF them returned to Mary's apartment and the inevitable letdown set in. Even Patricia was silent as, with a proprietary air, she used Mary's key to open the front door.

Jayne looked exhausted. She'd been marvelous with the press, composed and dignified, thanking them for their kindness and consideration, fending off their outrageous questions about the events leading up to these last moments, graciously smiling a sad little smile of refusal when they tried to press her about drugs and alcohol and even, incredibly, about Terry's relationship with Paul.

"My husband was all the good things Mr. Andrews said about him," Jayne answered. "There's nothing I can add."

"Is it true you're taking over your aunt's job at the station?"

Charlie stepped in. "Certain things are under discussion. If there's to be an announcement, ladies and gentlemen, this is hardly the place for it."

"Then it's true? What's Mrs. Morgan going to do?" They turned their attention to her. "There's a rumor you're leaving radio, Mary. What's the story?"

She could feel Christopher waiting for her to tell them. Felt Jayne and Charlie's eyes on her. Saw the discomfort on Stanley's face and the smug satisfaction on Patricia's as her sister waited for her to publicly abdicate her career. Not really knowing the effect of her words, she said, "My plans are still tentative. There are personal as well as professional considerations. As Mr. Burke told you, we'll have an announcement at a more suitable time."

She was hardly aware of the frustrated grumbling of the reporters, so conscious was she, suddenly, of Christopher tensing beside her, of the others looking at her with surprise. Without elaborating, she took Jayne's arm and led her to the limousine. Solicitous hands helped them all inside and not a word was spoken on the short ride home.

Inside the apartment, they stood uneasily in the foyer, the unspoken question she'd raised hanging in the air. Jayne finally broke the tension.

"I think I'd like to lie down for a while, if nobody minds," she said.

Patricia was instantly the solicitous mother. "Of course you should, darling. I'll go in and turn down the bed for you."

Mary and the three men remained standing until Charlie said, "Well, I'd better go on down to the office. In spite of everything, it's still a working day." He shook Christopher's hand. "You did a fine job. Just right. I know it wasn't easy."

"Thank you." Christopher was terse, distracted.

"I'm going to get some air," Stanley said. "Be back in a little while."

The door closed behind them and Christopher and Mary were alone. Nervously, she walked into the living room and he followed.

"Would you like a drink, darling?"

"No," Christopher said, "I'd like an explanation."

She nodded and sat down, almost primly, on a straight chair. "I . . . I don't know where to begin. I love you. I want to be with you, but . . ."

"But you can't give it up," Christopher finished for her. His voice held no reproach. "You can't give up your home and your job and the security of familiar people and things. You couldn't bring yourself to say, back there, that you were getting married and leaving it all. You don't want to, my dear. I realize it now. I suppose I've always known it but I wouldn't let myself face the truth. You're not meant to be an idle, dependent woman. You need something of your own, something more than being a pale reflection of me."

She looked as miserable as she felt. "What's wrong with me, Christopher? I adore you. I'd be so proud to be your wife. I've waited forever for someone like you, a strong, decisive, protective man. It's not you I doubt, or our love. It's myself. I want it all—you and our life together and my work. And I know that's not realistic. I have to choose and I don't know how."

He was very gentle. "You know how, darling. We had a lovely, special moment. A love affair built on wishful thinking, a storybook thing that hoped for an impossible happy ending."

She didn't want to hear it. "No. I'm not sure that's true. If you can only give me a little more time . . ."

Christopher shook his head. "We've been over that. I'm too old to be patient. Perhaps I wouldn't be patient even if I were young; youth is headstrong and eager, too. But the sad truth is, my love, we were never meant to be. I've refused to admit it, but I know you can't do all the changing. And that's what it would take, Mary. It's too much to ask. I'm too selfish, too settled in my ways, too vain, perhaps, to give you freedom to be yourself. Passion would dwindle with proximity. It would never disappear, not between us, but it would turn from a raging fire to a slow, steady flame. And you'd be restless and empty when days became routine. Being a wife and hostess isn't enough. Vicarious living is not your style. You need to be Mary, wrestling with demands, stimulated by problems, feeling alive and curious and productive every day of your life.''

She was weeping now. ''It's wrong. Those things don't matter. The only thing that matters is love.''

''For some women, sweetheart. For some just as fine as you, but differently oriented. You need love, Mary, but not to the exclusion of everything else. You say you want it all. You can have it. You *will* have it with the right man.''

She shook her head. ''Never. I'm a fool. Don't let me do this, Christopher. Don't let me throw away what we feel for each other. ''

He put his arms around her, raising her gently from her chair. ''You can't throw that away, any more than I can. What we feel is for all time, no matter what. There are all kinds of love, dearest, and we've known the best. It will live as long as we do, perhaps better in memory than in an uncertain future. We've had the blessing of knowing what great love is. We'll never forget that sweet, rare sense of having shared a dream.'' He held her close. ''Good-bye, my darling Mary. Don't regret, not for a moment.''

Before she knew what had happened, he was gone. Her heart felt as though it would, literally, break. Christopher, Christopher, her mind said, what have I done? How could I let you go? For what? Some insane unwillingness to trust my emotions? Some stupid fear that there are things I'll regret never having done? What things? What could possibly be more important than this overwhelming love I feel?

I could have changed, she thought. I could have learned to live as other, happier women do. I would have been fulfilled. Christopher's wrong. It would have been enough for me. But not for him, she realized. He saw that, even if I couldn't. He saw me in my own surroundings and recognized the difference. I'm not the clinging playmate of the cruise, the dazzled, happily obedient woman who adores him to the exclusion of all else. He knew I couldn't give him what he needs, and that he'd be miserable and guilty watching me try. He loves me too much to demand what he knows he must have in a wife, and what I'd never, wholeheartedly, be able to offer. He's putting my happiness ahead of his own, in his wisdom and his love for me.

I wish I were able to hope he finds the woman he needs. I can't. Not yet. The desolation is too terrible, the wound too open and sore. Not yet can I be that unselfish or even that certain that what we're doing is right.

A wave of nausea rose. Blindly, she stumbled toward the bathroom and was violently, wrenchingly ill.

When she came out of the bathroom, Patricia was lounging in a chair by the window, sipping a drink.

''Your boy friend leave?''

Mary cringed. ''Yes.''

''So what are your plans? When are you getting married?''

Mary sank slowly onto the couch. No use postponing it. ''We're not,'' she said.

Patricia sat up straight. ''You're not? What the hell does that mean? You're not getting married *now*? Or not *ever*?''

''Not ever. It's over. Finished. Christopher's going home.''

"What happened, for God's sake?"

Mary put her hands over her eyes. "I really don't want to talk about it." Especially to you, she added silently. Of all people, I don't want to talk about it to you. But Patricia wasn't going to let her off that easily.

"You damned well had better talk about it! I don't know how you've managed to mess it up, and I don't particularly care, but my daughter's involved in this. If you're not leaving, what does that do to Jayne's future? If you're going to stay in that job, where does that leave her? And me? We can't run a household and support a child on that lousy little receptionist's salary! She was counting on getting the program!"

"She'll get it," Mary said wearily.

"Oh, sure!" Patricia dripped sarcasm. "Sure she will. The minute Charlie Burke hears you're not going to Australia, all bets will be off for Jayne." Patricia began to pace the room. "What a lousy thing to do! You got that girl's hopes up and now you're going to kiss her off and say, 'So sorry, dearie, I've decided I want my job after all.' No wonder she detests you. You don't give a damn about anybody but yourself."

Mary looked up. "Jayne doesn't detest me, Patricia. She's been pretending to so I'd leave with an easy conscience, thinking she didn't want me around. She thought she was making it easier for me to do what I wanted. It was a wonderful, unselfish act, and it took me a long time to see through it."

"Bull! She knew who to turn to when she was in trouble—her mother, not her frustrated aunt who tried to take over. You've seen how close we've been these past two days. It's me she needs. Get that through your head! And I'm going to stay with her. This time you can't drive me away."

Mary was too drained to argue. "Believe what you want, Patricia, about me or Jayne or yourself. But start believing one thing—Jayne will never let you back in her life. She's done a good job of fooling both of us since you arrived. I've caught on, but apparently you haven't."

Patricia looked at her narrowly. "What are you up to? You divorced Michael to marry this dream man of yours and now, all of a sudden, it's over. He must have dumped you, and now you think you can pick up the pieces and go on as though nothing happened. You're trying to drive a wedge between my daughter and me. Again. I see it now. You'll keep on being the great Mary Farr Morgan and you'll take care of Jayne and my grandchild. You'd like that, wouldn't you? Having her depend on you. Hell, you'll probably take Michael back now so you can run his life again, too!"

"You're wrong about everything," Mary said quietly.

"Yes, Mother, you are." The voice from the doorway startled them. Jayne stood looking at the two women. "I've been eavesdropping. Aunt Mary's telling you the truth. She didn't leave Michael for Christopher. She took that trip to decide whether she could live with an unsatisfactory marriage. Meeting Christopher was a million-to-one shot. She'd have left Michael in any case." Jayne's voice sharpened. "Particularly when she came home and found out you'd been sleeping with him."

"Don't, Jayne," Mary said. "This isn't your problem. Don't get into it."

The girl sat down, facing them. "I have to get into it. A large part of it concerns me. I did try to make you feel I didn't need you, Aunt Mary. I was so sure you should go with Christopher. Not because of the job. I wanted that, I won't deny it, but I wanted the right thing for you even more.''

"I know,'' Mary said. "I don't know why it took me so long to see what your motives were.'' She managed a smile. "You're a good actress. You had me believing you couldn't wait for me to leave.''

"But you knew you couldn't.'' Jayne almost echoed Christopher's words.

"No. I didn't know it. Christopher knew it. In the end, he saw me more clearly than I saw myself.''

"God, I'm so sorry!''

Mary nodded. "So am I. It makes no sense from a practical point of view. Or,'' she added wistfully, "a romantic one. But the facts are there, Jayne. There's some kind of restlessness in me, some kind of drive that won't let me settle into a vacuum, not even with a man I adore. I hate it. I hate myself for it. But it's there, and there's no use kidding myself that it isn't.''

Patricia snorted. "I never heard such a ridiculous thing! Are you crazy, Mary? You could have a life without a worry in the world and you throw it away for some kind of stupid 'drive'? You'd rather work and struggle for another forty years than be rich and pampered and secure? I think you're out of your mind. I don't even think you're telling the truth. I think the guy walked out and you couldn't stop him, so you're handing out this great story about your 'restlessness.' Maybe you can fool a twenty-one-year-old girl, but I'm too smart to swallow that line.''

"I don't give a damn what you swallow!'' Mary flared. "I don't care what you think about me. What anybody thinks! All my life I've tried to please people. Mother and Father. Older Sister. Husband. None of you cared about me, but you were perfectly willing to use me. And I was dumb enough to let you. Well, that's over, Patricia, Nobody's going to use me ever again!''

Patricia looked scornful. "Use you? That's a laugh! You've had it your own way all your life. Picking the job you wanted. The husband. The life-style. Used you, Mary? Not for a minute. Let me tell you who's been used—me. Knocked up and forced to marry. Stuck in a dull, dreary life with a boring man. Seen my only child estranged by the wild ideas you put in her head. And now you're going to take her away again, aren't you? You're going to make her believe that I don't love her, that she's only an escape for me.''

"You said it, Patricia. Not I. You made your life. Don't blame other people for what it's become. Look at your daughter. You don't hear her blaming anyone for the unhappy situation she's in.''

"It wouldn't be such an unhappy situation,'' Patricia snarled, "if you were out of the picture!''

"Stop it!'' Jayne's voice was trembling. "Stop hurling accusations at each other! And stop using me as a pawn in all this! I can't stand it! I know what I feel for both of you. I'll make my own decisions and neither of you will make them for me.'' She looked from her aunt to her mother and said, more evenly, "I'm going to stay here in San Francisco and work. There's a future for me, even if it doesn't mean a top job right away. We were all dreaming, thinking I could take over Aunt Mary's. I'm not ready for it. We just wanted to believe

I was. In a few years, I'll have a job like hers. Maybe a better one. But for now I'm going to wait and learn and watch for my own opportunity; not one that's handed to me on a silver platter because Charlie Burke would do anything for Aunt Mary. Don't you think I know that's what it's been? I'm twenty-one, and green as grass. I'm a quick study, but there's no way I could handle this now. It's been scaring me to death, but I felt I had to take the chance. Not only for myself. For Aunt Mary. Well, I don't have to do that now. I can serve my apprenticeship and be ready when the time comes.''

Patricia stared at her. ''And meantime, Miss Noble, how do you propose to live and take care of a child?''

''The same way thousands of other women do, Mother. I'll stay in the same apartment. I'll find a Day-Care Center for the baby. It won't be luxury, but we'll manage. I believe in myself. I was willing to take care of Terry. I certainly am willing to take care of his child.''

''No, Jayne, you're wrong,'' Mary said. ''You *can* do my job. I want you to do it. I've made something of a name for myself in this town. It will be much easier for me to move on to the next thing. Television, maybe. I've had offers, but I couldn't bring myself to desert Charlie. Maybe this is the hand of God, pushing me forward. Telling me something. And don't believe you were picked as my successor out of sympathy or charity. You weren't. Charlie wouldn't do that. He has too much of a sense of responsibility toward his own job. You'll be ready to take over in August, as planned. And I won't starve, I promise you.''

Jayne looked uncertain. ''I'm not sure. I still think . . .''

''Trust me,'' Mary said. ''I'd never lie to you.''

''Very touching,'' Patricia said. ''Very convenient. You two will work out your lives to suit yourselves. I'm sure you don't care, Jayne, but where does this leave me?''

There was pity in her daughter's eyes. ''It leaves you where you should be, Mother—in your place as a wife to a man who loves you very much. You can't live with me. We'd both be miserable. You can't attach yourself to my life. It wouldn't work. I'm sorry. Sorry you're unhappy and frustrated. Maybe you *should* change your life. I don't know. I only know that if you can't live with what you have, *you'll* have to find some other way to make it different.''

Mary and Charlie sat by the bedside, looking fondly at the radiant girl.

''This is the damndest place I ever spent Christmas Eve,'' Charlie said. ''Not even a fireplace to hang a stocking.''

Jayne laughed. ''Santa Claus doesn't care. Why should *you*? He drops in at hospitals through the laundry chute, I suspect. And leaves the best presents of all in the maternity ward.'' She carefully opened the blanket wrapped around the bundle in her arms. ''Isn't she beautiful? Isn't Mary Theresa Spalding the damndest hunk of female you ever saw?''

''Sensational,'' Mary said. She glanced around her. ''So is this florist's shop you call your room. I never saw so many glorious bouquets. And you must have a thousand cards and letters and telegrams. Your fans love you, Jaynie. Is it permissible for me to say 'I told you so'?''

"She's made your ratings look like chopped liver these past five months." Charlie put his arm fondly around Mary. "Not that you're doing too badly on your own, much as I hate to admit it. I don't care for competition. Thank God your TV slot isn't opposite the Jayne Spalding radio show!"

"Big deal," Mary said. "I'm still local." She smiled. "And that's the way I like it. This is my town. The rest of the world can stay out there where it belongs."

"Speaking of the world"—Charlie glanced at his watch—"you stars can stay here celebrating if you like, but I'm a working stiff. Okay if I leave you here, Mary? I have to check out the six o'clock news."

"Sure. Meet you at Ernie's at eight-thirty."

He kissed them both lightly. "Hate to leave my two favorite women," he said. "Oops. Sorry. My *three* favorite women."

"Your harem will miss you," Jayne said. "Merry Christmas, Charlie, and God bless you."

They were happily quiet for a few minutes after he left. The two-day-old Mary was surrendered to a nurse, and Jayne settled back on her pillows, comfortably regarding her aunt.

"It's okay for you to say 'I told you so.' Things have worked out, haven't they? For both of us."

Mary nodded. "Not the way we thought, but yes, they have worked out."

"Those roses are from Michael," Jayne said. "Michael and . . . Rae."

"Pretty."

"Were you upset when he got married?"

Mary looked at the young woman. It was a blunt question but there was no malice in it. If anything, there was a tiny undercurrent of sympathy. "Upset? No, not exactly. There was a little pang when I read about it. Only natural, I suppose. Like seeing him that day at the funeral. He was so much a part of my life. Anything that happens to him, even a glimpse of him, makes me remember. Nice things, mostly." She seemed thoughtful. "Marriage to Rae isn't what I'd have wanted for him, given a choice. I'd have wished him someone softer, more in need of protection. But when I look back, I realize I was always trying to put him into a slot he neither fitted nor wanted. It was what I thought he should want. I had quite a habit of doing that, it seems."

"I know. It was true with Terry and me. It doesn't work." Jayne's face clouded. "I wish he could have seen his daughter, though. For her sake, as well as his."

"It wasn't meant to be, dear. Many things aren't. We have to think that's for the best, too."

Jayne knew she was thinking of Christopher, probably still wondering whether she'd done the right thing. "Do you hear from him?"

Mary didn't pretend. "Christopher? No. A thousand times I've been tempted to call him. I've written a hundred letters and torn them up. It's getting better now, as he said it would. Sometimes I go for a week and hardly think of him. I've discovered that memories are lovely things, but they belong to the past. Happy ghosts. There's today and tomorrow to concentrate on."

"Is Charlie in your tomorrow?"

There was a long pause. "We'll see. Charlie and I have everything in common, including a love of our work. We care deeply for each other, and we both need the kind of contentment we've never known. We might find it together one day. I don't know. It's too soon for me to make another big step, even with someone I've known so long and well. One day, maybe. If it's in my future, it will come."

"I didn't know you were such a fatalist."

Mary smiled. "Don't know that I am. But I spent too many years making things hard for myself. And for other people, too. This way seems easier."

Jayne looked troubled. "But you have no regrets, have you?"

Her aunt walked to the window and pretended to look out. Her words came over her shoulder, slowly, like slivers of pain. "Regrets? We all have regrets. Where is the perfect life, my dear? Who lives a flawless existence without doubts and tears and bad decisions? Not I, certainly. Nor you, or, for that matter, anyone who reacts from the heart." She came back to the bedside and took her seat again. "All we can do is put our mistakes behind us and try like hell not to repeat them. Learn from them, but not dwell on them or allow them to make us feel cheated. There's nothing constructive in the words 'if only.' We bury the past decently, Jayne, knowing we did the best we could, even though it wasn't perfect. We forgive ourselves, as well as others."

"Like I have, with Mother. I don't hate her anymore. I pity her."

Mary nodded. "Yes. It's what I've learned about my own parents. They give what they can. No more, no less. They're not gods to be pleased or devils to be exorcised. They're just there, and we can only hope they understand when we seem less than perfect. And try to understand, ourselves, when they're not all we'd like them to be."

"I'd like to take the baby back to New York to visit them sometime," Jayne said. "I'm never going to stay, but they should see her."

"Of course. Maybe I'll go with you when you do."

There was a little silence.

" 'I carry with me the sweet aroma of caring, a fragrance to linger the rest of my life.' Remember, Jayne?"

"Of course." The younger woman's eyes misted with tears. " 'Never doubt love,' " she repeated. " 'Never question its entrance or weep for its exit.' "

Each reached for the hand of the other. We've both lost so much, Mary thought. But we've won, too. In a way, we grew up together, through a shared and special time. Different days are ahead, but they're made all the more precious by those gone by. There's so much to be grateful for.

And so much to remember.

Sisters and Strangers

For my friend Jean, who generously shared
her time and her ''mile-high knowledge''

Chapter 1

LAURA'S FIRST THOUGHT when she awakened in the darkness of that pre-dawn October morning was that in two days she'd celebrate fifty years of marriage to Sam Dalton.

Fifty years. Half a century. Five decades with the same man. Perhaps she'd make a little speech about that at the party.

"Two score and ten years ago we brought forth upon this community a marriage created by convention, conceived in monotony and dedicated to the proposition that all wedlock is enchained and unequal."

She smiled, imagining how they'd all look at her if she said such a thing. Sam would think she'd taken leave of her senses. Her daughters would be shocked. No. Barbara and Alice would be shocked. Frances probably would think it was funny. The relatives would not understand. And the friends would feel embarrassed, as though she'd taken off her clothes in public.

Of them all, Sam would be closest to the truth. Sometimes she thought she was going crazy. Proper Laura Dalton, perfect wife and home-maker, pillar of the church, past-matron of The Eastern Star, mother of three, survivor of domestic disasters, keeper of the peace, tender of the flame of fidelity for fifty years. I have everything in the world to be grateful for, she told herself sternly. A paid-for house. Good health. A dependable, provident husband snoring beside me. I'm seventy years old, but in this day and age that's not "old," as it was when I was growing up.

Why, then, am I ticking off my blessings as though each one was a superstitious knock on wood? Why do I feel so unsatisfied, so trapped? My children are women. Not even young women. And for the first time in nearly thirty years they're all sleeping safely under one roof. My worrying days should be over. All the things that hurt so much when they happened are far behind me. Sam and I got through them together. No, not really together. We suffered them independently, though we pretended otherwise. All that trouble with Alice and Frances. Even Barbara's departure was a reproach, though she didn't intend it to be. But that's all in the past. The scars have healed. Or have they? Has each of us come to terms with what had to be? I don't know. I don't know my children any more. Or my husband. Or myself. Perhaps I never did. Never will.

All I know is that, all things considered, I've had a good life. A good marriage.

Day after tomorrow I'll prove that by accepting congratulations for having lived through eighteen thousand two hundred and fifty days of being Mrs. Samuel Dalton of Denver.

Sam stirred. "What time is it?"

"Six-thirty."

He grunted, sat up in the double bed and scratched his head in that irritating way she'd hated for fifty years. Why did he start every morning by scratching his head? To make sure the thick mane of hair, now so handsomely white, had not disappeared while he slept? Laura smiled, thinking what a ridiculous little thing it was to object to. But that's what marriage was about: loving so many important things about a man and hating so many trivial ones.

"Why do you always scratch your head when you wake up?" She wondered why she'd blurted that out after all these mornings.

"What?"

"For fifty years you've awakened, asked me what time it is and then scratched your head."

He looked at her as though she'd lost her mind. "What are you talking about? You're not making any sense."

"I know, dear. It just occurred to me that we all have funny little habits that never vary from year to year." She smiled at him. "What do I do that irritates you, Sam? I'd like to know."

He climbed out of bed, hitching up his pajamas at the waist.

"That, too," Laura said. "You always hitch up your pajamas that way. What do *I* do that's exactly the same every morning?"

He glanced at her over his shoulder as he headed for the bedroom door. "I never thought about it. I don't know what's gotten into you this morning, Laura. You don't sound like yourself."

She sat propped up in bed, the pink nylon nightgown with the fake lace discreetly covering her shoulders. The shoulders that, like her arms, were better hidden these days. She used to be so proud of her arms and shoulders and her long, unlined neck. No more. I may not feel my years, Laura thought, but once in a while the mirror reminds me. No, she didn't sound like herself this morning. Sam was right about that. She didn't feel like herself, either. She supposed it was the awareness of the oncoming golden anniversary. Or the fact that the girls were home and there'd be such a fuss going on in the next few days. Sam thought she was crazy with all this talk about sameness. He probably was right about that, too. He hadn't answered her question. Surely she must have habits that drove him mad. Or maybe not. Maybe he never noticed any more.

"I'm sorry," she said. "I'm just spouting nonsense. You'd better get into the bathroom if you want it first."

Sam shook his head as he left the room. Another time-worn gesture, that half-annoyed, half-indifferent motion he made when things puzzled him. The little shake of his head that clearly said, "I'll never understand women." Or, for that matter, present-day politics, sexual mores, taxes, the tactics of the Denver Broncos, the "young squirt" who replaced him in his old job at the telephone company. A long list of non-understandables. There was so much he refused to understand. He was a kind man at heart. A good man. But uncompromising and becoming more rigid every day, more narrow in his interests, less tolerant of a changing world. In the eight years since his retirement he'd become old. At seventy-three he was a being with no purpose, no aspirations, no particular interest in anything. It's no good for a man like Sam to retire, Laura thought for the hundredth time. On Sam's pension we're too poor to travel, too inflexible to move out of this dreary old house to some nice "Sun Belt Community" where we could make new friends, too bored with each other after fifty years to even try to communicate.

But we've never communicated. The realization was like a new thought. We've talked and argued and made love, but we've never spoken as one voice. Not when the children were growing up. Not when they needed the solid support and comfort we should have given them. If only Sam hadn't been such a biblical patriarch when Alice got into trouble. If I'd been more aware of Frances' restlessness. If both of us had discouraged Barbara's interest in politics. If only we'd broadened our horizons early on, been adventurous enough to see the world or even widen our circle of friends here, or if we'd taken up hobbies to occupy us in these declining years.

If. What a useless word. And what ridiculous thoughts plagued her these days. If only I had someone to talk to. There I go with my "ifs." There was no one. Not even the children. I don't understand my girls. I know so very little about the way they think, even the way they live. Don't even know whether they're happy or miserable, whether they love us or hate us, whether they're here out of desire or duty.

What on earth is happening to me?

She watched the light slowly sneaking through the window. Another day. More exciting than most because of the preparations for the party. But it was only a brief respite from sameness. It would soon be over, and within a week her daughters would be gone and the predictable way of life would return.

She sighed heavily.

It all seemed so pointless.

Frances opened her eyes and felt the old, familiar wave of apprehension waiting. The nonspecific, ugly one that greeted her every morning. It was always the same. Her first conscious moments were filled with unfocused fear, a suffocating depression she privately called her "insecurity blanket." She dreaded each new day and at the same time feared it might be her last. She'd tried everything—from tranquilizers to TM. Nothing helped. Not even geography. Denver or Deauville, anxiety claimed no nationality. She was as frightened coming back to life in her old room in her parents' house as she was in any apartment or hotel suite or chateau or manor house in the world. Why did she think it might be different here? *I'm* no different, she thought. I'm still Frances Dalton Mills Stanton de St. Déspres. Madame Dalton-Déspres. Social figure. Thrice divorced. Pointed, reluctantly, toward my fiftieth birthday. Sophisticate and super-failure. The prodigal returned for the celebration of Sam and Laura Dalton's golden wedding anniversary. She was back in the bed she'd left nearly thirty years before. Back in body, but not in spirit. The spirit, if she had one, was someplace else.

The house was very quiet. Alice glanced over at the other twin bed, half-expecting in this first waking moment to see Spencer and momentarily surprised to see, instead, the peacefully sleeping figure of her younger sister. Barbara still looks like a young girl, Alice thought, though she's forty. And Fran, in her own room next door, was a cleverly face-lifted forty-nine. And I'm a year younger and look old enough to be their mother. Especially in this unflattering half-light.

It wasn't true, of course. Alice Dalton Winters, like most middle-aged women in 1976, could have lied by ten years about her age and gotten away with it. Provided one didn't know she had a twenty-three-year-old son and a twenty-one-year-old daughter. But everyone did know, back in Boston where she lived and here in Denver where she'd come for the celebration. What most of them didn't know was about the other one. The one born in 1946. Johnny, she'd called him. The baby she'd given away.

She didn't want to think about him now. Didn't want to wonder where he was and what his life was like. And whether he was as curious about her as she was about him. She didn't want to think about any of her children, legitimate or otherwise. Or her husband or her home or her life back East. She wanted to be a girl again, a seventeen-year-old girl with everything to live for and nothing to hide.

It was strange to wake up in her old room. Stranger still to realize there was someone else there. Most mornings Barbara was alone, except when Charles could stay the night. And those sweet awakenings were rare and special occasions, moments when she could pretend that she, not Andrea, was Mrs. Charles Tallent.

She lay very still in the narrow twin bed, trying not to disturb Alice. Her big sister. She could still remember sharing this room in the little Denver house with a young, popular, pretty Alice Dalton. How she'd envied her, back in the mid-forties. How she'd envied both Alice and Frances, her "grown-up" sisters. It had made her angry to have arrived so late in her parents' life. At least it had seemed late. Eight and nine years, respectively, after Allie and Fran. She was still a "baby" when they were dating, and they treated her as a little pest, ignoring her adoration, blind to her desire to be not only a sister but a peer. Time had narrowed the distance. The three of them seemed of an age, now that they'd all crossed forty. But their worlds were as far apart as ever. Farther, really. Incredible they'd had no "reunion" in thirty years. Astonishing how little she knew of their lives, or they of hers. Sisters and strangers. We might as well be three uneasy house guests visiting two people we barely know.

Chapter 2

"I WISH YOU and Daddy had agreed to let us give you a party in some snappy place."

Laura looked at her eldest daughter who was smoking her fourth cigarette over her second cup of coffee at the big old oak table in the dining room. Frances looked, well, dissipated, her mother thought. For all the creaminess of her silk robe, the sleek cut of her hair, the carefully applied make-up (imagine doing one's face at eight in the morning!) she seemed like some world-weary visitor from a debauched realm beyond Laura's imagination. What kind of life must she lead? All those marriages and divorces, all that flitting around the world since she was nineteen. What has it done to my firstborn? Terrible things I'd guess, from the look of her.

"Your father and I thought it would be much nicer to have a little party at home. You girls were sweet to offer, but all our friends do it this way. It may not be grand, but it's suitable for us.''

Fran shrugged. If that was meant as a reprimand for her own extravagant way of life, she chose to ignore it. She could afford to give parties, big, lavish ones with orchestras and French champagne and clever, expensive florists' creations on small, chic tables set for ten. Not that one probably could produce such splendor in a Denver hotel, but surely the Brown Palace could turn out a smarter background than this shabby old house where nothing had changed in nearly thirty years. The party will be a middle-class horror, Fran thought, but that's the way they want it: dull, stolid and boring. She wished she hadn't come home. Memory was kinder to the scene of her youth than reality. She wondered how Alice and Barbara felt. Of course, they'd been back to visit and she never had. Probably the whole dreary little house wasn't such a total shock to them. And certainly their basis of comparison was less drastic. They'd "kept in touch." She hadn't. She wrote rarely, sent birthday gifts from Cartier in Paris and Christmas presents from Gucci in Rome. But she'd not come back since the night she eloped (what an extraordinarily old-fashioned word!) with that stupid young actor, Stuart Mills. She regretted many things about that first marriage, but she was grateful for one: It had gotten her out of this house and this town and this stultifying atmosphere of respectability.

"It's nice, the four of us sitting around the table like this." Alice smiled at them. "Can you believe how long it's been since we all had breakfast together?"

"If you can call it breakfast," Laura said. "You girls don't eat a thing! I'm glad your father was fed and out in the yard before you all came down. He'd have a fit, seeing you have nothing but coffee and juice. You know how he is."

Barbara laughed. "I can still hear him. The voice from our childhood. 'You girls eat your breakfast! Most important meal of the day. Got to stoke up after fasting all night.' Does he still feel that way, Mother? Does he still have his fruit and cereal and eggs and bacon and all those things?"

"You know he does. You saw him last year when you came out at Christmas. And he's right. The body can't go from dinner to lunch on nothing but caffein and nicotine."

"This one can," Fran said. "The only eggs I've been able to face in years are *oeufs en gelée* at lunch."

"Fran, you really are a pain in the behind," Barbara said suddenly.

"Beg pardon?"

"Oh, come on! You're home, remember? You're just Frances Dalton around here. Not Madame Dalton-Déspres! Get off our backs with that 'snappy party' stuff and your damned '*oeufs en gelée*.' For God's sake, look at you! The rest of us are in bathrobes and curlers, and you look like you're about to be photographed for *Town and Country!*"

"My, my!" Fran's voice was coldly amused. "Will you listen to the baby! The little kitten has grown up into a snarling pussycat. What's the matter, darling? You sound like a frustrated old maid. And I'm sure you're not *frustrated*."

"Not nearly as much as you, I'll bet!"

"Hey, cut it out, you two!" Alice spoke sharply. "What's the matter with you idiots? You're picking up right where you left off." She tried to make a joke of it. "Listen to them, Mother. The same as ever. They were always fighting, remember?"

"Only because Fran was always so full of phony airs and graces," Barbara said.

"And you were such a damned goody-goody!"

"I was only ten years old when you left, for God's sake!"

"Sure," Fran snapped, "and even then I could tell you'd be the prissy spinster in the family! You're just jealous because three men have married me and nobody has legalized your situation, whatever it is."

"Frances! Barbara! Stop this!" Laura's face was white with distress.

"Mother's right," Alice said. "You're both behaving like children! Can't you see how you're upsetting her? For heaven's sake, we're here for a happy time! What on earth is the matter with you?"

"I'm sorry," Barbara said. "It's just that . . ."

Alice nudged her under the table, as if to say, "Don't bring up a lot of things Mother doesn't know."

"I'm sorry, too, Barb," Fran said unexpectedly. "I don't know how we got into this silly ruckus. Probably it's my jet lag. And the altitude. I keep forgetting we're in the 'mile-high city.' When I got here yesterday I was so tired I was walking into walls. Air travel at best is like being cooped up in a Greyhound bus. I'll be in a better humor when I recover."

What would you know about Greyhound buses? Barbara was tempted to ask. But she said nothing. Maybe I do envy Fran, she thought. Maybe I envy her money and her freedom. Even her notoriety. Maybe I envy her those three rotten marriages—one for escape, one for money and one in sheer desperation. Do I somehow feel inadequate, being the only "single sister"? How crazy! In this day and age, there's no stigma to being single. No sign of "failure." It's a woman's option. I wouldn't marry Charles even if he were free to ask me. I love my job. I love Washington. I love my lover. I'm more my own person than either of my sisters. And, what's more, I suspect I'm happier than either of them.

Bolstered by her own thoughts, Barbara stretched and smiled. "Well, what's the program for today? Duty-calls on the relatives? Preparations for the party? Catch-up time with childhood chums? What do *you* want to do, Mother?"

The momentary crisis passed, Laura relaxed. "You needn't do any of those things unless you want to. You'll see your aunts and uncles and cousins at the party tomorrow. Uncle Fred and Aunt Mamie are flying in from Chicago. Uncle Earl's here, of course. I'm sorry Aunt Charlotte couldn't come from Boston, Alice. It would have been nice if she could have traveled with you."

"She's really too frail, Mother."

"I know. She's eighty. Imagine. My sister Charlotte eighty! Well, so much for my relatives. Fortunately your father's live in Denver."

"Aunt Mildred and Aunt Martha still sharing that gloomy old house on Race Street?" Barbara asked.

"Yes, dear. And very nice for them it is, since they're both widows."

"How are they?"

"Quite well for their age. They're both older than your father. Of course,

Mildred has trouble with her eyes and Martha doesn't hear too well, but th\
manage. This family really is blessed to have so many left on both sides. Mos\
of our friends have lost their brothers and sisters, but we're fortunate."

Fortunate, Fran thought. What's fortunate about a bunch of creaky old brothers
and sisters who probably do nothing but talk about their ailments, complain
about neglect by their children and spend most of their waking hours watching
soap operas and game shows on television? She didn't know that was the way
it was, but she'd have gambled she was right. She hadn't kept track of her aunts
and uncles. She'd almost forgotten their names. Sometimes when she got one
of those stilted letters from Laura she wasn't sure whether Aunt Mildred was
Daddy's sister or Mother's. Or whether Uncle Fred had two boys and a girl or
the other way around. What difference did it make? She hadn't seen any of them
in years and she wouldn't again until it was time to come home for her parents'
funerals. God! Just let me get through this week so I can hop on that big, shiny
"Greyhound bus" and get the hell out of here! But where then, Frances Dalton
Mills Stanton Déspres? Back to Europe, she supposed. There wasn't anything
there for her except an endless round of trips and parties, occasional brief affairs
and too many unadmitted nights with only a book for company. But there was
less here. She'd long since cut her ties with everything. With her family. Her
old friends. With America itself. She realized Laura was still going on in answer
to Barbara's question.

"As for party preparations," her mother was saying, "all I have to do is set
the table and get out the dishes and glasses, and it's almost easier to do it myself
than tell you girls where everything is."

"What about food?" Alice asked.

"Oh, everybody who's coming has her assignment. Some are bringing appetizers,
some the main course. Others will contribute salad and dessert."

Fran's eyes widened. "You mean the guests bring the meal?"

"Of course, dear. That's the way we've always done it for big affairs. Don't
you remember? I take whatever's requested when I go to somebody else's party.
It makes it all very easy and inexpensive when you divide it up that way."

"What can we contribute?" Alice persisted. "Liquor?"

Laura looked uncomfortable. "We're not much for hard liquor, Alice. You
know your father disapproves of it entirely. We'll have a little punch and soft
drinks. And tea and coffee, of course."

Barbara chimed in. "I know what we'll get: the wedding cake." She looked
at her sisters. "How about that? We'll get the most gorgeous five-tiered, rose-
decorated, goo-ey cake in town."

"Well, that would be nice," Laura said. "I admit I thought of having one,
but with Bernard Paige's wife offering to bring brownies, I gave up the idea."

Fran snapped to attention. "Bernard Paige? Buzz Paige? Don't tell me he's
still around!"

"Of course he's still around," Laura said tartly. "What did you think, Frances?
That all your old beaux committed suicide when you ran off? Bernard is a fine
man and very successful. He has a lovely wife and three handsome sons. We
don't see them much, of course. They're another generation. But I thought it
would be nice to invite some of your old friends and your sisters'. They're all
dying to see you again."

Good God! Buzz Paige! She'd thought herself in love with him when she was seventeen or eighteen. She'd even thought they'd get married. But that was before she met Stuart Mills. What would my life have been like if I'd stayed in Denver and married Buzz? Awful. He's, let's see, fifty-one or -two by now. Probably paunchy and balding and given to loud ties and a Kiwanis button in his lapel. Fran shuddered. She could picture his wife. A plain little woman, very housewifey. He probably had grandchildren. Damn. The whole thing made her feel old. She couldn't stand feeling old. She couldn't stand the idea of trying to make conversation with an overweight bore who'd once been a young and beautiful captain of the high school football team. She remembered they'd gone in for some very heavy necking in the back seat of his 1942 Chevrolet. But it had never gone beyond that. Maybe if it had, I'd have stayed, she thought wryly.

"You dragging up anybody else from our misbegotten pasts?" There was a slight edge to Alice's voice.

Laura pretended not to notice her middle-daughter's tone. "Just a few of the young men and women all of you used to be so close to. The ones who are still around, that is. So many of them moved away years ago." As all of *you* did, the sentence continued silently, accusingly. The youngest and the oldest couldn't wait to leave the nest. Only Alice was forced out. But Laura didn't want to think about that. It was the closest they'd ever come to disgrace. Still, it had worked out. Thank heaven for Charlotte in Boston.

An awkward silence came over the four women. Then Laura said briskly, "Why don't you girls go out for lunch today? Barbara still knows the town pretty well. I'll do my chores around the house and see you later this afternoon."

"Okay," Barbara said. "If you're sure you don't need us."

"No. Everything's under control. Go enjoy yourselves." She sounded suddenly wistful. "You're sisters. Maybe you can get to be friends."

Later, as she went to find her father and borrow the car keys, Barbara couldn't get those last words of her mother's out of her mind. It was sad, but Laura was right. We should be friends, the three of us. In our way, we're all nice people. Even Fran, much as she tried to be brittle and cynical, had a romantic streak she couldn't shake. Maybe I've been wrong, thinking she married for practical reasons. Maybe each time she fancied herself in love, thought she'd found the answer and ended up so hurt and disillusioned that she's wrapped herself in this hard shell of pseudo sophistication.

Of course, it wasn't easy to maintain a closeness with anyone who lived thousands of miles away and never came back even for visits. It was different with Allie. We could be closer, Barbara thought. Boston and Washington aren't that far apart. Less than two hours by plane. Yet we never visit each other, rarely even phone. There's no excuse for us. I haven't seen Allie's children since they were babies, and she doesn't have any idea that I'm somebody's mistress. I don't know what her life is like, any more than I know how Fran exists, except for what I read in the gossip columns. Is Allie happy with Spencer? After almost twenty-five years, is she content? To be so ignorant of your sisters' day-to-day lives was weird. More than weird. It was obscene. As though we're all ashamed of the paths we've chosen and don't want those we really love to know what stupid roads we've stumbled down in our search for happiness.

The morning sun was warm, but Barbara shivered. There was something ominous about all of them being together again. Why did she feel it was a trick of fate that brought them back for this presumably joyous occasion? Why did she feel this was a visit that would make a difference in the future? Jackass! she scolded herself. You and your bloody imagination! It wouldn't be like that at all. They'd spend this week in reasonably harmonious play-acting with their parents and relatives and friends from the past. They'd put on their "dutiful-daughter faces" even among themselves. And then they'd go away again, as they had before. Back to whatever separate, secret worlds they occupied. And that's the way it should be, Barbara thought firmly. It's too late for us to find each other again. Why should we even want to?

She forced herself to smile as she had at the breakfast table, pretending to be relaxed and untroubled as she came near her father. Sam, in old shirt and pants and a light pullover sweater with a hole in the elbow, was bending over a bed of yellow chrysanthemums, gently pulling weeds away from their roots.

"Good morning, Daddy."

He looked up. How much he's aged in these past eight years, Barbara thought. What a damned shame he had to leave the job he'd had long before she was born. He was withering away with boredom, rusting with disuse like an old car in a junkyard. She remembered how he used to go off to work each morning, full of confidence. The provider. The hunter out to kill for his family. Now, though he and Mother lived comfortably on his Social Security and his six hundred dollars a month retirement pay, in a house whose mortgage had long since been "burned," Sam Dalton must feel useless, displaced, missing the "business jungle" with the small challenges that, to him, had been so stimulating. Head of an accounting section for the phone company. What a dreary little job it seemed to Barbara, so used to the powerful men of Washington. Yet Sam had been proud of it. Proud to have worked his way up from clerk to "middle management" and eighteen thousand a year. Proud he'd gone to night school to study accounting and that for more than forty years he'd been "a boss." Now he was just another "old-timer," moved out to make room for younger men with more modern ideas and training. These men had to have their chance too. Had to know vacancies would come up as the long-ensconced managers took mandatory retirement at sixty-five. The policy probably was right for the company, right for business. But it was painfully wrong for the men who'd lived only through their jobs and who now had nothing better to do than weed chrysanthemum beds.

"Morning, Barbara. Sleep all right?"

"Just fine. I'm sure we all did. We were a tired bunch straggling in here yesterday."

"I know. You all came from so far away."

It was a simple statement and yet Barbara felt a pang of guilt, as she had when Laura had silently accused them of "running away." Why do they make me feel I've deserted them? Is it all right for the married ones to leave home but not "suitable" for me? I won't feel guilty. There's no need to. For all I know, the accusation may be in *my* head, not theirs. What accusation? I have a right to my own life too. She pretended not to notice Sam's subtle reprimand, if, indeed, it was one.

"Mother says she doesn't need us around here today, so Fran and Allie and I thought we'd go out to lunch. May I use your car?"

"Sure. The keys are on the dresser. Be careful. I take good care of that car, you know. I'm in no position to replace it if anything happens to it."

"What about us?" Barbara's voice was teasing. "Aren't you worried about replacing your daughters if there was an accident?"

"Don't talk crazy, Barbara." Sam got to his feet. His knee bones creaked in protest. "I don't know what's gotten into you women this morning. First your mother wants to know what she does to irritate me, and now you're talking foolishness about how I wouldn't care if something happened to you. I feel like I'm in the middle of a conspiracy."

Barbara laughed. "You're not used to having so many women around at one time any more, Daddy. We're just needling you. I know you'd care if we got hurt. You always cared. I remember how it was when we were kids." She paused. "You were always my hero. The best father in the world."

Sam turned away, embarrassed. She'd always been his favorite. He supposed he resented the fact that she preferred to live away from home. That's why he was gruff, not wanting her to know how much he wished she wouldn't go away again. Laura fretted that Barbara had never married. But he was only sorry she couldn't find her happiness at home.

"The keys are on the chain with the rabbit's foot," he said tersely.

"Right-o. We'll see you later." She kissed his cheek swiftly. "Your mums are gorgeous. This is such a pretty time of year. Everything's golden. Like your anniversary."

He didn't answer but watched her as she walked swiftly back to the house. Golden, he thought. It's all turned to tarnished brass. As Laura had early that morning, he determinedly counted his blessings. Health. Reasonable security. A good wife. Three handsome daughters. He'd long since stopped being unhappy that they'd not had a son. Or had he? Deep down, didn't it sadden him that there'd be no future Daltons? His sister's children were girls, too. Not that it would have mattered. They weren't named Dalton. Only he and Laura could have perpetuated the name, and they hadn't been able to. What difference did it make? There was nothing distinguished about the lineage. Let it die out. Who cared?

He pushed from his mind the thought that there was a male Dalton somewhere. Alice's illegitimate son. He had no idea where the boy was or what his adopted name was. If we'd let her keep the baby, there'd be a Dalton to carry on, Sam thought, but there'd been no way. No way at all.

He knelt again and viciously pushed a trowel into the soil, cutting too deeply into a root. Drat! He'd killed another one of Barbara's "golden things." No matter. He still had plenty left. More than enough of this "fool's gold" to leave behind.

Chapter 3

SQUASHED IN THE back seat of Sam Dalton's little 1974 Toyota, Alice felt more than physically uncomfortable. Whenever she came back to Denver it was as though she lived through 1946 all over again, the terror of it, the helplessness and rejection she'd felt on all sides. Those few awful weeks almost blotted out the seventeen happy years that preceded them. It was why she so seldom returned. Not more than ten times in thirty years, she realized. And then only out of a sense of duty, as though, even after what they'd done to her in their well-meaning way, she couldn't put her parents out of her life as Fran had been able to do.

I'm more like Barb, she thought. Neither of us can sever the emotional umbilical cord, much as we'd like to. What holds children to parents with whom they have nothing in common except the accident of birth? Maybe my Johnny is lucky, wherever he is. Or maybe his adopted parents are as unfathomable to him as mine are to me.

As Barbara expertly pushed the little car toward Larimer Square, Alice closed her eyes and reluctantly retraced the unhappy early days of her life.

She'd been so frightened when she found out. So ashamed. She and Jack Richards had known each other since they were children, had been "going steady" since she was fifteen and he seventeen. They were in love, they thought. Love. What did they know of love, babies that they were? But they were "unofficially engaged" and talked confidently of the day they'd marry, in three years, when Jack finished college. Allie was happy for most of those two years. Happy and yet miserable, made miserable by Jack's pleading, by her own desire. She could still hear the conversations they used to have, months of them before she agreed.

"Please, Allie." Jack's voice would be low and earnest. "Please do it. We love each other. We're going to be married."

She'd push him away, reluctantly, removing the fingers she allowed to reach inside her sweater and fondle her breasts. She'd be so excited herself at those times as he held her close in the front seat of his little car, gently easing his hand up under her skirt and inside the little panties to touch her. But she always moved away, straightening her clothes, trying to control the breathing that was as heavy as his own.

"We can't, Jack. Not till we're married."

"Why not? We're *going* to *be* married. Don't be scared, Allie. Nothing will happen. I'll take care of it."

"Something might. I might get pregnant."

"You won't. I promise. I have those things right in my pocket." He'd reach for her again. "You're afraid I won't respect you. You're wrong, sweetheart. I'll respect you all the more."

She'd shaken her head, knowing he'd now turn angry.

"Dammit, Allie, you're nothing but a tease! You don't have any idea what it does to me to get this close and not be able to go all the way!"

"Yes, I do," she'd said, almost in tears. "I know how *I* feel. I want to, Jack. I really do."

"Then, for God's sake prove it!"

"I can't. I just can't."

He'd turn away in disgust then, starting the engine and driving her home, dropping her off on South Carona Street, leaving her standing forlornly on the curb in front of her house at number 1016. She'd always say something placating through the car window before he left, half-promising that next time it would be different, begging him not to be mad, terrified that this time he'd go away and never come back. He seldom answered but he always came back, always accepted her frightened refusal. Until that night early in January.

It was a Saturday. She recalled it vividly. Every detail. He called for her after dinner as usual and she told her mother they were going to a movie. She really thought they were. But instead, Jack headed in a different direction.

"Where are we going?"

"My house."

"Your house? Why?"

"Because the family's away for the weekend and I have the whole place to myself."

Something in his voice told her he'd come to a decision. He sounded rougher, colder than she'd ever heard him. Allie was silent during the short drive. This was the long-avoided showdown. She'd either give him what he wanted—what they both wanted—or she'd lose him. She was as certain of it as she was of her name. She didn't need his words to confirm her thoughts.

"Make up your mind right now, Allie," he'd said. "Either we're really in love or I'm calling the whole thing off."

She'd pretended not to understand. "You know we're in love."

"Don't play cute. You know what I mean. I can't stand any more of these nights. We're not babies." He stopped the car in front of his house. "Decide now," he said more gently. "Either you're a woman or a child. I'll take you home, if that's what you want. But if you come inside with me, I'm going to take you to bed. Your choice, Allie."

She'd hesitated for a long moment, recalling all the things she'd heard about high school girls getting pregnant, all the disgraced families, the dangerous, ugly abortions, the "shotgun weddings."

"If . . . if something went wrong . . . That is, would you . . . I mean, what if . . ."

He'd put his arms around her. "I've told you a hundred times. Nothing will go wrong. But if you're still afraid it might, I promise we'd get married right away, Allie darling. I swear it."

She'd believed him. And that night, in Jack's bed, in his room with the college pennants and the pictures of his high school hockey team and the delicious smell of him all around her, she'd tremblingly discovered that sex was even more wonderful than she'd imagined. She had no way of knowing how inexpert they were. Not until much later did she learn there were nuances unknown to a nineteen-year-old boy and a seventeen-year-old girl. When he took her home at midnight, she crept into the room she shared with nine-year-old Barbara and lay wide-awake, reflecting on the gloriousness of it all. This, she thought, stroking her thighs under the covers, was what love was all about. This was what it was to be a woman. She supposed she should feel ashamed. It was wrong. Sinful. But she didn't feel shame at that time, and certainly no sense of sin. She was not one of those "easy" girls. She'd done what was natural and right with the man she would marry.

In the weeks that followed, they made love often in Jack's car, forgetting the cold, ignoring the discomfort of their cramped quarters. Alice hated the precautions, but was grateful. Though she knew he would have married her, she didn't want them to "have to marry." They'd have a family later on. For now they had passion.

And then, in April, she realized that what she feared had happened. When she told him, he looked horrified.

"Are you sure?"

"Pretty sure." She blushed. "I haven't . . . that is, I've missed."

"Have you seen a doctor?"

"No. Of course not. I don't even know one except our family physician."

"Well, you can't go to *him*. That's for sure. I'll get the name of somebody. Maybe it's a false alarm."

"And if it isn't?"

"Now, don't start worrying. Bet you a hundred dollars you aren't even that way."

She'd felt cold. Even now she could remember the awful, sick feeling in the pit of her stomach. She was pregnant. She knew it.

"You said we'd get married if this happened."

"Well, we will. Except I'm sure you're wrong. It couldn't be. I haven't taken any chances. You know that."

"But those things aren't always reliable, are they?"

"Allie, for God's sake! Wait until you see the doctor!"

A few days later she sneaked off to some out-of-the-way office and shortly after that the test came back. Positive. She was "about six weeks along."

"I don't see any problems, Mrs. Smith," the doctor said. He underlined the name as if to say he knew the story. "You're very young, but you're healthy. You should have a nice baby. Check with my nurse on the way out. She'll give you a date for your next appointment and some suggestions about diet and things."

She'd made the appointment, knowing she'd never keep it. She and Jack would get married right away and tell their families later. Lots of women had "premature" babies. It wasn't as they'd planned it. Jack still had three years of college. But they'd manage. They loved each other. She refused to think it would be any other way.

But it was. Jack, looking sheepish, said it just wasn't possible for them to get married. How could he support a family? He had to finish school and God knows they couldn't count on their parents to help out.

"Then, what shall we do?" She knew what he'd say and hated him even before he said it.

"Look. There's a guy at college who knows somebody. I'll get the name.

It's perfectly safe. It's a real doctor who just does this kind of thing on the side. We'll figure out how to get you away for a weekend and have it taken care of.''

Even then she was more mature than he. "Why can't you say the word? Abortion. You want me to go to some dirty place and have an abortion! I won't do it, Jack. I've heard about those places. Women die on kitchen tables. Or later, of blood poisoning. Or they bleed to death.''

"Don't be silly. It's done a thousand times every day.''

She began to cry. "No. No, I can't.''

"You have to, Allie. You know we can't get married. I'm not ready for that responsibility.''

Her tears stopped. "You lied,'' she said coldly. "You lied all the way. I wouldn't marry you now, Jack Richards, even if you begged me to. How could I have loved you? You're . . . you're nothing but an infant yourself!''

"Be practical. What choice do we have? I *do* love you. I just didn't think this would happen. We'll still get married. Later. Like we planned. This won't make any difference.''

"Maybe not to you. It's not your body. Or your life you're so willing to risk. You can't love me if you'd let me take such a terrible chance.'' She turned away from him. "I think I'd like to go home now,'' Alice said.

"Are you going to tell your folks?''

"Of course. I'll have to if I'm going to have a baby.''

"They'll raise hell! So will mine! Allie, you're being stupid!''

Maybe I was, an older, wiser Alice thought now, driving with her sisters to their "get-acquainted'' lunch. Maybe I was stupid not to have had the abortion. But I couldn't. It wasn't just a moral thing. I was too frightened. Too hurt. But maybe I'd have been less hurt if Johnny had never been born, if I hadn't had to part with a real, live child.

It had been terrible, telling her parents. Laura's stunned disbelief was worse than Sam's towering, patriarchal rage. I feel as though I've betrayed her, Allie had thought. As though I've canceled out all the things she tried to teach us, all the faith she had in us.

"I'm sorry, Mother.''

"Oh, darling, I'm sorry for *you!* My poor baby!'' Laura's initial shock turned to instinctive maternal protectiveness. "Alice, dear, we'll arrange things immediately. You and Jack must get married at once.''

She assumed Jack was the father. Why not? They knew Allie went out only with him. It also would never occur to Laura that there was any acceptable alternative to this situation. Sam Dalton's thoughts were the same as his wife's, though his reaction was not one of compassion but of anger. Anger initially directed at Jack.

"I'd like to kill him!'' her father said. "Damned little seducer! Wait till I get my hands on him! Young punk! I'll break his neck!''

"Daddy, it wasn't rape.'' Allie's voice was miserable. "He didn't force me. I'm as much to blame as he.''

Sam glared at her. "I know that too. Don't think I'm not just as furious with you, Alice. How could you do this to your mother and me? Haven't we taught you any sense of decency? Did we raise you to bring us this kind of shame? Look what you've done! Given away your most precious possession, your virtue! And look where it will take you: into a shotgun wedding at seventeen! How could you be so wanton?''

"Sam, please!" Laura tried to stop him. "Don't blame the children. What they did was wrong. But they're human. We mustn't hold this mistake against them. We must stand by them. We and the Richardses. The families will have to stick together, get these two married immediately.''

"No," Allie said. "I'm sorry, Mother, but Jack and I aren't going to get married.''

"What!" Sam exploded. "You mean he won't marry you? Well, he will! By God, I'll see to that!''

"He doesn't want to." Allie's chin went up. "And I don't want to marry him.''

Laura looked bewildered. "I don't understand . . .''

"He wants me to have an abortion. I'm afraid to. I won't. And even if he changed his mind, I wouldn't marry a man who'd suggest such a thing.''

They'd stared at her, open-mouthed, speechless. Sam recovered first.

"This is no time to be so high and mighty, young lady! Of course you won't have an abortion. But you'll get married. Never mind what either of you think you want. The fact is you're going to have a baby and he's the father and he'll do the right thing by you! I'll talk to his father. George Richards will agree with me. That boy won't get away with this. As for you, Alice, there's no other solution. You've sinned and maybe you'll pay for it, but you won't disgrace us with an illegitimate child!''

"I won't marry him, Daddy. No matter what you want. I don't love him.''

Sam snorted. "Fine time to think of that! Why didn't you reach that conclusion while you were behaving like a little tramp?''

"Sam! Stop it!" Laura broke in again. She turned to Alice. "We don't understand, dear. You're not thinking of having this baby with no husband, are you? What would people say? We'd be the talk of Denver! Allie, darling, be sensible. You and Jack must get married." Her voice was soothing. "It will work out. You'll see. Right now you're just hurt and frightened. You love each other. And certainly you want to give your baby a name, don't you? You wouldn't be that unfair to a helpless child.''

She hadn't thought of the child. She forced herself to say it. The bastard. Maybe they were right. Maybe she and Jack had to marry for the sake of the unborn baby.

"All right," she'd finally said, wearily, "I'll marry him. But I hate it. I hate the idea of someone having to marry me. I hate the idea of being married to someone who doesn't want me. But I'll do it.''

She didn't do it. Not because she wouldn't have, but because Jack Richards' parents did not agree with her own. There'd been an ugly scene in the Daltons' living room, with Alice and Jack sitting mutely by while their parents wrangled and shouted over their future, each blaming the other's child for this catastrophe. Terrible things had been said. The Richardses had painted Allie as an immoral girl who deserved no better than she got. The Daltons had responded that their spoiled, heedless son had taken advantage of an innocent child. It was unbearable. And it went on and on until, humiliated beyond endurance, Alice jumped up and screamed.

"Shut up! All of you shut up! It's our decision. Jack's and mine. You're acting like we're . . . objects! Like things you can push around to suit yourselves! Well, you can't! We've already made up our minds. A marriage we don't want is worse than any disgrace. It's obscene and I won't do it!"

She'd run sobbing to her room. Sometime later her mother had come in to find Barbara trying to calm her hysterical sister. Barbara, who had no idea what was going on. Who simply knew Alice was unhappy and who was trying to help. Laura had sat on the edge of Allie's bed and tenderly pushed the long black hair out of her daughter's eyes.

"It's all right, darling," she'd said. "Stop crying, Allie. We'll work something out."

Barbara hadn't said a word then nor later when the Daltons made hasty arrangements for Alice to go to her mother's sister, Aunt Charlotte, in Boston. It was years before Barbara and Alice discussed the episode. And in the meantime, Allie's baby boy was born and given away, to God knows whom.

"Where shall we go for lunch?" Barbara asked as they approached Larimer Square. "The two places I like best are The Promenade Cafe and LaFitte's."

"Since I've never been in this area," Fran said, "I wouldn't have a clue. What's the difference between them?"

"The Promenade is an outdoor place, and LaFitte's is dark and New Orleansy-looking."

"LaFitte's, without question," Fran pronounced. "To hell with the food. Give me that nice subdued lighting. Who needs to sit over lunch with your face hanging out in the sunlight? My God, I haven't been able to cope with that since I was twelve!"

The others laughed. "LaFitte's it is," Barbara said. "But I presume you could afford to explore The Square a few minutes before we duck into the darkness? It's interesting down here. A great restoration project, with lots of good little shops."

"Like Ghirardelli Square in San Francisco?" Alice asked.

"Kind of. On a smaller scale."

"They're doing the same thing in Boston with the Quincy Market development near Faneuil Hall. Fascinating, with all the old stalls and the brick and cobblestone walks. I'm glad it's happening all over."

"I wish I knew what language you two were speaking," Frances said.

"Serves you right for being an expatriate," Barbara answered. "But it seems to me I read they're doing something of the same in Paris, putting back an old section on the Left Bank of the Seine the way it was before it went entirely to pot. It's good to preserve old things."

Fran shrugged. "Okay if they're buildings, I suppose. A terrible idea if applied to people."

"I take it you don't approve of old age." Alice's voice was amused.

"I loathe it. I won't have it."

"Then you're obviously planning to die young." Barbara was teasing, but Fran took her seriously.

"I certainly am. I won't get old and wrinkled and ugly. Never. I'll take advantage of every kind of lift there is, face, bosom, buttocks—you name it. And when they don't work any more I'll use my saved-up sleeping pills."

Barbara was shocked. "You're kidding! Life is precious at any age."

They were walking slowly through the narrow little streets and arcades, passing the old black iron benches on the sidewalks, the carved sandstone Bear and Bull from Denver's original Stock Exchange transplanted over a doorway. Fran glanced with disdain at the restored façades and the ornate drinking fountain with its Victorian cherub on top.

"I can't bear things that are decrepit and quaint," she said. "Things and people should be young and vital. Your Larimer Square is like an old lady trying to be coy. Look at the names of some of these places. 'The Sobriety Sarsaparilla and Sandwich Shop,' for God's sake! And that plant store called 'Foliage Bergère'! The whole place proves how ludicruous it is to try to turn back the clock."

"I don't find it ludicrous," Alice said quietly. "I think the Square is charming and genteel and meaningful. As though a big busy city is determined not to forget its past. I like that. In cities and in people. Remembering is important."

"It's infantile," Fran snapped. "I'd think *you* of all people would agree with that."

There was a long moment of silence before Fran went on. "I'm sorry, Allie. Hell, all I've done this morning is put my foot into it and apologize!"

"It's okay. Neither you nor I have such pretty pasts, Fran. But that doesn't mean we should forget them."

"No, I suppose not. There's something to be learned from every experience, isn't there? At least, that's what people keep telling me. I hate that, too. Why does one have to suffer to mature? It's ridiculous. As though understanding is impossible without bad experiences. Who decided that good experiences don't teach anybody anything?"

"They do," Allie said. "It's just that we don't notice the good ones as much."

"Like headlines, you mean. Bad news sells newspapers. That kind of thing?"

"Precisely. A disaster is much more interesting and memorable than something dull and pleasant."

"Then your life and mine would make juicy copy," Fran said. "We seem to specialize in disasters. Not so our baby sister, however. She's revoltingly serene."

Alice smiled at Barb. "Maybe she just doesn't broadcast her mistakes the way we do."

Fran turned to Barbara. "Is that true, Barb? Do you have a secret life none of us knows about? What are the skeletons, past and present, in your closet?"

Barbara brushed aside the probing question. "My current secret is that I'm going to faint if we don't have lunch. Come on, philosophers, let's eat."

I wonder if I could tell them about Charles, Barbara thought. Would they understand my utter devotion to a married man? They wouldn't condemn me for it. Allie would probably feel sorry and sensibly try to talk me out of it. But Fran would tell me I'm nothing but a damned fool, wasting my life.

Maybe before this week is over I will tell them. I want so much to tell someone. That's the worst part of it: being in love and not able to let anyone know. Even if they think I'm crazy, it would be good to share the happiness I feel inside.

Chapter 4

"HOW ARE YOU going to feel when you see your old girlfriend?" Dottie Paige managed to make the question sound almost clinical.

Buzz lowered the pages of the *Rocky Mountain News* and looked innocently at his wife.

"What old girlfriend?"

"Really, Buzz! You know who I mean. Frances Dalton whatever-whatever. She's home for her parents' anniversary. We're invited there for the party. You know that."

"Oh, *that*."

"Well?"

"Well, what?"

Dottie was annoyed. Sometimes Buzz was so transparent. "How are you going to feel, seeing Frances again after all these years? You were crazy about her when we were kids. I used to be insanely jealous."

"That's nice. Are you still?"

"Should I be?"

"Honey, don't be ridiculous. I haven't seen Frannie for thirty years. Do you think I'm still lusting after her?"

"Could be. She's terribly glamorous. All those marriages and divorces and living in Europe. It really doesn't seem possible she's the same girl."

"I'm sure she isn't. Any more than I'm the same boy." He patted his slight paunch. "I'm a settled, contented, middle-aged grandfather. Not that jock she used to date. We probably won't even recognize each other. And I'll bore hell out of her, unless she happens to be interested in Ford dealerships."

"Some women are. I'm sure you haven't forgotten that!" She wished she hadn't said that. She'd promised never to again. She didn't add that from what she gleaned from the gossip columns, any presentable man was of interest to Fran, whether he sold Fords or owned Lincoln Continentals. She told herself Frances wouldn't try anything with Buzz. She wasn't like that other woman. It was just that Dottie knew, by comparison, she'd look like the little brown wren. The hometown girl Buzz married after he lost what turned into an international peacock. Peahen. Oh, blast, what difference did it make? She was nervous, thinking of seeing Frannie again. She wished she had something smarter to wear, wished she hadn't accepted Laura Dalton's invitation, wished, most of all, she hadn't volunteered to make those damned home-spun brownies. Why hadn't they offered to bring champagne instead? Because, idiot, the Daltons don't drink. Because nobody brings champagne to these local gatherings. Because you're behaving like a teen-ager instead of a woman who's been married to the same man for twenty-nine years. And that, at least, she thought, is more than one can say for Frances.

When he brought the second bloody mary, Fran eyed the waiter speculatively. Not bad. A kid, of course. Somewhere in his late twenties, which, to her, was a baby. But he'd looked at her in a way she recognized when he put her drink in front of her. The old "international invitation," she thought. She'd had it from bartenders in Madrid and croupiers in Nice. And usually, out of desperation, she accepted it. One-night stands. A few hours of pretended enchantment with some young, virile stranger. The fleeting satisfaction of feeling desirable. Sometimes they wanted money. Or the excitement of going to bed with a rich, social "older woman" whom they assumed, incorrectly, to be a nymphomaniac. She wasn't. She didn't care that much about sex for its own sake. It was admiration and reassurance she craved. Maybe even danger. One of those pick-ups could rob and kill her in whatever bed they occupied. Perhaps that made it all the more exciting. God knows it was a relief from loneliness or the sterile company of the unattached "gays" who were only too happy to squire her around.

She watched the waiter as he retreated to a corner of the restaurant near the ladies' room. He's done this before, too, Fran thought cynically. He's giving me a chance to excuse myself and make a date with him. Maybe I will. Anything to get through this week.

That's how I met Jacques, she remembered. I picked him up in the Carlton bar in Cannes. Of course, he wasn't a waiter. Just an opportunist with a phony title. Jacques de St. Déspres. He'd been thirty and she forty-two. They'd flirted openly, he from his table alone and she from her seat among her boring party of six: three rich divorcees and a trio of faggots. She'd been ready to cut out and go up to her room when she saw him. Dark, handsome, smiling his invitation. She'd gone to the ladies' room, discreetly dropping her calling card beside his chair, knowing he'd pick it up, sure he'd check with the desk clerk and find her room number, positive he'd keep calling the suite until she answered and invited him up.

They married a month later. She still wondered why. At the time it had seemed amusing to become a marquise. The Marquise de St. Déspres. For a little while, she'd thought the title was real, just as she thought Jacques' passionate protestations of love were real. But she supposed she knew, even at the start, that neither was genuine. Jacques' father was a Paris butcher, and the closest the family had ever come to a title was supplying racks of lamb to people with real family crests. She'd laughed when she found out. Laughed when Jacques blurted out the truth in the middle of one of their monumental fights. He'd thought it would humiliate her. It had only struck her funny.

They stayed together a year. She'd have gone on with it, out of inertia, if Jacques had not become so flagrantly unfaithful. Her pride couldn't take that. In that way, she remained "American." Even after all the years in Europe, she couldn't handle the upperclass European woman's relaxed attitude toward a husband's affairs; could never become sufficiently sophisticated to accept and ignore the fact that her husband had a mistress. Or perhaps it was because the mistress was twenty-eight years old.

Whatever, she divorced him and settled handsomely, giving him a sizable chunk of her second husband's money. "Share the wealth," she'd thought at the time. Arthur Stanton paid to get rid of me, and now I'm passing some of it along to get rid of Jacques. It seemed equitable, somehow, even though she'd gotten shortchanged. She never used the title, aware that the really elegant people knew it was a fake. So she hadn't even gotten that out of her third marriage. At least Stuart Mills had provided a way out of Denver. And Arthur had made her financially secure. But Jacques had given her nothing except some unusually expert French lovemaking in the beginning and a short-lived feeling that she still had the allure of a young woman.

Barb and Allie were chattering on. She paid no attention. She stared steadily at the LaFitte waiter, accepting his challenge.

"Back in a minute," Fran finally said. She sauntered toward the ladies' room, aware that heads turned as she passed. They didn't know the pants suit was custom-made St. Laurent, right out of the couture. Or that Boucheron made her jewels in Paris. But they knew she was Somebody. There was always satisfaction in that

She passed close to the waiter. "Give me your name and number when I come out," she said, barely moving her lips. "I'll be in touch."

Her sisters watched her progress, unaware of the exchange with the waiter.

"She's really something, isn't she?" Barbara shook her head. "Do you think she's as blasé as she tries to appear? Something tells me it's an act."

"I don't know," Allie said. "I do know she's an unhappy woman."

"I remember when she ran off with that actor, Stuart Mills. I was a kid, but I'll never forget it. It was the year after you left, Allie. Mother and Daddy were still so broken up over you. And then Fran got that job in summer stock at the theater in Elitch Gardens. We didn't even know what was going on. Everybody thought she was going to marry Buzz Paige until we woke up one morning and there was that note saying she'd left for New York and was going to marry Stuart Mills. And one telephone call, a week later, saying she had. Did you ever meet him, Allie?"

"Once. They came to Boston with a road company, and Fran called me at Aunt Charlotte's. She wouldn't come to the house. I met them at the Copley Plaza for a drink." Allie smiled. "At least they had a drink. I had tea. I was still such a kid, even though I'd had a baby." The smile faded and she was silent for a moment. "Anyway, Stu Mills was terribly good-looking, but Fran told me privately that the marriage wasn't working out. I didn't know she'd already met Arthur Stanton. He was much older, you know. A widower and one of the 'angels' of a show Stu had been in the season before. Fran married him six months later, but she never bothered to tell me. I read it in the papers."

"She called Mother and Daddy," Barbara said. "She just said she'd married a wonderful, wealthy man and was very happy. But she never brought him home. She never brought any of them home. In fairness, she did invite the three of us to New York when she was married to Stanton, but Daddy wouldn't go. So she never asked again. Not in that marriage or later. Daddy's so stubborn. He never forgave her for running off with Mills. And she's just like him. So she just disappeared. Except for occasional cards and gifts, none of us has seen her until last night. I'm surprised she came home for the anniversary."

"So am I. Maybe there comes a time when you'd like to recapture something. Maybe it's part of getting older."

Barbara looked worried. "Do you think she meant what she said when we were walking around? All that business about sleeping pills."

Allie shook her head. "I don't know, Barb. I don't know her well enough. I can't imagine anybody not wanting to live, no matter what." She gave a little laugh. "Funny. Last night I picked up a magazine Mother left in our room. Something called the *Colorado Woman's Digest*. There was an ad on the back. Some radio station, I think. It said something like 'Do not resent growing old. Remember, many are denied that privilege.' Maybe I should put it in Fran's room."

"I saw that. What a strange magazine for Mother to have. It's very 'liberated woman' stuff, I gather."

"Not entirely. It covers the spectrum, from jobs to politics, but it also has things like 'Community Care for the Elderly' and an amusing article on what to do with a husband who's retired. Anyway, you never know about Mother, do you? I often think there's much more to her than meets the eye."

"Much more to whom?" Fran slid back into her place on the banquette.

"To Mother," Barbara said. "We were just saying that she's not as uncomplicated as she seems."

"She's female," Fran said matter-of-factly. "When have you ever known an uncomplicated female? Let's order. I'm getting bored with this place."

They returned to the house on South Carona Street about four o'clock that afternoon. She'd been back once a year since she'd moved to Washington fourteen years before, but Barbara had never looked at her parents' home quite as appraisingly as she did this day. It really was a dreary place. Dreary but respectable. A two-story brick dwelling with three bedrooms, a front porch and those hideous stone urns on either side of the steps leading to it. Inside, nothing had changed in Barb's memory. It was all scrupulously clean and depressingly ordinary. The living-room furniture, including the cut-velvet "divan" and Daddy's big easy chair, stood exactly where they'd been placed fifty years before. Even the lamps and the few ornaments were the same as they'd been in her childhood. So was the dining-room "suite" with its big oak sideboard and its Tiffany lamp hanging precisely over the center of the table. It was as though time stood still. As though it was the late nineteen-thirties when Barbara Dalton was growing up in a middle-class house in a middle-class neighborhood in a middle-class family.

On her trips home these past years, she'd just taken it for granted. Now she supposed she saw it through her sisters' eyes as well as her own. How different Sam and Laura's surroundings were from her own sleek little apartment in Washington with its good modern furnishings. As different as they were from Allie's big house on Beacon Hill, which she'd visited once, years ago. Certainly different from Fran's Paris flat, which she'd never seen.

She felt suddenly homesick for her own place in Georgetown. That's where her life was. In that unobtrusive little converted brownstone with the landlady-owner on the premises, but no inquisitive doorman to note that Charles let himself in with his own key. She wouldn't let Charles pay the rent. He thought she was silly, but she'd been adamant about that from the start.

"I'll take your gifts and your flowers and as much of you as can spare," she'd said early on in their relationship, "but my home is my castle and I can maintain the moat."

He'd laughed. "I know you're a high-paid government official," he'd teased, "but this chic tenement is expensive. It's nineteen sixty-three, love. The age of Camelot. Everybody wants to live in Georgetown and the landlords know it. You are not a Kennedy, after all."

"But I am an able-bodied, twenty-seven-year-old woman working for a highly respected Colorado congressman," she'd said. "and I bloody well can afford to entertain one of his colleagues in my own paid-for apartment. So you just be quiet, Congressman Tallent, and don't trouble yourself about the cost of my turret."

"Okay. As long as you promise not to pull up the drawbridge one day."

"You could always set up a siege."

"Nut!" He'd taken her in his arms that night as he had so many nights in the thirteen years that followed. Thirteen years! Barbara thought. Where have they gone? I'm forty years old and Charles is fifty and we're as much in love as ever. She didn't want to think what would happen if her own boss did not get reelected. Or if the voters in Charles's state turned him out of office one day. Would he leave Washington? Could she follow him back to that midwestern country he came from? She lived with that fear at every election and so far they'd been lucky. The age of Camelot disappeared. Administrations changed. But Charles and her boss kept being returned to their seats in the House. Thank God. That's the way it would be. Anything else was unthinkable. I'd go crazy if I lost him, Barb thought. I'd be far more griefstricken than his widow would be if he died.

But Charles wasn't going to die. Any more than he was going to leave her. Or any more than he was going to marry her. Why did that thought keep popping up here in Denver? In Washington, where the reminders were much more prevalent, she was almost able to forget Charles's wife and his grown-up children and the house in Chevy Chase he shared with Andrea. She was content with her situation. Busy all day on Capitol Hill, occupied with theater at Kennedy Center or movies or restaurant dining with "girlfriends" on the nights Charles was fulfilling the social obligations of which she had no part. She shopped in Georgetown for food for the delicious little dinners she prepared on the nights he could get away: croissants and special cheeses from the French Market; Smithfield hams from Nimes; delicate veal from the Boucherie Bernard. My life is full and happy, Barbara thought again. God knows there are no marriages in my family to envy. Not Fran's three. Not even, she suspected, Allie's. There was something mysterious about Allie's marriage. Spencer was arriving tomorrow, but the children weren't coming. Allie had just announced that, giving no explanation. She'd also announced that she and Spencer would stay at the Hilton. Laura had been disappointed.

"Why? There's room here, dear. Barbara and Frances can bunk in Frances' room and you and Spencer can have the other."

"It's better if we go to the hotel, Mother. Spencer is a crank about his comfort. Not that we wouldn't love to sleep here, but, honestly, he'd go crazy without his own bathroom."

No word about her children, Christopher and Janice. No reason given for their failure to come for their grandparents' fiftieth wedding anniversary. Laura and

Sam hadn't seen them since they were teen-agers and Alice brought them for a visit on the way to Vail for a skiing holiday. Now they were twenty-three and twenty-one respectively. And obviously disinterested in family reunions.

I'm curious about that marriage, Barbara admitted to herself. Allie had stayed on in Boston after the baby was born. She'd worked at Filene's and lived with Aunt Charlotte until she was twenty-three. Then she'd met and married Spencer Winters in 1951. He'd given her two babies and, apparently, a comfortable, nearly rich life, thanks to his successful law practice. But had he given her happiness? Barbara sensed not. In fact, she suspected quite the contrary. Allie seemed quiet, almost fearful somehow. It was nothing one could define. There was simply an air of resignation and sadness about her.

I wonder if Spencer Winters knows about the other child? Not necessarily. Jack Richards' baby was adopted long before Alice met her husband. And she'd been in virtual seclusion in Boston during her pregnancy. That much Laura had later confided. But there was something not good about the marriage. Maybe, even thirty years later, Allie had never gotten over her first love.

If Jack Richards still lived in Denver, it was damned certain he wouldn't be invited tomorrow night. The Daltons and the Richardses had never spoken since their last confrontation. And Allie obviously had no desire to see the man who'd fathered her baby. She'd been home often enough over the years to have looked him up if she'd wanted to. Barb was sure she never had. No one ever mentioned his name, for that matter. It was as though he were dead. Or as lost as the son he'd never seen.

It wasn't Jack Richards who haunted Alice, but it might be a longing to know about their child. Or maybe Allie's tentative attitude had nothing to do with any of that. Maybe it was something entirely different.

Good lord, how her mind wandered, starting with her thoughts about this house! She was being snobbish about it. It was a nice house. A good house. The proper setting for the only happily married people she knew. Or were they? At seventy, something seemed to have come over her mother, something Barb had never sensed before. Restlessness. Or regret. She'd always thought of her parents as perfectly mated. But now she wasn't so sure. If it was difficult for her father to be idle, it must be equally difficult for her mother to have him underfoot twenty-four hours a day. It could be as simple as that. Or the normal anxiety that usually came with age, an anxiety underlined by the reminder of a golden wedding anniversary. So many years together. So much sameness in the way they lived, the people they saw, the things they did. The same unchanging, unchallenging life represented by the static state of this very house.

Were they bored? Could people at their age possibly begin to chafe at the pattern of a lifetime, suddenly realizing how limited it was, how much they'd missed? It seemed unlikely. Almost inconceivable. And yet Sam and Laura could have many more years to look forward to. Perhaps, Barbara thought, they don't really like what they see.

Or maybe they feel they failed all of us. If so, they're wrong. They shared all the things they believed in, tried to instill the values they were brought up to respect. It's not their fault they produced a trio of disappointing daughters who never fell into the safe little well-married roles they envisioned. If anyone's failed in this family, Fran and Allie and I have. We've never given Mother and Daddy what they really wanted: a part in our lives.

And it's too late now.

Chapter 5

ALICE MET THE United Flight when it arrived in Denver the next day bearing a predictably surly Spencer Winters. He didn't kiss her. It crossed her mind that at least he didn't hit her. Not that he would, in public. He only did that in the privacy of their home. And quite often. Spencer Winters was a wife-beater. Proper, prominent, conservative Spencer Winters regularly doled out his share of bruises and blackened eyes, and once even a broken arm.

He was not rare. There were thousands like him. Sadists who enjoyed physically punishing their wives. And all of them married to women like Alice, women who endured the cruelty out of fear or helplessness or, no doubt, masochism. She read about this phenomenon often, more often these days than ever, it seemed. She also read that many wives finally found the courage to "come out of the closet" and reveal what had been going on in their lives for years. There were organizations now to help such victims. Groups of other women willing to offer emotional counseling and practical assistance to those who wanted to escape this demeaning, brutal existence.

My good sense tells me I should be one of those, Alice thought. I should leave Spencer. I have no reason to stay. My children are grown and no longer in need of me, and I'd always find a way to support myself. I could come back here, to Denver. Or stay on after this "festive week" ends. But I won't. I'll go back to Boston. To the mental and physical cruelty I've known most of my married life. Why do I go on with it? Because I love Spencer? No. I haven't loved him for years. I never loved him. He was a way out of Aunt Charlotte's house: an escape from those self-righteous eyes that never stopped accusing me of my sin and reminding me of my lost child.

Johnny is why I stay. Even after all these years I must want to be punished for abandoning him. I suffer Spencer's beatings as I would a spanking from my father, knowing I've been a bad girl and compulsively determined to pay for it forever. I am a masochist. "Sick," the children would say. Sick in the head. There was no need for me to confess to Spencer about that schoolgirl mistake or the baby born of it. No reason he ever had to know. I wanted him to know. Wanted him to chastise me. And he's done so. He's used the knowledge like a whip, almost literally, every time I do something to annoy him. And I take it, feeling I deserve it. Feeling I'm not worthy of anything better.

If only I knew where Johnny was. If I could be sure he's well and happy, perhaps I'd get over this terrible guilt. But I never will. They wouldn't tell me who adopted him. I'm sure Aunt Charlotte knows, but she won't tell me either. She thinks I deserve to suffer. As Spencer does. As I do, myself.

In the taxi, she forced herself to smile at her husband.

"How was the trip, dear?"

"Boring."

"Are the children all right?"

"How should I know? Chris is dead, as far as I'm concerned. And Janice might as well be living with that man instead of just sleeping with him and coming home to change her clothes. Things haven't changed in two days, Alice," he said sarcastically. "Or did you think your absence might encourage your children to become paragons of virtue?"

She didn't answer that. "I've checked us in at the Hilton," she said instead. "We have a very nice room."

"I'll bet. Seen one Hilton you've seen 'em all. Couldn't you, for Christ's sake get us into some more civilized place? What's wrong with the old wing of the Brown Palace?"

"It was full. We're lucky to have gotten any accommodations." She hesitated. "Of course, we could still change our minds and stay with the family. There's room."

"Not on your life! My God, isn't it enough that I've made this idiotic trip? Do you expect me to stay in that stuffy little house as well? You really ask too much of me! You know I can't stand those people. Damned hymn-singing teetotalers! As for those sisters of yours! An international whore and a Washington swinger!"

"Spencer, you're not being fair! You hardly know any of them. You've met my parents three times and Barbara only once. And you've never met Fran at all!"

"Their reputations precede them. As yours did. No wonder your own children are so immoral. They take after their mother and their aunts."

"I don't understand you," Alice said slowly. "If you hate me so, why do you stay married to me? We have nothing, Spencer. No love. No sex. No companionship. And God knows we have no friendship. What *do* we have?"

"My reputation. My standing in the community. Not to mention my religion, which frowns on divorce."

"It's not *my* religion, though your children were raised in it. But with your influence, Spencer, you probably could get this twenty-five-year farce annulled."

"We were married in the Church."

"Yes, and I respect your church. I respect all religions. But I never converted. I'm sure you could find a way out."

"Forget it. My law firm is stuffier than any priest. You know how J.B. feels about divorce."

Yes, she did indeed know. J.B. The Senior Partner was a "veddy, veddy proper Bostonian" of the old school. Despite Spencer's more than twenty-five years with the firm, and a junior partnership, he was still an "outsider," a "newcomer from Chicago." Every move in the past and present was made with J.B. in mind. The choice of their friends, the right address, the correct club, the subscription to the symphony, the brilliant parties for which she was famous. All to enhance Spencer's future and raise him in the estimation of J. B. Thompson. I wonder how the old man would like it if he knew his "young associate" regularly punched his wife around? Alice thought. He'd not approve of the ungentlemanly violence, but he'd probably secretly be in favor of a man showing who's boss in his own home. Spencer was terrified J.B. would find out about

Alice's "lurid past" or discover how defiant and uncontrollable his own children were: Chris, considered "dead" since he brazenly told Spencer he was a homosexual; Janice, barely spoken to by her father since she took up with that art director from an advertising agency. Spencer was outraged, disgusted by both discoveries. Alice was saddened, heartsick about her son, but admiring of his honesty. As for Janice, the girl was only following her convictions. And, thank God, with more courage than her mother had shown.

My guilt is endlessly compounded, Allie thought. The children had been all too aware, most of their lives, of the anger in their house. They heard the screams and the angry shouting, saw the bruises she tried hard to hide. Chris had reacted with a violent hatred of his father and a fanatic devotion to his mother that even three years of psychoanalysis had not been able to change. She still saw him, outside of the house. He was a gentle young man and at least he had found happiness in his own way, revolting though it was to Spencer. Chris worried about her, begged her to leave, even suggested she move in with him and Peter. She'd sadly refused.

"I'm not going to spoil your life," she'd said. "Look, Chris, I won't pretend I don't wish you'd taken another path. But this is the one you want, the one that brings you contentment. Peter's a nice boy. I like him. But I'm not sophisticated enough to handle that household, even if I were selfish enough to intrude."

"You disapprove," Chris had said.

"Disapprove? No. That's too strong a word. I'm of another generation. It's hard for me to understand why you can't fall in love with some nice young woman. Hard for me to accept something no parent really wants to accept. But I love you. And who am I to set standards for others?"

"So you'll stay on in that house with that brute."

"I suppose so."

"Why, Mother?"

She couldn't tell him. Couldn't confess this thirty-year-old guilt that seemed to become more of an obsession as she grew older. He didn't know he had a half-brother somewhere. He'd never know. She supposed she kept quiet out of shame. She'd not be able to bear reproach in the eyes of one whose adoration was dearer than life itself.

She'd never told Janice either, though her daughter's attitude would have been much more casual. Janice still maintained a token residence at home, but she'd been "independent" for two years. When she spoke of her father it was as though she talked of some clinically disturbed case history she'd read about.

"He's weird. Talk about your male chauvinist pigs! Of course he's worse than most. The physical stuff, I mean. My God, I'd never stand for that! Why do you?"

Alice hadn't known how to answer but she flinched under Jan's obvious scorn for both of them. In Jan's eyes I'm no better than Spencer, she thought. She despises him for the way he treats me, but I think perhaps she has even less respect for me for putting up with it. She's right, of course. But I've never had her kind of strength. Not even when I was twenty-one. How I envy girls of today who don't even want to be referred to as girls. Women, they call themselves. Young women. Sisters. Persons. However they refer to themselves, the meaning is the same. They're individuals, free and honest, unburdened by the taboos I grew up with, untroubled by what other people think. Jan made no secret of her affair with her young art director, Clint Darby. They worked at the same advertising agency, ate their meals together, slept together. Spencer was right. She might just as well have moved in with him instead of keeping up the pretense of living at home. But Alice couldn't come out and ask her why she didn't. Jan might think she wanted her to leave. She didn't want that. Neither did Spencer, despite what he said. She supposed it was more selfishness than propriety that kept Janice theoretically at home. Home was a place where your underwear was done by the laundress, where Mother took care of your dry cleaning and had new heels put on your shoes, where the housekeeper tidied up your room and where Father paid your phone bills. Home was where you sulkily spent Christmas while Clint went back to Ohio to see his own parents. Home was a stopover, convenient and impersonal, where you checked in and out, counting on your mother's loving anxiety and your father's reluctant affection masked by the disapproval he felt compelled to register in his self-righteous way.

She saw Spencer frown as they pushed into the crowded elevator in the Denver Hilton, jostled by fat women in stretch pants and men with convention badges on the lapels of their ill-fitting brown suits. "Cowboy attire," complete with string ties and wide-brimmed hats, also abounded. She could feel his scorn. He was so intolerant. So damned superior and *Eastern*. He'd brought only an overnight bag, and when they entered their room she looked at it inquiringly.

"Traveling light, aren't you?"

"A couple of clean shirts. Some underwear. The usual. What did you think I'd bring for this great social event—white tie?"

I won't rise to the bait, Alice thought. "No. But for a week, I thought . . ."

"A week! You're not serious! You don't really think I could spend seven days here!"

"But we planned it. A week . . ."

"*You* planned a week. I said I'd come for this damned anniversary, and that's tomorrow night. After that, forget it."

"Spencer, that's so mean of you! We've almost never been here together. I thought just this once you could sacrifice a little of your precious time to be with me."

She saw the redness begin to creep up from his collar, the recognizable sign of rage. Don't let him, she prayed. Don't let him fly into one of those fits of uncontrollable anger. Not here. Not now.

"Goddamn you, Alice, you never appreciate anything! I've come all this way just so you could show your bloody relatives and friends that you have a real, live, legitimate husband. Well, they'll see me. Isn't that enough to prove your children have a father?" His voice was mounting. Surely the people in the next room could hear him. "You drive me insane! Never make an ounce of sense! You are the most infuriating, ridiculous . . ." He moved toward her, his fist raised. She backed away.

"No! Spencer, don't! My God, don't humiliate me this way! Not here. Please, Spencer!"

He lowered his hand. "Then stop nagging me! You can stay a week. Hell, you can stay a year! But not me. You should know better than to suggest it!"

"All right. I'm sorry. I realize it would bore you."

"Damned right it would. It bores me already." He opened his bag and threw a few things in the dresser drawer. "Call room service and order me a double scotch."

"There's an ice machine down the hall."

He turned and looked at her witheringly. "How nice. But I am not a traveling salesman, my dear. I do not go about with a bottle in my bag. Now will you kindly get on that telephone and tell them if they're not here in ten minutes there will be a scene the like of which they have not witnessed since they erected this convention hall they laughingly call a first-class hotel?"

"Drive me downtown, will you, Barb?"

"Sure. Something you want to buy?"

Frances smiled. "In a way. But first I want to rent a car."

"Rent a car? What on earth for? Don't tell me you're a sightseer."

"Hardly. I've been in Rome fifty times and I've never set foot inside the Vatican."

"Then what in the world do you want with a car? You planning to look up old friends? You can use Dad's car, if you are. Or I'll be glad to take you anywhere you want to go."

"For heaven's sake, Barbara, will you just shut up and do what I ask you? I want a car while I'm here. I get claustrophobic in this hellhole. I want to be able to move wherever and whenever the mood strikes me. Don't make a big deal out of it."

"Sorry."

"And don't look so damned injured." Fran smiled. "Listen, pussycat, your old sister never goes anywhere without looking for excitement. And excitement is synonymous with mobility. Get it? I'm not going to be stuck in this house for a week, or have to explain where I'm going and when I'll be back, which I'd have to do if I used the family car. No problem, right?"

"No problem. I'll drive you to a rental agency."

"Now, there's my dear little baby sister. Thanks."

Barbara didn't pursue it, but her mind was full of questions. Where was Fran planning to find "excitement" in a town she no longer knew? Surely, she wouldn't go out haunting the local bars alone at night. Or would she? Doubtful. She'd find them much too "provincial." And she didn't know anybody here any more. Except Buzz Paige. She'd perked up when Laura had mentioned him. It wasn't possible that Fran was planning to get in touch with her old beau! Maybe she already had. Maybe she'd arranged to meet him. But she'd had no opportunity unless she'd managed to call him at his office this morning. Certainly he must be listed in the phone book at a business address as well as a home one. But Fran wouldn't be so rotten as to start trouble with a happily married man. No? How about you, Barbara? That's different, she defended herself. Charles isn't happily married. Besides, with us it's a long-term arrangement, quite different from breezing into town for one week and disrupting a contented household just for kicks. Even Fran wouldn't do that. She half-smiled as she realized she'd thought "even Fran." As though Frances was so immoral she'd do anything. Well, maybe she was. Maybe she'd do anything outrageous and "amusing" to relieve a dull, dutiful stay in a place she obviously didn't want to be.

Driving downtown, she couldn't restrain herself.

"I don't mean to stick my nose into your business, Fran, but are you by any chance thinking of seeing Buzz Paige?"

Her sister's laugh was genuine. "Is that why you think I want the car? To set up an assignation with poor old Buzz Paige? Oh, Barbara, you really are ridiculous"

"You still haven't answered my question."

"Only because it's too silly to answer. Look up a tired middle-aged man who had the hots for me thirty years ago? What on earth for? No, darling, if I get into mischief I'll pick a stranger. So set your mind at ease. I'm not here to wreck homes, if that's what you're afraid of."

Barbara felt relieved. That would be all Laura and Sam needed: Fran coming back and creating another scandal in the community. So what did she have in mind?

Fran seemed to pick up her thoughts. "You're dying of curiosity, aren't you?"

"Frankly, yes."

"Okay, but keep your mouth shut. I have found someone here who may be momentarily diverting. He's young and sexy and available. I think he'll be good for a few laughs for a few days. Now are you satisfied?"

Barbara glanced quickly at her and looked back at the road. "Who is he? And where in the name of God did you find him? You haven't been out of my sight since you arrived."

"You're just not very observant. You or Allie. He's a waiter at LaFitte's. Name's Cary Venzetti. I picked him yesterday when we had lunch there. I'm meeting him tonight."

"Fran, you can't!"

"Why not? There's nothing special planned for tonight, is there? The party's tomorrow night. As far as I know, we have nothing more divine to look forward to this evening than meeting Allie's highly respectable husband. And my hunch is that I can do nicely without that."

"Mother will be upset if you're not with us for dinner. Allie and Spencer are taking us out."

"All right. If it's so vital, I'll arrange to meet the baby stud later."

Barbara felt a twinge of disgust. It was not only Fran's vulgar phrasing, it was her wild pursuit of someone to go to bed with. Anyone, it seemed. Picking up a waiter! My God, it was obscene, especially at her age. Never mind that it was dangerous. It was sickening. The revulsion turned to pity. Poor Fran. She had to keep denying the truth. She was so fearful of growing old, so desperately in need of reassurance that she'd accept it from anyone. Even from some calculating young man who probably expected to be well paid for his services this week. It was pathetic. Barbara wished she knew how to stop her.

"Hey," she said, "what do you need with that scene? Good lord, Fran, you'll only be here a week. Why not relax?"

"There's no such thing as 'only a week.' It's seven days and seven nights out of my life. Hours not to be wasted sitting around the living room listening to Daddy talk about his Masonic Lodge and watching Mother patiently resigning herself to old age. It's Allie, all matronly and settled. It's even you, my love, with your damned young face and your apparent secret happiness. What about you, anyway, Barb? What do you do with your life? Do you have a lot of lovers? Is there as much action in Washington as people say?''

"Very little. Not as much as you hear. It's really a small town grown big. You'd find it stultifying.''

"*You* don't.''

"I'm not you, Madame Dalton-Déspres.''

"And you're still not talking, are you?''

Barbara didn't answer. Then she finally said, "There's not much to talk about.''

Fran looked at her appraisingly. "You know, I somehow doubt that. Why don't you open up to your big sister?''

Barb laughed. "You've been reading to many sexy Washington novels.''

"Lots of spicy stories in the papers about congressmen these days. They even make the Paris papers.''

Barbara glanced at her sharply. Fran seemed to be looking idly out the window, but she was watching her sister in the glass. A shot in the dark. But dangerously close. Silly to be suspicious. Fran had never heard the name Charles Tallent. A few people did know about Barbara and him. It was nearly impossible to keep such a secret in Washington after so many years, no matter how careful they were. But the press mercifully had kept quiet about the liaison. It was local gossip exclusively.

Andrea Tallent knew, of course. That was inevitable. But Charles's wife seemed to accept the situation with equanimity, even nodding cordially to Barbara when they happened to run into each other at some cocktail party or charity event. Barb marveled at the way Andrea handled the whole thing. I couldn't be that unperturbed if it were my husband, Barbara often thought. I'd be wounded and furious. I'd demand he make a choice. But, according to Charles, Andrea had more "common sense" than that. When she first heard about Barbara— Lord! It was ten years ago!—she'd simply shrugged and said, "I don't really care what you do, Charles, as long as you don't publicly embarrass me or upset the children. If you must have someone else, and apparently you must, then I much prefer it be one intelligent woman rather than a series of vulgar little encounters.''

Barbara had been open-mouthed when Charles repeated the conversation to her. When he told her Andrea knew about them, she'd been glad, thinking they'd surely divorce and she'd become the second Mrs. Tallent. She'd wanted to marry then. But he'd made it clear that this never was to be.

"You know there'll be no divorce,'' he'd said softly. "I've been that honest with you from the start. There are the children to think of. Even though I don't love Andrea, I adore those kids. I couldn't walk away from them, Barb.''

She'd been terribly hurt. Resentful. "You love them more than you do me.''

"No, darling. I love them differently. I come from a broken home, Barbara. It's a sad and terrible thing to lose a parent. I'd never do that to my own. They're only eight and ten. They need the security of a mother and father.''

"But they must know you and Andrea aren't happy together! It's wrong to bring children up in a house filled with tension. Worse than letting them live with one peaceful parent. People who stay together 'for the sake of the children' aren't doing them any favor, Charles. You're probably warping their lives."

He'd been very gentle with her. He knew she was not pleading their case but her own. Though she might believe what she was saying, her motivation was not concern for his children's psyches but hope for her own happiness.

"There isn't any tension in our house, dear," he'd said. "Andrea and I never quarrel. We don't care enough to fight. The kids think they have perfect parents and Andrea and I never give them reason to suppose otherwise. They're very contented and secure. I won't destroy that. Neither will she."

"You even sleep together." She sounded like a petulant child herself.

He'd looked grave. "We share the same room. That's all. We don't sleep in the same bed. We haven't since the year after I met you. When I realized how deeply in love I was, I stopped having sex with Andrea. She soon knew something else was going on, of course. She's not a stupid woman. So she finally came out and asked me. And I told her about you. We agreed to stay married. I won't break that promise, darling. Not even for you. Andrea's given me a lot. She was with me through the hard years and she deserves the rewards."

"And what about me? What do I deserve?"

"Something better than what you have," Charles had said. "I know this situation is terribly unfair to you. I know how selfish it is of me. Monopolizing your time. Cutting you off from seeing other men. I think they call it 'taking the best years of your life.' Much as I love you, Barbara, I think you're foolish to go on with me. I wouldn't blame you if you didn't. It's a lousy life, sneaking around corners, spending all our time here in your apartment. God knows I'd be miserable if you stopped seeing me, but I'd understand. I'll understand whenever and if ever you decide that the little I can give you isn't worth all the sacrifices you make."

She'd held him close. "I don't want anyone but you," she'd said. "I never will. I don't need a gold band to feel married to you. I don't need anything but your love. I love my life. Our life. I love you because you're good and loyal and unselfish and more wonderful than anyone I could ever find."

Ten years ago, Barbara thought again. And nothing has changed, except Charles and Andrea and I are that much older and so are his children. They're eighteen and twenty now, old enough not to be "traumatized" by their parents' divorce, but in Charles's eyes they'll never be old enough for that. Not even when they're parents themselves. And with each year it probably seems more unfair to Charles to even consider leaving Andrea. She's his age: fifty. What happens to a lone woman of fifty used to the security and privileges of marriage?

No, it will never be different for us. We don't even discuss the possibility of his divorce any more. We haven't for years. I wonder if Andrea has found her own "outside consolation" in all this time? She must have. She's a healthy, attractive woman. Surely she couldn't go on year after year without physical satisfaction. But if she finds it, she's even more discreet than Charles and I. I've never heard an iota of gossip about Mrs. Tallent. And if Charles has, he's never mentioned it.

What would he do if the tables were turned and Andrea fell in love with someone the way her husband has with me? Unwillingly, Barbara didn't want to think about it. It was an unworthy suspicion, but she was afraid he'd not have his wife's cool attitude. She didn't want to believe it, but she couldn't dismiss the idea that if it came to that, Charles might trade his own affair for the cessation of his wife's. How terrible of me to think that way! He's a bigger man than that. He'd be glad if Andrea found the same kind of happiness he has. His male ego is not as great as his passion for me. I must believe that. I do believe it. But could he possibly believe Andrea has remained faithful to him, knowing what she knows? Perhaps. Men, even those as intelligent and understanding as Charles, usually are outraged when their wives do exactly what they're doing. By the standards of his generation, extracurricular sex, even freely admitted, is acceptable for the husband but an affront when practiced by the wife.

My God, how cynical I sound! It must be Fran's influence. She's been disenchanted since she was ten.

Chapter 6

LAURA CAREFULLY DESCENDED the stairs to the basement where Sam was puttering around his woodworking bench. She often wondered why he'd taken up this particular pastime since his retirement. He'd never been handy around the house. In forty-two years she'd hardly been able to coax him into hanging a nail on the wall for a picture. He had no interest in anything manual. He freely admitted he was "all thumbs," giving the deprecating phrase a strange little ring of pride when he said it in company, implying that the men in their circle were laborers at heart while he was the cerebral type with his mathematical skills and his staff of underling accountants.

But in the past eight years it was as though he considered his mind useless and all he had left were his hands. He was either in the garden during the day or down here with all these saws and hammers and chisels. And as far as Laura could see, it produced nothing, all this cutting and nailing and measuring. Not so much as a picture frame or a cabinet door. It was simply a pastime. A way to pass the hours that hung so heavily on Sam's inexpert hands.

A little wave of sympathy swept over her. He'd taken so quickly, so hopelessly, to the idea that he was old and good for nothing. She wished she could convince him otherwise. He could use his knowledge in so many ways. Probably become a volunteer teacher at one of the vocational schools, giving youngsters or adults the benefit of his accounting knowledge. There were interesting opportunities for a man with Sam's background, but he wouldn't even investigate them. In the beginning she'd tried to encourage him to see whether he could be useful at the Emily Griffith Opportunity School, which offered all kinds of classes for adults, but he'd dismissed the idea without even looking into it. Just as he'd brushed off all her other suggestions. He'd finally gotten angry one day, about two years before.

"Blast it, Laura, can't you leave me alone? I'm too old and tired to start trotting around looking for ways to be useful! I've been working since I was fifteen! Fifty-eight years! I'm retired. Think about the word. Retired. Slipped into the background. Disappeared into the shadows. Gone to bed. That's what retired means. It also means peace. No demands. For Lord's sake, woman, stop nagging me!''

So she had. She left him to his garden and his ''workshop'' and his television and his retreat from the world. But she hated seeing him this way. There was no need for it. She could hardly get him out of the house any more and she knew he was even dreading the party at home tomorrow night. She'd liked to have taken the girls up on their offer to have it at a hotel. It would have been something different. And secretly she supposed, though it was prideful of her, it would have been satisfying to have her daughters show the world how loving they were, how generous and thoughtful of their parents. But Sam wouldn't hear of it when Barbara wrote and said she and her sisters had corresponded and wanted to arrange a big celebration for the fiftieth year.

''Waste of money,'' he'd said.

''They can afford it, dear. They'd like to do it for us.''

''They can come home for a change. That's what they can do for us.''

She'd sighed and written to Barbara, thanking them but saying that she and Sam really would prefer a quiet little gathering at the house.

''It's enough of a 'party' for us,'' Laura said in her letter, ''to think of having the three of you home again. Please plan—all of you—to stay at least a week. And of course I hope and expect that Spencer and Christopher and Janice will come with Alice. We won't be able to house everybody, but I've already spoken to Aunt Mildred and Aunt Martha and they have plenty of room in their house. They can put up Uncle Fred and Aunt Mamie and Charlotte if she comes. You're a dear to take over the 'organizing' for yourself and your sisters, Barbara darling. It saves me writing three separate letters. Anyway, it will be a happy time for us and, I hope, for all of you.''

Maybe it will be a happy time, Laura thought, but certainly not quite as I pictured it. Frances is so changed. If I met her on the street I wouldn't know my oldest child. And it's disappointing that Alice's children won't be here. I suppose they don't want to spend a week with us ''old fogies.'' Can't blame them, I guess. It wouldn't be very exciting. Still, a golden anniversary is special. I'm afraid I feel Alice should have insisted. She hasn't really explained. I imagine she's a little embarrassed. Well, at least Spencer is arriving. We hardly know him, either. What a queer family this is!

She reached the bottom of the stairs and called out to her husband.

''Sam, dear, it's past four o'clock. Don't you think you should stop what you're doing and rest awhile before we get dressed? Alice called from the hotel. They've made a dinner reservation for six o'clock at the Continental Broker on Fillmore Street. They'll meet us there.''

He grunted. ''Darned foolishness, traipsing out to a restaurant. Why can't we have dinner here?''

She scolded him playfully. ''Don't be such an old grouch! It will do us good to go out. Besides, don't you think I'd like a night off from cooking? I still have a lot of last-minute things to do for the party tomorrow. It'll be nice to be waited on for a change. And Allie was sweet about the time. I told her you liked to eat early.''

"What time do she and her snooty husband usually eat? Ten o'clock?'' He was determined not to enjoy this. "Where are Barbara and Frances?''

"They should be back any minute. They went on some kind of errand.''

"In the car?''

"Yes, of course.''

"They didn't ask permission to use it.''

Laura couldn't contain her exasperation. "Really, Sam, you're just going out of your way to be difficult about everything! They're not children who have to ask for the keys to the car!''

"It's still my car. Only polite to ask.''

There was no use arguing with him when he was in this mood. "I've put your blue suit out,'' Laura said. "It will be ready when you decide to come upstairs.''

"My blue suit? Why do I have to wear my blue suit? I thought you wanted me to save that for tomorrow. Why do we have to get all fancied-up to go out to dinner?''

She was suddenly angry. "What do you want to wear? Your dirty old gardening clothes? Is this the way you're going to act the whole time the girls are here? If it is, I'm not surprised they come home so seldom. They'll probably never come back if you go on behaving so badly! What on earth is the matter with you?'' She stopped. "I know. It's Spencer Winters, isn't it? You never have liked him.''

"I don't trust him. Something shifty about him.''

"Sam! He's your son-in-law! Allie's husband! Your grandchildren's father! You've seen him three times in your whole life and one of those was at their wedding twenty-five years ago. How can you continue to dislike a man you hardly know?''

His mood changed suddenly from near-belligerence to anxiety. "Laura, have you taken a good look at Allie? She looks like she's suffering inside. It's that man. I know it. All that business about 'Spencer's comfort' and staying at a hotel! He's cruel to that girl. I just feel it. And why didn't their children come? Has Alice ever explained that? I think he doesn't even like his own kids. I think he's a terrible man and I wish he wasn't here.''

She was amazed at his perception. She had no idea he was aware of many of the same things that troubled her. They were both going on nothing more than instinct, but they had the same intuitive feeling that Allie's life was hell. Laura slowly nodded. "I feel as you do,'' she said, "but perhaps we're wrong, Sam. Maybe we're being unfair to him. It may just be his way.''

"I wish I could think so. I wish I could believe he's nothing worse than a stuffed shirt.'' He was silent for a moment. "I wish I felt all our girls were happy, but I don't think one of them really is.''

That, too! Her heart went out to him. Why did she think he was just a self-pitying, oblivious man? His senses were as keen as ever. His concern perhaps even greater. Above all else, he was a good husband and a loving father. Why did she think only mothers worried about their children, were attuned to them? In the brief time he'd spent with his daughters, Sam was as aware as she of the nuances, the undercurrent of unrest that seemed to be under the surface of all three.

Impulsively, she went over and kissed him. "I love you, Sam Dalton. After half a century you still surprise me."

He patted her lightly on the rear. "After more than half a century I still surprise myself. But it's true, Laurie. Those girls are in trouble. What are we going to do about it?"

"I'm not sure. It's probably too late to do anything now. Maybe we should have started long ago."

He shook his head in regret. "Yes. Maybe we should have, at that."

"Of all the ungodly hours to dine!" Spencer paid the cab driver as they arrived at the restaurant. "And I suppose I won't even be able to have a drink for fear of shocking your mother and father's sensibilities."

"Of course you can have a drink. I'm sure Fran will want one. Barbara, too, probably. Mother and Daddy don't expect other people not to drink. They don't serve liquor in their own house, but they don't impose their personal beliefs on others." Allie was distressed. "Please, Spence, be nice tonight. I know it's tiresome, but Mother's so excited about going out to dinner."

"You don't have to tell me how to behave. And for God's sake, stop calling me 'Spence.' You know I detest it."

"I'm sorry."

I *am* sorry, Alice thought. I'm sorry for so many things. For marrying this cold, cruel man. For staying with him. I'm sorry I let the family send me away "in disgrace" all those years ago. If they hadn't, I wouldn't have met Spencer. But if I hadn't, I wouldn't have Chris and Jan. And for all the heartaches they've brought, they're worth everything.

As they went down the steps to the restaurant, Alice saw Sam and Laura, Barbara and Frances already waiting. She rushed to them, apologizing for being late.

"Darlings, I'm sorry! Have you been here long?"

"No, dear, just a few minutes," Laura said.

"Sixteen, to be exact," Sam said.

"Forgive us. We had a little problem with cabs at the hotel."

"We should have come down and gotten you," Barbara said. Alice shook her head. "I have a mental picture of the six of us packed into Daddy's Toyota!"

Frances spoke for the first time. "We're a two-car family as of this afternoon. I rented one for the duration." Her eyes were on Spencer, standing silently behind Alice. "By the way, love, aren't you going to introduce us?"

"Fran, forgive me! This is my husband, Spencer. My sister, Frances Dalton-Déspres, dear. And of course you know Mother and Daddy and Barbara."

"Delighted to see you again," Spencer said formally. He turned to Fran. "And nice to meet the famous expatriate at last. I've heard a great deal about you, Mme. Dalton-Déspres."

Fran smiled icily. "I'll bet you have."

"Darling, you're being so formal!" Alice took his arm affectionately. " 'Madame Dalton-Déspres' indeed! She's Fran!"

Laura held out her hand. "It's good to see you, Spencer. It's been a long time."

"Yes, it has. You're looking well, Mrs. Dalton." He shook hands with Sam. "You, too, Mr. Dalton. Retirement obviously agrees with you." His gaze went to Barbara. "How are things in Washington?"

"Hectic, as usual. Everybody's edgy before an election."

"No, no politics tonight!" Alice said. "I hear enough of that at home! Let's go in to dinner, shall we?"

The dining room was already crowded, but Spencer's table for six was waiting. Sam immediately picked up the menu.

"Daddy, you don't mind if we don't order for a few minutes, do you?" Alice was obviously nervous. "I'm sure Barb and Fran would like a drink."

Laura answered for him. "Of course, dear. We're in no rush." She looked around. "Such an attractive place, Alice. It's sweet of you, Spencer, to ask us to dinner. It's a real treat."

"My pleasure, Mrs. Dalton."

Liar, Barbara thought. You hate the whole thing, you pompous ass. But instead she said, "You and Daddy have a harem tonight, Spencer. The Dalton women outnumber you."

"I'm sure we can handle it, don't you agree, Mr. Dalton?"

Sam grunted. "Always have before."

A pert little waitress approached the table for their drink orders. Spencer turned to Laura on his right.

"What will you have, Mrs. Dalton?"

Laura looked flustered. "Oh, I don't know. Ginger ale, I suppose."

"Why don't you try a virgin mary, Mother?" Alice asked.

"What's that?"

"It's the nonalcoholic version of a bloody mary. Tomato juice with spices and the vodka left out." Alice laughed. "Spencer, remember the time we had dinner with that priest who's a friend of yours? Father McLaughlin. I was dieting and wanted to order a virgin mary but I was afraid Father McLaughlin would be offended, so I asked for it by its other name, a 'bloody shame.' And when it got around to the priest, guess what he ordered."

"A virgin mary," Barbara said.

"Exactly. We broke up!"

"Alice, you're delaying everyone's order." Spencer's voice was cold.

"Oh, I'm sorry. Anyway, try one, Mother. You'll like it."

"All right, dear."

"One virgin mary," Spencer said to the waitress. "Same for you, Mr. Dalton?"

"No. I'll take a cup of coffee. Cream and sugar."

Spencer's face was impassive. "One coffee," he repeated. "Frances?"

"Double vodka on the rocks with a twist."

"Barbara?"

"Scotch and water, please."

"Mrs. Winters and I will have scotch and water, too," Spencer said. "White Label. Be sure. None of that bar scotch. You have all that?"

"Yes, sir. Three White Labels and water, one double vodka, one virgin mary and a cup of coffee."

There was an awkward pause as the girl departed. Laura turned her attention to her son-in-law. "How are the children, Spencer? I'm so sorry they couldn't come."

Alice held her breath, but Spencer, thank God, was going to play out the game.

"They're fine," he said. "They were sorry not to be here, but you know how young people are. Always a million 'unbreakable engagements.' Alice and I barely see them ourselves any more, even though we all live in the same city."

"They must be handsome," Fran said. "I've never seen them, but they must be beautiful. Do you have pictures of them?"

Barb glanced with amusement at her sister. Fran was being bitchy. She knew damned well a man like Spencer Winters would die before he'd walk around with pictures of his children in his wallet.

"No," Spencer said. "Sorry. No pictures." He turned abruptly to Sam. "I'm sure you must be enjoying your retirement, Mr. Dalton. Great to get out of the old rat race, isn't it? You're playing a lot of golf, I suppose."

"Don't play the game."

"Oh? You should take it up. Marvelous exercise."

"And where do you think I'd play?" Sam asked.

"Well, I don't know, I'm sure. I'm not that familiar with Denver, but there must be a country club."

"There's a country club all right. There are also a lot of big mansions above it in a place called Strawberry Hill. But we're not in that league. We're very simple folk, as you know. We get our fresh air in our back yard. Or once in a while we take a walk through Washington Park. It's city-owned and just a block from our house."

Alice leapt in nervously. "Washington Park! My lord, what memories that brings! Remember, Fran? We used to swim in the lake there. And we always cut through it on our way to South High. Good grief, South High School! It seems a thousand years since we went there!"

"It was," Fran said. "At least a thousand."

"I was so jealous of you two," Barbara said. "You were always going to the park with your friends and I was just an ugly little kid who wasn't allowed to tag along."

"Well, you have the last laugh," Fran said. "That eight or nine years' difference was on our side then, but it's on yours now."

Allie looked wistful. She was remembering those walks in the park with Jack Richards. Those precious young moments that led up to a nightmare. Those forever-lost days of happy innocence. "What's the park like now, Daddy? Has it changed much?"

"Yes, it's changed," Sam said. "Everything changes. It's very crowded now. Mostly full of ugly men in their underwear."

Laura explained. "Your father means it's a favorite place for runners and joggers. They also have tennis and volleyball and all kinds of things that weren't popular when you children were growing up. But it's still a pretty place, Alice. Dad and I go there sometimes when the weather's nice." She looked fondly at Sam. "We should go more often than we do, but it's hard to get your father away from his precious garden and his workshop in the basement."

"At least I know I won't get mugged there."

"Oh, Sam! The park's perfectly safe!"

"Denver's no different than other cities, Laura. Crime. Dope-users. Perverts. They're in every park in America." He shook his head. "Can we order now?"

They were halfway through their drinks and Fran desperately wanted another, but she could see that her father was anxious to eat his dinner and get away. Get home where he felt safe and at ease. God knows he wasn't at ease here. None of them was. You could cut the tension with a butter knife, she thought. What a motley crew. We have nothing in common. No more than I have with that crude little waiter I'm going to meet in an hour. But at least with him I won't have to make conversation.

Spencer looked as though he'd blundered into an episode of "All in the Family." Alice was nervous, sensing his disdain. Laura was trying too hard to be cheerful and chatty. Even Barbara seemed put off by this dreary conversation about parks and fear of crime.

"Good idea," Fran said. "Let's order. Sorry to be a party-poop, but I'm meeting a friend in an hour."

Her mother, surprised, opened her mouth to ask whom she was meeting, then closed it again. It's none of my business, Laura thought. She's a grown woman. But as Barbara had, she wondered where Frances could be going. Sam was less tactful.

"What friend?" he asked. "Who are you meeting at this time of night?"

Fran finished off the last drop of her drink. "Daddy, it's exactly seven o'clock. Hardly the witching hour! I ran into some old friends today and said I'd join them later. Any objections?"

Again, Laura answered. "Of course not, dear. Your father didn't mean to pry."

Like hell he didn't, Fran thought. He's always felt it was his privilege to know every place we went and everyone we saw. He never trusted us, the way Mother did. Maybe he was right at that. We weren't to be trusted, at least not Allie and I.

They ordered and ate quickly, forcing conversation, all as eager as Sam to be done with it. Once again, Laura felt sad. Her dreams of the "happy family gathering" were absurd. They weren't going to come together like a picture on a Christmas card. They were too far out of touch.

She worried about Frances. What on earth was she up to, this desperate-seeming, driven woman? And Alice, agitated and jumpy whenever that dreadful, condescending man spoke. Even Barbara was so private. Sweet and dear, but giving out nothing, hiding something. Sam's right, Laura thought. They're in trouble. All three of them. Each in her own way. And probably there's nothing we can do to help.

Chapter 7

BARBARA SAT SILENTLY in the back seat while Sam drove her and Laura home from the restaurant. She'd offered to be the "chauffeur" but her father had almost brusquely rejected her suggestion that he might not want to drive at night. She instantly realized she'd make a mistake.

"Nothing wrong with my eyesight," he'd snapped.

"I know, Daddy. I didn't mean there was. I just thought maybe you were tired."

"From what?"

"Now, Sam," Laura said, "Barbara didn't mean to hurt your feelings. She was just trying to be considerate. It has been an exhausting day."

"There wasn't anything wrong with the day. It was the dinner that was so terrible."

Laura protested. "Mine was delicious. Didn't you like your roast beef?" She looked over her shoulder. "How was yours, Barbara?"

"Just fine. It's a nice restaurant."

Sam snorted. "You know I wasn't talking about the food."

They lapsed into silence. Laura knew very well what he meant. Spencer Winters with his patronizing attitude toward Sam, his talk of country clubs and golf, his cutting remarks to Alice. And then there was Frances, who could hardly wait to escape to wherever it was she was going. Heaven help us tomorrow night, Laura thought, when everyone gathers for the party. She could imagine how supercilious Spencer Winters would seem, how nervous Alice would act, how unpredictable Frances would be.

Nothing more was said until they entered the house. Then Laura put her hand on her husband's arm and said, "I'm sorry you didn't enjoy the evening, dear. Tomorrow will be better."

"I'm going up to bed," he said. "You coming?"

She hesitated. She couldn't go to bed just yet. Couldn't lie there unhappily contemplating the anniversary, fearful it would seem "tacky" to her own children.

"I'm really not sleepy," she said. "It's only nine o'clock. I think I'll stay down awhile."

"I'll keep you company if you like," Barbara offered. "I'm not sleepy either."

Sam started for the stairs. "Don't sit up too late, Laura. You'll be worn out tomorrow."

"I won't, darling. Goodnight."

They stood for a moment, watching him laboriously make his way upstairs. Then, simultaneously, mother and daughter looked into each other's eyes, reading each other's thoughts.

"Poor Daddy. He's so upset."

"Yes. So am I, Barbara."

"About Spencer? Don't be, Mother. That's just the way he is, I'm sure. Allie must understand him after all these years."

"It's just not Alice and Spencer. It's Frances too. Where has she gone this evening? Do you know?"

Barbara hesitated. What would Laura say if she knew her eldest daughter had raced off to go to bed with a young stranger she'd picked up the day before? She'd be out of her mind with worry if she realized what Fran had turned into. To lie now wasn't wrong; it was merciful.

"She ran into somebody she knows when we were at lunch yesterday. She's going to meet him for a drink."

"Somebody she knows? Who?"

"I'm not sure of the name. Venzetti, I think. Something like that."

Laura wrinkled her brow. "Venzetti? We don't know anybody named Venzetti. I never heard of him."

"It might be somebody she met in Italy, Mother. Now stop worrying! She's a grown woman. She knows what she's doing."

"I hope so."

"Count on it," Barbara said cheerfully. "How about a cup of tea? We used to have some of our best conversations over a cup of tea at the kitchen table. Come on. This is the first chance we've had to talk. You haven't filled me in on the local gossip. It's been almost a year. What's going on in Denver these days? You still going to Eastern Star meetings?" Barbara laughed as she steered Laura to the kitchen. "My Lord, remember when the three of us were all members of Job's Daughters? I can still see those white robes and purple sashes! Fran got to be a Princess once. It killed her she never made Queen!"

"It was a fine organization for young girls. Job is a character one can relate to, poor man, with all his suffering. The Lord tested him. Like He tests all of us, every day."

Barbara glanced at her as she put the water on to boil. "You believe in the Bible, don't you, Mother?"

Laura looked shocked. "Of course! Don't you?"

"I don't know. I don't go to church, but I guess I still believe in something. The way I figure it, Mother, if there's a God, He'll judge us by the way we live and receive us accordingly. I mean, if we do the best we can, every day, that's about all there is, don't you think? If we try not to hurt other people. If we try to be decent human beings, that's religion to me. It doesn't require going into a building one day a week. I think God—if He's there—understands. And if He isn't there, it doesn't really matter, does it?"

"Is that what you do, Barbara? Try to be decent, try not to hurt?"

"Yes. I know what I am inside, so I figure He does too."

Laura slowly stirred the tea in front of her. "Something's troubling you, isn't it? Do you want to talk about it?"

No, Barbara thought. I don't want to talk about it. Not with you. You'd never understand the kind of life I lead. You'd be disappointed in me. Your "baby" stealing another woman's husband. Your youngest "living in sin" all these years. You'd never comprehend how pure and beautiful it is. You'd still like me to be a little "Job's Daughter" believing the things I learned in that all-girl junior offshoot of the Eastern Star. You can't believe I've outgrown all that.

"Tell me about your life," Laura suddenly said with surprising passion. "Please, Barbara, let me in. I feel so shut out. So alienated from all of you. Help me. Sometimes I think I'm going out of my mind, worrying about you and your sisters. You've never been a mother. You don't know what it's like to realize that your children think you're too stupid or too provincial or too strait-laced to understand and accept and, if need be, forgive. I can endure anything except this total ignorance you've all conspired to keep me in. I sense things, Barbara, but I can't put my finger on anything. It's becoming an obsession with me. As though everything I've done is meaningless. As though I were just a bitch who produced a litter of puppies and had no idea where they went.'' She wiped her eyes. "I know you love me. All of you. I know you want me to be happy and protected. But this isn't the way to do it. I'm a woman. Let me share the lives of the women who are my daughters. At least, darling, let me share yours.''

Barbara stared at her. Laura was right. They all thought of her as limited in understanding, in intelligence. But she wasn't. She had deep needs too. She'd been so undemanding all these years, letting them all go their own ways. What other woman would have asked so little? She's lonely, Barbara thought. Funny, I never thought of Mother as lonely, or introspective, or even unhappy.

"All right,'' Barbara said. "I won't speak for the others. I can't. I don't know that much about them myself. But I can tell you about me, Mother.''

She told her about meeting Charles Tallent a year after she went to Washington. She described their attraction for each other, explained truthfully that at first she'd run away, refused to see him, knowing he was married. It had seemed silly and pointless. He'd said from the start that he wouldn't get a divorce, couldn't leave his own children as his own father had left him.

"I couldn't picture myself in one of those 'Back Street' situations,'' Barbara said. "I was twenty-six years old and worried about finding a husband. In those days I still thought it was important to be married. And the way I grew up— the way you brought me up—I felt there was something shameful about being in love with a married man. Even an unhappily married one.'' She gave a rueful little smile. "Of course, I knew all along I was trying to talk myself out of what I wanted to do. I loved Charles as I'd never loved any other man. I still do. I'm happy, Mother. Much happier than most of the married women I know.''

Laura looked pensive. "Aren't you lonely?''

"Sometimes. Mostly on holidays when Charles has to be with his children. But by and large, no. I'm not lonely. I see him nearly every day, no matter how briefly. And the knowledge of him, of his love for me, warms me when he's away. He is my lover and my friend, my comfort and support. In every way, except legally, he is my husband.'' She paused. "Are you shocked, darling? Have I made you unhappy?''

Laura shook her head. "Neither. Of course I wish you were married, because to me that has always meant a woman is safe and secure. And I can't pretend to be enlightened enough to condone adultery. I'm the product of another time, as well as another world. But, Barbara, I have sense enough to know that each of us has to find his own way. If this is yours, then I pray it never brings you pain. My only hope is that you won't regret not having a husband and children of your own. My only fear is that circumstances might take your Charles from you.''

"Circumstances could, in any case,'' Barbara said, "even if I were married.

Husbands die. Or leave home. Or they're hell to live with. I wonder how many married women could say, after thirteen years, that they are blindly, ecstatically in love? I can say that, Mother. So can he. He's a wonderful man. I wish you two could meet. He gives me everything.''

"Except public recognition. Isn't that important?''

"Yes. I won't lie. I'd like that. I'd like to be seen with him. To show I'm loved. Keeping this kind of precious secret is hardest of all. I so want the world to know that I am the center of Charles Tallent's life and he of mine. But that's a small price to pay for the other things, the tender things, the kind of meeting of soul and spirit that most couples never have.''

Laura nodded. "I can understand that. But what of the practical side, Barbara? What happens when you're old? What if something happens to him?''

"When I'm old I'll probably be alone, like ten million widows. Marriage is no guarantee against that kind of loneliness. We mostly outlive men in any case and end up alone. And if you mean money, Charles has taken care of that. He's already set up a trust fund in my name that will take care of me. Not even Andrea can touch that.''

"Andrea? That's his wife? Does she know about you?''

"Yes.''

"Poor woman. What she must feel, knowing her husband cares for someone else.''

"I suppose. I try not to think about that. Charles is very good to her. Neither of us would ever publicly embarrass her or their children. She seems to handle it very well. She's civilized about leading her own life.''

For the first time, Laura looked disapproving. "You don't believe that. You couldn't. I don't condemn your love, Barbara, but I won't accept your hypocrisy. In your heart you know you're hurting another person. That can't be a very comfortable feeling, knowing you're depriving a woman and her children of a man's total devotion.''

"I'm not depriving them! If it weren't me, it would be someone else! Charles doesn't love Andrea. I didn't destroy their marriage. That happened long before we met.''

"Oh? Then this passion Charles feels for you might have gone to anyone. Is it possible you're really saying he hates his marriage more than he loves you?''

"No! That's not what I'm saying! You're twisting things, Mother. I never should have told you. You don't understand. You couldn't, living happily with one man for fifty years.''

"What makes you think I've been so happy? There've been bad times for your father and me too, but we're not such romantics that either of us went flying off to find someone else to build up our egos!''

Barbara was horrified. "Is that what you think Charles is doing? Using me to build up his ego? That's ridiculous! If that's all it was, we wouldn't have lasted all these years.''

"Please, darling, don't misunderstand. I'm not accusing Charles of anything. Or you. I know you must love each other or this couldn't go on. Unless,'' Laura said carefully, "it's a very easy, self-protective thing for both of you.''

"What do you mean? Mother, you're not going to say that old stuff about a man 'having his cake and eating it, too'!''

"*You* said it, Barbara. Not I. But no, I was thinking more of you. Perhaps you're really afraid of marriage. Some women are, you know. Afraid of the responsibility, afraid of the hurt. Afraid to make a life-long commitment. Are you, my dear?"

Barbara stared at her. Was this the naïve little seventy-year-old lady who thought about nothing but her husband and home and her "good works"? Was this the unsophisticated matron she'd always assumed Laura to be? If she doesn't know us, Barb thought, we know her less. Instinctively, Laura had reached in and pulled out the very core of her daughter's fears. One she hadn't admitted to herself for many, many years.

"Isn't there anyone you ever wanted to marry?" Laura went on. "Never a man at any time in your life whose name you wanted to carry? Whose children you wanted to bear?"

Barbara gave an embarrassed little laugh. "If I told you, you'd think I was stark raving mad."

"Tell me."

"The only man I ever idolized was Jack Richards. Are you ready for that, Mother? I was nine years old when he got Allie in trouble. I worshiped him. A kid, I was. But I've never forgotten him." She paused. "Now you know that's crazy! What does a little girl know about such things? She has a crush on her big sister's beau. A crush she remembers for thirty years! I remember being so jealous of Allie when she was dating Jack, and deciding even then that if I couldn't find someone like him, I'd never get married at all. I'll never forget the night all of you had the pow-wow about their future. I didn't understand everything that was going on, but I knew enough to see that one way or another everybody was miserable because the two of them weren't going to get married." She stopped. And then she said slowly, "Maybe I turned off marriage at that very moment. Maybe I saw it as some kind of necessity, rather than joy. Something a person was *expected* to do. I've always resented everything that was expected of me. Do you suppose it was because I was so sorry for two people I loved that I made up my mind never to be hurt as they were?" She tried to smile. "I probably should be with a shrink. Listen to me! Acting as though something that happened when I was a kid could have changed my outlook on life!"

"Perhaps it did," Laura said. "I don't understand such things. But, Barbara, there must be some reason you haven't married. Lord knows you've had chances. Instead, you've gotten mixed up with someone you can't possibly marry. Is that why you're satisfied with your present arrangement? Because you know Charles can't possibly make you his wife?"

Barbara grew stubborn. "Marriage is not impossible for us. Something could happen."

Laura gently touched her daughter's hand. "What are you saying? Are you wishing Mrs. Tallent dead?"

"No! What a horrible thing to say! Of course I don't wish her dead! I don't wish anyone dead! My God, Mother, what do you think I am?"

The older woman remained silent. Do I really wish that? Barbara wondered, appalled by the idea. No. I couldn't. But if Charles will never get a divorce, that is the only answer, isn't it? Wrong. Not the only answer. The answer is that I don't really want to marry him. I adore him, but I don't want to be his wife. I don't want to be anybody's wife. Why did I suddenly spout all that nonsense about Jack Richards and a schoolgirl crush? I barely remember him. I do remember thinking he and Allie would get married and they didn't. Just as I thought Buzz Paige and Fran would get married. But *they* didn't. At least not to each other. Did all that make me stop believing in anything? Did it make me feel that nothing is to be counted on? That vows are a joke? Have I always felt that faithfulness is a myth, whether it's to an ideal or another person? Did my sisters' lives going so wrong somehow affect me even in those early years?

Her head began to ache. It was all so unexpectedly distressing, this probing into influences that may or may not have made her choose the life she had. She hated remembering how she'd felt as a child. How she'd despised her parents for sending Allie away. How she'd been angry with Fran for abandoning a shocked and grief-stricken Buzz Paige. Yet, young as she'd been, she'd also sensed the weakness in both Jack Richards and Buzz. Why hadn't they fought for what they said they wanted? Why hadn't one shouldered his responsibilities and the other been man enough to stop a headstrong young woman from running out on him?

The minutes ticked by. I've no respect for any of them, Barbara realized. Not for my sisters or the "nice boys" I thought they'd marry. Not even for Mother and Daddy. Probably I have no respect for myself. Maybe I'm as shallow as they. Too shallow to pledge myself. "An easy, self-protective thing," Laura had called her long affair with Charles Tallent. Perhaps she was right. I don't want to think about it any more. I wish I'd never had this conversation. She pretended to yawn.

"I'm tired. I think I'll turn in. How about you?"

"Barbara, stop running away." Laura's voice was gentle.

Anger flared. "Running away! How can you say that to me? I'm the only one who stayed! Stayed until I was twenty-five years old, right in this house with you and Daddy! I was the 'dutiful daughter,' trying to be the child you wanted. Trying not to disappoint you. Trying to make up for the hurt that Fran and Allie caused. I stayed and watched my friends get married, watched you being apologetic that I hadn't, watched my life slipping slowly into a dull, dreary spinsterhood that was all this place had to offer me! I stayed until a new career and a new life opened up for me. My God, Mother, I'm the only one who's even bothered to come home regularly!"

"I know all that," Laura said. "I know how hard it was for you, how duty-bound you felt to make up to us for what your sisters never gave. I didn't begrudge you your freedom when you found a way to have it. I still don't. I didn't mean running away in the literal sense, darling. Like upstairs or back to Washington. I mean running away from your fears, whatever they are. Stop avoiding your duty to yourself. You're very special, Barbara. Too special to go on living the make-believe life you've described to me."

"What do you suggest?" Barbara asked sarcastically. "That I demand Charles get a divorce and marry me? Or should I dump him and go out looking for somebody who'll make me 'respectable'? I'm forty years old, Mother. Isn't it a little late for the vine-covered cottage and the patter of tiny feet?"

"It's never too late,"

"Oh, come on!"

"Don't pretend to be cynical, dearest. You're a romantic at heart. The dream world you're into proves that. It's unreal, unnatural for a woman like you to settle for second place. Unless you're afraid of first place."

"You don't understand. You don't have to *be* married to *feel* married."

"Perhaps not. I'm sorry, Barb. I shouldn't interfere in your life. You don't trust anyone to do that.' Laura rose. 'You're right. It's time to turn in." She paused at the kitchen door. "But I'm glad we talked. Even if we don't see things the same way, I'm glad we talked."

In the middle of Cary's passionate lovemaking, Fran suddenly thought, "Goddammit, I don't have a house key! I'll have to wake up the whole damned family when I go home."

It amused her to think that at the height of the sex act her mind would turn to something so routine. Amused and saddened her. She felt nothing for this young animal who was just another body on hers. What am I doing here in this shabby little room with a child I know nothing about? What am I hoping to find? Why do I pretend ecstasy and feel no satisfaction? It's sordid and stupid and terribly, terribly routine. All of them are. All these faceless, expert young men who think they're doing me a favor by going to bed with me. But they're not as stupid and sordid as I, who thinks one day the magic will return. The magic hasn't existed since I was a girl. It won't come again. All I can do is pretend and get it over with.

She moaned and gasped and cried out, play-acting as she'd done so often. And then she and Cary lay still.

"You're wonderful," he said. "Fantastic."

"So are you. I've never known anyone so exciting."

"Really?"

Ah, the infallible ego. Fran smiled. *"Really."*

"When will I see you again?"

Never, she said silently. You'll never see or hear of me again. I'm never coming back to this dingy one-room apartment with the rumpled, drip-dry bedsheets and cheap Picasso prints on the wall. You're not the answer, dear Mr. Venzetti. But don't be upset. There is no answer.

"Very soon," Fran lied in answer to his question. "I'll call you."

"Stay in Denver awhile. Please." She'd told him she was here only for a week. "Don't go away. I've never known anyone like you."

She slipped out of bed and began to dress. "Stay right there in bed," she said. "You look beautiful."

"How can I reach you?"

"You can't, my darling. But don't worry. I'll reach you."

"Promise?"

She came to the bed and kissed him lightly. "You have my word of honor."

She drove hesitatingly through the dark streets, not absolutely certain of her way back, annoyed that she'd forgotten to get a key. Careless. She hoped her parents wouldn't hear the doorbell and that Barb would let her in. That way there'd be no questions.

Funny, but she did remember the way home. She made only one wrong turn, and as she parked the car in front of the house it seemed only yesterday when she'd been sneaking in, hoping Mother and Daddy didn't hear. She could see the darkened windows of her own room, but next to it Barbara's light was on. Two in the morning. What was she doing still awake? Good. She'd be most likely to hear a discreet buzz at the door.

And then she remembered something else. She and Allie had often used Barb as an accomplice when they wanted to get in unnoticed. The Daltons didn't believe in latchkeys for fifteen- and sixteen-year-old girls. They wanted to know the time of their comings and goings. So sometimes she or Allie would throw pebbles at Barbara's window late at night and the kid would tiptoe down and let them in. She always was scolded for it, as they were, but it made Barb feel "grown-up," being part of the conspiracy. Maybe it would still work.

She picked up three or four little pebbles and aimed them at the lighted window. I feel like a jackass, she thought. Damned near fifty years old and standing in the yard pegging rocks at my sister's window! But she was relieved when Barb stuck her head out and waved. In a few seconds the front door quietly opened. Fran started to giggle.

"My God, it still works!"

"Hush! You want to wake everybody up?"

"Barb, you remembered." They spoke in whispers. "Thanks, baby."

"You're welcome, you bloody fool. Have a good time?"

"I got what I went for."

Barbara wanted to put her arms around her and comfort her. What a lost soul she was. If Mother thinks I'm running from reality, what would she think of Fran? She probably has a good idea without actually knowing.

"Go on up to bed, Fran. It's late."

"Right. Tomorrow's the big day. Whoopee." The voice was tired, disenchanted. "Tomorrow's the golden day." She stared listlessly at her sister. "It's all working out just swell, isn't it? We're all so thrilled to be here."

Barb pushed her toward the stairs. "Shut up," she said affectionately, "and get some rest. You look as though you need it."

Spencer slammed the door of their room.

"Christ! What a tacky two hours that was!"

Allie unfastened her pearls. "They enjoyed it, Spencer. You were nice to do it."

"Enjoyed it! Like hell they did! No more than I did. Not that I give a damn about them. What a family! Is your father always so defensive about his impoverished state?"

"He isn't impoverished. He's . . . he's middle America. He doesn't belong to country clubs and play golf and you know it. Why did you have to act so hoity-toity?"

Spencer laughed mirthlessly. "Hoity-toity? My God, Alice, you've even reverted to talking like them. That sounds like something your saintly mother would say! And your dear, 'social' sister Frances! A slut if I've ever seen one!''

"Spencer, stop it! I won't have you speak of them that way!'' She was angry and knew she shouldn't be. It was fatal to cross Spencer, who retaliated with physical force. I mustn't let him get into a rage, she thought. He'd love to hit me. He'd like to take out his fury about this evening on me. I can't have that. I can't show up at the party tomorrow with a black eye or a bruised throat. She deliberately calmed down, hoping he would. "It's once in a lifetime, dear,'' Alice said. "You were very patient and I could tell they were impressed. As they should be. You're the kind of successful, sophisticated man my parents only read about.''

He seemed slightly mollified. How easy it was if she could only be such an actress all the time. Sometimes the injustice welled up so strongly inside her that she fought back, knowing she couldn't win, preferring the black-and-blue marks to the demeaning acceptance of his hatred. But not tonight. Tonight, no matter what he said, she'd not be goaded into what he wanted: a battering whose evidence might be hard to conceal and impossible to explain.

She undressed and climbed into the king-sized bed. Why hadn't she insisted on a room with twin beds? She'd been so glad to get any hotel accommodations at all that she hadn't dared make special requests. It was years since they'd slept in the same bed. She lay as far as she could on one side, hoping to give him plenty of room, praying he wouldn't start in on her again for this "inconvenience.''

Fortunately, he didn't. He looked at the bed but said nothing, simply climbing into his side and turning his back to her. Allie almost literally held her breath as she said, "Goodnight.''

There was no reply.

Chapter 8

HE COULDN'T LET himself believe it. He shouldn't. It probably was just another false lead, a slim clue going nowhere, like the dozens of others he'd tracked down to no avail in the years he'd been searching for his mother. But something told him at long last this was it. He didn't know why he felt so sure it was she— this "prominent hostess'' described in the gossip column of the Boston *Globe*.

John Peck read it for the third time.

"That perennially inventive hostess, Mrs. Spencer Victor (Alice) Winters, did it again when she arranged one of the most imaginative dinner parties of the year to honor J. B. Thompson's fiftieth year as head of Thompson, Wallingford and McClean. (Insiders say it soon will be Thompson, Wallingford, McClean and Winters, but the expected announcement was not made at the 'purely social' gathering.) When they went in to dine on caviar and quail, Mrs. Winters' eighteen hand-picked guests found her Beacon Hill dining room transformed into a posh 'courtroom' complete with a 'judge's bench' for J.B. and Mrs. Thompson and 'defense table' for the Wallingfords and McCleans. Other guests occupied the 'jury box,' where they dined on special tables set with Waterford and Vermeil. Waiters were dressed as bailiffs and a 'court stenographer' recorded the tributes to one of Boston's most distinguished attorneys. Guests carried away small silver gavels as souvenirs and Mr. Thompson was presented with a gold humidor, suitably engraved.

"Mr. and Mrs. Winters leave this week for Denver to attend still another fiftieth anniversary, that of her parents, Mr. and Mrs. Samuel Dalton, who're marking half a century of marriage. Also, coming to the Colorado celebration will be Alice's sisters, Madame Frances Dalton-Déspres of Paris and Miss Barbara Dalton of Washington, D.C."

It was the last paragraph that intensely interested John. He'd known since he was ten that Wilbur and Sarah Peck had adopted him. Loving people, much older than his friends' parents, they'd carefully explained he was "special," that they'd chosen him to be their little boy, that he was more "wanted" than many children. He'd accepted this as the compliment it was meant to be, and even when unwittingly cruel playmates tried to torment him about not having "real parents," Johnny just smiled and said, "Your folks got you by accident. Mine went looking for me." He hadn't been sure exactly what that meant, but he knew it was good. Mother and Dad said so. He never thought of them as anything but his parents until he reached his late teens and full awareness and insatiable curiosity set in. Then he asked, time and again, who his real parents were, but Sarah and Wilbur stubbornly refused to give him that information.

Sarah had, in fact, seemed wounded that John even thought about the people who'd conceived him. She pretended not to know anything about them. All she'd say was that John had come to them soon after he'd been born, in Boston where the Pecks also lived.

"Was I born in a hospital?"

Yes, Sarah reluctantly admitted. Massachusetts General on November 10, 1946. But she insisted that was *all* they knew.

"Johnny, why do you care? Haven't your father and I been good parents to you? Haven't we loved you? Why do you want to find people who cared so little that they gave you away?"

He picked up quickly on that. "You *do* know who my real parents are. At least, you know they voluntarily put me up for adoption. I mean, I wasn't orphaned, or something like that."

Sarah bit her lip. She hadn't meant to reveal even that. She was hurt and angry. "All right, son. Your mother didn't want you. Isn't that reason enough for you not to think about her? We've been your family for eighteen years. Your mother is a stranger. How could you feel anything but resentment for a woman who could part with her own flesh and blood?"

He'd fallen silent. He didn't want to hurt Sarah. He loved her and Wilbur. But there was this passion to know about himself. What kind of people did he come from? Good stock or bad? What if there were some awful hereditary problem, physical or mental, he might pass on to his own children when he married and had a family? But most of all, what could they be like, these people who were his natural parents? Didn't they ever wonder what happened to him?

He longed to know, yet to pursue it seemed disloyal to the pair he thought of as Mother and Father. Forget it, he told himself bitterly. You weren't wanted. You probably still wouldn't be, even if you found them. Yet he couldn't shake this feeling of rootlessness, this desire to know. But without anything to go on, without even a name, there was nowhere to start. Sarah had spoken only of his mother. *She* didn't want him. *She'd* given him away. I'm probably illegitimate, Johnny reasoned. I probably was born out of wedlock and disposed of out of shame. It made him sick to think about it. Sarah was right. His loyalty was to those who took him in and loved him and gave him everything within their moderate means. At great sacrifice, they'd sent him to college, bought him a car, done everything for his happiness. And he wanted to repay them by looking for the mother who'd turned him away.

He now thought only in terms of his mother. Not his father. Probably because he was convinced that the woman who bore him had no husband. Otherwise, why would Sarah always say "she" and not "they"?

He tried once to talk to Wilbur about his curiosity, hoping to appeal to him, man to man. But the conversation produced no more concrete evidence than Sarah had given. Wilbur did not seem to share his wife's strong feeling of reproach, but he respected her wishes and said so.

"Johnny, your mother is deeply hurt by the way you feel. She thinks of you as her own. We both do. We tried for twenty years to have a family before we got you. Leave it alone, boy. What good would it do to stir up trouble after so many happy years?"

"But you know who my real mother is."

Wilbur's lips had tightened. "I didn't say that." He'd suddenly turned angry. "Dammit, why are you so selfish? Do you want to break your mother's heart? Can't you understand how emotional she is about all this? Don't bring it up again! We have nothing to tell you."

"All right, Dad," he'd said. And he'd done nothing more about it, though the wondering was always in his mind. He'd read that adoption records were sealed by law; that they could be opened only after a long, humiliating and expensive court hearing, and maybe not even then. Hospital records were impounded and birth certificates sealed to "protect" all the parties involved. He had no information, even if he were determined to instigate a search for his beginnings. Not even his mother's first name, much less her last.

And then on a Saturday morning when Johnny was twenty-one, the elderly Pecks climbed routinely into their car to go to the supermarket and do the weekend shopping. They never got there. A reckless young man in a souped-up hot rod sped through a stop sign and plowed into their old sedan. The boy came out with barely a scratch, but Wilbur and Sarah were dead on arrival at the hospital. They left everything to Johnny. The house, the insurance, a few stocks and bonds in the safe deposit box. And in the same box they left him his first clue to his past: their copy of his adoption decree.

For the first time he knew his mother's name was Alice Dalton. And his father was "unknown."

In the weeks of grief mixed with disbelief that followed, he barely realized the significance of what he now held. And when he did, he didn't know what to do with his information. Alice probably had another name by now. She could well live somewhere other than Boston, if, indeed, she were still alive. He looked up "Daltons" in the Boston telephone directory and called every one.

None had ever heard of an Alice. The hospital informed him that everything he wanted to know was on microfilm which, because he was adopted, he was not allowed to see. He attended a meeting of the Adoptees' Liberty Movement Association, an organization dedicated to helping adoptees find their parents, and though he was strangely comforted to learn that there were about five million adoptees in this country, and probably anywhere from two to five thousand children looking for their parents, he came up empty in terms of his own problem.

In the next six years he did everything he could think of to find his mother. He ran "blind ads" in the "personal columns" of newspapers in major cities asking for information as to the where' abouts of Alice Dalton. Several "Alice Daltons" responded, but they were never the right ones. He became even more obsessed with his search when, at twenty-five, he met Carol and fell in love with her. For two years they "dated," but Johnny was reluctant to marry, fearful of the unknown, for himself and her and the children they wanted. At last, Carol put her foot down.

"I've had enough of this, John Peck! You're not the only person in the world who doesn't know who his parents are! Good Lord, if there were some terrible reason you shouldn't marry, don't you think the Pecks would have told you? They might not have wanted you to find your own people, but they'd have warned you about something awful! They loved you *too* much *not* to! I think you just don't want to marry *me*. Okay. Why don't we call it off?"

It shook him. She probably was right. Mother and Dad would have said something to him if there'd been anything to say. And he wouldn't lose the third woman he cared so much about. In his mind, Carol was the third. His real mother was the first! Sarah was the second. And he'd lost both of them.

They were married in 1973 and Johnny reluctantly stopped his search. For the next three years, his life with Carol was happy. A commercial artist, she continued to work at free-lance advertising while he progressed in his career in banking. He was a branch manager now and slated for better things. When he got his next promotion, they agreed, it would be time to start a family. He was thirty and Carol twenty-eight. They didn't want to wait much longer.

"You've gotten over being afraid of our having children, haven't you, darling?"

"Yes. I know you're right about my background. There can't be anything terrible. And I love kids. Maybe more than most men, because I know how important it is to want them and make them feel secure. Not that I was an unhappy child. Don't misunderstand me. I had the best parents in the world. But I guess I always felt separate. Different. Like some part of me was incomplete." He'd tipped the pretty young face up to look into his. "You're a beautiful lady, Carol Peck. You'll have sensational kids."

"And you won't worry about anything?"

"Only the normal things. Will they kill themselves on their roller skates or break their necks on the playground swings. Just the everyday, parental fears."

He believed it true. He thought he had gotten over this hopeless, infantile yearning. And then he read her name in the Boston paper. Alice Winters, *nee* Alice Dalton. He showed the item to Carol.

"Do you think it could possibly be my mother?"

Carol was wide-eyed. "Mrs. Spencer Winters? You must be kidding! They're high society, darling."

"What does that prove?"

"Well, I mean, a woman like that . . . with her background and all . . . that is, I doubt that she'd . . . "

"Have a baby and give it up for adoption? Why not? We don't know whether she was born into society or married into it, and what difference does that make anyway? 'Nice girls' got into trouble thirty years ago, just as they do today. Of course, I don't know how old this Alice Dalton is, but she's bound to be about right. She's going to her parents' fiftieth wedding anniversary. So she could be in her late forties. Which means she could have had me when she was a teen-ager."

She tried to calm him. "Darling, don't get your hopes up. It says she's from Denver. You were born here."

"So what? Maybe she grew up here."

"Well, I don't know. What would she be doing in Boston if she was just a teen-ager?"

"I don't know, sweetheart. Something in my bones tells me she's the one." He stopped. "But now that I think I know, what do I do about it? Can I just call Mrs. Spencer Winters and announce that I think I'm her son? Hardly. It might not be so. Or Spencer Winters might not know about me. Or," Johnny said slowly, "even if it's true, she might not want to see me. All these years. She's never tried to find me."

Carol was troubled. Much as she knew Johnny wanted answers, she wished this had not happened. He'd just seemed to be settling down, putting the search out of his mind, and now he had his hopes up again. It was a long shot that this very social Alice Winters was his mother. And if it turned out to be true and she didn't want to see him, that would be a rejection too terrible for him to bear.

"Hey," she said lightly, "take it easy. Don't go jumping to all kinds of conclusions until we know more. You've heard of other Alice Daltons and they never matched the vital statistics. Let's go slowly, sweetheart, before we make any moves." She wrinkled her brow. "Spencer Winters. I know that name from the papers, but there's something else." She clapped her hand to her forehead. "Of course! My God! I know. Janice Winters!"

"Who's Janice Winters?"

"She's the daughter! And she's a copywriter at one of the agencies I do work for. Her boyfriend's the art director. I remember hearing that her father's a big-shot lawyer, but I didn't realize he was *the* Spencer Winters. Sure. He has to be. She couldn't dress so well unless she was loaded."

"Do you know her?"

"No. Not really. I've just been introduced to her. But I can double-check with Clint Darby. That's her fella. If Alice Dalton Winters is her mother, maybe we can find out something about you before we get into this with both feet."

Johnny shook his head. "Honey, I know you're persuasive, but I really doubt that Clint Darby would tell you about this, even if he knows anything. In fact, I'd be surprised if Janice Winters has any information. It's not the kind of thing women tell their children."

"Well, at least it's a lead." Carol was defensive. "It's a helluva lot better than going up to Beacon Hill and ringing the doorbell and identifying yourself as the baby she gave away. If she *did*. If you *are*. Oh, damn, Johnny, do you really think this could be it?''

"Yes, I do. I just feel it. And you know something else? I'm scared to death. I've wanted this so long, and now I'm almost sorry the search might be over. God, Carol, I couldn't stand it if my mother didn't want to see me!''

"I know. But you have to find out, don't you?''

Johnny nodded.

"All right. Don't do anything rash for a few days. There's nothing you can do anyhow. She's going to Denver. Let me nose around a little, okay?''

"Sure.''

"Listen, are you positive you want to belong to a woman who turns her dining room into a courtroom? Sounds pretty contrived to me.'' She was laughing at him now, trying to tease him out of his fears. "I can't imagine any mother of yours going in for such obvious apple-polishing with the boss!''

He smiled. "You're one step ahead of me. I can't imagine any mother of mine *period!* I've tried for years. I have no mental picture of her.'' Johnny looked troubled. "The only face I can see is Sarah's. That lady was a good mother to me, and if she didn't want me to know about the real one, she must have had a good reason. Maybe I'm not meant to know. Maybe I'm wrong to tempt fate.''

Carol yearned to encourage this thinking, to tell him he should forget it all, in deference to Sarah's wishes. But she couldn't. A child had a right to know about his parents. No matter what he found out.

In a way, she was glad this had come up right now. There was something else Johnny didn't know, something she'd been waiting for the right moment to tell him. She was pregnant. It was an accident, ahead of their "schedule,'' but she'd been happy when she found out last week. There was no need for them to wait for Johnny's next raise. They could manage nicely. She could work right up to the last minute. She'd planned to tell him the good news the very day he read about Alice Winters. Now she decided to wait a little. If he had a happy reunion with his mother, her announcement would only add to his joy. But if it was a false alarm or turned out badly, at least he'd have the compensation of discovering he was going to be a father.

Everything was timing, Carol thought. There must be a reason for Johnny to be "reborn'' just at the time he was going to learn about his own child.

She felt hopeful, optimistic, realizing that she, too, believed her husband had accidentally found his mother. She had to help him get at the truth. Maybe he was right that Janice Winters wouldn't know anything useful, but she was the only key. When she saw Clint Darby tomorrow she'd ask him to come to dinner and bring Janice. He wouldn't find that unusual. He'd heard Carol speak of her husband, and said they "must all get together sometime.'' Well, this was the time, unless Janice had gone to her grandparents' anniversary party too. But that seemed unlikely. If the Winters' daughter had been part of the Denver trip, the paper probably would have said so.

Now all she had to do was make Johnny hold still until they knew a little more.

Chapter 9

LAURA'S SILENCE NEXT morning was more telling than any questions she might
have asked. She'd been awake when Fran came in at two in the morning, heard
Barbara go down and let her in. She was angry with both of them.

Barbara appeared while her parents were still at the kitchen table. She was
full of cheer.

"Happy Anniversary! Well, it's finally here! The big day." She kissed both
of them. "Congratulations, darlings!"

Laura managed to smile. There was no reason for her to be annoyed with her
youngest. It was Fran who was so worrisome. Remembering last evening's
conversation with Barbara, her mother still felt unhappy about what she'd learned.
But she shouldn't feel angry because Barbara had conspired with her sister to
keep things from their parents. That's the way it always had been. Barb would
do anything to please the two older girls.

"Thank you, dear," Laura said, "though I don't know why people should
be congratulated simply for living together so long."

Sam's eyes twinkled. "You don't? I think they should get the Croix de Guerre
with orange blossom clusters. And maybe a purple heart for surviving the battle."
He was in a good mood. Barbara always put him in a good mood.

"Some battle!" Barbara teased. "A few skirmishes maybe, but no big conflicts
that I know of. You're a lucky pair."

"I know that," her father said. "I chose well."

Laura looked at him affectionately. "*We* chose well," she corrected.

Sam patted her hand. He was not one for public displays of affection. Never
had been. The few quiet words were as close as Barbara had ever heard him
come to expressing love for his wife. What do they say to each other in private?
It was hard to think of Sam as a passionate man or Laura as an ecstatic woman.
She supposed one always felt that way about one's parents; as though they had
no private lives, no secret comings-together, no moments of abandon when they
were simply a man and a woman filled with desire. What had they been like
when they were young and lusty? Children never thought of that. They must
have been happy and unhappy too. They must have had moments of anger and
disappointment about things that did not involve the daughters. How selfish
children are! We think our parents exist only for us. We merely think of them as
individuals. I hate their getting old, Barbara thought fiercely. I can't bear to
think of losing them.

"Where's your sister?" Sam asked.

"Still sleeping, I guess. You know Fran always hated getting up early, Daddy."

Laura flashed a look at her. Yes, the loyalty persisted. Barbara didn't know
her mother had heard the whisperings in the night. Where had Frances been until
all hours? I wonder if I dare ask. She wished Frances would confide in her as
Barbara finally had. She wished Alice would too. Small chance in either case.
Frances had been gone too long and too far. And despite her gentle ways, Laura
felt that Alice still harbored a terrible resentment toward her and Sam for what
they'd done so long ago. We were wrong, Laura thought again. We were wrong
to have handled it as we did. We were wrong the way we handled all of them.

Enough of this. There was too much to be done before the party tonight. Spilled milk, Laura thought. No use weeping over it now.

"Barbara, would you mind going out and getting Aunt Mamie and Uncle Fred at the airport? They arrive at noon."

"Glad to. Shall I wear a sign so they'll recognize me? I'm not sure I'll know them. I don't think I've seen them in twenty years."

"They'll recognize you," Sam said. "You haven't changed."

"Why, Daddy! what a compliment It's a terrible lie, of course, but I love you for it."

"It's no lie. You're still my little girl."

She blew him a kiss. "Maybe Fran will go with me. What else can we do for you, Mother? The cake should arrive from Child's early this afternoon. Wait till you see it! It's a Weight-Watcher's nightmare! About four million calories, give or take a million or two."

"Poor Dorothy Paige," Laura said. "Her brownies won't stand a chance."

"What's she like? I've never met her."

"Very nice."

"Oh, help! Deliver me from that dubious compliment! You mean she's dull. Is Buzz dull too? I remember him as such a hero."

Sam rose from the table. "You ladies will excuse me, please, but I have more important things to do than discuss the Paiges. You go on with your woman talk. I hear my garden calling. Dratted leaves are falling all over the place. Got to get them raked up before company comes."

They looked after him with amusement as he left the kitchen.

"Your father never could stand gossip," Laura said.

"Gossip? You mean what he calls 'woman talk'?"

Laura's eyes twinkled. It was un-Christian of her, she supposed, but she did enjoy a good tidbit now and then. "He's sure I'm going to tell you about the Paiges. They separated a couple of years back. The talk was that Bernard had taken up with some woman over on Bonnie Brae Boulevard. A rich widow who bought a car from him. Personally, I never put much stock in the whole story, but apparently Dorothy Paige was convinced he was having an affair with her. Anyway, Bernard moved out for a few months and Dorothy went into seclusion. They say she had a nervous breakdown and still sees a psychiatrist. She's always been a very high-strung girl. On the outside she seems calm as a millpond, but people who know her well say she's never been too stable. And she's insanely jealous." Laura hesitated. "I'm not sure I should have invited them tonight. She once told me she knew Buzz had married her on the rebound from Frances. Of course, I assured her that was nonsense."

"Is it?"

"Well, nobody would know that but Buzz, would they? But I doubt it. Dorothy was always a pretty little thing. She's given him three nice children, and personally I've never known her to be irrational. Anyway, I couldn't leave them out of the party. We see them often, mostly at church, and they'd have been hurt if they weren't asked. My Lord, Barbara, that high school romance of his with Frances is ancient history! It would be ridiculous to think Dorothy would be upset by her husband seeing one of his old girlfriends."

"How did they get back together? After the widow, I mean."

"I'm not sure. I guess Dorothy came to her senses. Like I said, I never felt we knew the whole story. They certainly seem happy enough now." Laura laughed. "I don't know what makes me go off on these flights of fancy! Imagine worrying that Buzz would still care about a girl he hasn't seen in thirty years. The last few days I've really been acting crazy." She lowered her voice. "You know, I even thought of asking the Richardses. Jack and his parents. It seemed like the moment to make things up, to let bygones be bygones. Of course I didn't. Your father would never hear of it."

Barbara stared at her. "Mother, you didn't! You didn't even *think* of asking Jack Richards! I don't believe it! Allie would die!"

"I know. It was a foolish notion. But it seemed kind of like Buzz and Frances. It was all so long ago. Oh, I quickly discarded the idea, of course. The thing with Jack was much more serious. But isn't it terrible, Barbara? Think of it. We live only a few blocks from the Richardses and we haven't spoken in thirty years. We didn't even acknowledge the death of Jack's wife when we heard about it. That was wrong, I think. I told Sam so. In times of sorrow, old feuds don't matter any more. Poor Jack. He was no more to blame than Alice for what happened. They were so young, Barbara. Do you remember?"

"Yes, I remember."

"It was a heartbreaking time, but people weren't so broadminded in those days. We did the only thing we could. It was the only decent thing. For everybody involved." She sounded as though she was begging for reassurance, and Barbara's sympathy went out to her.

"I'm sure it was, Mother. And Alice has long since forgiven you for it."

"Has she? I wonder. I wonder if I could forgive anybody who made me give up my baby."

"What about Jack? You said his wife died. Whom did he marry and what happened?"

"She passed on seven or eight months ago. The beginning of this year, right after you went home from your last visit. She had cancer, poor woman. I never knew her, of course, but I heard she was lovely. And so young. Only forty-five."

"Did they have children?"

"No. I heard she couldn't. But they say Jack adored her. He's done very well, by the way. Has a big insurance agency here. They say he was grief-stricken about his wife. Sold their house and took an apartment out in Stoneybrook. One of those new condominiums."

Barbara smiled. "For somebody who doesn't keep in touch, you sure keep in touch."

"Everybody who grew up in Denver knows everybody else. I hear lots of things indirectly. Of course I never mention anything about Jack to your father. He's never spoken the name Richards since the day Allie went to Boston. Barbara, do you think Alice is all right? Has she ever talked to you about . . . about anything?"

"We don't keep in touch as we should, Mother. I'm not sure why."

"Your father and I have a feeling she's not happy with Spencer."

Barbara tried to speak lightly. "Well, he's not exactly Mr. Warmth, I'll admit, but I'm sure she's content. Which reminds me, have you heard from her this morning?"

"No. I expect she'll call soon."

There was a pause before Laura said, "I wish you girls *would* stay more in touch. Particularly you and Alice. You live so close. Why don't you?"

"I don't know, Mother. It's just that our lives have taken such different paths."

"Does she know about your Mr. Tallent?"

Barbara smiled at the quaint phrasing. "No. Not that I'm aware of. Not many people know."

"Is that why you've cut yourself off from her? Are you ashamed, Barbara?"

"Of course not! Really, Mother! How did this whole conversation get back to me? Allie hasn't made any more effort to bring me into her life than I have to include her in mine! Why do you blame our lack of contact on me?"

"Don't get angry. I'm sorry. It's just unnatural that sisters don't see each other."

"There's nothing unnatural about it," Barb said more calmly. "We're three separate people who happen to be related. We're grown-ups with lives of our own. We have very little in common these days. If you're really sensible about it, there's no more reason for us to stay in touch than for me to try to sustain a friendship with some friend I grew up with here. We're an accident of birth, Mother, that's all. It doesn't mean we have to be buddies."

"I suppose not. I suppose your generation takes a different view of things. More realistic, probably, but still hard for me to understand." Laura began to clear the table. "My heavens, we've wasted half the morning again, just sitting around talking!"

Barbara felt a sudden surge of compassion. "It hasn't been wasted as far as I'm concerned. I think I've come to know you better in the past two days than I have in forty years. I hope you understand me a little more too."

Laura turned from the sink. Her eyes were full of tears. "I don't have to understand you, darling. Not any of you. I love you. That's enough."

The trouble was, Buzz thought as he drove to his office, that Dorothy had a peculiar way of building things up in her own mind and managing to put them into his. The prospect of tonight's party was a perfect example. He'd really meant what he'd said a few days ago about feeling nothing for Frances. It was ancient history and he'd almost forgotten that reckless, tantalizing girl he'd been in love with. But now he was apprehensive about seeing her in a few hours. Not that it would mean anything to either of them, but thanks to his wife's jealousy, he'd be ill at ease, conscious of every thing he did and said, knowing Dorothy's eyes would be on him every minute. Damn it, why was she so suspicious? It had been the same with that Stacy Donovan episode. There'd been nothing to it. Nothing at all. He'd simply sold the woman a car and gone to her house a couple of times when she called with minor complaints. But Dot had built it into a fullfledged affair in her mind. She'd carried on so that he'd finally moved out for a while, but not in order to see Mrs. Donovan. He'd never seen her again. No, that time he'd simply walked away from the last straw in a series of ridiculous accusations created out of his own life's own insecurity. He'd known he'd be back. He'd simply hoped to teach her a lesson. But in spite of psychiatrists and tranquilizers she hadn't really changed. She had no self-confidence and consequently no trust in him. It was like living with a volcano that could be dormant for months, years, and then suddenly erupt for no reason except that it couldn't contain itself.

Okay. He'd been wrong to marry her. He'd done it out of a feeling of injury when Fran ran off with that actor. As though he had to prove to the world that he hadn't been "jilted," as they said in those days. As though he had to prove he could get any woman he wanted. As though he believed Fran would hear and be sorry she'd let him go. What a bunch of bull! He'd regretted the marriage almost immediately, but his damned pride wouldn't let him admit his mistake. And then Dot got pregnant and suddenly he had a family and responsibilities and there was no way he could walk out on the whole thing.

Not that it had been all bad. If only Dorothy weren't so neurotic. If only she could believe in herself. He'd tried to make her happy and he supposed he'd done as much as any man could. He hadn't been all that unhappy himself, most of the time.

But it would have been so different with Fran. Stormy too, probably, but always exciting. He was sure of that. She'd also have driven him crazy. But it would have been because of her independence, her unpredictability, her greedy zest for living. She'd been that way as a girl. From what he'd heard, she'd stayed that way ever since.

He was suddenly excited about seeing her. Why? They were middle-aged people, not wild kids. I was right when I told Dot I'll probably bore her, Buzz thought. Maybe I'm going to hate that most of all.

Frances sulked in the front seat of Sam's car as Barb drove to the airport.

"I don't know why the hell we have to play shuttle-bus. Why couldn't they have gotten themselves into a taxi and over to the aunts by themselves?"

"Don't be such a grouch just because I rousted you out of bed at eleven o'clock. I didn't need you to come with me, but I thought if Mother asked me one more time why you weren't up, I was going to scream."

"So scream. Might be good for you. I do it a lot. It shakes up the liver."

Barbara ignored that. "You think we'll recognize Aunt Mamie and Uncle Fred?"

"Sure. They'll be the ones with the plastic clothes-hanger bags over their arms."

"Snob."

"Right. And getting worse every day." Fran stretched and yawned.

Barbara couldn't resist. "But not too snobbish for waiters. You're really done in this morning."

"Waiters don't count. Or truck drivers. Or masseurs. They're at least useful. Middle-class aunts and uncles bring out the worst in me, my love. In fact, this whole damn week brings out the worst in me."

"You could make an effort. For Mother and Dad."

"I will, I will! My God, I'm here, am I not? I'll be Saint Frances tonight, I promise you! I'll even be nice to dear Aunt Mamie and Uncle Fred and to those old relics Mildred and Martha when we drop the Chicago contingent off at their house. I'll be on my good behavior. Hell, I wasn't even rude to that uptight idiot Spencer Winters last night, was I?''

"Only moderately. Asking him if he carried pictures of his children! You know that was a put-down, Fran. He knew it, too.''

Her sister pretended innocence. "Is that the way it seemed? I thought all proud fathers carried snapshots in their wallets.''

Barbara couldn't help laughing. "You're impossible! Allie's children are in their twenties. Besides, you know damned well Spencer would consider himself far too chic to go in for anything like that, even if they were babies.''

"He's not chic. Under that veneer of pompous ass beats the heart of a pompous ass. He may have made a lot of money and established himself in Boston society—whatever *that* is—but he's still from nowhere. I'd bet on it.''

"Like *we* are.''

"Yes. Like we are. Except you have style, Barb. I don't know where you got it, but you do. And I think I've learned what real sophistication is all about, from rubbing elbows with so much of it.''

"And Allie?''

Fran lit a cigarette and exhaled before she answered. "Allie hasn't changed a bit. She's the only one of us who's produced babies, but she's the only true virgin in the lot. If they made a movie, Doris Day would play Allie. She's always been naïve. She still is. Anybody who stayed married to that pretentious boob would have to be.''

"I want to stop at the desk and see if I have any mail,'' Spencer said.

"Are you really expecting any? For such a short stay, I mean.''

"The office may have sent something.''

Allie waited in the lobby while he went over to check. He was right about the hotel. It really was a convention hall. People were signing in at booths set up for registration; groups of cigar-smoking men were exchanging boisterous greetings while their wives twittered in clumps nearby. But the hotel itself was pleasant enough. In spite of the things Spence complained about. He'd called twice about the air-conditioning, which couldn't be shut off even though it was too cool at night to sleep in it. He'd given the waiter hell because it took thirty minutes to bring their breakfast, and then the man forgot a knife and Spencer had to spread jelly on his toast with a coffee spoon. He's scared the maid half to death with his yelling about the lack of towels and facecloths and the fact that there were only three sheets of writing paper in the desk drawer. They were inconveniences, of course, but Allie wouldn't have complained. Spencer didn't seem to realize that this was a giant operation. He allowed for no unavoidable errors among such a big staff. For that matter, he allowed for no errors in anything, including his business or his personal life.

He returned and they took the escalator down to the street level. They were on their way to the Brown Palace for lunch. Spencer, needless to say, had wangled guest privileges at the hotel's private club. It seemed odd to be going to lunch with him. They never did that, unless they were away and there was nowhere more interesting for Spencer to go. Today he'd have gone anywhere to avoid the family. Bad enough, he said, that he'd have to face them tonight.

In the cab he handed her a letter. "Something for you."

Surprised, she opened it. There was a note in Aunt Charlotte's spidery handwriting.

> My dear Alice,
>
> I do hope you and Spencer have a pleasant visit, I feel quite sad about missing my sister's anniversary and hope you will give her and your father my fond regards. I am enclosing a little clipping from the paper about the dinner party you gave before you left. It sounds most original. I've not been feeling very well the past few days and I've heard nothing from Janice or Christopher since you left. Not surprising. Still, you would think they might call, if only to see if I'm alive. I daresay I'll hear from none of you until you return, but I trust you enjoy your visit.
>
> > Devotedly,
> > Aunt Charlotte

Allie sighed. She'd asked Chris to check on his great-aunt, knowing Janice couldn't be depended upon. Apparently Chris hadn't bothered either. It wasn't surprising, this cold yet self-pitying complaint from Charlotte. I'll call her tomorrow evening after the party, Alice thought, and she and Mother can talk.

She read the clipping, shuddering. It was so vulgar. It had been Spencer's idea, this fatuous fawning over the senior member of his firm. Her protests that a simple, elegant dinner would be in better taste had provoked nothing but anger and a terrible black-and-blue mark on her upper arm where he'd grabbed her to make his point.

"Damn it, don't tell me about taste! J.B. will be impressed that we've gone to special trouble to lay on a party that isn't just run-of-the-mill, and it will give the papers something to write about, since they think you're such an 'imaginative' hostess! If it weren't for me, they'd never know you were alive! I have to think up all the ideas. You don't know how to give a party you can't copy out of an etiquette book!"

So she'd done all that terrible, corny stuff with the courtroom atmosphere. And of course he'd been vindicated. As usual.

Alice handed over the clipping. "You were right. J.B.'s party got quite a write-up."

He read it, pleased.

"Who sent it? J.B.'s secretary?"

"No. Aunt Charlotte. Along with a note complaining that the children haven't called her."

He gave a derisive laugh. "What in hell made you think they would?"

Chapter 10

HE'D HAD KIND of a "funny feeling," as Laura would describe it, all day. Several times while he was raking the leaves, he'd had to stop to catch his breath. And his stomach felt queasy. I hope I'm not coming down with flu, Sam thought. Can't afford to get sick this week, not with the party tonight and all the out-of-town visitors here. He realized he lumped his daughters in with the "visitors," along with Laura's brother and sister-in-law. Well, why not? That's what his children were: Visitors. And rare ones at that.

It was wrong of him to reproach them for not coming home more often. There's nothing here for them, he reflected. They find it dull. The city. The house. Laura and me and our daily routine that becomes more proscribed with each passing year. Like now. He glanced at his watch. Twelve twenty-five. In exactly five minutes Laura would come to the door and summon him to lunch. Just as at five fifty-five she summoned him for dinner. At six-thirty we watch the news followed by our regular programs. And at ten o'clock we're in bed. You could set the clock by us, day in, day out.

He hadn't realized how monotonous life was nor how much he resented certain things. Other people of his and Laura's age had their children nearby, had grandchildren and even great-grandchildren to enjoy. But his daughters hadn't given him that. Quite the contrary. They'd gotten as far away as possible. And only one of them had produced children of her own, kids the Daltons never saw growing up, young people too remote and disinterested to even come to their grandparents' golden wedding anniversary.

"Sam! Lunch!"

He put down the rake and slowly went into the house. She'd made ham and cheese sandwiches. The sight of food made him nauseous. He knew he couldn't swallow a bite. He stood at the kitchen table looking at his plate.

"I think I'll skip lunch if you don't mind, my dear. I'm not really hungry."

If he'd said he was running off with another woman, Laura couldn't have looked more shocked.

"Skip lunch? Sam, what's the matter? Are you sick?"

"No, no. Just a little off my feed. In fact, I think I'll go up and rest a bit."

Second shock. "Rest? At this time of day?" Her face clouded with concern. "You *are* sick!" She felt his forehead. "I think you're running a temperature. Sam, you're not coming down with something, are you? I'd better call Dr. Jacoby. You must have picked up a bug. Oh, dear, what an awful time, with the girls here and the party . . . " She stopped abruptly. "I didn't mean that the way it sounded. None of that's important. It's you I'm concerned about. You never get sick! If you want to go to bed in the middle of the day, you must feel terrible!"

"Now, Laura, stop making such a fuss! I'm probably catching cold, that's all. Good Lord, I don't have a terminal illness! You know Jacoby gave me a thorough physical two months ago and said I was sound as a dollar." He managed to smile. "I'll just go up and lie down for an hour or so. I'll feel fine by this evening."

"You're sure?"

"Positive."

"I still think . . . ."

"I think you have enough on your hands getting ready for tonight. I told you: Stop worrying about nothing. I'll take a couple of aspirin and be okay."

"Can I fix you something? A cup of soup? Maybe some toast and tea?"

"Not a thing, dear. You just go about your business."

Reluctantly, she nodded. She supposed she was silly, making such a to-do over nothing. Except it was unheard of for Sam to admit he didn't feel well. In all the years at the phone company he'd never taken one "sick day." Maybe I should call the doctor, she thought. No. Sam would be furious. And he's probably just tired, as I am, from the strain of all this. It was more emotional than physical, this fatigue she felt. She didn't know why, but she'd been having a bad case of nerves ever since the girls arrived. As though she had to be on her good behavior, make them happy, try to keep them from being restless. How silly that was. They were her daughters, not acquaintances for whom one had to put on "party manners." Yet the tension was real and communicable. Perhaps Sam felt it, too. She never thought of him or, for that matter, any man, being nervous, but it could be he felt the same inexplicable anxiety.

A thought she did not wish to entertain came into her head: It's really much more peaceful without them. What an awful thing to think! To find one's own children upsetting, when she and Sam had been looking forward for months to their return! What had gotten into her these past couple of days? She was feeling the stress of these disparate personalities, making too much of an effort to recapture the "old days" when they really were a family. Yes, that was all that was wrong. And, yes, she faced the fact, she'd be relieved when everybody went home. You're a terrible mother, Laura Dalton, she scolded herself. No, I'm not, she answered the silent voice. I'm just realizing that we're too old to put up with "house guests" and even the minimum of entertaining. We're not parents any more, except in the legal sense. We're simply two quiet people unused to adjusting to our children's needs. We've not had to for so many years.

And yet they were good daughters in their way, she thought, smiling at the wedding cake Child's had delivered earlier. Barbara was right. It really was a "production." Three tiers of it, with pink icing—roses and the years 1926-1976 in gold letters at the base. There was even the inevitable, vapid bride and groom on top. It was a hideous cake and exactly right for the occasion. We never had anything this elaborate at our wedding. Only fitting we should have it now. She willed herself to be cheerful. It would be a nice party. It would be good to see Fred and Mamie again, and celebrate with all the friends and relatives. Childishly, she looked forward to the gifts too. Not that she expected anything grand. She simply loved presents. She hoped Sam would like his gold tieclip. She'd saved for it out of the household money he gave her. I wonder if he bought something for me? Laura wondered. We agreed we wouldn't give each other anything, but I hope he broke his promise, as I did. I'd like him to be a little more sentimental than usual on this day. There's so little romance in my life.

The idea of still craving romance almost made her laugh aloud. She'd never grow up. She'd never stop anticipating the kind of euphoria enjoyed by the leading ladies of soap operas and the heroines of Gothic novels. You fool! In your heart, you're still young and vain. Well, why not? No matter what the mirror said, she could still fantasize. She did a little waltz step around the kitchen, pretending she was a nineteen-year-old Laura Burrows, engaged to be married to a man who would smother her with love and shower her with gifts. And he had. Not the kind of dashing love she'd hoped for or the extravagant gestures she'd have liked. But Sam had been devoted. She lacked for none of the modest creature comforts.

And tonight would be the highlight of her life.

They began arriving a little after six.

Barbara, looking lovely in a blue chiffon tunic and wide-legged silk pants, went over to pick up Fred and Mamie and Mildred and Martha from the house where she'd dropped off the Chicago pair a few hours earlier. Alice, in black velvet, came by cab with Spencer, a big, interesting-looking, gift-wrapped box in her hands. Fran drifted down in a shockingly low-cut white crepe dress, slit up one side. Laura saw Sam look disapprovingly at his eldest daughter's décolletage. Thank goodness he seemed much better after his rest. He'd gotten up feeling perfectly okay, he'd said, much to Laura's relief. She hoped he wouldn't chide Frances for her revealing neckline or the expanse of leg. It was quite unsuitable, of course, but so like her. She was used to being the center of attention, and the arresting gown, not to mention the diamonds and emeralds at her ears and on her fingers, were designed to assure that.

Laura had bought a new, long, pale-pink dress for the party and knew she looked well in it. The color contrasted with her white hair and emphasized her still youthful complexion, and she was pleased when everyone complimented Sam on his "young and beautiful bride," and told her how lovely she was this evening.

They came in a steady stream. The neighbors deposited the "assigned" food where Laura directed—the clam dip and potato chips, the tuna casseroles and green salad, the rolls and biscuits. She'd baked a ham and filled the big cut-crystal bowl with fruit punch. Her table looked pretty, with the old lace cloth used only on special occasions, the china that had been her mother's, the silver she and Sam had received as their wedding gift from his family, and the wedding cake occupying a place of honor in the center.

There was a babble of greetings, of introductions and reunions, of kissing and hugging and exclamations of delight, particularly over seeing "the girls," most especially Fran, whom some had never met and others had not seen in thirty years. It was an atmosphere of warmth and affection. Even Spencer unbent enough to be polite to his wife's relatives and her parents' friends. Unlike Sam, however, who had enough control not to mention it, Spencer couldn't resist commenting on Fran's spectacular outfit.

"You're certainly stealing the show." It was a quiet aside, but his eyes went to her half-exposed bosom. "Is that the outfit *Vogue* recommends for black sheep?"

Frances looked at him with open dislike. "Naturally. Black and white. Isn't that the way everything is to you, Spencer?"

"What is that supposed to mean?"

She glanced at Alice in her conservative black velvet dress with the almost prim neckline and the strand of good pearls. "I'd think it was obvious. 'Nice' women wear careful clothes. 'Loose' ones wear flamboyant ones. That way everybody knows where they stand. It's all black and white. No gray areas. I'm sure there are none in your life, Spencer."

"Gray's an indecisive color."

"Exactly. And you're a decisive man, aren't you?"

"I hope so. A man should be decisive. And disciplined."

"And a woman? What should she be? Obedient and subservient? Above reproach?"

Spencer flushed. He suspected she was testing him to find out whether he knew about Alice's "past." He hadn't known when he married her. She'd deceived him. She and that damned old woman she lived with. If he'd had any idea that quiet little twenty-three-year-old girl had borne a baby out of wedlock he'd never even have taken her out, much less made her his wife. It had all come out during an angry quarrel. He remembered that night well. She'd been defiant, brazen about it. And he'd given her a beating she'd never forgotten. But Fran, he was sure, didn't know that. She knew about the baby, of course, but probably not that Alice had confessed. She didn't know about his violence either, he guessed. Alice would be too proud to tell anyone in her family about that. Too stubborn to admit she deserved it. He smiled coolly at Fran.

"Alice is all those things. I've taught her how to be a lady."

"Really? I thought she already knew." She saw Allie watching them even while she was making polite conversation with Aunt Mamie. She's wondering what Spencer and I have to talk about, Fran thought. She knows we despise each other.

At that moment she saw him come in. She recognized him immediately, even after all these years. Buzz Paige. Older, heavier, but surprisingly unchanged. Still handsome, still possessed of the smile that could melt icebergs, the smile he bestowed on Laura as he leaned down to kiss her gently on the cheek. Gentle. Buzz had always been gentle with women. Too gentle. That's why I didn't marry him, Fran thought. He wasn't tough enough to handle me. I knew I could always get my way, and that's always been the last thing I wanted. I need a man to dominate me. I've never found one. They've all turned out to be such miserable excuses for men.

She looked back at Spencer, so sure of himself, so egomaniacal. The cruelty showed in his eyes. You bastard, Fran thought. I should have married you. You wouldn't scare me the way you obviously do Allie. I would have served you right. And you're just about what I deserve.

"Excuse me," Fran said. "I just saw an old friend come in."

She approached Buzz and the attractive but rather faded-looking woman who stood with him. So that's his wife. Just about what one would expect. A dim bulb. A washed-out watercolor. Yes, that's what Buzz would have gone to after me: someone peaceful and placid and safe.

He hadn't seen her yet. She was at his elbow before he noticed her. Then he turned and looked into her eyes with an expression she couldn't read.

"Hello, Buzz. Long time."

He took both her hands. "Fran! You look wonderful!"

"Thanks. So do you. What's your secret?"

He laughed. "Clean living and tender loving care. Fran, you remember Dottie. She was Dottie Kravett when you knew her." He put his arm around his wife.

"Hello, Frances," Dorothy said.

"Dottie! My God, Dottie Kravett! Of course!" Fran kissed her, French-style, on both cheeks. "How marvelous! And you're married to Buzz! Imagine! All these years!"

"Twenty-nine, to be exact."

Fran pretended to shudder. "Don't say that. I can't bear to think how long ago it was when we were a gang of young lunatics tearing up this town!"

"I was never one of your crowd. We just knew each other from school." The voice was strained, taut.

"Fran means we all grew up together, honey," Buzz said. "And by God we did, though I'll never know how we didn't kill ourselves in the process. Remember that crazy old Ford convertible I had, Fran? It's a miracle it didn't turn us all into statistics!"

"Only because you drove it like you were Barney Oldfield!" Fran clapped a jeweled hand over her mouth. "I mustn't say things like that. Barney Oldfield! My God, that gives away my age!"

"It's no secret," Dottie said. "What are you now, Fran? Fifty? Fifty-one?"

The other two looked at her in surprise. The hostility was undisguised. Buzz reddened, embarrassed by his wife's rudeness.

"Darling," he said, "you know a lady never tells her age."

Dorothy smirked. "No. A *lady* doesn't."

Jesus! Fran thought. She's crazy. Crazy with jealousy, I suppose. That's crazy in itself. How could she be jealous of somebody from so far in the past? Poor Buzz. He really picked a loser. She decided to make light of the petty barb.

"That was no lady I saw you with," she said. "That was my high school girlfriend." Fran smiled. "We have no secrets, Dottie, have we? Fifty my next birthday. How *about* that?"

"You must tell us all about yourself," Buzz said quickly. "Are you still living in Paris?"

"Yes. I travel a lot, but that's officially home. I think Mother's looking for me. See you later."

"What's the matter with you?" Buzz turned angrily on his wife after Fran drifted off. "My God, Dottie, you were an absolute boor! Fran was merely trying to be pleasant. She was only showing us courtesy."

"Courtesy and everything else she has. You're such a fool, Buzz! Didn't you see the way she looked at you?"

"No, dammit, I didn't see anything but a woman who was trying to be gracious while you were downright insulting. Please, Dottie, don't behave this way. You're going to spoil the whole evening."

"Why shouldn't I? She's spoiled my whole life. You've never gotten over her, Buzz Paige, and you know it!" Her voice had risen. A couple of people nearby turned to stare. Don't let her make a scene, Buzz prayed. Not here. Not now. I was wrong to antagonize her. I know how volatile she is.

"Okay, honey. Forget it. Let's go talk to Mr. Dalton. We haven't had a chance to congratulate him."

Dottie didn't move, but she lowered her voice. "You're still in love with her, aren't you?"

He tried to soothe her. "Of course not! That was years ago, honey. We were kids. I had a crush on her, that's all."

The anger turned to resignation. "She was your first love. Nobody forgets his first love."

Buzz laughed. "Only in novels, sweetheart. What I felt for Fran wasn't love. It was schoolboy stuff. I fell in love when I found you. You're my first and only one."

She seemed mollified. "You won't let her take you away from me, will you?"

"What kind of silly talk is that? Come on. Let's circulate."

As they moved about, chatting with other guests, getting reacquainted with Barbara and Alice, meeting Spencer, being polite to the aunts and uncles, Buzz seemed to be relaxed and thoroughly at ease. But inside there was the old excitement. There'd never been anybody like Fran. Dottie was right. He'd never gotten over her. But what he still felt couldn't be called love. It was physical desire, tinged, he supposed, with the remnants of wounded pride and the memory of how sensual she'd been, even as a girl. She was even more provocative now with that cool assurance that made Dottie seem gauche.

He saw her glance at him as he and his wife went from group to group. He wondered what she was thinking. What she was remembering. Was the attraction still there for her, too? Helplessly, he wondered how to find out.

"Tell me about Washington. It must be a very exciting place."

Barbara started as her aunt spoke to her. Mamie stood in front of her, smiling. Barb realized she'd been daydreaming in the middle of the party, thinking about Charles, wishing he was here. She came back to the moment and smiled at the "Chicago aunt."

"I enjoy it. It's changed a great deal since I've been there. I hear Chicago has too."

"Oh my, yes. So much going on. The city is very progressive with all the new buildings and shopping areas. Michigan Avenue quite outdoes Fifth Avenue in New York, I hear. You should come and visit sometime, Barbara. It's been so many years since we've seen any of you girls."

"I'd like that, Aunt Mamie, but I don't get a lot of time off from my job. It's all I can do to get here once a year to see the family. It's a nice party, isn't it? Doesn't Mother look pretty?"

"Yes. She was always the best-looking of the three of us." Mamie made a little face. "And of course, being the baby, she was also spoiled rotten. She's six years younger than I am, you know. And ten years younger than Charlotte. Almost like you, Barbara, now that I think of it. The youngest of three girls, with quite a gap between the second and third. Sam and Laura spoiled you the same as our parents spoiled her. Frankly, I was surprised when she married your father. Not that he isn't a fine man. But Laura was always daydreaming about the 'Prince Charming' who was going to come into her life and take her off into some wonderful, glamorous life. Listening to her, I thought she'd never marry, because that kind of idealism can sometimes stand in the way of reality. It makes some women go through life seeking and yearning for the kind of relationship they never find. I never knew a spinster who hadn't had a chance to marry. I've only known those who never found the 'man of their dreams.' Pity. While they languish with their visions of a 'great love,' time slips by and they wake up to find themselves alone. I'm glad that didn't happen to Laura. Thank goodness she realized she wasn't a princess. She's had a good life. Fulfilling. It's wonderful to be here celebrating with her and Sam. Fred and I had our fiftieth two years ago. Laura and I are lucky. We still have our husbands. Poor Charlotte lost hers early, you know.'' Mamie's voice sank almost to a whisper. "He died the year before she took Alice. Sometimes I think all that business with your sister was God's will, terrible as it was. It gave Charlotte something to think about besides her loss. And it was salvation for poor little Alice. Just think, Barbara, if she hadn't gone to Boston she'd never have met that lovely, successful man and had two real children.''

"Real children?'' Barbara echoed. "What a strange thing to say, Aunt Mamie. Jack Richards' child was real.''

The plump little woman looked flustered. "Well, of course it was. That is . . . I mean it was real but it wasn't . . . you know what I mean. Anyway, I'm glad Alice is safely married. I wish Frances' husbands had turned out better.''

Barbara felt an anger that was difficult to control. How dare this smug, elderly matron stand here and patronize all of them? She and her talk about "safe marriages" and "yearning spinsters." And the omission of my situation is obvious. She's sniping at me. She thinks she's so subtle, reminding rne that I'm forty and unmarried, as though it were something idiotic or shameful. All that prattle about never finding one's "great love." She doesn't know I've found mine.

"Forgive me, Aunt Mamie,'' Barbara said, "but I think your standards are a little outdated. Marriage isn't the answer to everything any more. Some of us are single by preference.''

Mamie was unruffled. "Oh, dear, you liberated young women are missing so much. The Lord intended us to go two by two, Barbara.'' She patted her niece's cheek. "Never mind. At least you have a career. Poor Frances has nothing but money.''

Barbara clenched her teeth. Damned old biddy! I wish I'd left her at the airport.

Spencer, smiling like a loving husband, took Allie's arm and walked her into the deserted kitchen.

"How soon can we get the hell out of here? I can't stand much more of this. My God, what people! Can't we leave now?''

Allie was appalled. "Spencer, you know we can't! We have to stay until the very end. Mother and Daddy would be humiliated if we walked out in the middle of the party!''

"I've never been so bloody bored in my life. Damn it, I knew it was a mistake to come. I wish I'd stayed in Boston.''

Alice looked at him with hatred. "I wish so too," she said and walked out of the kitchen. I'll pay dearly for that, she thought. I don't care. I wish he'd go away now. I wish he'd go forever.

"Nice shindig, Sam," Earl Dalton said to his brother. "Almost makes me regret never having taken the plunge myself."

Sam smiled. "Now, that's the biggest whopper you've told in years. You never had any use for marriage and you know it."

"No, I guess not. You got the only girl I ever wanted. Laura's quite a woman."

"Yes, she is. A good wife. A good mother."

"And you have three beautiful daughters. You're a lucky man."

Mildred and Martha sat together on the sofa, surveying the scene. Sam's widowed sisters detested each other, as they detested a world that virtually ignored them.

"Get a look at the bookends on the couch," Fran said quietly to her mother. "They haven't missed a thing. My lord, what sour expressions! What are they waiting for—people to come and kiss the hem of their garments? Or are they merely constipated?"

Laura tried not to laugh. "Frances, you must be more respectful! They're very old and not very happy. It isn't easy to be alone in the world. After all, they both lost their husbands years ago and they're still quite disappointed that they don't get much attention from friends they had when they were married. I must say, I feel guilty about them myself. I try to visit now and then, but they're not much pleasure to be with. Your father's even less tolerant. He can't stand being around them. I have to bully him into it."

"Families," Fran said. "Don't you sometimes think they're more trouble than they're worth?"

"No," Laura said. "I never think that."

The party broke up soon after Sam and Laura opened their gifts. Or, more correctly, after Laura opened them. Sam stood back, letting her have the fun of untying the ribbons and gasp with pleasure as she took each present out of its box. She was like a child at Christmas, excited and flushed with pleasure, giving every donor the same grateful kiss of appreciation, whether the offering was extravagant or modest.

Our presents tell a lot about us, Barbara thought as she helped her mother with the wrapping and boxes. Fran's is costly and useless—two solid gold bars from Cartier, miniature pendants to be hung from chains around the necks of people who "have everything." Sam and Laura would never dream of wearing such things. The very idea of a necklace on a man would stun her father, and Laura would not understand that she'd received one of the year's status symbols. Alice and Spencer's gift was also expensive, as befitted their "station," but at least it had some possible use. It was a handsome Vermeil flower vase, far too elegant for the house on South Carona Street, much too ostentatious for the objects it would live among. Still, Laura could put her precious garden flowers in it.

At the very end, after all the gifts were opened and admired, after Sam had shown pleasure over his tie-clip and Laura had cried a little over the heart-shaped pin he'd bought for her, while the friends and relatives were being thanked for their gold-plated letter openers and gold-colored bookends and gilt picture frames and all the other well-meant, absurd mementos, Barbara sneaked out to the garage and returned with a wicker basket with a big gold bow on top.

"I saved mine for last," she said to her parents. "I hope you don't hate me for it."

Laura took the little basket and looked inside. Her expression turned from surprise to rapture as she lifted out a tiny creature. "It's a puppy!" Laura said. "Look, Sam! It's a darling little dog!"

"A dog!" Sam was startled.

"If you don't want him, we can take him back," Barbara said hastily. "I know he'll be a lot of trouble. He's only three months old and not housebroken, but I thought maybe he'd . . . he'd be company." She gave an embarrassed little laugh. "I fell in love with him when I passed the pet shop window this afternoon. And when I found he was a golden retriever, I couldn't resist." She looked anxiously at her parents. "I guess it was a silly idea. We've never had a dog in the house."

Laura held the puppy close to her face and its little pink tongue reached out to kiss her cheek. She snuggled it like a baby.

"Oh, Barbara darling, he's wonderful! He's beautiful! Isn't he, Sam?"

Anything his "baby" did was all right with Sam Dalton. Even something crazy like giving them a damned troublesome dog. "He sure is. And he'll grow up to be a beauty. Thank you, honey."

Most of the guests crowded around, enchanted by the tiny animal, petting and scratching him under his little jaws. Only Mildred and Martha stayed in their places, their eyebrows arched in identical disapproval at such foolishness. And Spencer Winters muttered to his wife that it was the dumbest present he'd ever seen. "What the hell do they need with a dog? For God's sake, is your sister out of her mind?"

"Maybe she wants to give them something faithful and loving and totally uncritical," Alice said softly. "Maybe she wants to bring new life into this old house."

"Oh, for Christ's sake, Alice! What nonsense is that?"

She didn't answer, but she watched her parents' faces. Barbara instinctively knew the moment was right to give them something to protect and care for and be completely loved by. Alice felt sad. A puppy was the grandchild they never were able to play with, a helpless thing that needed them as no other living creature did. How perceptive of Barb to sense that they needed some new purpose, some sense of responsibility for a life—even if it was only a dog's. Alice had cheated them of the only grandchildren they had. Chris would never give them a great-grandchild to love. And Janice had already announced she never planned to have babies, probably would never marry, for that matter.

Someday I'll be reaching out like that for something to love, Alice thought. Spencer would never understand that kind of emptiness late in life. Barb did. Even Fran seemed to grasp the deeper meaning of the gift. There was a suspicious moisture in her eyes.

A tear rolled slowly down Alice's face and she didn't wipe it away. She heard Spencer's exasperated sigh.

"Can we go back to the hotel now or are you going to stand there blubbering all night?"

"You go," Alice said. "I'm going to stay here, Spencer." She surprised herself by the sudden decision. "I'll come by the hotel tomorrow and get my things before you check out."

He stared at her. "Have you gone crazy too? What are you talking about? Why are you spending the night here?"

"You told me to stay in Denver as long as I wanted. I'm taking you up on it. Starting now."

"Come outside. Away from all these people. I want to talk to you."

"No. I'm not coming back to the hotel with you tonight."

"How will you explain that?"

"Maybe with the truth," Alice said. "Maybe after all these years I'll explain everything with the truth." She looked straight at him. "I'm not afraid of you any more, Spencer. I'm not afraid of your punishment. I don't need it. Maybe I never did."

He was too outraged to argue with her. Silly bitch! If she wanted to stay on with her family awhile, well, let her. Who cared?

"When will you be coming back to Boston?"

"I have no idea."

"For God's sake, Alice, what will I tell Janice? What shall I say to J.B.?"

"Tell Janice I love her and Chris. And tell J.B. to go to hell."

Chapter 11

BY ELEVEN O'CLOCK, they'd all gone, the friends and relatives, leaving only Sam and Laura and their daughters to survey the aftermath of the party. Laura sank into a corner of the sofa, the puppy in her arms.

"Would you believe twenty-five people could create such a mess?" She looked at the litter of tissue and ribbon and boxes, the plates and punch glasses on every surface, the overflowing ashtrays, the remnants of food on platters and the demolished wedding cake reduced now to one small slice on which the bride and groom were precariously perched.

"You go to bed, Mother," Alice said. "We'll clean up. You must be exhausted."

The others looked at her, the same unspoken question in their minds. Why had Spencer stormed off in a taxi, barely saying a civil goodnight to anyone? What was Alice doing here instead of returning to the hotel? Only Fran was bold enough to come right to the point.

"Is that why you decided to stay here tonight? To help us clean up?"

Alice hesitated. "I'll explain with the truth," she'd said to Spencer only moments before. But how could she? How could she tell her family she'd lived twenty-five years with a sadist? Could she say she wasn't willing to go back to Boston and the horrors and sadness it held for her? That maybe she'd never go back? They were waiting, looking at her, curious about this strange turn of events. She knew she could count on her mother's sympathy, her sisters' understanding. But what of Daddy? Would he remind her of her "duty" to her husband and children? He didn't like Spencer, that was obvious, but Sam Dalton had a curious code of ethics. You made your bed and you lay in it. You did the "decent thing," no matter what it cost you. That was Sam's attitude. He'd proved it to her many years ago.

"What is it, darling?" Laura's voice was kind. "Have you and Spencer had a fight? You can tell us, Alice."

I'm a coward, Allie thought. I haven't the guts to tell Mother and Daddy the truth. Not yet. Not tonight.

"Yes, we had an argument. That's all. I just decided I didn't want to go back to the hotel tonight. It's nothing," she lied. "Just your everyday domestic spat. But I didn't want to continue it. So I thought I'd stay here."

Laura seemed to accept that. Perhaps there'd been nights in her own life that she wished there were somewhere to go to get away from a quarrel for a while. But Sam was not so gullible. Husbands and wives did not sleep apart. Not unless there was something seriously wrong. He'd felt that ever since Alice had been at home. The man was no good. Allie's unexpected decision only verified his feeling that this was a bad situation.

"You going back to the hotel tomorrow?" he asked.

"To get the clothes and things I left there, Daddy. Spencer's returning to Boston tomorrow. He's too busy to stay the week. I'd like to, though, if it's all right with you."

"Of course it's all right," Laura said. "We expected you to stay. I'm sorry Spencer can't. You just tuck into your old room with Barbara tonight, dear. I'm sure tomorrow you and Spencer will iron out whatever it is that's bothering you."

Barbara and Fran exchanged knowing glances. Allie was lying about her little "domestic spat." Surely even her parents could see that. Sam's tight-lipped expression said clearly that he knew Allie wasn't telling the whole truth. Laura must know this was more than her daughter tried to make it sound, but she was putting a good face on it, at least for now. All right. If the three of them wanted to play out this little game, Fran and Barb would go along.

"Allie's right," Barb said in the small silence that followed. "You and Daddy go on up to bed, Mother. The three of us can clear up this cyclone in no time flat." She grinned as though everything was normal. "Where's the new baby going to sleep, by the way?"

"I thought we could make him a little bed in the kitchen."

"Give you odds he'll cry all night," Fran said.

"No, he won't," Barbara declared. "He's going to be a model child. And to make sure, I'll put an old alarm clock in his bed. They say the ticking reminds them of their mother's heartbeat and keeps them quiet."

"My sister the veterinarian," Fran laughed. "By the way, Mother, what are you going to call him?"

Laura cuddled the puppy. "I haven't the faintest idea. Anybody have a suggestion?"

"How about 'Spoiled'?" Sam said. "That sure is what he's going to be."

"Maybe 'Goldie'?" Alice suggested. "For the anniversary and his color?"

"He looks more carrot than gold right now," Barb said.

"But he's a fourteen-karat little beast." Fran smiled. "Why don't you call him 'Karat,' Mother? With a 'K' as in 'Killer.' "

"Or 'K' as in 'Krazy,' " Barbara added. "Which probably is what I am for giving you something that's going to be such a bother. Are you sure you and Dad want to keep him? I won't feel hurt if you decide not to."

Laura looked at her husband.

"Of course we're going to keep him," Sam said. He took the puppy from her. "Come on, Karat. Your old man's going to fix you a nice warm bed."

The three of them went about clearing up the living and dining room and kitchen after their parents went upstairs, Laura protesting that she really shouldn't leave them with all the work. They shoo-ed her off lovingly and changed into robes, except for Allie, who'd left hers at the hotel. "No matter," she said cheerfully. "I'll just stay in my bra and girdle and put one of Mother's aprons over me." The effect was hilarious. They laughed at Allie's girdled derriere exposed from the rear. They laughed at Fran in her two-hundred-dollar silk robe stacking dishes to carry to the sink. It was all suddenly warm and fun and girlish, as though they'd turned back the clock and were "the Dalton girls" of their youth. As they worked, they gossiped about the guests.

"Aunt Mamie is impossible," Barb said. "She had me cornered with a lot of self-righteous blather about the joys of marriage! Heaven help Uncle Fred. Imagine living with that!"

"How about the dour old aunts from Denver?" Fran asked. "Poor Mother. She has to cope with them. Daddy runs, I gather, even though they're his own sisters."

"And Uncle Earl," Barb said. "The perennial bachelor. Do you think he could possibly be gay?"

Fran collapsed with laughter, leaning against the kitchen table. "Gay? He wouldn't even know the meaning of the word! Listen to her, Allie. She's clearly out of her head."

Alice tried to join in the bantering, but she was much too troubled. Barb's flippant remark reminded her of Chris. Chris was gay. What would they think if they knew that? What would they think of Janice with her don't-give-a-damn attitude? Of Spencer with his psychotic behavior? What would my sisters say if they knew my whole life was a melodrama?

Fran was chattering on. "What did you think of that dreary little wife of Buzz Paige's? I remember her from school. She was always peculiar. Never did fit in. I wonder why on earth he married her."

"Oh, listen, Mother gave me a rundown on that," Barb said, suddenly remembering. She proceeded to tell them the gossip about the Paiges. Fran looked thoughtful.

"So he had an affair and left home once," she said. "That's very interesting."

Her sisters looked at her sharply.

"Fran, don't start anything," Barbara said. "You know we discussed that."

"That was before I knew all this. And before I saw him again. He's still damned attractive. And if you'll forgive my immodesty, I know he thinks I am too.''

Barbara was suddenly angry. "Don't you dare try any of your tricks with Buzz! For God's sake, Fran, you'll ruin his marriage and then take off to some other part of the world leaving a wrecked home and a couple of unhappy people! That's loathsome! That's more rotten than screwing around with a waiter!''

Alice looked Puzzled. "A waiter? What are you talking about?''

"Nothing," Barb said. "Forget it.''

"Oh, don't be such a damned prude, Barbara!" Fran was angry, too. "Allie's a big girl. I'm not ashamed to tell her.'' She turned to Alice. "Your little sister is referring to the fact that I picked up a waiter at LaFitte's and went to bed with him last night. Big deal. A one-night stand. What's so earth-shaking about that? I've had a hundred of them. A thousand. They don't mean a thing. They're more fun and less habit-forming than sleeping pills." She smiled. "Are you shocked, Allie? Barb is. Haven't you ever cheated on Spencer? Or am I the only immoral member of this trio?''

Her sister didn't answer. Finally, Barbara said, "Look, Fran, I'm not condemning you. I'm the last one to sit in judgment. But don't fool around with Buzz. You're not serious about him. You broke his heart once. Isn't that enough?''

"People's hearts don't break, pet. They just chip a little around the edges.''

"That's not true," Allie said slowly. "Mine broke when I had to give up Jack Richards and his baby.''

There was a long pause before Fran said with surprising gentleness, "Poor Allie. You've had it tougher than either of us, haven't you? You're still having it tough with old Spencer, aren't you? What's the story behind tonight? Have you left him for good?''

"I don't know. I'd like to. But there are so many things . . ." Her voice trailed off. "I can't talk about it just now. Maybe later. Maybe you two can advise me what to do about Spencer. And other things.''

Fran tried to lighten the atmosphere. "You certainly couldn't pick two better marriage counselors. One who'd had three strike-outs, and the other who's had none at all.''

"But you're both so much more determined than I," Allie said. "They couldn't have done to you what they did to me. Not that I blame them. It was my fault. I should have fought them.''

Who are "they"? Barbara wondered. Mother and Daddy? The Richardses and Jack? Aunt Charlotte? Or were "they" Allie's husband and children—that snob she married and the son and daughter none of them really knew anything about? Fran was right. Allie had had it tougher than the other two. And she was less able to handle it.

Fran's been bruised, Barb thought, but she's so basically selfish she's survived. And I've never had to go through anything that tore me to pieces. Her train of thought took her to Charles. Why hadn't he called since she'd been in Denver? They'd agreed she'd never call him. Certainly not at home. And not even at the office unless it was a real emergency. But it was strange she hadn't heard from him. She missed his voice. Even when they couldn't meet, he telephoned her every evening, telling her how much he loved her, how unhappy he was that he wasn't in her arms. It had been three whole days since she'd heard. That wasn't like him. Maybe he's ill, she thought, panicked. I'd have no way of knowing. My God, if he died, I'd read it in the papers! Pull yourself together. You're letting your imagination run away with you. He's probably been busy. He'll call tomorrow.

A strained silence had fallen after Allie's last remark. There was nothing to say. Not until she felt able to talk. Then we'll help her any way we can, Fran and I, Barbara thought. She's our sister. She's part of us.

John Peck couldn't keep his eyes off the young woman draped so casually in a chair in his living room, one trousered leg slung over the side. Janice Winters was pure class. She had the kind of assurance that came with money and breeding, the relaxed attitude of the rich who could afford to wear jeans and a sweater to dinner at the home of a stranger. He felt overdressed in his darkblue suit. Middle class. Even Carol's "hostess gown" seemed fussy and wrong. They were "squares" next to this easygoing, confident young pair.

Are you my half-sister? John wanted to ask. Do we have the same mother? Is something important going to come out of this. hastily arranged evening with Clint Darby and his girl? He felt terribly nervous. Carol didn't. At least she gave no sign of being ill at ease. She chattered brightly about the advertising business, about John's marvelous job, about everything except what he was dying to know: Was Alice Dalton Winters the woman who'd given birth to him and the exotic young creature across the room?

Not that he or Carol would come out and ask. But dammit, why didn't his wife steer the conversation toward some area that might produce a clue? She was in a better position than he to get into that without creating suspicion. Stop pressing, he told himself. Carol is right. Let the evening take its course. At some point we'll slide gracefully into the subject of Janice's family.

It was not until after dinner that the moment arrived, and then it was Janice who provided him with the opening he sought. While Carol and Clint discussed an upcoming advertising campaign, Jan turned her attention to her host.

"Is Boston your home?"

"Yes. I was born and raised here. You, too, I gather."

Jan nodded. "I'm a native. Not Mother and Dad, though. Mom comes from Denver and Dad's originally from Chicago." She laughed. "Not that he chooses to remember. He'd like everyone to think he was brought up with the Cabots and the Lodges. Old J. B. Thompson, the Lord High Executioner of my father's law firm, still firmly believes that no civilization exists west of Massachusetts. I think he's convinced that Illinois is still peopled by pioneers living in log cabins. So, darling Daddy has become more Bostonian than the baked bean."

"Have your parents lived here long?"

"Oh, sure. Forever. Mother came when she was seventeen. And Dad got his first job here, right out of law school."

Careful, John. Don't seem too interested. "Your mother was seventeen? What made her move to Boston at that age?"

"My Aunt Charlotte kind of adopted her. My great-aunt, really. Tiresome old lady. She's my grandmother's sister and she was widowed early with no children of her own. I think she talked Mother's parents into letting her raise their little Alice. Probably promised more 'advantages' than she could have in Denver. My grandparents aren't very well off. I mean, they're not poor, but I guess in those days, with three girls to raise, they probably thought they were doing the right thing for Mother, sending her to a rich relative.''

"I see. How long ago was that?''

Janice calculated. "Well, let's see. Mother's forty-eight, so it was about thirty-one years ago. Around nineteen forty-five or six. She married my father in nineteen fifty-one. They just had their twenty-fifth anniversary. I came along in nineteen fifty-five, two years after my brother Chris. He's gay, by the way.'' She tossed in that last, gratuitous piece of information as casually as though she were saying that her brother was six feet tall, or married, or a lawyer. Jan looked at him impishly and he realized she'd wanted to see whether he'd be shocked. John smiled.

"To each his own,'' he said easily.

Jan nodded approvingly. "Exactly. But you couldn't sell that to my father. Mother accepts it, more in sorrow than in anger, but the Old Man is outraged. He's practically disowned Chris. It's like an insult that this could happen to *his* only son.''

"So there are just the two of you. You and Chris.''

"Yep. What about you? Your parents living? Any brothers or sisters?''

"I'm an only child. At least I guess so. I was adopted when I was an infant. I was never told who my real parents were. The people who raised me were killed in an automobile accident when I was twenty-one.''

Jan's face softened with pity. "How awful for you!''

"It was a shock, but one gets over everything.''

"I meant about being adopted. Not that there's anything wrong with that, but it must be an odd feeling not to know anything about your real mother and father. I'm so sorry for people who'd like to know and can't find out. I think the laws are wrong. Records should be opened to adoptees when they're old enough to know. Don't you agree?''

He weighed his words carefully. "Yes. There's nothing worse than wondering. It used to bother me a lot.''

"I don't doubt it! It would drive me up the wall! Not that I'm so crazy about what I drew, but at least I know what kind of people they are.'' She realized he'd used the past tense. "It used to bother you,'' Jan repeated. "Doesn't it any more?''

"Sometimes. But you can get obsessed with that kind of thing if you don't watch it. The people who raised me were so good to me that it seems kind of disloyal to think about the others. My adopted mother, especially, was a wonderful woman. I was very close to her.'' He almost held his breath. "Are you close to your mother?''

"Not really. I mean, I like her a lot. She's a super lady. Pretty and kind and patient as hell with Dad and me, but I don't go along with some of her thinking.''

She obviously wasn't going to elaborate. At least I know that much about Alice Dalton, John thought. He was even more convinced this was the right one. He even imagined he saw some faint resemblance between this girl and himself.

And he knew now he had to see his mother. Even if she turned away, he had to meet her once, face to face.

"Didn't I read somewhere that your parents are in Denver?"

"Yes. Dad came home yesterday. Mother decided to stay a few days. They went out for her parents' fiftieth anniversary."

"You and Chris didn't want to go?"

"I think Chris would have liked to, but he isn't on speaking terms with The Pater. I couldn't care less about any of them. The Denver relatives, I mean. I don't even dig great-Aunt Charlotte. She's a whiny old lady who never lets you forget that her husband was *the* Carlton Rudolph, the architect who built so many of the old Back Bay houses. As if anybody cares."

Carlton Rudolph. Charlotte Rudolph raised Alice. John filed away the information carefully in his head. She might be the route to Alice. Alice who'd been sent to her rich aunt for "advantages." Alice who'd arrived in Boston the year John was born. It was too coincidental not to be the answer he'd searched for so long and hard.

"Telephone for you, Barbara," her mother called out late the next morning.

Thank God! It must be Charles. She hurried to answer, but another man's voice responded to her breathless "Hello."

"Barbara? I hope you remember me. It's Jack Richards."

She was incredulous. "Jack? Well, this is a surprise!" Even as she said it, Barbara thought that was the understatement of the century. As Laura said, since the day Alice left, no one had spoken that name. Even when Barb was growing up, she was forbidden to speak to him or his family, and of course she'd not attempted to contact them on her visits home in the past years.

"I'm sure you're wondering why I'm calling."

"Well, yes. Of course I am. It's been so long." She paused. "Mother told me about your wife, Jack. I'm sorry."

"Thank you. She was a lovely girl. I wish you'd known each other."

Barbara waited. What on earth was he getting at?

"I ran into Buzz Paige this morning at the bank. He told me you were home for your parents' anniversary party last night. You and Fran . . . and Allie." He sounded nervous. "I'd like to see her again. Allie, I mean. It's been so many years and I'm so ashamed of what happened. I'd like to try to make her understand why I let her down. Do you think you could arrange it, Barbara? Would you?"

She was puzzled. "I suppose I could, Jack. But why? What's the point? Allie's married, you know. She has two children by Spencer Winters."

"I know. Believe it or not, I've kept track of her."

"Then you must know she had to give your son up for adoption." Barbara's voice unconsciously hardened.

"Yes. That's part of what I want to talk about. I'm trying to make up for so many wrong things I did when I was young. Lucy's death hit me hard. She suffered so long before she died and she was so brave about it. It made me see what a weak, selfish man I've been all my life. How many rotten moments I've given other people. Allie most of all."

"Aren't you a day late and a dollar short? What good is your repentance now, Jack?"

"I want more than her forgiveness, Barb, if she can be big enough to offer that. I thought . . . that is, I hoped maybe I could find our child. Maybe do something for him, if he needs it. At least provide for him after I'm gone. I've done pretty well, and Lucy and I couldn't have children of our own. That boy, wherever he is, is all that will be left of me."

So that's it! Barbara thought. You don't want to make up for your mistakes. You want to enjoy a son you didn't care enough about to give your name to. My God! When she answered, it was coldly.

"Why are you calling *me*, Jack? Why don't you call Allie? I can't answer for her. I don't know whether she cares to speak to you again."

"That's just it. I was afraid she wouldn't come to the telephone. And I don't want to get her into trouble with her husband. I know he's here, too. But I'd like to see her. Just for a few moments. Please, Barb. You and I used to be such good friends. Won't you help me, for old times' sake?"

Such good friends. Barbara almost laughed. I worshiped you. I thought you were the most wonderful thing that ever drew breath. Even after you deserted Allie, I still felt sorry. Amazing. Even when I was nine I realized you weren't strong enough to fight the pressure your family put on you.

"I don't know," she said. "I don't think you should put me in the middle of this." She started to tell him that he could perfectly well call Allie; that Spencer had returned to Boston and her sister was right here at home. She'd already gotten her personal belongings from the hotel and come back to the house. In fact, she was sitting in the next room. But the wiser thing was to discuss it first with Allie. Barbara had no idea how she'd feel about seeing Jack Richards.

"Give me a number where I can reach you. I'll find out whether Allie wants to get in touch with you."

"Thank you, Barbara. I'm really grateful." He gave her his home and his office numbers. "I'll wait to hear from you or Allie. You've always had so much heart, Barb. Even when you were a kid you seemed to understand more than the grown-ups."

Sure, Barb thought as she hung up. I've always been the understanding one. The patsy. The fall guy. My big sisters manipulated me like a toy on a string. Even now, I'm the one who stays in touch with the family, pulls together the reunion for "us girls." And what do I get for it? Damned little. But what do I want for it? Nothing, really. Anything I've ever done I've done because I wanted to. So quit blaming the world, Barbara. You are the way you are.

She had no idea how to approach Allie on this. Straight out, she supposed, was the only way. Just repeat the conversation and hand over the phone numbers and let her make the decision. Jack Richards couldn't matter to her any more. But the child must. Maybe she's as anxious as Jack to find out what happened to their son. Or maybe she never wants to think about it. Perhaps she couldn't face that abandoned baby even if they were to find him. Could I, in her place? Could I stand the accusing eyes of a child I gave to strangers?

Damn. Why did this have to happen? Alice has enough problems with Spencer.

She doesn't need one more. She hasn't come out and said she wants to leave her husband, but that surely is in her mind. And she never talks about her children. Not really.

It's about time she leveled with us, Barb thought. We can't help her if she keeps us in the dark.

Chapter 12

HE WASN'T SURPRISED to see Fran drive up to the Ford showroom. It was as though he expected her this afternoon. They'd barely spoken last night after the initial encounter at the party, and yet Buzz knew she'd be here. Just as he knew there'd be a scene with Dottie when they left the Daltons'.

God how he hated arguments! And fighting with Dot was as unproductive as trying to reason with a drunk. She didn't listen. She stormed and cried and accused and heard nothing he tried to say. She knew he was going to go to bed with Fran, she'd said. Hadn't she seen for herself the way that woman looked at him? And the way he looked back? What did he think she was—a blind fool?

Buzz had protested gently at first. Her outburst was ill-founded. Of course he admired Fran. She was a beautiful woman. And, yes, he remembered how much he'd cared for her once. But it was over long ago.

"Dottie, dear, Fran and I have nothing in common any more." He tried to be reasonable. "There's no reason for you to be so insecure. I won't even see her again while she's here. You know that."

"I know nothing of the kind! You probably can't wait to get to the office tomorrow to call her!"

He finally exploded. "Don't be an ass! I have no intention of getting in touch with her. Or vice versa! You'll drive me crazy with your jealousy! Your damned possessiveness! Listen to yourself! Everything you're saying is a figment of your imagination!"

It was as though he hadn't spoken. She kept on and on for hours, comparing herself unfavorably to Frances, dragging up old wounds, including his supposed affair with Stacy Donovan, accusing him of a hundred infidelities he'd never even thought of, much less committed.

He finally put the pillow over his head, trying to shut out the sound of her voice. At that moment he could have killed her. And yet he felt sorry for her. She was so unknowingly self-defeating. The more she talked about her "old rival," the more Buzz thought about seeing Frances. Poor Dot. If she'd just stay cool, they'd both be happier. But she had to torture herself with these fantasies and put ideas in his head that probably wouldn't otherwise be there. She deserves what she gets, he thought savagely. It would serve her right if I did just what she expects. But he didn't plan to. What point pursuing something dead and buried? Why try to bring it back to life for the few days Frances would be in town?

But he knew, even as he denied it, that he would see Fran again. He'd not initiate it, but it would happen. Only this morning he'd told Jack Richards all about "the girls" being home. Which meant Frances was very much on his mind.

He almost expected the little rented car to pull up at dusk. She saw him through the big plate-glass window and lightly tapped the horn. He went outside and leaned on the open window on the driver's side.

"Hi," he said. "What brings you here?"

"Curiosity. How are you, Buzz?"

"Fine. That was a nice party. You looked gorgeous. I'm sure every woman in the room hated you."

Fran looked innocent. "Really? Anyone we know?"

He pretended not to understand. "*Everyone* we know. You made the rest of them look like last year's models."

"I presume you mean cars, not mannequins." She was flirting with him.

"Of course. Cars are my business. New and used."

They smiled at each other, their faces only inches apart. Buzz had an insane impulse to lean in and kiss her. Really kiss her. Not just a little social peck on the cheek. He pulled back. What the hell did she want? Diversion? A few kicks? Or did she need to prove she could still have him any time she wanted? It occurred to him that Fran, for all her glamor, might be as unsure of herself as the nervous little woman who was his wife. The anxiety of middle age, Buzz thought. The moment when we wonder whether we still have it. He knew the feeling. He'd experienced it lately himself. But Fran? With her money, her position, her three ex-husbands? What reason would she have to bother with a small-time car dealer from Denver? How could he possibly imagine she ever lacked confidence in herself? Still, she'd come looking for him. She hadn't been merely driving by. Come on, Frances, he thought. Make your move. Damned if *I* will.

"What time do you get off from work?"

He laughed. "Fran, dear, I'm not an employee. I own this franchise. I set my own hours. Sometimes I go home at four. Other times it's eight or nine."

She actually blushed. "I'm sorry. I didn't meant to sound patronizing."

"It's okay. How would you know?"

She drummed on the steering wheel with her long, perfectly manicured fingernails.

"I came by to see whether you'd buy me a drink. We didn't have a chance to talk at all last night."

He wasn't going to make it easy. He'd waited thirty years for this moment.

"I'd be glad to buy you a drink, but what do we really have to talk about? I'm sure you're not interested in what's been going on here since you left, and I certainly can't relate to the people you run around with now."

She sounded almost petulant. "You said last night you wanted me to tell you about myself."

"As I recall, I said you must tell *us*. Would you like to come to the house and have a drink with Dot and me?"

"Damn you, Buzz Paige!" Fran didn't hide her annoyance. "What do you want me to do? Come right out and say I'd like to spend some time with you? Say I still find you attractive? All right. If it gives you any satisfaction, that's the truth. I don't want to visit with you and your dreary little wife. I want to . . ."

"What?"

"I don't know. Get to know you again, I guess."

Suddenly he didn't want revenge. He spoke gently. "What's the matter, Fran?"

"Everything. Nothing. Never mind. It doesn't make any difference." She started the engine. "I was crazy to come here. Forget it, Buzz. It was nice seeing you."

"Fran, wait! We can be friends, can't we?"

She looked at him slowly. "No. We can't. I don't have men friends. They're either acquaintances or lovers. And you don't qualify as either." She'd regained her composure. "Now that I've made a fool of myself, I'll just take off and go home to the family. Thanks for putting me straight. I'm glad to know you've turned into such a faithful husband. It's nice to know somebody has one."

He reached in and took her face between his hands. This time he kissed her, deeply, passionately, not caring who saw. Slowly he released her and looked into her eyes.

"All right," Buzz said. "Do I qualify now?"

The answer came in a whisper. "Where can we go?"

It was semi-dark in the motel room. The only light came from the one he'd left on in the bathroom, enough light for him to see the quiet, naked figure beside him, enough to see by his watch that it was ten o'clock.

"You all right?" Buzz asked.

"Mmmm. Delicious. You?"

"Stunned."

"I take it that's a compliment," Fran said.

"You know damned well it is."

She reached over and touched him. "I was such a fool, darling. Why did I ever let you get away?"

"You didn't, remember? You were the one who left me."

"Stupid of me. But your fault, really. If you'd made love to me then I'd never have gone. Why didn't you? It would have changed the course of history."

"I wanted to marry you. I respected you."

Fran laughed. "Oh, my God! Buzz, my love, you were always much too good. Much too idealistic. Didn't you know I was sleeping around even before I ran off with Stuart Mills?" She suddenly sounded sad. "But I never loved any of them. Not then, not later. I never loved anyone but you."

"Then why did you leave me?"

"Who knows? Adventure, I suppose. I was afraid of getting married and settling down in a house like the one I grew up in. I had all kinds of delusions of grandeur. Thought I'd be a great actress, be rich and famous. Material things seemed more important than love."

"And now?"

"They're not worth a damn."

He smiled. "That's because you have them. I can't imagine you living here. Not any more. You'd hate this life. It would stifle you."

She was quiet for a moment. "Not if I had you. I'd be happy anywhere with you, Buzz. We wouldn't even have to live here, for that matter. I have plenty of money. We could travel. Live in Paris. Take the Concorde across the ocean. Oh, darling, it would be wonderful!"

He sat up on the side of the bed. "I can't, Fran. You know that. It's too late for us."

She snapped on the bedside lamp. Even tousled and with her lipstick smeared she was still ravishing.

"Too late? It's never too late."

"For us it is. I'm married. Good God, I'm a grandfather!"

"So what?"

"I couldn't walk out on Dot."

"You don't love her. You love me."

He didn't answer.

"Am I wrong about that?"

"No, you're not wrong. I don't love Dot, but I'll stay with her. She's helpless and unhappy and she needs me. I couldn't desert her."

She stared at him. "You don't love me after all, do you? What was this all about? Some kind of revenge? Why did you bring me here? Why did you make love to me? To show me what I missed? To laugh at me?"

"You know better than that. I love you. I wish I didn't. These past few hours have been more than I've ever dreamed of. You're like some kind of goddess to me. Unattainable. A creature beyond my grasp."

"Oh, for Christ's sake! You're talking like somebody in a Victorian novel! Buzz, don't you see? We've found each other again! We can have years of happiness. You're entitled to your life. You don't owe it to Dorothy. You've given her twenty-nine years. You even left her once before. What do you think she'd do if you left her again? Kill herself?"

He spoke very quietly. "Yes, I think she would. She tried it that other time."

"But she didn't make it. People who don't succeed at suicide don't want to die. They just want attention. Anybody will tell you that!"

"I'm sorry, dear. I couldn't take that chance. I couldn't live with that on my conscience."

"So you'd rather be half alive, is that it?"

"If that's what you think it is, yes. I guess I'd rather go on living as I have than be haunted every day of my life." He took her hand. "I'm not trying to be a martyr, my love. I just know myself. I'm fifty years old. I can't chuck my responsibilities and run off like some selfish, lovesick kid. It wouldn't work."

"I hate you." It came out in a monotone.

"You probably have every right. But I didn't propose marriage to you this time, Fran. I just wanted to go to bed with you. As you did with me. I'm sorry if you thought it was a commitment."

She began to laugh. "Oh, God, this is funny! The thousands of men I've been with just for sex, and I never took one of them seriously. It had to be you I wanted to believe in! The one I thought I was in love with!" She was almost hysterical. "No fool like an old glamor girl, is there? Nothing more pathetic than a washed-up beauty grasping at straws. How marvelous this must be for your vanity, Buzz. How you'll smirk over it later!"

"Fran, don't! It isn't like that at all."

"The hell it isn't! Get out of here. Go home to your damned dependent wife and your drooling grandchildren. Dear Dorothy doesn't have to worry about me. I never want to see you again as long as I live!"

"Fran, please! Calm down!"

"I'm calm. Boy, am I calm! Calm, cool and collected, that's me. Go home, Buzz."

"I won't leave you like this."

"Why not? I'm not the suicidal type. And I know how to let myself out of motel rooms. I've done it often enough before. But surely you've already thought of that."

He got up and slowly dressed. Fran lay still, staring at the ceiling, smoking a cigarette. When he was ready to go, he came to the bed and looked down at her.

"I do love you, you know, whether you believe it or not."

Frances shut her eyes. "As we say in Gay Paree, dear boy, *merde*."

"So you came home. What's the matter? Didn't she want you?"

His wife's voice assaulted him from the living room as soon as he opened the door. Buzz pretended innocence.

"What are you talking about? You know I had dinner with Al Farmer from Detroit. I called and told you I wouldn't be home."

"Don't lie. I can't stand it. You were with Frances."

"Don't be ridiculous." He yawned. "I'm beat."

"I'll *bet* you are."

Buzz didn't answer.

"Well, how was she?" Dorothy asked. "As marvelous as ever? Better, I should think, after all the practice she's had."

"Dot, I'm too tired for another fight tonight. I'm still tired from *last night's* fight. I'm going to bed. You coming up?"

"I tried to call you at the office ten minutes after you phoned me. Charley said you'd left half an hour before. He also said Al Farmer wasn't in town."

"How could Charley know? I don't report the visit of every company executive to my salesmen! What's this all about? It isn't the first time I've spent the evening with one of the people from Ford. All right, I called you from Al's room at the Hilton. I'm sorry I didn't make it clear that I wasn't calling from the office. What was on your mind? Why did you want to reach me?"

Her voice was calm. Dangerously calm. "What I wanted wasn't important. You weren't with Al Farmer at the Hilton. He isn't registered there or at any other hotel in town. I called them all." She paused. "And then I called the Daltons. Fran was mysteriously 'out for the evening' too."

"So what? What does Fran's social life have to do with me? As for the Hilton, they were wrong. Farmer is registered there. They just screwed up."

Dot narrowed her eyes. "All right, let's call him."

The bluff wasn't going to work, but he kept on with it. Anger was his best weapon. "Godammit, Dorothy, I'll do nothing of the kind. I'm not going to make an ass of myself by calling Al Farmer just so you'll believe he's there! What do you want me to say? That my wife is checking up on me? I've told you where I was. The subject is closed!"

"No, it isn't. You were with her, Buzz, weren't you? Where did you go? To some sleazy little motel? Did you lie there laughing at me? Was she very amused when you told her how jealous I am? It must have been a wonderful evening. Was she sympathetic? So sorry for you, having to live with a neurotic, nagging wife? 'Poor Buzz.' " Dorothy's voice dripped with sarcasm. " 'Poor, long-suffering Buzz, saddled with a dreary woman who can't control her emotions. How brave and noble you are. How self-sacrificing.' I can hear it now."

"You're crazy!" It was he who was yelling while Dorothy recited her accusations without raising her voice. "You're really crazy! I never heard such a bunch of circumstantial hogwash! You're so obsessed with the idea that Fran is after me that you've put a lot of crazy coincidences together and built a case of infidelity in your mind. Just as you've done before! I've had enough of this, Dorothy! I don't want to hear any more about it! As God is my judge, if you go on with this, I'll . . ." He stopped. He was getting dangerously near the breaking point. If he kept talking, he'd tell her the truth. He'd say that he'd give anything to leave her and go off with Frances. That he was tired of being patient and responsible. That his life was mediocre and his marriage nothing.

"You'll leave me?" Dot finished the sentence for him. "Is that what will happen if I go on with this? Well, why don't you? You did before."

Buzz forced himself to calm down. "Yes, I left once before. For exactly the same reason—your hysterical accusations. I can't live like this, always suspect in your eyes, always worried that some slight deviation from my everyday pattern is going to set off one of these outbursts. We're reliving that nonsense with Stacy Donovan. It's incredible! Have all these years of psychiatry been for nothing? Are you never going to stop this paranoid behavior? Every time I make a business engagement in the evening am I going to come home to this kind of inquisition?" His voice was rising again. "How much can I take, Dot? How often do I have to prove I'm faithful? How *can* I prove it when you choose not to believe it?"

"You can't prove it because it isn't true. You were unfaithful tonight. With Frances Dalton."

It was too much. Everything was too much. He didn't care.

"All right, I was! I've been in bed with her all evening! You're right. Now are you happy?" His rage was ungovernable. "And I'll tell you something else. She begged me to go away with her and I refused! I told her I owed you too much. That I couldn't leave you because I was afraid you'd harm yourself. That I wasn't able to walk out on my responsibility to you after twenty-nine years! Yes, I made love to Fran Dalton tonight and it *ended* tonight! She never wants to see me again. She thinks I'm a spineless hypocrite. And she's right. I am because you've made me one!"

In a split second, Dorothy changed. In one of her meteoric turnabouts, the coldness turned to sniveling fear, the sarcasm became a plea for survival. Tears spilled down her face as she choked out her words.

"I don't blame you," she sobbed. "I know what hell it is to live with me. I can't help it. I've tried to be different, but I love you too much. I'm so afraid. Always. Afraid of losing you. Afraid of being alone. I know I drive you to these things, Buzz, and I hate myself for it. I'm sorry. It's my fault, not yours. It's a vicious circle with no beginning and no end."

He was filled with remorse. "No, it's not your fault. I'm the one who should be sorry. And I am. I was wrong tonight, Dottie, and I beg your forgiveness. It won't happen again. I promise you."

She nodded. "We won't talk about it any more. You got it out of your system. I'm not a child. I knew you had to. I'm almost glad you did. And I'm thankful it's over."

It was impossible to believe she really meant that, but Buzz tried to tell himself it was true. One thing certainly was true. He wouldn't be with Fran again. But only because she made it clear she had no use for him. Maybe, he thought hopefully, Dot really is becoming mature. Maybe all the therapy is finally taking and she can handle the truth better than she can cope with lies. The confession was apparently more important to her than the fact of his unfaithfulness. He didn't understand, but he gratefully accepted this "new Dorothy." He felt tenderness for her for the first time in years. Crazy. He'd just left the passionate embrace of the woman he really loved and he was feeling warmth and gentleness toward the one he didn't.

I did the right thing, he thought. Right to have told Fran I couldn't leave my wife. Right to have confessed what I did tonight. Driving home, he'd regretted the first and had no intention of doing the latter. He'd called himself all kinds of a damned fool to throw away what Fran offered, had thought perhaps she was sensible in her appraisal of his situation. He'd almost turned back to the motel to tell her he'd changed his mind; that she was more to him than his damned code of ethics. He was glad now he hadn't. Just as he was glad he'd made a clean breast of it with Dorothy. Perhaps things would change at home after this. He'd behave himself. The funny part was, despite Dot's belief, he always had, until tonight. But in the future he'd be more caring, more considerate. If Dot could forgive, so could he. Besides, she couldn't live without him. And Fran could.

It was a good act, Dorothy thought, watching him from behind her handkerchief. He really thinks I blame myself. He believes I forgive him. I hate him. I hate them both. And I'll get even.

Chapter 13

BARBARA DECIDED TO wait until after dinner when the relatives left and Sam and Laura retired before she told Alice about the call from Jack Richards. She wasn't sure how her sister would react to the news that her childhood sweetheart wanted to see her again. Or, more surprisingly, that he wanted to search for the son he'd never acknowledged. As they cleaned up the dishes, Barb tried to lead up to the subject as easily as possible.

"Kind of a boring evening, wasn't it? We do have a batch of dreary aunts and uncles. No wonder all their kids moved away."

Allie smiled and didn't answer. She just kept washing plates and putting them into the draining rack for Barbara to dry.

"I think it was rotten of Fran to fink out on us," Barbara went on. "Mother and Daddy were really upset that she wasn't here. I'm sure they didn't believe her story about running into an old girlfriend and deciding to have dinner with her. Who'd buy that last-minute excuse? Honestly, she's hopeless. I can't help loving her, but she could drive you mad! Do you think she went back to that waiter? I can't believe the whole scene!"

"You know Fran," Allie said. "She's restless."

"And selfish."

"Yes, I suppose so. But in a way I envy her. She keeps trying to find something right for her. She doesn't seem to make it, but at least she never stops searching. I give her credit for that, even if it's sometimes selfish and thoughtless, like tonight."

"You've never been selfish and thoughtless in your life, have you?" Barbara spoke slowly, wiping a platter, not looking at her. "You're so good, Allie. So much nicer than Fran and I."

Alice turned abruptly from the sink. "Bull!" she said unexpectedly. "I'm anything but nice. I'm full of hate, Barb. I hate myself and other people. I nurse grievances and I put up with things no woman with an ounce of dignity would stand for. Nice? No, I'm not nice. I'm gutless." She suddenly pulled down the shoulders of her caftan. "You need proof? Look at this."

Barbara stared at the big, ugly, purple-green bruises on her sister's upper arms. "My God! Where did you get those?"

"Where I get them all. All the bruises and black eyes and broken arms. From Spencer. From my lovely, respectable husband. This morning when I went to the hotel to get my clothes, he beat me. But only around the shoulders so nobody will see the marks." Allie's lip curled. "Nice of him, wasn't it? He probably didn't want to 'embarrass me' in front of my family. That's why he showed such 'restraint.' Otherwise he'd have kicked the living hell out of me for staying here last night instead of going home with him."

"Allie! I don't believe this! He beats you?" Barbara was horrified. "Why? Why does he do such a terrible thing?"

"Because he's sick. That's a lot easier to understand than why I've put up with it all these years." She pulled the gown back up to cover the evidence of Spencer's sadism. "That's what I mean about being gutless, Barb. Why do I stay with a man who has so little regard for me that he treats me like a possession he can abuse at will? Why have I done that for so long?"

Barbara was almost speechless. "For your children? Have you stayed because of Christopher and Janice?"

"That's what I told myself in the beginning. But that was wrong, and I recognized how wrong it was even when they were small. It's a crime to bring up children in a house full of cruelty. I couldn't hide it from them once they reached the age of understanding. I did a terrible thing to them, letting them grow up in that atmosphere. The way they've turned out proves it. Chris despises his father and God knows he has no use for marriage. He's gay, Barb. And no matter what the doctors say, I'll always blame myself for shaping his character in that direction."

"You shouldn't. Nobody's ever proved that homosexuality is a result of environment."

"And nobody's proved it isn't. In any case, it's been his revenge on Spencer. He taunts him with it. It's the one thing he knows his father can't handle."

Barbara sighed. Christopher's sexual preferences did not shock her. They didn't even dismay her, except she knew that to Allie it must represent one more proof of her failure.

"What about Janice? She must hate Spencer too."

"It's not the same with her. She despises him, but she has more scorn for me as a woman. Jan's very 'together,' as they say these days. She goes her own way and doesn't brood about things the way Chris does. She's having an affair with a young art director named Clint Darby. She seems quite happy, as long as she doesn't have to spend too much time at home. And God knows she doesn't."

All this explains so many things, Barbara thought. Allie's obvious unhappiness. The fact that she's kept pretty much to herself, only visiting Denver every three years or so, discouraging contact between us even though we live quite close. She's ashamed. She hasn't wanted any of us to know. But it still doesn't explain why she hasn't left Spencer. Her children are grown. If there was nowhere else to go, she could always come home. Why does she put up with this? She's still attractive and she's not mercenary enough to stay for the "comforts" Spencer provides.

"Why, Allie? Why don't you divorce him?"

"Good question. Why do thousands of women stay with wife-beaters? There must be a different answer for each one. Maybe some really love these bastards. And some are afraid they can't make it on their own. And I suppose a few masochists enjoy the punishment. Or think they can reform the monsters. Who knows? I only know it's not rare. I used to think it was unique with a man of Spencer's intelligence and social standing. I thought wife-abuse was something confined to the poor and ignorant. Not so. The world is full of Spencers. Rich, smart, successful men. And it's also full of Allies. Willing victims for one reason or another." She shrugged. "All I know is that the beaten must be as demented as those who beat them."

"You're not demented."

"I think I am. This started when I told Spencer about Jack Richards and the baby. He was outraged. He felt he'd been tricked into marrying a tramp. Why did I tell him, unless subconsciously I wanted him to punish me?"

"But even if I accept that, Allie, even if I accept that as the motivation, does the punishment never end? Do you pay the rest of your life?"

"I was resigned to that until I got here. Being with you and Fran again, feeling I was with people who cared for me . . . well, it started me thinking, Barb. I wish we could all have more than a week together. That we could talk a lot. About life. About our lives. Maybe I'd get the courage I need to tell Spencer Winters to go to hell forever. I think I'm pushing out of the fog. Just a little. I can breathe here. I'm almost happy. I was happier those two days before Spencer arrived than I've been in years. It's you, Barb. You and Fran. You're my sisters. And my only friends. God, it feels so good to confide in somebody! I'm sorry to burden you with this, but I've been wanting to say it ever since we all arrived. I'm not looking for sympathy. Everything I've done is my own fault. What I'm looking for is strength. Some of yours and Fran's, if you're willing to lend it to me.''

Barbara put her arms around Alice. ''Willing? Need you ask? If I can help you now, you know damned well I'll do anything. So will Fran. I know she will. She may seem self-involved, but you were right in what you said earlier: She's a fighter. And she'll fight just as hard for you as she would for herself. You can count on both of us, Allie. We'll talk a lot. You need to get this thing out in the open. Fran can certainly stay on awhile. For that matter, so can I. My boss will understand a 'family emergency.' '' Barbara smiled. ''And nobody could say this isn't one.''

Allie was on the verge of tears. ''You don't know what it would mean to me. It's horribly selfish, but I don't know when the three of us will be together again.''

''Exactly. Good Lord, we've waited thirty years for this reunion! Wouldn't it be silly to end it in a few days?''

''You're really great, Barbara I love you.''

''I love you, too, silly.'' Forgive me, Charles, she thought silently. I want to be back with you more than anything in the world, but my sister needs me. We have years to be lovers, but she has only a few days to make up her mind about the rest of her life. If only Fran will help. But she will. There's a heart under that veneer. She'll be happy to make up for some of the neglect she's been guilty of too.

That thought brought Jack Richards back to mind. Absorbed in this startling story of Allie's life, Barbara had nearly forgotten about the man who really started it. The one who claimed he was anxious to atone. Was he serious? Could he help Allie now? Or would he only complicate her life and her thinking and make matters worse?

''Allie, I've been waiting all evening to tell you something.'' Barbara took a deep breath and told her about Jack's call. Her sister's face was a study in astonishment.

''Jack wants to see me? He wants to find our child?'' Allie was incredulous. ''Why? Why now?''

''I guess he's a changed man since the death of his wife. At least that's what he says. I don't know whether it's true, but somehow I believe him. Losing someone dear to you can do that, I imagine. Make you realize how precious life is and how sorry you are for your mistakes. But it's up to you. I have his phone numbers. I told him I couldn't make that decision for you.'' She watched Alice carefully and saw an almost ecstatic look come over her face.

''Oh, Barb, if you only knew how I've wondered about that baby! If you could imagine what it's like not to know whether he's well and happy! Whether he's even . . . alive.''

''I could guess,'' Barbara said quietly.

"I've thought about him every day since they took him away. Every single day. I know nothing. Not where he went or who the people are who took him. Aunt Charlotte handled the whole thing. I just signed papers. I was so young and dumb and scared. I knew I had to give him life, but I was too frightened to keep him. Girls didn't do that in those days, you know. Society is much kinder to them now." She looked at Barbara with hope in her eyes. "Do you think Jack could find him? How would he start? Aunt Charlotte won't tell him anything. To this day she won't tell me. Says it's history and should be forgotten. I'm not sure she even knows any more."

Old bitch! Barbara thought. How dare she refuse to tell a grown woman about her own child! She's punishing Allie, just as Spencer is. I could murder both of them!

"Maybe you should give Jack a chance" she said. "I don't see that you have much to lose."

"What if he finds Johnny and my son hates me?" Alice seemed frightened by the prospect of the very thing she'd prayed for.

"Darling, he won't hate you. Nobody could hate you. But let's face the worst. Suppose Jack can find him and you discover that he resents you, that he wants no part of you? At least you'll *know*, Allie. Isn't that better than spending the rest of your life wondering?"

"Yes." The answer came slowly. "Anything is better than that."

They heard the front door open. This time Fran had had the foresight to borrow a key from her disapproving parents. Barbara and Alice went into the hall. Fran looked terrible, as though she'd been crying.

"What's wrong?" Alice asked. "Are you all right?"

"Terrific." Fran quickly put on the mask of bravado. "What are you two doing lurking around the foyer?"

"We've been talking about important things," Barb said. She glanced at Alice, who nodded confirmation. "We need your help, Fran. Feel like listening?"

"Sure. I'm a whiz at other people's problems." She laughed, a brittle, disenchanted little laugh. "Shall we get into our 'jammies and make hot chocolate and talk about boys?"

While the mother and father he had yet to meet were separately considering a search for him, John Peck decided to make his own move. The evening with Janice Winters had reinforced his belief that he was the son of Alice Dalton Winters and some unknown man. It all fitted. Not only the name but the circumstances and time of her arrival in Boston, her own mysterious, unlikely "adoption" by a childless aunt. He surmised, accurately, that an unmarried Alice had "gotten into trouble" in Denver and been packed off to the East before people discovered her condition. She'd probably been unhappy and frightened. He felt sorry for this stranger whom he was prepared to love. But what of his father, whoever he was? Obviously, the man was not Spencer Winters, who married Alice five years after she came to Boston. Had he fathered her first child, he'd have married her then and there. Whoever my father is, John decided, he must be a sonofabitch to get a girl pregnant and not marry her. Maybe the man was already married when Alice took up with him. Or, more likely, he ran out on her when he found out about me.

Jan said her father had come home without Alice. Good. That meant John could look up Daltons in the Denver telephone book and call Alice at her parents' house without Spencer Winters' knowledge. His pulse raced as he realized that within a few minutes he could possibly be talking to his mother. But what if he was wrong? What if this was yet another false lead? Carol continued to urge caution, even after the meeting with Janice.

"There still isn't much to go on, darling," she said. "I know how much you want this to be it, but I can't stand to see you get your hopes up and be disappointed again. Isn't there anything else we can do before you call Denver? Any other confirmation we can get?"

"The only other link I have is an elderly lady named Charlotte Rudolph. She's Alice's aunt. The one she came to live with when she was seventeen. She'd know, of course, whether her niece had a baby here and gave it up for adoption." John shook his head. "I doubt she'd admit anything, though. She's Mrs. Carlton Rudolph, widow of the architect. If you think 'high-toned people' like the Winters wouldn't admit to all this, can you imagine the dowager Rudolph confirming it?"

Carol whistled. "You have picked the upper crust for a family, haven't you? Carlton Rudolph's widow! Spencer Winters' wife! Sure you can't tie yourself into the Saltonstalls? Or maybe the Kennedys?"

He had to laugh. "Honey, I haven't picked anybody. You're the first one to say this might be just another pipedream. But I don't think so. I'm approaching the truth. What the hell, maybe I'll have a go at 'Aunt Charlotte' anyway. She might surprise me. And then I could call Denver with some degree of confidence."

"What will you say to her?" Carol sounded worried.

"I'm not sure. I'll have to play it by ear."

The next day he called Mrs. Rudolph's residence in Back Bay. A woman answered the phone.

"May I speak with Mrs. Rudolph, please?"

"Whom shall I say is calling?"

"John Peck."

He held on while she went to inform her employer. In a few seconds she came back on the line.

"I'm sorry, Mr. Peck, but Mrs. Rudolph says she doesn't know anyone by that name. I'm her housekeeper. Could you tell me what it's about?"

If I did John thought humorously, you'd faint dead away. "I'm a friend of her great-niece, Janice Winters. It's purely a social call. I'd appreciate it if Mrs. Rudolph would spare me a minute or two."

"Hold on, please."

There was a period of silence and then an older, higher-pitched, more querulous voice came over the phone.

"This is Mrs. Rudolph."

He literally felt his knees knocking, but he tried to sound casual.

"Mrs. Rudolph, my name's John Peck. I'm a friend of Janice's."

"I already know that," Charlotte said tartly. "What is it you want?"

"I . . . I'm looking for some information about your niece, Mrs. Winters."

"Information? What kind of information? Who are you? Some government person from the tax bureau? Or are you selling something? What is your affiliation, Mr. Peck?"

"None," John said. "I mean, none of those things. That is, it's something personal. Mrs. Rudolph, could I come and see you? This is a very private matter and I'd rather not discuss it over the telephone."

"Come and see me? I don't entertain strangers, Mr. Peck. I'm a very old lady and in poor health, and even if I were not, I certainly wouldn't open my door to someone I've never heard of. I haven't the faintest idea what it is you're after, but if it has to do with Mrs. Winters, then I suggest you call her husband. Goodbye."

"Wait! Please don't hang up! Mrs. Rudolph, it's about something that happened thirty years ago. About a baby."

There was silence on the other end. John thought perhaps she'd already hung up.

"Mrs. Rudolph? Are you still there?"

"Yes. But I'm quite at a loss. I don't know what you're talking about."

"I think you do," John said quietly. "I'm the child Alice Dalton gave up for adoption."

"You're obviously mad, Mr. Peck." But the voice was less arrogant now. John felt a surge of joy. He'd shaken her. He was right. Her tone betrayed her surprise and dismay. He pressed his advantage.

"I think we should have a quiet talk, Mrs. Rudolph. Otherwise, my next call will be to Mrs. Winters at her parents' house in Denver."

This time he heard an intake of breath. But she was admitting nothing. She simply said, "I find this all quite extraordinary! Obviously a case of mistaken identity. However, if you wish to call at five o'clock I will receive you." She paused. "And I strongly advise that you do not embarrass yourself by calling my niece. There's no need to involve her in this mix-up."

"Of course. Thank you, Mrs. Rudolph. I'll be there at five."

She hung up without another word. John stood looking at the receiver in his hand. He couldn't help smiling. Aunt Charlotte was a tough old bird, but he'd have her eating out of his hand in another few hours.

Promptly at five, he rang the doorbell of the big old house on Huntington Avenue. A competent-looking woman in a white uniform, presumably the same person he'd spoken to on the phone, admitted him and ushered him into the drawing room, saying that Mrs. Rudolph would be with him in a moment.

While he waited, John looked about him, aware that this was his first real contact with his past. This is where she lived, he thought. This is where she hid out during her pregnancy. He imagined her sitting in this room with its stiff Victorian furuiture, all dark carved wood and red velvet upholstery. He touched the three-tiered walnut whatnot in the corner, covered with silver boxes and miniature paintings on tiny easels, wondering whether Alice had wandered around in boredom, touching them too. Had she gazed at the dark landscapes on the wall, dwarfed by their ornate gold frames? Or stood in front of the oil painting over the fireplace, examining the portrait of a man with kind eyes who'd posed stiffly in his "Prince Albert" morning coat? He was so absorbed that he didn't hear Mrs. Rudolph come into the room. He almost jumped when she spoke to him.

"Mr. Peck? I'm Charlotte Rudolph."

He turned to face a tiny woman with penetrating blue eyes. She wore a plain black dress and leaned heavily on a silver-headed cane. At her throat was a cameo, and her wrinkled hands were bare except for a plain gold wedding band. My God, thought John, she couldn't be a more typical matriarch if I'd ordered her from Central Casting! He gave an unaccustomedly formal little half-bow and said, "Thank you for seeing me. I wouldn't have imposed if it hadn't been terribly important."

Charlotte seated herself in an armchair and motioned him to the facing settee.

"Would you care for tea, Mr. Peck? I don't serve hard liquor."

"Nothing, thanks."

"Very well. Shall we get on with it? What is all this about you and my niece?"

He wondered how to approach her. As briskly and impersonally as she addressed him? Or should he try to ingratiate himself, play on her sympathy, beg for her help? Not that he really needed it now. He could always call Alice directly. But it would be easier if he had the background before he confronted his mother. No. No use trying to win over this hostile old lady. The best he could hope for was a few more scraps of information. He came right to the point. He told her about discovering his adoption papers after the death of the Pecks, how he'd searched for the Alice Dalton listed as his mother, how he'd finally seen the maiden name of Alice Winters in the society column and had met her daughter Janice. He told Charlotte of the meshing of dates and places and of his firm conviction that he was the child of Alice Dalton Winters.

Charlotte listened impassively, without interrupting. When he finished, she looked almost sympathetic.

"Poor Mr. Peck. What a sad story. How dreadful not to know who one's parents are. I was not blessed with children, but had I been I'd never have been so heartless as to part with them under any conditions. Nor," she said pointedly, "would *anyone* in my family. I'm sorry to disappoint you, but once again I'm afraid your search is futile. My niece came to live with me when she was a young girl because I was widowed and lonely and I could give her advantages my sister could not. Alice was introduced to the best people in Boston and eventually married well and had two children. But I assure you, Mr. Peck, she had no children before then, and she certainly gave none away for adoption. I'm sorry," Charlotte said again. The last words had the ring of dismissal. "I do hope you'll find your mother one day."

"I *have* found her, Mrs. Rudolph. I know she's your niece."

Charlotte flushed with anger. "Are you presuming to say I'm not telling the truth? Are you accusing me of falsehoods, young man?"

John spoke quietly. "I'm afraid I am. I know you're not the kind of woman who's accustomed to lying, but in this case I believe you'd resort to that to keep an old scandal buried. I can understand. You want to protect my mother's reputation. You don't know anything about me. For all you know, I might have come here to blackmail you. But please, Mrs. Rudolph, please believe that all

I want is to meet my mother. I don't plan to make a public outcry about any of this. I won't even tell Mr. Winters, if he doesn't know. Not anyone, except my wife. I don't want anything from you. Not even recognition by the world at large. I simply want to meet the woman who gave birth to me. To know about my father and the circumstances of that birth. I've lived all these years with questions. There'll be no peace for me until I get answers. Can't you understand that?''

"All I can understand is that you indulge in wishful thinking. You have nothing to go on but a not-too-unusual name and a series of unrelated events. I've never heard such nonsense! You had best leave now, Mr. Peck. And I warn you, if you have any ideas of stirring up trouble in this family we shall take steps to stop you.''

"You leave me no choice," John said.

"And what, exactly, does that mean?''

"You can't believe that I'm going to stop now. Not when I'm so close to the answers. I don't plan to 'stir up trouble,' as you call it, but I do intend to call Denver.''

Charlotte's eyes flashed. "And just where do you think that will get you? Mrs. Winters will no more confirm this silly supposition of yours than I will!''

"I hope you're wrong about that. I hope my mother will be happy to hear from me.''

"Stop that! She's not your mother! How many times must I tell you?''

"You could tell me a million times and I'd never believe it until I heard it from her. Maybe," John said sadly, "not even then, if she's as unwilling to accept me as you are.''

Charlotte stared at him. Somehow, she'd always known one day it would come to this. It was the thing she dreaded. One read about it every day in the newspapers: adopted children looking for their natural parents. She'd always feared Alice's illegitimate child might be one of those. That he'd turn up on their doorstep, demanding his birthright.

For that matter, it hadn't been easy after the first few years to keep Alice from trying to locate *him*. She wanted to find that Richards person's son as much as he now wanted to find her. Charlotte had had to be very firm, lying even then, denying she knew the name of the adoptive parents. Alice never believed that story, of course, but she had to accept it because her aunt was immovable.

And now it was here. All the old trouble, the old disgrace. This determined young man was dead-set on injecting himself into their lives, howling for his identity as loudly as he had howled with his first breath of life. Charlotte tried one last time.

"Look here," she said pleasantly. "I understand your obsession with your problem. I'm sure you're honestly convinced you're on the right track. But you could create some very upsetting gossip that would distress Mr. and Mrs. Winters. And to what avail? I assure you, Mr. Peck, my niece is not your mother. Why, after all this time, would I deny it if it were true? My heavens, it's so many years ago! If my niece had had you and given you up, there'd be no reason for her not to admit it to you. I'd admit it to you myself. Times have changed.

She's a middle-aged woman with grown children of her own. She's perfectly safe and secure, much too firmly entrenched in society to be bothered by a youthful indiscretion," Charlotte paused to let the next words sink in, "*if it were true*. But it isn't true. If you pursue this, you will force Mrs. Winters into a public denial which will be unattractive for her and humiliating for you. Take my word for it, Mr. Peck, and drop this whole pathetic idea."

"I'm sorry, I can't. I don't wish to embarrass anyone, least of all my mother, but I won't stop now."

Charlotte became angry again. "You've accused me of not telling the truth. Very well. I now accuse you. I think you know very well that this is a complete fabrication. You probably have read about Spencer Winters and somehow managed to meet his daughter. You have the ridiculous idea that you can blackmail us by threatening ugly publicity. You mentioned that very word when you arrived. Blackmail. I don't know why it took me so long to understand why you're really here. It's money you want, isn't it? You're nothing but a low, conniving thief! I should call the police. That's what I should do. But that would make distasteful headlines. That's what you're counting on. All right, Mr. Peck, or whoever you are, I'll give you money. I'll give you a check for a thousand dollars right now and you'll sign a paper saying Alice Dalton Winters is no relation to you. Then you'll go away and never bother us again."

John rose from the settee and stared down at her. She was a good bluffer but she'd overplayed her hand.

"Thank you, Mrs. Rudolph, for making that offer. You've finally told me what I needed to know."

Charlotte watched him walk out of the room. Too late, she realized her mistake. Offering money when she had no need to was all the confirmation John Peck needed that he'd stumbled on the truth. What an old fool she was! How could she have fallen so easily into a trap! Spencer Winters would be furious. He might not let Alice ever see her again. And Laura would be so upset that the secret was out after all this time. Heaven help her, what had she done? Why did she ever agree to see Alice's child? I'm too old for this, she thought. Too old and too tired. She crouched over like a frightened animal and wept with regret and frustration.

Chapter 14

IN HIS BEDROOM in Washington, Charles Tallent threw a clean shirt and a change of underwear into an overnight bag. Andrea watched him calmly, leaning against the door in that appraising stance he knew so well.

"I'll be back tomorrow night," he said. "It's only a two-hour flight, but the Candidate wants me to stay over."

"Do you think the rumor's true that he's going to offer you the job?"

Charles shrugged. "Secretary of Agriculture? I don't know. He's just interviewing possibilities. But you can't say he's not confident. Not even elected and he's already picking out his Cabinet."

"But he will be elected."

"Probably. All the polls point to a landslide."

"You'd be a very important and prominent man," Andrea said. "You'd have to change your lifestyle. Drastically."

"I don't see why. I'm already a public figure."

"Oh, Charles, for God's sake, stop acting! I'm not the only one who knows about your little Georgetown love nest. I'm sure the future President is well aware. In fact, I'm amazed he's even considering you. I hear he's going over possible appointees with a fine-tooth comb, looking for any *hint* of political or personal scandal. He can't afford to take chances. He's not going to name a man whose private life won't bear scrutiny."

Dammit, Charles thought, I've been wondering the same thing ever since I got the call. He must have heard about Barbara. It doesn't square with his pious image to choose a cabinet member with a mistress. It's probably just routine, this meeting. I don't have a chance. I'll be led to believe I'm "under consideration" because he wants my support in the House, now and later. That's all this is. Just window dressing. But I won't admit that. Not to Andrea, who must be getting great satisfaction out of knowing that my "outside interest" will do me out of something I'd give anything to have. She wouldn't mind being a Cabinet Wife. But she probably is enjoying her revenge even more.

"Well, we'll just have to see what the Senator has on his mind, won't we?" Charles sounded almost disinterested. "I'm sure as hell not flying to the Cape for a yachting trip at this time of year."

"Too bad you aren't meeting him in Denver."

Charles ignored her.

"I know where she is," Andrea went on. "I always know where she is. You've been home early every night for almost a week, so it's a fair guess your lady-love is not available. But I don't even have to guess at such things. Miss Dalton's landlady and I have become very good friends. She's quite meticulous about reporting to me. For a price, of course. She's a greedy, vulgar little woman, but she does have good eyes and ears."

He was furious. "That's disgusting! Spying on me as though I were some criminal! What for? You've known about this for years! I haven't lied to you. I haven't ever publicly embarrassed you. Why would you do this to Barbara?"

"Why would she do what she's done to me? *She's* had no scruples. Why should *I*? One day, my dear Charles, I'll get some information that will open your eyes. Believe me, I'll bet your precious paramour is not the faithful lover you imagine. No woman in her right mind would put up with that kind of situation forever. She'll stray. You'll see. And I'll be the first to know. And the most delighted to tell you."

"You miserable . . . ." Words failed him.

"It's a little absurd for you to play the injured party, isn't it? You're going to pay for the years that I've swallowed my pride and pretended to be above it all. What a pity your wonderful Miss Dalton is visiting her parents right now. It deprives you of the chance to strut like a peacock in front of her, instead of having only me to tell that the next President of the United States is interested in you." Andrea laughed. "Not that he is, of course. We both know that. This is a political ploy. You have too many strikes against you, Congressman. You'll flunk Agriculture. And every other important offer in your life. Because of her. I hope she's worth it.''

On the plane, Charles still felt the sting of her words. She was right, of course. He'd worried, every election, that some word of Barbara would get to his constituents back home. But it never had. Anyway, his people loved him. Even if they heard it, they'd never believe such gossip.

The Cabinet post was another matter. The Candidate had no blind devotion. He dealt in facts. Hard facts. And the fact was that even though Charles Tallent might be the best man for the job, he'd never get it while Barbara Dalton was in his life. Not Charles's qualifications nor his personal popularity would make the hard-nosed Yankee Senator lay himself open to criticism about the caliber of men he chose to surround him. But he must know, Charles thought again. What could he have in mind?

He found out within an hour of his arrival at the big old sprawling New England house where the Candidate rested briefly between his nonstop campaigning. The Senator and his wife and their five children greeted him cordially and then he was conducted to the study. His host offered him a drink and chair in front of the fireplace, where a bright blaze crackled more for atmosphere than for warmth on this October afternoon.

The nominee of his party smiled companionably, asked briefly after Andrea and then got right to the point.

"I'm going to be elected, you know."

"Yes. I have no doubt."

"Neither have I. That's why I want the team ready. From the Vice President all the way down."

Charles felt his heart leap. Tom Schneider was the vice-presidential candidate, but none of the "team" had been named. Wouldn't be until after the election, of course, but The Man was a planner. Between now and January, he'd act as though he were already elected and inaugurated. Every detail in place. The smoothest victory and transition the country had ever seen.

"Very wise of you," Charles said. "Gives you time to find the best people for the top posts."

"Exactly. I'd like you in one of those posts, Charles. Agriculture, I thought. That's where your strength is. With the farmers. You'd be a good Secretary."

Before Charles could answer, his companion went on. "You leave the rest of your competitors in the dust as far as political savvy is concerned. But there's something else. Something the press would jump on. Something that could embarrass both of us. I don't have to spell it out, do I?"

Charles reluctantly shook his head.

"Lovely girl, Barbara Dalton. Always found her amusing when we met at parties. But she's bad news for you. That's obvious. Hell, Charles, you're not the first man in government who's been indiscreet." He smiled. "Between us, there were a few incidents early in my life that I wouldn't exactly want publicized either. We all sow the proverbial wild oats at one time or another. The point is we can't still be sowing them when we go into high office. People will forgive the past, overlook the little indulgences and human weaknesses you've put behind you. Assuming they find out, which we'll try to avoid. But even if there's talk, it wouldn't matter a helluva lot, as long as the affair was over." He paused. "Unfortunately, it's not over, is it?"

"No."

"But it could be? If something really big came along?"

Charles hesitated. "I don't know whether you understand. This is not some fly-by-night thing. It's a long-standing relationship. Andrea knows about it. She and I haven't been man and wife in years. We only stay together for the sake of the children. I love Barbara. I'd marry her tomorrow if I could." He stopped. "What if I did? What if I got a divorce and married her?"

The Candidate frowned. "No good. Too late in the day. Too obvious. It's not a divorced man I'd object to. We've had a lot of those high up in government. But they don't get divorced and quickly marry another congressman's secretary just before a new President appoints them to the Cabinet. That would cause worse talk. No, Charles, that won't work. The post is yours if you want it. But it comes with the image of a long-time devoted husband and father. We'll try to keep the other thing quiet. The press has been damned good to you in the past. But you were only a congressman. This is something else. We'll hope it won't come up when we announce the appointment, but if it does, there won't be one bloody thing to link you now to another woman. They can speculate, but as long as you're clean they can't prove anything. I assume Miss Dalton could be counted on to keep her mouth shut? She seems like a decent girl."

Charles said nothing for a moment. Then, "Yes. She's a very decent girl."

"Good. Then it's worth the risk in order to have you with me. Assuming, that is, you want the job."

"I want it very much. I'm complimented that you want me, but . . ."

"But it's a high price to pay, giving up the lady? Yes, I suppose it is. It depends on where a man's priorities lie. What he hopes for in his own future. You're still comparatively young in this business. No telling where you could go in, say, another eight years."

"There's no way we could resolve this? Are you sure the divorce idea isn't practical? My children would get over it, and Andrea doesn't give a damn."

"No, the timing's wrong. Good Lord, man, you know the press! I couldn't have this coming down around me at this particular time! Every nervous housewife in the country would blame *me* for your leaving your family and marrying your mistress! Sorry, Charles, but it's either/or. A big political future without Barbara, or damned little future at all."

Charles was torn. "Can you give me a little time to think? This means a great deal to me. All of it. The appointment and Barbara."

"Sure. I'm sorry to be unfeeling. Sometimes it's tough to be a realist. But look at it this way. Maybe after a few years, when you're well-established in the new job, you *can* get a quiet divorce, wait awhile and marry again. It won't attract so much attention then." The Senator was compassionate enough to lie. "I know it's difficult, but I need a decision before you leave tomorrow."

"Yes. Of course. Thank you very much."

"I hope you'll make the right one, for both our sakes."

In the guest room Charles paced back and forth. Giving up Barbara was unthinkable. But so was refusing this great chance. "A few years " the Candidate said. What a laugh. As though Barbara would wait a few years, never seeing him. No. If he accepted the offer it was finished with the woman he loved. He couldn't imagine life without her. He couldn't bear to think how crushed she'd be. But she'd understand. She'd want this for him. She'd never stand in the way of his future. He might even be President. The Senator had hinted about "eight years"—implying that one day it might be Charles standing on that platform, listening to the cheers, accepting the party's acclaim. If only it could be Barbara and not Andrea standing next to him. But it couldn't, wouldn't be.

He knew his decision had been made even before he left the study. Andrea will be delighted on many counts, he thought bitterly. It solves all her problems. And she'll enjoy knowing what it cost me.

But what of Barbara? How can I face her? Can she understand that ambition sometimes is more compelling than love?

I'll fly out to Denver tomorrow, he decided. I've got to be man enough to tell her face to face, but I'm not strong enough to do it when we're alone in her apartment. There are too many memories there. Too many tender reminders of all the years. I couldn't stand saying goodbye to her in that dear, familiar place.

In the morning I'll tell the Senator I accept his offer. And I'll phone Andrea and tell her I'm going to Denver. And why. I don't give a damn what kind of fuss she makes. She's finally won. The Candidate has won. The loser is Barbara. And probably me.

The "loser," unaware of her impending loss, looked serious as she brought Fran up to date on the evening's developments. Allie sat quietly as her younger sister recounted the unexpected call from Jack Richards and her older one listened intently.

"So, he wants to find their son," Barb concluded. "He wants to see Allie again. He sounds like a changed man. Like he has a lot to make up for."

"You better believe it," Fran said. "More than a lot! But why the hell should he use Allie to purge himself of his sins? Why at this late date? For God's sake, it's been a closed chapter for a hundred years! Who needs him now? Him and his long-overdue remorse! I never heard such garbage! Tell him to get lost! Men! Always thinking of themselves! They don't give a damn how their actions affect anybody else as long as *they're* happy! If Allie sees Jack Richards again, she's a bloody fool. As for that crap about finding their 'long-lost child,' that's a convenient excuse if I ever heard one. He's probably bored and lonely and looking for a little heat from an old flame. I know the type. Probably thinks she's still in love with him, still wants him. And all *he* wants is some temporary action!"

Barbara stared at her, remembering the way Fran looked when she came home a few minutes earlier. She's not talking about Allie, she's talking about herself. Barbara was certain of it. Was it Buzz? Had Fran seen him tonight? Maybe made a play for him and been turned down? That's what this was all about. It had nothing to do with Allie and Jack. She opened her mouth to accuse Fran of voicing her own cynicism, but before she could say a word, Allie spoke up.

"I know you two are trying to help, but I get the feeling that I'm not in the room, the way you're discussing my problem. Look, my dears, it is *my* problem.

I have to make the decision. I don't mean to sound ungrateful, but you're turning this into a debate, as though I can't speak for myself.'' She smiled. ''I can, you know. You're both so strong, so sure of yourselves. I'm a mouse, but I can squeak when I choose to.''

The quiet voice temporarily silenced her sisters. Then Barbara said, ''I'm sorry, Allie. You're absolutely right. We are talking about you as though you aren't here. I guess . . . I guess Fran and I are seeing this from our viewpoints rather than yours. That's wrong, of course. Our attitudes aren't necessarily yours. What do you want to do about this?''

''I'm going to call Jack tomorrow.'' Alice's tone was firm. ''I do want to see him. Wouldn't you want to see someone you were once desperately in love with? Even if it was 'a hundred years ago'?''

Fran reddened. It was as though they knew about her and Buzz. What a complete ass she'd made of herself, throwing herself at him, sure he'd jump at the chance to leave his wife for her. And how humiliating it had been to be rejected. She shut her eyes, as if to blot out the memory of that scene in the motel room. It never happened, she told herself. I didn't mean any of it. I wouldn't have that stupid little car salesman on a bet! But she would. He seemed to represent all that was solid and sane in a world gone berserk. And he *was* solid and sane. So much so that he'd never get mixed up with her again. He's smart, Fran thought bitterly. He knows what he has. He's not going to take a chance on what he might get. He must have sensed her desperation and recognized it for what it was: the reach for the last chance; fear of loneliness, not love of him. She glanced at Barbara, who seemed equally thoughtful. What's Barb's life really all about? she wondered. In its own way I suspect it's as precarious as mine. Allie's wrong about one thing. She's as strong as we are. Stronger, maybe.

''Okay,'' Fran said, ''so you're going to see him. What then?''

''I don't know. Nothing, probably. Between us, I mean. But if he can help find our boy . . .''

''Oh, Allie, darling, don't count on that!'' Barbara was distressed. ''See him if you want. But don't hope for miracles about the other thing.''

''I live on hope,'' Allie said. ''I have for years. Hope that that baby is now a happy man. Hope that my other children will always be all right.'' An edge of bitterness crept in. ''I've even hoped that one day Spencer will change. Or that I will.'' She turned to Fran. ''I told Barb tonight what it's like to live with a man who beats you for any reason or for none at all. That's been my life for twenty-five years, Fran. Always in fear, always waiting for the unpredictable. Hiding the evidence, pretending my husband isn't psychotic, hoping, hoping he'll change. Or that I'll finally find enough courage to be done with it. I've been totally faithful to Spencer. I haven't so much as looked at another man since the day we got engaged. But this trip has made some kind of difference. Seeing Mother and Dad. Seeing you and Barb. Feeling cared about. It's renewed me. Strengthened me. And maybe seeing Jack will help restore some of the self-esteem I haven't had since I was a girl.''

Fran hardly heard the last part. ''Beats you? Spencer Winters beats you? And you stand for it?'' As Barb had been, Fran was horrified, outraged. ''Why, Allie? For God's sake, why?''

"It's too long a story for now. Let's just say he's a sick man. And I'm pretty mixed up myself to live with his sickness."

Fran took a deep breath. "You're not counting on Jack Richards to save you, are you? That's storybook stuff, Allie. The knight in armor riding in on the white charger to rescue the maiden in distress. Maybe you ought to settle one problem before you take on another."

"I told you I don't expect anything significant to happen between Jack and me. Nothing permanent or even momentary. But I do believe in fate, Fran. There must be some reason for his coming back into my life after all these years. Maybe our son is the reason. I don't know. I just know I'll see him, and whatever will be, will be." Allie gave an embarrassed laugh. "You must think I'm crazy, both of you. Talking about predestination. But I do believe in it. For all of us. I think heaven and hell happens right here in our lifetime, and that everything was meant to be." She sobered. "If I didn't believe that, I couldn't exist."

"Maybe so," Fran said. "But whoever drew up my plan was a lousy architect. And from what you've said, Allie, and from what I suspect about Barb, they should have gone back to the drawing board when they were mapping out our lives."

"Things could always be worse," Barbara said. "Bad as they may be, there are always people with more terrible troubles. Fran, nothing's perfect."

"Tell me," Fran mocked. "Listen, kid, I wasn't twenty years old before I discovered *that*. I've lived my life with one comforting piece of knowledge: There's always a broken window in the Taj Mahal."

The flippant remark broke the tension. Suddenly they were laughing, momentarily forgetting their disappointments and disillusionments, locked together in the warm and comforting embrace of womanly understanding. The same thought was in each mind: They're my sisters and they'll stand by me, no matter what.

It was a precious realization.

Upstairs, still awake in her bed, Laura Dalton heard the beautiful, sudden sound of her daughters' laughter. What good girls they are, she thought sentimentally. Warm and loving and devoted. True, they were not "dutiful" in the accepted sense. It was embarrassing sometimes to explain to friends why her children came home so seldom. Why, indeed, her eldest hadn't returned, until now, since the day she left. Why her youngest managed only an annual visit and her middle girl came to see her parents so infrequently. For that matter, it really was inexplicable. Not unique, perhaps, but rare, especially when families had not had an obvious "falling out."

She couldn't say to the world that Sam had virtually banished Alice and that the old wounds had never really healed. She couldn't admit that Frances had run from a "middle-class existence" of which she did not wish to be reminded and that she might never have come back if there'd not been a Golden Anniversary. One that Barbara had probably bullied or shamed her into attending. And Barbara herself was so involved with her congressman and her glamorous Washington life that she couldn't be expected to spend much precious free time in Denver, doing nothing.

I understand, the mother thought. And then, almost angrily, No, I don't. Why do I think of them as "devoted"? Because they send occasional letters and gifts and phone now and then? They're not devoted. Not the way other children are. They don't really want to see us. They stay in touch out of duty. Or, she shuddered, pity. They've made lives without us. Without our help or our approval. Almost in spite of us. They give us nothing. We seem more ancestors than parents.

Immediately, she was ashamed of herself. Those were the thoughts of a self-pitying, aggrieved mother. The stereotype of the deep-sighing, neglected parent. She had no right to think that way. She and Sam had no claims on these women simply because they'd given them life.

We gave them damned little else, Laura thought. We fed and clothed and housed them, but we didn't think it necessary to really know them or let them know us. We stayed aloof from them as human beings, even while we smugly assumed ourselves to be "good parents." We expected love. We didn't know we had to earn it.

And knowing that, they left us, not only physically but emotionally. Why *should* they come home? Because it's expected of them? Because it's the thing children are supposed to do? Where is it written that one must frequent scenes of boredom? We bore our children. She smiled at the unconscious little play on words. I bore them and we bore them. But it wasn't funny. It was sad. Parents and children should be friends. There should be a desire to see each other, to exchange ideas, compare worlds, have adult-to-adult conversations. But such congeniality was a two-way street, she told herself. And Sam and I know only one way.

It would be different, she supposed, if one of us were alone. If she died or Sam died, the girls would feel oblgied to pay more attention to the survivor. But that was wrong too. They're not responsible for us, Laura mused. I hope neither of us makes them feel that way, because we are as much to blame for the separation as they. Early on, they invited us to visit and we never did. Sam didn't want to. He felt they should come home. I suppose I did too. I'm as bound up as he in the conventional attitudes. I grew up in an age when respect was demanded and the elders received it. Or thought they did. Did I respect my own parents? Maybe not. Maybe not really. I never thought about it. I was so thoroughly conditioned to "honor" them that it never occurred to me it might be nice to like them as well.

And when my children were born, I made sure that Sam's parents and mine saw them often. "Duty calls." Aptly titled. We dutifully took the girls to see their grandparents. They probably hated it. Maybe that's why Alice doesn't insist her children come to see us. And of course Sam and I are too stiff-necked and thin-skinned to go and see them.

So, year after year goes by and I talk of my family and sometimes brag about them and always pretend I'm so "modern," that I accept their absence without hurt or question. But I don't. I wish I were more interesting to them. I wish we could share. I'm a little in awe of them, I suppose. All so efficient and poised and in charge of their lives. I wish they felt me worthy to enter the doors behind which they live.

The laughter stopped and she heard the sound of them coming upstairs, the whispered goodnights, the gentle closing of the two bedroom doors. Where was Fran earlier tonight? Why is Allie staying on without Spencer? What will become of Barbara if that married man leaves her one day? Where are my daughters headed in this life? So many questions. So few answers.

Sam snored loudly at her side. Lucky man, Laura thought. No nagging doubts nibble at his mind and disturb his dreams tonight.

Chapter 15

SPENCER WINTERS WAS still seething when his flight got into Boston's Logan Airport. The past two days had been full of surprises, and he didn't like surprises. They threw him off stride, took control of the situation out of his hands and Spencer didn't care for that. He hated it when it happened in the courtroom. When some unexpected witness for the prosecution appeared or some damned fool jury brought in an unlikely decision. Things were supposed to be predictable. Of all things, his wife was supposed to be. And she hadn't been, last night or this morning.

He felt his anger rising again as he remembered Alice's calm declaration, the night of the party, that she was staying at her parents' house. It had been humiliating to leave alone. She'd made an ass of him in front of other people, and even though there was no one there Spencer gave a damn about, he was still furious with her for that. This morning, he'd given her a little taste of what to expect when she came home. And she'll be home, he thought grimly. That uncharacteristic burst of independence won't last. She can't stay away from her precious children, for one thing. And for another, how would she get along? He'd not give her a red cent. She'd tire pretty quickly of living in her parents' run-down house without a penny to spend. God knows that dreary father of hers couldn't afford to support her. The man probably had a couple of hundred dollars a week, if that. And Alice wasn't likely to go back to work either. At her age, what would she do? Sell at the Denver Dry Goods? Hardly. After twenty-five years of luxury, she was far too spoiled.

Ungrateful bitch! She should be on her knees thanking God that a decent man had married her. Instead, she'd openly defied him at the hotel when she'd come to collect the few things she had there. He suddenly realized how few there had been. Allie had left most of her clothes at her mother's. She'd never intended, right from the start, to spend a week at the Hilton. She knew damned well he wouldn't stay in Denver, and all along she planned to be there without him. She was some actress! All that carrying on about his leaving early! Pretending she was disappointed he intended to go home the day after the party! She knew he would. She was hoping for it.

Well, she got her wish. And a few nice fat bruises to remind her that disobedience would not be tolerated. She'd get worse in a few days, when she came crawling back. Spencer would not soon forget the things she said the morning he left.

He'd started raising hell that morning, the moment she walked into the hotel room. He was still furious that she hadn't come back with him the night before, that she'd had the temerity to say he should tell J.B. to go to hell!

"You filthy little nobody!" Spencer had said. "How dare you behave as you did last night! Making a spectacle of me! What did those people think when I went home alone, a man whose wife preferred to sleep with her sister!"

Allie was dismayed to find he was still in the room. She thought he'd left. The desk said he'd paid his bill. "I don't think people noticed, Spencer." She tried to remain calm. "There was nobody there you cared about. Nobody important to you."

"That's not the point. Your place is with me."

"Why?" Her voice was flat.

Spencer was incredulous. "Why? Because, God help me, you're my wife. That's why! Because you belong to me. Because, like it or not, I own you."

"You really believe that, don't you?"

"You bet I believe it! I more than believe it: I *know* it! Every dress you put on your back, every mouthful of food you eat is thanks to me. Every person who knows you accepts you because you're Mrs. Spencer Winters, and don't you ever forget it!"

"I've never been allowed to. Not in twenty-five years" Her calmness only added to his anger. "You're going back to Boston with me this morning. Call your mother and tell her to pack your things. We'll pick them up on the way to the airport."

Allie stared at him. "Yesterday you said I could stay as long as . . ."

"Never mind what I said yesterday! Yesterday my wife was behaving like the dutiful, respectful woman she's supposed to be. Today I've changed my mind. I don't want you hanging around out here, letting those sisters of yours put ideas in your head. Oh, I know what happened. Don't think I'm a fool, Alice. They've encouraged you, those tarts! And you're so stupid you listened to them. I suppose you've told them everything about our life. About our pansy son and our immoral daughter. I'm sure you've even told them about our fights, without explaining that you deserve what you get!"

"I've told them nothing!" Alice's face was becoming as flushed as his own. "I'd be ashamed to tell them I'm married to a sadist. I'm not ashamed of our children, but I'm mortified for you. What kind of a man hits a woman? Any woman? And *deserve* it? My God, Spencer, even you can't believe you're entitled to beat your wife!"

He'd approached her then, his fists upraised. "It's the only thing you understand— a good whipping. You don't have brains enough to accept reasoning. Yes, I have a right to hit you anytime I damn well please because it's the only way to knock any sense into your head! Like now. You're going home. Willingly, if you're smart. Forcibly, if you make it necessary!"

Alice backed away. "No, Spencer. No, I'm not going. I'm staying here for a while. Long enough to decide what I should do."

He came closer. "It's not for you to decide. Do as I tell you."

"No." She was trembling, trying to step away from him, hopelessly looking for escape from the room. If only she could get to the door. But he'd come after her, follow her down the hall, maybe knock her around out there where anyone could see and hear. "No," she said again, placatingly. "Please, Spencer, let me stay. You said I could. I just want to visit with my family awhile. I'll come home in a few days. I promise. I didn't mean all that about deciding what I should do. I need a rest, that's all.''

"I'll give you a rest! In the hospital by God, if you don't stop this nonsense!''

He'd backed her up against the wall. She saw his clenched hands come down with terrible force, striking her shoulders. She covered her face tried to remain upright, but the strength of the attack knocked her onto the bed. She lay there; trying to shield herself as he struck her again and again on her upper body, accompanying every blow with a filthy word; calling her every kind of ugly name. She could only sob in pain and terror until he stopped. Then he straightened up and looked at her with disgust.

"That's all you know how to do, isn't it? Whimper and snivel. You misemble excuse for a woman! Beating's too good for you.''

Abruptly he turned away and picked up his overnight bag. Allie lay on the bed crying quietly, feeling the soreness begin in her arms and shoulders and yet also realizing a strange sense of victory. This time I won, she thought. I stood up to him for what I wanted. This time even his violence couldn't make me obey. Maybe I can make it, with the help of Barb and Fran and Mother. Maybe I never have to go back again.

She said nothing, nor did he. An almost unbearable sense of relief came over her as Spencer left, slamming the door behind him. She lay still for a few more minutes, fearful of his return, but nothing happened. At last she rose and slowly, painfully, packed her small bag. I could never tell them what he says to me, Alice thought. I couldn't use those words. But I'll tell my sisters about his cruelty. And I'll ask their advice. There must be some other way for me to live. I'm entitled to a life as free and independent as theirs. Coming back here has made me see things in a different light. I'd forgotten there was a world in which Spencer Winters is not king.

Spencer hailed a cab at Logan Airport and was home in a few minutes. To his surprise, Janice was in the living room.

"Well! To what do we owe this unexpected honor?''

His daughter smiled casually. "Hi, Dad. Just dropped in to pick up a few clean clothes. What are you doing home? I thought you were going to stay longer. Where's Mother?''

"Your mother is still in Denver. I permitted her to stay on for a few days.''

"You *permitted* her?'' Janice snorted. "My God, you make her sound like some kind of a galley slave! Why don't you get with it, Pops? It's nineteen seventy-six. Husbands don't *permit*; they *respect*. She's a person, too, you know. Not a possession of yours.''

"Don't call me 'Pops.' It's vulgar. As for the rest of your ridiculous conversation, Janice, I choose to ignore it. You're a silly child who doesn't understand a mature relationship.''

"I would if I saw one. I never have, around here.''

It was too much. First Alice defying him and now this impertinent girl telling him how to handle his own wife. Damn women anyhow! Damn all this new independence. He hated the way the world was going. He was only following the rules he grew up with in his own parents' house: Wives were submissive, and if they were not, they occasionally got a cuffing to keep them in line. Children were seen and not heard, and unfailingly respectful of their elders. Daughters were obedient and sons manly. The values he cared about and believed in, including the domination of the home by the father, were threatened, and Spencer Winters was infuriated by the knowledge.

"Janice, be quiet! I won't be spoken to that way!"

She grinned. "Aye, aye, sir. Yessir, Captain Bligh. Anything you say."

He wondered why he loved her. She was the only thing he did love. And yet she mocked him, ridiculed him, offended his "sense of decency" in every way. Spencer sighed.

"I suppose you're off again right away. You wouldn't consider having dinner here with me tonight?"

"Sorry, we can't. Clint and I are busy."

"I didn't ask Clint."

"Oh? I just assumed it. We come as a pair, you know. A matched set, like bookends." Janice was enjoying his discomfort. "When's Mother coming back, by the way?"

"I'm not sure. In a few days."

"How was the party?"

"You should have been there."

"It was that good, huh?"

"No, but it would have been respectful for you to show up."

"Hell, Dad, I hardly know those people! I wasn't about to fly all the way to Denver for a hokey reunion with some relatives I don't give a damn about."

"*I* did."

"Okay, I'm sorry." She smiled winningly. "You were a good sport to go. I'm sure Mother appreciated it."

He relaxed a little. "Anything happen around here?"

"Not much. Aunt Charlotte called a few minutes ago. She was looking for Mother. I reminded her you planned to stay a week. She'd completely lost track of time. She really is dotty, you know." Jan looked at him speculatively. "By the way, why didn't you stay? You and Mother have a fight?"

"Your mother and I don't fight, Janice."

"Oh, no, Dad. Neither does Muhammad Ali."

Shuffling through his phone messages, he pretended not to have heard. "Did your Aunt Charlotte want anything special?"

"I haven't a clue. She just said Mother was to call her as soon as she could. That it was urgent."

"I see. Well, maybe I'll give her a ring later and see what's on her mind. I know neither you nor your brother has checked in. There was a note when I was in Denver, saying you hadn't."

"Oh, for God's sake! She must have written it before Mother boarded the plane! I was going to call her tomorrow. Honestly, she's impossible!"

Charlotte sounded even more distracted than usual when he got her on the phone.

"Alice won't be home for a few days," he said. "Is there something you need?"

"No. That is, well, not really. I mean . . . Oh, dear, Spencer, I do think I've done something frightfully unwise." The moment she said it, Charlotte knew she'd made another mistake. She hadn't intended to tell Spencer anything about that upsetting visit from John Peck. Quite the contrary. She'd simply wanted to secretly warn Alice that the young man intended to make trouble. And now she'd given Spencer an opening he'd surely pursue until she told him the whole story. He'd be so angry with her, the way she handled it. Why was she so stupid! I'm old, Charlotte thought defensively. My mind doesn't work as quickly as it should any more. She heard her nephew-in-law's impatient intake of breath.

"All right, Aunt Charlotte, what have you done? Alice isn't here, so you might as well tell me."

She's probably done something idiotic, like firing the housekeeper, Spencer thought. Old fool! As though it wasn't difficult enough to get servants of any kind these days, and nearly impossible to find one willing to live in with an eighty-year-old woman. Why the hell didn't she answer him? He could hear her nervous breathing on the other end of the line.

"Aunt Charlotte? What is it? I asked you what you've done."

"Nothing, Spencer dear. Nothing important. It can wait until Alice comes back. No need to trouble you."

"I'm not sure exactly when Alice will be back." He was beginning to sound annoyed. "Now, you wanted something, surely. Otherwise, why the urgent call?"

She tried to think of a reasonable evasion but she was too upset. "It's John," she said. "He's looking for Alice."

"John? Who's John? What are you talking about?"

Once started, she blurted out the whole story. Spencer listened, trying to make sense out of the rambling account. For a moment he was too surprised to be anything but incredulous, and then the full impact hit him. Alice's goddamn illegitimate brat had turned up! He'd somehow found out where his mother was! And this ninny had thoroughly fumbled the situation, offering him money to go away and keep quiet, confirming that he'd stumbled on the truth! Spencer could have cheerfully wrung her neck. He tried to control himself. Tried to think how to handle it. It was too late for recriminations but he couldn't resist them.

"What on earth made you do such a damned-fool thing? Why did you receive him in the first place? Don't you realize how embarrassing this can be for all of us? My God, have you any idea the trouble this can cause?"

She'd begun to weep. "I know, Spencer. I knew you'd be angry. I was so frightened when he called. He sounded . . . evil. He was. He was threatening. I was in fear of my life!" She began to embroider the picture of a menacing, desperate man. "I . . . I thought a person like that would take a thousand dollars and go away without harming me. For all I knew, he might have had a gun!" She was whining now. "I'm an old, unprotected lady. Facing someone who might kill me. Don't you see, Spencer? I was terrified!"

"All I see is that you're even more stupid than your niece! How could you have made such a mess of things?"

"I'm sorry. I wish I'd gone to Denver! This never would have happened to me!"

To you, Spencer thought. Who the hell cares what happens to you? It's the future I'm thinking of. What will people say if they find out Alice has a bastard child? What will J.B. think? He'll think my wife is a whore. And he'll think me crazy for having married one. It's not fair. I've worked so hard for that partnership, and with a man like J.B. this could blow the whole thing. He won't tolerate scandal. None of us can forget how he fired Tyler Parke when he found out Parke's wife was an alcoholic. "Bad for the firm's image," J.B. said. Jesus! What will he make of this?

Be calm, Spencer told himself. Maybe you can solve it somehow. Think, man. There must be a way out. He forced himself to sound composed.

"All right, Aunt Charlotte. It's done. It can't be helped. What we have to do now is make sure this John Peck leaves us alone. He didn't take the money, is that right?"

"No." Her voice was almost a whisper.

"Too bad, in a way. I might have been able to threaten him with extortion. Scare him off with the idea of a criminal charge. But he's too smart for that, obviously. He's gambling for higher stakes."

"I think he just wants to find his mother," Charlotte said meekly.

"Don't be naïve! He thinks he's blundered into a good thing. We're not even sure he is who he claims to be. What proof does he have? Unfortunately, that's even less important than the trouble he threatens to make. It's the publicity we don't want, and he knows it."

"He said if he could just see Alice he'd never tell anyone."

Spencer turned sarcastic. "And of course we should believe him. He's just a poor little waif searching for his long-lost mother! Doesn't want a thing out of it except a kiss from her! Really, Aunt Charlotte! Even you couldn't swallow that!"

"I think I have to hang up now, Spencer. I'm feeling quite ill."

"Wait! Did he say where Alice could reach him?"

Charlotte searched her memory. "No. I don't think so. But there was something else besides the thing he read in the paper. Now, what did he say that made me think . . ."

"Try to remember! It's important that I have every detail."

"Just give me a minute, Spencer." There was a pause. "Oh, yes, I believe he mentioned Janice when he telephoned. Yes, he did. He said he was a friend of hers."

Spencer was stunned. "A friend of Janice? Are you sure?"

"Yes, quite sure. He began the conversation that way."

"But he didn't give you his address or telephone number. You're positive."

"No, he didn't. Perhaps Janice knows."

"We'll see. All right, Aunt Charlotte, I guess that's it for now."

"I'm so sorry, Spencer," she said again.

"You bloody well should be."

In his characteristically methodical way, Spencer went to his desk in the library and organized his thoughts on a yellow legal pad. In his precise handwriting he wrote on the left side of the page "Possibilities" and on the right "Solutions," numbering each:

POSSIBILITIES
1. Peck may be a fake.
2. P. may be A.'s child.

SOLUTIONS
1. Make him prove he isn't.
2. Have A. disclaim him. Tell J.B. we're being blackmailed.

Under this, Spencer made another heading:

PROCEDURES AND ALTERNATIVES
1. Inform Alice immediately.
2. Find out from Janice who P. is.
3. Say nothing and find him myself.

He studied the list carefully. Too bad this isn't a gangster movie, he thought. I could have a "contract" put out on this goddamned John Peck and end the thing forever. Sometimes the underworld had the right idea: move swiftly and silently and expeditiously to get rid of your enemies. He thought of Peck as an enemy. A threat to Spencer's well-ordered life and carefully planned future. Of course, murder was out of the question. Reason or, if necessary, threats would have to prevail with Peck. And force with Alice.

He realized he instinctively believed this intruder was his wife's child. God knows what the man actually said to Charlotte. Probably more than she remembered. He considered his options, immediately discarding the idea of telling Alice anything now. He was equally reluctant to question Janice. Perhaps she already knew about it. It seemed certain she did, if the man really was a friend of hers. Of course, he might not be. He could have also made up that part of the story if he'd "researched" the Winters family. He could have read Janice's name somewhere as easily as he'd read Alice's. But if that were true, how had he made the connection to Charlotte Rudolph? No. Peck knew Janice, all right. Not that that proved anything. How much does Janice know? Spencer wondered. She takes such pleasure in tormenting me. Maybe she knew all about this even while we were talking today. Maybe she was laughing inside, knowing what I'd hear when I called Charlotte. Damn that girl! I won't give her the satisfaction of asking her help. Not unless there's no other way.

He reached for the Boston telephone directory. There was a long list of "Pecks" and a number of "Johns" and "J.'s." I don't even know whether he lives in Boston, Spencer thought. He could be in a nearby town. Andover. Lexington. Concord. Anywhere they circulated the Boston *Globe*. I'll just have to assume he lives here. Tomorrow I'll have my secretary start calling every "J. Peck" in the book. She won't have to know what it's about. I'll simply have her ask for the gentleman who contacted Mrs. Rudolph.

If that doesn't work, I'll have to go to Janice. And I'd better move quickly. Peck said he was going to call Alice in Denver. I hope I can stop him before he does that. She'd be sentimental and crazy enough to see him, probably acknowledge him. It wouldn't matter a damn to her how that would affect me!

He paced angrily through the empty apartment, nursing the rage he felt once again at having been "tricked" into marrying what he thought was a virgin. What a young fool I was! I could have had any girl I wanted and I chose this one because I found her exciting. Exciting! You bet she was exciting! She had enough experience to know how to be. Good thing for her she isn't here right now when all this dirty business has come full circle. Yes, a damned good thing she isn't. I think I'd kill her.

Chapter 16

SHE WAS AS nervous as an animal in a windstorm. During the night, after the talk with her sisters and Allie's incredible admission of the abuse she took from that no-good Spencer Winters, Fran impetuously decided to leave Denver early. Get away from all of them. They made her feel so obligated: Allie with her marital problems, and now this business with Jack and the child; Mother with those damned haunting eyes that seemed to see right through her; Dad with his pathetic acceptance of old age. Even Barb, who had whispered to her on the way upstairs, "We may have to stay on a few days longer, Fran. Allie needs us."

The only one who didn't make her feel duty-bound was Buzz. He'd made her feel foolish, and that was even worse.

She'd lain awake until all hours, smoking cigarettes in the dark, thinking about them. And this morning she knew she wanted to run and wouldn't. Not from the family. Not from a man who'd rejected her. The nerve of him, that two-bit auto dealer! Men didn't do things like that to her. Ironically, she'd never felt about one as she did about Buzz. She wondered if, after all these years, she'd fallen in love for the first time. Idiotic fancy! And yet she'd never been so depressed over any lost lover. Perhaps because none had ever so gently but firmly pushed her away. His firm but tender dismissal only increased Fran's desire. She felt trapped and unable to free herself.

It had been almost dawn when she fell asleep, and after eleven when she woke. Barbara had written a note and shoved it under the door.

> Fran, dear, Allie spoke to Jack this morning. I'm driving her over to
> meet him. Borrowed your car. Hope it's okay. The Parents know *nothing!*
> (They've gone marketing.) See you later. Luv, B.

More nonsense! Fran thought. If Alice wanted to meet her old boyfriend, why on earth did she drag Barbara along? Obviously, Jack couldn't come here, but why didn't Allie drive herself? She probably needed "moral support." That was an apt phrase. Demure little Alice, the "weakest" of the three, turned out to be the one with the juiciest problems. God knows her pregnancy out of wedlock and her sordid married life were more dramatic than Fran's affairs and divorces. Probably more than Barb's life, too, whatever it was. Her "baby sister" was tantalizingly close-mouthed about her life in Washington. Well, I haven't gone into much detail about my own, Fran thought. Before we scatter, it would be interesting to swap stories. Who knows? It may be years before we see each other again.

The deserted house seemed shabbier than ever, its worn oriental rugs and frayed old furniture mercilessly spotlighted by the morning sun that streamed through the windows. Fran wandered out to the kitchen. They'd left coffee on the stove for her. While she drank it, hot and black, her mind went back to Buzz. He'd be in his office now. Was he thinking of her? Did he regret throwing away that second chance she'd offered? It would be easy enough to pick up the phone and find out. You can't really believe he doesn't want you, can you? she asked herself. No, she answered. I can't. I don't take kindly to defeat.

En route to Jack's apartment in Stoneybrook, Barbara chattered nervously to a silent, introspective Alice. "Every time I come back I remember so many things we all did together. It's amazing what stays tucked away in your head. Like 'special occasions' when Mother took the three of us to lunch at Daniels and Fisher's tearoom. Remember what a treat that was? These day's Mother goes to lunch at The Lookout Room at The May Company D and F, out in University. Once a week. With her 'girlfriends.' I think they even sneak a cocktail." Barb shook her head. "We grew up here a million years ago, didn't we? Everything's changed. Even the elm trees have died off from some kind of blight. . . ."

"Barb," Alice interrupted.

"Yes?"

"I know what you're trying to do: distract me. Get my mind off this meeting. Thanks, honey, but it really isn't working. I'm scared out of my mind. Even hearing his voice this morning gave me a sinking spell. I was so in love with him once. I'd have done anything for him." She gave a little laugh. "In fact, I did."

Barbara concentrated on the highway. "You were too young, Allie. Both of you. You made a mistake you couldn't handle. You can't go through life torturing yourself for it."

"I suppose so. I haven't had to. Spencer's done that for me."

They were silent for a moment and then Allie said, "I wonder what Jack is like now. He sounded the same on the phone." She looked at her sister. "Do you think I'm wrong, Barb? Going to see him, I mean? I don't know what I expect of this visit. I know he can't find our baby. I really do know that, in spite of what I said. I understand why he wants to see me. I guess that whole business has weighed on his conscience all these years. You wouldn't remember, but he behaved abominably. He lied to me, promised everything would be all right. What a dumb little thing I was to believe him! I was so disappointed in him I thought I hated him, but I never have. There's something about the first man in your life you never forget. Not even when he's also your first disillusionment. Women. We're such sentimental fools." She brushed at her eyes with the back of her hand. "Good Lord, I hope I don't start bawling when I see him! I mean to be calm and collected. I keep trying to imagine how Fran would handle this."

Barbara half-smiled. It was such a naïve statement. Fran would never find herself in such a spot. She'd always been too self-protective to be vulnerable to the kind of "sweet talk" that had been Allie's undoing. Fran was born knowing it all, Barb thought. I'm sure she was selfish in the sandbox. "You'll handle it better than Fran would," she said reassuringly. "You'll be yourself. Here's the turnoff to Stoneybrook. What was that number again?"

Allie consulted the little slip of paper in her hand. "South Yosemite Street. 8675. Apartment 108."

They pulled into the driveway and Barb switched off the engine. "Sure you don't want me to wait for you in the car? I don't mind. It might be easier for both of you if there's no third party present."

Something like panic came into Allie's eyes. "No! Please, Barb. You promised you'd be with me."

"I will, of course. I just thought . . ."

"That I'm a grown woman and should be able to handle this alone. I know. I am a grown woman. I shouldn't need support, but I do."

"Okay. You've got it."

They crossed a little stone path and climbed a flight of wooden steps to the front door of number 8675. The condominiums were more like small houses rather than apartments, each one with a "front porch" and an outside entrance. Alice hesitated for a fraction of a second and then rang the bell. The door was opened almost immediately and she stood looking up into the handsome face of Jack Richards. He's so much older! she thought involuntarily. The silly reaction made her smile. Of course he was. What had she expected? That nineteen-year-old who'd made love to her in the back seat of his car? He must be going through the same shock. But there was nothing but pleasure in his face as he reached out and took both her hands in his.

"Allie. I can't believe it. I'm happy to see you." The voice was the same. So were the clear brown eyes, though there were little crisscrosses of lines at the outer edges of them. He'd put on some weight and there was a touch of gray at the temples. But he hasn't really changed that much, Alice realized. He still has the magnetism that fascinated me from the day we met.

"I'm glad to see you, Jack. You're looking well."

"So are you. You haven't changed."

She was still smiling. "You're very gallant, but I know better." She gently extricated her hands. "You remember Barbara."

For the first time he noticed the other woman. "No! Not that kid who always wanted to tag along!"

Barb laughed easily. "If you say I haven't changed, I'll scream. Last time you saw me I had pigtails and braces on my teeth. But I'm still 'tagging along.' How are you, Jack?"

"Fine. Just fine. Come in, please. Both of you. This is wonderful!"

They followed him into a spacious apartment, the airy living room set three steps below the foyer. It was lovely, painted white, furnished with soft, flowered chintz sofas and chairs, the walls hung with delicate paintings and exquisite framed petit-point designs. Beyond, they glimpsed a small dining room and stairs leading to the bedroom floor of the duplex. It was all simple and cheerful and in impeccable taste.

"What a charming place!" Barbara said.

"It's nice, isn't it? Lucy was very talented. She did the paintings and the needlepoint herself." He spoke calmly but there was an undercurrent of pain. "I suppose it seems a little out of character for a man's apartment, but I haven't really wanted to change it."

No, of course you haven't, Alice thought. Lucky you. You must have been very happy here with your Lucy. "We were so sorry to hear . . . about your wife."

They were seated now, Jack and Alice on the couch, Barb in a chair pulled up beside it.

"Thank you. It was rough. She was so young. And she suffered so much." He stared at the floor. "She made me ashamed of my weakness. I was the one who fell apart when we knew she was dying. She was more concerned for me than she was for herself. You'd have liked each other, Allie. In many ways she was very like you." He looked up. "I told her about you. About the child. She always wanted me to get in touch with you, see if we could locate the baby. She couldn't have any and she'd have loved to have adopted mine. Ours." He stood up and began to walk back and forth. "I didn't think it made sense, so I didn't do anything much about it. Oh, it was easy enough to find out where you were. I hired a search outfit for that. But when I heard you'd had a boy and given him for adoption, I gave up. I figured it was too late." He stopped pacing. "No. That's a lie. The real truth is I wanted to forget the whole thing. I've always been so ashamed of the way I acted when all that happened. I couldn't face you. Not until Lucy died. That made me take a hard look at everything. It's what I told Barbara on the phone. I'd like to right some of the wrongs. I know you're married and have other grown children. I have no one. I was hoping I could find the son they made you give up, maybe make up to him now for what I should have done thirty years ago. Will you help me, Allie?"

She looked stricken. "I can't Jack. In the early days I tried to find out where he'd gone, but I never could."

"But there must be a way! He's grown now. He surely wonders who his parents were."

"I don't know," Allie said. "I don't even know whether he's alive."

"Of course he is! He has to be! Allie, I'll spend every nickel I have trying to find him. Tell me everything you know. Any clue may help us."

She shook her head. "I don't know much. He was born in Massachusetts General in Boston on November tenth, nineteen forty-six. He was a big beautiful boy and I named him John. After you. I only saw him once, right after he was born. They never let me see him again. I don't know where he is or even what he's called." Alice's eyes filled with tears. "Oh, Jack, why now? Why didn't you come for me when I needed you so?"

I can't stand it, Barbara thought. I don't belong here. Why on earth did I agree to come? I'm an intruder. It's indecent for me to be in the same room with these people who are torturing themselves and each other. They were oblivious of her presence, but that didn't help the way she felt. Quietly, unnoticed, she slipped out of the apartment and went to sit in the car. When she left, Jack and Allie had their arms around each other, she crying on his shoulder, he trying to comfort her.

It was almost an hour before he brought Alice out to the car. They were both red-eyed and subdued. And they were all embarrassed.

"I'm sorry, Barb," Jack said. "We didn't mean to make you uncomfortable."

"I shouldn't have come. It's too private a matter."

"It was my fault," Allie said. "I apologize, Barbara."

There was an awkward pause and then Jack helped Allie into the front seat. "Call you tomorrow," he said.

"Yes."

"'Bye, Barbara. And thank you for bringing her."

"Goodbye, Jack."

They drove for five minutes without saying a word. At last Alice said "I'm sorry I put you through that. I wasn't thinking how it might be for you."

"It's okay. It was dumb of me not to realize it myself."

"I told him everything, Barb. All about Spencer and me. He . . . he wants me to leave Spencer. He wants to marry me. He says we'll find Johnny."

Barbara almost drove off the road. "Are you serious? He's still in love with you? He wants you to marry him?"

"Is that inconceivable?" There was a faint smile on Allie's face. "Am I that far over the hill?"

"No. Of course not! But, my God, Allie, you were only together for an hour or so after all these years! He's a stranger, really. Isn't it a bit much to talk about marrying a man you haven't seen since you were a girl? You don't now anything about him. Not what he is today, I mean."

"I know as much about him as he does about me. But I haven't said I'm going to marry him. I just said he wants me to. Barb, dear, you know I'm much too timid to make such an important decision on the spur of the moment. That's the kind of thing Fran might do, but not me." Despite her quiet protest, Allie seemed more serene than she had since her arrival. "I'm going to see him again, though. Tomorrow. We have a lot of talking to do."

"Allie, he can't find your child. You must remember that."

"I know. I don't expect him to. For once I'm thinking of myself. Funny. I've felt all along there was some big purpose for this trip. Something made me stand up to Spencer for the first time in my life. It's as though I knew this was coming. Maybe it's a chance, Barb. Another chance."

"I hope so, dear. If that's what you really want."

"I don't know. I don't know what I want."

As the cab sped along the highway that skirted the Potomac River and wound its way past the Lincoln Memorial and up through Rock Creek Park toward his home, Charles Tallent thought he must be the world's most easily persuaded man. First it was the Candidate who made it all sound so logical and sensible to sacrifice his personal happiness for his eareer. Then it was Andrea on the phone, cool and dispassionate, pointing out that it would be unkind to Barbara to tell her in Denver that their affair was over. His wife had discussed the matter as clinically as though she were analyzing the problems of a stranger.

"If you have any feeling for that woman," his wife had said, "you won't humiliate her in front of her family. My God, Charles, you don't have an ounce of sensitivity! What makes you think it's right to burst on the scene out there and announce it's all over when her family probably doesn't know the whole thing exists? I hold no brief for Barbara Dalton. I should be the last to care how she feels. But if I were in her shoes, I certainly wouldn't want to be publicly renounced.''

"I wasn't planning to do it in front of the State Capitol,'' Charles said bitterly.

"No. You're just going to fly into town unexpectedly and call her. You'll meet in some bar and tell her. Terrific. What do you expect her to do? Go home, smiling bravely? I hate the woman. But I'd give my worst enemy a better shake than that.''

He'd wavered. It was weird. Why should Andrea give a damn for the feelings of her husband's mistress? He'd expected her to be angry that he planned to fly to Denver, but he'd not been prepared for this unlikely consideration of Barb's feelings.

"I don't get it,'' he said. "Why this sudden compassion?''

"Perhaps I know how it feels to be a victim,'' Andrea said. "Or maybe I can afford to be magnanimous in victory. Whatever. I simply know how any woman would feel in that situation. You'd be rotten to do it that way, Charles.''

Maybe she's right, he'd thought. God knows she has no reason to want me to postpone telling Barb. Quite the contrary. There must be a little milk of human kindness in her, a little sympathy for the woman who's been her enemy all these years. She's won. She has me back. She'll be a Cabinet Wife. She's picked up all the marbles. I suppose she feels sorry for Barbara, in a superior way. I don't understand the working of the female mind. If the tables were turned, I'd want her to rub the other man's nose in this kind of rejection.

"I think I owe it to her not to let her read about the appointment in the papers. The Senator will be making an announcement. She's been around Washington long enough to know what that means for us.''

Andrea sounded very patient. "Charles, you know he can't announce his Cabinet until he's elected. Presumably she'll be home long before. There'll be a more suitable time and place.''

"Why do you care?'' he asked again. "I can't understand your concern. Frankly, it isn't like you. Hell, it isn't like any woman!''

"I told you. You don't understand us. Come home, Charles, before you make a fool of yourself, as well as her.''

He'd reluctantly agreed, ashamed to realize he was grateful for a reprieve. There'd be no announcement for a few weeks. Meantime, he'd figure just the right words to say to Barbara. Thank God he'd made her financially secure. Not that she'd prefer a trust fund to him, but it was some consolation to know she'd be all right for money. Maybe it was all for the best. What kind of life was it for her, tied to a man who'd never marry her? Maybe some unselfish part of him had always known this was better for her. He simply didn't have the strength to let her go. It had to be taken out of his hands. Like a guy who doesn't have enough guts to kill himself and wishes someone would murder him. They'd done it for him, the Candidate and the Party. They'd probably done Barbara a kindness in the long run. He had to believe that. He loved her so much. But he supposed, human nature being what it was, he might even have come to resent her if he'd turned down this opportunity for her sake. I'm too old for idealism, Charles told himself. I've passed the stage where a man renounces everything for love. The bitter, ugly truth is that the only ultimate satisfaction is Power. It's been called the greatest aphrodisiac, and, God help me, it is.

I've pulled it off! Andrea was triumphant as she hung up the telephone. Charles was so weak, so manageable, so stupid, really. All he'd have to do is be in the presence of that woman and he'd probably change his mind about accepting the post. Barbara was smart. She'd use everything she had to talk him out of it if he went to see her. I know I would, in her place. This time, Andrea Tallent was going to outsmart her. Outsmart them both. Charles had been gullible, willing to believe she cared a hoot in hell about his mistress's feelings. How could he have fallen for that? Easy. He wanted to. There was a flash of unsettling comprehension. He was delighted to be off the hook, even temporarily. I gave him a way to postpone doing what he dreads. It really was funny in an unfunny way. Andrea frowned. She could end up outsmarting herself. By the time that bitch got back to Washington, Charles would have figured out some way to keep her *and* the job. He was no fool after all. Right now he was confused, upset, snowed by the Senator's flattery. He was ready to call off his affair and she'd stopped him. She'd been wrong. She should have let him go to Denver while he was fired up by the excitement of the big offer. Nothing Barbara could have said would have changed his decision. She saw that now, too late. But who knew what could happen when he'd gotten used to the idea of becoming Secretary? She'd given him time to scheme. Damn! The strategy she'd decided on when he said he was going had been a mistake. But she couldn't call him back and say she'd changed her mind. Not after the "humane" case she'd made.

He mustn't have a chance to think it through, and that's just what I've given him! He'll manage to keep Barbara tucked away somewhere, out of sight of the new President, away from the prying eyes of the press. When he's mulled it over, he'll never give her up. I blundered, Andrea thought. I acted on impulse, not reckoning with power of time to clarify things for Charles and let him get the whole situation in perspective. I can't let him spend these next few days figuring out how to get around a sticky situation. Because he will. I know he will. Unless I move first.

She went to her desk and pulled out a scrap of paper. Barbara's landlady had obligingly given her the forwarding address her tenant had left. Unhesitatingly, Andrea selected a piece of her personal notepaper and began to write.

"Buzz? This is your impetuous, headstrong friend."

The call surprised him. He'd been certain, after last night, that he'd not hear from her again.

"Hello, Fran. How are you?"

"Embarrassed. I don't usually make a fool of myself."

"You didn't. You were being sweet and honest. It was a wonderful few hours. I'll never forget them."

"Neither will I. I didn't mean it all to get so heavy." She laughed, a self-conscious little laugh. "I came on too strong. I guess I got carried away. Old longings. That kind of thing. Anyway, I called to apologize and tell you how much I admire you. You're terrific.''

He didn't answer for a moment. Then, ''No need for apologies. It was something we both wanted.''

''Yes, I suppose it was, but I almost wish it hadn't happened. What you haven't had, you can't miss.'' She paused. ''Oh, hell! There I go again. Sorry. I'd better quit before I make things even worse. 'Bye, Buzz. Take care.''

''Fran! Wait! Don't hang up!''

''What is it?''

''Look, we shouldn't leave it this way.''

''Do we have a choice?''

''Yes. Now that we both know where things stand, it would be different. For both of us. A few more hours while you're here, that's all. We're entitled to that.''

She pretended to hesitate. ''I don't know . . .''

''Please! We're not hurting anybody.''

''Well . . .''

''I'll be at the motel at six. Will you?''

''Yes,'' Fran said. ''I'll be there.''

Chapter 17

''I SUPPOSE I have to tell Mother and Dad.''

''Don't see how you can avoid it.'' Barbara parked Fran's rented car in front of their parents' house and sat still for a moment, looking at Alice. ''I don't know why you should even worry about it. It's not nineteen forty-six. You're not a kid living under their roof. For heaven's sake, you have a perfect right to do anything you please with your life, including marrying Jack Richards, if that's what you decide you want.''

''I know. Childhood hang-ups are hard to get rid of. Wouldn't it be nice if you could send old guilts out to The Thrift Shop, like old clothes?''

''You bet. We'd all have a helluva tax deduction. But I don't think it'll be as grim as you imagine. Dad may still harbor a grudge against the Richards family, but Mother doesn't. She told me so.''

''She did? When?''

Barbara repeated her earlier conversation with Laura and a smile of relief came over Allie's face. ''I'm so glad. It'll make things easier.''

''Easier still if you told Mother and Dad the truth about the way Spencer treats you.''

Alice shook her head. ''I don't want them to know about that. Why upset them any more than I will now? Spencer has nothing to do with this.''

''Like hell you say! If you had a happy marriage you wouldn't give Jack a second thought. And if they knew what you'd been living through all these years they'd have nothing but sympathy for this situation. They don't know anything about your life, Allie. They barely know Chris and Janice. And even though they've been tactful about it, I'm sure they're hurt and disappointed that your children didn't come out for their anniversary. To tell you the truth, I'm curious about that part myself.''

"I didn't encourage them," Alice said, "Jan didn't want to, but Chris would have. He'd really like to know his grandparents.''

"Then, why on earth didn't he come with you?''

"He and Spencer don't get along. Besides, I was afraid Mother and Dad would suspect.''

"Suspect what?''

"What he is. Oh, he isn't flagrant about it. I mean, he's not a stereotype. Anything *but*. He's strong and very manly. I don't suppose the casual observer would know, but I was afraid to chance it.''

Barbara was silent.

"I'm not ashamed of Chris," Allie went on. "I simply wouldn't want him or Mother and Dad or anyone to be embarrassed. I don't think the folks would understand. They haven't been exposed to that kind of thing.''

"It does bother you.''

"Of course it bothers me! My God, Barb, I'm only human. And I'm a mother, with a mother's natural instincts. Don't think I'm blithe about it. I've accepted it because it's his choice. Who has the right to decide what's 'normal'? Not I, of all people. No 'normal' woman would go on living with a wife-beater. No, I don't condemn Chris, but I do condemn myself. I told you before. Nobody will ever convince me that what he saw and heard at home didn't turn him off marriage forever.''

"Did it turn Janice off too?''

"Maybe. She's too thick-skinned to admit anything bothers her, but how could she not be affected? How could any child not react to such an environment?''

"Allie, you mustn't blame yourself.''

"Oh, but I must! I've done everything wrong all my life. I'm a born loser, Barb.''

"Don't be ridiculous!'' But even as she said it, Barbara reluctantly agreed. Allie did seem to make one mistake after another, always seemed to get the short end of things. Barbara wondered what the outcome of this reunion with Jack Richards would be. They didn't know him any more. What kind of man was he? As warm and kind as he'd seemed a little while before? Or was he playing some kind of game with Allie? The world had gone crazy. All this, and Fran's odd behavior and no word from Charles. None at all.

"We'd better go in the house," Allie was saying. "If they saw us arrive, they'll be wondering why we're sitting in the car so long.''

"Right. You plan to tell the family right away?''

"I guess so. Why postpone the inevitable?''

They found Laura and Frances having a cup of tea in the kitchen. Sam, fortunately, had gone back to his garden. It's better this way, Allie thought. Mother can tell Dad. I won't have to, God, I am "chicken''!

Fran looked up knowingly, a hundred questions in her eyes. But it was Laura who brought them to the subject.

"Well, where did you girls run off to? Fran said you borrowed her car for

Behind her mother's back, Fran silently mouthed, "I didn't say anything."

Allie took a chair at the table. "Mother, I have something to tell you."

Throughout the recital, Laura listened carefully, not interrupting.

"He wants to find our son," Allie said at the end. "He . . . he thinks we should get married."

Her mother exploded. "Married! Allie, you *are* married! What are you saying? My dear child, don't go searching for the past. You have a different life now . . ."

"A lousy one," Fran interrupted. "Mother, you don't know what Allie goes through with that maniac! He beats her, for God's sake! He's sadistic! Do you want her to stay with that?"

Laura's eyes widened. "Is that true, Alice?"

"Yes. I didn't want you to know. I'm terribly unhappy with Spencer. I have been, almost from the day we married. He's a sick man, Mother, just as his father was. He thinks of a wife as a possession he's entitled to abuse."

"And you've lived with that all these years? Oh, Allie, why? Why didn't you come home long ago?"

"I was ashamed. Also, soon there were the children to think of. And I wasn't sure you'd want me, after the disgrace I brought you."

Laura sighed. "We knew there was something wrong with your marriage. Your father and I sensed it. But in our wildest imagination we never pictured anything as terrible as this. My poor baby." She went around the table and hugged her daughter. "How can we ever make it up to you? If it hadn't been for us, these awful years wouldn't have happened."

The roles reversed, Alice began to comfort her mother. "You're not to blame, neither you nor Dad. You did what you thought was best."

"We were so wrong, so terribly wrong." Laura returned to her chair. "Don't go back to Boston, Allie. Stay here with us. Your children are grown and independent. You've been through enough. At least we can offer you peace."

"That's what Jack promises me." Alice gave a little laugh. "I don't know. I don't know whether I want peace. Maybe I don't deserve it."

Barbara jumped into the conversation. "That's crazy talk! Snap out of it, Allie! You've worn the hair shirt long enough. Mother's right. Stay here, at least until you decide about Jack. You can't go back to that life in Boston."

"Seems like I can't go back to any life. Mother says I shouldn't search for the past. What's here for me except the past?"

"How about a future?" Barbara asked. "That could be here, with or without Jack Richards."

Allie didn't answer.

"Do you still love him?" Laura's voice was gentle. "If so, Allie, you should go to him. I was wrong about searching for the past. Maybe you can find it together. You've both suffered so much. Perhaps it's the Lord's will that it comes out this way."

"I'm not sure how I feel about Jack. I don't want to use him as an escape from Spencer. That wouldn't be fair. And I don't want to be influenced by the hope of finding our son. I don't know. It's all so mixed up in my mind. I can't bear the idea of going back to Spencer, but I don't want to be separated from

Chris and Janice, either. They're my life, Mother. Just as we're yours. I don't want to leave them the way we left you."

"Your situation is quite different," Laura said. "You can't compare this separation to ours."

"I suppose not. I just don't want to hurt innocent people. Chris and Janice have their own lives, and yet I know they count on me. At least, I like to think so. Spencer and I gave them such a rotten childhood. They hate him. I don't know why they don't hate me, but they don't. In a funny way, they need me as much as I need them."

"I'm with Barb," Fran said. "You're talking crazy. Your children are adults. You're not deserting a couple of innocent babes. Good God, Allie, are you going to be martyred the rest of your life? It's dumb. Really dumb. The only thing to think of is yourself. Haven't you spent enough time repenting? What the hell do you think you are, some kind of saint? Stay here. See Jack Richards. Go to bed with him. Find out if the old magic is still there. And stop being such a pious bore!"

"Frances!" Her mother was shocked. "Don't talk to your sister that way!"

"Somebody had better talk to her that way," Fran said. "All this hand-wringing and sympathy aren't what she needs. What she needs is a damn good shaking up. A nice big jolt to make her see how stupidly she's behaved for years!"

"I won't have you say such things to her!"

"She's right, Mother," Allie said. "I have been stupid. My thinking is as warped as Spencer's. I wanted that punishment. I'd almost come to think of it as a way of life. Until I came here and realized how happy I was without him. I'm not going back. Not for a while. Maybe not ever. I'll explain it as best I can to Chris and Jan. They'll understand."

Barbara took her sister's hand. "What about Jack?"

"We'll have to see. I think Fran's advice is good." Allie smiled. "I've already had one affair with him. Why not another?"

Laura looked unhappy. "I don't know whether that's the answer Allie."

"Neither do I. But it's positive action for a change."

"Your father . . ."

"Will blow his top." Alice finished the sentence for her. "He won't have to know just yet. What's the point in upsetting him? We'll skip the gory details about Spencer, and we don't have to tell him anything about Jack. We can just say I've decided to stay on here for a while, can't we?"

"I don't know, dear. Your father is more aware than you might imagine. We'll have to give him some explanation."

"All right. We can say I'm unhappy with Spencer, without going into the sadistic part. And I won't let Jack come near the house."

"Denver's a small town in its way," Laura said. "It's bound to come out if you start seeing Jack."

"Not if we don't appear in public." Alice was suddenly filled with confidence. "I feel so free! Just thinking of the miles between here and Boston makes me happy. To be with my family. To have a breather. You can't imagine what a relief that is."

"You're safe here, darling," her mother said, "and welcome for as long as you want to stay."

"It's not going to work, you know," Fran said to Barbara when they managed a few minutes alone. "Grown-up daughters can't go back to living under their parents' roof. There's the conflict of two women, each used to running her own house. They'll drive each other mad in two weeks."

"Then what's the solution? She can't go back to Spencer."

"She could be on her own in some other city, the way you and I are."

"Fran, you know that's not possible. How would she live? You have money from an ex-husband and I have a job, but Allie isn't trained to support herself and she hasn't a nickel of her own."

"Then Jack Richards could keep her. What the hell, she doesn't have to marry him, she could just move in."

"Dad would die! Even Mother would have a fit! Allie 'living in sin' right under their noses? No way!" Barb paused. "Anyway, she's much too conventional for that. She's not like me."

Fran raised her eyebrows. "Am I to infer from that that you're being kept in Washington? And I thought you were the poor little working girl only Heaven is supposed to protect!"

"I'm not. Not being kept, I mean. But I've been involved for a long, long time."

As she had to her mother, Barbara confided her affair with Charles Tallent. When she'd finished, Fran sat back and looked at her.

"You're a bigger damned fool than any of us. Giving up your life for a guy who can never marry you? What kind of half-assed idea is that?"

Barbara's indignation made her sarcastic. "I didn't realize you were so moral! At least I don't go around picking up waiters for one-night stands!"

"That's a helluva lot smarter than tying yourself up permanently in some impossible situation."

"Look who's stumping for holy matrimony! It hasn't seemed to work out so well for you."

Fran laughed. "Touché. But that doesn't mean I don't believe in it. Listen, my little friend, no matter what you hear, marriage is still the most desirable state for women. It's convenient and comfortable. I know a lot of couples are living together without benefit of clergy these days. Fine. I wouldn't object if you were doing that, openly, but you aren't. You're playing second fiddle, Barb. You have all the disadvantages of marriage and none of the benefits. Hell, I wouldn't care if you didn't marry your congressman if you could live with him and be accepted. It's the dreary little catch-as-catch-can life that's such a nothing. You get the scraps from Mrs. Tallent's table. You're too damned good for that. I thought Spencer Winters was a selfish beast, but this one is worse. He's just plain greedy. And you're a dope."

"You don't understand," Barb said. "Charles often tells me how unfair this is. I'm the one who won't let go."

"Okay. Have it your way. Just be braced for the kiss-off when it comes. It always does in these deals."

"Not in this one," Barbara said stubbornly.

"Sure. You'll be the Romeo and Juliet of the geriatric set."

"How can you be so cynical? I'm sorry for you, Fran. I don't think you've ever loved anyone in your whole life."

"You know, I think I would have bought that until a couple of days ago." The tough mask dropped and Frances was suddenly soft and appealing. "Barb, I'm in love with Buzz Paige. We were together last night and we're going to be again tonight."

"Oh, no! Fran, you can't! I said it before: You'll get him crazy for you and then take off. That's terrible!"

"I don't mean to take off. Not alone, that is. I'm taking off with Buzz when I go."

"You're insane! His wife won't divorce him. I'd bet on it. Do you realize what you're saying? You're planning the very thing you've been criticizing me for: living with a married man."

"Wrong. He'll get a divorce and marry me. He doesn't think so now, but he will. But, okay, let's say he couldn't. I'm still better off than you. I'll be with him full time, not sneaking a few hours here and there. It won't be a secret, the way your affair is. We can have friends, go out together, be a 'couple' even if it's not legal."

"I don't believe he'll do it. He has too much integrity."

"Oh, come on, Barb! You sound like Buzz. He thinks that too. But I know something he doesn't: His strongest urges are not in his head. He's found something he won't be able to give up. Believe it. I may be forty-nine, luv, but I know how and where to hook a man. Just watch me."

"That's despicable."

"No, pet. That's life."

While she made conversation with her parents and her sisters the rest of that day, Barbara's mind was far away. Strange she hadn't heard from Charles. Why so strange? she asked herself. She'd been away only a few days, and he probably was wildly busy. Why was she making so much of this? It was an uneasy feeling. Almost a premonition that something was wrong.

Damn Frances! she thought. She and Mother make me think about things I don't want to dwell on. I know all the disadvantages of relationships like Charles's and mine, and it's still worth it. It was just that, at times like this, she wished she could call him at his office. But she'd have to give her name before the secretary would put her through, and it was foolish to be so indiscreet. Not that they didn't all know anyhow, no matter how careful she and Charles tried to be. But it still seemed ill-advised.

I'll hear soon. I'm sure of it. If I don't, I'll write to him, a letter marked "Personal," to say I'm staying on for a few more days. Barb realized she hadn't informed her own office of this change of plan. She'd better call in. For a few minutes she hesitated. She wasn't sure why she was staying on. It was pointless, really. There was nothing more to be done for Allie, now that she and Jack had gotten together. Those two adults could work it out.

She allowed her mind to drift to Jack Richards and her sister. It would be strange if they got together after all these years. Stranger still if they could locate their child. But more peculiar things did happen. Barb smiled, remembering what she'd told her mother about her schoolgirl crush on Allie's beau. It had been odd, seeing him again. She was almost as nervous about it as Allie. And he hadn't been a disappointment. He'd become an enormously attractive man, better looking now than he'd been in his youth. She felt a small pang of envy that Jack still worshiped Allie, that he wanted to marry her. Nobody wants to marry me, Barb thought.

What nonsense! Why am I feeling sorry for myself? I don't want to be married. Don't you? a little voice inside replied. Wasn't there a moment earlier today when you wished it was you Jack Richards loved?

The disloyal thought shocked her. How could she even entertain such an idea? She loved Charles. And Jack belonged to her sister. He wasn't interested in her now any more than he'd been when she was nine. It was Allie he wanted, and Barb was sure Allie ultimately would decide to marry him. That was probably as it should be. Probably? Wy on earth did she say "probably"? It was the rare "happy ending" that people only dream about: the long-lost-lovers' reunion. And they deserved it. Deserved to be together. If she was going to spend her time worrying about anybody, she should be worrying about Fran. This thing with Buzz was a hideous mistake. God knows where it would lead. Fran's so spoiled, she thinks she can have anything she wants. I don't believe Dorothy Paige will give up so easily, even if Fran convinces Buzz to go away with her.

Barbara recalled Dorothy as she'd been the night of the anniversary party. She'd seemed apprehensive, clinging to her husband's arm. It was not at all difficult to believe she'd had a nervous breakdown. Could Frances live with the idea that her actions might push this woman over the edge?

It was extraordinary, everything that had gone on since their arrival. No one could have foreseen that this "quiet family reunion" would create such highly charged side effects.

It's as though we were all brought here to act out a drama, Barb thought. As though we were programed. A slight shudder ran through her. I'm afraid, she realized. I'm scared to death of what's ahead. I don't know why, but I have an awful feeling the worst is yet to come.

Jack Richards paced the floor of his living room, also deep in thought. He'd been so sure of his course when he was talking to Allie, as though he somehow expected to find she was unhappily married, that it was the right moment to make contact with her. And now that he had, he didn't feel the elation that should have been part of his discovery. Alice was lovely. Kind, gentle and still beautiful. All a man could want in a wife. The right replacement for the dear creature he'd lost. But something was missing. Excitement. Alice represented peace, which is what she deserved, and what he'd promised her. But peace was not what he wanted. He still felt young, vital and eager for life, now that the pain of Lucy's death was diminishing. There'd be no heights with Allie. She'd gone through too much, been too beaten down for too long. She'd forgotten how to be gay and reckless. Why did I ask her to marry me? The silent question came on a note of panic. I want to find our child, but why did I think I wanted to marry his mother? I'm devoted to Allie but I'm not in love with her. I lied, out of guilt and remorse, out of the feeling I did her an injustice? Good God, what have I done?

Ashamed, he realized he hoped she wouldn't marry him. He needed someone brighter, more independent, younger. A playmate after all the months of agony, watching Lucy's life slip away. He longed for a companion to make him laugh aloud, after the long days of silently tiptoeing around a sick room; a passionate woman after so many nights with an invalid too frail to make love.

Allie isn't any of the things I want in a wife, Jack thought. But if she says yes, I'll marry her. I owe her that. Dammit, I owe her much more than that!

Chapter 18

NOW THAT HE was so close to the truth, John Peck was uneasy. His interview with Mrs. Rudolph had eliminated any lingering doubts he might have had about the identity of his mother. It was Alice Dalton Winters all right. No question. But instead of elation, he was experiencing a sense of anxiety. If his great-aunt was so dismayed by his appearance, would his mother also be appalled and frightened? I couldn't stand it, John thought again. Maybe I should leave well enough alone. Is there any real need to see her, even though I've dreamed of it all these years?

He did nothing for a full twenty-four hours after his meeting with Charlotte. He didn't even tell his wife he'd seen his great-aunt. Carol would be upset, angry that the imperious old woman had tried to buy him off. Strangely, John wasn't angry. He could understand the reaction even while he deplored it. It must have been a terrible shock to have the abandoned child appear out of nowhere, demanding to be recognized. Like some ghost rising from the grave, some creature they never expected to see again. Poor old Mrs. Randolph. He was sorry for her, but he was glad they'd met. At least he knew what to possibly expect when he saw his mother. He was glad, too, that Carol had insisted he wait until Mrs. Winters returned to Boston. She'd been instinctively right. This was not the kind of thing one announced in a long-distance call. He recognized that now.

Only a few days more. Janice had said her mother would be back soon. Janice, my half-sister. The idea seemed impossible but it was true. And Chris, the man she so flippantly said was gay, is my half-brother. I've suddenly walked into a full-fledged family. There's even a stepfather I know about, though I don't know my real father.

It was incongruous. He'd found them all and they probably wouldn't want him. Where would he find courage to intrude on these strangers? He was not an aggressive man. In a way, it was distasteful to push in where he feared he'd not be welcome. But I must, John thought. I won't rest until I've seen my mother, no matter what the outcome.

Janice was surprised to receive a call from her father. He never telephoned the office. It must be important.

"Yes, Dad?"

"Are you coming to the house this evening, Janice?"

"I hadn't planned to. Why? Is something wrong?"

"No, there's nothing wrong. I want to talk to you, that's all. Please make it a point to be here."

There was something going on. She could hear an unusual note of agitation in his voice.

"All right. I'll drop in after work."

"Fine." He hung up abruptly without saying goodbye.

Mr. Loveable, Janice thought. Mr. In-Charge. There's not a shred of affection in him. I might as well be some underling he's summoned for a business conference. She shrugged. Who cared? She'd long since given up the idea of having a father like other people's. He was a machine. Driven. Violent. Tyrannical. How did her mother stand him? Janice could never comprehend that. Since she'd been old enough to realize what went on, she'd been puzzled by her own family. Why had they married in the first place, these two incompatible people? And even more unfathomable, why did they stay together in an atmosphere of such open hostility? She shrugged, indifferently. It was their generation, she supposed. Early conditioning made them unable to recognize the fact that there was an alternative.

As she entered the house, it crossed her mind that this summons from her father might have something to do with Aunt Charlotte's "urgent" call. God, is he going to ask me to go see that old biddy? I can't stand her. Always patting my cheek and telling me what a lovely young lady I am, and how fortunate Mother is to have me. She makes me sick.

Spencer was already home. She saw the light in the library and went in. Her father was working at his desk, as usual. She dropped into a chair beside it.

"I'm here."

"So I see. Very generous of you."

Janice was impatient. "Come on, Dad. Does every conversation have to start out like World War III?" She lit a cigarette. "Can't we skip the sarcasm and get to the point?"

"Can't you say two words without lighting a cigarette?"

Jan sighed. "All right, I smoke too much. I'm going to die of lung cancer or a heart attack. Is that what you brought me here to say?"

"No. I need some information about a man who says he knows you. Peck. John Peck. Claims to be a friend of yours."

For a minute she couldn't remember who John Peck was, but then she recalled the evening with him and his wife. Dreary. She and Clint had decided not to see them again.

"I know him casually. His wife is a free-lance artist. Clint and I went to their house a couple of nights ago. He's not really a friend. More an acquaintance. Why do you ask?"

"I'm trying to find him. A business matter. Miss Perrone couldn't locate him through the phone book. I thought you might be able to give me his number."

Jan laughed. "Miss Perrone couldn't find the oars in a rowboat. I don't know why you keep such an incompetent secretary, just because she's been with you for twenty years. I take that back. I do know. Men resist change of any kind. They'll hang on to a useless secretary because it's too much trouble to break in a new one. Just as they'll stay in a loveless marriage because it's too much bother to end it. Women are much more adventurous and optimistic. They always think things could be better; men always presume they'll be worse. It's the difference between the sexes. *Vive la différence!''*

Spencer looked annoyed. "I fail to see what all this pseudo philosophy has to do with my question. I merely want to know if you know where to find John Peck."

"Of course I do. I told you I had dinner at his house. What kind of business matter would bring The Great You in contact with a lowly bank manager?"

"Never mind. That doesn't concern you. He lives in the city?"

"Yes."

"He must be unlisted. Miss Perrone called all the John Pecks in the Boston directory. She couldn't find the right one."

"Of course she couldn't. Honestly, how dense can she be? He works. So does his wife. Nobody would answer the phone during the day at his apartment. My Lord, she must have had a million 'don't answers' among her calls."

Spencer consulted the list in front of him. "Four, to be exact. That's very astute of you, Janice. I should have called myself, in the evening. I didn't think of it. However, since you know which of the four is your friend, I can spare myself that tiresome chore."

Her curiosity was rising. "Why do you want to find John Peck?" she asked again.

"I told you. A simple business matter."

"Then, why don't you reach him at his office?"

"It's personal."

"So why can't you tell me? If it's personal, you won't be violating any lawyer-client confidentiality."

He was reaching the end of his patience. "Janice, I do not choose to discuss my affairs with you. This has nothing to do with you, so stop playing childish games and give me Peck's number."

She took a wild guess. "Does it have to do with Aunt Charlotte's call to Mother?"

Spencer momentarily was taken off guard. His surprise showed in his startled reaction.

"How did you figure that out?"

Jan smiled her win-father-over smile. "I'm a witch. Didn't you know? Come on, Dad. If it's a family matter I'm a big enough girl to be let in on the secret. Maybe I can help with the problem, whatever it is."

Maybe she can at that, Spencer thought. She can charm her way into anything when she chooses. Or out of anything. Neither of the children knew about Alice's past. He'd die before he confided in Christopher. But this girl was something else. Maybe she knew something about Peck that would be useful. She might even be able to disprove his claim. Or talk him out of pursuing it if it were true. It was a gamble, but it might work.

"All right, Janice. I'm going to tell you something very few people know.

Your mother had a child out of wedlock before we were married. A boy. She gave it up for adoption. Of course I knew nothing of the matter until much later." There was a touch of righteous indignation in his voice. "It all happened thirty years ago and nothing has been heard of the matter since. Until this John Peck person went to see your Aunt Charlotte. He claims to be your mother's child."

Janice stared at him, open-mouthed. "You're putting me on! Mother had an illegitimate baby? I can't believe it!"

"Unfortunately, it's true. What we don't know is whether this man is that child or simply a con artist." He repeated Charlotte's rambling story of how John had tracked down "Alice Dalton." "I'm not sure the whole thing isn't a hoax," Spencer said, "but I can't afford to take a chance. That's why I must reach him before he starts any unpleasant publicity. I don't want your mother or anyone else to know about this, Janice. You do undersand that."

"I sure do," Janice said slowly. "I understand a lot of things I couldn't figure out before."

Spencer ignored that. "What kind of person is Peck? Does he seem like a smooth operator?"

"I hardly know him. We only talked a few minutes, but I got the feeling he was kind and honest. He spoke very warmly of his adoptive parents."

"I'm sure he tried to pump you about us."

"Maybe. He didn't seem to be prying, but I volunteered a lot of information. I didn't think anything of it at the time, but I told him a lot of things. About Mother's background and about Aunt Charlotte. I even told him about Chris."

"Good God! You set it up for him! You made it easy for him to approach Charlotte with that trumped-up story."

"Are you so sure it's trumped up?"

"No, but what difference does that make? Damn! I'm sure he's after money. Much more than Charlotte offered. Well, I have a surprise for him. I won't be blackmailed. I'm not going to buy his silence and be bled dry the rest of my life. Where do I reach him, Janice?"

Reluctantly she gave him the address. "I think he could be telling the truth."

"What if he is? You're being as sentimental and gullible as your mother would be if she heard about this. Thank you for your help. I'll take it from here."

She didn't answer. For once, Janice was subdued and thoughtful. This extraordinary disclosure explained a great deal about her parents. She could imagine a frightened young Alice, pregnant and "disgraced," coming to Boston. She saw how her mother might have married Spencer Winters to escape Aunt Charlotte. She realized now why her father was so cruel to his wife, and why she endured her punishment all these years. Poor lady, Jan thought. They brainwashed her into a low opinion of herself. She suddenly felt warm and loving toward her mother. It's unfair. She's suffered so much at so many hands. I wonder who fathered her child. Some "childhood sweetheart" in Denver who abandoned her, no doubt. She must have been remorseful ever since. I'd be. Guilty as hell if I gave away a baby. It's wrong to deprive her of this knowledge. If this man's her son, she has a right to know.

She tried to recollect John Peck's face. Did he look like her mother? Was there any family resemblance to her and Chris? No, as she recalled there was nothing in his appearance to tie him to Alice. Yet she was convinced he was telling the truth. It was gut reaction, but she was certain of it.

"What are you going to do?" she asked Spencer.

"See him. Set him straight before your mother returns. Let him know we're not frightened by this scheme. Get rid of him once and for all."

"What if he won't go away? Suppose he insists on seeing Mother?"

"He won't when I'm through with him. I'm used to crooks. I meet them every day in my business."

"Dad, I don't think he's a crook."

"Frankly, Janice, I don't care what you think. My instincts are better than yours. So is my judgment." Alarmed, he realized she might interfere, make things more difficult. It had been a mistake to tell her. "You stay out of this, do you hear? Don't go near John Peck. And don't say a word to anybody, least of all your mother."

The old, defiant Janice returned. "I'll do whatever I please. You can't order me around the way you do her!"

"I can and I will." Spencer's quick temper rose. "I won't tolerate impertinence from you, young woman. You'll do as you're told or . . ."

"Or what? You'll beat me up too? Mother's afraid of you. I'm not. You're a bully. I know the only way to handle bullies is to stand up to them. You won't touch me. I won't allow it."

In a quick movement, Spencer crossed the room and slapped her hard across the face. "You'll show some respect! You'll obey my orders! I'm head of this house and I'll take no nonsense!"

Janice stood very still. Her cheek stung but she didn't cry or move away from him. When she spoke, it was with scorn. "You're a big man, aren't you? It must make you feel wonderful, slapping women around. You're pathetic. So uncertain of your manhood you have to use force to prove how macho you are."

Enraged, Spencer raised his fist. Jan stared at him. Then she said, "If you hit me, I swear to God, I'll kill you. You're not dealing with Mother." She picked up a letter opener that lay on the desk and held it like a dagger. "I'm not kidding. You lay a hand on me again and I'll stick this in your rotten heart!"

He lowered his hand. "Get out!" he said. "Get the hell out of this house and don't come back!"

"Don't worry. I don't intend to." She started for the door, still holding the weapon. "I would have used this, you know. I wasn't bluffing. I'm going to get out of your house and out of your life, the way Chris has. And if I have any influence, I'll make Mother do the same."

She was gone before he could answer. Goddamn women! Spencer thought. I hate them all, the evil, conniving bitches. Good riddance to my ungrateful daughter. She'll go to her lover. Let her. She's nothing but a whore, the way her mother was, the way *my* mother was! Scheming whores, all of them, good for nothing but messing up a man's life. He glanced down at John Peck's address. There's the perfect example of the trouble women cause. Another inconvenience to be disposed of. I'm always washing Alice's dirty linen.

He reached for the phone and dialed Information.

Carol looked at John curiously when he came back from the phone. "Who was it?"

"Spencer Winters."

Her eyes opened wide. "Spencer Winters! Calling you? What's going on?"

John Peck sat down on the sofa and put his arms around his wife. "Winters wants to meet with me. Honey, I've been holding out on you. I didn't want to upset you."

He told her of his meeting with Charlotte Rudolph and, as he anticipated, Carol was furious with the old woman. She was also slightly annoyed with John.

"Don't you think you moved a little too quickly? I know we talked about Mrs. Rudolph, but I thought we agreed that you'd wait until your . . . until Mrs. Winters got back."

"We did, but after I got that lead from Janice I decided to follow it up. I said I might."

"But you didn't tell me you had." She looked hurt. "I didn't think we kept secrets. . . ." Abruptly Carol stopped and smiled. "I shouldn't say that. I've been keeping one from you. Johnny, we're going to have a baby."

"Are you serious?"

"Very. Almost three months serious. I held out on you too. I thought it would be compensation if you were disappointed about your mother again. Or a double celebration if Mrs. Winters turned out to be the one."

He kissed her. "Darling, it's wonderful! I'm so happy! And it is a double celebration!" He laughed. "My God, that lady has some surprises in store. Not only a son but a grandchild!"

Carol was very sober. "You're sure? That she's really your mother?"

"Completely. Mrs. Rudolph's performance confirmed it. And now this call from Winters. They're taking it seriously, that's obvious. I wonder what he'll have to say."

"When are you meeting him?"

"Noon tomorrow. At his office. I'll take an early lunch." He frowned. "It seems wrong to talk to him instead of my mother. Maybe I should call Denver."

Carol was about to advise against it when the phone rang again. This time Carol answered, and after a few seconds she called John.

"It's for you. Janice Winters."

He was trembling as he took the receiver. So much was happening so fast. The whole Winters family was in the act.

"I'd like to talk to you," she said without preamble.

"Of course." He couldn't tell from her voice whether she was friendly or hostile.

"I know everything that's happened," Janice went on. "You're going to be hearing from my father."

"I already have. I'm seeing him tomorrow."

"It figures. So we'd better talk tonight. May I come over now?"

"Certainly." He hesitated. "Janice, I don't intend to make trouble for anybody. I'm really not devious, though you might be thinking so. I did have something in mind when we asked you to dinner, but I hope you know it was just because I was so anxious to get at the truth."

"We'll talk about it when I get there. But meanwhile, put your mind at ease. I'm on your side."

He relayed the conversation to Carol. "She says she's on my side, whatever that means."

"I think she'll help you, darling. She's nice. And I'm glad she's coming over. You got an icy reception from 'Aunt Charlotte' and I doubt Spencer Winters will be better. Worse, probably. We can use a friend at court."

Chapter 19

LAURA DALTON CAME in with the mail. "Letter for you, Barbara," she said.

"Hallelujah!" It was here, the longed-for letter from Charles. She hugged it to her without even looking at it, smiled at her mother and disappeared to her own room to read, in private, the love words that had come at last. But the handwriting on the envelope was not Charles's familiar scrawl, though the return address was his. She sat down on the bed and slowly took the thin parchment paper from its envelope. Disbelieving, she began to read Andrea Tallent's message:

Dear Barbara,

This is a most awkward letter for me to write, but one of utmost importance to Charles and therefore worth the difficulty on my part and, I'm sure, the distress on yours.

Until this past week, we have all managed to be civilized and live with a distasteful but apparently unavoidable situation. The roles you and I have assumed have not been pleasant ones. You must feel a sense of shame equal to my humiliation, but we have both endured for the sake of a man we care for. You and I are enemies, Barbara, but we are also conspirators in the mutual effort to make Charles happy. Now we must collaborate to make him powerful and famous as well.

The Candidate, who is almost certain to be the next President, has offered Charles the Cabinet post of Secretary of Agriculture, with the proviso that he rid himself of the potential for scandal. You, of course, represent that potential in an administration which will pride itself on honesty and openness.

It is difficult for me, as a woman, to admit that the choice was a hard one for my husband. His devotion to you persists. And it is not easy for Charles to discard any obligation, particularly one of long-standing. However, he has decided to take the sensible and practical route which could lead him to a place in history, perhaps even, one day, to the highest office in the land.

You must be wondering why you learn this from me. Charles intends to tell you when you return to Washington, but my feminine intuition says that knowing what is in store may make you wish not to return to a place of haunting memories. It seemed kinder to let you make that decision now and avoid a wrenching scene whose outcome is already determined. Charles feels it is his duty to tell you his decision in person. He does not reckon, I fear, with the sensibilities of women's emotions. I have tried to put myself in your place. Were I in this situation, I would choose to close the book on a happy chapter rather than be left with a degrading finale. I cannot help but believe you will feel the same.

I bear you no ill will. Indeed, I feel sympathy for you. I do not doubt that you love Charles and that, given a choice, you would in any case have set him free to go on to the greatness of which he is capable. Like many other women in the backgrounds of important men, you will be comforted by the knowledge of the contribution you have made and, aware that the time has come to step aside, putting his and the nation's need above your own desires.

You will make things a great deal easier for Charles if you pretend you know nothing of this matter but have simply decided, given the perspective of time and distance, to end the relationship. It is a final kindness and one that will relieve his conscience and allow him to face his new responsibilities with a free mind and a lighter heart.

Sincerely,
Andrea Tallent

A numbness came over Barbara. It was cruel, unbearably cruel, to hear from her lover's wife that the only thing she existed for had been taken from her. I won't accept it! she thought. I don't believe it! It was a trick of Andrea's, cleverly contrived to get her husband back. But this was no threatening letter from an enraged wife. It would be too easy to disprove with a single phone call. It must be true. Charles has accepted the job and the conditions that go with it. The knowledge stabbed her. How could he? How could he give up the lifetime they planned to share? Could he put a job, no matter how important, above the happiness he found with her? Andrea's wrong. If he'd let me share in the decision-making I'd have made him see that no amount of fame can make him content if he doesn't have me. I'd have talked him out of it. Maybe I still can. I'll call him. I'll beg him to change his mind. Or I'll fly home tonight. I won't let him go. I can't.

But even as these thoughts raced through her head, Barbara knew it was useless. Even if she reached him, even if she persuaded him to decline the job, it had gone too far. The day would come when he'd hate her for depriving him of this chance. That would be worse than anything. Worse than this.

She threw herself down on the bed and let the tears come. Tears of misery and loneliness. Tears of regret for what would never be again. In her mind she relived their hundreds of times together, felt his touch as though he were in the room with her. I never thought it would end, she told herself. And it has, as suddenly and hideously as an amputation.

She stopped crying after a while and lay back, staring at the ceiling. Slowly, a feeling of resentment crept over her. Why didn't he come straight to her and tell her himself? Wasn't he man enough? Was her lover weak and cowardly, when she thought him strong and courageous? For a moment she felt revulsion, but it quickly passed. He didn't know about the letter. He did plan to break this news to her. It would have been terrible for him, but he'd have done it, trying to be gentle, hating himself for his ambition and begging her to understand.

And I'd have let him go, Barbara thought dully. I wouldn't have stood in his way. I know it. Andrea knows it too. We want for him everything he wants for himself. We want to make it easy for him because we both love him.

Strange that at this moment she felt a kinship with her old adversary. They worshiped at the same altar.

There was a tap on the door and she heard her mother's voice.

"Barbara? Are you all right, dear?"

She wiped her eyes and sat up. "Come in, Mother."

Laura approached the bed, a look of concern on her face. "Is anything wrong? You've been up here so long."

The sympathetic question brought a lump to Barbara's throat and she felt the tears coming again. Wordlessly, she handed her mother Andrea's letter. Laura fished in her apron pocket for her glasses and read, shaking her head as the meaning came clear, When she finished she put the pages down and faced Barbara, her own eyes swimming.

"My poor Barbara. My poor child."

"Don't. Please don't feel sorry for me, Mother. It only makes it worse. Tell me what a fool I've been. Tell me he isn't worth this pain. Tell me he's a weak, selfish man. That's what I need to hear."

Laura shook her head. "No, dear heart, I can't tell you that. If you loved him, he was all that you believed. You're unhappy now and disappointed in him, but if I know you, Barbara, you wouldn't have liked yourself if he stayed with you because you made him feel he should. Maybe in time you'd even have respected him less for running away from this awful choice. Or maybe he'd come to resent you for depriving him of a great future."

"I know. I've thought of that. But it's so hard, Mother. So terrible to think of life without Charles. I'm hurt. I can't help it. And I'm angry with myself for being such a fool all these years."

"You were no fool darling. You had more than a dozen years of joy. Even your sisters can't say that. All right, perhaps you would have been better off if you'd never met Charles, never tied up so much of your life to him. But you did and there's nothing to be gained by regretting. Remember the lovely times, Barbara. They can never be taken away from you. He was part of your experience and there's no such thing as a wasted experience, dear. We learn from everything that happens to us, good or bad. You've become a wiser, more tolerant, loving woman because of Charles. And I'm sure he's a better man because of you. Let him go gracefully, Barbara, without bitterness or hatred. You will let him go, won't you? You won't try to change his mind?"

Barbara shook her head. "No, I won't put him through that. Or myself, either. It would be wrong." She sounded wistful. "I think I could handle it better if I'd heard it from him, though."

"Possibly. But his wife says he plans to tell you." Laura sighed. "I wish I were Christian enough to think she meant well by writing that letter. I'm afraid it gave her pleasure. She's only human too. But I think her suggestion is right, if you're big enough to accept it. It would be a great gift to Charles if you wrote him, pretending to know nothing of this and breaking things off yourself."

"A gift to him? Letting him think I'm the one who's decided to end it? Good Lord, how much do you expect of me?"

Laura patted her head as though she were a child. "I expect a great deal of a woman as generous as you. I think you can do this one last thing in the name of love. Spare him, Barb. He must be in enough agony as it is."

"Agony of his own making. He didn't have to accept the post."

"You know that isn't true. He had to accept it for his own self-respect. He sounds like a man who couldn't turn his back on success. He'd be incapable of it. Washington's full of men like that, isn't it? If they didn't have drive, they wouldn't be there in the first place. It's not a god you love, Barbara, it's a human being torn between two different kinds of desire. If you could see this unemotionally, you'd know that the temptation would be too strong for him."

"Or his capacity for love too weak."

"I don't think you believe that," Laura said. "You're not a cynic. Don't let this make you bitter. We all suffer disappointments, some greater than others. But we keep our illusions and our belief in the basic goodness of people. He's made you unhappy, but that doesn't cancel out all the times he made you very happy indeed."

Barbara reached for her hand. "You're a wise lady."

"No. I've just lived a long time and seen a lot of grief. Some of it my own. You won't get over this today or next month, Barbara, but you'll get over it, and you'll be glad you handled it with dignity." Laura smiled gently. "I know that's easier said than done. You'll have some bad times, but they'll pass."

"I dread going back to Washington. I'm bound to run into him. Into them. Maybe I should stay in Denver."

"Don't make that decision quite yet. Your father and I would love to have you here, but that's something to think about when you're calmer. There's a lot of life ahead of you, and nobody pushing you to decide right now how to live it."

"Right now there doesn't seem to be very much to live *for*."

Laura was desperately sorry for her youngest. But Barb was right. It was no time for commiseration.

"Self-pity doesn't become you, Barbara. It's a trait the world quickly becomes weary of. You're an intelligent adult. You've had a bad shock, but you must have known this might happen one day." Her voice softened. "I'm sorry, darling. I hurt when you do. But I can only be glad this happened while you're still young enough to start over. It didn't have a future, that kind of relationship. It almost never does."

"Young enough?" Barbara's laugh was hollow. "Forty's hardly young, Mother."

"When you're seventy, it seems like nothing. You'll see."

Another thirty years of nothingness? God spare me, Barb thought. My job, my home, my life in Washington are meaningless without Charles. She allowed the tears to come again. I don't know what to do. I wish I were dead.

In contrast to the bleakness Barbara felt that morning, Fran's mood was optimistic. She was pleased with the way things were going with Buzz. Calling to "say goodbye" had been the smartest thing she'd ever done. It always worked with men. Just let them think you were going to walk away and they couldn't be without you. It was Buzz who was doing the pleading now. Buzz who, last night, had been grateful she'd agreed to meet him again, had begged her to give him a few hours every night as long as she stayed.

She'd shaken her head when he said that. "We can't, Buzz. Dorothy might find out. It's too risky. You've made it clear that you won't leave her. We'd better stop now, while we can."

He'd reached for her again. "No. There's no need. I know you're going to go away again. Let me store up as many memories as I can." He began to make love to her for the second time. "You're so incredibly desirable. I can't have you forever, but for now . . ."

Fran responded with genuine passion. She'd not expected him to be such an expert lover. I'm tricking him, she thought for a moment. I'm lulling him into a false sense of security. He really believes I'll let him go. The hell with it. I know what's best for him. All's fair . . .

This morning she was blissfully exhausted. They'd been very late leaving the motel, almost midnight. She'd been honestly concerned for him.

"Will there be trouble when you get home?"

"That's not for you to worry about, my love. Tomorrow night? Same time, same place?"

She laughed. "What do you think we are, teen-agers?"

"Yes. I feel like one. I haven't felt this young in years. Maybe never. I could make love to you all night."

"I'd like that." She allowed a wistful note to creep into her voice. "Do you think we'll ever have a whole night?"

Buzz hesitated. "I don't know why not. Why not a weekend? We could go to Vail or Aspen."

"Oh, Buzz, really? Could we? No. We couldn't. There's no way you could manage that."

It was all the challenge he needed. "I can manage it. This weekend, if you like. But what about you? How will you explain it to your family?"

"I don't have to explain, darling. There's no one to ride herd on me."

"Then it's a date."

"You're sure?"

"Damned right I'm sure. Dorothy doesn't know how lucky she is that I'm not taking off forever!"

Now Fran smiled, remembering last night, thinking of tonight and of the weekend. It was going perfectly.

"I'm glad somebody has something to smile about this morning."

Laura's voice surprised her. Her mother had come into the room, looking upset and unhappy.

"What's wrong? Are you still upset about Allie?"

"No, it's Barbara. I don't know whether she's told you about her friend in Washington. . . ."

"She told me. And I told *her* she's being an idiot. I didn't know you knew about it, Mother. But since you do, I'm sure you agree she's wasting her life."

"Not any more," Laura said. "She had a letter this morning."

Frances was aghast as she heard about Andrea Tallent's letter. "My God!

That poor kid! What a way to be brushed off! And that bastard Tallent! Not enough guts to tell her himself!''

"In fairness, he planned to."

"Oh, sure. I'll just bet he did. Like hell. He probably is behind the whole thing. I wouldn't be surprised if he suggested his wife write. What a smart move, loading the responsibility for his damned future onto Barb's shoulders! She's well out of it, is all I can say."

"I suppose she is, but it's hard for her. She loves him, Frances. He's been her whole life for a long time. I don't say it's right. I don't approve of any woman taking another woman's husband. But I feel sorry for her. She's almost destroyed by this. She's even talking of staying here, never going back to Washington. I think she'll change her mind about that, but right now she's at rock-bottom. Poor thing, she's paying for her sins."

"And he's getting off scot-free. A big important job. Back to the little woman and the kiddies. Where's the damned justice in this world? Isn't he supposed to pay for *his* sins? Or is it only women who get the short end of the stick?''

Laura shook her head. "No. They've both been wrong. I'm sure he's suffering too. He must be a fine man if Barbara loves him. This can't be easy for him."

"Oh, for God's sake, Mother! He's had all the kicks and none of the kicks-in-the-behind! He's not the one who's had to hide out. He hasn't had to sit by the phone like some damned beggar waiting for a handout. Barb's been a fool. She should have had better sense. But that's no reason why she should continue to make it all so easy for him. If she writes that letter, I'll kill her!''

"What would you have her do, Frances?"

"I'd make him sweat. I'd stop being such a pushover and give him and that smug wife of his a hard time. Damned if I'd let him off the hook so easily!''

Laura looked at her curiously. "And what would that prove? What good would it do to threaten a lot of trouble?"

"None, probably, but *I'd* feel better."

"You and Barbara see life differently," Laura said.

The implied criticism angered Fran. "Not all that differently, Mother. Neither of us has any qualms about going after a married man if he's what we want." She threw discretion to the wind. "While we're on the subject, I've been seeing Buzz Paige. I'm crazy about him and I'm going to take him away from that dreary wife of his."

"Frances! What are you saying?"

"I think it's pretty clear. I had first claim on him. He's never loved anybody but me. He only married that stupid girl because I left him. Well, I was wrong. I want him now and I'm going to get him. I'm sorry if that shocks you, Mother, but I only have one life and I'm going to get as much out of it as I can."

"Even if its means hurting an innocent woman?"

"Would you say that to Barb? She hurt one. She just wasn't smart enough to do the job thoroughly. I won't live any trashy little secret life with Buzz. The break will be clean. To me, that's more admirable than sneaking a few hours while you try to fool the public. I say, if you're going in for adultery, then for God's sake have the courage of your convictions. Otherwise, you end up like Barbara.''

Laura covered her ears. "I don't want to hear this! How can you be so hard? Frances, you mustn't break up Buzz Paige's marriage! It's wrong! It's a mortal sin!"

Fran quieted down. "I'm sorry, Mother. It probably was wrong of me to say those things to you. But, dear, I am going to do what I said. If Dorothy can't hold her husband, that's not my fault. Why should he stay in a marriage he doesn't want? I can make him happy, and I will."

"No, Frances. Please. Let him alone."

"Darling, I can't. I'm just as glad you know about it. Now I don't have to make up an excuse for going off this weekend. We're going to have a couple of days together to make sure we want to make it permanent."

Laura wrung her hands. "And Buzz agrees to this?"

"Yes. He doesn't know about it yet, but he agrees." Fran put her arms around her mother. "We give you terrible troubles, don't we? All of us. I wish we didn't. I wish we were what you deserve." She released Laura. "I think I'll go talk to Barb. Maybe my kind of selfishness is just what she needs."

Laura sank wearily into a chair. "Maybe so. I can't handle these things any more. I feel so totally useless. Your father and I. We're . . . we're outmoded. I used to think I was still part of today. I couldn't understand why he'd abandoned all the activity he used to love. But I feel that way now. You and Buzz. Allie and Jack Richards. Barbara and this married man. It's too much for me, Frances. I can't cope with it. I want to run away and hide."

"We'll be all right, Mother. You can't protect us, darling. No mother can shelter a child forever, much as she might like to. We don't live hermetically sealed, dear. We're going to have our tragedies, make our mistakes. We have in the past and we will in the future. Don't think it's a reflection on anything you have or haven't done. We're women, Mother, not girls, but don't think of us in terms of yourself. You'd never do any of the things we've done. You're much too good. You and Dad. Much too moral."

"Our friends' children haven't caused them such grief." Laura couldn't resist. "They stayed here, married, settled down, had children of their own. Most of your friends are grandmothers, Frances." She stopped. "That's wrong of me. I'm sorry. I'm trying to make you feel guilty because I'm guilty myself. You did what you had to do, all three of you. I'd give anything if you hadn't had to pay so dearly for it."

"It's okay," Fran said. "None of it's your fault."

Laura didn't answer. How I wish I could believe that, she thought.

Chapter 20

JANICE WAS HARDLY inside the Pecks' apartment when she came right to the point. "Are you on the level?" she asked John. "Did my mother have you before she was married?" But there was no hostility in the businesslike way she put her questions.

John answered in the same, unemotional vein. "Yes, I'm on the level. This

is no con game, Janice. I'm sure I'm the child Alice Dalton gave up for adoption.
I know Mrs. Rudolph believes it, and I think your father does too.''

"Aunt Charlotte's an addled old woman. Dad's something else. He'll demand
proof. Do you have any?''

"I have my birth certificate. I know my mother's name and the date and place
I was born. It all fits with the time of your mother's arrival in Boston.''

"It's damned slim,'' Jan said. "My father's a lawyer. He'll shoot holes in
that circumstantial evidence.''

"I'm sure he'll try. But how could I invent such a story? Besides, what about
your aunt? She practically admitted I was right. She even offered me money to
go away and not bother any of you again. She knows I'm the one. She knows
the Pecks adopted me.''

Jan shook her head. "I told you. She's a crazy old lady, and scared witless
of my father. He'll make her deny everything, and if it comes to that, it'll be
the word of a well-coached dowager and a prominent Boston attorney against
yours. Bad odds, John. You have no idea what you're dealing with when you
try to fight Spencer Winters. There's nothing he won't do to protect his bloody
'impeccable reputation'—including making mincemeat out of you and your story.''

John was silent for a moment and then he said, "You believe me. Why?''

"I'm not sure. Call it a hunch. No, it's really more than that. I don't think
you could invent it. And it explains some things I've never understood. Like
why he beats up on Mother. And why she stands for it.''

"Beats up on her?'' John was horrified. "You mean he literally hits her?''

"Always has. Knocks hell out of her. Maybe this is why. Maybe he's punishing
her for you, and she takes it because she's been conditioned to feel worthless.
I don't know. I don't have anything to go on. No more than you do. We're both
operating more from instinct than hard facts. But I do believe you. It's a shame
we don't look anything alike. That might help. You don't look anything like
Chris either.'' An idea struck her. "You wouldn't, by chance, have an identifying
birthmark, would you? Some nice heart-shaped thing on your shoulder that would
clinch it?'' Jan smiled. "If this were a mystery story, you'd dramatically open
your shirt and produce proof.''

He tried to return her smile. "Sorry. Nothing. Not a blemish on my beautiful
body.''

"Too bad. I don't know how you're going to make your story hold up. I don't
know much about adoption, John, but it even seems unlikely to me that Aunt
Charlotte would know the name of the people who took you. I thought that was
known only to the adoption agency and the court.''

Carol, who'd been listening quietly, suddenly spoke up. "I think that's true,
Janice. I haven't wanted to upset John, but I've wondered all along about that.
And yet, apparently, she does know. The way she reacted to John's visit indicates
that.'' She hesitated. "Unless . . .''

Her husband looked at her. "Unless what, honey?''

"Maybe you weren't placed through an agency at all. If they wanted to keep
everything so secret, maybe they managed it another way. Like through the
obstetrician. I've heard of that. Doctors sometimes know couples who're eager
to have a baby and can't get one through regular channels. Could the Pecks have

been one of those, John? Could they have gotten you through Mrs. Rudolph and the doctor who delivered you, without going through an agency? Was there any reason why they'd have been turned down if they'd followed the usual procedure?"

"No. They were good, honest, hard-working people. A lot older than the parents of my friends, but . . ."

"How much older?" Janice asked.

John realized what the question meant. "They were well into their fifties when they adopted me. Maybe more. My God, I never thought of that! They'd have been considered too old to adopt a newborn baby, wouldn't they? I haven't thought about it for years, but I remember my father telling me they'd tried to have their own children for twenty years before they got me! Do you think that's it? Could Carol be right? If they applied to an agency and were turned down because of age, maybe they paid the doctor to get them a baby! Sure. It makes sense. He'd have known the circumstances and put the proposition to Charlotte. He'd have told her about the Pecks! She could tell us who the doctor was. Or we could find him! That would prove it!"

"Slow down, darling," Carol said. "From what Janice says, Mrs. Rudolph's not likely to tell us anything. And it's been thirty years. The doctor could be dead by now."

His surge of hope disappeared. "I suppose you're right. It's just another unprovable idea that won't help with Spencer Winters."

Janice lit a cigarette and exhaled slowly. "I'm suddenly wondering why we're worrying about Dad and Aunt Charlotte. You don't give a damn whether they accept you or not, do you? There's only one person you want to convince. Seems to me we're making this too complicated. If you believe you belong to Alice Winters, why the hell don't you go and talk to her?"

"That's what I've wanted to do all along," John said, "but I guess I've been afraid. I keep looking for things to make sure she believes me."

"I've held him back," Carol said. "I was afraid he'd be disappointed again."

"He might be," Janice said. "We don't have a clue about how much Mother knows of what happened to you. She was a young, dumb kid when you were born. Maybe Charlotte dealt her out of the whole thing after she had the baby. But she's the only one who can answer your questions. Or, rather, the only one who *will*, if she can."

"Will she, Janice?" John sounded eager. "Will she see me and tell me what she knows?"

"She's a lady, whatever else she is," Jan answered. "She may be mixed up and full of guilts, but she's loving and honest. You get to her, John. Here." She pulled a scrap of paper out of her handbag. "I brought the address and phone number of my grandparents in Denver. Call Mother. Or get on a plane and go out there. The sooner the better. I don't know how long she's going to stay, and you sure don't want to meet her with Dad around."

"I'm supposed to see your father in the office tomorrow."

Jan laughed. "Forget it. Stand him up. It'll be good for him."

The plane came in low, making its approach to the Denver airport. John's face was pressed to the window, his eyes taking in this first impression of the land. It was checkerboarded from the air, like most countrysides, in brown and green squares that he assumed were farms, with an occasional speck of building dotted here and there. It seemed quite ordinary, almost dreary, until he saw the mountains. They rose in the distance, an imperious, snow-topped, breathtaking white-capped contrast to the drab flatness between. Like Sarah Peck's kitchen floor on the days she cleaned it—an expanse of unremarkable tiles edged with a dramatic border of billowing soapsuds. The unlikely comparison made him smile. Comparing the Colorado landscape to a Boston kitchen floor! I must be going mad, he thought. I *am* mad, flying here with no advance warning to the woman I plan to confront, telling no one except Carol and Janice what I decided in an instant to do. He glanced at his watch. Even now, Spencer Winters would be wondering what had happened to his twelve o'clock appointment. Let him. He'll probably call the apartment again, but Carol won't be home. And even if he suspects that Janice had a hand in this broken date, he'll have a hard time getting anything out of her.

He felt his anger rise again. The three of them had talked far into the night, and at some point Janice had told Carol and him about the earlier part of the evening when her father struck her.

"He's out of his mind," she said almost without concern. "I'll never see him again. Never speak to him if I can avoid it. I'm not going back to that house and I hope to God Mother won't either. You talk her out of it, John, when you see her. Make her understand there's no reason she has to live with that."

Make her understand, John thought now. There's so much I hope she understands before I get to that. He'd felt sick when he heard of Spencer Winters' cruelty. What possessed such a man?

"Does Chris know?" he'd asked.

"About Dad hitting me? No. Chris already hates him enough for what he's done to Mother. Why should I give my brother one more thing to be unhappy about? He's a nice fella. Much more like Mother than I am. You'll like each other."

The plane set down gently, and as he made the long walk from the gate to the taxi entrance, John realized he didn't even know where he was going to stay. He had only one piece of hand luggage. This wouldn't be a long trip. He couldn't stay away from his job more than a few days. Carol was going to call the bank and say he was sick. They'd thought of that, but they hadn't even discussed hotel reservations. Maybe I had an idea I'd call from the airport and be invited to my grandparents', John thought. Crazy! I have to check in somewhere and prepare my mother for this shock. He hailed a cab.

"Yessir. Where to?"

For an instant, he was tempted to give the Carona Street address, but instead he said, "I don't have a hotel reservation. Can you suggest one?"

"Town's pretty crowded. Always is, these days. We're getting to be a big convention center. Your best bet is the Hilton, I guess. They might have a single."

"Fine." John settled back as they pulled away from the airport. "By the way, how far is the Hilton from South Carona Street?"

"Fifteen, twenty minutes, maybe. The Hilton's right downtown. Carona's out near Washington Park."

"Nice neighborhood?"

"So-so. Not tops, but okay. Working people area, I guess you'd call it. You got friends there?"

"I hope so."

"How's that?" The cab driver looked at him in the rearview mirror.

"I mean I have relatives there. I've never seen them. John managed a laugh. "I sure *hope* they're friendly."

"Most people here are. It's a friendly town. If you can't get a room in the hotel you can always bunk in with your folks, right? Maybe you want to go there instead?"

"No. I'll try the Hilton."

Allie smiled nervously at the man across the luncheon table. "Barb suggested we eat here at the Promenade Cafe when she and Fran and I came to Larimer Square a few days ago, but we went to LaFitte's instead. This is pleasant."

Jack Richards nodded. He was as ill at ease as she. "It is nice. I like dining outdoors. What made you change your minds?"

"Fran changed them for us." Her smile broadened. "You know Fran. So conscious of her looks. She refused to sit in the sunlight."

"No, I don't know Fran. I haven't seen her since she was a girl, remember? I hadn't seen Barb either until yesterday."

Or me, Alice thought. You haven't seen any of us. Or we, you. We have to start all over. Can we? Is that what we really want? It was hard to believe this was the boy she'd loved, whose child she'd borne. He seemed a pleasant, attractive stranger. Yesterday's meeting had been emotional, dramatic for both of them. Today she sensed she was not the only one who was uncertain about a reconciliation.

"How is Barb, by the way?"

Alice hesitated. She didn't feel close enough to him to say that when she'd gone up to their room to dress for this luncheon date she'd found Barbara lying still as death on her bed. Alice had asked her what was wrong, but her sister had just smiled a pathetic little smile and said it was nothing, she wasn't feeling too well. It was an obvious lie, but whatever was troubling Barb, she didn't want to discuss it. I should have stayed and talked, Allie realized. I've been so absorbed in my own life I haven't even asked about hers. But Fran had come in just then, and her older sister had shaken her head as if to say, "Don't bother her now."

"I said, 'How's Barbara?'," Jack repeated.

"What? Oh, fine, I guess. She was resting when I left."

"You should have let me come to the house and pick you up. It was foolish for you to take a cab down here."

"I couldn't, Jack. Not yet. I don't know what Dad's going to say when he finds out you and I are meeting again." She seemed embarrassed. "Even Mother was upset when she heard, and she's much more sensible about ancient history."

He was quiet for a moment. "Your father's going to have to know, Allie. About us. You're not a child. He has no say in your life any more. Not like he did years ago."

"I know."

Jack suddenly reached over and took her hand. "You don't want to marry me, do you? Our reunion yesterday was romantic and nostalgic, but you're not sure you want to make it permanent, are you?"

She met his eyes squarely. "No, I'm not sure, Jack. I'm desperately unhappy in my marriage. I don't think, after this visit home, I can go on with it. But I don't want to make another mistake. That wouldn't be fair to either of us." A note of desperation crept into her voice. "I'm so afraid of everything. I wish I weren't. I long to be like my sisters, but I'm not. I can't make hasty decisions or take chances with your life or mine. You're lonely. You miss your wife. And I hate my husband. That's the truth of it. That's our bond."

"No, that's not all of it. You may be right. I won't try to rush you into anything, Allie. But you're overlooking the strongest tie beween us: our son. We both want to find him. We have that in common. We needn't decide about us. Not now, at least. But we have to resolve the other thing, or neither of us will ever know peace of mind."

"How, Jack? I want to find him as much as you do. I always have. But where do we begin? Realistically, how can we track down someone you never saw and I saw only once in my life? There's no place to start. No clues. It's hopeless."

"Nothing is hopeless. I'll get those private detectives again. They'll go back to the beginning. We'll find him. Doesn't your mother know anything? Didn't your Aunt Charlotte ever tell her who took the child?"

Allie shook her head. "I don't think so. Mother and Daddy didn't want to know. They left it up to her."

"Then, dammit, she's the key! She'll have to tell you."

"She won't. She's too afraid of Spencer. So am I. He'd be in a rage if my illegitimate child showed up and caused a scandal in his well-ordered life."

"To hell with him! He's there and you're here. He can't do anything to you, Allie. And what's he going to do to an eighty-year-old woman? We have to make her realize how important this is!"

"You just don't understand. She's kept the secret all these years. I'm not sure she even remembers the details any more. She's getting senile, Jack. Even if she wanted to tell us what arrangements she made thirty years ago, I'm not sure she could."

He looked grim. "I won't accept that. If we can't find out what we need to know through Charlotte, we'll do it some other way. People don't just vanish. Our son is out there somewhere, Allie, and I damned well am going to find him, with or without her help. And there's one thing more. We have to talk to your parents. I can't believe they still hold a grudge against me. And I can't believe they know nothing. It just isn't possible that they could wash their hands of the whole matter. Your mother, particularly. She has to have been told what was done with that baby. My God, that's her grandchild! Her flesh and blood! Wouldn't she have cared what happened to him?"

Allie looked at him hopelessly. "Tell me, Jack. Did you?"

He stopped. "That's a low blow, Allie."

"I'm sorry. I suppose it is. But it's true, isn't it? Everybody wanted to forget the whole thing. Your parents. Mine. Even you. Oh, I don't blame any of you.

I was the one who should have stopped it from happening. I wanted that child enough to have him. I should have been strong enough to keep him. I'm not surprised nobody inquired about what Charlotte did with Johnny. I never made much effort myself, and I was his mother.''

"Don't, Allie. Don't punish yourself this way."

"Who else should be punished? I caused the trouble by refusing an abortion. I thrust this problem on other people. I wasn't willing to go through with what I started."

"You were young. Frightened. Alone."

"That's no excuse. I asserted myself once in my whole life, and wouldn't you know I picked the wrong time? Insisting on having that child! What a stupid little fool I was. I should have known I'd never have enough backbone to take care of him. And I've spent the rest of my life repenting, and wishing I could see him, or even know he's alive."

Jack held her hand more tightly. "You will darling. You'll see him again. I make you a solemn promise. You'll see he's well and happy. Please don't cry. I don't know what will happen with us. We'll let that develop as it will. But we'll find your son. Our son. You believe that, don't you? Say you believe it."

She looked up, tears streaming down her face. "Say I believe in miracles? Is that what you're asking?"

"If that's what it takes, yes. But we won't trust to miracles. We'll make it happen. That's what I want you to believe."

"I'll try," Alice said softly. "I'll really try."

John Peck sat in his hotel room staring at the telephone. Just a local call. Dial nine and the number and you'll be talking to your mother. His palms were sweating as he picked up the piece of paper on which Janice had written the Daltons' telephone number and address. Very slowly he dialed and heard the telephone ringing in a house he'd never seen. It was three o'clock in the afternoon.

He felt as though he were choking as he asked, "Is this the Dalton residence?"

"Yes. Whom do you want?"

"Ah . . . Ah, I'm trying to reach Mrs. Winters. Mrs. Spencer Winters."

"This is Mrs. Winters. Who is this?"

The blood rushed to his head and he could feel his heart pounding. "It's John," he said. "John Peck." He stopped, wondering what to say next. The name would mean nothing to her. There was a pause and then Alice said, "I'm afraid I don't know anyone named Peck. You have the right number, but . . ."

"You don't know me." John was stammering. "That is, you do know me, but not really. I mean, it's all rather complicated."

There was a suspicious finality in the cool voice at the other end of the phone, yet the woman remained polite. "I don't understand. I'm sorry. Perhaps there's been a mistake."

"No! Don't hang up, please!" He was suddenly terrified, so frightened that he blurted out words he'd been prepared to lead up to carefully, cautiously. "It's John. I'm your son. At least I think I am. That is, I *know* I am. You haven't seen me for thirty years."

There was a terrible silence. My God! What have I done? John thought. Maybe she's fainted. Maybe I'm not even . . . I must be insane, telling a woman this kind of thing on the phone! He waited, cursing himself for his impulsiveness. Perhaps she had hung up. The silence after his outburst was almost unbearable, but finally Alice said, disbelievingly, "Johnny? You say you're Johnny?"

"Yes."

"But how . . .? Where . . .?" She sounded almost frightened and then her voice grew stronger. He could imagine her pulling herself together, wondering, no doubt, if this was some kind of hoax. "You believe we're related? What makes you think that?"

"It's a long story. A crazy set of coincidences. I've talked with Janice and Mrs. Rudolph . . . and your husband." Like Alice, he now struggled to sound calm, almost matter-of-fact. "I don't think there's any doubt," John said gently. "I'm sure I'm the child you gave up for adoption."

There was a quick intake of breath. "Where are you calling from?"

"I'm here in Denver. At the Hilton. I flew in today from Boston."

"Boston? You've been in Boston?"

"All my life. Since the day of my birth, November tenth, nineteen forty-six, at Massachusetts General."

"Oh, no!"

He couldn't tell whether she was happy or horrified. Or even whether she believed him. Probably she didn't know that herself. She was too much in shock, understandably unable to absorb the full impact of this incredible revelation.

"I'd like to see you as soon as possible," John said. He managed a little laugh. "That's an understatement. I've been waiting years to see you, Moth . . ." His voice trailed off. He didn't know what to call her. "Mother" was impossible to say, but he couldn't bring himself to call her "Mrs. Winters" or, even less suitably, "Alice." He hesitated, disconcerted, but finally he said, "Can we meet somewhere this afternoon?"

"I . . . I don't know." She sounded dazed, and John felt the return of his old fears. She didn't want to see him, didn't want him to exist. But then she said, "Yes, of course. I'd ask you to come here, but I think it's better that we talk outside the house. You're at the Hilton, you said? Why don't I come there? There's a little sort of cocktail lounge at the end of the lobby. Would that be convenient?"

"Perfectly. Thank you. I'll be waiting. Do you remember the name? It's Peck." He felt foolish saying that, but in her bewilderment she might have forgotten.

For the first time, she sounded half-amused. "I remember. I'll ask for you." There was another small pause. "I may bring someone with me. Jack Richards. Is that all right?"

No, John wanted to say. Come alone. If there's to be a reunion it's yours and mine, no one else's. He felt almost angry that she was being so cautious. Richards probably was her lawyer. She was bracing herself to cope with a possible phony, an impostor and extortionist, perhaps. "If you want to bring your friend, that's entirely up to you, but I assure you you're perfectly safe. I certainly mean you no harm."

"It's not that. If you are whom you say, you'll want to meet Jack Richards. He's your father."

It was John's turn to be stunned. He'd been so obsessed with finding Alice that he'd hardly given a thought to his other parent. Both of them? Here in Denver and presumably close? Good God! Who would have thought? He stammered something, hopefully civil, and hung up. In less than two hours he'd see her. *Them.* It was like a dream. Too nervous to sit still, he showered and changed, hoping he looked well, praying it would turn out right. He regretted their meeting in a public place, but there was little choice. She was right. He couldn't burst into his grandparents' house, and his modest hotel room was unsuitable, even if she were "chaperoned" by Jack Richards. He repeated the name to himself. Jack. Nickname for John. Alice had called her son after his father. I'm John Richards, Jr., he thought, staring into the mirror. I finally know who I am. Now I need to know how I came to be.

Alice gently replaced the receiver and sat gazing blankly into space. It couldn't be. It simply couldn't be that the child she and Jack had discussed finding would ring up an hour after their luncheon conversation about him. Things like that didn't happen. It was some dreadful mistake. Another disappointment in her life, which already seemed to have been a series of them.

And yet she dared to believe because she so desperately wanted the "miracle" she'd spoken of an hour before. Don't! she told herself. Don't get your hopes up! Things don't fall into place so easily. Not after thirty years. But how wonderful if it were true! What joy to be reunited with the child she'd given up! He'd surely accept her. Of course he would. If he wasn't prepared to forgive, he'd never have sought her out. And she yearned to put her arms around him, to try to make him understand the desperation of his young parents, to tell him he'd always been loved and wanted, despite how it must seem to him.

She glanced at her watch, silently giving thanks that none of the family was within earshot. She couldn't stand a skeptical, advance examination of this amazing development by anyone. Except Jack, who'd share her optimism and her joy. Quickly she dialed his office, and when he answered she said, "Something incredible has happened. Can you pick me up at four-thirty to go to the Hilton?"

"Sure." His voice was filled with curiosity. "What's going on?"

"We have an appointment at five o'clock." Suddenly she began to weep. "You won't believe it. I can't believe it!" The words came between sobs. "I've just had a phone call from Johnny. He's here, Jack. Our son has come to find us!"

From the moment she saw him, Alice knew this was her child. She and Jack approached the cocktail lounge at the hotel and Jack asked the hostess where Mr. Peck was. Before the young woman could answer, a tall, well-built stranger rose from a chair nearby and said, "I'm John Peck."

Alice's knees went weak. It was like looking at Jack Richards thirty years ago. There was no mistaking the resemblance. Even the smile was his father's. She stared at him, speechless, and then glanced at Jack, whose stunned expression confirmed her own instant reaction.

"My God!" Jack said as the three of them stood awkwardly looking at each other. The hostess gawked, openly curious. Crazy things went on every day in a hotel, but these people looked as though they'd all been struck by lightning. Finally, the young one regained his composure.

"Shall we sit down?" he asked courteously. "This nice young lady has been kind enough to save us a quiet corner over by the window."

The older couple followed him. In that first moment they'd simultaneously reached for each other's hands and they held on tightly as they made their way to the table. Even when they were seated, Jack and Alice's fingers remained entwined as though they were giving strength to each other. The hostess watched them. They all looked as though they were going to burst into tears. It seemed, she thought idly, like some kind of reunion, and yet they obviously were strangers. The young man had even had to introduce himself. It was a mystery. She saw the waitress take their drink orders and withdraw and finally, before she had to turn away, she saw they'd begun to talk. She was always telling her boyfriend about the nutty things that happened during her working day. The pick-ups, the arguments, the drunks, the solitary boozers, the silly groups of conventioneers, all were good for a laugh. But there was something sad and serious about this trio. Well, she'd never know. It probably was nothing at all. But why did they keep staring at each other that way, like skittish animals? Hell, who cared? It wasn't her business.

The hostess would have been even more intrigued if she'd managed to eavesdrop on that meeting. They gave their drink orders and sat silently for a long moment. Finally, Jack Richards cleared his throat nervously and said, "Let's get right to the point. What's this all about?"

Johnny couldn't take his eyes off his mother. She was so beautiful, so dignified, and yet she seemed frightened. He'd tried so long to picture this moment, imagined it full of drama, not sure whether it would be tears of joy or cold rejection but certain it would be emotional. And here they were, like three well-bred strangers, waiting for their cocktails, sizing each other up, finding it almost impossible to speak. They were going to leave it up to him to prove himself. Except for that first startled exclamation of Jack's, there'd been no outward indication that they were ready to accept what he knew to be true. All right. He'd carry the ball. Slowly, calmly, he began to tell the story of his search. Of finding the papers with Alice Dalton's name on them. Of tracking down a hundred futile leads. And of finally coming across the society item which led him to Janice and Mrs. Rudolph and a phone conversation with Spencer Winters and this precipitous flight to Denver.

"That's it," he ended, flatly, looking straight at Alice. "I've searched for you all my life. And now I've found you. I can't prove anything really. My adoptive parents are dead. To my knowledge, only your aunt knows the truth. Unless your parents do. Or unless we can find the doctor who delivered me and probably arranged the adoption 'under the counter,' so to speak." He kept looking at Alice. "But I know you're my mother. I knew it when you walked in. I think you know it too."

Alice was too overcome to answer, but Jack Richards made one more effort to be "businesslike."

"How can we be certain, John?" he asked not unkindly. "Just a few hours ago we talked about ways of finding our son. We had one. Alice has already told you that. We'd planned to explore every avenue that could take us to him, but to have you suddenly appear this way, so insanely coincidentally, is almost too pat. This is the most important thing in all our lives. We must be sure, all of us. Absolutely sure."

"Can you ever be?" Johnny answered. "Where will the proof come from? There's only one place I know: from Mrs. Rudolph, who can confirm that the Pecks took your baby. I know my mother's name is Alice Dalton." He smiled bitterly. "But there are a lot of Alice Daltons and I've contacted most of them in the past ten years. No, I can't prove who I am. I can only believe it."

Impulsively, Alice reached across the table and touched John's cheek. "You're Johnny," she said softly. "Look at you. Look at your father. Can either of you have any doubt?" Her eyes glistened with tears. "I don't need proof. I don't need a 'confession' from poor old Aunt Charlotte. I know you're part of me, part of us. I know it as surely as I'm sitting here. Oh, God, you don't know what this means to me! The years I've dreamed of you, the hours I've spent reproaching myself for ever letting you go, the wondering where and how you were. That was the worst, the not knowing. Johnny, Johnny, can you forgive me? I didn't want to let you go. I had no choice. I couldn't care for you. Nobody would help. I had to let them take you."

They were all weeping now, Alice openly, the men trying to brush away the tears with the backs of their hands.

"I want to know all about it," John said. "How it happened and why. But even before, I can tell you that there's never been any need for forgiveness. I always knew you wouldn't have given me up if you'd had a choice. I clung to that belief. It's why I never stopped searching. I wondered about you just as much as you did about me. I knew you'd be as sweet and warm as you are." He reached out and touched her cheek as she had his. "You're everything I dreamed you'd be. You're my mother."

They were so intent upon each other they nearly forgot the other person intimately involved. His voice brought them back to the moment.

"If there's any forgiveness, it must be for me," Jack said. "I'm the one who walked away. I'm the stupid, selfish kid who let her go through this alone. There are explanations, of a sort. Alice has found it in her heart to forgive me. I hope you will, too, when you hear the whole story. It's a long one, son. A terrible one, especially for you and your mother, but I want you to know it all, and I pray you'll understand and accept me. You see, I came late to this kind of love. So many years later than I should have. But that doesn't diminish what I feel . . . for both of you."

His parents looked at him, waiting for his answer. "You're my family," John said. "I finally know who I am, and I can only believe I'm lucky to belong to people like you."

"We're the lucky ones," Jack Richards said. "We have so much to talk about, Johnny. When you hear it, you'll realize how lucky we all are."

Chapter 21

LIKE ENVY, GREED or even misguided love, the desire for revenge is an ugly, all-consuming passion more destructive to the one who nurtures it than to its target. Seldom sweet, as popularly suupposed, revenge is, in fact, an empty, useless exercise in self-indulgence which feeds like a cancer on its carrier, destroying logical thought and discipline. There is a sick joy in the anticipation of it, but a sense of futility in its achievement. Yet there are those who cannot live deprived of hate. It sustains them, occupies their every waking thought, pervades their dreams and becomes as necessary as breathing.

For years, Dorothy Paige had nursed an irrational desire for revenge on "the Dalton girls." From adolescence she'd despised their beauty and easy confidence, their popularity and their strict but adoring parents. Her own mother and father were cold, undemonstrative people whose prime interest in Dorothy seemed to be in her scholastic achievements rather than her happiness. They approved her high marks in school, expected her to be (as, indeed, she was) valedictorian of her high school class. They did not see, or they chose to ignore, the fact that she had few friends and fewer dates and that her peers looked on her as a "grind," useful only when they faced a test for which they were not prepared and for which Dorothy had the answers. Eagerly, pathetically, she came to their rescue at such times, basking for a few moments in their admiration and friendship, hoping it would continue and knowing it would not. Frances Dalton was guilty of this unconscious cruelty time and again. So was Buzz Paige, for whom Dorothy had a secret, unrequited passion. She could not hate Buzz. But she grew to despise Fran and the sisters who were an extension of her: Alice, sought-after in her own group, with Jack Richards as a steady beau; even little Barbara, child that she was in those long-gone days, showed promise of being as pretty and popular as her older sisters. They seemed bathed in sunshine while Dorothy sulked in the shadows of loneliness and hated them.

Frances, of course, was an obsession, the focus of her envy. Fran and Buzz and their friends speeding by her house in his open car, en route to some picnic or party from which she'd been excluded. Fran and Buzz jitterbugging at the prom and dancing soulfully, cheek to cheek, as the band played "Goodnight, Sweetheart." Fran and Alice giving parties at the Dalton house for the "gang," sometimes inviting her out of pity but making no effort to see that she had a good time. Not that there was much they could have done about it. Dorothy was moderately pretty. She dressed as well as the others, did her hair and make-up in imitation of theirs, but she was shy and inarticulate and the boys found her boring.

Even when, once or twice, she talked her parents into letting her have a party of her own, it was a dismal failure. She had the same ingredients as Fran and Alice did—the latest phonograph records, the space cleared for dancing, the fruit punch into which someone would sneak a bottle of gin. But she was a nervous and inept hostess with no natural gift for entertaining, unable to project that indefinable enjoyment contagious to guests. Her parties broke up early and she went to bed in tears, knowing the others were off to a drive-in for hamburgers

and malteds, glad to escape from the heavy atmosphere of the Kravett house
and the stilted attitude of the Kravett daughter. She did not know then what was
missing in her. Even years later, when she had her "nervous breakdown" over
Buzz's imagined infidelity, she could not see what the psychiatrist tried to guide
her into discovering: she lacked the capacity for unselfish love. She wanted to
possess, to be totally necessary. She did not know she thrived on her injured
feelings. She thought she loved her husband and her sons, but in fact she did
not. She strove to be indispensable to them, playing on their sense of duty or
pity or guilt. And they responded with outward kindness and patience and with
hidden resentment of her devouring qualities.

When Fran ran off with her actor, Dorothy was the only person in town who
rejoiced. The Daltons were shocked and grief-stricken, unable to handle this
new blow coming so soon after Alice's disgrace. Buzz was like a man in a fog,
morosely moving away from the group of which he and Frances had been a part,
drinking to escape his memories, ripe for someone totally different from the girl
who'd betrayed him.

Dorothy was clever enough to know she could be that someone. She "moved
in" with gentle persistence, in the form of invitations to plays for which she'd
"accidentally" received tickets. She sent him notes and small, silly, thoughtful
gifts. Buzz was grateful for this unthreatening new companionship. He appreciated
her kindness, seeing her as he'd always seen her, an attractive but dull young
woman who people said was a born "old maid."

Later, he did not know how it happened, he went to her house one night for
a quiet evening and ended up seducing her on the living-room couch after her
parents had gone to bed. He'd been drinking heavily from the bottle he sneaked
in, and Dorothy was suddenly someone he'd never seen before—a passionate,
reckless girl who threw herself, literally, at him. Before he realized it, he'd been
aroused. She offered no resistance. On the contrary, she invited him to destroy
her virtue.

It was an inexpert and unsatisfactory coupling, for Dorothy was a virgin and
Buzz, for all his seemingly worldly ways, had had little experience. After it was
over, he was covered with remorse and yet he felt tenderness toward her, and
when she lay quiet, looking at him with her big eyes and saying, finally, "I
love you," he heard himself answering, "I love you too."

From that moment, she took it for granted that they were engaged. And Buzz,
too guilty to fight it and too unhappy to care, went along with her assumption.
They were married a few months later in a big church wedding at which some
of the guests privately remarked that the groom looked hangdog and the bride
had the smirk of a cat who'd devoured a canary.

It was, in the beginning, not too bad a marriage. Dorothy was not a sparkling
companion but marriage seemed to mellow her. She was a good wife, an excellent
homemaker and a surprisingly passionate bedmate who produced three strapping
sons, the joys of Buzz's life, in four years. He was never in love, but he was
reasonably content. His business flourished and kept him away from home for
long hours. He enjoyed his children and gradually slipped into the role of satisfied
husband, devoted father and active member of the business community, joining
all the businessmen's clubs, serving on the advisory committee of several charities

and taking an active role in church affairs. If his life was dull, he refused to think about what it might have been with Frances. And in time he could think of her almost without pain, as though she were some high-spirited shadow from his past. Only when he accidentally ran into the Daltons did he remember how much he'd adored their daughter.

It was not until she was forty that Dorothy reverted to the neurotic, withdrawn, frequently unpleasant creature of her youth. Whether the fact of becoming forty was traumatic, or whether she was undergoing premature ''change of life,'' Buzz did not know. She'd been angry when the boys married early, though they chose nice girls who wondered among themselves how that attractive Mr. Paige had ever chosen such a dreary wife. Whatever the reason, for the next few years Dorothy made life hell for everyone around her, culminating in her ungovernable jealous rage about her husband's supposed affair with the widow. He stood it as long as he could and finally moved out. It was a relief to be free of her. He'd have liked never to return, but the pressure came from all sides—from his parents and hers, from the sons who sympathized with him but felt sorry for their unhappy mother, from the daughters-in-law who had no love for her but saw the terrifying possibility of his children following in his footsteps someday. Most of all, the plea to return came from a seemingly chastened Dottie, who was dutifully undergoing therapy and apparently trying hard to change, vowing tearfully that she could and would.

So he went home and made up his mind to live with this still unpredictable woman whom he no longer even pretended to love. And he would have allowed this lethargy to carry him along forever if Frances had not come back into his life, offering herself and freedom and the kind of heady excitement he'd not known since the day she left. She was temptation incarnate. He could think of a dozen selfish reasons to run of with her: There were too few good years left to him. He'd always adored her. He'd fulfilled his obligations to his children, who now were grown men with families of their own. He'd been trapped into this sometimes dull, sometimes stormy marriage by his own youthful ignorance and Dot's shrewd, scheming mind. And Dot herself was still mentally unstable. But that last reason, which should have been the decisive one in favor of his defection, was, perversely, the same one that kept him from throwing caution to the winds and leaving town with Frances. He couldn't abandon Dorothy, he told himself. He couldn't be that cruel to a woman who was not responsible for her acts. And yet she drove him out of his mind with her nagging, her accusations, her air of being put-upon in every situation. He'd even been so undone that he'd confessed to sleeping with Fran! What had possessed him? And why had she reacted in that strange way, almost humbly and yet with a flicker of triumph, as though she was glad to have her suspicions confirmed. In a way, he wished Frances had never come back. And at the same time he gloried in knowing her as he never had, even if it was to be only a brief and dangerous interlude. She'd be leaving soon, but he was determined to arrange that weekend he promised. He wanted it as much as she. To wake up with her for two mornings was not too much to ask after a lifetime of longing. But this time he'd not indulge in some foolish confession. Dorothy wouldn't know. Nobody would. It would be a little difficult to invent a business trip over the weekend, but he'd manage.

And then suddenly he thought, Why does it have to be a weekend? Fran can come and go as she pleases and it will seem much more logical if I have to go out of town during the week. Mentally, he arranged it for Tuesday and Wednesday of the next week. They'd go to Phoenix. He'd find a small, romantic hotel where they'd make love and sleep and talk and be at ease instead of sneaking into a shabby motel room which they knew they must leave in a couple of hours. It's not wrong, Buzz told himself. Nobody will be hurt. And two people will be happy.

He underestimated the workings of Dorothy's warped mind. The confession of his infidelity which she appeared to accept only rekindled the fires of revenge which had simmered within her all these years. To have captured Frances' first love was not enough for Dorothy. Frances had to pay for her lifelong disregard of other people's feelings. God had brought her back to face her punishment for all the early hurts, and He'd appointed Dorothy His avenging angel. She felt almost euphoric. It was her duty to make Frances Dalton repent her wantonness, past and present. I'll have peace then, Dot thought. The peace that's always eluded me. In her troubled mental state she saw Fran's return as a sign from the Almighty. This was a new religion and it was called revenge.

She smiled calmly and nodded when Buzz told her he had to fly to Phoenix for a couple of days next week to look into a new dealership.

"How long will you be gone?"

"Oh, two, three days at the most. Will you be all right?"

"Of course. I'll visit the boys. And maybe have lunch with Laura Dalton." Dot's expression was innocent. "I imagine the girls will have left by then and she'll be feeling lonely. Besides, I should repay her for that nice party."

He glanced at her suspiciously. She and Fran's mother had had lunch before. They saw each other frequently at church. But even if this were coincidental, it would not do to have Dot get in touch with Laura and discover that Fran had gone away "for a couple of days." There was only one way. Fran would have to leave Denver for good when she went off with Buzz. She could fly back to Paris or wherever when they parted. That way, Dorothy could be assured that Frances really had left and Buzz's trip was legitimate. God, it was getting complicated! For a minute he wavered. Maybe all the cover-up wasn't worth it. It was too tricky. How did he know Fran was ready to leave Denver? But she was. She'd said she was only staying a week and it was almost that already. He'd tell her how it had to be when they met tonight at the motel. He couldn't bear to think of losing her again. But he had to. There was no future for them with the specter of Dorothy haunting him wherever he went. Fran accepted that. She was willing to settle for the only thing within reason. What a fabulous woman she's become, Buzz thought. Realistic but not cynical, passionate without possessiveness. There'd be regret, not for what they'd done, but for what they'd never have again.

Chapter 22

AFTER THE INITIAL, devastating effect of Andrea Tallent's letter, Barbara fell
into an uncharacteristic mood of helpless resignation. She seemed to have none
of her usual spirit or buoyancy, no instinct to fight back for what was dearest
to her. It was as though she'd always known one day it would come, this end
to her happiness, and now that it had, though not in the way she could have
imagined, she seemed to accept her defeat more in sorrow than in rage.

She stayed in her room that whole day and evening, feeling disembodied,
detached from reality. She knew now what people meant when they said that in
times of tragedy they felt they were outside of themselves, watching their own
grief in an almost clinical way as though this terrible thing was happening to
someone else. It was a protective trick of the mind, she supposed. A curtain
between the truth and one's unwillingness to face it. It was merciful, this feeling
of being dead. That's how she felt. Dead. Emotionless. Incapable of action or
even of anger.

After the tears, after the talk with her mother and later with Fran, she went
into this introspective state. She did not question the truth of what Andrea
reported. Not the fact of the probable appointment or the accurate reporting of
Charles's feelings. She was sure he was suffering the tortures of the damned,
looking for an "easy" way to end this with as little hurt as possible. Poor
Charles, mistaking cowardice for compassion. Like most men, he dreaded unpleasant confrontations. Barb could not hate him, could not summon up bitterness.
She understood why he was postponing the terrible moment when he'd have to
tell her the one thing neither of them wanted to hear.

If it hadn't been so terrible, it would almost have been funny, Barb thought.
Ironic. I thought I was the one in this family who "had it made." I pitied Allie
with her terrible husband and her awful guilts about the abandoned child. I saw
Fran's life as useless and petty, a lonely life in spite of its material comforts. I
even felt sorry for Mother and Dad, stuck in this mediocre existence with nothing
to look forward to. I thought I had it all: a man who adored me; a busy, interesting
life in the capital of the world; my independence and my tiny but nourishing
sense of importance. Now, in the space of a week, I've become the one with
no hope and no future and no one to cling to. The people I secretly patronized
are working out new lives while mine is coming to an end.

She walked to the window and saw Allie running down the front steps, her
movements as graceful and excited as a young girl's. Jack Richards waited in
a car at the curb. Four-thirty. Where were they going? And how had Alice
suddenly found courage to let Jack pick her up at the house? What difference
did it make? Alice had been reunited with the father of her baby. That was all
that mattered. He still cared for her. He could take her away from that awful
life in Boston. It was too much to hope they'd find their son, but they'd have
each other.

Barbara turned away. Even Fran has found something again, she thought. I
don't know how she really feels about Buzz or what she seriously plans to do
about him. But that doesn't matter either. Her ego has been restored. She knows

she's still desirable. She'll be able to take him, if she decides to. She'll hurt poor, pathetic Dottie Paige, but so what? In this world it's every woman for herself, Barbara thought bitterly. God knows I've found that out today.

She paced the room. Even Mother and Dad aren't the sorry creatures I once thought them. Their life seems unutterably boring to me, but why do I presume to put my feelings into their heads? They feel safe here where they've always lived. Comfortable with their house and their neighborhood and their friends and each other. Each other. That was the bottom line. That's what it eventually came down to: having someone to care about, some life to share. I should have realized that long ago. I thought I did, in my own, peculiar way. I thought Charles and I were the exceptions who could break the rules. We care for each other. But we never shared. Not really. Not, as Fran says, publicly. That still matters. Not marriage so much, but honesty. She's right. If I didn't want to marry, I should have had the wit to find a man who could openly be my lover. Why did I feel I could go on forever walking the tightrope, balancing an existence halfway between wife and mistress? I thought I was the smart one. The sensible one. And all the time I was a sloppy, sentimental dope. It is a laugh. A very bitter laugh. Well-adjusted Barbara is a bigger fool than her mousy sister or her cynical one. At least they recognize their failings. I've been so high and mighty, overconfident and stupid. Wonderful me. Miss Know-it-all. Advising everybody else. And now I don't know what to with my own life.

She heard noises in the next room, but she didn't want to see Fran again just then. Their earlier talk had only confused her further. It was so diametrically opposed to what their mother had said. Laura had urged her to step aside, to move off with dignity. Fran had taken just the opposite view when she'd come in to see her sister.

"Don't be a bloody damned fool!" Fran's voice was harsh. "Are you really going to hold still for this? Are you going to let him brush you out of his life like some piece of dirt that messes up his career? For God's sake, Barbara, where's your backbone? The man owes you!"

"He's . . . he's provided for me. We always thought, in case he died . . ."

Fran literally shook her. "I'm not talking about money! Hell, nobody likes it better than I do. I married for it once. I'd despise being without it. But you've never cared about it. You don't care about it now. He's 'provided for you,' you say. Well, I should hope so! But he hasn't provided for what you care about. He's used up most of your good years and now you're supposed to roll over and play dead because you're in his way. You're supposed to give up without a struggle. Be ladylike and well-mannered and subsist on the knowledge that you made some kind of contribution to his success. I never heard such garbage!"

Barbara looked at her helplessly. "I don't know what you think I should do. He's always said he couldn't marry me. He's been honest about that."

"But you never really believed it, did you?"

Her sister's shrewd insight startled Barbara. Fran knew her better than she knew herself. Inside, deep inside, she'd stifled the belief that somehow things would work out for her and Charles. She could deny it forever, even to herself, but it was true. She remembered how angry she'd been when her mother cautioned her. How vehemently she protested that she was content with things the way they were. But it was a lie she'd almost managed to make herself believe.

"All right, maybe I did hope. Unconsciously, at least. But what does that matter now? I have to let him go, Fran. I couldn't hold him even if I tried."

"No? My dear little sister, you are in a position to make things heavy for the good congressman. You could blow his life sky-high if you chose. He knows that. So does that bitchy wife of his. Listen, Barb, I can't stand to see you get the short end of this deal. You love him. And I suppose he loves you. A little less than power, maybe, but more than any other woman. Well, something's got to give. And why should all the sacrifice be on your side? To hell with Tallent's big cabinet job and his dazzling future! Don't accept this. Tell him when push comes to shove it's up to him to find a way out, but in any case you don't plan to disappear. Not now or ever."

Barbara was aghast. "I couldn't do that to him! My God, Fran, I wouldn't blackmail a man I love! And I'd never force myself on someone who didn't want me. What happiness could there be in that? He'd resent me forever."

"Oh, get off it, baby! Can't you see what that letter really means? Andrea Tallent is scared to death that her husband loves you so much he'll change his mind when he sees you. She's just dying to have you play the long-suffering heroine and kiss Charles off before he has a chance to realize what he's giving up. Well, you just beat her at her own game, kiddo. You get your fanny back to Washington pronto and remind the great man that it's damned uncomfortable to sleep with a cabinet post. You won't have to threaten him. I know that's not your way. It's unfortunate that this came up while you weren't around to stop it, but it's not too late. You want him, Barb. For God's sake get in there and fight for him. That's what I'm going to do about Buzz!"

Remembering, Barb shuddered. There was a great deal in what her sister had said. But she couldn't do it. It wasn't in her to scheme or demand or to play games. Charles was weighing the problem. She was certain of that. Nothing would happen until she either wrote the letter Andrea suggested or went back and made him tell her his decision in his own words.

I don't know whether to write the letter, Barbara thought. I can't really go with Fran's tough attitude. I won't keep him from the thing that will make him happiest, if only I were sure he knows what he wants. Fran doesn't think I should suffer because Charles is ambitious. Well, I don't think he should pay the price of my blindness, my childish, oblivious attitude toward the hard facts of life.

Absorbed as she was with her own problems, she suddenly recalled Fran's parting words about Buzz, a statement on which she'd not elaborated. Obviously, Fran *had* come to a decision about him, probably had a specific "game plan." I envy her the ability to justify everything she does, Barb thought. She's right. Grab what you believe belongs to you and don't think about the long-range results. I'd like to live for the moment, as Fran does. And then, contradicting herself, Barbara rejected that idea. She couldn't. Couldn't be blithe about destroying someone else's life for some selfish pleasure which might or might not endure. God knows, she was no saint. In her parents' eyes, she'd been "a fallen woman" all these years, but she'd never felt she was hurting anyone. Not even herself. She couldn't change now. Her automatic rejection of Fran's suggestion that she make things difficult for Charles came from a gut instinct. Much as I'd like to be a different kind of woman, Barb thought, I never will be. I might as well reconcile myself to that. As they grow older, people don't take on new attitudes; they only become more of what they've always been.

The acceptance of that made her suddenly stand very straight and tall, alone there in the room. Okay, Barbara Dalton, she told herself. Enough self-pity. You'll grieve. You'll regret. You'll damned near die. But you're your mother's child. Laura was right. It was time to let go, to do one last thing for someone she loved so much. Charles had been nothing but good to her. She wouldn't go out of his life with shrieks or whimpers. She'd leave quietly, knowing his memories would be as sweet and poignant as hers. The empty feeling would lessen in time as the anguish would diminish. Life wasn't over, as she'd so dramatically told herself. It might stop for a while, might seem futile and meaningless, but she'd endure. She didn't want pity from anyone. Not from Charles or from her family. Certainly not from herself. Before she could change her mind or be swayed by Fran's persuasiveness, she sat down at the desk where years before she'd done her homework and began to write the most difficult letter of her life.

My dearest Charles,

I've missed you so this week. There have been few moments when you have not been in my mind, as for all these years you have been in my heart and in my arms. You have given me hours of indescribable joy, a euphoric sensation of being endlessly submerged in happiness. You made me feel beautiful and invincible, as though nothing was wrong with the world and never could be as long as I was with you. You are an extraordinary man, the one I dreamed of and never hoped to find. A sensitive, brilliant, giving human being, your intuition is incredible in one so manly, so virile and strong. I've clung to you, Charles. I've grasped at you, clutched you to me fiercely to save myself from going under, from being swept away in a tide of loneliness.

I thought we could drift together, not wanting rescue, not wishing to step foot on the sands of reality. But since I've been home, I've seen that I have a need for firm ground and solid footing. I've watched my parents who've traveled fifty years over the rough road of marriage, clasping each other's hands, sharing the same triumphs and tragedies, holding their heads high, secure in the knowledge that they will be together in all things sad and wonderful. I want that too, Charles, for whatever time is left to me. This golden anniversary has made me think deeply about my own life. About you. About us, my darling. About the make-believe life we live.

It hurts to call those precious years 'make believe.' But they have been. They are. Our chemistry has no real continuity. Our passion no permanence. Our love no future. Not, at least in the sense of an enduringg commitment for all the world to see.

Coming home has made the ancient verities all too clear to me. I shall never have a fiftieth wedding anniversary, but selfishly I want a fifth, or a tenth, or even a first. The basic insecurity within me has come face to face with jealousy of those who have the security of an avowed love.

> The selfishness that has always been just under the surface can no longer settle for a secret love, deep and true as I know it is. Only a fool is compelled to state the obvious, but I am foolish enough to say I must give up something romantic because I need something real.
>
> I can see you now, my dearest love, reading these words with bewilderment. Or perhaps not. You have always known, I think, that someday I would want the whole of you I cannot have. You have understood my need better than I understood it myself. You have warned me about this very moment, even as I denied it would ever come.

Barbara paused in her writing. It was a blatantly unbelievable letter. Charles knew her too well to buy this story of "sudden realization." He'd recognize it as a tissue of lies and demand the truth. That's what I really want, she thought. I've put down this nonsense about the fiftieth anniversary bringing a flash of comprehension because I want him not to believe it, because I want him to tell me I'm a fool and reassure me that our love can go on. That's what I want. And that's what I must not allow. I must be more convincing. Fighting back the tears, she wrote the ultimate, convincing finale.

> You must be wondering, though, why my painful decision to end the thing between us comes so suddenly. You are entitled to know before anyone else that I've met someone here in Denver who wants to marry me and give me the kind of security and shelter a drifting, forty-year-old spinster should have. I cannot say I love him as I love you. No one will ever have that place in my heart. No one ever could. But he is a good man, a kind and patient one.

She stopped again, not knowing how to paint a convincing picture of this fictitious suitor. Tears forced themselves past her will to contain them, as she tried to think how to go on. Let me visualize someone, Barb thought. Anyone. Buzz Paige? No. Not even in imagination could she picture herself marrying Buzz. Jack. Yes, Jack Richards. Not that she could love him, or he, her, but he was a prototype Charles could understand. She began, again, to write.

> I've known this man since I was a little girl. I had a terrible "crush" on him even when he was taking out my older sister. He's a widower now and childless, as alone as I. He's intelligent and successful and devoted. I've told him there's been someone else in my life for many years. He does not condemn that. He is not interested in the past, only in a future which involves me. We will make our home here and travel a good part of the year. I do not expect the ecstasy you've taught me, but I hope for peace and serenity in the declining years which are coming all too quickly.
>
> Forgive me, my darling Charles. I could not bring myself to tell you this in person, coward that I am. Indeed, I will not be coming back to Washington at all. Am I afraid to risk seeing you? Of course I am. But

I know this is right for all of us, and the nearness of you must not cloud the clear course I am determined to follow.

I will be happy. I know you care about that most of all. And, dearest, you will be happy too, for the generosity of spirit which is so much a part of you will want what is best for me—as it always has. Just as I want all that is good and wonderful for you—and always will.

Barbara

She reread it, hoping against her real desire that Charles would accept it. She even prayed he'd be relieved, bitter as that thought was. It solved his problems and left no room for guilt.

Fran would think she was an utter fool. Perhaps she was. But this was how she had to handle it. Only this way could she live with herself, knowing she'd always have Charles's love even though she renounced it. The other way, Fran's way, was futile. She might get Charles but she'd lose his love, if not right away, certainly in time when he'd look back and regret the abandoned chance for a place in history.

Slowly, sadly, she addressed the envelope to his house. What did it matter if Andrea saw the letter arrive? But I hope she won't read it, Barb thought. I'd hate to think of her triumph, but even more, I'd hate to have anyone but Charles see these lying, loving words which are meant only for him.

"Where is everybody?" Sam Dalton looked curiously at the three empty places at the dinner table.

"You're really getting terribly spoiled," Laura teased. "We haven't had a full house in thirty years and now you expect one every night!"

"Well, dammit, those girls are only here a short time and I've hardly seen them. They don't seem to spend much time at home. I don't understand this younger generation. They finally come back for an overdue visit and all they do is gad around day and night! I thought the whole purpose was to see us."

"It is, dear," Laura said soothingly, "but you can't really expect them to be underfoot every minute. You're not around that much yourself, you know. You're either tinkering in the basement or working in the garden."

"I'm here at mealtimes and in the evening. And I see all the comings and goings. Who was that who picked up Allie this afternoon? Some man in a car."

Laura was genuinely at a loss. "I have no idea. I was in the kitchen about four-thirty when she called out and said she was going out for cocktails and might not be home until later."

"What about Frances? Where does she go until all hours? And why has Barbara been in her room all day?"

Laura hated lying to him. She never had, but she couldn't tell him about Buzz and Frances. Any more than she could let him know about Alice and Jack Richards, who, now that she thought about it, must have been the man who came for her today. Or Barbara with her smashed "illicit" romance. Dear Lord, it had all gotten so out of hand! Sam would never understand. He still thought of their middle-aged daughters as "the younger generation." He'd be outraged by all of it. He loved his girls and in spite of his actions, past and present, thought they were wonderful. It would break his heart if he found out what had happened to them, what tragedies they'd lived through, even those of their own making. And he'd go out of his mind if he had any idea of what had transpired this week. He wasn't young. It might affect him physically as well as emotionally. Heaven knows it had taken its toll on her. She felt a hundred years old.

"Well?" Sam was staring at her.

Laura tried to think how to answer him without outright lies. "Sam, dear, Frances has friends here. You remember the night Spencer took us to dinner? She was meeting one of them that evening. I suppose she's catching up with a lot of acquaintances." She hoped he wouldn't pursue the subject of Allie. She couldn't think how to avoid telling him about Jack Richards' renewed interest. "As for Barbara," Laura hurried on, "she hasn't been feeling well today. I thought she should stay in bed and rest."

"What's the matter with her?"

"Nothing serious. She'll be all right."

Sam didn't pursue it. Woman trouble, he supposed. Not the kind of thing he cared to discuss. Besides, he wasn't worried about Barbara. She was always fine, always cheerful. It was the other two he didn't understand. Alice staying on without her husband, and with apparently no intention of leaving. Frances out every evening. Laura was lying. Frances was up to something. She wouldn't have stayed this long in Denver if she wasn't. And he still fretted about Allie and that snob she was married to. He'd bet there was something really wrong in Boston. For a moment, he felt angry with all of them, with his daughters and his wife. He sensed the girls had confided more in Laura than she was willing to admit. Dammit, why didn't they think they could talk to him? Was he such an ogre? Did they think their mother was more understanding or more intelligent than he? Secrets! He hated them. He could smell them. And right now the scent of hidden knowledge was all over Laura Dalton. He knew her too well not to recognize when she had something on her mind. Something she was keeping from him. Sam was sure that was the case right now. His questions made her nervous. She kept picking at the bread crumbs on the table, avoiding his eyes when she answered. Hell, for all he knew there was something going on with Barbara too. He'd never known that girl to spend a day in bed since she was a child and had measles.

"Maybe I'll look in on Barb after dinner." He watched Laura's reaction. It was much too hasty.

"Oh, no! I mean, that isn't necessary, Sam. She's perfectly fine."

"Like the other two are fine?"

Laura didn't answer.

"Come on," Sam said quietly. "You might as well let me in on what's happening around here. I'll find out sooner or later."

It was an almost irresistible temptation to tell him everything. The burden of her knowledge was almost more than she could bear alone. Besides, he had a right to know. They were as much his children as hers. But she couldn't. Not just yet. Not until the girls found solutions to their problems. It would be much easier for everybody concerned if Sam stayed out of things right now. She could imagine his rushing over and telling Jack Richards to leave Allie alone. Or raging at Fran for her promiscuity with Buzz Paige. Or, worst of all, being faced with the fact that his favorite, his baby, had been involved in a long-term liaison with a married man. What would upset him more? Laura wondered. The fact of Barbara's affair or the knowledge that the man planned to walk out on her?

"There's nothing to get upset about," Laura finally said. "Really, Sam, I think your imagination is running away with you. These aren't babies we're dealing with, you know. They have a right to be out for dinner without your permission." She smiled. "You still think of them as little girls, don't you? Never mind. So do I. I guess we always will. No matter how old they get, they'll still be children to us." She came around the table and hugged him from behind. "Now you stop fretting, Sam Dalton! You'll just get yourself worked up over nothing."

He patted her arm. "All right, Mother, if you say so."

Chapter 23

IT WAS AS though some all-powerful playwright was building toward a third-act climax in the four separate dramas taking place in Denver that day.

For Alice he chose the moment of grateful happiness in the reconciliation with her son. For Barbara, frustration and a sense of unbearable loss. And for Laura, bewilderment, anxiety and a bad conscience about the secrets she kept from Sam. But it was for Frances that the director of our destinies reserved the moments of terrible tension which ultimately would propel her down a predetermined path of reckless destruction.

The evening began, as had those few before it, on a note of passion made all the more exciting by its illicit overtones. Within minutes of each other, Fran and Buzz slipped into the motel room and almost without words gave themselves to the devouring act of love. Each time there was more sexual satisfaction as each came to know the preferences of his partner. Each time there was less inhibition and more desire, a strengthening on Fran's part to have this man with her always, a mounting dread in Buzz at the thought of losing her.

When they finally rested, exhausted, Fran flung her arms over her head and sighed with contentment, stretching her still-beautiful body in sensuous relaxation.

"Darling, are we going away next weekend? Have you decided where?"

Buzz felt his muscles tighten. He'd known, driving to the motel, that he'd have to tell her of the change in plan. He assured himself once again that she'd accept the inevitable. God knows he didn't want it any more than she, but this thing had to end. Tentatively, he began to lead up to it.

"We have to talk about that, sweetheart." Stalling for time, he lit two cigarettes and gave her one. "The weekend thing isn't going to work too well, I'm afraid."

All of Frances' senses came alert but she didn't move. "Why not? You were the one who suggested it."

"I know. But it's getting pretty complicated. How about going off together for a couple of days in the middle of next week, instead? It doesn't matter which days, does it? I thought maybe we could fly down to Phoenix and lie around in the sun, like maybe Wednesday and Thursday. How does that suit you?"

She took a deep drag of the cigarette and exhaled slowly. Something was wrong. There was something more than a switch from a weekend to a midweek escape. Go slow, Fran, she warned herself. He's holding back. Whatever is making him nervous has to be carefully handled. She pretended to be perfectly amenable to the idea.

"Fine with me. Wednesday is as good as Saturday, but why Phoenix? I thought we were going to rough it in the mountains."

Lying next to him she could feel the tension in his body. She was right. This was no petty complication.

"Godammit, Fran, I can't lie to you. Dorothy's scaring hell out of me. She's too quiet, too agreeable. I recognize the symptoms. It's the calm before the storm. She knows we're still meeting. She has to. I've never been out night after night in our whole life. But she's never said a word since the first night. Not, that is, until I told her I had to go away for a couple of days. Then she said she'd probably have lunch with your mother, because, to quote her, 'Laura will be lonely with all the girls gone again.' She didn't mention you by name, but I know what that meant. She was fishing. She suspects I'm going away with you and she'll confirm it when your mother says you're out of town for a few days."

Fran propped herself up against the headboard. "I'm not quite following this, darling. Perhaps I'm dense, but I don't get the drift. I gather you decided on weekdays because they'd be less suspicious for a 'business trip' than a weekend. And I take it you chose Phoenix instead of Aspen or Vail because if you had to be reached, you conceivably could have business there. But I still don't see how all that changes anything. Mother will tell Dorothy I'm away at the same time you are." She paused. "Or do you expect Mother to lie and say I've really left town for good? That won't wash, you know. First of all, Mother won't lie. And second, when I come back to Denver, Dorothy will know it."

In the dim light, Buzz looked miserable. Finally he said, "Fran, darling, I know your mother won't lie. She'll be telling the truth. My idea is that you'll fly to Paris from Phoenix. Oh, Dorothy will still suspect that we've been together, but she'll accept it as she has this past week, knowing this was a last fling before your departure."

Frances stared at him in disbelief. "What the hell do you mean, 'a last fling before my departure'? Is that what this is to you? A fling? And what gives you the right to decide when I'll stay or go? Do you really think I'm going to arrange my life to suit that sniveling little creature you married? Do you honestly think I'm going to let her run me out of town? Tell me, Buzz, have you believed for one minute I'm going to give you up? I've known all along that one of us would have to be the heavy in this, and I knew when the chips were down it would be me. All right. If you're so damned scared of Dorothy, I'm not. I'll tell her we're in love and that we're going away together. I hadn't thought we'd have to break it to her quite so soon, but apparently we must. And since you can't, I will."

It was Buzz's turn to be startled. "What are you talking about? I told you I'd never leave her. I can't. I don't know what she'd do. Something desperate. I can't live with that on my conscience, no matter how much I want you. Fran, darling, we both knew from the start it couldn't last. We agreed to take our little bit of happiness and be grateful for it. I'll think about those days in Phoenix the rest of my life. I'll think about you the rest of my life. But that's all I can do— think and wish and dream.''

She pulled him to her, letting her body remind him again of what he was losing. "No, my love, that's not all you can do. Neither of us can live on wishes and dreams. There's too precious little time left. I won't let you martyr yourself this way. I won't let you throw away your happiness and mine for no reason." She kissed him gently. "I'm sorry I got so angry. I was hurt that you planned to push me out of your life this way. I realize you don't want to hurt Dorothy. I admire you for that. But you're too blinded by pity to see that you do the woman no favor by staying with her when your heart is somewhere else. What a wonderful, gentle man you are, dearest. You care for others so much you're willing to sacrifice yourself. But it's misguided loyalty. I promise you it is. You've given so much and gotten so little in return. This is your last chance, Buzz. Mine, too. I'll never want anyone except you.''

The persuasive voice flowed over him, the body pressed itself against his. She was so positive this was right. And he wanted it so much. He heard the soft words going on.

"Have you thought of me in this, dear heart? You know I'm not the hard-shelled creature the world thinks I am. I can be hurt too. Desperately hurt. Don't you care what will happen to me if you leave me? Dorothy has her children and her grandchild, her place in life. But until I found you, I had nothing. No roots. No love. No reason for being.'' She allowed a half-sob to escape. "I'd never threaten. That's not my style. I panicked when you told me you wanted me to leave. I won't go to Dorothy. You know that. That's your job, darling. A man's job to protect the woman he loves. And that's what I'm asking of you now. If I'm the woman you love, protect me. Live with me and love me forever. Let me make you as happy as you deserve to be.''

He felt he was in some kind of terrible war, the victim of a conflict not only between two women but of an even more frightening one within himself. He wanted to hear all the things Fran said. Wanted to believe them. Wanted to take charge of his life and hers. But there was Dorothy who'd have to pay the price for this selfishness. And how would she exact that price? On him? On their children? On herself?

As though she read his mind, Fran said slowly, "I know you fear what she might do if you leave her. We talked about that before. But she won't do anything, Buzz. I promise. I know women like that. They use their weakness as their strength. In her own way, she's more selfish than I. She's holding someone through the helplessness she pretends. She plays on duty and pity. That's a tenuous thread, but it can cut deep. I know it has cut into you all these years, dearest, and in time it will destroy you. I won't let that happen. I can't. I love you too much.''

For the first time that evening she heard hesitancy in his voice. "I don't know. I don't know what's the right thing to do. God knows I love you. It's taken every ounce of courage in me to say we've got to end it. I don't want to. You know that. But we can't go on this way, Fran. You can't stay on here, meeting me in motels, sneaking off for a day or two. That's no life for you. And I can't handle that forever either. As for Dot, I see the breaking point coming. I told you before. I'm frightened for her. I can't push her much further.''

"No, of course you can't. It would be cruel. Crueler than telling her the truth. You must tell her, darling. It will be hard for you, but it's best for everyone concerned. I give you my word. In the end you won't regret it. You only have one life, my love, and you've dutifully given most of it to your family. They don't need you any more. But I do. I need you beyond anything I can tell you. And you need me.'' Abruptly, Frances moved away from him and got out of bed. It was time for a change of strategy.

"Where are you going?''

"Home. To my parents' home, that is. But only for a few days. I'm not going to Phoenix, Buzz. Those two days will only haunt me if you go back to Dorothy. I'm going to leave you alone, darling. I won't see you or speak to you until you've had time to think things through once and for all. I'll wait a little, Buzz. But if you don't want to come to me totally and irrevocably, I won't wait forever. I'm strong, my love, but not that strong.''

He watched her dress, watched every gracefully calculated movement. Fran was the only woman who could put on clothes with more seductiveness than other women could take them off. Troubled as he was, he felt desire starting again as he looked at her. God help me, how I want this woman! She means more to me than anything. More than my conscience, my honor, my sense of right and wrong. I don't care what happens. I don't care about anything but her.

"Stop!'' he said suddenly.

Half-naked, she slowly turned to look at him, The Question in her eyes.

"You're right I can't let you go. Not now. Not ever.'' He held out his arms to her.

Triumphant and hiding her victory under easy tears of joy, Fran went to him, half-laughing, half-crying. And that night, as though to seal the bargain, neither of them went home at all.

The hours slipped by unnoticed as Alice and Jack talked with the stranger who was their son. To them and to John Peck, it was the fulfillment of an impossible dream. In one evening they could not hope to bring three lives up to date, much less fill in the searing background, but that did not matter. They had years ahead, they told each other. Years to be a family.

"Don't think I didn't love my adoptive parents,'' John said at one point. "I did. I loved them dearly. They were as good as any two people could be. It hurt them to know I wanted so much to find you, but I think they understood that everyone needs to know who he really is and where he comes from. Maybe they felt they were protecting me by not telling me anything. I don't know. But they never did. I didn't find the first clue until after they died.''

"Perhaps they weren't sure how you'd be received,'' Alice said reluctantly. "After all, how much confidence could anyone have in a woman who'd give up her child?''

"Don't,'' Jack Richards said softly. "Don't keep punishing yourself, Allie.

You've done that long enough. It's over, my dear. That part of your life is over. You've more than paid your dues.''

John nodded his agreement. "He's right. Janice told me what Spencer Winters has put you through all these years. It was because of me, wasn't it? He made you feel worthless, didn't he? That damned sadist! It's a wonder Jan didn't kill him when he tried the same . . .'' John's voice trailed off when he saw a look of horror come over Alice's face.

"Spencer threatened Janice? Oh, my God! He didn't hurt her, did he?"

"No, but he slapped her. I'm sorry. I didn't mean to tell you that. They had a terrible row when he was trying to find me, but Janice stopped him cold. That's when she came and told me where to find you. She's quite a girl.''

"He's mad,'' Alice said. "He's a maniac, but I never thought he'd lay a hand on Janice. She was the only one he ever cared about. Probably because she's the only one who wouldn't be intimidated by him. He drove Chris away and he made my life a living hell, but he could never get to Janice. She wouldn't let him dominate her. I think he admired that. Spencer admires strength, even when it gets in his way.''

Jack interrupted. "Forgive me, but I don't think this is a night to rehash Winters' mental problems. As far as I'm concerned, he's out of our lives. Not worth talking about. There's the future to think about now, isn't there? We want to meet Carol first thing. Imagine, Allie. We not only have a son but a daughter-in-law and a grandchild on the way!'' He shook his head. "It's almost beyond comprehension.''

Alice brightened at the reminder of the unknown other family in Boston. "Oh, yes, we can't wait to meet her, Johnny! Could she fly out right away?''

"I don't know. I really hadn't thought that far ahead. Lord, I haven't even called her! She doesn't know how everything's turned out. She must be frantic, wondering. Jan, too. They're the ones who really made this happen.''

"We'll get to a phone as soon as we leave,'' Jack said. They'd lingered for hours over dinner, hardly touching their food. "We can call from my place. By the way, wouldn't you like to move in with me instead of staying at the hotel? There's plenty of room for you and for Carol, if she comes.''

"Yes, I would. I'd like that very much.'' John waited. When would he be asked to meet his aunts and his grandparents? Alice had told him about them but there'd been no mention of a meeting. John realized this was a delicate area, at least where Sam and Laura Dalton were concerned. This was where he might not be so warmly received. It was understandable, he supposed. These were the people who'd sent his mother away when she was carrying him. But could they possibly resent him now? Yes, he answered himself, they could. That generation didn't change. To them, he'd probably be a reminder of an old "disgrace.'' During the course of the evening, he'd been amazed to learn that his mother and father had not seen each other for years and that Jack Richards had not entered the Dalton house since the day Alice left. It was incredible, the whole thing. He hadn't been surprised to discover he was an illegitimate child. He'd assumed that. But he hadn't known until tonight that his parents had not been in touch with each other for more than thirty years, that their reunion only slightly preceded his appearance. He wondered what they would do. Marry, finally? He couldn't repress a sudden smile. If his real parents got together after all this time, he might be his father's best man at his wedding to his mother. What was that old riddle from his childhood? "Brothers and sisters I have none, but this man's father is my father's son. Who is he?" And the answer of course was "Me." What unexpected turns this hoped-for discovery had taken! Childhood sweethearts meeting again. Long-lost children appearing out of nowhere. Grandparents nursing old grievances. Whole families, never dreamed of, springing into existence. It was more than any of them could grasp. But the wonderful thing, the blessed, almost inspirational thing, was that Alice Winters and Jack Richards had unquestioningly accepted him for what he was. They'd taken him on faith, welcomed him with an intensity of joy that matched his own. There still was no hard and fast evidence that he was their child, but they needed none. They knew. Just as John knew these were his real parents.

The minor things, and they were minor compared to the miracle of finding his mother and father, would sort themselves out. There were a thousand things to discover, a dozen difficult problems, large and small, to solve, and yet John knew that answers would come. How strange it all was. He didn't even know what to call them. All evening, he'd never directly addressed them, feeling awkward and unsure what they wanted.

"I'd like to ask you both something," he said almost shyly. "It seems silly, but I . . . well, I don't really know what you want me to call you. I mean, what's the precedent for this? When a thirty-year-old child suddenly meets his parents for the first time, does he call them by their first names?" He gave a little laugh. "I hardly can call you 'Mrs. Winters and Mr. Richards,' that's for sure. And it feels funny to say 'Alice and Jack.' I guess what I'm asking is whether it's okay to call you Mother and Dad. That is, if it doesn't bother you . . ."

Jack and Allie exchanged glances of understanding. It wasn't quite the ridiculous question it seemed. This sensitive young man was trying to tell them, politely, that it would have been different if they were a married couple. Knowing their strange story, he was diffident about linking them this way.

"Johnny, dear," Alice said, "we *are* your mother and dad. There were other people who had those titles for many years, but I'm sure they never wanted to hear them any more deeply than your father and I do."

"I've been waiting all evening to hear you call me that," Jack added. "I thought maybe *you* didn't want to. What your mother says is true. For years Mr. and Mrs. Peck were your parents. I was afraid you'd think we were trying to take their place if we suggested it." He sounded happy and slightly wistful. "Nobody's ever called me Dad. It has a mighty nice ring."

They sat silently for a moment. Such a little thing and yet so important to all three. It made it all real, somehow. Natural and warm and permanent. Allie's eyes were shining and Jack felt a suspicious moisture in his own. Brusquely, he cleared his throat, "Well, that's settled. Now, shall we go to my place and call Carol and Janice?"

Much later, Alice let herself into her parents' house and went quietly up the stairs. It was nearly midnight. There was no light under Fran's door. Maybe she's asleep, Allie thought. She's been out every night but she's always home and awake by now. She softly opened the bedroom door. The room was empty and the bed untouched. Allie felt a little let-down. She was so eager to share her wonderful news with both her sisters. I hope Barb's awake. She'll be amazed and delighted. And then she remembered the strange state Barb had been in earlier in the day. What a selfish thing I am! I've hardly given her a thought. It's been such a full day. First the revealing lunch with Jack and then, less than an hour later, the phone call that sent her rushing, not daring to believe, to the meeting with her son. But I should have found time to see whether Barb was all right. I shouldn't have dashed out this noon when there obviously was something wrong.

The room they shared was dark but Allie sensed that her sister was awake in the other bed.

"Barb?" she whispered. "You awake?"

"Yes. Hi."

"Mind if I turn on a light?"

"Go ahead. I haven't been asleep."

Alice switched on the lamp between the beds and sat down on her own. Barbara looked different, somehow. The usually cheerful face was expressionless as it turned to meet Alice's eyes. I know that look, Alice thought. It says everything's pointless and life is just one long, unfunny joke. I've seen it too often in my own mirror.

"What's wrong, baby? I knew something was going on when I left, but Fran shoo-ed me out before I had a chance to find out. What's happened, Barb?"

"I don't want to talk about it now, Allie. In the morning, okay? Did you have a good day? How's Jack?"

This was no moment to recount her own happiness. "My day was fine," Alice said quietly. "I'll tell you all about it. But right now, I want to know what's happened to make you look so miserable. Please tell me. Maybe I can help."

"Nobody can help."

"Don't be so sure."

Barbara sat up suddenly, almost angrily. "All right. Help me. Tell me how to solve this, if you're so smart!" She snatched Andrea Tallent's letter from the bedside table and threw it across the small space between them.

Alice read the cool, cruel words slowly, her heart sinking as she absorbed their meaning. When she finished she stared blankly at the woman who sat gazing into space. No wonder Barbara sounded so filled with hate! Right now she must hate the world, Allie thought. I know that feeling too.

"I'm so sorry." Such inadequate words, but she could find no others.

"Thanks. Me, too."

It was like listening to a stranger. Is this what the end of her love affair will do to Barbara? Allie wondered. Is she going to become hard and impossible to reach? Will this turn her into another Fran, embittered and distrustful of everyone and everything?

"I know how it hurts," Alice said. "I don't blame you for being angry. It's unfair. Hideously unfair. It's no consolation, but these things happen to nice women. It's the price you pay for giving so much of yourself, darling. All you can do is pick up and go on. And you will, Barb. You're not one to indulge in self-pity."

"You should be an expert on that! You've been pitying yourself for years!" Barbara stopped, aghast at what she'd said. "Oh, God, I must be out of my mind! Allie, forgive me. I didn't mean that. You know I didn't. You've been anything but self-pitying. You've been the bravest person I've ever known. I'm so sorry. I don't know what made me say such an awful thing to you, of all people. I thought I was under control. I even wrote a letter to Charles, pretending *I* was breaking off with him. I thought I was going to be able to handle it, for his sake. But I can't. I've been lying here for hours, going over everything in my mind, telling myself how I've been used and what a fool I've been and what an idiot I am to let him go. Fran thinks I shouldn't. She thinks I should make it tough for him, that I might even keep him if I fight." The words came tumbling out. "I don't know what to do, Allie. Should I send the letter? I'd convinced myself it was the only decent thing to do, but now I'm not sure. Everything seems so futile, so meaningless. You're right. I am drowning in self-pity and I should be killed for taking out my own stupidity on you. Please forget what I said. I'm not making any sense. You just happened to be the first target for all the spite and venom that's been building up inside of me tonight."

"It's all right. I understand. I truly do, Barb. There've been so many times I wanted to lash out at the first person I saw. Darling, I know how you feel about me. The same as I do about you. Those silly words aren't important. I'll never think of them again. What matters is you. I want you to come out of this the same generous, loving woman you've always been. I don't want to see you become disillusioned and distrustful of any relationship. And most of all, I want you to do what you know inside is right for you. Whether that means sending the letter or making a fight for Charles, I can't answer. Only you can decide what you can live with. That's what it finally comes down to, Barb. A compromise, at best, but hopefully an endurable one."

"I can't do it Fran's way. I have to let him go, Allie. But it's so hard. It's my whole life."

"I know," Alice said again. "I've been there. We all have, one way or another. But we survive." She went to Barbara's bed and stroked her head as she might have soothed Janice. "Try to get some sleep now, okay? We'll talk more tomorrow."

Barb nodded. "Thank you. I mean it. If you can live through what you have, I can live through this."

"You'll live. You may even come out the better for it, though I know you can't believe that now."

In the darkness, Alice lay awake, pitying the woman next to her. She'd never been through anything exactly like it, but in a way she'd felt the same terrible despair when Jack Richards deserted her for his own future. The situations were not comparable but each was terrible in its own way. It had taken years for Allie to shake her grief and her suppressed anger. In fact, she'd not felt truly happy until tonight, the night she'd been so eager to tell Barb and Fran about. God knows it was no moment to tell Barb how wonderful life had suddenly become.

That would have been rubbing salt in an open wound. Tomorrow, she thought. Tomorrow I'll tell them all, including Mother and Dad. I'll tell them about Johnny and about Jack. Except I don't know what to say about him. Do we love each other? Should we marry? Neither of us is sure. But I am sure of one thing: I'm never going back to Spencer. If I had any doubt that he's a madman, it was dispelled tonight.

Chapter 24

INSOMNIA WAS AN unusual affliction for Sam Dalton. Normally, he was a "good sleeper" even when he had things on his mind. Laura always marveled at his ability to rest soundly for nine or ten hours, not even waking during the night as she and most of their contemporaries did.

But this morning, the day after he'd tried to question Laura about the girls, Sam was up and in his garden at six o'clock. He'd had a terrible night. His mind simply wouldn't stop asking the questions his wife tried to make light of. She didn't fool him, though he let her think he was satisfied with her reassurances. As the hours crawled by he lay wide awake in the darkness, trying not to turn and toss and disturb Laura. Maybe he dozed off for an hour or so. He couldn't be sure. But at four o'clock he was wide awake and impatient to get out of this uneasy bed. He forced himself to stay put until five-thirty. Then he quietly slipped out of his side of the old four-poster, pulled on a sweater and pants and went down to make coffee.

The house was completely quiet, but Karat greeted him joyfully as he came into the kitchen. The puppy playfully nipped at Sam's gardening shoes and yapped happily as he ran in circles around his new master. Sam regarded him with sudden affection. He hadn't been too delighted with Barbara's gift, but he had to admit the little dog was a beauty.

"All right, Karat. Easy does it. Don't wake the whole household. You want to go outside? Okay. Come on. But don't get the idea I'm coming down here every morning at this ungodly hour!"

The early October morning air was chilly, but it felt good. He took a few deep breaths of it while Karat raced madly around the yard, finally stopping to "attend to his duties."

"Good boy!" Sam patted the dog's head. He hoped the little animal would be easily house-trained. The kitchen floor was covered with newspaper, much of it shredded by Karat, who'd obviously spent a good part of the night playing with the papers and tearing them into small pieces.

"You sure did more harm than good," Sam said wryly when they went back inside. "You're supposed to *use* the papers, dummy. Not tear them up! And how on earth did you manage to do your business wherever the papers *weren't?* Lord, what a mess!"

While the coffee perked, he cleaned up the kitchen floor and spread fresh paper. "There's where you go," Sam said, picking up Karat and setting him down firmly on the front page of yesterday's *Post*. "Until you learn to wait to be let out, you're supposed to use *these,* not the spaces in between!"

The small golden ball of fluff looked up at him so impishly that Sam couldn't help laughing. "You're a lucky little beast, you know. That lady upstairs is going to spoil you like a baby, and you'll take outrageous advantage of her. Everybody does, so why should you be different?" He finished his coffee. Breakfast would wait until Laura came down in an hour or so and fixed him a good meal. I'm spoiled too, he thought. I picked the best woman in the world. I wish our children had her serenity. Damn! The cloud of mystery that hung over his house made him uneasy. Why didn't they let him in on whatever was going on? Sam felt another surge of resentment. But in the next breath, he grudgingly admitted to himself that he hadn't always been the most sympathetic audience, especially where the girls were concerned. Not as understanding and forgiving as Laura, that was for sure. She'd have let Alice stay home and have her baby if I'd agreed. She'd have gone to visit Frances when we were invited, years ago. But I acted like some bloody biblical patriarch disowning an ungrateful child. Two ungrateful chidren. I tried to put them both out of my mind, and when I did think of them I made myself remember how they'd repaid us with immorality and selfishness.

He supposed he'd been unfair to all of them. Too strict, too demanding even while he was too much removed. He'd let Laura handle the children while he gave ninety per cent of his thoughts and energies to that damned job. He loved the girls, but he hadn't been much of a companion to them. It wasn't his way, even now. He felt so much affection inside, but he was incapable of projecting it as their mother was.

The stupid job. It had been his life. He resented anything that took his attention away from it: Alice's pregnancy, Fran's "unladylike" behavior. When circumstances demanded his attention, he felt put upon, impatient to be rid of family problems, anxious to find the easiest solutions with little thought of their consequences. He hadn't helped them when they needed it. Why did he think they'd come to him with their troubles now? Even Barbara didn't want him to know what was bothering her, and he was closer to her than he was to her sisters. By the time she was growing up, he'd mellowed a little. But, obviously, not enough.

So much for old mistakes. Sooner or later he'd find out what the mystery was all about. Nothing he could do about it now, but if these girls were in trouble he'd be more understanding, more compassionate. Funny. When you knew you were coming close to the end of your life you began to see the value of things you'd always taken for granted. Like the love and respect of your children. And the endless patience of your wife.

"You hungry, Karat?" Sam asked. "Me, too. Don't worry. She'll be down to feed us both soon."

He left the dog in the kitchen and went back outdoors. Six o'clock was a fine hour. You could feel the world waking up, yawning. There was almost nobody on the street. A paper boy down the block. A woman in curlers and a coat over her nightgown, walking a silly-looking little Yorkshire Terrier. He picked up the rake and started gathering fallen leaves into a neat pile near the front steps. I'm probably making a big fuss over nothing, he told himself, almost believing it. It's the whole business of having them all here at once after so many years. My routine is upset and I'm such a crusty old codger I can't stand having my pattern disturbed. Wild horses couldn't drag it out of me, but the honest truth is I'll be glad when they go away again. Too many women. Too many temperaments. They make me nervous.

He was so deep in his thoughts he didn't notice a car pull up to the curb. Fran was halfway up the walk when he saw her.

"Hi, Dad!" The voice was cheerful. "Lovely morning, isn't it?"

He was so surprised that, for a moment, he couldn't answer the breezy greeting. His eldest daughter was glowing. Fran never got up this early. What was she doing out at this hour? When had she left the house? And then he realized she was just coming home from wherever she'd spent the night. Sam's lips tightened.

"Where have you been, Frances? What is the meaning of this? It's six o'clock in the morning!"

"Is it? Good lord! So there really are two six o'clocks in every day. Imagine that!"

Her flippancy infuriated him. "Don't get smart with me! What will the neighbors think, seeing you come home at this hour?"

Fran refused to be ruffled. "What are the neighbors doing up at the crack of dawn? For that matter, Dad, what are you doing out so early?"

"Never mind me. It's you I'm interested in."

"Really? Ah, that's sweet, dear. I never thought you cared. Now, if it had been Mother . . . "

"Stop that! Answer me!"

Her smile faded. "Why, Dad? Why should I answer you? What business is it of yours where I spend my nights?"

"It's my business because you're under my roof! I won't have you disgracing us again with your running around! I don't give a damn how old you are, Frances, while you're in my house you'll behave like a lady, not like a tart!"

"Again?" she repeated. "Disgrace you *again?* Is that the way you feel? That I've disgraced you before?"

Angered, he snapped back at her. "Yes, that's the way I feel. Running off with that actor! Three divorces! All kinds of gossip about you in every unsavory newspaper! I hoped at your age you'd settled down. But no. You never will. You're as selfish and reckless as you were at eighteen. You don't care for appearances? Fine. That's your business when you're somewhere else. But in Denver, you'll behave yourself or, by God, you can just pack your bags and be off again!"

Frances leaned casually against the porch railing. "Nothing changes with you, does it? We were always guilty until proved innocent. You're doing the same things you did thirty-odd years ago. Jumping to conclusions. Damning me before you know the facts. What's so terrible about coming home at six in the morning? And why do you assume I couldn't have been spending the night with a woman friend? Or maybe alone in a hotel to get away from this stifling, dreary house? You're all over me like some bloody nemesis! And you don't even know whether I've 'disgraced' you or not!"

He was still furious but he tried to control his temper. "All right, Frances. Where were you?"

"I told you. None of your damned business! I can take care of myself. I always have. It's not *this* daughter you should be worrying about. Why don't you devote your righteous efforts to finding out why Allie is a battered wife? Or why Barbara has had an affair with a married man for the last dozen years? Why don't you take some interest in what's going on around you, Father dear? Or do you prefer to know nothing? Is it easier that way? Of course it is. Let Mother worry about us. That's always been your attitude." She stopped. Sam's face had gone gray and he suddenly looked old and helpless. "Oh, hell, I'm sorry," Fran said. "I had no right to go blabbing all those things to you just because I was so defensive about being questioned. I really am sorry, Dad. You're right. When we're in your house you have a right to know what we're doing. I'll tell you where I've been. You won't like it, but you're entitled. I spent the night with Buzz Paige."

Sam rallied. "You *what?*"

"I've been with Buzz. We're in love. He's going to tell Dorothy this morning. We're going away together. When she gets the divorce, Buzz and I will be married." She looked at him appealingly. "Please try to understand. He's the only man I've ever loved. I was foolish once, but I'm so fortunate to discover he still loves me. We're going to be happy, Dad. I've waited a long time to be happy."

"Get out!" Sam spoke quietly but his teeth were clenched in rage. "Go pack your bags and get out of this house right now! 'Tart' is too kind a word for you. You're a monster. An evil, conniving woman who's set out to destroy a good marriage. Well, I won't let you do that. Not while you're here. No child of mine will have my approval to wreck a happy home. I can't control what you do when you leave here, but I don't want you around one more day. Not one more hour! You've been trouble since the day you were born. You've broken your mother's heart. Enough is enough!"

Frances looked straight at him. "Yes. Enough is enough. You're certainly right about that. You've never attempted to understand the fuzzy areas of life. It's all good-versus-evil to you, and anything you don't approve of is evil. Poor Father. How incredibly naïve you are. 'Wreck a happy home.' Don't you know that's an impossibility? The unhappiness is already there, for God's sake! I couldn't take Buzz away from his wife if he hadn't been unhappy for years! But you wouldn't understand that, would you? My happiness doesn't mean a damn to you if it violates some middle-class, moralistic code. Yes," Fran said again, "I've had enough. Enough of wishing I had a father who cared more for me than for his damned pride. I'll leave. No problem. They still have hotels in this town. But I won't leave Denver until I leave with the man I love." She started for the door and then turned to face him once more. "I take it back. I'm not sorry I told you about Allie and Barb. Mother's out of her mind with worry about them, but she wouldn't let you know. She's used to protecting you from unpleasantness. Or perhaps she knows, as I do, that you and your moral judgments would only make things worse. Goodbye, Dad. I didn't say it before but I can this time. Goodbye and good luck."

He stood staring at the door after Fran vanished through it. He had to do something. Get to Buzz Paige before he talked to his wife. Jump in the car and go over there right now. Tell Buzz it was a mistake. That Fran left town.

Anything. But even as he thought it, he knew there was nothing he could do. He had no authority. He was not dealing with juveniles. Sam sat down weakly on the front steps. All those things Fran said about herself. About her sisters. About him. God help him, was that what the mystery was all about—Allie married to a wife-beater and Barb in love with a married man? Was he to blame for any of it or, somehow, for all of it? Dimly, he heard Laura's voice from the doorway.

"Sam? What's the matter? Are you all right?"

He turned slowly to look at her, to see the genuine concern in her eyes. He got up like a very old man and when he spoke it was with the voice of defeat.

"I think we'd better have a talk, Laura. There seem to be a few heavy crosses you've been carrying alone."

We were born fifty years too soon, Laura thought, as she finished her "confession" to Sam and saw the pained, incredulous look on his face. If only we could face these problems by today's standards, we wouldn't find it so horrifying that we have a thrice-divorced daughter about to run off with a married man. It happens every day. A man leaves his family for another woman, usually a younger one than Fran, but people accept it because it's become too prevalent to shock any group except us "senior citizens." She shuddered involuntarily at that phrase. Why do those of us in our late years have to call ourselves "senior citizens" or "gray panthers" or "elder statesmen" or anything except what we are—old people. We act as though it's indecent to have lived a long time. It isn't indecent. But sometimes it's damned inconvenient. We just can't accept the changes all around us. We cling to the old standards, the old values, stubbornly rejecting the new ones.

It's the same with Barbara and Alice's problems. These days, it's unsophisticated to be shocked when two mature people have an affair. Or even when it's discovered that your son-in-law is one of thousands of deranged men who regularly beat their wives. But Sam and I are old-fashioned. Such unorthodox behavior doesn't happen in our family. It's something you read about in magazine articles. Something that happens to other people. Like cancer or heart attacks or strokes. We don't believe they'll ever touch us. Scandal is in the same category, as far as we're concerned. Not so terrible, perhaps, but equally unacceptable.

And it is unacceptable. No matter how casually younger people treat infidelity and immorality, Sam and I cannot support it. Not when it comes to one of our own. Remembering her own anguish when she heard these stories from her girls, she was sympathetic to Sam's stunned reaction. It was like receiving a rapid series of body blows. You reeled from them, dazed, incapable of fighting back. Sam sat immobile at the kitchen table for a long moment after Laura's recital. And then he slowly shook his head in unmistakable bewilderment.

"What are we going to do?"

At least he isn't going to rant and rave. Laura thought with relief. It tore her apart to see him so defeated, but it was better than the monumental anger she'd expected when he finally found out what she'd known for days.

"I don't see that there's much we can do, dear. They're grown women. We can't direct their lives. We never could, really. Not even when they were young.

But certainly not now. All we can contribute is our presence, I suppose. Perhaps it helps to know that we love them, even if we don't really understand. We'd best stay quiet, I think. Let them work things out for themselves with our silent support.''

He gave a short, mirthless laugh. "Too late for that, at least where Frances is concerned. I caught her coming in at six this morning. She told me she'd been with Buzz Paige and that he was going to get a divorce and marry her. I told her to pack her bags and get out."

"Sam! You didn't!''

"Afraid I did. We had a whale of an argument. She said I'd never been much of a father to any of them. She's right. I never was. I never took time to find out what they were thinking. It didn't occur to me that they needed both of us. Maybe if it had, they'd have turned out differently.''

"That's nonsense," Laura said. "You've always been a good father, a good provider. You can't blame yourself for what's happened to them. If you believe that, you have to blame me even more. I was in a better position to influence them. You were busy. Your job was elsewhere. Do you blame me for the way they turned out?''

"No, of course not. You're a wonderful mother.''

"And you've always been a good father. Sam, dear, we tried to give them a good foundation. That was all we could do. All any parents can do. I don't hold with this business of people blaming their troubles on their early lives. I'm sure it's not always true. There comes a time when they have set their own course of action and they're influenced by all kinds of outside things.'' Laura sighed. "All you can do for children is try to teach them what you believe is right and decent. If they don't apply your standards to their own lives, it can't be helped. I love them as you do. I'm terribly disappointed in the way their lives have turned out. My heart breaks for them. But I can't solve their problems and neither can you.''

Sam frowned. "But I have to do something about Frances. What she's doing is wrong. Terrible. It makes me ashamed. But I took the wrong approach with her. I see that now. She might have responded to reason, but I didn't even try that.''

"I'll go up and see her," Laura said. "I'll explain that you were just terribly upset, and that we don't want her to leave this way. She'll understand. She's an intelligent, worldly woman.''

"No. You've been doing that for almost fifty years, making excuses for my stubbornness, smoothing over problems I've caused. I can't let you do that any more. I'll talk to Frances myself. Don't worry. I won't fly off the handle. I hate what she's doing because it is wrong. No one can convince me otherwise. But I have to let her know that no matter what she does she always has a home here. All of them do.'' He took a deep breath. "What's going to happen to the others? What's Barbara going to do now that that man has thrown her over? And Allie. We can't let her go back to that sadist.''

Laura patted his hand. Such a big hand with strong, blunt fingers roughened by endless work in the garden. Once Sam's hands were smooth and soft when they touched her. "White collar hands" they were, belonging to an executive.

Now they were as tough as a laborer's, and it had been a long, long time since they'd stroked her. Odd I should be dwelling on that now, she thought. Crazy that a woman in her "sunset years" should be thinking of romance long gone. It was simply that the change in Sam's hands reminded her of the changes in the man himself: As his will to live weakened, his body became stronger. Physically he had toughened, but emotionally he was spent. All this is killing him, she realized. In many ways he's more devastated than I, more filled with remorse.

"We're all going to survive," she said at last. "You and I and the children, as long as the Lord allows. The girls will find their way out of their situations. Ways they can live with. We just have to try to accept what they do." She smiled sadly. "We can't play God, Sam dear. We don't know enough to even try."

The slamming of dresser drawers in Fran's room a little after six in the morning awakened her sleeping sisters. Neither of them had slept well after their talk. Allie, almost ashamed of her new-found happiness, was sensitively reluctant to announce her good fortune when Barb was so miserable. That was silly, of course. No one would be more thrilled for her than her younger sister. Convincing herself of that, she'd finally drifted off to sleep.

Barbara dropped off at last from sheer exhaustion. She had no idea what time it was when she closed her eyes in merciful unconsciousness, but it must have been only a couple of hours before the racket next door awakened her. She and Allie sat up almost simultaneously when the noise began.

"What on earth is going on?" Allie asked. "What's Fran doing crashing around at this hour?"

For a moment, Barb forgot her own troubles. She got out of bed and put on her robe. "Let's go see."

The two of them entered their sister's room. All Fran's suitcases were out and she was feverishly packing, the contents of the closet and bureau making the place look like some elegant but disorganized dress shop. She didn't even look up when the other two came in.

Allie stared at the disarray. "What's happened? Where are you going?"

"To a hotel. I've had it with this house. I hated it before and I hate it now. I can't wait to get the hell away from all this goddamned middle-class morality!"

Barbara and Alice looked confused. Of course Fran wasn't at home here. Neither were they. But there was more than that to this precipitous departure.

"To a hotel?" Barbara repeated. "I don't understand." For the first time she noticed Fran's untouched bed. "You must have just gotten home. What *is* all this?"

"All this," Fran said acidly, "is that once again I'm getting out of here to live my own life without being told I'm a tramp and a tart and all those other attractive things. Who needs it? I'm going on fifty years old, for God's sake!"

"Calm down," Allie said. "Let's make some sense out of all this, Fran."

"Who can make sense out of a crazy old man who thinks he's still living in the nineteenth century? *Your* father is the same sanctimonious, self-righteous bastard he always was! He's ordered me out of the house. How do you like them apples? Caught me coming in a few minutes late again and did a rerun of 'Orphans of the Storm.' Too bad I'm not penniless or that there isn't a blizzard he can toss me out into!'' She sat down suddenly on the bed. "I'm sorry,'' she said more quietly. "I'm behaving like an Italian soprano. The fact is, I spent the night with Buzz. We're going to be married. I ran into Dad on my way in and told him. He's turned my picture to the wall. Again. It wasn't a very pretty scene on either side, but it was inevitable. Tom Wolfe was right: You sure as hell can't go home again. Anyway, I'm leaving, kids. Sorry to run out on you when you both have troubles, but I'll be sticking around Denver for a little while until Buzz can get his affairs in some kind of order, so we'll be able to meet away from here. That is, if you want to stay friendly with the black sheep of the family.''

"Don't, Fran,'' Barbara said. "Don't do it. It'll kill Mother to see you leave this way. You know Dad. He flares up. He'll come around when he's had time to think it through.''

"I'm sure he will,'' Fran said sarcastically. "Maybe he'll let me come back to celebrate his Diamond Jubilee. No, Barb. Sorry. No go. He doesn't want a 'fallen woman' under his roof. Might contaminate him, ruin his respectability. God forbid he should harbor a strumpet who sleeps with somebody else's husband! They'd probably drum him out of the Kiwanis!'' She stopped, seeing the pained expression on Barbara's face, remembering what she'd said to Sam. "Oh, Jesus, I've blown it for both of you too, I guess. I'm afraid I said more than I should have about Tallent and Spencer. He's probably getting the story of our lives from Mother right now and will come charging up here like the wild bull of the pampas. I'm really sorry about that. I shouldn't have involved anyone else.''

Alice was trying to absorb what she'd heard. Fran and Buzz Paige were going to be married? It was incredible. She had no idea her sister was contemplating such a thing. Apparently it was not surprising to Barbara.

"Are you sure, Fran? Sure this is right for you, I mean.'' Barb looked pleadingly at her sister. "It's a fierce responsibility you're taking, separating a man from his wife and children, asking him to chuck everything for you. Are you so sure he won't regret it? Or that you won't?''

She's thinking of herself, Fran recognized. She's decided to let that selfish congressman go because she's afraid he'll regret it later on if she doesn't. She was tempted to say something cutting to the younger woman, make some cynical crack about stupid self-sacrifice. Barb was wrong. She was too much the idealist, too considerate of others at the expense of her own happiness. Or maybe she was just too weak and frightened. But whatever the reason, Fran couldn't be cruel enough to add to her sister's misery.

"Who knows how any of us will feel in the future, Barb? We each have to do what we think is best at the moment. We don't have to agree, you and I. Our skins are not the same thickness, but that doesn't mean we don't respect and love each other.'' She stood up and put her arms around her sisters. "We're quite a trio, aren't we? The three sisters. Very appropriate title for us. Remember your Colorado history? In this neck of the woods 'The Three Sisters' refers to an avalanche area up in Loveland Pass!'' Fran laughed. "That's us, all right. Three avalanches crashing toward our individual ends. We're coming down from the mountains. Down to the flatlands in one hell of a rush!''

"I'm no avalanche," Barb said quietly. "Right now I feel more like a stagnant pool."

"You'll be okay. Time works wonders, honey." Fran was reassuring. "What about you, Allie? Which direction are you taking?"

This was the moment to tell them about Johnny. They'll be glad for me, she thought again. I haven't sorted out my life, not in terms of Spencer or Jack, but at least I'm at peace about the one thing that's haunted me all these years. "I have some news," Allie said. "Yesterday afternoon . . . " A knock on the door interrupted her.

"Frances? May I speak with you, please?" The voice from the hall was low-pitched, calm. Without waiting for an answer, Sam opened the bedroom door. "Oh, I'm sorry. I didn't realize you girls were in here. I wanted to talk to Frances for a minute. I can come back later."

"No, it's all right," Alice said. "We can come back when you're finished." She was actually relieved by the reprieve. It was still hard not to feel guilty about her good fortune amid so much misery. "Come on, Barb."

"Wait!" Fran's voice was cold. "There's no reason for you and Barb to leave. Everybody here knows the whole story. Whatever you came to say, Father, certainly can be said in front of all your children."

Sam took a deep breath. She wasn't going to make it easy for him, but perhaps she was right. He owed each of them an explanation, an apology. Perhaps through Fran he could speak to all three.

"Your sister is right. There've been too many secrets in this family. Too much you didn't want me to know. I'm not blaming you for that. You were right to think I wouldn't understand. I haven't had much time for understanding in the past. Or maybe no use for it. But I've been wrong and I hope I'm enough of a man to admit it. I want you all to know that I'm sorry I've been so rigid, so uncompromising, so sure my judgment was always right. I did a bad thing to Allie years ago. I couldn't find forgiveness in my heart when Fran ran away. Later I even resented you, Barbara, for wanting to leave me. Those things were wrong. Stupid and blind and un-Christian, and I regret them and all the things I've said and thought and done in the years since. I hope it's not too late to be a friend to you, even if I'm not much as a father. I want you to know that I love you and want you here if this is where you want to be. And if it isn't, I'll still try my best to see your side of things." He paused and looked first at Barbara. "I'm sorry about what's happened to you, child. I know you're miserable now, but as your mother says, you've had a lot of years of happiness. As for you, Allie, there aren't words to say how I regret causing you so much anguish." His gaze came to rest on Frances. "We had some hard words this morning. I'm not going to pretend I approve of what you're planning, any more than I can condone what Alice did years ago or what Barbara has been doing in Washington. But I'm going to try not to set myself up as judge and jury for you or your sisters. I hope you won't leave, Frances. Not like this. You are very dear to me. Very important. All of you. More important than the strict code of behavior I set for myself and tried to impose on you."

This extraordinary speech was met by silence from his children. They're not going to forgive me after all, Sam thought. One contrite confession, hard as it was to make, isn't going to wipe out all the resentment I've created. Why did I think it might? He turned to leave, but Fran caught his sleeve.

"Don't go," she said. "I know that was the hardest thing you ever had to do in your life. And maybe the best. We all love you, Dad. We do. No matter how we act, we couldn't stop being your daughters or admiring you more than any man we've ever known. Don't you see? Each of us has been searching for you in the men we chose. That young, lonely Allie thought Spencer had your dependability. And Barb saw the tenderness and consideration in Charles that she always got from you. And me, even crazy, mixed-up me, was always looking for someone with your sense of decency. I found it in Buzz. He's you. Honest and responsible and terribly guilty right now. As you would be in his situation. I think I can speak for all of us. We don't expect you to change your beliefs, Father, but we respect you for saying what we've always wanted to hear."

His gaze rested lovingly, lingeringly, on all his girls. Barb and Allie were crying softly, nodding their heads in agreement. He felt his own eyes fill with tears. I finally made it, he thought humbly. I finally found the humility to admit what a pig-headed tyrant I've been. He was suddenly overcome with emotion. He had to escape. He smiled and awkwardly threw them a grateful kiss before he left the room.

Laura was still sitting at the table when he went back to the kitchen. There was no need to voice the question.

"I did it," Sam said. "I talked to all three of them. Funny. It wasn't as hard as I thought it would be. The words just seemed to come tumbling out, almost like I couldn't have stopped them if I wanted to." He looked as though some terrible weight had been lifted from his shoulders. "I'm proud of them, Laurie. They're fine women. I said I couldn't approve of what they did, but I love them and I'd try to understand. And they—that is, Frances—said they loved me."

Laura was as relieved as he. She'd been afraid of what might happen when Sam went up to talk to Frances. They were so alike, these two. Stubborn, strong, opinionated. She'd been afraid there'd be another clash of wills. But it had turned out better than she dared hope, not only with Frances but with all their daughters.

"You've wanted to do that for a long time, haven't you? Tell the girls how much you care, I mean. I'm so glad you finally did. It means so much to all of us."

Sam nodded. "I wish I'd done it years ago. Why didn't I, Laura? Why couldn't I ever open up with them?"

"We do things when the time is right, I guess. There's no other explanation. But that's not important. What matters is that they know they have your sympathy and support. *Our* sympathy and support, whatever they do."

The daughters were quiet for a moment after he left the room and then, wordlessly, Frances began to put her clothes back in the closet.

Chapter 25

MARTHA PERRONE ENJOYED being the center of attention. Spencer Winters' drab middle-aged secretary pretended to disapprove of the curiosity the other secretaries were showing about her boss, but secretly she reveled in their attention. Usually, they paid little heed to her. She was older than most of the girls in the law firm and far more prim and proper. To know something they did not filled Martha with a heady sense of importance.

"Come on, Martha. What's turned that walking icicle into a towering inferno?"

"Yeah, Martha, what gives with Mr. Cool? Is he in hot water with the big boss? Or is it something juicier, like trouble at home?"

She looked at the interested faces of the secretaries to Wallingford and McClean. J. B. Thompson's secretary, lofty in her post as confidante of the senior partner, would not deign to join the group at Martha's desk, but Martha knew she was curious, equally intrigued by Mr. Winters' odd behavior in the past week. And J.B.'s secretary would love to find something she could report to the head of the firm.

"I'm sure I don't know what you mean," Martha said with just enough lack of conviction.

"Like hell! He's been in a rage ever since he got back from Denver. Snapping and snarling at everybody. And a while ago, he rushed out like his tail was on fire!" McClean's secretary lit a forbidden cigarette. All the executives were out of the office. "Come on, Mart. What's gotten into old Spence? You know he's always tried to win a popularity contest with the partners. He's even buttered-up us poor slaves, trying so hard to be the perfect heir to the throne! And now, all of a sudden, it's like he's mad at the world. We even hear him yelling at you these days, and Lord knows you don't deserve that," the girl said ingratiatingly. "You've always been the indispensable right hand."

It's true, Martha thought, nursing her injured pride. He has no right to be so mean to me just because he's having personal problems. I've given him years of loyalty and he repays me by calling me incompetent and stupid. It's not fair.

"Well," she said almost in a whisper, making sure she couldn't be heard by Thornpson's secretary, "it seems there is some trouble at home." She hesitated. It was unprofessional, unethical to tell anyone about Spencer Winters' private life, but the temptation to hold the spotlight was too strong. Besides, she really did feel put-upon. She didn't care what the widowed mother she lived with said about job security. She didn't have to take this kind of abuse.

"What kind of trouble?" Wallingford's secretary urged her on.

"It started the day he got back from Denver," Martha said. "First, he had me call every 'John Peck' in the phone book, trying to locate one who'd been in touch with Mrs. Carlton Rudolph."

"That's his wife's aunt, isn't it?"

Martha nodded. "Yes. She raised Mrs. Winters. Anyway, I couldn't find the right John Peck, and Mr. Winters was furious. He said I was incompetent and stupid. As though it was my fault, the man wasn't listed or was one of the ones who didn't answer the phone!"

The others looked sympathetic.

"But the next day I saw penciled in an appointment on his calendar for noon. It was just initials. 'J.P.' Of course I knew who *that* was."

"He sure wasn't making a date with a Justice of the Peace," Wallington's secretary said.

The other girl laughed. "Maybe it was a meeting with himself and he wrote in 'Just Perfect.' Go on, Martha. What then? Did John Peck appear? Who is he?"

"He didn't appear. Mr. Winters waited a whole hour and then he got his daughter on the phone. That's Janice, you know."

"Sure. The snappy one who lives with the art director."

Martha blushed. "I suppose she does. Anyway, Mr. Winters raised Cain with her and she was very fresh to him."

"How do you know?" McClean's secretary wagged a playful finger at Martha. "Don't tell me you listened in, you naughty girl!"

"Well, yes, I did. Mr. Winters wanted to know where John Peck was, and Janice said, 'How should I know? Am I my brother's keeper?' And then she laughed and said something about wasn't that funny, she never thought she'd be able to use that line and mean it."

Martha's audience was growing more intrigued, and she grew expansive under their rapt attention.

"The next thing I knew, there was a long-distance call from Mrs. Winters in Denver. That was just this morning. I never heard her sound like that. She's always so quiet, you know. Such a lady. But she was screaming at him, something about him beating up Janice the way he always beat *her!*"

The other two gasped. "You're kidding!" McClean's secretary said. "She actually said that? That he beats her? The sonofabitch! What a lousy hypocrite!"

"Shhh. Keep your voice down." Martha glanced nervously toward J.B.'s office. "I'm not so happy with Mr. Winters, but I don't want him reported to the head of the firm."

"Okay. Don't stop now. What else did she say?"

Spencer's secretary paused dramatically. "Then Mrs. Winters said—and her voice was enough to give you goose bumps—that she was never coming back to Mr. Winters because she'd found her long-lost child and she was going to make a new life for herself." Martha waited, enjoying the stunned reaction before she went on. She was having a fine time now. These snippy girls who made fun of her behind her back were truly impressed.

"You actually heard her say that? What do you think she meant, that stuff about a long-lost child?"

"I think," Martha pronounced, "that Mrs. Winters had another baby, not by her husband. I also think Janice knew something about it and wouldn't tell her father. That's why he hit her. And furthermore," Martha added, warming to her subject, "I think this mysterious John Peck knows something about it too. He was probably trying to blackmail Mrs. Winters through her aunt."

"Good God! It's better than a movie!" Wallington's secretary was fascinated. "No wonder old Spencer's been so steamed! Talk about scandal! J.B.'d toss him out on his can if he knew! Imagine, our teddibly respectable Mr. Winters a wife-beater! And that nice, sweet woman he's married to having an illegitimate kid!"

"Wait just a moment," Martha said. "I never said Mrs. Winters had an illegitimate child. I said I thought she had one by someone else. Maybe she was married before."

"If she was, why all this mystery about John Peck and Janice and blackmail? Why would she talk about a long-lost child? Come on, Martha. Don't try to pretend you think there are no skeletons in the closet."

Martha was silent. They were right, of course. She'd continued to eavesdrop on that phone call from Denver and there was much more. Things so terrifying she didn't dare repeat them. She'd probably said too much already. It had been foolish to let these nosey girls know any part of this. She'd been flattered by their attention, lured into telling things she had no right to disclose. She hoped they wouldn't repeat them. A dim hope. This was much too good not to be whispered around the office and it surely would get back to the big boss. Oh, Lord, what had she done? Mr. Winters would kill her!

The thought reminded her of the rest of that conversation, the part that really made chills run down her spine. When his wife said that about the child, he'd gone quite mad, calling her every kind of terrible name and then he'd said, evenly, "When I get my hands on you, Alice, I'm going to kill you. You and that goddamn bastard of yours. You've lied and cheated and made my life hell for too many years. You don't deserve to live."

Martha shuddered, remembering the cold, ominous quality of those words. I believe he could kill, she thought. He'd sounded insane with fury. But Mrs. Winters had calmed down and her level tone matched his own.

"You're not going to kill anyone, Spencer. You're much too cowardly, much too consumed with self-preservation. If you were going to murder me, you'd have done it long ago. But you always stopped just short of that. You may not think my life is worth anything, but you're too selfish to trade your own for the pleasure of destroying it."

"Don't be so sure of that. There's a limit to what a decent man can endure. And you've finally gone too far."

Alice hadn't answered that. She'd simply said, "Goodbye, Spencer. You'll hear from my attorneys."

That had been only a few hours ago. Immediately after the call, Spencer had slammed out of his office, only stopping long enough to say, "Miss Perrone, get me a plane ticket to Denver."

"Yes, sir. What day?"

"Tomorrow."

"Yes, Mr. Winters. Will you want a hotel reservation too?"

"No, I thought it would be more fun to sleep in the park. Of course I want a hotel, you idiot!"

She hid her resentment under the impassive face of the perfect secretary. "How long do you plan to stay? I have to tell the hotel."

"Oh, Christ, I'm not sure. One night. Two, maybe. That should be plenty of time."

"Yes, sir."

"And I probably won't be back in the office before I leave. Send the air tickets and hotel information to my house by messenger."

"Very well."

He'd shot out the door without another word, leaving her angry and frightened. "Plenty of time," he'd said. For what? To drag Mrs. Winters home? To settle things with her? Or, God forbid, to carry out his threat?

Automatically, Martha called the travel agent and specified his needs. Then she sat back and wondered what to do. Perhaps she should call Mrs. Winters at her parents' home and warn her. Or get in touch with Janice and tell her that her father might be on his way to do something terrible. But how could she do that without disclosing what she knew? And what if she was wrong? What if these theatrics were just Spencer's way of frightening his wife into submission? It's none of your business, Martha, she told herself. Don't get involved.

A short time later the girls had started asking questions. They'd seen Winters' angry departure, the culmination of several days of bad temper which, unusually, he hadn't bothered to hide. She'd told them as much as she dared. She couldn't bring herself to reveal the rest, though she'd liked to have asked their advice. Poor Mrs. Winters, she thought. Imagine having to live with that! Martha had had only a week of watching his Jekyll and Hyde personality. What could it have been like for Alice to have endured it for twenty-five years?

When the girls finally drifted back to their own desks, Martha picked up the morning paper and began to read the "Help Wanted" ads. She'd be sorry to leave this job, but she couldn't work for a monster. And she didn't want to be around when he finally, inevitably, cracked up.

Alice was trembling when she hung up on her furious husband in Boston. At the same time she felt an enormous sense of relief. It was over and done with, this nightmare life with Spencer. She'd declared herself, and though she feared the consequences, not only for herself but those most precious to her, she also had a sense of freedom and peace. Only now did she fully realize how much of her life had been devoted to needless self-reproach and contrition, how masochistic she'd been. Johnny was fine. Had been, all along. The fact did not absolve her from her feelings of guilt about letting him go, but it was comforting, at last, to know that he'd grown up in a good home and had turned into a son to be proud of. Another son. She'd always be proud of Chris too. And of her daughter. They had the courage of their convictions. More than she could say for herself, even now.

She frowned, troubled by thoughts of her future. It would be sensible to divorce Spencer, marry Jack Richards and settle down in Denver. Even though the children—hers and theirs—would be thousands of miles away, they'd be a family. Johnny would have the real parents he'd searched for, and her other two would be happy to see her safe and well-treated. But the truth was, she wasn't in love with Jack, and instinct told her his feelings toward her were more dutiful and nostalgic than romantic. They were both trying very hard to re-establish the old magic. And it wasn't working.

We're trying too hard, Alice thought. We've changed too much, or perhaps not enough. He's still weak, almost sanctimonious in this new, penitent role of widower. He's now trying to please a dead woman. Just as years ago he tried to please demanding parents. And I'm just as bad. I can't shake the habit of thinking first of what would make other people happy. I allowed myself to be sent away to accommodate my parents. Now I'm thinking of going into a life which will put my children's minds at ease.

It's wrong. Middle age is the time to start thinking of yourself. When you've done all you can for those who have real or imagined demands on you, it's time to be selfish. Healthily selfish. But what is it I really want? I want to be free, Alice told herself. Free as I never have been. I'd like to live in sunshine year round, after so many bitter New England winters. I'd like not to worry about housekeeping and social obligations and appearances. I'd like to be a slob when I feel like it. Sleep as late as I like, stay up all night reading if I decide to, eat a peanut butter sandwich for dinner if that's what I want. I'd like to be an old dropout. A late-blooming hippie. The idea made her smile. It was so totally unlike the proper Alice Winters the world knew.

She couldn't do it, of course. She had no money to support even a simple life. Neither could she return to Boston. But she didn't want to stay in Denver, though she knew her parents would gladly give her shelter. She'd made a move without thinking out a follow-up plan. She'd burned her bridges with Spencer and mentally rejected Jack, and she had no idea where she was headed. Oddly enough, she didn't worry. Perhaps, Alice thought ruefully, I have begun to believe in miracles. If Johnny could reappear as he did, anything is possible.

After they dropped Alice off, Johnny and his father talked most of the night in Jack's comfortable living room, shoes off, feet propped up on the coffee table, can after can of beer in hand. They'd told each other the stories of their lives, more like two friends than like father and son. It was a revelation to both men. Johnny had not expected the bonus of finding his father as well as his mother. And Jack was still filled with wonder at the return of his child.

"I'll be able to meet all the family while I'm here, won't I?" Johnny asked at one point.

"Of course. All your mother's family, that is. Her parents and her two sisters. I don't have any family left. I was an only child too, and my mother and father have been dead for years. But Alice makes up for it." Jack grinned. "She can trot out assorted, eccentric old aunts and uncles if you have need for such things."

"I wonder when she'll tell them about me."

"Remembering how close those sisters always were, I'd venture to say she's already told Barb and Fran, even if she had to wake them up to do it. She'll probably tell Mr. and Mrs. Dalton in the morning."

Johnny toyed with his beer can. "How do you think they'll take it?"

"The girls will be delighted and your grandmother is not the sort of woman to hold grudges. I suspect she'll be overcome with joy for you and your mother."

"But Mr. Dalton will be a problem." It was more a statement than a question.

"Could be," Jack said. "He's always been painfully righteous. He's a good man, Johnny, but unbending. Time may have softened him enough to let him accept the child he never wanted to see or hear of. But we can't be sure. Look, Son, I haven't seen any of those people in more than thirty years. Except your Aunt Barbara." An odd note came into Jack's voice. "She's lovely, Johnny. I can't understand why she's never married. She must have had dozens of chances."

John Peck glanced sharply at his father. He sounds like he's in love with Barbara! The unwelcome thought disturbed the younger man. He'd had it all worked out in his head. Alice would divorce that bastard Winters and marry her childhood sweetheart. He'd have a mother and father living together. He could bring his own child to visit his grandparents. More fantasy. Why did he think this whole thing was going to work out like a fairy tale, with everybody living happily ever after? He suddenly wondered whether Alice loved Jack Richards. He assumed she did. Was she going to be hurt again, after all she'd lived through? He felt himself becoming unreasonably angry, but he hid it under a seemingly casual question.

"Do you think you and Mother will get married when she's finally rid of Winters?"

Jack took a swallow of beer, stalling for time before he answered. "Getting rid of Spencer Winters isn't going to be all that easy. From what I know of the man, he could be vengeful, and your mother has your half-sister and half-brother to think of. Not to mention that poor old aunt of hers in Boston who's scared to death of the man, with good reason. Oh, Alice will eventually be free. We'll see to that. We're never going to let her go back into that situation again, but it may take a long time to work out."

He's deliberately ducked my question, Johnny thought. He's talked about the difficulties of the divorce, but nothing about remarriage. All right. It's none of my business. I can't tell them how to run their lives. It's enough that I've found them and that they're such good people. Other adopted people haven't been so lucky. He remembered the tales he'd heard, the stories he'd read. Some children were rejected by the parent or parents they finally found. Others discovered whores for mothers or drunkards for fathers. I'm blessed just knowing them, just finding out about myself. They've given me the identity I always needed. They owe me nothing more.

The Dalton girls were uneasy all morning, following Sam's unexpected emotional apology to them. It was not that they weren't happy about this new understanding, but each recognized that while unity was a supportive thing, the fact of its existence did not settle their individual problems.

Alice had not yet told them about Johnny. Even after she telephoned Spencer in midmorning, and then spoke to Jack and their son, arranging for them to come over late in the afternoon, she somehow couldn't find the right words to announce this wonderful news. What if they didn't believe Johnny was who he claimed to be? There was no proof. Just her instinctive certainty, and Jack's. She couldn't bear it if they doubted, and she was afraid they might. So she waited through the morning, longing to tell them and ridiculously afraid they'd try to burst her bubble.

Barbara dressed and came quietly downstairs, the letter to Charles in her hand. It was like issuing her own death warrant to put this final communication into the mailbox on the corner, but that's where she was headed. She slipped out of the front door and walked slowly down the familiar block, kicking at the fallen leaves in her path. She could imagine Charles's face when he read her words, but she could not hazard a guess as to his reaction. There'd be some response, of course. Either a vehement rejection of what she'd written or a sad but unwillingly thankful acceptance. There was nothing to do but wait for the next development. Wait in frozen despair for the verdict. But, bitterly, she was sure what it would be. She had no need to hazard guesses.

And what would she do then? Run? Hide? She didn't know that either. She couldn't anticipate her own course of action. Emotionally, she wanted to stay as far away as possible from any chance encounter with the man she loved. But sensibly, maturely, she should go back to her job in Washington. To her pretty apartment and her good friends. Life didn't end when a love affair did. Like millions of other disappointed women, she'd pick up the pieces and go on. But nothing would ever be the same. The realization stung her, and her hand trembled as she lifted the metal flap of the mailbox and slowly, reluctantly slid the envelope into its gaping jaws.

Fran paced her room, smoking endless cigarettes, waiting for the phone call from Buzz that would tell her he'd done what he promised. As the hours wore on, she became more apprehensive. What if he hadn't found the courage to tell Dorothy? What if that crazy woman had done something violent? My God, she was capable of anything! Maybe she had a gun. Maybe she'd killed Buzz! Nonsense. She, not Dorothy, was behaving like a lunatic. It took time, these things. After twenty-nine years you didn't just walk in the house, announce you were leaving forever and then run to the telephone and call your beloved. There'd be a lot of talking and arguing and angry accusations in the Paige household. Poor Buzz. Between his own conscience and the things that demented woman probably was threatening, he must be going through hell. Never mind. She'd make it up to him. For once in her life, she'd devote herself utterly and entirely to making a man happy. It had taken a long time and a lot of experiences she didn't even want to think about. But she'd come full circle. She was a woman in love. At last. Never mind if it took all day, she'd hear what she wanted to hear. There were years ahead to rejoice in this lovely new feeling of being a totally happy, totally fulfilled woman.

The five of them squeezed around the kitchen table for lunch, a reunited family. But only Sam seemed completely content, as though he'd purged himself of all the hatred and prejudices he'd held for years.

Men are so easily satisfied, Laura thought. It was wonderful beyond belief that Sam had been able to reach out to their daughters, to humble himself as she'd never seen him do. The fault wasn't all on his side, but he'd been willing to make it seem so, and she loved him for it. But having made one touching speech, he now acted as though all their troubles were behind them. And of course they weren't. All that had been accomplished was to keep Fran from leaving in anger, and assure her and her sisters that they could count on the devotion and support of both parents.

The girls were so quiet. Laura realized it was a troubled stillness, broken only by Sam's jovial monologue and his endless repetition of how wonderful it was that they all finally understood each other. She wished he'd be quiet. He was overdoing it with all those clichés about blood being thicker than water. Couldn't he see that his daughters were deep in their own thoughts? Why on earth did he have to rattle on so? She wanted to tell him, rudely, to shut up, but of course she wouldn't do that. He was so happy. So full of good will. She hoped they'd all hurry up and finish lunch so they could escape from this heavy atmosphere. Midway through the meal, Alice interrupted her father.

"Dad. Mom. All of you. I have something to tell you."

Sam stopped talking and four pairs of eyes fixed their attention on Alice. No one spoke until she finished the story of her reunion with John Peck. They listened, wide-eyed, as she told them the remarkable story of the past twenty-four hours. Only Sam did not know that Alice and Jack Richards had seen each other, but none of them was aware of how drastically Allie's life had changed since the previous day.

"They're coming over this afternoon," she said. "I want you all to meet Johnny and him to meet you. Jack's bringing him." Alice faced her father almost challenging him to go back on the generous words he'd spoken early that morning. "It's a blessing, Dad, that we all can count on your strength and understanding. It makes things so much easier to know you share my joy."

Sam Dalton's face went dead-white. It was one thing to try to forgive Fran for her selfishness in breaking up another woman's home, or attempt to understand how Barbara could have been involved in a love she was unable to deny. But welcome Jack Richards and the illegitimate child he'd fathered? Here, in his own house? No, Sam thought. That's asking too much. That man violated my young daughter. He brought us disgrace. And that boy! How dare he come back after all these years, demanding to be recognized! He felt them all watching him. Laura and the girls had not spoken, waiting for him to be first. They were happy, of course. Sentimental women. Ready to forgive and forget and have a good cry over a story with a "happy ending." Even Allie. How could she stand to look at the man who betrayed her or embrace a son who was a stranger to her? He looked at his middle daughter. Her eyes pleaded with him to remember what he'd said in Fran's bedroom. Sam gave a great sigh.

"That's wonderful, Allie dear!" he said. "Amazing! We'll welcome Jack and the boy."

As though he'd pulled a cork out of a bottle, the voices of the women bubbled forth, delirious with relief. Her mother and sisters kissed Allie and hugged her close, exclaiming in surprise and happiness, wanting to know more details, eager for every tiny scrap of the story. In their pleasure for her, they forgot their own difficulties and for a few minutes the kitchen was filled with the excited questions of Laura and the girls and the lyrical responses of Alice.

So be it, Sam thought. At least they wanted my approval. Only one thing's wrong. Nobody's mentioned what Spencer Winters is going to do about all this.

Chapter 26

IT HAS BEEN unreal, Jack Richards thought later. Unreal to walk into the old house on South Carona Street and find the living room exactly as he remembered it, down to the very last Maxwell Parrish print on the stucco walls. He'd shaken hands with a reserved but cordial Sam Dalton and a gently smiling Laura, and greeted Alice's sisters, a surprisingly subdued Barbara and a restless Frances. Most of all, it had been unreal to hear Allie introduce her family to her son.

The past blended with the present in those two awkward hours of "reunion." At one moment Jack was a callow kid, nervously hearing his parents and Alice's angrily accusing each other's child of immoral behavior. Even now, he remembered the horror on Allie's face that night so long ago. Fran, he recalled, had been out somewhere and Barbara was a little girl, banished to her room, out of earshot of this ugly exchange. It had been devastating. He'd wanted to speak out, say he was man enough to assume his responsibilities, young as he was. But he hadn't. He'd sat silently, letting his mother and father bail him out of the mess, letting Allie carry the burden alone. He'd been weak. He supposed he still was. Even Lucy had been stronger than he, not only in those last months when they knew she was dying, but all through their married life. Gentle, adoring Lucy had made his life easy, provided a quiet, comfortable home, bolstered him through his early struggle in business. It was Lucy, not he, who wanted to find the child he'd fathered, willing to accept another woman's baby because she could give him none. Yes, his wife had been strong and he missed her strength as much as he missed her love.

Allie had never really been strong, except in that one moment when she fled the scene, refusing to have any more of their undignified accusations. The only forceful thing she'd ever done was to reject the abortion and decide to have the baby without a father. That was her one moment of heroism, Jack thought. Before and after that she presented herself as a target for everyone's abuse.

I suppose that's why I never really loved her, never fought for her, he realized. It's why I don't want to marry her now. I need a strong woman. Not tough and brittle, like Fran, but confident and compassionate, like Barbara. Even as quiet and remote as she was this afternoon, Barbara exuded strength. She was like Lucy in many ways: composed, clear-headed. A woman a man could turn to for support and sensible advice.

He was nervous when the Daltons received him again and were introduced to their grandson. But John Peck handled himself well, not overeager or too deferential. In an awkward situation, he spoke easily and honestly, telling them how grateful he was to have found his parents and his mother's parents. He'd been warm and well-mannered, showing no sign of resentment or hostility toward any of them, not even toward Sam Dalton.

Alice had an almost worshipful attitude toward this young man who did her proud. Her eyes never left John's face as he told his grandparents and aunts of his early life, promising his adoptive parents as fine, upstanding people, smiling affectionately as he mentioned his wife and his forthcoming child. It was John who dominated the conversation and who was more at ease than his elders. Jack, for the most part, remained silent, uncomfortable in the presence of Sam and Laura, disquieted by Barb's stillness and Fran's inattentive attitude. He couldn't tell whether the sisters were distracted by their own thoughts or simply bored by this strange gathering. Fran's not a lovable woman, Jack thought, watching her fidget. Certainly not a serene one. She had none of Allie's kindness or Barbara's composure.

It's true that people don't change, he realized. In maturity, we continue to be what we always were. Fran was always volatile and Alice acquiescent. Barbara, even as a child, had grace and assurance. With every passing year, inherent characteristics become more pronounced: the nice get nicer, the selfish more self-involved.

On the whole, it had been a remarkably uneventful coming together of diverse individuals. They'd had tea and discreetly examined one another's reactions, subtly probing, seeking some common ground. There was none, really, except for this young man who'd torn a family apart before his birth and now sought to bring it back together for his parents' peace of mind and his own.

At the end of two hours, each of them was anxious to escape. The emotional intensity of Jack and Alice's meeting with their son was missing in this quiet, strained, "official" reunion. It was like a ritual they had to go through, and once done, they would go their separate ways, having merely tied up some loose ends. *Some,* indeed, Jack thought. John Peck had his own family, a wife and a child to come. Satisfied, after so many years of search, it was unlikely that he would stay close to any of them. It was too late, no matter what Allie thought, to become a "family." The senior Daltons seemed to accept this presentable young man, but it was clear from their courteous but restrained manner that they expected to see no more of him than they did of Alice's legitimate children. Fran would soon go on her wandering way, he supposed, and Barbara would return to her life in Washington. So much for loose ends. That left only him and Allie to decide where their futures lay. She couldn't return to Boston—not, at least, to Spencer. It would be sensible for all concerned if she'd stay here, remain with her aging parents, live quietly and contentedly, free from fear. It occurred to Jack that Allie, not Barb, should have been the unmarried, dutiful daughter. She was the best suited for it, the most passive and undemanding of the three. He wondered again what was really in her mind. He'd marry her, if that's what she wanted. She wasn't in love with him any longer. Maybe she never had been. But Alice needed protection, especially now when she'd found courage to tell Spencer Winters she was through with him. And Jack was her only recourse.

And what about me? Jack wondered. Marriage to Allie wouldn't be a bad life. Quiet, predictable, almost foreordained, as though it were a debt he was destined to pay. But it wasn't what he wanted. If only she were Barbara. The thought shocked him. He was attracted to Alice's sister. He'd marry her tomorrow if he could. He knew nothing about her life. He really knew nothing about her at all. And yet, after two brief meetings in their adult lives, he was half in love with her. Perhaps she was in love with someone else. She had to be, an attractive woman like that. And she hardly noticed Jack. She'd quickly left his apartment the day he and Allie talked and she'd barely glanced at him through these past

hours. He was thinking like a fool. Like the adolescent he still was. Barbara
Dalton had no interest in him, and God knows even if she had he couldn't pursue
it. Hadn't he hurt Alice enough?

At the end of the afternoon, Laura said, softly, "We all have so much to be
grateful for, haven't we? We have our health and we have each other." She
smiled at John. "And now we have a fine new grandson to take into our hearts."

For the first time, John Peck lost his composure. "I . . . I want to thank
you," he said. "All of you. I didn't know what to expect. I didn't dare hope
to find such warmth and kindness. That is, you've made me very happy, accepting
me this way. It's . . . well, it sounds trite, but it is a dream come true."

"For all of us, Johnny," Alice said.

Sam Dalton cleared his throat. "We hope you'll come back, John. Often.
You too, Jack. Bygones are bygones. We all made mistakes, but it looks as
though we've profited by them."

Laura glanced at him affectionately. It was as close as he could come to
apologizing to this fine young man and to the unhappy woman who'd been
separated from him. It was also his way of telling Jack Richards that he was
sorry for the years of bitterness that lay between then and now. There was a
moment of embarrassed silence and then Laura said, briskly, "Well, who's
hungry? My goodness, it's almost dinnertime! Just give me a few minutes and
I'll . . ."

"Why don't you let Alice and Johnny and me take all of you out to dinner?"
Jack said. "This certainly calls for a celebration, Mrs. Dalton. We don't want
you standing over a hot stove this evening."

Laura looked at Sam, but the older man shook his head.

"Nice of you, Jack, but I think not. It's been a good afternoon, but Mother
looks a little tired, and to tell you the truth, I am too." He smiled. "Guess
we're just not used to so much excitement. Maybe Frances and Barbara . . ."

"Sorry," Fran said. "I appreciate it, Jack, but I have to wait for a phone
call."

"I have to beg off too," Barb said. "It's sweet of you, but you three go
along and celebrate. How long are you staying, John? We'll see you again,
won't we?"

"I hope so. I'll be leaving in a day or two, I guess. Otherwise, I won't have
a job or a wife."

Alice sounded disappointed. "Carol can't come out?"

"Afraid not, Mother. She's working on a rush job for the agency. But she
sends her love and looks forward to seeing you and Dad in Boston."

The unfamiliar, intimate terms came as a shock to his grandparents and aunts.
It was startling to hear Alice and Jack referred to that way. More than anything
that had been said all afternoon, it established what they had been almost unable
to grasp. But Alice seemed blissfully unperturbed as she said, "I don't know
when we'll be in Boston, Johnny, but we'll see Carol. Certainly when the baby
comes, if not before."

"We," Jack thought as they prepared to leave. Well, that's what it is now,
isn't it? *We* have a son. *We're* going to be grandparents. We have to figure out
the next move.

*   *   *

Dorothy, fully dressed, was sitting in the living room when Buzz let himself into his house shortly after six o'clock that morning. He didn't see her as he quietly entered the hall and headed for the kitchen. The prospect of going up to their bedroom, of facing an enraged woman who would demand to know where he'd been all night was more than he could handle at the moment. He'd promised Frances he'd take the step he both wanted and dreaded, but the thought of speaking those final words made him almost physically ill.

His wife's surprisingly calm voice stopped him in his tracks.

"Good morning."

Buzz turned, startled, toward the living room and saw her in her usual chair, her face quite impassive except for a dangerous glint in her eyes. "Hello, Dottie. What are you doing up at this hour?" The words were so trite, so silly, but they came automatically.

She sat as though frozen. "I haven't been to bed. Too bad you can't say the same."

Buzz sat down in the chair facing hers. His chair. The one he'd sat in nearly every evening for twenty-nine years, reading his paper, having a small drink after work. He'd actually missed that chair when he'd moved out for a short time. He'd miss it when he left for good. It represented his place in the household, as comfortable and familiar as an old friend. Odd what trivial things one thought of at moments of crisis. He was about to break up his marriage, abandon his wife, probably alienate his sons and bring down the wrath of the community in which he'd lived all his life. And he found himself regretting the loss of a sagging piece of furniture.

"We have to talk," he said wearily. "I won't lie to you. I couldn't if I wanted to. You know where I've been, not only last night but every evening for a week. I'm sorry, Dot. I didn't mean to hurt you. I didn't mean it to go this far. It just happened."

"Affairs don't just 'happen.' " Dorothy's voice was scornful. "You wanted it to happen. So did she. You couldn't wait to get at her, like some prowling tomcat. I knew it before you saw her. I knew, just as I knew about that other woman. Men!" She made the word sound like a curse. "Evil, lecherous old fools, always running after something new and different, and then expecting to come home and find all is forgiven. How dare you do this to me? How dare you expect me to excuse you?"

"I don't expect you to. You'll never believe there was nothing between me and Stacy Donovan, but there wasn't. There's never been another woman in twenty-nine years. Until now. Until Frances."

Dorothy's control vanished. "Don't mention her name in this house! That whore! That disgusting, vulgar tramp! I never want to hear of her again! Never, do you hear?"

He'd never seen such hatred on anyone's face. The sight of Dorothy's twisted mouth and blazing eyes repelled him, even while he felt pity for her and shame for what he had to do.

"We have to talk about her, Dorothy. I . . . I want a divorce. Fran and I are going away together. There's no way to put it kindly. God knows I wish I could spare you, but I have to tell you the truth. Frances and I love each other. We're going to be married as soon as we can."

There was no answer. She simply stared at him for a long moment. She'd planned to make him pay for this insult. Planned to make Frances pay too, somehow, for sleeping with her husband. But she hadn't anticipated this. She hadn't really believed Frances would want Buzz permanently. She'd thought the woman would tire of the affair and take herself back to the glittering international world she preferred, leaving a chastened Buzz to be magnanimously but slowly forgiven. Divorce? A dazzled, flattered Buzz might think he wanted that, but it was wrong for him. In a few months Frances would leave him, as she'd left the others. She doesn't love this ordinary, middle-aged man, Dorothy thought. And I do. In spite of everything, I love him enough to save him from himself. The anger drained out of her. She felt like his mother, protective and much wiser than he. The rage generated by the affair gave way to a feeling of superiority as Dorothy realized she must keep her husband from making a fatal mistake.

"No, Buzz," she said gently. "No divorce. I'm not thinking of myself. I can't let you do such a foolhardy thing. Frances is not for you. Where would you fit in her world? Are you prepared to be a gypsy, never putting down roots anyplace? Can you handle her fancy friends? Speak their language? Will it make you happy to be a kept man? You'll live on her money, you know. You couldn't begin to earn enough to support her way of life, not even if you started over. You think you're in love. You're not. You're caught up in old memories, old dreams. You're a grandfather, Buzz. Not the dashing young man in the convertible. No," Dorothy repeated, "I won't divorce you. In fact, I won't even let you go. This is where you belong. Here, with your own kind. And here is where you'll stay." She rose from her chair. "I'll never forgive you for this humiliation, but I won't let you humiliate yourself by becoming a lapdog for a selfish, pampered, oversexed woman like Frances Dalton."

He couldn't believe his ears. This was not the unstable, emotional, hysterical Dorothy he knew. He'd expected a hideous scene, uncontrolled fury, threats. Anything but this clinical, almost dignified discussion of his future. What did it all mean? Dorothy was not the self-sacrificing, concerned person she was pretending to be. She was using the frighteningly clever deliberateness of a madwoman. Perhaps, at this moment, she really thought she was speaking the truth, but she was not. She was schizophrenic, and the role she was playing was the other side of Dorothy, the "authority figure" she sometimes practiced on her children, rather than the helpless, dependent personality she normally projected for Buzz.

He stood too, his face inches from hers. "I'm sorry, Dottie, but you can't keep me here. You may not divorce me, but there's no way you can make me stay."

There was a strange smile on her lips. "Isn't there? I think there is. I think I know how to save you from making a fool of yourself. Forget about marrying Frances Dalton. You never will."

Buzz sank slowly back into his chair when she left the room. He felt chilled, fearful of the unknown. He was dealing with a sick and devious woman. Her reasonableness was much more terrifying than the wild outburst he'd anticipated.

She's going to hurt Fran! he thought. She's crazy enough to try to kill her! For a moment he considered calling the Dalton house and warning Frances, but then he thought better of it. She'd think he was insane, would laugh it off and reasonably ask whatever had put such an idea in his head. He couldn't give a sensible answer to that. It was just something he felt. Some terrible threat that had no name.

He heard Dorothy in the kitchen. My God, she's preparing breakfast as though none of this ever happened! Suddenly he couldn't bear this house, couldn't bear the sight of his wife. Tired as he was, he went upstairs, showered and changed his clothes. He'd take a long drive up in the mountains and think things through before he called Frances. He had to be clear about this, had to try to make some sense out of Dorothy's implied threat. Fran was perfectly safe at her parents' house. She wouldn't be going out until she received his call. Nothing could happen to her. And he needed time to shake off this awful sense of impending doom. The crisp, fresh air made him feel better as he slowly drove along the winding roads. With each mile he put between himself and Dorothy, his terror receded until at last he told himself he was being stupid. Dorothy might not divorce him, but she couldn't keep him in Denver. He'd provide for her. He'd sell his agency and put the money in her name. He and Fran didn't care whose money they lived on. They were too mature for that. All they wanted was to be together and happy.

By noontime, he was in control of himself but exhausted. There'd not been much sleep the night before. The memory of those hours brought a smile to his face. They made love as though they were in their twenties. And they would, for a long, long time. But he wasn't twenty, and now he was weary.

Ahead, he saw a small, decent-looking motel. He pulled in and asked for a room. The owner looked at him dubiously.

"A room? For a few hours? You alone?"

Buzz laughed. "Believe it or not, I'm just tired."

It was dark when he awakened, and glancing at his watch he saw it was six o'clock in the evening. Good lord, Frances would be furious that he hadn't called her all day! He supposed Dorothy was wondering where he was too. That didn't matter any more. Still, he owed her the courtesy of checking in.

The man at the desk got Buzz's house on the line for him. To his surprise, his eldest son answered.

"Larry? What are you doing there?"

"Dad, where in God's name have you been? We've tried calling everywhere!"

Buzz felt his spine turn to water. "What's wrong?"

The younger man's voice broke. "It's Mother. She . . . she called me at noon and said I'd better come over as soon as I could. When I got here an hour later . . . ," the voice turned into a sob, "she was dead."

"Dead?" Buzz repeated the word stupidly. "She can't be dead."

Larry was crying openly now. "She hanged herself, Dad. I found her in the basement." He struggled for control. "The police were here. They've taken her away. I didn't let them see the note. It was sealed and addressed to you. Why did she do it? For God's sake, why did she kill herself?"

"I'll be home as soon as I can," Buzz said. "I'm a few hours away, but I'll be there, Son. I'm sorry you had to go through this, Larry. Finding her like that, I mean. I . . . I'd better leave now."

In a daze he raced back to the city, his mind accepting with terrible clarity what he'd not understood that morning. This was how Dorothy planned to keep him from marrying Frances. She knew him well. Knew there'd be no happiness for him with her rival while the specter of the suicide they'd caused hung over his head. The price of her own life was not too great for Dorothy to pay if it meant the final, ultimate revenge she was determined to have. He could not yet feel sorrow for her death. He did not know, would never know, that her deranged mind saw her final act as a sacrifice for him. He knew only, with bitterness, that the self-destructive destroy the lives of the living. Dorothy had destroyed his. No logic, no persuasion would take away his guilt. His whole life would be spent in self-reproach for the selfishness which had sent a woman to her last moments in the basement of their house.

He let out a great sob. The brief thread of happiness he'd reached for had turned into an ugly, unforgettable noose that would sway forever from the rafters of his mind.

After Allie and Jack and John Peck departed and Barbara wandered off to her room, Frances paced the downstairs of her parents' house, listening every minute for the phone, wondering angrily why she hadn't heard from Buzz all day. A little before six, she couldn't stand it any longer. To hell with what Dorothy thought. By now, if Buzz hadn't told her, she would. She dialed the Paiges' number and a young man answered.

"Is Mr. Paige at home?"

"No. This is his son. Who's calling?"

Frances hesitated. "I'm a friend. It's a personal call. Can you tell me where to reach him?"

"No, I can't. We've been trying to find him all afternoon ourselves. Who is this?" Larry asked again.

"I was Frances Dalton. Frances Déspres. I'm an old friend of your parents. If your father isn't there, may I speak to your mother, please?"

The voice shook. "I'm afraid that's impossible, Mrs. Déspres. My mother died suddenly this afternoon. That's why we're trying to locate my father. He doesn't know yet."

Fran was speechless for a moment and then she said, "Died? How can that be? She wasn't ill. What happened?"

"I'm sorry but I can't discuss it now. Please forgive me. Good-bye."

The phone clicked into place and Fran sat staring at the receiver. Dorothy dead? Had she had a stroke or been in an accident? And where was Buzz? Why didn't he know about this? Why hadn't he called her all day? What in God's name was going on? She flew up the stairs to Barbara's room and burst in. Her sister was sitting quietly in a chair by the window. One small light burned on the dresser but Barbara was gazing out into the darkness, lost in her thoughts.

"Barbara! I just called Buzz's house. Dorothy's dead!"

The younger woman turned, startled out of her reverie. "What are you talking about?"

"It's true. I just spoke to one of their sons. Buzz isn't there. He hasn't been home all day, apparently." Fran was suddenly conscious of the darkness. "For God's sake, why are you sitting here in the gloom? This room is like the black hole of Calcutta!" Fran quickly turned on two more lights. "There. That's better. What do you think could have happened?"

"I have no idea. It's terrible! I can't believe it!"

Frances suddenly looked frightened. "He was going to tell her about us. My God, you don't suppose they got into an argument and he killed her!"

"Frances! What are you saying? What a horrible idea! Of course that didn't happen! How could you even think such a thing?"

"Well, where is he? Why haven't I heard from him all day? Why is his family looking for him?"

"I don't know, but I know it isn't that. Buzz could never harm anyone. She must have had a heart attack, something totally unexpected like that."

"You mean as a result of Buzz saying he was leaving? That's all I'd need! Buzz blaming himself for her death. Oh, Jesus, why doesn't he call?"

"Pull yourself together!" Barbara's voice was commanding. "We don't know anything yet. We'll just have to wait until we hear. Let me get you a drink. Sit here quietly and try to compose yourself and I'll be back in a minute. You have a bottle in your room, haven't you?"

Fran nodded. "Top right-hand drawer. Thanks. I could use one."

As she got the whiskey from Fran's bureau, Barbara couldn't repress an actual feeling of dislike for her sister. She has no heart, Barb thought. Not an ounce of sympathy for that poor, dead woman. Only the fear that Buzz might be a runaway murderer or that Dorothy's death might somehow interfere with their plans. That's all she cares about—her own convenience. It's all she's ever cared about.

She took the drink back to Frances, who gulped it gratefully and sighed. "Maybe it's all for the best. Her dying, I mean. It solves a lot of problems, after all."

Barb stared at her in horror.

"You know what I mean," Fran went on. "I know Buzz didn't kill her. You're right about that. He could never do such a thing. And if she did have a heart attack, he won't be stupid enough to hold himself responsible. I'll see that he doesn't. That's an act of God, after all. No one can blame himself for that." She glanced up at Barbara. "You don't have to look at me that way. As though I'm some heartless monster. I can't pretend to be sorry she's gone. She contributed nothing to anyone, not even to herself. At least Buzz will be free, and I'll make him happy. I really will, Barb. You'll see. I love him."

"No," Barbara said slowly, "you don't. You don't love anyone. Not even yourself. In fact, I think you hate yourself, Fran. You've been on a self-destruct pattern all your life. I never realized it before, but everything you touch turns bad. You *make* it turn bad."

"What the hell are you talking about?"

"You don't give a damn how your running away from home affected Mother and Dad. You used your first husband to escape and married your second for money. And God knows what the third was like, but you must have driven him away too. Now you come back here and mess up the lives of some perfectly normal, contented people. You get Buzz crazy and worry Mother and Dad to death and now . . . '' Her voice trailed off.

"And now," Frances said angrily, "I suppose you think I'm somehow responsible for Dorothy Paige's death. Wonderful! What lovely, sweet, sisterly devotion! You probably wish Charles Tallent's wife would conveniently die. Oh, you'd never admit it! You're far too goody-goody for that! But you'd be just as relieved if that happened as I am right now, and if you had an ounce of honesty in you you'd admit it, instead of going through this nauseating self-sacrificing renunciation! Don't talk to me about loving! When I love, I take what I want. I'm not some hypocritical little martyr who sleeps with a woman's husband and hasn't enough guts to stand up and fight for him! Okay. I might be all the things you said, but I'm not the phony you are. I'm glad Dorothy Paige is dead. I'm glad I can have her husband. I'm goddamn grateful for the way it's worked out, for his sake and mine. And I don't feel guilty, little sister, for any part of it. Guilt is not an emotion I enjoy.''

Barbara turned away. "How could you enjoy it? You don't know the meaning of it.''

Fran walked to the door. "It must be lovely to be a living saint, but isn't it painful to have headaches from your halo?''

"Get out of this room!'' Barbara screamed. "Get out of my life! I'm ashamed that you're my sister!''

Chapter 27

THE CALL FRANCES waited for did not come until midmorning of the day after Dorothy Paige accomplished her "ultimate revenge." By the time Buzz telephoned, the morning paper already carried a small obituary notice, noting only the fact of his wife's death, "suddenly, at her home," and listing the surviving husband and children. Funeral services, it said, would be private.

At the breakfast table, Laura, who religiously read this page first, let out a gasp that made Sam look up from the sports pages.

"What's the matter?''

"I can't believe it! Dorothy Paige died yesterday!''

"You don't mean it! How?''

Laura shook her head. "It doesn't say. I can't imagine. How terrible, Sam! She was only forty-nine. Dear Lord, I wonder what happened! Poor Buzz!''

For a moment, both the Daltons had forgotten the Paiges' connection with Frances. The realization dawned almost simultaneously, and they looked at each other, the same question in their minds. Laura gave voice to it first.

"I wonder if Frances knows.''

"Doubt it.''

"She was awfully quiet at dinner last night. Hardly touched a bite of her food.''

"No more quiet than Barbara," Sam said, "but it did occur to me that except for the party it was the first evening Frances stayed home since she got here." He frowned. "I also thought she'd been drinking. Did you?"

Reluctantly, "Yes."

They sat in troubled silence for a few moments, communicating wordlessly in the way of people who've lived together most of their lives. Humanly, shocked and sorry as they were to hear about Dorothy, their thoughts were of their daughter. What would this mean to her? Would it clear the way, after a respectable period of mourning, for Buzz and Frances to decently marry? Was it, terrible thought, some kind of divine providence that would keep them all from another scandal? Each knew what the other was involuntarily thinking and was ashamed.

"I'd better tell Frances," Laura finally said.

There was, as she soon discovered, no need to tell Frances. Newspaper in hand, she walked into her daughter's bedroom and found her sitting up in bed, wide-awake and smoking a cigarette. The full ashtray beside her was mute evidence that she'd been awake most of the night. Before Laura could speak, Fran said, "I know about Dorothy Paige, Mother. I called the house yesterday afternoon, looking for Buzz, and his son told me."

Laura sat on the foot of the bed. "How did it happen? Had she been ill?"

"Not that I know of. I don't have a clue what happened. And Buzz hasn't had the good grace to call."

"Frances! What do you expect of him? The man's wife has just died, suddenly. He hardly could be expected to be on the telephone himself informing his friends!"

Frances stubbed out one cigarette and lit another. "I'm not exactly a 'friend,' Mother. Remember? I'm the woman he was leaving his wife for. That would seem to put me in a very special category, wouldn't you think?"

"I don't know what to think," Laura said. "I can't even imagine how this could have happened."

"There are all sorts of possibilities." Fran reached for her robe. "Anyway, I presume I'll hear something this morning."

Like Barbara, Laura was appalled by Fran's coldness. "How can you be so detached about this, Frances? A very nice woman has died too young. Her husband and children must be shocked and grieving. I know you and Buzz planned to go away together, but this puts a different light on things."

"Does it? Only a more respectable one, I'd think. Instead of running off, we can get properly married right away." Fran turned from the mirror where she was brushing her hair. "Or do you think we're going through those silly, outmoded gestures of waiting a year and pretending Buzz is mourning for a wife he didn't love and was ready to leave? Really, Mother! This isn't the turn of the century, you know. I'm sorry Dorothy's dead, but I can't pretend I consider it a great tragedy. And I'll be very surprised if Buzz turns out to be so hypocritical that he'll act the part of the bereaved husband."

"He's a decent man, Frances. He'll do what's expected of him."

"And what is that, may I ask? Should he go about weeping for twelve months, pretending Dorothy was the greatest woman who ever lived? God, if there's anything I can't stand it's the widow or widower who's been unhappily married and suddenly begins to act as though the person who died was a saint! I see it all the time, especially with women married to absolute stinkers. Just let those men die and you'd think they'd been paragons of kindness and virtue! It turns my stomach. Death doesn't automatically beatify a rotten human being. And Dorothy Paige was a rotten human being. If Buzz pretends otherwise, I'll spit in his eye!''

Laura was momentarily speechless. ''I've never heard such terrible talk!'' she finally said. ''How can you be so heartless?''

''It isn't heartless, Mother. It's realistic. People don't wear black and refuse invitations any more. Men especially. It's a good thing Buzz's future is already planned. If this had happened before I came back, every widow and divorcee in Denver would be after him twenty minutes after the funeral. And thirty minutes after *that* he'd be out enjoying his new role as an eligible man. It's a different world, dear. One you can't understand.''

''I suppose not. I'm not sure I want to. Do Barbara and Alice know what's happened?''

''Alice doesn't, as far as I know. She went out after that peculiar get-together yesterday, remember? But Barb knows. I told her, after I talked to Buzz's son yesterday.'' Fran shrugged. ''We had quite a set-to, as a matter of fact. She thinks I'm as much of a vulture as you do.''

''I never said anything of the sort, Frances.''

''Darling, you don't have to. I can read that anxious look from across the room. Don't worry. I'll play the game for a little while. I'll go to the funeral and look appropriately stricken if that makes everybody happy. I'll be respectful about my 'dear old high school friend' and no one will ever know what was in the works when she died. I'll put on a good show, but none of this changes Buzz's plans or mine.''

''I see. You're very sure of yourself and of Buzz, aren't you?''

''Of course. Why shouldn't I be? He doesn't have to live with his crazy guilt about leaving her. The one obstacle I feared has been providentially removed. I'd be a liar if I said I was sorry.''

''We still don't know how she died, Frances.''

''Does it matter? It must have been quick, an end all of us devoutly wish for ourselves. Buzz wasn't even home when it happened. Dammit, I wish he'd call!''

In midmorning he did, sounding totally unlike himself. When Fran picked up the phone, Buzz said without preamble, ''I know you've heard. Larry told me you called here yesterday evening.''

''Darling, I'm so sorry! I've been frantic, waiting to hear from you. Are you all right?''

''Yes. As well as could be expected.''

Oh, no, Fran thought, slightly annoyed. He's not going to pretend to be crushed. Not with me. She kept her tone gentle and solicitous. ''What happened, dear? I know you weren't there. Was it her heart?''

''No. She did it herself after I left the house. We talked. She didn't seem hysterical. In fact, she was reasonably calm but more determined than usual.

She said she'd never let me go. I was afraid she meant to do something to you. I never dreamed she planned . . . ''

Fran was suddenly shaken. She'd thought of everything from an accident or a massive stroke to the unlikely and quickly dismissed idea of murder. But suicide had never crossed her mind. It took a moment for the implications of such an act to sink in. Dorothy Paige knew what unbearable remorse her husband would feel. Much worse than if he'd left her. This was her way of making sure he'd never marry Frances. In her crazed mind, Dorothy conceived the one deterrent to Buzz and Fran's plans. If her husband felt he and his mistress were responsible for his wife's suicide, he'd never forgive himself. As for marrying "the other woman," the idea would be impossible. She'd be there every day, reminding him of the tragedy they'd precipitated. Damn you, Dorothy Paige! Fran screamed inwardly. Damn you to eternal hell! She willed herself to be calm. She was stronger than Dorothy alive, and she'd be stronger than Dorothy dead. She'd beat her yet.

"Buzz, dear, that's horrible! Horrible for you and your children. Thank God you knew she was not able to think rationally. The poor woman didn't know what she was doing. I'm so sorry for all of you, having to go through this. What can I do? Can I be of any help?"

"No. No, thank you. Everything's being taken care of. The boys and their wives have been wonderful. I'm afraid I haven't been good for much. But thank you for offering."

So polite. So distant. As though she were some old acquaintance offering sympathy and friendly assistance. Fran felt cold inside.

"I'd like to see you, as soon as you feel up to it."

"Yes, of course. In a few days when everything is . . . over."

"A few days when everything is over," Fran thought. My God, he's already dismissed me. Us. No. I won't let him. I'll give him time to come out of shock. Then I'll talk to him gently, sensibly. I've always been able to make him see things my way. I will again.

"Of course, dear. I understand. We'll all, the family I mean, see you at the services."

Buzz hesitated. "They'll be private, Fran. Just our family. But after that . . . well, I'll be in touch."

"I see. That's probably better. I'll wait to hear from you." She paused, uncertain whether to say it. "I love you, Buzz."

There was a moment of silence on the other end. Wrong, Fran thought. Wrong thing to say at this moment. Damn. She was stupid.

"Goodbye for now, dear," she said.

"Goodbye."

In Washington, Charles Tallent picked up the mail from the box outside his house and wandered back, sorting through the bills the "junk," the letters for Andrea, who kept up a voluminous personal correspondence with old friends. At the bottom of the stack was an envelope in familiar handwriting. He'd seen it hundreds of times on love notes left in the Georgetown apartment, little notes to greet him when he occasionally got there ahead of Barbara, messages pinned to his pillow on those rare times when he could stay overnight and awaken to find his darling making breakfast while he slept. The sight of the round, honest handwriting and the Denver postmark gave him a little jolt of joy, And then, almost as though he knew the contents were not happy, he dropped the other mail on the hall table, pushed the letter into the pocket of his robe and went into his study to read it in private.

He sat for a long time after he finished, trying to sort out his emotions. It was a phony. He knew it was. It came from Barbara, all right. No doubt about that. But it wasn't the truth. He knew her too well. This was not a woman who suddenly would have a "revelation" about her life, certainly not in the space of a week. She'd been home many times before, and the sight of her parents' companionship had never made her feel differently. If anything, those visits had only seemed to reinforce her happiness about her life with him in Washington. She'd always been so glad to come back, so lightheartedly grateful, in a kind way, to have escaped the dull, predictable routine of so many of her contemporaries in Denver.

"Thank God I got away!" Charles could hear her saying. "What if I'd married one of those hometown boys and been doomed to a life of diapers and drip-dry dresses!"

And now she was trying to make him believe that all she wanted was security and serenity with some nice middle-class life-companion. She was trying to fool herself. Or more likely, she was trying to fool him. For some reason, Barbara was making it easy for him. Could she conceivably have heard about the either-or offer of the Candidate? No way. No one knew except the Senator and his closest advisers. And Andrea.

Intuitively, he knew there was no "other man." No stalwart protector who'd suddenly come into her life to rescue her from a futile future. That was as much bunk as the nonsense about the happiness of her parents or the "make believe" world she and Charles had shared for years. The whole letter was a loving sham. Somehow Barbara did know how he was suffering over the selfish decision he had to make. This was her way of letting him off easily, caring for his happiness more than she did for her own. Someone had gotten to her, had made her feel it her duty to step aside, to spare him the terrible task of telling her that the wonderful thing they shared was over. Someone who knew she could not stand in his way because she loved him too much. And that same someone knew he might be unable to go through with the ending of his affair if he came face to face with the woman he adored.

There was only one person that knowledgeable, that devious and selfish. Only one that bitter. And he was married to her.

He started toward the door, to find Andrea and accuse her, but a rush of emotion stopped him. It would demean Barbara to discuss her letter with his wife. Damned if he'd give Andrea the satisfaction of knowing her plan had worked. And it was her plan. She knew where to reach Barb, and reach her she had, as certainly as his name was Charles Tallent. Who are you, Charles Tallent? he asked himself. Or, more aptly, *what* are you? Some wind-up toy who marches stiffly in any direction strong and clever people care to send you? Some helpless piece of putty to be manipulated to please others? It had pleased the Candidate, no doubt, to find him so quickly amenable to the idea of changing his whole life. It must have been sweet to Andrea to know that she had outwaited, outlasted and finally outmaneuvered Barb. My God, what is happening to me? Charles wondered. Am I so caught up in this power-crazed city that I'm willing to give up the only thing in the world that makes sense to me? What little shred of importance, or even what remote dreams of the future make me think that life is worthwhile without the only human being I really care for? Who could even remember the names of past Cabinet members? What real chance did he have of ever stepping into the Senator's shoes eight years from now? Damned little. He was a very low man on the big political totem pole. And even if he were not, how did all this stack up against what he'd pay for temporary prominence, or even for a possible place in history?

He knew suddenly why he'd let Andrea talk him out of going to Denver with her rational "Don't embarrass Barbara" arguments. He knew why he dreaded facing his love. It was wrong, and he'd known it all along. His whole life was wrong. A half-life which seemed enough until he was faced with losing even the small, wonderful part he had.

A feeling of peace came over him, as though he'd mercifully been relieved of a terrible burden. Andrea had done him a great favor. Ironic that her great coup had backfired. She must have spent so much time working out the convoluted, intricate scheme. He smiled. All he had to do was abdicate. Other men had given up much more for women they desired. What were those touching words spoken by a truly powerful man almost forty years before? Something about "I cannot faithfully discharge my duties without the help and support of the woman I love." I'm no king, Charles thought, but I know how he felt. It took courage. It would not be without some small twinge of regret for what might have been. But this was nothing compared to the knowledge of how lonely and pointless it would be with no one to share his triumphs, whatever they might be.

He glanced at the desk clock. Eight-thirty. Six-thirty in the morning in Denver. Too early to awaken a sleeping Dalton household, even for this. Besides, he wanted to put his declaration in writing, even if it were only on the yellow page of a telegram.

Charles picked up the phone. "I want to send two wires," he told the Western Union operator. "The first is to Miss Barbara Dalton, 1016 South Carona, Denver, Colorado. And the second is to Senator Wilson Derrnott, Horizon Manor, Burlington, Vermont."

Janice moved her head gingerly on the pillow, but the movement was enough to awaken Clint.

"Good morning." He reached out and tenderly stroked her brow.

Jan groaned. "A matter of opinion. Darling, would you mind not doing that? This morning, even my hair hurts."

"Hung over, huh? You deserve it."

"Thank you. I shall go to my grave remembering those sweet, understanding words."

"You're a terrible grouch when you wake up."

"Right now I wish I couldn't wake up for about forty-eight hours." But then she grinned. "It's worth it, though. That is, I'm trying to tell myself it is. It was a great evening, wasn't it? Super-special."

Clint Darby returned her smile. "It was an extraordinary evening, to say the least. You and I and your nice gay brother and his friend and your half-brother's pregnant wife all celebrating the reunion of your mother with her illegitimate child. Now that, I would say, is a rare combination of people and circumstances. I think that's what I love about you. You come up with such inventive gatherings. So sophisticated."

"Don't make it sound like something out of Noel Coward. It was sweet. The way Chris and Carol took to each other was nice. Really nice. I like her, you know. She's a helluva woman when you get to know her. She was so happy for John and Mother. I mean, we all were, but especially Carol. She is crazy for her husband. And so pleased about the baby. It's a damned shame she can't go to Denver and meet Mother. They'll get along like gangbusters when they do meet." Jan's voice trailed off. "Whenever that is."

Clint sat up on the side of the bed and stretched.

"Yeah. It doesn't sound like your mother's coming back, does it? I mean, not to that wonderful husband of hers anyway."

"No. And she shouldn't, God knows! She should have split years ago. Maybe she would have, if it hadn't been for Chris and me. It makes me feel terrible to think she might have gone through all she did just to keep a house together for us. We'd all have been better off if she'd had the guts years ago to tell him to get lost. You heard her on the phone when she and John called last night. She sounded so carefree. I haven't heard her sound that way ever." Janice sat up and let out another moan. "Oh, lord, that was a mistake." She slid down under the covers again. "I think I won't move for several days. It could be hazardous to my health."

"You're a nut." Clint looked at her soberly. "Jan, you mustn't think you were to blame for your mother's staying with Spencer. Some women do that kind of thing out of fear. Fear that they can't take care of themselves. Or they do it out of an irrational feeling of worthlessness. A need to be punished for imagined inadequacy. That was the case with Alice. We know that now. She had such terrible guilt about John. And now they're gone and she's free. Free of the inferiority. And free of that bastard, your father."

"Yes I know. I'm so glad for her, Clint. She's a nice lady. I only hope it isn't too late for her."

"How so?"

"Well, what's she going to do now? You know my father won't meekly give her a divorce. He's much too vicious for that." Jan frowned. "Is it sick to hate your father?"

"No, love. Not when he's a miserable sonofabitch. You're too intelligent to think you have to love him just because he's your father. Look at Chris. Chris openly hates him. And why not? Your brother may lead an 'unconventional' life, but his instincts are good all the way. Look how he took the news about John Peck. No 'disappointment' in his mother. Nothing but joy that she has another child to love. He's okay. He and John will like each other when they meet. My God, it's all too much happiness around here suddenly! Good thing I'm not a diabetic. I'd go into a coma from all this sweetness!"

"I'm still worried about Mother. I don't think Dad will give her a divorce. And if he does, what then? Will she stay in Denver and live with my grandparents? She won't have enough money to come back here and live."

"She has three kids who would gladly support her, Jan. Four, if you count me."

Janice looked at him lovingly. "That's dear. But I don't think she'd let us take care of her. She wouldn't live with Chris and David when they offered a long while ago. She certainly wouldn't move in with John and Carol. Or you and me. I don't know. I don't think she could be happy going back to her parents' home after all the years of running her own establishment. She's really displaced, isn't she? She's seen her dream come true, but where does she go from here?"

"Maybe she'll move in with Richards. Even if good old Spencer won't divorce her, she could live with John's father. He's alone too."

Despite the seriousness of it, Jan began to giggle. "It's almost too much. My quiet, proper little mother. I wouldn't have believed she wasn't a virgin when she married. Or that years later she'd tell her husband to go to hell. Or that we'd be discussing her 'living in sin' with the father of her child! I'm having a hard time adjusting to this new view of her. To me, she's a wife and mother. Period."

"Are they such awful things to be?" Clint took her hand and kissed the palm. "Lately I've been thinking of you in those roles. Maybe about time I made an honest, pregnant woman of you. What do you think?"

Janice stared. "Get married? Have a baby? Us?"

"Well, you don't have to say it as though I suggested we go out and rip off a bank! Is it such an awful idea? You don't have to stop working. I mean, just long enough to have the kid. Look at Carol. She's not planning to shrivel up and die because she and John are going to have a baby. Hell, we don't even have to rush into that part. Let's get married and see what happens."

"I didn't think you wanted . . . "

"And I didn't think *you* wanted. So we're even. But I want. Do you?"

Jan looked at him searchingly. "I don't think I knew until this moment how much I do. I thought marriage was superfluous. Kids, too. But in the last few days, seeing everything around me . . . "

"Sorry. That won't do. There's only one reason to get married."

"What's that?"

"It's called 'advertised love,' baby. It's wanting everybody in the world to know that we respect each other enough to share more than two names on the mailbox. It's old-fashioned, sentimental, corny, terrific, unchanging pride in announcing that the one person you think is perfect thinks the same of you." His handsome face was very serious. "We have a commitment, you and I. We don't need a paper to make it stick. But we need that piece of paper for our egos, believe it or not. Not for kids. Not for respectability, Jan. For us. For what we still believe in. Miss Winters, here in the sanctity of our premarital bed, will you do me the honor of becoming my wife?"

She sat up and kissed him gently. "Mr. Darby, I'd be delighted." A look of amazement crossed her face. "Hey, my hangover's gone! Can a proposal of marriage cure the morning-after blahs?"

"If so," Clint said solemnly, "we'll bottle it and make a fortune."

*   *   *

Midway in the process of throwing a clean shirt and his shaving equipment into an attaché case, Spencer Winters suddenly stopped. He had his first-class ticket to Denver and his hotel reservation efficiently dispatched the evening before by that sniveling secretary of his. But he hadn't been thinking clearly when he ordered them. What in hell was he rushing back to that hick town for? To bodily drag Alice home? To punch out that arrogant John Peck, who'd simply taken matters into his own hands and gone to find the woman he claimed was his mother? It was a stupid waste of time to fly thousands of miles to accomplish what was going to happen anyway. That screaming match on the phone with Alice, added to the nonappearance of her alleged son in Spencer's office and the final break with Janice had thrown his usually orderly mind into emotional chaos. This morning, things were clearer. It was beneath him to rush across the country like some hysterical, rejected husband. He was about to respond exactly as Alice wanted. It would please her to see him make a spectacle of himself in front of other people. As for that Peck person, Spencer would deal with him when he came back to Boston. He'd deal with Alice too. Because she'd come back. She had to. Where else would she go? It was easy enough, safely removed from him, to say the extraordinary things she'd screamed at him the day before. It was no trick to declare independence when a couple of thousand miles of telephone wire protected her. She wouldn't be so sure of herself when she walked back into his house. She was going to pay for this rebellion. And she was going to keep her mouth shut about the whole messy incident. "Long-lost child" indeed! Spencer grimaced. Somehow, he'd prove Peck was a phony, a clever opportunist trying to take advantage of a stupid woman like Alice.

No, there was no need to go charging out there to waste time on a silly woman who talked about "starting a new life for herself." He didn't love her. Privately, he'd be just as glad if she followed through with her nonsense about a divorce. But losing anything he possessed was foreign to Spencer's image of himself. And that included the approval of J. B. Thompson and the other partners in the firm. Alice was necessary to that image, which revolved around a steady, conservative home life with no hint of scandal. That's what the world thought he had. That's what he would keep. All he had to do was sit back and wait for his idiot wife to come to her senses. Bolstered by that trashy family of hers, she probably thought she *could* start over, as she'd said. But when she found herself without funds and removed from the comforts she was used to, she'd see there was no answer except to come home. And if nothing else she'd never be able to live away from those obnoxious children of theirs. If nothing else would bring her back to Boston, Janice and Christopher would. She was too fatuous to lose her daily contact with them.

He felt better. He'd been about to do something rash and oddly disorganized for a man who prided himself on his analytical powers. Damn these undisciplined people like Alice who could throw even the most rational man temporarily off base! No matter. All he had to do now was let nature take its inevitable course.

He called his office and told Martha Perrone to cancel his flight and his Denver hotel. He'd be in the office later.

"You've changed your plans, Mr. Winters?" Why did the woman sound relieved?

"No," Spencer said sarcastically. "I'm flying out on my Superman cape and staying at the governor's mansion. Obviously, I've changed my plans, Miss Perrone! I don't telephone you for the sheer pleasure of hearing your refined voice!"

He banged the receiver back into its cradle. Women! He was surrounded by foolish women—his wife, his daughter, even his secretary. What was that thing Hitler had once said? Oh, yes, "The greater the man, the more insignificant the woman." That was the damned truth. Old Adolf had had the right idea about that. Spencer had believed it all his life.

Chapter 28

As HE SLOWLY dressed in a dark suit and knotted his black four-in-hand tie, Buzz still couldn't believe it was true. He forced himself to say the words silently. "Dorothy is dead. Dorothy killed herself. She didn't want to live." For the tenth time, he reread the almost childish scrawl that had been her last message to him, the brief note Larry had considerately kept from everyone else's eyes.

> I don't have to explain this to you, Buzz. Life is over for me. You were a good husband, but you never loved me. I loved you, though. So much that I don't want to be around to see you belong to someone else. This is better for everybody. Kiss the children for me. And don't be sorry. Dorothy.

It crossed his mind, almost irrelevantly, that even in her final words she would not mention Fran's name. She'd been jealous of Frances since they were all teen-agers, never able to compete with her in any way, not in her whole life. She could compete only in death. And she'd won that last battle. She hadn't killed only herself. She'd destroyed Buzz's ceaseless obsession with her rival. It was finally over for him and Fran. No passion, no insane infatuation was stronger than the memory of despair. They'd killed a desperately weak woman who couldn't face the loneliness and rejection her husband and his mistress selfishly demanded she accept.

Standing there, waiting to go to the funeral, his body shook with sobs. He wept for Dorothy. Poor, inadequate Dorothy, who tried so hard, in her own way, to take another woman's place in his heart. She'd been irrational in the past, foolish and irritating and sometimes hostile. But yesterday morning she was none of those things. She knew exactly what she was doing when she made that noose and stood on a wooden chair and kicked it . . . Buzz stopped. He couldn't think about it. He refused to remember the way she looked when he went to identify the body. But he'd never forget it, much as he wanted to. She'd made that impossible. If only he could hate her for what she'd done to all of them. If only he could stop hating himself.

He was grateful that the boys, with a maturity of understanding beyond their years, had suggested that the final, awful business be completed quickly. The terrible night before, Larry had taken charge, his brothers and their young wives backing him up.

"Dad, I don't think we should make this a long, drawn-out thing." His son's voice had been firm but gentle. "Mother wanted to be cremated. We feel it should be tomorrow, if you agree."

Buzz had simply nodded, wondering how much they knew and whether they felt shame for what Dorothy had done or hatred for the father who'd caused it. As though Larry read his mind, the young man said, "She hadn't been herself for years. You know that better than anyone. Don't feel guilty, Dad. You were good to her always. It's rotten it had to end this way, but maybe . . . maybe it was inevitable."

Buzz had pressed his son's hand, unable to speak. If the children knew anything, they'd never say so. They wouldn't compound the sense of failure they recognized in him. They'd be kind and thoughtful as they were now. Larry's wife put her hand on his arm. "It's hard, Dad. We can only imagine how hard. But you'll be all right. Give it time."

He'd tried to smile. She was so sweet. So amazingly wise for a little thing in her early twenties. What would she think if she knew the truth? What would any of them think if they knew where he'd spent the night before Dorothy's death? He shuddered. He wasn't so foolish, even in this moment of shock, to think he'd never pick up his life again. He would. But not with Fran. Never with Fran. That, at least, would give some meaning to what Dorothy had done.

"Barbara, do you think it would be out of place for me to call on Buzz in the next few days?"

"Out of place? No, I don't think so, dear." Barb looked affectionately at her troubled mother. "You were always fond of him and you liked Dorothy. It's better to do what you'd ordinarily do under such circumstances."

"Yes, but . . . well, that business with Frances. Your father thinks it would be shameful for any of us to go near the Paiges. He's not taking this well. Not since we heard she . . . she died by her own hand."

"I think it would be worse if we acted as if we didn't care."

Laura sighed. "That's the way I feel. But Sam . . . " She hesitated. "Barbara, how do you think this will affect Frances? Her plans with Buzz, I mean, I don't mean to sound awful. That poor girl isn't even buried yet. But do you think the two of them . . . ?"

"No, Mother, I don't. Not now. Not because of Fran. Because of Buzz. I'm afraid he's going to blame himself."

Laura was silent. Nothing seemed to go right these days. She felt constantly fearful. Why was that? Last night she'd dreamed an awful dream. A nightmare. She'd been running around in a chicken yard, chasing three fluttering, frightened hens. She wanted to catch them, to put them back in their nests where they'd be warm and safe, but they kept slipping away from her. She went round and round the place for a long while, calling to them, reaching out to pick them up, but they wriggled out of her grasp. And then finally a man—she didn't know who he was—came out with a big axe and grabbed one of the hens, and Laura screamed that he mustn't kill her. The scream had been real, apparently. She'd been awakened to find Sam shaking her and commanding her to wake up, that she was having a nightmare. She'd been happy to. It had been so terrifying, and it made no sense. She'd been afraid to go back to sleep, fearful she'd have the same dream, but she hadn't. She'd merely slept fitfully the rest of the night.

"Mother?"

Laura came back to the moment. Barbara was looking at her quizzically. "You were a million miles away. We were talking about making a condolence call on Buzz. Do you want me to go with you? Not today, of course. Today's the funeral. Private, Fran says. But maybe tomorrow or the day after."

"I don't know. I mean, I don't know whether any of us should go. But if I do, I'd like you to go with me. How long will you be here, Barbara? I'm not trying to rush you. You know that, but I wondered about your job . . . and about Charles."

"I haven't made up my mind about the job, or Washington. I wrote and told them I needed some time at home." Barb paused. "I also wrote and broke it off with Charles."

"I see." The sadness of the world was in those two words. "You had to, of course. You're so strong, Barbara. So sensible. If only your sisters . . ."

Barbara tried to keep her temper. "If only they *what?* Had my common sense? My discipline? All those phony virtues everybody's constantly endowing me with?" She sounded weary. "I'm so tired of doing 'the right thing.' It's not the way I want to act at all. I want to throw myself on the floor and beat my fists and kick my feet! Does that surprise you, Mother? Of course it does. I'm so self-reliant, so pulled-together. Don't believe it. I'm as selfish as Fran and as frightened as Allie. Or I would be, if I ever allowed myself to show all of you the real Barbara. I'm bloody tired of hearing everybody worry about Fran and Alice. What about me, dammit?" Her voice had risen slightly and there was resentment in it. "Even Charles. Even the man I love expects me to understand that his needs come before mine." She laughed harshly. "And what's even worse, I almost make myself believe it. I'm not strong, Mother. I'm not sensible and forbearing. I'm scared and lonely and fed up with being the pillar of strength around here while Fran drives a woman to suicide and Allie wallows in absolution! It's not fair. It's never been fair!"

Laura didn't look at her. Staring at the floor, she said, quietly, "Nobody asked you to take that role, Barbara. Seems you chose it. Just as the other girls chose theirs."

It was more deflating than any surprise or protest her mother could have registered. Laura was right, of course. You made your own destiny shaped your own character. And, Barb thought ruefully, took your own licks.

"I'm sorry, Mother. You're right. We're all masochists, your children. Seems as though we each punish ourselves in our own way. What a sorry lot we are! What a trio of messed-up lives. And what heartaches we must give you." Barb smiled. "Never mind, dear. Fran will get over Buzz and I'll recover from Charles. As for Allie, who knows? I suppose she'll marry Jack and live more or less happily ever after. One out of three isn't such a terrific average, but it's better than none at all.'' She tried to change the subject. ''John Peck's a nice young man, isn't he? I'm glad about that. Imagine what it would have been like if he'd turned out to be some terrible, crude, unscrupulous man! That's the danger of letting children find their real parents, I suppose. It could be an invitation to blackmail in the wrong hands. It's not fair to deprive a person of the right to know his origins, but it's not fair to deprive the natural mother or father of his anonymity either.''

She realized she was babbling, trying to make Laura forget the earlier outburst. Her mother was only half-listening, though. Her mind was somewhere else. Had been, most of the time. ''What's wrong, Mother? You don't seem like yourself today.''

Laura was tempted to tell her about the dream. It must have meant something. It was like a fearsome omen. She didn't believe in such things, but this was so vivid. Even awake, she couldn't shake it, couldn't stop thinking that her unconscious was trying to tell her something, trying to warn her. Nonsense. Next she'd begin to think she had some sixth sense or other. It must have been that cheese she had at dinner. She never slept well after she ate cheese at night. You'd think after seventy years, she'd have sense enough to know that.

''Nothing's wrong,'' she said. ''That is, nothing you don't already know about. Heavens, that's enough to make me distracted, don't you think?'' Laura got up briskly. ''Time to get on with my work. Do you know it's nearly eleven o'clock? Your father will be wanting lunch soon. Will you be in? I suppose Fran will stay in her room. What about Allie?''

''She's getting dressed. I think she and Jack are taking John to lunch and then to the airport this afternoon. He has to get back to Boston.'' She paused before she said softly, ''Mother, do you wish we'd all go away? We're an awful lot of work and worry for you, aren't we?''

''Don't talk foolish, Barbara. You know your father and I love having all of you here. Even if it's not been quite the quiet reunion any of us expected.''

Barb couldn't help smiling. That, surely, was the understatement of the week. Of the century. They'd come home to celebrate an anniversary and everybody's life had changed in a matter of days. We have to leave, she realized suddenly. They love us, but our problems are too much for them. Sometimes separation is less distressing than having your loved ones' problems right under your nose. Even devoted parents can reach their limit. Laura had certainly reached hers. Sam probably had too, though most of the time he kept his thoughts to himself. I'll talk to Fran and Allie, Barb thought. Fran knows she's lost Buzz. She must know that. As for Allie, let her make up her mind about Jack. Stay here with him or find some other answer. But we've all got to get out of here and get on with our crazy destinies, whatever they are.

The phone rang again. It had been ringing all morning. First with Jack arranging to pick up Allie. Then Buzz with the terrible message Fran curtly reported before she went up to her room. Probably she's in there drinking, Barb thought. That didn't go well in this house either.

''I'll get it,'' Barb said.

''This is Western Union,'' the caller said when she answered. ''I have a telegram for Miss Barbara Dalton.''

She felt her knees begin to shake. "This is she."

"The message is from Washington, D.C. Shall I read it to you?"

Agony. Why didn't the disembodied voice get on with it? "Yes, please."

In the emotionless tones of a robot the operator began to recite. "Have your letter. Unacceptable due to changes in congressman who has come to his senses. Understand everything. Repeat everything. You are the world's loveliest liar. Come home. I need you and love you as never before. Charles." There was a pause and the voice said, "Shall I repeat that?"

"No. No, thank you."

"Would you like a copy mailed to you?"

Barbara was impassive. "That won't be necessary. I remember every word."

Her sisters stared at her as though she'd taken leave of her senses. In the late afternoon when Alice returned from the airport, still red-eyed from her emotional parting scene with Johnny, Barbara dragged her into Fran's room and firmly closed the door. Then she told them she thought it was about time they all got out from underfoot.

"We're overstaying our welcome," Barb said. "The folks aren't up to all the chaos we've created. I realized it today. I'm going to get going and leave them in peace, and I think it would be a good idea if you two did the same."

"Leave?" Alice asked incredulously. "Why? Why would they want us to?"

"Because they're no longer used to a houseful of people. They can't handle all this, Allie. It isn't just the extra work for Mother, though that can't be easy. It's that we upset their routine, give them things to worry about that they don't know about when we're not here. They're not ancient, but they're not young. I think they'd like nothing better than to be alone again."

"But we're their children!" Alice said. "I don't understand your thinking. If my children wanted to spend time with me, I'd be overjoyed! I don't think you know what you're talking about, Barbara. I think Mother and Dad are delighted to have us here. And it isn't as though we plan to stay forever. My lord, it's the first time they've had us all together in thirty years! I don't see what the rush is."

Barbara sighed. Why didn't Allie come out and say what she really was thinking? It wasn't that she was so anxious to stay in this house. It was that she hadn't made up her mind where she was going to go when she left it. Probably the same was true of Fran, who hadn't said a word so far. Barb turned to her older sister.

"What do you think, Fran? Don't you think it's time we moved on?"

"I don't know about you two, but I'm not leaving Denver. Not just yet. Maybe you're right about not staying in the house. I'll probably go to a hotel. Fact is, I'd rather. I always hated this place. But I'm sticking around town awhile."

The words were spoken very slowly, very deliberately. She's half-sloshed, Barb realized. She's probably been drinking all afternoon, sitting up here trying to figure out what to do about Buzz. Fran hadn't reported much about her phone call. Only that Dorothy's death was suicide and the services private, but Barbara knew there was more. It didn't take a genius to understand the remorse Buzz Paige must be feeling. Or the fact that he probably never wanted to see the woman who'd pushed him to Dorothy's breaking point. She isn't going to accept that, Barb thought sadly. She still thinks she's going to get Buzz if she stays around and waits for the shock to wear off. Both she and Allie are trying to buy time, just as I was. It was no good playing games with these women. Somehow they had to be made to face their situations. Barbara took a deep breath and plunged in.

"Listen," she said almost desperately, "we've all got to come to a decision. Allie, I know you're confused about the future. None of us wants to see you go back to Spencer, but if you don't, then you've got to make up your mind what you *are* going to do. Jack will marry you, if that's what you want. Hell, you can even go live with him until you get a divorce. And Fran, darling, you must be realistic about Buzz. He's probably going to take a long time to recover from this. Your staying around will only be agonizing for both of you. Why don't you go back to Europe? He'll come for you when he's ready." It was a kind lie. Barb hadn't the heart to say that Buzz undoubtedly wanted nothing more than to put Frances out of his life. Let her think that she was giving him breathing space; that when he'd gotten over this they'd be reunited.

But Frances wasn't buying it. "No way, kiddo. I'm camping right here in town for the so-called 'decent interval of mourning.' Buzz Paige wants me and now he's free to have me. The fact is, he can't wait! Oh, he may not know it right now, but he will. And soon. Do you think I'd be such a damned fool as to go off and let some of these local vultures get to him when he's at his most vul . . . vulnerable?" Her words were a little slurred. "Forget it. Butt out, babe. Allie and I are big girls. We can handle our own lives without a lot of unasked-for advice from you." She smiled unpleasantly. "Doesn't seem to me you've done so well with your own troubles. At least Allie and I haven't been kicked out by some quote wonderful, faithful lover unquote. What are you going to do, Sister dear, when you so nobly leave the nest again? Moon around Washington, hoping for a glimpse of the great man? Go into faith-healing? Maybe you can get a job on the *Post* writing a lovelorn column, since you think you're so damned good at it!"

Barbara's anger was greater than her compassion for this blind, self-indulgent woman. Her words came hotly, heedlessly as she struck back. "*I'm* not the one who's been kicked out, Fran. *You* are. Buzz will never want to set eyes on you again. If it hadn't been for you, Dorothy Paige would be alive today! You're a fool. A dangerous, blind fool! Don't you know Buzz must hate you as much as he hates himself?"

Fran smiled, a superior, condescending smile. "Darling little Barbara. Taking out her own disappointment on someone sensible enough not to play the martyr. A fool, am I? Well, we'll see. When I'm in a warm bed with Buzz Paige and you're at the movies with your girlfriends, we'll see who's a fool. You'll never understand men, dear girl. You never have. No doubt that's why you've never really had one of your own."

There was a moment of silence while Fran continued to smile and Barbara drew back, aghast at her sister's words and ashamed of her own. At last she said, "Fran, this is silly. We don't mean the things we've said. We're all upset. That's why we're carrying on like this. Come on. Let's talk about the situation calmly. We should leave here. Even you and I agree on that. You're probably right. I shouldn't presume to advise you two on what to do after that, but I'm sure Mother and Dad should have their nice, peaceful life back again. She turned to Alice, who'd been listening in horrified silence to the other two. "Allie? Don't you think we should all go?"

Alice looked at her helplessly. "I don't know. It's safe here and I don't know what would happen to me if I left. I'm afraid of Spencer. Of what he might do if I moved in with Jack. He might kill me, Barb."

"Oh, for God's sake!" Fran's impatience was now directed at Alice. "He hasn't killed you in twenty-five years. He's a bluff, can't you see that? A damned, egomaniacal bully! And you're as crazy as he is! What the hell's the matter with you, Allie? Jack Richards is willing to take you in. Where do think you'll get a better offer? Or do you want to go back to Boston and let Spencer treat you like the dirt you think you are? You make me sick. You're so bloody pious and timid. You're afraid of life, afraid to slug it out because somebody might harm you."

Alice didn't fight back. She simply said, "I can't argue with what you're saying, Fran. But there's something else. I don't know whether I love Jack. Or even whether he really loves me. I wouldn't want him to take me in out of pity or guilt. I wouldn't want to go that way either."

"Stop it, Fran" Barbara's voice was strong. "We're not solving anything by hurling accusations at one another."

Fran poured herself another drink. "I don't know. I think it's all rather refreshing. Healthy to say what we've always thought of each other. You think I'm a selfish fool. I think you're a spineless idiot. And Allie, well, poor little Allie doesn't think at all, do you, dear?"

Alice stood up. Suddenly there was a dignity about her that was in contrast to the frightened, confused woman who hadn't defended herself against Fran's ugly words. "I think a great deal," she said. "Perhaps that's been my trouble. I've thought too much of the past. I wanted so to come home, to be with my family. I thought I could find the comfort and help I needed. But it isn't here. It isn't anywhere except within myself. Yes, I'm afraid. Yes, I'm uncertain about many things. But I'm also at peace, Fran. At peace with my conscience. And that's more than you'll ever be."

Barb looked at Fran as Alice left the room. "You bitch," she said. "You utter, consummate bitch."

Chapter 29

FLYING BACK TO Boston, John Peck couldn't concentrate on the paperback he'd picked up at the airport. He put the book aside and sat back, letting his thoughts go, almost minute by minute, over the past forty-eight hours and allowing himself the luxury of self-congratulation. It had been worth it, the long search for his mother. To know, after all these years, what his heritage was gave him a sense of grateful contentment. He was a lucky man. Alice was the prototype of everything a mother is supposed to be: pretty, refined, gentle and loving.

It also was an enormous relief to know he'd pass on to his own child a healthy genetic background. He thought lovingly of Carol and the baby she carried. The secure, wanted baby whom Alice would also love. He'd done her a kindness with his persistence. She seemed to look ten years younger in two days, happy even while she cried at the airport when he boarded his plane. Only her last words to him as he was about to go through the gate hinted at the insecurity she still felt.

"I'll see you soon again, won't I, Johnny? We won't lose touch now that we've found each other?"

He'd put his arms around her and gently kissed her cheek. "Of course we'll see each other. You have to meet Carol. And the baby's coming, remember? You don't think I'm going to let you get away after I spent so much time looking for you?"

She'd nodded, smiling through her tears. "Give Carol my love. And Janice, when you see her. And, Johnny, please get to know Christopher. He's not like you, but in his own way he's just as sweet and sensitive."

He'd promised he'd do all those things. He wanted to ask about her own plans, but it seemed awkward to do so with Jack Richards standing silently by. He hadn't quite known what to do about his father. Though they'd spent two nights under the same roof, he didn't feel as close to Jack as he did to Allie, and he couldn't put his arms around him for a goodbye hug. He settled for a handshake and an exchange of smiles.

"Goodbye, Son," Jack said. "Take care of yourself."

"I will. You too."

Take care of *her*, Johnny wanted to say. Look after this nice woman you used to love. Even at that moment, the realization that he was thinking in the past tense surprised him. But it was true. A young Jack Richards had, perhaps, loved Alice. A grownup one did not. He cared about her, felt responsible for the trouble he'd caused, but he didn't love her. I'm not sure my father can deeply love anyone, Johnny thought. There's nothing wrong with the man. He's kind and decent, but he doesn't love his childhood sweetheart. And she no longer loves him. They were like two reconciled friends with an important shared experience. She won't marry him, Johnny knew in that instant. And he doesn't want her to.

The recognition of that fact troubled him as the plane droned eastward. What would happen to his mother? Now that she'd left Spencer Winters, where would she go? He couldn't imagine her staying in the South Carona Street house with her parents, or going to live with one of those dissimilar sisters. Perhaps she'd come to live with Carol and him. It would make more sense than going to Jan and Clint Darby or moving in with Christopher and his "roommate." He'd discuss it with Carol when he got home. Realistically, he wasn't sure Carol would be too thrilled about having her mother-in-law in residence, but she'd do it gracefully if it seemed the only answer. He was even less sure that Alice would take to the idea. She'd know it wasn't right for two generations of women to share the same house, especially when they didn't know each other.

It still seemed strange to have a whole family. Grandparents and aunts, as well as parents. Strange and splendidly solid. Everything would work out, now that they'd gotten this far. Peacefully, Johnny put his head back on the seat and fell into a light, happy sleep.

*   *   *

Almost at the moment her son dozed off, thousands of feet in the air, Alice was having the terrible confrontation with Fran. After she spoke her little piece about a clear conscience, she left her sisters and, fighting back the tears, half-ran out of the house she wasn't ready to leave for good. I must decide, she told herself. They're right. I must make up my mind where I'm going from here. Unthinkingly, she turned and headed for Washington Park. It was a beautiful evening and dusk was just beginning to fall. How many nights, long ago, she had walked through this park with Fran or Barb or the friends of her youth. How many times she and Jack had strolled here, stopping to kiss discreetly. It was all different now, of course. More "organized" with its tennis courts and recreation areas, but it was still beautiful and peaceful, and at this hour there were few people to interrupt her thoughts.

As she walked across the nearly deserted park, she was sure of only two things: She would never go back to Spencer and she did not want to live with Jack Richards. The Jack she remembered was no more. He had become a pleasant alien, no more to her than an old friend. Though she shared the joy of Johnny's return with him, she did not feel that Jack really was part of their child. He'd fathered him, but she'd carried him for nine months, seen him briefly as an infant, despaired when they took him away. Her life had been motivated by her guilt about the baby. Jack had thought of him rarely, had considered looking for him only because his wife had thought it might make him happy. And even then he'd refused. No, Jack was only a biological father. Just as he'd been only a hot-blooded, passionate young man without sensitivity in the beginning and without courage in the end. She'd been right all those years ago when she'd said she'd never marry such a man. She was still right thirty-one years later.

It was a long walk across the park, but Allie was unaware of the distance until she came to the other side and saw the little cottage she remembered. It was a designated landmark now, Laura had told her recently, carefully preserved in honor of the poet Eugene Field, who had lived there. It was the house in which he'd written the poem she'd often read to Janice and Christopher when they were children. A sweet little poem. What was it? Oh, yes. "Little Boy Blue." Alice stood pensively in front of the cottage, trying to remember it. How did it go?

> The little toy dog is covered with dust,
> But sturdy and staunch he stands;
> And the little toy soldier is red with rust,
> And his musket moulds in his hands.

She wrinkled her brow, concentrating, trying to remember the rest of it. Something about when the dog was new and the soldier was fair and Little Boy Blue kissed them and put them there.

Why had she read such a sad poem to her children? It was about death. About a little boy dying. She knew why. She didn't want to think about that. It was part of the nightmare years when she was afraid Johnny was dead.

The evening was warm but a chill came over her. It had become quite dark.

She could hardly make out the details of the house so painstakingly cared for by people who wished to preserve the memory of one of their famous citizens. She turned quickly. It was a long way back across the park and it was getting late. The family would be worried about her.

She'd gone only a few steps when she felt a presence behind her. Another evening stroller, she told herself. Nothing to be alarmed about. She quickened her pace and the stranger did the same. It was a man. She could hear his heavy tread. She began to be frightened, remembering her father's remarks about the park, no different from any park in any city these days, a place for perverts and muggers. People didn't go walking in lonely areas after sundown any more. Not in Boston or New York or any town. Not even in Denver. She felt panic rising. The man was following her, closing the distance between them. Frantically, Alice looked around, hoping to see someone, anyone. There was no one in sight. No one heard her gasp as the gloved hand came from behind and covered her mouth. No one saw her forced to the ground, her clothes roughly torn off her body. No one heard her pleading as she begged him not to do this. And no one heard her single terrified scream as the man finally raised a heavy stone and brought it crashing down onto her head. When Laura knocked on Fran's door shortly before six o'clock, there was no answer. She quietly opened it and saw her eldest daughter lying on the bed. Laura went over and shook her gently.

"Frances, dear, dinner's almost ready."

The woman stirred. Laura could smell the liquor even from a distance. She's drunk, Laura thought, dismayed.

"Frances, I'm about to put dinner on the table," she repeated. "You'd better get ready to come down."

Fran turned over. "Don't want any dinner."

"You must eat. You didn't have any lunch."

"No. Going to sleep. Leave me alone, Mother."

Laura sighed. It was useless. She went next door and rapped lightly. Barbara's voice told her to come in.

"You and Alice ready for dinner?"

"Alice isn't here, Mother. I heard her go out about an hour ago."

"Out? Out where?"

"I don't know."

Laura was annoyed. "Really, I do think that's inconsiderate. She could have let me know. It's not like her. She always tells me when she's not going to eat here. I don't know what's gotten into you girls, I really don't. Fran's in bed and refuses to get up and . . . and I'm sorry to say I think she's been drinking. And now Allie disappears without a word. She's never done that. Do you think she's all right, Barbara?"

"Of course. She'll probably call in a little while. Maybe she met Jack and decided to have dinner with him."

"Well, I guess it's just the three of us, then. You're coming down, aren't you?"

"Yes, I'll be right with you."

Barbara was not so unconcerned as she seemed. Laura was right. It wasn't like Allie not to say where she was going or when she'd be back. It was nothing to worry about, of course, but she'd been upset, and rightly so, by Fran's cruelty. Even I upset her, Barb thought, with that sudden business of all of us leaving. I still think we must, but it's harder for Allie than for Fran or me. At least we have somewhere to go.

She thought again of Charles's telegram. She'd told no one about it, not sure of what it meant. Had he figured out a way to continue his love affair with her, even though he'd accepted the new position? What did he mean that he understood "everything"? Somehow he must have found out about Andrea's letter. Obviously he recognized that Barb's dismissal of him was a pack of lies. He'd probably pieced it all together and wanted her to come home so they could talk. But what was this about "coming to his senses"? Did he mean the job or his marriage or the two of them? She'd been so happy when the telegram came. He loved her and wanted her. More than ever. But on what terms? At what sacrifice to himself and, yes, at what sacrifice to her?

I must go back, Barbara thought. Tomorrow. They'll all just have to cope here. Fran can do what she wants, and so can Allie. They're not my responsibility. I hope they'll leave, for Mother and Dad's sake, but I'm not saying one more word about it.

Her mind went back to Allie. Laura's concern was based on more than the anxiety of an aging woman. Where had Allie run to? Because she *had* run. Barb heard her dash down the stairs and out the front door as though she was being pursued. If she took a walk to clear her head, she should be back by now. It was getting dark.

Don't be silly, Barbara told herself. Nothing's happened to her. She probably called Jack from a phone booth and met him. They're together right now, feeling sad about their son's departure. Still, if they didn't hear anything from Allie in another hour it might not be a bad idea to call Jack's apartment. That was the only place she was likely to go.

When Barb called at seven o'clock, Jack answered. "No, Allie's not here. That last time I saw her was this afternoon. I brought her home after we took John to the airport. What's wrong, Barb?"

"Nothing, probably. I saw her after that, but then she went out after five and didn't say where she was going. We haven't heard from her and Mother's a little upset. I mean, it isn't like Allie to disappear without a word." She laughed. "You probably think we're crazy. Worrying about a grown woman who's only been gone less than two hours." Barbara lowered her voice. "But, to tell you the truth, Jack, I am worried. I keep having the nutty idea that Spencer Winters might have shown up. He's really a maniac and Allie's so frightened of him. You don't think . . . "

"No. Of course not. Think about it, Barb. If Spencer were in town he'd have called her, wouldn't he? And she didn't get a phone call before she left the house, did she?"

"No. We were all together, Allie and Fran and I. Then Allie left." No point telling him about the ugly argument.

"Well, then, she didn't go to meet Spencer. And I'm sure he's not the type

who'd be lurking in the bushes, waiting to kidnap her. She's all right, Barb. I'm sure of it. She'll probably be home soon. Maybe she went to a movie."

"How? She didn't take any money."

Jack was quiet. "Could she have gone to visit anybody?"

"I can't think of anybody except you. Oh, *look*, this is silly. She's somewhere. Maybe she's just taking a long walk to think things through. She has a lot on her mind these days."

"Yes. We all do. I agree with you that she's okay, but she shouldn't be walking around alone after dark. I don't like that idea very much. Listen, will you call me when she comes in? I'll sleep a lot better when I know she's home."

"Certainly. I'll call the minute she returns. And you'll call me if she shows up there, won't you?"

"Naturally. Don't worry, Barb. She's all right."

"Yes, I'm sure she is."

But by ten o'clock when there'd been no word from Alice, Barbara was as frantic as Laura. Sam, oblivious of the problem, had gone to bed and Fran presumably was still sleeping it off in her room.

"Barbara, I'm worried sick. Where could she be?"

"I honestly don't know, Mother."

"It's been five hours. Maybe we should call the police."

Barb hesitated. It seemed so drastic. Almost melodramatic. But in Alice's state of mind anything was possible. Not wanting to, Barb thought of poor Dorothy Paige buried only that afternoon. No. Allie would never kill herself. She was too considerate to inflict such punishment on those who loved her. Still, it was strange for her to be gone so long, and impossible to think where she'd been. Accidents did happen. She might have been walking and been hit by a car. She had no identification with her. Barb had quietly checked. Allie hadn't even taken a purse when she left the house. With no money, she couldn't even have made a phone call. She must have been in an accident. Even now she might be lying, unidentified, in some hospital. Laura was right. It was time to call the police.

On the phone, the desk sergeant was briskly impersonal. "How long has yo sister been missing, Miss Dalton?"

"About five hours."

Barbara could hear the policeman's small, exasperated sigh. "We can't cla her as a 'missing person.' Not for at least twenty-four hours." His voice be reassuring. "I wouldn't worry, if I were you. She probably went to visit fr or to a movie. She'll show up. She's not a child, after all."

Yes she is, Barbara wanted to say. She is like a defenseless, trusting In spite of Spencer's mistreatment, she's lived a sheltered life for a qu a century in that safe and privileged Boston where nothing violent hap "nice people." She doesn't know about terror in the streets. To her, I the "small town" of her early life, a place where we went anywhere, It's changed, like the rest of the world. I don't go out alone aft Washington. Even Frances wouldn't roam around by herself in Rom

Miserably certain of it, Barb knew something had happened to her sister. A lost, lonely, confused Allie was out there somewhere and in trouble. Barbara tried to be reasonable.

"I know you have rules, Sergeant, but Mrs. Winters hasn't been in Denver for a long while. She hardly knows her way around any more. She might have been in an accident and she has no identification with her. Couldn't you put out a call to try and find her?"

"Sorry, Miss Dalton. Not yet."

"Then what should we do?"

"If you're really worried, why don't you check with some of her friends?"

"I've done that."

"Well," the man said reluctantly, "you could call the hospitals. See if she's been taken sick on the street or . . . Wait a minute." She could hear him shuffling papers. When he spoke again, he sounded a little less certain. "I'm looking through the reports just in. Is your sister a female Caucasian between forty-five and fifty, wearing a navy-blue and white dress and blue shoes?"

Barbara couldn't breathe. "Yes. Yes, she is."

"Squad car found a woman answering that description in Washington Park at 7:22 P.M. They took her to Denver General Hospital at Sixth and Bannock." He read aloud. "Victim unconscious, suffering from head wounds. Presumed to have been sexually assaulted. No identification."

"Oh, my God!"

"Now hold on, Miss Dalton. Could be a lot of women answering that description. Doesn't have to be your sister."

"Is she . . ." Barb couldn't finish the question.

"She was alive when they found her. I guess she's being treated there right now, but I still say . . ."

"It's my sister," Barbara said. Suddenly she was angry. "Why haven't you tried to find out who she is? It's been more than two hours since she was picked up! Why weren't the police trying to locate her family? My God, what kind of inhumanity is this?"

"Take it easy, Miss Dalton. These routine things take time."

"Routine!"

"I mean, the report just reached me. Of course we're trying to locate her people, but the first thing is to take care of the victim. I'm sorry. You have no idea how many calls I get every night from people worrying because somebody's out for a few hours. Nine times out of ten . . ."

"I don't give a damn about nine times out of ten! My sister may be dying and you don't even care!"

Even as she screamed at the police officer, Barbara wondered why she was wasting time berating this man who saw Allie as only another anonymous casualty. She clutched at the hope that perhaps he was right. Maybe the injured woman wasn't Allie at all, but in any case she was losing precious minutes for no reason.

"I'm sorry," she managed to say civilly. "I know the details of every single incident can't be at your fingertips. Thank you."

"Good luck, Miss Dalton. I hope it's a false alarm. Your sister probably will walk in, just fine, in a little while."

Barbara was frantic as she hung up. She had to get to Denver General and she didn't want to go alone. Couldn't face it alone. Why was she so certain it was Alice lying there? She just was. It had to be, and yet there was always the slim hope that the sergeant might be right. It would be cruel to frighten Laura now, if it turned out to be a hoped-for "false alarm." But who else could go with her? Not her father. Sam was not even aware that Alice was missing. And not Fran, probably still drunk or totally passed out. Jack. Of course. Jack would go with her.

She called him and told him what she knew. There was alarm in his voice, but he tried to hide it. "It might not be Alice."

"I know. I pray not. But I'm sure it is. Will you meet me there as soon as you can?"

"Of course. Shall I come and get you?"

"No. I don't want Mother to know anything yet. I'll have to make up some excuse for going out at this hour. Please hurry, Jack. I need you."

"I'll leave right away."

Barb took a moment to compose herself and then walked into the living room where Laura sat staring at Allie's photograph.

"It's all right," Barb said. "I was just on the phone with Jack Richards. Allie's there now. In fact, I have to go and pick her up. His car won't start."

Laura shook her head. "Don't try to spare me, Barbara. I heard you on the phone. You were talking to the police first. Something's happened to Alice. Something terrible. Where is she?"

No use pretending. It wasn't fair. If, God forbid, Allie was dead or dying, her mother had to know. And if the unidentified woman in the hospital was someone else, there was nothing to lose but this momentary anxiety, even though it would be replaced, unfortunately, by continuing worry about Allie's disappearance.

Once again, Barbara repeated what she knew, but this time she echoed the words of Jack and the policeman. "It's a long shot, Mother. It may not be Allie. Probably isn't. But Jack and I are going to see."

"I'm going with you."

"No, darling, please don't. I'll call you the minute I get to the hospital."

"I'm going," Laura repeated. "Don't you see, Barbara? I have to know. That could be my child. I can't just sit here and wait to find out." It was she who was reassuring now. "I'll be all right, dear. No matter what. Don't be concerned about me. I'm stronger than you think. I may not seem so, but I really am."

Yes, Barbara thought, you are. You've lived through so much. Taken so many hours of sadness without whimpering. We think of you as a helpless, provincial woman who must be protected. But you're not. You're as strong as any of us. Stronger, maybe. You come from a generation of women who didn't scream about their "rightful place in the world" or blame everybody else for their hardships and disappointments. You've just gone on, patiently, quietly understanding that life isn't going to give us anything more than that to which we're entitled. And that we have to take the loneliness with the laughter.

Laura interrupted her thoughts. "Get your coat, Barbara. It's chilly out there."

*   *   *

The hospital was quiet, the visitors' hours over and the patients bedded down for the night by the time Laura and Barb arrived. Jack came in a few seconds after they entered the front door. He must have driven like a maniac, Barb thought idly. She took his hand gratefully and he pressed hers in reassurance before he went to the desk to make inquiries.

"Whoever it is is in intensive care," he said quietly when he returned. "But they'll let us go in for a minute to . . . to make an identification." He looked anxiously at Laura. "Mrs. Dalton, wouldn't you rather wait here while Barbara and I . . . "

"No. Thank you, Jack, but I'll go with you."

Mutely, they took the elevator to the area where busy doctors and nurses monitored the conditions of the critically ill. After a few whispered words from Jack, a nurse at the desk pointed toward a bed where a still figure lay, its head wrapped in bandages and its body sprouting tubes to overhanging bottles. Barb took her mother's arm as they walked silently to the bedside and looked down at what could be seen of the white, still face of Allie. Barbara let out an involuntary gasp and tightened her hold on Laura, but the older woman did not flinch. She simply looked sadly at her injured daughter, stood waiting as though she expected Alice to open her eyes and speak. She didn't expect that, of course. She knew Alice was near death, that she'd never open her eyes again, never speak. Yet Laura stood patiently, silently, as though she would will strength and life into her child, as though she refused to accept what she knew.

I can't bear it, Barb thought. This can't have happened to Allie! I can't stand Mother's heart breaking without a sound. I can't look at Jack's face. She saw him move away from the bed in response to a silent signal from the nurse. She saw him speaking with the woman, nodding his head, giving answers which she wrote on some kind of chart. He came back at last and said in a low voice, "They think we should leave now, Mrs. Dalton."

Laura seemed to come out of her trance. "Leave? How can we leave? I have to be here when she wakes up."

Jack looked at Barbara. "We'll just go to a reception room, dear," Barb said. "We'll stay close by. I'll call home and tell Dad where we are."

"I want to stay right here."

"You can't, Mother. They don't allow it. We'll sit and wait until she's conscious. Come on, darling. Please. They'll let us know the minute we can talk to Allie."

It was three in the morning before a young doctor came into the Visitors Lounge with the last of the bulletins they'd been getting every half hour. Sam was there, his face gray, his arm protectively around Laura as they sat and waited for news. Frances, looking destroyed, paced the room, drinking endless cups of black coffee from plastic containers. There had been almost no words spoken in hours, only the anxious questioning of the doctor when he appeared occasionally to say there was no change. They did not even have the heart to ask yet for details, though Jack disappeared at one point to talk to the police, who'd been notified of Allie's identity by the hospital and who had arrived to tell the whole ghastly story. He looked sick when he returned, but all he said was, "It was a rapist. In the park. They have no leads."

It was as though they were numb when the doctor finally said to Laura, "I'm sorry, Mrs. Dalton. We couldn't save your daughter. We did everything we could." And then, in unprofessional anger, he burst out, "Goddamn these savages on our streets!" He seemed surprised, embarrassed, by his own emotion. "I'm sorry," he said again. "We had her in surgery for over an hour, but we couldn't help. She . . . she never knew what hit her," he added lamely. "I hope that's some small consolation."

Jack and Barbara turned their heads away, and Sam broke into great, racking sobs. Only Laura and Frances moved. Fran ran from the room, but Laura rose and took the young doctor's hand. "Thank you," she said. "Thank you for caring."

Chapter 30

GUILT.

Like a creeping, poisonous vine, guilt took root in the Dalton household and its tendrils reached out across Denver and stretched as far as Boston, threatening to strangle those who, reasonably or not, felt themselves unwitting contributors to Alice Winters' death.

Whether the truly guilty party, the man who had raped and murdered, felt remorse, only he would ever know. The homicide men who pursued the case "came up empty," in their words. They were not surprised. Where did one start to look for a pervert sick enough to skulk around a park at nightfall, waiting to attack and kill an unsuspecting female with no "known enemies"? The next day, they routinely questioned the family and the woman's "boyfriend," looking for any detail that might provide a clue to the identity of this maniac. Considerate as they tried to be, it was agony for those who loved Allie, for it forced them to relive the event, regret the past and realize the depth of self-reproach each of them felt in varying degrees.

Frances, selfish, cynical Frances, was, of them all, most devastated by the tragedy. As the doctor gave his final, terrible news to the family, Fran had run blindly from the room. She hardly remembered getting into her car and driving downtown. She knew only that over and over in her head she heard the words, "I killed Allie. If it hadn't been for the fight with me, she'd never have left the house. I killed her as surely as if I'd been the monster who did the deed." At half-past three in the morning she found herself pounding on the door of Cary Venzetti's seedy little apartment.

The young waiter from LaFitte's finally opened the door a crack and peered out. He was astonished to see Frances. Astonished and shocked. She looked old, haggard, far from the elegant "older woman" he'd once been to bed with.

"Let me in." It was a command.

He hesitated. Was she drunk? Crazy? He'd not seen her since that one and only night.

"I said, let me in!" Fran's voice was harsh and angry. "Or do you already have company?"

"No. I'm alone." He opened the door and she came into the disorderly room. She barely looked at him but Cary, completely naked, reached for a pair of trousers slung on a nearby chair.

"Don't bother," Fran said. "I've seen it all before."

"Okay." Cary leaned against the door. "Mind if I ask what you're doing here?"

"What do you think I'm doing?" She was pulling off her clothes, dropping them on the floor. "You have any objections? You didn't before. And I paid you well enough, didn't I?" She was nude now, facing him, the trim, beautiful body somehow in terrible contrast with the wild-eyes, grim-lipped face. "Well? What the hell's the matter with you? Last time you couldn't wait. You were drooling, begging me to come back. So I'm here. What's the problem, sonny?"

He wondered why he wasn't excited. "I . . . I don't understand. I mean, all of a sudden, at this hour, you just appear."

"For God's sake, what are you? A dentist? Must I have an appointment? I want sex. Remember the word? S-E-X. It's good for the soul and the complexion."

She'd gotten into his rumpled bed and lay waiting for him. Cary didn't move. She was here, this poised, worldy creature, asking, no, *demanding* he make love to her, and he felt nothing but confusion and a slight sense of fear.

"Frances, what's wrong? You're not yourself."

"How would *you* know? How would you know what's myself? *I* don't even know that. All I know is I don't want to think about anything for a while. Is that too much to ask?"

"What happened?"

"My God, will you stop with the questions! Are you or are you not ready, willing and able?"

He came and sat on the edge of the bed. "None of them, I guess," he said slowly. "That other time was wonderful. I didn't even want your money. I wanted you. And I knew you wanted me. But tonight it could be anybody, couldn't it? There's something you're running from. Something terrible you have to forget, even for a little while. I don't amount to much, Frances, but I'm not a machine that you can turn on like you're pressing a switch. I don't think I can make it with you tonight. I'm sorry."

She was too surprised to answer for a moment, and then she began to laugh. It was a terrible sound, hollow and desperate, half laughter and half tears. "That's funny," Fran gasped. "I mean that's really, really funny! I've reached rock bottom. Begging a lousy little creep like you to take me! And being turned down at that!" She was hysterical. "What's the matter? Am I suddenly too old and too ugly?" Don't give me that crap about being a machine! That's exactly what you are: a machine in good condition, still new enough to turn out efficient work. And that's all I want from you. I didn't come here for some cocktail-party analysis of my motives! Don't go cerebral on me, baby. It's not your style!" Suddenly she shrugged, deflated. She pushed Cary aside, got up and began to put on her clothes. "That really ties it. Rejected twice in a week, once by a man and now by a dumb kid."

Cary looked up at her. "So that's it. Somebody you really want doesn't want you. You came here to forget him with me."

Fran shook her head. "No. I wasn't even thinking about him tonight. I was just running toward anything as far removed as possible from reality." She stood at the door, her hand on the knob. "You were right, Cary. It wasn't like the other time. That was fun and games. Tonight I wanted oblivion, and that other man couldn't give it to me, even if he were around. He was too close to the real thing." She gave a sad little smile. "Would you like to know why I really came here tonight?"

"Yes, if you want to tell me."

"Tonight I killed my sister."

"What? What in Christ's name are you saying?"

"I killed her. I said terrible things to her this afternoon. I called her pious and stupid and told her she made me sick. I drove her from the house. Into the park. And some fiend attacked her and she's dead."

He came toward her. "Frances, stop! *You* didn't kill her. It's horrible. Unbelievable. But *you* didn't do it!"

"Oh, yes, I did. I sent her out to be murdered. It's as though I did it myself." She began to cry. "Poor Allie. Poor, good, sweet, helpless Allie. Why is she dead and I'm alive? There's no sense to it. No sense at all."

Cary put his strong young arms around her, cradling her. "Frances, no. You're not responsible. Come back to bed. Let me hold you. You need comfort more than sex. You need to be with someone understanding. Someone who thinks you're wonderful."

She shook her head. "I have to go home. I shouldn't have come here. I don't know why I did, except it's the kind of thing I always do: look for some way to keep from facing myself. I have to go back and be with my family. They're probably already frantic, wondering where I've gone." She gently removed his arms. "There's so much about me you don't know, Cary." She thought of Dorothy Paige. "So much I don't ever want you to know because you're a nice young man. And I'm not a very nice lady." She kissed him lightly on the cheek. "Goodbye, little one. Thanks for turning me down. How did you know it was for all the right reasons?"

Before he could answer she was out the door and down the stairs. He heard the entry door close. She's gone forever this time, Cary thought. And tomorrow when I read the papers I'll finally know who she was.

The lights were burning when Frances let herself into the house a little past four. They were all there in the shabby living room, her parents and Barb and Jack Richards, and they looked up when she walked in.

"I hope I didn't worry you," Fran apologized. "I've been driving around, thinking of her, remembering all the good things."

"Yes," Laura said. "We've all been doing that. Thinking of our Alice. Wondering why God chose this for her." Her mother began to weep silently. "She was a good girl. She was always a good girl, even though your father and I made her feel she was bad. We'll never forgive ourselves for that."

"Don't, Mother," Barbara said. "That was all so long ago. Don't think about that. Think about how happy she was the last two days of her life when she was reunited with Johnny. She blossomed. The thing that haunted her all those years, her own guilt, was removed. Remember that, not the other.'' Barb brushed at the tears in her own eyes. ''If anyone should feel guilty, I should. I told her we should all leave here and give you and Dad some peace. Poor Allie. She didn't know where to go. She didn't want to leave. If only I hadn't said it! She wouldn't have gone rushing out of the house all upset. This never would have happened.''

''I was worse,'' Fran said, almost inaudibly. ''I was the one who really sent her out. I was cruel and terrible to her.''

Jack said nothing, but there was guilt in his heart too. Guilt he was sure Allie's sisters recognized. Why didn't I insist she marry me? I could have saved her. She'd have known where she belonged. He remembered what the police had told him: the rape, the brutal crushing of her skull, probably with a heavy rock. God! He couldn't stand to think about it. Allie alone and frightened and maybe begging for her life. Jack buried his head in his hands.

It was Sam Dalton, the one who had seemed most out of control at the hospital, who now spoke sadly but firmly. ''Blaming ourselves won't bring Alice back. Every one of us in this room wishes he could take back something, as though it would have changed anything. It wouldn't have. We don't understand why God moves as He does. We'll never understand. We just have to live with our faith and believe that it was His way of sparing that child from something worse to come. We have to hang onto that while we grieve for that innocent girl.'' His voice broke. ''I loved her so much. I never was able to show her. I'll regret that to my dying day.''

''She knew, Daddy,'' Barbara said. ''She knew you loved her, just as Fran and I know you love us and forgive us anything.''

Sam looked at his daughters. ''I do love you and I want you to be happy. Whatever you do, be happy.''

There was a long moment of silence as they thought of all that had been and might have been, remembering, regretting, trying to find some meaning in all this, searching for some shred of consolation in this senseless taking of a life. At last, Barbara spoke.

''Mother, I think you and Dad should get some rest. Lie down, even if you can't sleep. We're facing some hard days. You need your strength. It's almost five o'clock. In a couple of hours, things will begin to happen. There'll be the newspapers, I'm afraid. And . . . and we have to make arrangements.''

The others looked at her, knowing what was in her mind. Spencer would have to be notified. And Allie's children, including John Peck, who'd left her, happy, only a little more than twelve hours before.

Fran voiced their thoughts. ''I'll call Spencer. I don't know how to reach Janice and Chris, but I'll find out. Jack, will you call Johnny?''

He nodded, mutely.

''Charlotte,'' Laura said. ''Somebody has to tell Aunt Charlotte. I don't want her to hear it from Spencer.''

''I'll call her, Mother,'' Barbara said. ''And, Fran, I think I should call Spencer. You dislike him even more than the rest of us.''

''That's exactly why I should call. I hate his guts. If anyone is to blame for

Allie's death, it's that beast she married." She hesitated. "I'm afraid he's going to want to take her back to Boston. I'm sure Mother and Dad don't want that, and I'm the only one tough enough to tell him he can't."

"But he can," Sam said. "He is her husband. We can't stop him, even though we'd like to keep her here, near us."

Laura's soft voice interrupted this painful conversation. "I'm not sure Allie would want that, Sam. I think she'd want to be close to her children, and I think they'd like to know their mother was nearby. We lost her once, my dear, but wherever she rests she'll never be lost to us again. She came home and spent her last days here. To me, she'll always be here."

Again, that strength, Barbara thought. She's remarkable. What I would give for the special kind of wisdom Mother has! Even at this terrible time, when she must be dying inside, she's thinking of what Allie and her children might want, not what she and Dad would prefer.

Fran recognized the same unselfishness Barb saw. Allie was like Mother, she thought. She cared about people more than she cared about herself. She wouldn't want us to be petty and spiteful. Not even with Spencer. But I'm not sure I can please either of them. Not in this case.

"All right, Mother," Fran said. "I'll call Spencer and I'll try not to be rotten to him. Maybe I don't have to be. Let's hope he has enough of a conscience to be punished by it."

It was a half-truth. She would try to be civil to the man who'd made life a living hell for Allie, but she would not give in easily if he insisted on bringing his wife to Boston for burial. Her mother was wrong about that. Alice would want to be in Denver. She'd been a happy child here, and it was here she'd found her last moments of joy with Jack and Johnny. As for her children, there was no reason to think they'd want their mother nearby, as Laura believed. Janice sounded like a selfish little witch who didn't care enough to come to her grandparents' anniversary party. Christopher had his own, estranged life. Even the new-found son could not have formed such an attachment that he'd spend time at Allie's grave. But Sam and Laura would. It would comfort them. Fran didn't go along with the idea that it was meaningful to visit a cemetery. There was no one there under that smooth, grassy covering. But her parents didn't feel that way. They made regular trips to the family plots where their own parents were buried. They were of a generation that "paid their respects" to the dead. And if she could manage it, she'd see that they'd find the same solace in "visiting" the daughter they'd lost.

I don't know whether I can convince Spencer of that, Fran thought as she picked up the phone. But I'm damned well going to try, even if I have to blackmail him.

The shrill, persistent ringing of the telephone awakened two men in Boston almost at the same moment. And with almost the same foggy reaction, Spencer Winters and John Peck glanced at their bedside clocks as they reached for the jangling instruments. It was seven-thirty in the morning.

Spencer grunted with annoyance as he picked up the receiver. Who'd call at this ungodly hour?

"Yes?"

"Spencer? It's Frances."

For a moment it didn't register. "Frances? Frances who?"

"Déspres. Dalton. Your sister-in-law, remember?"

He came wide-awake. "Of course. Sorry."

"I have some bad news. It's about Allie."

He listened, incredulous, to the story. Alice dead? It wasn't possible. Raped and murdered? Unthinkable! For a moment he wondered if this was some sick joke. It was five-thirty in the morning in Denver. Frances, who so obviously hated him, must be drunk and looking for a way to torture him. But the tone of her voice, controlled but heavy with grief, told him otherwise. She was sober and telling the truth. As the realization hit him, he was stunned. There was no wrenching feeling of sorrow or loss. Only amazement and a terrible sense of distaste for the sordid details.

"I imagine you and your children will want to come out right away." Fran tried to choose her words carefully. If she could get him to agree while he was still in shock, one problem would be solved. "We'll make the arrangements here. There's room in the family plot for Allie and Barbara and me. The services will be day after tomorrow. I assume Janice and Christopher will come too. I'm sorry, Spencer. I know this must be a terrible shock for you. It's been a nightmare for all of us since ten o'clock last night."

Pettishly, he seized on her last words. "Ten o'clock? You've known since ten o'clock last night and you're only calling me now?"

Fool! Fran thought. Arrogant ass! She forced herself to sound repentent. "I'm sorry, Spencer. I suppose you should have been called, but we didn't know she . . . wasn't going to make it. We kept hoping all night that she'd pull through. She died at three this morning. It's been terrible for Mother and Dad, these past few hours. We've had our hands full, and there didn't seem to be much point in calling you at five o'clock in the morning. Forgive us. I guess we were wrong not to have let you know immediately. We really weren't thinking straight. We still aren't." Fran paused. "But Barbara and I are managing everything." The words were now genuinely reluctant. "We'll pick out the . . . the casket. And find the right thing for her to wear. You won't have to do anything but be here. You and your children. Will you let us know when you're arriving?"

Her overlong speech was a mistake. It gave Spencer time to collect himself and formulate his own intentions.

"That won't be necessary. I'll fly out this morning and bring her back. This was Alice's home. She'll be buried here, quietly and fittingly."

Here it comes, Fran thought. The showdown.

"We'd like the interment to be here, Spencer. It would mean a great deal to Mother and Dad. I hope you agree to that. It would be a kindness to a pair of elderly people. I'm sure you understand that generation's view of such things."

"No, I can't agree. Alice was my wife. She lived in Boston society. People would think it very strange if she died mysteriously and was quickly buried in Denver. I'm sorry, Frances, but I must insist. It's the only proper thing to do."

For whom? Frances wanted to ask. Proper for Allie? Allie didn't know. Proper for her children? Unlikely. Their generation certainly didn't hold with the macabre formality of drawn-out mourning and funerals. No, it's proper for you, Spencer, she thought. It's your chance to play the bereaved husband, to show off with a five-thousand-dollar casket and a fleet of limousines.

"I fail to see where it's any less proper for Allie to be buried here. And I seriously doubt anyone would find it strange." Fran's voice was cool and level, but she was revolted by this cat-and-mouse game she and Spencer were playing. God, it was like a tug-of-war over her sister's body!

"There's really no need to discuss it. I've made up my mind. I'll fly out today and bring the remains back to Boston. Alice had many friends here. It's only considerate that I allow them to pay their respects. Please give my sympathy to your parents and tell them I've decided to do what's right for Allie."

All right, you bastard, Fran thought. You've driven me to it. "Just as you always did what was right when you were married to her?"

"What?"

"You're very considerate of Alice and her friends now that she's dead. Too bad you couldn't have been as kind when she was alive. Listen to me, Spencer. You may be legally able to do this, but you'll pay for it. I know every damn gossip columnist in the world and I won't hesitate to tell them what you really are—a wife-beater, among other sadistic things. And I think they'd like to know about the illegitimate child Alice had before you were married. I gather you haven't been too anxious to advertise that piece of scandal to your very proper Boston friends."

Even over the miles she could feel his anger. "You'd do that? You'd sully your sister's reputation? What kind of woman are you?"

"Yes, I'd do that," Fran said grimly. "It can't hurt her now. In fact, it would be justice, even though she wouldn't know you were finally paying for all the unspeakable things you did to her. I think you and your children had better come out here, Spencer. Or do you want me to tell my newspaper friends you didn't even have the decency to attend your own wife's funeral?"

"Bitch!" Spencer slammed down the receiver.

Fran closed her eyes for a moment. She felt sick, but she'd done the right thing. It's for you, Allie, she thought. I couldn't let you spend eternity next to that creature.

When his telephone rang, John Peck couldn't remember for a moment where he was. So much had happened since he got home last night, He'd told Carol everything and shared her happy tears. He'd called Jan, who was delighted and who told him, almost shyly, that she and Clint had decided to "make it legal." They were coming over tonight and bringing Chris, who was eager to meet him. The phone continued to demand his attention. Sleepily, he reached for it.

"John? It's . . . it's your father."

"Dad? What in the world? It's five-thirty in Denver! Are you all right?"

"Yes. No. It's your mother."

Once again the horror story was told, this time to an incredulous and heartbroken listener. Jack was trying not to break down, but Johnny began to sob unashamedly. When, at last, he could speak, he said, "Why? Why her? She was the dearest, finest . . ."

"I know. We can't comprehend these things, Johnny. I blame myself. I should have protected her, should have sheltered her. If I had, she might be alive now." Johnny knew his father was also crying. He felt sorry for the man and suddenly angry as well. Yes, you should have, John thought. You should have looked after her. But he said merely, "We both should have. We were *too* selfish to realize how troubled she was, but we couldn't anticipate this. No one could."

Jack was breathing hard, taking in air in great gulps. "No, no one could imagine a thing like this. It's like a bad dream, Son."

"What . . . what are the plans?"

"I don't know yet. Frances is calling Spencer Winters now. I suppose he'll call Allie's other children. Maybe you'll want to reach them too. I'll get back to you later. When I know more."

"Yes. How are my . . . How are her parents?"

"Remarkable. They're unusual people, John. They're crushed, but they have faith to sustain them. I wish I had. I hope you have. We all need it now."

Johnny put the receiver gently back into its cradle. Faith? He had none of the kind his father meant. He was angry at God. Angry that a lovely woman was so savagely destroyed. Angry that he'd had so few hours of his life with her. But I did have that much, he thought. It was destiny that I found her in time. Almost as though God was good enough to give me a face and a voice and a touch to remember. And as though He knew Alice could rest in peace because she'd found her firstborn.

He threw himself back on the bed and wept bitterly.

The boys and their wives stayed overnight after the simple ceremony that preceded Dorothy Paige's cremation. It made Buzz feel a little better to see them that morning, all gathered around his breakfast table. Everyone was trying very hard to act normally. Larry, browsing through the morning paper as he drank his coffee, suddenly looked up.

"Dad, don't you know some people named Dalton?"

Buzz almost jumped. "Yes, of course. They're friends of your mother's and mine. Why?"

"Terrible thing. One of the Daltons' daughters was murdered while she was walking in Washington Park last night."

Buzz felt the color drain from his face. Fran. It must be Fran. Barbara and Alice weren't the type to go rambling around at any hour by themselves.

"Who . . . who was it?"

"Alice Dalton Winters. Somebody raped and killed her. Jesus, what is this world coming to?"

Alice. Sweet, soft, timid Alice. What was she doing there? How could such a thing happen? "May I see the paper, please?"

"Sure." Larry handed it over. "Say, was she the woman who called here?"

"No. That was another sister. Frances." Buzz read the second-page article. It was quite short. Violence was so rampant everywhere these days that muggings, rapes and murders didn't even make big headlines any more. It was just another unsolved crime.

BOSTON WOMAN KILLED IN PARK

At seven twenty-two last night, police discovered the unconscious body of Alice Dalton Winters, aged 48, in the bushes in Washington Park. The victim had been criminally assaulted a short time before. Police rushed her to Denver General Hospital, where she died of her injuries a few hours later. Identification was made by her parents, Mr. and Mrs. Samuel Dalton of Denver. Mrs. Winters had been visiting the city to celebrate the fiftieth wedding anniversary of Mr. and Mrs. Dalton, long-time residents. Police said they had no clues to the identity of the assailant who sexually attacked Mrs. Winters before crushing her skull with a heavy object.

Buzz lowered the paper. Those poor people. What was worse—the death of a woman so unhappy she willed it, or that of one who became its unsuspecting prey? No difference, he decided. The survivors were burdened with the same terrible cloak of sadness and guilt. The Daltons probably blamed themselves as much for whatever took Allie alone to the park as he blamed himself for the events that drove Dorothy down the cellar stairs. He sighed heavily. There was nothing but futility and gloom everywhere. Nothing seemed to matter any more.

Chapter 31

CHARLES TALLENT SWIVELED his big leather chair around and stared out the window of his office. Washington had never looked more beautiful than it did this October day, clear, with a bright blue sky and the first nip of autumn in the air. The kind of day Barbara loved, all fresh and invigorating and alive. Over the years they'd sometimes played "hookey" on days like this, driving down into Virginia to see the turning of the leaves, stopping at some little inn for lunch, returning, refreshed and happy to see their haven in Georgetown to make love in the afternoon. Before, Charles reminisced in bitter afterthought, he had to go home to Andrea and his "obligations."

Well, no more. He was through cheating himself and Barbara. Her letter had opened his eyes to a lot of things, including the realization of his own selfishness. How could he ever have considered giving her up? It would be like cutting out his heart. And he had no obligations to anyone but her. His children were grown, no longer babies to be "traumatized" by a broken home. Andrea was capable of making her own way without him, much as she'd dislike giving up her "official" prerogatives. The Candidate had responded in a gentlemanly fashion to Charles's telegram of regret that "for personal reasons" he could not accept the Cabinet membership so flatteringly offered. The Senator was an ambitious man, but a compassionate one. He understood. And Charles would work hard to get him elected, just as Charles would put even more effort into the committees he served on. In the long run, he probably could be more useful in the House than lost in the obscurity of a Cabinet post which changed with every administration. He had no worries about his own constituency. Even as a divorced man, the voters in his state would send him back to Congress term after term to do the good job he'd always done for them. With Barbara at his side, encouraging and loving him, he'd serve his country better. As a congressman he'd be remembered long after some frustrated Secretary of Agriculture was forgotten. As for the possible chance at the presidency one day, he'd been kidding himself. It had been momentarily tempting, but it was a long shot, a vague come-on, certainly not worth the destruction of his happiness and Barbara's.

All in all, he felt more at peace than he had in days. He hadn't told Andrea of his decision, neither the political nor the personal one. He'd not even mentioned Barbara's letter nor the part he suspected his wife had played in its writing. It hadn't been easy not to lash out at Andrea, to tell her she'd outsmarted herself. But he'd held his tongue, sent the telegram to Barbara and waited.

Only the waiting made him uneasy. It had been more than twenty-four hours since he'd sent his message and there'd been no reply from the woman he loved. For a moment, he was filled with terrible doubt. What if the letter was true? What if she had met someone she could care for? Suppose she really didn't intend to come back? No. His first reaction had been right. She was letting him out of his involvement easily and humanely. But why hadn't she answered his wire? It wasn't like her.

"Damn it!" He spoke the words aloud. This uncertainty was driving him mad. Ridiculous of him to sit here brooding. He fished in his desk drawer for the Daltons' phone number in Denver and dialed it on his private wire. It was eleven o'clock. Nine in the morning out there. They'd certainly be up.

Barbara wearily answered the phone. It had been ringing all morning, just as she'd predicted, with the press calling for information, asking for interviews and photographs of Allie. It was ghoulish. It was their job, but it was heartless. She'd protected Laura and Sam from this invasion so far, just as she'd spared them the shocked and sympathetic calls from friends and family. When Buzz Paige called, she hadn't known what to do. After accepting his condolences and offering her own for his loss, she hesitantly asked, "Do you want to speak to Fran?"

There'd been a pause before he said, "No. Don't disturb her. Just tell her and your parents how terribly sorry I am." There was another moment of silence before Buzz said, "Will the services be in Boston?"

"No. Here." Fran had reported the conversation with Spencer. "You're welcome, of course, Buzz. You're like family to us." She hadn't meant it as a reproach that he hadn't wanted any of them at Dorothy's funeral, but Buzz took it that way.

"I hope you understand why I couldn't . . . I mean, we thought under the circumstances it would be better if we kept yesterday private."

"Of course. And we'll understand if you're not here day after tomorrow. You've been through so much yourself."

"It isn't that. Not exactly. The fact is, I'm going away tomorrow, for a few weeks. I've got to get out of this house for a while. I'm going to visit my brother in San Diego."

"I see. That sounds like a good idea."

"Tell Fran for me, will you? And, Barbara, once again I can't tell you how shocked and grieved I am about Allie. It's a monstrous thing. Monstrous. God, it makes you wonder what life's all about. It's so crazy. Everything can change in a minute."

What about Fran? Barbara thought, it's certainly changed for her too. At that moment she hated Buzz Paige. He's blaming Fran for what happened to Dorothy. All right, she was partially responsible. But no more than he. Why won't he even speak to her? Hasn't he the guts to tell her there can't be anything between them ever again?

The thought brought her back, momentarily, to her own situation with Charles. She'd spent yesterday wondering what his telegram meant, debating what to do about it, and then this blow fell and for more than twelve hours her thoughts had been only with her family. It will have to wait, Barb thought. The whole thing will have to wait until this is over and I can try to sort my own problems. Death made even life unimportant. For a little while. She couldn't set Allie aside while she selfishly tried to interpret Charles's message. He'd understand when he finally heard why she hadn't answered.

It was almost eerie that the next voice on the phone should be his.

"Darling, is that you? I've been going crazy waiting to hear from you! Didn't you get my wire? Is something wrong?" He didn't wait for an answer. "Your letter was beautiful. Almost as beautiful as you. But I don't believe it, love. It isn't true, is it? There isn't anyone else. Tell me you still love me, Barbara. I adore you. I need you so much."

The warm rush of words, the outpouring of devotion, destroyed the control she'd been able to manage through the whole nightmare. Helplessly, she began to sob and no words could pass the aching lump in her throat. Just hearing him brought back all the yearning for him, all the hopelessness she felt without him.

"Sweetheart, what is it?" The alarm in his voice was somehow comforting. He cared, and she desperately needed someone to care.

Stammering, crying, she told him what had happened.

"Oh, my God! Barbara, darling! What can I say?"

She managed to calm down. "Nothing. There's nothing anyone can say. Or do. Just bear with me, Charles. Let me get through this and then we'll talk about . . . the rest."

"I'm getting the next plane out there."

"No! You can't! The idea's insane! What would people say if you suddenly showed up here?"

"I don't give a damn what people would say! I'm not going to let you struggle through this by yourself. I want to be right there beside you. That's where I ought to be. That's where I'm going to be, for the rest of our lives."

She protested feebly, but he brushed aside her words about Andrea and his place in the public eye.

"None of that matters. That's what my telegram meant. I've come to my senses. We won't talk about it now, but there's no way in the world you could keep me from coming to Denver, not unless there really is someone else. Someone you'd rather have with you."

"There's no one, dearest. No one in the world but you."

She heard his sigh of relief. "That's all you had to say. I'll leave here in a couple of hours. Be a brave girl. I'll be with you soon. I love you, Barbara. You'll never know how much."

Janice and Clint were asleep when Spencer called Darby's apartment. Clint answered and handed the phone to the young woman beside him, covering the mouthpiece with his hand.

"Guess who's calling. Your old man."

Jan shook herself awake. "My father? What does he want?"

"How should I know? He just barked for you."

She took the phone. "Yes, Father?"

"Your mother's dead."

Jan stared stupidly at the phone. "Dead? What do you mean, dead? What are you talking about?"

"Your mother died in Denver last night, Janice. She'll be buried there day after tomorrow. As soon as my office opens in half an hour I'll have Miss Perrone get three tickets on the one P.M. United flight. Please be good enough to call your brother and say we expect him to go with us. Tell him to be at the airport at twelve-fifteen. I'd do it myself, but I don't have his telephone number."

She couldn't believe it. Not the fact nor the cold way in which he was making plans, as though they were off on a family holiday. "Father, what happened to her? She was always in perfect health."

"She was murdered. Her sister called half an hour ago. Someone attacked her in a park and killed her." Spencer gave a mirthless little laugh. "It's a good thing I was in Boston, wasn't it? Otherwise, I'm sure I'd be the prime suspect."

Jan felt her whole body turn to ice. "My God, have you no feelings? How can you be so cold-blooded?"

"I am not a hypocrite, Janice, whatever else I may be. There's been no love between your mother and me for years. I'm sorry she died, especially in this cruel way, but you wouldn't expect me to make a spectacle of myself, would you?"

"No," Janice said bitterly, "I wouldn't even expect you to give a damn. And you obviously don't." She paused. "What about John Peck?"

"Who?"

"Your stepson. My half-brother. Mother's first child." Jan's voice was now as hard as her father's. "Has he been notified? Are you getting a plane ticket for him too?"

"Don't be absurd, Janice. John Peck is just some blackmailer who tried to frighten your Aunt Charlotte." Spencer dismissed him. "Which reminds me. I suppose I'd better call your great-aunt, though I have no intention of dragging her out to Denver."

The last words sparked something in Jan's mind. "Why is Mother being buried there? I'd have thought you would have insisted on bringing her here."

Spencer didn't skip a beat. "It seems more convenient this way. I'll see you at the airport."

"Are you going back to Denver, darling?" Carol Peck put her arms around her husband. "Shall I go with you?"

John shook his head. "No. I'm not going back. It would be an embarrassment for her family. And I don't want to be within striking distance of Spencer Winters. I might kill him. Jan and Christopher are going. They're the 'real' children."

"I think to her you were the most real of all."

John kissed her gently. "Yes, dear, I think I was, at that."

Barbara had a terrible time making Aunt Charlotte understand who she was. When she finally got through, she gently told her that Alice had passed away suddenly. No need to go into the sordid story with this old woman who seemed to grasp very little.

"Alice has passed away?" Charlotte did not seem sad, only a little puzzled. "That's strange. I certainly thought she'd outlive me. The young generation just doesn't seem to have the stamina we had. Poor little Alice. Thank you for telling me, young lady. I must hang up now. It's time for me to lie down before lunch. I always have a little rest between meals."

When Spencer called, the housekeeper told him that Mrs. Rudolph was resting.

"Wake her up," Spencer commanded. "This is important."

"Excuse me, sir, but is it about her niece?"

"Yes. Yes, it is."

"I believe Mrs. Rudolph already knows. She had a telephone call from Miss Barbara Dalton in Denver about an hour ago. Mrs. Rudolph told me her niece had passed away. I'm very sorry, Mr. Winters."

Spencer didn't acknowledge the sympathy. "She knows? Good. Then don't disturb her. If she asks, tell her I've gone away and will be back in a couple of days. Is she all right?"

"Oh, yes, sir. I don't think she quite comprehends things any more. The seriousness of them, I mean."

Lucky Charlotte, Spencer thought.

On the Boston-to-Denver flight, Janice and Christopher sat side by side in first class. Their father, across the aisle, was apparently absorbed in the current issue of *Fortune*.

"Look at him," Christopher said. "The sonofabitch has ice water in his veins."

Jan nodded. Spencer was unbelievable. He'd not spoken to Chris at the airport and had barely said half a dozen words to Jan since their telephone conversation. He seemed coldly angry, not just "normally' angry" as he always was with his children, but inwardly furious about something. It has to do with Mother being buried in Denver, Jan thought. He didn't want that, and somebody forced him into it. Somebody was able to make Spencer Winters do what he didn't want to, and he is enraged about it. His was not the silence of grief but of fury. It was in his eyes. It had even been in his voice when he told her that interment in Denver was more "convenient." Jan didn't believe that for a moment. Not that he'd give a damn where Alice was buried, but Jan knew her father well. It was not like him to give up the spotlight he'd hold during a period of mourning and funeral in his own town. Janice reached for her brother's hand.

"We'll miss her, Chris. God knows she and I didn't always see eye to eye, but I liked her."

She saw him swallow hard and felt his grip tighten on her fingers.

"I still can't accept it, Jan. It doesn't seem real."

"I know."

"I'm sorry for Grandmother and Grandfather. We hardly know them, but they must be going through hell. Her sisters too. We don't know them at all. Funny to have aunts you've never seen. For that matter, it's a damned funny family."

"Worse," Jan said. "It's no family at all, now that Mother's gone." She hesitated. "I wish I could have told her something that would have made her happy. I haven't told anybody except John Peck, but Clint and I are going to be married. Mother would have been pleased. She never made a fuss about my living with Clint, but I know she didn't like it." Janice reached for a tissue in her bag and dabbed at her eyes. "Damn it to hell! Why couldn't she have lived to see me become an honest woman?"

Christopher gently patted her cheek. "Let me be glad in her place. I'm happy for you, Jan. That's a nice guy you've got." He indicated Spencer. "You going to tell *him?*"

"Not now, certainly. Maybe not until after the ceremony. He's not going to force me into a big public wedding as a publicity gimmick. Clint and I will go quietly to City Hall one day soon, and I'll tell dear Father when the deed is done."

She realized what was in her mind even as she spoke. Spencer wasn't going to substitute an elaborate engagement and wedding for the vulgar funeral he'd have arranged if he could. It was a gruesome thought, but it was true. A terrible trade-off. She didn't want a big wedding, but even if she had, she'd have rejected it just to deprive him of the chance to show off. She shuddered.

"Are you all right?"

"Yes. I'm just thinking what a strange couple of days it's going to be. Strange and sad."

"I wish we'd come for the Golden Anniversary," Chris said slowly.

"Yes. I wish so too."

On another western flight, Charles Tallent gazed out of the window, seeing only the whipped-cream clouds below, thinking regretfully of the ugly scene he'd just left. Andrea had been like a madwoman when he'd told her what he planned to do. He'd never seen her so out of control. All the veneer was stripped away as she called him everything from a middle-aged fool to an incompetent politician who'd never be anything more than "a lousy little public servant from the sticks." He hadn't answered until his bag was packed and he was on the way to the front door. Even then he didn't raise his voice, didn't point out that in a way she'd brought this on herself with the ill-advised letter to Barbara. He didn't care enough to get into that. All he wanted was to leave and never come back to this vicious woman or this unhappy house.

"I thought you'd be more civilized about this," he'd said. "We don't love each other, Andrea. You'll be well provided for. The children are grown. They have their own lives. Before it's too late, I'd like to find some real happiness in the rest of my life. I wish the same for you.''

"Happiness!" She spat out the word. "You don't know the meaning of it! You're so juvenile you think you'll find 'happiness' in bed. My God! You'd give up position, recognition, maybe a place in history for that damned little tart? You must be crazy. You must be going through male menopause.''

He'd allowed himself one little flicker of nastiness as his parting shot. "If menopause means 'change of life,' " Charles said, "I'm not only going through it, I'm going to love every second of it.''

He smiled now, remembering. A change of life. Long overdue for him and the woman who waited for him in Denver.

Barbara and Frances drove in silence toward the funeral home. Theirs was a dreadful task: to see that Alice was properly dressed and arranged in her coffin before her parents and sorrowing friends and family came during the usual seven-to-nine o'clock "viewing hours" for the next two nights. The thought of it made both of them sick. Barb could not put her dread into words, but as they neared their destination Fran couldn't contain herself.

"It's barbaric! If you're around when I die, for God's sake don't let people come and look at me. Promise me, Barb. I want them to remember me alive and kicking. That's the way I want to remember Allie. I don't want to look at her all painted up like some doll in a box." She lit a cigarette nervously. "Must I look at her, Barb?''

"No. Not if you don't want to. I'll see that everything's in order.''

Perversely, Fran shook her head. "No, dammit, I will do it. We promised Mother we'd do it together. It's not fair to shove it off on you. It's just that I can't stand this kind of thing!''

Barbara couldn't help herself. "Then, for God's sake, why didn't you let Spencer take her back to Boston? Mother thought that was the right thing to do and I rather agreed with her. But no, you had to make sure Spencer wouldn't get his way. If the services had been back East you wouldn't even have had to go. I don't understand you, Fran.''

Her sister gave a joyless laugh. "Funny. That's more or less what somebody else said to me very early this morning. I told him he couldn't know me because I don't know myself.''

"Who is 'he'?''

"The Venzetti kid. I went there from the hospital.''

Barbara was genuinely shocked. "You went to that waiter? Last night? Right after we heard . . .''

"We all have our ways of trying to block out grief, Barb. That was mine. Only it didn't work. He turned me down. There was only one person I wanted to run to for comfort, and he didn't want me either. Buzz. I haven't heard a word from him today. Wouldn't you think he'd have the decency to telephone? He must know about Allie.''

"He knows," Barbara said slowly. "He phoned this morning.''

"And didn't want to speak to me.'' Fran's voice was flat.

"He's pretty badly broken up about Dorothy. You know that.''

"Sure. But not so broken up he couldn't speak to *you*. Oh, I know I've lost this battle. I thought, 'Give him a little time. He'll come back when the guilt and shock wear off.' But I guess I've known since the minute I heard about Dorothy that he'd never be able to look at me again.''

"He's going away tomorrow," Barb said. "To visit his brother in California. He told me to tell you. But he will come back. And maybe you're right. He loves you, Fran. Given enough time . . . ''

"No. No way. He'll marry some nice woman. Somebody he deserves." She paused. "Hell, Barb, maybe he'll marry you. You'd be good for each other. You're both decent people.''

"Me? Don't be crazy! Buzz Paige and I don't belong together! That would be a wild thought even if Charles . . . ''

"Even if Charles what?''

"He's coming this afternoon. I haven't told anyone. He wants to be here with me. I told him not to, but he wouldn't listen. I . . . I think he means to divorce Andrea. I don't know what's happening. Good God, this isn't the time to be thinking about ourselves, Fran! How can we even be discussing our own lives at this moment? It's dreadful! Allie's dead, and you and I are chewing over romances! We should be ashamed!''

Frances suddenly looked composed and wise. "There's no reason to be ashamed. It doesn't change things for Allie. I'm not heartless, Barb. I'm realistic. Life goes on. I'm glad it's going to go on well for you, at least. I'd be a rotten sister to begrudge you joy because I don't see much for myself. Allie would feel the same. I'm happy for you.''

"I told you, I don't even know what's happening. Only that Charles is coming.''

"You know what's happening, my dear. He's coming for you. He wouldn't show up here at this time if he weren't. You know that's true, Barb. Your Charles has finally come to his senses.''

A tear rolled down Barbara's face. "I've lived so long not daring to hope . . . I suppose I can't get used to the idea that the waiting might be over. What right have I, of the three of us, to be the only one things turn out right for? Allie's dead. You've lost the only man you ever really loved. How can I believe . . .''

"You can believe, little one. Allie saw her dream come true when she found Johnny. And who knows? My soulmate may be waiting in the wings. Don't ever feel unworthy of happiness, Barb. Don't be an Alice, God rest her soul, who thought she didn't deserve any better than she got. You've given Charles Tallent everything through the years. It's about time he paid some of it back. And, for God's sake, don't feel guilty because things are working out for you as they didn't for Allie and me! Just be damned glad one of us got lucky.''

Barbara managed to smile. It was good to hear her sister talking like the "old Frances." She was the true survivor among them. She and Laura. Strong women in different ways—the mother long on forbearance and faith; the daughter tough enough to take disappointments and romantic enough not to abandon the girlish ideals she hid under the cloak of cynicism.

"I love you," Barb said. "I'm sorry for some of the nasty things I said. I didn't mean them. They just came out because I was upset.''

"Forget it. I've heard a lot worse and deserved it all. 'Sticks and stones . . .' You know.'' Fran closed her eyes for a moment. "There's one good thing about me. I've discovered over the years that, as the old saying goes, 'I bruise easy but I heal quick.' " She opened her eyes and stared straight ahead. "Subject closed, at least for now. We have to take care of Allie."

Sam Dalton came into the kitchen and stopped short in amazement. His wife was on her hands and knees, scrubbing the kitchen floor.

"Laura! What in the name of heaven are you doing?"

She looked up at him, a wisp of gray hair falling down over her eyes. "I couldn't just sit any more. I was going out of my mind." She stood up, slowly, painfully. "Funny. I remember my mother doing the same thing. Whenever she had a terrible problem she scrubbed a floor or ran the carpet sweeper or rearranged the furniture. Sometimes it's the only thing that can get you through: hard, physical work that keeps you from thinking about what's happened." She sighed heavily. "I never thought about it before, but I suppose that's why you put in those long hours in the garden, isn't it? To keep you from thinking about how unhappy you are away from the job and how much you miss the people you worked with."

"It's not exactly the same," Sam said gently. "That's a different kind of unhappiness. A very minor one compared to this." He looked as though he were about to weep again. Please don't, Laura silently begged. Seeing a man cry, watching him being ashamed of his "unmanly" tears, was heartbreaking. And Sam had cried often in the past twelve hours or so. He tried hard to contain his tears, but they had to come. He's lucky, Laura thought. I haven't been able to cry. Not once. I wish I could. It would be such a relief from this awful numbness, this dreadful, strangling feeling of loss. Why can't I weep? she wondered almost angrily. When will the blessed, healing tears come? Later, I pray. Lord, give me the luxury of letting go. I've lost a child, a baby I pushed out of me, sweating and crying with pain, almost fifty years ago. Let me weep for her and the life she had. Let me weep for her father and sisters. For her children. And, Lord, let me weep for myself.

But she stayed dry-eyed, moving robot-like to empty the pail of sudsy water and put away the scrub brush. Automatically, she tidied her hair and straightened her dress.

"We'd better get cleaned up, Sam. Spencer and the children will be arriving soon. We don't want them to see us looking like this."

He made an effort to pull himself together. "Where are they staying?"

"I don't know. Frances just said they'd be coming today. They'll be at one of the hotels. I suppose they'll call when they get in."

"I don't want that man in my house." Sam's voice was suddenly strong. "I don't even think he should be allowed to receive people who come to pay their respects. Allie hated him. She wouldn't want him around, pretending to grieve."

"Dear, you said yourself he was her husband. He has his rights. He's a bad man, but I'm grateful to him now for letting us keep Allie nearby as long as we live. I thought at first it wouldn't be right, but I know it is. He wouldn't go to visit her grave. We will." Laura took a deep breath. "Besides, there are the children. We scarcely know them. I want them to feel we love them. No matter what we feel, Sam, we must be civil to Spencer for Janice and Christopher's sake."

He didn't answer, but he turned to go upstairs and "make himself presentable," as she'd suggested. Laura looked after him pityingly. She dreaded the sight of Spencer Winters as much as Sam did, but there was no way around it. She'd tell Frances and Barbara to keep the man away from their father. And from Jack Richards, too, she thought suddenly. What would Jack feel when he came face to face with Allie's husband? She was relieved that John Peck had sent a telegram of condolence and the news that he would not return. He was a sensitive young man. Laura knew he must want to be at the funeral of the mother he'd known so briefly. But obviously he realized how awkward that would be. She liked Alice's firstborn. In time she could have come to love him deeply, if things had not taken this tragic turn. Poor Johnny, she thought. The rest of them had had some part of Alice for years, but that child had seen his mother for only forty-eight hours. It was cruel. Cruel to have found her after all the years, only to lose her again, this time forever.

Laura stood in the middle of her kitchen thinking of John Peck. And the realization of his loss did what nothing else had been able to do. It brought the warm, gushing tears that streamed down her face and untied the horrible knot of agony in her breast. Sobs wracked her slender frame while she stood rooted, hands clenched at her sides, able at last to weep for them all.

Chapter 32

IT'S LIKE SOME eerie ballet, Christopher thought as he stood alone, almost unnoticed in a corner of the room. It's as though it's all been choreographed, our moves, our responses. An almost soundless ebb and flow of people following some unseen impresario's direction.

He'd never even been in a funeral home before, much less been a participant in the strange, prolonged ritual that preceded his mother's funeral. His eyes took in the room assigned to Alice Dalton Winters. What did they call it? A "slumber room." God! It was terrible beyond belief. The open-lidded container at the far end in which she lay; the cloying smell of flowers; the stream of curious callers who came and went, murmuring their hushed words of condolence which Laura acknowledged before she passed the visitor along to his grandfather and aunts and, in some few cases, to Christopher's father and sister and even to Chris himself.

He didn't know what to say to these people who pressed his hand and expressed their sympathy. He had no idea who they were. They usually identified themselves as an "old friend of your mother's," but they were nameless strangers. The sight and touch of them sickened him. The whole primitive process was endless torture and he felt alone and frightened. Even Janice seemed to manage as he couldn't. She was polite and subdued, gracefully composed. Occasionally, though, she glanced over at Chris, who was trying to lose himself in the far corner. He couldn't tell whether she understood his revulsion or whether she was annoyed that he did not play the game by the mysterious rules everyone else seemed to know.

What am I doing here? Chris wondered. I don't fit in among the conventions of death any more than I do among those of life. I loved my mother. She understood and accepted me for what I am. She'd know how I hate this. She'd hate it too. He hadn't been able to look at Alice. Had refused to, even though Spencer Winters ordered him roughly to. It was one of the few times Spencer had spoken directly to his son since they'd been together.

"Go pay your respects to your mother," Spencer commanded. "It's the last time you'll ever see her."

"No." Chris was surprised by his calm voice. "I'll see her forever. She'll always be alive to me." He was relieved that a roomful of people had prevented his father from shouting at him or dragging him bodily to the other end of the room. Spencer would have been capable of both if they'd been alone. Instead, the man stared at him scornfully and said, almost under his breath, "Damned little sissy. Not even enough guts to do that."

Chris didn't answer, and Spencer stalked away, ignoring Frances, who stood nearby, taking in the whole incident. As Spencer left, Chris's aunt approached her nephew. They'd been only briefly introduced. He'd had no more than a fleeting impression of a tall, handsome, quietly dressed woman who kindly but almost impersonally acknowledged her sister's child. Now she said, gently, "Let's take a little walk, Chris. I could use a breath of air. How about you?"

He nodded gratefully and they slipped quietly out. On the street they walked a few yards from the entrance before Frances stopped and leaned against a tree.

"I'm out of cigarettes. Do you have one?"

"Sure." He offered her the pack, took one himself and flicked his gold lighter. The small flame briefly illuminated Fran's big sad eyes, which stayed on him as she took the light and inhaled deeply. Chris nervously lit his own cigarette and waited.

"You loved your mother and you hate all this, don't you?"

"Yes to both questions. It's indecent. Everyone staring at her, and she unable to tell them she doesn't want them to." He took a long drag. "Does that sound crazy?"

"No. I share your feelings about this archaic business. That is, I did share them until now. Ever since I was introduced to this kind of thing I've thought it morbid and uncivilized. Outdated, at least. And cruel to the survivors. But, Chris, I've realized something in the past two days." Frances paused to make sure her words would have the impact she intended. "I've realized that for many people, perhaps for most people, this period which you and I find so excruciating is necessary. They need to look at death to accept it. They need this little time to recognize the truth—that someone they loved is dead. It is comfort rather than cruelty to most people. It occupies them and lets them adjust to the grief. Can you understand that?"

"No. I wish I could." His voice was sad in the darkness. "I think it's like cutting someone away piece by piece instead of making a clean amputation. I know Mother's dead. I don't have to see her that way or stand around making small talk like I'm at some ghastly cocktail party. I'm sorry, but to me it's bizarre."

Frances nodded, though he couldn't see her. "Yes, you'd feel that way because you're intelligent and aware and sensitive. But most people have to have time to understand that someone is gone forever. If everything's too quick, they can never really grasp it. Never make peace with themselves. It's . . . it's as though someone you love dies in a faraway country and you only hear that they've died. You never see them that way. You have to take someone else's word for it. Then, I imagine, it would never be real to you. You'd always feel that the person was just away on a trip, and that you'd be hearing from them or that they'd be coming back. That must be worse agony than this. If your mother had died and been buried here without your coming, perhaps you'd have had that sense of unreality, Chris. If we hadn't gone through this wake, your grandparents would be less able to adjust to the horror. I know," Frances said, "that's hard for you to believe. I never believed it myself before. But I do now. I promise you, it's true."

He was silent for a long moment. "I suppose I see what you mean," he said at last. "I don't know. I find it a difficult theory to buy, but I've never lived through anything like that, so I can't be sure how I'd feel. It's incredible to me that people have to mourn in public. That they have to be so organized about it."

"I know. It seems macabre. Masochistic, even. But have you watched the people here? They're drawing comfort from each other. And strength. Minute by minute, Allie's death becomes more real and thus less frightening. We only fear what we don't know, Chris. We can only accept what we can see. I see that sad but peaceful resignation on one face in particular: Jack Richards'. He loved your mother once. He felt he let her down years ago, and again during her last visit. I've seen the agony begin to disappear from his face. Oh, he still grieves. He will, for a long while. But he's coming out of the nightmare stage, the shock we all suffered. He may not know it, but he's beginning to accept. That's the purpose of all this, Chris. That's what you must accept emotionally, even if you reject it intellectually."

"Jack Richards." Chris repeated the name slowly. "Was he . . . ?"

"He was your mother's childhood sweetheart. He's the father of your half-brother. Haven't you met him?"

"I . . . I don't know. So many people have come up to me. Most of them don't even say their names. I'd like to meet him." There was pain in the young man's voice. "I'd like to meet a man Mother loved, and one who loved her. Will you point him out to me when we go back? I'd honestly like to tell him I'm glad he made her happy, even for a little while."

Frances stretched out her hand and found her nephew's. "I wish you were my child," she said.

Like her sister, Barbara deplored what Christopher called "a ghastly cocktail party." But, also like Frances, she knew it was necessary, particularly to people of her parents' generation—a time of confirmation and occupation. The let-down would come later when Allie was laid to rest; when the neighbors stopped coming by with vast quantities of food so the bereaved family would not have to trouble themselves with cooking; when there were no longer people to be polite to at the funeral home; when Barbara and Frances had left and Sam and Laura were alone. That's when they'd feel the full, hideous awareness of their loss. Until now, devastated as they were, the enormity of what happened hadn't really sunk in. It wouldn't until they had nothing but time on their hands. The dreadful days were still to come for Allie's mother and father, and there was nothing anyone could do about it. There was no way their grown daughters could come home to live with them. Frances would resume her pointless journey to nowhere. And I, Barbara thought, will be back in Washington, starting a new life with Charles.

She still felt selfish and irrationally guilty about her own good fortune. If only it had come sooner, or even later, she wouldn't have this apologetic feeling about the wonderful turn her own life had taken. It made no sense to feel that way, but the joy of her reunion with Charles had been overshadowed by the circumstances which surrounded it. She'd been torn between wanting him to come to Denver, bringing a strong shoulder to lean on, and wishing he'd stay away. It was almost indecent that at this moment of utter misery she should be introducing her long-time lover to her family. Not that Charles hadn't handled it with the utmost tact and understanding. He'd called from the Brown Palace when he checked in and said simply, "I'm here, darling. Whenever you're ready to see me, I'll come to you."

Bone-weary, just back from seeing that Allie was "properly arranged," her poor little head softly swathed in pale tulle to hide the ugly evidence, Barbara was tempted to tell him to go back to Washington. He didn't belong here. She couldn't handle this jarring note in the most intimate of family gatherings. He had no place in their sorrow, and for a moment Barbara didn't know what to say. She'd had no sleep since the night before last. None of them had. And they still had to face the awful days ahead. She yearned to be with him, to be held and comforted like a child, and yet, ambivalently, he seemed an added burden. Charles instinctively understood her silence.

"I don't want to make things harder for you, sweetheart. You must be going through hell. It's enough for me to be in the same city with you. At least you know I'm near if you need me. Would you rather I call you tomorrow? Would that be better?"

Her heart melted. He'd flown thousands of miles simply to be there if she wanted him. He asked nothing. He was willing to wait in the hotel for days, if she preferred. He sensed her distress, her divided feelings, and she loved him for it.

"I'll come down and pick you up," Barb said. "The family will be glad you're here. They'll be grateful." She broke down. "Oh, dearest, I'm so glad you're here. I love you so much. I need you terribly."

"Stay put," he said. "I'll be there as quickly as I can get a cab."

He arrived at the house within minutes and she ran into his arms. He held her close, looking over her shoulder at the three other adults in the hallway, nodding at them silently while Barbara tried to get herself under control. At last she separated herself from him and dried her eyes. Then she turned and said, "Mother. Dad. Fran. This is Charles. Charles Tallent."

Frances, the only one who knew he was coming, stepped forward and kissed his cheek. "How wonderful you're here," she said.

Laura looked stunned for an instant. Charles Tallent, the man Barbara loved, the one she thought she'd lost, was here in Laura's own house. What did it mean? What had happened? Never mind. What did it matter now? There'd be time for explanations later.

"We're glad to see you, Charles," she said, "Sam, dear, this is Barbara's friend, the congressman from Washington."

"Yes. Yes, of course." Sam extended his hand. "Good of you to come."

Charles returned the handshake. "Mrs. Dalton. Mr. Dalton. I can't begin to tell you how sorry I am. When Barbara told me what happened to your daughter, I just had to come. I hope it doesn't . . . embarrass you, my being here. I won't intrude. I simply wanted to be around in case there's anything I can do."

"You're welcome," Laura said simply.

Now, standing in the funeral home with Charles beside her, Barbara wondered what she'd have done if he'd not come. He'd been a tower of strength these past two days, running errands, keeping track of who sent what flowers, behaving like a family friend willing to take on any chore that needed doing. Their only concession to the awkwardness of his presence had been to agree among themselves that he'd be introduced as "Charles Tallent" or "Mr. Tallent." In Colorado, most people did not know he was a congressman and they accepted him as a friend of Barbara's from Washington. There'd be no publicity about a public figure. Only Spencer Winters sparked when he and Charles were introduced at the funeral home.

"Tallent? Charles Tallent? Are you by chance the congressman?"

Charles shot Barbara a baleful look as she left them. "Yes. I'm on The Hill."

"Well, well!" Spencer was visibly impressed. "Read a lot about you. You're a big man on the Foreign Relations Committee. Didn't know you knew my wife."

"Unfortunately, I never had the pleasure. I'm a friend of Barbara's. And, I hope, of the whole family now."

Spencer raised an eyebrow. "Oh, I see. Like to talk to you, Tallent, about some projects my firm is handling overseas. Get your advice about opening a few doors in Washington."

Charles did not try to disguise his distaste. "I'm amazed you can put your mind to such things at this moment, Mr. Winters."

Spencer was unsnubbable. "Naturally, I didn't mean *here*. I could run down and see you in your office one day."

"I'm sure we can schedule it sometime. Have your secretary call mine."

"Good." Spencer did not seem to even notice the rudeness. "We can probably do a little mutual back-scratching."

Charles walked away, not answering. "My God," he said when he reached Barbara's side, "what kind of a man was your sister married to? He was actually trying to talk business to me!"

"He's a terrible man," Barb said. "It was a terrible marriage."

"Ours won't be, darling. I promise you that." He put his hand gently on her arm. "No, don't turn away. I know this isn't the time or place to propose. I just want you to know I'm going to be free and I intend to make you happy."

She looked up at him with adoration. They hadn't been alone since he arrived. They knew without discussion, this was not the time for that. Charles had not even hinted at it, and Barb respected the delicacy that made him know physical lovemaking was not what she needed. He unselfishly gave her what she did need—undemanding comfort and strength through his presence. He represented security and reality, a promise of a sane future in a world gone mad. Sex was good with them and would be again, but it would have been almost agony for Barbara in this atmosphere of pain for the living and respect for the dead.

From his place on the other side of the room, Jack Richards watched Barbara and Charles Tallent in that brief but unmistakably loving communication. He'd been introduced to Charles by Frances, who whispered later, "Isn't it wonderful? They're so in love."

Jack was startled to feel a terrible sense of disappointment at those words. Startled and ashamed. Standing there, only a few feet from the body of the woman he should have loved, he admitted to himself that from the moment Barbara had brought Alice to his apartment he'd wanted her, not the sister. She'd been in his mind ever since. Even in his agony over Allie, he'd selfishly thought that perhaps, after a decent interval, he could begin to "court" Barb. He'd even dared hope she was attracted to him too. He fantasized that she might stay on in Denver with her parents, that they'd begin to see each other, that, in time, they would marry. She'd be the right woman for him—witty and bright and strong, capable of being wife and playmate. What an animal he was, allowing himself such dreams when Alice was not even in her grave! And, as it now turned out, what a stupid animal as well. He should have known someone as magnetic as Barbara would have a man in her life. How could he have deluded himself that she'd want him for a husband as much as he desired her for a wife?

He looked at Charles Tallent and hated him. Hated him for his good looks, his easy manner. Hated him most of all because he was the man Barbara loved and went to bed with.

It's all a big zero, Jack thought. Nothing works out the way it's supposed to. I've lost everyone. I'll probably never even see Johnny again. The boy didn't fool him. He'd been glad to find his father, but it was his mother who mattered to him. John Peck tolerated Jack. Perhaps he even felt some slight affection for him. But it was Allie their son cared about. Allie who'd borne the agony and frustration while Jack made a life of his own with little thought of the child he'd fathered. John Peck knew that. Deep down, Jack thought, he must resent me for not having taken care of his mother either in the early or late years of life. I meant well. I did. I'm just a selfish man. That's the way I'm made.

It was over. The brief eulogy delivered by the minister had been simple and moving, a good job since the man had never met Alice and had to rely on her sisters and her daughter for the bits of personal tribute, the references to her parents and sisters and husband and children, the citing of her charitable work in Boston and her goodness as a mother, wife and child. The clergyman had quietly but firmly denounced the violence that pervaded the world, the insanity that had caused the death of an innocent woman. But he urged those at the funeral to find mercy and forgiveness in their hearts, to see Allie's death as the work of a sick mind and to believe that God had taken her to a peaceful and happy place.

"We know that to forgive is divine," the young minister said earnestly. "We know too that it is the most difficult, as well as the most Christian, assignment a shocked and bereaved family can be asked to accept. But those who deeply and truly loved Alice remember her generosity of spirit, her lovely childlike belief in the basic goodness of people, her capacity for understanding and faith and compassion. May they find it with themselves to pray not only for her but also for the deranged soul who perpetrated this tragic act."

Damned young bleeding heart! Sam Dalton thought angrily. How would he know what it was like to have your daughter violated and murdered? How could he brazenly stand there and ask them to pray for some animal who was still loose and probably never would be brought to justice? It was insufferable. Sam considered himself a religious, God-fearing man. Not as good a church-goer as Laura, but as good as most. It would take a saint not to wish for vengeance. Pray for my daughter's killer? I pray for only one thing: that he's caught and made to pay for his crime.

That's what's wrong with the world, Sam thought. All this permissiveness, all this psychological mumbo-jumbo about rehabilitating criminals and finding something in their upbringing or their environment to explain the lawless things they do. Even the ministers are spouting it from the pulpit, as concerned with the redemption of evil men as they are with the eternal life of the good people who try to live by the Commandments. Whatever happened to "Thou Shalt Not Kill"? Do these young wearers of the cloth really believe rape and murder are understandable? Forgivable? Never in a million years!

He clenched his teeth in rage, and it was as though this fury brought him back to life. In the three days since Allie's death he'd been like a dead man himself, walking, talking, trying to eat and sleep, consumed with a grief so deep he could feel the physical pain of it. Now, even as he left the church with Laura, even as he climbed slowly into the limousine that would follow the hearse, his sorrow did not diminish, but he prayed that the beast-at-large would suffer in some monstrous way for his sins. Sam would never forget. How dare anyone ask him to forgive?

Late that afternoon, Laura answered the front-door bell and was surprised to find Janice Winters there. The young woman looked so utterly drained that, involuntarily, Laura held out her arms. Jan fell into them, her tears mingling with her grandmother's.

"Come in, Janice dear," Laura said at last. "I thought you'd gone back to Boston."

"We have a flight later this evening." She glanced around. "You aren't all alone, are you?"

"No. Your grandfather and aunts are upstairs trying to rest. I couldn't be still, so I came down to make myself a cup of tea. Would you like one?"

"Yes, thank you. I would."

"Let's have it in the kitchen. We always seemed to end up talking in there, Frances and Barbara and . . . and your mother. We had many a conversation around that table when the girls were young, and even in these past days when they were home for the anniversary.'' Laura was trying hard to act normally. ''Just sit yourself down there. The kettle's already boiling.''

Janice looked around the cheerful, old-fashioned kitchen. It was thoroughly out of date, with its four-burner gas range and refrigerator, its porcelain sink and plastic rack for draining dishes. It was a far cry from the one in Boston that Spencer had insisted be ''modernized'' with dishwasher and freezer and wall oven and miles of butcher blocks and stainless steel. The Boston kitchen did not invite sitting. It was cold and efficient. Like Spencer. This one was warm and cozy, welcoming, as though it had received fifty years of confidences and seen more than its share of tragedies and triumphs. Bright curtains hung at the windows and Laura's precious African violets bloomed on the ledge. There was a big round table and plenty of room for the once-reunited family of five.

''I love this room!'' Jan said. ''It makes me feel safe.''

Laura, returning with the tea things, nodded. ''Yes. It's always made me feel that way too.'' She poured the tea, waiting, but Janice seemed reluctant to say why she'd come. She sipped her tea took out a package of cigarettes and asked if Laura minded her smoking.

''No. Help yourself. I just hope you're not a fiend, like your Aunt Frances. I do worry about how much she smokes.''

What does this child want? Laura wondered. They'd all said goodbye at the cemetery. Sam had barely looked at Spencer, had not even shaken hands with the man, but she and Fran and Barbara had tried to be composed. Horror that Spencer was, he had been Allie's husband for twenty-five years and one had to acknowledge that. Besides, Allie's children were sweet, even if they'd been rather reserved. Only Fran had seemed to get close to young Christopher. She'd said he was sensitive, a nice boy. None of them knew much about Janice. Only that she was pretty and well-mannered. Why had she come here now? Laura thought again. There must be something she wants to say to me or to all of us.

As though she picked up Laura's thoughts, Janice suddenly spoke. ''I wanted to see you, Grandmother, before I left. I . . . I want you to know how much I regret never having been close to you. Any of you. Mother wanted me to come with her to your anniversary party and I didn't want to. It didn't seem to mean anything to me, coming all this way to see grandparents I barely remembered. She was disappointed. I guess I disappointed her in many ways. I loved her, and I think she knew that. But I'm sure she also knew that I didn't have much respect for her. Because she stayed with my father, I mean. Because she let him be so cruel to her . . . and to me and Chris.''

Laura said nothing. She was listening to a confession, a cleansing of the soul. Jan took a deep breath and went on.

''I didn't know, until John Peck turned up, how little respect Mother had for herself. And how wrong she was to feel she had to pay for that early mistake. I see now why she did what she did. Why she stayed with my father. She *was* punishing herself, but she was also making sure her other two children had a home, no matter how troubled a one. We, that is Chris and I, had no idea of her feelings. Chris was much closer to her than I was, even though he couldn't stay in that house, not even for her sake. He didn't understand why she didn't leave, any more than I did. But she wouldn't leave. Maybe she was afraid to.

Maybe she didn't know where to go. I don't know. I only know I didn't try to help."

Laura reached across the table and touched Jan's arm. "Don't blame yourself, Janice. You didn't know. None of us knew how she felt. We were all to blame in one way or another. We more than you, dear. Much more."

"I was glad when she didn't come back to Boston after your anniversary. Glad for her sake, I mean. And when John told me about their reunion, I was so happy. I thought maybe she'd marry his father and finally have some kind of life worth living. I helped get Mother and John together, you know." There was a little trace of pride in her voice. "It was a crazy coincidence, but I was the one who finally helped him sort out the clues and find her."

"Thank the Lord you did," Laura said. "It meant more to her than anything in the world."

"Yes. I know. And then to have it all blow up so suddenly, so terribly. All the good years she might have had at last." Jan began to cry again. "Maybe we'd have finally understood each other." She wiped her eyes. "I've been a smart-aleck most of my life, Grandmother. Very sophisticated. Very liberated. Very stupid. I wanted Mother to know that I'd finally grown up, that I'm going to marry Clint Darby, the man I've been living with. I want the conventional life I've always sneered at. I want it all. The wedding ring and his name and all that goes with it. I never had a chance to tell her any of that. Or to tell her how I finally realize what she sacrificed for Chris and me, and how grateful we are."

"I like to believe she knows," Laura said softly. She was crying now too. Crying for Alice and for this dear child who never gave herself a chance to know her mother. "I'm glad you have someone you love, Janice. Someone who loves you and wants you to marry him. He must be very proud of you. I think that's what it means when a man wants you to take his name—that he's proud of you and respects you, as he should. And as you should respect him. That's the way your mother would want it."

Jan looked lost. "I feel that I can almost speak to her through you. She was your baby. That's why I came today. To tell you these things and to ask you . . ."

"What? Ask anything you like, dear."

"I've been thinking. Clint and I decided to have a City Hall wedding. I won't let my father turn it into a circus, a chance to show how rich and successful he is. But since I've been here, I wondered, well, could we be married out here, from your house, Grandmother? I won't let Dad come. Just Chris and John and his wife. I want to be married in front of my family, and you and Grandfather and my two brothers are all I have. Doing it that way would make it seem as though Mother was here. May I, please? May I plan that?"

It seemed an eternity before Laura answered. "No one could pay your grandfather and me a bigger compliment, Janice. We'd be proud to have you married from our house. But it wouldn't be right, dear. I'm not your mother. I'm her mother. I'm too old to be a substitute mother for my daughter. Maybe you're too young to understand that. I can't replace her, dear. No one can. And just being married in the place your mother once lived doesn't mean you'll have your mother back.

This house is part of her past, not yours. Your place is in Boston, Janice. Where your friends are, where your roots are. Even where your father is. I know you have no love for him, nor have I. He was cruel to my child and that's hard to forgive. But he's still your father, and a father is entitled to give his only daughter in marriage. You can have your wedding any way you want it, but my advice is to have it there and let your father be part of it. He may not be what you deserve or want, but I suspect if there's anyone in the world he cares for, it probably is you. Men feel that way about their girl-children. No," she said as Janice started to protest, "don't tell me I'm wrong. Think about it. Try to understand that, wicked as he is, underneath he's a pathetic man, driven and insecure. He's been hateful, horrible, and none of us can forget what he did to Alice. But take pity on him, because no one else ever will."

"I can't. I can't be that magnanimous."

"At least consider it. And if you decide you want to be married here, we'll welcome you with open arms. But don't take revenge, Janice. And don't mistake the emotions of this moment for something more than they are. Just think it over, all of it. And let us know your decision. We'll abide by it, whatever it is." She kissed her granddaughter's cheek. "I love you. We all do. That takes no thinking over at all."

Chapter 33

IT WAS RAINING lightly. A quiet, thin but steady rain that blew red, yellow and orange leaves against the library window and reminded Charles that another brutal Washington winter was all too close. He looked up from his desk and took pleasure in the sight of Barbara curled up in a chair next to the small, crackling, wood-burning fireplace. A year ago he'd never hoped for this idyllic life. Last October he'd had a different wife, one for whom he felt nothing, and a mistress he loved who was now his wife. He felt a rush of affection for the woman he'd nearly lost in the temporary headiness of a political plum dangled before his greedy eyes. Thank you, God, he said silently. You do, indeed, work in wondrous ways.

"Anything interesting?"

Barbara looked up from her letter. "Everything's fine at home, Mother says. They're both all right and sorry we won't be there next week to celebrate their fifty-first."

"Do you want to go?"

"No. They've promised to come here for Christmas. I want them to see our new house. Do you realize they've never been to Washington? Dad will have a wonderful time grousing about the Administration, and Mother will love the sightseeing." Barbara smiled. "About as much as I'll hate showing another visitor the White House and the Jefferson Memorial for the nine-hundredth time. It ain't easy being a congressman's wife, old buddy. Sometimes I feel like a tour guide for the constituents."

For a moment he was troubled. "You don't regret it, darling, do you? All the extra work? This big house instead of your little apartment? Being a Washington hostess instead of a businesswoman? You're not bored, are you?''

"I hate every minute of it.'' Seeing the dismay on his face, she laughed. "You really are mad, Congressman. Regret it? It's like a dream, every second of it. Do you know, sometimes I wake up in the morning and watch you while you sleep? You're a lovely sleeper. Quiet, with a little smile on your face. It's still a new feeling to me, knowing where I belong, being part of you, helping a little.'' She became quiet. "I'm always afraid you're the one who might have regrets,'' she said softly. "You gave up so much to marry me. I never want you to be sorry.''

Charles left the desk to come over and kiss her. "Now who's the mad one? Oh, I suppose I should regret it,'' he teased. "What's so terrific about being married to the most beautiful, brightest, kindest, sexiest lady who ever lived? What's so great about a stepmother who's totally captivated my children and loves them in return? How could I possibly be happy in a warm, loving house? Or content to know I have a stronger voice in the future of the world than I ever could have had if I'd sat like a stick in Cabinet meetings worrying about government subsidies for hog growers? Regret? Lady, that word is missing from my vocabulary.''

In her Paris apartment, Frances pushed aside the remnants of her croissant and café-au-lait and propped herself higher on the frilly white pillows in the king-sized bed. Funny how she could read this letter and feel nothing. Buzz had written to say he was being married next month. Some friend of Dorothy's. He wanted her to know she'd always have a special place in his heart and he hoped she wished him happiness.

"I suppose it was never to be for us, Fran,'' he wrote. "For a little while I thought I could be what you wanted. That we had a second chance. But I know, as I suspect you do, that even if circumstances had not pulled us apart again, we'd not have been happy together for very long. You're a free spirit, my dear, eternally young and curious. I'm a quite dull, middle-aged homebody who enjoyed a brief moment of rapture and believed I could sustain it with you. I'd have disappointed you very soon. I wouldn't have fit in with your exotic life or your friends. It was a lovely dream, like something we used to see in movies before they became real and ugly. But I couldn't have supported that dream in any way. With a year to analyze it, I'm sure you know that too.''

She tossed the letter aside. He was right, of course. It had all been make-believe. She'd tried to recapture something that had intrigued a girl thirty years ago. She'd been swept up in nostalgia and foolish memories. And she'd been afraid of the future, fearful of the loneliness ahead, convinced she could buy back her youth. She was glad he was going to marry a replica of Dorothy, hopefully a saner and more predictable one, but with the same housewifely instincts, the same utter dependence he needed above all else.

There were two other letters from Denver in the morning mail. She opened Laura's first. They were both well, her mother wrote, and planning to be in Washington with Barbara and Charles for Christmas. Was there any hope she might be there too? It would be wonderful if she and Sam were with their two dear daughters.

No mention of Allie, who'd been dead almost a year. No need to mention her. She was never long out of their thoughts. She had, in a terrible way, brought them all closer together. At least they were all in touch now, a family reunited by a tragedy that nearly destroyed them all. Christmas in Washington sounded good. The Concorde could take her there in a few hours. She'd write to Barb and invite herself.

Idly, she opened the third letter, surprised to see it was from Jack Richards, a surprise he anticipated in the first sentence.

"You'll be startled to hear from me, I suspect, but I've thought of you often in the past year, Fran. A great deal has happened. Johnny and Carol have a beautiful little girl whom they named Alice. They're very happy, and I've visited them twice since Allie died. For the first time I feel like a father and, good God, a grandfather!

"I hope this doesn't sound terrible, but I want to be utterly selfish and travel a lot. I can afford it, and, like you, I have no obligations. I guess I was never made for obligations, the way most people are. I don't think you were made for them either, Fran. Maybe together we can enjoy the practical joke we know life really is. It's a helluva lot better to take a pratfall with a friend than to be safe and bored alone. Not that I think you're alone! You're probably so besieged with invitations and plans you won't want to bother with me. But I hope not. I'd like to see Paris and you. Could you spare some time to show a country boy what Europe is all about?"

She was smiling as she put the letter down. He was incredibly naive. Like a kid planning a holiday. But he was attractive, and he might be fun. She'd never let him know how few invitations she received. Even the young waiters and bartenders and lifeguards had begun to pall. At least Jack Richards was grown-up and willing to learn cosmopolitan ways, unlike Buzz, who never could. Why not? Why not enjoy the company of an honest-to-God intelligent male who thought she was glamorous? Who cared where it led or how long it lasted?

She wrote out a cable and reread it. "Adored your letter and applaud your attitude. Come ahead. Love and laughter. Fran."

Yes, that was the right, light touch. She was still smiling, but now with a touch of wistfulness. She raised her eyes upward and said aloud, "Is it okay with you, Allie? We no-good bastards probably deserve each other, don't you think?"

She felt foolish but better, somehow.

Martha Perrone carefully noted three dinner parties in her employer's engagement book and saw, penciled in his own hand, a weekend invitation at one of the great houses of Newport. "Cottages," she remembered they were called. Some "cottages"! Great mansions is what they were. She'd seen pictures of them. Spencer Winters spent a lot of weekends in Newport last summer. This was probably the offbeat idea of one of those crazy society women he ran around with, having an "out of season" weekend party. Funny he hadn't given her the invitation to note, as he usually did. She was turning into a social secretary.

Ever since his wife's death, Mr. Winters had been so in demand he could hardly keep up with the whirl. Martha sniffed. Widowers had it made. An eligible, available man could be out every night in the week. Men were always in short supply, even if they were old and dull. Not like single women or divorcees or widows. They could rot on the shelf after the age of thirty.

Not that Mr. Winters was so old, but he was dull. Snobbish. Pompous. Even more so now that his wife's aunt had died and left him all that money. Funny she didn't leave anything to any of her relatives, Mrs. Winters' family. Funny, that is, until she remembered that Mr. Winters himself had drawn up her new will last November.

Martha shrugged. She wasn't sure why she kept on working for him. His social and financial life had improved, but his disposition certainly hadn't. He'd been furious about the way his daughter got married. In one of his rare, unguarded moments, he'd said to Martha, "Damn, headstrong young people! Janice won't have a wedding suitable to her social standing. No. She has to be married in some crumby little chapel in Lexington. Someplace 'picturesque.' No big wedding. No reception. Nobody there. I'm surprised she's letting me come!" He'd stopped abruptly, annoyed that he'd shown such emotion in front of "the hired help." Martha hadn't said anything. She'd been too surprised. She simply stood there until Spencer said, "Never mind, Miss Perrone. Forget it. It doesn't matter."

"Certainly, Mr. Winters." But she hadn't forgotten it. It gave her a kind of satisfaction to know that in some things even the great Spencer Winters could be thwarted. Not many. He had everything now. Money, power, position. She wondered if he'd marry again. Maybe that strange October weekend in Newport was some kind of assignation. Well, it was none of her business. He was free to live any way he chose. Even the job wasn't so important to him now that he was independently rich. Probably Mrs. Winters would have inherited if she'd lived, poor thing. Not that she'd have seen the money anyway.

It was terrible the way Mrs. Winters died. All so strange. Martha had never found out what that whole business was about, a year ago when Mrs. Winters was in Denver. She remembered the phone calls she'd eavesdropped on. She'd never heard another word about the mysterious John Peck or figured out what Janice meant about being "her brother's keeper." Most of all, she'd never know what Alice Winters meant about "a new life" and "long-lost child." It would remain forever a mystery, just as, sadly, it would always be a mystery about who killed that nice lady. They'd never solved the crime. At least she never read that they had. When it happened it was in the Boston papers, but since then, nothing.

Mr. Winters hadn't spent much time grieving. That was for sure. What an awful man he was. No heart. Not a trace of one. He never even mentioned his wife after he came back from her funeral. It was as though she never existed. Martha wished her mother would stop harping on the "nice, secure job" Martha had, and pointedly asking all about Mr. Winters' life as a widower. She probably thought if Martha stayed there Spencer would one day "discover her," rip off her glasses and say, "My God, Martha, you're beautiful! I love you! Marry me!"

The idea made her snicker. If anything was far-fetched, that was. But she almost wished it would happen, like it used to in old Doris Day films. Plain girl becomes raving beauty. She knew just how she'd handle it. She'd look at him scornfully and say, "Yes, Mr. Winters, I am beautiful, but *you* are a pig!" And she'd walk out, leaving him heartbroken, his hopes dashed. He'd drink himself to death.

Martha giggled again.

"What's so funny?" Wallingford's secretary asked.

Martha's comic fantasy faded and she resumed her usual scowl. "Nothing's funny," she said. "Not a damned thing."

"Clint?"

"Um?"

"I've been thinking."

Darby put down his book and regarded his wife with amused interest. "That's pretty heavy. Cerebral activity, I mean. What's the topic?"

Jan was very serious. "Babies. Or, more correctly, the lack of them. Would you mind very much if we didn't have any?"

"You mean right away or never?"

"Never. We haven't actually talked about it lately, but I don't want children. Is that awful?"

"No. Not if you don't want them for the right reason. It's like wanting them for the wrong reason, if you follow me." He smiled. "That sounds pretty convoluted, doesn't it? What I mean is, I don't think there's anything worse than people having kids because they think it is expected of them. That's a wrong reason. Peer pressure. Family pressure. A parent who wants to be a grandparent. Wrong. Like having a baby in the hope it will hold a bad marriage together, or replace the love you're not getting from a husband. Also wrong. Now, there must be equally wrong reasons for *not* wanting a baby. And equally *right* ones. So if you don't want children, let's examine your reasons and find out if they're wrong or right. Am I making any sense to you?"

Janice returned his smile. "In your verbose way, yes. You're asking me why I don't want children. Period."

"Astonishing. You should have been an editor. Press on."

"I have several reasons. First, I don't really come on all-over dewy-eyed at the sight of babies. Somebody omitted the maternal instinct when they put the pieces of Janice Winters together. Second, I like our marriage the way it is, the free-to-be-you-and-me part, without the distinctions, worries and expense of kids. Third, I think the world is sufficiently overpopulated without people like us—at least like me who doesn't care—adding to future problems. Right reasons?"

Clint considered her arguments for a minute. "Sure. All the right reasons. Or are they *all?*"

"Meaning?"

"Meaning, Janice darling, are you leaving out one? Are you afraid of having a family because your own home life was so unhappy? I know you don't think I'll beat you, but are you being influenced by your mother's life? Do you still feel guilty because you think she stayed with her husband to keep a home together for you and Chris? Hell, I'm not trying to be a road-company Freud, but are

you worried that kids might somehow suffer if they belonged to you? The way
you suffered belonging to your parents? The way your mother suffered at the
hands of her parents? All I'm saying is, if you don't want babies because you
just plain don't want them, like you don't want canaries or goldfish, then I
respect that. I'm not that hung up on the subject either, to tell you the truth.
But I don't want you to be pressured into *not* having kids any more than I'd
want you to be pressured into *having* them. Oh, hell, this is getting awfully
complicated! I just mean this kind of decision should be based on us, our
relationship, our feelings. Not on anything you've seen or lived through in the
past.''

Janice looked thoughtful. ''I don't think any of that enters into it. I really
don't. For some people, like Carol, babies are the fulfillment of a lifetime desire.
For John too, who spent years searching for his real parents. But children aren't
necessary to my life. I'd have them if you really wanted them, Clint. And I
wouldn't mind. I'd love them and be good to them and try to understand them.
I'd probably make a damned good mother, believe it or not. But I truly have
no urge in that direction.''

''Nor have I. So that's settled. I guess it was about time we talked about it.
I hadn't really given it much thought. Which is a pretty good indication that I'm
no more the papa-bear type than you're the den-mother variety.''

She sighed with relief. ''It's not an irrevocable decision, of course. We have
plenty of time in case either of us changes his mind. I still have what is known
as a lot of 'child-bearing years' ahead. Or we could even adopt later on if we
felt we didn't want to add to the world's numbers.''

''Right.'' Clint grinned. ''But promise me that if we do adopt it will be some
little ghetto kid. Some child who needs a good home.''

''That's nice. That's as it should be. Unselfish and generous.''

''Well, not entirely. It would also give me pleasure to introduce your stuffy
old man to his only 'grandchild.' Think how thrilled he'd be.''

''Sadist!'' Jan gave him a playful shove. ''Now who's talking about wrong
reasons?''

Clint became very serious. ''All kidding aside, babe, it's a different world
than your mother's was. There's no stigma to having a childless marriage, just
as it's no disgrace for women not to marry at all. Or for men to choose their
own lifestyles, as Chris has. Don't feel you're failing anybody by preferring not
to have babies. Not me, not your grandparents, and certainly not yourself. I
married a woman, not a brood mare. Kids are for those who want them and all
that goes with them, and plenty of people do. But that's their thing. I respect
freedom of choice, as long as it's an honest choice.''

For a moment, Christopher was tempted to accept Barbara's invitation to go
to Washington for Christmas. His grandparents were coming from Denver, and
Frances from Paris, or wherever she happened to be at the moment.

''I've also written to Janice and Clint,'' his aunt wrote, ''and I'm going to
invite John and Carol and little Allie. It will be quite a houseful, but we can
manage. Foxhall Road is big enough for ten adults and a baby, though it may
feel more like a sardine can than a house! Anyway, Christopher, please try to

come. None of us had the heart for celebrations last year, but it would be lovely to have the family together. I know your mother would like it if she knew.''

Yes, Mother would like it, Chris thought. She was a frustrated traditionalist, if ever there was one. God knows she never had a chance to enjoy those storybook gatherings of family one reads about. Not in that hostile house with a constantly angry husband, a rebellious daughter and an unhappy son. A house to which her parents and sisters never came. A house which was open only to "important people" who could be useful to Spencer Winters. He hadn't stepped foot in that house in years, not since the day he'd left it and begged Alice to go with him. He hadn't seen or heard of his father since the funeral almost a year ago, and he had no wish to. He did regret not going to Jan's wedding, but he declined when she told him Spencer would be there to give her away.

"Why?" Chris asked. "You loathe him as much as I do! Why would you want him there?"

"I don't. I don't really want him within ten miles of me, and I'll probably never see him after this. But, well, I guess this is going to sound silly, but Grandmother asked me to do it. She asked me to be kind to him because no one else ever would.''

He'd been aghast. "Kind to him! After what he's done? After what he did to Mother?''

"Chris, I can't destroy myself with anger. It's over. It wasn't something of our making, and like it or not, he's our father. That's why I'm going to have him at the wedding. I don't forgive him, but I'm trying to understand what made hiin the way he is. There must be a great deal of self-loathing in him!.''

"Damned well hidden, if there is." Chris shook his head. "I love you, Jan. I'd like to be at your wedding, but I can't. Not with him there." He wanted to say it seemed like a betrayal of Alice, but he couldn't hurt Janice that way. She'd obviously made a promise to Laura Dalton, an irrational one in a moment of emotion, he supposed, and she was going to keep it despite the reluctance she must feel. Good for her, but he couldn't be that hypocritical, or maybe that big.

Jan accepted his decision. "I understand, Chris. John feels the same way. He and Carol won't come either. I'm not even going to ask anyone else of Mother's family. Not Frances or Barbara or even the grandparents, though I think they'd come out of deference to Mother." She paused. "I'll be honest with you. I hoped Father would refuse to take part in any wedding he couldn't mastermind. Then Clint and I could go to City Hall, the way we wanted. But he didn't decline, so I'm stuck with it. Look, it's no big deal. A couple of our friends from the office will stand up for us, and a few days later we'll have a party at the apartment to celebrate. You'll come to that, won't you? And bring Peter?''

"Sure. Of course we'll come." He felt terribly selfish. "I'm sorry, Jan. I know I'm letting you down. I just can't bring myself to . . . .''

"No need to be sorry. It's a silly commitment on my part, but I made it and it's something I have to do for a nice, elderly, sentimental lady.''

His grandmother had been pleased. Jan had shown him her letter and a check for fifty dollars, which was probably more than Sam and Laura could afford. For all her toughness, Clint thought, my sister is more sensitive than I. He wondered whether she and Clint would go to Washington for Christmas. Probably. Barbara had made it clear by omission that she had no intention of including Spencer. They'd probably all go and have the kind of gathering his aunt hoped for, full of gifts and love and nonsense.

But that's not the place for me, Chris thought. My family is Peter, and there's no way I could include him. It would only make things tense and awkward, spotlight the very situation I know Mother wanted to play down. She understood, but she knew my grandparents wouldn't. That's why I didn't go to their golden anniversary, though I wanted to. She never said why she didn't want me to go, but I knew. She didn't want to embarrass them or me by presenting a son who was gay. Ironic. They didn't know when I went out for the funeral. No one suspected. Not even Frances, who surely would have been the first to recognize what I am.

But they'd all know if I showed up in Washington with Peter, and I wouldn't go without him. He's made my life happy. Aside from Mother, he's the only one who ever cared.

God, how it must gall Father to know that the precious Winters name ends with me! This is the end of the line. Even if Jan has children they'll be Darbys. Well, good riddance is all I can say. It's appropriate in a way. Everyone waits for the end of Boston's cold, cruel winters.

Christopher smiled humorlessly at his own pathetic little play on words. In a way, it was terribly unfunny.

"Shall we accept Barbara's invitation for Christmas?"

"I wouldn't mind," John Peck said. "How about you?"

"I think it would be nice. They haven't seen Alice, any of them." Carol hugged her daughter. "Would you like to meet your great-grandparents, Allie? Want to let your great-aunts and -uncles make a fuss over you?"

If only the woman she was named for could see her, John thought. What high hopes we had when we said goodbye in Denver. She was looking forward to meeting Carol and so happy about the baby coming. I think she must have sensed Carol and I were her only hope for grandchildren. She knew Chris would never marry. And she probably suspected Jan wouldn't either. Or that she wouldn't want children if she did.

The old anger returned. Why? He'd asked himself that a thousand times in the past year. Why did my mother have to die? Why, after all the bad times, were she and I deprived of the good ones?

He hoped, childishly, that she forgave him for not being at her funeral. It would have stirred up too much talk, opened old wounds for her parents, maybe precipitated a confrontation with Spencer Winters. But, most of all, John knew he couldn't have borne it. He could live better with the memory of those two golden days.

He brought himself back to the present. "You haven't met my grandparents either," he said. "You'll like them, Carol. They're salt-of-the-earth people. And Frances will fascinate you. Not every family has its own Auntie Mame."

"If she's as nice as Barbara, I won't complain. They were lovely to come up when Allie was born."

John tickled his daughter. "Well, how about it, sweetheart? Want to spend your first Christmas in the bosom of your old dad's family?"

The baby gurgled.

"See?" Carol said. "Of course she does. She knows someday she's going back to Washington as the first female President."

"Wouldn't surprise me. Wouldn't surprise me a bit."

Chapter 34

ON THE MORNING of her fifty-first wedding anniversary, Laura Dalton opened her eyes and lay staring at the ceiling above the bed. Almost reluctantly, she allowed her mind to retrace the events of the past year, something she seldom did, not only because much of it was painful or incomprehensible, but because she was determined not to be one of those aging women who wallow in the past. She preferred to think of the tranquillity of the present and optimistically contemplate the future.

And there was something more. She was almost superstitious about the good and the bad of the months since last October. Funny how different the years were in one's life. Some of them passed swiftly, uneventfully, lulling one into a false sense of security. Others were like a newsreel, full of drama, with brief moments of joy and lingering periods of despair, disrupting the normal flow of things with unexpected twists and turns. Unconsciously, she crossed her fingers. Let Barbara's life go smoothly now. Give Frances some sense of peace. Let Sam stay well.

She'd been so terrified in January when he'd had his heart attack. Terrified and guilt-ridden that she'd allowed him to ignore those early-warning signs back in October. Thank God the attack had been mild, but there'd been a few terrible hours when she'd felt so alone, when she thought she was going to lose him. It all happened so swiftly in the middle of that bitter cold night. She remembered his waking her, almost apologetically, saying he had chest pains and felt nauseous. She'd phoned Dr. Jacoby, who'd sent an ambulance and was waiting at Presbyterian Hospital when they arrived. She remembered how helpless she felt sitting in the waiting room while Sam was rushed into intensive care. There was no one close. No one to call. Her daughters were thousauds of miles away, and though she knew they'd come to her, it would take many hours. It might even, she'd thought, be too late.

Recalling it now, she shuddered. Even then she'd been superstitiously glad they hadn't taken Sam to Denver General, where they'd lost Allie. She'd concentrated on the doctors' quick opinion that the attack was "slight," willing it true, wondering how she'd go on without him if it was not.

How selfish people are, Laura thought. I was frantic with worry about Sam, yet part of my mind was consumed with what would happen to me if he died. I was thinking as much of my loss as of his life. That's the way it works, I suppose, though it's a shameful thing to admit. In times of trouble, we're subconsciously absorbed with ourselves and the effect sickness and death have on us. Even Allie's tragedy was that way. The hateful truth is that, much as we grieved for the end of her life, we were pitying ourselves for our pain, desolate that such misery had been inflicted on us who loved her. Why are we like that? Is it because "every man's death diminishes us a little?" Do we see in it the inevitable reflection of our own?

She turned her thoughts away from this morbid introspection, remembering the relief she'd felt when Dr. Jacoby finally came and said Sam would be okay. She'd burst into tears, realizing how much she loved this man she'd lived with for more than fifty years, and how fortunate she was to have him for a while longer. Only then had she called Barbara, assuring her there was no need to come, grateful for the offer to cable Frances.

"You're sure you don't need me, Mother?"

I need you terribly, Laura had thought. But I have no right to disrupt your life when there's nothing you can do but hold my hand.

"No, everything's fine, dear. Your father is out of danger. There's nothing to worry about now."

"You should have called me hours ago." Barbara was reproachful. "I could have been there by now. I hate your having gone through this all alone."

"I'm fine," Laura repeated. "And so is your father. He'll just need time to recuperate. I'll take good care of him."

"You always have," Barbara said gently. "He's a lucky man."

"I'm pretty lucky myself."

I really am, Laura thought now, looking at Sam sleeping peacefully beside her. He was well now, better than he'd been in years, looking forward to going to Washington for Christmas. He'd been pleased, even enthusiastic, about Barbara and Charles's invitation. A quite different Sam. He'd begun to change when the girls were home last year. His daughters' tragedies had humbled him, and his own brush with death made him thankful for every new day.

That's another thing about us mere mortals, Laura mused. Sadness and regret can take one of two routes—either embittering the sufferer, or making him more gentle, more compassionate and considerate. Trouble had mellowed Sam Dalton. The self-righteousness and stubbornness that had been his only real flaws had given way to a new tolerance. He rejoiced with Laura when Barbara and Charles were married. In years past he'd have been the disapproving patriarch, frowning on Charles's divorce, perhaps even thinking of his youngest child as a "home wrecker." Not now. He was happy for her happiness, as though he savored every piece of good fortune even when it happened to others.

They didn't often speak of Frances, but when they did, Laura knew he was as troubled about her as her mother was, though, manlike, he could not grasp the roots of her restlessness. Only another woman could understand how much Fran hated growing old, losing her beauty and her desirability. She'll never be truly serene, Laura thought regretfully. She's the eternally lost soul, always seeking something or someone, in quest of the magic answer. Fran didn't know what she wanted. Not really. So it sadly followed that she'd not recognize happiness if she ever found it. She'd be an angry, hostile old lady. Lucky she has enough money that people will put up with her when she reaches that stage. Only the rich can afford to be impossible. Her unusually cynical analysis made Laura smile. I'm glad I won't be around when Frances reaches that stage. My pity might show. And pity is one thing Frances can't abide. She'd be outraged.

On Sam's side of the big old bed, Karat stirred and stretched. She saw the golden dog rise and nuzzle his master's hand. These days it was Karat who acted as Sam's alarm clock. Since the heart attack, Karat had attached himself firmly to Sam, as though he would protect him from whatever happened that January night when all "his humans" had rushed frantically from the house, leaving Karat to whine at the window, puzzled by the unusual desertion. They'd had to restrain him from leaping on Sam and covering him with ksses when he finally came home from the hospital. And since that day, Karat had been the man's constant companion. It was the only thing that dampened Sam's enthusiasm about going away for Christmas: leaving Karat. But Buzz Paige had kindly volunteered to look after him while they were gone.

The thought of Buzz made Laura wonder how Frances would take the news of his impending marriage. No one would ever know. Fran had her pride. She'd been vulnerable during her visit last October, more honest about her emotions than her mother had ever known her to be. But she was not a woman who easily exposed her hurt or, probably, forgave the one who hurt her.

Janice, Allie's child, was different. Laura was proud of her, knowing what a sacrifice it must have been for her to have Spencer Winters at her wedding. But she'd done it to please Laura. Bless that child, her grandmother thought. I can't wait to see her and meet her husband. Just as I can't wait to see John's wife and the baby who's been named for Alice. I want to hold her and tell her to grow up sweet and pretty and kind, like the grandmother she never knew. But she must be stronger. Not frightened of life. Not full of guilt. Not sad and lost as Allie was.

Sam mumbled and reached out to stroke Karat's shining head. He turned over and opened one eye.

"You been awake long?"

"A few minutes," Laura said. "I've just been lying here thinking."

"'Bout what?"

"Oh, I don't know. A little of everything. The children. The grandchildren. Even the great-grandchild we're going to meet."

"Oh." Sam sounded disappointed. "I thought you'd be thinking about us."

She pretended innocence. "Us? Any special reason?"

"Don't try to fool me. You know as well as I do that it's our fifty-first anniversary."

She went on with the game. "Why, so it is! Imagine my forgetting!"

"You're a fraud, Laura Dalton. Happy anniversary, dear." Sam leaned over and kissed her. "Happy gold-plus-one. Thanks for putting up with me all these years."

She patted his stubby cheek. "I hope we have another twenty-four. I'm already planning our diamond jubilee."

Sam sat up and scratched his head, stood, stretched and hitched up his pajamas. Laura smiled, remembering a year ago when she'd asked him what habits of hers got on his nerves. He'd been puzzled then. He'd be puzzled today. Men. They were basically uncomplex. And indispensable.

He addressed himself to Karat. "She's really crazy, you know, boy. Wants to be married for seventy-five years! Good Lord!"

Sam winked at her on his way out of the room.

Laura relaxed, content. Things would never be the same. Not after Allie. Not even after Dorothy Paige. She mourned for both those unhappy women. She'd never forget the past year, but a new one had begun. There'd be no party for this anniversary. The house would be quiet, peaceful. Maybe she and Sam would go out for dinner, but the day would be routine, unremarkable, the way they really liked it. You could love your children with all your heart, rejoice for them, grieve for them, try to help. But in the end, with luck, you were alone with the man you'd chosen to live with. And in the end, there was something to be said for the undemanding life that was a compensation for growing old. You had your regrets and disappointments, even a kind of haunting depression, knowing that any day it could all end. But mostly you gave thanks for what you had in the past and what you hoped for in the future, for health and serenity for yourself and the ones you loved. Life was more kind than cruel.

At least for Mrs. Samuel Dalton of Denver.

Always Is Not Forever

Introduction

EVERYTHING AROUND HER whispered money and taste. Whispered, because the homes of the old-established rich are carefully planned to look just a shade this side of shabby; quietly expensive as though their owners were far too secure to shout their status. Obvious is vulgar; understated is elegant. Be it furniture or feelings. It's as simple as that.

Susan settled herself more comfortably on the slightly frayed Louis XV chaise and plumped the little Porthault pillows in the small of her aching back. She drew a light, hand-woven throw over her legs to protect them from the coolness of the air-conditioned cocoon in which she rested like some delicate, pampered, embryonic butterfly.

The idea of herself as a delicate butterfly made her smile. ''Iron butterfly'' would be more like it. All the battering blows, the storms of anger and cold winds of despair would have crushed a creature whose wings were gossamer. Hers were not. They'd carried her to heights of joy and treetops of hope. And into valleys of desperation. But they did not fail, even when they faltered.

The merciless July sun scorched the street eighteen stories below, and the huffing, puffing New York traffic set up a symphony of irritable horn honking as screeching brakes were slammed on amid the angry curses of jacketless men in wilting shirts. But she heard and felt none of it. She was cut off from the heat and noise and ugliness of the world outside. She sat alone, rereading what she had written.

My darling, this is a love letter to you.

You will never read it, and perhaps that is just as well. I would not add to the pain you suffered or the lonely moments you endured, locked in the solitude of your personal, hidden hell.

Yet, selfishly, I would wish these words could reach you. Then you would know what you meant to me. What you mean to me still. Today, tomorrow and beyond. I think you do know. For what is transcribed on the heart transcends the petty human limitations of time and space. Apart we are together, you and I. Two who are one. Eternally welded by the links of the love we shared.

I hope you can remember those brief, shining hours. Gratitude is such a tiny word for a life that included your presence. But I am grateful to you. I mingled my tears with yours, echoed your laughter, joined in the delight you felt at your hard-won triumphs. I thrilled to your strength and cursed God for your burdens, wishing I could take them from you, seeking the courage to share and the wisdom to understand Why. Sometimes I succeeded, seeing the bright glimmer of solution in the blackness of the puzzle. Often I was more lost than you, failing you when you needed me most.

But even as I damned the Creator who made you as you were, I adored Him for the very fact of your being. My rage was as nothing compared to the thankfulness for His bringing you into life. My life.

What joy we found in that life! What happiness was allowed two people so alike and so different. Different. That was the word people used to describe you. But you were not different. You were so like the others, yet uniquely yourself. In the bad times you were stubborn and sulky, rebellious and angry, filled with frustration. But in the golden days you were tender and trusting, full of love and warmth and charm. That was the real you: neither angel nor devil, but with irresistible overtones of both.

You were not perfect, my darling. Not even in my enchanted eyes. And yet it seems, in retrospect, the very imperfections that threatened to break my heart were the ones that brought us closer together . . . to share the cruel hurts and savor the dreams that were always just beyond our reach.

The dreams were never to be. Such beautiful dreams. Even as I hoped for their fulfillment, I knew they were no more than the wishful thinking of this grown-up child. But I still believe in dreams, dearest. I've seen them come true for others who love as we loved, and have blind, abiding faith in each other as we did . . .

She stopped reading and stared sightlessly across the room, seeing none of the treasures in it. She saw, instead, the young woman who'd been herself in another time. A determined young woman, wrapped in the ignorant assurance of youth. How supremely confident of the future she'd been. How certain of her competence. No mountain of misunderstanding defied her. No hill of hatred was too tall to level. How could she know always is not forever?

And yet what a vulnerable thing she'd been. So easily wounded for all her façade of self-sufficiency and poise. I was such an incurable romantic, Susan thought. Emotion seemed more valid than experience, for I had so much of the former and so little of the latter. I thought I could deny the truths that offended me, rebel against an older, wiser world that waited, perhaps with regret, to bring me to my knees.

If arrogance is the heady wine of youth, then humility must be its eternal hangover.

I've drunk the wine and found it bitter. Yet I welcome this lifetime of mornings-after.

For they are strangely sweet on the tongue.

Chapter 1

LATER, WHEN SHE tried to make sense of everything, Susan realized that the first twenty-two years of her life in no way prepared her for those that were to follow. They had been uncomplicated, eternally trouble-free, naïvely happy in an almost mindless and pleasantly anonymous way.

She grew up, an only child, in a sprawling old house in suburban Bronxville, New York, a gentle Westchester community fifteen miles and twenty-eight minutes on the commuter train from Manhattan. Her parents, Wilson and Beatrice Langdon, were second-generation products of this moderately affluent area, childhood sweethearts who'd married in 1939 and produced the delicate blond, brown-eyed daughter a year later. Wilson had enlisted in the Air Force in World War II, though as a married man with a child he might have been exempt, and Susan carried dim memories of a father in uniform returning hale and handsome to the big house on Sunset Avenue. She had no traumatic recollection of the war or of Beatrice's anguish all through that terrible time. Her father and mother, it seemed to her, had always been there, loving her and each other, fitting gracefully into the Edwardian atmosphere of the village whose stable population was only about six thousand.

It had been the best of worlds. Near enough to New York to let a little girl enjoy the ease and freedom of "country living," with playmates and tree-houses and neighborhood "secret societies." Later there was golf at the Siwanoy Country Club and tennis at the Bronxville Field Club. She dated local boys and brothers of her classmates at Sarah Lawrence College, joined the Junior League, made a modest debut as befitted the daughter of a vice-president of the Chase Manhattan Bank, and, in 1962, at the age of twenty-two, got a job on *Vogue* as assistant to the Features Editor. ("Probably," she would say later, "on the strength of the fact that I come from the same town in which Kate Douglas Wiggin wrote *Rebecca of Sunnybrook Farm*. And Dorothy Thompson practically *commuted* to Berlin from Bronxville in the '30s!")

In any case, she adored her boss, Kate Fenton, loved the fashion magazine's zany atmosphere, made friends with other young women very much like herself who could afford to work for the glamour of the job rather than the modest salary. Her father subsidized her earnings when, after a year, she guardedly suggested she'd like to share an apartment in Manhattan with one of the other assistant editors. The Langdons hated to have her leave home, but they were realistic about it. Young women like Susan were entitled to freedom. Besides, they had faith in their daughter. She was a cheeful, levelheaded, knowledgeable young person, unlike so many young people in the '60s. They had (thank God) no worries about drugs or radical movements or other rebellious tendencies. She'd left their house, but the ties of affection and respect were strong, the contact continuous and their daughter's obvious delight with her new world was a constant source of pleasure for Wil and Bea Langdon.

But there were troublesome things about her independence that Susan kept from her parents. Liberal and understanding as they were, the "generation gap" existed. She did not want them to know that she was no longer a virgin, though she was not silly enough to believe that they did not suspect. Her "affairs" since she'd left home had not been casual. She was not a promiscuous girl. In many ways, she was surprisingly innocent and stubbornly idealistic, always believing herself in love, never accepting the popular attitude that sex was only an exciting temporary adventure. She could not separate the physical from the emotional, could not take love-making as a quick, insignificant encounter. She had slept with only two young men and secretly expected, in each case, that the relationship would be long-term and "meaningful." When it was not, she was heavyhearted and angry with herself for her old-fashioned outlook and her inability to handle sex in the matter-of-fact fashion of the 1960s. Almost apologetically, she discussed this "weakness" with her roommate and best friend, Evelyn Maxwell, a young woman of her own age and approximate background who also worked at *Vogue*. Evie was less sentimental, more experienced, yet gentle and understanding.

"Look, Sue, you've got to understand how *men* feel these days. We've declared our independence, financially and socially. They expect we've also taken the male point of view about our physical needs. This isn't your mother's day when sex, for girls like us, was an undeclared proposal of marriage. You meet a fellow, you dig each other and eventually you end up in bed, enjoying it. For a night or several nights or a few months. But it docsn't mean you're going to be with him for a lifetime, or that he loves you. Or that you should talk yourself into believing *you* love *him*."

Evie was right, of course, Susan told herself. She remembered Professor Higgins' song in *My Fair Lady* . . . something about "Why can't a woman be more like a man?" Today a woman could be. She had to be. It was outmoded, stupid to believe that intimacy between people need be more than a healthy, therapeutic release. Sex was more honest, more satisfying than the fumbling, frustrating "heavy necking" of her high school and college days. She was no longer a skittish teen-ager or a chaste debutante. She was a woman, with a woman's needs. Where was her perspective, her humor? Why did she make such a big deal of "giving herself"? Even the expression was wrong. Victorian women "gave themselves." A hundred years later their great-granddaughters took as much as they gave—and accepted the pleasure for what it was, without guilt or foolish hopes.

But she never really believed what she finally was logically obliged to accept: that passionate words and acts were momentary things. She didn't believe it then or for the rest of her life. The sense that her body and the sharing of it involved dignity and self-esteem stayed with her always. And those who knew her best knew Susan would never truly think otherwise.

Kate Fenton was one of those. Her assistant did not discuss these feelings with her superior at the magazine, but the Features Editor had developed an unusually personal attachment to and understanding of the young woman who'd been "handed to her" by the personnel department. Susan was unlike the long line of empty-headed, indifferent creatures who'd preceded her in the job. For one thing, she took it seriously and wanted to learn. She had perception and imagination, along with a willingness to work hard and an intuitive awareness of what interested the readers of *Vogue*. These were the same traits on which Kate prided herself. She's me as I was twenty-odd years ago, Kate often thought. But she won't end up like me, married to her job, though she has enormous potential. She's not one of those bored little idiots who drift through the halls of this magazine, marking time between their coming-out parties and their rigidly prescribed marriages to "suitable" young men. Susan could be a good editor. But, Kate thought cynically, she'll probably throw it all away for some young broker or banker who'll set her up in a house in Scarsdale and limit her mental capabilities to planning dinner parties for his clients. Oh yes, she'll marry. But I hope it's to someone who appreciates her. Not one of those selfish young studs I hear her talking to on the phone. Not one of those arrogant, overbearing males with whom she's been so enamored in the past two years, and who obviously let her down.

There was no need for Susan to tell Kate how she felt about her "romances." Kate knew. She'd been the same when she was in her twenties—open, giving, believing the "sweet talk' that always came to nothing. Realization had come early to Kate. She liked men. She simply didn't want to marry, and she refused the chances she had. For twenty-five years the magazine had been her mate, demanding all the passion and dedication of which she was capable. She was not dissatisfied with the alliance. She'd come a long way from "little Mary-Kate Fenton" of Selma, Alabama. She'd dropped the Southern accent aong with the first half of her name, had become a power in social and artistic circles, on a first-name basis with the great of the theatre, the concert halls, the "salons" of New York and Paris and Washington, D.C. She was known for her sophistication and her brittle wit and widely quoted among awed junior members of the staff, most of whom were terrified of her. Susan was not. That was another thing Kate liked about the girl. She was respectful but not fawningly deferential. For the first time in many years, Kate felt she was working with someone who genuinely admired her as a person rather than an "institution." She half-wished Susan would opt for a lifelong career, even while she doubted it. In any case, she was not the type to hang around as an assistant for twenty years until Kate retired and bequeathed her the job. If Susan kept on working, it would, sooner or later, be somewhere else. She was too bright not to want a number-one spot of her own, something she couldn't have at *Vogue* as long as Kate Fenton was alive. And Kate Fenton planned to stay alive for a long, long time. She came from a long line of iron-willed Southern women who lived forever, dominating their families while appearing helplessly "female," dictating to servants while oozing benevolence, doing "good works" to satisfy their vanities rather than giving selflessly of themselves. Kate hated her "genteel" background. "I never go south of the Mason-Dixon Line if I can help it," she often said. "For that matter, anything below Fiftieth Street gives me shudders."

Once, when they were lunching together, Susan shyly asked Kate why she'd never married.

"I'm sure you could have. You're so attractive and witty and bright. I hope I'm not stepping out of line, Kate, but didn't you ever want to?"

"Yes, I wanted to. When I was your age and for a few years more I positively wallowed in romantic fantasies—none of which came true. And then one morning I woke up and said, 'Kate,. old girl, unrequited love is a bore. You're never going to find that dream man, so forget it.' And I have forgotten it. Love and marriage, I mean. I've had my moments over the years. I still have them and I hope I will until I'm eighty-five and buying the services of some totally insincere but hungry young man fifty years my junior." Kate laughed. "That sounds as tough as I'm popularly supposed to be, doesn't it? But it's true, Susan. At least partly. The other part is that I can't bear making a fool of myself. I detest failure in any form, particularly my own. And I'm too selfish not to fail a husband . . . or I'd pick one who couldn't fulfill all those old Galahad dreams I still carry around. No, marriage isn't for me. I'm not bright enough to make it work." She speared a shrimp savagely, and without looking up from her salad, asked, "Are *you*?"

"I don't know. So far, it doesn't seem that way."

"Unrequited love," Kate repeated. "To you it's still tears and self-reproach. It takes a while to realize it's dreary. Oh hell, cheer up, kiddo! You may yet find that rare and exotic species who knows how to give as well as take. I'm rooting for you, you know. I don't recommend my way of life for anybody else. I hope you find the man you want, even if it means losing the best damned assistant I ever had."

Susan smiled. "You'll never lose me. Even if I find that 'rare and exotic creature' you'll be one of the best friends I ever had—or probably ever will have. I'll always be in your life, Kate. And I hope you'll always be in mine."

"You can lay odds on it." The older woman seemed suddenly embarrassed. "Listen, I want to charge this lunch on the expense account, so let's talk business to make it legitimate. In the editorial meeting this morning, we decided to do a feature on Richard Antonini. I think you should handle it."

"Antonini? The young one? The concert pianist? I heard him last year at Carnegie Hall. He's sensational!"

Kate arched an eyebrow. "So I'm led to believe. And not only at the keyboard. In the dear old South we used to call his kind 'lady-killers.' Well, why not? He's twenty-eight, handsome and a genius. A veritable young lion, from a long pride of lions. God! Papa Giovanni must be nearing seventy and still conducting major symphonies and minor infidelities. Brother Sergio, an upcoming conductor, is following Daddy's footsteps—in *every* way. But the word is that Richard's other brother, Walter, the composer, prefers the company of young men to that of his wife and children. Quite a family."

"Isn't there a sister, too?"

"Yes. Grace or Geraldine. Something like that. No. Gloria, that's her name. She's the ugly, untalented duckling. A big horsy dame who bosses everybody around, including her husband."

"Richard Antonini isn't married, is he?"

"No. He's the only chick Mama Maria has left, and from what I hear she damn well means to hold onto him. I've met the powerful Signora a few times. A combination of Lucretia Borgia and Hitler. Smooth and sinister. Sometimes known as 'the velvet knife.' Maria really runs the show. Manages the maestro's career. Dictates to the kids. And *their* kids. Richard's her baby *and* her favorite. Would you believe at twenty-eight he still lives with his parents in a big house on East Seventieth Street? That's where you'll interview him, by the way. Call him when you get back to the office. I have the unlisted number. Set up a date. We'll get Irving Penn to take the photograph later.''

"I'd better bone up on classical music. It's never been one of my better subjects.''

"I wouldn't worry, if I were you. Richard's a publicity hound. He'll feed you the answers without the questions. Then he'll probably make a pass at you.''

Susan laughed. "You must be kidding! Make a pass at *me* when all the rich, beautiful women in the world are throwing themselves at him? What would he want of a poor girl-reporter like me?''

"Now *that*,'' Kate said, "is one of the silliest questions I've ever heard you ask.''

Chapter 2

FROM THE OUTSIDE, the Antoninis' town house was typical of the relatively few remaining private residences of the New York rich. As Susan stepped out of the taxi, she took in the kitchen windows fronting the street level, the authoritative sign announcing the watchful private eye of Holmes Protection, the brilliantly shined brass and the forbidding black-lacquered door with multiple locks.

It was, she thought, like a fortress. Of course it had to be. Inside were precious people and, undoubtedly, precious possessions, both of which had to be guarded from the curious eyes of the public and the terrifying invasion of burglars. What was it like to be rich and famous? Fun, she supposed. But also laden with responsibilities, restrictive and probably quite dull at times.

She rang the bell, saw an eye through the tiny peephole before she heard the unbolting of locks and bolts. A pleasant young Chinese man finally opened all but one safety chain and said politely, "Yes, madam?''

"I'm Susan Langdon of *Vogue*. I have an appointment with Mr. Richard Antonini.''

The houseman nodded and opened the door.

"Come in, please. This way.''

She stepped into a long, mirrored foyer with a black and white marble floor. At its end, through an open door, she could see a huge dining room, heavy with dark, Italian-looking furniture and dominated by an enormous crystal chandelier. To her right was a winding staircase, richly carpeted, and beside it a small private elevator. Quite close by she could hear the sound of a piano.

"Mr. Richard is in drawing room on second floor. You go right up. You wish to take stairs or you prefer elevator?''

"I'll walk,'' Susan said.

Her guide led the way. With a reporter's instinct for detail, Susan noted the niches in the stairway wall, each with an impressive bronze bust of a music immortal—Chopin, Liszt, Beethoven, Brahms. A benevolent procession of the past pointing the way to the genius of the present. The phrase had a nice ring. She must remember it when she wrote her piece.

The music was louder now, crashing, thundering. At the top of the stairs, the houseman pointed to the closed double doors at the right.

"Mr. Richard working, but he left word he be interrupted." The man raised his hand to knock, but Susan stopped him.

"May I just stand here a moment to listen?"

"Certainly, madam." The impassive Oriental face broke into a small smile. I must look as awed as I feel, Susan thought. But it's magnificent. How many people are privileged to hear Richard Antonini outside the concert hall? She returned the smile. "You needn't wait, unless you're supposed to. I'll announce myself."

When the servant bowed and left, she stood for a full five minutes listening to the music. She had no idea what it was. Something obscure and complicated and thrillingly powerful. Even with her limited knowledge, Susan was sure it was a tour de force, perhaps a seldom-performed selection that the artist would present at his next concert. There was, finally, a pause and Susan tapped lightly at the door, heard footsteps approaching and then was face to face with the most attractive man she'd ever seen.

"Miss Langdon? Come in. Did Chang abandon you?"

"At my request. He brought me up but I wanted to stand and listen for a moment. Until now, I've only heard you from a distance. It was a treat to be this close."

He grinned boyishly. "What did you think?"

"I blush to say that I haven't the faintest idea what it was, but it was breathtaking."

"It was Schumann's Third Piano Sonata, the one he called 'Concerto Without Orchestra.' And don't feel embarrassed about not recognizing it. Few people do—including many professional pianists. I'm going to try it in my next concert. Somehow, people expect me to do unexpected, the 'undiscovered masterpieces' as well as the good old standbys. I do my best to please. But enough of that! I'm keeping you standing in the doorway like an Avon lady! Come in. Have a seat. Would you like a drink?"

"No, thank you. It's a bit early in the day."

"Tea, then? Coffee? Something soft?"

"Not a thing, thanks. I know you're busy. I don't want to take up too much of your time."

Richard gave the crooked little smile she was to come to know so well. "I have plenty of time. In fact, I'm delighted to have company. Gives me an excuse to relax and talk about myself . . . two of my favorite pastimes."

He was utterly disarming. Susan didn't know quite what she'd expected. Some conceited, pompous young man, she supposed, puffed up with his own importance, perhaps overtly condescending about these "tiresome, necessary interviews." She could see now why women fell in love with him. It was not simply his looks or his fame or even the aphrodisiac of greatness that drew them to him. He had warmth, a shade of humility and, thank the Lord, a nice, light touch of humor. She looked around her, wondering how to begin.

"What a beautiful room! Everything's a treasure!"

He followed her gaze. "My parents' doing. They're a good combination. Mother has taste and Father has money." He laughed. "Actually, they were very smart and very lucky. They were buying Picassos and picking up Renoirs before most collectors caught on. In the early days they invested in signed furniture and good art. Now the insurance costs more than they paid for the stuff forty or fifty years ago. Sometimes the maestro threatens to sell it all, including this mausoleum, but of course he won't. Mother wouldn't let him. And he doesn't really want to."

"But who *would* want to? Most people would give their souls to have a house like this! It would be like living in a museum!"

"If that's your ambition I suppose you could rent a vacant wing at the Metropolitan." He sounded amused and Susan realized she was gushing. She was angry with herself for being so obviously impressed; angry with Richard for the easy confidence that took all this for granted and made light of it. He seemed to sense her resentment.

"Don't misunderstand me, please, Miss Langdon. I respect beauty in all forms. I appreciate everything in this room, but most of all I love that big, fat, black lady by the window." He pointed to the grand piano. "To me, she's more interesting than paintings, more subtle than furnishings, more alluring than women with much better legs." The deep, blue-violet eyes turned suddenly serious. "Have you any idea what a miracle a fine piano is? It takes twelve months to make a great one. Longer than it would take you to make a baby, and, if you'll forgive me, the end product is infinitely more beautiful upon delivery." He warmed to his subject. "I think of my piano as a desirable woman—precisely formed, patiently molded, capable of soothing or exciting, responsive only when properly handled and unbearable when mistreated. She has feminine reactions—instantaneous and strong. She hurls and retrieves eighty-eight hammers at more than two hundred and twenty strings in fractions of a second. She has a wrest plank that can hold up under thirty-five thousand pounds of tension, yet she's so delicate that her soundboard is only eight millimeters thick in the middle and five at the edges. To me, she's the ultimate sex object, and controlling her is as exhilarating as making love." He laughed. "Sometimes more exhilarating. But I'm sure the readers of *Vogue* aren't interested in all that technical jargon about pianos."

Susan was scribbling furiously. "On the contrary. It's revealing. Your infatuation with the instrument and your seeing it in sexual terms." She hesitated. "I mean, particularly since everyone says . . ." Her voice trailed off.

"That I'm Don Juan and Frank Sinatra rolled into one? I assure you if half the things that are whispered about me were true, I'd never have time to perform at the piano. I'd be too tired to get out of bed. Not that I don't like women. I do. Very much. Especially bright and pretty ones."

Kate's half-serious words came back to her. When she answered, she sounded very cold, very professional.

"I'm sure you do, Mr. Antonini, but we leave those things to the fan magazines, We're not interested in your personal life . . . at least not the romantic side of it."

"What, then? Shall we have a heavy discussion about music? A Freudian one about my childhood? A boring one about my family?'' He was teasing her. "Name your weapons. I'm all yours.''

Damn the man. He was so sure of himself and yet she couldn't dislike him. She struggled for poise.

"Let's talk about Richard Antonini the person. Not the silly fan magazine stuff, like what you eat for breakfast or what you—wear to bed. Tell me. Are you at all a political creature? How do you feel about Viet Nam? Let's discuss the world in 1964 from a young man's point of view.''

It was his turn to sound cold. "What are you really asking me, Miss Langdon? Why, at twenty-eight, I'm not in the Army? You'll be disappointed by the answer. It wasn't money or influence that's kept me out. Not even a conscientious objection. Nothing more glamorous than a bad back that goes out every now and then and drives me up the wall and into a most repulsive brace. As for politics, I find them unutterably boring. Jack Kennedy was a nice fellow and I'm sorry he's dead. But all we had in common were some mutual friends and trouble with our spines.''

It was a not-too-subtle rebuff. Susan wanted to ask him what he thought about the morality of the young, the emerging role of women, subjects she'd planned to get into when she wrote this damned profile. But she was not going to get anywhere on that track. She went to safer ground, consulting the list of questions she'd prepared. "Let's talk about the very young you, about how you got into music, and what your day-to-day life is like.''

"Good diversionary tactic. Okay. I was born into a musical family. Father, brothers, all top-flight, as I'm sure you know. Climbed onto the piano stool at five and have spent at least five or six hours in the same spot every day since. I still take lessons—don't look so surprised, most pianists do—from a wonderful, miraculous, terrible ogre of a genius-lady on Central Park West. She's the Ilsa Koch of the keyboard and I adore her. When I'm not being a pupil, I'm practicing, either here or in the basement of Steinway Hall. And when I'm not doing that, I'm on the road more than half the year. Life isn't all Carnegie Hall for me. Not yet. It's also tank-towns and cold pizzas—as well as Los Angeles and Boston and Houston and the lush life. And when I'm not traveling and concertizing, I'm giving interviews like this. Or recording. Or accepting paralytically dull invitations to the homes of rich and influential people who can 'further my career.' Or, once in a blessed while, having dinner with a gorgeous lady and sometimes,'' Richard said wickedly, "scoring in the more vulgar sense of the word.''

In spite of her determination to be impersonal, Susan found herself smiling as she wrote.

"You're very close to your family, aren't you?''

"Very. As you see, I still live at home, which is not a case of arrested development but a matter of convenience since I'm in New York so little. I also go upstate to Pound Ridge where we have a big old place on which the brothers and sister and in-laws and offspring converge regularly. I'm an uncle six times and my alarmingly fertile sister is about to make it seven.''

"But you've never married? Why not?''

"Have you?''

"No."

"Why not?"

"Because I've never found anyone who loved me the way I loved him." Susan's frankness surprised her.

"Then you don't have to ask me that question, do you?" Richard said. "You can just echo your own answer." He reached out and took her hand. The fingers were long, slim, the grasp warm and firm. "Susan. May I say 'Susan?' This has become a sparring match, hasn't it? Practically everything we've talked about you could find in a publicity release my press agent could send you. Do you realize we're shy with each other? Isn't that extraordinary?"

"I'm not shy," she lied, defensively. "You're not an easy man to interview, Mr. Antonini, for all your apparent frankness."

"Why not try 'Richard'?"

"All right, Richard. You make it difficult. I don't quite know why, but you do."

"I'm sorry. It's not intentional. I want a good story. So do you. Ask me anything you like. I swear I'll answer truthfully."

Susan thought. "Let's go back to the fact that you're not married. Not *my* answer. *Yours*."

"I probably will marry one day. My parents are happily married. There's a good example for me. Maybe too good. Make of it what you will, for I'm sure it means something, but I have yet to meet a woman with the extraordinary qualities of my mother. I suppose you'd say she's the 'ultimate piano.' How's that for frankness?"

"Not bad." Susan felt in control now, so much in command that she was emboldened to ask another question on her list. "Your extraordinary dedication to music. Is it real or a defense? Family orientation surely has been very important in your life. Competition in a house full of geniuses must be enormous. A father who's a legend. Super-achieving older brothers with more years of fame. Are you trying to prove something to yourself or them? The Antoninis are a dynasty, with a strong matriarchal influence. Aren't you really a self-contained empire like the Roosevelts or the Kennedys?" She stopped, suddenly nervous about such intimate, probing questions. He'd probably order her out of the house. But instead he simply looked thoughtful.

"My dedication to my work is real," he said slowly. "Competitive? Probably, but in a healthy, extroverted way. A dynasty? We've been made to seem so in the press, but I don't think we're that different from many families. Close-knit. Protective of our own. Outside of our work we live quite ordinary lives, like any big tribe. You don't believe that, do you, Susan?"

"No," she said softly, " I'm not sure I do." She glanced at the French clock on the mantel and was amazed to see that an hour had passed. She had enough meat for her story and there was plenty of background. She stood up, put her notebook in her purse and extended her hand. "Thank you for your time. I'll try to do a good interview. For both of us."

"I'm sure you will. I'll look forward to it."

He took her to the door and kissed her hand formally. "You're a charming girl, Susan. I hope we'll meet again."

"I'll come to your next New York concert if I can get tickets."

"I'll send you a pair."

"Oh no! I didn't mean it that way. I wasn't hinting!"

Richard smiled. "I know you weren't. You wouldn't know how to be conniving. Perhaps, if I may say so for your own sake, you'd do well to learn."

She slept badly that night. It was not only because she felt she'd done a bad job on the interview. She thought she was well prepared, but she'd handled it so awkwardly that Richard had been compelled to save it for her. That was part of it. It was unlike her to be so unprofessional and she was annoyed. But another part of her restlessness was the ridiculous instant attraction she felt for the man himself. She told herself she was being stupid. She'd never see or hear from him again. Why should she? She was no more to him than a hundred other star-struck reporters, a hundred thousand worshipful followers. And yet she fantasized their falling in love, even marrying and having wonderful children. She saw herself the devoted, envied wife of a young genius, becoming part of the fabulous Antonini clan, catering, gladly, to her husband's needs, traveling with him, being with him and their family in some elegant town house of their own. I must be losing my mind, Susan thought in the dark hours. It's a schoolgirl crush on a movie star—infantile and impossible. And yet she couldn't forget the way he'd looked at her, taken her hand. And the strange remark about their being shy with each other. Was he trying to tell her that he also felt their meeting was important? He'd said he'd like to see her again. And what did all that add up to, for God's sake? Nothing. Absolute zero. Zilch. Yet no man had ever had such an impact on her. She remembered everything about him. The way he moved and smiled, the way his voice sounded when he spoke passionately of his music, loyally of his family, somewhat wistfully of his life. She tried to turn her thoughts away from Richard Antonini the desirable man and focus on what she'd write about him. It had been an interview with odd, indefinable overtones. And it would be difficult to translate into a good, meaty feature.

It was. Susan struggled at her typewriter for three hours the next morning, hating the way the piece kept coming out. Half a dozen times she ripped the paper out of the machine and wadded it into a ball which she threw angrily into the wastepaper basket. She felt Kate watching her, without comment but aware that this was not her assistant's usual easy, fluent style.

At one o'clock, Susan shoved her chair back from the desk and announced she was going to lunch.

"I take it the Antonini assignment is a bitch," Kate said calmly. "What's the problem?"

"I don't know. I can't get the essence of him. When we talked it seemed interesting, even 'intellectual' in spots. But when I try to write it, it keeps coming out like a cross between a fan letter and a Steinway piano brochure. It's terrible. Unprintable. Damn it, Kate, I really want to do a good 'think piece' on him. He's important and exciting and I keep making him sound like a plastic toy!"

"Why shouldn't you? That's essentially what he is. Gifted, yes. Perhaps even great. But still a creation of our times. I'm sure Richard is like all the Antoninis. None of them is real flesh and blood. They're romantic, improbable sex objects.

The press and the public hero-worship glamorous people with talent. We expect them to be above us. It's our society's subconscious wish for royalty. With no real kings and queens and princes, we try to turn our matinee idols into regal beings. We long to endow them with superhuman gifts—such as awesome intelligence and infinite wisdom. And all they have, outside of their God-given talent, is a well-cultivated flair for self-promotion. Hell, I told that bunch in the editorial meeting that young Richard wasn't serious feature material! He should be reviewed by our music critic or left to the society columns. I'm not surprised Prince Charming had nothing meaningful to say. I doubt that he ever thinks about anything but himself, his music and his women, in that order.''

Susan felt unreasonably annoyed. ''Then why did you agree to do the feature?''

''Dear girl, I am not THE editor. I am only AN editor. Contrary to what they say in the ladies' room, I do not win all my battles.''

''I still think there's something important here,'' Susan said stubbornly, ''He's a thinking, complicated artist with a lot to say. It's just that I don't know how to write it.''

''Take a suggestion? Stop trying to make Richard Antonini sound like Adlai Stevenson by Albert Schweitzer out of Marianne Moore. Tell it like it is. He's the gifted, hard-working, moderately intelligent, infinitely charming youngest son of a famous family. Make him human, Susan. Make every woman want to mother him. Play up his 'loneliness' and his little boy appeal. Give him the other-worldliness that's already his image . . . the dreamy, sensual bachelor, the idealistic child-man, the dedicated artist. Goop it up with culture and charisma. He has enough of both, and that's what people want to believe in. It's an unbeatable combination . . . the kind dreams are made of. And it'll make a piece that will be the most tear-stained page in the October issue.''

''I can't be phony about him.''

''Who's asking you? On the contrary, I'm advising you to tell the truth—not gloss him over with the veneer of cerebral greatness which is what I suspect you're struggling to do.'' Kate looked at her sharply, suddenly aware. ''You were really taken with Antonini, weren't you? Susan dear, you're only twenty-four but I thought you were much too worldly to be snowed by that practiced professional charm. Was I right? Did he make a pass at you? Is that what this is all about?''

''Good Lord, no! He was a perfect gentleman.''

''And you wish he hadn't been.''

''Yes. No. I'm not sure. Anyway, what does it matter? Even if he noticed me, it would only be more of the same. I'd make a fool of myself as usual. Especially with a man like that.'' She felt a need to unburden herself. ''Do you know, Kate, that I thought about him all last night? I even imagined what it would be like if we fell in love. Now *that* is crazy, even for me! I spend one hour with a charmer and I'm daydreaming myself into a lifetime romance! Next thing you know I'll be putting his picture up on my bulletin board—the way the secretaries all have photographs of Paul Newman!'' She managed to laugh. ''Okay. I feel better. I think I can get Antonini out of my head and onto paper after lunch. Join me? I might go wild and have a Bloody Mary to drown my sorrows.''

"You're on," Kate said. "I'll even pay."

They came back at three o'clock, a little high and a great deal more relaxed. They glanced at the messages their shared secretary had left on their desks. The second one Susan picked up made her catch her breath. Wordlessly, she handed it to Kate. It was marked 2:25. Kate read it aloud.

"'Mr. Richard Antonini called. Would like you to dine with him this evening at La Caravelle. Please call him at home.' "

"I don't believe it," Susan said. "It must be a joke."

"Played by whom? It's not my kind of thing. Besides, I was with you, remember?"

Susan didn't answer.

"You're going, of course."

"If I were smart, I wouldn't. I'd stop this whole thing right now, before it starts."

"So?"

Susan smiled. "I never was too bright."

Chapter 3

HE'D BEEN PLEASED but not surprised when Susan returned his call and accepted the dinner invitation.

"Lovely," Richard said. "I'm glad you're free. Give me your address and I'll pick you up. About eight?"

She gave him the number on Fifty-second Street and then added, "Just have the doorman ring up and I'll come right down."

Afterward, she wondered why she'd done that. She wasn't ashamed of the apartment. It was no Antonini mansion, but it was attractively furnished and suitable for two young working women. And it wasn't that she didn't want him to meet Evie, who was equally presentable and the last girl in the world who'd try to steal a roommate's date. I suppose I want to feel as though I'm stepping out into a whole new world, Susan thought. Like Cinderella taking the coach to the ball. I want to drift down and find Richard waiting for me. She hoped he'd be in a chauffeured limousine. She always said that owning one was her ultimate wish. Not sables or yachts or forty-karat diamonds, but her own private car and driver. She used to kid about it with her mother. "When I become rich and famous that will be my first important acquisition. Think of the advantages. You never have to own a winter coat, right? And I know it would add ten years to my life if I didn't have to worry about catching cabs, running from one corner to another like some crazed creature!"

Bea Langdon had smiled. "It's not a bad ambition, but you'll need a better-paying job or a rich husband to realize it."

Remembering, Susan told herself that she had gotten neither and was unlikely to. The few times she'd gone to business dinner-dances as the guest of rich manufacturers, she'd reveled in the luxury of a big black Cadillac, knowing it was waiting at the curb no matter what hour they left the party. She'd love it if

Richard Antonini provided the same elegant touch, even if it was equally temporary and she was sure it would be. They'd have one pleasant evening and he'd be on his way. She had to be sensible and believe that.

She wondered why this celebrity-bachelor had asked her out at all. Susan underrated her appearance, her charm, her unstudied sensuality. She was unaware of how extraordinarily attractive she was, and also how few totally alluring women there really were in this world. As she dressed, fretting over the appropriate thing to wear, she wished she'd had the will-power to refuse this last-minute invitation. It would have been smarter to play hard-to-get. Not be available on such short notice. Pretend her engagement book was so full she couldn't fit in a date with Richard for another week at least. That's the way the clever girls would have done it. But she never was clever about men. She persisted in believing that she could be honest and let a man she liked *know* she liked him. It never worked. She'd found that out. Still, she couldn't change, couldn't stop hoping that someone, someday, would understand and appreciate the foolishness of this eternal game-playing between the sexes.

A few minutes after eight the house phone rang and the doorman announced that Mr. Antonini was waiting. She started to leave immediately, calling good night to Evie, who was dressing for her own date. "See you later," Susan added.

Her roommate came to the door. "*Will* you?"

Susan paused in the act of pulling a little black silk shawl around her. It was a hot June night but restaurants were always arctically air-conditioned. "What do you mean, '*Will* you?' I may be late, but you're usually *later*."

"I meant will you be home *at all?*"

"What kind of dumb question is that? I'm just going out to dinner with a man I met once!"

"And have been mooning over ever since."

"I have not been mooning! Evie, stop this! You sound as mother-hennish as Kate! For your information, I am not planning to spend the night with Richard Antonini, even if he is after my lily-white body, which I very much doubt."

"Why doubt? You know his reputation. Everybody does. Not that it matters. I think it would be super to go to bed with a celebrity. A nice change from the sweet paupers who usually buy us a hamburger at P. J. Clarke's and want a return equivalent to a diamond bracelet. With Richard you might even *get* a diamond bracelet."

"I don't want one," Susan said crossly. "And I think the whole world's crazy on the subject of Antonini's sexual prowess. Isn't it possible that he simply wants to have dinner and talk?"

"Nope."

Susan gave an exasperated sigh. "Honestly! This is a helluva way to start an evening. I feel like I'm dating Young Bluebeard."

Evie turned away, flapping a languid hand. "I don't see you rushing to the house phone to send him away."

He was waiting on the sidewalk, the door of the hoped-for limousine open.

"Hello," he said. "I was getting worried. I thought maybe you weren't coming down."

"I'm sorry. A last-minute discussion with my roommate."

"No problem. You look sensational. I'm glad to see you again."

She nearly said, with her usual candor, "Why? What on earth made you call?" But for once she resisted, though there was no mistaking the look in her eyes when she said softly, "And *I'm* glad to see *you. Very* glad."

He liked the way heads turned and eyes watched them speculatively when they walked into the restaurant. He wasn't sure whether it was because they recognized him or because Susan was so beautiful. She stood out in this room of overdressed, overjeweled women. The scoop-necked, clinging black jersey dress showed off her lovely full bosom, her incredibly tiny waist. The dress hugged her, not too tightly but revealingly. For a moment, Richard wished he'd asked her to come to the house for a few drinks before dinner. The family was in Westchester for the summer.

"Signor Antonini!" The maître d' practically fell over himself. "An honor, sir! And Madame. *Bon soir*. Your usual table?"

"Yes, please."

They were led to a corner in the back. Susan was surprised. She'd only been in this ultraswank restaurant for lunch, but she knew the "right place" to sit was in the corridor between the front door and this room. Richard seemed to read her mind.

"Hope you don't mind not sitting up front. I really prefer a little privacy when I dine."

Susan smiled, flattered *he* knew *she* knew about the "best" tables. What he really meant was that he was so secure he didn't need to be stared at in restaurants.

"This is much nicer," she said, settling on the banquette. "I always feel as though I'm eating in a department-store window when I'm in that alleyway."

Richard ordered their aperitifs and, with her agreement, chose dinner for them. Then he sat back and regarded her appraisingly.

"When we met I thought you were pretty. I was wrong. You're beautiful. It's all right to say that, isn't it? Now that we're not 'on business'?"

"I never turn down a compliment."

"Tell me about Susan Langdon," he said.

"Turn-about is fair play? It's your turn to do the interviewing?"

He grinned, a boyish, disarming crinkling of the face. "Sure. Why not? You have me at a disadvantage. You know all about me and I know nothing about you."

"All right, though I warn you it's a boring biography."

She told him about her parents and her early life, her schooling and the "silly little debut." She was enthusiastic about her job and full of amusing anecdotes about her boss.

"That's about it," she said. "See? I told you it was boring."

"Not at all. I think you have a happy life, Susan. Normal. Full of people who love you."

She brushed it aside. "Compared to yours, it's bland. But yes, I'm lucky. Never really wanted for anything. In fact, sometimes I feel overprivileged, as though I don't give enough in return. I should do more active things outside my job."

"Don't tell me you're into a lot of 'do-gooder' stuff!"

"Don't look so scandalized. I'm not, but there's a need for it. The world is polluted, Richard. Not just ecologically, but socially, morally. People are hungry and discriminated against and used! Those of us who have so much have an obligation to make any contribution we can. Not just giving money or going to charity balls. We ought to speak out for those who can't speak for themselves. Really roll up our sleeves and go to work." She stopped. "I'm sorry. I'm doing what my roommate calls my 'soapbox number'—all talk and no action. Let's change the subject."

"You amaze me. I'd have thought you would be more interested in your own future. Most girls are."

"I like to think I'm not 'most girls,' " Susan said, softening the words with a smile. "My classmates are all married by now and most of them have a baby or two. They have mixed feelings about their old school chum: half pity that I'm not married; half envy that I have all this delicious independence."

"You honestly like the independence? Is that the real reason you haven't married?"

"No, I'm too young," Susan teased. Then she sobered. "I believe in the institution, though a lot of people don't these days. But I'm in no rush. And I told you, the famous 'Mr. Right' hasn't appeared. I'd like to be as certain as anybody possibly *can* be—which isn't really certain at all. I hope to get married one day. But if I don't, it won't be the end of the world. Thank God women don't live under those terrible social pressures any more!"

Don't they? Richard said silently. You should know my sister.

"You're a terrific girl," he said.

"Woman," Susan corrected.

"All right. Woman. Girl. Young lady. Business-person. Who cares? You're still terrific. I'm glad we're going to be friends."

"So am I."

He didn't try to make love to her that evening. He was almost more surprised by that than Susan was. It was not that she didn't attract him. She did. Enormously. The fact was, she frightened Richard a little. For the first time in his life, he felt genuinely eager to win the approval of a woman. It wasn't usually this way. In fact, never. Women had always responded to him immediately when he showed the slightest interest, cried a little when he went on to the next adventure but accepted the end of the affair and continued to adore him. For twenty-eight years he remained untouched, never truly in love. He sensed that with Susan it could be different, that it could even lead to marriage, and he wasn't sure he wanted that. Nor did he want to hurt her. It will be better if I don't see her again, he decided. She's too nice, too vulnerable. And I could get involved. It would get in my way. Marriage would stifle me, though it hasn't seemed to inhibit my brothers very much. But I'm not like my brothers. Or am I? Certainly Susan is not like my sisters-in-law. She's not like Gloria either, God knows. Or even Mother.

They stayed at Caravelle until eleven and then drove to the Carlyle Hotel to hear the pianist at the Café Carlyle. Susan enjoyed every minute of it. Shamelessly, she loved the deference everyone showed Richard. It *was* fun to be famous, with headwaiters sweeping you past dozens of people to the head of a waiting line, seating you at the best table though you had no reservation. It was amusing to have the entertainer wave from his place at the piano and later join them on the banquette in the middle of the crowded nightclub. It was exciting to realize that people recognized Richard and whispered their discovery to the others in their party.

And Richard himself was so dear. He held her hand quite openly, which made her feel proud and important. His touch excited her and she decided she would go to bed with him when he suggested it. She could handle it. It would be different this time. She knew better than to expect that a "seduction," especially by Richard Antonini, would have any long-range significance. That would keep her from being miserable when it ended. She would have had at least one glorious, unforgettable, unregretted night. Evie was right. It would be super to have sex with a celebrity. You didn't have to be in love. Not in this day and age. She had to get over that ingrained puritanical streak. She was grown-up and modern. How everything has changed, Susan mused, looking at Richard's handsome profile. I was brought up to believe that "nice girls" didn't even *kiss* on the first date. Now I'm quite calmly deciding that there's nothing wrong with immediate intimacy between consenting adults.

Consequently, she was surprised and actually disappointed when they left the club at 2 A.M. and Richard gave the driver her address. He'd told her, during the evening, that his parents were in the country and he was rattling around all alone except for the servants in that big house. She interpreted this as the buildup for their going there. Apparently she was wrong, and she felt an unreasonable sense of rejection. He was literally going to 'kiss her off.' It was quite clear the attraction was one-sided. Well, so be it, Susan thought philosophically. Probably better this way. He'll be easier to forget if I don't know him that well.

At the entrance of her apartment he kissed her lightly. "It was a great evening Susan. Thanks for coming."

She summoned all her dignity. "Thank *you*. I had a wonderful time."

"Hope I didn't keep you out too late."

Not late enough, she wanted to say. "Not at all. I adored every minute of it."

They stood awkwardly for a moment, he waiting to see her safely inside the building, she hoping he'd suggest another date. Finally she smiled and went inside, and Richard, with a little half-salute, turned and climbed back into the big car.

She didn't hear from him for two weeks, during which time it was impossible to forget him. Not only did she have to finish and polish the article about him, she also had to make arrangements with the photographer for his portrait session, discuss the layout with the art director, do a hundred and one things that reminded her of Richard. It seemed, too, that every paper she picked up had his name somewhere . . . in the music section in the society pages ("Richard Antonini pictured at the Southampton Junior League Art Show with debutante Ann-Marie Tillingham") and even in the gossip columns where his every dinnner date was reported with the importance of some world-shaking event. She became testier and more morose. She'd told Kate about her evening, saying with pretended lightness that it was "fun and platonic," but one morning in a particularly foul mood she literally hurled the *Daily News* across the office.

"Damn! I'm sick of Richard Antonini! Two weeks ago I was hardly aware of him, and now every place I look I see that face or read the name. He gets more publicity than Lyndon Johnson!"

Kate leaned back and lit one of her endless cigarettes. "Ever heard that old cliché about a woman who thinks she's pregnant? Suddenly every woman she sees on the street is pregnant."

In spite of herself, Susan laughed. "You're right. I can't get that idiot out of my mind. I wish I'd never told anybody I was going out with him. I didn't tell many. Only you and Evie and, unfortunately, Mother. At least you two have had the good grace to keep quiet about it, but every time I call home Mother asks if I've heard from him and then I get snarky and snap at her and hate myself for it. I don't know why I'm so uptight about somebody I've seen twice and won't ever see again. It's downright infantile."

"You're playing that favorite female game called wishful thinking," Kate said. "Perfectly natural. You keep imagining how terrific it would have been if something had come of all this. Rich, handsome, famous, unmarried young men do not come along every day. Can't blame you for being disappointed. 'All sad words of tongue or pen' . . . etc., etc. I'm sorry it didn't work out, Susan. At least I *guess* I'm sorry. I'm not sure how hurt you could have been if Richard had decided to play games."

"I know. All my common sense tells me I'm better off this way. And I'll recover faster. But damn it, Kate, he's special and I really thought he liked me. A lot. He acted as though he did all that evening. How *can* I be so naïve? I'm twenty-four years old, for God's sake! Am I never going to grow up and stop believing in men?"

"Probably not. Some women never do."

"Thanks heaps! *That's* a dismal future to contemplate."

"Torturous, maybe. But not dismal. People who stop getting hurt are only half alive, Susie. They lose their dreams, their illusions, their hope-springs-eternal quality. Look at me. Tough, cynical, self-protective. That's because I developed a hard shell early. You don't want to be like that."

"You're not really like that, Kate. You only pretend to be."

"Want to bet?"

"Well, if I ever run into that egomaniac again, you can bet I'll tell him what he can do with his phony charm!"

"I'll take odds on that one too," Kate said.

The attraction was not, as Susan believed, one-sided. Richard went about his professional and social activities as usual, but every morning he awakened thinking of Susan Langdon. More than once he was tempted to call, and each time something stopped him. He tried to assess his feelings about her. She was beautiful, but not the most gorgeous creature, by far, that he'd ever known. She was brighter than most. And perhaps that was actually a deterrent, for Richard knew quite well that his intellectual capacities were limited. His formal schooling had been negligible. Mostly he'd been privately tutored, with all the emphasis and most of the time spent on his advancement from prodigal to seasoned performer. Susan's seriousness about world affairs and her sense of responsibility were matters he rarely thought of and such talk made him feel inadequate and slightly inferior, new sensations, and not pleasant ones. He honestly didn't know why he was so drawn to this girl. She was sexy in a completely understated way and he knew she'd be satisfying in bed, but surely no more so than a hundred other women. Yet he recognized, without knowing how he knew, that he was already half in love with her. It made no sense at all and he tried as hard to put Susan out of his thoughts as she tried to forget about him. He wished she'd call him and relieve him of the responsibility of instigating the next move. Girls he dated once usually did. But this one had too much pride and dignity. Class. That was the word for it. Without great wealth or background, she was the classiest young woman he'd ever met. She'd be something to own. Richard wondered whether she'd allow herself to be owned, fleetingly or, God forbid, permanently. To hell with it! There was only one way to find out. Two weeks after their only date, he broke down and called her at the office.

"Susan? Richard Antonini."

There was a fraction of silence. Then, sounding almost amused at his announcing himself by his full name, she said, "Hello, Richard Antonini. How are you?"

"Fine. I've been thinking about you."

"Have you? That's nice."

Damn. She wasn't going to make it easy. "I wondered if you were free for dinner tonight?"

He would have felt much more sure of himself if he'd known what inner turmoil those words produced. There was a longer pause this time. Susan felt Kate listening, though the editor pretended to be deeply absorbed in a manuscript. Don't be eager, Susan, she told herself. In fact be smart and stay the hell out of it all together. You're just beginning to get him out of your head. A few more weeks of not seeing him and you won't feel that desperate unhappiness about "what might have been." That was sensible. That was logical.

"Yes, I'm free," she said.

He picked her up, as before, at eight. But this time when the doorman announced Mr. Antonini she asked that he be sent up. He admired the apartment, was charming to a charmed Evelyn, sat for fifteen minutes while the three of them had martinis on the rocks.

"Your driver probably thinks you've been kidnaped," Susan said.

"I'm without driver tonight. I have a cab waiting."

She was aghast. "Why on earth didn't you say so?"

"What difference does it make? He won't leave without us."

"I'll get my wrap," Susan said.

Evie followed her into the bedroom. "Now *that's* what it's like to be rich," her roommate said. "Not to let a ticking taxi meter give you palpitations. He's something else, Susie! And God, is he good-looking!"

Susan smiled. "I think I'm the world's biggest fool to even go out with him again."

"Don't be crazy. What have you got to lose?"

It was another wonderful evening. Another superb dinner, this time at Lutèce, where Susan had never been, not even for lunch. She loved the small, elegant dining room, the captain who, though less obsequious than at Caravelle, was equally impressed. She was fascinated by her menu, which had no prices on it—a "ladies' menu," as opposed to the man's, which listed the outrageous cost of the entrees.

During dinner they talked easily about inconsequential things. It was not until they got to their espresso and brandy that Richard turned suddenly serious.

"I don't know how you managed it" he said, "but you've had me crazy for two weeks. I kept hoping you'd call me."

Susan raised her eyebrows. "Telephones work both ways."

"I know." Suddenly he didn't seem the great celebrity, the confident, spoiled, uncaring darling of the columns. He seemed almost humble, appealingly uncertain. "I hoped you'd call me because I was really afraid to call you. I knew if I saw you I'd get involved. I know what you're thinking. I've been 'involved' hundreds of times. But not like this. Not emotionally. I could fall in love with you, Susan. And I have a feeling that might be terrible for both of us."

"Why?" Her voice was gentle. "Because I'd suffer so when you dropped me?"

"No. Because I don't think I could drop you."

"And that would be terrible?"

"It might be. After it was wonderful."

She didn't understand. She didn't want to. All she knew was that no matter how Richard felt she was in love, totally and irrevocably.

This might all be part of the techinque. She didn't care. She sat silently, stirring her coffee, not daring to look at him.

"There's so much about me you don't know," Richard said. "I'm a vain, meteoric, selfish clod who's never been able to remain faithful. Never wanted to. I don't know if I can, Susan. I don't know if I want to try."

The foolishness and wisdom of women in love came to her. Gently, she put her hand on his.

"Why don't we let things work themselves out as they will?" Susan asked. "Don't fret about what may or may not be. Let's enjoy what we have now."

He leaned down and kissed the back of her hand. Then he rose and draped the little black scarf over her shoulders. "Come on, pretty lady. Let's go home."

This time he gave the cabdriver his address. Alternately cursing and laughing, he fumbled with keys and burglar-alarm switches, finally letting them into the foyer. He opened the elevator door next to the staircase she had climbed two weeks before.

"This way, madam," he said lightly. "Fourth floor." He imitated the elevator operator in a department store. "Fourth floor. Bachelor boutique. Superstereos, built-in bars, adjustable rheostat lighting fixtures." He paused. "And king-sized beds."

Chapter 4

"I MUST SAY, I've never seen you looking better, Susie," Bea Langdon remarked a week later when Susan went to Bronxville to have Sunday dinner with her family. "Whatever you're doing, it agrees with you."

Susan blushed. What she'd been doing every night for a week was going to bed with the most glorious, exciting man in the world. Her affair with Richard filled her with such joy that she bloomed. Even away from him she could feel the touch of those extraordinary fingers on her body, the warmth of that seeking mouth on her willing one, the ecstasy they shared in that hidden-away room on the fourth floor. She was madly, passionately in love with Richard Antonini. She'd never felt so desirable, so complete, so happy. For though nothing more had been said about the future, Susan knew this was the man she would marry. He knew it too, though the words remained unspoken. The only specific hint of his "serious intentions" had been the invitation to go to the family house in Pound Ridge for the long Fourth-of-July weekend.

"I'd like you to meet the family." That's what he'd said last night as they lay together in his bed. "Can you go to the country with me next weekend?"

She'd turned on her side, pressing her body against his. "Darling, I'd go to the end of the world with you, and you know it."

He kissed her eager mouth. "Want to know something? I've never taken a girl up to meet the clan before."

They were the most thrilling words she'd ever heard. She thought of them now as she looked at her mother's contented face. If Richard thought his parents' marriage was a good example, hers was equally good, perhaps better. Certainly it was more peaceful. From time to time in the past week, Richard had spoken, seemingly with amusement, about his famous family, and Susan's impression was that everything Kate had told her was true and then some. Temperament and eccentricity were, apparently, the name of the game. He did not go into detail, but Susan read between the lines. He adored his family but acknowledged they were, to put it mildly, difficult. And now she was going to meet them. The idea frightened her. They'd be there for the holiday. She'd get the full impact of them en masse. It was a prospect designed to unnerve even the most self-assured young woman.

"Mother, I've been invited to the Antoninis' in Pound Ridge next weekend. I haven't mentioned it but I've been seeing Richard."

Beatrice looked interested. "So he *did* turn up again! You were getting so touchy about the subject I stopped asking."

"I know. I'm sorry I was beastly. It's just that I thought he didn't particularly like me, and I was, I don't know, feeling deflated and disappointed and all those stupid things. My ego was bruised for a while."

"And now it's healed." It was a flat statement, not a question.

"Completely. I'm terribly in love with him. And I'm sure he loves me. In fact," Susan hesitated, "I think he's going to ask me to marry him." She looked almost pleadingly at her mother. "That's the first time I've dared say that aloud. I'm superstitious about it. Scared that I'll jinx the idea by mentioning it. It's too good to be true. Richard Antonini in love with me! I can't believe it. He could have any woman in the world he wanted. Why me?''

Bea Langdon bristled. "Why *not* you, for heaven's sake? You have everything—youth, beauty, brains. And he's not a god, Susie. He may be a genius, but he's human.'' She frowned. "From the little I know about him and his family, *he'll* be the fortunate one if he persuades you to marry him.''

Susan laughed. "Darling, it won't take much persuasion. In fact *none*. More than anything in the world, I want to be Mrs. Richard Antonini. I'm only afraid I can't live up to it.''

"Live up to what? Why should you have to live up to anything?''

"You don't understand. They're all gifted. And rich. And famous.''

"Notorious" is more like it, Bea thought. Like most reasonably sophisticated people, she'd read and heard a great deal about this news-making family. She might be "only a suburban housewife," but she was not naïve. Where there was smoke there was more than a blaze of publicity. There'd been too much whispering about Richard's father and brothers and their affairs with all kinds of women and men. It was gossip only hinted at and almost indulgently excused because of their "genius," but it formed a picture of emotional instability. What must the wives of Sergio and Walter go through? What, indeed, had Maria Antonini put up with all these years? Bea felt troubled. Susan was not the kind of girl to shrug off a husband's unconventional behavior or retaliate with indiscretions of her own as at least one of the "Antonini women" was reputed to do. She wasn't thick-skinned, as the matriarch of that family presumably was. For all its wealth and glamour, this was not the kind of family Bea visualized her only daughter marrying into. She felt it would be wrong. Susan was too overwhelmed, too willing to see herself in an inferior role, too humbly grateful to be chosen by one of the 'elite.' And too blindly in love to see the pitfalls.

"Darling," Bea said now, "I do understand how flattering it must be to have someone like Richard Antonini in love with you. He's a great talent and I'm sure he's a fine young man. But don't rush into anything, Susie. You've only known him a few weeks. Your father and I want you to have whatever makes you happy, and that certainly includes the right husband, but make sure that you're not simply dazzled. Marriage is serious business. It isn't all fun and games. You're no child. You're nearly twenty-five years old with a mind and will of your own. Look at marriage to Richard from all angles, most of all from a selfish one. And never again let me hear you even *indicate* that you have to 'live up' to anything except your own standards!''

Susan knew what her mother was trying to say. To an outside observer she must, indeed, sound like a fatuous fool. But Bea didn't understand. She didn't know Richard—his tenderness, his concern for her happiness. In this week of intimacy I've come to know the real person under the veneer of the "spoiled brat," Susan thought. I know he needs me. I know I can make him happy. I know that life with a man like this won't be easy, but I'm mature and experienced enough to handle it.

She put her arms around her mother, comforting her as though their roles were reversed and Bea the anxious child.

"There's nothing to worry about," Susan said. "I know exactly what I'm doing. This is the only man for me, Mother. I've waited a long time for him. And in spite of how I must sound to you, I'm not downgrading myself. You and Dad gave me a good base of self-confidence. Believe me, I *know* Richard will be lucky to get me." She gave a litile laugh. "If, indeed, he *wants* me. I could still be wishful-thinking. He hasn't asked me to marry him, after all. I only *think* he will."

"And if he doesn't?"

Susan made a theatrical gesture of mock-despair. "No problem. I'll just kill myself."

The effort to clown her way out of a serious discussion did not deceive Beatrice. If Richard didn't marry her, Susan wouldn't literally kill herself, but if there were such a thing as a broken heart she'd have one. I want so much for her, Bea thought sadly. Everything beautiful. So does Wil. Lord, please make it right. Don't let this love destroy her. Don't even let it hurt too much.

Maria Antonini replaced the telephone receiver in its cradle and went into the library, where Giovanni was intently studying a score. She stood for a moment looking at him. He was so deeply absorbed in the music he wasn't even aware of her presence. Nearly seventy, Maria thought, and still as handsome as the day I met him. More handsome, in a way. For now the thick black hair was snow-white, the heavy, sensual features slightly softened with age and success, the uncertainty of the blossoming genius now replaced by the assurance of immortality. Giovanni Antonini. The maestro. The revered. And I made him what he is. I prodded and pushed and molded an adequate young conductor into a legendary figure. I put up with his erratic behavior, his childish susceptibility to women, his inability to cope with the mundane commercial and financial aspects of his professional life. I bore him four children, including three sons who one day will be as great as he, and whose children will continue the greatness. Because I'll see to it. God knows no one else in this family can.

"Joe," she said. "Joe, Richard was on the telephone."

He looked up reluctantly.

"He's bringing a young woman up next weekend."

Giovanni shrugged. "So? The house will be full, but certainly there's room for one more."

Maria sighed impatiently. Except for music, her husband was irritatingly unaware of the nuances of anything. He honestly thought she was concerned about where this unexpected guest would sleep. Someday he would drive her mad with this total lack of comprehension.

"Of course there's room," she said now. "That's not the point."

Knowing he could not escape, he gave her his full attention. Maria's flashing eyes, the way she tugged at her big diamond ring were signs of agitation he'd come to know all too well.

"All right, my dear. What *is* the point?"

"Richard's never brought a girl here before."

Giovanni looked honestly puzzled. "Forgive me, I still don't understand. He's bringing one now. As the young people say, 'What's the big deal?'"

"You simply refuse to understand your children, don't you? You've never tried to understand any of them. Especially Richard."

Giovanni's quick temper, usually reserved for the browbeaten members of a symphony orchestra and seldom displayed at home, suddenly flared.

"Will you please, for God's sake, tell me what you're talking about? What is this nonsense, Maria, about Richard and my refusal to understand things? What is it you want me to understand?"

"I want you to understand," she said slowly and deliberately as though she were speaking to a backward child, "that Richard obviously has found a girl he's interested in. The first one he's ever brought into a closed-family situation. I would like you to realize that your youngest son may be quite seriously involved with some young woman we know nothing about. He was quite emphatic about all of us making her feel welcome. Quite emphatic indeed," Maria said angrily. "As though we had to be taught manners! I didn't care for the tone of his voice."

At last Giovanini understood. She was frightened that some other woman had become more important to "her baby" than she. She hadn't been upset when Sergio introduced them to Mary Louise or when Walter finally presented Jacqueline. As for Gloria, Maria was unabashedly relieved when their only daughter finally found someone willing to marry her. Even if that someone was an impoverished lawyer who wanted the Antonini influence and money more than the Antonini heiress. Richard was another matter. Maria's attachment to him was more intense, her ambition for him fiercer than for any of the others. It was because he was the late, unexpected, even unwanted child, the result of too much champagne on a New Year's Eve in 1935. For years, except for that night, the Antoninis had not shared a bed. When Richard was conceived, Sergio was sixteen, Walter fourteen and Gloria eleven. Maria had long since decided that sex with Joe was over, that he had strayed once too often, and she wanted no more of him. God knows she wanted no more children! She was a cold woman, frigid, he supposed, and she did not miss love-making. Only the false sentimentality of the night and the unusual amount of wine she drank enabled him to come into her bed and leave the seed that was to be Richard Antonini.

How furious she'd been when she discovered she was pregnant! Giovanni still remembered her rage—at him, at God, at everything except her own weakness. Maria did not admit to weakness in herself. Even in this case she was, in her own mind, a victim of Giovanni's selfish, ungovernable lust, not a fallible human who, for once, abandoned her rigid self-discipline.

And yet, when the baby was born she loved him more than the others. He was more beautiful as an infant, more talented as a child. He came more quickly to fame than his brothers, his career cleverly maneuvered, as Giovanni's had been, by the sharp, shrewd mind of Maria. Richard was her creation and her private and personal possession. For twenty-eight years she had successfully discouraged any serious interest in other women. "Flings" were acceptable, for he was a man, with a man's animal needs. But love and marriage definitely were not.

Poor girl, Giovanni thought. Whoever you are. Heaven help you if Richard really has decided to marry you. Maria will make your life hell.

He tried to answer his wife, tried to make light of what she—probably accurately—

read into this unexpected turn of events. He couldn't say what he really thought: that Richard, for all his deference to her, was as stubborn as his mother. If he decided to marry he would do so, despite anything Maria might say. Richard was the only one, himself included, who dared cross Maria. Sometimes he got away with it. Sometimes he didn't. But, perversely, she loved and respected the rebel of the family more than those who bowed unquestioningly to her dictates.

"I wouldn't worry too much, my dear," Giovanni finally said. "This may mean nothing at all. Perhaps Richard would simply like a companion for the long weekend. It must be tiresome for him sometimes, being only a son, brother, in-law and uncle. Don't get yourself upset over imagined problems."

"I never imagine anything. I *know* Richard too well."

He attempted the impossible. He tried to reason with her. "So, what if you are right? What if Richard has found someone? Is that so terrible? She's probably a nice girl. Don't you want him to be happy?"

"Happy?" She turned her eyes, now fully ablaze, on him. "I've given my life to making Richard happy! And his happiness is his music, his career, his greatness! I've devoted myself to his comfort, catered to his every wish, provided everything he needed! There's nothing I haven't done for my son! No woman could do more!"

"One can," Giovanni said softly. "She can sleep with him and give him children."

Maria turned away, furious. "You are disgusting!" she said.

"All right," Susan said, "give me the rundown once more. I want to know exactly who's who, right down to the names of the family dogs."

Richard, expertly maneuvering the Lincoln convertible along the parkway, smiled indulgently. "Sweetheart, I've been over it half a dozen times with you. Anyway, you don't have to be so thoroughly briefed. You're *visiting* my family, not *interviewing* them."

More like the other way around, Susan thought. They'll be interviewing me, all right. It was not the July sun beating down that made her hands perspire. She was terribly anxious about this weekend, "Please," she said. "I don't want to confuse your sisters-in-law or get their kids mixed up. I want to make a good impression."

"As though you wouldn't anyhow."

"I love you for the vote of confidence, but I'd still like one more run-through."

Richard sighed. "Okay. You know about the parents. You know that Sergio's my eldest brother. He's a conductor, too. He's married to Mary Louise Ryan, called Mary Lou. They have two kids—Joseph (sort of named for my father) who's fifteen, and Patricia who's twelve. Walter, my other brother, is the composer, and he's married to Jacqueline, who's always called Jacqueline. She was a Calhoun from New Orleans. Very social. They have two boys—Calhoun, thirteen, and Charles, eleven. All right so far?"

Susan nodded. She was folding a finger under for each name he mentioned, keeping track of how many there were. So far, she'd reached six adults and four children.

"Then there's my sister, Gloria, and her husband Raoul Taffin. He's a lawyer.

They live in Pound Ridge year round and Raoul commutes to the city. They *also* have two kids. Raoul, Jr., is five and Maria, named for you-know-who, is three. Gloria and Raoul have only been married six years. My sister was a late bloomer. She was thirty-four when she trapped Raoul and she's been making up for lost time. She's pregnant again, and, God help us, they think it's going to be twins this time!''

"Fourteen people. Plus the two of us. Good grief!''

Richard laughed. "It's not as frightening as it sounds. It's a big place. Twenty acres. And each of us has his own house, so there's hope for occasional privacy.''

"Four houses?''

"Six, actually. Mrs. Lowman, the housekeeper, has her own. And then there's the pool house, which can accommodate four guests.''

"Is that where I'll stay?''

"I doubt it. You'll probably stay in a guest suite in the big house with Mother and Father.''

"I don't suppose I could stay with you?'' She made a face. "No, of course I couldn't. That would really blow my image, wouldn't it?''

"It would blow my mother's mind, that's what it would do.'' He took one hand off the wheel and caught hers. "Will you relax, darling? It'll be a fun weekend. A little frenetic, maybe, but you'll have a good time. We can swim and you can play tennis if you like. And there's certain to be a daily softball game organized by Gloria. She's very big on contact sports.''

"In her condition?''

"In any condition. My sister is the outdoorsy type. Always has been. That's *her* claim to fame. That and being fertility goddess of the century. Crazy lady. I think she'll probably end up with nine kids.''

"Richard! She's forty years old *now!*''

"Don't think Gloria will let a little thing like that stand in her way. She may not be as unflappable as Mary Lou or as glamorous as Jacqueline, but she's got 'em beat hands-down when it comes to endurance.'' Richard hesitated, "She also holds her husband on a tighter rein than they do.'' He gave a false little laugh. "Let me know if Serge or Walter tries to get too friendly. I'll take care of them.''

For a moment Susan was speechless. Surely he was teasing. His own brothers try to move in on him? Nonsense. But was he lightly trying to warn her? What they said about the Antonini men must be true, she thought. But not Richard. Never Richard. She responded in the same vein.

"Don't worry. I'll use my karate chop on them. Anyway, my love, I only have eyes for you. Or hadn't you noticed?''

He seemed to relax. "I've noticed. Eyes and other delightful things.''

"Lecher!''

Laughing, they pulled into the driveway of the estate and after some little distance up a winding private road arrived at the front door of the main house. "Country'' indeed! Susan thought. This is a millionaire's mansion. It looks like it was built for William the Conqueror!

"Nice little place your folks have here,'' she said wryly, looking at the three-story stone building, "Just a simple, rural, weekend retreat. What are the other houses like—the Petit Trianon and Monticello?'' She was being flippant to cover her nervousness and Richard knew it. He gave her a quick kiss before they got out of the car.

"You're such a hick,'' he teased, shaking his head in pretended despair. "I don't know. I just can't take you anywhere.''

Take me home, she felt like saying. I'm going to lose you here. I can't live up to this. I'm a stranger. And scared to death. Then she remembered Bea Langdon's words. Why was she worrying about "living up'' to anything? Richard loved her. It was no mere whim to bring her here. He must feel sure she'd fit into the family, that they'd all like each other. Suddenly she felt better. It was going to be all right. This wasn't the end. It was the beginning.

Chapter 5

THEY WERE THE last to arrive, for Susan, the only one with a "real job'' had not been able to get away as early as she hoped. When she and Richard walked into the living room, there seemed to be dozens of people waiting for them, people of all ages, all of them looking appraisingly at her, hopefully reserving judgment. A small woman, not more than five feet two and a hundred pounds, wearing a Givenchy pants-suit, came quickly toward them, hand outstretched in welcome, a "perfect hostess'' smile on her lips.

"Mother,'' Richard said, "this is Susan.''

Maria took Susan's hand in both of hers. "I would have known. Welcome, my dear! How chic you look! But of course you would. An associate editor of *Vogue!* I'm delighted to have you here, Susan. Richard has told me so much about you. I've been looking forward to this visit.''

Richard could hardly contain his amusement and his surprise. Maria was turning on her charm, had taken her "darling pills'' as the family referred to this façade of warmth and pleasure. The act always threw strangers off balance. Only the family knew that when Maria was this cordial she was covering an instant dislike or distrust of the person, or plotting his undoing inside her well-tinted, well-coiffed little head. "Beware of Mother when she gushes'' was the watchword in the family. "She's up to no good.'' Richard had witnessed this polished performance many times, played for all kinds of people, and had always found it transparently funny. But this time there was an added dimension of surprise. He had told her almost nothing about Susan beyond the fact that she worked on *Vogue*. Maria must have gone to the trouble of looking up Susan's title on the masthead of the magazine. He wondered what else Maria had discovered about his "friend'' in the few days since she'd first heard of her. Probably plenty. Maria's sources of information were good, from the servants in the town house, who undoubtedly knew of Susan's visits there, to her "social'' contacts who probably knew or were the bigwigs at *Vogue*. She smells trouble, Richard thought. And, from her point of view, she's probably right.

Susan was completely taken in by this gracious little woman. She breathed a sigh of relief at the apparently genuine welcome, which was almost as unexpected as Maria's physical appearance. She'd seen candid photographs of Richard's mother in magazines and newspapers, but she was usually snapped at the table at some charity dinner. They didn't show how tiny she was. Susan expected someone big and formidable, almost a Wagnerian type with an ample bosom and a booming voice. From her reputation as a tyrant, Susan had pictured Maria as physically overpowering. The last thing she anticipated was this fragile-looking little lady who seemed so pleased to meet her.

"I'm delighted to be here, Mrs. Antonini. It was kind of you to let Richard bring me."

"A great pleasure, my dear. Come. Everyone is eager to meet you." Still holding Susan's hand, she led her to a giant of a white-haired man. "This is my husband. Joe, dear, this is Richard's little friend Susan Langford."

"Langdon, Mother," Richard said. "Not Lang*ford.*"

"Of course, darling, how stupid of me! But no matter, really. We're all on a first-name basis here, aren't we?"

Giovanni made a small bow, smiling with real warmth. "And what a pretty friend she is!" The deep, resonant voice still held a trace of his Italian origin. "Welcome to our house, Miss Langdon. You pay it a great compliment."

Susan was entranced by the Old World courtesy and awed at finding herself in the presence of the great artist.

"It's a privilege to meet you, sir," she said. And then, almost shyly, "It's something one dreams about."

The handsome, aging face broke into an impish grin. "My dear child, lovely young women have long since stopped dreaming about me, alas. Except, perhaps, as a grandfather figure with a baton. But you are kind."

Maria interrupted. "Joe, dear, stop monopolizing our guest. Everyone else is waiting to greet her."

Like an ocean liner in the wake of a strong little tug, Susan found herself being steered around the huge room.

"This is my eldest son, Sergio, and his wife Mary Louise." Susan shook hands with a dark, broodingly handsome man and a small blond woman hardly bigger than Maria. "And these are their children." Joseph made a formal bow and Patricia actually curtsied. Susan was amazed. Did children really behave that way any more? Obviously, Antonini children did. Sergio looked like an older, more sardonic Richard. What had Richard said? Oh yes. There was almost seventeen years' difference between the oldest and youngest boys. That would make Sergio forty-five, a most attractive age for men. His wife must be about forty, Susan thought, though she seemed more girlish.

There was only time for a word of greeting before Maria moved her on. "And this is Walter and Jacqueline and Calhoun and Charles, who're being allowed to join us for dinner tonight." The boys, like their cousin Joseph, made "dancing-school bows." Maria smiled. "It's a special treat when I allow the grandchildren to dine with us," she said. "You feel terribly grown up, don't you, Calhoun? And you, too, Charles."

"Yes, ma'am." A dutiful chorus.

Walter laughed. "I'm afraid they consider it a dubious honor, Mother. They have to stay on their best behavior."

Susan smiled sympathetically. "It's probably more fun having dinner without the grown-ups, isn't it?" she asked them conversationally.

Maria allowed a shade of annoyance to cross her face before she answered for them. "They *adore* being permitted to come to table."

My first gaffe, Susan thought. Even though Walter had given her the cue, Jacqueline said nothing. She simply stood quietly by, an unreadable expression on her face. Was it scorn? Boredom? Resigned tolerance? Susan couldn't decide. And then she saw a corner of Jacqueline's mouth turn up ever so slightly, as if to say, "You're right, but it's a hopeless battle." Susan liked Walter and Jacqueline on sight. The second son seemed more gentle, more relaxed than his older brother. And his wife, so extraordinarily beautiful in her remoteness, was, Susan felt, the only woman in this family she might possibly relate to.

She was sure of that when they got to the final pair. "My daughter, Gloria Taffin," Maria said, "and her husband Raoul. Unfortunately, *their* babies are too small to join the dinner party." The way in which it was said was an unmistakable reprimand to Walter and Susan. Gloria was a big-boned woman, nearly as tall as her brothers and physically fit in spite of her obvious pregnancy. She shook Susan's hand with a strong grip. Her husband, slight and handsome, had great elegance and charm. They were a strange pair.

"I hear you have two beautiful children,' Susan said. "And congratulations on the upcoming event."

"Thanks," Gloria said tersely.

Raoul was more gracious. "Our little ones are very winning," he said, "but already they are *enfants terribles*. Still we adore them."

"You'd adore them less," Maria said tartly, "if you didn't have that good English nanny! Thank heavens I could find one for you. Gloria is hopeless as a functioning mother. She's much too busy winning blue ribbons in horse shows." Then she reverted to ber assumed softness. "Of course, we're very proud of Gloria's athletic accomplishments. And she certainly keeps all of us on our toes! Even me. The only one she can't convert to the great outdoors is my stubborn husband." She looked appraisingly but affectionately at her daughter. "Darling, you really must be careful of your skin. All that outdoor exposure! In another two years you'll positively have an alligator hide! Raoul, can't you control your wife? The women in my family have always been famous for their good complexions."

Richard spoke from behind her. "If not for their *tact,* Mother dear. Stop nagging Gloria. I think you're just jealous of her trophies. Besides, Susan doesn't want to hear the usual family squabbles the first twenty minutes she's in the house." His tone was bantering but he was annoyed, and Maria, to Susan's relief, subsided with an apologetic little laugh.

"Forgive me, Susan. I never can stop worrying about my children. Even when my babies are grown up and have babies of their own. Gloria understands. I only want her to stay pretty."

There was an awkward silence and then Richard said, "Why don't we all have a drink? I could use one and I'm sure Susan could, after working all day, driving up here and meeting twelve new people."

"Good idea." Jacqueline spoke for the first time, but Maria gently vetoed the idea.

"Richard darling, it's after five, and I'm sure Susan would like to settle in before dinner. Why don't we show her to her suite and meet, as planned, for cocktails at seven? Unless, of course, Susan really *needs* a drink . . ."

"Oh no, Mrs. Antonini. Not at all. I'll unpack."

"What a sensible young lady you've brought us, Richard dear," Maria said. "Shall I have one of the maids help you, Susan?"

"No thank you, Mrs. Antonini. I can manage."

In the guest suite to which Maria personally conducted her and left with a warm smile, after checking that she had everything she needed, Susan sat for a moment thinking about her introduction to this house, this family. There was no doubt who was in charge. It was Maria's domain, in every sense. It was always "I," or "my." Never "we" or "our." *I* am delighted to have you here. Richard has told *me* so much about you. These are *my* children. *I* found the nurse for the Taffin baby. It was as though Giovanni did not exist as a husband, only as an artistic possession of Maria's, an extension of herself. Susan could well believe all the things she'd heard about Signora Antonini. Until today, she'd thought most of it farfetched. No longer. From her highhanded manner with her family, Susan could imagine the made-of-steel little woman negotiating with managers, making financial deals, choosing the cities in which Giovanni appeared, the clothes he wore, the hotels he stayed in and the cuisine offered. I've never seen such a dominant woman, Susan thought. With sudden insight she sensed that Maria ran her husband's life and controlled her children, not for their sakes but for her own monumental ego, her insatiable need to be in charge of everything and everyone.

The terrible part was that she undoubtedlly was good at it, probably so often right that the family had realized the foolishness, as well as the futility, of trying to buck her. It was easier—and usually wiser—to give in, to pay the homage she demanded, to go along with her in matters from career development to child rearing. What the hell, the children probably said privately, she was spoiled rotten and had been, all her life and theirs. It was too late to start rebelling now. And besides she was so damned competent. She had intelligence and experience and a total lack of mawkish emotion that enabled her to view all problems clinically. The children probably thought they loved her. Susan suspected that it was more awe, even fear. She guessed, from the little she'd seen, that Maria's wrath could be formidable, her disapproval cold and devastating, a plague to be avoided. It seemed clear that "the children" and those they married deferred to Mother and probably reserved any true affection for the kind, smiling father who had withdrawn from all decisions, knowing he'd not be allowed to make them even if he tried. He'd seemed indulgent and tolerant of his wife's complete command of the situation. Certainly he uttered no words of protest. Perhaps he admired her strength. Susan doubted that Giovanni felt much love for his wife, but in his gentlemanly way the world would never know that.

She began looking around her temporary quarters. It was a beautiful suite, done in her favorite pink, white and green. A gay, flowered bedroom with ruffled bedspread, an inviting chaise longue, and an ample dressing table. The little sitting room had its own television set, a painted Italian desk well stocked with writing paper engraved "Six Corners," the name of the estate. There was a pile of new best-sellers on the table beside a deep, comfortable chair and ottoman, a bowl of peppermints and a box of cigarettes next to it. The bathroom was papered in green and white latticework paper and equipped with thick towels monogrammed "MSA." Maria's initials. Susan wondered what the "S" stood for. What was Maria's maiden name? Sanford? Sterling? Certainly not Smith. More like "Superwoman," Susan thought half-amused. Or "Simon-legree." She smiled at her own nonsense. Stop it! she told herself. You're making snap judgments based on twenty minutes of contact and twenty different malicious rumors. Give her a chance. If only because she's Richard's mother.

Susan looked out the window. She could see, at a distance, a series of small houses. Which one is his? I wish I were staying in it with him! I love him so. I wouldn't care if he came from a family of aborigines. She wondered if he were thinking of her now, wanting her as she wanted him.

Richard was, in fact, still downstairs in the same house. After the others had wandered off to change for dinner, Maria detained her younger son.

"Sit and talk with me for a moment, Richard. I haven't seen you for nearly a month since we've been staying up here. Is everything all right at the house? You're not too lonely?"

"Everything's fine, Mother." Was this her way of telling him she knew about Susan's visits to the town house? He waited.

"Your friend is charming. A bit outspoken with the children, I thought, but very attractive."

"You weren't exactly the soul of diplomacy yourself a couple of times. Those cracks about Gloria's kids. And the poor old girl's lousy complexion. Why don't you let her up?"

"My dear, what I say to your brothers and sister is only for their own good."

"Those might be the most awful words anybody ever says." Richard grimaced. "They're a license to lecture." He decided to plunge in. "All right, Mother, let's have it. You don't like Susan. Shall we talk about it?"

"That's utter nonsense. How could I dislike her? I don't even know her."

"Stop acting. The minute she walked in you were snide about how 'chic' she was. And all that going-on about being an associate editor of *Vogue*. Interesting that you checked that out. What *else* did you chcck out?"

"I haven't the faintest idea what you're talking about. You are a grown man, free to pick your own friends without interference from me. If I said something ill-advised about her appearance, I assure you it was unintentional. After all, entertaining a *Vogue* editor makes one feel quite provincial and dowdy."

If it hadn't been so annoying, it would have been funny. Richard felt himself growing angrier. What kind of idiot did she think he was?

"When you go into that 'I'm just a simple housewife' routine, Mother, it really breaks me up! You're about as provincial as Maria Callas. You're in Paris and Milan and Leningrad much more often than you're in Pound Ridge. As for the 'dowdy' part, you're very simple indeed in your Galanos gowns and your David Webb jewelry. Just the typical American homemaker, 'overcome' by meeting a fashion magazine editor. Hell, you're probably best friends with the wife of the man who *owns Vogue!*"

Maria looked at him speculatively. "You seem overly excited about nothing, Richard. I've met some of your lady-friends before, at parties. I'm sure I treated *them* no differently and you didn't seem so upset . . . Or," she said slowly, "is there something special about your little Susan? I'm not stupid, dear boy. This is the first young woman you've felt impelled to introduce to your family. And for a whole, private weekend at that. Should I read some unusual significance into this visit?"

Until that moment, Richard had not been absolutely sure that he was going to ask Susan to marry him. Sleeping with her was terrific. She was interesting to talk to. And he liked having such a beautiful young woman on his arm. But marriage? He hadn't totally made up his mind whether he wanted that. To anyone. God knows, he was surrounded by discouraging examples. There wasn't an ounce of marital happiness among the whole lot of them. And yet suddenly, perversely, he heard himself saying, "Yes, you should read something significant into it. I'm in love with Susan. I'm going to marry her."

Even when the words were out of his mouth he wasn't certain it was what he really intended. But it was done. He couldn't back down now. He wasn't sure he wanted to. He did love Susan. As much as he could ever love any one woman. There'd been ten good years of bachelor fun. Marriage might be very pleasant very comfortable, much easier than hopping from bed to bed. As though Maria were deaf, he repeated his words more loudly. "I said I'm going to *marry* her, Mother."

"I heard you, Richard."

"Well?"

"What do you want from me? Ecstatic squeals of delight? Congratulations and blessings? Or perhaps a simple case of hysterics would suit you better. I don't think I need to point out to you why you've decided to take this foolish step just at the moment when you're on the threshold of your best years."

This was Maria at her most devastating. Cold. Sarcastic. Puzzling. Richard stared at her.

"I'd be interested in your theories. Personally, I thought it was quite normal and natural to fall in love."

"For normal, natural people, perhaps." Maria was entering her persuasive pbase. "But you are an artist, Richard. Your talent puts you above ordinary behavior. You know that at this crucial stage of your development, the *last* thing you need is the distraction and responsibility of a wife and probably children! You need to be free to concentrate on nothing but your work. My dear, you're still young. There's plenty of time to think about marriage."

"You still haven't answered my question, Mother. Why do *you* think I'm marrying?"

There was a carefully calculated pause. "This is painful for me to say, Richard, but if, heaven forbid, you should not reach the eminence we all hope and believe you will, the time-consuming demands of a personal life would be a face-saving alibi. If you had a wife, there'd be someone to blame, wouldn't there? As there isn't now, when you're pampered, protected and totally self-indulgent. It will be different when you have a family of your own to worry about. There'll be domestic problems. Boring. Demanding. Your daily life will be quite altered.

Even the engagements you accept, the out-of-town appearances you're offered will be subject to your wife's opinions and some consideration of her needs. I think you're frightened, son. Afraid of failure. And looking for an acceptable scapegoat if such unlikely but possible disaster strikes.''

He was openmouthed. ''That's the most insane thing I've heard you say! Afraid of *failure?* For God's sake, I'm already a *success!* And even if I weren't, you're the last person in the world to single out a wife as a deterrent to a man's career! Look what you've done for Father!''

Maria smiled. ''This may be immodest, but Susan is not like me. I can tell. She'll hang onto you, burden you with demands for attention, depend on you for decision-making. You'll be irritated, Richard. And resentful of the intrusion into your working life. She's a nice girl. I have nothing against her. But she comes from a different world. Yes, I've done some checking up. You were right about that. She is the product of a solid, middle-class background, raised, I'm sure, to dedicate herself to a husband, but not necessarily to his work. There is no way she could understand you as I have always understood your father. You may love her. I'm sure you do. But she will not put your career first, above her own view of you as a 'couple,' and don't think for a moment she'll take a back seat to you. She's had a career of her own. Even if she's ready to forget it and start a new one as Mrs. Richard Antonini, she won't be any real help to you. On the contrary, she'll be a hindrance. But then, of course, as I started out by saying, it's always comfortable to have an alibi for failing to achieve what you know you should have.''

She'd always been able to shake him with this kind of glib, authoritative double-talk. For a moment, Richard was uncertain. Was she right? Was he subconsciously afraid of failure and looking for the ''alibi?''

Seeing the slight hesitation, Maria pursued her advantage. ''I know. You're thinking that marriage hasn't been a millstone around Sergio's and Walter's necks. You're wrong. Neither of them has attained the stature they could have if they'd not been forced to give part of every day to wives and pregnancies and stupid, domestic obligations that Mary Lou and Jacqueline persist in involving them in. It takes a very special kind of woman to submerge herself in the interest of art, Richard. A very strong one, willing to abandon her own personality and wise enough to find satisfaction in reflected glory.'' Maria smiled. ''I have no doubt that you're going to be a truly great man. The greatest of all my sons. I hoped you shared that conviction and were willing to make sacrifices for it.''

He was silent for a long time. Then he said, ''I'm sorry, Mother. You're wrong. I'm not looking for someone to pass the buck to if things go wrong. I'm looking for someone to share my life. Other artists have wives and children. I don't believe what you've been saying. I don't think you believe it, either.''

''I have always wanted only your happiness, Richard. Which is the same as wanting your success.''

''I know that, Mother. And I promise you'll get what you want. Susan will only enrich the gift.''

She was too clever not to know when she was beaten. Richard was so like her. Strong-willed, difficult (impossible, really) to manipulate when his mind was made up. And she could see that his mind was made up.

"Very well," she said. "You're of age. There's nothing I can do to stop your marrying Susan."

"I'd prefer your blessing."

"I can't be a hypocrite. I can only hope my instincts are wrong."

He smiled suddenly. "Wouldn't it be ironic if all this bridge-crossing was a waste of time? I haven't even asked Susan yet. She might turn me down."

"Not likely," Maria said.

No, he thought, it wasn't likely. He'd ask her tonight. He knew what her answer would be.

Dinner was a kind of delicate torture, a noisy meal that left Susan feeling more than ever an outsider. The family seemed to forget that she was there, though she sat at Giovanni's right with Richard beside her. As they always did when they gathered, the Antoninis threw themselves into a spirited discussion of topics which were far from Susan's frame of reference. "The boys" and Giovanni and Maria did most of the talking and most of it about music. There was a heated debate over the merits of Hindemith's *Mathis der Maler* and Prokofiev's *Piano Concerto No. 3*. Giovanni had a long pronouncement about Berlioz's *Damnation of Faust,* while Maria insisted that Beethoven's *Leonora Overture No. 3* was intensely significant.

Susan, with a layman's limited knowledge of the classics, had understood very little of it, a fact Richard realized. Occasionally, he squeezed her hand in encouragement. Once or twice, she caught Maria looking at her thoughtfully. She must know we're in love, Susan thought. And she's bound to disapprove. The knowledge made her feel weak. What if Maria talked her son out of this romance? She had such power over all her children. No. That wouldn't happen. Why wouldn't she want me for a daughter-in-law? I'm presentable, from a better-than-average background, with a fair share of intelligence and a reasonable education. What more could she want for Richard? Maybe a European princess or the daughter of a rich Greek shipowner, Susan answered herself. She looked at Mary Lou and Jacqueline. They were no better than she. But then, perhaps Maria considered Richard better than Sergio or Walter. Damn. Would this dinner never end?

It finally did and they trooped into the library, an enormous room with heavy oak beams, a vast fireplace and leaded glass windows. A huge concert grand dominated one end and there were floor-to-ceiling bookcases, filled with biographies of great musicians, textbooks, histories of composers, bound scores of symphonies, librettos of operas. This "country house" was more impressive, in its way, than the East Seventieth Street one. It reeked of solid position and "old money," and it was even more forbidding, somehow, in spite of its casual chintz fabrics and the masses of fresh flowers on every table.

They were served coffee and brandy by a white-coated houseman, one of the eight servants it took to run this enormous establishment, under Mrs. Lowman's crisply efficient direction.

Susan found herself standing next to Giovanni. "This is a marvelous house," she said. "Do you spend much time here?"

"Most of the summer. That is, Mrs. Antonini and I do. The children have their own places, of course. Except for Richard, However, we manage to gather regularly for many weekends and most holidays. My wife likes to have the whole family together as often as possible. It's difficult, you see. We are on tour a great part of the time.''

"It must be a glamorous life.''

The maestro shrugged his shoulders. "I suppose. One comes to take it for granted after so many years.'' He looked wistful. "In time, one symphony hall comes to look very much like another. Hotel suites have an extraordinary sameness. Even audiences are only bodies who own you, for a few hours, for the price of a ticket. The 'glamour,' my dear, is not without its boredom and its difficulties, as well as its rewards.'' His eyes twinkled. "As I'm sure you will soon find out.''

Susan looked at him sharply. Giovanni lowered his voice. "Mrs. Antonini whispered your little secret to me before dinner. I am very happy, dear Susan. You will make Richard a wonderful wife.''

Her surprise and momentary exhilaration gave way to annoyance. The arrogance of it! Richard had told his mother he planned to marry even before he proposed! Before she could say anything, she heard Richard's voice and saw him coming through the doorway, followed by the houseman bearing a tray filled with glasses of champagne. She'd been so interested in talking to Giovanni, she hadn't noticed Richard leaving the room. Now he stood beside her.

"My dear family,'' he now said loudly, "may I have your attention, please? I wish to propose a toast. Everyone have a glass? Good! Let us drink to the lovely new lady in our midst. My bride to be. To Susan, the future Mrs. Richard Antonini!''

There was a second or two of silence as the assembled group reacted to this sudden announcement. Then there was a babble of "To Susans'' and "Good wishes'' as they raised their glasses in her direction. Everyone saluted her except Maria, Susan noticed. The matriarch stood stony-faced and motionless, saying nothing. Richard waited, looking at Susan, a satisfied smile on his face. For a moment she felt outraged. How dare he be so sure of himself, so sure of her? How humiliating to have one's engagement proclaimed as a *fait accompli* before being privately asked! She flushed with instinctive anger. For a fleeting moment she wondered what would happen if she turned coolly to Richard and said, "I'm afraid you're mistaken, dear. No one has proposed to me yet.'' But she wouldn't, of course. This was what she had dreamed of from the first moment she'd set eyes on him. He was kissing her lightly now, laughing at her high color.

"Look!'' he called to the others. "Would you believe, in this day and age, a girl who can still blush?'' He was oblivious to the hurt and anger she felt at this hoped-for moment. "Happy, darling?'' he asked in a voice meant only for her ears.

What could she say? He was so pleased with himself, so utterly unaware that he'd deprived her of a precious private moment that could never come again, a moment alone when he would ask her to be his wife. She managed to smile. "Of course I'm happy.''

They were crowding around her now, the people to whom she soon would be related. The men kissed her and patted Richard on the back. Jacqueline and

Mary Lou hugged her, but Gloria only shook her hand, a bone-crushing grip as opposed to the limp one Maria finally offered. Richard's mother was tight-lipped, too well bred to show her displeasure, too proud to pretend happiness.

"You are getting a wonderful man, Susan," she said at last. "I count on you to make his life perfect."

What about my life? Susan wanted to say. Or isn't that important in the scheme of things? She knew the answer as far as Maria was concerned, and she savored a taste of triumph as she gazed steadily into her future mother-in-law's eyes and said, "I don't hope for perfection in anything, Mrs. Antonini, but I'm sure Richard and I will make each other happy."

"When's the wedding?" Jacqueline asked.

Richard answered for her. "As soon as possible. Right, darling?" He had his arm around her. "Early September, before I leave on the next tour. I want Susan with me."

"Not taking a chance on a long engagement, are you?" Sergio asked. "What's the matter, Richard? Afraid she'll change her mind?"

Richard only laughed confidently. "No way. No way at all."

And no way you've consulted me about that either, Susan thought. I'm not to be allowed even to pick the date of my own wedding. Now stop this! she scolded herself. Remember whom you're marrying! He didn't mean to slight her. It would not occur to him to consult her, or even dream that she might be piqued by having no voice in the matter. He's been so terribly spoiled all his life, so used to having his way. It will take time for him to realize that he now has a partner entitled to an equal voice in all decisions. None of that is important, I mustn't be so thin-skinned. So impatient. He'll adjust, as I will. For now, the only thing to do is go along, and not be so damned sensitive. Love will make the difference. Love will soften and mold Richard and bring out all his potential for sharing.

She smiled contentedly. "September sounds wonderful," she said. She looked across the room. Giovanni gave her a small, approving, conspiratorial nod of the head.

Chapter 6

BEA AND WIL LANGDON waited impatiently for the train to pull into the Bronx-ville station that hot Monday evening in July. Susan's mother was visibly agitated and Wil kept patting her hand reassuringly.

"It's going to be all right, darling. You heard how happy Susie sounded when they phoned us Saturday morning. And Richard is a gentleman. I liked the way he apologized for telling *his* family first. It was perfectly natural. After all, they happened to be with the Antoninis when they decided."

Bea was unconvinced. "And is it perfectly natural for him not to come out here with her this evening? My Lord, Wil, we've never laid eyes on him. You'd think he could spare the time to meet his fiancée's parents."

"Now, honey, Susie explained that. He has a meeting with his manager tonight."

"Maybe we're not grand enough for him," Bea said petulantly. "Maybe Susan's worried about introducing her dull family."

Wil laughed. "Come on. That's not like you. You know better. You're just a bundle of nerves. Typical mother-of-the-bride syndrome."

Even she had to laugh at herself. "I suppose you're right. It just seems so sudden. I wish they'd give it more time. Get to know each other a little better. September! That's only two months away! Who can get ready for a wedding in two months? I don't understand the big rush."

"Yes you do. Richard starts on tour. He wants his wife with him."

His wife. How strange the words sounded, even to his own ears. It was hard to imagine Susie married. And to someone so famous. To him, she was still his little girl, his adorable and adored child. But she was not. She was a woman. She'd waited longer than most of her friends to marry. It was like her, her father thought proudly, to wait until she found the right man. Not settle for some second-rate young squirt with a mediocre job and a dubious future.

And yet, though he'd die before he'd let her know, Wil Langdon shared his wife's reservations. He, too, would be easier in his mind if only they wouldn't rush into marriage after such a brief courtship. He did not wish to admit that they probably knew each other well, physically. Fathers didn't like to think about things like that where daughters were concerned. But even if they were intimate, it didn't mean they really *knew* each other. He was not privy to all the gossip about the Antoninis that reached Bea's ears, but he'd heard enough to make him nervous about the family. Not that he didn't think Susan could hold her own in any situation. She had such poise, such good common sense. But this was the Big League. Things would be expected of her that she might be unwilling, if not unable, to supply. She'll have to make so many concessions, Wil thought. More than most wives.

As though she read his mind, Bea said, "Among other things I can't imagine Susan telling me this morning that they want a big wedding! She's always been vehement about the wastefulness of an elaborate ceremony. 'Downright obscene' she always called those productions that cost thousands of dollars. And now on the phone she says they've decided on a full-scale event with all the trimmings. I'm sure it's not her idea! She must be doing it for Richard's sake. Or his family's. I was really surprised at her rattling on about bridesmaids and receptions as though that's the only way to get married. And it's downright inconsiderate. She could at least ask whether we can afford it!"

"Honey, if that's what she wants, we can afford it."

"That's not the point. She shouldn't just take it for granted. It's so unlike her. Everything is. Imagine marrying a man we've never even met!"

"Now calm down," Wil said. "This is the happiest moment of her life. You don't want to spoil it for her, do you?"

Bea subsided. "No. Of course not. And you know I won't. I'm just uneasy. I don't know why. I simply don't have a good feeling about all this."

He gave her a little kiss. "You'll feel better the minute you see her. Here comes the train. You want to stay in the car?"

"No. I want to be right there on the platform when she gets off. One look at her face and I'll know everything."

Susan stepped off the train. And they hugged and kissed and cried a little before they started for home, Bea listened carefully as her daughter talked nonstop. Susan was keyed up, chattering about the wedding plans. It was natural for her to be excited, but this was almost frenetic, as though she had to convince them and herself that everything was flawless. She's in a panic, Bea thought, alarmed. Happy, yes. But almost deliriously so. Almost frantically anxious to assure them how wonderful Richard was, how she looked forward to a beautiful wedding and a glorious life.

"This is pretty sudden, sweetheart, isn't it?" Wil said when they'd settled in the living room. "Your mother's going to have her hands full putting together a big do in two months. And you won't be much help. You'll have to give the magazine at least two weeks' notice. Maybe more. They've been very decent to you. You can't walk out on Kate tomorrow."

Bea looked at him gratefully. He was trying to help, after all.

"I know," Susan said. "I realize it's an imposition, but Richard starts on a concert tour in mid-September, and we want to squeeze in at least a week to ourselves before then."

"Why not wait until the tour's over and then get married?" Bea asked. "He won't be away more than a couple of months."

"Richard doesn't want to wait. And neither," Susan said almost defiantly, "do I."

Bea persisted. "But darling, it's really only a short time. It isn't years."

Susan suddenly seemed angry. "For God's sake, Mother, you sound like . . ." She stopped.

"Like Richard's mother?" Bea said gently.

"Well, yes, I'm sorry, Mom. I didn't really mean that. You could never sound like Mrs. Antonini."

They waited, but Susan apparently was not going to elaborate. They sat in silence for a few seconds until Bea finally said, "Well, dear, I know your mind's made up. But why don't we simplify it? A small wedding. Just the family at the church here in Bronxville and a few friends at the club after for a little reception. You always said that's the way you wanted it. And that, at least, we could cope with. You've always wanted to be married quietly, surrounded only by those you love and who love you. It would be nice, Susan. I promise. You know we want you to have a sweet wedding."

Susan looked appealing from one to the other. "Don't you understand? I didn't know when I said those things what was going to happen to me. Don't you understand I'm not marrying just *anybody?* I'm marrying *Richard Antonini.*"

Bea took a deep breath. "Yes, we understand, darling. We really do."

Not then, not until years later, could Susan explain what that Fourth-of-July weekend had been like. She had to live through things much more terrible before she could even discuss the lost feeling she'd had at what should have been her moment of utter joy. When at last she did talk about that visit, she was able to put it into perspective, to see it as a warning she'd recognized and chosen to ignore.

She had been annoyed by Richard's highhanded way of announcing their engagement and setting the date, but in her dazed happiness she'd quickly recovered from this unintended lack of thoughtfulness. It was not until the others had gone to bed and only she and Richard and Maria were left in the library that she felt the first full impact of Maria's strength and her own helplessness. She'd wanted so much to be alone with Richard, but he made no sign of their slipping away together, and his mother deliberately lingered until everyone else had finally drifted off. Then Maria, who'd been almost silent during the evening, decided to speak her piece.

"Sit down," she commanded. "I think the three of us had better have a talk."

Susan expected Richard to tell his mother that it could wait; that they'd like to be alone together now. She'd whispered to him in passing that they had to call her parents right away. But he did no such thing. Obediently, he sank into a sofa facing Maria's big chair, pulling Susan down with him.

Maria looked long and hard at her future daughter-in-law. "As you come to know me better," she said, "you will find that I am many things. Above all, I am direct. Like it or not, I've already told Richard that I do not approve of your marriage in September."

Susan misunderstood. "I know it seems a little hurried, Mrs. Antonini." She tried to make a joke of it, glancing at Richard. "I was a bit taken aback myself, hearing the announcement. But since Richard will be traveling for months, I agree. I want to go along."

"The timing is unimportant. Whether Richard marries in two months or two years is not the issue. Not the basis of my objection. Nor are you, personally, the reason I am against this." Maria spoke deliberately. "He chooses not to listen, but the practical fact is that Richard should not marry for some years. He is at a crucial stage of his career, a time when he needs to give his full attention and energies to his music. For all his 'fame and glory' he is at the threshold of emergence into the world of immortals. Every step, every word must be carefully planned, every rough edge smoothed for him. He needs no emotional or domestic distractions. The artist must be selfish, totally self-involved. Richard has had that privilege since he was five. The results are only now becoming evident. And now he is about to dilute his potential with the demands of marriage."

Susan stared at her, speechless, uncomprehending. For a moment the room was quiet. Richard slouched sulkily beside her while Maria sat erect allowing her words to sink in.

"I don't understand," Susan said finally. "You think I'll be a *handicap* to his career? That's incredible!" She felt anger rising. Anger at Mrs. Antonini's words. Anger at Richard's silence. "How could you believe such a thing, Mrs. Antonini? Don't you know that because I love Richard so much, because I have so much respect for his talent I would never, never do anything to distress or disturb him? On the contrary, marriage will give his work more feeling, more depth. He's not a priest, after all! He's a man!"

Maria smiled condescendingly. "I have never expected Richard to be celibate. He can have all the women he wants. Including you. But they need not carry his name. Or his children. They should not burden him with all kinds of unforeseen problems. A wife could make unwise utterances which might embarrass him in the press, or even create awkward social situations unsuited to his image. I know,'' she went on, ''you don't think those things are possible. You believe you will be a valuable addition, the 'good woman behind every great man,' the proverbial 'power behind the throne.' Richard thinks so, too. Right now. But you're both wrong. His brothers' wives have done nothing but distract them, impede their advancement. What makes you think you'd be different?''

As Richard had earlier, Susan made the obvious comparison. ''How can you, of all people, say such things? You who have been so important in your husband's career?''

''I was trained for my role, Susan. My father was a famous concert violinist. I grew up in a household where my mother's every thought and plan revolved around her husband's future. I know discipline *and* self-sufficiency. I know music is all. I recognize that the home of an artist is like a shrine, in which the idol must be protected and served. You think I dominate. No. I protect and serve at the expense of any possible desire for personal recognition. I live only through my husband's genius and that of my sons. I've learned to keep my mouth shut in public, and forego affection in private. Can you do the same?''

Susan's chin went up. ''I may not do it your way, Mrs. Antonini, but I will be as supportive of my husband as you've been of yours. Or your mother was of hers. I'm not stupid. I'm untrained in this kind of thing, but I understand what is required of Richard's wife.'' Her voice softened. ''And I can't believe you won't help me learn to be an asset rather than a liability.''

''Don't count on any help, Susan. Not from me or anyone. The rules for the life you're choosing can't be taught.''

Richard stirred. ''All right,'' he said, ''now that you two have gotten everything off your chests, can we put an end to this? I'm damned tired of sitting here listening to both of you discuss me as though I weren't in the room. Susan, you've heard Mother's opinion. And Mother, you've made your speech. Nothing has changed, but I hope you ladies feel better for it. As for me, I'm going to bed. Being the middle of a tug of war is exhausting.''

Maria rose with dignity, looking at Susan as though to say, ''See? See how impatient he is? How totally unconcerned with the important 'little things'?'' At the door, she paused. ''Since you are both determined, I shall say no more. Over the weekend we can discuss the details of the wedding, Susan, and of course I shall write to your mother.''

When she left, Richard pulled Susan into his arms and kissed her. ''Sorry about all that,'' he said. ''There's no stopping Mother when she gets her teeth into something. You were great, honey, but I think you can see that a long debate with La Belle is an exercise in futility. You'll learn what the rest of us know: you just let her go on and on and then do what you intended in the first place.''

She tried to be as blithe about it as he, but she was troubled. She hadn't expected Maria to welcome her with open arms, but this quiet, fierce opposition was more than she'd bargained for. What if Maria was right? What if lack of freedom would somehow hamper Richard's career? Suppose he did chafe under these new bonds? She'd not be able to bear it. But that wouldn't happen. It couldn't. They loved each other too much.

"I'll truly try to be the wife you deserve," she said, "I know there'll be enormous responsibilities, but you'll always come first." She was trembling. Richard held her close.

"Hey, you really *are* upset, aren't you?"

She nodded her head against his chest.

"Well, don't be. All that barking has very little bite. You'll see. You'll fit right into this family, just as Mary Lou and Jacqueline have. We're not a bad group, once you get used to us."

She needed more than the sound of his voice, the feel of his arms around her. She needed the closeness of him at this moment, the love-making that blotted out all the worrisome realities, the passion that enveloped her when they were together. "Can't we go to your house for a while?" she asked meekly. "I don't want to be alone."

He ran his hands along her body. "You tempt me greatly, madame, but let's cool it for this weekend, okay? We'll be back in New York Monday, away from all the alert eyes and ears that might inhibit my performance!" He laughed. "Darling, we have years in which to make love!"

She'd gone quietly to bed, but she lay awake thinking about Maria's words. There was so much she didn't understand, including Richard's parting words.

"We should call my family, darling," Susan had said. "And by the way, I've always wanted a small, quiet wedding. All right with you?"

"Fine with me, but I don't know whether we'll get away with it. Let's leave all that for tomorrow, sweetheart. I'm bushed and you must be, too. It's been quite a day." He gave her a quiet kiss and was out the front door before she could ask more questions. It was as though he was running away from an unpleasant subject.

She did not tell her parents of this brutal conversation with Maria. The Langdons would have been outraged. Better to let them think the Antoninis were delighted, as Richard told them on the phone next morning. She supposed most of the Antoninis were, if not exactly delighted, at least philosophical. Throughout the weekend, they treated her with offhand acceptance, not making any great effort to be warm but not making her feel unwelcome, either. No, that wasn't true. Gloria did overtly make her feel unwelcome. On Saturday afternoon when she joined the group at the pool, Richard's sister sarcastically remarked on Susan's beautiful, expensive new bikini.

"Well, will you look at Miss Vogue!" Gloria said. She was wearing a beat-up old white jersey tank suit that made her enormous stomach even more obvious. "Who are you expecting, Susan? Some of your fashion-photographer pals?"

The others smiled tolerantly at Gloria's biting remark. Apparently they were used to their sister's tart tongue, but Susan didn't know how to answer such rudeness. She felt herself blushing. It was an uncalled-for snub, and she was thankful when Richard came to her rescue.

"Your eyes are turning green, Glo," he said. "With that front bulge of yours no wonder you're jealous of anybody without an extra ounce of fat."

"*You* should be *dying* of jealousy in that case," Gloria answered. "Yours is all between your ears!"

"Touché," Sergio said. "That'll teach you not to meddle with The Mouth, Richard."

They were all so easy, so casually cruel to one another. Even Richard was unperturbed as he joined in the general laughter. They were used to this give-and-take that spared no one's feelings. Apparently they were secure enough to find insults funny among the family. Only Jacqueline was not amused.

"That's a smashing swimsuit, Susan," she said. "Don't pay any attention to these clods, just because they think it's smart to go around looking like a bunch of Salvation Army rejects."

Susan looked at her gratefully, but she noticed that Jacqueline, like the others, was wearing the kind of nondescript bathing outfit affected by people with generations of money and social standing behind them. Only the middle class really bothers much about "smart" clothes. When you're really confident, Susan thought, you don't give a damn. So I'm "overdressed." So what? I may not know much about being a snob at poolside, but damn it, I can show them up in the water!

Without a word, she stepped up onto the diving board and executed a clean, graceful arc into the pool. Effortlessly, she swam six lengths, knowing she looked good, pleased that they were all watching intently. She'd been on the swimming team at school and loved it, had spent hours practicing her dives and her long, smoothly co-ordinated strokes, never dreaming that one day this special skill would come to her rescue.

Richard was impressed as he offered his hand to help her out of the water.

"You're really good!"

Susan smiled. "Surprised?"

"Not really. It's just one more thing to admire."

Even Gloria was grudgingly complimentary, but the brief moment of glory was soon forgotten. At all other sports, Susan was a disaster. In the softball game she couldn't hit a thrown ball when she was at bat or catch one when she was in the outfield. She knew nothing about touch football and wisely declined to participate in the rough-and-tumble game. Fortunately, Richard played neither baseball nor football. He and Susan sat on the sidelines as Sergio, Walter, Gloria and their older children roughoused tirelessly throughout the afternoon. Jacqueline detested all strenuous activity and said so.

"You don't like games, either?" Susan asked Richard. "Your family seems to specialize in organized mayhem."

He laughed easily. "I was never allowed to go near 'contact sports.' Mother wouldn't permit it." He held out his hands. "These are supposed to be quite valuable. The private nightmare of all pianists is a broken finger."

"Of course. For a moment I forgot."

"I can't even play a game of tennis. Some of the others are going to have a go at a game this afternoon. Want to join?"

Susan shook her head. "I'll be the cheering section."

Later, she and Jacqueline watched Walter and Gloria play a fierce, driving doubles match against Maria and young Joseph. Richard wandered off to the piano. His mother looked like a girl on the court, her small, trim body moving swiftly to return shots even her grandson couldn't reach.

"She's amazing," Susan said.

"Which one? Maria with her years or Gloria with her belly?"

"Both of them. Where *do* they get their energy?"

Jacqueline lit one of her endless cigarettes. "I suspect it comes from sheer meanness. Or maybe they take out their frustrations in physical fitness. Who cares? I don't. You mustn't either."

"I could never be that competitive."

"Good. We don't need another one in the family."

Susan glanced at her. She seemed perfectly relaxed. Only the chain-smoking was a sign that Jacqueline was not as much at ease as she pretended.

"Was it hard, getting used to the family?" Susan asked.

"Not particularly. But then I haven't gone out of my way to try to make them love me. They don't respect anybody whose veins do not course with rich Antonini blood. That definitely leaves out Mary Lou, Raoul, me . . . and you."

Susan understood the friendly, tacit advice. Jacqueline was saying, "Don't try to become one of them. Accept your place as an in-law. Get along. And don't make waves." Somehow the few words of simple acceptance made it easier to swallow the bitter pill that came on Sunday: the total take-over of her wedding plans. It happened after Mrs. Antonini returned from church. She was the only one who attended, and she found Richard and Susan lounging in chaises on the lawn, contentedly browsing through the New York *Times*. Maria pulled up a chair.

"Since you'll be leaving late this afternoon, I think we'd better discuss the wedding. There are a great many plans to be made and very little time to make them."

"It will take a bit of doing," Susan agreed politely, "but I'm sure we can manage. It will be a very quiet, simple ceremony."

"Quiet? Simple?" Maria looked at her as though she was mad. "For Richard? My dear Susan, I don't think you understand. This marriage will not be buried in the society section of the newspapers. It will be big news. Surely you don't expect a celebrity to be married as anonymously as a shoe clerk! There are important guests to be asked, press coverage to be arranged. I'd think St. Thomas's would be the suitable church. You *are* Episcopalian, I believe? And the reception at the Colony Club, I suppose?"

"Mother, Susan *really* wants a modest wedding at her own church. She told me so again this morning. What difference does it make? After all, it *is* the bride's prerogative to have the kind of ceremony she wants."

Bless you, darling, Susan thought. But Mrs. Antonini was scandalized.

"What difference does it make?" Maria echoed. "Richard, have you taken leave of your senses? If you have no regard for what your family wants, then at least consider what you owe your public! You are an internationally known figure. You cannot simply skulk off to some little Bronxville chapel! How would it look? People would think you were marrying a nobody! They'd probably conclude we didn't approve! There'd be all kinds of unsavory gossip we couldn't control. No. It's impossible. If you insist on rushing into this marriage, then at least let it receive the attention suitable to your stature."

Susan waited for him to refuse, but instead he seemed to be considering.

"Well, you may have a point. Tell you what. Let's compromise. Since you don't like our timetable aud Susan doesn't like your conception, maybe we all have to give a little. Mother, you be graceful about the date and we'll go along with the dog-and-pony show." He turned to Susan. "That seems fair, doesn't it, darling?"

She stared at him in disbelief. He was overriding her wishes to suit his mother, his public and, probably in truth, himself. Is this how it will always be? Susan wondered. Will I be on the outside of every decision, large or small, giving way to the demands of public life and the power of Maria Antonini? If I start this way, can I ever turn back?

"No, darling," she said almost in a whisper, "it *doesn't* seem fair. You know how I feel. I'm not an untouched eighteen-year-old who comes trembling down the aisle in virginal white. It's hypocritical and pretentious. I've always hated the idea of a big wedding, even when I was very young. And I'm not a child-bride. I'm an adult, marrying an adult." Her eyes went to Maria. "Mrs. Antonini, I do realize how important Richard is. But this is my wedding, too. I don't wish to have it arranged by concert managers and press agents. It's a very personal and private thing, not a publicity stunt staged for the newspapers and the curious stares of strangers. Please understand. Both of you."

She was trembling as she stopped speaking. She knew she was fighting for something much bigger than the details of a wedding, She was in a struggle for independence—from Maria, from the Antonini name, even from Richard himself, who was beginning to consider the various aspects of this event as clinically as he would plan a concert. And she knew she was going to lose this battle as she would lose many more in the future. She knew it, even as she spoke. She saw the answer in Richard's face as he weighed the matter.

"Susan, love," he said finally, "I know how you feel. I happen to agree with you. But Mother *does* have a point. She's been through this before. It would look odd if we didn't give the world what it expects. Sweetheart, my publicity is something you're going to have to learn to live with, annoying as it is. And it starts for you the day we announce our engagement. Let's be practical, shall we? I know you're too intelligent to be inflexible. *How* we're married isn't what's really important. All that counts is that we'll *be* married. You do see the reasoning. I know you do. And it'll still be your show. A bit fancier than you'd planned, I realize, but you'll still be the star." I don't want to be a star, she thought. I just want to marry you, and if I refuse to do it your way—your mother's way—I might not be able to marry you at all. She nodded, finally, reluctantly.

"That's my girl!" Richard said. "I'm sure your parents will approve."

"If they don't wish to undertake the cost of a big wedding, Susan, Richard's father and I will, of course, be willing to . . ."

Susan could have slapped her. "That won't be a problem, Mrs. Antonini," she said coldly. "Thank you all the same, but my parents are well aware that the obligations are the bride's family's." At the moment she was the most dignified of the three. "They wouldn't have it any other way," she said proudly.

Maria nodded. "Very well. I'm glad you see the necessity for this."

Susan didn't answer. I wish I *couldn't* see it, she thought. One of the things she would like to change in herself was this damned ability to look at both sides of almost any question. She wished she could be more opinionated, less open to reason. People who could were infinitely less confused, probably much happier. She could understand, rationally, why Richard's wedding probably *had* to be elaborate, but she wondered what would have happened if she'd refused to go along with that fact. The question was academic. She *was* going along. She'd try to believe it was for the best. She'd even try to sound convincing to her mother and father when they heard of her change of heart.

Chapter 7

IT WAS CLEARLY impossible to put together, in a few short weeks, the kind of spectacular wedding she visualized for her son, but Richard's mother did it. Maria was used to accomplishing what other people thought hopeless. She had the drive and determination. She also had money, influence and "personnel." Once she faced the fact that she could not stop this marriage, she took it on as a personal project, enlisting Richard's manager, Paul Carmichael, and Richard's press agent, Gerry Carter, as full-time aides.

To Susan's amazement, and that of the Langdons, St. Thomas's was magically booked for the ceremony on unprecedently short notice. The Colony Club—to which Bea Langdon did not belong but Maria Antonini did—was reserved for the reception. Printers were bullied into getting out, overnight, engraved invitations which Maria's social secretary addressed and mailed, keeping a careful count of the RSVP acceptances which came back with the speed of a summons to the White House. Caterers were instructed, florists contacted, a fleet of limousines engaged, police barricades arranged for, to keep back the curious who would gather outside the church.

The Sunday after Susan's visit to her parents, her picture, taken by Bachrach, ("the *only* suitable potraitist," Maria said), appeared in the *Times,* under the headline "RICHARD ANTONINI TO WED." Beatrice was furious when she saw it. She had unwillingly but realistically turned over all the details, including the announcement, to the "professionals."

"I simply couldn't do what they can," she'd told Wil. "Not in eight *years,* much less eight *weeks!* It must be nice to have such clout." Now she rattled the paper angrily. "There's no doubt whose wedding *this* is, is there? I thought it was customary to feature the *bride's* name."

"Now, honey, you know none of this matters as long as Susie's happy."

"I know." Bea's eyes filled with tears. "I'm being petty. It's just that I always thought her wedding would be something we'd all put together with pleasure. I wasn't prepared for this three-ring circus."

"Sweetheart, don't fight it. You still have plenty to do. My God, the presents that are pouring into this house already! Cataloguing them will be a career in itself!" He looked at the array of silver tea services and porcelain demitasse cups and tissue-thin crystal goblets. "They're collecting a king's ransom of gifts from personal friends. Can you imagine what it will be like after this announcement? You'll be up to your ears in lists of who sent what!"

She wouldn't be comforted. "Any reasonably intelligent eighth-grader could do that. I'm surprised Mrs. Antonini hasn't sent one."

He tried again. "Come on. Stop pouting. In spite of their overwhelming efficiency, there are things only you can do. Look how quickly you got together that list of guests to be invited 'on the bride's side.' You stayed up two whole nights!"

"Big deal. I can imagine what the Antonini list will be like."

"All right, what about the really important things you have a say in? The wedding gown, for one. You and Susan go to Bendel's tomorrow to get that, don't you? And the bridesmaids' dresses?"

"On her lunch hour, for heaven's sake!" Bea said. "Why does she have to give Kate Fenton a whole month's notice? She's going to be absolutely exhausted, going to all the prewedding parties and working full time! And why doesn't she move home right away? It would be better to pay her share of two months' rent to Evie Maxwell and come back here to live until she's married."

Wil's patience began to wear thin. "Darling, it would be even more exhausting for her to commute right now. You know that! Take it easy. She'll still have a few weeks to herself after she leaves *Vogue*. You two will go trousseau-shopping and apartment-hunting and all those nice mother-daughter things."

"Apartment hunting," Bea repeated. "That's another ridiculous thing. They should be moving into their own place as soon as the tour is over. Not coming back to the fourth floor of the Antonini town house!"

Her husband counted to ten. "Okay. I agree with you. But it would be hard to find a place in a month. Staying with Richard's parents is only temporary. Maybe you and Susie *will* find the right apartment before she's married, but there's not much time. When they come back in December you and she can start looking in earnest."

"You know what I think? I don't think they're *ever* going to have their own place. I have a hunch Mrs. Antonini means for them to stay right there. She wants to hold onto Richard any way she can, even if it means putting up with his wife."

"Now why do you say a thing like that? You haven't even met Mrs. Antonini."

Bea was quiet for a moment. "I don't know. I just feel it, from the few things Susan says. And from the way Richard talked about his mother when the four of us had dinner last Thursday. She has an abnormal hold on that young man."

"*Abnormal?*"

"I don't mean anything *terrible*. Not incestuous! But he obviously think she's the Oracle of Delphi! Heaven help Susan. Your everyday, run-of-the-mill mother-in-law is enough to take, without having to cope with such a paragon. And from what I hear, the sister and in-laws also excel in everything from child-rearing to the three-minute mile! Not that I don't think Susan isn't as good as—or better than—any of them. But she'll have her hands full."

"Richard will take care of her," Wil said. "He's a strong character in his own right. And he adores Susie."

"Yes," Bea admitted, "I liked him. More than I thought I would. There were no 'airs and graces' when he came here." She finally smiled. "I am being silly. I know that. My nose is terribly out of joint."

"Your nose is beautiful. Like the rest of you. Of course, you're a little weird," Wil teased. "Most mothers would cut off their right arms to see their daughters making such a brilliant marriage. Admit it. Aren't you the envy of the Friday-afternoon bridge club?"

"Idiot!" But he was right. It was only human, after all, to take pleasure in your child's achievements. And becoming the fiancée of one of the world's most eligible bachelors certainly had to be rated as no mean feat. Bea's friends were wild with envy.

Kate Fenton had different worries. Along with the reservations she and Beatrice shared about the Antoninis, Susan's boss was not convinced that her promising young associate could be happy "doing nothing." She said just that to Susan when she was told of the girl's plans to leave the magazine.

"You love working," Kate said. "You like being important in your own right. What the hell will you do with your time?"

"A million things! I'll be getting our own place ready, when we find one. After we're settled, I probably can do some volunteer work while Richard's busy during the day. And, of course, there's all the traveling. He tours half the year. There's no way I could hold down a full-time job even if I wanted to."

"I suppose not. Not if you plan to go everywhere with him. What about children?"

"Not right away. We've agreed to wait a couple of years."

"Good decision," Kate said noncommittally. "You still could do some writing, Susan, Free-lance features or articles for me. Even for other publications. I hate to see you give up the one piece of yourself that's your very own."

"I might try. Later. Thanks, Kate. It's a good idea."

She knew Kate was happy for her, yet troubled about this totally new character she was about to assume. Susan could understand. She privately felt some of those misgivings. But nothing was perfect. It would be a difficult adjustment but she didn't doubt she could make it. She was sorry Kate had refused to be her maid of honor. The woman had looked startled and then burst out laughing when Susan asked her.

"Me? Maid of honor? You must be kidding! That's all you need—an aging spinster doddering down the aisle ahead of you, dressed in some outlandish rig and holding a bunch of flowers! Get Evie or one of your other friends, for God's sake! It's ridiculous!'

She didn't realize how hurt Susan was until the girl said, almost inaudibly, "It doesn't seem ridiculous to me. You're my dearest friend."

Kate was filled with remorse. "Susie, I didn't mean I wasn't honored by your wanting me. It might be the best compliment I've ever had. But my dear, that kind of role is for someone your own age. Now if, God forbid, I were married and could be your *matron* of honor, that might be different. But this just isn't a suitable role for me. I'll be right up front, on your side of the church, cheering. By the way, who are your attendants?"

"Well, I guess I'll ask Evie to be maid of honor since you won't. I'm having Richard's sister and his two sisters-in-law as bridesmaids. I'd planned on Evie as the fourth. Now I suppose I'll ask one of my old college chums."

As she spoke, she realized that she had almost no close women friends. Not that she didn't like women. She had simply drifted away from the Bronxville group and except for Evie hadn't been that close to any young women in New York. It had been easy and (inadmissible thought!) probably politic to ask Richard's female relatives to attend her. It went along with his brothers and brother-in-law being ushers and Paul Carmichael his best man. Who is the fourth usher? Susan wondered, surprised she didn't know. It'll be interesting to see whether Paul and Evie like each other when they meet. They're both very attractive and unmarried . . . She paused, smiling at herself. I'm thinking like all my newly-wed friends whose devout mission in life is to get everybody else married. Matchmaking was a diversion she'd always scorned in others. And here she was mentally doing the same thing. It was a switch, but not the only one. Whoever would have thought Susan Langdon would hold still for this incredible production of a ceremony? She could hardly wait for it to be over and she could be alone with Richard. They'd have only a week before Boston and his first concert of the fall season. They'd rented a fully staffed house on Cape Cod for their honeymoon, a wild extravagance since they had to take it for the whole month of September and would spend only seven days in it, but it was what they both wanted—someplace secluded and quiet, yet close enough to Boston so that traveling time would not cut into their precious free days. Susan had, however, protested the houseful of servants.

"I can take care of us for a week," she'd said. "I'm no Julia Child, but I can keep us fed. Please, Richard. We don't need a bunch of retainers underfoot. Certainly not *this* week, particularly!"

"Darling, I don't want you in the *kitchen* on our honeymoon." He'd smiled endearingly. "Or any other time, for that matter. From here on in, your full-time job is wife and lover, mistress of *me,* not of the *house."*

He meant it well and Susan did not argue, but it was another glimpse of things to come. She *wanted* to be mistress of her own house. They'd require help, of course, but not a huge staff.

"When we have our own apartment, I'll be mistress of that," she said. "Even if I'm only supervising a cleaning lady."

"One thing at a time, baby."

Sometimes he didn't understand Susan. She should have been thrilled at the thought of the luxury she was about to enjoy. She'd never known what it was like to be rich and waited on. It was as though she resisted the idea of having nothing to do. You'd think she'd be delighted to realize she could hire anybody she wanted for anything. Instead, she seemed troubled by the prospect. He was glad they could't rush into a place of their own. It was a good thing they'd live in his old bachelor quarters for a while. Susan would have a chance to get used to life in a big household, find out how to give orders to servants, learn from Maria how the well-oiled machinery of "gracious living" worked. Cleaning lady indeed! What was she thinking of? Even when they found their own place it would have to be something spectacular, a triplex, or maybe a town house, something that would require at least three in help. Susan was acting as though she saw them in a one-bedroom apartment with a dining area attached to the living room. Well, that was nothing to worry about for now. It would be months before they even considered their own establishment. There was the fall tour and a recording session scheduled for December and then the holidays. After that they'd be off for another series of recitals lasting well into the spring. With luck, he could postpone the departure from Seventieth Street for at least six months. Maybe more. Maybe even for a couple of years, until they had a child.

He supposed he'd misled Susan. She and her mother were looking for an apartment. No matter. They wouldn't come up with anything that suited him.

The 4 P.M. wedding was as storybook-beautiful as any ever seen by the hundreds who packed the church, the other hundreds who peered at the famous guests from behind police lines set up on the sidewalk, and the millions who gobbled up every gushing detail of the ceremony and reception on the six-and eleven-o'clock TV news that night, and in papers across the country next day.

Susan was glorious as she came toward the altar on her father's arm, regal in her ivory satin and lace gown with a little tiara of pearls holding her veil and a small bouquet of cream-colored roses crowning the white prayer book that Bea Langdon had carried at her own wedding twenty-six years before.

Gloria, Jacqueline, Mary Lou and Barbara Dudley, a childhood friend of Susan's, walked sedately down the aisle preceding Evelyn Maxwell, the maid of honor. In front of them were the ushers—Richard's brothers and brother-in-law and his young nephew, Joseph, Sergio's fifteen-year-old son. Susan had been surprised that the boy was chosen as the fourth usher.

"I thought you'd pick some old friend," she'd said to Richard when he told her.

"Thought I'd keep it in the family," he'd answered.

That wasn't true, Susan realized. The truth was that Richard had no close men friends except his manager. How strange that neither of us has contemporaries who are not related either to our families or our jobs. Even Barbara had been an almost "desperation" choice. Richard's background and mine are so different, Susan thought, and yet we're so much alike. Loners, really. He's been too occupied with music all his life to form any "outside attachments"; I've drifted away from my early ones. She hadn't seen Barb in nearly two years, not since her fourth bridesmaid's own wedding to Stan Dudley. She'd been surprised, rightly so, when Susan had asked her to be a member of the wedding, but she accepted with pleasure. The two had been inseparable as children, had gone to college together and then drifted apart when the one married and the other moved to New York and a job which absorbed her time and interests.

Susan's attendants were lovely in their ecru chiffon gowns, their arms full of yellow roses. Evie's dress was café-au-lait color, a dramatic touch between the bridesmaids' pale dresses and Susan's creamy satin. All the flowers in the church were in the bride's favorite tones—masses of yellow roses and trees of freesia, pale orange tulips and lemon-colored carnations. They gave the church a golden glow accented by hundreds of candles, and they filled it with the fragrance of springtime-past. It was like a beautiful oil painting, this stately parade, a moving masterpiece splashed with sunlight. Even the noticeable pregnant Gloria looked soft and serene, her floating gown for once diffusing the stocky outlines of the woman's figure.

In the front pew, Bea sighed with pleasure at the sight. And woman-like, she was glad she'd "gone overboard," as Wil insisted, in the choice of her own gown.

"You're the mother of the bride," he'd said. "The most important person there, after the bride and groom. Buy yourself something beautiful, darling. And don't look at the price tag!"

For once, she'd done just that. Her own outrageously expensive Stavropoulos chiffon gown in tones of pale blue shading to green was as beautiful as, maybe more beautiful than, Maria Antonini's gray silk-jersey Dior. True, she did not have the Antonini jewels, but she felt she did her daughter proud. We may not be rich, Bea thought, and this damned wedding is ten times what we can afford, but by God we won't be patronized by anybody! Neither, she thought proudly, would Susan. Watching her approach, so poised and dignified, Bea remembered her daughter's indignation as she recounted her refusal of Maria's suggestion that five-year-old Raoul Taffin and his three-year-old sister be ring-bearer and flower girl.

"I told her, 'No thanks,' " Susan reported. "My God, what does she think this is: The Coronation? Not enough to have a full choir and a fortune in flowers! She actually wanted to have that little boy come down the aisle with my wedding ring on a satin pillow and that baby toddle along strewing rose petals in my path! Can you believe it? Even Richard was with me on that one!" Susan laughed.

"He said he was damned if he was going to be at the mercy of a couple of scene-stealers barely out of diapers. I swear, Mother, Mrs. Antonini really *does* think they're the Royal Family!"

Bea had only smiled in reply. It was true, of course, she thought now. This is the wedding of a prince. Pay homage to the son of Maria. She and Mrs. Antonini had met twice, over tea in the town house, to discuss wedding details, and again the night before, when the entire wedding party had been Giovanni's and Maria's guests at an elaborate dinner at home. Like Susan, Bea had instantly taken to the maestro and was charmed by Jacqueline. As for the others, she found them polite but for the most part distant and even in some cases faintly sardonic. There was a great deal of the same almost cruel family teasing that Susan had seen in Pound Ridge, a strange undercurrent of rivalry among the sons and daughter as though each was constantly trying to outshine the others. Maria subtly fostered this, cleverly baiting them, pitting one against the other. What a ruthlessly ambitious woman she is! Bea thought. She doesn't love her children as a mother naturally does; she only wants them to win at everything. Richard was attentive to his fiancée's parents, and Paul Carmichael, whom Bea also liked immediately, was especially warm and considerate. Probably, she thought ruefully, because aside from Evie and Barbara and Stan Dudley, he was the only other "outsider." And even he was no stranger. As Richard's manager, he was as much a part of the family as anyone not born or married into it could be.

"Your daughter is marrying a great man, Mrs. Langdon," Paul had said. "He's the true genius in the family, aside from the Old Man, of course."

She'd smiled. "All I want him to be is a great husband. Susan deserves that."

He'd given her a serious, almost troubled look before he answered lightly, "Of course she does. We all love Susan. Every man here envies Richard his good luck."

Watching her husband and daughter come down the aisle, Bea thought fleetingly of that brief conversation. I hope they do love her, she prayed. But if they don't, don't let them destroy her.

The newlyweds fled the reception as early as possible, taking the limousine a few short blocks to the Pierre Hotel, where they'd spend the night before leaving next morning for the Cape. In the suite, Susan collapsed with a sigh of relief.

"My God, it's only eight o'clock!" she said. "I feel as though it's four in the morning!"

"You didn't eat anything at the reception. Hungry? Want dinner sent up?"

She shook her head. "No. But that bottle of champagne in the bucket looks tempting."

"Let's have some while we're getting comfortable."

While they got into robes, Susan began to laugh.

"What's so funny?"

"I was just thinking how nice it is to be alone—and legal."

"You think a piece of paper is going to make it better?"

"Yes," she said. "Isn't that crazy? But I do."

Richard pulled her to him. "Let's find out how crazy you are."

I was right, she thought much later, lying beside him, fingering the diamond band on her left hand. It *was* better. The best. As close to heaven as I'll ever come. How hopelessly conventional I really am! She hadn't realized it when they'd been in bed before. She'd thought then that she couldn't know greater passion, more eagerness than she had during their affair. But knowing she was Richard's wife made her feel free, uninhibited as she'd never been. And her abandon sweetened and strengthened his desire until they reached heights that left them both speechless with pleasure. It's as though we're discovering each other, Susan thought when they finally separated. She lay limp and satiated, happy beyond description. Then she reached over and began to caress her husband.

"Help!" Richard said weakly. "No more! Not yet!"

"I *was* right, wasn't I?"

He looked very serious. "Yes, sweetheart. Surprisingly you were. I hope it will always be this good."

"Better," she teased. "On our fiftieth aninversary it'll be *super!* Oh, darling, I love you so much!"

"And I you." He gave her a little slap on the rear end. "Hey, it's nearly nine-thirty. Think I'll call down and see if the first editions of the papers are in."

"You're kidding! Who gives a damn about papers?"

"We had a helluva press turnout."

"I know. I didn't think I'd ever get rid of those funny purple circles in front of my eyes from the flashbulbs."

"You'll get used to it," Richard said. "It comes with the territory."

While they waited for the papers, Susan chattered. "Did you ever see anybody cry as hard as my Aunt Clara? I thought her dress would melt! And your father was so darling. His toast to us was sweet. I'm glad Evie caught the bouquet. I aimed at her, of course. Do you think she and Paul liked each other?''

The doorbell buzzed before he could answer and a bellman handed Richard the *Times* and the *Daily News*. Susan made a face.

''I don't know why you give a hoot about a dumb picture of me in my wedding gown. They'll just run that along with the press release of who attended. I can recite that story to you in advance. The headline will say 'Susan Langdon weds Richard Antonini,' and then there'll be a dreary account of who wore what, and all the other canned information Gerry sent them a week ago. Bor-ing!''

Richard glanced at the papers, smiled, and passed them to her.

''There, my love, is your bor-ing little story.''

Susan's eyes widened. She'd expected an important account of her wedding on the society pages, but she'd not imagined it would be treated as news, rushed into print like some major, late-breaking story. The *Times* had a four-column picture of herself and Richard emerging from the church with the heading, ''Concert Pianist Richard Antonini Weds.'' The *News* went all-out, devoting the entire two-page center spread to photographs of the ceremony and the reception. There were not only candid shots inside the church, but pictures of Giovanni and Maria arriving, a shot of Sergio leaving, with Mary Lou barely visible behind him. There was a closeup of the newlyweds cutting the wedding cake and photographs of the great of the music world—opera stars, symphony conductors, violinists, pianists, impresarios. With its usual irresistible urge for puns, the paper had captioned the story ''DUET LOOK LIKE A SOLO FOR ANTONINI?''

Susan threw down the pages in disgust. ''It's obscene! They make it sound like Barnum and Bailey! It's so vulgar! Kids are dying in Viet Nam and blacks are being beaten up in Alabama, and the best use they can make of space is to report a wedding like it was big news! It reads like a bash at the court of Louis XIV! I'm surprised there isn't a picture of some fat soprano stuffing her face and saying, 'Let 'em eat cake'!''

He was not amused. ''It's probably vulgar, Susie, but it's good box office. You're just annoyed because you're surprised. I expected it. You'd better be ready for this and a lot worse when it comes to your precious privacy.'' Then he softened. ''Sweetheart, don't be upset. You belong to the world now, just as you belong to me.'' He held out his hand, smiling. ''You know what happens to bad little girls when they have temper tantrums, don't you? They get sent to bed. And you, thank God, are a bad little girl.''

In spite of herself, Susan laughed as he picked her up and carried her into the bedroom. But it was more than the outlandish publicity that bothered her, The biggest disappointment was that there'd been just the briefest mention of ''the bride's parents.'' For all anybody cared, she could have been an orphan.

In other houses and apartments around New York, other Antoninis sent out for the early editions.

''I do wish Richard would be more careful about camera angles,'' Maria said. ''He *knows* his right side is the better one.''

''Perhaps he had other things on his mind,'' Giovanni answered mildly.

''Jesus, I'm getting fat!'' Sergio said.

"Susan looked lovely, didn't she?" Jacqueline asked Walter.

In the guest suite on East Seventieth Street, Gloria threw her copy of the paper in the wastebasket. "No pictures of *us*. As *usual*." Raoul didn't answer. He was already asleep.

Chapter 8

THE WEEK THAT followed her wedding was one of surprises for Susan, most of them wonderful. Wonderful to awaken beside the man she loved, knowing it was her rightful place. Enchanting to discover the everyday little things that were all part of Richard—what foods he liked and what he hated; the television he preferred ("talk shows" primarily); his fascination with diets and exercise and all forms of physical fitness; his vast knowledge of musical lore. Every piece of trivia seemed a separate, interesting revelation. She did not see them forming a picture of a totally self-involved man, protective of his health and his youthful good looks, scornful and envious of other celebrities, educated only about his own field. She did not see him as ego-ridden and intellectually shallow. Through her infatuated eyes, he was not vain but artistic. His narrowness of interests she interpreted as dedication, his food-faddism as the eccentricity of genius. Even his flashes of male chauvinism seemed excitingly masculine and dominant, and as a lover he was expert and insatiable.

They rose late, breakfasted heartily, took long walks along the ocean, holding hands and stopping occasionally to kiss. Susan felt like the heroine in a soft-focus foreign film, as though she were drifting in the misty atmosphere of some perfect, unreal world. She chided herself for resenting the hours each afternoon when Richard left her for the piano. The first day, she protested when he said he had to practice.

"Oh, Richard, no! Not this week!"

"This week and *every* week, my darling. Can't afford to get rusty, especialiy when I have a performance seven days from now."

He was perfectly right, of course. This was no businessman on holiday. An artist could not let down for one moment. She tried not to be jealous of the hours he literally shut her out of his life. What a child I am, she thought, wanting every minute of his time, every second of his company. I will always have to share him with his music. It is the focus of his life. I'm only grateful that what's left over is so intensely, irrevocably devoted to me.

And she *was* proud and grateful the first time she heard him perform after their marriage. It was as though his brilliance was now partly her own. From her seat in the audience in Boston's Symphony Hall, she was so moved that tears literally ran down her face. She wanted to stand up and announce that he was hers, that this beautiful creature at the piano was her adored husband. Susan's eyes and ears and heart devoured him from the moment he made his entrance onstage. She felt she would burst with happiness when the audience stood and cheered, applauding wildly as he entered and faced them with a grave smile and a formal little bow.

He seated himself at the big Steinway, waited, showman-like, for the settling-in-seats to subside, the coughing to stop, the rustling of programs to cease. And then those wonderful hands that excited her began their seduction of the piano. She had heard him play in public before, but it seemed to her that there was new passion in his performance, as though it matched his love-making. There were gentle, caressing motions followed by great slashes of power. She felt the depth of emotion in his approach, the concentration on detail, the melodic shadings, the exquisite intricacies, the whispers of measures and the great surges, like thunder, relating them to his love-making. I've done something for him, she thought, awed. He's never been this great.

At intermission she went backstage, helped him into a complete change of clothing. He seemed to barely notice her as he stripped off his sweat-soaked morning coat and put on everything fresh from the skin out. She'd been amazed, as they left their suite at the Ritz-Carlton, to see how much they carried with them. Richard went to the auditorium in casual clothes and brought another, more conservative "street outfit" to wear when he left past waiting crowds. In addition, there were the two complete sets of formal wear, plus his own special brand of soap, deodorant and cologne, even the blow-dryer he used for his hair and Band-Aids to protect the little finger of each hand.

Susan had laughed. "You look as though you're going away for the weekend!"

He hadn't been amused. He hardly seemed to know she was there. He was already temporarily lost to her, deep in thoughts of his work, mentally rehearsing the music. It was the same at intermission. Paul Carmichael was also in the dressing room, acting as Susan did—as a quiet pair of hands, following orders, speaking little, aware that they must not break the intense concentration necessary for the second half of the performance and the encores. She wanted to tell her husband how superb he was, how extraordinary, but she sensed he would not hear her. This was the "performing Richard," as unaware of his wife as he would have been of a paid attendant. She was not hurt. She and Paul smiled at each other, knowing that this Richard was oblivious to everything but his music.

When he finished the final encore—the *Étincelles,* by Moszknowski—Susan unthinkingly stood with the rest, screaming, "Bravo!" as he took his bows and finally shook his head and made a little gesture of apology, as though to say, "I'd go on forever to please you, but I am exhausted."

Reluctantly, they let him go. Then Paul was at her side, protecting her as they made their way through the crowds that swarmed backstage, elbowing aside the throngs of admirers who hoped to get into their idol's presence.

"Excuse us," Paul kept saying. "Would you make way for Mrs. Antonini, please?"

The new words sounded wonderful. There would be many afternoons and evenings when Paul would guide and shelter her, clearing a path with the same polite but forceful request. But never again would she feel what she did that first time. She would come to recognize the more obscure music, anticipate the modest gestures Richard would make as he accepted the hysterical adulation. But she'd never recapture that first magic moment of awareness, that total revelation of Richard's unique gift. In the dressing room she hung back as people surrounded him, kissed him, suffocated him with compliments. He loved it. It was some time before he even saw her. Then, across the room he gave her a smile she interpreted as a special embrace, and she hugged it to her, content.

In Chicago and Minneapolis and Houston and Dallas and San Antonio, Richard repeated his triumphs. He practiced daily on the piano that was made available in each city . . . those concert grands pianists referred to by the numbers assigned by Steinway. When he was in the flower-filled hotel suite he was constantly surrounded by people: local VIP's, patrons of the arts, and the omnipresent press, shuttled in and out by Gerry Carter, who joined them in Boston and expertly manipulated the impossible demands of local papers and TV stations.

At one moment when she and Richard were dressing for a dinner party, Susan, wearing only a bra and panties, said, playfully, "Gerry does a fantastic job, doesn't she? I could almost be jealous of the way she takes you over."

He'd laughed. "She's a terrific press agent."

"So how come she wasn't around when I interviewed you for *Vogue?*"

"I don't know, darling. She's always busier when we're out of town. Maybe she was doing something else that day. Or maybe I had a hunch I'd want you all to myself."

"Now you're telling me you're psychic?" Susan grinned. "You want me to believe you knew I was going to be special?"

He'd come close to her, then, pressing his body against hers. "Could be. I can smell a sexy woman even over the telephone." He pulled the bra away and kissed her breasts. "You're delicious." His hands began to move.

"Darling, stop! We're due at dinner in half an hour."

"The hell with it. Let 'em wait."

She'd be glad to get home, even if home was the Antonini house. The trip was exciting but exhausting. She'd never realized how complicated it was to go on tour with a celebrity, and a demanding one, at that. Richard hated hotel food, so they took full suites with kitchens, which meant that Susan made breakfast the way her husband liked it, fresh and piping hot, not lukewarm from room service. He was fussy about his diet, so Gerry arranged in each city to have a chef come in to prepare other meals which Paul and Gerry usually shared. Occasionally, they went to a party in some elegant private home, but only if the hostess was rich and influential . . . someone who could not be offended because she was "important."

They did not go to many such events and Susan was not sorry. The dinner parties and cocktail receptions were stiff and formal, and though she did not begrudge the fact that Richard was the focus of attention, she felt merely tolerated.

They had, in fact, very little fun for the next three months. When he was not practicing or giving interviews or receiving people, Richard needed rest. He conserved his energy for concert and his charm for the press and public, He was still sexually greedy, but there were times when Susan felt his mind was somewhere else even when his body was over her own. Still, she was not unhappy. Her response to his touch was instant and as hungry as his. But she found herself restless with too much time on her hands. She did the local shops and museums and art galleries, and when he had time, Paul came with her. She grew fonder of Paul every day. He was becoming her closest friend, her only confidant. A lanky, somewhat rumpled, even-tempered young man of thirty, he was a marked contrast to the spectacular Richard. She was not physically attracted to him, but she loved his company and felt easy with him, to the point where she could discuss things with which she'd never dare bother her preoccupied husband. Things such as the letters that poured in wherever they went. Susan, in her new role as wife/lover/semiservant, had voluntarily taken on the chore of going through the daily mail. It surprised her to find that a classical musician inspired the same kind of manic devotion as a film actor or a rock star. The letters came on heavily engraved stationery and blue-lined pages of schoolgirls' notebooks. Some were pure "fan mail," shy and reverential or overly effusive. But many verged on the obscene, saying what they'd like to do to Richard or have Richard do to them. They were disturbing letters and, of course, never acknowledged.

"I can't believe what people write!" She and Paul were strolling through the Chicago Art Institute. "I've never read such uninhibited propositions! Good Lord, you'd think Richard had his own 'groupies'!"

Paul smiled. "He has. The sickies go for *any* celebrity, and to some people Richard's sexier at that piano than Elvis with his guitar. Don't *you* feel that sensuous quality when he plays?"

"Yes, of course. But my God, Paul, you wouldn't think that strangers presumably interested in the classics would have such thoughts about Richard!"

"Why not?" Paul's handsome face darkened. "They're still people who fantasize about being screwed by somebody famous. It's been going on for years, Susie. Since he was eighteen." He paused. "Frankly, I'm glad he's safely married."

She looked at him curiously. "Don't tell me Richard ever *responded* to any of these nymphomaniacs!"

"Honey, he's human, too. You must know Richard had quite a reputation with the ladies."

"Well, yes, but I thought . . ."

"You thought he was an ordinary bachelor, dating your kind of girls and sometimes taking them to bed."

Susan didn't answer. Yes, she had thought that, though she didn't want to think about any of it any more. She knew Richard had been far from a saint. He was attractive, unmarried and full of normal desires, but he was also discriminating and discreet. That's what she'd believed. That was understandable. Forgivable. After all, she'd been to bed with men before she met Richard. But she'd known and liked them, even thought herself in love with them.

"I don't mean to shock you," Paul went on, "but any famous man is subject to temptations the ordinary guy never runs into. Fame as an aphrodisiac works both ways, you know. Anyway, that's over, thank God. He has you now and he loves you very much. Don't pay any attention to the letter writers who're just dying to get on their backs for him. Or any other position he might suggest. In fact, if I were you I'd give up the secretarial duties. Leave the mail to Gerry or to me. We'll send it back to the office to be answered or destroyed."

"Don't be silly. I know it doesn't mean anything. Richard doesn't read it." She smiled. "Not any more."

"Then why should *you?* Or do you dig masochism?"

The words stayed with her. It was naïve to think that Richard could have resisted some of these titillating propositions. What man could turn away from the erotic opportunity to have any kind of sex he wanted, any time, in any way he chose, from people who worshiped him? All right. Forget it. That's past. And Paul was right. Reading all that nonsense *was* masochistic. Turn it off, Susan, she told herself. Your husband is an attractive, sought-after man who was once susceptible. But that's all over. And it was only an ego trip when it was happening. He doesn't need that kind of flattery any more. Nor does he have time or opportunity with me around, she thought wryly, somewhat startled by her own cynicism. Anyway, she still didn't believe that Richard had ever gotten involved with the kind of promiscuous, oversexed women who wrote to him, no matter what Paul implied. Richard could have his pick of the best. I wonder if he ever had an affair with Gerry? Susan thought suddenly. She was a striking divorcée, five or six years older than Richard, and wordly in a way that Susan was not. Gerry obviously was devoted to him, though she'd never given the slightest hint that theirs had been more tban a close business relationship. Could you be in love with a man, make love to him and then when he married, turn it off to become the perfect impersonal employee? It seemed hard to believe. Even Gerry wasn't *that* sophisticated. What kind of crazy thoughts were these? It came from reading that stupid, erotic mail, from watching women make fools of themselves when Richard was in a room, from seeing him be charming and attentive to pretty girls and chic women whose names he could not even remember. She'd never been a jealous woman and she wouldn't start now. But, Susan thought that day in Chicago, I'll be glad when we get back to New York where the spotlight momentarily dims.

The trip also made her realize how anonymous she felt and how much she needed some identity of her own. It was not enough for her to stay docilely in the background all the time. Kate was right. She'd do some writing when she got home. Face it. She got a kick out of seeing her name in print. Maybe she'd look into volunteer work as she'd also considered. The taste of "importance" she'd had on *Vogue,* however minor, was something she missed. Not that she intended to be a "career woman" ever again, but there was no reason why she couldn't be Mrs. Richard Antonini and still achieve things on her own.

They came back to New York early in December, the day before Gloria produced the expected twins whom she named Pierre and Claudette in grudging acknowledgment of Raoul's dead parents. Susan and Jacqueline went to visit Gloria in Doctors Hospital, where that untypical mother seemed almost disinterested in the whole affair. Even her sisters-in-law's enthusiasm for the adorable twins produced nothing but a yawn and the indifferent response that "they seemed healthy enough."

Over lunch in the Palm Court of the Plaza Hotel, Susan shook her head in wonderment.

"I don't understand Gloria. She acts as though she couldn't care less about those babies. Why on earth does she keep on having children? She doesn't even pay much attention to Raoul, Jr., or Maria. They're always with their nurse, I gather."

Jacqueline nodded. "Don't ask me to play curbstone psychiatrist, but I'll bet you a nickel Gloria will have at least one more.''

"For heaven's sake, *why?*"

"Two reasons. She's forty years old and determined to prove that age doesn't matter. And now she's even with Maria. They both have four kids, but Gloria still has time to top her.''

Susan stared at her sister-in-law. "You've got to be kidding! About outproducing Maria, I mean. That's insane!''

"Is it? She can't beat her mother at looks or charm or brains. She's not even that much better at sports, when Maria chooses to play well. But biologically she can practice one-upmanship on the old girl. She hates her, you know.'' Jacqueline made the pronouncement as calmly as if she were saying that Gloria detested spinach.

"Hates her own mother?''

"It may be unthinkable to you, Susan, because you love yours and more importantly, she loves you. Poor old Gloria's never had anything from Maria but grudging acceptance, and damned little of that. Maria can't forgive her for not being beautiful or talented or both, and she hasn't made much of a secret of it. For all that tough exterior, Gloria's dying for approval. She knows damned well nobody loves her. She wasn't even married for love.'' Jacqueline gave a brittle little laugh. "I'm not sure any of us was.''

Susan didn't answer.

"I'm not saying *Richard* doesn't love *you,*" Jacqueline said. "I was talking about Mary Lou and me. She won't admit that her husband is incapable of honest affection *or* fidelity. She just goes her chin-up way, buying clothes and jewelry in the hope that Serge will notice she's alive.''

"But if he didn't love her, why did Sergio marry her?''

"Good question. My hunch is he decided at twenty-nine his image called for a wife. Someone presentable, and tractable who'd wipe out the frivolous playboy stigma and make him appear a serious artist, like the father he envies. He'll never hold a candle to Joe as a conductor, but he doesn't know that. He wants to be *more* famous. And Maria's always encouraged him to believe he would be. Mary Lou is part of the picture of 'stability.' Sergio the husband and father. The family man. What a laugh! He travels alone, you know. And in every town there's some cute little thing waiting for him with open legs and a closed mouth. At least he likes to *think* it's closed. Everybody in the world knows what a tomcat Serge is.''

Susan's unspoken question hung in the air. Jacqueline looked at her, faintly amused.

"You're dying to know about Walter and me, aren't you?''

"No, of course not,'' Susan lied, "it's none of my business. Anyway, I don't believe Walter didn't marry you for love. You're so beautiful and poised and . . .''

"And I was twenty-four years old when I married Walter because I decided it was more glamorous and interesting being an Antonini than an aging post-debutante in New Orleans. I didn't love him, Susan. And he didn't love me. But when I deliberately got pregnant during our 'courtship,' there wasn't much he could do, being who he was. I refused to have an abortion and the Antonini family couldn't tolerate a scandal about their darling budding-genius-composer.

So we got married. It hasn't been bad. I like being Mrs. Antonini with a big Park Avenue apartment and a lot of amusing jet-set friends. Walter and I go our own ways, pretty much. We really like each other and the kids. It's an okay arrangement. He has his 'friends' and I have mine. There's been no marital sex in our household for ten years. I have two nice boys and an attractive husband and a not too rapidly shifting roster of lovers. So does Walter. But we keep up appearances. I don't embarrass him and he pays me the same courtesy. If people talk, the hell with them. They can't prove anything, and a little gossip adds to my glamour. Like being married to a bisexual does." She smiled. "Don't look so shocked. Ours is a good deal more honest than most marriages."

"You've never thought of divorce?"

"Thought of it? Once or twice when someone I was involved with began to get to me in more than a physical way. But I always came to my senses. Why should I divorce Walter when we can both have our cake, etc., etc.? The best thing about our marriage is the fact that it's cast-iron protection against making the same mistake twice. Walter and I both know that. We can back off from any entanglement with the excuse that we're already married."

"But aren't you ever jealous?"

"Susan, my dear, jealousy is an infantile emotion. The sentimental indulgence of unrealistic people who fancy that love lasts forever. Look at Maria. Joe had a hundred affairs when, you should pardon the expression, he was up to it. Did she care? Maybe the first or second time. I don't know. But for years she's been much too busy building a musical dynasty to give a damn what Giovanni does— or did—with his spare time. If outside sex made him a better conductor, I'm sure Maria would have acted as procuress. She knows all about her two sons' extramarital adventures, you can bet your life on that. But as long as there's nothing overt and messy, no blot on the family escutcheon by them or the daughters-in-law, she chooses to ignore *that* part of our lives. Thank God for small favors!"

Susan remembered Maria's "speech" the first time they met. Whether Jacqueline knew it or not, Mrs. Antonini did not consider her sons' wives helpful to their careers. Or had she said that only in the hope of discouraging *Richard's* marriage? And would she also ignore Richard's behavior if he followed the example of his father and brothers? Susan shuddered. It was unthinkable that her husband would want to make love to another woman. As unthinkable as her seeking another man. And if, God forbid, Richard ever was unfaithful, could she accept it in the casual way Jacqueline handled her own marriage? Never. She was repelled by what she'd heard. She was not an unsophisticated woman, but Jacqueline's jaded discussion of her own life and that of her in-laws *did* shock Susan. It was decadent. Her sister-in-law was no better than those horrible women who offered themselves by mail to Richard!

No. That was unfair. Jacqueline was honest realistic. She was a nice woman, strangely enough, though she gave herself no credit for being one. Perhaps she'd even lied about her "deliberate" pregnancy. Perhaps she'd loved Walter and might love him still. It was possible that she was simply making the best of a bad marriage, for her children's sake. What would I do in her situation? Susan wondered. It's wrong of me to judge her. I should judge those men, those

Antonini men whose need for blind adulation is stronger than their vows. She tried to match Jacqueline's offhand manner.

"And what about Raoul and Gloria?" she said. "Is that the same kind of marriage?" Susan answered herself. "No, of course it isn't. Not with all those babies coming along every minute."

Jacqueline raised an eyebrow. "It doesn't take long to make a baby. Gloria wouldn't stray. Who'd look at her? But Raoul? My dear Susan, he's an attractive Frenchman with a dreary wife whom he also did not marry for love. What do *you* think?"

I don't want to hear any more, Susan thought suddenly. I want to get out of here.

Jacqueline sensed her distress. "I'm sorry, Susan. I suppose I really shouldn't have gone into all this. But you're family now. It's pointless to pretend. Please don't think this has anything to do with you. Richard's sown his wild oats. He didn't *need* marriage; he *wanted* it, Your life won't be like any of ours. I'm certain of that."

"I am too. I know Richard. And I know myself."

We're both lying, Susan thought. Nothing is certain except my unswerving love for the man I married. But please, God, don't ever let him put my love to that kind of test.

Chapter 9

IN NEW YORK, Susan had little time to think seriously about the resolution she'd made in Chicago. The awareness that she would not be content without some degree of independent action remained in the back of her mind, but she was too busy with the holidays to explore the possibilities. Before Christmas, she talked on the phone with Kate and was ashamed to feel pleased when that outspoken woman complained bitterly that she still hadn't been able to find a good replacement.

"You're *sure* you couldn't come back to work?"

"You know I can't, Kate. We leave on another tour in February. I'm dying to tell you about that life! Nobody would believe the experiences of an artist on the road!"

"Maybe you should write a piece about it. Firsthand account."

Susan hesitated. "I don't know. I'm not sure Richard would approve."

"Do it and *then* tell him. I bet he'll be delighted. Forgive me, pet, but he *does* like publicity."

"Let me think about it."

The idea appealed to her and there was enough material to make an amusingly biting story. She'd have to be careful, though, that it didn't reflect badly on Richard. She could be satirical about the rigors of travel, the inanities of the 'cultured" people they met, the blatant social climbers and hero-worshipers. Even the incredible fan mail would be a revelation. And Kate was right. Richard did love publicity. Gerry was good at the "artistic" side of it, but no one except the celebrity's wife could tell the "behind the scenes" story. It could be handled with taste, tongue-in-cheek. Yes, it was worth thinking about, once she had Christmas behind her.

Christmas. It was certainly the kind an only child had never known, Susan thought, as she shopped feverishly for gifts. Nine adult Antoninis and Taffins and eight children! Not to mention twelve servants between the town house and Pound Ridge! And then there were her own mother and father, and Kate, Evie Maxwell, Paul and Gerry! Thirty-five presents to be found and wrapped . . . and so many of them doubly difficult because they were for people who "had everything." What on earth did one give the Senior Antoninis? Or, for that matter, the rest of the family?

She was ambivalent about Christmas in the country. There'd been no question that they'd go to Maria's. Richard hadn't even consulted her. He'd simply taken it for granted that Maria would have her "gathering of the clan." The idea of a big family, of the excitement of the children, of a country Christmas, maybe with snow, appealed to Susan's romantic nature. But part of her was sad to be away from her own parents, sad for herself and for them. It would be their first Christmas apart and even the premature celebration on December 23, when she and Richard went to Bronxville, was depressing, for all the attempted heartiness.

Bea cooked a wonderful, traditional dinner and they drank wine and opened their gifts under the same kind of tree Susan had had every year of her life. But in spite of the determined gaiety and the enthusiastic exchange of gifts, there was a wisful look in Bea's eyes and even Wil seemed unusually subdued. Susan and Richard did not exchange their presents that evening. That would be saved for the "real" Christmas. But they gave Beatrice an exquisite strand of cultured pearls with a diamond clasp, and Wil a handsome new set of the most expensive golf clubs.

"Such extravagance!" Bea said. "My dears, you shouldn't have!"

"Richard insisted," Susan bubbled, delighted they were pleased. "Do you really like them?"

"We love them, baby," her father said. "Thank you both."

"I'm afraid our gifts to you don't quite compare," Bea said, "but they come with all our love."

Susan eagerly unwrapped her present. It was a thin gold chain at the end of which was a small gold star inscribed, in minute letters, "Susan-Richard. First Christmas, 1964."

Tears came to her eyes as she kissed her parents. "It's beautiful. And you know what a pushover I am for sentimental things. Thank you, darlings. I'll wear it always."

"Hey, look at these!" Richard said, "You're not the only star in the family, my girl!" He proudly displayed star-shaped gold cuff links. "Thanks so much, Mrs. Langdon, Mr. Langdon! They're beautiful! And I really need them!"

Susan looked at him gratefully. Her parents would never know that he owned at least two dozen pairs of cuff links, gold and platinum, real pearls and diamond clusters. He was being darling, and she loved him for it.

"You went pretty far overboard yourselves," she said, "showering us with gold! We didn't expect all this after the enormous expense of the wedding."

"Sweetheart, your mother and I love you both." Wil put his arm around his wife. "The best gift is to see how happy you are together." He lifted his glass of champagne. "Here's to marriage. May yours always be as complete and rewarding as ours has been."

They drank solemnly and exchanged kisses. It was a gentle, tender moment. I feel as though I'm taking my vows all over again, Susan thought. And as though Mother and Dad are renewing theirs. Once again, she felt a little pang at the thought of her separations from them at the holidays. Then she smiled, hoping it was a bright, cheerful smile.

"What are you two doing for Christmas?" she asked.

"Going over to the Emersons' for dinner," Bea said. The Emersons were the Langdons' closest friends. "They're having their three children and five grandchildren for dinner that day. It will be a mob scene," Bea went on, "but I'm sure it will be fun."

There was no reproach in her voice, that the Antoninis hadn't asked them. Certainly Richard heard none as he said, "That sounds nice. Christmas is the time for mob scenes, I guess. But Lord knows how we'll get through that madness in Pound Ridge!"

He didn't mean to be unfeeling. He couldn't know how bereft Bea and Wil felt this year. Damn it. Maria *could* have asked them! Susan quickly changed the subject. After all, the Antoninis couldn't ask *all* the in-laws' families. She couldn't expect hers to be an exception.

"As soon as we get back, Mom, you and I will start apartment-hunting again, okay? We sure didn't have much luck in August, but we didn't have much time, either. It'll be almost two months before we have to leave again. I'm sure we'll find something perfect."

"We'll do our damnedest," Bea said, looking at Richard. Did she imagine he avoided her gaze? Did he have no intention of leaving Seventieth Street? If so, Susan was unaware of it. It's probably all in my mind, her mother thought. He's too sensible a young man not to realize that living with one's parents can be a dreadful mistake.

On the way home, Richard took one hand off the wheel and pulled Susan close to him.

"About that apartment business, honey. Don't you think we ought to let it go for a bit? After all, we're off on tour again so soon. Why not wait until we get back?"

There was no response.

"Susie?"

She answered very slowly. "You really don't want a place of your own, do you? I showed you a couple of good apartments before we were married and you found a million things wrong with them. Now you don't even want me to look. I don't understand."

"What's to understand? Of course we'll get an apartment, or maybe a house, but what's the big rush?"

"I don't want to live with your parents. It's as simple as that. We're like children, occupying the fourth floor. I want to run my own house, Richard. Not be a guest in someone else's."

"I'd think you'd be damned appreciative of your easy life." He was angry. "Not that we've been there enough for you to even *know* whether you like it or not!"

"I didn't marry you for an easy life. I married you because I love you and want to make a home for you."

"Well, goddammit, we have a home!"

"No. We only have an address. Your parents' address."

He went stony-silent, both hands on the wheel, eyes straight ahead, concentrating on his driving. The grim set of his mouth was Susan's answer. He has no intention of moving out, she realized. Not now. Not even soon. It's all too comfortable, too easy, too irresponsible. He can have his wife and his mother and his own bed. Life is very uncomplicated this way. He doesn't have to make a decision, except about his work. At least he has that. I have nothing to make me feel important. Not even a house to manage. Or children to raise. My darling is truly a Taurus baby. Stubbon beyond belief.

Her thoughts jolted her into the seemingly simple answer. There was only one way to escape. It was underhanded but necessary. Richard's suite wasn't big enough for them *and* a baby.

Katherine Antonini was conceived in February in a suite in The Everglades Club in Palm Beach during a free weekend, and born in the hotel-like atmosphere of New York's Doctors Hospital in November of 1965, fourteen months after Susan and Richard were married.

Looking at the little pink, squirming bundle they put into her arms at feeding time, her mother no longer felt guilty. Escape from one's in-laws was the wrong reason for having a baby, but now that Katie was here, Susan was so suffused with love for her that she was sure it had been the right thing to do, whatever the motive. She was no longer an excuse. She was an adored and welcomed daughter. Even Richard, once he'd gotten over the shock of Susan's announcement in April, had been satisfactorily enthusiastic about impending fatherhood and was endearingly proud of his beautiful child. He'd even (wonder of wonders!) canceled his November engagements to be in New York with Susan when she was due to be delivered.

Bless you, angel, Susan thought looking down at her baby. You've changed our lives. In the first months of her pregnancy, Susan was ashamed of her deliberate plot. She and Richard *had* agreed to wait two years before starting a family, and when she told him about "the accident' she was sorry to lie and not very proud of her devious plan. But if Richard had any idea of what was in her mind, he gave no sign of it. He agreed to the necessity of their own place and approved the duplex co-operative apartment she found in June at Sixty-first and Park Avenue. He amiably discussed renovation and decorating schemes with her, fussed over her endlessly, warning her not to "overdo."

There was so much structural work to be done in the ten rooms that they could not move in until late August. Susan, feeling wonderfully healthy, cheerfully agreed to spend the summer in Pound Ridge in "Richard's house," commuting to New York once a week to consult with workmen and decorators and check on the progress of her new home. Things were so good with her and Richard that even Maria's silently furious presence did not disturb her, nor did the "gaggle of Antoninis," as she thought of them, make her feel as insecure and inadequate as they had a year before. In time, she almost forgot she'd done a deceitful thing, just as she forgot Maria's icy reception of the news when they told her and Giovanni, adding that they'd be looking for a place big enough for them and the baby and a nurse.

"I see," Maria said. "Naturally, the fourth floor won't be suitable for you now that you have a family so quickly on the way."

She knows, Susan thought. She knows I deliberately got pregnant to get us out of here. She wondered whether she was blushing. She felt uncomfortable under her mother-in-law's steady gaze, but she said nothing. She would not say she was sorry they'd be leaving. Such a blatant lie would be too obvious.

"My ninth grandchild," Giovanni said proudly. "What shall we have? Another composer or conductor or piainst? Or shall we wish for a beautiful girl?"

Susan reacted immediately. "Why couldn't we have both?"

"Twins?" Giovanni twinkled. "You're going to compete with Gloria?"

She'd laughed. "No, Papa-Joe. But is it impossible for a *girl* to be a musical genius?" She'd easily fallen into the habit of calling him "Papa-Joe" as the grand-children did. She was unable to call Maria anything but "Mrs. Antonini." For that matter, she'd never been invited to. "There already are some female virtuosos," Susan went on. "And there'll be many more by the time our child grows up."

The maestro had smiled in agreement. "Of course, of course, my dear. You are quite right. Antonia Brico was the first woman to conduct the Berlin Philharmonic back in 1930. I remember Schweitzer, Klemperer, Bruno Walter, Sibelius all giving their support. Pity, though, it didn't last. I believe she gives piano lessons now."

"What about Lili Boulanger's *Faust et Hélène* that won the Grand Prix de Rome in 1913?" Richard asked. "And how about her sister Nadia? She conducted the New York Philharmonic in 1939 and again for a week three years ago." He was enjoying the little game, pleased to show his father that he, too, was scholarly.

"Quite right," Giovanni said again. "And don't forget Sarah Caldwell up in Boston. Or Rosalyn Tureck. She also led the Philharmonic, though it was from the keyboard, which doesn't literally qualify as conducting. Well, now, Susan. Perhaps your daughter will be a famous musician." He patted her head. "That is, unless you have a son. Then it will be a certainty."

"Maybe she'll be a great pianist, like her father," Susan said. "Don't forget about Gina Bachauer."

"Such nonsense!" Maria snapped. "The musical talents of women lie primarily in their voices. Anyway, it seems rather a waste of time to speculate on the child's future before it's born."

"You have a point, Mother dear. Let's get him *or* her born healthy and then see what happens." Richard was appeasing Maria. "I'll take a chance on the Antonini heritage."

Susan had been ridiculously pleased by her husband's defense of women and Giovanni's contribution to the subject. Maria was more antifeminist than any of them. How strange, Susan thought, when she is such an achiever. But of course it's not achievement for herself she wants. It's for the men in her family.

"I adore you," Susan said that night when she and Richard were in bed. She touched him and felt him respond.

"Shouldn't I be a little careful of you?" he'd asked, almost nervously.

Susan laughed. "Not for months, my darling. And then not for too long!" She patted her belly proudly. "Look. Three months and I don't even show!"

He touched her already swelling breasts. "You do here. And it's marvelous, Maybe I should always keep you pregnant if you're going to be this sexy."

It had been, except for fleeting moments, a wonderful six months, Susan mused now as Katherine greedily attacked one of those full breasts. She loved the apartment, was never bored for a moment, not even when Richard went off in September for six weeks without her. She'd missed him terribly, of course, but it had been fun to catch up with Evie Maxwell and Barbara Dudley for "girl lunches." She had a great deal of time with Bea and Wil, spending nights in her old room in Bronxville and having them stay in town sometimes with her. She'd been able to dine often with Kate, who was still urging her to write.

"I can't do it now," Susan had said again. "I'm much too busy getting the apartment in shape."

"Bull," Kate had said bluntly. "You don't want to. You're afraid Richard won't like it."

"Don't be silly!" She told Kate about the support of women musicians Richard had voiced in the spring. "He's no chauvinist. He'd be *glad* if I did something on my own."

"*That* is what *I* told *you* months ago," Kate reminded her.

"Well, I'll get around to it. After the baby."

Kate shrugged. "How's lovely Maria?"

"All right, I guess. I haven't seen anything of the family since Richard's been away. Except for Jacqueline. We have lunch together often, and talk on the phone nearly every day."

"Nice *somebody* in that family keeps in touch."

"I hear from Richard almost every night," Susan said defensively.

"*Almost?*"

"Yes. My Lord, Kate, he can't call every minute! You have no idea what a frantic thing a tour is!"

"I'd know if you wrote it."

"Oh, shut up," Susan said affectionately.

But it had troubled her that sometimes she didn't hear from him for a night or two. There was always time to make a phone call, no matter how busy one was. She put her uneasiness down to her "condition" and tried to dismiss the things Jacqueline had told her about Sergio's behavior on the road. Maybe I should have gone along, she thought. And then, how absurd to even let such a thing enter my head! Richard wouldn't be unfaithful. Not when I'm carrying his child! Not *ever!* Not every man strayed. She had to be sensible. Men just didn't think about keeping in touch the way women did. They didn't live for a note or the sound of a voice on the phone, for reassurance that they were always in the heart and mind of the beloved.

"You're an ass, Susan Langdon Antonini," she said aloud when these little fears came to her in the middle of the night. "You're a ponderous, slow-moving, dim-witted elephant!" And for the most part, that took care of the uncertainties and she fell peacefully asleep, dreaming of Richard's return and the arrival of his baby.

Chapter 10

ALMOST FROM THE day he had learned he was to be a father, a change came over Richard. He was gentle and considerate of Susan during her pregnancy and quite obviously mad about his daughter when she was born. He hadn't been sure, in the first hours after Susan told him, whether he was glad about it. He'd have preferred to wait, and he'd have been happier if they'd decided this together. But his doubts soon turned to anticipation and when he saw Katie his delight was genuine. "Look at those fingers!" he said. "By God, she *is* going to be a musician, Susie! Just like you said!"

When he could, he took to haunting the nursery, playing with the baby under the eagle eye of Bridie Grey, the nurse Susan had been fortunate enough to find. The two women watched with amusement as the famous big fingers placed tiny ones on the keys of the miniature piano he bought as her first toy.

"I wouldn't have believed it," Susan told Kate Fenton. "He's positively dotty about your namesake! I expected him to love her, but I had no idea he'd take to parenthood with such enthusiasm!"

Kate hid her doubts. People did not change so drastically overnight. Richard the selfish lion did not magically become Richard the sentimental lamb. He's showing off, Kate thought, as he always does. He's playing a new and amusing game, preening in a starring role with the supporting actress who's a reproduction of himself and a boost to his ego. But she said nothing, hoping it was true, hoping Richard really had matured with the arrival of this new, dependent life.

Even Paul thought he was witnessing a small miracle. It was amazing how "settled" Richard seemed. In all the years Paul had managed him, he'd seen Richard as the temperamental artist, the petulant ex-prodigy, the careless Casanova, but never as an understanding and incredibly, faithful man. He'd not strayed since his marriage, and though they were on tour for months without Susan, he did not so much as look at another woman.

Even when they started the East Coast tour in April, a tour Susan had planned to accompany, Richard gracefully accepted her unexpected change of heart about making an extended trip. She came to Washington to meet them, but after three days she went home, apologizing that good as Bridie was, she didn't feel easy leaving Katie alone. Paul expected Richard to be angry, jealous, but he was not. Nor did her husband notice that Susan seemed nervous and distraught as though she had something terrible on her mind. Paul did, but he didn't comment on her hasty departure. Instead, he said, "Things are a lot different these days, aren't they? You've really become a family man. No offense, but I didn't expect it. That is, I know you. Or I should say, I *knew* you, and I wouldn't have believed . . ."

"That I'd turn out to be a pillar of respectability?" Richard laughed. "Tell you the truth, neither did I. I love Susie, but I never figured to be faithful. I guess the baby's made a difference. I want her to be proud of me. That sounds nuts, doesn't it? A five-month-old kid! As though she'd know! I can't really explain it to you, or myself, Paul. I suppose because Katie's so perfect I'm trying to be better for her sake, and for Susie who gave her to me. I know it sounds maudlin, but for the first time in my life I'm thinking about the future . . . watching my kid grow up, not wanting her to know about me the things I knew about my own father. He's a great man, but it was never a secret that he gave Mother a bad time with women. I think it influenced all our lives. We loved him. We still do. But none of us ever respected him as a father. We didn't listen to him or confide in him. Mother was the one for that. I don't want the same thing for Katie. I want her to have as much faith in me as she has in Susie. And she won't have if I go on behaving like the perennial juvenile. Do you understand what I'm saying, Paul? Susie has become more important to me because she's Katie's mother. And Katie—beautiful, flawless, enchanting Katie—is something I've produced. Susie had her, but it was my seed." He broke off suddenly. "I must sound like a maniac."

"No," Paul said carefully, "I admire you. And I'm glad for all of you."

Richard smiled. "You don't miss the good old days when you and I had a different broad every night? Not that you still couldn't. This mad metamorphosis of mine has nothing to do with you. In fact, I've been meaning to speak to you about that. Don't think you have to tie yourself to me while we're on the road. Hell, man, you're a handsome bachelor! Get out and grab what's right there waiting! Nobody will understand better than I."

"Don't worry about me. I was never the prize package. Who cares about an artist's manager? But if I wanted to carry on our old traditions, I would. I know there's plenty there for the taking. Even for me. Being this close to the throne gives me a certain clout with women. Funny. This new life of yours makes sense for me, too. Sooner or later we'd have both worn ourselves out with those mattress gymnastics. I can wait for New York. I have a couple of reliable phone numbers there."

"Have it any way you like," Richard said. "I just wanted you to know that I don't expect you to embrace my voluntary celibacy. With me it's temporary. I still have a sexy wife to go home to."

He had no idea how the words hurt. Paul's longing for his friend's wife had grown stronger every day and he despised himself for it. He'd known he was in love with Susan from that first tour when they'd spent so many hours together, when she'd been so unsure of her new life. He'd found her a warm, bright human being and every time he saw her, even when she was radiant and content in Richard's love, the hunger grew.

At the beginning, ashamed of his own thoughts, he'd hoped the marriage wouldn't last, that he'd have his chance. He reasoned that a selfish Richard would eventually betray her, or tire of her, or both. And he'd be waiting. But now that unworthy hope had disappeared. The change in Richard seemed real and both he and Susan were happy. Paul tried to be glad, but he envied Richard. No one person should have so much—talent, looks, money, fame, a wonderful wife and now this beautiful child. It's unfair. But at least he appreciates his blessings and that makes it better for Susan. I'm glad she isn't traveling with us very much any more. That means I only rarely have to see her, and that's a good thing. I might accidentally or compulsively let her know how I feel. She'd only be gentle and sorry for me and I couldn't stand that. I couldn't stand her pity.

Susan did not tell Richard her real reason for hurrying home from Washington. Only she and Bridie Grey shared the knowledge of the tragedy that had come to Katherine Antonini and her parents.

Susan became aware of it only two days before she was to leave to join the East Coast tour. The baby's nurse came into the master bedroom that morning and said, nervously, "May I speak with you, Mrs. Antonini?"

Oh, God, Susan thought she's going to quit. Employees always quit when they came in asking to speak to you. I thought she was happy with us. She adores Katie. Maybe it's money. If so . . .

"Of course, Bridie. What is it?"

"It's Katie, madam."

"Katie?" Susan jumped up, alarmed. "Has something happened to her?"

"No. That is, not exactly." Bridie's sweet Irish face wrinkled up and she looked as though she were going to burst into tears. "It's . . . Oh, God, save us, it's that for the last couple of days . . . I mean, I didn't want to alarm you, madam . . ."

Susan shook her by the shoulders. "What is it? Bridie, what on earth is it?"

"I . . . I don't think she hears, Mrs. Antonini. I think Katie is deaf." The woman began to cry.

Susan stared at her stupidly. Katie deaf? Her baby deaf? No. It was impossible. The nurse must be wrong. Her Irish imagination was playing tricks on her, that's all it was. Susan fought for control.

"What makes you think such a thing?" She was surprised to hear her own voice sounding so calm. "Hush, Bridie! Setttle down and tell me about it."

Between sobs, Bridie told her. Two days before, she'd accidentally dropped a heavy pan right behind Katie, who lay on her stomach in the playpen. The baby hadn't looked up or begun to cry as a normal child would when such a loud, frightening noise happened so close to her ear.

"I didn't think too much about it," Bridie said, "but then I began to notice other things. When I shook her rattle behind her, she didn't look around for the noise. When she happened to *see* it she crowed—you know the way she does when she sees something bright colored—but she didn't hear it. At first, I thought it was just because she's so little. But I've cared for babies all my life. I know this is different." Bridie's voice broke. "I know she can't hear."

"You're wrong," Susan said firmly. "Those little tests of yours don't mean anything. Katie's perfectly normal."

"I pray to the good Lord she is." Bridie wiped her eyes. "But you'd better take her to the doctor, Mrs. Antonini."

Without answering, Susan ran to the nursery. Katie was lying in her crib, smiling radiantly at the bright-colored mobile which dangled over it. The sight of her made Susan feel better. There's nothing wrong with this baby, she thought. Bridie's being an alarmist. With Katie's gaze still turned to the ceiling, Susan stood a little behind the crib and clapped her hands loudly. The child continued to look upward. Susie did it again and again, with no results. She felt a sickness start in the pit of her stomach and she literally screamed, "Katie!" Her daughter continued to look up at the mobile, undistracted by the loud voice.

Blindly, Susan picked her up and held her close. Katie clutched at her hair, her earrings, gurgling with pleasure as her mother carried her into her own bedroom and sat in a chair, cuddling her and making little crooning noises. Bridie watched with an anguished expression.

"You'd better call the doctor," she said again.

"Yes. Yes, of course."

Still holding the baby, she tremblingly dialed the pediatrician's office. He was not in, but his nurse was helpful.

"I expect Dr. Ashley shortly," she said. "Is it an emergency?"

"No. Yes. I don't know." Susan was almost hysterical, "Yes, of course its an emergency! There's something wrong with Katie, and I have to go away to meet my husband in Washington, and . . ." She realized she was babbling incoherently. "I must see Dr. Ashley today! Please! What time may we come in?"

The nurse recognized the panic in her voice. "All right, Mrs. Antonini. Bring Katherine as soon as you can. I'll work you in."

"Thank you," Susan said. "Thank you very much."

Dr. Ashley did not make light of her fears as Susan hoped he would.

"I can't really tell about Katherine. Normally, babies begin to hear about thirty-six hours after birth, Mrs. Antonini, but the only way to tell whether this little one has a hearing impairment is to have her scientifically tested." He jotted down the name and address. "I want you to call the New York Eye and Ear Infirmary. I'll ask them to give you an immediate appointment. Their otologists can tell you for sure in an hour. Try not to worry," he said kindly. "It could be nothing, She may respond when she decides to. You remember that old story about the child who didn't speak for seven years? Then one morning at breakfast he said, 'This oatmeal is too hot.' Naturally his parents were delighted and asked him why he hadn't spoken before. And he said, 'Up till now, everything's been *perfect*.' It may be the same thing with Katherine."

Susan couldn't even smile at the well-meant little joke. Instinctively she knew, and no halfhearted reassurance from the pediatrician could dispel the terrible certainty that her baby didn't hear.

Next day the tests confirmed her worst fears. She stood by numbly as the doctors attached metal electrodes to Katherine's hands and feet and administered a series of tiny electric shocks with a machine formidably called a psychogalvanic skin response audiometer. There was much testing with batteries of earphones and twirling of dials and knobs, and Katie cried and the diagnosis was made.

"The child has a slight degree of hearing only in her right ear. Very slight. almost none at all."

To Susan, the words were a pronouncement of doom. She knew what they meant. Her gay, laughing, alert little daughter was destined for a life in which she would hear nothing. And if she could not hear, she could not speak. Deaf and mute. It was unbearable. Tears slowly began to stream down her face as she stood with a now quiet Katherine in her arms.

"What can we do? Please. Whatever it takes, what can we do?"

The doctor in charge was very gentle. "There are two choices for the prelingual deaf child, Mrs. Antonini. One is to put her, as soon as she's old enough, into a school for the deaf where she'll be among others like her. She'll learn sign language and be able to communicate through it. The other, which is more difficult, is to try to bring her up in a hearing world. That means, in time, fitting her with hearing aids and trying to teach her to lip-read and speak intelligibly. But I must warn you that if you choose that course of action, it will be your whole life. Yours and your husband's. Katherine will need speech therapists and, even more importantly, constant, and I emphasize *constant,* at-home training. You will have to talk, talk, talk. Incessantly. You will say one word over and over a hundred times until she begins to imitate the shape of the word she sees on your lips. It's not an easy thing, I regret to say. I must tell you that most parents find it too frustrating, too heartbreaking, as well as too time-consuming. You and the child would go through torture for years, and even then no one can promise you'll succeed."

"You're telling me we shouldn't even try."

"No, I'm not saying that. Many parents have chosen this way and found it worth all the agony to see their child grow up like other children. It's possible. In all probability, her impairment has nothing to do with her I.Q. That's why we object to the awful phrase 'deaf and dumb.' She is deaf and mute, but she seems bright and chirpy. I'm simply warning you, Mrs. Antonini, that it takes an incredible amount of patience and devotion, an almost fanatic dedication to achieve results. You'll give your life to it. Some people, and no one blames them for it, just can't cope with that burden."

"What about *her* burden, Doctor?"

He shook his head sympathetically. "There is a school of thought that believes the deaf-mute child, like the mentally retarded one, is happier among her own kind. In a way, that life can be less painful for her than one in which she is asked to behave like other children, to compete in areas for which she lacks the equipment. It's a terrible decision for you and your husband. Think about it carefully, for her sake as well as your own. Your husband is the pianist, isn't he?"

"Yes."

"I think you should take that into consideration. I imagine he travels a great deal. That means most of the burden of training will be on you. Bringing up Katherine 'normally' is an every-waking-hour job that really requries the efforts of both parents. Usually, the mother, at home, works with the child during the day while the father picks up the process at night. Give it a lot of thought before you decide. You have time. She couldn't be put into school or even fitted with hearing aids until she's about two years old. Meantime, why not investigate some of the help you could call on?"

Susan left with a list of books to read and the names of institutions to contact. The John Tracy Clinic in California, founded by Spencer Tracy and named for his own hearing-impaired son, offered on-the-spot training or a correspondence course which helped parents to learn how to handle not only their child but themselves. The Volta Bureau in Washington, D.C., founded by Alexander Graham Bell, also was an organization for the parents of handicapped children, using shared experiences as training and consolation. The same was true of the New York League for the Hard of Hearing, which offered lectures by psychologists, doctors and prominent guests. Eleanor Roosevelt, herself the victim of a hearing defect, had been one of the speakers many years ago.

Susan stayed up all night reading the literature of these organizations. When she brought Katherine home from the testing, she told only Bridie what she'd learned.

"I don't want anyone else to know just yet," Susan said.

"Will you tell Mr. Antonini when you see him in Washington tomorrow?"

Susan looked startled. She'd completely forgotten she'd planned to join Richard. I can't go now! was her first reaction. I can't leave my baby. And there's too much to think about before I tell him about Katie. I must have all my facts marshaled. Even then she realized that she'd already made her decision. No matter what it took, she wanted Katie brought up as a child, not a *deaf* child. But if Richard did not immediately agree, she'd need all the arguments she could muster.

"I'm going to cancel my trip," she said. "I don't want Mr. Antonini upset while he's on tour, and I'm not a good enough actress to keep the news from him if I see him. This is no moment to go away. Besides, I have so much research and thinking to do." She stopped. She was behaving as though she was alone in this problem, as though she had to handle it by herself. As though she was sure Richard would be no help. Katie was also Richard's child and he adored her. What was she thinking of? He had a right to know, an equal voice in the decision. "On second thought," Susan said, "I guess I will go down to Washington. He's expecting me. But I'm not going on with him to Richmond and Atlanta as planned. I'll come home after the concert at Constitution Hall."

On the Eastern shuttle next morning, she rehearsed what she'd say, but by the time the plane landed at National Airport she knew she couldn't tell him. Not now. He'd be heartbroken, distraught, maybe unable to go on with this series of concerts. There's no reason to rush, Susan rationalized. Nothing can be done for a while, one way or the other. I'll keep the secret until he gets home, keep it from him and everyone. I'll have a couple of months to become informed about these children and how to handle them. I can put up a front for Richard for a few days. There are other doctors. Maybe a corrective operation. She swallowed a terrible lump in her throat. Oh, Katie, my precious, beautiful baby, why did this have to happen to you?

For those three days she tried to act as though nothing was wrong. Richard, his mind on his music, did not notice her tension. Only Paul was aware that Susan was deeply troubled about something, and that she was nervous and sometimes so deep in thought that she jumped when she was unexpectedly spoken to.

Whatever the problem is, Paul thought, it's a killer, and she's trying hard to fool all of us. He was sure Richard knew nothing. If he had, the pianist would have behaved differently, probably would have blurted out something to give it away. Susie was going through some kind of private hell and making the awful trip by herself.

Chapter 11

MUCH AS SHE longed to talk to Kate or her mother, Susan stuck by her decision to tell no one of Katie's handicap until she had discussed this wrenching blow with Richard. Keeping quiet about the worst disaster of her life was the hardest thing she'd ever had to do. She wanted to run to Bea Langdon for comfort, to ask Kate's sensible advice, but it would be unfair to Richard. He'd have enough pain without discovering that he was one of the last to know.

Instead, she spent the next two months reading everything she could find on the subject, taking the baby to two more specialists, writing to the Tracy Clinic for information. It was all disheartening. The books she got from the library turned her blood to ice water. They warned that the parents of deaf children sometimes began to hate them for the way they shuffled their feet made disgusting noises when they ate, behaved more like animals than children. Susan slammed the books shut and refused to believe such possibilities. Unfortunately, she had to accept the fact that Katie's condition was inoperable. She wished she had gone to the Volta Bureau when she was in Washington, but she knew why she hadn't. Going there was admitting that Katie was handicapped, and though she knew that in her heart, she was not yet ready to affirm it by joining one of these groups.

It was still hard to believe, looking at her daughter, that she was anything but perfect. Just as it was nearly impossible to make cheerful replies to inquiries about her, to tell people who asked that "The baby is marvelous!" Susan thought her resolve would melt when Bea came to town and spent happy hours playing with her grandchild, unaware of Katie's condition. But she hung on. Only a few more weeks, she told herself. Then Richard and I will make our plans and it will be easier to break the news to our families when we've already decided on the solution.

When he did return, elated by his triumphant appearances, Richard burst into the apartment full of high spirits, shouting, "Hey! I'm home! Where are my two gorgeous women?" Susan ran to meet him and flung herself into his arms, holding onto him as though she'd never let go, covering his face with kisses. All discipline left her, all the bottled-up control was unleashed. Bridie had been a comfort but no substitute. Only Richard could share the anguish she'd borne alone. Startled by the ferocity of her embrace, he returned her kisses, holding her close and wondering what this frantic welcome meant. At last he disentangled himself and looked into eyes swimming with tears.

"That's even a bigger reception than I expected! I know my homecoming is a major event, but did you miss me *that* much?"

She could barely speak, merely nodded and hugged him again before she said, "Oh, Richard, I've needed you so!"

"Well, I've needed you, too, baby. It's been a long, lonely spring. But I'm home now, and no more traveling until fall. Just a lot of time to spend with you and Katie. Where is she? In the nursery? Let's go see her. How is my beautiful heiress?'' He started toward the baby's room, but Susan grabbed at his arm.

"Wait. Please. There's something we must talk about.''

"Can't it keep until I've seen Katie?''

"No. It's about her.''

He felt the beginning of fear. "What's wrong? She's sick! My God, Susan, don't tell me something's happened to her and you didn't let me know!''

"She's all right, dearest. I mean, she's not really sick.'' Susan took his hand and pulled him into the living room. "Let's sit down for a minute.'' She held his hand tightly as she told him the whole story, fighting back the fresh tears as she took him, step by step, over the events that had been her living nightmare since the morning Bridie first came into her room. "So you see, darling,'' she concluded, "we have an enormous responsibility. It will be hard on us, worse for Katie, but we can do it. I know we can. I've been studying everything I can find on the subject, and there are some marvelous success stories. Girls and boys who've learned to lip-read and speak quite well. Children who go to regular schools, colleges even. Some have married and have children of their own. They lead perfectly normal lives.''

He was in the same kind of disbelieving state of shock Susan had suffered earlier. At first he said nothing, simply staring at her, trying to take in what she'd told him. Then the full, terrible impact of it hit him and his face went dead white. "Deaf and dumb,'' he said. "My child is deaf and dumb!''

"Don't think of it that way. She can't hear and she'll have to be taught to speak and understand, but she can. She will. Thank God we have the money to get her the best speech therapist. We can make it much easier for her than most parents.''

"She's deformed. A freak.'' His voice was hopeless.

"Richard! That's not true! She's the same bright, alert, happy baby she always was. She'll be a beautiful, cheerful young girl, a lovely woman. She'll have the same kind of life any other child has. It's true. I swear it. She has a handicap. But she has a good mind and if we're willing to make sacrifices it won't matter that much that she doesn't hear. She'll be able to function like other people.''

He turned to her, eyes blazing. "Are you crazy? Haven't you ever seen deaf and dumb people, all vacant-looking and unco-ordinated? I can hardly look at them, shuffling along, making grunts instead of words, trying to communicate with their fingers.'' He jumped up and started out of the room. Susan was frozen with horror.

"Where are you going?''

"To the bathroom. I'm going to be sick.''

Unable to move, she waited for him to return. She'd expected him to be devastated, as she had been, but she hadn't anticipated this revulsion, this instant rejection of the baby he adored. It's only the shock, she told herself. He's reacting without thinking it through. Once he realizes how much can be done, he'll adjust to the situation, sad as it is. She remembered her own first days of knowledge. She, too, had been almost insane with grief. That's how it is with Richard, she thought. He can't accept this yet. But he will. He loves Katie so much. When he sees her and we sit down quietly to discuss our plans, it will be all right.

He came back in a few minutes, red-eyed. He'd been weeping, Susan realized. He left the room because he couldn't bear to let me see him shed "unmanly' tears. Her heart went out to him.

"I'm sorry," he said in a low voice. "I don't know what made me flare up like that. I realize you wanted to spare me as long as you could. It must have been hell for you, Susie, all these weeks, knowing and not telling me." He tried to smile. "Let's go see the princess, shall we?"

As Susan had when she was filled with fear, he gathered Katie in his arms and began to talk to her. "Hello, beautiful," he said. "Your old man's home from the wars. Glad to see your daddy?"

The baby smiled and gurgled, her little head turning from side to side, the big violet-blue eyes, so like Richard's, looking all around the room, her gaze finally coming to rest on her father's face. In an inquisitive gesture, she reached out and put her tiny fingers on his mouth. Richard involuntarily drew back. Susan knew they shared the same sad thought. This is what Katie deliberately would do later when she tried to recognize and imitate unheard words. It was accidental, of course, but it was eerie. In a second, Richard recovered and kissed the little pink fingertips before he put the infant back in her crib.

Arms around each other, they left the nursery. In their bedroom, Richard said, "I still can't believe it."

"I know."

"I talked to her but she didn't hear me. She'll never hear me. She'll never hear voices, or music. She'll be in a world of her own, cut off from us, as we're cut off from her."

"It won't be like that, darling. I told you. It's possible to raise her in a hearing world."

"I don't think so. From what you've told me, it means total dedication to her. There wouldn't be any life for you, and damned little for me when I'm home. You'll never be able to leave her, to travel with me. We'll be prisoners, the three of us, locked in a world of silence."

"But other people have done it!"

"We're not other people, Susan. I'm an artist, in the public eye. Things are demanded of me that aren't demanded of a businessman. And things are demanded of you, as my wife, that aren't required of the average housewife. From what you've told me, the at-home training is as important as the help she can get from speech therapists. That's not the kind of life I can handle."

She knew what he was leading up to, but she had to hear him say it. "What's the alternative?"

"You know the alternative. The doctor told you. When she's old enough, she can be sent to a special school for the deaf. Live with children like her. She'll be happier than she would be trying to grow up in a family of healthy, boisterous cousins with whom she can't keep up."

Susan stared at him in horror. "You want to send her away? You want to discard her like some imperfect piece of equipment that needs repair? She's not an object, Richard, she's flesh and blood. Our flesh and blood! No! If you're not willing to do whatever it takes, I am! She's my baby and I want her. I can't just put her out of my life."

He tried to soothe her. "Sweetheart, it will be best for her. That's what I'm thinking of. I know." He paused. "I've never told you this, but we've had firsthand experience. Sergio and Mary Lou had a child between Joseph and Patricia. A little girl, Frances, born in 1950, a year after her brother. When she was three, they discovered she was retarded. She's been in a special school ever since. She's happy there. Mary Lou goes to see her often. She says Frances is content. She looks fifteen years old but her mind hasn't grown past five. She plays with dolls and she can read a little and the staff is very good to her. I was seventeen when they made the decision and I remember how hard it was for them, but they knew it was the only way. She could never be a normal child and it would have been cruel to to watch her try to handle herself in a normal family and a normal world. We're going to have to face this with Katie. Much as we love her, we have to do what's best for her."

"No!" It was a scream of pain. "Katie isn't retarded. I don't care if it takes every minute of my life, I'm going to keep her with me." She looked at him, not willing to admit what she suspected. Richard was ashamed of having a child who was not perfect. She was an embarrassment to him. He wanted her out of sight and, if possible, out of mind. He loved her when she was everything he found beautiful, but his love had no room for a child whose presence was an affront to the sensibilities. How could this be? How could this man she adored beyond reason be so selfish, so unfeeling? She could imagine Sergio sending his little Frances away. He was shallow and cold, and she'd never liked him. She could even understand how Mary Lou, anxious to please the family, might have gone along, unprotestingly, with the decision. For that matter, Susan was not sure she wouldn't have done the same, had Katie been mentally deficient and totally beyond help. But Katie was neither of those things. All she asks of us is our time, Susan thought. And Richard is unwillng to give it. He wants to hide her. He's unwilling to admit to the world, as Sergio obviously was, that an Antonini produced a "defective" offspring.

"You think I don't love her," Richard said as though he read her mind. "You think I want her out of the way because I don't want the problems or the publicity. That's not it Susie. We can't cope. We'll fail and do her a terrible injustice."

"Yes, that's exactly what I think. Not that we'll do her an injustice, but that it will be inconvenient for you. Your damned public might find out, is that it? Or maybe your mother won't approve. You can't stand the idea of some reporter telling the world that you fathered a deaf-mute! 'Do what's best for her!' I know what's best for her. To stay with the parents who love her, to go to school with children who have no such handicap, kids who'll accept her because she's bright and sweet and wonderful." Susan was trembling. "No, Richard. I won't let you send her away. Not even," she said slowly, "if it means leaving you and taking Katie with me."

He stared at her. "You won't do that. You couldn't. We love each other."

"Katie is part of that love. Please see this as it really is. It's no disgrace, Richard." Shamelessly she played on his weakness. "If anything, it would only make people admire you more, knowing what a loving father you are to this helpless child. They'll admire your courage, your determination."

For a moment she thought he was going to buy this obvious ploy. God knows she didn't want to leave him, but she couldn't send her little girl away. She wanted them both. She'd do anything to keep them.

Richard hesitated, mulling over her words, but then he shook his head. "You don't believe me, Susie, but I'm not thinking only of us. I really am trying to do what's best and easiest for Katie." He sighed. "Look. I'm tired. We both are. There's nothing to be done immediately. Let's give this a little time."

It was something. At least a small concession. He'll come around to my way of thinking, Susan told herself. He has to get used to the idea. He hasn't lived with it, as I have. He's reacting from shock, from sadness and disappointment. In a few days he'll see that keeping her with us is the only possible thing to do. Everyone will back me up. I know they will. Mother and Dad. Paul. Jacqueline. Papa-Joe. They'll all see that Katie needs constant love from us. Even Maria, impossible as she is, has a soft spot about "her own." Since Katie's birth, Maria had been, if not cordial, at least more tolerant of Richard's family, even conceding that his baby was one of the prettiest newborn gandchildren she'd ever had. Maria will see that this is not another Frances. For once she'll agree with me.

Blindly confident that things would work out, Susan smiled and nodded. "You're right, darling," she said. "We'll give it a little more time." She held out her arms to him, inviting his love-making. "I've missed you so. I want you so much." Her voice was a seductive whisper.

She expected him to react as he always did, but he turned away. "Not tonight, Susie. I'm done in."

She couldn't believe it. They'd not seen each other in weeks. What was happening? Did he find it tasteless of her to think of sex at this time, as though Katie's future had already begun to affect their intimacy? One thing has nothing to do with the other, Susan thought. If anything, we need the touch of each other more tonight than we ever have. She wanted her husband to hold her, comfort her, as she would comfort him, She wanted an affirmation that their desire for each other could not be dampened, not even by tragedy or the quarrels that unhappiness produced.

"I don't understand," she finally said. "It's been so long. So much has happened."

"Exactly. My God, after the last hour do you really think I can be in the mood for romance?" He wasn't angry. Worse, he was indifferent to her. Is this to be my punishment until I see things his way? she wondered. Is the battle of wills to be fought in the bedroom?

With all the dignity at her command she answered him calmly. "No. I suppose not. I couldn't have made love to you the night *I* found out."

It was a lie. She'd gone to Washington two days after she'd learned about Katie. They'd made passionate love, she in her misery, Richard in his blissful ignorance. We view sex differently, Susan thought. Richard thinks of it only as lusty physical fulfillment when things are going well. To me, it's also spiritual nearness and peace, strength and solace when the rest of the world threatens my very existence.

Richard gave her a perfunctory kiss and climbed into bed, lying as far away from her as possible. They both lay sleepless, staring into the darkness, wrapped in their separate, tortured thoughts.

It was weeks before they made love again, though it was only hours before Susan knew she had lost her battle. She was to find no support for her decision anywhere, not even from her own parents, who were the first to be told.

Bea Langdon looked at them and began to weep with pain for her daughter and her grandchild. Wil had taken Susan in his arms, his own eyes wet, while Richard stood by, miserable and inarticulate. Only Susan had been able to speak at that moment.

"I've been doing a lot of studying," she said firmly, "and I know we can bring up Katie to be like other little girls. We can get the best speech therapists and in time she'll have her hearing aids. I'll work with her day and night. Other people have done it successfully."

The Langdons looked at Richard.

"I wish I could agree," he said, "but I can't. Susan doesn't realize she'd have the burden of this alone most of the time. I have to work and travel. I can't give this what it takes. At best, it would be a ninety-ten arrangement. I've read everything Susan's gathered about bringing up a deaf-mute child at home. It's admirable, what some parents have done together, but in our circumstances, we're not equipped for it."

Susan waited for her mother and father to dispute this. They adored Katie. They'd see why she couldn't be consigned to a silent, abnormal world. She thought she wasn't hearing correctly when Wil Langdon said, "I suppose you're right, Richard. If yours were a different life, if you could really share the burden, I might feel otherwise, but it's too much for a woman alone, or virtually alone."

"Daddy!"

"I know, sweetheart. I can imagine what you're feeling. God knows what agony you've both gone through! Your hearts must be breaking! But you must also be realistic, Susie darling. You can't run the risk of ruining Katie's life and your own."

"I wouldn't ruin her life! I can do it. I know I can!"

"You're a strong woman," Wil said, "and I know you believe that. Maybe you're right. Maybe you could do it. But what will you do to Richard, to yourself, to your marriage? How can such an undertaking possibly succeed unless both parents are willing and eager to take a long chance?"

Susan was hurt, bewildered. She turned to her mother. "Mom, *you* understand. You'd do it my way, wouldn't you?"

Bea looked tortured. "Darling, I don't know. I have a husband who can always be at my side. That makes a difference."

Susan felt the bottom dropping out of her world. "You both think Richard's right." Her voice was flat. "You really think his way is best for Katie. I wouldn't have believed it."

Bea took her hand. "No one loves that baby more than we do. No one loves *you* more. But you must think of her first, Susan. You're sure you can singlehandedly make her a normal child. I'd give anything, anything in this world to feel that way too. But you're speaking from a mother's natural emotions, darling, not from terrible reality. What will you do if you send her to a regular school and her classmates ignore her or laugh at her? How will you heal those wounds?

What will you feel when you see an angry child having temper tantrums because she can't hear or make herself understood? Forget your marriage. If it's good, it might even survive the absences and your total preoccupation with this problem. I think it *is* strong enough to survive those things. But think about your little girl, Susan, and what will happen to her. Where will she be when other young girls are going out on dates, giggling on the telephone, falling in love, doing all the things you and your friends did? Will you be able to bear that loss for her? Don't think of yourself, my darling. Don't even think of how you'd die a thousand times every day if you weren't with her. A mother's true love is always sacrifice, willing sacrifice, as long as it's best for the child.''

Susan began to cry. "You think I'm being selfish."

"No, sweetheart," Wil said. "You're acting from the most unselfish of motives. You're literally offering to give your life to Katie. What could be more unselfish than that? But if that well-meaning sacrifice only results in forcing a child into a lonely half-world, you'll have destroyed everyone. Susie, baby, it's a terrible decision, but you know you have to make it. You'll be able to visit Katie at her special school, even have her home some of the time. And you'll have other children.''

She looked at her parents with momentary hatred. They'd betrayed her. And then the anger was replaced by sorrow. They didn't understand, any of them. They were desperately trying to be unemotional about something that couldn't be treated as a dispassionate problem. They believed what they were saying, but they were wrong.

"If we send her away, I'll never go to see her," Susan said in a mechanical voice. "I couldn't bear it. And I'll never have another child."

"You don't mean that," Bea said, her voice soft with sympathy. "Of course you'll see her. And you'll be glad to see her happy and contented, not torn apart with frustration. As for other babies, you'll have them, darling. It's important that you do. For many reasons."

"No, I'd never risk it again." She looked at Richard and her eyes were empty. "You win," she said. "If this is what my family feels, I know how yours will react." She began to laugh hysterically. "Aren't we all marvelously civilized? So sensible. So intelligent! How could I have been so stupidly sentimental? My God, Richard, I thought your ego was monumental, but mine must be colossal! Imagine my presuming that I could handle this! What an insane idea to entertain!''

She was out of control and the three people with her were frightened. Richard tried to calm her.

"Easy, darling. We're not talking about tomorrow."

Susan looked at him, but he felt she didn't see him. "Oh, but we are," she said. "I want you to take her away right now. There must be a fine, expensive institution that will care for her since I can't. The sooner the better, so we can get on with our lovely, untroubled lives." She was laughing and crying. "What do you think I'm made of? Wood, like your precious piano? Do you think I can stand seeing her for another two or three years, knowing every day brings us closer to the time we'll be torn apart? No, no. Take her. Take her right now so everybody can forget she ever existed."

Richard shook her. "Susie! Darling! Stop this!"

Bea was sobbing openly and Wil looked as though he wanted to die. As quickly as Susan's hysterics had begun, they subsided.

"I'm all right," she said quietly. "Just leave me alone. All of you."

She would not go with Richard when he told his parents. She went to bed after the visit to her family and refused to get up. She wouldn't go near the nursery nor allow Bridie to bring Katie in to her. She simply lay there, saying nothing, except to ask Richard, after a week, whether he'd made arrangements for a place to send Katie.

He was nearly out of his mind. The terrible news that had greeted him was compounded by Susan's withdrawal from him, from the world. She refused to see anyone, picked listlessly at the meals the cook set in front of her. She simply lay like dead, staring at the ceiling.

"Yes," he said now, in answer to her question. "There's a lovely school up on the Hudson. They usually don't take children until nursery age, but they'll make an exception for us. It's beautiful honey. I went up there yesterday. I wish you'd go see it with me."

There was no answer.

"Susan darling, we must get you some help. This thing has been more than any woman could handle. I want to have the doctor in."

"When can they take Katie?"

"Any time," Richard said sadly. "But we don't have to think about that right now. Let's get you on your feet first. Please see the doctor. If not for yourself, for me. For everybody who's so worried about you."

"I'm not the one they should be worrying about."

He kept quiet, but he was running out of patience, unused to dealing with emotional problems of this kind. Nor was he helped by Maria's cold reception of the news. Giovanni had looked mortally wounded, but Maria's reaction had been unreasonable outrage.

"This must come from Susan's side of the family! Nothing like this has ever been known in ours!"

Richard flared up. "What about Frances? I suppose that was Mary Lou's fault?"

"I have no doubt it was."

"Mother, how can you? This is a terrible thing! My child is hopelessly handicapped and my wife is having a nervous breakdown. My God, have you no compassion?"

"Of course I have. I'm bitterly disappointed that Katherine is not normal. And I'm sorry Susan is so weak she can't hold up under the strain. But I fail to see how my carrying on like a madwoman can help things. I prefer to do something constructive, Richard. Such as finding a suitable place for the child. And in one thing Susan is right. It should be as soon as possible."

"What am I going to do about Susan? I think she's losing her mind."

"You'll get her a psychiatrist, obviously. And you'll be sure to keep all of this very, very quiet. I mean *all* of it, Richard."

"Like Sergio did," he said bitterly.

"Precisely. Can you imagine the field day the tabloids would have with your deaf and dumb child and a crazy wife?"

He'd gone home numbly. Two days later Maria used her influence at the place he'd since gone to see. The sight depressed him unutterably. From babies to adults, those who lived there were mute. The terrible silence was all-pervasive. Yet the people seemed cheerful, conversing in rapid sign language, and the surroundings were more than comfortable. It was as luxurious as it was expensive.

In September, when she was ten months old, he and Bridie took little Katie to the place where she'd probably live most of her life.

Susan did not even kiss her goodbye.

CHAPTER 12

IT WAS KATE FENTON who, late in October, finally broke through the invisible wall that Susan had built between herself and the reality she was unable to face. A month after little Katie went away, the baby's godmother barged, unannounced, into Susan's bedroom and stood glaring at the wan, closed-eye figure under the coverlet.

"What the hell do you think you're doing?"

Susan opened her eyes and stared lifelessly at her unexpected visitor.

"Remember me?" Kate asked. "I'm part of the living. You look like a candidate for Morticians' Award of the Year!"

Susan didn't answer.

"No, I take that back," Kate went on. "You're more eligible for the title of 'Woman Sorriest For Herself.' Susan, I'm disappointed in you. I'm more than disappointed; I'm mad as hell at you! You're behaving abominably. Making a lot of innocent people suffer with your self-pity. I thought you had more guts than that. Or if not more guts, at least more consideration. Your poor mother! She's beside herself!"

"I'm sorry," Susan said.

"Are you now? Well, isn't that big of you! Listen, dear girl, you've had one lousy kick in the teeth, but does that give you the right to punish the world? Don't you think all of us who love Katie are in enough agony without going crazy with worry over you?"

"I can't help it."

"Don't you dare say that to me! You don't *want* to help it! If you did, you'd behave like a normal human being instead of a zombie. You'd get out of that bed and start living again. I don't care whether you want to or not, you owe it to the people who care about you, your friends and parents, and, most of all, your husband."

Susan's face darkened at the mention of Richard. "Don't talk to me about him," she said. "If it weren't for Richard, I'd have my baby with me. He's the one who didn't want her here. I think he never wanted her at all. He's probably glad this happened."

Kate sank into a chair. "For God's sake, will you listen to yourself? Have you forgotten how pleased he was when you were pregnant? How crazy he was about the baby? Whether you believe it or not, he did what he thought best, what everybody except you thought best. I don't know if they're wrong and you're right, Susie, but I do know you can't proceed to slowly kill yourself and everybody around you because your vote was overruled. You're not thinking about Katie. You're much too involved in what's happened to you."

Tears began to roll down Susan's face. "That's not true. There's not a moment I don't think about her. I dream of her. I didn't even dare say goodbye to her, Kate. I knew I couldn't let them take her if I saw her again." The tears came faster. "Oh, Kate, what am I going to do? That little thing, that baby, separated from her family, all alone with strangers! I can't bear it! It's wrong. It was evil of Richard!"

Kate felt so sorry for her she had to choke back her own tears. But it wouldn't do to show pity. She had to take a tough line. Solicitous as she felt, she knew Susan had to be shocked and angered into moving again.

"Now you listen to me," Kate said firmly. "You're not the first person this has happened to. Neither is Katie. And you won't be the last. It's tragic, yes. It's a terrible trick of fate. But that's what it is, Susan. Fate. You can't fight it and you can't change it. You have no choice but to accept it. I can guess what you're going through, not only because of Katie's handicap but because you want to take care of her and can't. But you *can't*. If you went back to the doctor who examined her and asked him what your chances are of doing the job alone, of bringing up that child virtually singlehandedly, he'd tell you again it's not a one-person job. The kindest thing for Katie is to let her be with trained people who'll enable her to make the adjustment millions of others have. You think only you can help her. Sorry. Not true. You are not indispensable. In fact, in your efforts to help her, you'd probably maim her for life. And then, by God, you'd have *reason* to want to die!"

Susan looked like a whipped child. "You really believe that?"

"I really do. This is the biggest sacrifice you'll probably ever be called on to make. Make it with grace. Make it out of love for Katie, if nothing else."

"I don't know. I still think . . ."

"No," Kate said. "No more thinking. It's time for action. Get up. Get going."

"If only Richard would work with me." It was almost a whimper.

"He can't," Kate said flatly. "What do you want him to do, stay home and give piano lessons? That's not fair. And even if he gave up his career, what kind of house would Katie grow up in? Richard would come to hate you. He'd hate his child. You'd spend the rest of your life in guilty misery, trying to make two unhappy people happy. Is that what you want for this baby you love so much? To have her used as a reason to wreck two other lives? I don't think so. When you reason it out, Susan, you can only come to the same conclusions everyone else has. Let that baby have the life she was born for. In time the pain will ease for you and Richard. It's not as though you've given her up for adoption. You'll be able to see her. Perhaps, when she's older, she can even come home. But for now, she must learn to function within her limits. And so must you." Kate paused. "I'm not big on amateur psychiatry, but any fool can see that right now you hate Richard. You have to get over that hurdle, too. You need professional help. Someone uninvolved to talk to. We'd like you to have some sessions with a good doctor."

She expected resistance, but she received none. Susan didn't even have the will to fight, "All right," she said listlessly, "if that's what everybody wants. But it won't help."

"It won't if you go into it with that attitude! Susan, how much do you expect of people? How long do you think we'll go on tiptoeing around your martyrdom? Even those who who love you best are getting impatient. It's a cynical thing to say, but nobody wants to listen to the same old troubles month after month. Not even your parents. And not your husband. For better or for worse, remember? You took a vow to share everything. Let Richard share your grief, and you share his. He has plenty of it. It's his child, too. You've put him through enough. You've put *yourself* through enough."

Susan held out her hand. "Thank you, Kate."

"I'm not shaking the hand of any road-company Camille. Get up and start getting dressed. *Then* I'll shake your hand. Hell, I might even kiss you!"

For the first time, Susan smiled.

The sessions with the doctor went on for many weeks, and if Susan did not come out of them reconciled, she at least began to have a better understanding of herself. She saw that her pity for her daughter was as real as her love. But she also painfully recognized that her own ego was involved. In the family of giants she'd married into, she'd always felt unimportant. Her beautiful baby was a personal triumph, something she did not owe to any Antonini but one. Now she was unconsciously seeing Katie's imperfection as a symbol of her own failures, a reflection of her inadequacy. These were not pleasant things to discover. She was not even sure she entirely believed them, and though she began to behave "normally," there was an unusual reserve, a lingering inability to recapture the old laughing, loving Susie.

She tried hard to become once again the young woman Richard had fallen in love with, but it was not until the next spring, just before he went on tour, that they resumed their marital relations, and even then it was a near disaster.

Richard had wanted her to make the West Coast trip with him, to Seattle, Portland, San Francisco and Los Angeles, but Susan was deep into her sessions with Dr. Marcus, and though she would have been glad for an excuse to end them, Richard agreed it was better that she stay in New York and continue with the psychiatrist.

"He's helping you, sweetheart, isn't he?"

"I suppose so."

'Then we can sacrifice a little more time together, can't we? I hate leaving you, but I expect to return to the girl I love."

"You can't. She doesn't exist any more."

Suddenly he was angry. "Goddammit, Susan, what do you expect of me? I lie here night after night, hungry for you, not daring to touch you, afraid you'll shatter like some piece of glass if I so much as say one wrong word! What about me? What do I have to look forward to?"

He was right. Susan knew what she was doing to him. She still loved him. He'd been wonderful, kind and patient all these months, a different Richard from the undisciplined man she married. If only I could feel, she thought. If only I could desire as I used to.

"I still love you, you know."

"Do you? Richard asked. "Then prove it."

He moved against her, caressing her tenderly. The response that used to come instantly did not appear and it infuriated him. Uncaring, he tore off her nightgown and threw her onto the bed. Afterward, he was covered with remorse. "My God, how could I have done that? How could I rape my own wife? I'm an animal! No better than my own father! Can you ever forgive me?"

She didn't know what he meant about Giovanni but instead of resentment, she felt release. "I should be outraged," she said quietly, "but I'm glad you did it. If you hadn't, the gulf between us might have widened hopelessly. You didn't 'rape me,' Richard, You did what was necessary to bring me to my senses. I was afraid to have you touch me. Afraid my anger was still there. It is. But so is my desire. And my love. I've asked more of you than I had a right to. This was no 'violation,' as though you were some sex fiend attacking me in an alley. You're my husband. Thank God you shocked me out of my numbness."

He could't believe what he heard. She liked it! Maybe it was true that some women fantasize about sex by brute force. Or maybe Susan had to be brought back to reality with this uncontrollable evidence of his craving for her. Whatever, he wasn't going to probe for reasons. That was the doctor's job.

When he left three days later, it was with a light heart. They'd made love, good, passionate love, every night and morning since. He was filled with well-being, his old confident self again. She came to him willingly now, almost fiercely ecstatic at her climax. And then she held him until he fell asleep, making little sounds of love as she might to a baby. He didn't recognize them as such. He only knew he felt restored and virile. He was a little ashamed that he hardly thought of Katie these days, but he told himself that life had to go on. His life. And Susan's. Things were okay again. His body made her forget, just as hers gave him back his temporarily lost feeling of manliness. Sex, Richard thought. Old Freud was right. It's the basis of everything.

"That's quite a smile you're wearing," Paul Carmichael said when Richard got into the car to go to the airport. "You look like your old, cocky self."

Richard grinned more broadly. "Susie's fine again."

At first, Paul didn't know what he meant. "You mean she's through with the doctor? Will she be joining us?"

"No. Her head isn't back to normal, but everything else is, thank God."

Paul felt a flush of jealousy. You ass! he told himself. She's his wife.

"I'm glad. For both of you."

"You'd better believe it," Richard said. Then he frowned. "Trouble is, it only happened the last few days. I'm like a sailor rescued from a desert island. I don't know how I'll get through the next few weeks without more of that."

This time Paul understood only too well what he was saying. You bastard. We all marveled at the change in you. There's been no change at all. He could almost read Richard's mind. He's like a child who's been very, very good for a long time. Now he thinks he deserves anything he chooses as a reward for that behavior. It's going to be like the old days before he was married. He'll be hellbent on proving himself all over again. Well, he can do it alone. One of us will be ridiculously faithful to Susan.

"Do you think I should see my baby, Dr. Marcus?"

"Do you want to, Mrs. Antonini?"

"I'm not sure. That is I want to see her, but I don't know whether I could stand it."

"Do you want to see her for her sake or yours?"

Susan thought for a moment. "She won't know me, will she? I'm only indulging myself. Being masochistic."

He didn't answer.

"It's pointless isn't it? I'm not ready to handle that and it won't mean anything to her."

"I think that's probably true. How are you getting along with your husband away?"

"I miss him."

"What do you miss about him?"

"Everything. His presence. His music. Even his love-making."

"*Even?*"

"I didn't mean that. I love sex with Richard. Why did I say 'even'?"

"I don't know. Why do you think you did?"

She pondered. "Because that's only a small part of what I think love and life and marriage should be? I don't think it's a 'necessary evil' Doctor. I enjoy it. It's not something to 'submit' to. Except that once."

"Then why do you mentioned it as the third thing?"

Susan was quiet for a moment. "Maybe that's all my life has really been for the past three years. This crazy sex urge of ours. Maybe I thought it was enough. I've been nothing but Richard's bedmate, haven't I?"

"Some women find that enough."

"You mean *I* don't."

"I can't say. Apparently you have some doubts."

"Yes," Susan said slowly. "I have to feel important. My job made me feel important." She swallowed hard. "So did Katie. And now they're both gone. I need something more, don't I?"

"It's worth thinking about, Mrs. Antonini."

Maria slammed the evening paper down in a rage. "I don't believe it," she said. "I simply do not believe it!"

In the gathering darkness of the early evening, Giovanni looked across the living room at his wife. "What is it you don't believe, my dear?"

"Susan is writing a column! Why wasn't I told about this?"

"Perhaps because we've been away," he said mildly. "Let me see. What kind of column?"

She handed it to him. "Some trash called 'The Woman's Way.' I thought Gloria was joking when she called this morning to say that Susan was writing regularly for a newspaper. Apparently it started two weeks ago. What on earth would possess that girl to do such a thing?"

Giovanni was busily reading. "Doesn't seem so bad to me," he said. "She writes well. Amusingly. And the material is inoffensive, if this is an example.

'The Private Life of an Idol's Wife.' That's rather appealing. She's simply talking about women who leave careers to marry celebrities.'' He smiled. '' 'Sometimes the second fiddle is the most important instrument in the orchestration of a marriage.' Quite a well-turned sentence, don't you think?''

"No, I certainly don't think!" Maria snapped. "She's making a laughingstock of us."

"Oh, come now," Giovanni said placatingly, "I don't see it that way. Sounds as though she's making a good case for the status of a full-time wife. A refreshing change from all the propaganda about how terrible it is to be married."

"It's trash," Maria said again. "She's such a fool she can't see that they're simply exploiting her name! Richard Antonini's wife is no ordinary homemaker.' The world will think she's speaking for him, whatever she writes. It's dreadful. A newspaper column! Whoever heard of such a thing?"

Giovanni couldn't resist. "I seem to recall Eleanor Roosevelt. 'My Day' it was called, wasn't it?"

"Yes," Maria said. "And everyone knew she was using the column to glorify the political policies of that despicable husband of hers. You only prove my point. People read nonsense like this believing it reflects the husband's views. Do you think this column would exist if Susan's name were Smith?"

"I still don't understand what harm it can do. She's not going to write anything damaging to Richard. Maria dear, I'm sorry for Susan. She's been through so much, with the baby and now the doctor. It must be lonely for her, not being able to travel with Richard. At least this gives her something to do."

"What she should do is stop pampering herself! Bad enough she produced a defective child and left the solution up to Richard and me while she lay like a lump in her bed! Not enough that she's still running to psychiatrists, and heaven help us if *that* ever gets out! Now she's going to air her private life so every chambermaid can read what it's like to be married to an Antonini!"

"I think you're making too much of this, my dear. I see it as a good sign. At least she's coming back into the world, poor little thing."

"Poor little thing indeed! She's always been headstrong and scheming." Maria thought of the pregnancy which had gotten Susan her own home. "She's devious and unpredictable. Who knows what she might write about us?"

"Maria, be sensible! She's not writing a gossip column about us. She's taking current subjects and discussing them from the viewpoint of an intelligent woman."

"She's always had you fooled. From the first minute she knew how to flatter your ego. You don't understand women like this. I said she was an unsuitable choice for Richard. But he wouldn't listen."

Giovanni sighed. "All in all, she's been a good wife to Richard."

"That's debatable. She's been a terrible daughter-in-law to *me*. And this column business is the last straw. If Richard were here he'd put a stop to it. Since he isn't it's up to the family."

He made one last try. "Don't you think it should wait until Richard comes home? You're tampering with a matter that should be between husband and wife, Maria." Not that you don't always, he thought.

"I know my son," she said loftily. "He has no idea what's going on. I'm sure of that. She's taken advantage of his absence to indulge her selfish need for personal publicity. I'll see her tomorrow and straighten her out. Idiot! I could kill her!''

God knows you're trying, the maestro said silently. But it's not Susan's death you really want. It's the murder of a marriage you're plotting.

It was a terrible scene, one that left Susan in despair. Maria phoned and invited her to lunch and she dutifully accepted. They were alone in the library afterward when the older woman got right to the point.

''Susan, I don't know how you ever got into this business of writing for the newspaper.''

Unaware, Susan smiled. ''It was just luck. I needed something to do, Mrs. Antonini, and my old boss, Kate Fenton, happened to have lunch with a publisher who was looking for a woman to write about today's problems from a female angle. Kate suggested me and to my amazement I was hired. I can't wait to tell Richard! I know he'll be pleased that I'm occupied and interested.''

''So Richard doesn't know. I thought not.''

''No. I want to surprise him when he comes home.'' She found herself eager to confide in her mother-in-law. ''It's really been a lifesaver for me, having this work to do. I thought when Katie . . . when she went away . . . I thought I didn't want to live any more. I thought I had no purpose.'' Susan smiled. ''This silly little column isn't much, but it makes me feel part of things. It's a first step.''

Maria looked at her coldly. ''It's a wrong step. And you must stop it immediately.''

Susan was uncomprehending. ''Why? What's wrong with writing little essays a couple of times a week? It's good therapy. The money isn't important but it gives me something to think about. Dr. Marcus says . . .''

''I'm not interested in what Dr. Marcus says. Nor in your therapy. I am interested in your husband's career and the possible embarrassment to him.''

''I don't understand. This can't hurt Richard.''

''Don't be naïve, Susan. In your position, everything you write will be interpreted as a personal insight into your life and your husband's. It's unseemly for you to go about expressing views with which he may not agree.''

Susan suddenly understood. It wasn't Richard's agreement that was at issue. It was Maria's angry conviction that Susan was competing with him. That was taboo. *Verboten.* Antonini wives stayed in the background, spoke when they were spoken to, behaved as decorative and decorous appendages. They didn't have careers of their own. Or, except for Maria, even thoughts of their own. At least none that were expressed in public. They stayed out of sight like Mary Lou. Or lived separate lives, like Jacqueline. They didn't write columns or give revealing interviews or reach for any kind of personal identity. Well, she wasn't going to go along with that. She was a person with a mind of her own. Richard would be the first to agree with that.

''I'm sorry you think I'd ever embarrass Richard or any of you,'' Susan said. ''I hoped you'd give me credit for more taste and intelligence. I even hoped you'd understand this helps fill an important need for me.''

''You! Always you!'' Maria was angry. *'Your* taste and intelligence. *Your* needs. I don't give a rap about your needs! You have only one obligation: to make Richard's life serene so that nothing interferes with his work. You have usefulness only in that you can try to pick up where I left off and devote your life to his genius. Haven't you worried him enough? Haven't you distracted him to the point where I fear for his career? I won't stand by and let you destroy him with your selfishness. You're making a fool of yourself with this 'job' of yours and you'll make a fool of him with your pushy ways! You must stop this immediately, Susan. No more columns. No more items such as the one I saw this morning in *Newsweek*. No more pictures in *Time*. You are not a public figure to be photographed and interviewed and gossiped about. I'm appalled by what's happened! You are Richard Antonini's wife and you will conduct yourself as such.''

Susan was surprised by her own calmness in the face of this tirade. ''You seem to have done a great deal of research since you got back from Europe two days ago. How clever of you to have assembled such a dossier. You must give me the name of your clipping service.''

''Your levity is as inappropriate as your disrespect. But it is no more than I expect from you. Be as discourteous as you like. I don't care, as long as you stop this unacceptable behavior.''

''I don't intend to stop, Mrs. Antonini. Only Richard could possibly make me stop and he wouldn't try. It's innocent and gives me a little pleasure. You're making it sound like a plot to upstage the entire family and harm my husband! How ridiculous! Nothing could be further from the truth. Richard will find your attitude as funny as I do.''

Maria was furious. ''You're sure of that, aren't you? Very well. Let's find out. Why don't we call Richard in Los Angeles right now and see what he says?''

Susan hesitated. To refuse to call would seem an admission that she doubted his reaction. But this was not something she wished to discuss with him on long-distance, and certainly not with his mother hovering in the background waiting a chance to have her say.

''Well?'' Maria asked. ''What about it? Shall we call?''

''No. This is a private matter between Richard and me. I'm sticking to my original plan to tell him when he comes home.''

The other woman smiled knowingly.

''I'm not afraid to call him in front of you,'' Susan said defensively. ''I just don't think this concerns you.'' She knew it sounded weak, frightened, and the knowledge depressed her because it was close to the truth. She wasn't sure how Richard would react. She had been, before Maria had delivered her vehement ultimatum. But now Susan wasn't as confident. Richard might agree that her tiny emergence into the public eye was unsuitable. ''Do it and tell him later,'' Kate once said. Had she been wrong? He doesn't like competition any more than his mother does, Susan thought with discouragement. And if she gets to him before I do, she'll certainly persuade him to make me stop writing the column. She flirted with the idea of begging her mother-in-law not to interfere, to let Susan handle it her own way, but that would be as demeaning as it would be futile. I won't beg, she decided. I won't grovel. Not to her or any of them.

But even as she wondered how to make Richard see this situation her way, she knew she'd been beaten once again. She was, as always, no match for Maria.

CHAPTER 13

JACQUELINE SETTLED HERSELF comfortably on a banquette in the front room of La Côte Basque and gazed around appraisingly before she turned her attention to her sister-in-law. "This really is a most civilized restaurant," she said. "Say what you will about how Madame Henriette rules it like a benevolent despot, what with all that nonsense about not admitting ladies in pants, you must admit she keeps up her standards. No blue-denimed slobs in here, thank God! Just beautiful people. I do like beautiful people. Even though under those Trigère dresses beat little hearts of pure steel."

Susan looked around as though she'd never been there before, trying to see the assembled lunch crowd through Jacqueline's eyes. They were mostly beautiful. And mostly famous. Albert, the official host, was hovering over a rich and impossible social-climbing widow, making polite conversation about Paris, where she'd soon be buying couture clothes and he'd be ordering his winter supply of fine wines. "Madame" herself was chattering in French to a former Presidential aide of JFK all the while keeping an eye on the orderly destruction of the "cold dish table" near the door, where the waiters rapidly depleted the artistic array of cold baby lobsters, fresh salmon, artichokes, and *oeufs en gelée*. A famous cosmetician faced them across the room and a film star and her current lover occupied the table reserved for the Duke and Duchess of Windsor when they were in town. It was all elegant and expensive and sleek, the province of a very small and influential segment of New York.

"This is Maria's favorite restaurant, isn't it?" Susan asked.

Jacqueline laughed. "Yes, but I like it nonetheless." Then she sobered. "I hear you had quite a little dust-up with our sainted mother-in-law over that column you're writing. Is that why you suggested lunch—to talk about it?"

Susan was surprised. "As a matter of fact, yes. I do need your advice. But how did you hear about it so quickly? It only happened yesterday."

"Darling girl, everybody in the family has heard about it. Maria was on the phone to Mary Lou and Gloria and me five minutes after you left. Not that that's surprising. She's on the phone to me every day of her life when she's in the vicinity."

"Every day? Maria calls you every day?"

"Like clockwork."

"For heaven's sake, why?"

"To give me advice about the children. What else? You'd think that Calhoun and Charles were hers, with all the instructions she gives about their care and feeding. We all get it. As though none of us had the mental capabilities to run our lives and handle our own children. Do you mean she doesn't call you every day?"

"No. Almost never. Unless it's about something like the column."

"Well, I guess she wouldn't call you at that," Jacqueline said thoughtlessly, "since you don't have children for her to manage." She stopped abruptly. "Oh, Susan, I'm so sorry! How careless of me! For a moment I forgot . . ."

"It's all right."

"No, it isn't. I'm an insensitive boor. How is Katie? Have you been to see her?"

Susan shook her head. "I'm afraid to go. I know she's well taken care of, but I don't think I could stand seeing her being brought up by strangers, no matter how capable, kind and well paid they are."

Jacqueline was silent.

"I've never really discussed that with you," Susan said. "I have a feeling you think I did the wrong thing."

"Not the wrong thing, I don't suppose. That is, I don't blame you for buckling under all the pressure. Maybe it was sensible. Everybody seemed to think so."

"Except you."

"I'm not sure," Jacqueline said. "I keep wondering what I'd do in your place. Of course, the situation's a little different with me. Physically estranged as I may be from Walter, he *is* there. The kids feel as though they have both parents. In your case, with Richard away so much of the time, I don't know." She lit a cigarette. "Hell, I don't know what I'm talking about. We probably wouldn't have had the determination and the patience to cope with an un-hearing child either. It must be a monumental job."

"I wanted to do it."

Jacqueline looked at her almost angrily. "Then why didn't you? Nobody could have forced you to send Katie away. It's just like this damned column. Maria's having a fit over it and Richard's going to back her up when he comes home and you're going to give in again. My God, Susan, you can't let them have their way in all things! Where's your backbone? What are you afraid of—losing your husband? You'll lose him anyway, the route you're going. Richard's a bully. All the Antoninis are basically bullies. And the only way to survive in their world is to be as tough as they are. Look at me. I may not be much of an example, but damn it I live my own life in spite of them. And Walter accepts it. He knows they're all going to get back what they give, selfishness for selfishness. Our marriage would have broken up long ago if I hadn't been just as pig-headed as the rest of his 'wonderful family'. I want to stay married. So do you. But you won't if Richard thinks he can use you for a door mat."

"What about Mary Lou? She never crosses Sergio or Maria."

"Don't kid yourself. You ever see Mary Lou's jewelry? In her quiet way, she makes Sergio pay for every fling. A Buccellati bracelet for every extracurricular roll in the hay—that's Mary Lou's method. She acts meek as a lamb, but she's learned how to get her revenge on the Antoninis. She hits Serge where he lives—in his wallet."

"But what about her child? She put Frances in a home."

"True. The difference is, Mary Lou wanted to. She had to, if only for the sake of the son she already had. Remember, Frances is retarded. There's no hope for her. It wouldn't have been fair to Joseph and, as it turned out later, to Patricia to have raised those normal kids in a household with a sister who simply couldn't keep up. And it would have been miserable for poor little Frances."

"That's what I was told about Kate."

"Except you have no other children to worry about. If you wanted to put all your energy into Katie's development you could, without depriving others."

"So you really do think I was wrong," Susan said slowly.

"All right. Yes, I think you were wrong. Something went out of you when you let them take that child away, Susan. It was the beginning of total submission. Now you're at the second step. I know you're going to stop writing this column you really enjoy doing. And for what? To please Maria? To make Richard happy? Bull! You're quitting because you've lost the will to fight."

"I haven't said I was quitting the column."

"Well, aren't you?" Jacqueline softened. "I don't mean to be so hard on you. I know you love Richard. I know his happiness is everything to you. That there's none for you unless he's content. But *you* matter, too. It can't be all giving and no taking. Nobody loves a jellyfish. Sorry, but that's the God's truth. They're drinking your blood, Susan, these damned Antoninis. They'll keep doing it till you're drained lifeless. They'll turn you into a stupid little robot who'll put up with anything. A faceless creature who doesn't make waves. And when that's accomplished, Richard will find you so boring that he wouldn't even *pretend* to be faithful." Jacqueline was so intense she didn't think what she was saying. "My God, from what I hear he's already . . ." She clapped her hand over her mouth. "Oh, Jesus, I didn't mean to say that!"

Susan went deathly pale. "He's already what?"

"Nothing. Forget it. A stupid piece of gossip. You know how people talk. Come on, let's order lunch. I think I'm going to have the rack of lamb. It's divine here."

"No," Susan said. "We won't order until you tell me what you meant."

"All right. Maybe you should know. The word is that Richard's picked up his old affair with Gerry Carter on this trip. They're sleeping together all over the West Coast, I hear. You know, of course, they had a thing going when Richard met you. I'm sorry, Susan. I had no right to tell you, I suppose. But I can't stand your giving up everything *you* want in life while Richard has it all *his* way! This doesn't mean he doesn't love you. It's just another side of his life. He doesn't want to marry Gerry. If he had, he would have long ago. He married you. He didn't have to. He *wanted* to. But now that he's so sure of you, so sure you'll do exactly as he tells you, he thinks he can get away with anything. That's why you've got to be independent. Demand what you want, whether it's your work or your baby or both. Fight him. Make life tough for him. It's the only way he'll respect you. And the only way you'll survive. Believe me. I know the Antonini men. And the Antonini women."

The bottom dropped out of the world. Susan's mind jumped to bits and pieces of the past. She'd wondered about Gerry, intuitively sensing there'd been something there, but supremely confident that it was over. She thought of her newly revived sex life with Richard before he left on tour, of the way he'd demanded her body, of the insatiability of his physical needs. She instinctively knew that once he'd resumed his sexual activities with her, he'd not be content to go for weeks without a woman. Any woman. She'd have to decide now. Make a life of her own, as Jacqueline advised, or devote herself to her marriage, do whatever

Richard wanted, travel with him, put career and children out of her mind forever. She wondered why she felt so certain Jacqueline was telling the truth about her husband and his publicity woman.

"How did you hear about . . . about Richard and Gerry? Was it Paul? Has Paul been in touch with you?"

Jacqueline shook her head. "Paul? He'd be the last one to tattle, especially about Richard. Paul's a loyal darling. He may know what's going on, but wild horses couldn't drag it out of him. No, my information comes from a friend of mine in San Francisco. She says the whole of California knows, because Gerry's making sure of it. She was humiliated when Richard dumped her for you. Everybody thought he'd marry her." Jacqueline laughed bitterly. "My God, they sure don't know the Antoninis, do they? Imagine Maria letting Richard marry an 'employee'! Not that he ever intended to, but Gerry kidded herself that he did. Anyway, I suppose this is her revenge, proving she can get him back any time she wants him, even on this basis. Or maybe she loves him. I don't know, Susan. I'm only sure of one thing: Richard's reverting to his old role as a naughty spoiled brat and you'd better nip this in the bud."

"But how? By doing everything he forbids me to?"

"Exactly. Get your baby home. Rehire Bridie and in a year or two you can start teaching Katie to live in the real world. Even without Richard's participation, I believe you can do it. Meantime, keep on with the column. Who cares whether he and Maria hate the whole thing? Try being selfish for a change. It's the only way you'll make it." She shook her head. "I have some nerve, handing out this gratuitous advice. You'll probably hate me, and I'd be sorry about that because I'm really terribly fond of you, Susan. You're the best thing that's happened to the Antoninis in years. You're the only one in the whole damned family I can relate to. And, if you'll forgive the immodesty, I rather think that goes both ways."

"It does," Susan said. "Even at this moment." She tried to laugh. "It's not easy to be fond of someone who knocks the props out from under you, but I suppose it's better. At least now I know I have to decide what to do." There was a muffled catch in her throat. "Maybe I should leave him," she said sadly. "Maybe I should divorce him, get a job, bring Katie to Mother's."

"You don't want to do it that way," Jacqueline said. "And you don't have to. You can make this work. Remember you're dealing with a man, not a superbeing. He's like all men, complete with the irresistible urge to see exactly how far you'll let him go. Like a child testing your patience. He knows damned well you'll hear about Gerry. Maybe in an infantile way he'd like you to. I'll bet he really wants you to be the independent, no-pushover young woman you used to be. I don't pretend to read his mind. Right now I could cheerfully murder him. And yet, I like him. In fact, of all the brothers I think he's probably the only one really worth saving." She beckoned for a menu. "If I haven't entirely spoiled your appetite, shall we order lunch?"

One look at his face when he came into the apartment told Susan that Richard already knew about the column. Whether Maria had called him or whether he'd seen it in the paper or heard about it from a friend, she didn't know. It didn't matter. He barely said hello, didn't kiss her, slammed into the bedroom and began taking off his traveling clothes. Susan followed him silently.

"Would you like a drink?" she asked.

"I'd prefer an explanation."

"I presume you mean about the column."

"Exactly. What the hell do you think you're doing, Susan? Are you crazy? I have to deal with the press every day of my life! What kind of position do you think this puts me in, when my wife is one of them? I simply don't understand you! You're not well enough to travel with me, but you're in such good shape that you can take a stupid job writing a bunch of idiotic drivel! Who put you up to this? That damned, meddlesome Kate Fenton, I suppose. Or was it your shrink who thought you should have an 'outside activity'?"

"Kate got me the interview," Susan said quietly, "but I got the job on my own. Obviously you know your mother doesn't approve."

"You bet she doesn't! And she's dead right! It's embarrassing beyond belief! You'll quit it. And right away."

Susan felt her anger rising, but her voice was under control. "And what will you quit, Richard? What will you give in return?"

He stared at her. "What does that mean?"

"Don't pretend. I know about Gerry."

He turned his back to her and fiddled with the buttons on his shirt. Finally he faced her. "All right. You've heard. Goddamn people's big mouths! I'm sorry. I didn't mean it to happen."

She didn't answer.

He became suddenly defensive. "In a way, you know, you're just as much to blame as I. You should have been where you belong, with your husband. Not skulking around New York, crying all over that bloody Marcus and letting that bitch Kate Fenton con you into doing something stupid! You should know, of all people, that if you'd been around I wouldn't have needed anybody else to screw!"

The coarseness of it made her cringe. "Is that all you need? Someone to screw? Funny, I thought it was love you wanted. Tenderness. Something more than you can get from a call girl . . . or even a press agent. Apparently I don't matter to you as a wife. I've been part servant, part mistress. For a little while I was also part of your ego when I was carrying your child. And now you want me to be a combination of legal whore and watchdog, is that it? You want me to give up everything I want in order to tag along after you and make sure you stay out of any bed but mine. Well, I won't do it, Richard. I'll go with you, gladly, anywhere, but not as a deterrent to your tomcat instincts. I can't make you faithful to me unless you want to be, so don't stand there and tell me it was my fault you were with Gerry or God knows who else! You could always find a way to cheat on me if you wanted to, even if I shared every room in every hotel suite from here to Timbuctoo! Don't try to transfer your guilt to me by saying I'm to blame because I wasn't where I belong. Where *do* I belong, Richard? on a scale of one to ten, would I rate a possible seven . . . maybe one step above your manager and three steps under your piano tuner, your mistress and your mother?"

For once, he was openmouthed, struck dumb. And then in one of those meteoric changes of attitude he came toward her and tried to take her in his arms.

Susan pulled back. "No. No more getting eveything you want that way. Let's straighten this out right here and now. You speak of the embarrassment of my writing a column. What of my humiliation having the world know you've picked up with your ex-mistress? What of the abuse I've taken from your mother? What about you and your family taking our child away against my wishes? What is a little job compared to all this, for God's sake? How dare you come in here giving me orders about the only thing I've done on my own in the past two years?" She was erupting with anger. "You're killing me, Richard, and I don't want to die! I did once, but no more. I intend to live, hopefully as half of you. If not, I'll live on my own."

He couldn't believe this was his adoring, obedient Susan. And yet he liked it. This was the spunky, sure-of-herself young editor he'd found so attractive, the only woman worth marrying, the one he'd felt had Maria's strength tempered with compassion.

"I don't want to kill you, darling," he said quietly. "I want you to live forever, with me. I'm sorry, Susan. I'm truly sorry about the thing with Gerry. It just happened. I didn't plan it. I was so happy when I left you. I suppose I was still hungry, and you weren't there. I'm not blaming you," he added hastily. "That was a stupid thing to say. I was wrong. I beg your forgiveness and I promise it won't happen again." He paused. "As for the column, perhaps I'm making too much of it. If it makes you happy, what the hell. How much harm can it do? I trust your taste and discretion. Who knows? Maybe it will be helpful." He smiled. "They say Eleanor's column was the most useful propaganda FDR ever had. What's good enough for a President should be good enough for me."

Now it was her turn to stare. Jacqueline was right. Her beloved was a bully and only understood those like him. How quickly he would trade his objection to her writing for her "forgiveness" of his lapse of faith. How easy it was to get one's own way if you stood your ground. More than standing your ground, you had to attack. The knowledge saddened Susan. It was not the way she thought, and she resented the necessity for it, but there was too much at stake not to press her advantage.

"There's something else, Richard," she said.

"What's that?"

"I want to bring Katie home."

His reaction was violent and instantaneous. "No! We're not going to go through that again. It's out of the question. Everyone has told you so. I won't have you giving up your life to a hopeless cause!"

"It's my life. You have yours." She was amazed at her own strength. "I want our child here. I'm going to bring her home, whether you agree or not. If it's too painful for you, I'll try to spare you as much as I can and I won't ask you to help. I won't neglect you, Richard. I love you. I want us to be happy. I'll plan things so I can travel with you some of the time." Susan paused. "And when I can't I'll try to trust you. Again."

"You're really making me pay for one stupid lapse, aren't you?' His tone was bitter.

"It's not a question of payment. Or vengeance. I think I've known all along that I was trying to play a role I wasn't suited for."

"What role is that?"

"Jellyfish," Susan said, remembering Jacqueline. "Nobody loves a jellyfish."

Bea went with her when they drove up to get Katie. Susan's mother was worried about her. Worried about how thin she'd become this past year, more worried still about the grim set of her daughter's mouth, the unreadable expression in her eyes. Susan, who'd always been so gay, so outgoing, now seemed, if not bitter and cynical, something closely approaching that frame of mind. And she'd been so uncommunicative of late. Even when she called to ask Bea to go with her to the school where Katie lived, she hadn't explained. She'd merely said tersely, "I'm going to get Katie. Will you come?"

Bea hadn't hesitated. Of course she would go, in spite of her reservations about this move. She would do anything for her child. Lie, steal, even kill, she supposed. It crossed her mind that even now she might be part of a 'kidnap plot,' that Susan was taking her baby over Richard's objections. Not that such an action really would be kidnaping. Susan had as much right to remove Katie as the Antoninis had to put her there. But her daughter's tense attitude on the drive upstate increased Bea's feeling that the decision was not one made happily or in accord with her husband.

As they crossed the George Washington Bridge, Bea glanced out of the car windows, looking right and left, up and down the Hudson River. It was so beautiful in this area, so near tumultuous, dirty Manhattan, and yet one felt a million miles removed, as though the serene countryside had not changed since the Dutch created their settlements in the seventeenth century. She loved the quiet, peaceful vista of mountains, the winding roads with signs that pointed to towns called Garrison and Fishkill and Cold Spring. It was remote and lovely.

"You have the directions?"

Susan nodded. "Bridie remembered them very well. She went with Richard."

"Bridie gave you the directions. I see. Then Richard doesn't know you're doing this. I rather thought not." Bea sighed. "Susan, is it wise to bring Katie home without his approval?"

"I don't care what's wise. I know what I'm doing. You were wrong, all of you, to agree with him. I know you meant well. I don't blame you or Dad or Kate. If anyone's to blame, it's I. I didn't put up a fight. I was too much in shock. Now that I'm all right I know what must be done."

She explained her plan to her mother. Bridie had been re-engaged to look after the baby. When Katie was old enough she'd start with a speech therapist. There'd be constant, meticulous training for years to come, but Susan was determined to make it work. "I've signed up for the correspondence course at the Tracy Clinic. I'll find the right prenursery school for her, one with normal children. I know what I'm in for, but it's the only answer. Katie has her rights and I'm going to see that she gets them. I have to. I brought her into the world."

"I," Bea thought. All this without Richard's co-operation. Worse, with his disapproval. She thinks she can do it alone. She's gambling her marriage, her child's future, even her own sanity. And yet I understand. I'd probably do the same. It's not possible to be coldly clinical where your baby is concerned.

She felt such sadess for Susan and Katie. She even pitied Richard. He'd been through hell in that awful period of discovery, and it was not he who insisted the child be sent away immediately. It was Susan who, in her anguish, had made that hasty decision. But now that it was done, Richard was determined to stick by the heart-rending choice, still believing it the only viable alternative. What will this do to the two of them? Bea wondered. How far apart have they already drifted?

As though Bea communicated her thoughts, Susan suddenly said, "I may leave Richard, Mom. I may have to."

"Darling, no! You love each other. He'll adjust to having Katie home if that's what you truly want."

"It isn't just Katie." Susan's whole body tensed. She wanted to tell her mother about Gerry, but she couldn't bring herself to do it. "It's . . . well, a lot of things. He doesn't really want me to do the column, though he finally agreed. He doesn't need me, but he doesn't want me to have any life of my own. I don't know. We don't seem to share anything lately."

"That will change," Bea said. "You've both been through a terrible, stressful time. And there's been too much separation. That's no good for any marriage. Promise me, Susan, that even when you have Katie back you'll still arrange to travel with Richard as much as possible. You're wrong, dear. He needs you. You need each other."

"Do we? I wonder."

The owner of the school for the deaf was surprised to hear that Mrs. Richard Antonini had arrived. In all the months since Mrs. Giovanni Antonini, the child's grandmother, had made the arrangements with him, Mr. Pomeranz had never once laid eyes on Katherine's mother. The father, the famous pianist, had brought the baby, had looked as though he were in actual pain as he left her, had seemed, understandably, near tears.

"It's kind of you, Mr. Pomeranz, to make this exception. I know you normally don't take children before school age, but my wife is ill and we thought it best that it be done at once."

"I understand, Mr. Antonini. Your mother explained the circumstances. Katherine will have her own quarters and a special nurse until she's old enough to be with the others. We've never done this before, but you may be assured that we will give your daughter the best of care." He did not mention the enormous "contribution" Maria had made over and above the exorbitant annual "tuition." It had been sizable enough to make Pomeranz more than willing to bend his rules. Since that day, no one had come. Mrs. Antonini, Sr., telephoned occasionally and so did the child's other grandmother, Mrs. Langdon. Brief conversations in which they ascertained that the child was well. Other than that, silence. Until today, when the receptionist announced Mrs. Richard Antonini. Suprised and vaguely troubled, Mr. Pomeranz hurried out of his office to meet her.

Susan introduced herself and her mother.

"We've spoken on the telephone," Bea said. "I'm Mrs. Langdon. Katherine's grandmother,"

"Yes, yes, of course. Happy to meet you both. Very happy to know you, Mrs. Antonini. You've come to see Katherine? That's fine. You'll find her well and happy."

Susan shook her head. "I haven't come to see her, Mr. Pomeranz. I've come to take her home."

"Take her home? But Mrs. Antonini said . . ."

Susan interrupted him coldly. "*I* am Mrs. Antonini. My mother-in-law does not speak for me. I'm removing Katherine. She belongs at home."

"But your husband told me this was a permanent arrangement."

"You are mistaken. It was only until I was well again. Now, if you'll be good enough to show me where my daughter is, we'll be on our way."

The owner hesitated. The twenty-five-thousand-dollar "gift" had been made with very explicit instructions. It was all highly irregular, this sudden change of plan. And, for that matter, how did he know that this cool, beautiful young woman was who she presumed to be? He'd never seen her or the woman who allegedly was Mrs. Langdon. They might be impostors, kidnapers intent on stealing the baby! He'd be responsible! My God, Pomeranz thought, I could be in terrible trouble! The Antoninis were influential people. Even if this is the child's mother she might be taking Katherine against her husband's wishes. I could be charged with neglect. Maybe sued. My school taken away. My license revoked. A few frozen seconds ticked by before he answered.

"Mrs. Antonini, this is all very sudden. I've had no instructions to release your daughter."

"What instructions do you need?"

"Well, that is, you were not the one who made the arrangements or brought her. I really feel . . . I mean some authorization . . . I'd have thought we'd have had notice . . . " Pomeranz was stammering, wondering how he could ask this woman to identify herself.

She did it for him.

Susan's voice was approving and sympathetic when she answered. The cold, hostile attitude disappeared and she smiled kindly. "You need to be sure of who I am. Of course. You should be. I'm delighted you're so cautious. For all you know, I could be here to kidnap the baby." She fished her wallet out of her handbag. "Here's my driver's license, Mr. Pomeranz. And a bank card with my picture. And here's the best proof of all. It's a photograph of me holding Katie only a couple of months before she came to you. My husband took it. I'm sure you recognize us both."

The man examined everything carefully. She was who she claimed to be, all right, But that didn't mean the family wanted the baby released to her. The wrath of the Antoninis could still come down on his head.

"I'm sorry," he said placatingly. "I didn't mean that I doubted your identity, but we have to be very careful."

"Naturally. I told you I approved of that. Now, may we see Katherine?"

"Of course. Right this way."

He led them up the winding, carpeted stairway, wondering how he could reach someone who would authorize this curious development. Perhaps he could stall the woman long enough to reach her husband or her mother-in-law.

"Katherine has quite a few things," he said. "It will take a few minutes to pack them. Perhaps meantime you'd like to inspect some of the classrooms and play areas? That is, you might wish to have your little girl return here when she reaches school age?"

"No," Susan said. "She'll be going to regular nursery school with hearing children."

"I see. Well, in any case, you'll excuse me for a few minutes? There are certain release forms for you to sign. I'll see to it." He paused outside a closed bedroom door. "Katherine is in there with her nurse. I'll be back right away."

Pomeranz scurried down the hall. Susan and Bea looked at each other with the same thought in mind: he was going to telephone Richard or Maria.

"Let's move fast," Susan said.

Bea hesitated. "Susie, don't you think we should visit now and come back later for Katie after you and Richard have talked more about it? It seems a lovely place and they obviously are very conscientious. Perhaps . . ."

"No. I've come for her and I'm taking her home."

She opened the door and moved swiftly to the playpen where a smiling Katie was engrossed in inspecting a pink plush elephant. At the sight of her, Susan's determination strengthened. She was so beautiful, so charming in her serious study of the little toy. Ignoring the startled nurse, Susan scooped up the baby and held her close, hugging and kissing her, laughing with joy.

"Hello, angel," she said. "Hello, my darling. Mummy's here. We're going home. Isn't that wonderful? Katie's going home!"

Katie smiled and grabbed for Susan's earring. The nurse was on her feet, reaching for her charge.

"It's all right," Susan said. "I'm Katherine's mother. We're taking her with us. Mr. Pomeranz is getting the release papers. We're to meet him in his office."

Without another word she strode out of the room, carrying Katie, a worried Beatrice at her heels. Susan headed directly for the front door.

"Susan! Are we going to leave like this? Aren't you going to sign the forms?"

"There aren't any forms, Mother. You know that. He's stalling until he reaches Richard or Maria, and when he does, he won't let Katie leave. Come on. Hurry up. I want to be out of here before Pomeranz tries to stop me."

"Darling, you're crazy! What will Richard say?"

Susan glanced at her briefly over her shoulder as she opened the front door. "He'll say just what you said: that I'm crazy. Only he'll mean it."

Chapter 14

IT HADN'T BEEN easy, but it hadn't been as drastic as Susan expected. Yet the blind determination that fortified her when she went to get her baby slowly weakened as she and her mother drove back to the apartment in uneasy silence. Silently she rehearsed what she'd say to Richard, tried to think how to defend herself against Maria's inevitable, angry participation. When she let herself in her door she felt terribly alone and frightened, and she hugged Katie tightly, as though "they" would drag the child out of her arms by force.

Bea had offered to come in with her, but Susan shook her head.

"Thanks, Mom, but I have to do this part alone. It's between Richard and me. I'm so grateful to you for going with me, but I have to face the rest of it by myself."

She'd stood for a moment, watching her mother walk slowly down Park Avenue toward her own car. At the corner Bea turned and looked back and then made a "thumbs up" gesture of encouragement. Susan nodded and managed to smile, thinking, God bless her. She does understand.

The apartment was very still as she walked in. Perhaps Richard isn't home, she thought hopefully. Perhaps Mr. Pomeranz couldn't reach him. She prayed for a little more time, dreading the moment she'd have to stand up to him, but as she went toward the nursery, Katie toddling beside her, he opened their bedroom door and stood silently looking at her.

"So you did it."

"Yes. I know you're angry, but I had to. Don't be too hard on Mr. Pomeranz, Richard. Please. He tried to keep me from taking her, I don't want him to suffer for this."

He exploded in a mirthless laugh. "Pomeranz! Who the hell cares about Pomeranz? Who's even thinking about that little nobody at a time like this? Susan, in God's name, what have you done? I thought you were just beginning to accept the inevitable and now you're starting all over again!"

"I could never accept it. At first it was almost bearable because it was unreal. I knew it and wouldn't believe it. But now I know I was right all along. Katie belongs with us. She's worth every bit of pain and sacrifice." She held the child by the hand. "Look at her, Richard. Look at your daughter. She's as much a part of you as your arms or legs. You can't amputate her from your life."

He stared down at the little face, saw the dark, curly hair, the big, trusting eyes, the features so like his own. "Oh, Christ," he said, almost like a prayer. "Susan, you know we can't. We can't handle this." But even as he protested, she heard his surrender.

"Yes we can, darling." Susan's voice was joyful. "I swear to you I'll make it right for all of us. We'll forget everything that's happened. Everything. It will be better than ever for us. I won't neglect you for the baby, I promise. There's room for both of you, enough love to go around." She pushed Katie gently into his arms. "Hold her, dearest. She needs her father as much as I do."

He took Katie reluctantly, remembering the delight he'd felt when she was born, recalling the first months before they knew. How changed he'd felt then! How much he'd wanted to be the father of this beautiful little girl, to be close to and proud of her. And now it couldn't happen. They'd never have the parent-child happiness he'd imagined. She'd never hear. Not his voice or his music. And if she spoke it would be gutturally, in nasal tones offensive to his ears. Involuntarily he shuddered, thinking ahead, hating himself for lacking the kind of blind faith Susan had, unable to believe, as she did, that this helpless little thing could be what her mother dreamed. He should insist, right now, that Katie go back. But he couldn't. The depth of love in Susan's eyes wouldn't let him.

She had to have her chance, even if it was only for a little while. Gently, he stroked his child's head.

"All right," Richard said sadly. "We'll try."

Susan, weeping with relief, put her arms around both of them. "Thank you, dearest. Thank you. You'll never regret it."

I wish I were sure of that, he thought as he kissed her. I wish I could believe that this demanding child will never come between us.

For almost a year, he nearly did believe it. Despite Maria's outrage, Gloria's scorn for his "weakness" and Sergio's older-brother advice based on the experience with his own Frances, Richard defended Susan's choice. He also found a new kind of peace in her return to "normalcy," her renewed sexual passion for him, and he was aware of the extra effort she made to ensure he was not disturbed by the mute presence of Katie. Strengthened by Paul's approval of his actions, fortified by Jacqueline's compliments and the Langdons' gratitude, he almost came to believe that the situation was manageable. Once again he returned to the voluntary faithfulness he'd chosen after Katie's birth. Even when, on rare occasions, he made a trip without Susan, he entered into no intimacy with other women. Gerry had departed even before Katie came home, given a handsome severance the very day after Susan had told him she knew about the resumption of the affair. He'd been so guilty then, so remorseful that he never wanted to see his publicity agent again. Susan had not commented on the dismissal. Gerry had understood.

"I knew it couldn't last," she said. "Susan was bound to find out, and you care about her too much to hurt her again." She couldn't resist a cyincal smile. "At least with me."

'With *anybody*,'' Richard had said firmly, and believed it. There was no lover like Susan when she was happy, no one who satisfied him so completely and who was so obviously satisfied in return. There were even long stretches when he nearly forgot about Katie s handicap. She was walking but had not yet reached the "talking stage" and to all outward appearances she was a contented, cheerful busy child, secure in the devotion of her mother and her nurse. He did not spend much time with her, so she was not a constant reminder of the imperfection he hated in all forms. For all that he saw of her, she might almost have becn away at the school. Unconsciously, he refused to think what would happen when she was fitted with hearing aids, when the speech therapy began, when she went "out into the world." For now life was good. He was playing better than ever, His ego gratified by public acclaim, his physical needs well taken care of by his wife, his position as "best in the family" confirmed by his growing reputation over Sergio and Walter. Even Maria was less sharply critical of his actions, though she reinforced her disapproval by barely speaking to Susan and never coming to see her granddaughter, The first summer after Katie's return, the Richard Antoninis took a house in Southampton. By tacit agreement, they knew they could not spend months in Pound Ridge with the child Maria refused to acknowledge. Instead, with little discussion, Richard went alone to his parents' house for occasional visits. He would simply say, "I think I'd better go to

Mother and Father next weekend.'' And Susan would nod, answering merely, ''We'll miss you, darling. Give everyone our love,''

In a sense, though she bitterly resented Maria's stubborn refusal to see Katie, it was almost a relief not to be in the midst of the supercharged Antoninis. Susan appeared, dutifully, at dinner in New York when they were invited to the town house or to Walter's and Jacqueline's, but those times were rare and she got through them without great distress, even though her mother-in-law's presence was like a cold wind that chilled her to the bone. Giovanni was always dear to her, asking after Katie, making it plain that he felt no ''stigma'' in having a grandchild unlike the others. Susan was grateful to him, as she was grateful to Jacqueline, for making her feel welcome. Sergio and Mary Lou, like Gloria, sided with Maria, They thought Susan a fool for insisting upon raising a ''deformed'' baby, and Richard an ass for allowing it. When the family was all together she was almost pointedly ignored. She no longer cared, and made less effort than ever to be part of the conversation. She'd come a long way from that first anxious weekend when she'd so desperately wanted to be accepted by Richard's famous family. She had her husband and child now. Her own home. The friendship of Jacqueline and Kate Fenton. And the unswerving support and devotion of Bea and Wil Langdon.

She'd given up writing the colunm which had been such a bone of contention. She told herself she didn't need that ''ego trip'' any more, and it was a small enough concession for Richard's reluctant compliance with her much more important wish. She said so to Kate one afternoon after an elegant lunch at Quo-Vadis. They strolled down Madison Avenue, looking in the window of boutique after boutique, pausing to inspect Jolie Gabor's spectacular jewelry shop, dropping into Boyd's, the only place in New York where one could get any kind of domestic or imported cosmetics, browsing through the little gift and card shop near Fifty-eighth Street, picking up always-needed birthday greetings and ''get well'' cards like two secretaries on their lunch hour.

''This is such mindless fun,'' Susan had said as they came out into the sunshine clutching their little paper parcels. ''I don't envy you, Kate dear, having to go back to the office and face deadlines.''

''Don't you? I thought you enjoyed doing that column.''

''I did. But Richard hated the idea. And he's been so patient about Katie, the least I can do is do something to please him. He was so relieved when I quit, and it doesn't matter that much to me. Not any more.''

''Not since you've decided to spend your whole life being slobberingly grateful to your husband for allowing you to keep your own child, and his?''

''Kate! That's cruel!''

''Sorry. But it's true, isn't it? You've really abdicated any identity of your own. Pity. Hate to see a good mind go to waste. No need for it. For God's sake, Susan, you don't have to repay Richard for something that's as much his doing as yours! You didn't create Katie singlehandedly and you shouldn't feel the sole responsibility for her! All this nonsense about 'pleasing Richard.' I never heard such rot! He should be down on his knees to you in gratitude for putting up with his family and his temperament and his infidelity.''

Susan stared at her, amazed.

"Oh hell, don't look so surprised. Everybody knew he was back with that trashy Girl Friday of his last year. At least he had the good taste to get rid of her professionally as well as personally."

Susan flushed. "He was going through a terrible time, Kate. You know that. You saw how I was."

"Bull. He was just plain horny and you know it. I don't say you shouldn't have forgiven him. Gad, if every wife divorced an unfaithful husband there wouldn't be a marriage left in America. I just say that all the 'bigness' hasn't been on Richard's side. Not by a damn sight. So if you really wanted to write that column, you shouldn't have stopped. In fact, I think it was a lousy idea to stop. You're living in too small a world now, Susie. Your whole life is Richard's comfort and Katie's future. That's not enough. Not for someone as vital and interested in things as you."

"I have my interests. You named them."

"Okay. I'll shut up."

"No. I'm glad you always speak your mind to me and I can speak mine to you. It's terribly important to have a woman to talk to. I know I can say anything to you. You and Jacqueline. She was the one who told me about Gerry. I've never even mentioned it to Mother." Susan paused. "I'm not kidding myself, Kate. I don't know what will happen now that Katie's intensive training has begun. Up to now she's been no problem to anyone. But from here on . . . I don't know. I've got to give myself to both of them. It's been easy enough for me to travel sometimes with Richard. The baby didn't even miss me when I was away. But now that the daily teaching has started how can I leave her? And if I'm not with Richard . . ."

Kate finished the sentence for her. "There may be another Gerry or a string of Gerries."

"Yes. But I have to take that chance."

"You still seeing Dr. Marcus?"

"No. He helped me a lot but I don't need him any more. He gave me strength and some understanding. I doubt I'd be sane today if it weren't for him, and for you who insisted I go see him." She looked pleadingly at Kate. "It's going to be all right, isn't it, Kate?"

"You want soothing lies?"

Susan shook her head.

"Then how can I tell you it's going to be all right? Nobody knows. The only thing I know is that you will do what your heart tells you. That's the way you are, Susie. Incredibly durable in some ways, pathetically hurtable in others. And incurably romantic in this calculating age. You'll blunder through, my girl, I have no doubt. But the path you've chosen, like our wonderful city streets, is not without it's neck-breaking potholes. Try not to fall into too deep a one."

That fall, the nightmare of turning Katie into a functioning person began. A woman weaker than Susan, one less fiercely determined, would have admitted defeat, but from somewhere Susan found a superhuman kind of strength created out of love for her child and, admittedly, a stubborn refusal to admit that nearly everyone thought she'd taken on an impossible task.

There were days, many of them, when Susan herself wearily thought it impossible. Katie had, for such a small child, a strong will of her own. At the doctor's advice, Susan had given her a doll fitted with two hearing aids like those she now wore. "It will help her communicate," he'd said. "Watch her try to talk to that doll. She'll identify with it." But sometimes she loved the doll, and other times she hated it, as though she instinctively knew that it, too, was "different." Contrarily, she seemed to sense that her own hearing aids were her link to the world. Every morning, Bridie reported, as soon as she awoke, Katie toddled to the bureau and pointed to the devices, which she wore uncomplainingly and without interruption until bedtime. Five mornings a week Susan took her to Edith Chambers, a speech therapist, a vivacious, enthusiastic young teacher. And in the afternoons, following instructions from the Tracy Clinic and others, Susan spent hours with the child. Crouching down to Katie's level, Susan repeated one word over and over, a hundred times, a thousand times, keeping her face in a strong light so Katie could see her mother's lips clearly and hopefully begin to imitate the words she saw forming there. When Susan tried, Bridie took over for hour after hour of this endless task, exhausting for "teacher" and "pupil," seemingly fruitless as Katie neared her third birthday.

Worse still, as Katie's need for Susan increased, Richard had begun slowly and not unexpectedly to withdraw. He took no part in the training. Not that Susan asked him to. She'd vowed, when he'd reluctantly acquiesced to Katie's return that she'd not ask of him something he'd be unwilling, probably unable, to do. Still she hoped he might want to participate, that his paternal love might be stronger than his inherent distaste for this slow, seemingly futile process. Once she coaxed him into the nursery to watch as she went through the patient repetition of one word. After fifteen minutes, he left.

"I'm sorry. I could never do that. I haven't the patience."

Forgetting the agreement she'd made with herself, Susan flared with anger. "Why not? You can do the same stupid scale a thousand times with pleasure. Isn't your daughter as important as your damned piano?"

"That's unworthy of you," he said.

"Unworthy! Richard, this is your child!"

"Yes, and you're my wife. I haven't forgotten either thing. Have you?"

She'd turned back to Katie, no longer angry but miserably unhappy. It was true. She hadn't shared her time and attention as she'd promised herself and him. She couldn't. Katie needed these hours of training now. She'd still need her mother for many years, no matter how well she progressed. Susan thought of the lecture she'd attended at the Parents Group of the New York League for the Hard of Hearing. She remembered the pathetic account of one mother who told how her twelve-year-old daughter had come home one day, thrown her hearing aid on the floor and screamed, "I don't want this! It's your fault! What are you going to do about it?" What would *she* do if, after all the effort and training Katie blamed her? I would't care, Susan told herself. If she could speak those words, I wouldn't care, as long as she was talking. But it frightened her, all of it. The present and the future. She felt trapped between husband and child. She loved them both and they loved her, possessively, jealously, demanding she make a choice. There could be only one choice, she realized sadly. She had to stay with the helpless one, the little one, even at the risk of losing the other.

Desperately, in the late hours of the night she tried to make up to Richard for her preoccupation with Katie the rest of the day. She made love to him as expertly and passionately as she knew how. There was a kind of wildness in her when they were together, as though she knew she had only one way to hold him, as though she had to make her body indispensable while her mind was elsewhere. It was tearing her apart and she thought of going back to Dr. Marcus for help. But there was no time. Just as there was no time to travel with her husband, or spend leisurely mornings in bed with him as she used to, or even to go to those hated weekends in Pound Ridge which meant so much to him. Not that she wanted to visit Maria, nor was she even welcome, except insofar as Richard's wife was dutifully welcome, but his parents and brothers and sister were important to him and she knew he resented Katie for interfering with the old order of things.

Sometimes she thought again of leaving him, of setting him free, and the irony of it was exquisite. She hadn't left him when he sent Katie away, nor when she'd discovered he'd been sleeping with Gerry. Now she was considering it in a spirit of kindness rather than revenge. But she didn't want to leave him. She prayed for some kind of miracle that would save her marriage. Perhaps when Katie began to talk, when she went to school, when her constant need for her mother's presence diminished, perhaps then things would be serene again and she'd lose this awful feeling of failing Richard.

And it was not all hopelessness. Edith Chambers was encouraging, full of accounts of successful "case histories," and Bridie was endlessly devoted and optimistic. Bea and Jacqueline spurred her on when her courage failed and even Kate Fenton, though she disapproved of Susan's limited horizons, was generous in her admiration for her young friend's tenacity. But the staunchest ally of all was Paul. Richard's manager dropped in almost every afternoon, sitting quietly in a corner of the nursery, watching as Susan went through the teaching routine, often with an inattentive, bored and restless child. Sometimes he even took over the job, scrunching his long, lanky frame down next to Katie, his gentle mouth saying, over and over, one simple word. Observing him, Susan sometimes wondered whether Katie thought this was her father. Certainly she saw more of him than she did of Richard. Susan was grateful to Paul, yet a little worried about her husband's reaction to this devotion which was not only for Katie. Paul said nothing to her that could be construed as a hint of love. Still, she knew he was in love with her. Sometimes she half-returned the feeling. He was so kind, so tender with the baby. I wish I'd met him first, Susan thought at difficult moments. Life would have been so much easier if I'd married him. But she knew this was only tired, discouraged thinking. She was in love with Richard. She loved Paul. It was quite different.

"You and Richard are off to Houston next week," she said one afternoon. "I'll miss you both."

He smiled. "Can't you come along, Susie? It's only for ten days. It would do you good, and Bridie can handle this little minx."

She shook her head regretfully. "I'd love to, but I can't. Next week is the big moment. Katie's starting nursery school."

Even he seemed suddenly uncertain. He frowned. "Are you sure that's the thing to do? I mean, can she manage with . . . with the others?"

"Edith thinks she can. So do I. It's only two days a week. I've talked with the teachers there. They say it will be good for her to be with other children." Susan smiled. "Kids don't need words to communicate. They have a language all their own. Besides, Paul, I think she's about ready to break through. I honestly do. She's beginning to imitate sounds. Of course, only Edith and I understand them, but it's a start. I'm so encouraged!"

She was breaking his heart with her bravery. Thank God she doesn't know why I really want her with us, Paul thought. Richard was back to his old ways again. There'd been that affair with the socialite in Philadelphia which had quickly ended when her husband found out. But the movie actress on the Coast was promising (threatening?) to meet Richard in Houston. It was insane. They were both too well known to carry off a clandestine affair. Somebody was bound to pick it up—a friend, or a gossip columnist. Susan doesn't need that again, Paul thought angrily. Goddamn Richard! Why does he have to salve his wounded ego with other women just because he can't have a hundred per cent of his wife?

"I'm sorry about the timing. For your sake, I mean."

She looked at him penetratingly. "Is there something special about this trip?"

"No. Of course not. I just thought you could use a change."

Susan smiled. "I could. You're right about that. But I wouldn't miss the sight of Katie in a real school. I've dreamed of this day, Paul." She paused. "I know what you're thinking. I should be with Richard more. I know it, all too well. Maybe I can be, soon. When Katie's mind is on finger-painting and block-building, and her new little friends. Then I'll be able to leave her. To set her free."

I'm using the same words I've thought about in relation to Richard, she realized. Setting *her* free! Setting *him* free. I'm such a hypocrite! I don't want either of them not to need me.

"You're the boss," Paul said.

The film star was sleeping quietly beside him at the Warwick Hotel in Houston when the phone rang in the middle of the night. For a moment Richard didn't know where he was. Then he remembered the evening. Glamorous Sylvia Sloan had flown in from Hollywood, her blond hair jammed under a disreputable-looking hat, her recognizable face half-obscured by oversized dark glasses. She'd registered as "Mrs. Charles Robinson" and taken a single room which she left immediately for the comfort of Richard's suite. They'd had dinner sent up, had drunk quantities of champagne and laughed over the art on the hotel walls, discovering it really was true that if you removed a painting it left a big space with letters that announced an expensive oil had been taken away. It was an ingenious way to protect good art in a world of light-fingered travelers, and they'd found it hilariously funny. Later there'd been some pretty wild sex and now Sylvia slept like dead while the phone rang on and on.

Richard switched on the bedside light and looked at his watch. Four A.M. Good God, who'd call at this unearthly hour? He lifted the receiver and said, fuzzily, "Yes?"

Sergio's words came through without preamble. "Richard? Cancel the concert and come home immediately. Mother's had a stroke. We think she's dying."

Chapter 15

NOBODY IN THE family believed it, but Maria Antonini had absolutely no intention of dying. She lay in New York Hospital, in a private room overlooking the East River, paralyzed on her left side unable to speak and furious about it. It was insupportable, this business of being unable to move or talk when your mind was so clear. Her bright little eyes glittered with anger as the doctors and nurses fussed over her and Giovanni and the children crept in reverentially, as though she were already dead. When Richard appeared, she was outraged. They'd called him back from Houston obviously made him cancel an important concert! And to make it worse, he'd shown up with Susan. Susan, who must take a fiendish delight in seeing her mother-in-law as mute as her child! Except that *I* can hear and I'll speak again, Maria thought. Katherine is a cripple, which I refuse to be. Her frustration was enormous. Why didn't they all stop hovering? Didn't they know her? Didn't they know she wasn't going to go until her children had reached the heights she planned for them? They're idiots, all of them, she fumed. Without me, they'd be nothing. That's why I have to get well.

"What are her chances, Doctor?" Giovanni had asked the specialist as they stood in the hospital corridor.

"To survive? Good. She's a strong woman, despite her age. For full recovery? I can't answer that, Mr. Antonini. The stroke was relatively mild, but recovery will depend on her determination as much as the therapy we'll begin as soon as she's able. The will to return to a normal life is as important as anything we in the medical profession can do."

Giovanni smiled. "In that case, my wife will fully recover. She has an indomitable spirit."

The doctor nodded, pleased. "Fine. Our job will be easier."

Returning to his wife's room, the maestro permitted himself a rare moment of introspection. Yes, Maria's will to survive was good. For *her*. Even for him, he supposed. He'd learned to depend completely on her in all things personal and professional. It used to irritate him in the early days, having her take over his life. But for many years, since he'd resigned himself to it, his wife's decisiveness and efficiency had made everything easier. In a way, it was pleasant to make no decisions, to be spared the annoyance of dealing with details, to have, face it, his life run for him. Even when he'd strayed, Maria had taken it in stride, waiting out his "romances," knowing he'd always come home.

But Giovanni wasn't certain that Maria was the best thing for their children. She'd turned Sergio into a ruthlessly ambitious egomaniac who cared nothing for his wife or children and who saw his brothers only as opponents to be bested. Walter had retreated into a nonperforming world, knowing he could not measure up to the flamboyant brothers on either side. Poor Walter. He'd never really wanted to be a composer. Everyone but Maria realized that. Yet he'd be a great one. Walter's and Jacqueline's "marriage of convenience" turned up in Giovanni's thoughts. His daughter-in-law was too strong for such a weak husband. For a long time they'd lived separate lives, but one day Jacqueline might leave him. And for all his pretended sophistication, Walter would come apart under that final admission of inadequacy.

As for Gloria, hers was the saddest example of Maria's obsession with achievement. In her mother's eyes, the girl had nothing. No talent, no looks, not even social graces, How she must loathe Maria! Giovanni thought. How she must have always longed for a mother like Susan's—adoring, uncritical, companionable. Gloria had made the best of it. Even marrying a man who couldn't possibly be in love with her, just to prove to Maria she could get a husband. But she was bitter as, underneath, the others also were bitter. Strange that Maria never recognized her daughter's anger. Or did she? If so, she'd not admit it.

Giovanni's eyes went to Richard and Susan standing quietly at Maria's bedside. Maria was right to put her faith in her youngest as her hope for immortality. He was the most gifted of them all. But she'd made him self-centered and narcissistic. She'd schooled out of him the ability to give of himself in any deep and lasting way. He could only use people. He couldn't return the healthy love of that nice girl he'd married. Perhaps, in fairness, he wanted to. There'd been fleeting signs of it. But as long as Maria lived, her influence would keep Richard from loving. And from facing his own flaws. She'd taught him to look into an altered mirror and see nothing but a perfect, irreproachable image.

Giovanni stared at the motionless figure of his wife and sighed deeply. He wanted her to live. He, alone, was most confident she would. And yet, God forgive his terrible thought, most of her family would be better off if she left them alone at last.

Hearing his sigh, Susan left her husband and came to his side.

"Are you all right, Papa-Joe? Can I do anything for you?"

He smiled gratefully. Susan was the only one who'd shown any concern for him. "No, my dear. Thank you. I'm all right."

"Why don't you come home with Richard and me? You don't want to be alone in that big house. We have plenty of room."

He shook his head. "That's kind of you, Susan, but I'm better off in my own bed. The servants are there. I'll manage." He looked at her affectionately. "How are you? I haven't seen you in a long while. How's my little Katie?"

"She's doing so well! She started nursery school this week."

"And?"

"So far, so good. The other children have accepted her beautifully. They're very kind to her, as though they know, young as they are, that she needs special protection. I'll never again believe that children are basically cruel to each other, the way I've always heard. It just isn't true."

"I'm happy for her. And for you. I know it hasn't been easy, Susan. You've done a wonderful job."

She actually blushed. "Thousands of other mothers have done the same and more. And most of them don't have the financial advantages I have. It must be terrible to have an afflicted child and no money for the best doctors and therapists and private nursing schools, and no one like Bridie to help."

But they have husbands to help in an even more important way, Giovanni wanted to say. They get the kind of moral support and physical assistance Richard is unable to give you.

"If you need anything, Susan . . . anything at all." Giovanni seemed suddenly embarrassed. "I'm afraid the family hasn't been very attentive." His voice trailed off and involuntarily he looked over at Maria. Thank God she couldn't hear this conversation spoken in whispers.

Susan followed his eyes. "It's all right," she said. "It's understandable. I'm sorry about Mrs. Antonini. She's the last person in the world I'd have imagined this happening to. How she must hate being helpless! But she'll be all right, won't she?"

"I think so." What an extraordinary young woman you are, Giovanni thought. You really are sorry, after all she's done to you. Most people would see it as retribution, God's punishment for Maria's arrogant impersonation of Him. Funny. He'd never thought of it quite that way before, but Maria had always acted as though she were the Almighty, directing people's lives, ordaining their futures, almost presuming the power of life or death over them. Her frequent anger was like a thunderbolt from heaven, her rare approval like the warmth of a June day. God must hate that. He made us in His own image, but He didn't intend us to usurp His infinite wisdom. Giovanni was surprised by his musings about God. He'd never been a formally religious man. He left the churchgoing to Maria, but he wondered whether the Lord was so irritated by Maria's righteousness that He'd struck out at this cheeky daughter of His, "smote her with His wrath," as they said in the Bible. The idea was so ridiculous he laughed aloud. Richard looked over at him.

"Father? What is it?"

"Nothing," Giovanni lied, knowing Maria could hear him. "I was just thinking what hell your mother will give us when she gets around to it. We're behaving as though this is more than what she'd call 'a temporary inconvenience.' She'd want you to fly back to Houston today, Richard. She's probably furious that you came at all. I'm sure you can still keep the concert date. They probably haven't even had time to announce the cancellation."

They looked at Maria, who was trying to tell them that for once in his life her husband was absolutely right.

"I agree with your father," Susan said. "That's what your mother would want most. We'll all be here with her every minute, Richard. You should go back for the concert."

He hesitated. Sylvia would have returned to Hollywood, and just as well. When she'd suggested joining him, he'd known it was a mistake. A one-night stand was one thing, but having a nymphomaniac around for days before he performed was too distracting. He wouldn't make that mistake again. He wondered what drove him to these women he really didn't give a damn about. The urge for variety? Monogamy was not man's natural state, after all. Or was it pure pique because Susan chose to stay with the child rather than be with him? He was jealous. He admitted it. He almost hated her for all her bloody, uncomplaining self-sacrifice. Like now. Self-sacrifice, hell! She probably would be relieved if he'd go away again so she could devote herself to Katie.

"All right," he said finally. "If you think that's what Mother would like." He stroked Maria's cheek tenderly. Did he imagine a look of satisfaction in those amazingly alert eyes?

When word of Maria Antonini's illness got out, the press had a field day. For forty-eight hours after the first story, the family could hardly get in and out of the hospital for the crowd of reporters camped at the entrance. It was not so much the matriarch's condition that interested them as it was the chance to report on the suffering of the lofty Antoninis, to put the agony of the famous under a microscope for the "little people" to examine and enjoy for the price of a newspaper or the flick of a television dial.

In the beginning, the stories were more or less routine coverage: photos of a gray-faced Giovanni entering his limousine without comment; quotes from a willing-to-talk Sergio, saying their faith was sustaining them and asking for the public's prayers; daily bulletins from the hospital and live TV interviews with the big-name specialists who'd been called in for special consultation. Though they were not allowed into the hospital the reporters pestered nurses and orderlies for details of Mrs. Antonini's daily routine. Had she spoken or moved? Was it true she'd had her own furniture moved in? Who was allowed to visit? What famous names had sent flowers? The President and the First Lady? Mr. and Mrs. Vladimir Horowitz? Beverly Sills? Terrific!

But in a couple of days, interest in the subject waned and the Antoninis would have been left in relative peace except for the doggedness of one woman reporter who worked for a weekly "scandal sheet." Her name was Carlyn MacKenzie, and her nationally distributed paper, which outsold *Time* and *Newsweek* combined, was a gossipy sheet called *Open Secrets*, specializing in rumors, speculation and sometimes outright misrepresentation of the private lives of well-known personalities.

Carlyn was a tough reporter who could "smell a scandal a mile away." She knew the Antoninis' closets rattled with skeletons. She'd been doing a lot of quiet digging and her sources were numerous and reliable.

"I'd like your okay to do a series on America's number-one musical family," she told her city editor. "There's a lot of juicy stuff the Antoninis have managed to hush up."

"Such as?"

"Such as the fact that big brother Sergio has a fifteen-year-old retarded daughter hidden in a mental home. And young Richard and his wife tucked away a deaf-mute kid in a ritzy school upstate. And get this. Susan Antonini had a nervous breakdown when Richard put the child there. She went to a psychiatrist. And she also went up and took the baby out of the school without her husband's permission. I have a contact who works in the place. She says there was hell to pay when Pomeranz, the owner, had to explain to Richard and his mama how that happened."

The editor was getting interested. "Keep going, MacKenzie. Anything else?"

"Plenty. That caper damned near broke up the marriage. They've stayed together, but Richard's been consoling himself elsewhere ever since." She paused dramatically. "Sylvia Sloan was with him in Houston when Maria Antonini had her stroke. He left her in the bed while he flew home to mother."

"Sylvia Sloan the movie actress?"

"None other. And there's more. I can't prove it yet, but I hear the other brother, Walter, is AC-DC. How about that? Him and his supposedly sexy jet-set wife!"

"I'm sold. Go to it. Just try to avoid libel suits."

"No problem. The facts are there. Some of them have even been hinted at, but nobody's done the full exposé."

Three days later the series began. The first article was headlined "Antonini's Baby Will Never Hear Father Play." Carlyn wrote luridly of Katie's affliction and the repercussions, including a mawkish account of the day Richard and Bridie brought the infant to the school.

"The young pianist's handsome face was ravaged with grief as he carried his deaf-mute baby into the silent, secret world to which he'd doomed her. For a moment he seemed to hesitate, as though he couldn't do it. He held little Katherine tightly while Bridie Grey, the baby's nurse, looked pleadingly at him, her eyes begging him not to give her tiny charge to these strangers. But he did not relent, even though those nearby saw tears in his eyes when he handed his daughter to a waiting attendant. 'Goodbye, Katie,' he said. 'We love you,' and then he walked away, not looking back."

It went on to describe Susan's breakdown and therapy and her eventual headstrong decision to retrieve her child. "What the future holds for the Richard Antoninis, for their marriage and their handicapped child, acquaintances refuse to speculate. Those close to them believe, however, that the clash of wills between the glamorous couple has done irreparable harm to the storybook union of the charming prince of the concert hall and his Cinderella bride."

At the end of the story there was a "teaser" for the next one. "How is Richard consoling himself? And with whom? Next week: The continuing tragedy of the Antonini family."

"Good piece, MacKenzie," the editor said.

"Thanks. Wait till you see the follow-ups."

Kate Fenton rang up Susan. "You see this week's *Open Secrets?*"

"You know I never read that rag! It was bad enough when I had to, in case there was something *Vogue* should know. Now that I'm a free woman I don't waste time on that drivel."

"You'd better read this issue, Susan. You and Richard and Katie are the first of a continuing series on the Antoninis." Kate's voice trembled with rage. "Those bastards! They're a disgrace to journalism. Not that you could call this journalism. More like writing on the walls of a public toilet."

Susan tried to stay calm. "What did they say?"

"Everything. The commitment, the 'kidnaping,' your psychiatric care, difficulties between you and Richard. The works. And frankly, even *that* isn't as gruesome as what I suspect is going to follow." She read the "sign off" paragraph. "Sounds like they've got plenty on Richard. I hope there isn't too much, for his sake and yours." Kate probed gently. "Is he still acting up, Susie?"

Her friend's long silence was confirmation. "You know there've been things. You remember about Gerry. But that's over. It happened when I was so depressed and unresponsive. In a way, I couldn't blame Richard. There was nothing for him at home. But things are fine now. They really are."

Kate knew better. She, too, had her sources. There was no point in worrying Susan with the things she'd heard. Kate only hoped that terrible bitch who was writing the series didn't know about all the others, including Sylvia Sloan.

"They've probably shot their bolt," Kate lied. "You know how these sensation-seekers operate. Lots of snide suggestions but no substance. I just thought you ought to know before your phone starts ringing. By the way, how's Maria?''

Susan guessed how Kate's mind was working. ''She's making great progress. Improved a thousand per cent in the past few weeks. Now that Richard's home he sees her every day, but she's still not allowed many visitors. And of course no newspapers.''

''Good. Keep it that way.''

They'd barely hung up when Jacqueline called to discuss the same subject.

''Nasty stuff,'' Jacqueline said. ''You'd think they could find something better to write about than our family secrets! Don't let it get to you Susan. It's ugly but it's no disgrace.''

''Kate's worried about what's to come. She read me the announcement of the next article.''

''Yes,'' Jacqueline said slowly. ''The series could be sticky for all of us. I wonder how much they know about things we'd rather not air. I don't give a damn myself, but I'd hate to have my boys disillusioned about their father.''

It was Susan's turn to comfort. ''It may just die down after they get through speculating about Richard and Katie and me.''

''I hope so, but I'll admit I'm worried. Once those bloodhounds pick up the scent, there's no stopping them until they've advertised every stupid mistake any of us has ever made. Maria won't know. But I feel sorry for Joe.'' I feel even sorrier for you, she added silently. God knows what will happen when you read this lurid, lipsmacking account of yourself and your husband and child. And if they really start detailing Richard's sexual exploits it'll be devastating. Who knows what they've got on *all* of us? Probably plenty. She tried to sound unconcerned once again. ''Oh hell, we're probably getting wrought up over nothing! Let's be nonchalant when our 'dear friends' call. Don't react to this garbage, Susan. That's the wrong thing to do.''

''All right.''

''Maybe it won't be too bad,'' Jacqueline added feebly.

''I hope it won't. I'm going to run over to Lexington Avenue now and pick up the paper.'' She gave a troubled sigh. ''I can guess what it says. I've read enough of their stuff to know how piously vicious they can be.''

Chapter 16

''I THINK WE'D better have a family conference, Richard.'' Gloria's voice was business-like. This was her third call. She'd already reached Sergio and Walter and made arrangements for all of them to meet at their parents' house that afternoon.

''What for? Mother isn't worse, is she?''

''It isn't about Mother. That is, not directly. I take it you haven't read the story in this week's *Open Secrets.*''

''Story? What story?'' Richard was getting impatient. ''Get to the point, Gloria? What's in that yellow sheet that necessitates a summit meeting?''

She told him. ''Serge and Walter agree with me that we have to plan a strategy.

God knows what those people are going to come up with about any of us! This Katie thing is only the beginning. They've already promised to discuss your extracurricular romantic activities next week.'' Gloria's voice was sarcastic. *''That* should endear you to all those proper Bible Belt dowagers who think you're Little Lord Fauntleroy. And you can bet you're only the *first* target. Wait till they take off on Sergio's life and his idiot child, and Walter and Jacqueline's peculiar marital arrangements! My God, do you think they'll dare say he's gay? We'd better damned well get some good counterpublicity in the works before the Antoninis sound like a family of degenerates! They'll probably drag out those hundred-year-old stories about Father and his 'conquests.' I doubt that even I'll be spared, though they can't compare my life with any of yours.''

Several thoughts crashed headlong into each other in Richard's mind as he listened to his sister. The first almost irrelevantly, was how much she sounded at this moment like Maria. No doubt she saw herself in the role of ''family commander'' now that the real one was wordless and immobile. In spite of his distress, he felt a grudging admiration for Gloria. She might hate Maria but she also envied her. She really wants to be like her, Richard thought. And she foolishly thinks this is her chance.

The idea of a story about his child angered and upset him. He tried to love her, but he couldn't get over the feeling that Katie's handicap was somehow a ''disgrace,'' a reflection on him, and he'd hoped that it would go forever unnoticed by the world. It would have, damn it, if Susan had left well enough alone. If she hadn't sneaked up there and taken the child out of school, nobody would ever have known he had a daughter who wasn't like other children.

Susan. He still loved her, but she was so little his these days. Everything had changed. They barely communicated, each feeling wronged by the other. How much did *Open Secrets* really know about what he did when he was away? He dreaded next week's revelations. Dreaded them for what they'd do to his image as well as his marriage. Sergio and Walter must be just as nervous, Richard thought. Gloria was right. ''Idols'' as they were, the public would accept only so much before, feeling ill-used, they turned the wrath of their moral indignation on the Antoninis. He wondered what plans his sister had. If only Maria were functioning!

''All right,'' he said finally, ''I suppose we should put our heads together. This afternoon? At the family's? Okay. Shall I bring Susan?''

''God, no! None of the wives is coming. Just the four of us, Richard. Father will be at the hospital. I haven't told him a word of this. Not even about the newspaper article. Oh, I did think I'd ask Paul Carmichael to be here. He's like one of the family and he has good ideas. Lord knows we can use some!''

Richard hung up and wandered disconsolately through the apartment. It was Saturday and Susan had left an hour before to take Katie to the Children's Zoo in Central Park. She'd poked her head into the library to say they were leaving. Not even a question as to whether he'd like to join them. She knew better.

''We'll be back by lunchtime,'' she'd said, ''but if you get hungry Lily can fix you something.''

He'd nodded and smiled at Katie, who smiled and waved back automatically. He couldn't reach her as Susan could. Mother and daughter seemed to have an understanding that did not involve words or gestures, but he was an outsider, a strange man whom he supposed Katie thought of as an occasional visitor. Or did four-year-old Katie think at all? How could one think or dream without sounds to relate to? Today the world knew all about his lost child and he felt ashamed. He wondered, suddenly, whether Susan had heard about the article. She hadn't mentioned it. He hadn't told her of Gloria's call or of the afternoon meeting. Perhaps she didn't even know the secret was out. No, she couldn't. She'd have said something.

But when his aimless roaming took him into the library he saw that Susan did know. A copy of *Open Secrets* lay on a table. He picked it up and read the purple prose. God, it was even more disgusting than he'd imagined! He sounded like a monster and Susan sounded crazy. And those last couple of lines. Jesus! He'd like to get his hands on that MacKenzie bitch and on whoever had given her that inside information! Who could it be? Who knew that much about all of them? It was no one in his family, that was for sure. Susan's parents wouldn't have discussed any part of this. Besides, they didn't know about his "consolations." Paul knew everything, but Paul wouldn't talk. It must have been Gerry. Yes, it had to have been Gerry. Hell hath no fury . . .

Angrily he tossed the paper aside and went to dress for "the meeting."

Like Richard, Sergio did not discuss the planned conference with Mary Lou. Whatever his wife's part in Gloria's "counterplot," Mary Lou would go along as long as he made it worth her while. He supposed they'd get around to Frances, those devils at the paper, damn their souls, and probably find out about some of his women, too. Well, what the hell. They couldn't destroy the Antoninis. They were artists and every artist since the beginning of time had been offbeat, even scandalous. The public would soon forget. He didn't worry about these things the way his mother and Gloria did.

Jacqueline answered the phone when Gloria called to ask for Walter. She knew instantly what was on her sister-in-law's mind, and she couldn't resist baiting her.

"Looks like we're all going to get quite a going-over in the press, doesn't it, Gloria? I assume you've seen *Open Secrets.*"

"Yes. It's disgusting."

"Poor Susan. She doesn't need this."

"Poor *Susan!*" Gloria's tone was shrill. "What about the rest of us? Do you imagine for one moment your husband's peculiar life-style won't be subject to the same ugly scrutiny? Or Sergio's? Or Father's? They have something to lose by bad publicity. What does Susan have to lose? Thank God Mother doesn't know about this! After all she's done to build the Antonini name!"

"Your concern for your mother is touching," Jacqueline said acidly. "Still, you must be relieved that *your* name is Taffin. They may overlook you and Raoul when the rest of us are rolling around in the mud."

Gloria was almost speechless. She loathed this cool, superior wife of Walter's. With effort she restrained herself from taking the bait. Jacqueline always knew how to get at her: by reminding her subtly that she was the "unknown Antonini."

"May I speak with Walter, please?"

"Of course. I'm sure he's around somewhere."

When Walter came back from the phone, Jacqueline looked at him with amusement. "Gloria must be in seventh heaven taking Maria's place during this family crisis. Does she have a master plan? Or should I say a master *key* to keep Pandora's box securely locked?"

Walter couldn't help smiling. Though they had nothing together any more, he liked and admired Jacqueline more now than he had in the days he'd made himself believe he could love her or any woman. They were really friends. She was worldly and sensible and he could always talk to her, knowing she liked him, too, in spite of his late-blooming homosexuality.

"My dear sister has called a conference," he said, "to decide how we should combat this bad publicity and worse that's bound to follow."

"It figures. That's what Maria would have done. Except Maria would already have the answers, and I doubt Gloria has. Who's sitting in?"

"Serge and Richard and I, And Paul Carmichael."

Jacqueline nodded. "No Giovanni. And no wives."

"Correct."

"And typical. Maria would have done it the same way." Jacqueline laughed. "Isn't it incredible? Gloria detests her mother, but she's even more jealous of her. She's going to prove she's as smart and strong as the old lady, and that none of you really needs Maria as long as her daughter is around. Gloria's finally gotten her chance to shine. Well, God bless! But wouldn't the Signora be in a rage if she knew her bumbling daughter was making a power play while Maria is flat on her back?"

Walter frowned. "I don't think it's quite like that, Jacqueline. Not a power play, I mean. Gloria's really worried. And she's right. Stories like this can do terrible harm. Somebody has to organize a defense."

His wife shook her head. "You're all such a bunch of babes in the woods, poor darlings. What defense, for God's sake? So far they haven't printed anything they'd have to retract and I'll bet they won't, no matter how far they go. The only thing that surprises me is that we've all escaped as long as we have. Well, have fun at your meeting, old boy. Put your little heads together. Me, I'm going to hand mine over for a restyling at Mr. Kenneth's, which I daresay will be infinitely more productive."

The family gathering, as might have been expected, developed into a shouting match, with brother accusing brother of "crimes" more heinous than his own. It was all going nowhere until Paul, who'd been sitting quietly by, cleared his throat and said, "As an outsider, may I make a couple of suggestions?"

"Please do," Gloria said with undisguised relief. This meeting, which she'd imagined would be as calm and orderly as one Maria might have called, had disintegrated into a series of personal defenses and unproductive outbursts of anger. "Shut up, everybody, and let's hear what Paul has to say."

He'd smiled at her easily from the big chair, his feet propped on an ottoman, his glasses pushed up onto his forehead. "Let's review where we are. First, *Open Secrets* has printed a very unpleasant but true story about Richard and Susan and Katie. Unfortunate, but it had to come out sooner or later, and it's no crime to have a deaf-mute child no matter how embarrassing some of you may find it.''

Richard interrupted. ''I suppose you wouldn't be embarrassed to be pictured as a man who cried over a baby, nor one whose wife had to go to a psychiatrist?''

''No, frankly, I wouldn't. And I don't think people are going to feel anything but sympathy for you and Susan and your child. It's sad and human. And thousands, maybe million of people who could never identify with the untouchable genius at the keyboard will now feel a kinship with the man who's been struck by such an understandable tragedy.''

There was silence as they tried to absorb this new way of looking at the problem. Paul went on.

''We don't know what they're going to say next. About Richard's 'amourous adventures.' Or any of the rest of you. Let's don't kid ourselves, there's plenty to say, but we don't know how much they have or what they can prove. Seems to me, the biggest problem will not be with Richard's public, but with his wife. If a lot of things Susan isn't aware of suddenly come to light we can't predict how she'll react. We can only hope she'll stand by and give a lie to the rumors by her presence and her seemingly unbelievIng response to 'a pack of vicious lies.' ''

Paul sounded calm, but he hated himself for suggesting that Susan play the role of loyal, loving wife. He wasn't sure she would. In his heart, he felt she shouldn't. Or was that part of the old wishful thinking? In any case, it would be the only way to take some of the curse off Richard's philandering.

''You'll have to make a clean breast of things with Susan,'' he said, ''before she reads about it. And then, friend, you'll have to shape up. No more fooling around. You'll have to be living proof of that nice lady's faith in you.''

Gloria snorted. Paul ignored her.

''I imagine they'll go after you next, Serge. Same thing applies in both cases, really. Properly handled, your retarded child will create sympathy. And Mary Lou will come on strong as the devoted wife and mother. Maybe both you fellows will have to buy the silence of a few ladies with whom you've been indiscreet. Let's hope that can be done in secrecy.'' Paul took a deep breath. ''Strangely enough, you're in the best spot, Walter, if there is one. You're not literally ''onstage,'' but even more importantly, you and Jacqueline are already known as a couple of the 'beautiful people' and your freewheeling life-style is pretty well accepted for the unconventional thing it is. Still, it won't hurt for you to cool it with your 'friends.' Be seen more with your wife and children. Create a 'chic family' impression. Make it all look modern but 'normal.' ''

They were subdued now, impressed by Paul's clinical analysis.

''What about Father?'' Gloria sounded almost meek. ''Will they drag him in?''

''Maybe, but not likely. He's The Maestro and he's untouchable. A living legend with a gravely ill wife. Nobody will have the bad taste to drag up his indiscretions.'' Paul smiled. ''Past or, for all we know, present.''

He felt the tension in the room easing. Goddamn these egomaniacs! Show them how they can save their skins and they suddenly get happy and secure again. What do they care how their wives and children will suffer, as long as they come out with their adulation intact and their bloody careers undamaged.

"You're terrific," Richard said, "My God, Paul, you're the best friend anybody ever had! You've solved it all, just like that! Why couldn't we see it ourselves? Hell, we've been in an uproar over nothing! Talk about making lemonade out of lemons! This damned ugly series may end up making us all look better than ever—humble and human. It's genius!"

"Hold it," Paul said. "It's not that easy. Your wives will have to go along with all this, and they're not without pride themselves. Do you think Susan is going to easily forgive you when she knows the facts, Richard? Will she submit to interviews about her 'happy married life?' Will she let Katie be photographed and seen for the happy child she is? Those things will be necessary. And what about Mary Lou? Will she start doing active work for retarded children? That should be part of it, too. Part," he said bitterly, "of this sympathy-creating act the Antoninis will have to work like hell at."

"She'll do it," Sergio said. "For a new sable coat Mary Lou will do anything."

Richard was quiet. "I think Susan will go along," he said finally. "She cares about my career."

"Mother will be wild," Gloria said. "She's always been vehement about not publicizing Frances and Katherine."

"I'm afraid Mrs. Antonini doesn't have a choice," Paul said politely. "Unfortunately, even if she has a better solution she's in no position to give it to us."

As they left the house, Richard put his arms around his manager's shoulders. "Thanks again, Paul. In a pinch this family behaves like a bunch of Italian tenors. You really saved the day."

"That remains to be seen. All I did was make some cheap, self-serving suggestions. Whether they work, or what *Open Secrets* has up its sleeve, none of us knows."

Richard was full of confidence. "If we all follow your advice, things will turn out fine."

Will they? Paul wondered as they parted. How could Richard be so blithe about confessing his sins to Susan? Would she consent to this dishonest game-playing which involved not only herself but the exploitation of her child? Was Richard's career worth that? Paul shook his head. I've never been as disgusted with anybody in my life as I am with myself right this minute, he thought. But I had to try to help them. It's part of my job. What a lousy job! I should chuck *it* and *them* and this whole degrading mess. I would if I had a shred of self-respect. No. I would if I weren't so hopelessly in love with Richard Antonini's wife.

As he walked down Park Avenue, Richard's momentary vision of an easy salvation began to fade. Paul was right. Nobody knew what *Open Secrets* actually was going to print. Just as no one could predict Susan's response when he told her some ugly truths and asked her to stand by him. Maybe, he thought for a moment, I shouldn't jump the gun. All the paper may know about is the thing with Gerry, and Susan already knows about that. It would be ironic if he ran through a list of his misdoings only to find out later that they need never have been exposed to her at all! Still, he couldn't take a chance. Paul was right. He'd have to tell Susan everything so there'd be no surprises for her in next week's paper. He'd have to throw himself on her mercy and if necessary beg for her support. Beg, hell! He was entitled to that! Even the wives of common criminals were always shown at their accused husbands' sides, vowing belief in their men's innocence. Susan can do no less for me, Richard told himself virtuously. I've done plenty for her.

But he felt less confident when he let himself into the apartment that late afternoon. Susan was reading in the library and she looked up from her book, smiling quizzically when he came into the room.

"You're so late, Richard! I was beginning to worry about you. You haven't even touched the piano today! Where were you, dear? Visiting your mother?"

He shook his head. "I was at the house with Serge and Walter and Gloria and Paul. We thought we should discuss that article in *Open Secrets*. I know you saw it. Where is it now?"

"In the trash where it belongs." Susan's voice was bitter. "I didn't want to discuss it. How dare they, Richard? How dare they say those things about us?"

"You can't keep the press from printing the truth, Susan. You should know that." He hesitated. "And as you read, there's more to come. I think we should talk about that before it appears in the paper. That's what we were meeting about today. We all have to level with each other now and stand together. We're a family, Susie. Families have to protect themselves and make sacrifices so the world will continue to admire them."

She saw what he was getting at: a united defense against next week's promised disclosures about his extramarital sex life. She didn't really delude herself about what had been going on in recent months. She didn't honestly believe, no matter what she said to Jacqueline, that Gerry had been Richard's only mistress since their marriage. She simply preferred not to think about his lack of control. Or she made excuses for it when she did. It was a kind of desperate self-protection. Her concern for Katie was so intense that she couldn't handle another area of distress. She'd avoided speculating about Richard's behavior, hoping, foolishly, that that problem would go away by itself. It hadn't, of course. And now it was all going to come out. Richard had some kind of plan, worked out with his family, in which she undoubtedly was expected to participate. She waited, quietly, for him to explain all this talk about "families standing together." What "sacrifices" was she to be asked to make?

Gently, remorsefully, he told her what he presumed *Open Secrets* knew. The affair with the Philadelphia socialite. The liaison with the film star. "I didn't want you to know, ever," Richard said. "They've all been meaningless, impulsive physical acts that have nothing to do with our marriage or my love for you. But I couldn't let you be shocked by finding out about them in that filthy paper."

"I see," Susan said. She was surprised by how unmoved she was. "So now I know. What am I supposed to do? Forgive you? Pat you on the head and say, 'There, there, little boy. Don't be upset. You couldn't help it?'" Awareness suddenly dawned. "Oh, no. I see what's wanted. You and the family want me to stand by, bravely refusing, in public, to believe a word of this. You need me to be the loving, trusting wife. To help squash scandal by my unswerving faith in you. That's it, isn't it? You probably want me to give interviews denying you are anything but the perfect husband. We'll be seen together more in public, right? I'll suddenly emerge as the only woman you adore. That's the name of the game, isn't it? I suppose Mary Lou will do the same for Sergio when *his* time comes, And Jacqueline will make an extra effort to be portrayed as the blissful wife. It's all you can do, isn't it? All any of you Antonini men can do now is depend on the women you married. If it wasn't so dreadful, it would be funny!"

He didn't answer right away. Then he said, "There's more, Susie. Even more I need of you."

"What more? Shall I get pregnant again to prove how devoted we are?"

"No. But I hope you'll let the other papers and magazines take pictures and do stories about Katie. Maybe you could take part in some fund-raising endeavor for deaf-mute children. In any case, please speak out as often as possible about the love and devotion we've given this child."

She stared at him, momentarily speechless. "Have you gone mad or have I?" she finally asked. "*You*, who always wanted to hide Katie as though she were some terrible disgrace, now want to push her into the foreground? You want me to talk about her disability and the love and devotion 'we' have given her?" Again she saw the answer. "Of course. It's out in the open now. So we might as well capitalize on it. Let's use our daughter's handicap to create sympathy for her father, to make the world judge him less harshly. My God, Richard, is there no end to your selfishness?"

He didn't fight back. It would have been easier if he had. "I can't argue with anything you say, Susan. I only ask you to help. I don't think you really want to see this filthy gossip sheet destroy everything my brothers and I have worked for. I've been wrong about a lot of things. I'm not as strong as you. Not as honest. I don't blame you for being disgusted, but I've never known you to lack compassion for the weak."

The surprising humility disarmed her, but she was not yet ready to agree. "Whose expedient little plan is this?" she asked. "It sounds like something Maria would have thought of. It can't be your father's idea. He has too much self-respect. And your brothers and sister wouldn't have reasoned this through so systematically. None of you has been allowed an original thought since the day you were born!"

He took her scorn without flinching. "It was Paul. Gloria realized we needed counterpublicity, but it was Paul who outlined how to proceed. He's also advised Sergio to have Mary Lou become active in some kind of work for the retarded, talking about Frances the way I hope you will about Katie."

Susan gasped. "Paul! I don't believe it! It's monstrous! Paul wouldn't use people this way! You're lying, Richard!"

"Ask him yourself. Susan, try to understand. As a family, we haven't been a very admirable lot. We thought we could get away with anything. Hiding our affairs and our imperfect children. We believed we were beyond reproach. Above the power of the press. All our lives it's been drilled into our heads that we're special, privileged. That anything we did was okay because we are Antoninis. We never dreamed that one spiteful, ambitious reporter could bring our world down around us. Paul understands that. Still, rotten as we may be, we have something precious to give the world: our music. If we lose the respect and affection of the public, we lose the right to share our talent with them. And in the long run their loss might be greater than ours.''

Susan was suddenly deflated. She didn't believe what Richard was saying, but she believed in Paul Carmichael. If he felt these lies and pretenses were worthwhile, then they must not be as shameful as they seemed to her. Paul had integrity. He would abandon it only in a good cause. But this! To ask her to counteract the sordid stories by putting herself and her child on display as proof of Richard's goodness! No, she couldn't. Not to save her husband's career or the Antonini name. Not even if it took Richard years to live down his offensive behavior, his unfeeling attitude toward his child and his unfaithfulness toward his wife. Besides, she doubted the articles would do that much harm. People were used to ''celebrity sex scandals.'' They did not affect the guilty one's career as they might have even twenty years before. Richard would survive. They all would. In a few months the series would be forgotten but the damage she could do to Katie would be irreparable. Even if Paul thought it was the thing to do, she'd have no part of it.

''I'm sorry, Richard. I can't go along with any of this.'' Her voice was quiet. ''I care about your career. Strangely enough, I even still care about you. But I won't have Katie's life turned into a circus to divert attention from your mistakes.''

He tried once more. ''Will you talk to Paul? He can explain the reasoning better than I.''

''No. I won't talk to Paul. I'll go on as we are for now, if you like. Living in the same house, I mean. But that's all. No interviews, no pictures, no speeches or joining causes. Let Mary Lou do that if she can stomach it. I can't.''

Abruptly he was enraged. ''It must be wonderful to be so pure, so holier-than-thou! I've made concessions for you, Susan. One of them is right there in that nursery instead of in an institution where she belongs. If it hadn't been for your damned willful act of getting her out, none of this probably would have been stirred up! All right. Take your goddamn principle and your righteous indignation and get the hell out of my life! I don't want you here, accusing me with every look! You won't help? Okay. Then move out. Add a little more fuel to the fire. Prove everything they say is true by leaving me. Who cares? I'm a lousy father and a lecher and a fool. That's what you believe. Why not let the world believe it too?''

He stormed out of the apartment and Susan suddenly knew, helplessly, that she couldn't leave him. He was her husband and she loved him. For all the agony he'd brought her, she was still his wife and he needed her. I must talk to someone, Susan thought. Someone who knows Richard as well as I do. Paul? No. She was hurt and disillusioned by his uncharacteristic expedience. Her mother? Bea would be too emotional. And Kate would be too cynical and Jacqueline too involved. Whom can I turn to who has gentleness and wisdom and knowledge? There was only one. Slowly she dialed a number.

''Papa-Joe, it's Susan. Are you alone? May I come and talk with you?''

Chapter 17

HE DIDN'T FEEL like talking to anyone. Not even to Susan, whom he infinitely preferred over his other daughters-in-law and certainly over his own daughter. Gloria, in fact, was the most tiresome of all. She'd just left, after reporting, in boring detail, the family plan to counteract some stupid publicity in a paper he'd never heard of. He'd half-listened to her agitated talk. How momentous everything is when one is young, Giovanni thought. Not that Gloria was *that* young. But compared with him, she was a child. He smiled. And compared to Arthur Rubinstein, he thought wryly, *I'm* a child. It's all a matter of degree.

His mind came back to Richard's wife. She'd never, in all the years of her marriage, sought out her father-in-law. He knew what prompted this unexpected call, asking if she could come to see him. He welcomed her, of course. He truly liked Susan. It was just that spending hours at the hospital every day was such a strain and he was so tired from sitting beside Maria who silently but unmistakably resented her illness. He was weary of conducting bedside monologues, full of false heartiness for her benefit. Damn, he thought, why couldn't it have been me who had the stroke? Maria would be much better able to cope with my illness than I am with hers. She'd probably be better able to cope with Susan's problem too.

He was shocked to see how white and drawn Susan looked, almost ill. Giovanni kissed her on both cheeks and motioned her to the chair facing his.

"Drink?" he asked. "I'm going to have one."

"No, thank you. I won't stay long, Papa-Joe. I know you must be tired. How is Mrs. Antonini today?"

"Coming along remarkably. You've been very sweet about visiting so often, Susan." He cleared his throat as though the words were difficult to say. "I know she hasn't always been kind to you. She's not an easy woman. But I'm sure she's grateful for all the thoughtful things you do."

Susan shrugged off the compliment. "She's been very sick. One doesn't hold grudges at a time like this."

"No." Giovanni took a sip of his scotch. "Well, now. What brings you here, dear Susan? I daresay it's not to discuss Maria." The piercing brown eyes seemed to bore into her. "It's Richard, I suppose." Vague snatches of Gloria's conversation came back into his mind. "Yes, of course. That nonsense about a series of articles. Gloria told me about it a little while ago. Can't say I pay too much attention to such things. People love to gossip but they quickly forget. Can't think why the children are making such a fuss over nothing."

"It isn't exactly nothing," Susan said. "What is, I agree with you. The best thing to do would be to ignore it, but the others don't think so." She took a deep breath. "Richard and I just had a terrible fight over it. I don't know what to do. I'm sorry to burden you, Papa-Joe, but I don't know where to turn for advice."

In spite of his impatience, Giovanni felt pleased. It was the first time any of them had come to him for advice. Even Gloria, telling him what they planned, hadn't been asking his opinion; she'd simply been informing him of a decision, the way Maria would have done. For that matter, if Maria were around they'd have left it up to her to inform him, if she thought it necessary for him to know. I should have listened more carefully to Gloria, he thought. I would have, if I'd had any idea my views would matter.

"Let me hear your version of all this, Susan," he said gently. This time he'd listen, knowing it was important.

She told him, straightforwardly, about the first article and the one already announced. She spoke of what was bound to follow. She recounted Richard's "confession" to her about the women he'd been with. "I hate it" Susan said, "but, crazy as it sounds, it's not his faithlessness that makes me so miserable. I have to take part of the blame for that. A contented married man has no impulse to cheat." She forced a smile. "At least not on so regular a basis." Then the sad look returned. "What I can't accept is Richard's asking me to publicize our 'happy marriage' and use Katie as the device. He wants me to expose her not as his beloved daughter but as a cross we've had to bear together. He's begging me to make speeches and join groups devoted to helping the parents of deaf-mute children. He wants to generate sympathy to overshadow the things that will be written about us. Mary Lou's going to do that with Frances, but I'm not able to. I told him so tonight, and he told me to get out. He says I owe him this, Papa-Joe. Do I? He's your son. You must understand him. What shall I do?" Susan wiped her eyes. "I don't want to leave him. I still love him. But how can I endure this exploitation of our child?"

Giovanni searched desperately for the right words. It was a new role for him, this business of being approached as an oracle. How would Maria handle it? he wondered. She'd probably remind Susan of her duty to her husband, tell her to stop being so unworldly and do what she was told. But she'd be wrong. Susan wouldn't obey orders. She'd proved that before. She had to be reasoned with, approached like the intelligent woman she was. In any case, Giovanni thought with satisfaction, she'd never come to Maria with this problem. She'd know Richard's mother would automatically take his side. He felt ridiculously proud that Susan had brought her troubles to him. Such a little triumph, and so late in life. Yet it made him feel more a man than he had in years. He hoped he could be as wise as this young woman believed him to be.

"Susan, my dear, let's look at this as objectively as we can. You always wanted Richard to openly acknowledge Katie, not be ashamed of her. You took it hard, rightly so, when he sent her off to be, let's face it, hidden away. You defied him by bringing her home, getting help for her, sending her to nursery school with hearing children. You've never made a secret of a handicap she can't help. On the contrary, you've wanted, more than anything, for her to be part of the world. Am I correct?"

"Yes, but . . ."

"Let me finish. Now he *is* anxious to acknowledge her. Granted, for the wrong reasons. But is that not less important than the fact that he is coming forward, with you, to tell people that he has a deaf-mute child and considers it no disgrace? This is what you've always hoped for, Susan. It's not the *way* you hoped for it, I admit, but what difference if the end result is good? Is it asking too much for you to make a few little talks, pose for a few photographs in exchange for having your husband at your side, helping you raise your child instead of your trying to do it alone? And you'll have your own identity. The world will applaud you. You've *won*, Susan. In a strange way you've won. And the irony is that Richard doesn't realize it.''

She stared at him. Won? If so, it was a hollow victory, achieved not through Richard's compassion or fatherly love but through his fear, his weakness. It didn't make him love Katie. It didn't make him want her. Giovanni didn't understand. What on earth had possessed her to come to this sweet ineffectual man whose world was as limited as his son's? For the first time, she almost sympathized with Maria. They'd both married children who were unwilling or unable to assess the true value of things.

Giovanni took her silence for agreement. "I knew you'd see it sensibly, Susan dear. A little role-playing, some humane forgiveness for Richard's past mistakes, that's all that's involved here. Now that everything's out in the open, your marriage will be better than ever. When you've been married as long as I have, you come to learn that life's path is full of tiresome little detours. This is one of them, child. And the road will be all the smoother for it. I promise you.''

She wanted to cry out that he hadn't understood anything of her problem. He couldn't comprehend that the strain of publicly pretending to be delighted with her life was an unbearable prospect. This wasn't the kind of "identity" she wanted. And he couldn't envision what the sudden thrust into the limelight might do to Katie, who was only beginning to find her way. Lord knows I'm not looking for applause! He grasped none of it. None of the dishonesty, the deliberate use of innocent people. He was not an evil man. Simply an incredibly sheltered one. Susan stood up.

"Thank you for talking with me, Papa-Joe. It helped. It really did.'' She gave him a soft kiss on the cheek.

"You're a bright young woman, Susan. You won't find this as hard as you imagine. Besides, consider how much you'll be helping other parents with handicapped children! By speaking out, you may save more marriages than just your own.''

Save my marriage, Susan thought as she walked slowly home. That's what it comes back to, always. Is it just foolish pride that makes me unwilling to admit I was wrong in marrying Richard? Was I? Did I go into it too quickly, as Mother and Dad said? I still can't believe that. But how much can I swallow while I look for the happiness I thought this life would bring?

But maybe, in a crazy, contorted way, Giovanni was right. She had always wanted Richard to share her pride in Katie, to let the world know that there was nothing "disgraceful" in having a handicapped child. Maybe this was the way, distasteful as it was, Maybe it would let some light into the dark corners of their marriage. To be able to talk about Katie freely would release some of her own long-suppressed frustration and make her feel a better person. Perhaps it was fate. This publicity that was being forced on her could be the very tool she needed to convince Richard that they were not unique in their problem, that hundreds of thousands of others lived with it and were strengthened by their resolve to give an extraordinary child an ordinary life. Maybe this would, as his father said, bring Richard to her side. Maybe the end did justify the means. She didn't know the answers. She simply knew that her choice was to go along with the scheme or refuse and risk losing everything she cared about. If this disaster produced a constructive change in Richard, then it would be worth it no matter how vulgar or difficult the role. And was it all that difficult, really? A few pictures, some interviews and speeches. They probably wouldn't hurt Katie. They might even, in the long run, help her.

By the time Richard came home she'd come to terms with the situation. She'd play the game as carefully as possible, protecting Katie as best she could. She even rationalized that, as his wife, she owed him something. But it was the kind of indulgence a woman owed a little boy who looked to his mother to get him out of a nasty scrape. That's what I really am, Susan thought sadly. I'm really the mother he has to have. He never needed a wife. Maria always reached him. In this case, she can't. So it's up to me.

"I'm here," she called from the library, where she'd been sitting for hours in the dark.

He came in, switched on the light, looking at her warily. The anger had left him and he seemed uncertain.

"I thought you'd be gone."

"I'm not going. We'll get through this together. I'll do what all of you want. We'll work it out."

He seemed to crumble with relief. "I'm sorry I said those things, Susan. I didn't mean them. I know how you hate . . ."

"Never mind," she said.

It was as grotesque as she'd imagined. More so. The second article in *Open Secrets* pulled no punches about Richard Antonini's success with women. Apparently MacKenzie had well-documented proof of his affairs, those he'd told Susan about and a few others he'd neglected to mention. Susan read the story with a feeling of nausea and it took every ounce of strength she could muster to sound unconcerned when Bea Langdon called, almost weeping with pity for her child.

"Darling, what are you going to do?" Bea wailed. "It was terrible enough when they wrote about Katie. But this! Is it trne, Susan? Is this how Richard has been behaving? Why didn't you tell me? How *could* he? No wonder you had to go to Dr. Marcus."

"Mother, stop it! You're getting everything wrong. It's not true. None of it. Do you think I'd put up with it if it were? This is simply a bunch of lies. They run stories like this all the time about famous people! And for heaven's sake, you know I saw Dr. Marcus when Katie was taken to that school, not because Richard was being unfaithful to me!"

Apparently she sounded convincing. Or Bea was simply anxious to believe her. Whichever, she calmed down. "I know what your father will say: Demand a retraction. If they won't give it, sue them! They shouldn't be allowed to get away with such mudslinging. I'm sure Richard and his family agree with us."

"No, they don't. Neither do I. Mother dear, people don't pay attention to retractions buried on page forty-two after the damage has been done on page one. The best thing to do is simply ignore it. In fact," Susan continued to lie, "it's an odd coincidence, but Richard's new press agent made arrangements only yesterday for *House and Garden* to photograph Katie and Richard and me here in the apartment. They've been wanting to do it for a long while, but I've been too busy. It's good timing now, to show how secure and happy we are as a family. I'm going to do more of that, I think. It's the best way to put these revolting rumors to rest."

Beatrice Langdon was not a stupid woman. The "odd coincidence" was, she realized, part of a hastily constructed plan based on the Antoninis' nervousness about this projected series. She felt hurt that Susan chose to pretend with her, as though she were a stranger, but she kept quiet. All she said was, "I'm sure you know best. What else are you planning to do?"

Susan tried to sound enthusiastic.

"Richard and I are going to join the Parents' Group of the New York League for the Hard of Hearing, You remember. I investigated it when we first found out about Katie."

"I also remember that Richard wanted no part of any of that."

"Yes, I know. I still don't think he'll have time to be very active, but I wlll. They'd even like me to speak. It's really worthwhile, Mother. I'll probably start doing a lot of speaking on the subject of handicapped children. I'm excited about it. You know how much I've wanted to do something, make some kind of contribution."

"You always said you hated public speaking, Susan. You said it scared you to death, Remember when you were on *Vogue* and the Fashion Group asked you to speak at a meeting? You wouldn't do it. Said you'd be too nervous."

Why doesn't she stop? Susan thought. She knows this is a game I have to play, so why can't she make it easier for me? "That was different. I was just a kid and terrified of all those lady executives. Now I have something valuable to say. Something really meaningful. And I'm going to do more tours with Richard. We hate being apart so much. Besides, it's good for his image as a serious musician to have his wife with him, giving interviews to the women's pages in the cities where he appears."

Bea couldn't contain her sarcasm. "What a sudden change of heart we've had! Extraordinary! And to think it just 'accidentally' happened at the same time as this bad publicity."

Susan gave in. "All right, Mother. I'm sorry. I shouldn't insult your intelligence this way. You know we have to do everything we can to lessen the effect of this bad press. I can do much more for Richard than he can do for himself." It was a relief to speak the truth. "I hate it. I wanted to do something on my own, but I've never wanted to be a 'celebrity.' Certainly not this way. It's so phony. But it has to be done."

"What about Katie?"

"She'll be all right. I'll draw the line at certain things. She won't be personally involved in appearances and things like that. And she's well and happy at school and content and safe with Bridie at home. Even the speech therapy has gone faster than we dared hope. I can leave her more often now without worrying about it."

Bea sighed. "Are you sure you know what you're doing, darling? You're going to put yourself under a terrible nervous strain, traveling and speaking and doing all these things you hate. Is it really necessary, Susan? Do you love Richard so much you can let him do this to you?''

She didn't answer the last question. She merely repeated, "It's necessary, Mother, or I wouldn't do it.''

"You're becoming a household word," Kate Fenton said. "Every time I pick up a paper or a magazine, there you are. You and Richard in *Town and Country,* looking unutterably silly at the Swan Ball in Nashville. You and Katie posing for a mother-daughter fashion spread in the Sunday *Times Magazine* section. You giving interviews to *Cosmopolitan* about the 'joys' of being married to a genius, and sounding off on handicapped children in *Good Housekeeping.* I know this was the deal you made a year ago, but aren't you overdoing it? What are you bucking for—sainthood?''

Susan unsmilingly finished her third martini.

"And that's another thing." Kate scowled. "When did you corner the world market on vodka? Three drinks at lunch? My God, Susie!''

"It keeps me going. You can't imagine how tired I am.''

"Then why the hell don't you slow down? You've done everything possible to counteract that *Open Secrets* series, so how about relaxing? The damage is done and you can't undo it. None of it. Not even including the windup on that Hollywood tart. I know, Richard confessed everything before it got in print so the gory details didn't come as a shock to you. You took it. All this time you've been making wifely noises to disprove the whole mess. MacKenzie had her day, but it's *over.* The whole damned Antonini family survived. Including, to my surprise, you. Except you're not going to survive much longer if you don't stop killing yourself with booze.''

"It never lets up, Kate. Once Maria found out about it—and I could kill Gloria for telling her—she saw how she could use the Antonini wives to build up the eternal flame in front of the family shrine. She pushes us all the time. It's too damned bad, God forgive me, that she recovered." Susan's speech was a little slurred. "I think I'll have another vodka martini.''

"You don't need one. You didn't need the last two.''

"My! Haven't we gotten moral!''

"My!" Kate mimicked. "Haven't we become a jackass!''

The sharp words momentarily sobered Susan. She looked around, half dazed. Everything was strange these days. Even this out-of-the-way restaurant. A year ago, they'd have been lunching where they'd see and be seen. Now Susan wanted to hide whenever she could. So they faced each other across a checkered tablecloth at a tiny table in the rear of Billy's, a First Avenue neighborhood saloon-turned-restaurant where well-known people carne for late-night hamburgers and steaks but almost never for lunch. The turn-of-the-century place had a certain studied charm, having retained its long oak bar with the brass footrail, its shirt-sleeved bartenders and aproned waiters, its original gaslight fixtures, now electrified, and its simple menu posted on the wall. I came here often before I knew Richard, Susan remembered. It was fun then, noisy and informal in the evenings. Evie and I used to have dinner here alone or with dates when we roomed together.

It seems a hundred years ago. Such an exciting, carefree time. Now I come because I don't want to be stared at because I can't bear to pick up another copy of *Women's Wear Daily* and read about myself in "The Eye."

"Nothing's turned out the way I expected," Susan said.

"Things seldom do. Is that any excuse for getting sloshed in the middle of the day?"

Susan didn't answer. She *was* drinking too much. She didn't need Kate to tell her that. Of course she was unhappy. Who wouldn't be? She was so weary of pretending. No one seemed to understand how she hated being a "prominent person," how displaced she felt, how continually, totally inadequate under an exterior that seemed so poised and "sophisticated." How could they understand? Hadn't she always maintained she had to have an "identity" of her own? Hadn't she even tried for it, early on, with the short-lived column? They couldn't see how different this identity was, how "tolerated" she felt by Richard and Richard's family, how fragile the structure of her life really was. All the appearances as Mrs. Richard Antonini, all the graceful speeches and tasteful interviews she gave were like well-rehearsed lines from a play on which the curtain never mercifully descended so the leading lady could relax and "be herself." She was never herself any more. She was what Richard wanted—a suitable wife and a willing bed partner. What Maria wanted—an available spokeswoman for "the best of the Antoinis." She supposed she was even what Paul Carmichael wanted, since it was he who'd cynically cast her and the other wives into their prominent roles as social, civic and charitable leaders.

Mary Lou and Jacqueline didn't seem disturbed by it all. They'd easily adjusted to the new and greater demands on them. Jacqueline and Walter had made it a point to tone down their separate lives, had become more discreet than ever about their continuing affairs. Mary Lou had plunged wholeheartedly into her work for the retarded. Incredibly she seemed to enjoy taking about Frances after nearly fifteen years of shamed silence. The image of "wonderful people" that Maria had tried so long to project to her family was now coming true. Her sons had achieved new respect, greater fame through the campaign launched in retaliation for the scandal-sheet series. Maria herself was as physically whole as she'd been before her stroke and even more demanding. She'd been toughened by an experience that would have humbled weaker women. Her ambition for her "boys" was now insatiable and her standards more rigid than ever. The slightest sour note in a critique of Richard's performance sent her into a rage, not at the critic but at the man who'd played with something short of perfection. A damning written word about Sergio's conducting brought a tirade of accusations about her eldest son's sloppiness. And just as a poor composition by Walter evoked her scorn, so now did any lapse of activity by Susan or one of the others provoke her anger. A dynasty, powerful and impregnable, was what Maria wanted, and her obsession to see it created before she died was reaching manic proportions. She was increasingly into every facet of their lives, from the highly publicized public appearances they made to the theoretically private way they raised their children.

Why am I the only one who finds this so shattering? Susan wondered. She's only more of what she's always been. The difference is that she used to ignore me. Now she's involving me, and I haven't had years of getting used to it, the way the others have. If only Richard would stand up to her. If only he'd say we have the right to our own lives. But he won't. None of them will.

Richard. On the surface their marriage seemed firm. There'd been no more affairs after Sylvia Sloan. At least none she knew of. That had been the most sordid of all somehow, cheap and ugly. Whether Richard was now faithful by choice or because she was so seldom out of his sight, Susan didn't know. She traveled almost constantly with him now, hating it more than ever, loathing the pat conversations with reporters, the earnest little speeches at luncheons for parents of the deaf-mute where she sounded off on the needs of other handicapped children while she neglected her own.

That, above all, was the source of her greatest unhappiness, her most deep-seated guilt. She had so little time with Katie these days. The beautiful little six-year-old was closer to her nurse and her speech teacher than she was to her own mother. Even when Susan was in New York, she sometimes could spend no more than an hour with her daughter each day, for the mother's time was filled with "do good" duties and social, cultural events that enhanced the father's professional image.

Sometimes Susan felt as though she was in the eye of a tornado, dead-center in a whirling funnel of ceaseless activity, spinning like a giant cone toward some awful eventuality. Why didn't she, as Kate sanely suggested, slow down? What could they do to her—kill her if she stopped doing all these torturous things? They're not pushing me, Susan suddenly realized. I'm pushing myself. I'm trying so hard to believe this is the only way my marriage can survive. I'm too proud to admit I'm not cut out for this pattern of overachievement. I'm a pygmy among giants, a dumb marigold in a hothouse of orchids. I'm not even good at what I'm trying to be. Why can't I face that?

"I feel as though I'm lunching alone," Kate said. "You haven't said a word in five minutes."

Susan was apologetic. "I'm sorry. I got off on a whole stream-of-consciousness thing inside my head. It's your fault really, for asking me why I didn't slow down. I was trying to figure out why I didn't."

"And . . . ?"

"The jury is still out on that one."

"Susan, I'm worried about you. Look at you. Your hand is shaking. You're skinny as a rail. Not just chic-skinny, more sick-skinny. How long since you've seen a doctor?"

"I'm fine, Kate. Nothing wrong with me that a week at Maine Chance couldn't cure."

"Then why don't you have one?"

"Sitting around with all those overweight ladies would drive me mad. I'm not the spa type, sinfully luxurious as it would be to do nothing but sleep, get massaged, facialed and whipped into shape. I don't really want to go to a health farm, not even Elizabeth Arden's," Susan said slowly, "but I could use a little time to myself. If I could just get away for a few days alone to think things out. No, it's out of the question. My damned schedule is too full."

"What are you, the indispensable woman?"

"On the contrary, everything really important would go on just fine without me."

"Then for God's sake take a vacation! You must! And do something completely different, something no Antonini would ever do."

Susan smiled, but she was intrigued. "Like what?"

Kate thought for a minute. "I don't know. Have you ever been to Las Vegas?"

Susan burst out laughing. "Las Vegas! No, and I don't think I want to go. I hear it's terrible! Honky-tonk. Men in short-sleeved shirts and white socks and dumpy women with curlers in their hair playing the nickel slot machines! You really are crazy, Kate. Las Vegas!" she said again. "Can't you just see Richard's face if I told him I was going there?"

Kate shrugged. "Okay, then how about Palm Springs or Palm Beach? They're in the Antonini tradition—rich, exclusive and more of the same."

"You're serious about Las Vegas, aren't you?"

"Sure I am. I think more than anything you need to forget the world you know, and the one that knows you. I'd even use a different name. Just be sure it matches the initials on your luggage. Let's see. 'A' How about 'Armstrong?' By the way, do you gamble?"

Susan shook her head. "Never even tried."

"It's fun. I remember the Casino in Monte Carlo. Not that Vegas is anything like that I'm sure. Still, there's a kind of Never-Never-Land feeling about rooms full of people staking everything on the roll of the dice or the turn of a card. Hell, you might become a roulette addict! Or have an affair with a blackjack dealer. Who knows? Where's your spirit of adventure?"

"It's the wildest suggestion I've ever heard! Of course, I would love to see it. They say it's indescribable." Susan was beginning to toy with the idea. "I could go to Palm Springs for a few days and then maybe nip over to Nevada without telling anybody." Her eyes suddenly began to sparkle. "Kate, do you really think I could?"

"I think it would be the best thing in the world for you."

Susan continued to plan. "I wouldn't have to tell anybody where I was going. Only Bridie, in case Katie needed me. Richard would understand Palm Springs. He knows I'm tired. If he found out about Vegas, I could always say I just had the idea on the spur of the moment when I was out there. How would he find out anyway? I could call him every night." She was getting excited now, more like the old, enthusiastic Susan. "Oh, Kate, it's an insane, marvelous idea! Only you would have thought of it! I do need to hide out in some place just like that. Some place where they've never heard of Stravinsky or Tchaikovsky or Liszt's *Transcendental Études!*"

Kate nodded approvingly. "Better still, some place they think Antonini is the name of an Italian shoemaker or the owner of a pizza parlor."

Susan threw back her head and roared with laughter. It felt absolutely marvelous.

Chapter 18

GOING AWAY NEXT month for a week? By yourself?" Bea Langdon looked hard at her daughter. *"Why, Susan?"*

"No special reason, Mom. I suddenly realized I desperately need a holiday and Richard's too busy to take any time. Even when he's home, he works six or seven hours every day. Much more than he ever did before.''

"I should think as he got more famous he'd need to practice less.''

Susan smiled. "It doesn't work that way.''

"What about Katie?''

"Bridie's better with her than I am. Do you know she's reading? Isn't that incredible? Six years old and she's picking whole sentences out of her picture books. What's even more amazing, she's learning to say words! God bless Edith Chambers! What a marvelous teacher she is. She must be to Katie what Anne Sullivan was to Helen Keller.''

Involuntarily, Bea cringed. She hated being reminded of her only grandchild's tragedy. It broke her heart every time she saw that dear little thing with her hearing aids and listened to the strange speech that was incomprehensible to Bea. She adored Katie, but she wished Susan would have another baby, a heathy, bouncing one. Susan loved children. What was more, a pregnancy could release her from all her exhausting activities, the way Katie's conception had gotten Susan and Richard out of Maria's house. But there'd be no more grandchildren for the Langdons. Susan had already made that clear.

"I wouldn't risk something going wrong again,'' she'd said before, when Katie was taken away.

You wouldn't. Bea had wondered then. Or is it Richard who wouldn't? She still wondered about it, just as she fretted secretly over the whole status of her daughter's marriage, Now this trip alone. Was she running away? Had something else happened between Susan and Richard?

"Don't look at me like that, Mother. I can read your mind. Nothing's wrong. Richard's on his good behavior and perfectly happy for me to get a rest. I'm going to Palm Springs, not to Reno for a divorce.'' Susan smiled. "Now that I think of it, does anybody go to Reno for a divorce these days? I suppose not. Not with Mexico offering 'quickies.' Don't look so serious! Lots of couples take separate vacations. They say it strengthens the marriage.''

Does yours need strengthening? Bea wanted to ask. Strange. Close as they were, Susan didn't talk much about her private feelings. Perhaps she confides in Kate, Bea thought with a twinge of jealousy. Maybe she thinks I wouldn't understand, being so blessed in my own marriage. All that awful scandal last year. And all the things they were still doing to present a "united front." It wasn't natural. Susan was showing the strain. Probably a week to herself was a good idea at that.

"Well, it sounds like fun, dear,''

"I'm not looking for fun. Just peace.''

There it was again. That little hint of unhappiness.

"When do you leave?'' Bea asked.

"In about three weeks. Richard's playing in Washington week after next. When he comes back, I'll take off.''

"You're not going with him to Washington?''

"Not this trip. It's just a short one. Only three days. I need to get a few new clothes, and with him away I'll be free to organize myself and spend some time with Kit-Kat.'' She smiled as she used the child's nickname. She was Kit-Kat only to Susan. To everyone else, she was Katie. Except to Maria, who, when she referred to her at all, called her Katherine. "I wish I could take her with me. She'd have fun in the desert. But I can't let her miss school."

She really meant it. She'd happily have taken Katie to Palm Springs and stayed there, forgetting that nonsense about Vegas and assumed names. But it would be selfish to uproot her, even for a week, when she was doing so well in school. She mustn't miss her classes. Or her lessons with the speech therapist. Or any of the other things I can't do for her, Susan thought, feeling a little pang of self-pity. I'm not nearly as important any more as the company of her peers and the help of her teachers. I've lost touch with her since I've been on this merry-go-round. She doesn't need me so much any more. But I need her. She's the only tangible thing in my life.

Damn that MacKenzie woman and what she'd done to them with her stories! Even after a year the gossip went on. About Richard and his women. And Sergio and his. And Walter and his young men. And the poor children, Frances and Katie. Just when we think everything's quiet, somebody rehashes it all in a magazine article or on a talk show. Sometimes she suspected Sylvia Sloan kept the whole thing alive for her own purposes. Richard hadn't seen her again. Susan was positive of that. But who'd believe it?

Who'd believe any of this? Susan thought cynically. Who'd believe I go on, week after week, trying to make sense of my life? I *must* change. When I come back, I will.

Richard watched his mother in complete fascination. Looking at her, listening to her, even he found it hard to believe that a year ago she'd lain mute and helpless in a hospital bed. Most people would be left with some sort of difficulty after a seizure such as hers, but not even those who knew her best could detect the slightest trace of an aftermath. She walked erectly and had regained full use of her hands. God knows she'd sweated to accomplish that. She'd worked harder than the doctors recommended, exercised furiously, doubled, tripled the amount of therapy they'd suggested for a woman of her age. She'd been fanatic about it. "I won't be p . . . p . . . itied," she'd said the first moment her speech returned. "I'll g . . . get well. Make a f . . . full . . ." She seemed to be groping for a word that eluded her. The patrician brow wrinkled in frustration for a few seconds before she completed the sentence. "I'll make a f . . . full recovery!"

And to their admiration and amazement, she had. True, the stroke had not been as severe as it first seemed, but Richard knew that was not the reason she was now facing him in full command of her movements and her speech. She'd simply refused to let this defeat her. At the beginning of her recovery she'd had trouble speaking without hesitation, had sometimes seemed unable to find a word she wished to use. Even this limitation outraged her. She would not have it. She would not go through life stuttering and stammering like an idiot.

She'd gotten a speech therapist immediately, adding those lessons to the physical exercise, working day and night on every part of her afflicted body. And it had turned out as she was determined it would.

Most women, most men for that matter, would not have come out of this so totally intact. Some, Richard thought, might even have used a handicap as an added weapon in their arsenal of power, wielding a cane to make a point or demanding even more service, using as an excuse a hand or leg that never came back to full strength. But not Mother. She didn't need these devices to reinforce her domination. Indeed, she would have none of them, lest they be construed as weakness. She'd fooled them all, and she presented a smug expression of condescension as the doctors congratulated her on an extraordinary rehabilitation.

"You had me counted out, didn't you?"

"It *is* a remarkable recovery, Mrs. Antonini."

"Not for me, it isn't."

Richard smiled, remembering the sight of the big specialists being reduced to silence by this tiny, indomitable woman. They'd been like embarrassed schoolboys proved wrong by the teacher. He felt a little like a schoolboy himself right now, as Maria raised her eyebrows and said, "Susan's going to Palm Springs alone in February? How very odd, Richard."

"Not really, Mother. She deserves a holiday. She's worked her tail off for the family this past year. She's tired."

"I see." She didn't at all, of course. "Would she like to look up some of my friends there? I know a number of people with charming houses."

"I don't think so, thanks. She says she plans to sleep twenty hours a day."

Maria shrugged. "Well, it's your business . . ."

"Yes, it is, dear. Susan's and mine."

Maria ignored that impertinence and changed the subject. "Richard, how do you think your father looks?"

"All right. Why?"

"I don't think he's well, That awful flu. It took him two weeks to get over it!"

"Darling, everybody takes time to get over flu. And Father's getting along. People don't bounce back so fast as they get older." He looked at her pointedly. "Most people, that is. Thank God you're made of iron."

She smiled, pleased.

"Susan's going away alone for a week," Jacqueline said.

"Good for her." Walter kept on reading the morning mail. "Where's she going?"

"Palm Springs."

"She could get a divorce in Mexico in twenty-four hours."

Jacqueline laughed. "Haven't you heard? Antoninis don't get divorces. It makes for messy publicity. You really don't like Richard very much, do you?"

"Nope. Not very much." Walter looked up. "Mostly because he's not honest. At least we know where we stand, but he keeps trying to fool himself and Susan."

"I thought he was behaving."

"You obviously haven't heard the gossip about the Senator's daughter."

"Oh no! Not again!"

"Susan's going to Palm Springs. Without Richard," Mary Lou said.

Sergio looked mildly interested. "Really? I didn't think she had the guts."

"You didn't tell me Susan was going away by herself for a week." Raoul said. "I ran into Richard and *he* told me."

"Who cares?" Gloria replied.

On Friday afternoon as the plane came in low over the Jefferson Memorial, Richard nudged Paul. "You can see Kennedy Center. Ugly damned thing, isn't it?"

"But the fee they're paying makes it beautiful."

"Christ, Paul, don't you ever think about anything but money?"

"Sometimes. I'd think of it less if I were as rich as you."

Richard look at him sharply. Even after all the years together, he was never quite sure when his manager was serious or when he was subtly making a joke at Richard's expense. For that matter, close as they were, Richard often felt he really didn't know Paul Carmiehael. He spent more time with him than he did with his brothers or even, for that matter, with Susan. Paul knew all about his employer's continuing activities, but he kept his mouth shut. And in the past year he always somehow managed to disappear when Richard suggested a night of 'innocent fun' with the out-of-town ladies. Paul never voiced outright his disapproval of Richard's affairs, but it was clear that he did not wish to participate, even remotely, in the unfaithfulness to Susan. He cares more about her feelings than he does about me, Richard thought jealously. He's turned into a damned prig. Sometimes I think he's in love with my wife. But that doesn't make sense. If Paul wanted Susan, he'd encourage me to get into trouble, hoping the marriage would blow up and he could have her for himself. Instead, he always tries to smooth things over, though lately he's made it a point not to know what I'm doing. Like tonight. I'll bet he won't have any part of the evening's plans. He'll pretend he doesn't know Dolly Johnson exits.

The airplane touched down with a series of gentle bumps at Washington's National Airport. Involuntarily, Richard gave a sigh of relief. He was not an "easy flier," just as he was not a relaxed passenger in a car. It made him nervous to know that his life was in someone else's hands. The tenseness went out of him as they rolled safely along the ground. Even the crazy ideas he'd had about Paul in the past few minutes disappeared. He's totally loyal, Richard thought. God knows he's proved himself time and again. I'm more than his meal ticket; I'm his best friend. And he's mine.

Walking toward the exit, Richard genially approached the subject of this evening. "What are your plans for dinner?"

Paul shrugged. "Nothing special. I'll probably hit the sack early. I have to be at the Center early in the morning to check out things before your rehearsal."

"You still have to eat."

"I'll probably have something sent up from room service." Paul hesitated. "What about you?"

"I promised to take Dolly Johnson to dinner. You remember her. The Senator's daughter. The one who's divorced. She's picking me up at the hotel at seven. She knows some nice little place in Virginia where the food and drinks are good. We'll probably go back to her apartment at the Watergate for a nightcap."

Richard sounded offhand. "Just a quiet evening. I'm sure she could get a friend for you."

"No, thanks. I'll take a rain check."

The feeling of annoyance returned. "You think I'd be smarter to dine upstairs too, don't you?"

"You're a big boy. Do what you like."

"Goddammit, Paul, you're a pain in the ass lately! You never used to be so pious about my having a few laughs with a beautiful woman."

"You never used to be married."

Richard exploded. They were in the rented limousine waiting for the driver to return from the claim area with their bags. In the privacy of the car, Richard raised his voice. "What the hell do you want from me? What do you *all* want from me? Have I ever missed a concert? Given a bad performance? Flubbed an interview? Jesus, don't I deserve something more than eight hours a day of practice, a martyred wife who hates being a public figure and a mother who's never let up on me since I was old enough to reach the keyboard? Am I not entitled to *any* relaxation, *any* freedom? I'm no ribbon clerk who works from nine to five and forgets the job at the end of the day! I'm always under pressure of one kind or another! You used to understand that. All of a sudden you've turned into a approving watchdog!"

Paul turned an equally angry face toward him. "I'm not a watchdog, Richard. Nor a lapdog. If you want to justify your stupid behavior by saying you need 'relaxation,' be my guest! But goddammit don't expect me to keep on getting you out of trouble with your public *or* your wife! I don't need that. I don't want any part of it. What the hell is it you're trying to prove? 'Martyred wife,' for Christ's sake! If there was ever anybody who isn't a martyr, it's Susan! She's been a damned good sport about what we've asked her to do. And she's been a thousand times more forgiving than any ordinary woman would be. But that's not enough, is it? You're starting all over again with the broads, showing yourself and the rest of us that you can make your own rules because you're an artist, a genius or whatever you've come to believe from reading your own publicity. Well, the hell with you and your needs or your freedom or whatever you choose to call it! I think we've come to the end of the road, Richard. You don't need a manager, you need a pimp! I've had all I care to put up with. Find yourself a new boy. After this tour I'm through."

Richard was stunned. "You're quitting me? You can't do that!"

"Why not? I don't have a contract. Just a 'gentleman's handshake' agreement. The fact is, Richard, I can't stand you lately. I hate what you're doing to Susan. I even hate what you're doing to yourself. And God knows I hate what you've done to me and what I've done to a lot of other people as a result."

The chauffeur returned and they started toward the city. Richard lowered his voice.

"All right, you sonofabitch. You don't know the meaning of loyalty or gratitude. That's fine with me. Any manager will be glad to handle me, but how many artists will want you when they hear I've gotten rid of you?"

Paul smiled grimly. "That's exactly how you'll release the news, isn't it? True to form. Nobody ever rejects Richard Antonini. He proposes and disposes, whether it's a woman, a manager or a child he'd like never to see."

"You no-good bastard!"

Paul looked out the window. He'd said everything that had been bottled up inside. Richard might be right. He might have a hard time finding someone as famous and lucrative to represent. But to hell with all the Antoninis and their willful, selfish ways! He'd not miss any of them. Except Susan. For her sake, he hoped she wouldn't guess the real reasons for his sudden departure.

Susan was still up, puttering around the bedroom, getting clothes organized for her trip, when the telephone rang at eleven o'clock that night.

"Mrs. Richard Antonini? This is Harry Penza of the Washington *Post*. We'd like to know when you're arriving in Washington and what your reaction is to the accident. Is Dolly Johnson a friend of yours? Did you know your husband was with her this evening? Do you think he'd been drinking?"

Susan stared stupidly at the receiver. No sound came from her.

"Mrs. Antonini? Are you there? May we have a comment from you, please?"

"I don't know what you're talking about." Susan began to stammer. "What . . . what accident? Has something happened to my husband? Where is he? Where's Paul . . . Paul Carmichael?"

Penza sounded sympathetic. "I'm sorry. I was sure you'd been informed. Your husband was in a car crash on the road from Alexandria this evening. He's apparently not hurt, but his passenger Mrs. Dolly Johnson, is pretty badly banged up. They're both in Washington Hospital Center out on Irving Street. The police won't say anything except that Mr. Antonini was driving and apparently lost control and hit another car head-on." The reporter paused. "Unfortunately, the other car was driven by a man who had his wife and two children with him. The woman and a little girl were killed."

Susan closed her eyes. "Oh, my God!" She began to shake violently. "Was my husband's manager, Mr. Carmichael, with him?"

"No, ma'am. Just Mrs. Johnson. Mr. Carmichael's at the hospital, but he's not giving out any statements. About Mrs. Johnson, the Senator's daughter," the man said again. "Is she a friend of yours *and* your husband's? Will you be coming down tonight? Do you know whether Mr. Antonini's mother and father will come with you?"

"I . . . I don't know anything. That is, I have nothing to say. Please get off the phone, Mr. . . . ."

"Penza. With a P as in Post."

"Please hang up, Mr. Penza. I'm sure Mr. Carmichael is trying to reach me."

"What about the concert? I suppose it will be canceled."

"I don't know. I suppose so. Please excuse me but I'm going to hang up now."

She turned away in a daze. Why hadn't Paul called her? What was this all about? Thank God Richard wasn't hurt, but those other people, those poor, unfortunate people in the other car. She thought of calling someone. Her parents. Richard's. Perhaps she could find Paul at the hospital. Yes, that was best. She'd get more facts before she spoke to anyone else. Just as she was about to pick up the phone it rang.

"Susan, I have some bad news. Richard's been in an accident, but he's all right," Paul said hurriedly. "Hardly a scratch on him. Just shook up. They're keeping him in the hospital overnight for observation. This is the first chance I've had to call."

"I know. A reporter from the Washington *Post* phoned. He told me. Paul, he told me about the people in the other car, too. It's terrible! How did it happen?"

"I'm not sure of the facts yet, Susan. It only happened about an hour ago. Richard had them call me at once."

"I'm coming right down."

"No point in starting out tonight. It would be practically impossible at this hour anyway. You can come tomorrow. Listen, Susan. Call the Antoninis and tell them. Be sure to say Richard's perfectly okay, but warn them not to talk to any reporters. And don't you talk to any either. What did you tell the *Post* guy?"

"Nothing. I was too shocked. He wanted to know about somebody named Mrs. Johnson. Whether she was a friend of mine."

There was a small pause. "What did you say?"

"I told you: nothing. Who is she, Paul?" She stopped. "Never mind. I'm sure I can guess."

If Carlyn MacKenzie's editorial pursuit of the Antoninis had been agony, the press coverage of Richard's accident was a crucifixion. The story had all the ingredients of sensational reporting and unlimited innuendoes: the famous, married concert arrist in the company of a rich divorcée whose father was a United States senator and whose reputation, on her own, was none too savory; the late-night drive; the mysterious "loss of control" of the car; the death of two innocent people, leaving a working-class widower and one motherless child. Once again, the recklessness of the country's number-one musical family was rehashed as "background material" for this latest escapade of its youngest member. Nothing and no one would be spared in the weeks ahead. Not only would the investigation of the accident and the consequent hearing be reported in minute detail, but the nation's diligent reporters would dig back into the morgues of their newspapers for photographs of Susan and (God, how Susan regretted having permitted them!) Katie, who, ironically, was the same age as Jenny, the little girl who died in the crash.

Frank Olmstead, the press agent who'd replaced Gerry, accompanied Susan to Washington the morning after the accident. They took a 7:00 A.M. Eastern shuttle, hoping to arrive unnoticed. It was a futile hope. The press had stationed itself at the airport at dawn to meet every incoming New York flight and when Susan emerged they set upon her, still cameras flashing, TV cameras grinding, reporters shouting questions as she and Frank tried to make their way to a waiting car.

"Look this way, Mrs. Antonini!"

"Are you and Dolly Johnson friends?"

"Was your husband drinking?"

"Will you and Richard attend the Armstrong funeral?"

"Just one more, Susan! Look this way!"

Susan kept walking toward the entrance, not answering the shouted questions, looking straight ahead, her face expressionless. Frank acted as a shield, elbowing them through the crowd, saying over and over, "Mrs. Antonini has no comment.

She's anxious to get to her husband. Please let us through. We'll have a statement later.''

Only when they were in the car on their way to town did Susan bury her face in her hands for a moment. Then she looked up, her eyes full of tears.

"I can't bear it Frank. It's like a zoo!''

"I'm afraid it's only the beginning.''

Or the end, Susan thought. I really thought Richard had learned his lesson. All we've done to project the image of a solid, loving family has gone down the drain in the dirty water of another of his escapades. She'd heard about Dolly Johnson. Her name was constantly in the columns, always linked with some glamorous escort, in Washington or Acapulco or St. Tropez. In an earlier age they'd have called her a "madcap heiress,'' the thrice-divorced, ungovernable only child of a millionaire Oklahoma senator. It didn't take a vivid imagination to see how Richard would appeal to her. And vice versa. Or why they'd been together on that highway in Virginia.

They pushed their way through more reporters in the lobby of the hospital and made their way up to the room where Richard, fully dressed, was sitting in a chair at the window. Paul Carmichael straddled a straight chair on the other side of the room. Both of them got to their feet when Susan came in. She looked at Richard but didn't go to him.

"Are you all right?'' she asked.

"Yes. They just kept me here overnight for observation.''

"He's been signed out,'' Paul said, "but I thought it would look better if we waited for you to arrive so you and Richard can go to the hotel together.''

"And how is Dolly Johnson?'' It was a clipped, pointed question.

There was an uneasy pause. "She has a broken arm,'' Richard said. "Nothing serious. We were lucky.''

Susan stared at him.

"I mean, I could have had my hands smashed up, Susie! Hell, I could have been killed! Look, I know it's awful about that Armstrong woman and the child. But it was an accident! My God, I didn't mean to do it! You don't have to look at me as though I'm a murderer! I'll make some kind of settlement on the husband. I'm sorry. I'm terribly sorry. But it was unavoidable. Something went crazy with the steering mechanism. I couldn't control the car. It wasn't my fault.''

She looked at Paul, who was staring at the floor, avoiding her eyes. Even Frank Olmstead, who did't know them as well, shifted his feet restlessly as Richard poured out his defensive story. In your mind, nothing's ever your fault, Susan thought. And there's nothing that can't be solved with influence and money. Nevertheless, she felt half sorry for him. He was frightened under the bravado. He'd never been involved in anything as serious as this. But he'd get away with it. The Antoninis would provide the best legal talent to defend him against a charge of reckless driving or involuntary manslaughter or whatever they accused him of. The Antoninis would pay off to avoid a damage suit, buy off the widower, who might accuse their darling boy of killing the man's wife and child. Everybody would pitch in again to protect Richard. They'd expect her to stand by him, to give still another performance as the loving, trusting wife. I can't do it, Susan thought. I won't do it any more.

"Shall we go?" Paul finally broke the silence.

A sudden question crossed Susan's mind. Weren't people taken to the police station and booked when they were involved in fatal accidents? Wouldn't charges be preferred?

"Are we free to?" she asked. "Can Richard just go back to the hotel?"

"Yes. He's released on his own recognizance, pending a hearing. He's already given a full statement to the police. He'll have to appear later, but he's free to come and go as he pleases until then." Paul cleared his throat. "In fact we're not canceling the concert. The lawyers advised us it would look much better if everything appeared as nearly routine as possible. We'll have the full rehearsal today and the performance Sunday afternoon as planned."

"We'd better schedule a press conference," Frank said. "Richard and Susan together. Later this morning, I think. When's the funeral, Paul?"

"I don't know. Tuesday, probably."

"They'll have to show up for that of course."

Susan couldn't believe what she was hearing. They were expected to talk to the press, look lovingly into each other's eyes, holding hands, no doubt. Richard would go onstage, a modest and saddened figure, while she sat bravely in the first row. They were to go together to the funeral of the woman and her child, appearing pained but innocent. The machinery was rolling, set in motion by the family and run by the people who were well paid to operate it. She felt sick, repulsed by the cold-blooded step-by-step plan in which it was assumed she would co-operate. It was grotesque.

She said nothing until she and Richard were alone in the suite at the Hay-Adams. Paul had gone to Kennedy Center to see about the afternoon rehearsal. It was a final gesture. He'd leave no loose ends and Richard knew it. Frank was setting up the press conference for noon. There'd been another mob of reporters in the hotel lobby, but they'd gotten through in a repetition of the scenes at the airport and the hospital. The telephone operators had been instructed to put no calls through. Susan sank into a chair and said, dully, "You'd better call your parents. Your mother was very upset when I talked to her last night."

"In a minute. Susan, I want to explain about Dolly Johnson."

"You don't have to. I don't care."

"But it isn't what you think! We just went out for dinner. Paul was in a snit and wouldn't go with us, otherwise I wouldn't have been alone in the car with her. I know it looks suspicious, but I swear to God there was nothing to it!"

Susan looked at him wearily. "Don't think I'm an idiot, Richard. You took her out to dinner a couple of hours after you arrived in Washington. Do you really expect me to believe that wasn't preplanned?"

"All right, it was planned. But it was still innocent. You know how I hate eating alone in strange towns. Yes, I called her from New York and asked her to have dinner. Is that a crime? She's an amusing woman. You'd like her."

Susan began to laugh, almost hysterically. "Like I liked Gerry? Like I probably would like Sylvia Sloan and all the others? You're absurd, Richard! You don't fool me. You did once. I loved you. I made myself believe in you. I excused your behavior because I thought you couldn't help yourself. I blamed Maria for spoiling you rotten, giving you your phony values. But it's you who are hopelessly egocentric and thoroughly satisfied to be that way. I can't live with it. I'm coming to pieces under the strain. I won't go through this latest farce nor any that come after it. I'm not going to be at the press conference or the concert or the funeral of that poor woman and her child. You do it. You and your press agent and your whole damned arrogant family! Let *them* come down here and be at your side. I'm catching the next flight back to New York.''

''You don't know what you're saying!'' There was panic in his voice. ''You've got to stand by me through this! How will it look if you run back to New York? My God, that's all I need! People will be sure there was something going on with Dolly Johnson and me.''

''Then people will be right, won't they?'' Susan went over to the bar and poured a stiff scotch. Her hands were shaking as she added a little water. ''Richard, I'm not just leaving you now. I'm leaving you forever. I'm taking Katie and moving out. I've had it up to here with everything. I guess I've known it for a long time. Since the day you took Katie away. But I loved you so. I thought I was always failing you somehow. I tried to be everything I thought you wanted and needed, but no woman could be. When they made Maria, they broke the mold. She's the only woman you respect. And you don't even love her, because you can't love anyone except yourself.''

Unexpectedly, uncharacteristically, he began to cry. Deep, painful sobs he tried to muffle with his handkerchief as he turned his back to her.

Don't! Susan thought. Don't play on my sympathy again. I don't believe your tears. She walked to the window and stood looking down on Sixteenth Street, watching the slow Saturday morning traffic move by, trying desperately not to hear him. In a few minutes he became quiet and she turned to see him sitting on the sofa, his eyes on her.

''You're right,'' he said. ''I'm a façade. Nothing happens underneath. Except when it comes to you. That's the one place you're wrong. I do love you. Don't walk out on me, I beg you. I'll give you anything you want, any amount of freedom. I won't let everyone make demands on you, the way they have this past year. I'll change. I swear it. Please. One more chance. I'm on my knees to you. I've never been on my knees to anyone.''

''I can't. Don't ask me to.'' She held up the glass in her trembling hand. ''Look at me. I'm turning into a drunk! I need liquor to get me through every day. A few drinks, no, a *lot* of drinks for courage to live a life I hate with a man I don't understand. I'm lost, Richard. I'm frightened and lost and bone-tired. I'm going on nervous energy and booze. The next step will be a real nervous breakdown, not the one I was on the brink of when you took Katie away. Your life, your world is killing me! God help me, I wish I could be like Jacqueline. I wish I did't care so deeply for you. I'd like to match you affair for affair, hurt for hurt. I wish I could playact and be content. But that's not my style. I'm not a sophisticate like Jacqueline, nor mercenary like Mary Lou. I'm wrong for you, Richard. As wrong as you are for me, the sooner we end it the better.''

He sounded defeated. ''If that's what you really want. Just see me through this. One last favor. Then you can get a divorce. I won't fight it. You deserve more than I can ever give you, and I love you enough to want you to have it.''

How could she refuse? She knew she was being used again, but he'd been her lover, the father of her child and he was in deep trouble. It wasn't his fault if she wasn't tough enough to protect herself from his selfishness or the high-handedness of his family.

Wearily, she nodded. "All right. I'll go through the motions one more time. But when this is over, I'm through."

"Thank you," Richard said humbly. "I'm grateful." He hesitated. "I suppose you'd like to take the second bedroom? Paul can bunk in with me."

"Yes." She felt a wrench. He'd accepted defeat, but she didn't feel victorious. She felt empty and miserable and confused. It was like before. Like abandoning a child who needed you. But this time I must, Susan thought. This time I must save myself. He's not a little boy for whom I'm responsible. He's a man who could drive me insane. "I'm sorry," she said from force of habit.

"You have nothing to be sorry about. You're doing the right thing."

Chapter 19

SHE CALLED NEW YORK and canceled her Palm Springs and Las Vegas trip, thinking ruefully of her conversation with her mother, wondering whether the nonsense she'd spouted about a Reno divorce might have been some kind of omen. Where *would* she get her divorce, and how soon would she be able to leave without stirring up another cloud of notoriety? She told no one of her plans to leave Richard. Paul recognized the significance of the bedroom arrangements, but the announcement, even within the family, would have to wait until this dreadful period following the accident was over. Just as the announcement of Paul's defection would.

It was a nightmare. It took every ounce of her strength to get through the press conference, to look subdued but calm, to answer the questions with lies and evasions. Yes, of course she knew Dolly Johnson, she said. She's an old and dear friend of my husband's and mine. Certainly I knew they were dining together. No, of course Richard wasn't intoxicated. My husband is a moderate drinker.

A sharp-eyed young woman reporter brashly picked up this subject. "What about you, Mrs. Antonini? There've been reports that you've had some problems in that area."

Richard, under control, answered. "My wife and I enjoy an occasional cocktail, if that's what you mean. I have no idea where you could have heard such a silly rumor."

"From some of the best headwaiters in New York," the girl answered brazenly.

"I assure you they're as misinformed as you."

Throughout the exchange, Susan tried not to look stricken. There is no privacy, she thought. None at all. Even when I have a few drinks at lunch the whole world knows it.

"Shall we get back to the point of this conference?" Frank Olmstead interjected.

"Will you tell us exactly how the accident happened, Mr. Antonini? Just as you told it to the police." The questioner was a local television commentator.

"Certainly. Mrs. Johnson and I were on the way back from dinner. I was driving her car. Something apparently went wrong with the steering mechanism and I lost control. Tragically, Mr. Armstrong's car was approaching from the other direction and we hit head-on."

"Have the police checked the steering mechanism in Mrs. Johnson's car?"

"I couldn't say," Richard answered coldly, "but when they do they'll find it exactly as I've described."

"Will you attend Mrs. Armstrong's funeral?"

Richard looked at Susan. "Yes, my wife and I will be there, if Mr. Armstrong wishes us to be. We don't know the family, of course, but any moral support we can give at this terrible time is the least we can do."

"Is it true that Armstrong is suing you for five million dollars?"

"I have no knowledge of that."

The reporter who'd asked Susan about her drinking put another question. "Mrs. Antonini, don't you find it sad that the child who died is the same age as your own daughter?"

This time Susan looked her in the eye. "As a mother, I find it unbearable."

There were a few final questions about the concert.

"Over the phone last night Mrs. Antonini, you said the concert would be canceled," Harry Penza said. "What changed the plans?"

"You're Mr. Penza?"

"Yes."

"Then you know you were the one who first told me of the accident. Obviously, I had no idea of the plans."

"Well, why *is* your husband playing? Doesn't it strike you as rather disrespectful?"

Frank spoke again. "On the contrary, it's very courageous of Mr. Antonini to perform. He is doing so against his doctor's advice, but he's an artist who believes his first obligation is to the people who stood in line all night before the tickets went on sale, waiting to buy a seat. Mr. Antonini never has and never will disappoint his public. He comes from a family steeped in that tradition."

"Speaking of your family, Mr. Antonini, how are they taking this?"

"They are saddened as my wife and I. We all want to do everything we can for Mr. Armstrong in his loss."

"Does that mean you'll make a settlement out of court?"

"I told you," Richard said evenly, "I've heard nothing of claims in this matter."

"I think that's about it," Frank said. "I'm sure you have everything you need."

"Just one more question," a voice in the back row called out. "Mrs. Johnson told friends before the accident that you were planning to get a divorce and marry her. Any truth to that?"

Richard reddened. "You heard my wife, Mrs. Johnson is a close friend of both of ours."

"That's not exactly a denial, sir."

Richard lost his temper. "What filth is this? My marriage is happy and secure, and always will be!"

"Okay," Frank said hurriedly. "That's it, people. Thanks very much."

They fed out of the suite, comparing notes among themselves.

"Jesus!" Richard said. "What a pack of vultures!"

"Dolly Johnson is news in this town," Frank said. "Don't worry. It was rough, but you did fine. The worst is over."

But it wasn't. The critical reviews of Richard's performance were generally poor, though the reservations about certain faulty passages were explained in the notices by the fact that "the pianist was obviously under unusual strain, due to his accident less than forty-eight hours before." There were photographers waiting as Susan entered the hall, and she felt as though every eye in the house was on her as she sat through the concert, trying to look composed and absorbed in the music.

Worse still was the double funeral of Mrs. Armstrong and Jenny.

"I don't understand why we're going," Susan said. "We're invading their privacy! Surely Mr. Armstrong can't want us there!"

"He's a little man," Frank said. "A bricklayer. People like that are sometimes strange, Susan. This one is. Even while he blames Richard for his loss, it gives him some kind of weird stature to have the celebrity appear in a secondary role. Besides, from our angle, it shows how stricken you and Richard are, how much you care. A vase of flowers would seem impersonal. People would think Richard was brushing off the whole thing."

"I don't believe it. I think it's indecent for us to show up." She appealed to Paul, who stood by silently through this exchange. "You agree with me, don't you?"

"My instincts are yours, Susan, but I think we'd better defer to Frank. He knows more about public relations than we do."

She said no more. Silently, she endured the drive to the little church in Maryland, suffered the stares and the flashbulbs that went off in her face as they went in and out, stood respectfully in the second row at the cemetery as the big and little coffins were positioned at the modest Armstrong plot. Neither she nor Richard spoke to the reporters, but after it was all over she impulsively approached the widower and his remaining child, Richard behind her. She put her hand gently on eight-year-old Christopher's head, and her eyes brimming with tears, looked at his father.

"I am so sorry, Mr. Armstrong," Susan said. 'It's hard to accept God's will."

The man stared at her stonily. "Harder still to know that some folks have everything and others have nothing."

"We want to help you," Richard said. "We'll do everything we can. My attorneys are going to be in touch."

The man didn't answer, but Susan thought she'd never seen such contempt on any face.

The hearing was the following day. Richard told his story and a deputized statement given by Dolly Johnson from her hospital bed corroborated his account. The police confirmed that the steering wheel was defective and the inquiry was closed.

"Cut and dried," the Antoninis' lawyer said as they left the courthouse. "Let's just hope Armstrong lets it go at that."

"What do you mean?" Richard asked. "I'm not legally responsible. I was cleared. It was an unavoidable accident."

"You never know what some shyster will advise him to do. You being who you are, they might just threaten to bring a multimillion-dollar damage suit, knowing you'll settle out of court to avoid the publicity."

Susan couldn't resist. "Richard, you did tell him you'd do everything to help. You even said your lawyers would be in touch."

The attorney looked surprised. "Did you? Did you say that to Armstrong?"

"Well, hell, yes I did. I thought we'd have to. Listen, I wouldn't mind giving the poor guy a few dollars to help him out right now. Even though I wasn't at fault, I feel rotten about it."

"Let's see what happens." The lawyer frowned. "That steering wheel really *was* defective, wasn't it?"

"Things were just as I said," Richard repeated, "but wouldn't it be smart to give him some money anyway and get rid of him once and for all? If he takes a settlement, he can't come back at us ever, can he?"

The lawyer hid his disgust. He was paid for this, but he hated it. He'd bet the overprivileged bastard was lying. He probably rammed the car because he was drunk. But Antonini was afraid of that kind of publicity. That's why he was so anxious to pay off. It wasn't conscience money. It was self-protection.

"I'll go out and see Armstrong tomorrow and tell him of your generosity. How generous are you feeling?"

"I don't know. About twenty-five thousand dollars' worth, you think?"

Sonofabitch. "I'd say more like fifty."

"Okay," Richard said. "Give fifty."

Paul Carmichael returned to New York right after the funeral. There was no need for him to hang around Washington for the inquiry. Better he didn't. Better he get as far away as possible from all of them. Thank God it was over. All the years of playing nursemaid were behind him. He and Richard had spoken only once about Paul's resignation. That was on Sunday afternoon.

"You've changed your mind, Paul, haven't you? I mean, all that crap you said in the car Friday about quitting. Hell, buddy, you don't want to leave me any more than I want you to leave! We both lost our tempers."

"I meant it. I'm through, Richard, as of now."

Richard's face darkened. "You're a bloody fool."

"Possibly. But better that than some of the other things I've been."

Back in his own apartment in the brownstone on East Sixty-third Street Paul relived the past few years, relieved they were over. His only regret was leaving Susan. She'd been so distressed when he said goodbye. He felt pain at the thought of her. He loved her so deeply, so futilely. He wondered how much of his decision to quit Richard had been based on an almost subconscious hope that it would free him to tell her how he felt. He'd felt joyful when she took the second bedroom in the suite. It was an unmistakable sign that things were seriously wrong between her and her husband. Just as the planned vacation alone had been a danger signal he understood, even if no one else seemed to. Maybe now that he owed no loyalty to the man who paid him, he could say what had been in his heart since the beginning. He wanted Susan and her child. He loved Katie, too. She grew more endearing every day, a wide-eyed, always-smiling cherub who didn't need words to communicate affection. She was like her mother, outgoing, full of warmth and trust. How could Richard push her away from him? How could the man help but adore this brave little thing who seemed determined, even at this early age, to be like other children?

Paul knew that Susan worried about spending less time than she should with Katie. Damn it, that was his doing! If only he hadn't suggested she and the others become "more visible" when that *Open Secrets* mess started! The whole family had become involved in the plan just as he'd outlined it. It didn't bother the others, but it was destroying the very one he wanted most to protect.

Angrily, he threw himself down on his couch. He'd been on the verge of suggesting to Susan that she could ease up on all the "image making" activities now that the series was long over. And then Richard pulled the Washington stunt and started the tongues wagging again. He wondered if she'd stand by this time. She'd canceled her Western trip, but she'd said nothing about the future, at least not to him.

He'd been in his apartment barely ten minutes when the phone rang and Maria Antonini's voice, strong as ever, came over the wire.

"I just spoke to Richard and he told me you'd returned," she said without preliminaries. "How is everything down there? Will there be trouble from the authorities or that Armstrong man?"

For the hundredth time he marveled at her quick mind.

"Eveything's going to be all right," Paul said. "There's nothing to worry about, Mrs. Antonini."

She snorted. "In this family there's always something to worry about." Then her tone became almost plaintive. "Why can't they lead more orderly lives, all of them? Bad marriages, scandalous affairs, ridiculous scrapes like this latest thing with Richard? How can they expect to be taken seriously as artists when they have so little regard for their personal obligations? I don't know, Paul. I want so much for them. I've tried so hard . . . ." As abruptly as she let down her guard, it went up again. "Well," Maria said briskly, "I hope everything was properly taken care of in Washington. I should have gone down, I suppose. Richard is so helpless, and heaven knows Susan is no good at this kind of thing! I'm glad you were there. The publicity was terrible, but it probably would have been worse if you hadn't been around to advise Richard. I don't have much use for that Olmstead man. Gerry was much better. I'll never know why Richard let her go."

There are a lot of things you'll never know, Paul thought.

"This Johnson woman," Maria continued. "Dreadful type. Pushy. Trying to cash in on Richard's prestige, no doubt. I know the family. Vulgar, *nouveau riche*. Oil money, I believe. Let's hope we've heard the last of her!"

Why is she going on like this with me? Paul wondered. It wasn't like Maria to be so open with anyone, particularly with someone "outside the family." There's something more on her mind. When will she get to it?

"Paul, I'd like to ask a favor of you," she said at last. "You're Richard's closest friend, as well as his manager, and Susan seems to trust you more than she does any of us."

He wanted to tell her that he was no longer either of those things to Richard, but he waited, curious to hear what was on her mind.

"I'm troubled about that marriage. It's all the things I feared—distracting to Richard's work, demanding of his time and interest. It was a mistake to bring that child home. I know she's always a worry to him, whether he admits it or not. As for Susan, she's really quite unstable. So emotional! I hear things. Hear she's drinking too much. Hear she's restless. And that solitary trip she planned! Such nonsense! You know very well there'd be all kinds of talk if she went off by herself!"

He waited. What was she going to ask of him? To talk to them about their marriage? To save it or break it up? To convince them that Katie belonged in a special school? What did she think he was, a marriage counselor? But it turned out to be quite different.

"I'd like you to arrange an extended tour for Richard," Maria said. "Right away. To Japan, perhaps. I hear they pay astronomically for the appearance of American artists. Or if not there, at least to Europe. Somthing that will get him away for three or four months."

Paul was surprised. "I don't quite understand, Mrs. Antonini. There's nothng wrong with the idea of such a tour, from a career standpoint but what's the urgency?"

"It should think it's obvious," she said tartly. "This past year has been most distressing. Actresses, divorcées. Rumors about my son's irresponsible behavior and his wife's peculiarities. It would be wise to remove them from the scene for a prolonged period. My dear Paul, you read those notices of Richard's concert in Washington, He's *never* gotten such poor reviews! Perhaps he deserved them, but more likely they were colored by his behavior, just as everything that will be written about him in this country for the next few months will also have some sly reference to his personal life. I want all this speculation to die down. It is having a serious effect on his professional reputation. No matter how brilliantly he performs in American cities, the press will find some reason to link his sloppy private life with his work. Fotunately, people forget. In a few months they'll have forgotten this unpleasantness in Washington. But we can't let him be badly and unfairly reviewed in the interim. It could damage his entire future."

So that was it! She didn't give a damn about Richard's personal happiness or Susan's. It was those unexpectedly bad reviews. She was only concerned that a snide press would confuse the man with the artist. She saw her life's work being destroyed by the critics. But why come to me? Paul wondered. Why doesn't she simply tell Richard that he has to disappear for the time being? God knows she's never been reticent before about directing his career.

As though she read his mind, Maria said, "You're probably wondering why I don't just go straight to Richard with this solution. I'll tell you frankly, Paul. Richard's always been the most difficult of all my children, and he's worse since his marriage. He's defensive and stubborn. If the suggestion came from me, he might be just mulish enough to reject it so he could try to prove me wrong. Susan has too much influence over him. I told him long ago what complications marriage brought. Look at that business with Katherine! He should never have permitted that child to be taken out of the school. He even thinks Susan has

done more for him than he has for her. He told me so himself. I'm having a
very hard time getting through to him lately and I don't wish to engage in an
argument with him about this. Coming from you, he'll accept it. From me, he'll
think it's overreaction.''

Paul couldn't have been more surprised. It was totally out of character for
Maria to admit she might fail in some demand on her children. I can't imagine
her accepting the idea that someone else could be more influential! How angry
she must be that Richard's work could be questioned. But how much more she
hates Susan. She's never gotten over that marriage. In the end, everything comes
back to that. She doesn't really blame Richard for anything. She honestly thinks
that Susan and Katie have caused all his troubles. How extraordinary that people
see only what they wish to see, believe only what reinforces their own convictions.

"Mrs. Antonini, I'm sorry I can't do what you want. I gather Richard hasn't
told you that I've resigned. The trip to Washington was my last one.''

There was a moment of stunned silence. "Resigned? Paul, you can't mean
that! Richard needs you!''

"Thank you, but he'll get along. There are any number of good managers
who'd be delighted to handle him.''

"But you've been much more than a manager. You're like family.''

God forbid, Paul thought. "I'll be sorry to leave him, Mrs. Antonini, but it's
really for the best.''

"But why? Is it money? If so, we surely can set that straight.''

"No, it's not money.''

"Then what? You never had problems all the years you worked together. It's
Susan, isn't it? She's interfering, is that it? We can put a stop to that, Paul. I've
suspected all along she's had too much say in Richard's business decisions.
That's not a wife's job. She'll have to be made to understand that.''

He was glad this was a telephone conversation so she couldn't see his face.
Of all people to talk of a wife staying out of her husband's career, Maria was
the last one to criticize. She'd manipulated Giovanni through most of his life.
But we don't see ourselves, Paul thought again. Not as we really are. No
imperfections show. Interfere? Susan? It was laughable. All she wanted was
anonymity, especially where Richard's career was concerned. Everything had
been forced on her. By them. By me.

"Susan isn't the problem. In fact," he lied, "neither is Richard. It's simply
that I need a change. I've only had one job in my whole life, Mrs. Antonini.
It's time I moved on.''

"Is there nothing I can do to change your mind?''

"I'm afraid not. It's flattering of you to ask.''

"Richard must be terribly upset.''

"No," Paul said. "He took it quite well. In the long run, he knows it will
be best for all concerned.''

He heard anger creep into her voice. "I must say, Paul, I think you might
have told me this before I confided so trustingly in you! It wasn't very honorable
to let me expose my anxieties and my plans, knowing you were going to leave.''

"You needn't worry, Mrs. Antonini. I've had a great deal of experience in
being discreet these past years. Your secrets are quite safe with me.''

"Goodbye, Paul," she said, and hung up before he could answer.

He slowly hung up the receiver on his end. Poor Susan, he thought. I've added another burden to those she already has. Now she'll be blamed for still another inconvenience: my leaving. There'll be one more black mark against her in Maria's book. Goddammit, why does everything I do end up backfiring against the only woman I've ever cared for? He wondered again what Susan would do. If only she'd leave that bastard! If only she'd give me a chance. He wondered how Maria would sell Richard on the idea of an extended tour. She'd find a way. He had to admit it was a good idea for Richard to keep a low profile for a while and this was a neat solution. Let the smoke die down. Let the Dolly Johnsons and Sylvia Sloans be forgotten. Let the beautiful couple travel together around the world. Paul shook his head. What was the point? It would be only a temporary reprieve. Richard has been on his good behavior before, but he was incapable of staying on it. They could send him to Outer Mongolia and he'd get into trouble. He must enjoy the danger and defiance. He was a complex, quixotic human being, this talented creature called Richard Antonini. In his own crazy way, Paul grudgingly admitted, the damned fool probably loved his wife even while he was being unfaithful to her. The other women had no real meaning. He supposed Susan knew that. He supposed it was why she stayed with him in spite of all the terrible things he'd done to her.

Or maybe, Paul forced himself to admit she was so much in love with Richard that she couldn't do anything about it. He tortured himself with visions of her moving back into the bedroom with her husband, fantasized her passionate response to sex, seeing himself in Richard's place. He knew how she would feel in his arms, how soft and fragrant her skin would be, how gentle but eager her touch. They would come together slowly, rapturously . . .

"Susan!" he said aloud in the empty apartment. The sound of his own voice startled him. God help me, they've got me talking to myself! I'm right to make the break now, before it gets worse. I hope I never see the Antoninis again. *None* of them.

Chapter 20

"THE WASHINGTON AFFAIR," as many of those involved came to think of it, had unexpectedly far-reaching effects. It reinforced the bitterness of some, saddened others, forced at least one to do some deep and painful soul-searching.

Paul Carmichael and Leon Armstrong, in different ways, viewed the circumstances of the accident with heightened cynicism. To Paul, it was confirmation of the rightness of his decision to resign. After he'd blurted out the angry words in the car, he'd been almost sorry, During the evening, before the frantic message from Richard, he'd thought seriously of reconsidering. Maybe he was a fool to throw away this good life in which he'd invested so many years. But after the Dolly Johnson business, he knew he had to get away from the man.

To Leon Armstrong, the discreet payment of fifty thousand dollars by Antonini's lawyers was proof of the pianist's guilt, proof it would otherwise have been almost impossible for the widower to substantiate. He was sure Richard was drunk, but there was no way to prove it. The man and woman in the other car had been whisked away by ambulance while Armstrong was in shock. At the inquiry, Leon could not honestly testify to anything that disputed Richard's story. But he knew. He knew people like that got away with things the average man could not. Money could not replace the loss of his wife and child, but it could ensure the remaining boy's education and ease some of the financial pressure Leon had labored under all his life. He knew it was "hush money" but it was a windfall of undreamed-of proportions and he took satisfaction in knowing that it was motivated by fear of disclosure. He took the payoff sullenly, realistically, smiling inwardly at the idiocy of the man who paid it.

Susan found it all painful and sad. She only guessed at the truth. She didn't ask, didn't want to know for certain. Strangely, she was not angry about Dolly Johnson, not even hurt as she'd been when she learned of Richard's other women. She supposed she'd reached the point where nothing surprised her. A kind of numbness had set in. All she felt was this heavy despair, this utter weariness as she contemplated the future. She'd meant it when she told Richard she was through. How much humiliation and unhappiness was she expected to endure? And yet it was as though she was incapable of making a move, too drained to go forward with her plan to divorce him, too exhausted to figure out where she and Katie would live afterward, how she alone would set up a household that revolved around a child who needed so much special care. For the next few weeks she did nothing. Wordlessly, she moved into the guest room in the apartment, spoke politely and almost impersonally to her husband when the need arose. She moved like one in a dream and she drank more than ever, recognizing the need to escape, welcoming the oblivion, not particularly caring who knew. Paul's departure added to her unhappiness. She realized how much she depended on him, how much she liked him and would miss his comfort and understanding. She thought of going to see him and decided against it. What would she say to him? That he shouldn't leave Richard when that was precisely what she, herself, planned to do? She knew how Paul still felt about her. It was the kind of thing a woman sensed. She didn't know how she felt about him. She found him enormously appealing, but that wasn't love. God help me, Susan thought, I'm still in love with Richard, even knowing what a faithless, self-involved, thick-skinned creature he is. In the strict moral sense of the word he is even—she flinched from the idea—guilty of murder. Accidentally or not, he's responsible for the death of a woman and a child the same age as his own. Why do I go on living with such a man? Why can't I stir myself to leave him? What am I waiting for? A miracle? Richard seemed so subdued these days, so chastened. But I mustn't be deceived by that. It's only temporary, as his other periods of "repentance" have been. He won't change. He can't.

She would have been heartened if she'd known the self-examination Richard had been going through since the accident. Instead of fading from his mind, as other scrapes had, he lived with a steady recollection of that dreadful night. He relived the horror in his dreams, thought about it even when he was awake. It was more terrible than anything that had ever happened to him. The affairs he'd had since his marriage had been wrong, of course. They'd hurt Susan and he was sorry about that. But never before had he been responsible for taking the lives of innocent people, and never before had he stopped to take a harshly critical look at himself. He didn't like what he saw: a playboy pianist who was no longer a boy and who had no right to play games with the lives of others. It's time you grew up, Richard, he told himself. Time to be a man and a serious arrist. Time to assume your responsibilities as a husband and a father. You've been the "little prince" too long. It was unbecoming, at thirty-five, to go on being carefree and thoughtless. He was no longer the "debutantes delight,' as he'd still unconsciously thought himself to be until the Washington affair. I deserve to lose Susan, he thought. I don't know why she's put up with everything as long as she has. But he prayed she wouldn't leave him. She was the only woman who mattered to him, the only one who ever had or ever would. Maybe he could convince her that he was determined to change, if only she'd stay. Maybe she'd give him and their marriage one more chance if he could somehow prove to her that he could be dependable and considerate, that he was more her husband than Maria's son.

It was strange. He felt awkward in his wife's presence these days, unable to tell her what was on his mind. Her remoteness did not help. Neither did her drinking. He understood both and blamed himself, yet he was incapable of revealing his thoughts, of asking anything more of her. He wished there were someone in whom he could confide, someone who could even speak for him before it was too late. To whom would Susan listen? Her mother? Possibly. But more likely she'd pay attention to Kate Fenton, knowing her friend would be more dispassionate in her understanding. I don't know whether I dare approach her, Richard thought. I've never felt she liked me. Why would she come to my rescue now? No. It can't be Kate. Who then? Jacqueline? Of course. Susan was close to her sister-in-law and Jacqueline was more likely to believe in Richard's change of heart.

He went to see her the next day. It was the first time they'd met since the accident, and Jacqueline was surprised to see how unhappy her brother-in-law looked. She found herself feeling sorry for him, an unusual emotion where Richard was concerned. More surprising still, she was touched as he told her his thoughts about himself and Susan, and almost humbly asked her help in saving his marriage. Nonetheless, she had reservations.

"I don't think anyone can talk to Susan for you," she said dubiously. "I believe you. I really do. It took something drastic to snap you out of your adolescent behavior, but I'm sure this kind of thing would bring anyone to his senses. It was a terrible piece of carelessness, Richard. You'll live with that guilt forever. But some good came out of it. It forced you to take a hard look at yourself. I'm sure it wasn't an admirable view. I don't know whether people will believe it's changed you. I'm not certain Susan will. But you're the only one who can convince her. Nobody can be your proxy. If Susan wants to talk to me after you've told her the same things you've said here, then I'll back you all the way. But I won't plead your case. People have been shouldering your responsibilities far too long. This problem is of your creation and if you're serious about changing you'll see that the solution is also up to you."

"Yes, it is. You're right. I've always let other people bail me out of tight spots, whether it was Susan or Paul or Mother. I can't think that way any more."

Jacqueline nodded. "You'll make it. By the way, speaking of Maria, she tells me you're not going to play in the States for a while. Says you're going to do a long tour out of the country. Will Susan go with you?"

Richard shook his head. "Mother's wrong. She wants me to make a long trip, but I've already told her I won't. I'm through with running away. That's what it amounts to: lying low until people forget the gossip. I've done enough of that to last me a lifetime. No. I'm going to play the concerts already booked in this country. If the critics are influenced by my personal difficulties, I'll have to live with that. I'll just have to try to be so damned good at my work that they'll have nothing to harp on, at least about my performance."

"Good! About time you stopped acting like a windup toy that Maria can send in any direction she chooses! Does Susan know? I'd think that would be good evidence that you intend to be your own man."

"I haven't discussed it with Susan. I haven't had courage to talk to her about anything." He gave an almost embarrassed little laugh. "I guess I'm afraid that if we have a serious converation she'll tell me when she's leaving. It's the one thing I can't bear to hear."

"You have to face it sometime," Jacqueline said gently. "You can't live in suspense forever. Neither can she."

"I know. It's postponing the inevitable."

"Maybe not. Wasn't Susan going to take a little holiday alone just before that mess in Washington?"

Richard nodded. "She was going to Palm Springs for a rest."

"Why don't you encourage her to go now? Put her on a long leash, Richard. Let her get away from you and everything for a few days. I believe she'll think things out in the desert. Tell her what you feel. Ask her to take time to be alone and gather her thoughts. I have a hunch she'll come back to you."

He was almost pathetically eager to believe her. "Do you really think so, Jacqueline? Do you think she'll give us another chance?"

"She's hungry for honesty from you. God knows it's worth a try." She hoped she sounded more convinced than she felt. She wasn't at all sure Susan would try again. She'd had so many disappointments, suffered so many wounds. She's not as tough as I, Jacqueline thought. The only kind of marriage for her is an old-fashioned one. I don't know whether she'll believe Richard capable of that. Hell, I'm not sure I believe it. I want to, but deep down I'm wondering if he's sincere. He thinks he is, but can a man like that really repent? Maybe the Antoninis are all alike: constitutionally incapable of being good husbands. What makes me think this one is different from his father or his brothers? Just because he's momentarily humbled, maybe a litile scared, doesn't mean he's undergone a permanent transformation. I'm afraid that's what Susan will think, too. Can't blame her if she does. It would all be so easy if they could live as Walter and I do, separate but equal. But they can't. At least Susan can't.

Richard was getting ready to leave.

"Thanks, Jacqueline, for the good advice. I'll talk to Susan tonight, and I hope she'll come to see you after."

"Call me Ann Landers," she said flippantly. And then she sobered. "Good luck, Richard. I hope everything works out for you and Susan. If it does, you'll be the one who makes it happen. You'll have to do all the changing." She looked at him sharply. "It won't be easy."

"I know. But I want this."

We all want things we can't have, Jacqueline thought. You're finding that out for the first time, late in life. It must be a shattering experience.

"Can we talk?"

Susan looked at him over the rim of her after-dinner brandy glass. She was a little high, but not drunk. "Of course. What do you want to talk about?"

"Us," Richard said. "You and me and Katie. Our future together."

"Do we have one?"

"I hope so. I want us to very much, Susan."

"Really? That comes as news."

He began to pace the living room nervously. "I've given you a rotten time, right up to and including that business in Washington. I've been a lousy husband, a failure as a father. I told you that you were right to leave me. I guess you still are, but I'm hoping you'll change your mind. I've been doing a lot of thinking, a lot of growing up. I haven't slept much, going over my whole life, realizing how impossibly selfish I've been, thinking how much damage I've done. Susan, I want to be different. I intend to be. If you'll let me, I'll show you I can change, that I can be the kind of husband you deserve. I love you and I love Katie. I've come close, more than once, to blowing everything that matters. Maybe I've already blown it but I'm asking you, begging you for another chance. Things have become clear to me. Things I never even thought about before. Sure I've been influenced. By Mother. By a worldful of fawning idiots who made me feel like Superman. But I know now how I've wallowed in self-delusion. I see how impossible to live with I've been. I don't know how you've stood it this long, but I give you my solemn oath that I won't fail you again." He came and knelt down beside her. "Please. Please say we can try to make it work. Please believe I mean every word."

There's nothing I'd rather believe, Susan thought, but how can I? How do I know this isn't just another act you're putting on to get your own way as usual? I want to believe you so much, my darling, but I'm afraid you've destroyed my faith forever. Like that other little boy, you've cried "wolf" too often.

"I think you mean what you're saying," she answered. "At least right now. At this moment I know you're utterly sincere. But you speak of self-delusion. How do I know this isn't more self-delusion, Richard? You have the ability to convince yourself of anything you want to believe. Anything expedient to your own comfort. Where will all the lofty resolutions be a year from now? A month from now? When your remorse has faded, your remorse about me and, I'm sure, about those poor people who died, will you still feel the way you do right now? How can I believe that? Why should I feel so sure you've changed?"

He took her hand, looking at her pleadingly. "Because I have. I swear it."

Susan pulled back. "You've sworn so many things." Her voice was harsh. "What is your oath worth when you can put your hand on a Bible in court and swear to a pack of lies?" She felt him cringe. "I'm sorry," she said. "That was cruel. I didn't mean to say that."

"It's all right. It's only the truth. It was one of the things that made me stop and think. I was still saving my hide, Susan. I admit it. But no more. Even Mother can't make me crawl back into that protected, unreal life." He told her of Maria's plan for the tour and his rejection of it and the reasons for his rejection. "It isn't much," he said, "but it's something. A start. A few months ago I'd have jumped at the chance to avoid a lot of unpleasantness with the gossipmongers across the country. It was a big step for me, not to take the easy way out. It would be routine for most people to face the music, but it's never been routine for me. I'm not bragging about such a little accomplishinent. I'm only telling you because you know the old Richard couldn't have done it. I'm hoping it proves something to you."

She was surprised. He was quite right. The "old Richard" would have been obedient to his mother, would have been all too eager to run from hostility, public disapproval or criticism. It *was* something, she admitted. But was one gesture enough to erase the doubts in her heart and mind? Yes, said her emotions, No, said her reason. "I'm glad you made that decision," Susan said slowly. "It is a hopeful sign. But again, how long will this new strength last? How can I expect a metamorphosis in you? Can I repledge my life on the basis of one brave, manly move? I don't see how that's possible. Even as gullible as I am, I've been disappointed too often to believe in your rebirth."

"Give me time to prove it. Just say you won't get a divorce, at least for a while. Let me show you it's true. If I go back to my old ways, I swear I'll never ask for another chance. You can leave me and have anything you want. But you won't, darling, I'm betting my life on it. Because I'm going to earn your respect. I've never had that. Love, yes. But not respect. I've never been dependable, strong and protective. I'm going to be, if you'll let me."

Susan wavered. It was almost impossible to think he didn't truly mean what he said. "I don't know . . ."

Richard leaped at this first sign of hope. "Darling, at least think about it. Go on a little holiday alone as you planned. Rest and relax. Bridie will take good care of Katie while you're away. I'll even have a chance to get to know her. I want that, too. A week or so in Palm Springs will do you a world of good. And I'll be here waiting for you."

Some impulse made her say, "I didn't plan to go to Palm Springs. I was going to Las Vegas."

He looked startled. "Las Vegas? Why would you pick that place?"

"It was Kate's idea. She thought I should do something absolutely out of character for an Antonini. I agreed with her. I wasn't going to tell you where I'd be. I don't know why I have now. Maybe it's because I can't bear the idea of any more lies between us, not even over something as trivial as that."

"Las Vegas, Palm Springs, Los Angeles, who cares? Go where you want, any place, any time. I want your happiness, Susan. I want you back, dearest, so I can make up for some of the pain I've caused."

She'd never been able to refuse him anything when he was like this. "All right. I'll go for a week and make a decision. But I really want to be left alone, Richard. I'm not even going to use my real name. In fact, Kate and I decided I'd call myself . . ." She stopped, horrified by the coincidence.

He was in good spirits again. "Call yourself what? Or am I not allowed to know?"

"You have to know," Susan said slowly. "You might need to reach me in an emergency. I was going to call myself Mrs. Armstrong."

There was a moment of heavy silence. How strange Kate had picked out of thin air the name of the woman who, so soon after, was to die because of Richard. Susan was first to speak again.

"Kate said I should choose an initial that matched my luggage." She sounded dazed. "How horrible. Like an omen." I can't call myself that, she thought shuddering. My husband took her life and, God help me, I was going to take her name as well!

Richard understood. "I'm sorry, darling." He was very gentle. "How about another 'A' like Anderson or Allen?"

She shook her head. Dr. Marcus would probably say she was punishing herself. Maybe it was masochistic, but she didn't want to forget the real Mrs. Armstrong. She mustn't forget. It was important that she remember. "No," Susan said unexpectedly, "I'll stay with the first choice. Maybe if she'd lived, Mrs. Armstrong would have enjoyed going to Vegas in style." Her voice was bitter. "After all, what's in a name? *She* has no use for it any more."

The stewardess, pencil poised over clipboard, leaned over their seats in the first-class section of the plane. "Your name, please?"

Susan looked up from her book "Armstrong," she said firmly.

"First initial?"

"S."

"Thank you, Mrs. Armstrong." The young woman with the polished practiced smile (did she rehearse it every morning in front of the bathroom mirror?) turned to the man in the aisle seat.

"Tanner," he said. "Martin."

"Of course, Mr. Tanner. Nice to have you with us again. We'll be airborne in a few minutes. Would you care for a cocktail before lunch?"

Tanner silently deferred to his seatmate. Good-looking woman, he thought. Classy. It wasn't just the trappings that spelled money, the Hermes handbag, the Vuitton tote at her feet, the well-tailored, obviously expensive suit. Any rich broad could acquire those things with the help of *Harper's Bazaar* and a charge account at Saks Fifth Avenue. No, he'd drawn a real lady to sit next to on the flight to Vegas, She hadn't spoken a word since they boarded at Kennedy, had studiously applied herself to her reading, hadn't even looked up when he slipped into the place beside her. He was glad she wasn't one of the chatty traveling companions he sometimes cursed the airlines for pairing him with on the trip he took so often. He sometimes had to be downright rude to those talkative types. Not this one, Martin thought. I'd like to talk to *her,* but she's making it very obvious that the feeling isn't mutual, He noticed the diamond band on her left hand. Where is Mr. Armstrong? Maybe there wasn't one. Maybe she was widowed or divorced. He rather hoped so. It would be pleasant to have a companion like Mrs. Armstrong for a change. He was fed up with Vegas show girls. Hell, what was he thinking of? He was going to gamble and probably lay some gum-chewing, bare-breasted, mindless dame who worked in one of the clubs. He had no time for this cool customer, even if she was available.

"I'll have a double vodka on the rocks," Susan said.

Well, well. Eleven o'clock in the morning. Maybe the lady drank a little, Martin thought. Maybe she drank a lot.

"Scotch and water," he said, sitting tensely in his seat. The new issue of *Time* lay in his lap, but he didn't open it. He never really relaxed until the plane got off the ground. He'd heard that the first two minutes of any flight were the most dangerous. He only felt easy when the "No Smoking" sign went off. That meant the pilot felt they were up there to stay. Unobtrusively he crossed his fingers. He was superstitious. All gamblers were, and Martin Tanner made his living as a professional gambler. A good if somewhat erratic, living.

His companion had returned to her reading. She obviously was not a "white knuckle flier" as he was. Relaxed, withdrawn, composed. Not a care in the world he supposed. But why did she have those faint circles under her eyes? Maybe the lady was not as content as she seemed. He felt the plane gather speed, tensed as it left the ground, took a deep breath as it gained altitude and slowly unclenched his fists as it headed west and the warning signs were turned off. Almost immediately the stewardess brought their drinks, and as Susan reached over to accept hers, she looked directly for the first time into the eyes of Martin Tanner.

As he had appraised her as "classy," she now involuntarily thought of him as "dangerous." He was almost too good-looking, too expensively, casually dressed, too sure of himself, as he courteously took her vodka from the tray and handed it over with a faint knowing smile. She smiled politely in return, coolly, uninvitingly. She had no wish to start a conversation with this attractive man. For that matter, she wanted to talk to no one. She was seeking anonymity. She'd even used that spine-chilling alias to avoid recognition by anyone who might have heard of her or Richard or any of the Antoninis. She yearned only to be alone, to live an uncomplicated existence for the next week while she made up her mind about the rest of her life.

It was ridiculous to think her traveling companion could intrude on that plan. What was the matter with her? He hadn't spoken a word to her. Probably couldn't care less whether she talked or not. Certainly their paths would never cross when they left the airplane. Yet there was something in his eyes, in that half-smile that contradicted her rational thoughts. She felt, oddly, that he could see through her. Not just into her mind but right through her clothes. How crazy! She had the sensation of sitting naked next to a stranger! Sipping her drink, she went back to her book, but her mind was no longer on the printed page. She was aware that he was watching her and she felt an unwilling thrill of excitement. Automatically, she turned the unread pages, looking up only when the stewardess reappeared with menus.

"I don't care for lunch," Susan said, "but I would like another drink, please."

"You, too, Mr. Tanner?" the stewardess asked.

"No, thanks. I'll have the beef. Very rare." As she left he turned to Susan. "Don't blame you for hating airplane food," he said companionably. "Pure cardboard. Even at these prices."

Susan smiled politely, not raising her eyes.

The hell with her, Martin thought. Who does she think she is? Some damned society bitch, going slumming in Vegas. Probably going where she can stay drunk without anybody knowing or caring. He was so annoyed with her that perversely he refused to be rebuffed.

"Been to Vegas often?" he asked.

Susan looked up. "No. My first trip."

"Is that so? Where do you usually do your gambling?"

Her impulse was to end the conversation with a pleasant smile and a return to her book, but good manners prevailed. "I don't gamble. I'm going simply for a rest."

He gave a good-natured laugh. "A rest? Now that's what I call a switch! It's a twenty-four-hour marathon, don't you know that? Nobody sleeps there. There literally isn't a clock in the whole damned town! Forgive me. I know it's none of my business, but why in God's name would you pick Vegas for a *rest?*"

You're right, Susan thought. It's none of your business. She took her second drink, noticing he'd barely gotten through half of his first one. Why am I bothering to talk to you? I don't want to speak to anyone. She was surprised to hear herself answering pleasantly. "I've heard it's one place where nobody pays any attention to other people. That can be more restful than going to a health spa where one is constantly being fussed over, or a smart resort where you're bound to run into friends-of-friends. The fact is, Mr. . . ."

"Tanner. Martin Tanner."

"The fact is, Mr. Tanner, I don't intend to talk to anyone except waiters for the next week. I probably won't leave my hotel room. I won't even have to answer the phone because I don't know a soul in Las Vegas."

"I see. Sorry. Didn't mean to intrude." He picked up his magazine and began riffling through the pages.

God, how boorish I sound! Susan thought. The man is only trying to be pleasant. I'm so damned touchy these days. He just wants to pass the time in a little innocent conversation and I've come on like an utter snob. Or was there something more? There was something magnetic about Tanner, something excitingly different. It was the first time in years she'd met someone who exerted such physical appeal, who was so unmistakably sexy. She'd not felt like this since she met Richard. It was insane, but she knew why she was being so reserved. Martin Tanner had an animal-like quality to which she responded. It frightened her. As she had before, she thought, He's dangerous. But now she silently added, And I'm vulnerable.

"Forgive me," Susan said, "I know that sounded terribly rude." She held out her hand. "I'm Susan . . . Armstrong."

He took her hand. His was strong, warm as he held hers briefly. "Nothing to forgive," he said. "You've paid for your seat and your privacy. To tell you the truth, I don't even know why I imposed. Usually I hate talking to people on airplanes. Bloody bores, most of them. Traveling alone has its disadvantages that way, don't you agree?"

"I wouldn't know. I seldom travel alone. I'm usually with my husband."

"Oh. I see."

No, you don't, Susan thought. You don't see at all. "Actually, this is the first time I've been anywhere without him in more than six years. I needed a holiday and he . . . he couldn't get away just now." She gave a nervous little laugh. "They say separations are sometimes good for a marriage. Brief ones, I mean. Do you think that's true?"

You're in trouble, lady, Martin thought. You're running away, probably from a marriage you can't decide whether or not to continue. You're a sitting duck for a big adventure, whether you realize it or not. But when he spoke, his tone was deliberately offhand.

"I don't know. My only marital separation was permanent. Ended in divorce four years ago. Maybe my wife and I should have tried vacations alone first, if you believe that 'absence makes the heart grow fonder.' Personally, I've always leaned more toward the theory of 'out of sight, out of mind.' Who knows? Every case is different."

"Yes. I suppose it is." She felt more relaxed now. The second double vodka was beginning to take effect. "Do you have children?"

"No. Just a niece I'm crazy about. You have kids?"

"A little girl. Katie. Six last November. She's beautiful."

"Of course. She'd have to be."

Susan actually blushed. "She's in New York with her father and her nurse. She's being well taken care of while I'm away."

Martin looked at her carefully. Why was she feeling so guilty that she had to explain the child was in good hands? What was it with this beautiful woman who'd seemed so remote at first and now was almost overeager to talk? The drinks, he supposed. The infallible tongue-looseners. She was sipping the dregs of her vodka when the stewardess put his unappetizing lunch tray in front of him.

"You're right to turn down this food," Martin said again. "I should have done the same." He looked at Susan's empty glass. "Would you like another drink?"

"I really would, but isn't two all they'll serve?"

"You can have my second one. Besides, no problem. I'm a regular on this flight. The girls will bend the rules for me."

He watched as she downed her third cocktail. Three double belts before lunch! Jesus! It was enough booze to put a strong man under the table, but aside from making her less formal, all that alcohol didn't seem to have much effect. She was still clear-eyed and she spoke distinctly. She was used to plenty of booze, no doubt about that. The lady is a lush, Martin told himself. Too bad. What would make a woman like that drink so heavily? What was she trying to forget? She intrigued him. Maybe, he thought, she doesn't want to be alone quite as much as she says. Maybe this could turn out to be an interesting week after all.

Chapter 21

MARTIN'S WORLD WAS as totally alien to Susan as Richard's had once been; two spheres in which she'd suddenly set foot, knowing little about either. First the snobbish, inbred world of the arts, and now the wide-open slightly unsavory milieu of the professional gambler. She'd always assumed she'd live an orderly life, economically comfortable and intellectually middle-of-the-road. Instead, marriage had catapulted her into the realm of the rich and famous, an arena in which she was ill-equipped to do battle and one which had driven her to despair and, literally, to drink. She'd never fitted into Richard's world. It was as though everything conspired to keep her from becoming an accepted part of it. She did not have Maria's iron will, Jacqueline's worldliness, Mary Lou's self-absorption. She hadn't been able to cope with the demands, understand the eccentricities, adjust to the prerogatives of money and status as they were bestowed on the Antoninis.

Nor, she thought, would she ever feel at ease in Martin's atmosphere, as foreign to her in a totally different way as the one she'd left behind. She'd never seen anything like Las Vegas. The whole city seemed to be one huge playground, a tacky, tawdry, vulgar amusement park devoted to pleasure yet underlined with the grim and serious business of flirting with luck.

By the time they landed, Martin took it for granted she'd spend her trip with him, and she did not disabuse him of that idea. Why not? she'd thought defiantly, a little drunk. He's attractive and he knows his way around. Why should I sit moping in a hotel room, chewing over problems I'll never know how to solve? I don't know why I came here. In retrospect, Kate Fenton's idea of an "unlikely vacation" seemed stupid in the light of all that had happened since her friend originally suggested it. I could come to this decision as easily on Park Avenue as I could in a room at the Flamingo Hilton, Susan told herself. So, what the hell? As long as I'm here I may as well find out what this place is all about. And if anybody can show me, Martin Tanner can.

And what did Martin Tanner want in return? Three guesses, she thought. This was not the kind of man who'd settle for a platonic friendship. He wasn't desperate for companionship. He seemed to know everybody, from the croupiers and pit bosses in the gambling casinos to the maître d's in the special hotel dining rooms set aside for the convenience of the "big spenders." He'll expect me to go to bed with him. Will I? Can I? Do I want to? She didn't know. It had been easy enough to avoid it the night of their arrival. She'd been able to laugh off his suggestion that he come in for a nightcap as he took her to her room at three in the morning.

"Be a good boy," she'd said. "I have jet lag and I'm already drunker than I should be! See you tomorrow."

He hadn't made a fuss. He was quite sober, though he'd had a great many drinks during the evening, and he kissed her hand with exaggerated politeness.

"I'll accept that," he'd said. But then he'd given her his little smile and added, "For tonight." There was no misunderstanding the words. Tomorrow night there'd be no acceptable excuses.

And "tomorrow night" is here, Susan thought as she ran a tub and prepared to dress for dinner. Decision time.

She made a drink and took it into the bath with her, thinking irrelevantly how convenient it was that the oversized marble tub was shaped with armrests on which she could put the glass of vodka. She tried to relax, stretching full length in the warm water, slowly sipping the liquor and reviewing the past twenty-four hours.

Las Vegas, she mused, looked and sounded like a giant pinball machine, all bells and gongs and flashing lights. From the time the cab drove up "The Strip," flanked by garish hotels with their huge signs announcing the appearance of big-name entertainers, to the moment they'd entered her hotel lobby (which was barely a lobby as she knew one, but more an anteroom to the huge casino straight ahead), Susan had been openmouthed. She'd never seen so many people, heard such a constant buzz of voices and a current of strange noises. As far as she could see, there were blackjack and crap tables, roulette wheels, rooms for keno and rows of slot machines greedily awaiting anything from a nickel to a silver dollar. The loudspeaker never stopped paging someone. Grandmothers clutching paper cups full of dimes and quarters went through a bizarre ballet: drop in a coin, pull the lever, wait impassively for a winning combination, start over if it did not appear. ordinary-looking men and women sat motionless on high stools at the blackjack tables, conducting their serious play with few words. The big spenders threw dice and placed bets at the roulette wheels, sometimes, Martin told her, winning or losing thousands of dollars in an hour. Tired-looking young girls in short shirts made change for the slot-machine addicts and brought free drinks to the other players who accepted them without looking up from their "work." It was all intense and rather frightening and compulsive.

Martin was staying at Caesars Palace, but he had brought her to the Hilton and had taken her for a quick tour before she checked in. He watched, amused, as she surveyed the scene.

"It's incredible!" Susan said. "It's the middle of the afternoon!"

"Same at any hour. I told you. There are no clocks. Time doesn't mean anything here. Gamble when you can, eat when you must, sleep only when you're ready to drop. That's life in Vegas."

"But the people! Most of them look as though they can't afford to gamble."

"Most of them probably can't. They're dumb amateurs. Always sure they're going to make a killing. They don't know the odds. Or don't want to. Poor slobs. They save all year to come here and get rich. They refuse to believe it won't happen. Still," Martin said, "they love it. It's a helluva vacation. They gamble, see entertainment they'd never be able to see anywhere else for the price of a dinner, go home and tell the neighbors they really lived it up in Vegas! In their minds they've rubbed elbows with Frank Sinatra and Sammy Davis. They probably think they'll run into Howard Hughes playing roulette at The Sands." Martin laughed. "It's the Great American Dream Machine and even suckers are entitled to a go at it."

"Is it honest?"

"If you mean are the games rigged, they're not. No need to be. The odds are all with the House. Nobody gets cheated here, Susan. Nevada's damned sticky about protecting the greatest ongoing gold mine in the U.S.A."

She shook her head. "I can't get over it. It's unreal."

"Not for me," Martin said. "It's my living."

She stared at him.

"I gamble, lady. It's my profession. Do you mind?"

"No. Of course not. I mean, what business is it of mine how you earn your money? It's just that . . ."

"You've never known an underworld character before." Martin finished the sentence for her. "That's what you're thinking, isn't it? That I'm some kind of Legs Diamond or Bugsy Siegel? That I'm a mobster and you're my moll, like in the old movies?" Martin laughed again. "Don't worry. I'm so bloody respectable you can't stand it. I don't know what Mr. Armstrong does for *his* daily bread, but if he uses computers I use cards. It's just another kind of business and I'm damned good at it." He patted her cheek lightly. "Come on. You'd better check in and unpack. Take a little nap. I'll pick you up about eight-thirty and give you another look at life in Las Vegas."

He'd done just that. They'd dined quietly and elegantly in the reserved area at his hotel. "No tourist traps for us," Martin had said as they passed long lines of people waiting to get into the big showroom. "The peasants queue up for hours waiting to sit at long tables with thirty or forty strangers from Mule Shoe, Nebraska, and eat indifferent food while they gawk at the overpriced talent." He shuddered, "No way! If there's some special show you must see, we'll go at midnight. I have a special pass that will get us right in, not that I use it much. I prefer a quiet meal in a civilized room before I settle down at the tables. Will it bore you to watch me play?"

"No. I'll be fascinated."

"Maybe you'll bring me luck."

Susan sighed wistfully. "Don't count on it."

During the evening while Martin gambled, she wandered off from time to time, drink in hand, watching the people, inspecting the shops that sold everything from ugly souvenirs to expensive jewels and furs. She felt removed, almost disembodied. For fun she put five dollars' worth of quarters in a slot machine, won a few times, eventually put the whole lot back. That's what Martin means about the odds, she thought. If you stay at it long enough, you're bound to return whatever you win.

At three in the morning, he got up from the roulette table.

"That's it," he announced. She saw him hand some money to the croupier. The man nodded his thanks.

Martin casually put his arm around Susan, steering her out of the casino.

"Sure you weren't too bored? It must be dull when you don't gamble."

"I wasn't bored. Did you win?"

He nodded. "A couple of thousand."

She gasped. "A couple of thousand! Do you always do so well?"

"No. Sometimes I lose. Particularly if I get careless."

"You must make a lot of money every year." She stopped. "I'm sorry. That's rude of me."

"It's never rude to talk about money," Martin said. "It can buy you anything you want." He smiled. "Where would you like to go now?"

"I think I'll call it a night, if you don't mind. It's been a long day."

That's when they'd had the little exchange at the door of her room. It had been graceful, lighthearted. But it won't be again, Susan thought, as she lay in her tub. Tonight when he's through gambling Martin will have other ideas. I wish I knew whether I have courage for an affair. It would be so easy. One week. I'll never see him again. Jacqueline would think it a good idea. Therapeutic.

And God knows I owe Richard no fidelity after all he's done! I'm a grown woman. It could hurt no one. Maybe it could even make me feel something again. It's been so long since I've thought of myself as anything except Richard's wife, the mother of his child. Martin Tanner doesn't even know who I am. For all he knows, I could be an expensive whore. The thought amused her. In a way, she supposed, that's what she was to her husband: a sexy body he'd bought with his charm. Certainly he'd never really shared a life with her. On the surface, yes. But she didn't know the meteoric man she'd married. She didn't really comprehend his motivations or understand his constantly changing attitudes. She'd seen him in so many incarnations in a few short years. How real is this latest one? Susan wondered. Has he really "reformed?" Is there any chance for us at all?

I still love him, Susan thought hopelessly. I still want to believe in him, in spite of his lies. But something inside me also wants to hurt him, to pay him back for hurting me.

She climbed out of the tub and dried herself with a thick towel, looking critically at the image reflected in the big bathroom mirror. Hers was a young body, slim and firm, not even showing signs that she'd given birth. As though she were inspecting a nude in an art gallery, she took in every detail of the rounded breasts, the flat stomach, the well-shaped thighs. Naked, she walked into the bedroom and poured another drink. Maybe if she had enough vodka she'd lose her stupid inhibitions. Out of nowhere the thought crossed her mind that she wished it were Paul Carmichael with whom she probably was going to be unfaithful. Paul loved her, had always loved her. Gentle, patient understanding Paul should be taking advantage of this moment of defiance or weakness or desperation—whatever it was. It should be Paul who would be the instrument of revenge; not some stranger Richard would never know about.

I must be losing my mind, Susan thought.

"What do you hear from your wife?"

Richard looked at his mother from his place on her right at his parents' dining table. "She's only been gone three days," he said patiently.

"Hasn't she telephoned?"

"Yes, she called when she arrived to say she'd gotten there safely."

"And she hasn't been in touch since? Isn't she concerned about that child of hers?"

"*Ours*, Mother. Katie is *our* child, not just Susan's." Her needling annoyed him. "Damn it, can't you use their names? Must you always refer to them as impersonal objects?"

Maria arched her eyebrows. "Really, Richard, you're frightfully testy. I've never seen you so on edge. I'm afraid to open my mouth to you!"

From the other end of the table, Giovanni chuckled. His wife shot him an angry look but Richard smiled grimly. He knew all too well what his father was thinking. When Maria said she was afraid to "open her mouth" it was the prelude to a sermon delivered "for your own good." He followed the long-established format.

"I'm sorry, Mother."

"I should think you would be!" But she was mollified, ready to launch into a discussion of Susan's "abandonment" of him. "I can't think what's gotten into that young woman, running off to that dreadful place, leaving you to cope with her responsibilities! For that matter, Richard, I can't understand your permitting it! And she doesn't even care enough to find out what is happening in her own home while she's gallivanting about doing God knows what shocking things!"

He kept his temper. "I wanted her to have this little holiday, Mother. I told you that. I know Susan. She's much too good to do anything 'shocking' as you put it. I could have called her last night, but I don't want her to feel I'm checking up. She's earned a little peace and privacy, and she knows very well that between Bridie and me things are under control. She needed to get away. It's been hard for her these past years, and that mess in Washington was the last straw." In spite of his best efforts he felt himself getting angry. "My God, she hasn't *left* me! She's taking one lousy little week for herself. Is that so terrible? I suppose you'd like me to divorce her for desertion and have her declared an unfit mother!"

Maria was quiet for a moment. Then she said, "You said it, Richard; I didn't."

Her son and husband stared at her in disbelief. Giovanni was the first to recover.

"My dear, I'm sure you don't mean that the way it sounded. You may not be overly fond of Susan, but you must admit she's been a loyal wife to Richard and a devoted mother to little Katherine."

"I also admit she's a troublemaker," Maria retorted. "She's connived to alienate her husband from his family, to embarrass us all by requiring psychiatric care. She's insisted upon this ridiculous burden of keeping a deaf-mute child at home. She's courting some ugly publicity by running off to Las Vegas alone. And," Maria went on bitterly, "as if all that weren't enough, the whole world knows she's become an alcoholic and God knows what she'll do next! I've tried to get along with her, but she makes it impossible. She's brought Richard nothing but unhappiness. She's the one who's forced him into some of those impetuous, ill-advised acts. If he had a suitable wife and healthy children, things like that unpleasantness in Washington never would have occurred. I knew the first minute Richard brought her up to the country that she was all wrong for him. But he wouldn't listen. She had him hypnotized, even then. Just as I'm sure she's influenced him in this unwise decision to continue with his concerts here instead of taking a long tour out of the country. I believe she gets a fiendish pleasure out of making people gossip and laugh at us behind our backs!"

Richard abruptly pushed his chair back from the table and stood up, trembling with rage. "Stop it!" he shouted. "Stop it right now, Mother! I won't listen to any more of this! You're talking about my wife. The mother of my child. You hate her because she wants us to have a life of our own. You can't stand anyone trying to wriggle out from under your thumb. You're furious that I won't run away from criticism. That's what this is all about, isn't it? You're offended by anyone who has the guts to go against your wishes!"

"Richard!" Giovanni interrupted. "Calm down! I won't permit you to talk to your mother that way! She's devoted her life to her family. She wants what's best for you."

"No, Father, she wants what she *thinks* is best for me. For all of us. She didn't want me to marry, or leave home or be anything but her little boy. She'd like to turn me into you, Father—dependent on her for every thought and action. She knows she's met her match in Susan and it's driven her wild. It's also damn near destroyed us. She made me believe that I wasn't subject to the rules other people live by. Susan won't stand for that. It's taken me a long time to see that she's right.''

Maria slowly rose from her place. The color drained from her face and her voice cut like a knife. "This is the thanks I get for bearing you," she said slowly. "This is the reward for all the years of devotion. I think you'd better go home, Richard. I don't think I want to see you again for a long, long time."

The ingrained habit of submission took over; the implanted guilts returned as Richard heard the quiet words. My God, he thought, I must be a monster! How could I talk to her like that after all she's done for me! She meant well. She still does. What kind of ingrate am I? I forget she's getting old, that she's been desperately ill, that she loves me so much she refuses to believe, even now, that anything rotten I do is my own fault. He went to her side, penitent as a small boy.

"Forgive me," he apologized. "I didn't mean to hurt you. I'm going to straighten things out, Mother. You're right: Susan should come home. I'll call her tonight. And I'll think about scheduling that tour. It's probably wise."

"Don't do things to please me, Richard. It's not my future I'm concerned with. I have very little left."

"Don't say that. Look at the recovery you made. Besides, I'm not doing this for you. I'm doing it because I want to. I'll work it out," he said again. "I promise."

She turned away without answering. Neither her son nor her husband saw the tiny flicker of a triumphant smile on her face.

It was eleven o'clock New York time when Richard entered his apartment. Eight in the evening in Las Vegas. He placed a call to Susan Armstrong. Her voice sounded strange when she answered, as though she were expecting someone else.

"Susan? Darling? How are you?"

There was a pause as though she were gathering her thoughts, and then she said, "Richard? Why are you calling? Is something wrong? Is Katie all right?"

"Everything's fine, except I miss you. Are you having fun?"

No, she thought, I'm not having fun. I'm hating myself. I loathe what I did last night. Loathe the memory of Martin Tanner's body on mine. Loathe the fact that it was glorious and I loved it. At the moment. Today I'm ashamed and disgusted with myself. And yet I'm dressing to meet him again. He was an expert lover, Martin Tanner. For a little while he'd made her forget everything— Richard, Katie all the things that mattered. For a while she'd been primitive, an animal and very drunk. But not so drunk she didn't know what she was doing. Not so drunk she couldn't remember every sensuous gesture, every tempting, tingling motion, every second of the ultimate fulfillment. And, shamed as she was, she wanted more. She supposed she knew now how Richard felt when he went to bed with a woman. It had no deep meaning. There was no love. It was blatantly physical, exquisite in its variety, tantalizingly dangerous. She saw how an act could be regretted and repeated. Weirdly, her unfaithfulness to Richard made her understand him for the first time. Made her, in a strange way, love him more. A sob rose in her throat.

"Susan? Are you there?"

"Yes. I'm here." Her voice was blurred. Even these few words come out with difficulty.

She's drunk, Richard thought unhappily. God help us, she's probably been locked in that hotel room all this time, drinking herself senseless.

"I asked whether you were having fun."

"No. Not fun. Have you been having fun?"

"No, sweetheart. Anything but. Susan, come home tomorrow, won't you? I know it's selfish, but I want you here. The apartment is terrible without you." He tried to laugh. "I'm getting a taste of what it's like for you when I go away. No good, love. I'm rattling around in all this space."

"How is Katie?" she asked again.

"I told you. She's fine. Bridie took her to the Children's Zoo in Central Park. She had a wonderful time."

"Why didn't *you* take her? *I* always take her. I wish you'd spend more time with her, Richard. She needs you."

"I know. I will, darling. I'm going to do a lot of things differently. We're going to have a different life. Please believe that. Don't take any more time to think about it. Just come home to me. Forgive me for all the awful things I've done. I know you can, sweetheart."

Yes, I can, Susan thought. But can I forgive myself?

"All right" she said slowly. "I'll come home tomorrow."

He was jubilant. "Wonderful! Call me when you've booked your flight. I'll meet you."

"That will be nice."

"Have a good evening, darling, and get to bed early."

It was so unconsciously ironic she nearly laughed aloud.

Martin looked baffled when she told him at dinner that she was leaving in the morning.

"Has something happened? Why are you cutting your trip short?"

Susan smiled. "Yes, something happened, Martin. *We* happened."

He took her hand. She looked so beautiful in this low-cut beige chiffon dress. She was a desirable, sensuous woman and she'd been wild in bed. He didn't want her to go. Not that he had any long-range plans. He was adept at extricating himself from sticky situations with women who fell in love with him. He'd never marry again. But Susan Armstrong was someone he'd planned to see more of, not only here but in New York. He hoped she hadn't read any romantic meaning into last night. He assumed this was not her first affair. Mr. Armstrong, whoever he was, must have had other rivals for his wife's affection. Still, why was she running away? He returned her smile.

"We 'happened' very good, as I remember."

She was straightforward. "It *was* good. You're a marvelous lover, by my limited ability to judge. You're only the fourth man I've ever slept with, Martin.

Two boys before I was married. And since then, no one but my husband.'' She withdrew her hand. ''Don't look so upset. You didn't seduce me. I wanted to be with you. I still do. But I won't be again. I can't handle this kind of thing. God knows I'd love to be modern and 'sensible' about it! I'd love to enjoy sex for its own sake. My husband always has. I never understood before how he could want to be with anyone but me, because I know he loves me. I can understand it now, but that doesn't wipe away my guilt. And it probably won't make it any easier for me to forgive him if he does it again. Maybe you've made me a little more 'liberated' in my thinking, and I thank you for it but I don't *want* to get used to this new freedom. It confuses me. And I don't need that. I'm mixed up enough. I had to see you and say 'thank you.' It's been wonderful. If I were unattached I'd follow you from Las Vegas to San Juan. But that's not the way it is, or ever will be. Goodbye, Martin. Take care of yourself.''

''Wait!'' he said as he stood up. ''Where do I find you in New York. I want to see you again, Susan. You want to see me, too.''

''I may want to, but I won't. And you can't find me.''

She left the restaurant abruptly, before he could answer, and went back to her room. The telephone rang half a dozen times during the evening but she didn't answer. She couldn't trust herself not to let him come up for one last forbidden night. Methodically, she drank her way through half a fifth of vodka and finally, sometime after midnight, fell into a deep sleep, looking forward to tomorrow and half-welcoming, half-dreading it. She dreamed she confessed her adultery to Richard and when he answered he'd turned into Maria, who grabbed Katie and vanished with her into the night, the child screaming her mother's name. She woke in a cold sweat, turned on the bedside light and looked at the clock. Four A.M. She already had a terrible hangover. She tried to forget the nightmare. How insane that she should have dreamed of Katie screaming her name. Little Katie, who could barely make a coherent sound! She considered taking a sleeping pill and decided against it. She had to be up early to catch the plane to New York. Richard was waiting. They were all waiting.

Chapter 22

SHE SAW BOTH of them the minute she came through the doorway from the plane. Richard was searching for her in the crush of people racing toward the baggage area as though they actually expected their luggage to get there ahead of them. She waved at him and he returned the signal, then pointed down to a tiny figure beside him, almost invisible in the crowd. He'd brought Katie to the airport. Susan was unreasonably delighted. It seemed a good omen, as though his willingness to appear in public with his child indicated a change of attitude about many things.

Susan rushed to them, kissed Richard swiftly and then picked up Katie, holding her so their faces almost touched.

''Hello, my love,'' she said clearly. ''Remember me?''

There was a big smile. ''Muh-muh.''

"Yes, Kit-Kat. Yes, darling. Mama. Mama is home. Did you have a good time with Daddy?"

"Day-de," Katie said confidently. "Purg."

Susan looked inquiringly at Richard. "Park? She's saying park."

"Right. We went this morning."

"You and Katie?"

He laughed. "Don't look so amazed. You told me we should. As a matter of fact it was fun. That brat of ours is absolutely fearless. She led me a merry chase, up and down rocks and around trees. Damned if I know how you and Bridie keep up with her!"

She was touched. "Thank you for doing that."

"Don't thank me. I should have done it long ago. I must confess, though, I was afraid to face it alone. I took Bridie along for moral support."

Susan wondered why she felt relieved. Didn't she trust the child with her own father? What nonsense! She had to start thinking of them as a threesome. If they were to start over, Katie would have to be a shared project. She understood that now. Just as she felt she understood a great many other things that had eluded her. When she'd heard Richard's voice on the phone she'd known that she wanted to come back to him, no matter what. She deeply regretted the night with Martin Tanner. No. She didn't. I learned something from that, she thought. I learned that unfaithfulness can happen from boredom or disappointment or hostility. That it's a means of blotting out other things. Like liquor is. I also learned it isn't for me, but the experience has made me less self-righteous.

A long, long time ago, her roommate had tried to tell her that female sexual attitudes had to change, along with other demands for equality. Evie was right, she supposed. Yet I won't do it again, Susan vowed. I can't handle it. Right now I feel terribly guilty. I wish I could confess to Richard, but he'd never understand. He's still a double-standard man.

She could see why married people so often felt compelled to admit their affairs. It was a selfish thing, as though by telling the injured party it became his problem, shifting the weight of guilt from the wrongdoer to the wronged.

Whether he intended to or not, that's how Richard had made her feel when he told her about his infidelities. She'd been angry and hurt, but her primary emotion had been a sense of failure, as though she weren't enough of a woman to keep him satisfied. I've always felt inadequate, Susan thought as the three of them walked through the airport Richard chatting easily about trivial things. Perhaps I've even blamed myself for Katie, for giving Richard a flawed child. Her grip tightened on Katie's small fingers contentedly entwined in her own. That's stupid. I'm not at fault. No one is. Why have I been punishing myself and punishing Richard? We're both simply human. I can thank Martin Tanner for teaching me that. I knew I wasn't tackling an easy project when I married this man. Did I really think I could change him? How young and foolish I was! He's been bad, but why did I expect him to be good?

"I got a lot of things straightened out in my head on this little trip," Susan said suddenly.

He didn't ask what they were. Her tone told him she was home to stay. That was enough.

In a way, it was as though they turned back the clock to the early days. Susan recognized her potential drinking problem and took pains to control it so that her senses, no longer dulled, responded to Richard's heightened affection. She almost put the Martin Tanner episode out of her mind and devoted herself contentedly to her husband and child. She would not dwell on the past—not Richard's or her own.

These were good days, the best ever. Together, they took Katie to the park, enjoyed prebedtime romps with her. One day, Susan even talked Richard into going to the nursery school to see how well Katie fitted into this environment. Another day, they had had a long talk with Edith Chambers, who was highly encouraging.

"Katie's doing remarkably well," the speech therapist said. "I know it seems slow to you, but believe me she's making exceptional progress."

"Will she ever speak normally?" Richard asked.

"Probaby not, Mr. Antonini. Not in the way you mean. But she'll become more and more intelligible. She'll manage nicely. Her lip-reading is extraordinary. You've done a great job on that with the home training. I think she understands as much, maybe more, than most hearing children her age."

"But she'll never hear." Richard sounded resigned.

"No. At least very little." The teacher hesitated. "I know what you're thinking. Music is your life."

"Music is my career," Richard said. "My wife and child are my life."

He seemed depressed after that visit. "I let that woman give me credit for something I don't deserve. I haven't helped Katie at all. I try, Susie. But I don't do well at it. I don't think I ever can. It just doesn't come naturally to me."

"It doesn't come naturally to any of us. We expect people to react and respond in the way Katie can't. But you're doing so much better. I know how you're trying."

He shook his head. "It's no good. I'll never be a good father to a child who requires so much patience and understanding." He tried to smile. "Well, it could be worse. At least we get A for effort even if we struck out at our first and only time at bat."

He wasn't talking about the failure he considered they'd had with Katie. He was saying there'd never be another baby. I didn't want another one either at first Susan thought. But I do now. I want to give Richard a child he can relate to. It must be terrible for him to realize that the best he has to offer literally falls on deaf ears . . . that the one he most wants to be proud of him can never hear his music.

She was about to discuss the idea of a second baby, but she stopped. He'd never consent to it even though the doctors had assured her the odds were good that she'd have a normal child next time. Do I dare, Susan wondered? He seemed so happy about Katie in the beginning. A whole, healthy child would bring us such joy. He might be upset at first, but later he'd be delighted to have that "little musician" they'd hoped for.

Six weeks later the doctor confirmed she was pregnant. She was delighted and simultaneously worried about how to tell Richard. She chose a quiet moment in bed after love-making, knowing he was deliciously weary and full of tenderness for her.

"Darling, I have some good news."

"He lay still, eyes closed. "What?" He was half-asleep.

"I'm pregnant."

He sat bolt upright. "Pregnant! Susan, you can't!"

"Why not? There's no medical reason why we should't have another child. The odds are all in our favor. It will be wonderful for us and for Katie, too. She should have brothers and sisters. I'm so happy about it. Please, you be happy too."

He stared at her in the dim light. "You didn't even discuss it with me. You know how I feel about that risk!"

"I know. I should have discussed it with you, but I was sure you'd never agree. Have faith in me, Richard. I'm so certain this child will be perfect. I want to do this for you more than any other reason. I want to give you someone who perhaps will carry your genius as well as your name. We're really getting our life together after so many disappointments. Things are going to be good for us, better when we have another baby."

He sank back on his pillow, half-disturbed, half-happy. It was true he'd like to have a child he was proud of. But how could Susan be so sure they'd not have another like Katie? They couldn't stand that, either of them. It was foolhardy. Even the slightest chance of a repetition was too much. He imagined what Maria would say when she heard, especially since he'd half-promised to make the tour she was so dead-set on. That idea would have to be canceled now. He couldn't leave a pregnant wife and he couldn't drag one halfway around the world. Damn!

"Richard?" Her voice was almost timid.

He turned and looked at her. "I wish you hadn't done it, Susan."

A tear rolled down her face and it was like a reproach. He took her in his arms. "All right, baby," he said. "I trust you. Scared as I am, I'm glad, too. Just keep injecting me with doses of your faith. God knows I need 'em!"

She clung to him, feeling relieved and confident. There was no medical reason for him to resist another child, but he had every right to be angry that she hadn't consulted him. He'd been upset about that. It was only natural. Or was it? Was there something more, something she didn't know? Was there something in his family he hadn't told her? Some history of this kind of thing that he'd kept secret? Was that why he was so afraid?

"I do not believe it," Maria said flatly.

"It's true, Mother. Susan and I are going to have another child. And we're delighted."

"You're insane. Both of you."

They were alone in her drawing room. Richard tried to placate her. "The doctors assure us there's only the remotest possibility this baby will be impaired."

"Doctors are asses. So, it seems, are concert pianists."

Irritated, he blurted out the truth. "As a matter of fact, I didn't know Susan planned to get pregnant again. It came as a total surprise to me."

Maria raised her eyebrows. "I might have guessed. So you've been tricked again, have you? Just as I was. Like mother, like son. Your wife is as devious as your father. Incredible how you refuse to recognize that, Richard! The first pregnancy was deliberately done to get you out of this house. Now I suppose this one is to keep you from going on that long tour. Very clever of her. Very stupid of you to allow it.''

"Susan doesn't even know I was reconsidering the tour. Anyway, I didn't promise. I only said I'd think about it.''

"Don't quibble over terms. You were going to go before this happened.''

"Maybe so. What difference? I can't go now.''

"No,'' Maria said, "obviously not. Unless, of course, you come to your senses and insist Susan terminate this selfish pregnancy. I don't quite know why she's done this to you. Perhaps she was afraid of losing you.''

"That's not true, Mother. We've been closer than ever since I convinced her to come home for good. It was I who was afraid of losing her when she went to Las Vegas.''

"Don't be a fool, Richard. She never had any intention of divorcing you, not any of the times she pretended she did. Pity she didn't, instead of putting one impediment after another in your way. She doesn't want you out of her reach. Any moderately intelligent person could see how she operates. Unplanned pregnancies, psychotic behavior, alcoholism. My God! How much can you put up with?''

Richard's face darkened. "How much can I put up with? How much has *she?* Susan didn't wish for Katie's condition! What woman would't have been on the verge of a breakdown when we took her child from her? What woman wouldn't have turned to drink or drugs or anything she could find to give her courage when we asked her to mouth a lot of embarrassing statements to protect the family name? Tell me, Mother, what woman wouldn't have long ago given up on a husband who couldn't keep his hands off of anything in skirts?''

Maria's voice was scornful. "I'll tell you one woman who wouldn't. *This* one." She let the words sink in. "You know some of the things I've gone through. But I had discipline and intestinal fortitude. I was willing to make sacrifices for your father and for all of you. I didn't think about my own precious 'happiness.' There were bigger things at stake. I knew that. Susan refuses to learn it and you refuse to hear what I've been saying for years. If you permit her to saddle you with another child, handicapped or not, you're a blind, spineless, unintelligent caricature of a man. You deserve to be tricked into fatherhood over and over again. You deserve to be bogged down with a domineering wife and a houseful of demanding children. Go ahead. Play father. Play devoted husband. But don't also expect to play genius. Those things don't go together.''

As always, she could outtalk him, muddy his mind with reminders of the past and dire predictions of the future. She could make him feel small and foolish and inarticulate in the face of her strong opinions and facile phrases. He was so torn. Who was right? Who was wrong? Music was everything to him, he told himself. Far more than babies who were begun without his knowledge or consent. Babies who didn't hear or speak. He didn't need them. Why was he giving in so easily to Susan's idea of a "perfect marriage?" Damn her, anyway! Why was he taking himself into something he didn't want? He didn't have to. He was Richard Antonini.

Troubled, he walked slowly home, considering the things Maria had said. It was true. Susan hadn't consulted him on either conception. His children were as unwanted as he had been. And his wife had been a problem in so many ways. Defying him by bringing Katie home when she should have been left where she was, in a safe and secure atmosphere. That was wrong. It had always been wrong. Just as it had been wrong of her to constantly threaten to leave him, making him nervous. In his mind, she was responsible for those bad notices in Washington after the accident. Susan with her accusations and her damned injured pride! He wouldn't be surprised if Paul knew what a bad influence she was on Richard's work. He'd probably seen the handwriting on the wall and left before he found himself handling a failure.

It was all irrational and meteoric, but disquieting thoughts grew from the seeds Maria had planted over the years. Hell, even yesterday's recording session had been a near-disaster. It had taken frustrating hours to complete, something that never used to happen. Normally, he would have sailed though it easily and confidently. But he'd faltered time and again, made errors a first-year student wouldn't have. And all because his mind was on what he'd learned the night before. He was full of fears about another child, full of resentment at Susan for doing this to him. He saw that now. Goddammit, the personal side of his life *was* interfering with the artistic one. That had to stop. His mother was right. The wife of an artist had to bear up under inconveniences and eccentricities. It was her job to nurture a special talent, not go to pieces under every damned little pressure, the way Susan had all their married life. Jacqueline and Mary Lou never gave Walter and Sergio the problems Susan gave him. His brothers hadn't chosen neurotic, unmanageable wives. Why had he? Why did he have to fall in love with a woman who wouldn't conform? No longer afraid of rejection, he felt suddenly determined. No more babies. No more giving in to Susan on things he didn't agree with. No more being used. If anyone did the using, it would be he.

The innocent victim of his rage was lying contentedly on a chaise, reading, when Richard barged into the bedroom. Susan looked up at him lovingly.

"Have a good visit, darling?"

He didn't answer. He was looking at her as though he hated her. The familiar knot in her stomach told her there was a storm brewing. She pretended not to notice his expression.

"How are your parents? Did you tell them our news?"

His voice came out as a vicious accusation. "Why do you always start a baby without asking me? I've been thinking about it. My first instinct was right. We can't have another child."

For a moment she was speechless. These past weeks had been so good. Even two nights ago he'd seemed reconciled to her pregnancy. True, he'd had doubts. But she'd thought they were momentary. Of course. Maria. She of the powerful influence, the insatiable jealousy. Maria had put her son into this new and terrible mood. She tried to answer quietly.

"What happened? I thought you were happy about the baby."

"You haven't answered my question. Why didn't you consult me?"

"You know why. I was afraid you'd say no. And I wanted to give you another child. One you could be close to. One who'd appreciate your artistry. It's as simple as that.''

"Simple? Nothing with you is simple! You make decisions for both of us. You must have your own way, no matter how it affects me. You must raise a handicapped child yourself. You must be free of my family. You must make demands on me that destroy my concentration, drive me out of my mind with worry about your drinking and your mental state and your threats of divorce! And now this! Another 'simple pregnancy' you knew I wouldn't want. One that could produce another misfit!''

Angry counteraccusations rushed into her mind. What of his selfishness, his unfaithfulness, his lack of sensitivity to her needs? What of his weakness in the face of Maria's sick domination? She got up and closed the bedroom door. No need for the servants to hear this ugly quarrel. No need to broadcast their unhappiness. She stood quite still, looking at his flushed face, his wild, tormented eyes. How could he be so manipulated? And yet Maria could only light the fires of discontent. It was Richard who willingly warmed himself at the flames.

"Well?'' he shouted. "Are you just going to stand there? Aren't you going to say anything?''

Her voice was almost a whisper. "What do you want me to say? That you're right? That everything wrong with our marriage is my fault?'' She shook her head. "No. I take the blame for my share of our troubles, but I don't accept the picture you've painted. Any more than I accept your convenient forgetfulness of your part in our problems.''

"Whatever I've done, you've made me crazy enough to do!''

She flinched. It was unreal. Perhaps he was a little crazy. Certainly he needed help. But he'd never understand that. Never admit such a need. God knows what Maria had said to get him worked up that way. No doubt she'd goaded him about losing his "manhood,'' allowing another child, implanting fears that all this "permissiveness'' was somehow affecting his work and that he was letting his wife run his life. As though his mother didn't, Susan thought cynically. As though she hasn't always called the shots and still does.

"What is this all about?'' Susan asked. "The baby will be all right. I know it will. Please, Richard, don't let your fears distort your thinking about us. We were doing so well. I was truly happy. I thought you were. I don't know what's been said to turn you so against me, but I don't believe you mean those things. I *can't* believe it. Darling, only you and I count in this. You and I and Katie and the new baby.''

"No! You can't have this child. We can't risk it. I can't work with this worry in my mind. I knew that from the first, and when I talked to Mother . . .'' He suddenly stopped. His voice faltered and he seemed to crumple. "All right, I know you think she has too much influence over me, but in this case she's right, Susan. You must have an abortion. Now, while it's still safe.''

"An abortion?'' she was incredulous.

"It's our only hope. You said it yourself: We were happy. But we'll never make it with this hanging over our heads. Don't worry. We'll find a good man. There are plenty of them as long as you can afford the best. And we'll get the best.''

"No."

He was genuinely amazed. "But you must! Haven't you heard anything I've said?"

"I heard *everything* you said, and the answer is still no. Because it doesn't make sense. I won't give up the child to pamper you, Richard. To free your mind and leave your concentration undisturbed. A human life means more than that to me. I'm not some poor, forsaken kid who has to get rid of a baby. I want this child and I'm going to have it. If you can't cope with that, then you're not the person with whom I choose to spend my life."

His anger turned to pleading. "Please, Susan. I know what you believe, but I can't feel the same. I want you, but not the terror of another seven months of wondering and fearing. I didn't mean those things I said about you. I know you've tried hard to make things work. You've been wonderful."

She laughed. "Wonderful? Hardly. I've been a damned fool, self-deceiving and masochistic. I'm sorry, Richard. Sorry for you. Sorry for myself. Sorry we failed at something that could have been wonderful."

He was furious again. "Failed? I haven't failed! I'm not responsible!"

"No," Susan said. "That's just it. You never have been."

Chapter 23

GIOVANNI HAD NOT been present the day before when his wife and youngest son had the discussion that brought Richard and Susan close to the breaking point. He frowned when Maria reported the gist of it to him next morning over the breakfast table.

"Imagine!" she said. "That young woman deliberately getting pregnant again! And without letting Richard know what she planned! Unthinkable for them to have another child! So like her to use Richard's infatuation to make sure she holds him. It's the last straw among all the destructive things she's done! Never mind. I think I finally made him see her for what she is. There'll be no more unwanted babies in that household!"

He knew her so well. Without having heard the words he could imagine how she'd worked on Richard, played on his fears, made him feel the injured party, the innocent victim. She would have pulled out all the stops. And Richard, poor, weak Richard, probably went home full of righteous indignation and raised hell with that nice, patient girl. For all anyone knew, Maria's clever manipulation might have worked this time. She'd been hell-bent on destroying that marriage from the start, and from the satisfied look of her this morning, she may well have finally made it. There must be a limit to what Susan would take, Giovanni thought. He pretended to be oblivious of the "minor crises" within his family, but the maestro was more aware than he seemed. He knew the strain Susan had been under, was sure she'd thought more than once about chucking the whole thing. She wasn't like his other daughters-in-law, any more than his sons were like him. He felt uneasy, listening to Maria rattle on about how she'd "straightened out" Richard. The sensitivity that was so much a part of his nature told him that this was something to seriously worry about.

There was something else to worry about, too. Something he'd not told anyone, not even his wife. The "routine" prostate operation he'd had six months before had turned out not to be routine at all. He'd made the surgeon promise to tell him, and only him, if there was a malignancy. Giovanni felt there was. And he was right.

"But at your age," the doctor said, "it won't kill you. Try to forget about it. It's a slow process and, frankly, a man of your years probably will succumb to natural causes before this takes over. I don't mean to sound heartless, Mr. Antonini, but you are seventy-six years old, and at your time of life this kind of carcinoma is less dangerous than the inevitable passing of time. We think we have your problem under control, in any case. The side effects of your treatments should be minimal."

And they were. So minimal that he was able to keep the results of the biopsy from everyone. But Giovanni knew he did not have long to live. The knowledge did not particularly distress him. He had had his "glamour." Standing ovations from his audiences, slavish devotion from the men and women to whom his name was second only to God's. He'd had his share of beautiful women, good food and wine, satin sheets for his bed and silken words for his ego. He'd missed very little. He'd even had the outward appearaace of a "perfect" family—a supportive wife, talented children, a gracious home in which they'd fostered the Antonini "dynasty."

He knew his dying would scarcely disrupt that home life. To call Maria "self-sufficient" was a gross understatement. And his children were self-confident and not, for that matter, so close to him that his passing would cause any deep and lasting grief. He had no need to worry about them. None except Richard, the only vulnerable one of the four. For all his selfishness, his outrageous conceit, this youngest son was the one for whom Giovanni felt most concern, as Maria did, but in a different way. She expressed her love by dominating, almost consuming, the late, unwanted child. Giovanni appeared unconcerned and remote, yet he recognized that Richard was not strong enough to make it alone. While Maria was alive, he could cling to her, defer to her, as he was doing now. But Maria would not live forever. Richard had instinctively chosen the right wife, the one he could depend on always, the one he needed now, even while his mother lived. Giovanni could not stand by silently and let his wife destroy Richard's future happiness and security. And there was so little time to save the boy from her.

Maria scarcely noticed the uneasy silence with which Giovanni received her account of this latest development in Richard's life. She was used to him, too. To his lack of response, his "ivory-tower disinterest" in the day-by-day emergencies. She knew him less well, though, than he knew her—a fact which would have surprised her considerably. She did not dream he cared deeply for his family, that he regretted nothing except having been a withdrawn and apparently unreachable "father figure" to his children. It was the only thing in his life he wished he'd done differently. But Maria's strength and, he admitted, his own selfishness had made it easier to abdicate parental responsibilities. He'd been the poorer for it. And so, he feared, had his sons and daughter.

It was too late to do anything about Sergio and Walter or Gloria. But there was still time to help Richard and Susan. Or at least still time to try.

He finished the last of his coffee and looked over at Maria, who was going through her mail.

"You don't think you might be meddling in Susan and Richard's lives with all this well-meant advice?"

She raised her eyes, surprised. "Meddling? What a peculiar word to use, Joe. Of course I'm not meddling. Richard always talks things over with me. He needs a sounding board. You don't think he'd have come here yesterday if he hadn't been concerned about his marriage, do you?"

"From what you said originally, I thought he came to tell you he was pleased about the baby."

"Nonsense! He was never pleased. That was simply an excuse to see me. He knows the trouble he's in. He needed reinforcement."

"Reinforcement for what?"

"For what he had to do about that headstrong girl, of course! To stop her from complicating their lives further with another child."

"That's true? You weren't making one last stab at breaking up that marriage?"

Maria's mouth tightened. "That's a stupid suggestion and you know it. I've never tried to destroy the marriage. I've only ttried to make it acceptable for Richard."

"And what about Susan? Doesn't she matter?"

His wife sighed. "I can't think what's gotten into you this morning. What does Susan mean to you?"

"Quite a lot," Giovanni said mildly. "I think she's the best thing that ever happened to Richard."

Maria stared. "You must be getting senile! She's been unsuitable from the start."

"To whom? To Richard or to you?"

Before she could answer, the maid announced that Mrs. Antonini was wanted on the telephone.

"It's Mr. Richard, madame."

Maria nodded and gave Giovanni a smug little smile of vindication. "I daresay he's going to tell me he asserted himself."

She was back in a few minutes, looking complacent. "I was right. Richard laid down the law to her and she's threatened to leave him. *Again.* She won't, of course, even though he's foolish enough to believe her. He told her he didn't want the baby and she flatly refuses to have an abortion. Naturally, she will have one. She's not going to let go of a good thing like Richard."

"Isn't he terribly upset?"

Maria shrugged. "For the moment. But he'll get over it. He's a child himself. He can't see she's simply going through one of her acts."

"Are you sure she is?"

"Of course I'm sure. Joe, you don't understand devious people. You never have. You haven't a clue to how to handle things like this. I don't even know why I tell you about them. Leave this to me."

"When does Susan say she's going to leave?"

Maria shrugged. "I have no idea. Richard said something about their discussing it today. Presumably she expects him to make some financial arrangements for herself and Katherine. But what difference does it make? It's academic. She won't leave. She's played this same scene before. She was going to leave him after that business in Washington, and she didn't. She won't now. Not that I'd care, to tell you the truth. I've tried very hard to help Richard make his marriage work, but she's a stumbling block. The proverbial millstone. He could move better and faster without her and in his heart he knows it. But he's stubborn. Like all the Antoninis. He won't admit he's made a mistake, so the only thing he can do is make her see that he won't put up with all her nonsense. I think I got that across to him yesterday." She gave a self-satisfied little nod. "Yes, I think Miss Susan has finally realized that Richard won't knuckle under to her demands any longer."

Giovanni pushed his chair. "I'm going for my walk," he said. It was his habit to walk two carefully counted miles every morning after breakfast. It was his "thinking time," an hour when he could escape from everything, from the boredom of Maria's overorganized household, even from the work he loved. He enjoyed these solitary strolls. Sometimes he walked down Lexington Avenue, past rows of tacky boutiques and cut-rate drugstores, losing himself in the crowds of harried shoppers who didn't recognize him. He found the hustle and bustle somehow restful, liked the idea that he appeared to be just another elderly gentleman window-shopping in front of Alexander's. Sometimes he walked home by way of Third Avenue, passing the elbow-to-elbow movie houses where the "Ticket Holders Only" lines were forming for the noon perfonnance. Who on earth went to the films at this hour? he wondered. Bored housewives? Salesmen who should have been making calls on customers? Out-of-work men who had nothing to do between job interviews? He was curious about a world that was not his, speculating on the people who stood at open-air counters eating hot dogs and pizzas, wondering who bought the ugly clothes and bad art and fake antiques in the shops that lined these avenues. Maria thought he was quite mad.

"How can you bear to be shoved around in the middle of that mess?" she'd ask when he told her the sights he'd seen. "It's become Coney Island! Hippies and freaks! For heaven's sake, Joe, can't you walk up Fifth Avenue and look at Central Park? Or Madison where at least the shops are chic?"

Sometimes he did take those more "respectable" routes. Once in a while he ambled along Park Avenue where there was nothing more interesting to look at than high-rent apartment houses and expressionless doormen, and where, unfortunately, well-dressed matrons sometimes stopped him to gush over his latest triumph at Philharmonic, He was always polite, but the "smarter areas" bored him. Trashy as they were, First, Second, Third and Lexington Avenues pulsed with life. Fifth, Madison and Park were sterile and "suitable."

As "suitable," he thought this morning, as Maria would like Susan to be. She'd like to see all the life taken out of that young woman. He winced at the unintentionally literal comparison. Maria wanted Susan to give up her unborn child, to be docile and proper in her role as Richard's wife. He wasn't surprised that Susan would agree to none of that. She was not selfish, but she was proud and, in her own way, stubborn, too. As stubborn as Maria, really, and as strong. But with much more heart and much less arrogance.

I must help her, Giovanni thought again. For her sake and Richard's. I must get to them before Richard destroys everything by playing the ventriloquist's dummy, with Maria mouthing the words. But how? I can't openly tell Richard not to listen to his mother. I can't suddenly become a concerned father after all these years of tacit acceptance of Maria's child-rearing rules. Richard would never understand. But Susan would, if only I could get her alone.

As though something or someone was guiding his steps he found himself on East Sixty-third Street between Park and Lexington. Someone he knew lived on this block, but who? He stood for several moments gazing sightlessly at the Miró and Picasso prints in the window of Pocker's Picture Framing Store until it came to him. Paul Carmichael lived somewhere around here. He'd never been to Richard's former manager's apartment, didn't even know the exact address, but he was sure it was Sixty-third. Paul. Maybe Paul was the way to reach Susan. He'd always liked her, Giovanni knew. Sometimes he suspected that Paul was even a little in love with her. Perhaps that forbidden attraction was the reason he'd left Richard. In any case, Paul was a gentleman and he was Richard's friend, his *only* friend as far as Giovanni knew.

He found a public telephone booth on the corner and looked up Paul Carmichael in the directory. He was only three houses away. Not knowing what he was going to say, Giovanni dropped a dime in the slot and dialed the number.

Kate Fenton listened attentively as Paul told her the involved, incredible story. Every now and then she shifted the telephone to her other ear, holding it with her shoulder as she lit a cigarette. She said almost nothing as Paul talked for ten minutes, telling her what was happening to Susan and Richard, reporting Giovanni's surprising visit to him that morning, and now asking her help.

"The old man wants to get to Susan without Richard knowing it," Paul said. "He's determined not to let Maria wreck that marriage and he thinks he can help if he can talk to Susan alone. I don't know what his plan is, Kate. I'm not sure *he* knows. But he cares about Susan, as you and I do."

Kate heard the pain in his voice. Yes, you care, she thought. You always have.

"So Papa-Joe came to ask you to get Susan out of the apartment so he could talk to her."

"Yes," Paul said, "that was his original thought. But I explained that I wasn't the right one. If I called there, Richard might pick up the phone. Even Susan would wonder why I'd turned up after all these months. It seemed to me you were the logical person to get hold of her for Mr. Antonini. You're her dearest friend. You could tell her you wanted to see her right away and she'd come."

"Maybe she's already left," Kate said. "Maybe she's gone to her parents'. He could try getting hold of her there. Her mother might be a better go-between. I've been out of town on an assignment. Just got back this morning. I haven't spoken to Susan in weeks. My God, I didn't even know she was pregnant!"

"I don't think she could have left yet, from what Mr. Antonini tells me. I'm sure she means to, but she's sensible enough not to walk out until she knows Katie and the new baby will be provided for. And that will take some wrangling with Richard. She probably will try to pin down the arrangements quickly, but Richard will stall. I don't know if the maestro can save the day, but he thinks he can, and he's damned determined to try! Surprising old bastard, isn't he? We always had the idea he never thought of anyone but himself."

"Surprising is hardly the word. Stunning is more like it. But I wonder if he's right. I wonder if that rocky marriage *should* be saved. Susan might be better off without it." Kate paused. "Seems to me you're being pretty unselfish about all this, Paul."

He knew what she meant. It must have been obvious to everybody how he felt about Susan. How he still felt. And he'd thought no one suspected. Kate did. So did Giovanni. He supposed Susan knew. I must be a lousy actor, he thought. Evidently I don't have a sleeve big enough for the heart I carry on it.

"I care about Susan. *And* Richard," he said carefully. "But I'm something of a fatalist, Kate. If things are to be, they'll be."

She snorted. "If you really believed that, you'd stay the hell out of this, as you should. As *I* should. But we won't, of course. I don't have any more sense than you. All right, I'll call her. What's the plot?"

"Ask her to meet you for lunch today. Your apartment. Mr. Antonini will be there. He's calling me back in thirty minutes to see if that works out."

"I think we've all gone crazy," Kate said. "Do you really think a woman who's about to move out bag and baggage is going to stop in the middle of everything to keep a lunch date?"

"I think Susan will. Especially with you. She probably is desperate to talk to someone, and you're the only candidate. I'm sure she needs you a lot right now. She'll come. I'd bet my life on it."

Kate sighed. "Okay. I'll get back to you." She lit another cigarette, swiveled around in her desk chair and stared pensively out the window at the New York skyline. What a mess! That bloody Richard and his rotten, scheming mother. Poor Susie. What will happen to her next? The last time they talked was just after her return from Vegas, just before Kate left on assignment. Susan had confessed about what's-his-name, Tanner. She'd been remorseful, unnecessarily swearing Kate to secrecy, terribly ashamed of what she'd done. And yet she'd seemed more relaxed. Purged, somehow. She'd said she was determined to make a go of it with Richard, that she honestly felt they'd both changed. She'd seemed more in control of herself, more optimistic than she'd been in a long while. But, Kate thought ruefully, she must have carried that euphoria too far. Pregnant! Dear Lord, how did she dare? For a moment, she had the sinking fear that this child might be the product of that fling in Vegas. No. Susan was such an honest little idiot she'd have stupidly told Richard if that were the case. And from what Paul said, that was not the reason Susan was being pressed to have an abortion. It was simply Richard's "normal fears." And Maria's, of course. Kate was the only one who knew about Tanner.

With a heavy heart, she made her phone call. A subdued but grateful-sounding Susan said yes, she'd love to come for lunch. She had a lot to tell her. Kate didn't say she already knew.

Fortunately for Giovanni, Maria had left the house when he returned from his walk. He breathed a sigh of relief. He never went out for lunch. How would he have explained this mysterious appointment? He told the servants he wasn't hungry and wouldn't take his usual one-o'clock meal. He'd be working in his study and didn't wish to be disturbed. He closed himself into the quiet room and thought of what he'd say to Susan. What would convince her not to leave Richard? He was not an eloquent man, but he'd have to find the words. They were there, in his heart, if only he could use them to reach Susan's own.

The subject of all their thoughts sipped vodka and tonic as she dressed to meet Kate. It had been a terrible morning. First thing, she'd been sick to her stomach. Odd. She'd never had morning sickness with Katie. Nerves, of course. She'd hardly slept all night. She lay awake on the "emergency bed" in Katie's room, the one kept there in case Bridie needed to be near her charge. She'd been afraid to move for fear of waking the child, not realizing at the time how absurd that was. Katie without her hearing aids could not have been disturbed by a herd of elephants. Sometimes I forget, Susan thought. She seems so complete to me that I forget.

She wondered if the new baby would be all right. It worried her more now, knowing she'd be having it alone, knowing she'd have the sole responsibility of raising and educating two children. She'd tried to talk to Richard about that this morning, t   he'd brushed her off and left the house. She couldn't go until they decided the financial things. She wanted nothing for herself, but Katie's care was frighteningly expensive. She'd never been able to earn enough to support the private schools and the therapist and all the things the little girl had to have. And what if, God forbid, the second one needed the same help? She could stay with her parents until she had her baby, but then she'd have to get a job. Could she go back to *Vogue?* Could she afford to? Realistically, she had little choice. She was trained for nothing but magazine work and it would be hard to make ends meet on the salary she'd probably earn, but she'd have to. Even if she had to ask Bea and Wil to let the three of them and Bridie stay in Bronxville indefinitely. Her parents would be more than willing, of course, but it would be a tight squeeze, taking four more people into the house. It would be hard on everybody, getting Katie into town for her lessons, caring for the infant, to say nothing of paying Bridie's salary. Richard would *have* to help. She'd force him to, even if it took "blackmail" in the form of threatened sordid publicity.

She shuddered. It could all be so easily solved. She could agree to the abortion, forget the terrible things Richard had said, try for a marriage as loveless and "sensible" as Jacqueline's and Walter's. But it would be total prostitution of everything she believed in. An empty, let's-pretend life.

She fixed another drink, even while she was thinking she should take it easy. If anyone had dared suggest she was an alcoholic, she would have vehemently denied it. She wouldn't admit her drinking was a form of escape, a necessary buffer against life's rough edges. She was convinced she could give it up completely. Hadn't she drunk practically nothing for the few weeks when she thought everything was all right between her and Richard? Didn't that prove she wasn't hooked? Anyone in her present situation would need something to bolster them. She was about to end her marriage, to start over with Katie and a baby whose father didn't want it. And incredibly, no matter what he did, she was in love with her husband. There seemed to be no way she could stop loving him. It was a sickness for which she had no cure.

Thank God Kate had called. There was ESP between them. Kate was the one person she could talk openly to; the friend who understood and invariably sensed when she was needed. She hadn't been appalled or disapproving when Susan told her about Martin Tanner. Not as Bea Langdon would have been. Mother would have forgiven me and tried to understand, Susan thought, but she couldn't be analytical and unemotional about her own child. No mother could be. I'm not. Not about the one I have or the one I'm going to have.

Kate had been matter-of-fact about the Tanner affair. All she'd said was, "You had to get it out of your system, kiddo. It was a way of paying Richard back. You realize that, don't you? Put it out of your mind. I assume you're never going to see Tanner again."

"Of course not. He doesn't even know my real name."

Kate had nodded. "Leave it that way. It was immoral, sure. Wrong, probably. But maybe it will help you understand how these things can happen to the best of wives. *And* husbands."

She'd felt better after their talk, more loving toward Richard. Too loving, she thought bitterly, thinking of the child she'd meant to be a special gift. What will Kate say when I tell her what's happened? What do I expect her to say?

She was a little drunk when she arrived at Kate's duplex penthouse on East Fifty-second Street. She'd always loved this crazy little "upside-down" apartment with its big, fabric-draped bedroom on the lower floor and its small, chic living room at the top of the curving staircase. She smiled, remembering her amazement the first time she saw it. "It's topsy-turvy!" she'd said. "Bedrooms are supposed to be upstairs and living rooms *down!*"

"I know. Whimsical, isn't it? But there's a valid point. The big terrace with the view is upstairs. That's why the living room is there, for the view."

It was a spectacular view. The apartment faced the East River on one side, the United Nations building on another and the jagged outlines of the Empire State and Chrysler buildings on the third. It was designed to make guests gasp with pleasure.

The friends hugged as Kate opened the door.

"I'm *so* glad to see you!" Susan said.

"Me too. There's someone else who's anxious to see you. Come on upstairs."

"Someone else?" Susan was disappointed. "Who?"

"A friend of yours."

Giovanni was waiting at the top of the stairs, his handsome face serious but his eyes full of sympathy.

"Papa-Joe?" Susan was incredulous. "What are *you* doing here?"

"I'm afraid we tricked you, but I had to talk to you, away from the family. Miss Fenton was kind enough to arrange it."

"With Paul Carmichael's help," Kate said.

Susan looked from one to the other. "What is this all about? You and Kate plotting? And Paul? I don't understand."

"Come and sit down and I'll try to explain," Giovanni said.

Kate gave her a little shove. "I'll be downstairs if you need me." She patted

Susan's arm. "We'll talk later. Right now, Mr. Antonini has a few things to say to you."

Obediently, Susan took one of the big chairs at the fireplace. Giovanni faced her in its twin.

"There are things you should know, Susan," he began. "Things that I hope will make you reconsider your decision to leave Richard."

"Papa-Joe!" Susan was incredulous. "What are *you* doing here?"

"Hush, please, dear Susan. Hear me out before you make up your mind. I love you very much, you know. As much as I love my son. That's why we must talk together. Like loving people."

And so he began.

Chapter 24

SUSAN WAS NEVER to forget that afternoon in Kate's apartment, an hour that ultimately started a whole new chain of events.

She'd always been fond of her father-in-law. For all his fame, he was a lonely man, taken for granted and virtually ignored by his family. At first, his lack of involvement in their activities puzzled her, but eventually she decided he was above competition, that he didn't care to be part of the plots and counterplots that swirled around him. The only conversational area in which he showed any animation was that of music. Here, his was the voice of authority and he enjoyed holding forth. In other areas he seemed to be a man of intellectual narrowness, with no interest in worldly affairs and little insight into the behavior of others.

That day she learned how wrong she'd been. Giovanni was attuned to the complexities of people, surprisingly tolerant and analytical. He proved to be a clever man and as he'd said, a loving one.

"I've come here to beg you not to leave Richard," he said bluntly. "I know something of what's been going on and I can guess at the rest. His mother wants only what she honestly believes is best for him but sometimes her judgment works against the boy. Unfortunately, he's easily influenced by her. Always has been. You know that better than anyone, of course. But perhaps you don't know the basis of her extraordinary hold on him, the simple thing that motivates some of his reactions and makes him so pathetically insecure."

Susan looked at him curiously. "Richard insecure? Immature, perhaps, but insecure?" She smiled sadly. "I'd hardly call him that."

"I know. But it's true. As it's true of anyone who discovers he was an unwanted child."

The words came slowly from Giovanni's tightly set lips. Susan stared at him for a long moment.

"Unwanted? You didn't want him? I can't believe that. But even if it's so, how did he find out?"

"His mother told him long ago." Giovanni's voice was bitter as he related the events of that long-ago New Year's Eve. "Maria and I had not lived as husband and wife for years until that night. She was repelled, and I suppose rightly, by my infidelities. But that night there was champagne and sentiment and perhaps a kind of anger in me. In any case, Maria acquiesced, but in her memory of it, she was raped. Or, at least tricked. So, Richard was conceived, twelve years after Maria thought she'd had her last child. It's a paradox. She loves Richard more than any of her children, yet she's never forgiven me for siring him. What she really hates, of course, is herself, for having been vulnerable enough to forget her 'principles' for one passionate moment. It was the first, and probably the last, time she was not completely in control of her own feelings.''

"But I don't understand why she would tell Richard such a thing." Susan was horrified. "Who'd tell a child he wasn't wanted? Who'd be so cruel, and for what purpose?" In her agitation she went to the bar and poured another drink. "Make something for you?" Giovanni shook his head, waiting until she sat down again. Then he answered her question.

"I've wondered that same thing over all these years. I'm not a student of psychology, but I've thought a great deal about it. I believe telling him was my wife's way of getting back at me for that night. Letting Richard know he was an 'accident' has somehow made him feel apologetic about being alive. It's kept him from loving me as I love him. When a child knows his father was unfaithful for years and then 'seduced' his mother and conceived him out of lust, what could he feel except resentment? He's felt all his life, the need to please Maria as though he owed her something. His anger at me has been her revenge, and his 'guilt' her weapon. She uses it to this day to make Richard do anything she wants.''

"That's insane!" Susan said. "I could understand a child feeling irrational guilt if his mother died giving birth to him, I could even see how he might hate his father. But to feel those things because he was conceived in a careless moment? No. I can't believe it. Richard's too bright for that."

"The brightest people get caught in emotional traps, especially when they're up against a clever woman like Maria, who knows how to subtly play on a feeling of 'obligation.' Of course, it's insane! Logically, Richard knows his mother is a strong woman who doesn't need protection. He also knows that if it hadn't been for my 'selfishness' that particular night he wouldn't even be here! But he isn't logical where this matter is concerned. He's always been more bound to her than the other children. His brothers and sister defer to her, but in the end they are independent. Only Richard feels obliged to make up for something that was done years ago, as though he needed to justify his existence by pleasing her in every way. He's never been allowed to forget the infidelities that were a prelude to the circumstances of his birth. There's that too. He's outraged by the attraction women have always had for me." Giovanni smiled. "And, of course, vice versa."

Susan's head began to reel from the several drinks she'd had and from the strange story her father-in-law told. She had a sudden sharp pain in her stomach. She winced and ignored it. "But in many ways he's irritated you," she said. "He's been unfaithful over and over, as you admit you were. He once even forced himself on me, and much more literally than you did on Mrs. Antonini. He attracts women and responds to them. Papa-Joe, he's more like than you than any of your children!''

"Exactly. But he doesn't see that. Or doesn't wish to. He can't admit he shares my craving for admiration, a need that leads us into meaningless outside relationships. He won't face the fact that we're both easily influenced by others, or that we have the same God-awful feeling that we don't deserve our success.'' The old man sighed. ''Yes, he's very like me, Susan, except that I don't carry his burden. I was not an unwanted child. At least, if I was I never knew it.''

''I still don't understand.'' Susan's words were a little slurred. The pains were worse now. They were coming steadily. ''Why is he so angry with me because I'm going to have a baby? He seemed happy at first, As he was with Katie. Now he wants me to have an abortion. And he isn't really close to Katie. He's tried, but he can't accept her because she isn't perfect, and he doesn't want this one because he's afraid it won't be perfect either. I've told him there's practically no risk. I only want to give him a child he can love.''

Giovanni realized she was quite drunk. If she hadn't been, she'd have seen the point of his story. Slowly, patiently, he tried to sum it up.

''Susan, my dear, listen carefully. Richard was happy about both children until Maria pointed out to him that he had no part in planning either of them. To him, they represent the same kind of unwanted child he was. He blames you for 'forcing' them on him, just as I 'forced' him on Maria. He sees it as her life in reverse. he's unconsciously identifying with his mother. She's made him feel that in the conception of your children he was used—that he was not in control, as my wife was not in control years ago. She's told him you are conniving, selfish and devious, and reminded him that once again you took a major step without his permission. She has practically insulted his manhood, making him feel tricked, as she felt tricked. It's sad. He was just at the point of learning to love his first 'unplanned child' when you presented him with the fact of another.''

''By why does Mrs. Antonini do this? Why does she hate me so?''

''She doesn't hate you. No more than she'd hate any woman Richard loved. She simply refuses to give up her hold on him.''

Susan refilled her empty glass. Maybe another drink would help the pains go away. ''It's hopeless, isn't it? I'm right in knowing I have to leave him.''

''No,'' Giovanni said, ''it isn't hopeless. There's time to make it right. Richard loves you. He loves you so much he took his first defiant steps because of you. He married you in spite of everything Maria tried to do. He left home because you wanted it. He's managed more independence of action in the past eight years than he's ever shown in his life. You've won most of your battles, whether you realize it or not. But you can't win when you strike at the very thing that has always eaten at Richard. You cannot have this child or any other you don't plan with him. It comes down to that.''

Her eyes widened. ''You, too? You think I should have an abortion?''

He answered reluctantly. ''Yes. I hate the thought of it. Even more, I hate the irrational reason for it. But it's there, and it won't go away. You're young. You can have more children. Babies you *and* Richard decide to have. But not this one. This one will destroy your marriage.'' He paused. ''And, selfishly, I know that will destroy my son.''

''But he doesn't want me! All the cruel things he said . . .''

Giovanni shook his head. ''You didn't hear Richard. You heard his mother. He's the product of the last person he talks to. Especially if that person is my wife. Didn't he apologize? Didn't he swear he didn't mean the accusations he must have made?''

She nodded miserably.

"I'm sure he regretted his outburst. He always regrets them. He's telling the truth, He doesn't see you as Maria does. He loves you, Susan, and I beg you to help him.''

"I can't. I can't get rid of my baby." Suddenly she was angry. "Why should I? What about me? Haven't I some rights?''

"Of course you have. But you and Richard have time to set things straight. Unfortunately, I haven't.' He hesitated. "I didn't want to use emotional blackmail, Susan. I hoped I could convince you without asking a personal favor, but I'm reduced to anything that will save my boy. I'm dying. And I can't die knowing my son's life has been ruined by this madness of his mother's. I can't abandon him to her. When you came along, I thanked God. I thought, He's all right now. He won't be a lifelong penitent with no will of his own. But if you leave him, Susan, his mother will own him again, body and soul, as she did before. He'll be a great man but a lonely, useless one.''

Susan heard the words, but everything was overshadowed by the hideous knowledge that Giovanni was dying. The shock momentarily sobered her.

"You can't! You can't die! What do you mean you're dying?''

"Hush! Miss Fenton will hear. I don't want anyone to know. I've known for some months that I have cancer, but I've told no one. I don't plan to tell anyone. I wouldn't have told you, except that I'm a desperate, bumbling old man trying to do one last, good thing." He sighed. "It's too bad you're not a different sort of woman. This would have been so easy if I could just have offered you a million dollars to stay with Richard, But you can't be bought. I know that. And still I'm not above trying to buy you by appealing to your compassion. It's the only thing I want: to die in peace knowing the children I love are safe. I'll go to any lengths for that.''

She stared at him. "But you won't tell them? You won't let them be close to you for whatever time is left? That's selfishness, not love. You must tell them. They deserve to know.''

"For what? So they can pity me? So they can pretend at long last to love me? I haven't earned their love. Why should I expect the obligatory gentleness and concern one shows a dying man? No. You must keep my secret. That kind of dutiful devotion is ugly. As ugly as disease. More ugly than death itself.''

She wanted to cry for this lonely man, trying to put things in order before the cancer killed him. Too proud to seek comfort. Too frightened, perhaps to talk about it.

"You must tell the family," Susan repeated. "You think they don't love you, but they do. It's only that you're so withdrawn. You've made yourself unapproachable. Give them a chance to show how much you mean to them, how important you are to all their lives. Please. I beg you. Don't be unfair.''

"Unfair?'' Giovanni managed a smile. "When have I been known for my fairness? What good would it do for them to know? It would only be a burden and it wouldn't help me.''

"I think it *would* help you. I think you'd see you have the affection you've always wanted.''

He wavered. "I'm not sure. I suppose I really don't know my own children very well. I've always been too busy or too preoccupied to think much about them since they've been grown. Only Richard. Because he was the baby. And at home." He looked at her with pathetic eagerness. "You think they care? You honestly think they love me?"

"I know it."

"Well, we'll see. Right now I'm more concerned with you and Richard."

She looked away from him. "I'll stay with Richard. I'll have the abortion."

"I'm grateful," he said slowly, "and ashamed. You're a fine young woman, A good person. Maybe too good. It's wrong of me to ask this of you, knowing you wouldn't refuse."

It was she who was ashamed. She wasn't good in her own eyes. She was difficult. She drank too much. She'd never been the kind of "professional wife" a performer needed. She'd even broken her marriage vows. Oh, she could make excuses for all those things. She could blame them on the shabby treatment she'd had from Richard and most of his family. On the fact that she'd never felt needed. But that wouldn't wash. What she'd done she'd done out of weakness or willfulness or both. She had reacted like a human who'd been hurt. But that didn't excuse her. And it certainly didn't deserve praise.

"I'm not staying because of you, Papa-Joe. I'm staying because I love my husband."

Giovanni accepted the half-truth. "Thank you for that, Susan. Thank you for everything. I know the sacrifices you're making. I'm sorry.

There was a lump in her throat. Why you? Why does it have to be you who's going to die?

He kissed her hand and tred to slowly descend the stairs. He seemed old and fragile, a man who felt himself a failure despite all his success. For a moment, Susan wondered whether it was all a clever ploy. Could Giovanni have made up this extraordinary tale just to keep her from leaving Richard? No. It was too bizarre to have been invented. She suspected even Richard did not know how deep his guilts and resentments went. Her husband was not an introspective person. She felt sure he'd never come to grips with the obsession Maria had instilled and nurtured over the years. In this area he was, as his father said, a "penitent," a robot programmed for remorse. Why does Giovanni think I can save him? she wondered. Why do I even try? Is Richard's future worth trading for the life I'm going to destroy? Why did I agree to an abortion and another try at this marriage? Because a pitiful, dying man asked it of me? Or because, deep down, I know I shouldn't bring an unwanted child into the world? Am I punishing myself for my own mistakes?

She was so mixed up. So utterly lost in a world that was more than she could cope with. The Antoninis are selfish and heartless, she thought. Even Giovanni, using the sentimental, vulnerable side of her nature. Damn them all! Damn Richard for ever coming into her life. Damn the conscience and, yes, the love and pity that kept her from walking away from him. Damn her own stupidity!

She heard Kate bidding Giovanni goodbye at the front door, heard her friend climb the stairs to where Susan stood looking at the afternoon sun coloring the tips of the spires of St. Patrick's Cathedral. I wish I were a religious person,

Susan thought. I wish I could ask God for help and believe I'd receive guidance and absolution. The pains were more intense now. She clutched her stomach, almost bent double with each spasm. She straightened up. What were these violent cramps that came and went with the ferocity of labor pains? She turned and saw Kate staring at her.

"You knew, didn't you?" Susan asked. "You knew the whole story before I got here."

"Some of it. Paul told me everything Giovanni told him." She explained how the meeting had been arranged. "So where do you go from here?"

"Back to square one." Susan laughed mirthlessly. "Back to Richard and his family and Katie. Back to a life that's totally pointless." It was her turn to explain. She told Kate everything. How she'd been touched by Richard's nervous efforts to be a father to Katie. How she'd believed she could make him happy with another child. How hideously it had all backfired because of Richard's twisted, unshakable beliefs. "And now Giovanni's dying," she said. "Dying in anguish over his son's future if I leave him. I promised him I wouldn't." Her voice was flat and hopeless. "I told him I'd get rid of the baby. That I wouldn't have another one unless Richard and I planned it together." She was quite drunk now. "Richard thinks I used him!" She giggled. "Isn't that insane? My God! I only wish I were smart enough to!"

Kate watched her carefully. Susan was on the verge of hysterics. Drunken hysterics. She literally staggered as she started toward the bar.

"I hate to be a nag," Kate said quietly, "but don't you think you ought to lay off that stuff? You look terrible. Are you all right?"

Susan unsteadily poured a stiff drink. "Not to worry. I can handle it."

"I wouldn't say so. Susan, that isn't going to do any good. Booze won't solve your problems. You've got to keep a clear head. Sit down. Let's talk. I don't know whether you want to leave Richard, but I'm damned sure you don't want an abortion. It's your body. You have a right to do with it what you want; not give in to Richard's wishes or even let a clever old man twist you around his finger. Has it occurred to you that Giovanni may be using you? Maybe he'd like you to stay with Richard just to spite Maria. Who knows how these people think? He's got to harbor a lot of resentment toward her, Susan. Maybe he's the opposing force, trying to keep the marriage together because he knows she wants it to come apart."

Another searing pain shot through Susan and this time she cried out. She waited to tell Kate she'd rejected that idea. Richard's father was good. He loved his son. But she couldn't speak for the hot, grinding agony in her stomach.

"Susan! What is it?" Kate sounded frightened.

"I . . . I don't know. Terr . . . terrible pain." She held onto the edge of the bar. The room spun around. And then it was all black.

She awoke wondering where she was. It was an unfamiliar room, a hard, narrow bed. She remembered the spasmodic cramps and a feeling of something warm and sticky between her legs. She supposed she'd fainted. She opened her eyes wider and saw the gentle, concerned face of her mother.

"Hello, darling," Bea said. "How do you feel?"

"Awful."

"I'm sure. You had a dreadful experience, but you're all right."

"What happened?"

"A miscarriage, sweetheart. Kate got an ambulance and brought you to Doctors Hospital. I'm sorry, Susie." Bea looked as though she'd been weeping. "It's terrible to lose a baby, but thank God you're all right."

"God takes care of drunks and fools."

"Don't talk like that." Bea hesitated. "Maybe it was a bad seed. Maybe it wasn't meant to be born."

Susan turned her head away wearily. "No, I'm sure it wasn't."

"It happens that way sometimes you know. It's nature's way of solving a problem, making sure you couldn't go full term with a . . ."

Susan interrupted her. "Don't, Mother! Please. It's gone and I'm glad. I don't want to talk about it. Where's Dad?"

"Just down the hall, with Richard and Kate. We've been waiting for you to wake up," She tried to smile. "You took long enough, I must say. Shall I send Richard in now?"

"No. Kate first."

Bea didn't understand any of this. How could Susan be glad about the miscarriage? Why didn't she want to see her husband at this sad moment? But apparently it wasn't sad. Bea didn't know what was happening, but she didn't question her child. She did say, "All right. As you like. But Richard's been so worried . . ."

"Kate, please, Mother." Richard worried? Hardly. He must be delighted. Everything always works out for him, Susan thought. Even this. I wonder if it's possible to subconsciously will a miscarriage? Maybe I did, to avoid the abortion. What would Dr. Marcus say about such a neat solution? As she waited for Kate, Susan decided the whole thing was an analyst's delight: Richard's brainwashing by his mother; Giovanni's "dying request"; the miscarriage of a fetus nobody except herself had ever wanted. How much of our destinies do we control? she wondered. How much can we make happen?

"Susie?" Kate's voice was anxious. "You okay?'

She turned. "I'm fine."

"Well, I feel like killing myself! I shouldn't have been so rough on you. I didn't know you were in agony."

"You couldn't know, Kate. I didn't know, myself, what was happening when it started, long before you began giving me hell. I had pains while I was talking to Papa-Joe, but I thought it was nothing serious." She half-smiled. "It could easily have been the beginning of an ulcer. Seems to me I'm ripe for one between the aggravation and the drinking." Susan turned serious. "You were wrong about Papa-Joe, though. He wasn't using me. He really cares."

"I'm sure. You know me. Given to half-baked theories. Anyway, my dear, sad as it is, you no longer have the problem of an unwanted child. I suppose it's for the best. You can have others. The doctor told us so."

There was no humor in Susan's voice. "That must have thrilled Richard."

Kate didn't answer.

"I've been lying here wondering whether I could have willed it. Do you suppose I actually provoked an act of God?"

"No. It was nobody's fault, Susan."

"I suppose not. Nothing ever is. Thank you for taking care of me, Kate. I'm grateful to you. I'm always grateful to you."

Richard took her home two days later. In the hospital they spoke only briefly of the miscarriage and, as though by tacit agreement, they did not discuss the implications of the loss of the child. At least, Susan thought, he's not hypocritical enough to say he's sorry. I don't think I could forgive him that.

Her husband was gentle and affectionate, seeing that she was tucked safely into their big bed, bringing Katie in to hug her mother, making Susan promise that she'd take it easy. There was no talk of the ugly quarrel that preceded all this. No discussion of her leaving. It was as though Richard took it for granted they'd pick up their life together in the way he wanted it.

She told him nothing of her conversation with Giovanni. It was obvious he didn't know his father had been at Kate's, just as it was apparent he knew nothing of the man's illness. Susan wondered when, or if, Giovanni would do as she asked. Maybe he won't tell them, she thought. He hadn't really said he would; only that he'd think it over. What difference did it make? What difference did anything make these days? She felt as empty and as fragile as a shell, emotionally drained, too defeated by the circumstances of her life to do more than go through the motions of living.

It was strange. She tried not to think about the baby she'd lost. Most of the time it seemed as though it had never happened, and yet there were moments when she wondered what it would have been. A handsome, gifted boy like Richard? A happy, carefree little girl like Susan had been? Or would it have been another Katie—mute and pathetic, another "bad seed?"

When such thoughts came to her, she reached almost automatically for a drink. But she was drinking less these days. Only at the really bad moments did she escape into the blessed fog of liquor, for though she had no real will to assume her old life, she knew she would. She'd promised Giovanni she'd stay with Richard and she meant to keep that promiise as long as the old man lived. In truth, she wanted to stay. Crazily, she still hopcd they could recapture the happiness they'd once had. And there was Katie. Katie was her real reason for being.

Despite the emptiness inside her, she forced herself back to something near normalcy. Her sexual relationship with Richard resumed in a more stable, even a more meaningful way. For now she knew his secret and she was able to be tender with him, understanding, though he did not know she did, the awful demon that plagued him. She was glad Giovanni had told her. It made many things that were once strange and infuriating explainable. She felt sorry for Richard, driven by his guilt. She could even halfway pity Maria for her twisted outlook, though she could never forgive her for what that warped vengeance had done to her son and her husband, nor what the woman's scheming mind still wished to do to her son's marriage.

As Susan regained her strength, she resumed her role as wife, hostess, mother. She made the proper appearances, gave the little dinner parties attended by the "right people," shared Richard's pleasure when such events produced favorable newspaper publicity. And all the while, she waited for Giovanni to keep his part of the "bargain."

It was two more months before they were summoned to the Senior Antoninis', all the children and those they'd married. It was a 'no excuses accepted' invitation for 9 P.M. issued that morning on the phone by a strangely subdued-sounding but very firm Maria.

"Mother, we can't make it," Sergio had said. "We're going to a sit-down dinner at the Leonard Bernsteins'."

"Cancel," Maria said tersely. "And don't ask questions."

"I'm leaving the Hunt at the crack of dawn tomorrow," Gloria protested. "We can't come all the way in town tonight!"

"You can and you will."

"What's this all about?" Walter asked. "Sounds like a command performance."

"That's exactly what it is," Maria answered.

"Darling, if it's about Susan and me, everything's fine," Richard said.

"It's not about you, except indirectly. I don't wish to explain, Richard, but all the family will be here."

He'd hung up puzzled. "What the hell do you think that's all about? Mother's demanding a tribal powwow. No notice at all. I wonder what's up."

Susan didn't answer; she knew. He's finally told Maria and now he's going to tell them all, just as he promised. She felt heartsick, knowing what lay ahead. How would Papa-Joe handle it? With calm and dignity, she answered herself. Please let them respond as I assured him they would. Please let them come out of their selfish shells to be loving children. Don't make him wish he hadn't told them.

It had been a long while since she'd been in the house on East Seventieth Street, but nothing had changed. It was exactly the way it had always been, the way it was the first day Susan ever saw it as a quite nervous magazine writer come to interview the famous young pianist. More than seven years ago, she thought. What dramas we've lived through since those rose-colored days!

They were all prompt. Maria insisted upon that. Always had. "To keep others waiting is an insult, as though you think their time is less precious than yours." Susan had heard her say it more than once in the course of "schooling" her grandchildren in the conduct of "ladies and gentlemen." It was one of the few things she and Maria agreed on. Susan hated to be kept waiting, too. She knew enough psychiatry to know tardiness was a sign of hostility. At two minutes past nine, the eight adults were seated in the drawing room. One minute later, Giovanni and Maria came in.

She looks more ill than he does! Susan thought. For the first time she honestly felt that this cool, distant woman loved her husband, within the bounds of her capability to love. She must be devastated, knowing she's going to lose him. Theirs was a strange marriage by ordinary standards, but there were more than fifty years of shared memories, good and bad, mutually enjoyed or endured. It must be like losing part of yourself. Even a part you unthinkingly accepted on a day-by-day basis. Maria was not weeping, but she looked infinitely sad, and in the only clinging gesture they'd ever seen her make, she held tightly to Giovanni's hand. There was not a sound in the room as they entered, a far cry from the usual babble.

Giovanni seemed unusually tender toward his wife, seating her courteously in a chair before he turned his face to his silent "audience."

"You're very sensitive people," he said without preamble. "You know your mother and I have something serious to say, so I will be quick to say it." He cleared his throat. "I've known for some time that I have cancer."

There was an almost simultaneous intake of breath from his children, a shocked horrified response to the bald words. Susan saw Jacqueline's eyes fill with tears, Mary Lou's mouth fall open in surprise, Gloria wince as though she'd been struck. "The boys" made no motion, but terror was written on their faces. Terror and a kind of stunned disbelief.

"I hadn't planned to tell anyone," Giovanni went on. "Not even your mother. I'm the product of a generation that was almost ashamed of having cancer. In my day, we didn't speak of it. Perhaps we superstitiously hoped that by not talking about it it would cease to exist. But mostly it was a kind of disgrace." He smiled. "I guess you'd say it wasn't an 'elegant' disease. Anyway, that's the way I was brought up and that's the way I'd intended to handle it. But something happened to make me see how wrong and selfish of me that was." He carefully did not look at Susan. "Someone made me realize that you, my dearest ones, had a right to know. And that I had an obligation to tell you.

"I haven't been a 'model father' and because of that you've not been 'model children.' I wish we'd been closer, more outgoing toward one another. I wish we'd been able to share things. I wish I could have helped you more. My fault. My choice, really. But I've loved each and every one of you—my children since the days of your happily awaited births, my children-by-marriage since you honored us by becoming part of the family. You make me proud, as your mother makes me proud. I respect you as I do her. Life owes me nothing. All I've hoped for and dreamed of has come true in you—in your talents, your grace and your beauty."

He looked slowly, tenderly at each of them in turn. "Don't be sad," he said. "God has been good to me. Exceptionally good. Possibly better than I deserve."

The silence that followed seemed interminable. Susan closed her eyes. Why doesn't someone say something? Don't his children realize how hard this is for him, how much courage it took to even discuss it? What are they thinking? That he should have told each of them privately? Are they being competitive even at a time like this? Or are they reacting as he was afraid they would: repelled by disease denying their father's death because it brought them one step closer to the inevitability of their own? How would I feel if it were my own father standing there telling me he was going to die?

In the end, it was not "one of his own" who spoke first. Jacqueline finally asked softly, "How long do we have, Joe?"

"We," she'd said. Susan blessed her for that. Not "How long do *you* have?" Jacqueline was doing what her sister-in-law hoped; telling this almost diffident-sounding man that they wanted to share every moment that was left.

Giovanni shrugged, "The doctors think it could be quite a while. They think old age will get me before the cancer does. That seems highly possible." It was said lightly, but his tone told them he didn't believe it. "In any case, the odds are in my favor. I'm playing on the Lord's money, so to speak. I passed my limit long ago. From here on, it's poverty poker in this game."

Susan looked up, startled. Why on earth was Joe using the jargon of gamblers, a manner of speaking totally foreign to him? For a crazy moment he sounded like Martin Tanner, using the slang of thc casiino. She realized he was looking directly at her, a little smile on his face. Is he telling me that he knows about Vegas? Did he know about it when we talked, but wouldn't use that as a weapon any more than he'd have tried to bribe me with money? If he knew, what must he think of my moral tone, discussing his infidelities and Richard's and never confessing my own! She reddened. But did he really know, or was it pure coincidence that he'd chosen to discuss his life expectancy in gambling terms? She'd never be sure. Giovanni went on, looking now at the others.

"Life's a gamble from the day we're born, Some of us play out the game until the end, trying to bluff our way through it. And some of us go through our days holding nothing but winning hands. I've becn one of those lucky ones. I intend to go on being lucky. I'm not depressed. In fact, I'm declaring a holiday. Your mother and I are going to take a real vacation. We haven't had one in years and it's high time we traveled for fun."

"A vacation!" Sergio was incredulous. "Is that wise, Father? Shouldn't you be near your doctors?"

"No need. They've done all they can."

"But we don't want you to go away from us now!" This from Gloria, the one who'd always seemed the least caring. "We should all stay close, Papa, for as long as we can."

"She's right," Walter said. "Don't deprive us of the time we have."

He looked as though they'd given him a gift. "We won't stay away too long," he said. "I want to be with all of you, too. But I also want some time with your mother. She's been so busy with my career and yours that we've not had much time alone. I have many things to tell her, most of them long overdue."

Susan was aware that of all the children Richard was the only one who'd not spoken. Was he going to say nothing? Until that day at Kate's, she'd had no idea he bore a grudge against his father. There'd always been the outward appearance of "normalcy" between them, as "normal' as Giovanni's relationship with any of his family, but now Richard's silence struck her as significant. She wondered what he was feeling, whether he regretted what he'd always secretly felt. He simply sat there, expressionless, as the others began to chatter nervously, crowding around Giovanni and Maria, trying to pretend nothing had changed as they spoke of mundane things.

Maria, for once, was as quiet as her youngest son. Susan had never seen her like this—answering in monosyllables, obviously distracted, her eyes rarely leaving her husband's face and her hand once again in his. Susan felt an involuntary flicker of pity for her. Ruthless, ambitious and cold as she was, Maria had once known ecstasy with this man, and even through all the time beyond those early, passionate days she had been loyal and faithful to him. In many ways, she'd made him happy, Susan supposed, happier perhaps, than he'd made her. Happier than I've been able to make Richard. Maria was not a woman who inspired pity but at this moment Susan felt sorry for her. She'd go on as dominant and opinionated a widow as she'd been a wife. But she was losing the one person who'd always depended upon her strength. Susan knew it. She might have nothing else in common with Maria, but she could identify with the need to be needed.

Chapter 25

IT WAS QUITE a joke, Giovanni thought as he opened his eyes that last morning in the spring of 1972. Doctors! They always figured out a way to be right. Last fall when they told him old age would get him before the cancer did, he should have realized there was no way they could be wrong. In another month he'd be seventy-eight years old. Who could say at that age what they'd list as "cause of death?"

He didn't know how he knew this was the final day. He felt no worse than usual. He'd been lucky. There'd been no hideous suffering, not even much disability beyond the normal slowing down of a man who'd lived hard for nearly eighty years. And yet he sensed there'd be no tomorrow. Odd. He wasn't frightened. Almost curious and quite satisfied.

In these past months he'd behaved normally. That is, he'd kept several already-scheduled engagements, conducting the New York, Boston and Philadelphia symphonies, telling no one outside the family of his illness and showing no signs of it at the performances. He was proud of that.

He was also proud of his sudden ability to communicate with his wife. he and Maria had gone off for their holiday alone, and though it was no rapturous thing, it had been a peaceful two weeks in Jamaica. They kept to themselves, sunned on the beach and talked long hours into the night. Giovanni could hardly remember their ever talking so much before. Not since the first days of their marriage. Terrible how people drifted apart. He mourned for how much they'd missed and he told her so.

She'd nodded as if to say, "I know," when he said he'd always loved her, in spite of his unfaithfulness and the distance it had put between them. He told her that he was grateful for the wife and mother she'd been, and aware of what she'd contributed to his success. It felt good to say these things, and better still to mean them. She was far from perfect, and he said that, too. But she was a strong and determined woman and he knew that any "shortcomings" she had were brought about by the need to survive with him.

"And your warts aren't a patch on mine," Giovanni had said, smiling. "For every flaw in you, my dear, there are twenty in me. How could you have put up with me all these years?"

She'd looked young then, soft, like the girl he'd married almost fifty-five years before.

"I loved you," Maria said. "I still do." She'd smiled back at him. "I've done some selfish things, too, Joe. Other kinds. But we can't help how we're made, either of us."

He wondered whether she was thinking of Richard, whether he should ask her to let go of the boy. Boy, indeed! Incredibly, Richard was thirty-eight years old. Too late now to change his thinking. Or Maria's. At least, Richard seemed content these days. Susan was doing a good job. She was more than keeping her word about standing by. Richard would be a great man and, thank God, not an empty one.

They'll be all right, Giovanni thought as he rose that morning and went about his meticulous grooming routine. All my headstrong, difficult children will be. As he shaved and showered he thought of them. Sergio was a fine conductor, but he'd never achieve Richard's stature. And Richard would never achieve Walter's. That was another curious circumstance. Walter, the most "different" of his sons, would undoubtedy be the immortal. Performers and conductors, the best of them, were eventually almost forgotten. But Walter's music would live on for other artists to interpret. In generations to come, as in the past, the names of composers were eternal, while those who conducted their works or gave them expression faded into dim memory. Walter, the least competitive, the least publicity-conscious, the least aggressive of the boys, would be the Antonini future generations would revere and remember. Fate did have its way of being whimisical.

As he put on his clothes, Giovanni thought of Gloria, the frustrated, "untalented" child who produced nothing. But that wasn't true, of course. She produced a complete, well-organized life for a husband and four beautiful children. Giovanni hoped it was also happy. He wished they'd had a more usual father-daughter relationship. In most families, the girl was "Daddy's favorite," especially when she was the only girl. But Gloria had always been too fierce, somehow. Too unfeminine. He supposed she felt she had to fight to be noticed among her glittering brothers. But she'd never allowed herself to be loved for her own qualities. And, in fairness to her, neither he nor Maria had spent much time looking for the qualities in Gloria that were unique.

Too late for that, Giovanni sighed. He was grateful to have glimpsed Gloria's tenderness the night he told them he had cancer. He was glad to know some love was there, regretting he hadn't realized earlier how much she'd wanted to reach out to him.

He walked slowly downstairs to the big room dominated by the concert grand. He settled himself in his favorite chair and picked up the new score Walter had left the night before. It was a piano concerto, incredibly difficult, nearly impossible but thrilling and unbearably beautiful. Walter hoped Richard would perform it, but before giving it to his brother, he wanted his father's opinion.

I'll be able to tell him it's more than good, Giovanni thought. It's genius. A challenge no pianist could resist. Richard will perform it brilliantly. The family will be proud.

He let the sheets of paper fall into his lap. He was so tired. His last thought was that he must tell Richard this was his brother's most important work. He could hear it in his head, soaring, torrential, carrying him with it. He rushed along with the passages and felt a strong surge of power within himself that matched the music—a great outpouring of hope and triumph that reached a final, crashing crescendo.

And it was over.

Where was the constrained, pathetic woman who had clung to her husband's hand a few months before, when he told his family of his illness? Watching

Maria organize Giovanni's final tribute, Susan felt she must have imagined that soft clinging creature. Certainly she bore no resemblance to the dry-eyed, straight-backed, calm widow who directed every phase of the elaborate procedure. It was Maria who found him that morning, Maria who called the children and announced, with no show of emotion, "Your father is dead." And it was Maria who supervised every detail from there on in, giving directions for the kind of spectacular "farewell appearance" Giovanni Antonini deserved.

Observing Maria in action, seeing her children jump to do her bidding, Susan marveled again at the strength of this petite martinet. And listening to her give crisp concise orders, Susan realized, uncomfortably, that Maria must have been planning this since the day she learned her husband was dying. The efficiency of it gave Susan cold chills. It was only practical, she supposed, to plan for the inevitable, especially where a man as famous as Giovanni was concerned, but it seemed so impersonal, so cold-blooded.

"Your mother is incredible," she said to Richard at one point. "What strength she has! She looks so frail but she's more composed than any of us. I haven't even seen her cry."

"And you never will. She's a lady to her fingertips."

Intentional or not, Susan felt the terse comment was a slap at her own emotional nature. She looked at Richard, trying to read his thoughts, but his face was impassive. She mustn't be so thin-skinned. They were so controlled, all of them. Not just Maria, but her children and those they'd married. Why couldn't she be like that? But she couldn't. My God have they no feelings? Don't they grieve for him at all? Was it "unlady-like" to shed a tear for the loss of a dear one?

She watched and listened, fascinated, as the business of the moment went on, orchestrated by Maria. There would be a private funeral service and a public tribute. Giovanni's closed casket would lie on the bare stage of Carnegie Hall and the greats of the music world would come to hear Sergio deliver the eulogy.

"Sergio is the one to do it," Maria said. "If we asked someone outside the family there'd be no end of hurt feelings. They'll all be there, of course. Giovanni's peers. Ormandy. Stern, Heifetz, Horowitz, Menuhin, Iturbi . . . all of them. Best to let Serge do it. He's the oldest son. I wonder if Beverly Sills is in town. I'd like her to sing something. Walter, try to reach her, will you? And Jacqueline, my dear, call Bergdorf and have them send over three or four black dresses for me to choose from. Gloria, be sure the invitations are *hand-delivered*. And Richard, you'd better arrange for the flowers. There'll be millions, of course, but the family will want a blanket. Red roses, I think. They'll look best against the black velvet curtain. Mary Lou, you take care of the seating in the hall. A ticklish bit of protocol, but you've had some experience at that with Sergio's concerts."

Susan, aghast at the performance of a woman who'd been widowed only a few hours, could also not help noticing that she and Raoul Taffin were the only ones to whom Maria did not assign duties. She's always found Raoul hopelessly weak, Susan thought. As for me, it's a calculated way of showing I'll never belong. Damn her. I won't let her exclude me.

"What may I do to help, Mrs. Antonini?"

Maria looked at her as though she was surprised to find her there. Then she frowned. "I think everything's in order, thank you. The papers have the obituary up to date in their files, of course. I don't know, Susan. Perhaps you could help with the children. They're all pretty well grown up, except for Gloria's little ones. You might keep an eye on them at Carnegie Hall. I don't suppose you'll want Katherine to attend."

"Why not? She's going on seven. Only a year younger than the twins."

"Well, yes. But I don't think it would be meaningful to her, my dear. She'd find it very disturbing, I'd imagine, not being able to hear."

Susan set her lips firmly. "Katie is deaf but she's mentally alert. I want her to remember what a great man her paternal grandfather was."

Maria shrugged. "As you like."

It went exactly as planned—the gathering at Carnegie Hall attended by every important figure in the arts. The crowds on West Fifty-seventh Street, held back by police barricades, strained to see the celebrities enter and leave, nudged each other and clicked their cameras as they recognized composers and conductors, violinists, pianists and opera stars. When Maria stepped out of her limousine, escorted by her three tall sons, a murmur ran through the crowd and a few sentimental women wiped tears from their eyes. "How brave she is," they told each other. "Isn't she dignified! She's up in her seventies, you know, but look at that figure! I bet she doesn't wear more than a size six. What a marvelous woman."

The "marvelous woman" looked neither right nor left as she mounted the steps, head high, showing just the right amount of awareness of those who came to gawk and comment. She was, in fact, loving every minute of it. She was sorry Joe was dead, but she'd had time to get used to the idea of his dying. We all have to go sometime, she reasoned, and how many of us leave this world so universally mourned? Joe would like being surrounded by his adoring fans. He always had. Just as she liked being the center of public attention and seldon was. For once, the spotlight was hers alone. She was the symbol of the family, widow and mother of great men, the keeper of the faith. She intended to play that role to thc hilt.

Sergio spoke movingly (Thank God Richard's publicity man had been able to write a eulogy that was neither too impersonal nor too mawkish!) and Beverly Sills's glorious voice singing the *Ave Maria* filled the hall and was amplified to the hushed crowd outside. As prearranged, one by one the musical greats came forward at the end of the ceremony. Slowly, the living legends crossed the stage in silence, paused a moment before Giovanni's casket, then moved on, heads bowed, faces showing their genuine grief. Joe would have liked that, Maria thought, watching from her front row seat. He always cared about the recognition of his peers. He always appreciated a good piece of showmanship.

"That was quite a production Maria put on." Kate Fenton's voice was matter of fact. "You have to hand it to her. She's a born impresario. I'm surprised she didn't walk behind the hearse from Campbell's Funeral Chapel to Carnegie Hall."

Susan, seated beside her friend on a banquette in the art-deco atmosphere of Maxwell's Plum, looked slightly shocked. Sometimes Kate could be so callous. Not that it wasn't true. Maria had turned her husband's funeral into an event the world would not soon forget. And yet it managed to be more impressive than tasteless, more tribute than three-ring circus. What it lacked, Susan knew, was heart. They'd all been so well bred, so composed. Oddly, the only one who wept uncontrollably was Gloria. She'd been pathetic, this big, athletic woman crying like a child for a father she must have loved more than she ever dared show.

"Your silence is stunning," Kate said. "What's the matter? Did I speak out of turn or are your eggs Benedict covered with curdled hollandaise?"

Susan smiled. "Sorry. I was just thinking about Gloria. Of everyone at the funeral, she was the only one who showed any honest emotion. I guess it surprised me, seeing how deeply she felt. She's always been so . . . I don't know, I guess 'formidable' is the word."

Kate nodded. "It would be helpful if we all had X-ray eyes. Then we'd know what was really going on inside people. Or maybe it wouldn't. We're probably better off not knowing." She deliberately changed the subject. "You know, I like this restaurant. All the marvelous stained-glass décor and *art nouveau*. We should come here more often. I keep forgetting about it. It's kind of off the beaten path over here on First Avenue."

"Not off the beaten path for half the world," Susan said. "It's packed."

"Yes, but not with the same old faces from *Women's Wear Daily,* thank God! I get awfully bored with so-called socialites who have nothing better to do with their lives than decide between sole amandine and beef Wellington. And speaking of people who don't know what to do with themselves, where do you go from here?"

"Bloomingdale's, I think. I need curtains for the kitchen."

"Very funny. That's not what I mean and you know it. I'm talking about what you're doing with your life. Joe's gone and your promise to him is canceled. My goddaughter is at the stage where she doesn't need you every minute. Here you are, kiddo, light years married and no prospects, I assume, of a bigger family. You're at a kind of crossroad, aren't you? Are you ever again to do something on your own? Or are you always going to be a shadow of Richard? Whither the hell are you drifting? Are you content to abandon all your potential? Can you really sublimate the need to accomplish something more satisfying than a well-planned dinner? You can't just mark time, Susan. That's not enough for you. You're a giver, a doer, a bright lady. Kitchen curtains, for God's sake!" Kate impatiently lit a cigarette. "I'm sorry. It's probably none of my damned business, but you've been in limbo too long. Isn't there anything you'd really like to do?"

"Yes," Susan said slowly. "I'd like to be needed. I know that sounds insane, but it's true. Katie's doing so well, I can't really contribute much more to her life than a mother can to any bright, busy little girl. Not that I'm not happy about it! It's what I've prayed for. Edith Chambers and Katie's teachers at school assure me she can go to college when she's ready. They say she'll be able to drive a car and engage in sports and get married and be like her friends in every way. Think of it, Kate! Isn't it a miracle what these people have done?"

"You were the one who always believed it could happen. Never forget that."

"I know. I'm glad for that. Glad I made that decision." She sounded wistful. "Even though it really was the beginning of the end for Richard and me."

Kate was silent for a moment. Then she said, gently, "What about Richard?"

"I love him," Susan repeated. "And in a strange way he loves me. But we don't share anything, Kate. He doesn't need me. He has his work, his success, more family obligations now that his father's gone."

Kate snuffed out her cigarette angrily. "You mean Maria is more demanding of his time than ever. Naturally! The widow's clinging to her baby boy. God! It's obscene! It's really sick! If you tell me you've agreed to spend the summer with her, I swear I'll kill you!"

Susan smiled. "No. Fortunately, she hasn't asked us. She'd love to have Richard there, I'm sure, but that would mean Katie and me, as well. She still wants no part of that. As a matter of fact, we're going to take a house in East Hampton. I've seen a lovely one, right on the beach, and Richard's agreeable."

"So you *are* going to stay with him, even though Joe's gone. You still think you can make it work."

Susan looked away. "I want it to work. Maybe I'm looking for another miracle, but I can't get away from the fact that he's the only man I've ever loved."

"Or you still have the guilts about the Vegas episode."

"No. I've almost forgotten that. That had nothing to do with love. That was part of my insane period. Like the heavy drinking. I hope you notice I'm not doing that any more, either. Something good will happen this summer, Kate. I just feel it will. Maybe Richard and I can get really close again. Maybe it will be like our honeymoon on the Cape. He needed me then. Not just physically. It was a spiritual thing. We were one person. Maybe we can recapture some of that when we're alone."

Her friend didn't answer. No need to tell Susan she was still dreaming dreams, trying to believe that everything that happened in the past could be wiped out by one idyllic summer that had no chance of coming true. True romantic that she was, Susan always kept coming back for more. It was such a waste. Especially when there was someone who cared so much for her, someone who'd devote his life to making her happy. Why couldn't she face the fact that Richard would *never* need her? Why did she cling to this impossible hope?

"Paul keeps calling me to ask how you are."

Susan looked at her curiously. "How is Paul? I saw him for a minute at Carnegie Hall."

"He's fine. Has his own flourishing business. Represents half a dozen artists."

"I'm glad. I was always so sorry he left Richard."

"You know why he did, of course."

"Yes. That dreadful Washington business. I don't blame him. He couldn't be a party to any more of that."

"Oh, come on, Susan! Who the hell do you think you're kidding? Paul left because he was in love with you. He still is. You know that! If you had a grain of sense you'd give up this business with Richard and grab a terrific guy who's mad for you. And, I might add, for Katie!"

"I'm not in love with Paul. I wish I could be."

"Well, maybe you ought to try! Maybe you should stop behaving like a schoolgirl and get wise to the fact that you can have a pretty damned good life with someone who's anxious to give more than he takes! This isn't *True Romances*, Susan. It's life. When are you going to get over being sixteen years old?"

"Is *that* what you think I should do with my life—marry Paul?"

"Not necessarily, but it isn't such a bad idea. I just want you to do something besides chase rainbows! I don't care if you get a job or write a book or take up good works, but for God's sake get off your ass! They've drained all the spirit out of you. They're making you a blob!"

Susan straightened and her eyes flashed fire. "Damn you, Kate, how dare you say such things to me? Who do you think you are? What have you done with *your* life that's so terrific? I don't think being a hotshot editor with no personal life exactly qualifies you for Woman of the Year! Have you ever known what it is to love a man so much you could suffer torture and still want to be with him? Have you ever hated yourself for your weakness in staying and yet be unable to leave? What do you know about spirit? Don't you think it's taken spirit to cope with the whole damned Antonini family—Richard included?" She stopped, aghast at the words that had come pouring out. Why was she attacking her best friend—the only person who cared enough to see that she had become a woman with no will of her own? For Kate was right, of course. She was drifting, purposelessly waiting for that miracle. It wasn't going to come. Richard would never be faithful or unselfish or truly in need of her. She was such a fool. Why couldn't she face that? She blinked back the tears. "Kate, forgive me. I'm crazy. I know you're right. I don't know what made me say those hateful things to you."

But Kate was grinning. "Well, it's about time! I figured you were still a spunky kid, but I didn't think I'd ever break through that shroud of martyrdom!"

"You're not angry?"

"Angry? I'm delighted to find they haven't removed your spine!"

Susan managed a little laugh. "But I still don't know where I'm going."

"Maybe not. But at least now I have hope that you won't be too blinded with self-pity to follow the road when you do find it!"

Chapter 26

WHEN THEY FINISHED lunch and Kate hopped into a cab at Sixty-fourth Street and First Avenue, Susan went off to do her errand at Bloomingdale's. Though it was a few blocks out of her way, she decided to cross town on East Fifty-seventh Street, past the "spit and polish" apartment buildings between First and Second Avenues, past the odd little antique shops and bookstores and the "discount fashion outlet" where "Name Designer Clothes" could sometimes be found for less than the regular price. She glanced at the marquee of the Sutton Theatre, and into the windows of Schrafft's, and ambled west toward Lexington Avenue, admiring the antique crystal chandeliers in Nesle's elegant shop and stopping to inspect the astounding household gadgets displayed by Hammacher Schlemmer. At Lexington, she turned north again, toward her destination. The going was more difficult on this avenue. It literally swarmed with people. Young men and women in jeans and T-shirts; nervous matrons with blue-dyed hair and purses firmly clutched; young housewives in pants-suits and dark glasses; crazy, raggedy old people mumbling to themselves; wild-eyed, raggedy young people peddling ugly homemade jewelry from folding stands illegally set up on the sidewalk. The atmosphere was carnival-like, the smells of food from open-to-the-street lunch counters downright nauseating. And yet there was something fascinating about it all. She thought, as she so often did these days, of Giovanni. He'd adored this part of town, loved to prowl the streets, marveling at a city that was such a study in contrasts. She understood that fascination. In a five-minute walk, one could leave the liveried-doorman-guarded block that housed New York's senior United States senator and his social wife and be in an area that was dirty, shabby and unabashedly commercial. "Bloomie's," as New Yorkers called the department store, was a kaleidoscope of its surroundings. The neighborhood had "grown up around it" in the past fifteen years, with new high-rise apartments and tall office buildings. Bloomie's was the mecca for rich women and couturier clothes. It was also the place for basement bargains and "in" clothes the secretaries loved, and "far-out" fashions that attracted high-school kids and homosexuals and hookers. Susan responded to the electricity of it. Crowded and confusing as it was, she found it a "miniature New York" with all that was beautiful and tawdry and tough and chic and throbbingly alive. No other store offered such infinite variety of selection, nor such disparity of social and financial status among its shoppers. Even finding what you wanted and getting waited on was a challenge only for the stouthearted, strong-winded shopper. Bloomie's was no kinder to models and movie stars than it was to mothers' helpers.

As she pushed her way onto the escalator, Susan felt ridiculously at peace amid the chaos, marvelously self-sufffficient as she put up her own battle in the crowds. She even began to smile as she thought of the conversation with Kate. Dear Kate. Deliberately making her defend herself, forcing her to think about the future, daring her to prove she'd not become a nothing of a person. The confrontation had been good for her. She'd been runnning away from remembrance of the past and stubbornly unwilling to make decisions about the years to come. Kate had made it impossible for her to duck the issues any longer.

What was it she really wanted? "To be needed," she'd said. What a stupid, pat answer! Everybody wanted to be needed. Ridiculous of her to sit back and hope for Richard to suddenly realize he couldn't function without her. He could. All too well. Giovanni had been wrong. It wasn't necessary for her to "save" her husband from a life of emptiness; it was more to the point that she save herself.

As she picked through the rows of kitchen curtains, hardly seeing them, she mentally listed all the things that had plagued her throughout her marriage. In the beginning, it had been unjustified jealousy over the strange women who literally threw themselves at Richard when he was on tour. Later, the jealousy and hurt had been real as she learned about film stars and socialites and senators' daughters and other women in her husband's life. There'd been the great periods of loneliness when she gave up traveling with him because of Katie's need of her. And, indeed, there was Katie herself. No plague this. This was her pride and joy, adorable Katie, whom she'd literally snatched back to her bosom from the exile that Maria had decreed and Richard—with his irrational desire to please her—had imposed. Katie, whom her father simply could not love.

We've survived so many things, Susan thought. The Washington fiasco and its aftermath. Her foolish, well-meant second pregnancy, so "conveniently" terminated. Giovanni's death and Maria's now greater-than-ever hold on her youngest son. Nothing, Susan told herself, has turned out as I thought. A spoiled, sought-after thirty-eight-year-old didn't magically become a paragon. Marriage didn't terminate women's interest in him, or his in them. He wouldn't lose his ego or his love of attention because he had a wife. I should have known he wouldn't have the patience for any part of Katie's upbringing. What an utter dreamer I am! And what am I hoping for now? A magic reconciliation? A metamorphosis in Richard? Kate must think me infantile. Everyone must. How they'd laugh if they knew what I'm secretly hoping: that this summer Richard and I might decide together to have another child. What nonsense! You'll never have a "normal" marriage. So forget it, Susan! Grow up! Kate's right. You've come to a crossroad. Put up or shut up. Live with Richard as he is and stop whining or concentrate on accomplishing something for yourself, with or without him. This time *you've* got to have breathing room. You're suffocating in boredom.

"May I help you, madam?"

Susan came back to reality with a start. She realized she'd been standing with the same pair of curtains in her hand for God knows how long. She smiled and blushed.

"Yes, thank you. I'll have these. Charge and send."

The girl produced her sales book. "You have your charge plate?"

"No. Sorry. The name is Antonini. Mrs. Richard Antonini. That's A-n-t . . ."

There was the usual wide-eyed reaction.

"You don't have to spell it. I'm a concert buff. I think your husband is simply wonderful, Mrs. Antonini!"

"Yes, he is," Susan echoed automatically. "Simply wonderful."

"I'm worried about Susan," Bea Langdon said.

Wil reluctantly switched off Walter Cronkite. "Any special reason?"

"We hardly ever see her. She doesn't even phone often these days."

"Honey, she's been through a bad time. She was very fond of the maestro. And don't forget she also had a miscarriage not too long ago."

"That's another thing. She never talks about the baby."

Wil sighed. If he lived to be a hundred, he'd never understand women. "Bea, dear, isn't it healthy that she's not brooding? Besides, it wasn't a real baby. I mean, she was only two months pregnant."

"You wouldn't understand. Any life inside a woman is real from the moment she knows it's there. Losing it, deliberately or accidentally, is traumatic. The normal reaction would be for Susan to unburden herself, to cry over her loss, instead of acting as though it never happened."

"So she's a strong girl. Good head on her shoulders."

Bea's glance was withering. "That girl's in trouble. You mark my word. She's tight as a drum. I know she just doesn't want to worry us, but there are things she's bottling up inside. I feel it, Wil. I'm frightened for her. I want to help and I can't reach her."

He came and sat next to her on the sofa. "She'll be all right. I know Richard has his faults, but Susie has a husband to turn to. The marriage has lasted almost eight years. It must be solid enough, my dear, even with all its ups and downs. Try to relax. They're going to have a good summer in East Hampton, In that atmosphere, problems have a way of disappearing. I suppose the vastness of the sea really does point up the insignificance of our petty little lives." He played his trump card. "Besides, Grandma, think what a swell time your Katie's going to have!"

Bea smiled and stroked his cheek. "What would I do without you, Wil Langdon? You make my world so safe and sane."

"My job, lady. And I love it."

Don't ever leave me, she silently begged him. I'm no Maria Antonini. I couldn't go on without you.

As she opened the apartment door, Richard called out to her from the terrace. "Susan? Come on out and soak up some spring sunshine."

She found him stretched out on a chaise, Walter's concerto carelessly tossed on a table beside him as though it had been thrown there in disgust or anger. She looked at the messy sheets as she sank gratefully into a chair.

"Lord, I've walked my legs off! It feels good to sit. Have you been home all afternoon? How's it going with the concerto?"

He scowled. "To answer your last question: lousy. I'll never master the damned thing!"

"Of course you will. You said yourself it was brilliant."

"More like diabolical. I swear to God I think Walter set out to write something Horowitz couldn't play! I wouldn't be surprised if he deliberately did it to drive me up the wall!"

Susan smiled. He sounded so like the angry child he was. He'd conquer it, of course. If only to prove that his brother couldn't get the best of him.

"Come on," she said teasingly. "You know you're as good as Horowitz."

Richard relaxed. "Not yet. But I will be. He has a thirty-year head start on me. It'll take another year or so to catch up."

She was pleased to find him in such a good humor. "Be a sport. Give yourself two years."

Richard laughed. "Okay. Two years. So how was Kate? Abrasive as ever?"

Susan refused to be ruffled. It was too nice a day. They were having a rare, "married people" kind of easy conversation. She wouldn't spoil this relaxed moment by getting uptight over the little crack at Kate.

"Of course. That's Kate's personality. Abrasive but interesting. She's fine. As you know, she goes to Europe in July, as usual, to do fashion features for the magazine. She says she's bored with it, but she never will be. After all these years, she still loves that by-line. She'd miss the excitement of dealing with people and the stimulation of feeling important. She'd be lost without applause. Kate needs recognition.''

Richard was quiet for a moment, and then he said, ''Who are you talking about, Susie? Kate or yourself?''

She looked at him in surprise. It was rare for Richard to be so perceptive. He was right. She hadn't consciously realized it as she spoke, but she was describing herself. That was one thing she missed: the ego-building. She had, in fact, determined that very day to find some form of it again.

''I was talking about both of us,'' she admitted finally. ''I didn't realize I was so transparent. But I've been thinking about it all day. I don't like what I've become. Or what I've *not* become. I'm not sure how to solve the problem, but I've still got to find something that's uniquely mine. Can you understand that?''

''Yes, believe it or not, I think I can. Any idea what you'd like to do?''

''No. Not a clue.' She felt very cheerful. ''But by the end of the summer I'll come up with an idea.''

''I think you should. I've been doing a lot of thinking too, Susie. I've been unfair to you. I took a lively, confident career woman and tried to make her an ambitionless 'second-rate citizen' for my sake. That's wrong. I guess I've always known you shouldn't be expected to change while I went on exactly as I always have.'' He smiled. ''The knowledge has come a little late, but I *can* see you must have something of your own. An 'identity,' I think they call it. I want you to know I'm all for it, and I know it won't hurt our marriage. It might even help it.''

She could hardly believe what she was hearing. Richard urging her to find outside interests? Richard admitting he'd been wrong about her role as an ''Antonini woman?'' Hating herself for her suspicions, she wondered what had produced this sudden insight. She could hear Giovanni's voice. ''Richard's the product of the last person he talks to.'' Whom had he been talking to? That was unfair. Why couldn't he simply have been thinking about her, recognizing that she, too, had needs? He couldn't have been untouched by his father's death. Perhaps he saw in Maria what happened to a woman when a cause to which she'd been devoted for years was taken from her. He must be relating that to us, Susan thought. He must have been thinking all these weeks, what my status would be if something happened to him. I've given up every outside interest. She felt very close to him. He'd shown so little outward emotion over Giovanni's death, but he must be overwhelmed with sadness for all the resentment-filled past. Death can sometimes bring other truths sharply into focus. Perhaps he's remorseful about depriving me of children. Her thoughts were interrupted by the sound of her husband's voice.

''Maybe you should go back to work for the magazine,'' he was saying. ''At least on a part-time basis. It would put you back in touch with people, give you the activity and self-importance you need.'' He stopped as though something had just occurred to him. ''Why don't you go to Europe with Kate? That's an idea! She's always wanting you to do some writing. And if *Vogue* won't pay for it you can go anyway. The money's no problem. Especially now. We're very rich, Susie. Father was a multimillionaire and he left it equally to Mother and all of us. She was telling me at lunch . . . '' He stopped abruptly. ''Anyway, darling, why not discuss it with Kate? Maybe you don't have to search for something to do. Maybe you can go back to doing what you loved when we met.''

In that instant it was all blindingly clear. Maria. Always Maria. She knew about *Vogue* covering the collections. She wanted Richard with her for this first summer she didn't wish to face alone. It was *her* idea to get rid of Susan temporarily so she could have her "baby" for six weeks in Pound Ridge. She could hear Maria subtly making Richard think this was his own brainstorm. Anger welled up in Susan. All that talk about ''understanding her need for identity'' was just so much convenient hogwash! Richard didn't give a damn. This time she wouldn't fall into the trap. She wouldn't let Maria have her way.

Pretending surprise, Susan looked at him innocently. ''Go to Europe? Give up a wonderful summer with you and Katie in East Hampton? Darling, I wouldn't dream of it! That's so dear of you. So generous! But nothing could make me sacrifice those weeks we've been looking forward to. No. Don't you worry. I'm just so thrilled you understand that I have to get busy again! But *Vogue's* not the answer. In the fall, I'll find the right thing to do. You'll see. You'll be proud of me, Richard. Just as I'm so proud of you for your unselfishness.''

He looked confused. ''Well, of course,'' he said finally. 'It was only a suggestion.''

''And a wonderful one, darling. Thank you for thinking of it.'' She rose casually. ''I'll go check on Katie. She must be home from school by now. Oh, by the way, I ran into one of your fans today. She sells curtains at Bloomingdale's. I didn't even have to spell my name for her. She knew it well.'' She gave him a bright smile. ''You see, sweetheart, there are compensations, being married to a celebrity!''

Inside the living room, out of his sight, she felt as though she were going to be actively ill. Would this cat-and-mouse game never end? She straightened up and the moment of disgust gave way to determination. Damn you, Maria. It's really come to a pitched battle now, hasn't it? With Giovanni gone, you want more of Richard than ever. Well, you won't have him. You're quite an actress, but I can be an actress too. I just proved that.

She felt very different from the indecisive young woman who'd sat on the banquette at Maxwell's Plum a few hours earlier. Kate was right. She still had spine. She was still Susan Langdon, no matter what. And a dozen Maria Antoninis weren't going to destroy her. How could I ever have felt sorry for her? Susan wondered. There's never a moment when she isn't scheming or playing a part. I don't believe she was even deeply touched by her husband's illness or his death. She simply portrayed what was expected—a shocked and saddened wife and a brave, grief-stricken widow. I don't think she can feel much of anything. People see her as strong and courageous, but all she is is totally self-involved. I made the mistake of thinking of her in terms of my own mother, who knows how to love deeply and unselfishly. I imagined what Mother would feel if something happened to Dad. Susan shuddered. It was an idea she refused to entertain. A morbid, unacceptable thought. Both her parents were in good health, thank God. And of course they were years younger than Richard's.

Still, I shouldn't neglect them as I have lately, Susan told herself. Except for each other, I'm all they have. I've been so deep in my own problems, I've hardly given a thought to them. Not that they've complained. They never would. All my life they've been understanding, easy to talk to. She felt an urge to talk with them now. Bea, especially. It was a need, she realized, to be part of a happy, giving, unselfish family, a childish wish, perhaps, to go back even for a little while to an atmosphere that was safe and undemanding. I really trust Mother more than anyone, Susan thought, somewhat surprised by her discovery. She's not as worldly as Kate nor as cynically realistic as Jacqueline. They're wonderful but I'm Mother's flesh and blood. I could tell her anything and she'd accept and forgive me because she loves me without reservation.

I'll call tomorrow and make a date to go to Bronxville for dinner. If Richard doesn't want to come along, he doesn't have to. She faced her feelings squarely. In fact, Susan thought, I hope he won't.

She made her way toward Katie's room. I hope my daughter always feels as much need for her mother as I do for mine. I hope we never lose the precious emotional reaction that's more sustaining than any amount of logical dissection. With Kate I can be honest and know I'll get a sensible, analytical appraisal and good advice. But with Mother I can be comforted even when I'm wrong.

He'd never debated so long over anything. For days Martin Tanner had tried to decide whether to call the woman he knew as Susan Armstrong, the woman who had, for God's sake, turned out to be Susan Antonini. Mrs. Richard Antonini. Socialite, patron of the arts, wife of one of the world's most famous concert pianists! The discovery had rocked him. He'd known she was hiding something. He'd suspected she was using a phony name. But he hadn't expected her to be a celebrity, vulnerable to publicity, even blackmail if she'd been unlucky enough to run into the wrong guy.

What was she? A nymphomaniac? A nut? Or didn't she give a damn? Running off to Vegas, staying stoned out of her mind most of the time, going to bed with a stranger she picked up on a plane. What kind of madness was that? Other women, ordinary women, might do those things, but the wife of a public figure was insane to run such risks with her husband's reputation, even if she didn't care about her own.

And obviously she didn't, Martin reasoned. It was ridiculous to think he was her only affair since her marriage, no matter what she said. And yet he wasn't sure. There was something about her half-fright, half-bravado that had gotten to him. She wasn't your usual bored wife out for a good time. He'd felt it then. He'd been almost surprised when she let him make love to her. For that's what it had been. She'd responded, but initiated nothing, as though she was holding back, out of guilt or fear or shame.

He had to admit she piqued his curiosity. Even after she left Vegas so precipitously, he hadn't been able to get her out of his mind. There weren't many women who left such a deep impression. He'd looked up Armstrongs in the New York phone book when he returned, but there were dozens who could have been possible. It was a silly idea. He didn't even know her husband's first name. And it was clear she didn't want to see him again, even though she'd told him, with a disarming lack of coyness, how much he attracted her, how she'd pursue him if she were free to. But she wasn't free and she obviously wasn't the kind of married woman who had the stomach for the sordid little hidden affair. He'd almost dismissed her until he saw the pictures of Giovanni Antonini's funeral service at Carnegie Hall. There, on the steps, was Susan, holding the hands of two little girls while a small boy about the same age stood nearby. Three children? He remembered her mentioning only one. No matter. It was Susan, all right. Unmistakably. His heart unexpectedly leaped at the sight of her and he remembered the soft, supple body, the deep, intelligent eyes, the voice that was so gentle, so full of suppressed wishes and a certain sweet sadness.

The caption under the picture identified her as Mrs. Richard Antonini, daughter-in-law, leaving the hall with her own daughter, Katherine, and her niece and nephew, Claudette and Pierre Taffin. He'd dropped the paper and gone back to the telephone directory. No Richard Antonini there, of course. They were too well known to be listed. But that was easy. It was his business to know where the rich and famous were at all times, especially the ones who had a weakness for no-limit poker games or dollar-a-point gin rummy. "Celebrity Service," to which he subscribed, wouldn't give out a private phone number, but his friend in the sports department of the *News* probably could wangle it out of one of the society columnists. His friend could indeed. In ten minutes, Martin had Susan's telephone number. For days he looked at it, once dialed half of it and then replaced the receiver. What the hell was the point? No reason to think she'd feel any differently now than she had in Vegas.

And yet on this beautiful late spring morning, he suddenly was overcome with a longing to see her. She had liked him. Very much. Maybe things had changed. She was unhappy enough when he met her. She could be even more in need of comfort now. It was chancy to call her house. Concert pianists, like gamblers, obviously didn't leave for the office in the morning. Suppose her husband answered? Well, what if he did? Martin would give odds that Richard Antonini had never heard the name Martin Tanner. Susan was not the kind of hysterical female who'd come home and confess all.

A soft voice he recognized answered the phone.

"Hello, Mrs. Armstrong. Martin Tanner. I called to say I'm sorry about your father-in-law."

He heard a quick intake of breath, and then with a remarkable composure, Susan said, "Well, hello! What a surprise to hear from you."

"Is it?"

"Yes, of course. When did you get into town?"

"I'm always in town, remember? I live here. I'm even in the phone book under my own name, which is more than I can say for you." He paused. "Susan, I'd like to see you. Would you like to see me?"

"That would be pleasant, to catch up, but I'm not sure I could manage it. We're going away for the summer and I have a million things to do."

She sounded so determinedly casual he realized she wasn't alone. The husband must be in the room. Or a servant. Or maybe the child.

"I gather you can't talk."

"That's right. It would have been fun. I'm so sorry. Ring up again when you're in New York, Richard and I would love to see you."

"I'll be having lunch at La Croisette tomorrow at one o'clock," Martin said.

"It's a nice restaurant but nobody seems to know about it. Fifty-eighth Street and First Avenue. I like it because you never see anybody you know. I'll be the guy in the back room at the corner table. Goodbye, Susan."

"Thanks for calling. Goodbye."

He wondered if she'd come. Yes, she'd be there. But for what reason he couldn't be sure. She knew very little about him, in spite of their fleeting intimacy. She might come out of fear. She might be afraid he planned to blackmail her or put pressure on her to be with him. If so, she'd try to appeal to his "better nature." She might come because she was attracted to him and was excited by the prospect of seeing him again. Or she might still be as reckless and unhappy as she was in Vegas, still running away from something. He hoped that was not the case. He didn't need a complicated, screwed-up female in his life. Not even one he was as drawn to as he was to Susan.

Why did I bother? Why didn't I leave well enough alone? He was almost sorry he'd called her. Maybe he wouldn't show up at Croisette himself. That would be the end of it. She'd never call him. He remembered something his Jewish grandmother used to say. "He who has no trouble makes himself trouble." Martin laughed aloud. That was him, all right. Risk-taking was his business. It was in his blood. He couldn't resist. He'd be there tomorrow.

And so, ninety-nine chances to one, would Susan.

Who was that on the phone?" Richard asked.

"An old beau," Susan said lightly.

"Oh?"

"I haven't seen him for a long while. He just found out I was married to you."

"*How* old a beau?"

She laughed. "I think you're jealous!"

"Don't be ridiculous," Richard said.

Chapter 27

AS SHE PAUSED inside the doorway of the restaurant, Susan wondered why she'd never noticed the place before. She'd actually walked past it only two days before, after she left Kate. It was attractively done, with a tiny bar, comfortably spaced tables and walls covered with murals of the South of France, in particular that stretch known as La Croisette. She'd never seen the Côte d'Azur, but she recognized the Riviera from photographs of the "playground of the rich"— Cannes, Nice, Cap Ferrat, Juan les Pins, all the expensive, exciting locales she associated with F. Scott Fitzgerald and the "Reckless Twenties."

I could see those places this summer, she thought suddenly. All I'd have to do is tell Richard I'd decided to go to Europe with Kate. I could hop down there from Paris. The exotic names were like music. Cap d'Antibes, Beaulieu, St. Tropez, Villefranche, Monte Carlo . . .

"May I help you, madam?" The smiling captain gave a little bow.

"Yes. I'm meeting Mr. Tanner. Martin Tanner."

"But of course. Monsieur Tanner is already here. This way, if you please."

Martin was right. There were only three other tables occupied. She felt sorry for the proprietors but relieved that it apparently was as he'd said, an "undiscovered" restaurant. She followed the captain down the length of the room, past a large fish tank where several mournful trout swam aimlessly back and forth, waiting to be chosen for someone's lunch or dinner, and into the square "back room," which was totally empty except for the man who waited for her.

He's even more attractive than I remembered, Susan unwillingly thought. She felt awkward and self-conscious as he greeted her with one of those meaningless little kisses on the cheek that are as usual to sophisticated New Yorkers as handshakes are to casual acquaintances in other cities.

"I'm glad you came. I was afraid you wouldn't."

She took a deep breath and tried to relax. "But you knew I would, didn't you?"

Martin grinned. That dangerous, exciting, sure-of-himself expression. "There's no such thing as a 'sure thing.' That much I've learned in my business. But yes, I would have given odds you'd come, Susan. I saw no reason why you shouldn't."

"That's right. No reason at all. This isn't the Victorian age. Even a married woman is entitled to have lunch with an old friend, isn't she?" God, she sounded so inane! In her nervousness she was prattling like a frightened virgin. Martin pretended not to notice.

"What will you drink? Vodka?"

"Nothing, thank you."

His raised-eyebrow surprise was comical. For the first time since she arrived, Susan smiled. "I don't blame you for being startled, but I'm hardly drinking at all these days. You go ahead, though. Please don't let me stop you. I'll have tomato juice, if I may."

He ordered scotch for himself, tomato juice for her, told the waiter they'd look at the menu later. Then he sat back and stared at her, shaking his head in pretended amazement.

"Mrs. Richard Antonini," he said. "My, my! Who would have thought it! My lovely little companion from Vegas turns out to be part of the most publicized family since the Kennedys. Little did I know I was rubbing, uh, elbows with such a famous lady."

Susan ignored the innuendo. "I'm not famous," she said. "Not at all. My husband is, and his family. But not me."

"I think you're overly modest. Antonini is a name every shopgirl knows. Even uneducated, culturally underprivileged gamblers read about all of you in the columns. We may not read concert reviews, but we're very big on gossip sheets like *Open Secrets*. Or even reputable papers like the Washington *Post*. Funny, I must have seen your picture dozens of times in the past few years and I didn't recognize you in Vegas. It didn't click until that photo of you leaving Carnegie Hall. Then I realized who your husband is. The Don Juan of the symphony set. The bad boy of good music. No wonder you have to break loose once in a while."

She should have been angry, but she wasn't. He was too close to the truth.

Or what used to be the truth. It's different now, Susan thought. At least that part of it. I'm quite sure Richard's been faithful since I went to Vegas. That in itself is ironic, she thought, looking across the table at the man who for one night had been her lover.

"I'm not sure what you're driving at, Martin. I suppose you're saying that because Richard's affairs have been so flagrantly publicized I have every right to go around leaping into beds. Is that it?"

"Not exactly, darling. You're not the type for the promiscuous stuff, but you're sure as hell entitled to some kicks of your own when your famous husband is so well known for his extramarital activities. All I'm saying is that I understand what happened in Vegas a little better now. I couldn't quite figure it before. You were too classy, I thought, for that pushover scene."

"And now you think I'm not."

"Let's just say I still think you have class, and I find you more interesting than ever."

"So you'd like to pick up where we left off."

He reached for her hand. "Wouldn't you? Why shouldn't you?"

She let her hand stay in his, but there was no thrill to his touch. Now that he knows about Richard, he's sure I'm available. He could never understand that the Vegas thing was unique; that I don't want anyone but my husband. Why shouldn't he think as he does? I did go to bed with him. I did tell him he attracted me and I wished I were free to follow him. It was true at that unhappy, confused point in my life, right after that terrible Washington episode. He can't know that in spite of Richard's behavior and mine, I cherish fidelity more than I seek diversion.

"Martin," she said quietly, "listen to me. I don't blame you for what you think I am. You have every reason to assume I'd be the most likely woman in the world to embrace a single standard. But I'm not. You met me in a strange period. I liked our love-making. Even more than I wanted to. But I'm working at my marriage. So is Richard. We lost a baby a few months ago." She swallowed hard. "I'm not drinking much these days because I don't need liquor to get me through. I still have problems. Lots of them. But you or someone like you isn't the answer. I can't blot things out any more. I have to stay sober and fight for my life. My life with my husband and my child. I didn't lie to you when I told you that you were the only man I'd been with since my marriage. You are. I think you always will be." She smiled. "You're great in bed. It's a pity I'm so hopelessly old-fashioned. I can't 'take my fun where I find it' as the cliché goes.'

"Not even when your husband can?"

"Not even then."

He shook his head. "Why did you come today? Were you afraid I'd make trouble for you if you didn't?"

"No. You like to picture yourself as a rough diamond but I know you're a gentleman. I wasn't afraid of what you'd do or say. You'd never hurt me. I came because I wanted you to know that my life is better now, partly, I think, because of you. You made me feel alive and wonderful, Martin. It was what I needed—to feel wanted that way. But I can't handle the price. I realized that when I came home and looked at my husband and my child.'' He started to interrupt but she stopped him. ''You're going to remind me again of Richard's ability to have a marriage and sex outside of it. But that's the male mentality, my dear, I know. These days women are supposed to be just as free and guiltless and independent of the institution of marriage as their husbands are. I know we're supposed to take sex as men always have—as something apart from love and emotion. God bless the women who can be so 'sensible.' They're probably absolutely right. I think I envy them. I just can't emulate them. I was born a little too early to think it doesn't matter who knows me intimately or that coupling isn't really all that big a deal. To me, it is.''

''You don't make sense. You even told me you could understand your husband's flings better, after ours.''

''I know I did. And it's true. Even though, strangely enough, he seems to have settled down in that department.''

He was impatient. ''For how long, Susan? Christ, everybody knows his reputation!''

''That still has nothing to do with the way I handle my own. Perhaps it should, but it doesn't.''

''You're worried about your kid, aren't you? You're afraid she'll hear some gossip about you. That must be a big part of this.''

''Not really. I'd never want her to be ashamed of me, but my child doesn't hear. She barely speaks. She's a deaf-mute, Martin.''

He was stunned into silence. Then he said, ''I'm sorry. My God, that's terrible!''

''It's hard for her and sad for us, but it's not terrible. She's being brought up like any other little girl. She'll have a nearly normal life. She already wants everything her nonhandicapped friends have. She's a spunky kid,'' Susan said, echoing Kate's words, ''and she's going to be a happy woman.''

''But the burden of that on you! And that guy you married who's given you nothing but trouble! What kind of life can you have? Even those supercharged in-laws I've read about!''

She looked at him gratefully. He'd virtually forgotten himself and his own desires in this real concern for her.

''My life's okay,'' she said. ''I'm no object of pity, but thank you for caring, Martin. You're a nice man.'' She hesitated. ''I don't think we should see each other again. I wish we could be friends, but we can't. The attraction is much too strong.''

He managed to smile. 'Well, thanks for that much, anyway. All right. Do it your way. Don't let me or any other guy make you miserable. And I would. Because I couldn't see you without wanting you. You're one hell of a lady.''

It was her turn to thank him. And then she said, almost in embarrassment, ''By the way, did you by any chance ever run into my father-in-law?''

''Are you kidding? Where would I have met a man like him? What makes you ask?''

''It's not important. Just a crazy idea. Once I thought he was trying to tell me indirectly that he knew about us. It was just a wild notion. My guilty conscience plaguing me, I suppose. Pure coincidence. Forget it.''

"Come on, you can't leave it at that! Don't you think I have any curiosity?"

"You're right. It's not fair." She told him about the night Giovanni had disclosed his illness, the night so soon after she'd come home. "He used expressions I'd never heard from him. Gambling terms I didn't even think he knew." Telling it now made it seem all the more ridiculous. "You can see how silly I was to think it was deliberate. He was simply equating his life with the odds. Perfectly natural. I'd never have noticed it if you hadn't been so fresh in my mind." She looked thoughtful. "Funny. I'm almost sorry he didn't know. I think in a way he'd have been glad to know I had that much spirit. Even if it meant I was cheating on his own son."

"They say he had his share of fun," Martin said. "I've heard he was quite a ladies' man in his day. Didn't *his* wife ever try to get back at him?"

"She got back at him every day of his life," Susan said, "but not by being unfaithful. Not the way I tried to punish Richard. Her way was more insidious, more evil, really."

"Sounds like a rough broad."

It was such an unlikely description of the well-bred Maria that Susan laughed.

"I guess that's just what she is, in a very smooth way."

Martin looked uncomfortable. "What you said a minute ago, about being unfaithful to punish your husband. Was that all it meant to you, Susan?"

"That's the way it started," she said honestly. "But my feelings changed very quickly. You know that. I'm glad I decided to leave while I still could. We'd never be right for each other, Martin."

"Speak for yourself," he said roughly.

Richard Antonini felt very put-upon these days. He was always bored and restless at this time of year, facing a summer in which he played no concerts and heard no applause. But this period was worse than any he could remember. He felt trapped by Susan, realizing she'd somehow outwitted him, that she was no longer worshipful. He loved her, he supposed, but this sudden feeling that she saw through him and was laughing at him disconcerted him and made him angry. Damn it, what did she want? What was all this constant crap about "something of her own?" She had plenty of her own! A big apartment, all the money she could spend, the opportunity to be as social as Jacqueline, as acquisitive as Mary Lou, even as prominent as Maria, if she wanted to. But she didn't want to. What she wanted was to possess him, to build some kind of stupid "togetherness" probably involving more children and a regimented, predictable existence like the one her parents had.

Well, she couldn't have it. God knows she should have realized that by now. She was married to an artist, and artists didn't make middle-class commitments to a stiff, structured life. He'd tried, after Washington, to change. But he chafed under domestic demands. Responsibility wasn't for him.

Even Maria was driving him crazy, always wanting him near her, nagging him about his work, implying he "owed it to her" to be great. What the hell *did* he owe her? Was it his fault she'd gotten knocked up damned near forty years ago? Obviously, he was glad she had, even if she'd been stupid about it. How had she managed all these years to make him feel so apologetic about his birth? The others weren't made to feel they'd been unwelcome. She didn't make *them* feel guilty. And he'd bet they weren't "planned," either. For that matter, aside from occasional meddling in the upbringing of their children, Maria didn't interfere much with Serge and Walter and Gloria. Only me, Richard thought. I couldn't feel more responsible for her if I were an only child.

He was so edgy. If only there were someone to talk to. He missed Paul. His new manager, George Reagan (Richard still thought of him as "new" even after all this time), was capable enough, but there was no personal closeness there, the way there'd been with Paul. He thought wistfully of the good times they'd had, the road tours, the women, the laughs. Since Paul had left, the tours were all work and little play. Oh, there was always a girl if he wanted one, and sometimes he did. But George had no part in that side of his life. He wasn't the type. And Richard wouldn't have trusted him to keep his mouth shut anyway.

He paced the apartment, stopping now and then to pick up Walter's blasted concerto and throw it down again. He couldn't concentrate, he was so bored. And it would be worse in a few weeks when they moved to East Hampton. There'd be hours of nothingness, endless practice interspersed with a few dumb parties at the big houses on Lily Pond Lane and a lot of hokey socializing at the Maidstone Club. Susan was looking forward to the summer. She still thought they'd rediscover something. That "one-happy-little-family" dream again. Susan's dream. *His* nightmare. He'd be running back and forth to Pound Ridge, pacifying Maria, trying to keep Susan happy and hating himself, always hating himself, for his inability to love a child with whom he couldn't communicate.

What damned rotten luck to have a daughter who was like a reproach. Another yoke around my neck, he thought. My life seems to be full of them. In no time I'll be forty. Forty! It seemed like the end of the line. The beginning of middle age with nothing to look forward to. He thought of all the times Susan had been ready to leave him. He almost wished he'd let her go, so he'd be free and desirable again. But his vanity wouldn't permit him to admit he'd failed at his marriage. He wanted it both ways: a wife and a series of sexual adventures. The way his father had had it. If the old man had beenn able to get away with it for years, why couldn't he? Because Maria never really gave a damn, as Susan does, Richard realized. She never really loved Giovanni. And she was right. Romantic love was a pain. What had somebody once called it? "A sweet folly." That just about summed it up.

The apartment was so bloody quiet it unnerved him. Susan was out somewhere, probably doing one of those endless housewifely chores of hers. He wondered whom he could call. Not the family. He was in no mood for any of them. He'd liked to have called Paul, but that was impossible. He'd never make the first move toward that ungrateful bastard. I haven't any friends, Richard realized. Not male or female. I only have an ex-friend and a lot of ex-lovers, like Dolly Johnson. The memory of Washington and the accident was still bitter, but the thought of the Senator's "madcap daughter" brought a smile to Richard's lips. She'd been a good sport, Dolly. Ready for anything. A girl of the moment who didn't thumb her nose at the future but simply pretended it didn't exist. He needed someone like that now. A Dolly Johnson. Or a Gerry Carter. Or even that dizzy little Hollywood actress who'd been with him in Texas when Maria had her stroke. What was her name? Sylvia. Sylvia Sloan. He hadn't thought about her in a long time, hadn't even heard her mentioned. She'd dropped from sight. He supposed the career had gone sour, the way careers often do with not-too-talented actresses.

It would be fun to see Sylvia again. He hadn't been in touch with her since that morning so long ago when they'd called him and he'd torn out of the hotel in Houston, hardly saying goodbye to her.

He went to his desk and fished out the little address book he kept buried in the back of the middle drawer. There it was. Sylvia Sloan. Impulsively, with nothing special in mind, he dialed the number. A sleepy voice answered.

"Sylvia?"

"Yeah. Who's this?"

"Richard Antonini."

She became instantly alert. "For Christ's sake! Richard! Where are you?"

"In New York. I was just thinking of you and wondered how you were."

"Well, if that's not the damnedest thing! After all this time! Last I saw of you, you were streaking out of the Warwick with your shirttail practically flapping out of your pants!"

Richard laughed. She made him feel young and carefree.

"I read your mother got over her stroke okay. I was sorry to hear about your father."

"Thanks."

"How's everything else?"

"I've been working hard."

"*That* I know, dummy! You're not exactly an obscure figure. That was some mess you got yourself into in Washington a while back. Really juicy! But you're still married. I have to hand it to you, pal. You do keep your women."

"Do I! I haven't kept you."

"You haven't exactly knocked yourself out trying."

'What about your life, Sylvia?"

"The acting career went down the toilet. I didn't really care. I got married to a rich old jerk from Oklahoma, mostly so I wouldn't have to get up for those studio calls at five in the morning. We were divorced three months ago and the settlement is just fine. I'm living it up in a big house in Beverly Hills."

"Oh? I thought you were in the same apartment. The phone number's the same."

"That's *all* that's the same, buddy. I'm a loaded divorcée now. Why don't you come out and see how the idle rich do it in California?"

"I wish I could," Richard said, "but I don't see how I could work it. Maybe I'll see you in the fall. I'm scheduled for an appearance at your Music Center."

'We may all be dead by fall. Or I may have found another sucker to marry. Oh well. It was a good idea, but you've obviously become a solid, settled citizen. Too bad. I always had a big thing for you. You used to be the sexiest kid on the block."

She couldn't have said anything more challenging.

"I don't know why I couldn't run out there for the long Memorial Day weekend," Richard said suddenly. "Might be a good idea. I could check out the fall concert."

"Terrific! That's next weekend. I'll plan a bash!''

"Don't do that, Sylvia. I'll want to keep my visit reasonably quiet. You can understand why."

"Oh, sure. Just a few discreet friends, okay?"

"Sounds good. I'll see you Thursday. Oh, by the way, you'd better give me your new address."

She gave him a number on Rodeo Drive. "It's close to the Beverly Wilshire. I assume you'll check in there, though I don't expect you to spend much time in your suite. The room service here is much better, if you know what I mean."

He hung up, laughing. She was really terrible. Brash and vulgar. But she'd make no long-term demands on him. She never had, He wasn't sure why he'd suddenly decided to go. It was sophomoric, as though he couldn't resist a dare. No, it was more. He needed it, this kind of unplanned, spur-of-the moment adventure. It was a good idea. One of those "why-not" inspirations. The kind he'd often had when he was a bachelor. Just pick up and go. He was *entitled,* Richard told himself, before the long, dutiful damned summer descended upon him.

Susan accepted, without question, his evasive announcement that he had to run out to the West Coast on business the following weekend. She was almost too understanding these days, Richard thought uncomfortably. As though she knew he was up to something and didn't really give a damn. He found himself giving a much too elaborate explanation for his trip, a dead giveaway that there was something out of the ordinary about it. He realized, to his amazement that he felt guilty. The awareness only angered him. Damn them! They really were turning him into a solid, settled citizen. He wasn't ready for that. Not for a long, long time. Maybe not ever.

"You don't seem to mind my leaving." His tone was almost petulant.

"Of course I mind! But I know you wouldn't go, especially over a holiday, unless you had to." Susan seemed absolutely serene. "Richard dear, it isn't the first time we've been separated, for heaven's sake! Why would you think I'd be upset about a short trip?"

Maria was another matter. "I don't understand," she said. "Why on earth do you have to go to California in May for a concert scheduled in October? For that matter, why do you have to go at all? That's what your manager is for. To check into details." She tapped her foot impatiently. "Really, Richard, it's most inconvenient! You know I planned to have all the family in Pound Ridge for the Memorial Day weekend. Even your wife and child."

"They can come without me. I'm sure Walter and Jacqueline will bring them if Susan doesn't want to drive."

Maria looked at him as though he were crazy. "Are you being funny? You know very well your wife will be thrilled to have an excuse to avoid the family. I was surprised she agreed to come in the first place. I suppose she felt she had to do it for your sake. This gives her a marvelous out. I'll bet *she* wasn't a bit perturbed about your going away."

Why didn't I see that? Richard wondered. Of course. Susan wasn't upset about his sudden trip because it meant she didn't have to spend the weekend with

Maria. It had been a pitched battle to get her reluctant agreement. She didn't suspect anything. No wonder she was so cool. She'd gotten a reprieve.

"That's not it at all, Mother. She was looking forward to it." He hoped he sounded convincing.

"Oh, please, Richard! It's bad enough to disappoint me. Don't play me for a fool as well!"

"I'm sorry. About the weekend, I mean. I wouldn't go if I could avoid it."

She tried another tactic. "It's all right, dear. I shouldn't be upset. It's just that it's the first holiday we won't all be together. It will seem strange, not having your father there. And now you won't be there, either. Never mind. It really isn't important. I'm just being a foolish, sentimental old woman."

For a moment he considered canceling. It was rotten selfish of him, he supposed. Maria watched him carefully.

"Please forget what I said, Richard. Of course you must go if it's necessary. Your work comes first. It's the most important thing in your life. And mine."

He felt like a heel, but the mental picture of a wild weekend with Sylvia and her friends was too tempting. To hell with it. Maria had her other children and all the grandchildren. Susan had already said she'd take Katie to Bronxville for a long-overdue visit with her parents.

"You're a darling," Richard said. "I can always count on you to understand. I'll make it up to you. We'll have plenty of other weekends. Maybe you'll come spend some time with us in East Hampton."

"Of course," Maria said, making it perfectly clear in two words that she had no intention of doing anything of the sort.

"Richard and Susan won't be coming to Pound Ridge for the weekend," Mary Lou said. "He's going to California."

Sergio looked surprised. "California? What the hell for?"

"Your mother says it's business. Something to do with his appearance there next fall."

Her husband laughed. "If she buys that, I've got a great piece of underwater land in Florida I'd like to discuss with her."

"You mean he's lying?"

"When did you ever hear of a pianist going five months ahead of time to set up arrangements for a concert in a hall he's played a dozen times?"

"Well, what's he doing?"

"I have no idea. But I'll bet if it's business, it's monkey, not music."

Jacqueline turned around so Walter could zip up the back of her evening dress. "Lucky Susan," she said. "Richard's going to California Thursday, so she doesn't have to go up to the Antonini Olympics."

"California? What's out there?"

"*He* says the Dorothy Chandler Pavilion."

"And what do *you* say?"

"A woman. Or a weekend party. Or both."

"Now why would you think that? Richard's been on his good behavior for a long time."

"That's exactly why I think that. Too good. Too long."

"Come on, Jacqueline. That's pretty farfetched. Hell, if he wanted to fool around he wouldn't have to go all the way to the West Coast."

She shrugged. "Maybe you're right. But who does business on a holiday?"

"Your brother-in-law Richard and his darling wife won't be with us at Mother's next weekend," Gloria said.

"How come?"

"He has to go to Califomia."

"That's too bad."

"Don't be stupid, Raoul. It's great. She's the world's worst party poop. And Richard's not a barrel of laughs these days, either. Personally, I think it's a break."

"You and Katie coming for the weekend? Oh, darling, I'm delighted! I'm sorry Richard can't come, though."

"He's sorry, too. Mother. Something came up unexpectedly about his appearance in Los Angeles next fall. But we'll have a chance for a really good gossip."

"Would you like me to plan anything? Anyone you'd like to see?"

"Just you and Dad. No festivities, please. I want to fall apart. It's been a hectic period."

"Yes, I know," Bea said. "Your father and I were discussing that just the other evening. Are you all right, Susie?"

"Never better. I think I've really gotten my act together again. But I need a sounding board. And you and Dad are the best ones I know."

Susan hung up, frowning. It was true. She had been feeling more optimistic lately. Even slightly victorious that she'd won out about her "banishment" to Europe. And she'd handled the situation with Martin Tanner like an adult. Things seemed to be going well with her and Richard. Despite Maria's best efforts, she thought they were finally settling into a reasonably, contented, harmonious life, beginning at long last, to understand and accept each other's frailties.

And now this.

He was patently up to something. It had to be another woman. The story about business would have been laughable if it hadn't been so upsetting. He's cooked up something, Susan thought. I feel it in my bones. God knows what he's up to. The only thing I do know is that he's lying. And the only satisfaction is *he* knows I know he's lying. Methinks you do protest too much, dear husband. If you're bored and restless, why couldn't you just say you need a few days alone, the way I did when I went to Vegas? No, that would be too easy.

Not that she thought for a moment he simply intended to be alone. Not Richard, who'd always been only fleetingly faithful.

Why am I so suspicious of him? Well, why shouldn't I be? I can love him, desire him, respect his genius. But I can never trust him, Why don't I accept him for what he is—an unpredictable, self-centered, hypnotieally attractive man who needs injections of outside adulation? He'll be immature and insecure as long as he lives. And still I want to live with him. I mustn't let foolish pride make me so possessive. I've got to give him a long lead, knowing, no matter whom he meets, he'll always come back. The way I did.

Chapter 28

THERE WERE A few frightening days following his return from California, days threatening enough to subdue even Richard. But by mid-June he dared relax and put thoughts of Beverly Hills and Sylvia Sloan out of his mind.

He'd agreed with Susan that the big, weather-beaten old house in East Hampton really was more than they needed for themselves and Katie, Bridie and two other servants. It was a huge establishment with nine bedrooms, a pool and tennis court. But it was luxurious and lovely, set high on the dunes, with stairs leading down to a private beach, and it had a sweeping view of the ocean. The deciding factor, though, was the vast, air-conditioned living room, which could be kept at the carefully controlled temperature necessary for his piano. Not too many houses at the beach provided such an important feature for his precious possession, which was trucked out from New York by the local "Home Sweet Home" moving company. It was this room that sold him. Rapid changes of heat and cold or moisture and dryness were a constant threat to the fine instrument. Changing climatic conditions called for endless tuning, and on humid days the felts of the piano could stick annoyingly. The room's controlled temperature, in which he could practice and refine the works for his upcoming fall concert, was the deciding factor in their choice of this house.

He sat there now, running his fingers lovingly over the keys as he thought about the future. He intended to be more brilliant than ever in his upcoming concerts and he spent hour after hour appraising his own work, perfecting an already near-perfect technique. Some of the unfriendly criticism of the recent past still rankled. One reviewer had dared call his performance "a bland, superficial display, unworthy of the artist who used to make audiences feel he was afire." He'd show them. He'd give them the old, dazzling Richard Antonini. And later he'd play that damned concerto of Walter's, which he still hadn't mastered to his satisfaction. But he would, by God, if it killed him.

His old confidence had returned. He'd really come to terms with his life with Susan. He glanced out of the window and saw her on the beach with Bridie and the child. They presented a peaceful picture on this hot July afternoon. He'd been unfair to them, he supposed. It had taken that horrifying weekend with Sylvia to make him appreciate the sanity and security he had at home.

God, what a scary experience that had turned out to be! Lucky Susan had not asked much about the trip or its aftermath. Experienced liar that he was, he really wasn't very good at it.

His thoughts wandered back to those few days. He'd checked into the Beverly Wilshire Hotel, feeling adventurous and free, and been greeted by the assistant manager, an old friend, Bud Porter.

"Keep the press off my back, will you Bud?" he'd asked. "I just want to relax. It's a quiet personal visit, Sorry to disappoint your publicity lady, but I'll make up for it when I come back in a few months.''

"Of course. Anything we can do for you?''

"Not a thing. I'll be out most of the time with friends.''

What an understatement that had been! Sylvia had almost devoured him, never wanting him out of her sight, sexually demanding when they were alone, embarrassingly possessive when she allowed a few intimates to join them in her big, vulgar, overdecorated mansion in Beverly Hills. For the first twenty-four hours, Richard had enjoyed the attention and the intense passion of a woman whose bizarre sexual practices were titillating but almost shocking, even to him. At first, he hadn't even minded the high-handed way she behaved when her few friends were around, as though he was her personal possession. But by Saturday, he began to feel uncomfortable, uneasy. Sylvia was not the carefree, amusing "sex symbol" he'd known in Houston. He was sure she was heavily into drugs. She'd even lost the lush blond beauty that had first attracted him. In fact, she was haggard, dissipated-looking. She seemed desperate, somehow, pressing too hard. On Sunday night, physically exhausted and troubled by her state of mind, he tried, diplomatically, to talk to her about her behavior.

"Let's keep things in perspective, Syl,'' he said. "You know I'm fond of you, but there's never been anything long-term between us. I don't think you should give friends the idea that this is a serious affair. I don't even know when I'll see you again. This trip was a spur-of-the-moment thing and I've enjoyed it. You're really terrific, but I'm married, you know. There can't be anything for us except some laughs once in a while.''

She didn't seem to understand what he was saying.

"Then why did you come back to me? Why did you leave your wife to fly out here and be with me? You love me. I know you do.''

"No,'' Richard said kindly, "I don't love you. You sounded gay and amusing on the phone, and I remembered what good times we had in the past. No strings attached. I was anxious to see you again and it's been great. But I didn't 'come back to you,' Sylvia, because in spite of Houston, you and I know there was never anything to come back to. You're a beautiful woman,'' (what harm in a compassionate lie?) "and right now you're feeling a little displaced after your divorce. But you'll meet another man. You're young and marvelously sexy and you're a famous name.'' He tried to sound relaxed and casual. "You don't need a married piano player who lives three thousand miles away, for God's sake! All you have to do is crook your finger and half the studs in Southern California will come running! Come on, where's your sense of humor? It isn't like you to turn a simple, sexy weekend into a heavy commitment. You know better than that. You're the glamorous Sylvia Sloan, the beautiful lady of Beverly Hills!''

Her response was a mirthless laugh. "More like the whore of the Hollywood Hills,'' she said. "I thought you were going to make me come alive again, Richard. I thought you were the answer after all the months and years of screwing around with guys who didn't give a damn. I have nothing. Don't try to be kind. It's all gone. My looks. My career. The marriage I thought was 'safe.' Even what you call my 'glamour.' Nobody gives a damn for me. Nobody ever has. Until you. I thought you did, coming back in spite of that scandal. I wanted to believe you could give me something to live for.'' The despondent, droning voice suddenly turned loud and accusatory. ''Who the hell asked you to start this up again? What was I supposed to think, after all this time, when you called? You sonofabitch! You're like all the rest! All you want is the only thing I have left: a body. The only difference between you and the rest is that you're willing to fly three thousand miles for a good lay while the others are only willing to drive twenty minutes!''

Richard was stunned and shaken. ''My God, I didn't mean to mislead you! I thought you knew where we stood. Where we've *always* stood. I didn't realize how unhappy you are. Or how lonely.''

She screamed at him. ''I'm not lonely! I'm surrounded by people who eat my food and drink my booze and share my bed! The public still adores me! You're right. Who needs *you?* Get the hell out of my house and don't come back until you have something more to offer than one of your 'simple, sexy weekends!' Get out! Now!''

He'd gone back to the hotel, puzzled and faintly disgusted. He felt sorry for her, but the woman was a lunatic. He'd never given her a hint that he wanted her as permanent fixture in his life. Jesus, he thought, if I'd known what I was getting into! Poor Sylvia. He hadn't realized how unloved she felt, how hopelessly she clutched at any ridiculous dream. But he couldn't save her. He had no wish to. She had no reason to think he could.

He called American Airlines and booked a 1 P.M. flight to New York next day. Before I leave, I'll send her something expensive, he decided. A good piece of jewelry, maybe. She'd like that. It occurred to him that she'd probably tell the world it had been a present from her ''adoring lover'' Richard Antonini. He frowned. So what? Let her, if it gave her any comfort. Besides, who'd believe her? By this time all of Los Angeles must know she's out of her head, living on pills and liquor. Pathetic. What a waste. She'd sure gone downhill since the days in Houston.

At three in the morning his phone rang. He answered groggily. It was Sylvia and she was crying.

''I'm sorry,'' she stammered. ''I don't know what got into me. I know you don't love me Richard. It's just that I need someone. So much. So very much.''

He tried to shake himself awake. ''It's all right,'' he said. ''Don't worry about it. I understand. You had a little too much to drink.''

''No you don't understand. I love you. I always have. I never thought I could have you, but when you called and came out, I thought . . .''

''I know. It was foolish of me. I didn't think how it would seem to you, Stay well, Sylvie. Take care of yourself. And, I don't mean to sound heartless, but try to forget about me, will you?''

''Yes. Thank you. Goodbye, Richard.''

''Good night, my dear. Get some sleep.''

''I will. I promise.''

''Good girl. And let me know how you are.''

''Yes,'' she said again. ''I will.''

He was thankful to be safely back in the apartment Monday evening, deserted as it was. He called Susan at her mother's.

"I'm home and glad to be here! How are you, darling? How's Katie? When are you coming back?"

"We're fine. We'll be in tomorrow morning. Have a good trip?"

Was there a coolness in her voice? Richard wasn't sure.

"It was okay. Pretty uneventful. I got a lot of details firmed up for the fall."

"Good." There was a pause. "Sad about that actress, wasn't it?"

"What actress?"

"The one you used to know. The one *Open Secrets* made so much of. Sylvia Sloan. She took her life sometime early this morning. It was on the six-o'clock news. Sleeping pills, they said."

He was near panic. Susan had put two and two together, adding up Houston, and his quick trip, and this. But she couldn't prove anything. Nobody could unless, God forbid, that insane woman had left a note! He made himself sound deliberately remote though sorry.

"Good God, that's terrible! Sylvia Sloan! I haven't thought of her in years!"

There was silence at the other end of the line.

"You know what I mean," Richard said. "Not since that foolishness in Texas. I always regretted that, Susie. You know I did."

"Of course." The voice was calm. "That's one of the things we've put behind us, isn't it? I certainly had no love for her, but it's sad when such a beautiful, talented young woman wants nothing more than to go to sleep forever."

The words were chilling. The last thing he'd said to Sylvia early that morning was "Get some sleep and let me know how you are." She'd agreed so meekly. She must have known exactly how she was going to keep both those promises.

"Well," Richard said, "those things are beyond understanding. You're right, it's sad, but some people are beyond help. Okay, dear, I'm going to turn in. See you tomorrow. Sleep well." He paused. "I love you."

"Good night."

He raced to the television set and turned on the ABC eleven o'clock news in time to hear the commentator say, "Friends of Sylvia Sloan, the former Hollywood star, were shocked to learn of her death early this morning in her Beverly Hills home. Cause of death was an overdose of sleeping pills accidentally or deliberately administered. Miss Sloan, recently divorced from millionaire Harley Custin, was discovered by her maid, who went in to awaken her at noon, Los Angeles time. Police say no note was left by the actress, who starred in such films as . . ."

Richard switched off the set. No note. Thank God. Thank God, too, that Monday was a legal holiday. The good jewelers were closed, and he hadn't been able to send her the gift he planned. Sweat poured over his body at the thought of a delivery turned over to the police. They couldn't involve him in this sordid story now. Not unless some of those creepy friends of her chose to tell the world he'd been with them over the weekend. And they might. They were all publicity-mad. He'd deny it, of course, but much good that would do! Susan would be certain and the world would be suspicious. Those bloody reporters who caused him so much trouble would be on his tail again. Goddammit! What a stupid idea the whole weekend had been!

But surprisingly, nothing more happened. Sylvia Sloan was no longer important enough to rate more than a TV glimpse of the simple funeral service for the actress, who, it was officially decided, accidentally ended her life. The millionaire, probably a conservative pillar of his community and loath to have the details of his ex-wife's lurid life exposed, must have hushed up the "hangers-on," Richard concluded. The man sensibly wanted no sensational publicity. Thanks, Harley Custin, whoever you are, Richard thought as the days went by and there was no mention of the old scandal. You not only saved your reputation and Sylvia's, you also rescued mine.

On the surface, Susan seemed as calm and contented as Richard did, but inwardly she agonized over her husband's latest escapade. It didn't take a genius to figure out that Richard had been off to some adventure when he left so precipitously for California. Her comment about Sylvia Sloan had been a shot in the dark, but the moment she heard his tone of voice she knew that Richard's trip and Sylvia's overdose were no coincidence. She tried hard not to think that the young woman's death had anything to do with Richard, but with a wife's instinct she felt he was directly involved. It was such an intolerable suspicion that she could discuss it with no one, least of all with him. I don't want to hear another of his confessions, she thought. I couldn't bear having this terrible certainty confirmed. If it's true, if he somehow drove that pathetic creature to her grave, how in God's name can he live with it? For that matter, how can he be so extraordinarily serene, so enthusiastic about his work, so loving and tender toward me? He even seemed slightly less subservient to Maria these days. It was incredible, as though a new Richard had returned from California, a more appreciative and contented Richard, at peace with himself.

She tried to put it out of her mind, rationalizing that no one isolated incident drove a person to suicide. If the actress had taken her life, it couldn't have been because of one weekend with Richard. Such things were the result of a long buildup of despair and loneliness and fear, the final act of a mind that had been sick for a long, long time. But it was a mental state that Susan, for all her moments of terribly personal tragedies, could not fully comprehend. Even at her lowest point when her child was taken away, she had not wished to die. Oh, she might have said so, but she'd never reached the point of not wanting to live. Life was often hard, sometimes nearly insupportable, but it was precious and never totally devoid of hope. She wondered, heartsick, how it felt to be so utterly despondent that death could be the only release. She'd retreated after her own sorrows, withdrawn, turned to drink, even sought solace in infidelity, but she'd never considered ending her life. It chilled her to know that such misery was possible. I'm lucky, she thought. In spite of everything, I'm much luckier than that golden girl who seemed to have everything—beauty, success, public adoration. And yet she had nothing because, obviously, she lacked something to live for, someone to love her.

Had Sylvia loved Richard? Did she die for impossible love of him? Susan could not accept that. Sylvia Sloan died because she was mentally ill. Too many other women had survived their dismissals by Richard Antonini. She was sure they'd wept, probably pleaded or threatened. But they did not destroy themselves at the dapper clay feet of the idol.

As the weeks wore on, the memory of a woman she'd never even met dimmed, and, like Richard, Susan was more tranquil than she'd been in a long time. Another scandal, if there was one, never surfaced. Richard seemed happy. He was working hard and well, enjoying the beautiful summer days, even making fewer and fewer "duty trips" to his mother's country house. They lived quietly, accepted few invitations. Walter and Jacqueline came for a weekend and so did Kate and the Langdons, and it was all easy and congenial. Their only argument came over Susan's stubborn refusal to go to a big party with him. Richard didn't really enjoy most of them, but this was one he wanted to attend. Susan begged off.

"Why?" Richard asked. "It's *the* big party of the year. There'll be lots of people we know from the city. I think it'll be amusing. We could do with a little outside stimulation."

"I'm sorry. I just don't feel like it. I hope you don't mind."

"Well, I *do* mind! How will it look, my showing up without my wife?"

"It won't be the first time." Susan's voice was icy.

He glared at her. "Are we starting that all over again?"

"No. Sorry. I lost my temper. I just meant I saw no reason for you to stay home because I know I wouldn't have a good time." She knew she was making an issue over nothing. She was simply tired of doing what he wanted. The party and the people giving it bored her. For once, she would please herself. It was one of those small gestures that every now and then she felt compelled to make . . . a pathetically insignificant rebellion that somehow made her feel independent of Richard. She was being foolish, but she stuck to her decision, though she softened her attitude.

"Darling, *do* go to the party! It'll be fun for you. And honestly, I'm dying to do some more work on the book. I want you to go. Please, You can always say I have a cold."

"Well, all right. But I still say it's crazy."

"It probably is, but you know you married a crazy lady."

His thoughts went back to Sylvia and he remembered being thankful that his wife was so sane. "You're the most levelheaded female in the world," he said, smiling, "even if you do go off half-cocked once in a while."

"Then you *will* go?"

"Yes, I'll go and leave you in the company of the Muse. How's the book going, by the way?"

"Agonizingly, but I love doing it."

"The old identity search again, right?"

She smiled back at him. "Afraid so. But it's more than that. It's also a labor of love."

Starting the book had been one of the most unexpected and joyful events of her life. It had happened quickly and completely out of the blue. Soon after they arrived in East Hampton, she and Richard had gone to a small dinner party at the home of a famous publisher. At table, Susan was seated next to an attractive young man named Rhett Wilson, one of the host's senior editors.

"You obviously belong in publishing," Susan said lightly, "with a name like yours."

He winced, pretending pain. "Did you have to?" he asked. "You seem so bright and pretty I was hoping you'd be one of the rare ones who wouldn't ask whether my mother was reading *Gone with the Wind* during her pregnancy.''

Susan laughed. ''Was she?''

''Of course, damn it. I can only give thanks that she hadn't the bad taste to marry a man named Butler.''

Susan found him amusing, rather whimsical and yet completely professional. She was so relaxed that, after having told him about her job on *Vogue*, she confessed, with embarrassment that the ambition of her life was to write a book. ''I know that's the cliché of all time,'' she said. ''Every person who's ever written a magazine article or a newspaper piece or an ad thinks he could become an author. It's nonsense, of course. Even I know that writing a book is far different from doing a short feature. It must take enormous discipline, not to mention talent.''

Wilson seemed suddenly cool. ''Yes, it does,'' he said, and then quite deliberately changed the subject to talk about tennis, which he claimed was his overwhelming passion.

Susan felt foolish and rebuffed. He must think me a typical opportunist, taking advantage of a social situation to get an ''in'' with an important editor! I'm sure every other person he meets attacks him with a silly idea about writing a book. He must be bored out of his mind with it. She hid her discomfort, and throughout the rest of the dinner chatted about other things, still finding him a delightful companion. He'd rented a small house in Bridgehampton for the summer, he told her, and was there every weekend. He hoped she and her husband would ''come slumming'' one afternoon.

''We'd love it,'' Susan said. ''And you must visit us.'' She scribbled the phone number and address on her card. ''Please call when you feel like it. I'm a poor tennis player and Richard won't touch a racket because of his hands, but we do have a court and I'm sure we could get a game for you.''

Next week in the mail she received a current best-seller and a note from Rhett Wilson saying he'd enjoyed talking with her. The week after, he sent two more books, and that weekend she called him.

''I should write you a proper thank-you note,'' Susan said, ''but I thought I'd make it an invitation instead. You've been so kind to send the books and we'd love to see you again. Can you come for lunch on Saturday? There'll just be Richard and me.''

''Be delighted. By the way, how did you enjoy the books?''

She hesitated. ''Honest answer?''

''By all means.''

''I liked the novels but I was disappointed in the nonfiction account of the woman in the Peace Corps. It's nervy of me to say so, but I didn't think it was awfully well written. She had a chance to turn a moving experience into a meaningful account of the suffering and fears of the lepers in India. How they affected her, I mean. I think she missed the boat. There wasn't enough heart in it.''

She could imagine him smiling at her audacity, but instead he said, ''My reaction exactly, though I haven't said so because it wasn't my book, I mean, I wasn't the editor, and we don't like to criticize our colleagues' projects. You're right, I think. It should have been great and it was only medium-good.''

Susan felt pleased and even more delighted when he said, "You know, I had a hunch. I sent you those books for a purpose. Just to see how astute a critic you are. Now I know you understand writing, so maybe we ought to talk about *your* trying a book. Do you have an idea?"

"No. Not really. I was just fantasizing that night at dinner."

"Well, think about it. And we can talk Saturday."

She was feverishly excited when she reported the conversation to Richard. Surprisingly, he seemed to take to the idea.

"Why not? You're a good writer and this could be the thing you've been searching for ever since we were married. It's something you can do at home or even when we're on tour. Sounds like a good idea to me. What would you write—a novel?"

"I don't know. I'm not sure. Listen, don't let me get carried away, will you? I mean this is a far cry from having a book under contract. I don't want to get all steamed up and be disappointed when nothing happens. It's purely exploratory. Probably won't amount to a damn."

He teased her. "You don't believe that for a moment and you know it. I can see that glint in your eye. You *know* you'll be the next Jacqueline Susann."

Chapter 29

RHETT WILSON SEEMED dubious when Susan told him her idea for a book.

"I don't know," he said. "It's a touching story, this account of your and Richard's determination to bring up Katie in a hearing world and having it all turn out so successfully. It's just that, commercially, it might not sell. People, by and large, don't like to be reminded of the handicapped. Even if I could get you a contract, there'd be a ridiculously small advance. Probably not more than, say fifteen hundred dollars, based on projected sales. Would you want to waste your time for that?"

"The money isn't important," Susan said. "I know that sounds terribly snobbish, but I really don't care what I'm paid for it. Whatever I get I'm going to donate to one of the organizations that help deaf-mute children and their parents. The thing that matters to me is to tell people that it can be done. That they don't have to hide their children or condemn them to a silent, abnormal existence. And," she admitted, "I guess there's something of an ego trip involved here, too. As I told you the first night we met, anybody who's ever been paid to put pen to paper is secretly hungry to see his name on a book jacket. But the main thing is to give encouragement to others. God knows we received precious little of it ourselves in the beginning!"

"I'm sure of that. Look, Susan, I'll be perfectly frank with you, If I can get the publishing board to accept this idea, one of the reasons will be because you are Mrs. Antonini. That means automatic publicity. Would you be willing to promote at publication time? Would you go on TV talk shows and make personal appearances in book departments around the country and give interviews to the press? It's hard work, but it moves copies. Frankly, I think that's the best way I can sell this idea to my people."

She was quiet for a long moment. This was not at all what she expected. She hadn't thought about trading on her husband's name. She simply wanted to tell her story as a mother, no different from thousands of mothers faced with the same wrenching decision. When the family was frantic for good publicity they'd encouraged her to speak out about Katie, but she was sure their attitude would be quite different now that there was no "crisis." She hadn't even told Richard she planned to write about their child. He still thought she was going to do some kind of novel. He'd be upset even by the idea of this book. And he'd have a fit if she was all over the country selling it, "letting her name be used" so blatantly and commercially. As for Maria's reaction, the temporary truce would end and the war with her mother-in-law would start up again, probably more intense than ever. She remembered how Maria had carried on years before when Susan began to write a relatively impersonal column. She had killed that idea, innocuous as it was. Wait until she heard this one!

Rhett correctly guessed some of what was going through her mind. "Why don't you give it some thought? It's the kind of thing you'll want to discuss with your husband, I'm sure. Let's face it, Susan, we'd be taking advantage of the Antonini name, and Richard may object to that. I think you could do a good and useful book even under a pseudonym, but the commercial facts of life still exist. More people are going to buy a book by Susan Antonini than one by Susan Nobody. We all have to accept that right up front. It doesn't downgrade your talent as a writer. It's just the way things are."

Richard had left them alone after lunch while he went into the house to practice. She could hear him now, going over and over the same passage, toying with the phrasing, striving for perfection, seeking his own interpretation of the music, bringing his emotions to the world. That's what I want to do, Susan realized. I really want to tell the world what I believe about the power of love and its miraculous ability to strike down obstacles. These are *my* emotions and my public tribute to a brave little girl. I can't help how Richard and his family feel. I'm proud of Katie, and grateful to those who've helped her. And I damned well am going to say so.

"You're very understanding," she said. "And quite right in assuming that the Antoninis don't like their name exploited. But I still want to do the book, Rhett, if your company will accept it. And I'll do as much promotion as I can without neglecting my husband or my child."

"You're sure? You could try a novel that wouldn't call for such soul-baring. I'm sure you're imaginative and you must have a lot of experience to draw on. Maybe you should consider that, instead of the nonfiction story of Katie."

"No," Susan said firmly. "I want to write a love letter to my daughter. That's what this really is, you know."

He nodded. "I think I can understand that. By the way, that's not a bad title if we can clear it: *Love Letter to My Daughter*. But I'm getting ahead of myself. First we have to get a contract."

He explained the procedure. She'd have to give him a detailed outline of the book and write the first hundred pages of it with no guarantee of acceptance. "I know you've been a magazine writer," Rhett said, "but to us you're an 'unpublished author.' We have to get an idea of your style, see how you organize the first few chapters. When that's done, I'll present the whole package and hope for the best. Let's see. This is the first week of July. Think you could get something to me around mid-August?''

Susan mentally calculated. Six weeks. Forty-two days. Even if she did only three pages a day she should easily be able to meet that deadline. On *Vogue* she'd been used to much more "rush assignments."

"I'll try," she said. "I think I can."

"Good. I'll be looking forward to it." He glanced at his watch. "Good Lord, I've got to run! Say goodbye to Richard for me, will you? And thanks for the lunch."

"Thank *you*. I'm really excited about this, Rhett."

"Believe it or not, so am I. I think you'll write a helluva book that probably would sell without the hoopla. But the promotion will be added insurance. Do a good job, Susan, and call me if you need help along the way. I'm looking forward to being your editor. It's always a vicarious thrill to discover a new talent."

She wandered into the house, smiling, already plotting the outline in her head. Richard came out of the living room when he heard the screen door slam.

"How did it go?"

She was radiant. "Wonderfully! Darling, I have to do an outline and a hundred pages by mid-August and then Rhett will see whether he can get me a contract!"

"Good for you!" He seemed genuinely pleased. "Now that you've talked to 'your editor' are you going to break down and tell me what the novel will be about?"

"It isn't a novel. It's a nonfiction book. About how we're raising Katie."

Richard's expression changed from indulgence to dismay. "A book about Katie! Are you mad, Susan? You can't seriously be thinking of putting the intimate details of our life into the hands of every shopgirl on the subway! I won't hear of it! You led me to believe you were going to write some innocuous little novel. Something to fill your time. And now you propose to go into the sordid story of our deaf-mute child. Absolutely not! I forbid it!"

She went rigid. "You *forbid* it? How dare you say that to me! Don't give me orders, Richard. I've had enough of that! I'm your wife, not an employee!"

"Damned right you're my wife. And I won't permit you to flaunt the sordid story of our unfortunate parenthood!"

"That's the second time you've used that word," Susan said passionately. "You *do* find it sordid, don't you? You always have. Well, I don't. I find it beautiful and inspirational and something to be proud of. Katie is all those things, even if we're not. It's *her* story, Richard, not *ours*. You don't have to worry," she said nastily. "I'd already planned to leave out the part about your rejecting her. I'm going to pretend we chose this course together, worked on it together and rejoiced together in the happy outcome. I won't destroy your precious image, have no fear. I'd never let the world know how you've tried to ignore your child most of her life. You'll come out smelling like a rose, if only because one day Katie will read this book and I want her to be proud of her father as a father, not just as an artist."

He was livid. "How can you be so insensitive? Using your own child! Embarrassing yourself and me! Publicizing the most private part of our life!"

"You seem to forget I did it once before. For your sake and your family's. You've conveniently forgotten that thanks to the gossip about you, I was forced to speak publicly about this problem to portray the Richard Antoninis as a close, devoted family. It was all right *then*, when you wanted to counteract the filth about your affair and your brothers' lives. But now, when I want to pay a loving compliment to an extraordinary little girl, it's suddenly 'sordid' because *you* don't need it. Well, *I* need it. And I'm going to do it. You can scream and yell all you want, but I'm going to write this book. It's important to me. In a way it's my therapy."

"If you need more therapy, why the hell don't you go back to your precious Dr. Marcus? At least that's privileged information!"

"I'm not the one who needs professional help, Richard. If anyone does, it's you!" She stopped, appalled, sickened by the terrible things they were yelling at one another. Yet she couldn't apologize. Everything she'd said was true. And in spite of Richard's fury she was going to write the book. "I wish you weren't so angry about it," she said slowly. "I wish you understood. This is something I have to do. I've lived with the fear and sadness so long that it just has to come out. I'll try to do it with taste. I promise there'll be nothing in it to offend you. Please, Richard, back me up, even if you don't approve."

Her measured voice calmed him. At least he stopped shouting and tried reasoning with her. "What good will it do to drag all this up again? Katie's doing fine. We're all adjusting. Things are peaceful and good between us at last. Why do you want to stir it up, Susan? There must be other kinds of books you can write."

She felt like a traitor. She couldn't logically refute his arguments. She just knew this was meant to be. It was as though fate had put her beside Rhett Wilson at that dinner table. It was the only legacy she alone could leave Katie. Richard could leave her money and a name that opened any door. But only her mother could bequeath the warm and lasting inheritance of love.

"I could write a different kind of book," Susan said, "but that would be meaningless to me and that child. And it wouldn't help other people with heartaches like our own."

He turned away, shaking his head, recognizing defeat. He knew Susan well enough to recognize that, pliable as she was, when she really made up her mind to do something, nothing could stop her. She'd shown that when she virtually kidnaped Katie from the school. He believed she'd have killed anyone who tried to stop her. It was far different than the times she threatened to leave him and allowed herself to be talked out of it. Even today, Richard thought, she's never tried to find out about Sylvia Sloan, though he was certain she suspected his part in the story. Susan fought for the vital things, the changeable things. Mostly, she fought for her child. But sometimes, as now, she also fought for herself.

Susan left the room. It was an unhappy victory, as all her victories seemed to be, and yet she felt strong and sure. Richard loved her, even when he couldn't control her. A mischievous smile appeared on her lips. How I'd love to be a fly on the wall when he tells Maria about this! Then she frowned. Maybe he won't have to. Maybe they won't accept the book and all this will have been for nothing. She realized she hadn't said a word about the "promotion" that would be involved if her "love letter" were published. God knows it was no time to add *that* fuel to the fire! Time enough later to break that news to Richard if it was necessary. And maybe by then, when he'd read the book and seen how gently she handled it, he'd be less upset. He might even be proud of me, Susan thought. I want him to be proud of me.

From that moment, she religiously spent four hours every morning at her typewriter, struggling with the outline and then beginning the engrossing business of telling what it was like to discover that the beautiful, cheerful baby they adored could neither hear nor speak.

She and Richard had no further discussion about the book. They maintained a reasonably harmonious relationship, conversed, made love, acted as though she was simply answering mail or doing household accounts when she disappeared after breakfast into the little room she'd set up as her "office." From lunchtime on, she tended her domestic duties, overseeing the menus, driving into Southampton to shop for groceries at Herbert's or clothes at Saks or knicknacks at Cal Alexander's. Bridie stayed on the beach with Katie while Richard practiced. And on the surface, everything was normal.

She told no one else what she was doing. Not even her mother or Kate knew. It would be too disappointing if the book were rejected, but a lovely surprise if it were not. She was sure Richard had not confided in anyone either, but for a different reason. He must be secretly wishing hard that the publishers would turn it down and he'd not have to face the "embarrassment" of it or the ordeal of breaking the news to Maria.

At the beginning of August, two weeks ahead of her deadline, she'd finished the material Rhett needed. She was not completely satisfied with it, but she knew from experience that she'd never be thoroughly satisfied with anything she wrote. No use worrying it like a dog with a bone. There was just so much revising and polishing one could do at this point, otherwise a year from August she'd still be rewriting and probably making it worse instead of better. Nervously, she called Rhett at his office and told him that the outline and hundred pages were done.

He was delighted. "Terrific! You're ahead of schedule! My heart leaps with joy at the thought of an author who actually turns in work ahead of deadline! I'll be out this weekend. Shall I drive over and pick it up?"

"Please do. I won't sleep a wink until you've read it and given me your opinion. Can you come Saturday? We'll give you lunch or a drink."

"A drink will be great. About six?"

"Perfect. Thank you, Rhett."

"Save that for the big moment when we notify you you've become a full-fledged author."

"From your mouth to God's ears, as we used to say on Seventh Avenue."

He laughed, "It's going to be good. I feel it in my bones."

He arrived, tanned and handsome, promptly at six on Saturday, accepted a drink and said, "I hope I remembered to tell you to make a carbon copy! Not that I won't guard your manuscript with my life but it's madness for you not to have a duplicate in case I get killed driving home!"

"I have one." Susan smiled, but she seemed uneasy. "I'm sorry Richard can't join us. He isn't feeling too well."

"Nothing serious, I hope."

"No. Just a bad headache. Too much sun, I guess." She wondered whether Rhett knew it was a lie. The truth was that Richard had flatly refused to see their guest. He hadn't made a scene, he'd simply said, "I don't feel kindly enough toward Mr. Wilson to have a drink with him. Make my apologies."

Rhett seemed to accept the falsehood without question. "Sorry I missed him. Next time." He picked up the Manila envelope with her life's blood in it. "I'll try to read this tomorrow and phone you. I know writers. Nervous wrecks until they hear. Of course, you'll only be getting my opinion. And even if it's enthusiastic—which I expect—I still have to let a few other people read it and take it to the meeting. So don't start donating your royalty checks quite yet. It will take a couple of weeks, at least, to get the final decision."

He called the next afternoon. Susan literally held her breath until she heard him say, "It's *really* good, Susan! I cried twice and that's the test. I'm taking it into the office tonight and I'll start circulating it tomorrow. You'll hear from me."

On the fifteenth of August, she received a telegram. "Dear Susan. You are now a full-fledged Doubleday author. *Love Letter* passed publishing committee with flying colors. Congratulations. Rhett."

She read it three times and burst into tears. She wasn't sure whether she was crying with joy or nervousness. She felt something of both as she ran down the long flight of stairs to the beach and picked up Katie, whirling the nearly-naked, bronzed little girl round and round.

"Kit-Kat darling," she said distinctly, "I've written a book and it's about you. All about how I love you."

Katie smiled and stroked Susan's cheek. She read the words on her mother's lips but she wasn't sure she understood exactly what they meant. It didn't matter. Something had happened that made Mummy very happy.

Holding the precious telegram, Susan went silently into the room where her husband was working. She curled up in a chair, waiting for a break in the music before she spoke to him. He seemed unaware of her presence, deep into an intricate Liszt polonaise which would be part of his fall program. It was a good ten minutes before he stopped playing, looked up and saw her sitting there, watching him.

"What do you think?"

She smiled. "It's wonderful. Breathtaking."

"I'm not sure. Maybe the Tchaikovsky concerto in B-flat minor . . ."

"Richard, it's been accepted."

"What has?"

"My book." She held up the telegram. "They're going to publish my book."

She waited, holding her breath. Let him be happy for me. Just for once let him show the bigness of spirit I still believe he has.

Without a word he came over and took the piece of yellow paper from her hand, reading it impassively.

"I was hoping they wouldn't, you know. I was putting out all the negative thought-waves I could."

She didn't answer.

And then with one of those meteoric changes of mood that were part of his nature, he leaned down and kissed her. "I'm glad for you, Susie, I know you want this more than anything. There should be room in the Antonini family for another talent. Will you let me read what you've done, now that it's a *fait accompli?*"

She was going to cry again, damn it. But this time with relief, with gratitude that Richard's generosity was bigger than his ego, stronger than his aversion to anything that might reflect unpleasantly on the image he spent his life building. The tears she couldn't contain fell on his soft silk shirt as she put her arms around him and wept with happiness. He held her tenderly, her face against his chest, glad she couldn't see the annoyance he felt. He hated the vanity that made him unwilling to share glory with anyone, but it was ingrained in him. He was jealous when Sergio was praised for his conducting, angry when his damned faggot brother Walter wrote a piece of music that defied even the enormous talent of Richard Antonini. He knew it was petty, but he'd lied when he said there was room for another talent in the Antonini family. There wasn't. In his mind, history had reserved space only for him.

Not that Susan's little book was likely to make history. Not that it was in any way a threat to his superiority as an artist or a man. As he held her, he knew it was infantile to wish she'd been denied any recognition beyond that of being his wife. Still that was how he felt. Despite the words that made Susan so happy, he damned the day Rhett Wilson had come into their lives. He didn't want Susan independent in thought or deed. He wanted her to need him for her identity as well as her material comforts and her social and sexual satisfaction. Richard could not tolerate less than total ownership of his wife. He hated her self-sufficiency and was frustrated when she exerted it. Had he been wise enough to recognize it, he would have seen that one reason for marrying Susan had been to squelch that quality in her and make her dependent upon him for her happiness. And had he been schooled in the workings of the human mind, he also might have recognized that he sought a wife as totally unlike his mother as any woman could be. He would have seen that, pretending to love women, he really feared them, that the devotion he thought he felt toward Maria was resentment of the knowledge that he needed her. He preferred to believe he needed no one except as a satellite orbiting around the glow of his greatness.

Susan was looking up at him now, the old adoration in her eyes. At last she answered his question.

"Darling, I can't *wait* to have you read what I've done! It isn't really very good, I'm sure. Not great writing, but straight from my heart. From yours, too, I hope." She seemed almost timid. "Richard, I'm so glad you've taken this attitude. I was afraid . . ."

"That I'd fly into another rage when I heard they'd bought the book? No. As I said, I'd have preferred they didn't. I still don't take to the idea of hanging out the wash for public scrutiny. I never will. But I can't be so rotten that I'm not pleased for you. I had my tantrum when this whole thing started and," he said ruefully, "it didn't do me a damned bit of good. So what's the point of my screaming now?" He smiled. 'The only thing I *should* do is make *you* break the news to Mother. I'm sure you know how *she's* going to feel."

Susan took him seriously. "I don't mind telling her. Why don't we both go to see her? That is, if I'm welcome."

He shook his head. "You're welcome any time. Don't be silly. But it'll go better if you're not around when I give her the word. I'll do it this weekend. No use postponing the hysterics. But let me read it before I try to sell it to her, will you?"

"Of course. I have a copy. Don't move!"

She ran to her office and brought back the outline and first five chapters.

"I'm sure they'll want me to make changes, but this is the stuff they bought." There was almost a wistful, little-girl tone in her voice as she said, "I hope you like it."

Bea Langdon was ecstatic when Susan phoned to tell her the news.

"Imagine! Selling a book on the first try! Susie darling, it's marvelous! I'm so proud of you. We've always known how talented you are, but *this*! Why, I've heard that writers get a hundred turndowns before anything is ever published! Wait until your father hears. He'll burst!"

"It was luck, Mother. Really. If Rhett Wilson hadn't been at that dinner party . . ."

"Nonsense! I'm not saying it wasn't lucky he was there, but if you hadn't had the talent and the discipline, nothing would have happened. I swear, I don't know how you do it! Managing that enormous place, spending time with Katie, catering to Richard and still finding time to write a book! You're marvelous!"

Susan laughed. "And you're wildly prejudiced. Anyway, it isn't written yet. I have a long way to go."

"When will it be published?"

"Fall, seventy-three, Rhett said when I spoke to him this afternoon. That is, if I can finish it by December."

Bea sounded disappointed. "Fall seventy-three! That's more than a year away. I was hoping it would be sooner."

"These things take time, Mom. I'll try to explain it to you—as much as I understand it—next time we get together."

Kate, when she heard, was equally delighted and even more impressed with the "instant success." "Thank God," she said on the phone. "At last you're doing something more intellectually stimulating than squeezing cantaloupes at the market!"

"Much you know," Susan teased. "At Herbert's you don't squeeze the merchandise. You just accept it reverently and pay through the nose. Seriously, Kate, I *am* excited."

"Why not? I'd be, too. How about the Boy Wonder? Can he cope with the competition?"

"He's been wonderful. Oh, he doesn't really like the idea of my writing about Katie and he raised holy hell when the idea came up, but now he's darling. He's going to Pound Ridge this weekend to inform You-Know-Who."

"*Bonne chance* to him," Kate said. "By the way, I haven't heard you mention the Scourge of East Seventieth Street lately. How is that dear lady?"

"Unsinkable. Going stronger than ever, Richard reports. I don't see her at all in the summer. She won't come here. Says she hates the beach. I also get the feeling she's not exactly bereft that I haven't been to Westchester. We're cordial on the phone when we accidentally speak, but I imagine our little détente will end when she hears about the book."

"Who cares? With a mother-in-law like that, it's too bad you don't belong to one of those tribes that puts a limit on the time anyone can spend with the parent of a spouse. I'm much more interested in the public acceptance of your book, and in the way you'll feel. You're overdue for a little recognition. You've had none of your own for damned near eight years. Which reminds me. You have an anniversary coming up soon."

"Next month. I think I'll plan a party. I feel so good about everything these days. Not just the book. Everything."

"Things are going well."

"Yes," Susan said. "Oh, we fight. But what married couple doesn't? But mostly we're behaving like adults. It's so peaceful here, Kate. Sometimes I think I'd like to stay forever. It's so undemanding. Richard works well in this atmosphere and so do I. And Katie is flourishing. It's a remarkably cloudless horizon."

She didn't mention the nagging doubts about Richard's trip to California and the coincidental death of Sylvia Sloan. She'd said nothing to anyone about that. Apparently, the case was closed. If he'd been involved, no one had suspected. Or at least been able to prove it.

"Is it all right if I tell people about the book?" Kate asked. "Friends, I mean."

"Such as."

"Well, Paul for one. I know he'll be delighted. We keep in touch and he always wants to know how you are."

"By all means tell Paul. I've never stopped being fond of him. I wish he were still Richard's manager. I think Richard wishes so too, though he'd never admit it."

"Funny you should say that. I get the same feeling when I talk to Paul. Pity those two are so stubborn. They were a great team."

"More than that," Susan said. "Paul was the best man-friend Richard ever had."

"The only one, you mean."

"Yes, I'm afraid that's true."

Paul called over the weekend to congratulate her. Susan wondered whether Kate had offered the gratuitous information that Richard would be away, visiting his mother. They spoke briefly but warmly. Susan was tempted to invite him to East Hampton. Maybe she could effect a reconciliation. No, she mustn't meddle in Richard's affairs. That was Maria's kind of thing, not hers.

Chapter 30

RICHARD DROVE BACK to East Hampton, Maria's tirade still ringing in his ears. She'd been as angry about Susan's book as he'd expected, and as sarcastic about his ability to control his own wife. I should be used to it by now, he thought wearily. Women. My whole life has been shaped by them in one way or another. Especially the strong ones, like Mother and, yes, Susan. They were more determined, when they put their minds to it, than any man, but their strength was the thing that attracted him. He saw it in different forms in Gloria and Jacqueline and Mary Lou and begrudgingly admired it in Kate Fenton. Even Susan's mother was strong in her seemingly soft way. Spineless women were those who fawned over him or, like Sylvia, killed themselves for "love" of him. He despised them, as he loathed anything or anyone he could dominate. His mind went back to his first interview with Susan and he remembered telling her how passionately he felt about a piano. In this reflective mood he sensed that he adored this object because he could never truly control it. It constantly challenged him. As Maria and Susan did. It was not passive and obedient, as were many of his past bedmates. Nor dependent, as was his handicapped child.

He frowned, thinking of Katie and the years ahead. No matter what Susan believed, Katie never would be self-sufficient. He cared about her, dutifully, because she was part of him, but he also was irrationally angry with her. Every time he saw the healthy children of his brothers and sister, he pitied his own misfortune. He supposed, reluctant as he was to admit it even to himself, he also felt a sense of shame. Not simply because she was "different" or because there was always the lingering doubt that his genes might have contributed to Katie's condition (though the doctors flatly said this disfunction was not inherited) but more because he knew he hadn't carried his share of the burden these past seven years, He left that to Susan, who had long since stopped hoping he'd be a father in anything but name.

He'd felt guilty when he read the first pages of Susan's book, She wrote well and touchingly about the first months of Katie's life. It was not a maudlin, syrupy account, but it had great tenderness. It was factual and yet it was not true, for she'd changed the description of Richard's attitude and had left out any mention of the baby being sent away. The reader would believe that Susan and Richard together had taken on this monumental task of raising Katie as though she were any little girl, and that they shared equally in the slow, tedious process of drawing her into a hearing world. He appreciated that. He wasn't proud of how he'd resisted and finally withdrawn, and God knows his real attitude would make him a villain in people's eyes. He wished that what Susan had written was true: that he really was that kind of father. But he wasn't. The best he could manage was resigned tolerance and an occasional, forced show of affection for his child. At least that was better than the downright revulsion he used to feel.

So let Maria scream, he thought crossly as he pulled into the parking area next to his summer house. I can't stop Susan from doing this book, and when Mother finally reads it she'll see that it's really good publicity for me. He'd tried to tell her that, but she wouldn't listen. All she could see was that a family flaw was to be advertised, unnecessarily, once again.

"I thought we'd reburied those skeletons!" she'd said when he finally told her on Sunday. "You don't see Mary Lou still running around talking about Frances, do you? She was willing to discuss it when it was necessary, but she has better sense than to keep *reminding* everyone that Sergio has a retarded child! One would think your wife would realize that this situation is precisely the same."

"But it isn't," Richard had protested. "There's nothing wrong with Katie's mind. She's bright as any child her age. She's nothing to be ashamed of, Mother!"

"That's your point of view. Some people think there's no shame in having a retarded child, either. I happen to think neither is something one wishes to shout from the housetops." Maria, dressed in golf clothes, rose to end the discussion. "Since there's nothing I can do to stop your wife, I see no point in continuing our talk, Richard. I have a golf date in fifteen minutes, so I'll say goodbye to you and hope you'll come soon again."

He'd kissed the remarkably unlined cheek. As he made the automatic gesture, it came to him that he couldn't remember Maria ever kissing him or any of the others on the mouth. He couldn't recall her ever holding them lovingly, as Susan held Katie. She was always there, a figure of dependability, but a cold one. Some head-doctor would say he'd spent his life looking for the tender mother-love he'd missed. That they *all* had, probably. Bull! What had set him off on that psychiatric hogwash? Mother was Mother. Period, paragraph, full stop. And none of them had turned out badly for lack of sloppy cuddling.

He let himself into the East Hampton house and called Susan. She came out of her "office," eyebrows arched in an unspoken question.

"It went just as I anticipated," Richard said. "Mother would gladly skin you alive."

"I'm sorry she gave you a hard time."

He shrugged. "I expected it. What did you do over the weekend?"

"Nothing much. Took Katie into the village for ice cream. Worked, mostly. Oh, by the way, Paul called."

"Paul? What did he want?"

"Kate told him about the book. He phoned to congratulate me." Susan paused. "Richard, I'd love to ask him here for a weekend before we go back to town. He was always such a good friend to us. It's a pity to lose him."

"I didn't lose him. I kicked him the hell out."

"But you once said it was just because you lost your temper. You even indicated you regretted it."

"Damn it, Susan, get off my back! I don't want to see that ungrateful louse, so let's drop it! I've been through enough this weekend because of the bloody book. Now you're starting a crusade about getting Paul back! Forget it!"

Susan didn't answer. All she said was, "I'll tell Cook you're here. Dinner in about thirty minutes, okay?"

"Sure. Listen, I'm sorry I flew off the handlle. It's been a tough couple of days. But I don't want to get involved with Paul again. You can't pick up relationships with people as though nothing ever happened. Paul and I agreed to disagree. You understand that, don't you?"

"Yes, I suppose I do. But I can't really accept it. Not if two people still have some feeling for each other."

"Well, I accept it. So, no more Paul."

You should be glad I don't believe that old ties never can be reestablished, Susan thought as he left to shower and change. If I believed that, you and I wouldn't be together. Even with all that's happened to us, I still think it's possible to forgive and forget and pick up a relationship that, by your standards, should have been smashed beyond repair. She wondered exactly what Maria had said about the book. Not that she couldn't guess. Kate said it: Who cares? To hell with her. At least Richard was being more supportive than she'd dared hope. And the writing was really going well. She loved every moment of it.

It was broiling hot that first day of September when Susan drove into the center of East Hampton to pick up a few packages of typing paper and carbon. It was incredible how she seemed to eat up supplies now that she was nearly two hundred pages into the book. She was surprised she did not find it painful to relive the past years. Probably, she thought, it's because I'm making the story what I've always wished it really was. All the things about Katie were true, all the wrenching moments of discovery, the sympathetic but doom-laden pronouncements of the doctors, the hours of endless, painstaking work, even the child's remarkable, blessed progress. But the implication of Richard's unselfish participation was a tissue of lies. And even that was forgivable, Susan told herself. He couldn't help being the way he was, and it would have been unnecessarily spiteful to show him in his true light. People who didn't know the influences that had molded him wouldn't understand his turning away. Even more importantly, for those with similarly afflicted children, it was vital to stress that the cooperation of both parents was imperative if they hoped to succeed. She'd been lucky to have gotten this far without Richard's assistance. From talking to other parents, she knew that few made it alone. For the hundredth time she thanked heaven for the patience of Bridie and the skill of a dedicated Edith Chambers. They'd been the support other women found in their husbands. By the time Katie was old enough to understand the book, she'd have forgotten how withdrawn her father had been for most of these formative years.

Susan had a sense of well-being as she drove down Main Street, passing the local library where she'd recently spent hours checking things in medical books, glancing at Guild Hall, the cultural center of East Hampton with its museum and summer theatre and its endless program of art exhibits and other "old-money" sponsored events. As always, she found herself smiling indulgently as she skirted the charming, meticulously maintained Village Green, zealously protected by the Ladies Village Improvement Society. It was a nice town, a different atmosphere from the blatantly expensive environs of Southampton or the determinedly "arty" aura of Bridgehampton with its colony of well-known writers and what were once called "jet setters." East Hampton had a feeling of wealth and permanence. Many of its inhabitants lived there year round, as opposed to the influx, no matter how chic, of the "summer people" who boasted of their modern houses and sixteen-thousand-dollar tennis courts in the other nearby villages. This whole area of Long Island, a hundred miles, give or take, from Manhattan, had a charm of its own, however, and Susan was in love with all of it. She almost dreaded the return to the city right after Labor Day. Not that she didn't love New York, but it was demanding, dirty and supercharged. She already missed this quiet place where she could be more alone with Richard, could write her book in peace and watch her child happily and safely at play.

Thinking now of Katie on the beach with Bridie, she stepped up her pace, eager to get home to them. I have the "end of summer blues," she thought as she made her purchases and got back into the car. No use moping. There's always next year.

Richard's thoughts as he sat at the piano were quite different than Susan's as she hurried through her errands. He was glad the summer was ending. It had gone well enough, but he was getting restless, anxious to plunge back into the pulsing tempo of the city and more anxious still to begin the fall tour. Anonymous living did not suit him for long. He blossomed in the spotlight, grew taller to the sound of applause. Only another ten days, he thought, and we'll be back in the apartment. He was pleased that Susan was planning a big cocktail-buffet party a week after their return, in celebration of their anniversary. It would be fun to see "his kind" of people again, to talk of his upcoming concerts and accept compliments on his becoming tan. He and Susan had been too much alone out here. Her wish more than his. True, most of the people were boring, but he'd have welcomed a little more social activity. Susan s.emed to want almost none. All her foolishness about that damned party! It had been amusing. The people were rich and civilized and made a well-bred fuss over him. Still, he hadn't gone out often alone. There were too many pretty young girls, too much temptation. And East Hampton was too small a village not to immediately hear of any "unacceptable behavior."

With ingrained discipline, he put these wandering thoughts out of his mind and went back to his practicing. He was still fighting Walter's concerto, but coming closer now to interpreting it in his own way. He could taste the sweetness of the victory, savor the idea that his big brother wasn't after all, capable of presenting him with a challenge he couldn't meet.

A persistent tapping at the door broke his concentration. Who'd dare disturb him now? Susan was in the village, and even she rarely interrupted when he was working. Irritably, he called out, "Yes? What is it?"

The door opened a crack and Bridie's timid face appeared. She looked green.

"I'm sorry to disturb you, sir, but may I ask you a favor?"

He answered impatiently, "Come in! Come in!"

The nurse entered, holding Katie by the hand.

"I'm feeing awfully sick," Bridie said. "I tried to wait until Mrs. Antonini got back, but I just can't. I think it's food poisoning. What I came to ask, sir, was would you mind keeping Katie for a little while? Just until Madam returns. I'm sorry to disturb you, but . . ."

She really did look as though she'd be violently ill at any moment.

"Isn't there anyone else who could watch her? Where are the others?"

"It's Thursday. The rest are out for the day."

Richard sighed. "All right. Leave her with me. She can sit in that chair over there and be quiet."

"Thank you, sir." She led Katie to a chair and said slowly and distinctly, "Sit here and be a good girl, darling. Your daddy will take care of you."

Katie nodded as her nurse's lips moved, then she looked at Richard and smiled. The sight of her in her little red swimsuit, sitting with her legs straight out, so small and silent in the big armchair, made Richard uncomfortable. I don't even know how to talk to her, he thought. He smiled back and returned to his music as Bridie left the room, but he couldn't keep his mind on his work. He could hear Katie stirring restlessly, making little crooning sounds to the doll she held in her arms. That damned doll, fitted with hearing aids. He wanted to smash it. He'd never had any faith in the idea that a toy pretending to have her impairment would help her adjust. It was grotesque.

He suddenly felt very nervous. It was strange, being alone with his daughter, and the responsibility made him uneasy. Besides, he couldn't concentrate while she was moving and making those undecipherable noises. How in God's name did Susan stand it day after day? He got up from the piano, picked up the sheet music and went over to Katie. Crouching down, as he'd seen Bridie and Susan do, he looked into her face and spoke rapidly in a shout.

"Let's go down to the beach until your mother comes back. I'll study my music and you can play in the sand."

A look of bewilderment crossed the child's face and Richard remembered it did no good to speak loudly. One had to speak in a normal tone, forming every word with care. He tried again.

"We will go to the beach. You and I."

The smile returned and she climbed down out of the chair and trustingly took his hand. It was so small and soft, that little hand, so confidently holding his own. She looked up at him adoringly.

"Du-de. Katie. Beach."

He felt her tearing at his heart. She was his. So brave and so sweet. So proud to be with him.

"That's right. Daddy and Katie will go to the beach."

They carefully descended the steps to the sand where Katie had left her pail and shovel and Bridie her canvas folding chair. Richard settled himself in it and said, "You play."

She nodded and went busily about her lonely, fruitless digging in the sand. Richard watched her for a few minutes, shaken by the unexpected tenderness he'd felt at that first moment of contact. She was a sweet child and well behaved, but he could never be around her for long periods of time. It was too heartbreaking to watch. How terrible life will be for her, Richard thought. What will she ever do? What man will ever want her? Susan was insane with all that talk about college and marriage. Katie was hardly any better off than Frances. Worse, maybe, because Frances would never grow up, and this exquisite little thing would become an unhappy woman, all too aware of the pleasures she never could have. Oh, he knew there'd been cases when children like this turned into functioning adults. Once or twice in the beginning, Susan had tried to tell him what miraculous things were possible, but he'd cut her short.

"That's wishful thinking," he'd said curtly. "Can't you face the truth?"

Watching Katie now, he knew, sadly, he was right. This was reality: a human being who'd never be independent, never truly desired, never a whole person. A cheerful little robot would grow into a bitter adult. He felt an unaccustomed lump in his throat. It was so unfair. So goddamned unfair. To her. To all of them.

To shake such thoughts, he picked up Walter's concerto and let the bliss of total involvement take over. Later, as he went back over and over the scene in his mind, he realized that he was engrossed for only five or six minutes, ten at the most, before he looked up and saw nothing but an empty beach.

When Susan returned thirty minutes later and saw the Fire Rescue Squad truck, a police car and another vehicle parked at her house, her legs turned to water. She could hardly find strength to jam on the brake and throw the gearshift into "park." She flung herself out of the seat and ran frantically to the house. A hysterical Bridie was waiting inside the door.

"Bridie! What is it? What's happened? My God, is it Katie?"

The woman was almost unable to speak. Susan caught snatches of words. "Sick. My fault. Mr. Richard. Undertow." Susan brushed by her and ran into the living room, where she heard the sound of low voices. Richard, his clothes soaking wet, sat in a chair, his head buried in his hands. Nearby, looking miserable, were several members of the fire department and a sad-faced young policeman. And on the big couch, unmoving, lay Katie.

Susan screamed as she ran to her child, holding her, shaking her as though she could shake her back to life.

"Katie! Katie, angel! Mummy's here! Katie!"

She felt strong hands behind her, gently lifting her from her kneeling position beside the sofa. She fought them off, holding onto her around. She looked into the sympathetic eyes of the local doctor.

"I'm sorry, Mrs. Antonini. Everybody got here as quickly as possible after your husband pulled her out of the water. We did everything we could. But it was too late."

She stared at him. "No! I don't believe it! It's not true! Not my Katie."

"I'm sorry," he said again. "It's hideous and it happens too often. That damned undertow out there has taken much stronger swimmers than your child. Your husband made a superhuman effort to get to her, but no one could have helped. When those big waves come in . . ."

"Stop it!" Susan's voice was a scream of pain. She stared at Richard, who'd raised his head. Tears were streaming down his face.

"Susan, I only took my eyes off of her for a minute. She was playing in the sand. I didn't know she'd go in the water. I was studying Walter's concerto and I . . ."

"You killed her! You and your goddamn selfishness! You and your stupid music!" Her own tears came now. She did not ask how he'd happened to be alone with their child on the beach. Those questions would come later. All that possessed her now was a demonic rage intermingled with shock and overwhelming grief. "You let my baby drown! You didn't care! You've never cared!"

"No. It wasn't like that, Susan. I swear. I tried to get to her, but I couldn't reach her in time." His sobs matched her own. "My God, what kind of monster do you think I am that I wouldn't try to save my own child! I'd have given my life! You must believe that!''

The strangers in the room, with the exception of the doctor, went quietly out the door, pitying the bereaved parents, embarrassed by the scene.

"Let me give you something so you can rest, Mrs. Antonini. It's a terrible, tragic accident and you're in shock. Let's go to your room where you can lie down.''

"No! I won't leave my baby!''

The doctor was very gentle. "There's nothing more you can do for her. Please. Come with me.''

Susan felt as though she were going to faint. There was a terrible weakness in her whole body and she sagged against the doctor. "My mother,'' she said. "I've got to call . . . to tell her to come.''

"We'll call her. Your husband can tell us who should be notified.''

"I'll call, Susan.'' Richard's voice was almost inaudible. "I'll get your mother. Please do what the doctor says. I'll take care of things here.''

She turned on him, making a snarling sound like a wounded animal. Like you took care of them when I was away! she wanted to scream. Like you took care of the baby you never wanted! But no words came out. She simply looked at him in terrible accusation, and the eyes that had flashed hatred were now vacant except for unmistakable contempt. And then, because it was too much to bear, her mind mercifully held out the salvation of unconsciousness and she collapsed in the doctor's arms.

She barely remembered the next twenty-four hours. She knew that Bea and Wil Langdon came and that next morning her mother helped her dress for the drive back into the city where Kate Fenton waited at the apartment. She was heavily sedated, only dimly aware of Richard moving like a restless ghost in and out of her room. People spoke to her and she didn't answer. They brought her food and she didn't eat it. Only when Bridie came into the room did Susan hold out her arms to the crushed woman and try to comfort her as others were trying to comfort Susan. They clung together, the two women whom Katie had loved and who had loved her as though she was the child of both. It was from Bridie that Susan finally heard the whole story. Bridie, who blamed herself for leaving her charge, who felt responsible for the whole hideous accident.

"I never should have left her,'' the nurse sobbed. "If I hadn't left her, she'd be here today.''

"Hush,'' Susan said. "You mustn't blame yourself. You were sick. There was no one else. Why wouldn't you turn a child over to her own father to watch after for a few minutes? Dear Bridie. You're not at fault. It's not you who must live with the guilt. You were everything to Katie. Closer to her than I. She loved you so much. She wouldn't want you to do this to yourself,''

"I should have known better. Mr. Richard never took care of her alone before. He didn't know you couldn't take your eyes off her for a minute on the beach. He didn't know how she loved that dangerous water. Don't blame him, madam. He hadn't been around her enough to realize that when she faced the beach she couldn't hear the sound of those big waves coming in behind her, like the one that . . .'' The nurse couldn't go on.

"You didn't know he was going to take her to the beach," Susan said. "You thought she was safe in the living room."

Trying to comfort someone who was as brokenhearted as she gave Susan the strength to face the ordeal ahead. Dry-eyed, superhumanly controlled, she indicated to her mother and Kate what she wanted done. No prolonged period before the burial service, no morbid "viewing" at Campbell's, and as little publicity as possible, though that, of course, was too much to hope for. The accident had already made headlines and the press was all over them once again, trying fruitlessly to get at Richard or Susan or Bridie or anyone even remotely close to them. There was no way to stop the newspaper stories, but at least the family would not reveal the time of the service, in the hope that the curious "celebrity watchers" could be avoided.

Susan remembered the spectacle of Giovanni's "tribute" and shuddered. Perhaps the great man would have wanted it the way Maria had arranged it. As a public figure, it was the proper way for him. But Katie was only a baby. She'd been sheltered from the curious for most of her life. She'd have the same protection in death, as far as her mother could manage it. The service would be quick and private.

"I'd like Edith Chambers to say a few words," Susan told Bea.

"All right, dear, though I thought perhaps Kate might be the one. She was Katie's godmother."

"No. Kate couldn't do it. She was too close. Besides, Edith taught Katie to speak. It seems only right that she should say the last words about her."

Bea marveled at the reserve of strength Susan had found. I couldn't do it if it were my child, she thought. She's more in control now than she was when they took Katie away from her the first time. I don't know how she can handle this. She must be dying inside.

Kate Fenton was less sure that Susan was really in control. True, she did go about the arrangements quietly, did seem almost fatalistic about it after her initial outburst, the details of which Richard unexpectedly confided to Kate. But Kate watched her friend apprehensively. She was too calm, too disciplined. It was unnatural and frightening. Susan spoke to Maria and to the members of Richard's family who appeared at the apartment uttering appropriate condolences, but she did not speak to Richard. She hadn't, he told Kate, since that first afternoon. He was almost crazy with grief and guilt, and it was to Kate, of all people, that he unburdened himself. She supposed he could not face Bea Langdon's natural resentful anguish or, conversely, his own mother's blind defense of him. He didn't want to be "forgiven" by a biased Maria who would assure him that he was not at fault. He knew he was, and he was willing, almost eager, to be punished for it, as though suffering was as necessary as it was natural.

"I don't blame Susan for refusing to talk to me," he told Kate. "Why should she ever talk to me again? My God, Kate, how can I live with this? Is this retribution for all the rotten things I've done? If so, why this way? Why did it have to come through that innocent child?"

"I don't know," Kate said. "I couldn't possibly answer that. No one could." It was impossible not to blame him, but equally impossible not to feel some pity. He'd been stupid and careless. Tragically so. His only defense was, as

Bridie had pointed out to Susan, the fact that he had no idea how carefully Katie had to be watched. And even that was his own fault, Kate thought bitterly. If he'd taken the slightest interest in his daughter's upbringing, he'd have realized she was an easy victim of any menace she couldn't hear. Like the sound of an oncoming car or the wail of a speeding ambulance or, Kate shuddered, the booming roar of a huge, enveloping, shore-bound wave. There was no comfort for Richard. The best he could hope for from Susan was pity and the resigned acceptance of his folly. Slim consolation and a thin thread on which to continue a marriage.

"I won't be silly enough to tell you not to blame yourself," Kate said. "You *were* to blame. Only a fool would pretend otherwise. What can I say to you, Richard? That I understand? I don't. I never have. But perhaps, in time, Susan will. She's always been able to understand you better than anyone, and perhaps she'll be able to accept the 'mitigating circumstances.' All you can do is wait and hope. It was a terrible lesson learned at incalculable expense. If there's any good that possibly could come out of this horror it will be a long-overdue awareness of your own selfishness and your disinterest in the problems of other people."

"Do you think Susan will stay with me?" It was a plea for reassurance, a desperate grasp at something to live for.

"I don't know. No one knows what's going on in her head at this moment. I doubt she knows that herself."

Chapter 31

FOR THE SECOND time in one year, the families sat together at the last goodbye for one of their own. Aside from Edith Chambers, the only "outsiders" at the simple service at Campbell's were Kate, Bridie, Evie Maxwell and Paul Carmichael. Susan had told Kate to ask Paul to come.

"He was the only man, aside from Giovanni and my father, who loved Katie," Susan said in the flat, lifeless tone in which she'd spoken since the day of the accident. "In the early days, I believe she thought Paul was her father. I want him there."

"Will Richard . . . ?"

Susan's expression was hard. "I don't care what Richard wants."

Paul was touched by Susan's request and equally certain Richard had played no part in the decision. He sat far back in the funeral chapel, removed from the others, a voluntary outcast from the Antoninis. From his seat he could see only the backs of heads, but he recognized them all. Richard's nieces and nephews were the only ones drastically changed since the days when Paul first was involved with the family. Sergio's and Walter's children were so grown-up. Joseph was twenty-three and playing guitar, to his grandmother's horror, in a rock group in Greenwich Village. His sister Patricia was twenty and in college. Walter's Calhoun had graduated from Harvard in June, and his younger brother was there in his junior year. Even Gloria's children, except for the twins, who were nearly eight, were leaving "babyhood." Raoul, Jr., was thirteen and Maria eleven. It was hard to believe the third generation of Antoninis were all young adults, or nearly so. Where had the years gone? It seemed only yesterday that Richard had introduced "his girl" to his parents and his brothers and sister and their pack of overactive kids. Pierre and Claudette Taffin weren't even born then, and now here they were at "the age of reason." The age, Paul thought despairingly, that Katie had not lived to see. Anger welled inside him. Goddamn Richard! Damn him to hell for this and a thousand other heedless acts!

He could see the faces of Bridie and the closest members of the family as they entered last and took their places in the front pew. Ironic that Maria should be among them, the grandmother who literally had no use for her youngest son's child. The tiny figure, straight and youthful at seventy-three, came in first. Richard, looking destroyed, followed her. Susan moved like a wooden doll, her uncovered face a study in controlled agony. Behind her came Bea and Wil Langdon, Bea veiled to hide the tears she knew she'd not be able to restrain; Wil gray and drawn; Bridie openly weeping.

Paul suffered for the last four. Even for Richard, though part of him wanted to kill the man who'd let this happen. But his heart went out to the woman he loved. He wanted to take Susan in his arms and comfort her, hold her as he'd often seen her hold the one who now lay in the small coffin under a blanket of sweetheart roses and baby's breath. He'd sent the same flowers. A tiny basket of them, suitable for a child. On the card he'd written simply, "To Katie from her friend Paul." Susan would know how much love was in that message.

The service was mercifully brief. A clergyman spoke a few words and said appropriate prayers and then Edith Chambers walked to the podium and began. Her soft voice filled the chapel but her words were for Susan.

"I speak for Katie. For Katie who was learning to speak for herself. For Katie whom God chose to afflict, but whom He also chose to place in the tender, patient hands of those who loved and believed in her.

"Hers was such a brief life. But filled with so many things. In less than seven swift years she knew more suffering and frustration and bewilderment than most of us know in a lifetime. Yet she knew more joy, was more loving, more giving, more instinctively understanding than we who are seven times seven, or ten times that number.

"Katie was a child who did not hear and barely spoke. But she was not a silent child. She did not need speech to communicate happiness. She had no need of words to express her cheerfulness, Man-made sounds were not necessary to convey her generosity of soul and spirit. She was a brave little girl. And we loved her.

"For each of us, she had special gifts. For me, her teacher, it was the delight of touching a responsive chord, of seeing her awaken to the everyday pleasures of life. For her little friends it was the company of a gay, uncomplaining schoolmate who asked no special consideration. And for her family, most of all, she gave the special gifts of unending adoration expressed in the radiant smiles, the small, surprisingly competent hand always outstretched to touch the faces of the ones she loved.

"Young as she was, I think Katherine took nothing for granted. Everything was new and wonderful. To recognize a word in a book, to identify a flower, to utter a first, small, hesitating sound and be understood. She did not know these things were her due. To her, every moment was a discovery, every day a great adventure. She was not handicapped in the sorrowful way we are wont to use the word. For Katie was not deaf to the nuances of love nor speechless in her gratitude for them. She heard and spoke with her heart.

"We mourn. And there is cause to mourn the death of one so young. But there is cause to rejoice in her life. She heard her own music, this elfin child. She danced through a storybook world bathed in sunshine that defeated the dark and ugly clouds. She made her own place, a little kingdom, a tiny Camelot filled with shining moments. And we were allowed to enter and fleetingly share the magic with her, to see goodness through her innocent eyes.

"She left us rich in recollections of her enchanted world. She left us strength and hope and serenity through our sadness. She took from us our golden moments of glory. But their blessed memory remains."

Bridie and Bea were sobbing uncontrollably as Edith sat down, and Richard's head was buried in his hands as it had been when Susan saw him that terrible day in East Hampton. Only Maria and Susan were dry-eyed, the former apparently unmoved, the latter so devastated she could not find merciful release in tears.

We've lost the two best ones within months of each other, Paul thought. The oldest and the youngest Antonini. He closed his eyes and sent forth a silent prayer. "Let her survive this, God. Above all, let Susan survive."

Susan and Richard returned from the cemetery to a silent and empty apartment. Only Bridie rode back in the car with them and not a word was uttered on the long trip home. Richard gazed sightlessly out of the window of the limousine and Susan stared at the driver's back. Bridie crouched in a corner, quiet feeling out of place in this car with her employers. She would not be with them much longer, she supposed. They had no need of her now. The realization brought tears to her eyes once again. It was not finding a job she worried about. Competent baby nurses were always in demand. It was simply that after nearly seven years she couldn't imagine being anywhere else or taking care of any other child. Katie had been almost as much hers as her mother's, Just as Mrs. Antonini had said. And no matter how many reassurances she offered, Susan would never convince Bridie that she did not bear the blame for their loss.

It was not until they were entering the apartment that Susan turned to the nurse and took her hand.

"You'll stay with us, Bridie, won't you? At least for a while. Until things are settled."

Bridie knew what she meant. She'd wondered whether this unhappy couple would stay together. If only they could. It was times like these when a man and a woman needed each other. She found that out when her late husband Patrick (May he rest in peace,) saw her through the agony of their stillborn child so many years ago. She could never have another and she was sure she couldn't have survived without Pat to comfort her and share the misery. After he passed on she turned to taking care of other people's children. She loved them all dearly. All her little charges over the years. But she'd felt about none as she had about Katie.

Of course, though they both were nearly crazy with sorrow, Mr. and Mrs.

Antonini's problem was different than hers and Pat's had been. Here there were also guilt and bitterness, along with the memories of seven years of a living child. They needed each other but they had other terrible feelings to overcome before either could offer or accept comfort.

"I'll stay as long as you want me," Bridie said.

"Thank you. There's a lot . . . There are things to be done."

Bridie knew what she was trying to say, though Susan couldn't get the words out. Katie's nursery had to be dismantled and Katie's clothes and toys given away. Even in her dazed state in East Hampton, Bridie had had enough presence of mind to hide the doll with the hearing aids. Mrs. Antonini had never seen it since that day, and she never would. It was safely out of sight in the back of Bridie's closet, where it had been since she smuggled it back to New York in her suitcase. But there were all the other reminders to be gotten out of the apartment. Susan couldn't face that. Bridie would do it.

"Yes, madam," she said quietly. "I'll see to them."

"I don't understand why Susan wouldn't let us come with her." Bea's swollen-with-tears face mirrored her distress as Wil drove toward Bronxville. "She shouldn't be alone now."

"She has her husband, dear."

Bea stared at him. "Do you know what you're saying? Her husband! My God, Wil, she can barely look at him, much less speak to him! I'd be less worried if she were really alone than with that man!"

"You're wrong, my love. Yes, this terrible tragedy was Richard's fault. Directly. But indirectly, Susan is to blame, too."

"Wil!"

"I'm sorry, sweetheart, but it's true. If Richard hadn't been permitted to abdicate all responsibility toward his child, things might have been different. Susan let him drop out. Maybe, in a strange way, she was so possessive about Katie that she never really wanted him to participate. I know that's shocking to you, but put yourself in her place. Would you have stood for it if I'd flatly refused to have any part in our daughter's upbringing? Would you have turned a nursemaid into that child's other parent? Damned right you wouldn't! You'd have yelled and screamed and forced me to do my duties as a father. And don't give me all that stuff about Richard being 'different' because he's an artist. He's still a man, a husband and he was a father. Why did Susie permit him to stay aloof from a mutual problem they should have been sharing all these years?"

Bea was indignant. "Have you forgotten how he behaved from the moment he knew Katie was handicapped? How he and that mother of his took the baby away and Susan and I had to kidnap her to bring her home? Have you blocked out all the embarrassment he's caused Susie with his women and his wild escapades? I don't understand you, Wil. It's unthinkable that any of the blame for this could fall, even indirectly, on that girl. She did nothing but try to raise Katie singlehanded, without an iota of interest from Richard!"

"You've just said the viable words. 'She did nothing.' She did everything for Katie, and I admire her for that, but for years she did nothing to make Richard part of it. If she was going to raise Katie as a single parent, then she should have left her husband and really become one. But she wanted it both ways. No, dear. Richard can't be blamed for all of this. Any more than you could blame a child for burning down the house if you hadn't told him what could happen with matches." Wil's voice trembled. "God knows I hold no brief for Richard. He should have had enough common sense to know you have to watch any small child near the water. But most children *can* be ignored for a few minutes. The trouble is, Richard was able to avoid the fact that Katie wasn't 'most children.'"

The stern set of Bea's lips told him that she refused to believe a word of what he said. In her mind, Susan was a saint and Richard a devil. It wasn't as easy as that.

"Look," Wil said, "nobody in this world—including you—loves Susie more than I. Nobody is more heartbroken over what's happened to her. But she hasn't been a hundred per cent right in this. I hate to think of how she's going to go on punishing that poor bastard who's already in hell."

Bea snapped at him. "I honestly think you feel sorry for him! It's incredible! Men really do stick together, even at a time like this! He's responsible for the death of your grandchild and you're worrying about his suffering! What about Susan's suffering?"

"I worry about that, too. Believe me I do. But I also pray she has enough compassion and charity in her to understand her role in this. It was an accident, Bea. It happened so fast! It could have happened to anyone. It could even have happened if Susan had been reading a book on the beach or Bridie had nodded off in her chair. Except that neither of them would have done that because they were well instructed in the care of a nonhearing child. Richard was not, And he's paying heavily for his ignorance."

"It was ignorance he chose."

"Yes," Wil said, "but it was an option he should never have been allowed."

"I suppose Susan really will leave Richard now," Jacqueline said. "I'm sorry. Until this happened, I think they were really beginning to make a go of it."

"I know. And it had to be my damned concerto he was so wrapped up in. It really makes me feel partially responsible."

"Don't be ridiculous. It could have been Mozart."

"Do you think Susan will stay with Richard?"

Sergio looked at his wife. "Would you have left me if I'd let one of our kids drown?"

Mary Lou considered that. "I don't know. I don't know how much any woman can forgive a man she loves."

Gloria and Raoul went back to Maria's house with her. For once, Gloria was sincerely sympathetic.

"I feel so sorry for them," she said. "My God, it must be terrible to lose a child. And especially that way."

"I hope it won't affect Richard's work," Maria said. "He has a very heavy schedule. An important tour. He'll have to get over this by next month."

"Could I ask you a favor?"

"Of course, Kate," Paul said. "Name it."

"Would you mind spending the rest of the day with me? I have a feeling I'm going to get terribly, terribly drunk and cry a lot."

I wish I could have said it better, Edith Chambers thought as she returned to her office. It was like walking on thin ice. I couldn't mention Susan and ignore Richard. I couldn't mention Richard without reminding everyone of the circumstances. And I loved that child so much. I had such hopes for her. She would have made it. Damn it! She blew her nose hard and wiped her eyes before she sat down at the desk and picked up a folder marked "Katherine Antonini." She supposed she should keep it. It was valuable research. But her emotions were stronger than her professional assessment. Almost in anger, she ripped the file in two and threw it in the wastebasket. Goodbye, Katie. I'll miss you. The buzzer on her desk sounded.

"Your two-o'clock appointment is here, Miss Chambers. George Drue."

Another silent two-year-old with his mother. I can't bear it, Edith thought. How often can they break my heart?

"Thanks, Penny. Send them in."

The silence was everywhere and it was killing Richard. A week after the funeral, and Susan had not spoken to him. Not a single word, though they faced each other at the dining table each night their only meal together. Susan had moved into the guest room, not even discussing it with him, and had her breakfast sent in there. She was never home for lunch. He did not know where she went and dared not ask. He waited for her to say what was going to happen to them, and she said nothing. It was eerie. As though she had assumed the role of the deaf-mute child, Susan did not hear or speak.

He spoke to other people, his family and his business associates, but he only half-listened and automatically responded. They assumed he would go on the tour as planned, leaving in three weeks. He did not tell them he couldn't even think about performing, that he had not, in fact, touched the piano in the ten days since he left it to take his child to the beach.

Several times in the past week, alone in the apartment except for the servants, he'd gone into the room where he usually practiced, had sat in front of the keyboard and stared at the music on the rack. But his hands lay quiet in his lap, and after a few minutes he'd gotten up and walked away.

I must get back to work, he told himself fiercely on this clear September morning. It's all I have. I must pick up my life. I must go on with my music. All of them said so. Mother, Serge, Walter, Frank Olmstead, George Reagan. All except Susan, who's as silent as the grave. The rest talk to me, but hers is the only voice I want to hear. I need her, Richard thought almost in surprise. I need her and I've lost her forever.

The realization was unbearable. He'd given lip-service to his marriage, taking all and giving as it pleased him, certain of Susan's devotion, even when she'd threatened to withdraw it. Now her love had died with the child, and there was none left for him at the moment he could not live without it.

From somewhere in the back of his mind, he remembered some much-quoted lines from Shakespeare. How did they go? "If music be the food of love, play on." What was the rest of it? Compulsively, he went to the library and found the anthology of Shakespearean quotes. There it was. *Twelfth night*. Alone, he read the passage aloud:

> If music be the food of love, play on;
> Give me excess of it, that, surfeiting,
> The appetite may sicken, and so die.

He closed the book and went back to the piano. Take the plunge, he told himself. Start with Walter's concerto. Don't think. Just begin where you left off. He raised his arms and nothing happened. His fingers were like ten sticks of marble, inflexible, unmoving. Frantically, he tried to warm the stony hands, rubbing them against his chest, placing one stiff set of fingers over the other. Nothing. He stared at them in disbelief. Only a moment ago he'd been thumbing through the pages of a book. Now, in one hideous instant, he had no use of his hands. The terrible word burned in his brain. Paralysis. My hands are paralyzed. I can't move them. Inside he was screaming, but no sound came out. Susan found him three hours later, still sitting at the piano, staring at the lifeless fingers which lay like accusatory pointers on the black and white keys.

The diagnosis was "hysterical paralysis." The specialists were cautiously optimistic. The top men in the country were called in for consultation and they nodded their heads solemnly and said yes, indeed, it was psychosomatic. Nothing physical involved. Thoroughly understandable. They felt it would go as quickly as it came. One day, when Richard had worked out his grief and guilt, his hands would move again, as swiftly and magically as ever. But he must go into therapy, they said. Psychotherapy. Not the kind that got muscles moving after a stroke, as Maria's therapy had done, but the healing of a mind that had brought upon itself the worst kind of punishment, one it unconsciously sought. This was delayed shock, they opined. There was no organic problem. It was a case for a psychiatrist.

The doctors explained it carefully to them—to a stunned and frightened Richard, a sick-at-heart Susan and an almost belligerent Maria, who called it all "hogwash."

"It's impossible," Maria said firmly. "I will not accept that diagnosis. There must be a physical reason and we'll consult every doctor in the world until we find out what it is. 'Hysterical paralysis,' indeed! Richard has never been hysterical in his life. He has too much control for that. He's a disciplined man. My son has been through a trying time, I'll grant you that, but until now he's functioned well, as he's been trained to do."

The doctors glanced at each other as the feisty little woman spoke. "A trying time," they thought. A man sits by while his child drowns and she calls it a "trying time"! Good God, the woman wasn't stupid, she was simply blind!

They hoped Richard and his wife would override this refusal to accept the facts. If not, Antonini had no chance. All the exercise and massage in the world wouldn't help. Somewhere in the dark corners of his mind he didn't want to play again, didn't want to relive the moment when he'd resentfully left the piano to care for his daughter. Couldn't Mrs. Antonini see that? The man was in mental agony. Probably had subconsciously been suffering for years. The tragedy only triggered a breakdown which inevitably would have come sooner or later. Child prodigy. Driving mother. Genius father. Competitive family. Too much fame and adoration all his life. Not a normal existence in any sense. And now this. This terrible guilt that cried out for unspeakable revenge. Lucky he has a sensible wife, the doctors said among themselves. His mother is a raving maniac.

Susan knew what they were thinking. Her own days with Dr. Marcus had given her a layman's insight into Richard's problems, particularly as they related to her own. Because of the psychiatrist she'd survived eight years of this turmoil-filled marriage. Because of the doctor and her own solid background, her quite ordinary and happy childhood, her own understanding and devoted parents, she'd kept her sanity. Giovanni had helped her understand other things. She'd even kept her love for Richard. Until he let Katie die. Then nothing helped. She couldn't forgive him. Couldn't speak to him. Thought of nothing but how and when she could get away from this self-involved, heedless man.

Yet when she found him dazed and stricken, deprived of all he cared for, she wept for the first time since Katie's death. She'd gone to him, this man she didn't recognize, and thoughts of escape left her mind as she held him and comforted him and saw her own tears drop on the immobile fingers. It was more than pity. It was a sad realization that they lived as strangers, not daring to expose their real feelings, hiding behind arrogance and anger and false pride. It was all such a waste, such a farce.

She saw in him the same withdrawal she'd felt when Katie was taken to the school. She remembered the unwillingness to be part of the world, the retreat into a shell where no reality could penetrate. He must get help, too, she thought.

How many years of resentment and fury and disgust with himself must lie behind this hideous tangible evidence of guilt! How many things must have been pushed far back in his mind, hidden behind the facile smile, the confident air, the consuming self-interest. How much he must have suffered while refusing to face his suffering, hiding his uncertainty from himself, from me, from everyone. Susan tried to speak to him and he didn't answer that first day. Only later, after he'd listened to the doctors and smiled sardonically at Maria's rejection of their diagnosis, did he agree to try psychoanalysis.

"It's a bitter joke, isn't it?" he said to Susan. "I was so scornful of your need for help. I must have tempted fate just a little too far."

If it's a joke, it's a terrible one, she thought. It's heartbreaking self-punishment. Even more than he deserves.

Chapter 32

"YOU'RE NOT VERY pleased to be here, Mr. Antonini, are you?"

Richard shifted uneasily in the chair facing Dr. Beekman's desk. "No, not particularly. But nothing else has worked. I've been through all kinds of physical therapy in the past month and it does no good. I still can't move my hands." A bitter expression crossed his face and his voice was suddenly angry. "My mother recovered completely from a stroke. I've had nothing as serious as that and yet I'm more a cripple than she. I have a manservant to dress me, a chauffeur to open car doors, and a wife to cut up my food and feed me. And now I have you, Doctor, to massage my mind. You're my last resort. Not pleased to be here? That's the understatement of the century. I hate being here. I have no hope that you can help."

"I see. That makes things a great deal more difficult for both of us. Most patients come because they no longer can cope with life. They know they're sick, and they're hoping I can help them find their own cure. An unwilling patient is not one I usually accept, Mr. Antonini." The young doctor was kind but very serious. "If Dr. Marcus, whom I respect so highly, had not asked me to take you, I don't think I would have. You see, you're not a genius to me. You're just another human being with all the stresses and rages and guilt of lesser mortals. I hope I can help you help yourself. But I'll need your co-operation." He paused. "Can I count on that?"

"I'm here," Richard said listlessly. "And I'll be here five afternoons a week until I'm cured. Or until we mutually decide that I'm a lost cause. I'll try to co-operate, Doctor."

"Very well, then. Let's start from the beginning."

Susan sat in Paul's apartment, her feet propped up on a big ottoman, a glass of club soda in her hand. She'd been there many afternoons in the past weeks. Since Richard's paralysis, she had most meals with her husband, feeding him as though he were a child, talking quietly to him, gently urging him to get professional help. It had taken a month to get past his stubborn resistance, a resistance abetted by Maria, who shot down every argument the doctors and Susan presented. But finally even Richard could see that the physical therapy was useless, and, over Maria's last, lingering protests, he'd begun to see Dr. Beekman every afternoon. He'd been in therapy only a month, too soon to expect results, yet every day Susan thought she could see him beginning to scratch at the bars of the cage he'd inhabited all his life. He talked a little more freely to her about the doctor, conceding that the man had a way of making him recognize things he hadn't realized were bothering him. Yet even with these small admissions, he remained a disbeliever.

"But what good is it if I still can't move my fingers?"

"Richard, you can't expect an overnight cure! Whatever caused this probably was years in the making. How could it go away so quickly? Give it time."

"I know what caused it. What I did to Katie. Will that go away, Susan?"

"No," she said slowly, "it won't go away. Not the fact of it. But you'll come to see why it could have happened; why, perhaps, your whole life had been moving inexorably toward that moment.''

''And then I'll be able to forgive myself? You'll be able to forgive me?'' The words were a challenge.

Susan felt so weary. ''I'm no doctor. I can't answer that.''

''You're a woman. You're my wife.''

''Yes, I'm both those things, but I still can't answer for you, or for myself.''

''Will you ever love me again?'' His voice was desperate.

She turned away. She wanted to tell him that she'd always loved him, that she'd spent long hours searching for understanding and forgiveness for them both. But she knew that until he reached the full depths of knowledge about himself, theirs was nothing but the façade of a marriage.

''Susan, I can't live without you.''

God, how she once would have sold her soul for those words! How desperately she'd longed to be needed by him. All the single-minded devotion to Katie had been more than mother-love. It had also been compensation for Richard's independence. The dependent child had, in a peculiar way, taken the place of the indifferent partner. They were two different kinds of love, hers for her husband and her daughter, yet at the bottom of both was this crying out for someone on whom to shower love, to indulge her need to be indispensable. I used you, Katie, she thought. I adored you, but I used you for the fulfillment I wouldn't find with your father. What colossal ego I must have! What is this consuming wish to be all-important?

''I won't leave you,'' she said quietly. ''I know you need me. I need you, too.''

The relief in his face was evident, But a second later the pleased expression turned to a scowl as he looked at his immobile hands. ''Need me?'' He almost spat out the words. ''Who needs a husband who can't make you feel what you used to feel? Who needs a goddamn wooden Indian who has to be dressed and fed and even taken to the bathroom, for Christ's sake?'' He was getting terribly worked up. ''Without my hands I don't want to live! Why couldn't it have been my eyes? I'd have been better off blind. At least I could have worked! I could have made love. My God, I wish I were dead!''

She tried to soothe him. ''You're going to be all right,'' she said firmly. ''The doctors all say so.''

''Doctors! Quacks! What do they know?''

''They know a great deal. Your case is not unique. Hysterical paralysis is not all that uncommon, Richard. They know how to deal with it. Please believe that.''

He'd subsided and gone to the big chair by the window, sitting there quietly, looking at nothing, his useless hands hanging motionless at his sides.

Susan sighed, thinking of a dozen other episodes like it in the past weeks. She'd turned to Paul for comfort after Katie's death. Every afternoon that he was free she left her apartment and walked to his, like a lost soul seeking refuge. He was the only person with whom she found true peace these days. Kate, Jacqueline, Bea—all the women she felt close to were ready to offer advice and companionship. But though they talked *to* her, *at* her, trying to help, none had the serenity of this man. Sometimes she and Paul sat for an hour or two, never exchanging a word. Often he worked at his desk while she simply rested nearby, lost in her thoughts. She'd given up drinking entirely. She was confused enough without living in an alcoholic fog.

No one knew of these frequent visits. No one would have believed them platonic. Paul had never done more than give her a kiss on the cheek, or put his arms around her when she unexpectedly burst into tears, as she often did these days. Sometimes she wondered whether she came here subconsciously hoping he'd make love to her. She missed physical satisfaction. She was a sexy woman and there had always been a strong atttraction between her and Paul. And yet neither of them made a move, understanding without words that she was not seeking an affair but a haven.

There was in this period no sex with Richard, an unspoken agreement as much for his pride as for her still ambivalent feelings about him. There had been, a week after the funeral, a note from Martin Tanner, a properly written message of condolence. Had she wished to, Susan could have picked up with him. But it was as though she was in limbo. Even her capacity for passion was suspended. If she had been able to seek forgetfulness in a man's arms, Susan knew she would have reproached herself, been ashamed that the grief she morbidly hugged to her could be even momentarily forgotten.

But then why do I keep running to Paul? she asked herself. If I'm not hoping for affection, why am I here? It wasn't fair to him. She knew how he'd felt about her since the day they met. What right did she have to use his devotion when she wasn't ready to return it?

My God, Susan, she thought, you really are loathsome! Here is someone who wants you, needs you in a healthy way, and you play games with him, treating him like a "big brother," expecting him to keep his distance. She could not contain these thoughts. It was dishonest and insulting to someone as kind and generous as Paul Carmichael. Hesitatingly, she cleared her throat and he looked up from the correspondence he was studying.

"You ahem-ed, madam?"

'Afraid I did. Can we talk or are you too busy?''

"Never too busy for you. Glad to take a break, in fact. You all right?'' He glanced at her empty glass. "Want a refill?''

"No, nothing.'' Susan paused. "I was just sitting here wondering why you let me impose on you this way.''

He raised an eyebrow. "Impose? It's no imposition. I'm flattered. You know that. I'm glad there's somewhere you want to come. I'm glad I'm the one you want to come to.''

"But I sit here afternoon after afternoon, sometimes not even talking. It must be a bore for you—me and my tragic act! I'm feeling guilty about taking so much of your time, Paul. It's life-sustaining for me, but what's in it for you?''

"Does there always have to be 'something in it' when friends help each other?''

"That's just the point. I'm doing all the taking. I draw strength from you, and contentment. For a few hours I'm away from all the unhappiness at home. I can almost forget there are questions without answers; you reassure me that there is still sanity and solidity in this world. But I give back nothing. We're not 'friends helping each other.' It's one friend—*you*—helping a very unsatisfactory me.''

He moved away from the desk and perched on the edge of the ottoman. ''You give everything back,'' he said, ''Just by being here. I know what you're thinking, Susan. You think you should return my hospitality by going to bed with me. You know that's what I've always wanted and you're feeling guilty because you sense how strong that desire is. And it is. Every minute we're in the same room I want to make love to you. But my dear, you're not ready to make love to me, and you don't have to be sorry about that. I want you, Susan. I damned well do. But I'm not one of those high-school boys you used to know who tried to get to you by telling you how painful it was to suppress a strong sex urge. Don't feel sorry for me. Or worried that you're causing me physical or mental anguish. I've lived with the mental anguish for eight years. As for the physical, I wouldn't let you try to ease that unless you wanted to. If someone goes to bed with me, I sure as hell don't want it to be out of pity. Right now, being near you is enough. I can hope for more, one day, but time wili have to resolve that.'' He leaned over and patted her cheek. ''Dearest Susan. Don't you know you're not the only one who finds pleasure in giving? Other people need to be needed, too.''

She took his hand and held it tightly. ''Oh Paul, I do love you.''

''I know you love me, Susan. I'm waiting to see if I'm your *true* love.'' He disengaged his hand. ''Meantime, don't stop coming here. You need it just the way it is. And so do I.''

The simple matter-of-fact words had a peculiar aphrodisiacal effect upon her. For a moment she felt the quickening of desire, the urge to kiss him deeply, to touch him and be touched. As though he sensed it, Paul walked away.

''Time for me to kick you out,'' he said flatly, ''before I start giving you a line like your old high-school dates. Go home, friend. And come back tomorrow.''

When the door closed, Paul angrily kicked the wastebasket, overturning it, ignoring the trash that fell on the floor. Who the hell do you think you are? he asked an invisible Susan. How much longer can you put me through this? Come to me or stay away forever, but for God's sake don't torment me with your blasted unplanned seductiveness! What do you think I'm made of? And then he laughed at himself. What a pack of lies he'd just told her to relieve her mind. It was agony for him when she was here. Agony to want her and know nothing was going to happen, to be almost afraid to speak, lest one ill-chosen word end her visits forever. I can settle for crumbs, Paul thought. I'd rather have her around this way than not see her at all. And I *am* one of those high-school kids. I physically ache with desire. If it can't be Susan, it'll have to be someone else.

Deliberately, he called and made a dinner date, knowing where he would spend a mindless night.

Three days before Christmas, Kate and Susan had their annual preholiday lunch. In years past, Susan had looked forward to this event. She was childish about Christmas, the gifts, the gaiety, the warm and loving spirit of it that made even grumpy New Yorkers smile at each other on the street. But this year there was no joy in her. She had no heart for any of it. There were too many memories. Even the good ones hurt.

"Let's be really corny and go to the Edwardian Room at the Plaza," Kate had said on the phone. "It's so damned Dickensian with its old-fashioned trimmings and fur-bearing tourists. I love it, I'll get us a nice, sedate table near the window where we can look at Central Park and the horse-drawn carriages and Bergdorf Goodman done up in Christmas lights. Okay?"

"Sure."

"I'm overwhelmed by your enthusiasm," Kate said tartly. "What are you rehearsing for—the road-company role of Scrooge?"

"I'm sorry. I know I'm not much fun these days." Susan tried to sound brighter. "It's a good idea. The Plaza, I mean. I couldn't stand looking at all those jaded faces at Caravelle."

"Not too many of them around. They've all fled in horror to Palm Beach. But I agree. To my dying day I will fight the efforts of the effete to make Christmas chic."

As she came through the revolving doors at the Fifth Avenue entrance and entered the crowded lobby of the hotel, Susan's heart sank. It seemed everywhere she looked there were women of her age, many of them holding the hands of bright-faced, excited children, chattering in high-pitched voices which their mothers tried to still. Don't hush them, Susan thought. Be glad you have them, well and happy.

Kate was already in the dining room. Susan saw there was a small package at the other plate and a bottle of champagne in a silver wine cooler standing next to the table. She clutched the big box that was her gift to Kate—a pale beige, hideously expensive Ultrasuede dress from Halston. It seemed strange to be giving a magazine editor a dress for Christmas, but it was the newest, chic-est "status symbol," the fabric introduced only that fall and the designer already a favorite of Jackie Onassis and all the rich New York ladies. Besides, Kate never bothered much about clothes for herself. She loved them, but the stubborn streak in her made her dress almost dowdily in contrast to the fashion editors who pounced on every new trend the minute it came on the market. It had seemed a good gift for Kate, a change from the usual expensive handbag or perfume or jewelry of which her friend already had too much, Now Susan wasn't sure. Maybe Kate would think Susan was being patronizing about the way she dressed. Maybe the damned thing would be construed as an insult. Standing in the doorway, Susan toyed with the idea of pretending the dress was her own, apologizing that she hadn't had time to buy Kate's gift, rushing to Tiffany after lunch to find something "safer." No. Kate will like it, Susan thought. Why am I so indecisive about everything these days?

They exchanged perfunctory kisses and Susan sat down, the box leaning against her chair. She smiled warmly at her friend. It was good to be with Kate again. She hadn't seen much of her lately. It was unfair to burden even your nearest and dearest with your depression. Except Paul, she thought fleetingly. Paul didn't mind. At least he said he didn't.

Susan glanced at the champagne. "Heavens! How festive!"

"Why not? Christmas attacks us only once a year."

"Do you know I haven't had a drink in months? I'm not sure I should even now."

Kate shrugged. "Suit yourself. God knows I don't want to enlarge the membership of AA. I was one of the early complainers about your drinking, remember? But I don't think a couple of glasses of champagne will hurt you. Might even cheer you up. It's that heavy stuff I object to. The five-martini lunch scene. Unless you have a real drinking problem, Susie, I can't see how a little wine in moderation could do much harm."

" 'Moderation,' " Susan echoed. "That's the key to everything, isn't it? I don't seem to understand the word. I love too much, hate too much, grieve too much, expect too much." She gave a little laugh. "Who was it who said, 'I'm moderate about everything except moderation'?"

"I don't remember. W. C. Fields, maybe. Or Dorothy Parker. Who cares? The point is, can you handle a little bubbly or would you rather have an appropriately named Virgin Mary?"

"Champagne," Susan said. "I don't expect I'll go straight from the Plaza to Skid Row."

Kate grinned. "For a minute you sounded like a girl I used to know. Open your present. I love watching people open presents. Except for some of those bitches at the office. You know how their greedy little eyes light up every time a messenger brings in a hunk of a loot from a grateful manufacturer. I'm secretly delighted that things have changed since your day, Susie. Remember the gold goodies we used to get? Now it's more likely to be a box of Godiva chocolates or a fifth of scotch. The pickings aren't what they used to be. Seventh Avenue is in a much more frugal period these days and we're no longer covered in caviar and Cartier baubles. Things have changed. Santa Claus has a smaller tote bag." She signaled the waiter to pour the wine and lifted her glass to Susan. "Here's to change. The good and the bad of it. At least it isn't stagnation."

Susan raised her glass in return, saying nothing. She took a sip and opened her package. Inside was a charming little hand-enameled Battersea box, delicately engraved "Remember the Giver."

"Oh, Kate it's beautiful! But so extravagant! You shouldn't have!"

"What the hell. It's only a week's pay."

"You're trying to make that a joke, but I know better. It *is* a week's pay! These antique English boxes are superb. And outrageously expensive. But I love it. Not only the box, but the message. As though I could ever forget the giver." Susan almost shyly handed the big Halston box to her friend. "Merry Christmas. I hope you'll like this. It's exchangeable if you don't."

"A sable coat," Kate teased, untying the ribbon. "Susan, you *know* I find sable ostentatious and fat-making." She pulled aside the tissue and her face lit up with pleasure. "Well, did you ever? An honest-to-God Halston Ultrasuede! How on earth did you know I was dying for one and too damned cheap to buy it for myself? Speaking of extravagant! Thank God you have a rich husband!"

"I'm so glad you like it. I was afraid . . ."

"That I'd think it was a commentary on my usual unsnappy style? Don't be crazy. Those ladies at the office will faint when I turn up in this. Probably think I'm being kept. Hah! I should live so long! Even a hundred years ago when I used to get gifts from some poor benighted guy it was never anything this grand. I'm the only slob in New York who had to buy her own mink coat. No, now that I think of it, there was one other. But she looked like an orangutan by a gargoyle out of *The Hunchback of Notre Dame*. No hope for her, poor dear."

Susan was laughing now, actually wiping the tears from her eyes as Kate went on and on with nonsense about the magazine ("Did I tell you the office manager has given us all a new paint color called 'merciful oblivion'?") and stories about some of the people she'd recently interviewed ("There was this old movie star whose hair was so lacquered it wouldn't have moved in a hurricane. She kept assuring me it wasn't true she'd had her face lifted, while I sat there looking at enough scars to turn Zorro green with envy."). It was a gay lunch, Kate making light small talk, Susan even managing to counter with an absurd story of a cook, recently hired and fired, who thought the kitchen was full of demons and accused Susan of putting a curse on her.

But even as she told her little anecdote, Susan realized how restricted her life had become. Obsessed with Katie's death and Richard's infirmity, living a private, hidden life (for Richard wanted no one to know what had happened to him), she felt very narrow, very dull. Even the "old days" when she'd found the tours so boring and Richard so unpredictable seemed preferable to these endless days and nights of nothingness. Dear Lord, I have nothing interesting to say. My most lilting contribution is a stupid story about a domestic. I'm thirty-two years old and I'm as dreary as a dowager. Drearier. At least a dowager can talk about social events and charities. And children.

Kate watched sadness come over the face of the young woman she loved like a daughter. All the pretended gaiety was ridiculous. They couldn't sit here like casual strangers and make idle chitchat, even though she'd come to lunch determined to keep it light, to avoid talking about Susan's troubles.

"How goes it, really?" she asked. "Things are rough, aren't they?"

Susan nodded. "I don't know what I'm going to do."

"The doctor helping Richard?"

"I think so. There's no physical evidence of it, but I see slight changes in him. He's much more introspective these days, much more absorbed with himself."

"Is that news? Richard's always been absorbed with himself!"

"This is different. He always was automatically selfish, not broodingly obsessed with his actions. Therapy does do that to you sometimes. Makes you examine every move and motivation. I know. I've been through it. Even his attitude about Maria is slightly different, He seldom calls her. She does all the telephoning. He's still deferential, but it's not the same."

"That sounds like progress to me! God knows, if he'd kick his mama hang-up that would be a big step!"

"It's not as simple as that, Kate. It's going to be a long pull. He's thirty-eight years old. He has a lot of lifelong hang-ups to kick, and quite a few more recent ones. Like the collapse of his career."

"But that will be resumed in time."

"Maybe. Hopefully. But when? He doesn't want anyone to know what's happened to his hands. We've put out word in the press that he is in temporary retirement following the death of his daughter. We had to make up some excuse when the tour had to be canceled, and we certainly don't want to indicate he may never play again. I think the use of his hands will come back, but what of the state of his mind? He's bitter and angry and pathetic and remorseful all at the same time. He says he can't live without me. Imagine, Kate. The very thing I used to dream of when I thought he didn't care.'' She paused. ''But how real is it? Will he feel that way when he's well again? Or will the old Richard return? And if not, do I want this dependent one? God, I'm so mixed up! I know part of this is my fault. I tried to change him. Always a fatal mistake. And I was angry when I couldn't. And now I have a child leaning on me and I don't want that, either.''

Kate was quiet, letting her spill out the doubts and fears that tormented her.

''I've been spending time with Paul,'' Susan said.

''Oh?''

''It's not an affair. I've been going to his apartment almost every afternoon since Katie died. Sometimes we don't exchange a dozen words, but it's so peaceful just to be there. He's a marvelous human being, Kate.''

''He's more than that, Susie. He's in love with you.''

''I know.''

''Are you in love with him?''

''I don't know. I'm not sure. He's so unlike Richard. He's the kindest. gentlest most undemanding man I've ever known. Yet he's so strong. He makes me feel protected, as though nothing could ever hurt me again.''

''But you're not in love with him.''

Susan seemed to rouse herself from this dreamy recital, ''Damn all this talk about being in love! I was so crazy in love with Richard I would have died for him! And what has it gotten me? A few happy hours and more misery than anyone in her right mind could bargain for! If that's what being in love is all about, I don't want to ever feel that way again! Maybe Paul *is* the right one for me. Maybe I should take the safe line I'm lucky enough to be offered.''

''Don't be an ass! You're talking nonsense! No one is a bigger admirer of Paul than I, but he's not for you. You're too old for a security blanket and too young for placid companionship. You're a strong woman, Susan. You don't want to be wrapped in cotton wool. You need a man who'll challenge you; not an adoring protector! Why do you think you've stayed with Richard all these years when he's done everything unspeakable? Because it's been exciting, terrible as it is, to live with an ego like that! And why are you questioning your love now? Because the challenge has gone. He's changed. He's admitted his need of you. You've won. And you never wanted to win!''

Susan stared at her. ''You're crazy, Kate! That's not true. I stayed with Richard because I was in love with him, even though he wasn't what I hoped for in a husband.''

''Wrong. He was not what you hoped for but he was what you had to have. The very independence you hated was what intrigued and held you. That was the romantic, unrealistic side of you, always looking for a mountain to climb, a star to reach. Richard was your adversary and you played the game, pretending to despise it. Well, the game's over. You have a man now, with human weaknesses, with needs, and with the guts, finally to see what he's been missing. You think the thrill is gone. It isn't, Susie. It's just been replaced by more honesty on both sides. If you want my opinion—and you'll get it, wanted or not—you and Richard can finally love each other as sharing people, not as individuals constantly spoiling for a fight. Richard grew up overnight. When are you going to begin?''

Chapter 33

JACQUELINE WATCHED SILENTLY as her mother-in-law stood impatiently in front of the big fireplace, her fingers drumming an annoyed tattoo on the big mantel. Maria was in a terrible mood and making no effort to hide it. Ever since Jacqueline and Walter had arrived late that morning of Christmas Eve with their children, followed in minutes by Sergio and Mary Lou and Gloria and Raoul with theirs, Maria had been in a foul humor. Even more brusque than usual, she'd dismissed all inquiries about what was troubling her.

"Are you feeling all right, Mother?" Walter had asked solicitously after she'd given all of them the same cool reception.

"Of course I'm feeling all right! Why shouldn't I be?"

"No reason. You just seem . . . preoccupied."

"I have things to be preoccupied with," Maria snapped. "Perhaps you think it's easy to put together a Christmas for sixteen people, but I assure you it's not!"

"Seventeen," Sergio corrected. "Joseph is bringing a friend, remember? Besides, it never used to faze you if there were seventy people in the house. What's wrong, old girl?"

"Nothing is wrong! And I'll thank you, Sergio, to remember that I'm your mother and do not care to be addressed in such vulgar terms."

"Sorry." Sergio suppressed a smile. It was heresy to make even a flippant reference to Maria's years. Not that she was that old. These days, seventy-three was still a vigorous age and there was no one more vigorous than she. Her family was still amazed at the complete recovery she'd made from that stroke. "A miracle," they called it, and Maria had agreed.

"It was God's will," she'd said. "His will and the strength He gave me to be healed."

Maybe so, Sergio had thought at the time. Maybe God is on her side. She pays Him enough attention in church-time and money. But I don't think God could have stopped Mother from getting completely well even if He'd wanted to, She's the toughest creature, man or woman, I've ever met. She's a survivor, pure and simple. She'll bury us all.

"Well," he said now, "as long as everybody's here except Joseph and his young lady, who's for the woods to cut down our Christmas tree?"

All hands shot up in the air with the exception of Jacqueline's. "Count me out," she said. "Tradition or no tradition, I'm not playing lady-pioneer in a blizzard. You maniacs go ahead. I'll stay and keep your mother company while we wait for Richard and Susan." She gave Maria a steady, meaningful look. That was what was making her mother-in-law so testy: waiting the arrival of her precious and uncomfortably altered youngest son. Strange no one else realized why Maria was so edgy. But they wouldn't. They were all much too concerned with themselves.

"Say, you're right! Richard hasn't arrived." Gloria seemed genuinely surprised. "They coming by train or car?"

"The chauffeur is driving them."

"Oh, of course. I keep forgetting about Richard's hands. Well, maybe it's just as well they're late. It might be embarrassing for Richard, knowing he couldn't help with the tree-cutting."

There was unconcealed rage in Maria's response to her daughter's remarks. "Gloria! You are the most insensitive girl I've ever known! Forget about your brother's troubles? How could you? How could you possibly forget we're witnessing the interruption of the greatest musical career in history!"

Gloria sounded like a sulky, chastised child. "I didn't mean I *forget*, Mother. Just for that *moment* I did. Anyway, Richard never did join us when we cut down the tree. Always afraid he'd get a splinter in his precious fingers,"

"And rightly so," Maria said coldly. "And when he's recovered, he still will have sense enough to guard those priceless hands."

There was a tense silence. What are Walter and Sergio thinking? Jacqueline wondered. How can she so unfeelingly dismiss their talents and refer to Richard's that way? "Interruption," she said. I wonder whether she really believes Richard will regain the use of his hands. I'm sure she does. She's counting on God's help again. God's help and Richard's determination, which she likes to think is as great as her own. only it isn't. Richard is weak and insecure, thanks in no small part to Maria herself. And Gloria. How does she endure the constant contemptuous scolding? Forty-eight years of being the awkward ugly duckling in a family of talented swans. How she must hate all of them!

"Let's go," Sergio said as though nothing had happened. "Everybody set? It's snowing like crazy. Be sure you're all prepared for it."

There was a scramble for heavy coats and boots and mittens and then all of them, including Gloria's twins, streamed out the door, shouting and shoving with good-natured exuberance. Maria gave a small sigh of relief as they departed and she and Jacqueline were left alone in the big living room, but signs of her nervousness remained—the slight scowl and the incessant drumming of her fingers.

"Don't worry about the storm," Jacqueline said. "They'll make it all right. Phipps is a good driver."

"I'm not worried. You know I simply detest tardiness."

A lie. She was worried, but not about the driving. Nor the lateness. She was worried that the doctor she had opposed was alienating her son, influencing him as even Susan had been unable to do. Jacqueline and Susan had talked often in these past months and it was clear that the analysis was forcing Richard to examine his whole life, including his relationship with his mother. As she had to Kate, Susan mentioned to Jacqueline that Maria now instigated all the contact between herself and her son, hinted that Richard seemed almost unwilling to be in his mother's company these days. Maria was no fool. She sensed the change. She must be secretly frantic, Jacqueline thought. To see the dreams disappear, to lose control of the only one who could fulfill those dreams. I wonder if she ever takes any of the blame for this on herself? Of course she doesn't. The scapegoat would be Susan. Susan and her rebellion. Susan and her tragic child.

Susan who interfered with Maria's methodical plans for Richard's life. Susan who convinced her husband to enter the therapy which presumably was separating him from his mother.

Jacqueline was relieved to hear the sound of a car pulling up to the front door. They were here at last thank God. Maybe Maria would relax now.

"That must be Richard and Susan now," she said.

"Yes. I suppose it is." Maria did not stir from the fireplace, made no move to go and greet them. Typical. They'd have to come into The Presence, figuratively tugging at their forelocks, apologetic about keeping her waiting.

The old feeling of anxiety came over Susan as it always did when she entered this house. Not that she'd been here often in recent years, but the memory of that first weekend stayed with her. How young she'd been! How overwhelmed by the beauty of Richard's big handsome family, the Old World courtliness of the maestro, the hypocritical temporary graciousness of a welcoming Maria. It hadn't taken long to be disillusioned about most of them, she recalled. She knew almost from the start that she had only two true friends among the Antoninis: Giovanni and Jacqueline. And now one of them was gone and sorely missed by his daughter-in-law. She was glad he hadn't lived to see the tragedy of his grandchild or the professional and personal decline of his son.

As she watched Richard dutifully kiss his mother's cheek and apologize for their being late, she thought how much he'd changed in these past few months. There seemed to be no spark in him, he who'd always been the epitome of energy. He moved slowly, as though he were old and tired, his stiff hands hanging hopelessly at his sides. But he was more handsome than ever. The face had a drawn, ascetic quality that made him appear more sensitive, and the touches of gray that had appeared overnight at his temples gave him the look of a distinguished personality rather than a boyish matinee idol.

She could not dismiss that last luncheon with Kate. Was her friend right? Was there, perhaps, a masochistic streak in her, a need not to be needed but to be mastered? Had Kate touched on some facet of Susan's character that had eluded her even in her days with Dr. Marcus? Had she fallen in love with Richard because he was so full of assurance, even conceit? Did she love him less now that the overblown ego had been punctured by his losses?

Strange how she lumped the losses as though they were of equal importance: a child's life and the end of a career. As though the latter had any comparable importance. But it did. With the paralysis, Richard had lost his reason for being. Just as she had lost hers when Katie died. We've both been deprived of the things we love, Susan thought, and now we're alone though we're together. Love. Was it always such a lonely thing? Did one pay for every ounce of pleasure with a pound of pain?

Even while she searched for answers she went through the motions of "a well-brought-up girl," greeting Maria politely, adding her apologies to Richard's; kissing Jacqueline; even inquiring where the others were.

"In the woods, cutting down the Christmas tree," Maria said in answer to Susan's question.

"Such an exhausting group," Jacqueline added. "It makes me tired just to watch them."

Maria ignored the remark, her whole attention concentrated on Richard.

"Did you bring your valet, son? If so, I must make arrangements for his sleeping quarters."

"My *male nurse*, you mean, Mother. No. Susan generously offered to take over for the next couple of days. She's very good at being my surrogate hands."

"It's only temporary, dear."

Richard looked at her insolently. "Is that so? I didn't know you had a degree in psychiatry, Mother."

It was the first time Susan had ever seen Maria unsure of herself, almost frightened. She seemed startled by the rude remark, but she quickly recovered.

"One doesn't need to be a doctor to predict the outcome of this." She smiled confidently. "One needs only be a mother."

What an actress she is! Susan thought. What an accomplished performer. As though that ended the whole subject, Maria now chattered about the family. "Would you believe, Richard, that Sergio's Joseph has asked a girl up for the holiday! Dear heavens, I can't believe he's old enough to even think about girls!"

"He's twenty-three, Maria," Jacqueline said. "I imagine he's been thinking about them for quite some time. Who is she, by the way?"

"I haven't the faintest idea, but she can't be much. Any girl of a good family certainly wouldn't be anywhere but in her own home at Christmas. I don't know what Sergio's thinking of to let that child become involved at his age!"

"He's no child," Richard said flatly. "He's a man."

"Well, perhaps. Legally. But twenty-three-year-old boys aren't like girls of that age. They're immature until they're thirty or so, really. They should have time to find themselves before they seriously think of settling down."

"What makes you think Joseph is serious?"

"Richard dear, what a question! *You* know very well when any member of this family brings a *stranger* for a holiday it's more than a passing fancy."

Susan flushed. There was no mistaking the intent of that last remark. She was reminding Richard of that long-gone Fourth-of-July weekend. Damn her. She never gave up.

"May we go up to our room, Mrs. Antonini?" Susan asked quietly. "I'd like to unpack our things."

"Of course. But there's no need for Richard to go, is there? It's been such a long time since I've had a chance to chat with him, and there probably won't be another moment of peace after this." She looked appealingly at Richard. "Stay and talk a few moments, won't you, dear? There's so much I want to catch up on. I'm sure Susan doesn't mind. Jacqueline can help her get settled."

The daughters-in-law went up to the room Richard and Susan would share. Jacqueline flopped on one of the twin beds while Susan opened suitcases. One was completely filled with gifts, nearly two dozen of them for the family and staff.

"Christmas is a nightmare in a family this size, isn't it?"

Susan nodded. "An exercise in insanity. We should really stop exchanging gifts except for the children."

"I agree. That would cut the list down to nothing. They're all grown except Pierre and Claudette," She stopped, distracted by the look of pain on Susan's face.

"I'm sorry, Susan. I can imagine what you must be feeling this Christmas. I didn't mean to remind . . ."

"It's all right. You didn't do anything wrong. As for reminding me, nobody need worry about that. I never forget. Not for a single waking moment."

"How's Richard? I mean, *really*."

"Discouraged. Depressed. Guilt-ridden. Confused." Susan shook her head. "I don't know what's going to happen to him, Jacqueline. I'm over my irrational hatred for him, the way I felt when it . . . first happened. Now I feel sorry for him. Imagine anyone feeling sorry for Richard Antonini. But I pity him. He's so helpless, in every way."

"Do you think he'll come out of the paralysis? Have you talked to his doctor?"

"Yes to both questions. I think he will recover the use of his hands, but no one can say how it will happen or when. Dr. Beekman is optimistic, though he says Richard is as complex a problem as he's seen since medical school." Susan gave a little laugh. "You'd know that would have to be so, wouldn't you? Richard Antonini was never one for an uncomplicated life." She paused. "Kate says that's what attracted me to him in the beginning. Do you think that could be so?"

"I wouldn't discount it. We're all rather alike in that way. Look at my crazy life with my once bisexual, now thoroughly homosexual husband. Look at Mary Lou with that arrogantly unfaithful Serge. Look at you, marrying a notoriously spoiled mama's boy. What do we all think? That we can change these men? Are we so conceited we still consider their flaws some challenge we'll eventually overcome? Probably. Women like us are so damned strong ourselves that we believe we can alter our husbands' personalities. What colossal nerve!"

"But you've accepted Walter's way of life," Susan said. "And Mary Lou has learned to live with Serge's cheating. You've both given up trying to change them."

"Only on the surface, my dear. We put up good fronts, but deep down we're still engaged in hand-to-hand combat with our stubborn spouses. You were too, until last September. What now? Are you still attracted to the docile, well-tamed Richard? *You* didn't accomplish the change in him. Does that make the victory hollow?"

"You sound as though you've been comparing notes with Kate."

"No. We both just know you. And love you." Jacqueline spoke the last words almost shyly.

"I love you, too," Susan said. There was a slight, embarrassed pause before she said, "Oh Lord, I don't have a gift for Joseph's girl!"

"Not to worry. You and I will run into town tomorrow and pick up some perfume or something. It would have been nice if Mary Lou had bothered to let us know her son was bringing someone." Jacqueline rose. "I'll leave you to your chores. You still haven't answered my question, though. *Is* the victory hollow?"

"I don't know," Susan answered. "I don't even know whether it's a victory."

In the living room, Maria gazed indulgently at her favorite child. "I think you've been avoiding me, Richard," she said playfully.

"Not really. I haven't felt like seeing anyone."

"Except the doctor."

He sighed. "Look, Mother, I know you don't approve, but he's the only thing that's kept me from suicide these past three months. Don't nag me about the analysis, please. I don't want to have an argument with you."

Maria looked hurt. "Nag you? I've never nagged you in my life! What a terrible thing to say!"

There was no response. Maria kept control of herself.

"Why can't we talk together any more?" she asked. "We used to be so close, dear."

"Too close, perhaps," Richard said quietly. "And we never talked together. You talked and I listened."

"Richard!"

"It's true, Mother. I'm sorry to say it, but I've discovered that I spent my life trying to please you. Trying to atone for being born. I hated my father because of what I thought he'd done to you. I had no life except music because that's what you wanted. Oh, I wanted it, too. I still do. But I want it in perspective, as part of my life, not the whole of it. And God knows whether I'll ever have it again. Ironic, isn't it?"

Maria couldn't believe what she was hearing. "What kind of ridiculous talk is this? Atoning? I've never asked that of you! I simply acquainted you with facts! And because I recognized genius and encouraged you, does that make me an ogress? Because I didn't want you to saddle yourself with a wife and keep a handicapped child at home, does that make me a terrible mother? And I was right. Events have proved that! You don't know what you're saying. You're parroting all that stupid psychiatric jargon! You've been brainwashed by that doctor and, yes, by that selfish, hostile woman you married. You should get down on your knees and thank God for the background you've had. For the talent He gave you. And you should beg Him to give you another chance to use it. Turn to the real God, Richard, not to some white-coated charlatan who tries to impersonate Him!"

Suddenly he was no longer calm. "Listen to yourself! You still don't care about me. You never have. It was always my goddamned career that mattered. And even that wasn't for me. That was for you. So you could be the woman who gave birth to the famous man! So you could bask in the reflected glory and to hell whether there was any personal happiness in my life! You liked it when I had my 'little affairs.' They kept me from seriously devoting myself to any one woman. You hated the idea that a wife might steal some of the attention from you. You were ashamed to be the grandmother of a deaf-mute." He was raging now. "What a pity all your children turned out to be so second-rate, Mother! The least one of us could have done would have been to become President so you could ride down Pennsylvania Avenue in state!"

"Richard, I forbid you to speak to me that way!"

"You forbid me nothing! You've done your last forbidding. You've damned near wrecked everything with your interfering. You've given me a lifetime of guilt and a terrible feeling of inferiority that I tried to cover up by being Superman! No more, Mother! Not one more second of it! Don't push me one more inch or I'll say all the terrible things I feel!"

"What more terrible than what you've already said?" Maria's fury matched his own.

"One thing more terrible! I hate you. I've always hated you!"

He stopped aghast. The blood drained from his face and he was trembling. But there was something else. He was almost afraid to look terrified to trust his own eyes. But it was true. In his agitation and anger he was steadily clenching and unclenching his fists.

Chapter 34

THROUGH THE WINDOWS behind Dr. Beekman's desk, Richard could see Central Park and the skyline of the East Side of New York. It was beautiful, this day after Christmas. The sky was crisp, clear blue and the buildings silhouetted against it stood proud and tall, like a row of sentinals guarding the sacred city. We live on the wrong side of town, he thought irrelevantly. The "unfashionable" West Side has the spectacular view while the "silk stocking district" pays dearly for the privilege of looking toward grubby Tenth Avenue.

"I beg your pardon?"

"I said, 'And what happened then?' " the doctor repeated.

"It's hard to remember. I recall seeing my hands moving and being surprised. Not even excited or happy. Just surprised. And then everybody was crying and talking all at once. Even I was crying, I think. Just sitting there, looking at my hands and crying like a damned fool."

"There's nothing foolish about tears, Mr. Antonini. They're a sign of some emotion: sadness or sometimes happiness. Or rage. Even children seldom cry without a reason."

"I wouldn't know. I was never a child."

Dr. Beekman didn't answer.

"Did you ever play that game where people sit around at parties and try to see who never did the things most kids do?"

"No. I don't think I know that one."

"I always won," Richard said. "Nobody believed me, but I was always the only male adult in the room who'd never played ball or tinkered with the engine of a hot-rod or gone away to camp. I might have hurt my hands, you see," he explained carefully. "Mother lived in deathly fear of that." He looked thoughtful. "I was also the only one, usually, who'd never been spanked or even slapped."

Dr. Beekman waited.

"You were asking me about Christmas Eve, weren't you? When my hands started to work again. Yes. Well, let's see. There was a kind of 'slow take' about it all. It took me a few seconds to realize what had happened and I remember seeing Mother's face change from anger to astonishment. And then I guess I yelled for Susan and she came running downstairs and saw me moving my

fingers. And Jacqueline came in and all the crying started, along with the hugging
and kissing and shouting. We were like crazy people. Like we'd won the Irish
Sweepstakes or struck oil in the back yard.'' Richard smiled sheepishly. ''We
must have looked like a bunch of lunatics, all of us.''

''All of you?''

Richard frowned. ''No. Not all of us. I remember being dimly aware that
Mother didn't move. She was crying, I know that. But she didn't hug or kiss
me. She just sat there looking at me as though I were a stranger.'' He reached
for a tissue from the box next to his chair and blew his nose hard. ''At that
moment I didn't even remember the fight we'd had. I was so damned happy I
didn't hate anybody. Not even Mother, though I'd just told her I did.''

The doctor made a note. ''And then?''

''Then I realized what I'd done. The things I'd said to her, I mean. I went
over to her chair and tried to embrace her, but she pushed me away. She pushed
me away,'' Richard repeated, ''and then she got up and walked out of the room.
She never said a word. Not a single, solitary word.''

''What did you expect her to say?''

Richard thought for a few seconds. ''I don't know. Was I waiting for her to
compliment me?''

''She always did whenever you accomplished something great.''

''Yes. That's stupid, isn't it? I didn't accomplish anything this time. It just
happened.''

''Why do you think it happened?''

Richard bristled. ''You always said it probably would. It just did, that's all.''

''You really think that's all, Mr. Antonini?''

The belligerency disappeared. ''No. Of course not. All the while Mother and
I were talking, this thing kept building up inside of me, like a steam valve that
was going to blow. Nothing in the world could have stopped me from saying
what I did. I didn't want to hurt her, I just couldn't help myself.'' He paused.
''That's not true. I did want to hurt her. I wanted to punish her for everything
she'd ever done since she went to bed with my father thirty-nine years ago. It
all came boiling out, all the disappointments of my life, all the things I've been
deprived of, all the bloody damned years I tried to be what she wanted. I was
so angry. Angrier than I can ever remember being. I hated her. I hated that smug
assurance that things would turn out exactly as she believed. I guess I always
felt this hideous resentment. A few times in my life I came near to telling her,
but I always backed off. I took my frustration out on something, or someone,
else.'' He shook his head. ''You know, Doctor, in a way you were directly
responsible for what happened two nights ago. I've put up with her maneuvering
and her slurs about people I love, but when she started attacking these sessions
with you, mouthing platitudes about God and forgiveness, I realized she was
the most coldly conniving, selfish woman who ever lived. I felt I had to protect
myself from her, stand up to her because I'd never survive if I didn't. I knew
if I let her talk me out of seeing you, I'd never make it. God! It's weird! I came
here not believing in you or anyone like you. And you end up being the one
thing I won't let my mother take away from me. When I think how I resisted
the need for this therapy! I wanted to live with my guilt. I thought the paralysis
was my punishment for letting Katie die.''

"And now?"

"Now I suppose that tragedy was the match that finally lit the stick of dynamite that's been inside me for years." Richard spoke slowly. "I didn't lose the use of my hands just to punish myself for the neglect of my child, did I? I lost it to punish Mother, too. I wanted her to suffer, not for me but for herself. I wanted to take away the one thing she cared about. Is that possible? Is that what I really did? Was this paralysis as much revenge as guilt?"

"It's possible."

"But I still feel such terrible guilt about Katie! I wanted to be working and I was saddled with her that day." Richard's eyes misted. "Yet I remember feeling quite happy about being with her. She was so trusting, so adorable. It was the one time in her whole little life that I felt close to her. It didn't surprise me that I couldn't play after she died. I had to pay for her death. I couldn't look at the piano without seeing her face in the keys." He began to waver. "Maybe I was right in the first place. Maybe I couldn't move my hands because of that day, not because of all the resentment toward Mother."

"If that is so," Dr. Beekman said, "why do you think movement in your hands came back at the very height of the attack on your mother? Was it coincidence? Why not sooner? Or later? Or never? You'll always be remorseful about Katie. So if you've been punishing yourself for that alone, what caused your recovery? In these sessions, Mr. Antonini, I haven't encouraged you to absolve yourself of blame for that tragic accident. We've talked about almost everything else in your life."

"But it's fashionable to blame everything on one's parents, isn't it?" Richard's voice was bitter. "Maybe that's all I'm doing now: looking for someone to blame for what I am. Child prodigies develop strangely. Look at stage kids or baby movie stars. They're screwed up, take drugs, kill themselves. And people always point the finger at a pushy parent. Maybe I'm trying to unload the mistakes of my whole loused-up life on Mother and convince myself that I could't get well until I told her I hated her."

Beekman was sympathetic though he tried to remain unemotional about his patients, objective and impersonal. It was the only way he could survive this daily onslaught of misery, these endless tales of self-recrimination and frantic searching by bewildered, unhappy people. He knew what Richard was going through; ashamed that he did not love and honor his parent, wishing he could deny what he now knew to be true. Look at the sudden reversal of thinking. Look at the still desperate desire to be a "good son." Poor bastard.

"You told your mother you hated her," the analyst said quietly. "You accused her of selfishness, of interference, of blind ambition that could be achieved only through you. Think about it now, Richard" (It was the first time, he realized, that he'd ever used his famous patient's first name.) "and tell me honestly how you feel."

The words seemed to come sadly and realistically from somewhere deep inside Richard. "She is a selfish, interfering, blindly ambitious woman, but I don't hate her. I can't love her. I can't even like her as a person. But I suppose she did what she thought she had to do. She's always seen herself as the strong one in the family, the one who made the decisions and set down the rules. I can't really know her motives, can I? Maybe this is her kind of talent, making us all rich and famous. She grew up the daughter of a genius. She married one. Should I condemn her for expecting more of all her children than we possibly could give? She's a child herself, isn't she? A spoiled, demanding child to whom we've all catered, my father, my brothers and sister, and, most of all, me. We let her run our lives. If she's run them badly, should we blame her for doing it or ourselves for permitting it? She's been wrong, Doctor. But so have we.'' He straightened in his chair. "I hope I haven't alienated her forever. She's my mother and I'd like her to be my friend. I won't apologize for the things I said, because they were true. But I simply didn't see that all this suppressed anger toward her was also anger at myself for being less than a man. I've failed her, in her eyes. But I failed Susan and Katie in worse ways. I've disappointed friends like Paul Carmichael, and God knows I've failed myself. I *was* punishing myself for Katie. Nothing will ever make me believe otherwise. But I was also punishing myself for being stupid and superficial. The anger that ate at me is gone, Doctor. It came out of me like vomit. The knowledge of a thousand blunders remains, but at least I'm beginning to recognize them.''

"That's what it's all about, Richard.''

"Yes, I suppose it is.''

"And now?''

"I have work to do. I have to try to make my wife love the 'real' me. I have to pick up my career, maybe in a less frantic way. I have to mend fences, eat crow, face the music. Choose your cliché. I have to do all of them, don't I?'' The famous smile appeared, but this time it was more than a surface gesture. "I'm grateful to you, Dr. Beekman.''

"Are you discharging yourself?''

"No. I don't feel ready for that. I'm going to need your help for a long time to come. I have enough sense to realize that there are a helluva lot of hurdles still to clear, a frightening number of things I still don't understand about myself or other people. My father, for one. All my family, for that matter, not just Mother.''

"I'm glad you feel that way about continuing the therapy. You must be the one who decides when you're well. But won't you start touring again? How can you see me and be away for months at a time?''

"I thought about that last night. I'm not sure I want to go on performing as regularly, now that the obsession is clear to me. We'll have to see. In any case, it will take months of practice to get back to playing as I used to.'' He smiled again. "The old hands have rusted with disuse. I'm not sure they'll ever be the same. Funny, it doesn't bother me that I might not be the big 'idol' again. There's so much more I want. I thought I had everything and I've missed a lot that really matters.''

"You're still a young man.''

"You mean there's time to catch up. Yes, I think so. God knows, I hope so.''

"Tell me exactly what happened,'' Bea Langdon said.

Susan described their arrival at Maria's on Christmas Eve and the few tense minutes that followed before she and Jacqueline went upstairs.

"I'd just unloaded all the gifts and Jacqueline had left when I heard Richard frantically calling. I rushed down and he was opening and closing his fists, staring at his hands as though they weren't part of him. Oh, Mother, you'll never know how I felt at that moment! So full of joy and gratitude that I couldn't stop crying. Richard was crying, too. And Jacqueline when she came in."

"Mrs. Antonini must have been beside herself with happiness."

"She was crying," Susan said, "but she was the most tragic figure I've ever seen."

"Tragic? Why on earth would she be tragic at a time like that?"

Susan recounted most of the bitter exchange as Richard had told it to her in the car on the way back to New York less than an hour later. "I didn't know until we were on the road home what had happened. Richard quietly told me to get our things, that we were leaving. He seemed so distraught I didn't even question our abrupt departure. I just did as he asked. I hadn't even opened our personal suitcases. I left the gifts there on the bed, called Phipps and we were on our way. The others hadn't even come back from the tree-cutting."

"Did she say goodbye or anything?"

"Mrs. Antonini? No, she left the room while the three of us were jumping around for joy. I didn't see her again. Later I found out why of course."

"Poor woman," Bea said. "I can't help feeling sorry for her. How terrible to have your child say you've ruined his life; that he hates you." She shuddered. "I know everything Richard said was true, but it must have been unbearable for her to hear, and just as hard for Richard to say."

"But he had to say it, Mother. It was what was eating at him. I'm sure the paralysis was partly Katie and partly the result of all that pent-up fury. Just as all the irresponsible things he did in his youth were more to defy his mother than to gratify himself. Even in our marriage he's been more concerned with her approval than with mine. God knows we saw that when she convinced him to take Katie away! And she kept him separated from his child even when the baby was home. For almost seven years, he acted as though Katie didn't exist, simply because Maria made him feel ashamed of a handicapped daughter!"

Bea was quiet for a moment. "There's something I want to tell you, Susan," she said at last. "Perhaps Richard or even Mrs. Antonini is not entirely to blame for that isolation from Katie." She repeated the theories Wil expounded the day they drove home from the funeral. "Your father loves you so much, but he can be more objective than I. I don't think it was deliberate, but perhaps, with reason, you were overly possessive about Katie. Maybe you shut Richard out of her life more than he might have really wanted, given a second chance. Darling, this is hard for me to say. You've always had all my sympathy, all my support. You still have it, from your father and me. But Susie, my dear child, perhaps you were unconsciously self-righteous about your situation. Oh, I know you tried in the beginning to involve Richard and you were terribly hurt when he wouldn't go along with your convictions about the right way to raise your child. I can't blame you for that. But you never tried to understand his side. You didn't work at the problem. When you saw he was unable to give of himself the way you could, you gave up trying. It wasn't fair to him or Katie. It wasn't even fair to yourself.'' Bea looked troubled. ''It's easy to be wise in hindsight. Perhaps we should have raised you to be more sympathetic toward those who haven't your strength. You're so competent yourself that you have a low level of tolerance for those who are weak and easily influenced. We fostered independence in you. Perhaps in this case it backfired.''

Susan was aghast. This, from her own mother? Was this how people saw her? The shock turned into anger.

''I can't believe you and Daddy feel such things! Shut Richard out? Mother, you saw it all! He shut himself out. I never wanted it that way. I wanted him to love Katie. I wanted us to be a family!''

''On your terms, darling. Without much thought of what was going on inside Richard, You didn't know all his private demons. You didn't really try to find out the real reasons for this unnatural rejection of one's child. It was easier to blame it on his mother, on his selfishness and vanity. It was easier to abdicate responsibility for marriage and pour everything you had into your utter devotion to Katie.''

With horror, Susan realized what Bea was really saying: If Richard had been forced to understand Katie that awful carelessness on the beach wouldn't have happened. No! It wasn't true!

''You're blaming me for the accident!''

''No, darling, of course not. I'm just saying . . .''

''You're saying I was the one with the overblown ego,'' Susan interrupted. ''You're saying I should have demanded that Richard love his child. That I should have made him participate in her upbringing. That if he'd known how to handle her she'd never have drowned! Don't you think I tried? You saw it yourself. It was impossible. He didn't want to hear any of that, Mother!''

Bea was in physical pain, but she went on. ''It doesn't matter what he wanted to hear. He would have heard. He would have known to watch her every minute, even if he didn't want to. Blame you for the accident? Of course no one blames you! But it's not right to blame Richard entirely, either. He didn't feel responsible for Katie's care. He didn't even know what he was supposed to do. I'm not excusing him, Susan. It was despicable for him to let his mother be horrible to you. It was wrong that he went along with her in most things. But you were guilty of unwitting bad judgment, too. Your assuming sole responsibility for your child was a kind of self-indulgence. You had faith only in yourself. None in Richard. I know. He's never done much to inspire faith. Quite the contrary. But you didn't even try to trust him or urge him to be trustworthy. You couldn't believe in him so you walked away. It's understandable. You didn't know he needed help as much as Katie did. How could you? But the truth is you were defying Richard and his mother as much as you were following your own heart. No one's all right in this, my dear, but no one's all wrong. A hard lesson. But life's full of hard lessons.''

Susan was quiet for a moment, digesting the words that Bea found so painful to say. She didn't want to accept this surprising theory, but she could not dismiss it. She'd simply never thought of it that way. Maybe I did cop out. Maybe I was so resentful of their opposition, so hurt and angry about all the things Maria and Richard did that I kept the biggest weapon for myself. Katie. Maybe I used that child as proof of my own capabilities. Evidence that I didn't need anyone. Not even Richard.

"Don't hate me, Susie." Bea's voice was soft and sad. "I'm thinking of the future. Yours and Richard's. He's trying to change. Don't let him feel alone. Let him know you understand. Let him see you've changed, too. Be patient, darling. Be loving and mature. You are, you know."

"Am I?" Susan was wistful. "I wish I could believe that. Perhaps you're right, Mother. Could be I *liked* being the only one Katie looked to for her life. Could be I enjoyed the secret revenge, the bittersweet knowledge of owning something the Antoninis couldn't touch, even if they wanted to. God, it's all gone so wrong! Everybody has made so many awful mistakes!"

"They can't be rectified," Bea said. "But they need not be repeated. Richard's in the process of purging himself. You love him still, Susan. And he loves you. Make it right this time. Make a few changes in yourself. If he can, you can."

Susan tried to smile. "Can I? You and Kate. Always making me look at my warts. Kate thinks I'm masochistic. And you see me as some kind of self-ordained avenging angel. I'm quite a creature, according to my two best friends."

"Darling, you *are* quite a creature. Quite a wonderful, human, fallible creature, thank heavens! I'd be terrified to think I'd given birth to a saint!"

"No danger of that," Susan said. "No danger at all."

On that Christmas Eve, for the first time since she was a little girl, Maria Antonini had wanted to hide. She heard the car pull away, knew Richard had left her house, maybe forever. Not that he could have stayed after the terrible, bitter words between them, ungrateful words she never dreamed she'd hear from her son's lips. He hadn't come looking for her, to apologize, after she'd walked out of the room. He must have known it would be useless. She'd never forgive him. She washed her hands of him.

Hands. Richard had regained the use of his hands. She knew he would. She knew the Almighty would see to it in His own good time. Hadn't she just told Richard that? She lay on her bed, thanking her personal God for this blessing, unsurprised it had been granted.

She'd have to tell the others about the miracle. But how would she explain Richard's sudden departure? I can't face them, she thought. I can't face that sea of inquisitive faces. But I must. My family is waiting for me. She rose and dressed carefully taking special pains with her make-up. The Givenchy. Yes, she'd wear the new bright red Givenchy. It was beautiful, expensive and elegant, as she was. I look very well, she thought dispassionately. Not at all like a woman whose child has just told her that he hated her, that she was selfish and scheming.

For a moment she sat down, weakly. More than half a century ago, another man had said much the same to her. Her father had lashed out in much the same way when she'd announced she was going to marry Giovanni Antonini. She could still hear the words, still see the scornful look on his face.

"So you're going to marry the young Antonini, are you, Maria? Why? He's a nobody!"

"I love him, Papa."

"Love? Phah!" He'd spat out the word. "You don't love anyone. You're marrying him because he's weak-minded and manageable and you can get whatever you want through him. Silly young fool, he can't see how selfish and crazy for power you are! It wouldn't do to pick a strong man like your papa, would it? Not for you. You're too much like me, Maria. You must have your own way. You won't be like your mama. She is gentle woman as women are meant to be! Her pleasure in life is making her husband happy. Giovanni Antonini," he repeated. "You'll make him famous and miserable, won't you? Probably do the same to your children. You'll never make anyone happy. Not even yourself."

She'd run from him and hidden, as she wanted to hide now. He knew her so well. She was ambitious even then, and shrewd enough to choose a talent she could mold. She'd never have her adored father's genius, but she could have her own kind of fame if she worked things right. She'd be a celebrity's wife and the mother of celebrated children. It frightened her that her father understood her so completely, recognized his own ambitious, ruthless nature in her, knew how she despised her mother's complacent self-effacement. Papa knew she found power more desirable than love. Why not? So did he.

"I did it, Papa," she said aloud. "I made Joe immortal and turned my sons into great men. I was as strong and tough and successful as you."

Why, then, did she feel so empty and alone?

Susan picked up the telephone.

"I'm a little late," Paul said, "but Merry Christmas, Susan. I heard about Richard's recovery. That must be the best present any of you could have gotten."

Susan realized she hadn't thought about Paul for a single moment in these last three days. She'd told Bea and Kate the good news, but she hadn't even remembered to call the man who'd been her greatest comfort through it all. She was distressed and ashamed. She'd been so involved in examining her own reactions to this sudden change in her life that she hadn't considered the person who might also be drastically affected by it.

"Paul, I'm sorry I didn't call you right away! It was unforgivable of me."

"It's all right." (Was there a touch of reproach in his voice?) "Kate rang up this morning. I'm happy for Richard."

"Yes. Did Kate tell you how it came about?"

"Most of it, I guess. How's he doing?"

"It's been hard on him, but it had to come. It's been brewing for a long time. You know that even better than I. I'm only grateful that he finally got up enough courage to tell Maria the truth. He's free of her, Paul. It's saddened him, but there's also an obvious feeling of relief."

"And how are you?"

She understood what he meant. Now that Richard was self-sufficient again, what was she going to do?

"I'm all right," Susan said noncommittally. And in the next breath, "No, I'm not really all right. I've had to put myself under a microscope lately and the picture looks pretty damned unattractive."

"I find that hard to believe."

"It's true. My self-imposed halo is giving me a headache."

Paul laughed. "How's your time? Want to come by tomorrow? I'll be working at home. We could have a pre-New Year's Eve Coke, or a post-Christmas one. That is, if you're still on the wagon. Otherwise, I'll chill a bottle of champagne."

She hesitated. She wasn't sure she was ready to see Paul. It had been easy enough when she was feeling ill-used, when the future looked hopeless. But now she was at a crossroad and Paul knew it. It was the first time he'd ever issued a special invitation to visit instead of waiting for her to drop in when she needed to get away from home. At their next meeting there'd be no long, undemanding stretches of silence. She was free to make a decision now, and Paul had every right to expect one.

"Chill the champagne," she said lightly. "I had some with Kate before Christmas and I didn't go straight to perdition."

She hung up, thinking about the conversation, feeling confused and troubled. "Pre-New Year's Eve," he'd said. She'd almost forgotten it was only three days off. They'd made no plans this year, for obvious reasons. What will Richard want to do? she wondered. How will he wish to welcome in 1973?

Chapter 35

JACQUELINE CALLED THE next morning.

"How are things?"

"Pretty good here. How were they in Pound Ridge after we left?"

"Not to be believed! Maria swept down, done up in Hubert's latest Paris creation and announced that you and Richard had gone back to town so he could check with his doctor about the recovery which she of course, knew was nothing short of an act of God! Everybody was stunned about Richard's hands, but not a damned one of us believed her story about your hasty exit. What doctor works on Christmas Eve? What *did* happen?"

Susan told her about Richard's terrible confrontation with his mother. "I didn't know, myself, why we were leaving so suddenly. We had to, of course. Those two couldn't look at each other. I'm not sure they ever will again."

"Lucky Richard," Jacqueline said. "Lucky you. Such a divorce from Maria should only happen to Walter and me."

"Was Christmas bearable?"

"Scarcely. Everybody was dying to know what really happened and nobody dared ask. So we played out the charade, complete with overpriced, useless gift-giving. You never saw so many blue Tiffany boxes in your life! We were Gucci-ed and Pucci-ed up to our eyebrows. I have your presents and Richard's here, by the way. And I distributed the ones you brought. And I even got a bottle of Weil de Weil for you and Richard to give Joseph's girl. You owe me seventeen fifty."

"Thanks so much. I'll send you a check. By the way, how was Joseph's girl?"

"Cute as a button. Maria hated her."

Susan smiled. It never stopped, did it? Any female competition was abhorrent to Maria. She only tolerated women and not even then if they threatened her.

Why on earth would she care one way or another about a girl her grandson was interested in?

"Was there anything to hate?"

"I couldn't find anything, but don't go by me. I'm not programmed like our dear mother-in-law. But going back to Richard and her, I can see why she was so preoccupied the whole time we were there. Mutiny against Lady Bountiful! Dear me! And led by the most submissive member of the crew at that! Who'd have thought it! That doctor must be a magic man if he gave Richard courage to tell Maria what he really thinks of her. We'd all like to do that but nobody has the guts. Maybe the rest of us should start with a shrink. Make it in an organized rebellion."

"I only hope it sticks," Susan said.

"Meaning?"

"It's hard to change the patterns of a lifetime."

"You think he'll go crawling back?"

"I don't know. I don't want to think so. But she's so powerful, Jacqueline. So difficult to anticipate. She'll do anything to get him back."

"I think you're wrong there. She'll never make the first move. It isn't her style. Too proud. Too haughty. She'd cut her tongue out before she'd say she's sorry for what she's done to him. For that matter, what she's done to them all. And I don't think Richard will back down either. He's stubborn in his own way when he chooses to be. As though I had to tell you! But from what you've said, I think he's burned his bridges and he's probably much too relieved to rebuild them. The others would be more likely to buckle under in this situation than Richard would be."

"Speaking of the others," Susan said, "I'm surprised we haven't heard from Sergio or Gloria. You'd think they'd ring up and say they're happy about his recovery. You already knew. You were there and Richard knew how delighted you were. But there hasn't been a word from the rest."

There was a long pause before Jacqueline said reluctantly, "Listen, Susan, I don't know that they're so all-fired happy, any of them. Except Walter and me."

She was incredulous. "I can't believe that! Anyone would be happy for him. Even a stranger!"

"More likely a stranger. A stranger hasn't had to compete for the last thirty years with Mama's little darling. My dear, Sergio and Gloria have always been consumed with jealousy over Richard's talent and Maria's obvious preference for him. I won't say they were glad when his paralysis put him out of business, but I can't honestly say I think they were sorry. I know that's almost too sick for you to accept, but you haven't known them as long as I have. They knew damned well that without his music Richard was only a minor threat. He wouldn't be more famous than Sergio or more loved than Gloria. Mama would love them as much as she did her baby boy. And then, by God, he goes and recovers! They don't know about the big fight. All they can see is that he also goes right back to being the center of Maria's universe. I'm sure they're sulking in their tents, rotten little beasts that they are."

"That's horrible! Their own brother!"

"Well, how would *you* explain their silence? Fortunately, Walter doesn't have those hang-ups. He's mixed up in a lot of other ways, but he doesn't crave fame or a pat on the head from Herself. He wanted to call you and Richard when we got home yesterday, but I thought we should let you catch your breath, particularly since you already knew how happy I was."

"I see," Susan answered. But she didn't see at all. It was hard to believe that children of the same parents didn't love each other. More than that, were jealous of each other. She supposed it was because, as an only child, she had no frame of reference for what was called "sibling rivalry." Until now, it had been a textbook phrase to her. Even throughout her marriage the one thing she'd been convinced of was the clannishness of the Antoninis, like an inbred mutual-admiration society. Wrong again, she thought. They put on a great show of solidarity for the public, even for "outsiders" such as I. But they have no real loyalty or affection, not even for their blood relatives.

She wondered whether Richard felt the same about them. Was the constant bickering between him and Sergio only brotherly teasing? And he'd been so fiercely determined to master the difficult concerto Walter had written. As though he was fighting an enemy.

What strange, pathetic people they were. For all the advantages they had, they were petty and insecure even among themselves. The Antoninis as a dynasty are no more than a myth perpetuated by public relations, Susan thought. They're not a close-knit family. They're a bunch of talented, scared-to-death individuals who fight each other for recognition. They don't even like their own.

Jacqueline was rattling on. "Any chance of you and Richard coming to us for New Year's Eve? I know you haven't been going anywhere, but maybe now . . . We're only having a few friends, about twenty, including Walter's newest, a very nice young man who does *not* wear yards of gold chains. We'd love to have you."

"I'll ask Richard. I'm not sure what he wants to do that night."

"Well, come if you can. The Sergios and Taffins are not, underline *not*, invited! It's a buffet so you can let me know later."

"Thanks, I will."

She moved slowly down the hall toward Richard's bedroom. Since their return from East Hampton they'd occupied separate sleeping quarters. For the first few days it was because Susan could hardly bear the sight of him. Later, the man who took care of a partially paralyzed Richard had to have constant access to him, so there was no question of their returning to a shared room. Had they stayed at Maria's, it would have been the first time they'd slept in the same room in months. But, at the time, the fact hadn't disturbed Susan, even though she would still physically reject him. Not that it mattered. He was too proud to come near her in his less-than-perfect state. He wouldn't have touched her while he was a "cripple," even if she'd wanted it. And in the few days since his recovery, there'd been no move on either side to change the arrangements.

She tapped lightly on the door and was told to come in. He was still in his pajamas, reading the *Times* and having a cup of coffee. He looked up at her and smiled, and Susan thought again what a beautiful specimen he was.

"Look!" he said. "Isn't it sensational? I can turn the pages of the paper and lift my own coffee up! Would you ever imagine a grown man could find such pleasure in little things?"

"It's wonderful, Richard."

"I swear I'll never take anything for granted again." He was suddenly very subdued. "Every time I turn a doorknob or eat a meal or strike a chord, I'll remember the days when I couldn't."

Will you? she wondered. Time has a way of dimming the memory of pain. When they're well and happy, people forget how sick they once were, or how sad. The old cliché about childbirth being the worst pain in the world and the most easily forgotten is true. Would Richard go back to being the way he was, before the paralysis, before Katie?

"I'm continuing with Dr. Beekman. Did I tell you?"

"Yes. I'm glad." She hesitated. "That was Jacqueline on the phone. She'd like us to come there New Year's Eve. Would you like to?"

"It's fine with me if you want to. But I hoped . . ."

"Hoped what?"

"I hoped we might spend it together. Just the two of us. It's a very special night this year. I'd like to celebrate quietly, if you wouldn't mind." He sounded almost embarrassed by his unusual sentimentality.

"I'd like that very much," Susan said formally.

"We have a lot to talk about."

"I'll tell Jacqueline." At the door, she paused. "Don't you think it's strange we haven't heard from Serge or Gloria?

His voice was calm. "No. I didn't expect to. By now Mother probably has hinted that she wants no more to do with me. They'll take her side in any estrangement no questions asked."

"But why? They're your brother and sister!'

"No, they're my mother's children. Maria's puppets. They belong to the lady who pulls the strings."

Her knees were shaking as she rode the rickety little elevator up to Paul's apartment. One side of her was eager to see this man who loved her, but another side dreaded the encounter. It was not because she didn't want to hurt him, though that was part of it. It was because she wasn't sure of the rightness of her choice. If she had an ounce of intelligence she'd run to Paul, now that in good conscience she could. He would care for her, give her other children, never be mercurial and infuriating. He was strong and sane and sweet and she loved him. But not enough, Susan thought sadly. He'd never have the whole of me.

Damn it, what was this irrational, ungovernable hold Richard had on her? Why did she go back, time and time again, for more punishment? She supposed she was not unique by any means. The world was full of women in love with men they should never have chosen and were incapable of leaving. And the other way around. There was no explaining it. Call it masochism, as Kate did. Or call it love, as Susan preferred to. Whatever, Richard was the right man for her. And the wrong one, too. I must be one of those women who are fatally attracted to rotten men, Susan thought. And Richard may still be rotten. I can't yet make myself believe in that quiet person who says he'll be forever grateful for any motion he can make with his hands. Why do I grasp at the hope that he won't go back to being what he was? That he might not go back to Maria? Why can't I face the fact that this may be another mirage? That he may be physically healed but still emotionally disabled?

She felt a rush of affection for Paul, who stood waiting for her. But it was only affection. No excitement, no breathless, eager desire. She hugged him and stepped inside. The champagne was there and after he helped her out of her coat he opened the bottle and poured two glasses. Curled up in the corner of the sofa, Susan accepted one and waited for him to speak.

"What shall we drink to? A new year? A new life?"

He knows, Susan thought. He had only to look at my face to know I do not love him less but Richard more.

"I'll drink to you, Paul. To the finest, dearest, kindest man I know."

He did not respond to her toast. He simply gazed down at her steadily and said, "But not the man for you. That's it, isn't it, Susan? I knew it when you walked in. I'm not really surprised. I've always known it. There'll never be anyone for you except Richard."

Her voice was almost a whisper. "There can't be."

"Then I drink to you. To the happiness you hope for and the contentment you deserve."

Her eyes were full of tears. "Oh, God, Paul I wish it were different! We'd be so right. I know that."

"We'd never be right." There was no bitterness. Simply resignation. "I told you I'd wait to see if I were your true love. I'm not. There's no 'rightness' about being in love, Susan. It doesn't come with a built-in guarantee of happiness. That's for fairy tales. And you and I are too old for fairy tales."

"And too old for happy endings?"

"Not really. One man's happy ending is another man's letdown. Or vice versa. I don't delude myself about perfect happiness. There's no such animal. It's all compromise and making the best of what we have. It's adult acceptance of reality. I've avoided it too long. So have you. It's time we grew up and faced the facts of life. Real life. It's never going to be all we want; all peaches and cream and strawberry sodas. Not for either of us. Not even for Richard. But we'll all be where I suppose we're meant to be in the scheme of things. We'll make do."

"Why can't I get over him, Paul?" Her voice trembled. "What's wrong with me?"

"Nothing's wrong with you. You just don't know what it is to take the easy way out. And you'd hate it if you did. You're a fighter, dear Susan. And love is really war." He pulled her to her feet. "You'd better get out of here while I'm still being so damned brave and noble."

The question framed on her lips would not come out. Paul smiled.

"You're afraid to ask if we can still be friends, aren't you? Ever the avoidance of the obvious! Yes, dear, we'll be friends forever, but don't come here again to test my strength of character. Or your own. Go home to your husband, Susie. That's what you want. But do me one last favor, will you?"

"Anything."

"Start working on your book again. You can do it now. And it's important for you."

She cringed. "I can't, Paul. That's one thing I can't do. I want to forget those years."

"You can't forget and you mustn't. You can't run from the memories of Katie as though they were something terrible. They were beautiful. *She* was beautiful and so was the life you gave her. Put it on paper, Susan. For her. For other people. For yourself. Put into it all the faith and tenderness you felt for that little girl, and all the love and courage she returned. Give her a memorial that means something. And give all your bottled-up hurt a chance to come out. Promise me you will."

She looked into the serious, pleading face that mirrored such concern for her. Concern greater than his own disappointment.

"All right," she said. "If you think I should, I'll try. I don't know if I can, but I'll try."

Rhett Wilson was delighted when she phoned and said she thought she was ready to get back to the book. She hadn't even spoken to him since September. He understood and hadn't pressured her.

"I'm so glad to hear it! I haven't wanted to bother you, of course, but I'm delighted, for many reasons, that you feel able to go on with it. It's important, Susan. It really is. It will be comforting to a lot of troubled people."

"That's what a friend of mine says."

"Your friend is right. We'll extend your deadline a few months. Plan publication in the fall of seventy-four instead of this coming year. I don't want you to feel pushed. Take it slowly. I know it won't be easy for you." His voice was full of compassion. "I'm so sorry about Katie. I hope the writing will give you a sense of release. It often helps to put things on paper."

She went almost fearfully to the dresser drawer where she'd shoved the beginning of the manuscript. She remembered that awful day in East Hampton, trying to pack a few personal things for the sorrowful return to New York. She recalled picking up the folder from her desk, moving like she, too, was no longer alive. She'd thought of destroying it, but she'd literally not had enough strength to rip the pages to pieces, Instead, she'd tossed them into a suitcase and later, in unconscious imitation of Bridie's movements with Katie's doll, had hidden them away, out of sight and hopefully out of mind.

Slowly, reluctantly, she began to read what she'd written with such optimism, with such a feeling of dedication. The tears began again and she brushed them away. There were other little girls to think of, other parents and children to help if she could. Their stories might come out better than hers.

On the afternoon of New Year's Eve, Susan was restless and uneasy. She'd spent the morning trying to write and it came hard. Richard didn't know she was working on the book again. She'd been almost afraid to tell him, not sure what his reaction would be. They still lived as harmonious, though wary, strangers, uncertain of each other. He might think she was resuming the story to punish him. That wasn't true. Forgiveness was not perhaps, the proper word for what she felt. Shared regret was more like it. Or Paul's "adult acceptance of reality," including her own shortcomings.

I'll tell him about the book tonight, she thought. He'll see it's a step toward our new life, a reminder not to forget our child but to rid ourselves of bitterness and guilt.

She felt increasingly nervous and sad as the hours wore on. She tried to tell herself she always felt this way on the last day of any year. There was something gloomy about it, as there was about fall, when everything withered and died. No good reminding herself that things were reborn in the spring, or that the old year made way for the new. She still hated the end of anything. That about sums up my character, she thought. I can't bear to see things end: seasons, years, lives, marriages. I seem to want them to go on, even when they're worn out and useless. I didn't want to stop seeing Paul. I wanted it both ways, and that's impossible. I'm like Richard, who thought he could have his affairs and his marriage, his freedom and his commitment. We should have taken different vows: "Love, honor, and betray." She smiled mirthlessly. "Till life do us part."

Soaking in a foamy bath, seeking relaxation in the warm, scented bubbles, Susan knew that part of her nervousness was caused by the prospect of spending this New Year's Eve alone with her husband. "We have a lot to talk about," he'd said. Like what? The past? The present? The future? Can we really communicate again? "Again" is the wrong word. We've never communicated, not even in our happiest hours. We've shared the same roof but not the same thoughts. We've made love, but only our naked bodies have touched. We've never truly bared our souls.

She glanced at the little clock on the bathroom shelf. Half-past six. Richard was never this late getting back from the doctor. Where was he? With a woman? He was a physical person and now that he could enjoy sex again perhaps he'd gone seeking the satisfaction he no longer found at home. I'm jealous, she realized, God help me, it's starting all over! No. I mustn't feel that way. But where could he be? Maybe with Maria? The thought came over her like a black wave. What if he'd decided to start the new year by making things right with his mother? It's sinful of me to want them estranged, but I do.

She was startled to hear his voice calling to her through the bathroom door. He'd not been in her bedroom since their return.

"Susie! Come out! I have some great news!"

"In a minute!"

She dried herself slowly, postponing the "great news," It's Maria. I know it's Maria. Wrapped in a thick, terry robe, she came out. Richard was barely visible in the darkness of the late winter afternoon. She could only make out the outline of him perched on the edge of the bed. She snapped on a lamp and saw the happiness in his face. Susan stood quietly, a little way from him.

"What's your news?" She tried to speak naturally.

"I've been thinking about it for the last few days, but I didn't want to tell you. I was afraid it couldn't work out. Or that you might not approve if it did."

Oh, dear God, no!

"But today I discussed it with Dr. Beekman and for once he broke down and told me he thought I'd made a good decision,"

Would he never come to the point? It was like waiting for a bomb to fall . . . an explosion you knew would wipe you out.

"Come on," she said lightly. "This suspense is killing me."

"Susie, I've decided to handle my career differently. Spend less time away giving concerts, and more at home. I'm fed up with airports and lousy hotel food and literally sweating out every appearance. I'll take a few important bookings every season. I have no intention of retiring. But I'll do more recording. And," he broke into a big grin, "here's the best part. This afternoon I went to the Mannes College of Music and made them a proposition. I said I didn't want to join the faculty, but I'd be glad to take any really promising students who weren't already working with other teachers. I'd like to be responsible for developing talent. I won't take money for it and I won't accept anyone who doesn't show signs of tremendous promise. Maybe only two or three a year, carefully screened. They jumped at the idea, and I can't wait! Think of the satisfaction of seeing kids develop and knowing you've helped! God, I'm so excited! If it works out, I could do the same thing with Juilliard or the Manhattan School of Music. Maybe both. Of course, I'll need a few months of work myself before I begin. I need a lot of limbering up after such a long layoff." He was bubbling like a child. And then he abruptly subsided. "You do agree, don't you? You never liked touring. And we have no money problems. I'll still earn plenty, not that we need it. Father left us well fixed. It's okay with you, isn't it? You're not angry that I didn't tell you what I was going to do?"

She sank down on the bed beside him, too relieved and stunned to speak for a moment. The idea that Richard would not go back to his old life in music was the furthest thing from her mind. She was happy but bewildered, hardly able to believe it.

"Agree?" she said. "Of course I agree. It's fantastic! But I'm so surprised. I don't really understand. I thought you couldn't live without the constant applause, the endless excitement of performing. I thought you needed that limitless admiration. It's been your whole life, Richard. Thirty years of hard work to become one of the world's greatest artists. And now you've decided to give it up and teach?"

"I'm not giving it up. I'm simply cutting back to some degree of sanity. I told you, I'll still appear. I'm proud of my work. I'm young. I don't want to be forgotten. I won't be. But I don't want to be so driven, so possessed, that everything else is secondary to the next concert. I don't think that's necessary. I don't blame you for being surprised. The applause and admiration and all those things you mentioned have always been like food and drink to me. In a way, they still are. I like being famous. I'm not ashamed to admit that. But I don't like the one-dimensional life I've lived. I want to be more than a symbol. I'd like to try being a person, not the instrument of someone else's ambition." He stood up and began to pace the room. "Sometimes it takes a terrible shock to make you open your eyes to what you really are. Or what you thought you were. I thought I was the best of the Antoninis. The best of the best. I had to have the best treatment, the best publicity, even the best wife. I thought it was coming to me. When I heard about Katie's handicap I wallowed in self-pity. Yes. More pity for myself than for her. I didn't have the best child. I asked myself over and over how that could have happened to me. To me! Incredible! And even when she . . . died, my remorse was clouded with a sense of the injustice of it all. How dared you and Bridie saddle me with a job I didn't know how to handle!

Even then, Susan, I was angry. It wasn't only the end of her life that paralyzed me, it was the unwilling recognition of still another failure."

"Don't!" Susan said. "Don't torture yourself this way! It's not true. Especially the part about Katie. Nothing on God's earth could make me believe you didn't feel grief and remorse about her!"

"I felt grief. And certainly remorse. I was that human. I regretted a lot of things I'd done. And hadn't done. Of course I felt guilt for her death. Terrible guilt. But I also felt I'd been cheated somehow, and I didn't know by whom." He spoke slowly, carefully. "All this fall, with Dr. Beekman, I've been trying to get to the bottom of all this. And in the end, the answer was so simple: I've never known how to love. I thought success was a replacement for it; that you and Katie and, yes, Mother should be content with the only thing I could offer: the privilege of living in the shadow of the great man's triumphs. It was enough for Mother. It was all she wanted, because she doesn't know how to love either. But it wasn't enough for you, Susan. And in the end it wasn't enough for me."

She held her breath and let him continue, uninterrupted.

"You know all about my hang-ups. You recognized, long before I did, how they colored my life. I thought I hated my father. I didn't. I wanted him to worship me, too, the way Mother did. Or pretended she did. I had the insane idea that I could be to her all that he wasn't." Richard laughed. "Good old classic Oedipus. And even when I realized how crazy I was to blame myself for being born, even when I thought I hated Mother for making me feel guilty all my life, even then I knew I hadn't really gotten at the answer. I don't hate her. I don't think she realized how empty my life was because I didn't know how to give. She's a taker. Perhaps she'd be surprised if she found out how good it feels to do something for someone besides yourself. The teaching is the only way I know to begin. That and trying to show you that I can love you."

He really means it, Susan thought. He doesn't yet realize the monumental step he's taken or all the reasons why. This is more than a break with Maria's values. More than a fresh start with me. He may not know it, but he's also doing this for Katie, to make up to young people for the attention and help he was never able to give his child. I write a book and Richard molds talent, and both are for Katie. She corrected herself. Not entirely for Katie. This is also for himself and for me. And, most importantly, for us.

He stood in front of her, waiting for her response. "I need you, Susie. I need to get back your love."

"You never lost it," she said simply. "God knows you tried. We both did. But nothing could make me stop loving you." Without thinking, she held out her arms and he knelt and held her.

"Happy New Year, darling," he said.

She reread the opening words.

"My darling, this is a love letter to you."

The book was finished. The book she'd written for Katie. *To* Katie. I do believe she knows, Susan thought. She must know how much at peace we are. As she is.

She looked down at her swollen belly. Another baby conceived like Richard, on New Year's Eve. But this one in happiness, in harmony and in desire. A new life, inside and out. Another child, welcomed and wanted and shared. A new chance in a new world.

Thank you, Katie, she said silently.

Thank you for the lessons you taught in the time you were here.

Thank you for helping us find ourselves. Forever.